Hans Christian Andersen

Hans Christian Andersen's

COMPLETE FAIRY TALES

Translation by Jean Hersholt
Translation of "The Tallow Candle" by Compass Languages

Canterbury Classics

San Diego

Canterbury Classics
An imprint of Printers Row Publishing Group
10350 Barnes Canyon Road, Suite 100, San Diego, CA 92121
www.thunderbaybooks.com

Printers Row Publishing Group is a division of Readerlink Distribution Services, LLC.
The Canterbury Classics name and logo are trademarks of Readerlink Distribution Services, LLC.

All correspondence concerning the content of this book should be addressed to Canterbury Classics, Editorial Department, at the above address.

Publisher: Peter Norton
Publishing Team: Lori Asbury, Ana Parker, Laura Vignale
Editorial Team: JoAnn Padgett, Melinda Allman, Traci Douglas, Dan Mansfield
Production Team: Blake Mitchum, Rusty von Dyl
Cover and endpaper design by Ray Caramanna

Library of Congress Cataloging-in-Publication Data

Andersen, H. C. (Hans Christian), 1805-1875.
  [Tales. English.]
  Hans Christian Andersen's Complete Fairy Tales/translation by Jean Hersholt.
      pages cm
Includes bibliographical references and index.
  ISBN-13: 978-1-62686-099-5 (alk. paper)
  ISBN-10: 1-62686-099-8 (alk. paper)
  1. Fairy tales—Denmark—Translations into English. 2. Children's stories, Danish—Translations into English. [1. Fairy tales. 2. Short stories.] I. Hersholt, Jean, 1886-1956 translator. II. Title.

  PZ8.A54Her 2014
  741.5'973—dc23

                                                    2013044919

Printed in China
19 18 17 16 15 3 4 5 6 7

CONTENTS

"Life itself is the most wonderful fairy tale."

INTRODUCTION

THE WORLD OF HANS CHRISTIAN ANDERSEN

The Little Mermaid," "The Emperor's New Clothes," "The Princess on the Pea"—even for those who have not read the originals, the stories and themes in the work of Hans Christian Andersen resonate with us, repeated in movies, television, and pop culture. But Hans Christian Andersen wasn't just a writer of *eventyr*, or fairy tales: He was also a novelist, playwright, travel writer, and ardent Scandinavian nationalist. These works reflected the world Andersen lived in, and so no appreciation of Denmark's foremost writer can be complete without an understanding of his own character, his life, and the times he lived in.

Understanding Andersen's education and adolescence are especially important in understanding his writing. The collection you hold in your hand contains not just all of Andersen's major *eventyr*, but also a recently discovered work of juvenilia, "The Tallow Candle." Although Andersen's mature style is still undeveloped in this early short story, it nonetheless shows many of the same themes that mark his greatest works. To fully appreciate Andersen, we must examine all his work in its proper context, and this volume, containing this once-lost tale, allows us to trace the development of his themes and style. Chief among these themes are those of self-fashioning, of inner beauty as compared to the indifference and superficiality of the world, of the redemptive power of suffering, of longing for love, and, most of all, of the idea of self-transformation and ultimate triumph—themes that are rooted in Andersen's own experience.

These themes clearly mark Hans Christian Andersen as a product of the early nineteenth century. The world Andersen lived in had seen some remarkable changes in the generation before his birth, and would see even more during his lifetime. The balance of power in European society was shifting to the middle classes, and, with the shift came a new way of looking at childhood and new emphases in literature. Andersen fully took part in these changes, as his writing, and his life, reflect.

ANDERSEN AND ROMANTICISM

Andersen was born into a Europe that had recently seen turbulent change: In the chaos following the French Revolution, Napoleon had taken over France and proceeded to conquer a continental empire that included Denmark amongst its allies. In so doing, he spread the ideas of the French Enlightenment—democracy, freedom to choose one's own path in life, patriotism, and the rights of peoples to live in sovereign nations and for nations to determine their own fates—all through Europe. Even after the emperor's final defeat and exile to St. Helena, these ideas lingered. The grand theme of the nineteenth century was the idea of the self-made man who would, by innate virtue, climb the social ladder to a position of respectability. Along with this came ideas of nationalism, democracy, and equality—that all members of the nation-state were fundamentally equal and that one's place in society should be decided by merit, not accidents of birth. These ideas existed tenuously with renewed political and emotional investment in the ruling houses of Europe, which were increasingly characterized as national, populist monarchies, in the years after Napoleon's defeat.

Along with the ideas of hard work and self-discipline inherent to middle-class social mobility came repression of sexuality. A young man of good family could not marry until he was earning enough to support his wife (who would, of course, not work) and children. Later marriage also meant fewer children, with more time, energy, and money invested in cherishing, raising, and educating each of them. Childhood as we know it today was thus the product of nineteenth-century middle-class values—a special time in which the young person should be protected from the cruelty of the world and prepared for future roles in the adult struggle for existence. This was reflected in the creation of special clothes for children (as opposed to dressing them like miniature adults, as had been done previously), the repression of children's gender identity, and the birth of "children's literature"—a literary representation of what childhood was supposed to be about.

Some of the great themes of this literature for (or, rather, about) children included the shaping of character in childhood, self-fashioning, the search for authentic national culture in an imagined past, and the democratic belief in the fundamental equality of all members of the nation. In Germany, the Grimm Brothers had collected *Kinder und Hausmärchen* (Children's and House-Tales) to recover the primal volksgeist, or spirit, of the German people, which they saw as being passed on from women to children in a domestic setting. Likewise, both Andersen's invented stories—his *Eventyr, fortalte for Børn*, or *Fairy Tales, Told for Children*, from 1835—and the way he presented his life fully shared in these ideas—although he, of course, had his particular take on things, which included healthy doses of humor and satire. Nonetheless, he was careful to play up how life in his rural hometown had followed the "old ways" unknown in cosmopolitan Copenhagen, and how he had soaked in the stories told to him in his childhood.

Along with the "invention" of childhood and the other ideals of the middle class came the cultural tendency that we call Romanticism. While, as a movement, Romantics had no credo or manifesto, and their beliefs ranged from the revolutionary sentiment of the French novelist Victor Hugo to the reactionary politics of the German composer Wilhelm Richard Wagner, all shared certain commonalities. In the words of the Yale historian Peter Gay, Romanticism aimed for the "re-enchantment of the world." In its focus on emotion (particularly romantic love), personal subjective experience, and authenticity of feeling, it was the antithesis of the cold, rational Enlightenment and the new world of industrial capitalism it had birthed. Rather than scientific atheism, Romantics were religious, even mystical. Instead of understanding the world with intellect, they sought to understand it with feeling. Rather than machines and ordered cityscapes, they loved nature and wild beauty. Rather than a perfected future, they looked to an imagined past, the idea of authentic national culture, and the brotherhood of all members of the nation-state, for inspiration. In other words, Romanticism was simultaneously the opposite and complement of the world of industrial capitalism: it was the social style subscribed to by those who invested in and maintained this world; yet, even as it forwarded its ideologies, it was the very antithesis of it.

Hans Christian Andersen certainly reflects the paradox of Romantic ideas. The themes of the transformation of the true self and the discovery of hidden talent in Andersen's stories would have been unthinkable in an earlier age, when people were born into a social caste and had little room to change their fate. Charles Perrault's seventeenth-century Cinderella is ultimately a comedy (in the classical sense) about rewarding virtue, paying back evil, and people being returned to their proper social class. The stories collected by Andersen's elder contemporaries Jacob and Wilhelm Grimm are often tragedies about immutable character flaws leading to inevitable denouements. However, Andersen's tales, whether comedic or tragic, often have the idea of transformation and social advancement at their heart—particularly, advancement through romantic love. Virtue is not always rewarded, but cleverness is. The nineteenth century—the world Napoleon had created—was a time when a young man of talent but no breeding could, at least in theory, remake himself and climb the social ladder.

Andersen's own life reflects the theme of transformation—a poor boy receiving an education thanks to saintly benefactors and becoming his nation's best-beloved writer—and his autobiography, *My Enchanted Life*, is an exercise in reinforcing this myth, spinning the author's education as an ugly-duckling story. Andersen describes himself as a Romantic hero, the boy writer who tries to work with his heart rather than his mind. In the end, of course, he triumphs. In this sense, both Andersen and his tales belong firmly to the middle-class social milieu—the very same social stratum that consumed Romantic literature.

Of course, Andersen's work encompasses other themes. Never feeling entirely at home either among the middle class or the aristocracy, Andersen felt free to mock the better classes of society. Many of his tales are satirical. In "The Princess On the Pea," a seeming commoner is revealed as a princess by her extreme sensitivity (which, in a typically Andersen manner, is the sign of true nobility). In the pièce de résistance, the pea is then put in a museum. In a similar manner, the nobility is played for fools in "The Emperor's New Clothes."

Andersen's stories were also much more Christian in orientation than the Grimms'. In them, we can find Karl Marx's appraisal of nineteenth-century religious feeling as "at one and the same time, the expression of real suffering and a protest against real suffering . . . the sigh of the oppressed creature, the heart of a heartless world, and the soul of soulless conditions." Andersen's characters often suffer in a protest against the suffering of the real world. They are welcomed into Heaven since there is no justice in this world, save for what we create ourselves. His is, however, a very emotional religion of love and forgiveness, not one of sin and retribution—a Romantic Christianity steeped in the Lutheran tradition of a forgiving, loving God, but interpreted in a uniquely nineteenth-century way.

Andersen also uses religion to give even his most tragic stories a "happy ending." Unlike the Grimm's terrifying punishments, Andersen's tragedies often befall innocents ("The Red Shoes" being a notable exception). The Little Mermaid neither achieves the love of her prince nor recovers her mermaid form by killing him, but throws herself into the sea and dissolves into foam—not as a punishment for hubris or curiosity, but seemingly as a direct result of her sacrifice, love, and compassion. The Steadfast Tin Soldier does not gain his ballerina, but is melted with her in the fire.

There are numerous mawkish compositions, such as "The Dying Child" and "The Little Match Girl," on the theme of dead children that exploited the new middle-class sentimentality towards the young. Yet, in a sense these stories do have happy endings: Andersen always tells us that the good are rewarded in Heaven. Even the Little Jewish Maiden, in what was perhaps an early groping towards egalitarianism, is received into Heaven even though she could not be baptized in this world. (In the case of the Little Mermaid, in a coda he added later, he blackmails his juvenile audience into behaving by telling them that their good deeds would earn the protagonist time off from limbo!)

It would seem that cruelty of the world is reflected in Andersen's stories. After all, the nineteenth century was not known for its compassion; it was a time when children really would freeze to death and there was little or no social welfare. But in many ways, they are also the heralds of a new mentality—they evoke in the reader the desire to alleviate suffering. Today, Demark, Sweden, and Norway are some of the most liberal social welfare states in the world. The Little Match Girl would not freeze to death in today's Denmark.

LIFE AND TIMES

Hans Christian Andersen was born on April 2, 1805, in the town of Odense. His father, also named Hans, was a cobbler, neither wealthy nor well educated, while his mother, Anne Marie, worked as a washerwoman. Despite his own lack of formal schooling, the elder Andersen imbued his son with a taste for literature by sharing Danish legends and the *Arabian Nights* with him. Unfortunately, Hans Christian's beloved father died in 1816, leaving his wife and only child impoverished.

Andersen was an awkward child, tall and gangly, with a large nose. Worse, he was a dreamer who failed at no less than three apprenticeships—the usual vocational training for working-class children. It was clear he was good for nothing but telling stories, going to Odense's theater, and pretending to be an entertainer. The one thing that Hans Christian had working in his favor was that he had an excellent singing voice—so good that when he escaped his beloved but illiterate mother and ran away to Copenhagen to become an actor at the age of 14, his voice earned him an appointment with the Royal Danish Theatre. Here, one tragedy and one bit of good fortune befell him: First, his voice changed, ending his singing career. To act or dance were out of the question for the awkward youth, and he was hopeless at manual work. However, Andersen did meet Jonas Collin, one of the theater's directors. Hans Christian had written a play that, while not good enough for the stage, showed enough potential that Collin secured funding from the king to send Andersen to school. (The fact that the king paid for Andersen to be educated in exclusive schools later fueled the rumors that he was descended from nobility—perhaps that he was even the illegitimate son of King Christian VII. The allegations have never been substantiated.)

Hans Christian went to school first at Slagelse and then at Helsingør, the famous "Elsinore" from Shakespeare's *Hamlet*. Andersen later recalled school as one of the worst periods of his life. Lacking formal education, he had to begin at the next to lowest grade at Slagelse. Furthermore, Hans Christian's teachers universally discouraged him from writing (or so he later recounted). Worst of all, in his opinion, was Simon Meisling, under whose personal supervision Collin had placed him. Andersen later recalled Meisling as a strict man who bullied him, disparaged him at every opportunity, and did his best to discourage him from becoming a writer. The sensitive Hans Christian soon entered into a deep depression and almost totally ceased to write poetry.

Such was the story Andersen later told. After all, every Romantic hero needs a villain to triumph against. In all fairness, neither Andersen nor history has been kind to Meisling. The other side of the coin was that the schoolmaster was a serious scholar of middling social class and strict classical tastes who had taken on the decidedly odd, royally sponsored pupil as both a special project and a way to achieve his worldly ambitions. For instance, his connection with Collin was probably part of the reason for the move to Helsingør—Meisling, making the most of the connections Andersen afforded him, had successfully applied to become the headmaster at the more prestigious school. Andersen accompanied him, and even boarded at his house. No matter what the reality, the kindly Jonas Collin, who believed in Hans Christian's talent, later removed Andersen from Meisling's clutches and arranged for a private tutor. Finally, in 1828, at the advanced age of 23, Andersen managed to pass the examination to enter Copenhagen University.

It was in school, probably in the 1820s, that Andersen wrote "The Tallow Candle." This work was rediscovered by chance in 2012 in the Plum family dossier, which resides in the Funen, Denmark branch of the Danish National Archives, by a couple researching their family history. Esben Brage, a local historian, noticed Andersen's signature and realized it might be an original document. "The Tallow Candle" is dedicated to Madame Bunkeflod, a vicar's widow, childhood neighbor, and benefactress of the young Andersen; the Plums and Bunkeflods had been friends, which explains how the manuscript wound up in the Plum dossier.

The tallow candle begins with a good start in life, having inherited fine physical characteristics from its mother, a sheep, and a craving for bright, shining fire from its father, a melting pot. However, the uncaring world sullies the candle, not understanding it and only marking its outside with grime and dirt. Although the candle remains pure and untainted underneath its blemishes, it begins to despair. It is not until the candle finds a tinderbox—a soulmate who understands it better than it understands itself—who sees its true self and lights its ardent flame. In an overtly sexual metaphor, the fat drops of melted wax, which Andersen calls the physical and spiritual result of this "marriage," drip down its side, covering the old grime. The candle goes on to burn and light the way for its true friends for many years.

The candle's longing to belong and to be useful was surely a mirror of Andersen's own life. Contemporaries saw Andersen as an awkward man-child, uncomfortable in social settings, not brilliant in conversation, and immune to subtle cues. When writing about himself, however, Andersen chose to emphasize what he saw as his inner light. We have in "The Tallow Candle" a variant of the theme in "The Ugly Duckling": the misunderstood genius, whose innate virtue goes unrealized by a cold, uncaring, and conventional world. Finally, he meets someone who recognizes his true beauty, a helpmate who will enable to him realize his true value and his own special talent, and achieve his rightful place in the world. The story thus mirrors both Andersen's flair for pathos and somewhat self-absorbed belief in his own specialness and eventual success, even if it lacks the wry humor of his later fairy tales.

Despite his obsession with romantic love in both this story and in later works such as "The Naughty Boy," the awkward Andersen never met his own tinderbox. He at various times equivocated between swearing himself to celibacy—again, the bourgeois obsession with sexual discipline—and falling passionately in love. His diaries and personal correspondence reveal that he yearned for unobtainable women throughout his life, including a girl named Riborg Voigt; on his deathbed, Andersen clutched a long letter from Riborg next to his heart. He also fell in love with Jonas Collin's daughter Sophie and with Jenny Lind, the famous Swedish opera singer. Like the others, Lind rejected Andersen's proposal of marriage, saying that she loved him like a brother.

EARLY CAREER AND TRAVELS

In 1829, Andersen's fantastical short story "A Journey on Foot from Holmen's Canal to the East Point of Amager" was published to some small acclaim. He followed it up with poetry, a short piece for the theater, and an account of a trip to Germany. These were well enough received that, in 1833, following his graduation from college, King Frederick granted Andersen some money to travel through Europe. His journeys through Switzerland and Italy were extremely artistically productive, inspiring his breakout novel, *The Improvisatore*.

Andersen did not begin publishing the work he is best known for, his *Fairy Tales Told for Children*, until 1835. It was not an immediate success. Critics disliked his sense of humor, lack of didactic morals, and informal style, which Andersen had made similar to everyday conversation. Andersen nonetheless published three installments of *eventyr* from 1835 to 1837, and then had them collected in a single bound volume. His greatest success in the genre would not come until the 1840s, when English translations were published—notably, "The Little Mermaid" in the prestigious *Bentley's Miscellany*. Andersen continued to release fairy tales in installments until 1872.

In the same period as he wrote his first *eventyr*, Andersen published two further novels, *O.T.* and *Only a Fiddler*. The latter was unfavorably reviewed by Søren Kierkegaard, who later became a giant in nineteenth-century philosophy. Kierkegaard felt that Andersen's prose lacked a single, forceful ideal. In other words, Andersen put too much into feeling and describing; Kierkegaard felt that fierce determination, reflected in a strong narrative, was key. Yet, each man, in his own way, reflected the anxieties and thought of their age.

Andersen made his first trip to Norway in 1837. From then on, he was also a fervent believer in Scandinavianism, the idea that the three linguistically and culturally related Scandinavian countries—Denmark, Sweden, and Norway—should come together in unity. Only by such integration could the Scandinavian people achieve their true destiny as a nation-state. The three already had much in common: a common origin in the Viking past, and even political entanglement—Denmark had ruled Norway until 1814; later that same year, Sweden and Norway were unified under King Charles

XIII. In 1839, Andersen wrote his poem, "I am a Scandinavian," as an attempt at a national anthem; it never achieved great success. Sandanavianism itself never led to political unity, although the three countries, along with Finland and Iceland, did cooperate extensively up until World War II.

Andersen first visited England in 1847, where he met Charles Dickens at a party hosted by the Countess of Bessington. One would think that the two writers would have become fast friends—after all, they both used many of the same concepts and themes in their work, such as social mobility based on inner virtue and the use of sentimentality to dramatize and provoke sympathy for the life of the poor. Likewise, they shared a common background, having risen from poverty to become their countries' most prized writers. Anderson certainly adored Dickens—ever the ardent fan, he apotheosized Dickens in his diary and presumably was no less puppyish in person. On the other hand, Dickens, the proper Englishman, kept the adoring Dane at arm's length.

Things went rather less well on Andersen's second visit: Dickens had written Andersen saying that he simply must visit, with the result of the latter descending upon Dickens' house at Gad's Hill in the summer of 1857. He stayed for five weeks and was as awkward and unbearable as ever, or, as Dickens' daughter Kate later recalled, "He was a bony bore, and stayed on and on." When he finally left, Dickens wrote on the mirror in the guest room, "Hans Andersen slept in this room for five weeks—which seemed to the family *ages*!" Dickens later read of Andersen's Danish account of the visit, in which he lauded the English author, his wife, and his happy home life, excerpted in *Bentley's*. This was the last straw. Although Andersen's praise was sincere, *Bentley's* published the piece with intentional irony, since it was well known that the Dickenses had ended their unhappy marriage by separating shortly after Andersen's visit. Finally convinced the awkward Andersen was a hopeless case, Dickens ceased all correspondence with the Danish author. Andersen, for his part, continued to admire Dickens—even if the latter never answered his letters.

LATER CAREER AND DEATH

Andersen continued writing through the 1840s and '50s. While his attempts to write for the stage did not go well, his travel writing met with a great deal of success. So, too, did his fairy tales—Andersen's second series of *eventyr* was begun in 1838, and the third in 1845. Another success was 1840's *Picture-Book without Pictures*, which is framed as a series of stories told to the narrator by the Moon.

The sixty-seven-year-old Andersen's health began to decline after he fell out of bed in 1872—the year of the last publication of his stories. Shortly thereafter, he began to show the symptoms of the liver cancer to which he succumbed on August 4, 1875. Even before his death, Denmark had already begun to commemorate its most famous writer. Ever mindful of his public, Andersen gave directions that the tempo of the music for his funeral procession keep time with the small steps of the children who would attend.

Ken Mondschein, PhD

PUBLISHER'S NOTE

In this volume, the years that appear after each story's title indicate the original date of publication (in any language) for that story. Most were published by Andersen (in Danish) during his lifetime as serials in magazines or as books, but the last few tales were published posthumously by Jean Hersholt.

Andersen's earliest work, "The Tallow Candle," lay unknown to scholars and the public for almost two centuries before it was discovered among papers donated to the Danish National Archives. Historians have confirmed it is one of Andersen's first stories, written in his teens before his true authorship began. We have placed it at the beginning of this book to retain as much chronological order to Andersen's writing as possible.

Jean Hersholt (1886–1956) was born in Copenhagen, Denmark, to parents who were actors in the Danish Folk Theater. He grew up in show business, touring and performing onstage before focusing his career on film acting. In 1913 he emigrated to the United States, and a year later he moved to Hollywood, where he quickly became a premier radio and film actor. One of his most popular radio characters, Dr. Christian, was named directly for his favorite author, Hans Christian Andersen. During his career, Hersholt's philanthropic endeavors earned him a knighthood from King Christian X in Denmark, three Academy Awards for charity work, and a permanent place in the hearts of many in the entertainment industry.

An avid collector of Andersen editions, Hersholt's fascination with his fellow countryman's work culminated in *The Complete Andersen*, published as six volumes in 1949. The books contain Hersholt's English translations of over 160 of Andersen's fairy tales. Some stories were found in private letters and papers Hersholt had acquired, and were previously unpublished—not even in Danish—by Andersen. These translations are consistently rated as the best English representation of Andersen's work.

Hersholt's grave in Glendale, California, is marked by a statue of Klods-Hans (Clumsy Hans), an Andersen character who left home to find his way in the world, much as both Andersen and Hersholt did. Hersholt's memory is honored in the entertainment industry by the Academy of Motion Picture Arts and Sciences Jean Hersholt Humanitarian Award.

Canterbury Classics would like to thank the Hans Christian Andersen Museum in Odense, Denmark (museum.odense.dk/en/museums/hans-christian-andersen-museum), and the Hans Christian Andersen Center website (www.andersen.sdu.dk) for their invaluable assistance with the Hersholt translations. We are proud to offer the most complete volume available of Andersen's beloved fairy tales, and we hope it will become a treasured classic in your collection.

THE TALLOW CANDLE (1820s)

There was sputtering and sizzling as the flames played under the pan. This was the tallow candle's cradle, and out of the warm cradle slipped the candle—perfectly shaped, all of a piece, shiny white and slender. It was formed in a way that made everyone who laid eyes on it believe that it must promise a bright and glorious future. Indeed, it was destined to keep that promise and fulfill their expectations.

The sheep—a pretty little sheep—was the candle's mother, and the melting pot was its father. From its mother, it had inherited its dazzlingly white body and an intuitive understanding of life; but from its father, it had acquired the desire for the blazing fire that would eventually reach its very core and "shine the light" for it in life.

That is how it had been made and how it cast itself, with the best and brightest of hopes, into life. Here it met an amazing number of fellow creatures with whom it had dealings, since it desired to get to know life and thus perhaps find the most suitable niche for itself. But the candle saw the world in too benevolent a light, while the world only cared about itself and not about the tallow candle at all. The world was unable to understand the true nature of the candle, so it tried to use it to its own advantage and handled the candle improperly. Black fingers made bigger and bigger spots on the white color of innocence, which little by little totally disappeared, to be covered with the filth of an outside world that had been far too harsh and come much closer than the candle could bear, since it had been unable to distinguish between the pure and the impure—but deep inside, it was still innocent and unspoiled.

That is when the false friends realized that they could not reach its innermost part. In anger, they threw away the candle, considering it a useless thing.

The outer black layer kept away everybody good—they were afraid of becoming contaminated by the black color, of getting spots on themselves, so they kept a distance.

Now, the poor tallow candle was lonely, abandoned, and at its wit's end. It felt cast off by what was good and discovered that it had been nothing but a blind tool used to advance what was bad. It felt so terribly sad because it had lived its life without purpose—perhaps it had even tarnished some good things by its presence. It could not grasp why and to what end it had been created, why it was put on this Earth where it might destroy itself and even others.

More and more, increasingly deeply, it pondered the situation, but the more it thought, the greater its despondency, since it could not find anything good at all, no real meaning for itself—or see the purpose it had been given at birth. It was as if the black layer had also thrown a veil over its eyes.

That was when it met a small flame, a tinderbox. The tinderbox knew the light better than the tallow candle knew itself, for the tinderbox saw everything so clearly— right through the outer layer, and inside it found so much good. Therefore, it went closer, and bright hopes emerged in the candle. It lit up, and its heart melted.

The flame shone brightly—like a wedding torch of joy. Everything became bright and clear, and it showed the way for those in its company, its true friends—and helped by the light, they could now successfully seek truth.

The body, too, was strong enough to nurture and support the burning flame. Like the beginnings of new life, one round and plump drop after the other rolled down the candle, covering the filth of the past.

This was not only the bodily, but also the spiritual gain of the marriage.

The tallow candle had found its true place in life—and proved that a true light shone for a long time, spreading joy for itself and its fellow creatures.

THE TINDERBOX (1835)

There came a soldier marching down the high road—*one, two! one, two!* He had his knapsack on his back and his sword at his side as he came home from the wars. On the road, he met a witch, an ugly old witch, a witch whose lower lip dangled right down on her chest.

"Good evening, soldier," she said. "What a fine sword you've got there, and what a big knapsack. Aren't you every inch a soldier! And now you shall have money, as much as you please."

"That's very kind, you old witch," said the soldier.

"See that big tree." The witch pointed to one nearby them. "It's hollow to the roots. Climb to the top of the trunk, and you'll find a hole through which you can let yourself down deep under the tree. I'll tie a rope around your middle, so that when you call me, I can pull you up again."

"What would I do deep down under that tree?" the soldier wanted to know.

"Fetch money," the witch said. "Listen. When you touch bottom, you'll find yourself in a great hall. It is very bright there, because more than a hundred lamps are burning. By their light, you will see three doors. Each door has a key in it, so you can open them all.

"If you walk into the first room, you'll see a large chest in the middle of the floor. On it sits a dog, and his eyes are as big as saucers. But don't worry about that. I'll give you my blue-checked apron to spread out on the floor. Snatch up that dog, and set him on my apron. Then you can open the chest and take out as many pieces of money as you please. They are all copper.

"But if silver suits you better, then go into the next room. There sits a dog, and his eyes are as big as mill wheels. But don't you care about that. Set the dog on my apron while you line your pockets with silver.

"Maybe you'd rather have gold. You can, you know. You can have all the gold you can carry if you go into the third room. The only hitch is that there on the money-chest sits a dog, and each of his eyes is as big as the Round Tower of Copenhagen. That's the sort of dog he is. But never you mind how fierce he looks. Just set him on my apron and he'll do you no harm as you help yourself from the chest to all the gold you want."

"That suits me," said the soldier. "But what do you get out of all this, you old witch? I suppose that you want your share."

"No indeed," said the witch. "I don't want a penny of it. All I ask is for you to fetch me an old tinderbox that my grandmother forgot the last time she was down there."

"Good," said the soldier. "Tie the rope around me."

"Here it is," said the witch, "and here's my blue-checked apron."

The soldier climbed up to the hole in the tree and let himself slide through it, feet foremost down into the great hall where the hundreds of lamps were burning, just as the witch had said. Now he threw open the first door he came to. Ugh! There sat a dog glaring at him with eyes as big as saucers.

"You're a nice fellow," the soldier said, as he shifted him to the witch's apron and took all the coppers that his pockets would hold. He shut up the chest, set the dog back on it, and made for the second room. Alas and alack! There sat the dog with eyes as big as mill wheels.

"Don't you look at me like that." The soldier set him on the witch's apron. "You're apt to strain your eyesight." When he saw the chest brimful of silver, he threw away all his coppers and filled both his pockets and knapsack with silver alone. Then he went into the third room. Oh, what a horrible sight to see! The dog in there really did have eyes as big as the Round Tower, and when he rolled them, they spun like wheels.

"Good evening," the soldier said, and saluted, for such a dog he had never seen before. But on second glance, he thought to himself, "This won't do." So he lifted the dog down to the floor, and threw open the chest. What a sight! Here was gold and to spare. He could buy out all Copenhagen with it. He could buy all the cake-woman's sugar pigs, and all the tin soldiers, whips, and rocking horses there are in the world. Yes, *there* was really money!

In short order, the soldier got rid of all the silver coins he had stuffed in his pockets and knapsack, to put gold in their place. Yes sir, he crammed all his pockets, his knapsack, his cap, and his boots so full that he scarcely could walk. Now he was made of money. Putting the dog back on the chest, he banged out the door and called up through the hollow tree:

"Pull me up now, you old witch."

"Have you got the tinderbox?" asked the witch.

"Confound the tinderbox," the soldier shouted. "I clean forgot it."

When he fetched it, the witch hauled him up. There he stood on the high road again, with his pockets, boots, knapsack, and cap full of gold.

"What do you want with the tinderbox?" he asked the old witch.

"None of your business," she told him. "You've had your money, so hand over my tinderbox."

"Nonsense," said the soldier. "I'll take out my sword, and I'll cut your head off if you don't tell me at once what you want with it."

"I won't," the witch screamed at him.

So he cut her head off. There she lay! But he tied all his money in her apron, slung it over his shoulder, stuck the tinderbox in his pocket, and struck out for town.

It was a splendid town. He took the best rooms at the best inn, and ordered all the good things he liked to eat, for he was a rich man now because he had so much money. The servant who cleaned his boots may have thought them remarkably well worn for a man of such means, but that was before he went shopping. Next morning, he bought boots worthy of him, and the best clothes. Now that he had turned out to be such a fashionable gentleman, people told him all about the splendors of their town—all about their king, and what a pretty princess he had for a daughter.

"Where can I see her?" the soldier inquired.

"You can't see her at all," everyone said. "She lives in a great copper castle inside all sorts of walls and towers. Only the king can come in or go out of it, for it's been foretold that the princess will marry a common soldier. The king would much rather she didn't."

"I'd like to see her just the same," the soldier thought. But there was no way to manage it.

Now he lived a merry life. He went to the theater, drove about in the king's garden, and gave away money to poor people. This was to his credit, for he remembered from the old days what it feels like to go without a penny in your pocket. Now that he was wealthy and well dressed, he had all too many who called him their friend and a genuine gentleman. That pleased him.

But he spent money every day without making any, and wound up with only two coppers to his name. He had to quit his fine quarters to live in a garret, clean his own boots, and mend them himself with a darning needle. None of his friends came to see him, because there were too many stairs to climb.

One evening when he sat in the dark without even enough money to buy a candle, he suddenly remembered there was a candle end in the tinderbox that he had picked up when the witch sent him down the hollow tree. He got out the tinderbox, and the moment he struck sparks from the flint of it, his door burst open, and there stood a dog from down under the tree. It was the one with eyes as big as saucers.

"What," said the dog, "is my lord's command?"

"What's this?" said the soldier. "Have I got the sort of tinderbox that will get me whatever I want? Go get me some money," he ordered the dog. *Zip!* The dog was gone. *Zip!* He was back again, with a bag full of copper in his mouth.

Now the soldier knew what a remarkable tinderbox he had. Strike it once, and there was the dog from the chest of copper coins. Strike it twice, and here came the dog who had the silver. Three times brought the dog who guarded gold.

Back went the soldier to his comfortable quarters. Out strode the soldier in fashionable clothes. Immediately his friends knew him again, because they liked him so much.

Then the thought occurred to him, "Isn't it odd that no one ever gets to see the princess? They say she's very pretty, but what's the good of it as long as she stays locked up in that large copper castle with so many towers? Why can't I see her? Where's my tinderbox?" He struck a light and, *zip!* came the dog with eyes as big as saucers.

"It certainly is late," said the soldier. "Practically midnight. But I do want a glimpse of the princess, if only for a moment."

Out the door went the dog, and before the soldier could believe it, here came the dog with the princess on his back. She was sound asleep, and so pretty that everyone could see she was a princess. The soldier couldn't keep from kissing her, because he was every inch a soldier. Then the dog took the princess home.

Next morning when the king and queen were drinking their tea, the princess told them about the strange dream she'd had—all about a dog and a soldier. She'd ridden on the dog's back, and the soldier had kissed her.

"Now that was a fine story," said the queen. The next night, one of the old ladies of the court was under orders to sit by the princess's bed, and see whether this was a dream or something else altogether. The soldier was longing to see the pretty princess again, so the dog came by night to take her up and away as fast as he could run. But the old lady pulled on her storm boots and ran right after them. When she saw them disappear into a large house, she thought, "Now I know where it is," and drew a big cross on the door with a piece of chalk. Then she went home to bed, and before long the dog brought the princess home too. But when the dog saw that cross marked on the soldier's front door, he got himself a piece of chalk and cross-marked every door in the town. This was a clever thing to do, because now the old lady couldn't tell the right door from all the wrong doors he had marked.

Early in the morning, along came the king and the queen, the old lady, and all the officers, to see where the princess had been.

"Here it is," said the king when he saw the first cross mark.

"No, my dear. There it is," said the queen, who was looking next door.

"Here's one, there's one, and yonder's another one!" said they all. Wherever they looked they saw chalk marks, so they gave up searching.

The queen, though, was an uncommonly clever woman, who could do more than ride in a coach. She took her big gold scissors, cut out a piece of silk, and made a neat little bag. She filled it with fine buckwheat flour and tied it onto the princess's back. Then she pricked a little hole in it so that the flour would sift out along the way, wherever the princess might go.

Again the dog came in the night, took the princess on his back, and ran with her to the soldier, who loved her so much that he would have been glad to be a prince just so he could make her his wife.

The dog didn't notice how the flour made a trail from the castle right up to the soldier's window, where he ran up the wall with the princess. So in the morning, it was all too plain to the king and queen just where their daughter had been.

They took the soldier, and they put him in prison. There he sat. It was dark, and it was dismal, and they told him, "Tomorrow is the day for you to hang." That didn't cheer him up any, and as for his tinderbox, he'd left it behind at the inn. In the morning he could see through his narrow little window how the people all hurried out of town to see him hanged. He heard the drums beat, and he saw the soldiers march. In the crowd of running people, he saw a shoemaker's boy in a leather apron and slippers. The boy galloped so fast that off flew one slipper, which hit the wall right where the soldier pressed his face to the iron bars.

"Hey there, you shoemaker's boy, there's no hurry," the soldier shouted. "Nothing can happen till I get there. But if you run to where I live and bring me my tinderbox, I'll give you four coppers. Put your best foot foremost."

The shoemaker's boy could use four coppers, so he rushed the tinderbox to the soldier, and—well, now we shall hear what happened!

Outside the town, a high gallows had been built. Around it stood soldiers and many hundred thousand people. The king and queen sat on a splendid throne, opposite the judge and the whole council. The soldier already stood upon the ladder, but just as they were about to put the rope around his neck, he said the custom was to grant a poor criminal one last small favor. He wanted to smoke a pipe of tobacco—the last he'd be smoking in this world.

The king couldn't refuse him, so the soldier struck fire from his tinderbox, once, twice, and a third time. *Zip!* There stood all the dogs, one with eyes as big as saucers, one with eyes as big as mill wheels, one with eyes as big as the Round Tower of Copenhagen.

"Help me. Save me from hanging!" said the soldier. Those dogs took the judges and all the council, some by the leg and some by the nose, and tossed them so high that they came down broken to bits.

"Don't!" cried the king, but the biggest dog took him and the queen too, and tossed them up after the others. Then the soldiers trembled, and the people shouted, "Soldier, be our king and marry the pretty princess."

So they put the soldier in the king's carriage. All three of his dogs danced in front of it, and shouted "Hurrah!" The boys whistled through their fingers, and the soldiers saluted. The princess came out of the copper castle to be queen, and that suited her exactly. The wedding lasted all of a week, and the three dogs sat at the table, with their eyes opened wider than ever before.

LITTLE CLAUS AND BIG CLAUS (1835)

In a village there lived two men who had the self-same name. Both were named Claus. But one of them owned four horses, and the other owned only one horse; so to distinguish between them, people called the man who had four horses Big Claus, and the man who had only one horse Little Claus. Now I'll tell you what happened to these two, for this is a true story.

The whole week through, Little Claus had to plow for Big Claus and lend him his only horse. In return, Big Claus lent him all four of his horses, but only for one day a week, and that had to be Sunday.

Each Sunday, how proudly Little Claus cracked his whip over all the five horses, which were as good as his own on that day. How brightly the sun shone. How merry were the church bells that rang in the steeple. How well dressed were all the people who passed him with hymnbooks tucked under their arms. And as they went their way to church, to hear the parson preach, how the people did stare to see Little Claus plowing with all five horses. This made him feel so proud that he would crack his whip and holler, "Get up, all my horses."

"You must not say that," Big Claus told him. "You know as well as I do that only one of those horses is yours." But no sooner did another bevy of churchgoers come by than Little Claus forgot he mustn't say it, and hollered, "Get up, all my horses."

"Don't you say that again," Big Claus told him. "If you do, I'll knock your horse down dead in his traces, and that will be the end of him."

"You won't catch me saying it again," Little Claus promised. But as soon as people came by, nodding to him and wishing him "Good morning," he was so pleased and so proud of how grand it looked to have five horses plowing his field, that he hollered again, "Get up, all my horses!"

"I'll get up your horse for you," Big Claus said, and he snatched up a tethering mallet, and he knocked Little Claus's one and only horse on the head so hard that it fell down dead.

"Now I haven't any horse at all," said Little Claus, and he began to cry. But by and by, he skinned his dead horse and hung the hide to dry in the wind. Then he crammed the dry skin in a sack, slung it up over his shoulder, and set out to sell it in the nearest town.

It was a long way to go, and he had to pass through a dark, dismal forest. Suddenly a terrible storm came up, and he lost his way. Before he could find it again, evening overtook him. The town was still a long way off, and he had come too far to get back home before night.

Not far from the road he saw a large farmhouse. The shutters were closed, but light showed through a crack at the top of the windows. "Maybe they'll let me spend the night here," Little Claus thought, as he went to the door and knocked.

The farmer's wife opened it, but when she heard what he wanted, she told him to go away. She said her husband wasn't home, and she wouldn't have any strangers in the house.

"Then I'll have to sleep outside," Little Claus decided, as she slammed the door in his face.

Near the farmhouse stood a large haystack, leading up to the thatched roof of a shed, which lay between it and the house. "That's where I'll sleep," said Little Claus when he noticed the thatch. "It will make a wonderful bed. All I hope is that the stork doesn't fly down and bite my legs." For a stork was actually standing guard on the roof where it had a nest.

So Little Claus climbed to the roof of the shed. As he turned over to make himself comfortable, he discovered that the farmhouse shutters didn't come quite to the top of the windows, and he could see over them. He could see into a room where a big table was spread with wine and roast meat and a delicious fish. The farmer's wife and the sexton were sitting there at the table, all by themselves. She kept helping him to wine, and he kept helping himself to fish. He must have loved fish.

"Oh, if only I could have some too," thought Little Claus. By craning his neck toward the window he caught sight of a great, appetizing cake. Why, they were feasting in there!

Just then he heard someone riding down the road to the house. It was the farmer coming home. He was an excellent man except for just one thing. He could not stand the sight of a sexton. If he so much as caught a glimpse of one, he would fly into a furious rage, which was the reason why the sexton had gone to see the farmer's wife while her husband was away from home, and the good woman could do no less than set before him all the good things to eat that she had in the house. When she heard the farmer coming, she trembled for the sexton, and begged him to creep into a big empty chest, which stood in one corner of the room. He lost no time about it, because he knew full well that her poor husband couldn't stand the sight of a sexton. The woman quickly set aside the wine and hid the good food in her oven, because if her husband had seen the feast, he would have asked questions hard to answer.

"Oh dear!" Up on the shed, Little Claus sighed to see all the good food disappearing.

"Who's up there?" the farmer peered at Little Claus. "Whatever are you doing up there? Come into the house with me." So Little Claus came down. He told the farmer how he had lost his way, and asked if he could have shelter for the night.

"Of course," said the farmer, "but first, let's have something to eat."

The farmer's wife received them well, laid the whole table, and set before them a big bowl of porridge. The farmer was hungry and ate it with a good appetite, but Little Claus was thinking about the good roast meat, that fish and that cake in the oven. Beside his feet under the table lay his sack with the horsehide, for as we know, he was on his way to sell it in the town. Not liking the porridge at all, Little Claus trod on the sack, and the dry hide gave a loud squeak.

"Sh!" Little Claus said to his sack, at the same time that he trod on it so hard that it squeaked even louder.

"What on Earth have you got in there?" said the farmer.

"Oh, just a conjuror," said Little Claus. "He tells me we don't have to eat porridge, because he has conjured up a whole oven-full of roast meat, fish, and cake for us."

"What do you say?" said the farmer. He made haste to open the oven, where he found all the good dishes. His wife had hidden them there, but he quite believed that they had been conjured up by the wizard in the sack. His wife didn't dare open her mouth as she helped them to their fill of meat, fish, and cake.

Then Little Claus trod upon the sack to make it squeak again.

"What does he say now?" asked the farmer.

"He says," Little Claus answered, "that there are three bottles of wine for us in the corner by the oven."

So the woman had to bring out the wine she had hidden. The farmer drank it till he grew merry, and wanted to get himself a conjuror just like the one Little Claus carried in his sack.

"Can he conjure up the devil?" the farmer wondered. "I'm in just the mood to meet him."

"Oh, yes," said Little Claus. "My conjuror can do anything I tell him. Can't you?" he asked and trod upon the sack till it squeaked. "Did you hear him answer? He said 'Yes.' He can conjure up the devil, but he's afraid we won't like the look of him."

"Oh, I'm not afraid. What's he like?"

"Well, he looks an awful lot like a sexton."

"Ho," said the farmer, "as ugly as that? I can't bear the sight of a sexton. But don't let that stop us. Now that I know it's just the devil, I shan't mind it so much. I'll face him, provided he doesn't come near me."

"Wait, while I talk with my conjuror." Little Claus trod on the sack and stooped down to listen.

"What does he say?"

"He says for you to go and open that big chest in the corner, and there you'll find the devil doubled up inside it. But you must hold fast to the lid, so he doesn't pop out."

"Will you help me hold it?" said the farmer. He went to the chest in which his wife had hidden the sexton—once frightened, now terrified. The farmer lifted the lid a little, and peeped in.

"Ho!" he sprang back. "I saw him, and he's the image of our sexton, a horrible sight!" After that, they needed another drink, and sat there drinking far into the night.

"You must sell me your conjuror," said the farmer. "You can fix your own price. I'd pay you a bushel of money right away."

"Oh, I couldn't do that," Little Claus said. "Just think how useful my conjuror is."

"But I'd so like to have him." The farmer kept begging to buy it.

"Well," said Little Claus at last, "you've been kind enough to give me a night's lodging, so I can't say no. You shall have my sack for a bushel of money, but it must be full to the brim."

"You shall have it," said the farmer. "But you must take that chest along with you, too. I won't have it in the house another hour. He might still be inside it. You never can tell."

So Little Claus sold his sack with the dried horsehide in it, and was paid a bushel of money, measured up to the brim. The farmer gave him a wheelbarrow, too, in which to wheel away the money and the chest.

"Fare you well," said Little Claus, and off he went with his money and his chest with the sexton in it. On the further side of the forest was a deep, wide river, where the current ran so strong that it was almost impossible to swim against it. A big new bridge had been built across the river, and when Little Claus came to the middle of it, he said, very loud so the sexton could hear him:

"Now what would I be doing with this silly chest? It's as heavy as stone, and I'm too tired to wheel it any further. So I'll throw it in the river, and if it drifts down to my house, well and good, but if it sinks, I haven't lost much." Then he tilted the chest a little, as if he were about to tip it into the river.

"Stop! Don't!" the sexton shouted inside. "Let me get out first."

"Oh," said Little Claus, pretending to be frightened, "is he still there? Then I'd better throw him into the river and drown him."

"Oh no, don't do that to me!" the sexton shouted. "I'd give a bushel of money to get out of this."

"Why, that's altogether different," said Little Claus, opening the chest. The sexton popped out at once, pushed the empty chest into the water, and hurried home to give Little Claus a bushel of money. What with the farmer's bushel and the sexton's bushel, Little Claus had his wheelbarrow quite full.

"I got a good price for my horse," he said when he got home and emptied all the money in a heap on the floor of his room. "How Big Claus will fret when he finds out that my one horse has made me so rich, but I won't tell him how I managed it." Then he sent a boy to borrow a bushel measure from Big Claus.

"Whatever would he want with it?" Big Claus wondered, and smeared pitch on the bottom of the bushel so that a little of what he measured would stick to it. And so it happened that when he got his measure back, he found three newly minted pieces of silver stuck to it.

"What's this?" Big Claus ran to see Little Claus. "Where did you get so much money?"

"Oh, that's what I got for the horsehide I sold last night."

"Heavens above! How the price of hides must have gone up." Big Claus ran home, took an ax, and knocked all four of his horses on the head. Then he ripped their hides off, and set out to town with them.

"Hides, hides! Who'll buy hides?" he bawled, up and down the streets. All the shoemakers and tanners came running to ask what their price was. "A bushel of money apiece," he told them.

"Are you crazy?" they asked. "Do you think we spend money by the bushel?"

"Hides, hides! Who'll buy hides?" he kept on shouting, and to those who asked how much, he said, "A bushel of money."

"He takes us for fools," they said. The shoemakers took their straps, and the tanners their leather aprons, and they beat Big Claus through the town.

"Hides, hides!" they mocked him. "We'll tan your hide for you if you don't get out of town." Big Claus had to run as fast as he could. He had never been beaten so badly.

"Little Claus will pay for this," he said when he got back home. "I'll kill him for it."

Now it so happened that Little Claus's old grandmother had just died. She had been as cross as could be—never a kind word did she have for him—but he was sorry to see her die. He put the dead woman in his own warm bed, just in case she came to life again, and let her lie there all night while he napped in a chair in the corner, as he had done so often before.

As he sat there in the night, the door opened, and in came Big Claus with an ax. He knew exactly where Little Claus's bed was, so he went straight to it and knocked the dead grandmother on the head, under the impression that she was Little Claus.

"There," he said, "You won't fool me again." Then he went home.

"What a wicked man," said Little Claus. "Why, he would have killed me. It's lucky for my grandmother that she was already dead, or he'd have been the death of her."

He dressed up his old grandmother in her Sunday best, borrowed a neighbor's horse, and hitched up his cart. On the back seat, he propped up his grandmother, wedged in so that the jolts would not topple her over, and away they went through the forest.

When the sun came up, they drew abreast of a large inn, where Little Claus halted and went in to get him some breakfast. The innkeeper was a wealthy man, and a good enough fellow in his way, but his temper was as fiery as if he were made of pepper and snuff.

"Good morning," he said to Little Claus. "You're up and dressed mighty early."

"Yes," said Little Claus. "I am bound for the town with my old grandmother, who is sitting out there in the cart. I can't get her to come in, but you might take her a glass of mead. You'll have to shout to make her hear you, for she's deaf as a post."

"I'll take it right out." The innkeeper poured a glass full of mead and took it to the dead grandmother, who sat stiffly on the cart.

"Your grandson sent you a glass of mead," said the innkeeper, but the dead woman said never a word. She just sat there.

"Don't you hear me?" the innkeeper shouted his loudest. "Here's a glass of mead from your grandson."

Time after time he shouted it, but she didn't budge. He flew into such a rage that he threw the glass in her face. The mead splashed all over her as she fell over backward, for she was just propped up, not tied in place.

"Confound it!" Little Claus rushed out the door and took the innkeeper by the throat. "You've gone and killed my grandmother. Look! There's a big hole in her forehead."

"Oh, what a calamity!" The innkeeper wrung his hands. "And all because of my fiery temper. Dear Little Claus, I'll give you a bushel of money, and I'll bury your grandmother as if she were my very own. But you must hush this thing up for me, or they'll chop off my head—how I'd hate it."

So it came about that Little Claus got another bushel of money, and the landlord buried the old grandmother as if she'd been his own.

Just as soon as Little Claus got home, he sent a boy to borrow a bushel measure from Big Claus.

"Little Claus wants to borrow it?" Big Claus asked. "Didn't I kill him? I'll go and see about that." So he himself took the measure over to Little Claus.

"Where did you get all that money?" he asked when he saw the height of the money pile.

"When you killed my grandmother instead of me," Little Claus told him, "I sold her for a bushel of money."

"Heavens above! That was indeed a good price," said Big Claus. He hurried home, took an ax, and knocked his old grandmother on the head. Then he put her in a cart, drove off to town, and asked the apothecary if he wanted to buy a dead body.

"Whose dead body?" asked the apothecary. "Where'd you get it?"

"It's my grandmother's dead body. I killed her for a bushel of money," Big Claus told him.

"Lord," said the apothecary. "Man, you must be crazy. Don't talk like that, or they'll chop off your head." Then he told him straight he had done a wicked deed, that he was a terrible fellow, and that the worst of punishments was much too good for him. Big Claus got frightened. He jumped in his cart, whipped up the horses, and drove home as fast as they would take him. The apothecary and everyone else thought he must be a madman, so they didn't stand in his way.

"I'll see that you pay for this," said Big Claus when he reached the high road. "Oh, won't I make you pay for this, Little Claus!" The moment he got home, he took the biggest sack he could find, went to see Little Claus, and said:

"You've deceived me again. First, I killed my four horses. Then I killed my old grandmother, and it's all your fault. But I'll make sure you don't make a fool of me again." Then he caught Little Claus and put him in the sack, slung it up over his back and told him, "Now I shall take you and drown you."

It was a long way to the river, and Little Claus was no light load. The road went by the church, and as they passed, they could hear the organ playing and the people singing very beautifully. Big Claus set down his sack just outside the church door. He thought the best thing for him to do was to go in to hear a hymn before he went any further. Little Claus was securely tied in the sack, and all the people were inside the church. So Big Claus went in too.

"Oh dear, oh dear!" Little Claus sighed in the sack. Twist and turn as he might, he could not loosen the knot. Then a white-haired old cattle drover came by, leaning heavily on his staff. The herd of bulls and cows he was driving bumped against the sack Little Claus was in and overturned it.

"Oh dear," Little Claus sighed, "I'm so young to be going to Heaven."

"While I," said the cattle drover, "am too old for this earth, yet Heaven will not send for me."

"Open the sack!" Little Claus shouted. "Get in and take my place. You'll go straight to Heaven."

"That's where I want to be," said the drover, as he undid the sack. Little Claus jumped out at once. "You must look after my cattle," the old man said as he crawled in. As soon as Little Claus fastened the sack, he walked away from there with all the bulls and cows.

Presently, Big Claus came out of church. He took the sack on his back and found it light, for the old drover was no more than half as heavy as Little Claus.

"How light my burden is, all because I've been listening to a hymn," said Big Claus. He went on to the deep wide river, and threw the sack with the old cattle drover into the water.

"You'll never trick me again," Big Claus said, for he thought he had seen the last splash of Little Claus.

He started home, but when he came to the crossroads, he met Little Claus and all his cattle.

"Where did you come from?" Big Claus exclaimed. "Didn't I just drown you?"

"Yes," said Little Claus. "You threw me in the river half an hour ago."

"Then how did you come by such a fine herd of cattle?" Big Claus wanted to know.

"Oh, they're sea cattle," said Little Claus. "I'll tell you how I got them, because I'm obliged to you for drowning me. I'm a made man now. I can't begin to tell you how rich I am.

"But when I was in the sack, with the wind whistling in my ears as you dropped me off the bridge into the cold water, I was frightened enough. I went straight to the bottom, but it didn't hurt me because of all the fine soft grass down there. Someone opened the sack, and a beautiful maiden took my hand. Her clothes were white as snow, and she had a green wreath in her floating hair. She said, 'So you've come, Little Claus. Here's a herd of cattle for you, but they are just the beginning of my presents. A mile further up the road, another herd awaits you.'

"Then I saw that the river is a great highway for the people who live in the sea. Down on the bottom of the river, they walked and drove their cattle straight in from the sea to the land where the rivers end. The flowers down there are fragrant. The grass is fresh, and fish flit by as birds do up here. The people are fine, and so are the cattle that come grazing along the roadside."

"Then why are you back so soon?" Big Claus asked. "If it's all so beautiful, I'd have stayed there."

"Well," said Little Claus, "I'm being particularly clever. You remember I said the sea maiden told me to go one mile up the road and I'd find another herd of cattle. By 'road' she meant the river, for that's the only way she travels. But I know how the river turns and twists, and it seemed too roundabout a way of getting there. By coming up on land, I took a shortcut that saves me half a mile. So I get my cattle that much sooner."

"You *are* a lucky man," said Big Claus. "Do you think I would get me some cattle too if I went down to the bottom of the river?"

"Oh, I'm sure you would," said Little Claus. "Don't expect me to carry you there in a sack, because you're too heavy for me, but if you walk to the river and crawl into the sack, I'll throw you in with the greatest of pleasure."

"Thank you," said Big Claus, "but remember, if I don't get a herd of sea cattle down there, I'll give you a thrashing, believe me."

"Would you really?" said Little Claus.

As they came to the river, the thirsty cattle saw the water and rushed to drink it. Little Claus said, "See what a hurry they are in to get back to the bottom of the river."

"Help me get there first," Big Claus commanded, "or I'll give you that beating right now." He struggled into the big sack, which had been lying across the back of one of the cattle. "Put a stone in, or I'm afraid I shan't sink," said Big Claus.

"No fear of that," said Little Claus, but he put a big stone in the sack, tied it tightly, and pushed it into the river.

Splash! Up flew the water, and down to the bottom sank Big Claus.

"I'm afraid he won't find what I found!" said Little Claus as he herded all his cattle home.

THE PRINCESS ON THE PEA (1835)

Once there was a prince who wanted to marry a princess. Only a real one would do. So he traveled through all the world to find her, and everywhere things went wrong. There were princesses aplenty, but how was he to know whether they were real princesses? There was something not quite right about them all. So he came home again and was unhappy, because he did so want to have a real princess.

One evening, a terrible storm blew up. It lightninged and thundered and rained. It was really frightful! In the midst of it all came a knocking at the town gate. The old king went to open it.

Who should be standing outside but a princess, and what a sight she was in all that rain and wind. Water streamed from her hair down her clothes into her shoes, and ran out at the heels. Yet she claimed to be a real princess.

"We'll soon find that out," the old queen thought to herself. Without saying a word about it, she went to the bedchamber, stripped back the bedclothes, and put just one pea in the bottom of the bed. Then she took twenty mattresses and piled them on the pea. Then she took twenty eiderdown feather beds and piled them on the mattresses. Up on top of all these the princess was to spend the night.

In the morning they asked her, "Did you sleep well?"

"Oh!" said the princess. "No. I scarcely slept at all. Heaven knows what's in that bed. I lay on something so hard that I'm black and blue all over. It was simply terrible."

They could see she was a real princess and no question about it, now that she had felt one pea all the way through twenty mattresses and twenty more feather beds. Nobody but a princess could be so delicate. So the prince made haste to marry her, because he knew he had found a real princess.

As for the pea, they put it in the museum. There it's still to be seen, unless somebody has taken it.

There, that's a true story.

LITTLE IDA'S FLOWERS (1835)

My poor flowers are quite dead," said little Ida. "They were so pretty last evening, but now every leaf has withered and drooped. Why do they do that?" she asked the student who sat on the sofa.

She was very fond of him because he told such good stories and could cut such amusing figures out of paperhearts with dancing ladies inside them, flowers of all sorts, and castles with doors that you could open and close. He was a rollicking fellow.

"Why do my flowers look so ill today?" she asked him again, and showed him her withered bouquet.

"Don't you know what's the matter with them?" the student said. "They were at the ball last night, that's why they can scarcely hold up their heads."

"Flowers can't dance," said little Ida.

"Oh, indeed they can," said the student. "As soon as it gets dark and we go to sleep, they frolic about in a fine fashion. Almost every night, they give a ball."

"Can't children go to the ball?"

"Little daisies can go. So can lilies of the valley."

"Where do the prettiest flowers dance?" Ida asked.

"Haven't you often visited the beautiful flower garden just outside of town, around the castle where the king lives in the summertime? You remember—the place where swans swim close when you offer them bread crumbs. Believe me! That's where the prettiest flowers dance."

"Yesterday I was there with my mother," said Ida, "but there wasn't a leaf on the trees, or a flower left. Where are they? Last summer, I saw ever so many."

"They are inside the castle, of course," said the student. "Confidentially, just as soon as the king comes back to town with all of his court, the flowers run from the garden into the castle and enjoy themselves. You should see them. The two loveliest roses climb up on the throne, where they are the king and the queen. All the red coxcombs line up on either side, to stand and bow like grooms of the bedchamber. Then all the best-dressed flowers come, and the grand ball starts. The blue violets are the naval cadets. Their partners, whom they call 'Miss,' are hyacinths and crocuses. The tulips and tiger lilies are the old chaperones who see to it that the dancing is done well and that everyone behaves properly."

"But," said little Ida, "doesn't anybody punish the flowers for dancing in the king's own castle?"

"Nobody knows a thing about it," said the student. "To be sure, there's the old castle keeper, who is there to watch over things. Sometimes, he comes in the night with his enormous bunch of keys. But as soon as the flowers hear the keys jangle, they keep quiet, and hide, with only their heads peeking out from behind the curtains. Then the old castle keeper says, 'I smell flowers in here.' But he can't see any."

"What fun!" little Ida clapped her hands. "But couldn't I see the flowers either?"

"Oh easily," said the student. "The very next time you go there, remember to peep in the windows. There you will see them, as I did today. A tall yellow lily lay stretched on the sofa, pretending to be a lady-in-waiting."

"Can the flowers who live in the botanical gardens visit the castle? Can they go that far?"

"Why, certainly. They can fly all the way if it suits them. Haven't you seen lovely butterflies—white, yellow, and red ones? They almost look like flowers, and that's really what they used to be. They are flowers who have jumped up off their stems, high into the air. They beat the air with their petals, as though these were little wings, and so they manage to fly. If they behave themselves nicely, they get permission to fly all day long, instead of having to go home and sit on their stems. In time, their petals turn into real wings. You've seen them yourself. However, it's quite possible that the botanical garden flowers have never been to the king's castle and don't know anything about the fun that goes on there almost every night. Therefore, I'll tell you how to arrange a surprise for the botanical professor. You know the one I mean—he lives quite near here. Well, the next time you go to the garden, tell one of his flowers that they are having a great ball in the castle. One flower will tell the others, and off they'll fly. When the professor comes out in the garden, not one flower will he find, and where they've all gone, he will never be able to guess."

"How can a flower tell the others? You know flowers can't speak."

"They can't speak," the student agreed, "but they can signal. Haven't you noticed that whenever the breeze blows, the flowers nod to one another, and make signs with their leaves. Why, it's as plain as talk."

"Can the professor understand their signs?"

"Certainly he can. One morning, he came into his garden and saw a big stinging nettle leaf signaling to a glorious red carnation, 'You are so beautiful, and I love you so much.' But the professor didn't like that kind of thing, so he slapped the nettle's leaves, for they are its fingers. He was stung so badly that he hasn't laid hands on a stinging nettle since."

"Oh, how jolly!" little Ida laughed.

"How can anyone stuff a child's head with such nonsense?" said the prosy councillor, who had come to call and sit on the sofa too. He didn't like the student a bit. He always grumbled when he saw the student cut out those strange, amusing pictures—sometimes a man hanging from the gallows and holding a heart in his hand to show that he had stolen people's hearts away; sometimes an old witch riding a broomstick and balancing her husband on her nose. The councillor highly disapproved of those, and he would say as he said now, "How can anyone stuff a child's head with such nonsense—such stupid fantasy?"

But to little Ida, what the student told her about flowers was marvelously amusing, and she kept right on thinking about it. Her flowers couldn't hold their heads up, because they were tired out from dancing all night. Why, they must be ill. She took them to where she kept her toys on a nice little table, with a whole drawer full of pretty things. Her doll, Sophie, lay asleep in the doll's bed, but little Ida told her:

"Sophie, you'll really have to get up, and be satisfied to sleep in the drawer tonight, because my poor flowers are ill. Maybe, if I let them sleep in your bed tonight, they will get well again."

When she took the doll up, Sophie looked as cross as could be, and didn't say a word. She was sulky because she couldn't keep her own bed.

Ida put the flowers to bed, and tucked the little covers around them. She told them to be good and lie still, while she made them some tea, so that they would get well and be up and about tomorrow. She carefully drew the curtains around the little bed, so the morning sun would not shine in their faces.

All evening long, she kept thinking of what the student had said, before she climbed into bed herself. She peeped through the window curtains at the fine potted plants that belonged to her mother—hyacinths and tulips, too. She whispered very softly, "I know you are going to the ball tonight."

But the flowers pretended not to understand her. They didn't move a leaf. But little Ida knew all about them.

After she was in bed, she lay there for a long while thinking how pleasant it must be to see the flowers dance in the king's castle. "Were my flowers really there?" she wondered. Then she fell asleep. When she woke up again in the night, she had been dreaming of the flowers, and of the student, and of the prosy councillor who had scolded him and had said it was all silly nonsense. It was very still in the bedroom where Ida was. The night lamp glowed on the table, and Ida's mother and father were asleep.

"Are my flowers still asleep in Sophie's bed?" Ida wondered. "That's what I'd like to know."

She lifted herself a little higher on her pillow and looked toward the door that stood half open. In there were her flowers and all her toys. She listened, and it seemed to her that someone was playing the piano, very softly and more beautifully than she had ever heard it played.

"I'm perfectly sure that those flowers are all dancing," she said to herself. "Oh, my goodness, wouldn't I love to see them." But she did not dare get up, because that might awaken her father and mother.

"I do wish the flowers would come in here!" she thought. But they didn't. The music kept playing, and it sounded so lovely that she couldn't stay in bed another minute. She tiptoed to the door, and peeped into the next room. Oh, how funny—what a sight she saw there!

No night lamp burned in the next room, but it was well lighted just the same. The moonlight streamed through the window, upon the middle of the floor, and it was almost as bright as day. The hyacinths and the tulips lined up in two long rows across the floor. Not one was left by the window. The flowerpots stood there empty, while the flowers danced gracefully around the room, making a complete chain and holding each other by their long green leaves as they swung around.

At the piano sat a tall yellow lily. Little Ida remembered it from last summer, because the student had said, "Doesn't that lily look just like Miss Line?" Everyone had laughed at the time, but now little Ida noticed that there was a most striking resemblance. When the lily played, it had the very same mannerisms as the young lady, sometimes bending its long, yellow face to one side, sometimes to the other, and nodding in time with the lovely music.

No one suspected that little Ida was there. She saw a nimble blue crocus jump up on the table where her toys were, go straight to the doll's bed, and throw back the curtains. The sick flowers lay there, but they got up at once, and nodded down to the others that they also wanted to dance. The old chimney sweep doll, whose lower lip was broken, rose and made a bow to the pretty flowers. They looked quite themselves again as they jumped down to join the others and have a good time.

It seemed as if something clattered off the table. Little Ida looked and saw that the birch wand, that had been left over from Mardi Gras time was jumping down as if he thought he were a flower, too. The wand did cut quite a flowery figure with his paper rosettes and, to top him off, a little wax figure who had a broad trimmed hat just like the one that the councillor wore.

The wand skipped about on his three red wooden legs, and stamped them as hard as he could, for he was dancing the mazurka. The flowers could not dance it, because they were too light to stamp as he did.

All of a sudden, the wax figure grew tall and important. He whirled around to the paper flowers beside him and said, "How can anyone stuff a child's head with such nonsense—such stupid fantasy?" At that moment, he was a perfect image of the big-hatted councillor, just as sallow and quite as cross. But the paper flowers hit back. They struck his thin shanks until he crumpled up into a very small wax mannequin. The change was so ridiculous that little Ida could not keep from laughing.

Wherever the sceptered wand danced, the councillor had to dance too, whether he made himself tall and important or remained a little wax figure in a big black hat. The real flowers put in a kind word for him, especially those who had lain ill in the doll's bed, and the birch wand let him rest.

Just then, they heard a loud knocking in the drawer where Ida's doll, Sophie, lay with the other toys. The chimney sweep rushed to the edge of the table, lay flat on his stomach, and managed to pull the drawer out a little way. Sophie sat up and looked around her, most surprised.

"Why, they are having a ball!" she said. "Why hasn't somebody told me about it?"

"Won't you dance with me?" the chimney sweep asked her.

"A fine partner you'd be!" she said, and turned her back on him.

She sat on the edge of the drawer, hoping one of the flowers would ask her to dance, but not one of them did, She coughed, "Hm, hm, hm!" and still not one of them asked her. To make matters worse, the chimney sweep had gone off dancing by himself, which he did pretty well.

As none of the flowers paid the least attention to Sophie, she let herself tumble from the drawer to the floor with a bang. Now the flowers all came running to ask, "Did you hurt yourself?" They were very polite to her, especially those who had slept in her bed. But she wasn't hurt a bit. Ida's flowers thanked her for the use of her nice bed, and treated her well. They took her out in the middle of the floor, where the moon shone, and danced with her while all the other flowers made a circle around them. Sophie wasn't at all cross now. She said they might keep her bed. She didn't in the least mind sleeping in the drawer.

But the flowers said, "Thank you, no. We can't live long enough to keep your bed. Tomorrow we shall be dead. Tell little Ida to bury us in the garden, next to her canary bird's grave. Then we shall come up again next summer, more beautiful than ever."

"Oh, you mustn't die," Sophie said, and kissed all the flowers.

Then the drawing room door opened, and many more splendid flowers tripped in. Ida couldn't imagine where they had come from, unless—why, they must have come straight from the king's castle. First came two magnificent roses, wearing little gold crowns. These were the king and the queen. Then came charming gillyflowers and carnations, who greeted everybody. They brought the musicians along. Large poppies and peonies blew upon pea pods until they were red in the face. Blue hyacinths and little snowdrops tinkled their bells. It was such funny music. Many other flowers followed them, and they all danced together, blue violets with pink primroses, and daisies with the lilies of the valley.

All the flowers kissed one another, and that was very pretty to look at. When the time came to say good night, little Ida sneaked back to bed too, where she dreamed of all she had seen.

As soon as it was morning, she hurried to her little table to see if her flowers were still there. She threw back the curtain around the bed. Yes, they were there, but they were even more faded than yesterday. Sophie was lying in the drawer where Ida had put her. She looked quite sleepy.

"Do you remember what you were to tell me?" little Ida asked.

But Sophie just looked stupid, and didn't say one word.

"You are no good at all," Ida told her. "And to think how nice they were to you, and how all of them danced with you."

She opened a little pasteboard box, nicely decorated with pictures of birds, and laid the dead flowers in it.

"This will be your pretty coffin," she told them. "When my cousins from Norway come to visit us, they will help me bury you in the garden, so that you may come up again next summer and be more beautiful than ever."

Her Norwegian cousins were two pleasant boys named Jonas and Adolph. Their father had given them two new crossbows, which they brought with them for Ida to see. She told them how her poor flowers had died, and they got permission to hold a funeral. The boys marched first, with their crossbows on their shoulders. Little Ida followed, with her dead flowers in their nice box. In the garden, they dug a little grave. Ida first kissed the flowers, and then she closed the box and laid it in the earth. Adolph and Jonas shot their crossbows over the grave, for they had no guns or cannons.

THUMBELINA (1835)

There once was a woman who wanted so very much to have a tiny little child, but she did not know where to find one. So she went to an old witch, and she said:

"I have set my heart upon having a tiny little child. Please could you tell me where I can find one?"

"Why, that's easily done," said the witch. "Here's a grain of barley for you, but it isn't at all the sort of barley that farmers grow in their fields or that the chickens get to eat. Put it in a flower pot, and you'll see what you shall see."

"Oh, thank you!" the woman said. She gave the witch twelve pennies, and planted the barley seed as soon as she got home. It quickly grew into a fine large flower, which looked very much like a tulip. But the petals were folded tight, as though it were still a bud.

"This is such a pretty flower," said the woman. She kissed its lovely red and yellow petals, and just as she kissed it, the flower gave a loud *pop!* and flew open. It was a tulip, right enough, but on the green cushion in the middle of it sat a tiny girl. She was dainty and fair to see, but she was no taller than your thumb. So she was called Thumbelina.

A nicely polished walnut shell served as her cradle. Her mattress was made of the blue petals of violets, and a rose petal was pulled up to cover her. That was how she slept at night. In the daytime, she played on a table where the woman put a plate surrounded with a wreath of flowers. Their stems lay in the water, on which there floated a large tulip petal. Thumbelina used the petal as a boat, and with a pair of white horsehairs for oars, she could row clear across the plate—a charming sight. She could sing, too. Her voice was the softest and sweetest that anyone ever has heard.

One night as she lay in her cradle, a horrible toad hopped in through the window— one of the panes was broken. This big, ugly, slimy toad jumped right down on the table where Thumbelina was asleep under the red rose petal.

"Here's a perfect wife for my son!" the toad exclaimed. She seized upon the walnut shell in which Thumbelina lay asleep, and hopped off with it, out the window and into the garden. A big broad stream ran through it, with a muddy marsh along its banks, and here the toad lived with her son. Ugh! He was just like his mother, slimy and horrible. "Co-ax, co-ax, brek-ek-eke-kex," was all that he could say when he saw the graceful little girl in the walnut shell.

"Don't speak so loud, or you will wake her up," the old toad told him. "She might get away from us yet, for she is as light as a puff of swansdown. We must put her on one of the broad water lily leaves out in the stream. She is so small and light that it will be just like an island to her, and she can't run away from us while we are making our best room under the mud ready for you two to live in."

Many water lilies with broad green leaves grew in the stream, and it looked as if they were floating on the surface. The leaf that lay furthest from the bank was the largest of them all, and it was to this leaf that the old toad swam with the walnut shell that held Thumbelina.

The poor little thing woke up early next morning, and when she saw where she was, she began to cry bitterly. There was water all around the big green leaf, and there was no way at all for her to reach the shore. The old toad sat in the mud, decorating a room with green rushes and yellow water lilies, to have it looking its best for her new daughter-in-law. Then she and her ugly son swam out to the leaf on which Thumbelina was standing. They came for her pretty little bed, which they wanted to carry to the bridal chamber before they took her there.

The old toad curtsied deeply in the water before her, and said:

"Meet my son. He is to be your husband, and you will share a delightful home in the mud."

"Co-ax, co-ax, brek-ek-eke-kex," was all that her son could say.

Then they took the pretty little bed and swam away with it. Left all alone on the green leaf, Thumbelina sat down and cried. She did not want to live in the slimy toad's house, and she didn't want to have the toad's horrible son for her husband. The little fishes who swam in the water beneath her had seen the toad and heard what she had said. So up popped their heads to have a look at the little girl. No sooner had they seen her than they felt very sorry that anyone so pretty should have to go down to live with that hideous toad. No, that should never be! They gathered around the green stem that held the leaf where she was, and gnawed it in two with their teeth. Away went the leaf down the stream, and away went Thumbelina, far away where the toad could not catch her.

Thumbelina sailed past many a place, and when the little birds in the bushes saw her, they sang, "What a darling little girl." The leaf drifted further and further away with her, and so it was that Thumbelina became a traveler.

A lovely white butterfly kept fluttering around her, and at last alighted on the leaf, because he admired Thumbelina. She was a happy little girl again, now that the toad could not catch her. It was all very lovely as she floated along, and where the sun struck the water, it looked like shining gold. Thumbelina undid her sash, tied one end of it to the butterfly, and made the other end fast to the leaf. It went much faster now, and Thumbelina went much faster too, for of course she was standing on it.

Just then, a big May bug flew by and caught sight of her. Immediately, he fastened his claws around her slender waist and flew with her up into a tree. Away went the green leaf down the stream, and away went the butterfly with it, for he was tied to the leaf and could not get loose.

My goodness! How frightened little Thumbelina was when the May bug carried her up in the tree. But she was even more sorry for the nice white butterfly she had fastened to the leaf, because if he couldn't free himself, he would have to starve to death. But the May bug wasn't one to care about that. He sat her down on the largest green leaf of the tree, fed her honey from the flowers, and told her how pretty she was, considering that she didn't look the least like a May bug. After a while, all the other May bugs who lived in the tree came to pay them a call. As they stared at Thumbelina, the lady May bugs threw up their feelers and said:

"Why, she has only two legs—what a miserable sight!"

"She hasn't any feelers," one cried.

"She is pinched in at the waist—how shameful! She looks like a human being—how ugly she is!" said all of the female May bugs.

Yet Thumbelina was as pretty as ever. Even the May bug who had flown away with her knew that, but as every last one of them kept calling her ugly, he at length came to agree with them and would have nothing to do with her—she could go wherever she chose. They flew down out of the tree with her and left her on a daisy, where she sat and cried because she was so ugly that the May bugs wouldn't have anything to do with her.

Nevertheless, she was the loveliest little girl you can imagine, and as frail and fine as the petal of a rose.

All summer long, poor Thumbelina lived all alone in the woods. She wove herself a hammock of grass, and hung it under a big burdock leaf to keep off the rain. She took honey from the flowers for food, and drank the dew that she found on the leaves every morning. In this way, the summer and fall went by. Then came the winter, the long, cold winter. All the birds who had sung so sweetly for her flew away. The trees and the flowers withered. The big burdock leaf under which she had lived shriveled up until nothing was left of it but a dry, yellow stalk. She was terribly cold, for her clothes had worn threadbare and she herself was so slender and frail. Poor Thumbelina, she would freeze to death! Snow began to fall, and every time a snowflake struck her it was as if she had been hit by a whole shovelful, for we are quite tall while she measured only an inch. She wrapped a withered leaf about her, but there was no warmth in it. She shivered with cold.

Near the edge of the woods where she now had arrived, was a large grain field, but the grain had been harvested long ago. Only the dry, bare stubble stuck out of the frozen ground. It was just as if she were lost in a vast forest, and oh, how she shivered with cold! Then she came to the door of a field mouse who had a little hole amid the stubble. There this mouse lived, warm and cozy, with a whole storeroom of grain, and a magnificent kitchen and pantry. Poor Thumbelina stood at the door, just like a beggar child, and pled for a little bit of barley, because she hadn't had anything to eat for two days past.

"Why, you poor little thing," said the field mouse, who turned out to be a kind-hearted old creature. "You must come into my warm room and share my dinner." She took such a fancy to Thumbelina that she said, "If you care to, you may stay with me all winter, but you must keep my room tidy, and tell me stories, for I am very fond of them." Thumbelina did as the kind old field mouse asked, and she had a very good time of it.

"Soon we shall have a visitor," the field mouse said. "Once every week, my neighbor comes to see me, and he is even better off than I am. His rooms are large, and he wears such a beautiful black velvet coat. If you could only get him for a husband, you would be well taken care of, but he can't see anything. You must tell him the very best stories you know."

Thumbelina did not like this suggestion. She would not even consider the neighbor, because he was a mole. He paid them a visit in his black velvet coat. The field mouse talked about how wealthy and wise he was, and how his home was more than twenty times larger than hers. But for all of his knowledge, he cared nothing at all for the sun and the flowers. He had nothing good to say for them, and had never laid eyes on them.

As Thumbelina had to sing for him, she sang, "May Bug, May Bug, Fly Away

Home," and "The Monk Goes Afield." The mole fell in love with her sweet voice, but he didn't say anything about it yet, for he was a most discreet fellow.

He had just dug a long tunnel through the ground from his house to theirs, and the field mouse and Thumbelina were invited to use it whenever they pleased, though he warned them not to be alarmed by the dead bird that lay in this passage. It was a complete bird, with feather and beak. It must have died quite recently, when winter set in, and it was buried right in the middle of the tunnel.

The mole took in his mouth a torch of decayed wood. In the darkness, it glimmered like fire. He went ahead of them to light the way through the long, dark passage. When they came to where the dead bird lay, the mole put his broad nose to the ceiling and made a large hole through which daylight could fall. In the middle of the floor lay a dead swallow, with his lovely wings folded at his sides and his head tucked under his feathers. The poor bird must certainly have died of the cold. Thumbelina felt so sorry for him. She loved all the little birds who had sung and sweetly twittered to her all through the summer. But the mole gave the body a kick with his short stumps, and said, "Now he won't be chirping any more. What a wretched thing it is to be born a little bird. Thank goodness none of my children can be a bird, who has nothing but his 'chirp, chirp,' and must starve to death when winter comes along."

"Yes, you are so right, you sensible man," the field mouse agreed. "What good is all his chirp-chirping to a bird in the winter time, when he starves and freezes? But that's considered very grand, I imagine."

Thumbelina kept silent, but when the others turned their back on the bird, she bent over, smoothed aside the feathers that hid the bird's head, and kissed his closed eyes.

"Maybe it was he who sang so sweetly to me in the summertime," she thought to herself. "What pleasure he gave me, the dear, pretty bird."

The mole closed up the hole that let in the daylight, and then he took the ladies home. That night, Thumbelina could not sleep a wink, so she got up and wove a fine large coverlet out of hay. She took it to the dead bird and spread it over him, so that he would lie warm in the cold earth. She tucked him in with some soft thistledown that she had found in the field mouse's room.

"Good-bye, you pretty little bird," she said. "Good-bye, and thank you for your sweet songs last summer, when the trees were all green and the sun shone so warmly upon us." She laid her head on his breast, and it startled her to feel a soft thump, as if something were beating inside. This was the bird's heart. He was not dead—he was only numb with cold, and now that he had been warmed, he came to life again.

In the fall, all swallows fly off to warm countries, but if one of them starts too late, he gets so cold that he drops down as if he were dead, and lies where he fell. And then the cold snow covers him.

Thumbelina was so frightened that she trembled, for the bird was so big, so enormous compared to her own inch of height. But she mustered her courage, tucked the cotton wool down closer around the poor bird, brought the mint leaf that covered her own bed, and spread it over the bird's head.

The following night, she tiptoed out to him again. He was alive now, but so weak that he could barely open his eyes for a moment to look at Thumbelina, who stood beside him with the piece of touchwood that was her only lantern.

"Thank you, pretty little child," the sick swallow said. "I have been wonderfully warmed. Soon I shall get strong once more, and be able to fly again in the warm sunshine."

"Oh," she said, "it's cold outside, it's snowing, and freezing. You just stay in your warm bed, and I'll nurse you."

Then she brought him some water in the petal of a flower. The swallow drank, and told her how he had hurt one of his wings in a thorn bush, and for that reason couldn't fly as fast as the other swallows when they flew far, far away to the warm countries. Finally, he had dropped to the ground. That was all he remembered, and he had no idea how he came to be where she found him.

The swallow stayed there all through the winter, and Thumbelina was kind to him and tended him with loving care. She didn't say anything about this to the field mouse or to the mole, because they did not like the poor unfortunate swallow.

As soon as spring came and the sun warmed the earth, the swallow told Thumbelina it was time to say good-bye. She reopened the hole that the mole had made in the ceiling, and the sun shone in splendor upon them. The swallow asked Thumbelina to go with him. She could sit on his back as they flew away through the green woods. But Thumbelina knew that it would make the old field mouse feel badly if she left like that, so she said:

"No, I cannot go."

"Fare you well, fare you well, my good and pretty girl," said the swallow, as he flew into the sunshine. Tears came into Thumbelina's eyes as she watched him go, for she was so fond of the poor swallow.

"Chirp, chirp!" sang the bird, at he flew into the green woods.

Thumbelina felt very downcast. She was not permitted to go out in the warm sunshine. Moreover, the grain that was sown in the field above the field mouse's house grew so tall that, to a poor little girl who was only an inch high, it was like a dense forest.

"You must work on your trousseau this summer," the field mouse said, for their neighbor, that loathsome mole in his black velvet coat, had proposed to her. "You must have both woolens and linens, both bedding and wardrobe, when you become the mole's wife."

Thumbelina had to turn the spindle, and the field mouse hired four spiders to spin and weave for her day and night. The mole came to call every evening, and his favorite remark was that the sun, which now baked the earth as hard as a rock, would not be nearly so hot when summer was over. Yes, as soon as summer was past, he would be marrying Thumbelina. But she was not at all happy about it, because she didn't like the tedious mole the least bit. Every morning at sunrise and every evening at sunset, she would steal out the door. When the breeze blew the ears of grain apart, she could catch glimpses of the blue sky. She could dream about how bright and fair it was out of doors, and how she wished she would see her dear swallow again. But he did not come back, for doubtless he was far away, flying about in the lovely green woods.

When fall arrived, Thumbelina's whole trousseau was ready.

"Your wedding day is four weeks off," the field mouse told her. But Thumbelina cried and declared that she would not have the tedious mole for a husband.

"Fiddlesticks," said the field mouse. "Don't you be obstinate, or I'll bite you with my white teeth. Why, you're getting a superb husband. The queen herself hasn't a black velvet coat as fine as his. Both his kitchen and his cellar are well supplied. You ought to thank goodness that you are getting him."

Then came the wedding day. The mole had come to take Thumbelina home with him, where she would have to live deep underground and never go out in the warm sunshine again, because he disliked it so. The poor little girl felt very sad that she had to say good-bye to the glorious Sun, which the field mouse had at least let her look out at through the doorway.

"Farewell, bright Sun!" she said. With her arm stretched toward it, she walked a little way from the field mouse's home. The grain had been harvested, and only the dry stubble was left in the field. "Farewell, farewell!" she cried again, and flung her little arms around a small red flower that was still in bloom. "If you see my dear swallow, please give him my love."

"Chirp, chirp! Chirp, chirp!" She suddenly heard a twittering over her head. She looked up, and there was the swallow, just passing by. He was so glad to see Thumbelina, although, when she told him how she hated to marry the mole and live deep underground where the sun never shone, she could not hold back her tears.

"Now that the cold winter is coming," the swallow told her, "I shall fly far, far away to the warm countries. Won't you come along with me? You can ride on my back. Just tie yourself on with your sash, and away we'll fly, far from the ugly mole and his dark hole—far, far away, over the mountains to the warm countries where the sun shines so much fairer than here, to where it is always summer and there are always flowers. Please fly away with me, dear little Thumbelina, you who saved my life when I lay frozen in a dark hole in the earth."

"Yes, I will go with you!" said Thumbelina. She sat on his back, put her feet on his outstretched wings, and fastened her sash to one of his strongest feathers. Then the swallow soared into the air over forests and over lakes, high up over the great mountains that are always capped with snow. When Thumbelina felt cold in the chill air, she crept under the bird's warm feathers, with only her little head stuck out to watch all the wonderful sights below.

At length, they came to the warm countries. There the sun shone far more brightly than it ever does here, and the sky seemed twice as high. Along the ditches and hedgerows grew marvelous green and blue grapes. Lemons and oranges hung in the woods. The air smelled sweetly of myrtle and thyme. By the wayside, the loveliest children ran hither and thither, playing with the brightly colored butterflies.

But the swallow flew on still farther, and it became more and more beautiful. Under magnificent green trees, on the shore of a blue lake, there stood an ancient palace of dazzling white marble. The lofty pillars were wreathed with vines, and at the top of them, many swallows had made their nests. One nest belonged to the swallow who carried Thumbelina.

"This is my home," the swallow told her. "If you will choose one of those glorious flowers in bloom down below, I shall place you in it, and you will have all that your heart desires."

"That will be lovely," she cried, and clapped her tiny hands.

A great white marble pillar had fallen to the ground, where it lay in three broken pieces. Between these pieces grew the loveliest large white flowers. The swallow flew down with Thumbelina and put her on one of the large petals. How surprised she was to find in the center of the flower a little man, as shining and transparent as if he had been made of glass. On his head was the daintiest of little gold crowns, on his shoulders were the brightest shining wings, and he was not a bit bigger than Thumbelina. He was the spirit of the flower. In every flower there lived a small man or woman just like him, but he was the king over all of them.

"Oh, isn't he handsome?" Thumbelina said softly to the swallow. The king was somewhat afraid of the swallow, which seemed a very giant of a bird to anyone as small as he. But when he saw Thumbelina, he rejoiced, for she was the prettiest little girl he had ever laid eyes on. So he took off his golden crown and put it on her head. He asked if he might know her name, and he asked her to be his wife, which would make her queen over all the flowers. Here indeed was a different sort of husband from the toad's son and the mole with his black velvet coat. So she said "Yes" to this charming king. From all the flowers trooped little ladies and gentlemen delightful to behold. Every one of them brought Thumbelina a present, but the best gift of all was a pair of wings that had belonged to a large silver fly. When these were made fast to her back, she too could flit from flower to flower. Everyone rejoiced, as the swallow perched above them in his nest and sang his very best songs for them. He was sad, though, deep down in his heart, for he liked Thumbelina so much that he wanted never to part with her.

"You shall no longer be called Thumbelina," the flower spirit told her. "That name is too ugly for anyone as pretty as you are. We shall call you Maia."

"Good-bye, good-bye," said the swallow. He flew away again from the warm countries, back to faraway Denmark, where he had a little nest over the window of the man who can tell you fairy tales. To him, the bird sang, "Chirp, chirp! Chirp, chirp!" and that's how we heard the whole story.

THE NAUGHTY BOY (1835)

Once upon a time, there was an old poet—one of those good, honest old poets. One evening, as he was sitting quietly in his home, a terrible storm broke out— the rain poured down in torrents—but the old poet sat warm and cozy in his study, for a fire blazed brightly in his stove and roasting apples sizzled and hissed beside it.

"There won't be a dry stitch on anybody out in this rain," he told himself. You see, he was a very kindhearted old poet.

"Oh, please open the door for me! I'm so cold and wet!" cried a little child outside his house. Then it knocked at the door, while the rain poured down and the wind shook all the windows.

"Why, the poor little child!" cried the old poet as he hurried to open the door. Before him stood a naked little boy, with the water streaming down from his yellow hair! He was shivering, and would certainly have perished in the storm had he not been let in.

"You poor little fellow!" said the poet again, and took him by the hand. "Come in, and we'll soon have you warmed up! I shall give you some wine and a roasted apple, for you're such a pretty little boy."

And he really was pretty! His eyes sparkled like two bright stars, and his hair hung in lovely curls, even though the water was still streaming from it. He looked like a little angel, but he was pale with the cold and shivering in every limb. In his hand, he held a beautiful little bow-and-arrow set, but the bow had been ruined by the rain, and all the colors on the arrows had run together.

The old poet quickly sat down by the stove and took the little boy on his knee. He dried the child's hair, rubbed the blue little hands vigorously, and heated some sweet wine for him. And pretty soon the little boy felt better; the roses came back to his cheeks, and he jumped down from the old man's lap and danced around the old poet.

"You're a cheerful boy," laughed the old man. "What's your name?"

"My name is Cupid," was the reply. "Don't you know me? There lies my bow, and I can certainly shoot with it, too. Look, the storm is over, and the moon is shining!"

"Yes," the old poet said, "but I'm afraid the rain has spoiled your bow."

"That would be a shame," replied the little boy as he looked the bow over carefully. "No, it's already dry again, and the string is good and tight. No damage done. I guess I'll try it." Then he fitted an arrow to his bow, aimed it, and shot the good old poet right through the heart!

"Do you see now that my bow is not spoiled?" he said laughingly, and ran out of the house. Wasn't he a naughty boy to shoot the good old poet who had been so kind to him, taken him into his warm room, and given him his delicious wine and his best apple?

The good poet lay on the floor and wept, because he really had been shot right through the heart. "What a naughty boy that Cupid is!" he cried. "I must warn all the good children, so that they will be careful and never play with him. Because he will certainly do them some harm!" So he warned all the good children, and they were very careful to keep away from that naughty Cupid.

But he is very clever, and he tricks them all the time. When the students are going home from the lectures, he runs beside them, with a black coat on and a book under his arm. They don't recognize him, but they take his arm, thinking he is a student, too, and then he sends his arrows into their hearts. And when the girls are in church to be confirmed, he is likely to catch them and shoot his darts into them. Yes, he is always after people!

In the theater, he sits up in the big chandelier, burning so brightly that people think he's a lamp, but they soon find out better. He runs about the king's garden and on the rampart, and once he even shot your father and mother right through the heart! Just ask them, and you'll hear what they say.

Yes, he's a bad boy, this Cupid—you had better never have anything to do with him, for he is after all of you. And what do you think? A long time ago, he even shot an arrow into your poor old grandmother! The wound has healed up, but she will never forget it.

Saucy Cupid! But now you know all about him, and what a naughty boy he is!

THE TRAVELING COMPANION (1835)

Poor John was greatly troubled, because his father was very ill and could not recover. Except for these two, there was no one in their small room. The lamp on the table had almost burned out, for it was quite late at night.

"You have been a good son, John," his dying father said, "and the Lord will help you along in the world." He looked at his son with earnest, gentle eyes, sighed deeply, and fell dead as if he were falling asleep.

John cried bitterly, for now he had no one in all the world, neither father nor mother, sister nor brother. Poor John! He knelt at the bedside, and kissed his dead father's hand. He cried many salty tears, until at last his eyes closed, and he fell asleep with his head resting against the hard bedstead.

Then he had a strange dream. He saw the sun and the moon bow down to him. He saw his father well again and strong, and heard him laughing as he always laughed when he was happy. A beautiful girl, with a crown of gold on her lovely long hair, stretched out her hand to John, and his father said, "See what a bride you have won. She is the loveliest girl in the world." Then he awoke, and all these fine things were gone. His father lay cold and dead on the bed, and there was no one with them. Poor John!

The following week, the dead man was buried. John walked close behind the coffin; he could no longer see his kind father, who had loved him so. He heard how they threw the earth down upon the coffin, and watched the last corner of it until a shovel of earth hid even that. He was so sad that he felt as if his heart were breaking in pieces. Then those around him sang a psalm that sounded so lovely that tears came to his eyes. He cried, and that did him good in his grief. The sun shone in its splendor down on the green trees, as if to say, "John, you must not be so unhappy. Look up and see how fair and blue the sky is. Your father is there, praying to the good Lord that things will always go well with you."

"I'll always be good," John said. "Then I shall go to join my father in heaven. How happy we shall be to see each other again! How much I shall have to tell him, and how much he will have to show me and to teach me about the joys of heaven, just as he used to teach me here on earth. Oh, what joy that will be!"

He could see it all so clearly that he smiled, even though tears were rolling down his cheeks. The little birds up in the chestnut trees twittered, "Chirp, chirp! Chirp, chirp!" They were so happy and gay, for although they had attended a funeral, they knew very well that the dead man had gone to heaven, where he now wore wings even larger and lovelier than theirs. They knew that he was happy now, because here on Earth he had been a good man, and this made them glad.

John saw them fly from the green trees far out into the world, and he felt a great desire to follow them. But first, he carved a large wooden cross to mark his father's grave. When he took it there in the evening, he found the grave neatly covered with sand and flowers. Strangers had done this, for they had loved the good man who now was dead.

Early the next morning, John packed his little bundle and tucked his whole inheritance into a money belt. All that he had was fifty dollars and a few pieces of silver, but with this, he meant to set off into the world. But first, he went to the churchyard, where he knelt and repeated the Lord's Prayer over his father's grave. Then he said, "Farewell, father dear! I'll always be good, so you may safely pray to our Lord that things will go well with me."

The fields through which he passed were full of lovely flowers that flourished in the sunshine and nodded in the breeze, as if to say, "Welcome to the green pastures! Isn't it nice here?" But John turned round for one more look at the old church where as a baby he had been baptized, and where he had gone with his father every Sunday to sing the hymns. High up, in one of the belfry windows, he saw the little church goblin with his pointed red cap, raising one arm to keep the sun out of his eyes. John nodded good-bye to him, and the little goblin waved his red cap, put his hand on his heart, and kissed his finger tips to him again and again, to show that he wished John well and hoped that he would have a good journey.

As John thought of all the splendid things he would see in the fine big world ahead of him, he walked on and on—farther away than he had ever gone before. He did not even know the towns through which he passed, nor the people whom he met. He was far away among strangers.

The first night, he slept under a haystack in the fields, for he had no other bed. But he thought it very comfortable, and the king himself could have no better. The whole field, the brook, the haystack, and the blue sky overhead, made a glorious bedroom. The green grass patterned with red and white flowers was his carpet. The elder bushes and hedges of wild roses were bouquets of flowers, and for his wash bowl he had the whole brook full of clear fresh water. The reeds nodded their heads to wish him both "Good night," and "Good morning." The moon was really a huge night lamp, high up in the blue ceiling where there was no danger of its setting fire to the bed curtains. John could sleep peacefully, and sleep he did, never once waking until the sun rose and all the little birds around him began singing, "Good morning! Good morning! Aren't you up yet?"

The church bells rang, for it was Sunday. People went to hear the preacher, and John went with them. As he sang a hymn and listened to God's Word, he felt just as if he were in the same old church where he had been baptized, and where he had sung the hymns with his father.

There were many, many graves in the churchyard, and some were overgrown with high grass. Then John thought of his own father's grave and of how it too would come to look like these, now that he could no longer weed and tend it. So he knelt down to weed out the high grass. He straightened the wooden crosses that had fallen, and replaced the wreaths that the wind had blown from the graves. "Perhaps," he thought, "someone will do the same for my father's grave, now that I cannot take care of it."

Outside the churchyard gate stood an old beggar, leaning on his crutch, and John gave him the few pieces of silver that he had. Happy and high-spirited, John went farther on—out into the wide world. Toward nightfall, the weather turned dreadfully stormy. John hurried along as—fast as he could to find shelter, but it soon grew dark. At last he came to a little church that stood very lonely upon a hill. Fortunately, the door was ajar, and he slipped inside to stay until the storm abated.

"I'll sit down here in the corner," he said, "for I am very tired and need a little rest." So he sat down, put his hands together, and said his evening prayer. Before he knew it, he was fast asleep and dreaming, while it thundered and lightninged outside.

When he woke up, it was midnight. The storm had passed, and the moon shone upon him through the window. In the middle of the church stood an open coffin and in it lay a dead man, awaiting burial. John was not at all frightened. His conscience was clear, and he was sure that the dead do not harm anyone. It is the living who do harm, and two such harmful living men stood beside the dead one, who had been put here in the church until he could be buried. They had a vile scheme to keep him from resting quietly in his coffin. They intended to throw his body out of the church—the helpless dead man's body.

Why do you want to do such a thing?" John asked. "It is a sin and a shame. In Heaven's name, let the man rest."

"Stuff and nonsense!" the two evil men exclaimed. "He cheated us. He owed us money that he could not pay, and now that he has cheated us by dying, we shall not get a penny of it. So we intend to revenge ourselves. Like a dog he shall lie outside the church door."

"I have only fifty dollars," John cried. "It is my whole inheritance, but I'll give it to you gladly if you will solemnly promise to let the poor dead man rest in peace. I can do without the money. I have my healthy, strong arms, and Heaven will always help me."

"Why, certainly," the villainous fellows agreed. "If you are willing to pay his debt, we won't lay a hand on him, you can count on that."

They took the money he gave them and went away roaring with laughter at his simplicity. John laid the body straight again in its coffin, folded its hands, and took his leave. He went away through the great forest, very well pleased.

All around him, wherever moonlight fell between the trees, he saw little elves playing merrily. They weren't disturbed when he came along because they knew he was a good and innocent fellow. It is only the wicked people who never are allowed to see the elves. Some of the elves were no taller than your finger, and their long yellow hair was done up with golden combs. Two by two, they seesawed on the big raindrops, which lay thick on the leaves and tall grass. Sometimes the drops rolled from under them, and then they tumbled down between the grass blades. The little mannequins would laugh and made a great to-do about it, for it was a very funny sight. They sang, and John knew all their pretty little songs, which had been taught him when he was a small boy.

Big spotted spiders, wearing silver crowns, were kept busy spinning long bridges and palaces from one bush to another, and as the tiny dewdrops formed on these webs, they sparkled like glass in the moonlight. All this went on until sunrise, when the little elves hid in the buds of flowers. Then the wind struck the bridges and palaces, which were swept away like cobwebs.

John had just come out of the forest, when behind him, a man's strong voice called out, "Ho there, comrade! Where are you bound?

"I'm bound for the wide world," John told him. "I have neither father nor mother. I am a poor boy, but I am sure the Lord will look after me."

"I am off to the wide world, too," the stranger said. "Shall we keep each other company?"

"Yes indeed," John replied. So they strode along together.

They got to like each other very much, for both of them were kindly. But John soon found that he was not nearly so wise as the stranger, who had seen most of the world, and knew how to tell about almost everything.

The sun was high in the heavens when they sat down under a big tree to eat their breakfast. Just then, an old woman came hobbling along. Oh! She was so old that she bent almost double and walked with a crutch. On her back was a load of firewood she had gotten from the forest. Her apron was tied up, and John could see these big bunches of fern fronds and willow switches sticking out. As she came near the two travelers, her foot slipped. She fell down, and screamed aloud, for the poor old woman had broken her leg.

John suggested that they carry the woman to her home right away, but the stranger opened up his knapsack and took out a little jar of salve, which he said would mend her leg completely and at once, so that she could walk straight home as well as if her leg had never been broken. But in return, he asked for the three bunches of switches that she carried in her apron.

"That's a very high price!" The old woman dubiously nodded her head. She did not want to give up the switches, but it was not very pleasant to lie there with a broken leg, so she let him have the three bunches. No sooner had he rubbed her with the salve than the old woman got to her feet and walked off much better than she had come—all this the salve could do. Obviously, it was not the sort of thing you can buy from the apothecary.

"What on Earth do you want with those bunches of switches?" John asked his companion.

"Oh, they are three nice bundles of herbs," he said. "They just happened to strike my fancy, because I'm an odd sort of fellow."

When they had gone on for quite a distance, John remarked, "See how dark the sky has grown. Those are dreadfully dense clouds."

"No," his comrade said, "those are not clouds. They are mountains—splendid high mountains, where you can get clear above the clouds into perfectly fresh air. It is glorious, believe me. Tomorrow we shall certainly be far up in the world."

But they were not so near as they seemed to be. It took a whole day to reach the mountains, where the dark forests rose right up to the skies, and where the boulders were almost as large as a whole town. To climb over all of them would be heavy going indeed, so John and his companion went to an inn to rest and strengthen themselves for tomorrow's journey.

Down in the big taproom at the inn were many people, because a showman was there with a puppet show. He had just set up his little theater, and the people sat there waiting to see the play. Down in front, a burly old butcher had taken a seat, the very best one too, and his big bulldog—how vicious it looked—sat beside him, with his eyes popping as wide as everyone else's.

Then the play started. It was a very pleasant play, all about a king and a queen who sat on a velvet throne. They wore gold crowns on their heads and long trains to their costumes, all of which they could very well afford. The prettiest little wooden dolls, with glass eyes and big mustaches, stood by to open and shut all the doors so that fresh air might come into the room. It was a very pleasant play, it wasn't sad at all. But just as the queen rose and swept across the stage—heaven only knows what possessed the big bulldog to do it—as the fat butcher was not holding him, the dog made a jump right onto the stage, snatched up the queen by her slender waist, and crunched her until she cracked in pieces. It was quite tragic!

The poor showman was badly frightened, and quite upset about the queen, for she was his prettiest little puppet, and the ugly bulldog had bitten off her head. But after a while, when the audience had gone, the stranger who had come with John said that he could soon mend her. He produced his little jar, and rubbed the puppet with some of the ointment that had cured the poor old woman who had broken her leg. The moment the salve was applied to the puppet, she was as good as new—nay, better. She could even move by herself, and there was no longer any need to pull her strings. Except that she could not speak, the puppet was just like a live woman. The showman was delighted that he didn't have to pull strings for this puppet, who could dance by herself. None of the others could do that.

In the night, after everyone in the inn had gone to bed, someone was heard sighing so terribly, and the sighs went on for so long, that everybody got up to see who it could be. The showman went straight to his little theater, because the sighs seemed to come from there. All the wooden puppets were in a heap, with the king and his attendants mixed all together, and it was they who sighed so profoundly. They looked so pleading with their big glass eyes, and all of them wanted to be rubbed a little, just as the queen had been, so that they too would be able to move by themselves. The queen went down on her knees and held out her lovely golden crown as if to say: "Take even this from me, if you will only rub my king and his courtiers."

The poor showman felt so sorry for them that he could not keep back his tears. Immediately, he promised the traveling companion to give him all the money he would take in at the next performance, if only he would anoint four or five of the nicest puppets. But the traveling companion said he would not take any payment, except the big sword that hung at the showman's side. On receiving it, he anointed six of the puppets, who began to dance so well that all the girls, the real live girls who were watching, began to dance too. The coachman danced with the cook, and the waiter with the chambermaid. All the guests joined the dance, and the shovel and tongs did too, but these fell down as soon as they took their first step. It was a lively night indeed!

Next morning, John and his companion set off up the lofty mountainside and through the vast pine forests. They climbed so high that at last the church towers down below looked like little red berries among all that greenery. They could see in the distance, many and many a mile away, places where neither of them had ever been. Never before had John seen so many of the glories of this lovely world at once. The sun shone bright in the clear blue air, and along the mountainside he could also hear the hunters sounding their horns. It was all so fair and sweet that tears came into his eyes, and he could not help crying out, "Almighty God, I could kiss your footsteps in thankfulness for all the splendors that you have given us in this world."

His traveling companion also folded his hands and looked out over the woods and towns that lay before them in the warm sunlight. Just then, they heard a wonderful sound overhead. They looked up and saw a large white swan sweeping above them and singing as they had never before heard any bird sing. But the song became fainter and fainter, until the bird bowed his head and dropped slowly down dead at their feet—the lovely bird!

"Two such glorious wings!" said the traveling companion. "Wings so large and white as these are worth a good deal of money. I'll take them with me. You can see now what a good thing it was that I got a sword." With one stroke, he cut off both wings of the dead swan, for he wanted to keep them.

They journeyed many and many a mile over the mountains, until at last they saw a great town rise before them, with more than a hundred towers that shone like silver in the sun. In the midst of the town there was a magnificent marble palace, with a roof of red gold. That was where the king lived.

John and his companion did not want to enter the town at once. They stopped at a wayside inn outside the town to put on fresh clothes, for they wanted to look presentable when they walked through the streets. The innkeeper told them that the king was a good man who never harmed anyone. But as for his daughter—Heaven help us—she was a bad princess.

She was pretty enough. No one could be more lovely or more entertaining than she—but what good did that do? She was a wicked witch, who was responsible for many handsome princes' losing their lives. She had decreed that any man might come to woo her. Anybody might come, whether he were prince or beggar, it made no difference to her, but he must guess the answer to three questions that she asked him. If he knew the answers, she would marry him and he would be king over all the land when her father died. But if he could not guess the right answers, she either had him hanged or had his head chopped off. That was how bad and wicked the beautiful princess was.

The old king, her father, was terribly distressed about it, but he could not keep her from being so wicked, because he had once told her that he would never concern himself with her suitors—she could do as she liked with them. Whenever a prince had come to win the princess's hand by making three guesses, he had failed. Then he was either hanged or beheaded, for each suitor was warned beforehand, when he was still free to abandon his courtship. The old king was so distressed by all this trouble and grief that for one entire day every year, he and all his soldiers went down on their knees to pray that the princess might reform; but she never would. As a sign of mourning, old women who drank schnapps would dye it black before they quaffed it—so deeply did they mourn—and more than that they couldn't do.

"That abominable princess," John said, "ought to be flogged. It would be just the thing for her, and if I were the old king I'd have her whipped till her blood ran."

"Hurrah!" they heard people shout outside the inn. The princess was passing by, and she was so very beautiful that everyone who saw her forgot how wicked she was, and everyone shouted "Hurrah." Twelve lovely maidens, all dressed in white silk and carrying golden tulips, rode beside her on twelve coal-black horses. The princess herself rode a snow-white horse, decorated with diamonds and rubies. Her riding costume was of pure gold, and the whip that she carried looked like a ray of sunlight.

The gold crown on her head twinkled like the stars of heaven, and her cloak was made from thousands of bright butterfly wings. But she herself was far lovelier than all these things.

When John first set eyes on her, his face turned red—as red as blood—and he could hardly speak a single word. The princess was the living image of the lovely girl with the golden crown, of whom he had dreamed on the night when his father died. He found the princess so fair that he could not help falling in love with her.

"Surely," he thought, "it can't be true that she is a wicked witch who has people hanged or beheaded when they can't guess what she asks them. Anyone at all may ask for her hand, even though he is the poorest beggar, so I really will go to the palace, for I cannot help doing it!"

Everyone told him he ought not to try it, lest he meet with the same fate that had befallen the others. His traveling companion also tried to persuade him not to go, but John felt sure he would succeed. He brushed his shoes and his coat, washed his face and his hands, and combed his handsome blond hair. Then, all alone, he went through the town to the palace.

"Come in," the old king said when John came knocking at his door. As John opened it, the old king advanced to meet him, wearing a dressing gown and a pair of embroidered slippers. He had his crown on his head, his scepter in one hand, and his orb in the other. "Just a minute," he said, tucking the orb under his arm so that he could offer a hand to John. But the moment he heard that John had come as a suitor, he fell to sobbing so hard that both the orb and scepter dropped to the floor, and he had to use his dressing gown to wipe his eyes. The poor old king!

"Don't try it!" he said. "You will fare badly like all the others. Come, let me show them to you."

Then he led John into the princess's pleasure garden, where he saw a fearful thing. From every tree hung three or four kings' sons who had been suitors of the princess but had not been able to answer the questions she put to them. The skeletons rattled so in every breeze that they terrified the little birds, who never dared come to the garden. All the flowers were tied to human bones, and human skulls grinned up from every flower pot. What a charming garden for a princess!

"There!" said the old king, "You see. It will happen to you as it happened to all these you see here. Please don't try it. You would make me awfully unhappy, for I take these things deeply to heart."

John kissed the good old king's hand, and said he was sure everything would go well, for he was infatuated with the princess's beauty. Just then, the princess and all of her ladies rode into the palace yard, so they went over to wish her good morning. She was lovely to look at, and when she held out her hand to John, he fell in love more deeply than ever. How could she be such a wicked witch as all the people called her?

The whole party went to the palace hall, where little pages served them jam and gingerbread. But the old king was so miserable that he couldn't eat anything at all. Besides, the gingerbread was too hard for his teeth.

It was arranged that John was to visit the palace again the following morning, when the judges and the full council would be assembled to hear how he made out with his answer. If he made out well, he would have to come back two more times, but as yet, no one had ever answered the first question, so they had forfeited their lives in the first attempt.

However, John was not at all afraid of his trial. Far from it! He was jubilant, and thought only of how lovely the princess was. He felt sure that help would come to him, though he didn't know how it would come, and he preferred not to think about it. He fairly danced along the road when he returned to the inn, where his comrade awaited him. John could not stop telling him how nicely the princess had treated him, and how lovely she was. He said that he could hardly wait for tomorrow to come, when he would go to the palace and try his luck in guessing. But his comrade shook his head, and was very sad.

"I am so fond of you," he said, "and we might have been comrades together for a long while to come, but now I am apt to lose you soon, poor, dear John! I feel like crying, but I won't spoil your happiness this evening, which is perhaps the last one we shall ever spend together. We shall be as merry as merry can be, and tomorrow, when you are gone, I'll have time enough for my tears."

Everyone in the town had heard at once that the princess had a new suitor, and therefore everyone grieved. The theater was closed; the women who sold cakes tied crepe around their sugar pigs; the king and the preachers knelt in the churches; and there was widespread lamentation. For they were all sure that John's fate would be no better than that of all those others.

Late that evening, the traveling companion made a large bowl of punch, and said to John, "Now we must be merry and drink to the health of the princess." But when John had drunk two glasses of the punch, he felt so sleepy that he couldn't hold his eyes open, and he fell sound asleep. His comrade quietly lifted him from the chair and put him to bed. As soon as it was entirely dark, he took the two large wings he had cut off the swan, and fastened them to his own shoulders. Then he put into his pocket the biggest bunch of switches that had been given him by the old woman who had fallen and broken her leg. He opened the window and flew straight over the house tops to the palace, where he sat down in a corner under the window that looked into the princess's bedroom.

All was quiet in the town until the clock struck a quarter to twelve. Then the window opened and the princess flew out of it, cloaked in white and wearing long black wings. She soared over the town to a high mountain, but the traveling companion had made himself invisible, so that she could not see him as he flew after her and lashed her so hard with his switch that he drew blood wherever he struck. Ah, how she fled through the air! The wind caught her cloak, which billowed out from her like a sail, and the moonlight shone through it.

"How it hails! How it hails!" the princess cried at each blow, but it was no more than she deserved.

At last she came to the mountain and knocked on it. With a thunderous rumbling, the mountainside opened, and the princess went in. No one saw the traveling companion go in after her, for he had made himself completely invisible. They went down a big, long passage where the walls were lighted in a peculiar fashion. Thousands of glittering spiders ran along the walls and gave off a fiery glow. Then they entered a vast hall, built of silver and gold. Red and blue blossoms the size of sunflowers covered the walls, but no one could pick them, for the stems were ugly poisonous snakes, and the flowers were flames darting out between their fangs. The ceiling was alive with glittering glowworms, and sky-blue bats that zapped their transparent wings. The place looked really terrible! A throne in the center of the floor was held up by four horse skeletons in a harness of fiery red spiders. The throne itself was of milk-colored glass, and its cushions consisted of little black mice biting each other's tails. The canopy above it was made of rose-red spider webs, speckled with charming little green flies that sparkled like emeralds.

On the throne sat an old sorcerer, with a crown on his hideous head and a scepter in his hand. He kissed the princess on her forehead, and made her sit with him on the costly throne as the music struck up. Big black grasshoppers played upon mouth harps, and the owl beat upon his own stomach, because he had no drum. It was a most fantastic concert! Many tiny goblins, with will-o'-the-wisps stuck in their little caps, capered around the hall. Nobody could see the traveling companion, who had placed himself behind the throne, where he could see and hear everything. The courtiers who now appeared seemed imposing and stately enough, but anyone with an observing eye could soon see what it all meant. They were mere cabbage heads stuck upon broomsticks, which the sorcerer had dressed in embroidered clothes and conjured into liveliness. But that didn't matter, for they were only needed to keep up appearances.

After the dance had gone on for a while, the princess told the sorcerer that she had a new suitor, and she asked what question she should put to him when he came to the palace tomorrow.

"Listen to me," said the sorcerer, "I'll tell you what; you must think of something commonplace, and then he will never guess what it is. Think of one of your shoes. He won't guess that. Then off with his head, and when you come tomorrow night, remember to fetch me his eyes, so that I may eat them."

The princess made a low curtsy, and promised not to forget about the eyes. The sorcerer opened the mountain for her, and she flew homeward. But the traveling companion flew behind her and thrashed her so hard with his switch that she bitterly complained of the fearful hailstorm, and made all the haste she could to get back through the open window of her bedroom. The traveling companion flew back to the inn, where John was still asleep. Taking off the wings, he tumbled into bed, for he had good reason to feel tired.

It was very early the next morning when John awoke. When his comrade arose, he told John of a very strange dream he had had about the princess and one of her shoes. He begged him to ask the princess if she didn't have one of her shoes in mind. This, of course, was what he had overheard the sorcerer say in the mountain, but he didn't tell John about that. He merely told him to be sure to guess that the princess had her shoe in mind.

"I may as well ask about that as anything else," John agreed. "Maybe your dream was true, for I have always thought that God would look after me. However, I'll be saying good-bye, because if I guess wrong, I shall never see you again."

They embraced, and John went straight through the town and up to the palace. The whole hall was packed with people. The judges sat in their armchairs, with eiderdown pillows behind their heads because they had so much to think about, and the old king stood there wiping his eyes with a white handkerchief. Then the princess entered. She was even lovelier than she was the day before, and she bowed to everyone in the most agreeable fashion. To John she held out her hand and wished him, "Good morning to you."

John was required to guess what she had in mind. She looked at him most charmingly until she heard him say the one word "shoe." Her face turned chalk-white, and she trembled from head to foot. But there was nothing she could do about it. His guess was right.

Merciful Heavens! How glad the old king was. He turned heels over head for joy, and everyone applauded both his performance and that of John, who had guessed rightly the first time.

The traveling companion beamed with delight when he heard how well things had gone. But John clasped his hands together and thanked God, who he was sure would help him through the two remaining trials. The following day he was to guess again.

That evening went by just like the previous one. As soon as John was asleep, his comrade flew behind the princess to the mountain and thrashed her even harder than before, for this time he had taken two scourges of switches. No one saw him, but he heard all that was said. The princess was to think of her glove, and he told this to John as if he had dreamed it.

Naturally, John had no trouble in guessing correctly, and there was unbounded rejoicing in the palace. The whole court turned heels over head as they had seen the king do on the first occasion. But the princess lay on her sofa, without a word to say. Now everything depended on John's answer to the third question. If it was right, he would get the lovely princess and inherit the whole kingdom after the old king died. But if he guessed wrong, he would forfeit his life, and the wizard would eat his beautiful blue eyes.

That evening John said his prayers, went to bed early, and fell serenely asleep. But his comrade tied the wings to his back, buckled the sword to his side, took all three scourges of switches, and flew off to the palace.

The night was pitch black. A gale blew so hard that it swept tiles from the roofs. In the garden where the skeletons dangled, the trees bent before the blast like reeds. Lightning flashed every moment, and thunder kept up one unbroken roar the whole night through. The window was flung open, and out flew the princess. She was deathly pale, but she laughed at the weather and thought it was not bad enough. Her white cloak lashed about in the wind like the sail of a ship, and the traveling companion thrashed her with his three switches until blood dripped to the ground. She could scarcely fly any farther, but at last she came to the mountain.

"How it hails and blows!" she said. "I have never been out in such weather."

"One may get too much of a good thing," the sorcerer agreed.

Now she told him how John had guessed right a second time, and if he succeeded again tomorrow, then he won, and never again could she come out to him in the mountains. Never again could she perform such tricks of magic as before, and therefore she felt very badly about it.

"He won't guess it this time," said the sorcerer. "I shall hit upon something that he will never guess unless he's a greater magician than I am. But first, let's have our fun.

He took the princess by both hands, and they danced around with all the little goblins and will-o'-the-wisps that were in the hall. The red spiders spun merrily up and down the walls, the fiery flowers seemed to throw off sparks, the owl beat the drum, the crickets piped, and the black grasshoppers played on mouth organs. It was an extremely lively ball.

After they had danced awhile, the princess had to start home, for fear that she might be missed at the castle. The sorcerer said he would go with her, to enjoy that much more of her company.

Away they flew through the storm, and the traveling companion wore out all three scourges on their backs. Never had the sorcerer felt such a hailstorm. As he said goodbye to the princess outside the palace, he whispered to her, "Think of my head."

But the traveling companion overheard it, and just at the moment when the princess slipped in through her window and the sorcerer was turning around, he caught him by his long black beard, and with the sword he cut the sorcerer's ugly head off, right at the shoulders, so that the sorcerer himself didn't even see it. He threw the body into the sea for the fishes to eat, but the head he only dipped in the water, wrapped it in his silk handkerchief, and took it back to the inn, where he lay down to sleep.

Next morning, he gave John the handkerchief but told him not to open it until the princess asked him to guess what she had thought about.

The hall was so full of people that they were packed together as closely as radishes tied together in a bundle. The judges sat in their chairs with the soft pillows. The old king had put on his new clothes, and his crown and scepter had been polished to look their best. But the princess was deathly pale, and she wore black, as if she were attending a funeral.

"Of what have I thought?" she asked John. He at once untied the handkerchief, and was quite frightened himself when he saw the sorcerer's hideous head roll out of it. Everyone there shuddered at this terrible sight, but the princess sat like stone, without a word to say. Finally, she got up and gave John her hand, for his guess was good. She looked no one in the face, but sighed and said:

"You are my master now. Our wedding will be held this evening."

"I like that!" the old king shouted. "This is as things should be."

All the people shouted "Hurrah!" The military band played in the streets, the bells rang out, and the cake women took the crepe off their sugar pigs, now that everyone was celebrating. Three entire oxen stuffed with ducks and chickens were roasted whole in the center of the market square, and everyone could cut himself a piece of them. The fountains spurted up the best of wine. Whoever bought a penny bun at the bakery got six large buns thrown in for good measure, and all the buns had raisins in them.

That evening, the entire town was illuminated. The soldiers fired their cannons, and the boys set off firecrackers. At the palace, there was eating and drinking, dancing and the clinking of glasses. All the lordly gentlemen and all the lovely ladies danced together. For a long way off, you could hear them sing:

Here are many pretty girls, and don't they love to dance!
See them hop and swing around whenever they've a chance.
Dance! My pretty maid, anew, till the sole flies off your shoe.

But the princess was still a witch, and she had no love for John at all. His comrade kept this in mind, and gave him three feathers from the swan's wings, and a little bottle with a few drops of liquid in it. He said that John must put a large tub of water beside the princess's bed, and just as she was about to get in bed, he must give her a little push, so that she would tumble into the tub. There he must dip her three times, after he had thrown the feathers and the drops of liquid into the water. That would free her from the spell of sorcery, and make her love him dearly.

John did everything his companion had advised him to do, though the princess shrieked as he dipped her into the water, and struggled as he held her in the shape of a large black swan with flashing eyes. The second time, she came out of the water as a swan entirely white except for a black ring around its neck. John prayed hard, and as he forced the bird under the water once more, it changed into the beautiful princess. She was fairer than ever, and she thanked him with tears in her beautiful eyes for having set her free from the sorcerer's spell.

In the morning, the old king came with all his court, and congratulations lasted all through the day. Last of all came John's traveling companion; he had his stick in his hand and the knapsack on his back. John embraced him time and again, and said that he must not leave them. He must stay here with John, who owed all his happiness to him. But the traveling companion shook his head. Gently and kindly, he said:

"No, my time is now up. I have done no more than pay my debt to you. Do you remember the dead man whom the wicked men wanted to harm? You gave all that you had so that he might have rest in his grave. I am that dead man." And at once he disappeared.

The wedding celebration lasted a whole month. John and his princess loved each other dearly, and the old king lived on for many a happy day to let their little children ride astride his knee and play with his scepter. But it was John who was king over all the land.

GOD CAN NEVER DIE (1836)

It was a Sunday morning. The sun shone brightly and warmly into the room, as the air, mild and refreshing, flowed through the open window. And out under God's blue heaven, where fields and meadows were covered with greens and flowers, all the little birds rejoiced. While joy and contentment were everywhere outside, in the house lived sorrow and misery. Even the wife, who otherwise always was in good spirits, sat that morning at the breakfast table with a downcast expression; finally she arose, without having touched a bite of her food, dried her eyes, and walked toward the door.

It really seemed as if there were a curse hanging over this house. The cost of living was high, the food supply low; taxes had become heavier and heavier; year after year the household belongings had depreciated more and more, and now at last there was nothing to look forward to but poverty and misery. For a long time all this had depressed the husband, who always had been a hard-working and law-abiding citizen; now the thought of the future filled him with despair; yes, many times he even threatened to end his miserable and hopeless existence. Neither the comforting words of his good-humored wife nor the worldly or spiritual counsel of his friends had helped him; these had only made him more silent and sorrowful. It is easy to understand that his poor wife finally should lose her courage, too. However, there was quite another reason for her sadness, which we soon shall hear.

When the husband saw that his wife also grieved and wanted to leave the room, he stopped her and said, "I won't let you go until you have told me what is wrong with you!"

After a moment of silence, she sighed and said, "Oh, my dear husband, I dreamed last night that God was dead, and that all the angels followed Him to His grave!"

"How can you believe or think such foolish stuff!" answered the husband. "You know, of course, that God can never die!"

The good wife's face sparkled with happiness, and as she affectionately squeezed both her husband's hands, she exclaimed, "Then our dear God is still alive!"

"Why, of course," said the husband. "How could you ever doubt it!"

Then she embraced him, and looked at him with loving eyes, expressing confidence, peace, and happiness, as she said, "But, my dear husband, if God is still alive, why do we not believe and trust in Him! He has counted every hair on our heads; not a single one is lost without His knowledge. He clothes the lilies in the field; He feeds the sparrows and the ravens."

It was as if a veil lifted from his eyes and as if a heavy load fell from his heart when she spoke these words. He smiled for the first time in a long while, and thanked his dear, pious wife for the trick she had played on him, through which she had revived his belief in God and restored his trust. And in the room the sun shone even more friendly on the happy people's faces; a gentle breeze caressed their smiling cheeks, and the birds sang even louder their heartfelt thanks to God.

THE TALISMAN (1836)

A prince and a princess were still celebrating their honeymoon. They were extremely happy; only one thought disturbed them, and that was how to retain their present happiness. For that reason, they wished to own a talisman with which to protect themselves against any unhappiness in their marriage.

Now, they had often been told about a man who lived out in the forest, acclaimed by everybody for his wisdom and known for his good advice in every need and difficulty. So the prince and princess called upon him and told him about their heart's desire. After the wise man had listened to them, he said, "Travel through every country in the world, and wherever you meet a completely happily married couple, ask them for a small piece of the linen they wear close to the body, and when you receive this, you must always carry it on you. That is a sure remedy!"

The prince and the princess rode forth, and on their way, they soon heard of a knight and his wife who were said to be living the most happily married life. They went to the knight's castle and asked him and his wife if their marriage was truly as happy as was rumored.

"Yes, of course," was the answer, "with the one exception that we have no children!"

Here, then, the talisman was not to be found, and the prince and princess continued their journey in search of the completely happily married couple.

As they traveled on, they came to a country where they heard of an honest citizen who lived in perfect unity and happiness with his wife. So to him they went, and asked if he really was as happily married as people said.

"Yes, I am," answered the man. "My wife and I live in perfect harmony; if only we didn't have so many children, for they give us a lot of worries and sorrows!"

So neither with him was the talisman to be found, and the prince and the princess continued their journey through the country, always inquiring about happily married couples; but none presented themselves.

One day, as they rode along fields and meadows, they noticed a shepherd close by the road, cheerfully playing his flute. Just then, a woman carrying a child in her arm, and holding a little boy by the hand, walked toward him. As soon as the shepherd saw her, he greeted her and took the little child, whom he kissed and caressed. The shepherd's dog ran to the boy, licked his little hand, and barked and jumped with joy. In the meantime, the woman arranged a meal she had brought along, and then said, "Father, come and eat now!" The man sat down and took of the food, but the first bite he gave to the little boy, and the second he divided between the boy and the dog. All this was observed by the prince and the princess, who walked closer, and spoke to them, saying, "You must be a truly happily married couple."

"Yes, that we are," said the man. "God be praised; no prince or princess could be happier than we are!"

"Now listen then," said the prince. "Do us a favor, and you shall never regret it. Give us a small piece of the linen garment you wear close to your body!"

As he spoke, the shepherd and his wife looked strangely at each other, and finally he said, "God knows we would be only too happy to give you not only a small piece, but the whole shirt, or undergarment, if we only had them, but we own not as much as a rag!"

So the prince and the princess journeyed on, their mission unaccomplished. Finally, their unsuccessful roaming discouraged them, and they decided to return home. As they passed the wise man's hut, they stopped by, related all their travel experiences, and reproached him for giving them such poor advice.

At that, the wise man smiled and said, "Has your trip really been all in vain? Are you not returning richer in knowledge?"

"Yes," answered the prince, "I have gained *this* knowledge, that contentment is a rare gift on this earth."

"And I have learned," said the princess, "that to be contented, one needs nothing more than simply—to be contented!"

Whereupon the prince took the princess's hand; they looked at each other with an expression of deepest love. And the wise man blessed them and said, "In your own hearts, you have found the true talisman! Guard it carefully, and the evil spirit of discontentment shall never in all eternity have any power over you!"

THIS FABLE IS INTENDED FOR YOU (1836)

Wise men of ancient times ingeniously discovered how to tell people the truth without being blunt to their faces. You see, they held a magic mirror before the people, in which all sorts of animals and various wondrous things appeared, producing amusing as well as instructive pictures. They called these fables, and whatever wise or foolish deeds the animals performed, the people were to imagine themselves in their places and thereby think, "This fable is intended for you!" In this way, no one's feelings were hurt. Let us give you an example.

There were two high mountains, and at the top of each stood a castle. In the valley below ran a hungry dog, sniffing along the ground as if in search of mice or quail. Suddenly, a trumpet sounded from one of the castles, to announce that mealtime was approaching. The dog immediately started running up the mountain, hoping to get his share; but when he was halfway up, the trumpeter ceased blowing, and a trumpet from the other castle commenced. "Up here," thought the dog, "they will have finished eating before I arrive, but over there, they are just getting ready to eat." So he ran down, and up the other mountain. But now the first trumpet started again, while the second stopped. The dog ran down again, and up again; and this he continued until both trumpets stopped blowing, and the meals were over in both castles.

Now guess what the wise men of ancient times would have said about this fable, and who the fool could be who runs himself ragged without gaining anything, either here or there?

THE LITTLE MERMAID (1837)

Far out in the ocean, the water is as blue as the petals of the loveliest cornflower, and as clear as the purest glass. But it is very deep, too. It goes down deeper than any anchor rope will go, and many, many steeples would have to be stacked one on top of another to reach from the bottom to the surface of the sea. It is down there that the sea folk live.

Now don't suppose that there are only bare white sands at the bottom of the sea. No indeed! The most marvelous trees and flowers grow down there, with such pliant stalks and leaves that the least stir in the water makes them move about as though they were alive. All sorts of fish, large and small, dart among the branches, just as birds flit through the trees up here. From the deepest spot in the ocean rises the palace of the sea king. Its walls are made of coral and its high pointed windows of the clearest amber, but the roof is made of mussel shells that open and shut with the tide. This is a wonderful sight to see, for every shell holds glistening pearls, any one of which would be the pride of a queen's crown.

The sea king down there had been a widower for years, and his old mother kept house for him. She was a clever woman, but very proud of her noble birth. Therefore, she flaunted twelve oysters on her tail while the other ladies of the court were only allowed to wear six. Except for this, she was an altogether praiseworthy person, particularly so because she was extremely fond of her granddaughters, the little sea princesses. They were six lovely girls, but the youngest was the most beautiful of them all. Her skin was as soft and tender as a rose petal, and her eyes were as blue as the deep sea, but like all the others, she had no feet. Her body ended in a fish tail.

The whole day long they used to play in the palace, down in the great halls where live flowers grew on the walls. Whenever the high amber windows were thrown open, the fish would swim in, just as swallows dart into our rooms when we open the windows. But these fish, now, would swim right up to the little princesses to eat out of their hands and let themselves be petted.

Outside the palace was a big garden, with flaming red and deep-blue trees. Their fruit glittered like gold, and their blossoms flamed like fire on their constantly waving stalks. The soil was very fine sand indeed, but as blue as burning brimstone. A strange blue veil lay over everything down there. You would have thought yourself aloft in the air with only the blue sky above and beneath you, rather than down at the bottom of the sea. When there was a dead calm, you could just see the Sun, like a scarlet flower with light streaming from its calyx.

Each little princess had her own small garden plot, where she could dig and plant whatever she liked. One of them made her little flower bed in the shape of a whale, another thought it neater to shape hers like a little mermaid, but the youngest of them made hers as round as the Sun, and there she grew only flowers that were as red as the Sun itself. She was an unusual child, quiet and wistful, and when her sisters decorated their gardens with all kinds of odd things they had found in sunken ships, she would allow nothing in hers except flowers as red as the Sun, and a pretty marble statue. This figure of a handsome boy, carved in pure white marble, had sunk down to the bottom of the sea from some ship that was wrecked. Beside the statue, she planted a rose-colored weeping willow tree, which thrived so well that its graceful branches shaded the statue and hung down to the blue sand, where their shadows took on a violet tint, and swayed as the branches swayed. It looked as if the roots and the tips of the branches were kissing each other in play.

Nothing gave the youngest princess such pleasure as to hear about the world of human beings up above them. Her old grandmother had to tell her all she knew about ships and cities, and of people and animals. What seemed nicest of all to her was that up on land, the flowers were fragrant, for those at the bottom of the sea had no scent. And she thought it was nice that the woods were green, and that the fish you saw among their branches could sing so loud and sweet that it was delightful to hear them. Her grandmother had to call the little birds "fish," or the princess would not have known what she was talking about, for she had never seen a bird.

"When you get to be fifteen," her grandmother said, "you will be allowed to rise up out of the ocean and sit on the rocks in the moonlight, to watch the great ships sailing by. You will see woods and towns, too."

Next year one of her sisters would be fifteen, but the others—well, since each was a whole year older than the next, the youngest still had five long years to wait until she could rise up from the water and see what our world was like. But each sister promised to tell the others about all that she saw and what she found most marvelous on her first day. Their grandmother had not told them half enough, and there were so many thing that they longed to know about.

The most eager of them all was the youngest, the very one who was so quiet and wistful. Many a night she stood by her open window and looked up through the dark blue water where the fish waved their fins and tails. She could just see the moon and stars. To be sure, their light was quite dim, but looked at through the water, they seemed much bigger than they appear to us. Whenever a cloudlike shadow swept across them, she knew that it was either a whale swimming overhead or a ship with many human beings aboard it. Little did they dream that a pretty young mermaid was down below, stretching her white arms up toward the keel of their ship.

The eldest princess had her fifteenth birthday, so now she received permission to rise up out of the water. When she got back, she had a hundred things to tell her sisters about, but the most marvelous thing of all, she said, was to lie on a sand bar in the moonlight, when the sea was calm, and to gaze at the large city on the shore, where the lights twinkled like hundreds of stars; to listen to music; to hear the chatter and clamor of carriages and people; to see so many church towers and spires; and to hear the ringing bells. Because she could not enter the city, that was just what she most dearly longed to do.

Oh, how intently the youngest sister listened. After this, whenever she stood at her open window at night and looked up through the dark blue waters, she thought of that great city with all of its clatter and clamor, and even fancied that in these depths she could hear the church bells ring.

The next year, her second sister had permission to rise up to the surface and swim wherever she pleased. She came up just at sunset, and she said that this spectacle was the most marvelous sight she had ever seen. The heavens had a golden glow, and as for the clouds—she could not find words to describe their beauty. Splashed with red and tinted with violet, they sailed over her head. But much faster than the sailing clouds were wild swans in a flock. Like a long white veil trailing above the sea, they flew toward the setting sun. She too swam toward it, but down it went, and all the rose-colored glow faded from the sea and sky.

The following year, her third sister ascended, and as she was the boldest of them all, she swam up a broad river that flowed into the ocean. She saw gloriously green, vine-colored hills. Palaces and manor houses could be glimpsed through the splendid woods. She heard all the birds sing, and the sun shone so brightly that often she had to dive under the water to cool her burning face. In a small cove, she found a whole school of mortal children, paddling about in the water quite naked. She wanted to play with them, but they took fright and ran away. Then along came a little black animal— it was a dog, but she had never seen a dog before. It barked at her so ferociously that she took fright herself, and fled to the open sea. But never could she forget the splendid woods, the green hills, and the nice children who could swim in the water although they didn't wear fish tails.

The fourth sister was not so venturesome. She stayed far out among the rough waves, which she said was a marvelous place. You could see all around you for miles and miles, and the heavens up above you were like a vast dome of glass. She had seen ships, but they were so far away that they looked like sea gulls. Playful dolphins had turned somersaults, and monstrous whales had spouted water through their nostrils so that it looked as if hundreds of fountains were playing all around them.

Now the fifth sister had her turn. Her birthday came in the wintertime, so she saw things that none of the others had seen. The sea was a deep green color, and enormous icebergs drifted about. Each one glistened like a pearl, she said, but they were more lofty than any church steeple built by man. They assumed the most fantastic shapes, and sparkled like diamonds. She had seated herself on the largest one, and all the ships that came sailing by sped away as soon as the frightened sailors saw her there with her long hair blowing in the wind.

In the late evening, clouds filled the sky. Thunder cracked and lightning darted across the heavens. Black waves lifted those great bergs of ice on high, where they flashed when the lightning struck.

On all the ships the sails were reefed, and there was fear and trembling. But quietly she sat there, upon her drifting iceberg, and watched the blue forked lightning strike the sea.

Each of the sisters took delight in the lovely new sights when she first rose up to the surface of the sea. But when they became grown-up girls who were allowed to go wherever they liked, they became indifferent to it. They would become homesick, and in a month, they said that there was no place like the bottom of the sea, where they felt so completely at home.

On many an evening, the older sisters would rise to the surface, arm in arm, all five in a row. They had beautiful voices, more charming than those of any mortal beings. When a storm was brewing, and they anticipated a shipwreck, they would swim before the ship and sing most seductively of how beautiful it was at the bottom of the ocean, trying to overcome the prejudice that the sailors had against coming down to them. But people could not understand their song, and mistook it for the voice of the storm. Nor was it for them to see the glories of the deep. When their ship went down, they were drowned, and it was as dead men that they reached the sea king's palace.

On the evenings when the mermaids rose through the water like this, arm in arm, their youngest sister stayed behind all alone, looking after them and wanting to weep. But a mermaid has no tears, and therefore she suffers so much more.

"Oh, how I do wish I were fifteen!" she said. "I know I shall love that world up there and all the people who live in it."

And at last she too came to be fifteen.

"Now I'll have you off my hands," said her grandmother, the old queen dowager. "Come, let me adorn you like your sisters." In the little maid's hair she put a wreath of white lilies, each petal of which was formed from half of a pearl. And the old queen let eight big oysters fasten themselves to the princess's tail, as a sign of her high rank.

"But that hurts!" said the little mermaid.

"You must put up with a good deal to keep up appearances," her grandmother said.

Oh, how gladly she would have shaken off all these decorations, and laid aside the cumbersome wreath! The red flowers in her garden were much more becoming to her, but she didn't dare to make any changes. "Good-bye," she said, and up she went through the water, as light and as sparkling as a bubble.

The sun had just gone down when her head rose above the surface, but the clouds still shone like gold and roses, and in the delicately tinted sky sparkled the clear gleam of the evening star. The air was mild and fresh and the sea unruffled. A great three-master lay in view with only one of all its sails set, for there was not even the whisper of a breeze, and the sailors idled about in the rigging and on the yards. There was music and singing on the ship, and as night came on, they lighted hundreds of such brightly colored lanterns that one might have thought the flags of all nations were swinging in the air.

The little mermaid swam right up to the window of the main cabin, and each time she rose with the swell, she could peep in through the clear glass panes at the crowd of brilliantly dressed people within. The handsomest of them all was a young prince with big dark eyes. He could not be more than sixteen years old. It was his birthday, and that was the reason for all the celebration. Up on deck, the sailors were dancing, and when the prince appeared among them, a hundred or more rockets flew through the air, making it as bright as day. These startled the little mermaid so badly that she ducked under the water. But she soon peeped up again, and then it seemed as if all the stars in the sky were falling around her. Never had she seen such fireworks. Great suns spun around, splendid fire-fish floated through the blue air, and all these things were mirrored in the crystal clear sea. It was so brilliantly bright that you could see every little rope of the ship, and the people could be seen distinctly. Oh, how handsome the young prince was! He laughed, and he smiled and shook people by the hand, while the music rang out in the perfect evening.

It got very late, but the little mermaid could not take her eyes off the ship and the handsome prince. The brightly colored lanterns were put out, no more rockets flew through the air, and no more cannons boomed. But there was a mutter and rumble deep down in the sea, and the swell kept bouncing her up so high that she could look into the cabin.

Now the ship began to sail. Canvas after canvas was spread in the wind, the waves rose high, great clouds gathered, and lightning flashed in the distance. Ah, they were in for a terrible storm, and the mariners made haste to reef the sails. The tall ship pitched and rolled as it sped through the angry sea. The waves rose up like towering black mountains, as if they would break over the masthead, but the swanlike ship plunged into the valleys between such waves and emerged to ride their lofty heights. To the little mermaid, this seemed good sport, but to the sailors, it was nothing of the sort. The ship creaked and labored, thick timbers gave way under the heavy blows, waves broke over the ship, the mainmast snapped in two like a reed, the ship listed over on its side, and water burst into the hold.

Now the little mermaid saw that people were in peril, and that she herself must take care to avoid the beams and wreckage tossed about by the sea. One moment, it would be black as pitch, and she couldn't see a thing. Next moment, the lightning would flash so brightly that she could distinguish every soul on board. Everyone was looking out for himself as best he could. She watched closely for the young prince, and when the ship split in two, she saw him sink down in the sea. At first, she was overjoyed that he would be with her, but then she recalled that human people could not live under the water, and he could only visit her father's palace as a dead man. No, he should not die! So she swam in among all the floating planks and beams, completely forgetting that they might crush her. She dived through the waves and rode their crests, until at length she reached the young prince, who was no longer able to swim in that raging sea. His arms and legs were exhausted, his beautiful eyes were closing, and he would have died if the little mermaid had not come to help him. She held his head above water, and let the waves take them wherever the waves went.

At daybreak, when the storm was over, not a trace of the ship was in view. The sun rose out of the waters, red and bright, and its beams seemed to bring the glow of life back to the cheeks of the prince, but his eyes remained closed. The mermaid kissed his high and shapely forehead. As she stroked his wet hair in place, it seemed to her that he looked like that marble statue in her little garden. She kissed him again and hoped that he would live.

She saw dry land rise before her in high blue mountains, topped with snow as glistening white as if a flock of swans were resting there. Down by the shore were splendid green woods, and in the foreground stood a church, or perhaps a convent; she didn't know which, but anyway it was a building. Orange and lemon trees grew in its garden, and tall palm trees grew beside the gateway. Here the sea formed a little harbor, quite calm and very deep. Fine white sand had been washed up below the cliffs. She swam there with the handsome prince, and stretched him out on the sand, taking special care to pillow his head up high in the warm sunlight.

The bells began to ring in the great white building, and a number of young girls came out into the garden. The little mermaid swam away behind some tall rocks that stuck out of the water. She covered her hair and her shoulders with foam so that no one could see her tiny face, and then she watched to see who would find the poor prince.

In a little while, one of the young girls came upon him. She seemed frightened, but only for a minute; then she called more people. The mermaid watched the prince regain consciousness, and smile at everyone around him. But he did not smile at her, for he did not even know that she had saved him. She felt very unhappy, and when they led him away to the big building, she dived sadly down into the water and returned to her father's palace.

She had always been quiet and wistful, and now she became much more so. Her sisters asked her what she had seen on her first visit up to the surface, but she would not tell them a thing.

Many evenings and many mornings, she revisited the spot where she had left the prince. She saw the fruit in the garden ripened and harvested, and she saw the snow on the high mountain melted away, but she did not see the prince, so each time she came home sadder than she had left. It was her one consolation to sit in her little garden and throw her arms about the beautiful marble statue that looked so much like the prince. But she took no care of her flowers now. They overgrew the paths until the place was a wilderness, and their long stalks and leaves became so entangled in the branches of the tree that it cast a gloomy shade.

Finally, she couldn't bear it any longer. She told her secret to one of her sisters. Immediately, all the other sisters heard about it. No one else knew, except a few more mermaids who told no one—except their most intimate friends. One of these friends knew who the prince was. She too had seen the birthday celebration on the ship. She knew where he came from and where his kingdom was.

"Come, little sister!" said the other princesses. Arm in arm, they rose from the water in a long row, right in front of where they knew the prince's palace stood. It was built of pale, glistening, golden stone with great marble staircases, one of which led down to the sea. Magnificent gilt domes rose above the roof, and between the pillars all around the building were marble statues that looked most lifelike. Through the clear glass of the lofty windows one could see into the splendid halls, with their costly silk hangings and tapestries and walls covered with paintings that were delightful to behold. In the center of the main hall a large fountain played its columns of spray up to the glass-domed roof, through which the sun shone down on the water and upon the lovely plants that grew in the big basin.

Now that she knew where he lived, many an evening and many a night she spent there in the sea. She swam much closer to shore than any of her sisters would dare venture, and she even went far up a narrow stream, under the splendid marble balcony that cast its long shadow in the water. Here she used to sit and watch the young prince when he thought himself quite alone in the bright moonlight.

On many evenings, she saw him sail out in his fine boat, with music playing and flags aflutter. She would peep out through the green rushes, and if the wind blew her long silver veil, anyone who saw it mistook it for a swan spreading its wings.

On many nights, she saw the fishermen come out to sea with their torches, and heard them tell about how kind the young prince was. This made her proud to think that it was she who had saved his life when he was buffeted about, half dead among the waves. And she thought of how softly his head had rested on her breast, and how tenderly she had kissed him, though he knew nothing of all this nor could he even dream of it.

Increasingly, she grew to like human beings, and more and more, she longed to live among them. Their world seemed so much wider than her own, for they could skim over the sea in ships, and mount up into the lofty peaks high over the clouds, and their lands stretched out in woods and fields farther than the eye could see. There was so much she wanted to know. Her sisters could not answer all her questions, so she asked her old grandmother, who knew about the "upper world," which was what she said was the right name for the countries above the sea.

"If men aren't drowned," the little mermaid asked, "do they live on forever? Don't they die, as we do down here in the sea?"

"Yes," the old lady said, "they too must die, and their lifetimes are even shorter than ours. We can live to be three hundred years old, but when we perish, we turn into mere foam on the sea, and haven't even a grave down here among our dear ones. We have no immortal soul, no life hereafter. We are like the green seaweed—once cut down, it never grows again. Human beings, on the contrary, have a soul that lives forever, long after their bodies have turned to clay. It rises through thin air, up to the shining stars. Just as we rise through the water to see the lands on earth, so men rise up to beautiful places unknown, which we shall never see."

"Why weren't we given an immortal soul?" the little mermaid sadly asked. "I would gladly give up my three hundred years if I could be a human being only for a day, and later share in that heavenly realm."

"You must not think about that," said the old lady. "We fare much more happily and are much better off than the folk up there."

"Then I must also die and float as foam upon the sea, not hearing the music of the waves, and seeing neither the beautiful flowers nor the red Sun! Can't I do anything at all to win an immortal soul?"

"No," her grandmother answered, "not unless a human being loved you so much that you meant more to him than his father and mother. If his every thought and his whole heart cleaved to you so that he would let a priest join his right hand to yours and would promise to be faithful here and throughout all eternity, then his soul would dwell in your body, and you would share in the happiness of mankind. He would give you a soul and yet keep his own. But that can never come to pass. The very thing that is your greatest beauty here in the sea—your fish tail—would be considered ugly on land. They have such poor taste that to be thought beautiful there you have to have two awkward props that they call legs."

The little mermaid sighed and looked unhappily at her fish tail.

"Come, let us be gay!" the old lady said. "Let us leap and bound throughout the three hundred years that we have to live. Surely that is time and to spare, and afterwards we shall be glad enough to rest in our graves. We are holding a court ball this evening."

This was a much more glorious affair than is ever to be seen on earth. The walls and the ceiling of the great ballroom were made of massive but transparent glass. Many hundreds of huge rose-red and grass-green shells stood on each side in rows, with the blue flames that burned in each shell illuminating the whole room and shining through the walls so clearly that it was quite bright in the sea outside. You could see the countless fish, great and small, swimming toward the glass walls. On some of them, the scales gleamed purplish-red, while others were silver and gold. Across the floor of the hall ran a wide stream of water, and upon this the mermaids and mermen danced to their own entrancing songs. Such beautiful voices are not to be heard among the people who live on land. The little mermaid sang more sweetly than anyone else, and everyone applauded her. For a moment her heart was happy, because she knew she had the loveliest voice of all, in the sea or on the land. But her thoughts soon strayed to the world up above. She could not forget the charming prince, nor her sorrow that she did not have an immortal soul like his. Therefore, she stole out of her father's palace, and, while everything there was song and gladness, she sat sadly in her own little garden.

Then she heard a bugle call through the water, and she thought, "That must mean he is sailing up there, he whom I love more than my father or mother, he of whom I am always thinking, and in whose hands I would so willingly trust my lifelong happiness. I dare do anything to win him and to gain an immortal soul. While my sisters are dancing here, in my father's palace, I shall visit the sea witch of whom I have always been so afraid. Perhaps she will be able to advise me and help me."

The little mermaid set out from her garden toward the whirlpools that raged in front of the witch's dwelling. She had never gone that way before. No flowers grew there, nor any seaweed. Bare and gray, the sands extended to the whirlpools, where like roaring mill wheels the waters whirled and snatched everything within their reach down to the bottom of the sea. Between these tumultuous whirlpools, she had to thread her way to reach the witch's waters, and then for a long stretch, the only trail lay through a hot seething mire, which the witch called her peat marsh. Beyond it, her house lay in the middle of a weird forest, where all the trees and shrubs were polyps, half animal and half plant. They looked like hundred-headed snakes growing out of the soil. All their branches were long, slimy arms, with fingers like wriggling worms. They squirmed, joint by joint, from their roots to their outermost tentacles, and whatever they could lay hold of, they twined around and never let go. The little mermaid was terrified, and stopped at the edge of the forest. Her heart thumped with fear, and she nearly turned back, but then she remembered the prince and the souls that men have, and she summoned her courage. She bound her long flowing locks closely about her head so that the polyps could not catch hold of them, folded her arms across her breast, and darted through the water like a fish, in among the slimy polyps that stretched out their writhing arms and fingers to seize her. She saw that every one of them held something that it had caught with its hundreds of little tentacles, and to which it clung as with strong hoops of steel. The white bones of men who had perished at sea and sunk to these depths could be seen in the polyps' arms. Ships' rudders, and seamen's chests, and the skeletons of land animals had also fallen into their clutches, but the most ghastly sight of all was a little mermaid whom they had caught and strangled.

She reached a large muddy clearing in the forest, where big fat water snakes slithered about, showing their foul yellowish bellies. In the middle of this clearing was a house built of the bones of shipwrecked men, and there sat the sea witch, letting a toad eat out of her mouth just as we might feed sugar to a little canary bird. She called the ugly fat water snakes her little chickabiddies, and let them crawl and sprawl about on her spongy bosom.

"I know exactly what you want," said the sea witch. "It is very foolish of you, but just the same, you shall have your way, for it will bring you to grief, my proud princess. You want to get rid of your fish tail and have two props instead, so that you can walk about like a human creature, and have the young prince fall in love with you, and win him and an immortal soul besides." At this, the witch gave such a loud cackling laugh that the toad and the snakes were shaken to the ground, where they lay writhing.

"You are just in time," said the witch. "After the sun comes up tomorrow, a whole year would have to go by before I could be of any help to you. I shall compound you a draught, and before sunrise, you must swim to the shore with it, seat yourself on dry land, and drink the draught down. Then your tail will divide and shrink until it becomes what the people on Earth call a pair of shapely legs. But it will hurt; it will feel as if a sharp sword slashed through you. Everyone who sees you will say that you are the most graceful human being they have ever laid eyes on, for you will keep your gliding movement and no dancer will be able to tread as lightly as you. But every step you take will feel as if you were treading upon knife blades so sharp that blood must flow. I am willing to help you, but are you willing to suffer all this?"

"Yes," the little mermaid said in a trembling voice, as she thought of the prince and of gaining a human soul.

"Remember!" said the witch. "Once you have taken a human form, you can never be a mermaid again. You can never come back through the waters to your sisters, or to your father's palace. And if you do not win the love of the prince so completely that for your sake he forgets his father and mother, cleaves to you with his every thought and his whole heart, and lets the priest join your hands in marriage, then you will win no immortal soul. If he marries someone else, your heart will break on the very next morning, and you will become foam of the sea."

"I shall take that risk," said the little mermaid, but she turned as pale as death.

"Also, you will have to pay me," said the witch, "and it is no trifling price that I'm asking. You have the sweetest voice of anyone down here at the bottom of the sea, and while I don't doubt that you would like to captivate the prince with it, you must give this voice to me. I will take the very best thing that you have in return for my sovereign draught. I must pour my own blood in it to make the drink as sharp as a two-edged sword."

"But if you take my voice," said the little mermaid, "what will be left to me?"

"Your lovely form," the witch told her, "your gliding movements, and your eloquent eyes. With these, you can easily enchant a human heart. Well, have you lost your courage? Stick out your little tongue, and I shall cut it off. I'll have my price, and you shall have the potent draught."

"Go ahead," said the little mermaid.

The witch hung her caldron over the flames, to brew the draught. "Cleanliness is a good thing," she said, as she tied her snakes in a knot and scoured out the pot with them. Then she pricked herself in the chest and let her black blood splash into the caldron. Steam swirled up from it in such ghastly shapes that anyone would have been terrified by them. The witch constantly threw new ingredients into the caldron, and it started to boil with a sound like that of a crocodile shedding tears. When the draught was ready at last, it looked as clear as the purest water.

"There's your draught," said the witch. And she cut off the tongue of the little mermaid, who now was dumb and could neither sing nor talk.

"If the polyps should pounce on you when you walk back through my wood," the witch said, "just spill a drop of this brew upon them and their tentacles will break in a thousand pieces." But there was no need of that, for the polyps curled up in terror as soon as they saw the bright draught. It glittered in the little mermaid's hand as if it were a shining star. So she soon traversed the forest, the marsh, and the place of raging whirlpools.

She could see her father's palace. The lights had been snuffed out in the great ballroom, and doubtless everyone in the palace was asleep, but she dared not go near them, now that she was stricken dumb and was leaving her home forever. Her heart felt as if it would break with grief. She tiptoed into the garden, took one flower from each of her sisters' little plots, blew a thousand kisses toward the palace, and then mounted up through the dark blue sea.

The sun had not yet risen when she saw the prince's palace. As she climbed his splendid marble staircase, the moon was shining clear. The little mermaid swallowed the bitter, fiery draught, and it was as if a two-edged sword struck through her frail body. She swooned away, and lay there as if she were dead. When the sun rose over the sea, she awoke and felt a flash of pain, but directly in front of her stood the handsome young prince, gazing at her with his coal-black eyes. Lowering her gaze, she saw that her fish tail was gone and that she had the loveliest pair of white legs any young maid could hope to have. But she was naked, so she clothed herself in her own long hair.

The prince asked who she was and how she came to be there. Her deep blue eyes looked at him tenderly but very sadly, for she could not speak. Then he took her hand and led her into his palace. Every footstep felt as if she were walking on the blades and points of sharp knives, just as the witch had foretold, but she gladly endured it. She moved as lightly as a bubble as she walked beside the prince. He and all who saw her marveled at the grace of her gliding walk.

Once clad in the rich silk and muslin garments that were provided for her, she was the loveliest person in all the palace, though she was dumb and could neither sing nor speak. Beautiful slaves attired in silk and cloth of gold came to sing before the prince and his royal parents. One of them sang more sweetly than all the others, and when the prince smiled at her and clapped his hands, the little mermaid felt very unhappy, for she knew that she herself used to sing much more sweetly.

"Oh," she thought, "if he only knew that I parted with my voice forever so that I could be near him."

Graceful slaves now began to dance to the most wonderful music. Then the little mermaid lifted her shapely white arms, rose up on the tips of her toes, and skimmed over the floor. No one had ever danced so well. Each movement set off her beauty to better and better advantage, and her eyes spoke more directly to the heart than any of the singing slaves could do.

She charmed everyone, and especially the prince, who called her his dear little foundling. She danced time and again, though every time she touched the floor she felt as if she were treading on sharp-edged steel. The prince said he would keep her with him always, and that she was to have a velvet pillow to sleep on outside his door.

He had a page's suit made for her, so that she could go with him on horseback. They would ride through the sweet-scented woods, where the green boughs brushed her shoulders and where the little birds sang among the fluttering leaves.

She climbed up high mountains with the prince, and though her tender feet bled so that all could see it, she only laughed and followed him on until they could see the clouds driving far below, like a flock of birds in flight to distant lands.

At home in the prince's palace, while the others slept at night, she would go down the broad marble steps to cool her burning feet in the cold sea water, and then she would recall those who lived beneath the sea. One night, her sisters came by, arm in arm, singing sadly as they breasted the waves. When she held out her hands toward them, they knew who she was, and told her how unhappy she had made them all. They came to see her every night after that, and once far, far out to sea, she saw her old grandmother, who had not been up to the surface this many a year. With her was the sea king, with his crown upon his head. They stretched out their hands to her, but they did not venture so near the land as her sisters had.

Day after day, she became more dear to the prince, who loved her as one would love a good little child, but he never thought of making her his queen. Yet she had to be his wife, or she would never have an immortal soul, and on the morning after his wedding, she would turn into foam on the waves.

"Don't you love me best of all?" the little mermaid's eyes seemed to question him, when he took her in his arms and kissed her lovely forehead.

"Yes, you are most dear to me," said the prince, "for you have the kindest heart. You love me more than anyone else does, and you look so much like a young girl I once saw but never shall find again. I was on a ship that was wrecked, and the waves cast me ashore near a holy temple, where many young girls performed the rituals. The youngest of them found me beside the sea and saved my life. Though I saw her no more than twice, she is the only person in all the world whom I could love. But you are so much like her that you almost replace the memory of her in my heart. She belongs to that holy temple; therefore, it is my good fortune that I have you. We shall never part."

"Alas, he doesn't know it was I who saved his life," the little mermaid thought. "I carried him over the sea to the garden where the temple stands. I hid behind the foam and watched to see if anyone would come. I saw the pretty maid he loves better than me." A sigh was the only sign of her deep distress, for a mermaid cannot cry. "He says that the other maid belongs to the holy temple. She will never come out into the world, so they will never see each other again. It is I who will care for him, love him, and give all my life to him."

Now rumors arose that the prince was to wed the beautiful daughter of a neighboring king, and that it was for this reason he was having such a superb ship made ready to sail. The rumor ran that the prince's real interest in visiting the neighboring kingdom was to see the king's daughter, and that he was to travel with a lordly retinue. The little mermaid shook her head and smiled, for she knew the prince's thoughts far better than anyone else did.

"I am forced to make this journey," he told her. "I must visit the beautiful princess, for this is my parents' wish, but they would not have me bring her home as my bride against my own will, and I can never love her. She does not resemble the lovely maiden in the temple, as you do, and if I were to choose a bride, I would sooner choose you, my dear mute foundling with those telling eyes of yours." And he kissed her on the mouth, fingered her long hair, and laid his head against her heart so that she came to dream of mortal happiness and an immortal soul.

"I trust you aren't afraid of the sea, my silent child," he said, as they went on board the magnificent vessel that was to carry them to the land of the neighboring king. And he told her stories of storms, of ships becalmed, of strange deep-sea fish, and of the wonders that divers have seen. She smiled at such stories, for no one knew about the bottom of the sea as well as she did.

In the clear moonlight, when everyone except the man at the helm was asleep, she sat on the side of the ship gazing down through the transparent water, and fancied she could catch glimpses of her father's palace. On the topmost tower stood her old grandmother, wearing her silver crown and looking up at the keel of the ship through the rushing waves. Then her sisters rose to the surface, looked at her sadly, and wrung their white hands. She smiled and waved, trying to let them know that all went well and that she was happy. But along came the cabin boy, and her sisters dived out of sight so quickly that the boy supposed the flash of white he had seen was merely foam on the sea.

Next morning, the ship came into the harbor of the neighboring king's glorious city. All the church bells chimed, and trumpets were sounded from all the high towers, while the soldiers lined up with flying banners and glittering bayonets. Every day had a new festivity, as one ball or levee followed another, but the princess was still to appear. They said she was being brought up in some faraway sacred temple, where she was learning every royal virtue. But she came at last.

The little mermaid was curious to see how beautiful this princess was, and she had to grant that a more exquisite figure she had never seen. The princess's skin was clear and fair, and behind the long, dark lashes, her deep blue eyes were smiling and devoted.

"It was you!" the prince cried. "You are the one who saved me when I lay like a dead man beside the sea." He clasped the blushing bride of his choice in his arms. "Oh, I am happier than a man should be!" he told his little mermaid. "My fondest dream—that which I never dared to hope—has come true. You will share in my great joy, for you love me more than anyone does."

The little mermaid kissed his hand and felt that her heart was beginning to break. For the morning after his wedding day would see her dead and turned to watery foam.

All the church bells rang out, and heralds rode through the streets to announce the wedding. Upon every altar, sweet-scented oils were burned in costly silver lamps. The priests swung their censers, the bride and the bridegroom joined their hands, and the bishop blessed their marriage. The little mermaid, clothed in silk and cloth of gold, held the bride's train, but she was deaf to the wedding march and blind to the holy ritual. Her thought turned on her last night upon earth, and on all she had lost in this world.

That same evening, the bride and bridegroom went aboard the ship. Cannons thundered and banners waved. On the deck of the ship, a royal pavilion of purple and gold was set up and furnished with luxurious cushions. Here the wedded couple were to sleep on that calm, clear night. The sails swelled in the breeze, and the ship glided so lightly that it scarcely seemed to move over the quiet sea. All nightfall, brightly colored lanterns were lighted, and the mariners merrily danced on the deck. The little mermaid could not forget that first time she rose from the depths of the sea and looked on at such pomp and happiness. Light as a swallow pursued by his enemies, she joined in the whirling dance. Everyone cheered her, for never had she danced so wonderfully. Her tender feet felt as if they were pierced by daggers, but she did not feel it. Her heart suffered far greater pain. She knew that this was the last evening that she ever would see him for whom she had forsaken her home and family, for whom she had sacrificed her lovely voice and suffered such constant torment, while he knew nothing of all these things. It was the last night that she would breathe the same air with him, or look upon deep waters or the star fields of the blue sky. A never-ending night, without thought and without dreams, awaited her who had no soul and could not get one. The merrymaking lasted long after midnight, yet she laughed and danced on despite the thought of death she carried in her heart. The prince kissed his beautiful bride, and she toyed with his coal-black hair. Hand in hand, they went to rest in the magnificent pavilion.

A hush came over the ship. Only the helmsman remained on deck as the little mermaid leaned her white arms on the bulwarks and looked to the east to see the first red hint of daybreak, for she knew that the first flash of the sun would strike her dead. Then she saw her sisters rise up among the waves. They were as pale as she, and there was no sign of their lovely long hair that the breezes used to blow. It had all been cut off.

"We have given our hair to the witch," they said, "so that she would send you help, and save you from death tonight. She gave us a knife. Here it is. See the sharp blade! Before the sun rises, you must strike it into the prince's heart, and when his warm blood bathes your feet, they will grow together and become a fish tail. Then you will be a mermaid again, able to come back to us in the sea, and live out your three hundred years before you die and turn into dead salt sea foam. Make haste! He or you must die before sunrise. Our old grandmother is so grief-stricken that her white hair is falling fast, just as ours did under the witch's scissors. Kill the prince and come back to us. Hurry! Hurry! See that red glow in the heavens! In a few minutes the sun will rise and you must die." So saying, they gave a strange deep sigh and sank beneath the waves.

The little mermaid parted the purple curtains of the tent and saw the beautiful bride asleep with her head on the prince's breast. The mermaid bent down and kissed his shapely forehead. She looked at the sky, fast reddening for the break of day. She looked at the sharp knife, and again turned her eyes toward the prince, who in his sleep murmured the name of his bride. His thoughts were all for her, and the knife blade trembled in the mermaid's hand. But then she flung it from her, far out over the waves. Where it fell the waves were red, as if bubbles of blood seethed in the water. With eyes already glazing she looked once more at the prince, hurled herself over the bulwarks into the sea, and felt her body dissolve in foam.

The sun rose up from the waters. Its beams fell, warm and kindly, upon the chill sea foam, and the little mermaid did not feel the hand of death. In the bright sunlight overhead, she saw hundreds of fair ethereal beings. They were so transparent that through them she could see the ship's white sails and the red clouds in the sky. Their voices were sheer music, but so spiritlike that no human ear could detect the sound, just as no eye on Earth could see their forms. Without wings, they floated as light as the air itself. The little mermaid discovered that she was shaped like them, and that she was gradually rising up out of the foam.

"Who are you, toward whom I rise?" she asked, and her voice sounded like those above her, so spiritual that no music on Earth could match it.

"We are the daughters of the air," they answered. "A mermaid has no immortal soul, and can never get one unless she wins the love of a human being. Her eternal life must depend upon a power outside herself. The daughters of the air do not have an immortal soul either, but they can earn one by their good deeds. We fly to the south, where the hot poisonous air kills human beings unless we bring cool breezes. We carry the scent of flowers through the air, bringing freshness and healing balm wherever we go. When for three hundred years we have tried to do all the good that we can, we are given an immortal soul and a share in mankind's eternal bliss. You, poor little mermaid, have tried with your whole heart to do this too. Your suffering and your loyalty have raised you up into the realm of airy spirits, and now in the course of three hundred years, you may earn by your good deeds a soul that will never die."

The little mermaid lifted her clear bright eyes toward God's Sun, and for the first time, her eyes were wet with tears.

On board the ship, all was astir and lively again. She saw the prince and his fair bride in search of her. Then they gazed sadly into the seething foam, as if they knew she had hurled herself into the waves. Unseen by them, she kissed the bride's forehead, smiled upon the prince, and rose up with the other daughters of the air to the rose-red clouds that sailed on high.

"This is the way that we shall rise to the Kingdom of God, after three hundred years have passed."

"We may get there even sooner," one spirit whispered. "Unseen, we fly into the homes of men, where there are children, and for every day on which we find a good child who pleases his parents and deserves their love, God shortens our days of trial. The child does not know when we float through his room, but when we smile at him in approval, one year is taken from our three hundred. But if we see a naughty, mischievous child, we must shed tears of sorrow, and each tear adds a day to the time of our trial."

THE EMPEROR'S NEW CLOTHES (1837)

Many years ago, there was an emperor so exceedingly fond of new clothes that he spent all his money on being well dressed. He cared nothing about reviewing his soldiers, going to the theater, or going for a ride in his carriage, except to show off his new clothes. He had a coat for every hour of the day, and instead of saying, as one might, about any other ruler, "The king's in council," here they always said, "The emperor's in his dressing room."

In the great city where he lived, life was always gay. Every day, many strangers came to town, and among them one day came two swindlers. They let it be known they were weavers, and they said they could weave the most magnificent fabrics imaginable. Not only were their colors and patterns uncommonly fine, but clothes made of this cloth had a wonderful way of becoming invisible to anyone who was unfit for his office, or who was unusually stupid.

"Those would be just the clothes for me," thought the emperor. "If I wore them, I would be able to discover which men in my empire are unfit for their posts. And I could tell the wise men from the fools. Yes, I certainly must get some of the stuff woven for me right away." He paid the two swindlers a large sum of money to start work at once.

They set up two looms and pretended to weave, though there was nothing on the looms. All the finest silk and the purest old thread that they demanded went into their traveling bags, while they worked the empty looms far into the night.

"I'd like to know how those weavers are getting on with the cloth," the emperor thought, but he felt slightly uncomfortable when he remembered that those who were unfit for their position would not be able to see the fabric. It couldn't have been that he doubted himself, yet he thought he'd rather send someone else to see how things were going. The whole town knew about the cloth's peculiar power, and all were impatient to find out how stupid their neighbors were.

"I'll send my honest old minister to the weavers," the emperor decided. "He'll be the best one to tell me how the material looks, for he's a sensible man, and no one does his duty better."

So the honest old minister went to the room where the two swindlers sat working away at their empty looms.

"Heaven help me," he thought as his eyes flew wide open, "I can't see anything at all." But he did not say so.

Both the swindlers begged him to be so kind as to come near to approve the excellent pattern, the beautiful colors. They pointed to the empty looms, and the poor old minister stared as hard as he dared. He couldn't see anything, because there was nothing to see. "Heaven have mercy," he thought. "Can it be that I'm a fool? I'd have never guessed it, and not a soul must know. Am I unfit to be the minister? It would never do to let on that I can't see the cloth."

"Don't hesitate to tell us what you think of it," said one of the weavers.

"Oh, it's beautiful—it's enchanting." The old minister peered through his spectacles. "Such a pattern, what colors! I'll be sure to tell the emperor how delighted I am with it."

"We're pleased to hear that," the swindlers said. They proceeded to name all the colors and to explain the intricate pattern. The old minister paid the closest attention, so that he could tell it all to the emperor. And so he did.

The swindlers at once asked for more money, more silk and gold thread, to get on with the weaving. But it all went into their pockets. Not a thread went into the looms, though they worked at their weaving as hard as ever.

The emperor presently sent another trustworthy official to see how the work progressed and how soon it would be ready. The same thing happened to him that had happened to the minister. He looked and he looked, but as there was nothing to see in the looms, he couldn't see anything.

"Isn't it a beautiful piece of goods?" the swindlers asked him, as they displayed and described their imaginary pattern.

"I know I'm not stupid," the man thought, "so it must be that I'm unworthy of my good office. That's strange. I mustn't let anyone find it out, though." So he praised the material he did not see. He declared he was delighted with the beautiful colors and the exquisite pattern. To the emperor he said, "It held me spellbound."

All the town was talking of this splendid cloth, and the emperor wanted to see it for himself while it was still in the looms. Attended by a band of chosen men, among whom were his two old trusted officials—the ones who had been to the weavers—he set out to see the two swindlers. He found them weaving with might and main, but without a thread in their looms.

"Magnificent," said the two duped officials. "Just look, Your Majesty, what colors! What a design!" They pointed to the empty looms, each supposing that the others could see the stuff.

"What's this?" thought the emperor. "I can't see anything. This is terrible! Am I a fool? Am I unfit to be the emperor? What a thing to happen to me of all people!—Oh!

It's *very* pretty," he said. "It has my highest approval." And he nodded approbation at the empty loom. Nothing could make him say that he couldn't see anything.

His whole retinue stared and stared. One saw no more than another, but they all joined the emperor in exclaiming, "Oh! It's *very* pretty," and they advised him to wear clothes made of this wonderful cloth especially for the great procession he was soon to lead. "Magnificent! Excellent! Unsurpassed!" were bandied from mouth to mouth, and everyone did his best to seem well pleased. The emperor gave each of the swindlers a cross to wear in his buttonhole, and the title of "Sir Weaver."

Before the procession, the swindlers sat up all night and burned more than six candles, to show how busy they were finishing the emperor's new clothes. They pretended to take the cloth off the loom. They made cuts in the air with huge scissors. And at last they said, "Now the emperor's new clothes are ready for him."

Then the emperor himself came with his noblest noblemen, and the swindlers each raised an arm as if they were holding something. They said, "These are the trousers, here's the coat, and this is the mantle," naming each garment. "All of them are as light as a spider web. One would almost think he had nothing on, but that's what makes them so fine."

"Exactly," all the noblemen agreed, though they could see nothing, for there was nothing to see.

"If Your Imperial Majesty will condescend to take your clothes off," said the swindlers, "we will help you on with your new ones here in front of the long mirror."

The emperor undressed, and the swindlers pretended to put his new clothes on him, one garment after another. They took him around the waist and seemed to be fastening something—that was his train—as the emperor turned round and round before the looking glass.

"How well Your Majesty's new clothes look. Aren't they becoming!" He heard on all sides, "That pattern, so perfect! Those colors, so suitable! It is a magnificent outfit."

Then the minister of public processions announced: "Your Majesty's canopy is waiting outside."

"Well, I'm supposed to be ready," the emperor said, and turned again for one last look in the mirror. "It is a remarkable fit, isn't it?" He seemed to regard his costume with the greatest interest.

The noblemen who were to carry his train stooped low and reached for the floor as if they were picking up his mantle. Then they pretended to lift and hold it high. They didn't dare admit they had nothing to hold.

So off went the emperor in procession under his splendid canopy. Everyone in the streets and the windows said, "Oh, how fine are the emperor's new clothes! Don't they fit him to perfection? And see his long train!" Nobody would confess that he couldn't see anything, for that would prove him either unfit for his position or a fool. No costume the emperor had worn before was ever such a complete success.

"But he hasn't got anything on," a little child said.

"Did you ever hear such innocent prattle?" said its father. And one person whispered to another what the child had said, "He hasn't anything on. A child says he hasn't anything on."

"But he hasn't got anything on!" the whole town cried out at last.

The emperor shivered, for he suspected they were right. But he thought, "This procession has got to go on." So he walked more proudly than ever, as his noblemen held high the train that wasn't there at all.

THE GALOSHES OF FORTUNE (1838)

I. A BEGINNING

It was in Copenhagen, in one of the houses on East Street, not far from King's Newmarket, that someone was giving a large party. For one must give a party once in a while, if one expects to be invited in return. Half of the guests were already at the card tables, and the rest were waiting to see what would come of their hostess's query: "What can we think up now?"

Up to this point, their conversation had gotten along as best it might. Among other things, they had spoken of the Middle Ages. Some held that it was a time far better than our own. Indeed, Councillor of Justice Knap defended this opinion with such spirit that his hostess sided with him at once, and both of them loudly took exception to Oersted's article in the *Almanac*, which contrasted old times and new, and which favored our own period. The Councillor of Justice, however, held that the time of King Hans, about 1500 AD, was the noblest and happiest age.

While the conversation ran pro and con, interrupted only for a moment by the arrival of a newspaper, in which there was nothing worth reading, let us adjourn to the cloak room, where all the wraps, canes, umbrellas, and galoshes were collected together. Here sat two maids, a young one and an old one. You might have thought they had come in attendance upon some spinster or widow and were waiting to see their mistress home. However, a closer inspection would reveal that these were no ordinary serving women. Their hands were too well kept for that, their bearing and movements too graceful, and their clothes had a certain daring cut.

They were two fairies. The younger one, though not Dame Fortune herself, was an assistant to one of her ladies-in-waiting, and was used to deliver the more trifling gifts of Fortune. The older one looked quite grave. She was Dame Care, who always goes in her own sublime person to see to her errands herself, for then she knows that they are well done.

They were telling each other about where they had been that day. The assistant of Fortune had only attended to a few minor affairs, she said, such as saving a new bonnet from the rain, getting a civil greeting for an honest man from an exalted nincompoop, and such like matters. But her remaining errand was an extraordinary one.

"I must also tell you," she said, "that today is my birthday, and in honor of this, I have been entrusted to bring a pair of galoshes to mankind. These galoshes have this peculiarity, that whoever puts them on will immediately find himself in whatever time, place, and condition of life that he prefers. His every wish in regard to time and place will instantly be granted, so for once, a man can find perfect happiness here below."

"Take my word for it," said Dame Care, "he will be most unhappy and will bless the moment when he can rid himself of those galoshes."

"How can you say such a thing?" the other woman exclaimed. "I shall leave them here beside the door, where someone will put them on by mistake and immediately be the happy one."

That ended their conversation.

II. WHAT HAPPENED TO THE COUNCILLOR OF JUSTICE

It was getting late when Councillor Knap decided to go home. Lost in thought about the good old days of King Hans, as fate would have it, he put on the galoshes of Fortune instead of his own and wore them out into East Street. But the power that lay in the galoshes took him back into the reign of King Hans, and as the streets were not paved in those days, his feet sank deep into the mud and the mire.

"Why, how deplorable!" the Councillor of Justice said. "The whole sidewalk is gone, and all the street lights are out."

As the moon had no yet risen high enough and the air was somewhat foggy, everything around him was dark and blurred. At the next corner, a lantern hung before an image of the Madonna, but for all the light it afforded him, it might as well not have been there. Only when he stood directly under it did he make out that painting of the mother and child.

"It's probably an art museum," he thought, "and they have forgotten to take in the sign."

Two people in medieval costumes passed by.

"How strange they looked!" he said. "They must have been to a masquerade."

Just then, the sound of drums and fifes came his way, and bright torches flared. The Councillor of Justice stopped and was startled to see an odd procession go past, led by a whole band of drummers who were dexterously drubbing away. These were followed by soldiers armed with long bows and crossbows. The chief personage of the procession was a churchman of rank. The astounded councillor asked what all this meant, and who the man might be.

"That is the Bishop of Seeland," he was told.

"What in the name of heaven can have come over the bishop?" the Councillor of Justice wondered. He sighed and shook his head. "The bishop? Impossible."

Still pondering about it, without glancing to right or to left, he kept on down East Street and across Highbridge Square. The bridge that led from there to Palace Square was not to be found at all; at last, on the bank of the shallow stream, he saw a boat with two men in it.

"Would the gentleman want to be ferried over to the Holm?" they asked him.

"To the Holm?" blurted the councillor, who had not the faintest notion that he was living in another age. "I want to go to Christian's Harbor on Little Market Street."

The men gaped at him.

"Kindly tell me where the bridge is," he said. "It's disgraceful that all the street lamps are out, and besides, it's as muddy to walk here as in a swamp." But the more he talked with the boatmen, the less they understood each other. "I can't understand your jabbering Bornholm accent," he finally said, and angrily turned his back on them. But no bridge could he find. Even the fence was gone.

"What a scandalous state of affairs! What a way for things to look!" he said. Never had he been so disgruntled with his own age as he was this evening. "I think I'd better take a cab." But where were the cabs? There were none in sight. "I'll have to go back to King's Newmarket, where there is a cab stand, or I shall never reach Christian's Harbor."

So back he trudged to East Street, and had nearly walked the length of it when the moon rose.

"Good Heavens, what have they been building here?" he cried as he beheld the East Gate, which in the old days stood at the end of East Street. In time, however, he found a gate through which he passed into what is now Newmarket. But all he saw there was a large meadow. A few bushes rose here and there, and the meadow was divided by a wide canal or stream. The few wretched wooden huts on the far shore belonged to Dutch sailors, so at that time the place was called Dutch Meadow.

"Either I'm seeing what is called Fata Morgana, or I'm drunk," the Councillor of Justice moaned. "What sort of place is this? Where am I?" He turned back, convinced that he must be a very ill man. As he walked through the street again, he paid more attention to the houses. Most of them were of wood, and many were thatched with straw.

"No, I don't feel myself at all," he complained. "I only took one glass of punch, but it doesn't agree with me. The idea of serving punch with hot salmon! I'll speak about it severely to our hostess—that agent's wife. Should I march straight back and tell her how I feel? No, that would be in bad taste, and besides, I doubt whether her household is still awake." He searched for the house, but wasn't able to find it.

"This is terrible!" he cried. "I don't even recognize East Street. There's not a shop to be seen; wretched old ramshackle huts are all I see, as if I were in Roskilde or Ringstedt. Oh, but I'm ill! There's no point in standing on ceremony, but where on Earth is the agent's house? This hut doesn't look remotely like it, but I can hear that the people inside are still awake. Ah, I'm indeed a very sick man."

He reached a half-open door, where light flickered through the crack. It was a tavern of that period—a sort of alehouse. The room had the look of a farmer's clay-floored kitchen in Holstein, and the people who sat there were sailors, citizens of Copenhagen, and a couple of scholars. Deep in conversation over their mugs, they paid little attention to the newcomer.

"Pardon me," the Councillor of Justice said to the landlady who came toward him, "but I am far from well. Would you send someone for a cab to take me to Christian's Harbor?"

The woman stared at him, shook her head, and addressed him in German. As the Councillor of Justice supposed that she could not speak Danish, he repeated his remarks in German. This, and the cut of his clothes, convinced the woman that he was a foreigner. She soon understood that he felt unwell, and fetched him a mug of water, decidedly brackish, for she drew it directly from the sea-level well outside. The councillor put his head in his hands, took a deep breath, and thought over all of the queer things that surrounded him.

"Is that tonight's number of *The Day*?" he remarked from force of habit, as he saw the woman putting away a large folded sheet.

Without quite understanding him, she handed him the paper. It was a woodcut, representing a meteor seen in the skies over Cologne.

"This is very old," said the councillor, who became quite enthusiastic about his discovery. "Where did you get this rare old print? It's most interesting, although of course the whole matter is a myth. In this day and age, such meteors are explained away as a manifestation of the northern lights, probably caused by electricity."

Those who sat near him heard the remark and looked at him in astonishment. One of them rose, respectfully doffed his hat, and said with the utmost gravity:

"Sir, you must be a great scholar."

"Not at all," replied the councillor. "I merely have a word or two to say about things that everyone should know."

"*Modestia* is an admirable virtue," the man declared. "In regard to your statement, I must say, *mihi secus videtur,* though I shall be happy to suspend my *judicium.*"

"May I ask whom I have the pleasure of addressing?" the Councillor of Justice inquired.

"I am a bachelor of theology," the man told him in Latin.

This answer satisfied the Councillor of Justice, for the degree was in harmony with the fellow's way of dressing. "Obviously," he thought, "this is some old village schoolmaster, an odd character such as one still comes across now and then, up in Jutland."

"This is scarcely a *locus docendi*," the man continued, "but I entreat you to favor us with your conversation. You, of course, are well read in the classics?"

"Oh, more or less," the councillor agreed. "I like to read the standard old books, and the new ones too, except for those 'Every Day Stories' of which we have enough in reality."

"Every Day Stories?" our bachelor asked.

"Yes, I mean these modern novels."

"Oh," the man said with a smile. "Still they are very clever, and are popular with the court. King Hans is particularly fond of the *Romance of Iwain and Jawain*, which deals with King Arthur and his Knights of the Round Table. The king has been known to jest with his lords about it."

"Well," said the councillor, "one can't keep up with all the new books. I suppose it has just been published by Heiberg."

"No," the man said, "not by Heiberg, but by Gotfred von Ghemen."

"Indeed! What a fine old name for a literary man. Why, Gotfred von Ghemen was the first printer in Denmark."

"Yes," the man agreed, "he is our first and foremost printer."

Thus far, their conversation had flowed quite smoothly. Now one of the townsmen began to talk about the pestilence that had raged some years back, meaning the plague of 1484. The councillor understood him to mean the last epidemic of cholera, so they agreed well enough.

The freebooter's war of 1490 was so recent that it could not be passed over. The English raiders had taken ships from our harbor, they said, and the Councillor of Justice, who was well posted on the affair of 1801, manfully helped them to abuse the English.

After that, however, the talk floundered from one contradiction to another. The worthy bachelor was so completely unenlightened that the councillor's most commonplace remarks struck him as being too daring and too fantastic. They stared at each other, and when they reached an impasse, the bachelor broke into Latin, in the hope that he would be better understood, but that didn't help.

The landlady plucked at the councillor's sleeve and asked him, "How do you feel now?" This forcibly recalled to him all of those things that he had happily forgotten in the heat of his conversation.

"Merciful heaven, where am I?" he wondered, and the thought made him dizzy.

"We will drink claret wine, and mead, and Bremen beer," one of the guests cried out, "and you shall drink with us."

Two girls came in, and one of them wore a cap of two colors. They filled the glasses and made curtsies. The councillor felt cold shivers up and down his spine. "What is all this? What is all this?" he groaned, but drink with them he must. They overwhelmed him with their kind intentions until he despaired, and when one man pronounced him drunk, he didn't doubt it in the least. All he asked was that they get him a *droschke*. Then they thought he was speaking in Russian.

Never before had he been in such low and vulgar company! "One would think that the country had lapsed back into barbarism," he told himself. "This is the most dreadful moment of my life."

Then it occurred to him to slip down under the table, crawl to the door, and try to sneak out, but just as he neared the threshold, his companions discovered him and tried to pull him out by his feet. However, by great good luck they pulled off his galoshes, and—with them—the whole enchantment.

The Councillor of Justice now distinctly saw a street lamp burning in front of a large building. He knew the building and the other buildings nearby. It was East Street as we all know it today. He lay on the pavement with his legs against a gate, and across the way, a night watchman sat fast asleep.

"Merciful heavens! Have I been lying here in the street dreaming?" the Councillor of Justice said. "To be sure, this is East Street. How blessedly bright and how colorful it looks. But what dreadful effect that one glass of punch must have had on me."

Two minutes later, he was seated in a cab, and well on his way to Christian's Harbor. As he recalled all the past terror and distress to which he had been subjected, he wholeheartedly approved of the present, our own happy age. With all its shortcomings, it was far preferable to that age into which he had recently stumbled. And that, thought the Councillor of Justice, was good common sense.

III. THE WATCHMAN'S ADVENTURE

"Why, I declare! There's a pair of galoshes," said the watchman. "They must belong to the lieutenant who lives up there on the top floor, for they are lying in front of the door." A light still burned upstairs, and the honest fellow was perfectly willing to ring the bell and return the overshoes. But he didn't want to disturb the other tenants in the house, so he didn't do it.

"It must be quite comfortable to wear a pair of such things," he said. "How soft the leather feels." They fitted his feet perfectly. "What a strange world we live in. The lieutenant might be resting easy in his soft bed, yet there he goes, pacing to and fro past his window. There's a happy man for you! He has no wife, and he has no child, and every night he goes to a party. Oh, if I were only in his place, what a happy man I would be."

Just as he expressed his wish, the galoshes transformed him into the lieutenant, body and soul, and there he stood in the room upstairs. Between his fingers, he held a sheet of pink paper on which the lieutenant had just written a poem. Who is there that has not at some time in his life felt poetic? If he writes down his thoughts while this mood is on him, poetry is apt to come of it. On the paper was written:

IF ONLY I WERE RICH

If only I were rich; I often said in prayer
When I was but a tiny lad without much care
If only I were rich, a soldier I would be
With uniform and sword, most handsomely;
At last an officer I was, my wish I got
But to be rich was not my lot;
But You, oh Lord, would always help.

I sat one eve, so happy, young and proud;
A darling child of seven kissed my mouth
For I was rich with fairy tales, you see
With money I was poor as poor can be,
But she was fond of tales I told
That made me rich, but—alas—not with gold;
But You, oh Lord, You know!

If only I were rich, is still my heavenly prayer.
My little girl of seven is now a lady fair;
She is so sweet, so clever and so good;
My heart's fair tale she never understood.
If only, as of yore, she still for me would care,
But I am poor and silent; I confess I do not dare.
It is Your will, oh Lord!

If only I were rich, in peace and comfort rest,
I would my sorrow to this paper never trust.
You, whom I love, if still you understand
then read this poem from my youth's far land,
Though best it be you never know my pain.
I am still poor, my future dark and vain,
But may, O Lord, You bless her!

Yes, a man in love writes many a poem that a man in his right mind does not print. A lieutenant, his love, and his lack of money—there's an eternal triangle for you, a broken life that can never be squared. The lieutenant knew this all too well. He leaned his head against the window, and sighed, and said:

"The poor watchman down there in the street is a far happier man than I. He does not know what I call want. He has a home. He has a wife and children who weep with him in his sorrows and share in his joy. Ah, I would be happier if I could trade places with him, for he is much more fortunate than I am."

Instantly, the watchman was himself again. The galoshes had transformed him into the lieutenant, as we have seen. He was far less contented up there, and preferred to be just what he had been. So the watchman turned back into a watchman.

"I had a bad dream," he said. "Strangely enough, I fancied I was the lieutenant, and I didn't like it a bit. I missed my wife and our youngsters, who almost smother me with their kisses."

He sat down and fell to nodding again, unable to get the dream out of his head. The galoshes were still on his feet when he watched a star fall in the sky.

"There goes one," he muttered. "But there are so many, it will never be missed. I'd like to have a look at those trinkets at close range. I'd especially like to see the Moon, which is not the sort of thing to get lost in one's hands. The student for whom my wife washes says that when we die, we fly about from star to star. There's not a word of truth in it. But it would be nice, just the same, if I could take a little jaunt through the skies. My body could stay here on the steps for all that I'd care."

Now there are certain things in the world that we ought to think about before we put them into words, and if we are wearing the galoshes of Fortune, it behooves us to think twice. Just listen to what happened to that watchman.

All of us know how fast steam can take us. We've either rushed along in a train or sped by steamship across the ocean. But all this is like the gait of a sloth, or the pace of a snail, in comparison with the speed of light, which travels nineteen million times faster than the fastest race horse. Yet electricity moves even faster. Death is an electric shock to the heart, and the soul set free travels on electric wings. The sunlight takes eight minutes and some odd seconds to travel nearly one hundred million miles. On the wings of electricity, the soul can make the same journey in a few moments, and to a soul set free, the heavenly bodies are as close together as the houses of friends who live in the same town with us, or even in the same neighborhood. However, this electric shock strips us of our bodies forever, unless, like the watchman, we happen to be wearing the galoshes of Fortune.

In a few seconds the watchman took in his stride the 260,000 miles to the Moon. As we know, this satellite is made of much lighter material than the earth, and is as soft as freshly fallen snow. The watchman landed in one of the numerous mountain rings that we all know from Doctor Maedler's large map of the Moon. Within the ring was a great bowl, fully four miles deep. At the bottom of this bowl lay a town. We may get some idea of what it looked like by pouring the white of an egg into a glass of water. The town was made of stuff as soft as the egg albumen, and its form was similar, with translucent towers, cupolas, and terraces, all floating in thin air.

Over the watchman's head hung our Earth, like a huge dull red ball. Around him, he noticed crowds of beings who doubtless corresponded to men and women of the earth, but their appearance was quite different from ours. They also had their own way of speaking, but no one could expect that the soul of a watchman would understand them. Nevertheless, he did understand the language of the people in the Moon very well. They were disputing about our Earth, and doubting whether it could be inhabited. The air on the Earth, they contended, must be too thick for any intelligent Moonman to live there. Only the Moon was inhabited, they agreed, for it was the original sphere on which the people of the Old World lived.

Now let us go back down to East Street, to see how the watchman's body was making out. Lifeless it lay, there on the steps. His morning star, that spiked club that watchmen carry, had fallen from his hands, and his eyes were turned toward the Moon that his honest soul was exploring.

"What's the hour, watchman?" asked a passerby. But never an answer did he get. He gave the watchman a very slight tweak of the nose, and over he toppled. There lay the body at full length, stretched on the pavement. The man was dead. It gave the one who had tweaked him a terrible fright, for the watchman was dead, and dead he remained. His death was reported and investigated. As day broke, his body was taken to the hospital.

It would be a pretty pass if the soul should come back and in all probability look for its body in East Street, and fail to find it. Perhaps it would rush to the police station first, next to the Directory Office where it could advertise for lost articles, and last of all to the hospital. But we needn't worry. The soul by itself is clever enough. It's the body that makes it stupid.

As we said before, the watchman's body was taken to the hospital. They put it in a room to be washed, and naturally the galoshes were pulled off first of all. That brought the soul dashing back posthaste, and in a flash, the watchman came back to life. He swore it had been the most terrible night he had ever experienced, and he would never go through it again, no, not for two pennies. But it was over and done with. He was allowed to leave that same day, but the galoshes were left at the hospital.

IV. A GREAT MOMENT, AND A MOST EXTRAORDINARY JOURNEY

Everyone in Copenhagen knows what the entrance to Frederic's Hospital looks like, but as some of the people who read this story may not have been to Copenhagen, we must describe the building—briefly.

The hospital is fenced off from the street by a rather high railing of heavy iron bars, which are spaced far enough apart—at least so the story goes—for very thin interns to squeeze between them and pay little visits to the world outside. The part of the body they had most difficulty in squeezing through was the head. In this, as often happens in the world, small heads were the most successful. So much for our description.

One of the young interns, of whom it could be said that he had a great head only in a physical sense, had the night watch that evening. Outside, the rain poured down. But in spite of these difficulties, he was bent upon getting out for a quarter of an hour. There was no need for the doorman to know about it, he thought, if he could just manage to slip through the fence. There lay the galoshes that the watchman had forgotten, and while the intern had no idea that they were the galoshes of Fortune, he did know that they would stand him in good stead out in the rain. So he pulled them on. Now the question was whether he could squeeze between the bars, a trick that he had never tried before. There he stood, facing the fence.

"I wish to goodness I had my head through," he said, and though his head was much too large and thick for the space, it immediately slipped through quickly and with the greatest of ease. The galoshes saw to that. All he had to do now was to squeeze his body through after his head, but it wouldn't go. "Uff!" he panted, "I'm too fat. I thought my head would be the worst difficulty. No, I shall never get through."

He quickly attempted to pull his head back again, but it couldn't be done. He could move his neck easily, but that was all. First, his anger flared up. Then his spirits dropped down to zero. The galoshes of Fortune had gotten him in a terrible fix, and unluckily, it did not occur to him to wish his way out of it. No, instead of wishing, he struggled and strove, but he could not budge from the spot. The rain poured down; not a soul could be seen in the street; and he could not reach the bell by the gate. How could he ever get free? He was certain he would have to stay there till morning, and that they would have to send for a blacksmith to file through the iron bars. It would take time. All the boys in the school across the way would be up and shout, and the entire population of "Nyboder," where all the sailors lived, would turn out for the fun of seeing the man in a pillory. Why, he would draw a bigger crowd than the one that went to see the championship wrestling matches last year.

"Huff!" he panted, "the blood's rushing to my head. I'm going mad! Yes, I'm going mad! Oh, if I were only free again, and out of this fix, then I would be all right again."

This was what he ought to have said in the first place. No sooner had he said it than his head came free, and he dashed indoors, still bewildered by the fright that the galoshes of Fortune had given him. But don't think that this was the end of it. No! The worst was yet to come.

The night went by, and the next day passed, but nobody came for the galoshes. That evening, there was to be a performance at the little theater in Kannike Street. The house was packed, and in the audience was our friend, the intern, apparently none the worse for his adventure of the night before. He had again put on the galoshes. After all, no one had claimed them, and the streets were so muddy that he thought they would stand him in good stead.

At the theater a new sketch was presented. It was called "My Grandmother's Spectacles" and had to do with a pair of eyeglasses that enabled anyone who wore them to read the future from people's faces, just as a fortune-teller reads it from cards.

The idea occupied his mind very much. He would like to own such a pair of spectacles. Properly used, they might enable one to see into people's hearts. This, he thought, would be far more interesting than foresee what would happen next year. Future events would be known in due time, but no one would ever know the secrets that lie in people's hearts.

"Look at those ladies and gentlemen in the front row," he said to himself. "If I could see straight into their hearts, what stores of things—what great shops full of goods would I behold. And how my eyes would rove about those shops. In every feminine heart, no doubt I should find a complete millinery establishment. There sits one whose shop is empty, but a good cleaning would do it no harm. And of course some of the shops would be well stocked. Ah me," he sighed, "I know of one where all the goods are of the very best quality, and it would just suit me, but—alas and alack—there's a shopkeeper there already, and he's the only bad article in the whole shop. Many a one would say, 'Won't you walk in?' and I wish I could. I would pass like a nice little thought through their hearts."

The galoshes took him at his word. The intern shrank to almost nothing, and set out on a most extraordinary journey through the hearts of all the spectators in the first row. The first heart he entered was that of a lady, but at first, he mistook it for a room in the Orthopaedic Institute, or hospital, where the plaster casts of deformed limbs are hung upon the walls. The only difference was that at the hospital, those casts were made when the patients came in, while these casts that were kept in the heart were made as the good people departed. For every physical or mental fault of the friends she had lost had been carefully stored away.

He quickly passed on to another woman's heart, which seemed like a great holy cathedral. Over the high altar fluttered the white dove of innocence, and the intern would have gone down on his knees except that he had to hurry on to the next heart. However, he still heard the organ roll. And he felt that it had made a new and better man of him—a man not too unworthy to enter the next sanctuary. This was a poor garret where a mother lay ill, but through the windows the sun shone, warm and bright. Lovely roses bloomed in the little wooden flower box on the roof, and two bluebirds sang of happy childhood, while the sick woman prayed for a blessing on her daughter.

Next, the intern crawled on his hands and knees through an overcrowded butcher shop. There was meat, more meat, and meat alone, wherever he looked in this heart of a wealthy, respectable man, whose name you can find in the directory.

Next, he entered the heart of this man's wife, and an old tumbledown dovecote he found it. Her husband's portrait served as a mere weathervane, which was connected with the doors in such a way that they opened and closed as her husband turned round.

Then he found his way into a cabinet of mirrors such as is to be seen at Rosenborg Castle, though in this heart, the mirrors had the power of magnifying objects enormously. Like the Grand Lama of Tibet, the owner's insignificant ego sat in the middle of the floor, in admiring contemplation of his own greatness.

After this, he seemed to be crammed into a narrow case full of sharp needles. "This," he thought, "must certainly be an old maid's heart," but it was nothing of the sort. It was the heart of a very young officer who had been awarded several medals, and of whom everyone said, "Now there's a man of both intellect and heart."

Quite befuddled was the poor intern when he popped out of the heart of the last person in the front row. He could not get his thoughts in order, and he supposed that his strong imagination must have run away with him.

"Merciful heavens," he groaned, "I must be well on the road to the madhouse. And it's so outrageously hot in here that the blood is rushing to my head." Suddenly, he recalled what had happened the night before, when he had jammed his head between the bars of the hospital fence. "That must be what caused it," he decided. "I must do something before it is too late. A Russian bath might be the very thing. I wish I were on the top shelf right now."

No sooner said than there he lay on the top shelf of the steam bath. But he was fully dressed, down to his shoes and galoshes. He felt the hot drops of condensed steam fall upon him from the ceiling.

"Hey!" he cried, and jumped down to take a shower. The attendant cried out too when he caught sight of a fully dressed man in the steam room. However, the intern had enough sense to pull himself together and whisper, "I'm just doing this because of a bet."

But the first thing he did when he got back to his room was to put hot plasters on his neck and his back, to draw out the madness.

Next morning, he had a blistered back, and that was all he got out of the galoshes of Fortune.

V. THE TRANSFORMATION OF THE COPYING CLERK

The watchman—you remember him—happened to remember those galoshes he had found, and that he must have been wearing them when they took his body to the hospital. He came by for them, and as neither the lieutenant nor anyone else in East Street laid claim to them, he turned them in at the police station.

"They look exactly like my own galoshes," one of the copying clerks at the police station said, as he set the ownerless galoshes down beside his own. "Not even a shoemaker could tell one pair from the other."

"Mr. Copying Clerk!" said a policeman, who brought him some papers.

The clerk turned around to talk with the policeman, and when he came back to the galoshes, he was uncertain whether the pair on the right or the pair on the left belonged to him.

"The wet ones must be mine," he thought, but he was mistaken, for they were the galoshes of Fortune. The police make their little mistakes, too.

So he pulled them on, pocketed some papers, and tucked some manuscripts under his arm to read and abstract when he got home. But as this happened to be Sunday morning, and the weather was fine, he thought, "A walk to Frederiksberg will be good for me." And off he went.

A quieter, more dependable fellow than this young man you seldom see. Let him take his little walk, by all means. It will do him a world of good after so much sitting. At first, he strode along without a wish in his head, so there was no occasion for the galoshes to show their magic power. On the avenue, he met an acquaintance of his, a young poet, who said he was setting out tomorrow on a summer excursion.

"What, off again so soon?" said the clerk. "What a free and happy fellow you are! You can fly away wherever you like, while the rest of us are chained by the leg."

"Chained only to a breadfruit tree," the poet reminded him. "You don't have to worry along from day to day, and when you get old, they will give you a pension."

"You are better off, just the same," the clerk said. "How agreeable it must be to sit and write poetry. Everyone pays you compliments, and you are your own master. Ah, you should see what it's like to devote your life to the trivial details of the courts."

The poet shook his head, and the clerk shook his, too. Each held to his own conviction, and they parted company.

"They are a queer race, these poets," thought the clerk. "I should like to try my hand at their trade—to turn poet myself. I'm sure I would never write such melancholy stuff as most of them do. What a splendid spring day this is, a day fit for a poet. The air is so unusually clear, the clouds so lovely, and the green grass so fragrant. For many a year, I have not felt as I feel just now."

Already, you could tell that he had turned poet. Not that there was anything you could put your finger on, for it is foolish to suppose that a poet differs greatly from other people, some of whom are far more poetic by nature than many a great and accepted poet. The chief difference is that a poet has a better memory for things of the spirit. He can hold fast to an emotion and an idea until they are firmly and clearly embodied in words, which is something that others cannot do. But for a matter-of-fact person to think in terms of poetry is noticeable enough, and it is this transformation that we can see in the clerk.

"What a glorious fragrance there is in the air!" he said. "It reminds me of Aunt Lone's violets. Ah me, I haven't thought of them since I was a little boy. The dear old girl! She used to live over there, behind the Exchange. She always had a spray or a few green shoots in water, no matter how severe the winter was. I'd smell those violets even when I was putting hot pennies against the frozen window pane to make peep holes. What a view that was—ships frozen tight in the canal, deserted by their crews, and a shrieking crow the only living creature aboard them. But when the springtime breezes blew, the scene turned lively again. There were shouts and laughter as the ice was sawed away. Freshly tarred and rigged, the ships sailed off for distant lands. I stayed here, and I must forever stay here, sitting in the police office where others come for their passports to foreign countries. Yes, that's my lot! Oh, yes!" he said, and heaved a sigh. Then he stopped abruptly. "Great heavens! What's come over me. I never thought or felt like this before. It must be the spring air! It is as frightening as it is pleasant." He fumbled among the papers in his pockets.

"These will give me something else to think about," he said, as he glanced at the first page. *"Lady Sigbrith, An Original Tragedy in Five Acts,"* he read. "Why, what's this? It's in my own handwriting too. Have I written a tragedy? *The Intrigue on the Ramparts, or The Great Fast Day—a Vaudeville.* Where did that come from? Someone must have slipped it in my pocket. And here's a letter." It was from the board of directors of the theater, who rejected his plays, and the letter was anything but politely phrased.

"Hem, hem!" said the copying clerk as he sat down on a bench. His thoughts were lively and his heart sensitive. He plucked a flower at random, an ordinary little daisy. What the professor of botany requires several lectures to explain to us, this flower told in a moment. It told of the mystery birth, and of the power of the sunlight that opened those delicate leaves and gave them their fragrance. This made him think of the battle of life, which arouses emotions within us in similar fashion. Air and light are the flower's lovers, but light is her favorite. Toward it the flower is ever turning, and only when the light is gone does she fold her petals and sleep in the air's embrace.

"It is the light that makes me lovely," the flower said.

"But," the poet's voice whispered, "the air enables you to breathe."

Not far away, a boy was splashing in a muddy ditch with his stick. As the water flew up among the green branches, the clerk thought of the innumerable microscopic creatures in the splashing drops. For them to be splashed so high was as if we were to be tossed up into the clouds. As the clerk thought of these things, and of the great change that had come over him, he smiled and said:

"I must be asleep and dreaming. It's marvelous to be able to dream so naturally, and yet to know all along that this is a dream. I hope I can recall every bit of it tomorrow, when I wake up. I seem to feel unusually exhilarated. How clearly I understand things, and how wide awake I feel! But I know that if I recall my dream, it will only be a lot of nonsense, as has happened to me so often before. All those brilliant and clever remarks one makes and one hears in his dreams are like the gold pieces that goblins store underground. When one gets them, they are rich and shining, but seen in the daylight, they are nothing but rocks and dry leaves. Ah me," he sighed, as he sadly watched the singing birds flit merrily from branch to branch. "They are so much better off than I. Flying is a noble art, and lucky is he who is born with wings. Yes, if I could change into anything I liked, I would turn into a little lark."

In a trice, his coattails and sleeves grew together as wings, his clothes turned into feathers, and his galoshes became claws. He noticed the change clearly, and laughed to himself.

"Now," he said, "I know I am dreaming, but I never had a dream as silly as this one."

Up he flew, and sang among the branches, but there was no poetry in his song, for he was no longer a poet. Like anyone who does a thorough job of it, the galoshes could only do one thing at a time. When he wished to be a poet, a poet he became. Then he wanted to be a little bird, and in becoming one, he lost his previous character.

"This is most amusing," he said. "In the daytime, I sit in the police office, surrounded by the most matter-of-fact legal papers, but by night, I can dream that I'm a lark flying about in the Frederiksberg Garden. What fine material this would make for a popular comedy."

He flew down on the grass, twisting and turning his head, and pecking at the waving grass blades. In proportion to his own size, they seemed as large as the palm branches in North Africa. But this lasted only a moment. Then everything turned black, and it seemed as if some huge object had dropped over him. This was a big cap that a boy from Nyboder had thrown over the bird. A hand was thrust in. It laid hold of the copying clerk by his back and wing so tightly that it made him shriek. In his terror, he called out, "You impudent scoundrel! I am the copying clerk at the police office!" But this sounded like "Peep! peep!" to the boy, who thumped the bird on its beak and walked off with it.

On the avenue, this boy met with two other schoolboys. Socially, they were of the upper classes, though, properly ranked according to their merit, they were in the lowest class at school. They bought the bird for eight pennies, and in their hands the clerk came back to Copenhagen, to a family who lived in Gothers Street.

"It's a good thing I'm only dreaming this," said the clerk, "or I'd be furious. First I was a poet, and now I'm a lark. It must have been my poetic temperament that turned me into this little creature. It is a very sad state of affairs, especially when one falls into the hands of a couple of boys. But I wonder how it will all turn out."

The boys carried him into a luxuriously appointed room, where a stout, affable lady received them. She was not at all pleased with their common little field bird, as she called the lark, but she said that, for one day only, they could keep it in the empty cage near the window.

"Perhaps Polly will like it," she said, and smiled at the large parrot that swung proudly to and fro on the ring in his ornate brass cage. "It's Polly's birthday," she said, like a simpleton. "The little field bird wants to congratulate him."

Polly did not say a word, as proudly he swung back and forth. But a pretty canary bird who had been brought here last summer from his warm, sweet-scented homeland, began to sing at the top of his voice.

"Bawler!" the lady said, and threw a white handkerchief over his cage.

"Peep, peep. What a terrible snowstorm," the canary sighed, and with that sigh, he kept quiet.

The clerk, or, as the lady called him, the field bird, was put in a cage next to the canary's and not far from the parrot's. The only human words that the parrot could say, and which at times sounded quite comical, were, "Come now, let us be men." All the rest of his chatter made as little sense as the twittering of the canary. However, the clerk, who was now a bird himself, understood his companions perfectly.

"I used to fly beneath green palms and flowering almond trees," the canary bird sang. "With my brothers and sisters, I flew above beautiful flowers, and over the smooth sea where the plants that grow under water waved up at us. We used to meet many brilliant parrots, who told us the funniest stories—long ones and so many."

"Those were wild parrots!" said Polly. "Birds without any education. Come now, let us be men. Why don't you laugh? If the lady and all her guests laugh at my remark, so should you. To lack a sense of humor is a very bad thing. Come now, let us be men."

"Do you remember the pretty girls who danced in the tents spread beneath those flowering trees?" the canary sang. "Do you remember those delicious sweet fruits, and the cool juice of the wild plants?"

"Why, yes," said the parrot, "but I am much better off here, where I get the best of food and intimate treatment. I know that I am a clever bird, and that's enough for me. Come now, let us be men. You have the soul of a poet, as they call it, and I have sound knowledge and wit. You have genius, but no discretion. You burst into that shrill, spontaneous song of yours. That's why people cover you up. They don't ever treat me like that. No, I have cost them a lot, and, what is more imposing, my beak and my wits are sharp. Come now, let us be men."

"Oh, my warm flowery homeland!" said the canary. "I shall sing of your deep green trees and your quiet inlets, where the down-hanging branches kiss the clear mirror of the waters. I shall sing of my resplendent brothers and sisters, who rejoice as they hover over the cups of water in the cactus plants that thrive in the desert."

"Kindly stop your whimpering tunes," the parrot said. "Sing something to make us laugh. Laughter is a sign of the loftiest intellectual development. Can a dog or a horse laugh? No! They can cry, but as for laughter—that is given to mankind alone. Ho, ho, ho!" the parrot chuckled, and added his, "Come now, let us be men."

"You little grey bird of Denmark," the canary said to the lark, "have they made you a prisoner too? Although it must be very cold in your woods, you have your freedom there. Fly away! They have forgotten to close your cage. The door of the top is open. Fly! fly!"

Without pausing to think, the clerk did as he was told. In a jiffy, he was out of the cage. But just as he escaped from his prison, the half-open door leading into the next room began to creak. Stealthily, with green shining eyes, the house cat pounced in and gave chase to him. The canary fluttered in his cage. The parrot flapped his wings and called out, "Come now, let us be men." The dreadfully frightened clerk flew out of the window and away over the streets and houses, until at last he had to stop to rest.

That house across the street looked familiar. He flew in through one of its open windows. As he perched on the table, he found that he was in his own room.

"Come now, let us be men," he blurted out, in spontaneous mockery of the parrot. Instantly he resumed the body of the copying clerk, who sat there, perched on the table.

"How in the name of heaven," he said, "do I happen to be sleeping here? And what a disturbing dream I've had—all nonsense from beginning to end."

VI. THE BEST THAT THE GALOSHES BROUGHT

Early the next morning, before the clerk was out of bed, someone tapped on his door. In walked his neighbor, a young theological student who lived on the same floor.

"Lend me your galoshes," he requested. "It is very wet in the garden, but the sun is shining so gloriously that I'd like to smoke a pipeful down there."

He pulled on the galoshes and went out into the garden, where there was one plum tree and a pear tree. But even a little garden like this one is a precious thing in Copenhagen.

It was only six o'clock. As the student walked up and down the path, he heard the horn of a stagecoach in the street.

"Oh, to travel, to travel!" he exclaimed, "that's the most pleasant thing in the world. It's the great goal of all my dreams. If only I could travel, I'm sure that this restlessness within me would be stilled. But it must be far, far away. How I should like to see beautiful Switzerland, to tour Italy, and—"

Fortunately the galoshes began to function at once, or he might have traveled entirely too much to suit him or to please us. Travel he did. He was high up in Switzerland, tightly packed in a diligence with eight other travelers. He had a pain in his head, his neck felt tired, and the blood had ceased to circulate in his legs. His feet were swollen, and his heavy boots hurt him. He was half-awake and half-asleep. In his right-hand pocket, he had his letter of credit, in his left-hand pocket, he had his passport, and sewn into a little bag inside his breast pocket, he had a few gold pieces. Every time he dozed off, he dreamed that he had lost one or another of these things. Starting feverishly awake, his first movement would be to trace with his hand a triangle from right to left, and up to his breast, to feel whether his treasures were still there.

Umbrellas, hats, and walking sticks swung in the net above him and almost spoiled the magnificent view. As he glanced out the window, his heart sang, as at least one poet has sung in Switzerland, these as yet unpublished words:

This view is as fine as a view can be.
Mount Blanc is sublime beyond a doubt,
And the traveler's life is the life for me—
But only as long as my money holds out.

Vast, severe, and somber was the whole landscape around him. The pine woods looked like patches of heather on the high cliffs, whose summits were lost in fog and cloud. Snow began to fall, and the cold wind blew.

"Ah," he sighed, "if only we were on the other side of the Alps, then it would be summer weather and I could get some money on my letter of credit. Worrying about my finances spoils all my enjoyment of Switzerland. Oh, if only I were on the other side."

And there he was on the other side, in the middle of Italy, between Florence and Rome. Before him lay Lake Thrasymene. In the evening light, it looked like a sheet of flaming gold among the dark blue hills. Here, where Hannibal beat Flaminius, the grape vines clung peacefully to each other with their green tendrils. Pretty little half-clothed children tended a herd of coal-black pigs under a fragrant clump of laurels by the roadside, and if we could paint the scene in its true colors, all would exclaim, "Glorious Italy!" But neither the student nor his companions in the stagecoach made any such exclamation.

Poisonous flies and gnats swarmed into the coach by the thousands. In vain, the travelers tried to beat them off with myrtle branches. The flies stung just the same. There was not a passenger whose face was not puffed and spotted with bites. The poor horses looked like carcasses. The flies made life miserable for them, and it only brought them a momentary relief when the coachman got down and scraped off swarms of the insects that settled upon them.

Once the sun went down, an icy chill fell upon everything. It wasn't at all pleasant. However, the hills and clouds took on that wonderful green tint, so clear and so shining. Yes, go and see for yourself. That is far better than to read about it. It was a lovely sight, and the travelers thought so too, but their stomachs were empty, their bodies exhausted, and every thought in their heads was directed toward a lodging for the night. But where would they lodge? They watched the road ahead far more attentively than they did the splendid view.

Their road ran through an olive grove, and the student could fancy that he was at home, passing through a wood of gnarled willow trees. And there stood a lonely inn. A band of crippled beggars were camping outside, and the liveliest among them looked like the eldest son of Famine who had just come of age. The rest either were blind, or so lame that they crawled about on their hands, or had withered arms and hands without any fingers. Here really was misery in rags.

"*Eccelenza, miserabili!*" they groaned, and stretched forth their crippled limbs. The hostess herself went barefoot. With uncombed hair and an unwashed blouse, she received her guests. The doors were hinged with string; half of the bricks of the floors had been put to other use; bats flew about the ceiling; and the smell—

"It were better to have supper in the stable," one traveler maintained. "There one at least knows what he is breathing."

The windows were opened to let a little fresh air come inside, but swifter than the air came those withered arms and that perpetual whine, "*Miserabili, eccellenza.*" On the walls were many inscriptions, and half of them had little good to say for *la bella Italia.*

Supper was served. Supper was a watery soup flavored with pepper and rancid oil. This same oil was the better part of the salad. Dubious eggs and roasted cockscombs were the best dishes, and even the wine was distasteful. It was a frightful collation.

That night, the trunks were piled against the door, and one of the travelers mounted guard while the others slept. The student stood the first guard mount. How close it was in there! The heat was overpowering, the gnats droned and stabbed, and outside, the *miserabili* whined in their dreams.

"Traveling," said the student, "would be all very well if one had no body. Oh, if only the body could rest while the spirit flies on without it. Wherever I go, there is some lack that I feel in my heart. There is always something better than the present that I desire. Yes, something better—the best of all, but what is it, and where shall I find it? Down deep in my heart, I know what I want. I want to reach a happy goal, the happiest goal of all."

As soon as the words were said, he found himself back in his home. Long white curtains draped the windows, and in the middle of the floor, a black coffin stood. In this he lay, sleeping the quiet sleep of death. His wish was fulfilled—his body was at rest, and his spirit was free to travel. "Call no man happy until he rests in his grave," said Solon, and here his words proved true again.

Every corpse is a sphinx of immortality. The sphinx in this black casket that confronts us could say no more than the living man had written two days before:

> Stern Death, your silence has aroused my fears.
> Shall not my soul up Jacob's ladder pass,
> Or shall your stone weight me throughout the years,
> And I rise only in the graveyard grass?
>
> Our deepest grief escapes the world's sad eye!
> You who are lonely to the very last,
> A heavier burden on your heart must lie
> Than all the earth upon your coffin cast!

Two figures moved about the room. We know them both. Those two who bent over the dead man were Dame Care and Fortune's minion.

"Now," said Care, "you can see what happiness your galoshes have brought mankind."

"They have at least brought everlasting rest to him who here lies sleeping," said Fortune's minion.

"Oh, no!" said Care. "He went of his own free will. He was not called away. His spiritual power was not strong enough to undertake the glorious tasks for which he is destined. I shall do him a favor."

She took the galoshes from his feet. Then the sleep of death was ended, and the student awakened to life again. Care vanished, and she took the galoshes along with her, for she probably regarded them as her own property.

THE DAISY (1838)

Now listen to this! Out in the country, close by the side of the road, there stood a country house; you yourself have certainly seen many just like it. In front of it was a little flower garden, with a painted fence around it. Close by the fence, in the midst of the most beautiful green grass beside a ditch, there grew a little daisy. The sun shone just as warmly and brightly on her as on the beautiful flowers inside the garden, and so she grew every hour. Until at last one morning, she was in full bloom, with shining white petals spreading like rays around the little yellow sun in the center.

The daisy didn't think that she was a little despised flower that nobody would notice down there in the grass. No, indeed! She was a merry little daisy as she looked up at the warm sun and listened to the lark singing high in the sky.

Yes, the little daisy was as happy as if this were a grand holiday, yet it was only a Monday, and all the children were in school. While they sat on their benches, learning things, the daisy sat on her little green stalk and learned from the warm sun and everything about her just how good God is. The daisy couldn't talk, but high above her, the lark sang loudly and beautifully all the things that the little flower felt, and that made the daisy very glad. The daisy looked up at the happy bird who could sing and fly, but she wasn't envious because she couldn't do those fine things, too.

"I can see and hear," the daisy thought, "and the sun shines on me, and the forest kisses me. How gifted I am!"

Inside the fence stood all the stiff, proud flowers, and the less scent they had, the more they seemed to strut. The peonies blew themselves out and tried to make themselves bigger than the roses, but size alone isn't enough. The tulips knew that they had the brightest colors, and held themselves very straight, so that they could be seen more plainly. None of them noticed the little daisy outside, but the daisy could see them and thought, "How rich and beautiful they are! I am sure the pretty lark flies across to them and visits them. Thank God that I stand close enough so that I can see them!" But just as she thought that—*keevit*—down came the lark!

But he didn't come down to the peonies or the tulips! No, indeed, he flew right down into the grass to the poor daisy, who was so overjoyed that she didn't know what to think.

The little bird danced around the daisy and sang, "How soft the grass is here, and what a lovely little flower! With gold in her heart and silver on her dress!" You see, the yellow heart of the daisy looked like gold, and the petals around it were silvery white.

How happy the little daisy was no one can conceive. The bird kissed her with his beak, sang to her, and then flew up again—into the bright, blue air. It was at least a quarter of an hour before the daisy could recover from her joy! Then, almost ashamed, yet sincerely happy, she peeped over at the flowers in the garden, for they had seen the honor and happiness that had come to her, and would understand her joy. But the tulips stood up twice as stiff as before, and looked very haughty and very red in the face because they were very annoyed. The fatheaded peonies were jealous— bah!—and it was lucky they couldn't speak, or the daisy would have received a good scolding. The poor little flower could see they were not in a good humor, and that made her very sad.

Just then a girl with a great, sharp, shining knife came into the garden, went straight up to the tulips, and cut them off, one after the other. "Oh my," sighed the little daisy, "that's dreadful! It's all over with them now."

Then the girl took the tulips away, and the daisy was glad that she was only a poor little flower that nobody would notice out in the grass. Yes, she felt very grateful indeed. The sun went down, and the little daisy folded her leaves and went to sleep, and dreamed all night about the sun and the pretty bird.

The next morning, when the flower again happily stretched out her white petals, like little arms, toward the early sun, she recognized the voice of the lark, but this time the song was mournful and sad. Yes, the poor lark had good reason to be sad.

You see, he had been caught, and now sat in a cage close by an open window of the house. He sadly sang of the free and happy roaming he used to do, of the young green corn in the fields, of the glorious journeys he used to make on his wings high up through the air. The poor bird was very unhappy, for there he was, a prisoner—in a cage!

How the little daisy wished she could help him! But what could she do? Yes, that was difficult to figure out. She quite forgot how beautiful the world was, how warm the sun shone, and how wonderfully white were her own petals. She could only try to think of the poor little bird and how powerless she was to help him.

Suddenly, two little boys came out of the garden, and one of them was carrying a big, sharp knife like that which the girl had used to cut the tulips. They went straight up to the little daisy, who could not understand what was going on.

"Here we can cut a fine piece of turf for the lark," said one of the boys. Then he began to cut out a square patch of grass around the daisy, so that the little flower remained standing in the middle of it.

"Tear off that flower!" said the other boy.

And the daisy trembled with fear! To be torn off would mean losing her life, and she wanted so much to live now, and go with the turf to the captive lark.

"No, leave it there," the other boy said. "It looks pretty." And then the daisy, in a little patch of sod, was put into the lark's cage.

But the poor bird was complaining about his lost liberty and beating his wings against the wires of his prison; and the little daisy couldn't speak, couldn't console him however much she wanted to. And thus the morning passed.

"There is no water here!" cried the captive lark. "They've all gone away and have forgotten to give me anything to drink. My throat's dry and burning. I feel as if I had fire and ice within me, and the air is so close! Oh, I must die! I must leave the warm sunshine, and the fresh green, and all the splendor that God has created!"

But when he thrust his beak into the cool turf to refresh himself a little, his eye fell upon the daisy, who was trying so hard to speak to him. He kissed her with his beak, and said, "You must also wither in here, poor little flower. They've given me you and your little patch of green grass instead of the whole world that was mine out there! Every little blade of your grass shall be a green tree for me, and every one of your white leaves a fragrant flower. Ah, seeing you only tells me again how much I have lost!"

"Oh, if I could only help him and comfort him!" thought the daisy.

She couldn't move a leaf, but the scent that streamed forth from her delicate leaves was far stronger than a daisy ever gave forth before. The lark noticed it, and though in his thirst and pain he plucked at the blades of grass, he did not touch the flower.

The evening came, and still nobody appeared to bring the bird a single drop of water. At last, the lark stretched out his pretty wings and beat the air desperately; his song changed to a mournful peeping; his little head sank down toward the flower and his little bird's heart broke with want and yearning. And the flower couldn't fold its leaves and sleep, as she had done the night before; she too drooped sorrowful and sick toward the earth.

It wasn't until the next morning that the boys came; and when they found the bird dead, they wept many tears and dug him a neat grave, adorned with leaves and flowers. They put him into a pretty red box, for the poor bird was to have a royal funeral. While he was alive and singing, they forgot him and let him sit in a cage and suffer; but now that he was dead, he was to have many tears and a royal funeral.

But the patch of turf with the little daisy on it was thrown out into the dusty road; and no one thought any more of the flower that had felt the deepest for the little bird, and had tried so hard to console him and help him.

THE STEADFAST TIN SOLDIER (1838)

There were once five-and-twenty tin soldiers. They were all brothers, born of the same old tin spoon. They shouldered their muskets and looked straight ahead of them, splendid in their uniforms, all red and blue.

The very first thing in the world that they heard was, "Tin soldiers!" A small boy shouted it and clapped his hands as the lid was lifted off their box on his birthday. He immediately set them up on the table.

All the soldiers looked exactly alike except one. He looked a little different as he had been cast last of all. The tin was short, so he had only one leg. But there he stood, as steady on one leg as any of the other soldiers on their two. But just you see, he'll be the remarkable one.

On the table with the soldiers were many other playthings, and one that no eye could miss was a marvelous castle of cardboard. It had little windows through which you could look right inside it. And in front of the castle were miniature trees around a little mirror supposed to represent a lake. The wax swans that swam on its surface were reflected in the mirror. All this was very pretty, but prettiest of all was the little lady who stood in the open doorway of the castle. Though she was a paper doll, she wore a dress of the fluffiest gauze. A tiny blue ribbon went over her shoulder for a scarf, and in the middle of it shone a spangle that was as big as her face. The little lady held out both her arms, as a ballet dancer does, and one leg was lifted so high behind her that the tin soldier couldn't see it at all, and he supposed she must have only one leg, as he did.

"That would be a wife for me," he thought. "But maybe she's too grand. She lives in a castle. I have only a box, with four-and-twenty roommates to share it. That's no place for her. But I must try to make her acquaintance." Still as stiff as when he stood at attention, he lay down on the table behind a snuffbox, where he could admire the dainty little dancer who kept standing on one leg without ever losing her balance.

When the evening came, the other tin soldiers were put away in their box, and the people of the house went to bed. Now the toys began to play among themselves at visits, and battles, and at giving balls. The tin soldiers rattled about in their box, for they wanted to play too, but they could not get the lid open. The nutcracker turned somersaults, and the slate pencil squeaked out jokes on the slate. The toys made such a noise that they woke up the canary bird, who made them a speech, all in verse. The only two who stayed still were the tin soldier and the little dancer. Without ever swerving from the tip of one toe, she held out her arms to him, and the tin soldier was just as steadfast on his one leg. Not once did he take his eyes off her.

Then the clock struck twelve and—clack!—up popped the lid of the snuffbox. But there was no snuff in it, no—out bounced a little black bogey, a jack-in-the-box.

"Tin soldier," he said. "Will you please keep your eyes to yourself?" The tin soldier pretended not to hear.

The bogey said, "Just you wait till tomorrow."

But when morning came, and the children got up, the soldier was set on the window ledge. And whether the bogey did it, or there was a gust of wind, all of a sudden, the window flew open, and the soldier pitched out headlong from the third floor. He fell at breathtaking speed and landed cap first, with his bayonet buried between the paving stones and his one leg stuck straight in the air. The housemaid and the little boy ran down to look for him, and, though they nearly stepped on the tin soldier, they walked right past without seeing him. If the soldier had called, "Here I am!" they would surely have found him, but he thought it contemptible to raise an uproar while he was wearing his uniform.

Soon, it began to rain. The drops fell faster and faster, until they came down by the bucketful. As soon as the rain let up, along came two young rapscallions.

"Hi, look!" one of them said, "There's a tin soldier. Let's send him sailing."

They made a boat out of newspaper, put the tin soldier in the middle of it, and away he went down the gutter with the two young rapscallions running beside him and clapping their hands. High heavens! How the waves splashed, and how fast the water ran down the gutter. Don't forget that it had just been raining by the bucketful. The paper boat pitched, and tossed, and sometimes it whirled about so rapidly that it made the soldier's head spin. But he stood as steady as ever. Never once flinching, he kept his eyes front and carried his gun shoulder-high. Suddenly, the boat rushed under a long plank where the gutter was boarded over. It was as dark as the soldier's own box.

"Where can I be going?" the soldier wondered. "This must be that black bogey's revenge. Ah! If only I had the little lady with me, it could be twice as dark here for all that I would care."

Out popped a great water rat who lived under the gutter plank.

"Have you a passport?" said the rat. "Hand it over."

The soldier kept quiet and held his musket tighter. On rushed the boat, and the rat came right after it, gnashing his teeth as he called to the sticks and straws:

"Halt him! Stop him! He didn't pay his toll. He hasn't shown his passport." But the current ran stronger and stronger. The soldier could see daylight ahead where the board ended, but he also heard a roar that would frighten the bravest of us. Hold on! Right at the end of that gutter plank, the water poured into the great canal. It was as dangerous to him as a waterfall would be to us.

He was so near it he could not possibly stop. The boat plunged into the whirlpool. The poor tin soldier stood as staunch as he could, and no one can say that he so much as blinked an eye. Thrice and again the boat spun around. It filled to the top—and was bound to sink. The water was up to his neck, and still the boat went down, deeper, deeper, deeper, and the paper got soft and limp. Then the water rushed over his head. He thought of the pretty little dancer whom he'd never see again, and in his ears rang an old, old song:

> Farewell, farewell, O warrior brave,
> Nobody can from Death thee save.

And now the paper boat broke beneath him, and the soldier sank right through. And just at that moment, he was swallowed by a most enormous fish.

My! How dark it was inside that fish. It was darker than under the gutter plank, and it was so cramped, but the tin soldier still was staunch. He lay there full length, soldier fashion, with musket to shoulder.

Then the fish flopped and floundered in a most unaccountable way. Finally, it was perfectly still, and after a while, something struck through him like a flash of lightning. The tin soldier saw daylight again, and he heard a voice say, "The Tin Soldier!" The fish had been caught, carried to market, bought, and brought to a kitchen where the cook cut him open with her big knife.

She picked the soldier up bodily between her two fingers, and carried him off upstairs. Everyone wanted to see this remarkable traveler who had traveled about in a fish's stomach, but the tin soldier took no pride in it. They put him on the table and—lo and behold, what curious things can happen in this world—there he was, back in the same room as before. He saw the same children, the same toys were on the table, and there was the same fine castle with the pretty little dancer. She still balanced on one leg, with the other raised high. She too was steadfast. That touched the soldier so deeply that he would have cried tin tears, only soldiers never cry. He looked at her, and she looked at him, and never a word was said. Just as things were going so nicely for them, one of the little boys snatched up the tin soldier and threw him into the stove. He did it for no reason at all. That black bogey in the snuffbox must have put him up to it.

The tin soldier stood there dressed in flames. He felt a terrible heat, but whether it came from the flames, or from his love he didn't know. He'd lost his splendid colors, maybe from his hard journey, maybe from grief, nobody can say.

He looked at the little lady, and she looked at him, and he felt himself melting. But still he stood steadfast, with his musket held trim on his shoulder.

Then the door blew open. A puff of wind struck the dancer. She flew like a sylph, straight into the fire with the soldier, blazed up in a flash, and was gone. The tin soldier melted, all in a lump. The next day, when a servant took up the ashes, she found him in the shape of a little tin heart. But of the pretty dancer, nothing was left except her spangle, and it was burned as black as a coal.

THE WILD SWANS (1838)

Far, far away where the swallows fly when we have winter, there lived a king who had eleven sons and one daughter, Elisa. The eleven brothers, princes all, each went to school with a star at his breast and a sword at his side. They wrote with pencils of diamond upon golden slates, and could say their lesson by heart just as easily as they could read it from the book. You could tell at a glance how princely they were. Their sister, Elisa, sat on a little footstool of flawless glass. She had a picture book that had cost half a kingdom. Oh, the children had a very fine time, but it did not last forever.

Their father, who was king over the whole country, married a wicked queen, who did not treat his poor children at all well. They found that out the very first day. There was feasting throughout the palace, and the children played at entertaining guests. But instead of letting them have all the cakes and baked apples that they used to get, their new stepmother gave them only some sand in a teacup, and told them to make believe that it was a special treat.

The following week, the queen sent little Elisa to live in the country with some peasants. And before long, she had made the king believe so many falsehoods about the poor princes that he took no further interest in them.

"Fly out into the world and make your own living," the wicked queen told them. "Fly away like big birds without a voice."

But she did not harm the princes as much as she meant to, for they turned into eleven magnificent white swans. With a weird cry, they flew out of the palace window, across the park into the woods.

It was so early in the morning that their sister, Elisa, was still asleep when they flew over the peasant hut where she was staying. They hovered over the roofs, craning and twisting their long necks and flapping their wings, but nobody saw them or heard them. They were forced to fly on, high up near the clouds and far away into the wide world. They came down in a vast, dark forest that stretched down to the shores of the sea.

Poor little Elisa stayed in the peasant hut, and played with a green leaf, for she had no other toy. She made a little hole in the leaf and looked through it at the sun. Through it, she seemed to see her brothers' bright eyes, and whenever the warm sunlight touched her cheek, it reminded her of all their kisses.

One day passed like all the others. When the wind stirred the hedge roses outside the hut, it whispered to them, "Who could be prettier than you?" But the roses shook their heads and answered, "Elisa!" And on Sunday, when the old woman sat in the doorway reading the psalms, the wind fluttered through the pages and said to the book, "Who could be more saintly than you?" "Elisa," the book testified. What it and the roses said was perfectly true.

Elisa was to go back home when she became fifteen, but as soon as the queen saw what a beautiful princess she was, the queen felt spiteful and full of hatred toward her. She would not have hesitated to turn her into a wild swan, like her brothers, but she did not dare to do it just yet, because the king wanted to see his daughter.

In the early morning, the queen went to the bathing place, which was made of white marble, furnished with soft cushions, and carpeted with the most splendid rugs. She took three toads, kissed them, and said to the first:

"Squat on Elisa's head when she bathes, so that she will become as torpid as you are." To the second she said, "Squat on her forehead, so that she will become as ugly as you are, and her father won't recognize her." And to the third, she whispered, "Lie against her heart, so that she will be cursed and tormented by evil desires.

Thereupon the queen dropped the three toads into the clear water, which at once turned a greenish color. She called Elisa, made her undress, and told her to enter the bath. When Elisa went down into the water, one toad fastened himself to her hair, another to her forehead, and the third against her heart. But she did not seem to be aware of them, and when she stood up, three red poppies floated on the water. If the toads had not been poisonous, and had not been kissed by the witch, they would have been turned into red roses. But at least they had been turned into flowers, by the mere touch of her head and heart. She was too innocent and good for witchcraft to have power over her.

When the evil queen realized this, she rubbed Elisa with walnut stain that turned her dark brown, smeared her beautiful face with a vile ointment, and tousled her lovely hair. No one could have recognized the beautiful Elisa, and when her father saw her, he was shocked. He said that this could not be his daughter. No one knew her except the watchdog and the swallows, and they were humble creatures who had nothing to say.

Poor Elisa cried and thought of her eleven brothers, who were all away. Heavy-hearted, she stole away from the palace and wandered all day long over fields and marshes, till she came to the vast forest. She had no idea where to turn. All she felt was her sorrow and her longing to be with her brothers. Like herself, they must have been driven out into the world, and she set her heart upon finding them. She had been in the forest only a little while when night came on, and as she had strayed from any sign of a path, she said her prayers and lay down on the soft moss, with her head pillowed against a stump. All was quiet, the air was so mild, and hundreds of fireflies glittered like a green fire in the grass and moss. When she lightly brushed against a single branch, the shining insects showered about her like falling stars.

She dreamed of her brothers all night long. They were children again, playing together, writing with their diamond pencils on their golden slates, and looking at her wonderful picture book that had cost half a kingdom. But they no longer scribbled sums and exercises as they used to do. No, they set down their bold deeds and all that they had seen or heard. Everything in the picture book came alive. The birds sang, and the people strolled out of the book to talk with Elisa and her brothers, but whenever she turned a page, they immediately jumped back into place, to keep the pictures in order.

When she awoke, the sun was already high. She could not see it plainly, for the tall trees spread their tangled branches above her, but the rays played above like a shimmering golden gauze. There was a delightful fragrance of green foliage, and the birds came near enough to have perched on her shoulder. She heard the water splashing from many large springs, which all flowed into a pool with the most beautiful sandy bottom. Although it was hemmed in by a wall of thick bushes, there was one place where the deer had made a path wide enough for Elisa to reach the water. The pool was so clear that if the wind had not stirred the limbs and bushes, she might have supposed they were painted on the bottom of the pool. For each leaf was clearly reflected, whether the sun shone upon it or whether it grew in the shade.

When Elisa saw her own face, she was horrified to find it so brown and ugly. But as soon as she wet her slender hand and rubbed her brow and her eyes, her fair skin showed again. Then she laid aside her clothes and plunged into the fresh water. In all the world, there was no king's daughter as lovely as Elisa. When she had dressed herself and plaited her long hair, she went to the sparkling spring and drank from the hollow of her hand. She wandered deeper into the woods without knowing whither she went. She thought of her brothers, and she thought of the good Lord, who she knew would not forsake her. He lets the wild crab apples grow to feed the hungry, and he led her footsteps to a tree with its branches bent down by the weight of their fruit. Here she had her lunch. After she put props under the heavy limbs, she went on into the depths of the forest. It was so quiet that she heard her own footsteps and every dry leaf that rustled underfoot. Not a bird was in sight, not a ray of the sun could get through the big heavy branches, and the tall trees grew so close together that when she looked straight ahead, it seemed as if a solid fence of lofty palings imprisoned her. She had never known such solitude.

The night came on, pitch black. Not one firefly glittered among the leaves as she despondently lay down to sleep. Then it seemed to her that the branches parted overhead and the Lord looked kindly down upon her, and little angels peeped out from above His head and behind Him.

When she awoke the next morning, she did not know whether she had dreamed this, or whether it had really happened.

A few steps farther on, she met an old woman who had a basket of berries and gave some of them to her. Elisa asked if she had seen eleven princes riding through the forest.

"No," the old woman said. "But yesterday I saw eleven swans who wore golden crowns. They were swimming in the river not far from here."

She led Elisa a little way to the top of a hill that sloped down to a winding river. The trees on either bank stretched their long leafy branches toward each other, and where the stream was too wide for them to grow across it, they had torn their roots from the earth and leaned out over the water until their branches met. Elisa told the old woman good-bye and followed the river down to where it flowed into the great open sea.

Before the young girl lay the whole beautiful sea, but not a sail nor a single boat was in sight. How could she go on? She looked at the countless pebbles on the beach, and saw how round the water had worn them. Glass, iron ore, stones, all that had been washed up, had been shaped by the water that was so much softer than even her tender hand.

"It rolls on tirelessly, and that is the way it makes such hard things smooth," she said. "I shall be just as untiring. Thank you for your lesson, you clear rolling waves. My heart tells me that someday you will carry me to my beloved brothers."

Among the wet seaweed, she found eleven white swan feathers, which she collected in a sheaf. There were still drops of water on them, but whether these were spray or tears, no one could say. It was very lonely along the shore, but she did not mind, for the sea was constantly changing. Indeed, it showed more changes in a few hours than an inland lake does in a whole year. When the sky was black with threatening clouds, it was as if the sea seemed to say, "I can look threatening too." Then the wind would blow, and the waves would raise their white crests. But when the wind died down and the clouds were red, the sea would look like a rose petal.

Sometimes it showed white, and sometimes green, but however calm it might seem, there was always a gentle lapping along the shore, where the waters rose and fell like the chest of a child asleep.

Just at sunset, Elisa saw eleven white swans, with golden crowns on their heads, fly toward the shore. As they flew, one behind another, they looked like a white ribbon floating in the air. Elisa climbed up and hid behind a bush on the steep bank. The swans came down near her and flapped their magnificent white wings.

As soon as the sun went down beyond the sea, the swans threw off their feathers, and there stood eleven handsome princes. They were her brothers, and, although they were greatly altered, she knew in her heart that she could not be mistaken. She cried aloud and rushed into their arms, calling them each by name. The princes were so happy to see their little sister. And they knew her at once, for all that she had grown tall and lovely. They laughed, and they cried, and they soon realized how cruelly their stepmother had treated them all.

"We brothers," said the eldest, "are forced to fly about disguised as wild swans as long as the sun is in the heavens, but when it goes down, we take back our human form. So at sunset, we must always look about us for some firm foothold, because if ever we were flying among the clouds at sunset we would be dashed down to the earth.

"We do not live on this coast. Beyond the sea, there is another land as fair as this, but it lies far away, and we must cross the vast ocean to reach it. Along our course, there is not one island where we can pass the night, except one little rock that rises from the middle of the sea. It is barely big enough to hold us, however close together we stand, and if there is a rough sea, the waves wash over us. But still we thank God for it.

"In our human forms, we rest there during the night, and without it, we could never come back to our own dear homeland. It takes two of the longest days of the year for our journey. We are allowed to come back to our native land only once a year, and we do not dare to stay longer than eleven days. As we fly over this forest, we can see the palace where our father lives and where we were born. We can see the high tower of the church where our mother lies buried. And here we feel that even the trees and bushes are akin to us. Here the wild horses gallop across the moors as we saw them in our childhood, and the charcoal-burner sings the same old songs to which we used to dance when we were children. This is our homeland. It draws us to it, and here, dear sister, we have found you again. We may stay two days longer, and then we must fly across the sea to a land that is fair enough, but not our own. How shall we take you with us? For we have neither ship nor boat."

"How shall I set you free?" their sister asked, and they talked on for most of the night, sparing only a few hours for sleep.

In the morning, Elisa was awakened by the rustling of swans' wings overhead. Her brothers, once more enchanted, wheeled above her in great circles until they were out of sight. One of them, her youngest brother, stayed with her and rested his head on her breast while she stroked his wings. They spent the whole day together, and toward evening, the others returned. As soon as the sun went down, they resumed their own shape.

"Tomorrow," said one of her brothers, "we must fly away, and we dare not return until a whole year has passed. But we cannot leave you like this. Have you courage enough to come with us? My arm is strong enough to carry you through the forest, so surely the wings of us all should be strong enough to bear you across the sea."

"Yes, take me with you," said Elisa.

They spent the entire night making a net of pliant willow bark and tough rushes. They made it large and strong. Elisa lay down upon it, and when the sun rose and her brothers again became wild swans, they lifted the net in their bills and flew high up toward the clouds with their beloved sister, who still was fast asleep. As the sun shone straight into her face, one of the swans flew over her head so as to shade her with his wide wings.

They were far from the shore when she awoke. Elisa thought she must still be dreaming, so strange did it seem to be carried through the air, high over the sea. Beside her lay a branch full of beautiful ripe berries and a bundle of sweet-tasting roots. Her youngest brother had gathered them and put them there for her. She gave him a grateful smile. She knew he must be the one who flew over her head to protect her eyes from the sun.

They were so high that the first ship they sighted looked like a gull floating on the water. A cloud rolled up behind them, as big as a mountain. Upon it, Elisa saw gigantic shadows of herself and of the eleven swans. It was the most splendid picture she had ever seen, but as the sun rose higher, the clouds grew small, and the shadow picture of their flight disappeared.

All day, they flew like arrows whipping through the air, yet, because they had their sister to carry, they flew more slowly than on their former journeys. Night was drawing near, and a storm was rising. In terror, Elisa watched the sinking sun, for the lonely rock was nowhere in sight. It seemed to her that the swans beat their wings in the air more desperately. Alas, it was because of her that they could not fly fast enough. So soon as the sun went down they would turn into men, and all of them would pitch down into the sea and drown. She prayed to God from the depths of her heart, but still no rock could be seen. Black clouds gathered, and great gusts told of the storm to come. The threatening clouds came on as one tremendous wave that rolled down toward them like a mass of lead, and flash upon flash of lightning followed them. Then the sun touched the rim of the sea. Elisa's heart beat madly as the swans shot down so fast that she thought they were falling, but they checked their downward swoop. Half of the sun was below the sea when she first saw the little rock below them. It looked no larger than the head of a seal jutting out of the water. The sun sank very fast. Now it was no bigger than a star, but her foot touched solid ground. Then the sun went out like the last spark on a piece of burning paper. She saw her brothers stand about her, arm in arm, and there was only just room enough for all of them. The waves beat upon the rock and washed over them in a shower of spray. The heavens were lit by constant flashes, and bolt upon bolt of thunder crashed. But the sister and brothers clasped each other's hands and sang a psalm, which comforted them and gave them courage.

At dawn, the air was clear and still. As soon as the sun came up, the swans flew off with Elisa, and they left the rock behind. The waves still tossed, and from the height where they soared, it looked as if the white flecks of foam against the dark green waves were millions of white swans swimming upon the waters.

When the sun rose higher, Elisa saw before her a mountainous land, half floating in the air. Its peaks were capped with sparkling ice, and in the middle rose a castle that was a mile long, with one bold colonnade perched upon another. Down below, palm trees swayed and brilliant flowers bloomed as big as mill wheels. She asked if this was the land for which they were bound, but the swans shook their heads. What she saw was the gorgeous and ever-changing palace of Fata Morgana. No mortal being could venture to enter it. As Elisa stared at it, before her eyes the mountains, palms, and palace faded away, and in their place rose twenty splendid churches, all alike, with lofty towers and pointed windows. She thought she heard the organ peal, but it was the roll of the ocean she heard. When she came close to the churches, they turned into a fleet of ships sailing beneath her, but when she looked down, it was only a sea mist drifting over the water.

Scene after scene shifted before her eyes until she saw at last the real country whither they went. Mountains rose before her beautifully blue, wooded with cedars and studded with cities and palaces. Long before sunset, she was sitting on a mountainside, in front of a large cave carpeted over with green creepers so delicate that they looked like embroidery.

"We shall see what you'll dream of here tonight," her youngest brother said, as he showed her where she was to sleep.

"I only wish I could dream how to set you free," she said.

This thought so completely absorbed her, and she prayed so earnestly for the Lord to help her that even in her sleep she kept on praying. It seemed to her that she was flying aloft to the Fata Morgana palace of clouds. The fairy who came out to meet her was fair and shining, yet she closely resembled the old woman who gave her the berries in the forest and told her of the swans who wore golden crowns on their heads.

"Your brothers can be set free," she said, "but have you the courage and tenacity to do it? The sea water that changes the shape of rough stones is indeed softer than your delicate hands, but it cannot feel the pain that your fingers will feel. It has no heart, so it cannot suffer the anguish and heartache that you will have to endure. Do you see this stinging nettle in my hand? Many such nettles grow around the cave where you sleep. Only those and the ones that grow upon graves in the churchyards may be used—remember that! Those you must gather, although they will burn your hands to blisters. Crush the nettles with your feet and you will have flax, which you must spin and weave into eleven shirts of mail with long sleeves. Once you throw these over the eleven wild swans, the spell over them is broken. But keep this well in mind! From the moment you undertake this task until it is done, even though it lasts for years, you must not speak. The first word you say will strike your brothers' hearts like a deadly knife. Their lives are at the mercy of your tongue. Now, remember what I told you!"

She touched Elisa's hand with nettles that burned like fire and awakened her. It was broad daylight, and close at hand where she had been sleeping grew a nettle like those of which she had dreamed. She thanked God upon her knees, and left the cave to begin her task.

With her soft hands, she took hold of the dreadful nettles that seared like fire. Great blisters rose on her hands and arms, but she endured it gladly in the hope that she could free her beloved brothers. She crushed each nettle with her bare feet, and spun the green flax.

When her brothers returned at sunset, it alarmed them that she did not speak. They feared this was some new spell cast by their wicked stepmother, but when they saw her hands, they understood that she labored to save them. The youngest one wept, and wherever his tears touched Elisa, she felt no more pain, and the burning blisters healed.

She toiled throughout the night, for she could not rest until she had delivered her beloved brothers from the enchantment. Throughout the next day, while the swans were gone, she sat all alone, but never had the time sped so quickly. One shirt was made, and she set to work on the second one.

Then she heard the blast of a hunting horn on the mountainside. It frightened her, for the sound came nearer until she could hear the hounds bark. Terror-stricken, she ran into the cave, bundled together the nettles she had gathered and woven, and sat down on this bundle.

Immediately, a big dog came bounding from the thicket, followed by another, and still another, all barking loudly as they ran to and fro. In a very few minutes, all the huntsmen stood in front of the cave. The most handsome of these was the king of the land, and he came up to Elisa. Never before had he seen a girl so beautiful. "My lovely child," he said, "how do you come to be here?"

Elisa shook her head, for she did not dare to speak. Her brothers' deliverance and their very lives depended upon it, and she hid her hands under her apron to keep the king from seeing how much she suffered.

"Come with me," he told her. "You cannot stay here. If you are as good as you are fair, I shall clothe you in silk and velvet, set a golden crown upon your head, and give you my finest palace to live in." Then he lifted her up on his horse. When she wept and wrung her hands, the king told her, "My only wish is to make you happy. Someday you will thank me for doing this." Off through the mountains he spurred, holding her before him on his horse as his huntsmen galloped behind them.

At sundown, his splendid city with all its towers and domes lay before them. The king led her into his palace, where great fountains played in the high marble halls and where both walls and ceilings were adorned with paintings. But she took no notice of any of these things. She could only weep and grieve. Indifferently, she let the women dress her in royal garments, weave strings of pearls in her hair, and draw soft gloves over her blistered fingers.

She was so dazzlingly beautiful in all this splendor that the whole court bowed even deeper than before. And the king chose her for his bride, although the archbishop shook his head and whispered that this lovely maid of the woods must be a witch who had blinded their eyes and stolen the king's heart.

But the king would not listen to him. He commanded that music be played, the costliest dishes be served, and the prettiest girls dance for her. She was shown through sweet-scented gardens and into magnificent halls, but nothing could make her lips smile or her eyes sparkle. Sorrow had set its seal upon them. At length, the king opened the door to a little chamber adjoining her bedroom. It was covered with splendid green embroideries, and looked just like the cave in which he had found her. On the floor lay the bundle of flax she had spun from the nettles, and from the ceiling hung the shirt she had already finished. One of the huntsmen had brought these with him as curiosities.

"Here you may dream that you are back in your old home," the king told her. "Here is the work that you were doing there, and surrounded by all your splendor here, it may amuse you to think of those times."

When Elisa saw these things that were so precious to her, a smile trembled on her lips, and the blood rushed back to her cheeks. The hope that she could free her brothers returned to her, and she kissed the king's hand. He pressed her to his heart and commanded that all the church bells peal to announce their wedding. The beautiful mute girl from the forest was to be the country's queen.

The archbishop whispered evil words in the king's ear, but they did not reach his heart. The wedding was to take place. The archbishop himself had to place the crown on her head. Out of spite, he forced the tight circlet so low on her forehead that it hurt her. But a heavier band encircled her heart, and the sorrow she felt for her brothers kept her from feeling any hurt of the flesh. Her lips were mute, for one single word would mean death to her brothers, but her eyes shone with love for the kind and handsome king who did his best to please her. Every day, she grew fonder and fonder of him in her heart. Oh, if only she could confide in him, and tell him what grieved her. But mute she must remain, and finish her task in silence. So at night she would steal away from his side into her little chamber that resembled the cave, and there she wove one shirt after another, but when she set to work on the seventh, there was not enough flax left to finish it.

She knew that the nettles she must use grew in the churchyard, but she had to gather them herself. How could she go there?

"Oh, what is the pain in my fingers compared with the anguish I feel in my heart!" she thought. "I must take the risk, and the good Lord will not desert me."

As terrified as if she were doing some evil thing, she tiptoed down into the moonlit garden, through the long alleys, and down the deserted streets to the churchyard. There, she saw a group of vampires sitting in a circle on one of the large gravestones. These hideous ghouls took off their ragged clothes as they were about to bathe. With skinny fingers, they clawed open the new graves. Greedily, they snatched out the bodies and ate the flesh from them. Elisa had to pass close to them, and they fixed their vile eyes upon her, but she said a prayer, picked the stinging nettles, and carried them back to the palace.

Only one man saw her—the archbishop. He was awake while others slept. Now he had proof of what he had suspected. There was something wrong with the queen. She was a witch, and that was how she had duped the king and all his people.

In the confessional, he told the king what he had seen and what he feared. As the bitter words spewed from his mouth, the images of the saints shook their heads, as much as to say, "He lies. Elisa is innocent." The archbishop, however, had a different explanation for this. He said they were testifying against her, and shaking their heads at her wickedness.

Two big tears rolled down the king's cheeks as he went home with suspicion in his heart. That night, he pretended to be asleep, but no restful sleep touched his eyes. He watched Elisa get out of bed. Every night, he watched her get up, and each time, he followed her quietly and saw her disappear into her private little room. Day after day, his frown deepened. Elisa saw it and could not understand why this should be, but it made her anxious and added to the grief her heart already felt for her brothers. Her hot tears fell down upon her queenly robes of purple velvet. There they flashed like diamonds, and all who saw this splendor wished that they were queen.

Meanwhile, she had almost completed her task. Only one shirt was lacking, but again she ran out of flax. Not a single nettle was left. Once more, for the last time, she must go to the churchyard and pluck a few more handfuls. She thought with fear of the lonely walk and the ghastly vampires, but her will was as strong as her faith in God.

She went upon her mission, but the king and his archbishop followed her. They saw her disappear through the iron gates of the churchyard, and when they came in after her, they saw vampires sitting on a gravestone, just as Elisa had seen them.

The king turned away, for he thought Elisa was among them—Elisa, whose head had rested against his heart that very evening.

"Let the people judge her," he said. And the people did judge her. They condemned her to die by fire.

She was led from her splendid royal halls to a dungeon, dark and damp, where the wind whistled in between the window bars. Instead of silks and velvets, they gave her for a pillow the bundle of nettles she had gathered, and for her coverlet the harsh, burning shirts of mail she had woven. But they could have given her nothing that pleased her more.

She set to work again, and prayed. Outside, the boys in the street sang jeering songs about her, and not one soul came to comfort her with a kind word.

But toward evening, she heard the rustle of a swan's wings close to her window. It was her youngest brother who had found her at last. She sobbed for joy. Though she knew that this night was all too apt to be her last, the task was almost done, and her brothers were near her.

The archbishop came to stay with her during her last hours on earth, for this much he had promised the king. But she shook her head, and by her expression and gestures begged him to leave. This was the last night she had to finish her task, or it would all go for naught—all her pain, and her tears, and her sleepless nights. The archbishop went away, saying cruel things against her. But poor Elisa knew her own innocence, and she kept on with her task.

The little mice ran about the floor, and brought nettles to her feet, trying to help her all they could. And a thrush perched near the bars of her window to sing the whole night through, as merrily as he could, so that she would keep up her courage.

It was still in the early dawn, an hour before sunrise, when the eleven brothers reached the palace gates and demanded to see the king. This, they were told, was impossible. It was still night. The king was asleep and could not be disturbed. They begged and threatened so loudly that the guard turned out, and even the king came running to find what the trouble was. But at that instant the sun rose, and the eleven brothers vanished. Eleven swans were seen flying over the palace.

All the townsmen went flocking out through the town gates, for they wanted to see the witch burned. A decrepit old horse pulled the cart in which Elisa sat. They had dressed her in coarse sackcloth, and all her lovely long hair hung loose around her beautiful head. Her cheeks were deathly pale, and her lips moved in silent prayer as her fingers twisted the green flax. Even on her way to death, she did not stop her still unfinished work. Ten shirts lay at her feet, and she worked away on the eleventh. "See how the witch mumbles," the mob scoffed at her. "That's no psalm book in her hands. No, there she sits, nursing her filthy sorcery. Snatch it away from her, and tear it to bits!"

The crowd of people closed in to destroy all her work, but before they could reach her, eleven white swans flew down and made a ring around the cart with their flapping wings. The mob drew back in terror.

"It is a sign from Heaven. She must be innocent," many people whispered. But no one dared say it aloud.

As the executioner seized her arm, she made haste to throw the eleven shirts over the swans, who instantly became eleven handsome princes. But the youngest brother still had a swan's wing in place of one arm, where a sleeve was missing from his shirt. Elisa had not quite been able to finish it.

"Now," she cried, "I may speak! I am innocent."

All the people who saw what had happened bowed down to her as they would before a saint. But the strain, the anguish, and the suffering had been too much for her to bear, and she fell into her brothers' arms as if all life had gone out of her.

"She is innocent indeed!" said her eldest brother, and he told them all that had happened. And while he spoke, the scent of a million roses filled the air, for every piece of wood that they had piled up to burn her had taken root and grown branches. There stood a great high hedge, covered with red and fragrant roses. At the very top, a single pure white flower shone like a star. The king plucked it and put it on Elisa's breast. And she awoke, with peace and happiness in her heart.

All the church bells began to ring of their own accord, and the air was filled with birds. Back to the palace went a bridal procession such as no king had ever enjoyed before.

THE GARDEN OF PARADISE (1839)

There was once a king's son; no one had so many beautiful books as he. In them, he could read of everything that had ever happened in this world, and he could see it all pictured in fine illustrations. He could find out about every race of people and every country, but there was not a single word about where to find the Garden of Paradise, and this, just this, was the very thing that he thought most about.

When he was still very young and was about to start his schooling, his grandmother had told him that each flower in the Garden of Paradise was made of the sweetest cake, and that the pistils were bottles full of finest wine. On one sort of flower, she told, history was written, on another geography, or multiplication tables, so that one only had to eat cake to know one's lesson, and the more one ate, the more history, geography, or arithmetic one would know.

At the time he believed her, but when the boy grew older and more learned and much wiser, he knew that the glories of the Garden of Paradise must be of a very different sort.

"Oh, why did Eve have to pick fruit from the Tree of Knowledge, and why did Adam eat what was forbidden him? Now if it had only been I, that would never have happened, and sin would never have come into the world." He said it then, and when he was seventeen, he said it still. The Garden of Paradise was always in his thoughts.

He went walking in the woods one day. He walked alone, for this was his favorite amusement. Evening came on, the clouds gathered, and the rain poured down as if the sky were all one big floodgate from which the water plunged. It was as dark as it would be at night in the deepest well. He kept slipping on the wet grass, and tripping over the stones that stuck out of the rocky soil. Everything was soaking wet, and at length, the poor prince didn't have a dry stitch to his back. He had to scramble over great boulders where the water trickled from the wet moss. He had almost fainted, when he heard a strange puffing and saw a huge cave ahead of him. It was brightly lit, for inside the cave burned a fire so large that it could have roasted a stag. And this was actually being done. A magnificent deer, antlers and all, had been stuck on a spit, and was being slowly turned between the rough-hewn trunks of two pine trees. An elderly woman, so burly and strong that she might have been taken for a man in disguise, sat by the fire and threw log after log upon it.

"You can come nearer," she said. "Sit down by the fire and let your clothes dry."

"There's an awful draft here," the prince remarked, as he seated himself on the ground.

"It will be still worse when my sons get home," the woman told him. "You are in the cave of the winds, and my sons are the four winds of the world. Do I make myself clear?"

"Where are your sons?" the prince asked.

"Such a stupid question is hard to answer," the woman told him. "My sons go their own ways, playing ball with the clouds in that great hall." And she pointed up toward the sky.

"Really!" said the prince. "I notice that you have a rather forceful way of speaking, and are not as gentle as the women I usually see around me."

"I suppose they have nothing better to do. I have to be harsh to control those sons of mine. I manage to do it, for all that they are an obstinate lot. See the four sacks that hang there on the wall! They dread those as much as you used to dread the switch that was kept behind the mirror for you. I can fold the boys right up, let me tell you, and pop them straight into the bag. We don't mince matters. There they stay. They aren't allowed to roam around again until I see fit to let them. But here comes one of them."

It was the North Wind who came hurtling in, with a cold blast of snowflakes that swirled about him and great hailstones that rattled on the floor. He was wearing a bearskin coat and trousers; a sealskin cap was pulled over his ears; long icicles hung from his beard; and hailstone after hailstone fell from the collar of his coat.

"Don't go right up to the fire so quickly," the prince warned him. "Your face and hands might get frostbite."

"Frostbite!" the North Wind laughed his loudest. "Frostbite! Why, frost is my chief delight. But what sort of 'longleg' are you? How do you come to be in the cave of the winds?"

"He is here as my guest," the old woman intervened. "And if that explanation doesn't suit you, into the sack you go. Do I make myself clear?"

She made herself clear enough. The North Wind now talked of whence he had come, and where he had traveled for almost a month.

"I come from the Arctic Sea," he told them. "I have been on Bear Island with the Russian walrus hunters. I lay beside the helm and slept as they sailed from the North Cape. When I awoke from time to time, the storm bird circled about my knees. There's an odd bird for you! He gives a quick flap of his wings, and then holds them perfectly still and rushes along at full speed."

"Don't be so long-winded," his mother told him. "So you came to Bear Island?"

"It's a wonderful place! There's a dancing floor for you, as flat as a platter! The surface of the island is all half-melted snow, little patches of moss, and outcropping rocks. Scattered about are the bones of whales and polar bears, colored a moldy green, and looking like the arms and legs of some giant.

"You'd have thought that the sun never shone there. I blew the fog away a bit, so that the house could be seen. It was a hut built of wreckage and covered with walrus skins, the fleshy side turned outward, and smeared with reds and greens. A lovely polar bear sat growling on the roof of it.

"I went to the shore and looked at birds' nests, and when I saw the featherless nestlings shrieking, with their beaks wide open, I blew down into their thousand throats. That taught them to shut their mouths. Further along, great walruses were wallowing about like monstrous maggots, with pigs' heads, and tusks a yard long."

"How well you do tell a story, my son," the old woman said. "My mouth waters when I hear you!"

"The hunt began. The harpoon was hurled into the walrus' breast, and a streaming blood stream spurted across the ice like a fountain. This reminded me of my own sport. I blew my sailing ships, those towering icebergs, against the boats until their timbers cracked. Ho! How the crew whistled and shouted. But I outwhistled them all. Overboard on the ice they had to throw their dead walruses, their tackle, and even their sea chests. I shrouded them in snow and let them drift south with their broken boats and their booty alongside, for a taste of the open sea. They won't ever come back to Bear Island."

"That was a wicked thing to do," said the mother of the winds.

"I'll let others tell of my good deeds," he said. "But here comes my brother from the west. I like him best of all. He has a seafaring air about him, and carries a refreshing touch of coolness wherever he goes."

"Is that little Zephyr?" the prince asked.

"Of course it's Zephyr," the old woman replied, "but he's not little. He was a nice boy once, but that was years ago."

He looked like a savage, except that he wore a broad-rimmed hat to shield his face. In his hand he carried a mahogany bludgeon, cut in the mahogany forests of America. Nothing less would do!

"Where have you come from?" his mother asked.

"I come from the forest wilderness," he said, "where the thorny vines make a fence between every tree, where the water snake lurks in the wet grass, and where people seem unnecessary."

"What were you doing there?"

"I gazed into the deepest of rivers and saw how it rushed through the rapids and threw up a cloud of spray large enough to hold the rainbow. I saw a wild buffalo wading in the river, but it swept him away. He swam with a flock of wild ducks that flew up when the river went over a waterfall. But the buffalo had to plunge down it. That amused me so much that I blew up a storm, which broke age-old trees into splinters."

"Haven't you done anything else?" the old woman asked him.

"I turned somersaults across the plains, stroked the wild horses, and shook coconuts down from the palm trees. Yes indeed, I have tales worth telling, but one shouldn't tell all he knows. Isn't that right, old lady?" Then he gave her such a kiss that it nearly knocked her over backward. He was certainly a wild young fellow.

Then the South Wind arrived, in a turban and a Bedouin's billowing robe.

"It's dreadfully cold in here," he cried, and threw more wood on the fire. "I can tell that the North Wind got here before me."

"It's hot enough to roast a polar bear here," the North Wind protested.

"You are a polar bear yourself," the South Wind said.

"Do you want to be put into the sack?" the old woman asked. "Sit down on that stone over there and tell me where you have been."

"In Africa, dear Mother," said he. "I have been hunting the lion with Hottentots in Kaffirland. What fine grass grows there on the plains. It is as green as an olive. There danced the gnu, and the ostrich raced with me, but I am fleeter than he is. I went into the desert where the yellow sand is like the bottom of the sea. I met with a caravan, where they were killing their last camel to get drinking water, but it was little enough they got. The sun blazed overhead and the sand scorched underfoot. The desert was unending.

"I rolled in the fine loose sand and whirled it aloft in great columns. What a dance that was! You ought to have seen how despondently the dromedaries hunched up, and how the trader pulled his burnoose over his head. He threw himself down before me as he would before Allah, his god. Now they are buried, with a pyramid of sand rising over them all. When someday I blow it away, the sun will bleach their bones white, and travelers will see that men have been there before them. Otherwise, no one would believe it, there in the desert."

"So you have done nothing but wickedness!" cried his mother. "Into the sack with you!" And before he was aware of it, she picked the South Wind up bodily and thrust him into the bag. He thrashed about on the floor until she sat down on the sack. That kept him quiet.

"Those are boisterous sons you have," said the prince.

"Indeed they are," she agreed, "but I know how to keep them in order. Here comes the fourth one."

This was the East Wind. He was dressed as a Chinaman.

"So that's where you've been!" said his mother. "I thought you had gone to the Garden of Paradise."

"I won't fly there until tomorrow," the East Wind said. "Tomorrow it will be exactly a hundred years since I was there. I am just home from China, where I danced around the porcelain tower until all the bells jangled. Officials of state were being whipped through the streets. Bamboo sticks were broken across their shoulders, though they were people of importance, from the first to the ninth degree. They howled, 'Thank you so much, my father and protector,' but they didn't mean it. And I went about clanging the bells and sang, 'Tsing, tsang, tsu!'"

"You are too saucy," the old woman told him. "It's a lucky thing that you'll be off to the Garden of Paradise tomorrow, for it always has a good influence on you. Remember to drink deep out of the fountain of wisdom and bring back a little bottleful for me."

"I'll do that," said the East Wind. "But why have you popped my brother from the south into the sack? Let's have him out. He must tell me about the phoenix bird, because the princess in the Garden of Paradise always asks me about that bird when I drop in on her every hundred years. Open up my sack, like my own sweet mother, and I'll give you two pockets full of tea as green and fresh as it was when I picked it off the bush."

"Well—for the sake of the tea, and because you are my pet, I'll open the sack."

She opened it up, and the South Wind crawled out. But he looked very glum, because the prince, who was a stranger, had seen him humbled.

"Here's a palm-leaf fan for the princess," the South Wind said. "It was given to me by the old phoenix, who was the only one of his kind in the world. On it he scratched with his beak a history of the hundred years that he lived, so she can read it herself. I watched the phoenix bird set fire to her nest, and sat there while she burned to death, just like a Hindu widow. What a crackling there was of dry twigs, what smoke, and what a smell of smoldering! Finally it all burst into flames, and the old phoenix was reduced to ashes, but her egg lay white-hot in the blaze. With a great bang it broke open, and the young phoenix flew out of it. Now he is the ruler over all the birds, and he is the only phoenix bird in all the world. As his greetings to the princess, he thrust a hole in the palm leaf I am giving you."

"Let's have a bite to eat," said the mother of the winds.

As they sat down to eat the roast stag, the prince took a place beside the East Wind, and they soon became fast friends.

"Tell me," said the prince, "who is this princess you've been talking so much about, and just where is the Garden of Eden?"

"Ah, ha!" said the East Wind. "Would you like to go there? Then fly with me tomorrow. I must warn you, though, no man has been there since Adam and Eve. You have read about them in the Bible?"

"Surely," the prince said.

"After they were driven out, the Garden of Paradise sank deep into the earth, but it kept its warm sunlight, its refreshing air, and all of its glories. The queen of the fairies lives there on the Island of the Blessed, where death never comes and where there is everlasting happiness. Sit on my back tomorrow, and I shall take you with me. I think it can be managed. But now let's stop talking, for I want to sleep."

And then they all went to sleep. When the prince awoke the next morning, it came as no small surprise to find himself high over the clouds. He was seated on the back of the East Wind, who carefully held him safe. They were so far up in the sky that all the woods, fields, rivers, and lakes looked as if they were printed on a map spread beneath them.

"Good morning," said the East Wind. "You might just as well sleep a little longer. There's nothing very interesting in this flat land beneath us, unless you care to count churches. They stand out like chalk marks upon the green board."

What he called "the green board" was all the fields and pastures.

"It was not very polite of me to leave without bidding your mother and brothers farewell," the prince said.

"That's excusable, when you leave in your sleep," the East Wind told him, as they flew on faster than ever.

One could hear it in the tree tops. All the leaves and branches rustled as they swept over the forest, and when they crossed over lakes or over seas, the waves rose high, and tall ships bent low to the water as if they were drifting swans.

As darkness gathered that evening, it was pleasant to see the great cities with their lights twinkling here and spreading there, just as when you burn a piece of paper and the sparks fly one after another. At this sight, the prince clapped his hands in delight, but the East Wind advised him to stop it and hold on tight, or he might fall and find himself stuck upon a church steeple.

The eagle in the dark forest flew lightly, but the East Wind flew more lightly still. The Cossack on his pony sped swiftly across the steppes, but the prince sped still more swiftly.

"Now," said the East Wind, "you can view the Himalayas, the highest mountains in Asia. And soon we shall reach the Garden of Paradise."

They turned southward, where the air was sweet with flowers and spice. Figs and pomegranates grew wild, and on untended vines grew red and blue clusters of grapes. They came down here, and both of them stretched out on the soft grass, where flowers nodded in the breeze as if to say: "Welcome back."

"Are we now in the Garden of Paradise?" the prince asked.

"Oh, no!" said the East Wind. "But we shall come to it soon. Do you see that rocky cliff, and the big cave, where the vines hang in a wide curtain of greenery? That's the way we go. Wrap your coat well about you. Here the sun is scorching hot, but a few steps and it is as cold as ice. The bird that flies at the mouth of the cave has one wing in summery and the other in wintry air."

"So this is the way to the Garden of Paradise," said the prince, as they entered the cave.

Brr-r-r! How frosty it was there, but not for long. The East Wind spread his wings, and they shone like the brighest flames. But what a cave that was! Huge masses of rock, from which water was trickling, hung in fantastic shapes above them. Sometimes the cave was so narrow that they had to crawl on their hands and knees, sometimes so vast that it seemed that they were under the open sky. The cave resembled a series of funeral chapels, with mute organ pipes and banners turned to stone.

"We are going to the Garden of Paradise through the gates of death, are we not?" the prince asked.

The East Wind answered not a word, but pointed to a lovely blue light that shone ahead of them. The masses of stone over their heads grew more and more misty, and at last they looked up at a clear white cloud in the moonlight. The air became delightfully clement, as fresh as it is in the hills, and as sweetly scented as it is among the roses that bloom in the valley.

The river that flowed there was clear as the air itself, and the fish in it were like silver and gold. Purple eels that at every turn threw off blue sparks frolicked about in the water, and the large leaves of the aquatic flowers gleamed in all of the rainbow's colors. The flowers themselves were like a bright orange flame, which fed on the water just as a lamplight is fed by oil.

A strong marble bridge, made so delicately and artistically that it looked as if it consisted of lace and glass pearls, led across the water to the Island of the Blessed, where the Garden of Paradise bloomed.

The East Wind swept the prince up in his arms and carried him across to the island, where the petals and leaves sang all the lovely old songs of his childhood, but far, far sweeter than any human voice could sing. Were these palm trees that grew there, or immense water plants? Such vast and verdant trees the prince had never seen before. The most marvelous climbing vines hung in garlands such as are to be seen only in old illuminated church books, painted in gold and bright colors in the margins or twined about the initial letters. Here was the oddest assortment of birds, flowers, and twisting vines.

On the grass nearby, with their brilliantly starred tails spread wide was a flock of peacocks. Or so they seemed, but when the prince touched them, he found that these were not birds. They were plants. They were large burdock leaves that were as resplendent as a peacock's train. Lions and tigers leaped about, as lithe as cats, in the green shrubbery that the olive blossoms made so fragrant. The lions and tigers were quite tame, for the wild wood pigeon, which glistened like a lovely pearl, brushed the lion's mane with her wings, and the timid antelopes stood by and tossed their heads as if they would like to join in their play.

Then the fairy of the garden came to meet them. Her garments were as bright as the sun, and her face was as cheerful as that of a happy mother who is well pleased with her child. She was so young and lovely, and the other pretty maidens who followed her each wore a shining star in their hair. When the East Wind gave her the palm-leaf message from the phoenix, her eyes sparkled with pleasure.

She took the prince by his hand and led him into her palace, where the walls had the color of a perfect tulip petal held up to the sun. The ceiling was made of one great shining flower, and the longer one looked up, the deeper did the cup of it seem to be. The prince went to the window. As he glanced out through one of the panes, he saw the Tree of Knowledge, with the serpent, and Adam and Eve standing under it.

"Weren't they driven out?" he asked.

The fairy smilingly explained to him that Time had glazed a picture in each pane, but that these were not the usual sort of pictures. No, they had life in them. The leaves quivered on the trees, and the people came and went as in a mirror.

He looked through another pane and there was Jacob's dream, with the ladder that went up to Heaven, and the great angels climbing up and down. Yes, all that ever there was in the world lived on, and moved across these panes of glass. Only Time could glaze such artistic paintings so well.

The fairy smiled and led him on into a vast and lofty hall with walls that seemed transparent. On the walls were portraits, each fairer than the one before. These were millions of blessed souls, a happy choir that sang in perfect harmony. The uppermost faces appeared to be smaller than the tiniest rosebud drawn as a single dot in a picture. In the center of the hall grew a large tree, with luxuriantly hanging branches. Golden apples large and small hung like oranges among the leaves. This was the Tree of Knowledge, of which Adam and Eve had tasted. A sparkling red drop of dew hung from each leaf, as if the tree were weeping tears of blood.

"Now let us get into the boat," the fairy proposed. "There we will have some refreshments on the heaving water. Though the rocking boat stays in one place, we shall see all the lands in the world glide by."

It was marvelous how the whole shore moved. Now the high snow-capped Alps went past, with their clouds and dark evergreen trees. The Alpine horn was heard, deep and melancholy, and the shepherds yodeled gaily in the valley. But soon the boat was overhung by the long arching branches of banana trees. Jet-black swans went swimming by, and the queerest animals and plants were to be seen along the banks. This was New Holland and the fifth quarter of the globe that glided past, with its blue hills in the distance. They heard the songs of the priests and saw the savages dance to the sound of drums and trumpets of bone. The cloud-tipped pyramids of Egypt, the fallen columns, and sphinxes half buried in the sands, swept by. The northern lights blazed over the glaciers around the pole in a display of fireworks that no one could imitate. The prince saw a hundred times more than we can tell, and he was completely happy.

"May I always stay here?" he asked.

"That is up to you," the fairy told him. "Unless, as Adam did, you let yourself be tempted and do what is forbidden, you may stay here always."

"I won't touch the fruit on the Tree of Knowledge," the prince declared. "Here are thousands of other fruits that are just as attractive."

"Look into your heart, and, if you have not strength enough, go back with the East

Wind who brought you here. He is leaving soon, and will not return for a hundred years, which you will spend as quickly here as if they were a hundred hours.

"But that is a long time to resist the temptation to sin. When I leave you every evening, I shall have to call, 'Come with me,' and hold out my hands to you. But you must stay behind. Do not follow me, or your desire will grow with every step. You will come into the hall where the Tree of Knowledge grows. I sleep under the arch of its sweet-smelling branches. If you lean over me, I shall have to smile, but if you kiss me on the mouth, this paradise will vanish deep into the earth, and you will lose it. The cutting winds of the wasteland will blow about you, the cold rain will drip from your hair, and sorrow and toil will be your destiny."

"I shall stay," the prince said.

The East Wind kissed his forehead. "Be strong," he said, "and in a hundred years we shall meet here again. Farewell! Farewell!" Then the East Wind spread his tremendous wings that flashed like lightning seen at harvest time or like the northern lights in the winter cold.

"Farewell! Farewell!" the leaves and trees echoed the sound, as the storks and the pelicans flew with him to the end of the garden in lines that were like ribbons streaming through the air.

"Now we will start our dances," the fairy said. "When I have danced the last dance with you at sundown, you will see me hold out my hands to you, and hear me call, 'come with me.' But do not come. Every evening for a hundred years, I shall have to repeat this. Every time that you resist, your strength will grow, and at last you will not even think of yielding to temptation. This evening is the first time, so take warning!"

And the fairy led him into a large hall of white, transparent lilies. The yellow stamens of each flower formed a small golden harp that vibrated to the music of strings and flutes. The loveliest maidens, floating and slender, came dancing by, clad in such airy gauze that one could see how perfectly shaped they were. They sang of the happiness of life—they who would never die—and they sang that the Garden of Paradise would forever bloom.

The sun went down. The sky turned to shining gold, and in its light, the lilies took on the color of the loveliest roses. The prince drank the sparkling wine that the maidens offered him and felt happier than he had ever been. He watched the background of the hall thrown open, and the Tree of Knowledge standing in a splendor that blinded his eyes. The song from the tree was as soft and lovely as his dear mother's voice, and it was as if she were saying, "My child, my dearest child."

The fairy then held out her hands to him and called most sweetly:

"Follow me! Oh, follow me!"

Forgetting his promise—forgetting everything, on the very first evening that she held out her hands and smiled—he ran toward her. The fragrant air around him became even more sweet, the music of the harps sounded even more lovely, and it seemed as though the millions of happy faces in the hall where the tree grew nodded to him and sang, "One must know all there is to know, for man is the lord of the earth." And it seemed to him that the drops that fell from the Tree of Knowledge were no longer tears of blood, but red and shining stars.

"Follow me! Follow me!" the quivering voice still called, and at every step that the prince took his cheeks flushed warmer and his pulse beat faster.

"I cannot help it," he said. "This is no sin. It cannot be wicked to follow beauty and happiness. I must see her sleeping. No harm will be done if only I keep myself from kissing her. And I will not kiss her, for I am strong. I have a determined will."

The fairy threw off her bright robe, parted the boughs, and was instantly hidden within them.

"I have not sinned yet," said the prince, "and I shall not!"

He pushed the branches aside. There she lay, already asleep. Lovely as only the fairy of the Garden of Paradise can be, she smiled in her sleep, but as he leaned over her, he saw tears trembling between her lashes.

"Do you weep for me?" he whispered. "Do not weep, my splendid maiden. Not until now have I known the bliss of paradise. It runs through my veins and through all my thoughts. I feel the strength of an angel, and the strength of eternal life in my mortal body. Let eternal night come over me. One moment such as this is worth it all." He kissed away the tears from her eyes, and then his lips had touched her mouth.

Thunder roared, louder and more terrible than any thunder ever heard before, and everything crashed! The lovely fairy and the blossoming paradise dropped away, deeper and deeper. The prince saw it disappear into the dark night. Like a small shining star, it twinkled in the distance. A deathly chill shook his body. He closed his eyes, and for a long time, he lay as if he were dead.

The cold rain fell in his face, and the cutting wind blew about his head. Consciousness returned to him.

"What have I done?" he gasped. "Like Adam, I have sinned—sinned so unforgivably that paradise has dropped away, deep in the earth."

He opened his eyes and he still saw the star far away, the star that twinkled like the Paradise he had lost-it was the morning star in the sky. He rose and found himself in the forest, not far from the cave of the winds. The mother of the winds sat beside him. She looked at him angrily and raised her finger.

"The very first evening!" she said. "I thought that was the way it would be. If you were my son, into the sack you would certainly go."

"Indeed he shall go there!" said Death, a vigorous old man with a scythe in his hand and long black wings. "Yes, he shall be put in a coffin, but not quite yet. Now I shall only mark him. For a while I'll let him walk the Earth to atone for his sins and grow better. But I'll be back someday. Someday, when he least expects me, I shall put him in a black coffin, lift it on my head, and fly upward to the star. There too blooms the Garden of Paradise, and if he is a good and pious man, he will be allowed to enter it. But if his thoughts are bad and his heart is still full of sin, he will sink down deeper with his coffin than Paradise sank. Only once in a thousand years shall I go to see whether he must sink still lower, or may reach the star—that bright star away up there."

THE FLYING TRUNK (1839)

There once was a merchant so wealthy that he could have paved a whole street with silver and still have had enough left over to pave a little alley. But he did nothing of the sort. He knew better ways of using his money than that. If he parted with pennies, they came back to him as crowns. That's the sort of merchant he was—and then he died.

Now his son got all the money, and he led a merry life, went to masquerades every night, made paper dolls out of banknotes, and played ducks and drakes at the lake with gold pieces instead of pebbles. This makes the money go, and his inheritance was soon gone. At last, he had only four pennies, and only a pair of slippers and a dressing gown to wear.

Now his former friends didn't care for him anymore, as he could no longer appear in public with them, but one of them was so good as to send him an old trunk, with the hint that he pack and be off. This was all very well, but he had nothing to pack, so he sat himself in it.

It was no ordinary trunk. Press on the lock, and it would fly. And that's just what it did. *Whisk!* It flew up the chimney, and over the clouds, and away through the skies. The bottom of it was so creaky that he feared he would fall through it, and what a fine somersault he would have made then! Good gracious! But at long last, he came down safely, in the land of the Turks. He hid his trunk under some dry leaves in the woods and set off toward the nearest town. He could do so very well, for the Turks all wear dressing gowns and slippers, just as he did.

When he passed a nurse with a child, he said, "Hello, Turkish nurse. Tell me, what's that great big palace at the edge of town? The one that has its windows up so high."

"That's where the Sultan's daughter lives," said the nurse. "It has been foretold that she will be unhappy when she falls in love, so no one is ever permitted to visit her except in the presence of her mother and father."

"Thank you," said the merchant's son. Back he went to the woods, sat in his trunk, and whisked off to the roof of the palace. From there, he climbed in at the princess's window.

She lay fast asleep on a sofa, and she looked so lovely that the merchant's son couldn't help kissing her. She woke up and was terribly frightened, but he told her he was a Turkish prophet who had sailed through the air just to see her. This pleased her very much.

As they sat there side by side, he told her stories about her eyes. He said they were beautifully dark, deep lakes in which her thoughts went swimming by like mermaids. He told her about her forehead, which he compared to a snow-covered mountainside with its many wonderful halls and pictures. Then he told her about the stork, which brings lovely little children from over the sea. Oh, they were such pretty stories! Then he asked her to marry him, and the princess said yes, right away.

"But you must come on Saturday," she told him, "when my mother and father will be here to have tea with me. They will be so proud when I tell them I am going to marry a prophet. But be sure you have a really pretty tale to tell them, for both my parents love stories. My mother likes them to be elevating and moral, but my father likes them merry, to make him laugh."

"I shall bring no other wedding present than a fairy tale," he told her, and so they parted. But first, the princess made him a present of a gold saber all covered with gold pieces, and this came in very handy.

He flew away, bought himself a new dressing gown, and went to the woods to invent a fairy tale. That wasn't so easy. However, he had it ready promptly on Saturday. The Sultan, his wife, and the whole court awaited him at the princess's tea party. They gave him a splendid reception.

"Won't you tell us a story?" said the Sultan's wife. "One that is instructive and thoughtful."

"One that will make us laugh, too," said the Sultan.

"To be sure," he said, and started his story. Now listen closely.

"There once was a bundle of matches, and they were particularly proud of their lofty ancestry. Their family tree—that is to say, the great pine tree of which they were little splinters—had been a great old tree in the forest. As the matches lay on the kitchen shelf, they talked of their younger days to the tinderbox and an old iron pot beside them.

"'When we were a part of the green branches,' they said, 'then we really were on a green branch! Every morning and evening, we were served the diamond tea that is called dew drops. We had sunshine all day long, and the little birds had to tell us stories. It was plain to see that we were wealthy, for while the other trees' garments lasted only the summer, our family could afford to wear green clothes all the year round. But then the woodcutters came, there was a big revolution, and our family was broken up. The chief support of our family got a place as the mainmast of a fine ship, that could sail around the world if need be. The other branches were scattered in different directions, and now our task is to bring light to the lower classes. That's the reason we distinguished people came to this kitchen.'

"'My lot has been quite different,' said the iron pot, who stood next to the matches. 'From the moment I came into this world, I've known little but cooking and scouring, day in, day out. I look after the solid and substantial part, and am in fact the most important thing in the house. My only amusement comes when dinner is over. Then, clean and tidy, I take my place here to have a sound conversation with my associates. But except for the watering pot, who now and then makes excursions into the yard, we always live indoors. Our only source of news is the market basket, and he speaks most alarmingly about the government and the people. Why, just the other day, an old conservative pot was so upset that he fell down and burst. That basket is a liberal, I tell you!'

"'You talk too much,' the tinderbox flashed sparks from his flint. 'Let's have a pleasant evening.'

"'Yes, let's talk about who among us is most aristocratic,' said the matches.

"'No. I don't like to talk about myself,' said the earthenware crock. 'Let's have some entertainment this evening. I'll begin. I'll tell you the sort of things we already know. That won't tax our imaginations, and it is so amusing. By the Baltic sea, by the beech trees of Denmark—'

"'That's a very pretty beginning,' the plates chattered. 'That's just the kind of story we like.'

"'There I passed my youth in a quiet home, where they polished the furniture, and swept the floor, and hung up fresh curtains every fourteenth day!'

"'How well you tell a story!' said the broom. 'You can hear right away that it's a woman who tells it. There's not a speck of dirt in it.'

"'Yes, one feels that,' said the water pail, and made a happy little jump so the water splashed on the floor.

"'The crock went on with her story, and the end was as good as the beginning.

"All the plates clattered for joy. The broom made a wreath of parsley to crown the crock, because she knew how that would annoy the others. And the broom thought, 'If I crown her tonight, she will crown me tomorrow.'

"'Now I'll do a dance,' said the fire tongs, and dance she did. Yes, good heavens, how she could kick one of her legs up in the air! The old chair cover in the corner split to see it. 'Will you crown me too?' said the tongs, so they gave her a wreath.

"'What a common mob,' said the matches.

"The teapot was asked to sing, but she had a cold in her throat. She said nothing short of boiling water could make her sing, but that was sheer affectation. She wished to sing only for the ladies and gentlemen in the drawing room.

"On the window sill was an old quill pen that the servant used. There was nothing remarkable about him except that he had been dipped too deep in the ink, but in that difference he took pride.

"'The teapot can sing or not, as she pleases,' he declared. 'In a cage, outside my window, there's a nightingale who will sing for us. He hasn't practiced for the occasion, but tonight we won't be too critical.'

"'I find it highly improper,' said the teakettle, who was the official kitchen singer, and a half-sister of the teapot. 'Why should we listen to a foreign bird? Is that patriotic? Let the market basket make the decision.'

"'I am most annoyed,' said the market basket. 'I am more annoyed than anyone can imagine. Is this any way to spend an evening? Wouldn't it be better to call the house to order? Everyone take his appointed place, and I shall run the whole game. That will be something quite different.'

"'Yes. Let us all make a noise,' they clamored.

"Just then, the servant opened the door, and they stood stock-still. Not one had a word to say. But there was not a pot among them who did not know what he could do, and how well qualified he was. 'If I had wanted to,' each one thought, 'we could have a gay evening. No question about it!'

"The servant girl took the matches and struck a light with them. My stars, how they sputtered and flared!

"'Now,' they thought, 'everyone can see we are the first. How brilliant we are! What a light we spread.' Then they burned out."

"That was a delightful story," said the Sultan's wife. "I felt myself right in the kitchen with the matches. My dear prophet, thou shalt certainly marry our daughter."

"Yes, indeed," said the Sultan. "Thou shalt marry her on Monday." They said "Thou" to him now, for he was soon to be one of the family.

So the wedding day was set, and on the evening that preceded it, the whole city was gay with lights. Cookies and cakes were thrown among the people. The boys in the street stood on tiptoe. They shouted, "Hurrah!" and whistled through their fingers. It was all so grand.

"I suppose I really ought to do something too," said the merchant's son. So he bought firecrackers and rockets and fireworks of every sort, loaded his trunk with them, and flew over the town.

Pop! went the crackers, and *swoosh!* went the rockets. The Turks jumped so high that their slippers flopped over their ears. Such shooting stars they never had seen. Now they could understand that it was the prophet of the Turks himself who was to marry their princess.

As soon as the merchant's son came down in the woods, he thought, "I'll go straight to the town to hear what sort of impression I made." It was the natural thing to do.

Oh, what stories they told! Every last man he asked had his own version, but all agreed it had been fine. Very fine!

"I saw the prophet himself," said one. "His eyes shone like stars, and his beard foamed like water."

"He was wrapped in a fiery cloak," said another. "The heads of beautiful angels peeped out of the folds of it."

Yes, he heard wonderful things, and his wedding was to be on the following day. He went back to the woods to rest in his trunk—but what had become of it? The trunk was burned! A spark from the fireworks had set it on fire, and now the trunk was burned to ashes. He couldn't fly anymore. He had no way to reach his bride. She waited for him on the roof, all day long. Most likely, she is waiting there still. But he wanders through the world, telling tales that are not half so merry as that one he told about the matches.

THE STORKS (1839)

On the roof of the last house in a little village was a stork's nest. The mother stork sat in it with her four young ones, who stuck out their heads with their little black beaks. (You see, their beaks had not yet turned red as they would in time.) And a little way off, all alone on the ridge of the roof, stood Father Stork, very upright and stiff. He was really a sentry on guard, but, so that he would not be entirely idle, he had drawn up one leg. My, how grand he looked, standing there on one leg! So still you might have thought he was carved from wood!

"It must look pretty fine for my wife to have a sentry standing by her nest!" he thought. "People don't know I'm her husband; they'll think I'm a servant, ordered to stand here on guard. It looks very smart, I must say."

So he went on, standing on one leg.

A crowd of children were playing down in the street, and as soon as they saw the storks, one of the boldest boys, followed by the others, began to sing the old song about storks. They sang it just as their leader remembered it:

Stork, stork, long-legged stork,
Off to your wife you'd better fly.
She's waiting for you in the nest,
Rocking four young ones to rest.
The first he will be hanged,
The second will be stabbed,
The third he will be burned,
And the fourth will be slapped!

"Just listen to what they are saying!" cried the little stork children. "They say we're going to be hanged and burned!"

"Don't pay any attention to that," replied the mother stork crossly. "Don't listen to them, and then it won't make any difference."

But the boys went on singing and pointing mockingly at the storks with their fingers. Only one boy, whose name was Peter, said it was a shame to make fun of the birds, and he wouldn't join the others.

The mother stork tried to comfort her children. "Don't let that bother you at all," she said. "Look how quietly your father is standing, and only on one leg, too!"

"But we're very much frightened!" insisted the young storks, and they drew their heads far back into the nest.

Next day, when the children came out to play and saw the storks, they began their song again:

The first he will be hanged,
The second will be burned!

"Are we really going to be hanged and burned?" asked the young storks.

"No, certainly not," replied their mother. "You're going to learn to fly! I'll teach you. Then we'll fly out over the meadows and visit the frogs; they'll bow down to us in the water and sing, 'Co-ax! Co-ax!' and then we'll eat them up. That'll be a lot of fun!"

"And then what?" asked the young storks.

"Then the storks from all over the country will assemble for the autumn maneuvers," their mother continued. "And it is of great importance that you know how to fly well then, for if you can't, the general will stab you dead with his beak; so when I start to teach you, pay attention and learn well."

"Oh, then we'll be stabbed, just the way the boys say! And listen, there they go, saying it again!"

"Never mind them; pay attention to me," said Mother Stork. "After the big maneuvers, we'll fly away to the warm countries, oh, so far away from here, over mountains and forests. We'll get to Egypt, where they have four-cornered houses of stone that come up to a point higher than the clouds. They call them pyramids, and they're even older than a stork could imagine. They have a river there too, that runs out of its banks, and turns the whole land to mud! We walk about in that mud, eating frogs."

"Oh!" cried the young storks.

"Yes, indeed. It's wonderful there. You don't do anything but eat all day long. And while we're so comfortable there, back here, there isn't a green leaf left on the trees, and it's so cold that the clouds freeze to pieces and fall down in little white rags."

She meant snow of course, but she didn't know any other way to explain it to the young ones.

"And do the naughty boys freeze to pieces, too?" asked the young storks.

"No, they don't quite do that," their mother replied. "But they come pretty close to it, and have to sit moping in a dark room. But we, on the other hand, fly about in foreign lands among the flowers and in the warm sunshine."

Some time passed, and the young storks grew large enough so that they could stand up in the nest and look at the wide world around them. Every day, Father Stork brought them beautiful frogs and delicious little snakes and all sorts of dainties that storks like. And how they laughed when he did tricks to amuse them! He would lay his head entirely back on his tail, and clap his beak as if it were a rattle. And then he would tell them stories, all about the marshes that they would see someday.

At last one day, Mother Stork led them all out onto the ridge of the roof.

"Now," she said, "it's time for you to learn to fly." Oh, how they wobbled and how they tottered, trying to balance themselves with their wings, and nearly falling off the roof!

"Watch me now," their mother called. "Hold your head like this! Move your legs like that! One, two! One, two! That'll help you get somewhere in the world!"

Then she flew a little way from the roof, and the young ones made a clumsy attempt to follow. Bumps! There they lay, for their bodies were still too heavy.

"I don't want to fly," complained the youngest one, creeping back into the nest. "I don't care about going to the warm countries at all!"

"Oh, so you want to freeze to death here when the winter comes, do you?" demanded his mother. "You want the boys to come and hang you and beat you and burn you, do you? All right, I'll call them!"

"Oh, no! Don't do that!" cried the little stork, and hopped out on the ridge again with the others.

By the third day, they could fly a little, and so they thought they could soar and hover in the air without moving their wings, but—when they tried it—bumps!— down they fell! They soon found they had to move their wings to keep up in the air.

That same day, the boys came back and began their song again:

Stork, stork, long-legged stork!

"Shall we fly down and pick their eyes out?" asked the young storks eagerly.

"Certainly not," replied their mother promptly. "Let them alone. Pay attention to me. That's much more important. One, two, three! Now we fly around to the right. One, two, three! Now to the left around the chimney. That was very good. That last flap of the wings was so perfect that you can fly with me tomorrow to the marshes. Several very nice stork families go there with their young ones, and I want to show them that mine are much the nicest. Don't forget to strut about; that looks very well and makes you seem important."

"But can't we take revenge on those rude boys first?" asked the young storks.

"Oh, let them scream as much as they like," replied their mother. "You'll fly with the clouds, and way off to the land of the pyramids while they'll be freezing. There won't be a green leaf or a sweet apple here then."

"But we *will* have our revenge!" the young storks whispered to each other, and went on practicing their flying.

Now, among the boys down there in the street, the worst of all was the boy who had begun the teasing song. He was a very little boy, hardly more than six years old, but the young storks thought he was at least a hundred, for he was much bigger than Mother and Father Stork, and how could they know how old children and grown-ups can be?

The young storks made up their minds to take revenge upon this boy, because he was the first to start the song, and he always kept on. As they grew bigger, they were determined to do something about it. At last, to keep them quiet, their mother had to promise them that they would be revenged, but they were not to learn about it until the day before they left the country.

"First, we'll have to see how you behave at the big maneuvers," she warned them. "If you don't do well, so that the general has to stab you with his beak, the boys will be right, at least in that way. We'll see."

"Yes, you'll see," replied the young ones, and my! How they worked! They practiced every day, until they could fly so neatly and lightly that it was a pleasure to watch them.

At last the autumn came on, and all the storks began to assemble before flying away to the warm countries to get away from the winter up here. What a review that was! All of the young storks had to fly over forests and villages to show how well they had learned, for they had a very long journey before them. And the young storks did so well that their report cards were marked, "Remarkably well, with frogs and snakes!" That was the highest mark, and meant that they could eat frogs and snakes as a prize. And that is what they did!

"Now we will have our revenge!" they cried to their mother.

"Yes," their mother agreed. "What I have thought of will be just the right thing to do. I know the pond where all the little human babies lie until the storks come to take them to their parents. The pretty little babies lie in that pond, dreaming more sweetly than they ever dream afterwards. All parents want a little baby, and every child wants a little sister or brother. Now, we'll go to that pond and bring a little baby sister or brother for each of the children who didn't sing that wicked song or make fun of us. But those that did won't get any."

"But that naughty, ugly boy who began the song?" demanded the young storks. "What shall we do with him?"

"In that pond," said his mother slowly, "there is a little baby that has dreamed itself to death; we'll bring that to him. And then he'll cry because we've brought him a little dead brother. But don't forget that good little boy who said it was a shame to make fun of us! We'll take him both a brother *and* a sister! And since his name is Peter, you shall all be called Peter, too!"

It was done just the way she said. And all the young storks were named Peter, and all storks are called Peter to this very day.

THE ROSE ELF (1839)

In the midst of a garden, there grew a rosebush, quite covered with roses, and in the most beautiful of them all there lived an elf—an elf so tiny that no mortal eye could see him. But he was as well made and as perfect as any child could be, and he had wings reaching from his shoulders to his feet. Behind each petal of the rose, he had a tiny bedroom. Oh, how fragrant his rooms were, and how bright and transparent the walls, for they were the beautiful pale pink petals of the rose! All day long, the little elf rejoiced in the warm sunshine as he flew from flower to flower or danced on the wings of the fluttering butterflies and measured how many steps he would have to take to pass along all the roads and paths on a single linden leaf. You see, what we call the veins on a leaf were highroads and byways to him. It was a long journey, and he had begun it rather late, so before he finished, the sun had gone down!

It turned very cold, dew fell, and the wind blew, so now it was high time he went home. He hurried as fast as he could, but to his dismay, he found that the rose had closed its petals for the night! Not a single rose stood open! He couldn't get in! Now, the poor little rose elf was terribly frightened, for he had never been out at night before; he had always slumbered sweetly and safely behind the warm rose petals. This would surely be the death of him!

Suddenly, he remembered that at the other end of the garden there was an arbor of lovely honeysuckle, those flowers that looked like big painted horns. In one of them, perhaps, he could go down and sleep safely till morning.

Swiftly he flew to the far end of the garden. But suddenly he stopped! Quiet! There were already two people in the arbor. The loveliest maiden and a handsome young man. They sat closely together and wished they might never, never part. They loved each other, even more than the best child can love its father and mother.

"Yet we must part," the young man was saying. "Your brother doesn't like me, so he is sending me on a long journey, far over distant mountains and oceans. Farewell, my sweetest bride, for that you will always be to me!"

Then they kissed, and the young maiden wept and gave him a rose. But first, she pressed on it a kiss so warm and tender that the rose petals opened, and then the little elf slipped quickly inside. As he leaned his tiny head against the delicate, fragrant walls, he could hear, "Farewell! Farewell!" and he felt that the rose was being placed on the young man's heart. Ah, how that heart beat! The little elf couldn't go to sleep for its beating!

But not long did the rose rest undisturbed on that throbbing heart. As the young man walked lonely through the dark wood, he took the rose out and kissed it so often and so warmly that the little elf was almost crushed. Through the petals, he could feel the young man's burning lips, while the rose itself opened as if under the strongest midday sun.

Suddenly, another man appeared. It was the pretty maiden's gloomy and wicked brother! He drew out a long sharp knife, and while the young man was kissing the rose, this wicked one stabbed him to death! Then he cut off the head and buried head and body in the soft earth beneath the linden tree.

"Now he's dead and forgotten!" the evil brother thought. "He'll never come back again. He was supposed to have left on a long journey where a man might easily lose his life—and so he has lost his. No, he won't come back, and my sister won't ever dare ask me about him." Then he kicked dry leaves over the loose earth and went home in the darkness of the night.

But he was not alone, as he thought. The little elf was with him. For, as he dug the grave, a dried, rolled-up linden leaf had fallen in his hair, and the rose elf was in that leaf. Now the man's hat was placed over the leaf, and it was very dark in there where the little elf trembled in fear and anger at the wicked deed.

In the early morning, the evil man reached home. He took off his hat and went into his sister's bedroom. There lay the pretty maiden, dreaming of her beloved, whom she thought far away traveling over mountains and through the forests. The wicked brother leaned over her and laughed—the hideous laugh of a devil—and the withered leaf dropped from his hair onto her bed cover. But he didn't notice, and pretty soon he left her room to get a little sleep himself.

Now the little elf crept quietly out of the withered leaf, slipped into the ear of the sleeping girl, and told her, as in a dream, the dreadful story of the murder. He described the spot in the woods where her brother had killed her sweetheart, and the place under the linden tree where the body was buried, and then whispered, "And so that you may not think this all a dream, you will find a withered leaf of the tree on your bedspread!" And when she awoke, she found the leaf.

Oh, what bitter, bitter tears she shed! Yet to no one did she dare betray her grief. All that day, her window stood open, and the little elf could easily have escaped to the roses and all the other flowers of the garden, but he could not bear to leave the sorrowing girl.

In the window stood a bush that bore roses every month, and he found a spot in one of those flowers from where he could watch the poor girl. Often her brother came into the room, merry with an evil mirth, and she dared not say a word of the grief in her heart.

When night came, she stole out of the house and into the forest to the place where the linden tree stood. She brushed away the leaves, dug into the earth, and so at last came to the body of her beloved. How she wept then, and how she prayed to God that she too might die! She would gladly have taken the body home with her, but since that would be impossible, she took up the pale head, with its closed eyes, kissed the cold mouth, and with a trembling hand brushed the dirt from the beautiful hair.

"This, at least, I can keep," she wept. Then she buried the body again and scattered the leaves once more over it. But the head, together with a little sprig from a jasmine bush that bloomed in the wood where he had been killed, she took with her to her home.

As soon as she reached her room, she brought the biggest flowerpot she could find, and in this she laid the dead man's head, covered it with earth, and planted the sprig of jasmine.

The little elf could no longer bear to see such grief. "Farewell, farewell," he whispered, and then he flew out to his rose in the garden. But it was withered and faded now, and only a few dry leaves clung to the bush. "Alas!" sighed the elf. "How soon everything good and beautiful passes away!" But at last, he found another rose and made his home in safety behind its delicate, fragrant petals.

But every morning, he would fly to the poor maiden's window, and he always found her there, weeping over the flowerpot. Softly her bitter tears fell upon the jasmine spray, and every day as she became paler and paler, the sprig grew fresher and greener. New shoots appeared, one after another, and little white buds burst forth, and these she kissed.

When her wicked brother saw her do that, he scolded her and asked why she acted so silly. He didn't like it and didn't understand why she was always weeping over the flowerpot. He did not know what closed eyes were there, and what red lips had there returned to dust.

And the pretty maiden leaned her head against the flowerpot, and the little elf found her there, fallen into a gentle slumber. So he crept again into her ear and whispered to her of that evening in the arbor and of the scent of the roses and the loves of the elves. Then she dreamed so sweetly, and while she dreamed, her life passed gently away. She died a quiet death and was in Heaven with her beloved. And the jasmine flowers opened their big white bells and gave out their wonderful sweet fragrance. It was the only way they knew to weep for the dead.

When the wicked brother saw the beautiful blooming plant, he took it for himself as an inheritance from his sister and put it in his bedroom close beside his bed, for it was glorious indeed to look at, and its fragrance was sweet and fresh. But the little rose elf went with it, and flew from blossom to blossom; in each lived a tiny soul, and to each he told the story of the murdered man whose head even now rested under the earth beneath them. He told them of the evil brother and the poor sister.

"We know it!" replied each little soul in the flowers. "Did we not spring from those murdered eyes and lips? We know it! We know it!" they repeated, and nodded their heads in an odd way. The rose elf could not understand how they could be so quiet about it, and he flew out to the bees gathering honey and told them the terrible story about the wicked brother. So they reported it to their queen, and the queen commanded all the bees to kill the murderer the very next morning.

But the night before, the first night after his sister's death, while the evil brother was asleep in his bed beside the fragrant jasmine, the flowers opened, and out of each blossom came a tiny spirit—invisible, but armed with a sharp little poisoned spear. First, they crept into his ears and told him wicked dreams; then they flew across his lips and pierced his tongue with their poisoned darts.

"Now we have avenged the dead man!" they cried, then flew back again into the white bells of the jasmine.

When the morning came, and the windows of the bedroom were opened, the rose elf and the whole swarm of bees with their queen swept in to kill him.

But he was already dead, and people stood around his bed and said, "The scent of the jasmine has killed him!" Then the rose elf understood the vengeance of the flowers and told it to the queen, and she and her whole swarm of bees ceaselessly hummed around the flowerpot and could not be driven away. When a man picked up the pot, a bee stung him on the hand, so that he let it fall and it broke into pieces. Then the people saw the whitened skull and knew that the dead man on the bed was a murderer.

So the queen bee hummed in the air and sang of the vengeance of the flowers and about the rose elf, and how behind the smallest leaf there dwells one who can disclose and repay every evil.

WHAT THE MOON SAW (1839–1840)

INTRODUCTION

It is a strange thing, that when I feel most fervently and most deeply, my hands and my tongue seem alike tied, so that I cannot rightly describe or accurately portray the thoughts that are rising within me; and yet I am a painter: My eye tells me as much as that, and all my friends who have seen my sketches and fancies say the same.

I am a poor lad, and live in one of the narrowest of lanes; but I do not want for light, as my room is high up in the house, with an extensive prospect over the neighboring roofs. During the first few days, I went to live in the town, I felt low-spirited and solitary enough. Instead of the forest and the green hills of former days, I had here only a forest of chimney-pots to look out upon. And then I had not a single friend; not one familiar face greeted me.

So one evening, I sat at the window in a desponding mood; and presently, I opened the casement and looked out. Oh, how my heart leaped up with joy! Here was a well-known face at last—a round, friendly countenance, the face of a good friend I had known at home. In, fact it was the Moon that looked in upon me. He was quite unchanged, the dear old Moon, and had the same face exactly that he used to show when he peered down upon me through the willow trees on the moor. I kissed my hand to him over and over again, as he shone far into my little room; and he, for his part, promised me that every evening, when he came abroad, he would look in upon me for a few moments. This promise he has faithfully kept. It is a pity that he can only stay such a short time when he comes. Whenever he appears, he tells me of one thing or another that he has seen on the previous night, or on that same evening. "Just paint the scenes I describe to you"—this is what he said to me—"and you will have a very pretty picture book." I have followed his injunction for many evenings. I could make up a new *Thousand and One Nights*, in my own way, out of these pictures, but the number might be too great, after all. The pictures I have here given have not been chosen at random, but follow in their proper order, just as they were described to me. Some great gifted painter, or some poet or musician, may make something more of them if he likes; what I have given here are only hasty sketches, hurriedly put upon the paper, with some of my own thoughts interspersed; for the Moon did not come to me every evening—a cloud sometimes hid his face from me.

FIRST EVENING

"Last night"—these are the Moon's own words—"I glided through the clear sky of India and reflected myself in the Ganges. My rays struggled to force their way through the thick roof of old sycamore trees that arched beneath me like the shell of a tortoise. From the thicket, a Hindu maiden stepped out, graceful as a gazelle and beautiful as Eve. There was something truly spiritual, and yet material, about her, and I could even make out her thoughts beneath her delicate skin. The thorny liana plants tore her sandals, but she walked rapidly forward. The wild beasts that came up from the river after quenching their thirst fled away in fright, for the maiden held a lighted lamp in her hand. I could see the blood in the delicate fingers arched into a shield over the flame of the lamp. She walked down to the river, then placed the lamp on the surface, and it drifted away with the current. The flame flickered back and forth, as if it wanted to expire, but still it burned as the maiden's dark, sparkling eyes followed it, with a soulful gaze from beneath the long, silken lashes of her eyelids. She knew that if the lamp should burn as long as her eyes could follow it, her lover would still be alive; but if it went out, he would be dead. As the lamp burned and trembled, the heart of the maiden burned and trembled. She knelt and prayed. Beside her, a deadly snake lurked in the grass, but she thought only of Brahma and of her bridegroom.

"'He lives!' she shouted joyfully, and the echo answered from the mountains, 'He lives!'"

SECOND EVENING

"It was yesterday," the Moon told me, "that I peeped into a little courtyard, enclosed by houses; there was a hen there, with eleven chickens. A pretty little girl was playing around them, and the hen clucked and spread out her wings in fright over her chicks. Then the little girl's father came and scolded her, and I passed on, thinking no more of it.

"But this evening, just a few minutes ago, I again peeped into the same yard. It was very quiet there, but soon the little girl came out, crept cautiously to the henhouse, lifted the latch, and stole softly up to the hen and chickens. They clucked loudly and fluttered about, with the little girl running after them! I saw it plainly, for I peeped through a hole in the wall. I was very angry with the naughty child, and was glad when the father came and caught her by the arm and scolded her, still more sternly than yesterday. She bent her head down, and her big blue eyes were filled with tears.

"'What are you doing here anyway?' he asked.

"'I wanted to go in and kiss the hen and beg her to forgive me for yesterday,' she wept. 'But I was afraid to tell you.' Then the father kissed the innocent child's forehead. I kissed her eyes and lips."

THIRD EVENING

"In the narrow lane close by—it is so narrow that my rays can slide down the walls of the houses for only a moment, and yet in that moment, I see enough to understand the little world stirring below—I saw a woman. Sixteen years ago, she was a child, and out in the country, she used to play in the old parsonage garden. The rosebush hedges were old, and their blossoms had fallen. They had run wild, and grew rankly over the paths, twisting their long branches up the trunks of the apple trees. Here and there a rose still sat on her stem, not so lovely as the queen of the flowers usually appears, but the color was still there, and the fragrance, too. The clergyman's little daughter seemed to me a much lovelier rose as she sat on her stool under the straggling hedge and kissed her doll with the caved-in pasteboard cheeks.

"Ten years later, I saw her again; I saw her in a splendid ballroom, and she was the beautiful bride of a rich merchant. I was happy over her good fortune, and sought her again in the silent nights—alas, no one then heeded my clear eye, my trusty watch! My rose also grew up in rank wildness, like the roses in the parsonage garden. Life in the everyday world has its tragedies too, and tonight I witnessed the final act.

"In the narrow street, deathly ill, she lay upon her bed, and the wicked, rough, and cruel landlord, now her only acquaintance, tore away her blanket. 'Stand up!' he said. 'Your cheeks are enough to frighten anyone! Dress yourself! Get some money, or I'll throw you into the street! Get up, and hurry!'

"'Death is in my breast!' she cried. 'Oh, let me rest!' But he dragged her up, painted her cheeks, put roses in her hair, set her at the window with a lighted candle beside her, and went away. I stared at her; she sat there motionless, though her hand fell down into her lap. The wind pushed against the window until it broke a pane, but still she did not move. The curtain fluttered about her like a flame—she was dead. There at the open window sat the dead one, as a preachment against sin—my rose from the parsonage garden!"

FOURTH EVENING

"Last night I saw a German play," the Moon said. "It was in a small town, where a stable had been converted into a theater; that is to say, the stalls were still there, but had been fitted up as boxes, and all the woodwork was covered with colored paper. From the low roof hung a small iron chandelier; an inverted tub was fastened over it so that, as in a real theater, the lights could be drawn up when the prompter's bell tinkled.

"'Ting-a-ling,' and the little iron chandelier skipped up half a yard; this was the sign that the play was about to begin.

"A young nobleman and his lady who happened to be passing through the town were present at the performance, and consequently, the house was filled to capacity. The space directly under the chandelier, however, was as clear as a small crater; not a soul sat there, for the candles of the chandelier dripped down—drip, drip!

"I could see everything that happened, for it was so hot that the windows were left open, and at every window, the servants could be seen peeping in from the outside, though the constables were posted inside the door and threatened the intruders with their sticks. The young noble pair sat close to the orchestra in two old armchairs, which were usually occupied by the burgomaster and his wife. But tonight, they had to sit on the wooden benches, like the rest of the townspeople. 'Aye, look there now,' one woman whispered to another, 'one sparrow hawk in turn outflies another!' Everything took on a more dignified aspect on this memorable occasion. The chandelier hopped; the mob outside got their knuckles rapped, and I—yes, the Moon was present too through the whole performance."

FIFTH EVENING

"Yesterday," said the Moon, "I looked down on the busy city of Paris—and my gaze penetrated into the apartments of the Louvre. An old grandmother, poorly clad, for she belonged to the class of beggars, followed one of the attendants into the great, empty throne room. She had to see it, and it had cost her many a little sacrifice and many a fawning word before she had managed to make her way this far into the palace. She folded her scrawny hands and gazed around as solemnly as if she were in a church.

"'It was here!' she said. 'Here!' And she approached the throne, from which the rich, gold-edged velvet covering hung down. 'There!' she said. 'There!' And she fell to her knees and kissed the purple hanging. I believe she wept.

"'It wasn't this velvet,' said the attendant, a smile playing on his lips.

"'But it was here!' said the woman. 'And it looked the same then!'

"'The same, and yet different,' replied the man. 'That day, the windows were smashed in, the doors burst open, and the floor was red with blood. Yet you may truthfully say, "My grandson died upon the throne of France!"'

"'Died!' repeated the old woman.

"I don't believe another word was spoken, and they soon left the hall. The evening twilight faded, and my beams streamed with greater brilliance on the rich velvet hangings of the throne of France. Now, who do you think the old woman was? I shall tell you a story.

"It was during the Revolution of July, near the close of the evening preceding the most brilliant day of victory, when every house was a fortress, every window a barricade. The people stormed the Tuileries, even women and children fighting among the combatants; the mob forced its way through the halls and the apartments of the palace. A poor, ragged, half-grown boy fought bravely in the ranks of his older comrades. Mortally wounded with several bayonet thrusts, he sank to the floor. This happened in the throne room, and the bleeding body was laid on the throne of France; his blood streamed over the royal purple hangings that partly covered his wounds. There was a picture! That magnificent room—the mob of fighting rebels! A broken standard lay on the floor, while the tricolor waved over the bayonets; and on the throne lay the beggar lad, with his pale, glorified features, his eyes turned heavenward, his limbs stiffening in death; his naked breast and his ragged coat were half hidden by the rich velvet hanging with its silver lilies.

"Perhaps at the boy's cradle it had been prophesied, 'He shall die upon the throne of France!' and the mother's heart had dreamed of a second Napoleon. My rays have kissed the wreath of immortality on his grave; my beam last night kissed the brow of the old grandmother, when she saw in a dream the picture you may draw here—the poor ragged beggar boy on the throne of France."

SIXTH EVENING

"I have been to Upsala," the Moon told me. "I looked down on the great plain covered with coarse grass and on the barren fields. I saw my image in the river Fyris, while the steamer frightened away the fishes into the rushes. The clouds chased one another beneath me, throwing their long shadows upon the graves of Odin and Thor and Freya, as the hills there are called. The names have been cut in the thin turf that covers the hills; here, there is no memorial stone where the traveler can engrave his name, no rock wall whereon he can paint it. So the visitor cuts it into the turf, and the bare earth along the range of hills is covered with a network of letters and names—an immortality that lasts until the next growth of turf.

"Upon the hilltop, a man stood, a poet. He emptied a mead horn decorated with a broad silver ring, and whispered a name that he charged the breezes not to betray; but I heard it, and I knew it. The coronet of a count sparkled above it, and therefore he did not name it aloud. I smiled. For the crown of a poet sparkles above his! The name of Eleanora d'Este is with Tasso's. I too know where the rose of beauty blooms...."

Thus the Moon spoke, but then a cloud passed between us. Oh, that clouds might never come between the poet and the rose!

SEVENTH EVENING

"A fresh and fragrant grove of oaks and beeches, visited by a hundred nightingales with each return of spring, stretched along the seashore. The broad highway lies between this grove and the ocean, the ever-changing ocean. One carriage after another rolls past, but I do not follow them; my gaze rests mostly on one spot—a Viking's grave. Blackberry and sloe grow between the stones. Here is the true poetry of nature. How do you think people interpret it? Listen, and I shall tell you what I heard last evening and during the past night.

"First, two rich landowners came driving along. 'What splendid trees!' said one of them. 'Every tree should give at least ten cartloads of firewood,' answered the other, 'and we're going to have a hard winter. Last year, remember, we got fourteen dollars a load!' And then they were gone.

"'What a terrible road!' said another man as he drove past in his carriage. 'It's all because of those confounded trees,' his companion answered. 'The only way for the air to get in is from the sea!' And they rolled on.

"The stagecoach also came by, and during this loveliest part of the journey, all the passengers were fast asleep. The driver blew his horn, but he said only to himself, 'I blow well indeed! It sounds fine right here! But what do those sleepy people inside care about it?' Then the stagecoach disappeared.

"Now two young lads galloped along on horseback. Here are the fire and spirit of youth, I thought. They also glanced with a smile at the moss-green hills and the dark grove. 'I should certainly like to go for a walk in here with Christine, the miller's daughter!' said one of them, and off they rode.

"The fragrance of flowers was very strong; every breath of wind was still; the ocean seemed almost a part of the heaven that overhung the deep valley. A coach with six passengers rolled by. Four were asleep; the fifth was thinking of how his new summer coat would fit him, and the sixth popped his head out of the window to ask the coachman if there was anything remarkable about the heap of stones beside the road.

"'No,' said the driver. 'That's nothing but a heap of stones; but the trees over there—they're really worth looking at!'

"'Tell me about them.'

"'Yes, they're most remarkable,' said the man. 'In the winter, when the snow is so deep that nothing can be seen, those trees are signposts to me; I follow them and keep from driving into the sea. You see, that's why they are so remarkable!' And then he drove on.

"Now a painter came by. His eyes sparkled; he didn't say a word; he only whistled. Each nightingale sang more loudly and sweetly than the other. 'Stop that noise!' he cried, and then he carefully examined all the colors and tints in the landscape. 'Blue, purple, dark brown—what a beautiful painting this would make!' His mind took it all in, just as a mirror reflects a picture, and meanwhile he whistled a Rossini march.

"The last to come by was a poor girl. She sat down upon the Viking's grave to rest, and laid down her bundle. Her pale, lovely face turned toward the grove, and she listened; her eyes brightened as she raised them over the ocean toward heaven. Her hands were clasped, and I believe she said the Lord's Prayer. She herself did not fully understand the feeling that moment and the scene around her will in her memory be invested with colors more beautiful and richer than the artist's accurate colors. My rays followed her until the dawn kissed her brow."

EIGHTH EVENING

Dark masses of clouds covered the sky, and the Moon did not come out at all. In my little chamber, I stood more lonely than ever and gazed up into the sky where he should have appeared.

My thoughts flew far away, up to my great friend, who each evening showed me such lovely pictures and told me stories. What has he not experienced! He has floated above the waters of the deluge, and smiled down on Noah's ark, as now he does on me, and brought the consolation that a new world would bloom again. When the children of Israel wept beside the rivers of Babylon, he looked in sorrow through the willows where they had hung their harps. When Romeo climbed up the balcony and the kiss of love rose like a cherub's thought from the earth, the full Moon hung half hidden in the thin air behind the dark cypresses. He has seen the hero at St. Helena looking forth from the lonely cliff toward the ocean, while great thoughts stirred within him. Yes, indeed, what cannot the Moon tell? The history of humanity is to him a book of adventures. Tonight I cannot see you, old friend, and cannot sketch any picture in memory of your visit.

Then as I dreamily looked toward the sky, it brightened; there was a beam of light from the Moon, but it vanished, and black clouds glided by; still, it was a greeting, a friendly "good night" sent to me by the Moon.

NINTH EVENING

Again the sky was clear; several evenings had passed, and the Moon was in his first quarter. I again got an idea for a sketch. Listen to what the Moon told me.

"I followed the polar bird and the swimming whale to the eastern coast of Greenland. Bare rocks—covered with ice and mist—encircled a valley where twining willows and whortleberry bushes were in their fullest blossom, and the fragrant lychnis exhaled its sweet perfume. My rays were faint, my face pale as the leaf of a water lily torn from its stem and driven for weeks upon the water. The aurora borealis flamed; its ring was broad, and from it, strange pillars of fire, changing from red to green, shot forth in whirling columns over the whole heavens.

"The inhabitants here had assembled for a dance and various kinds of merriment; but the splendor of the scene did not excite wonder in their accustomed eyes. 'Let the souls of the dead play ball with the walrus head!' they thought, according to their superstition; they had thought and eye only for the song and dance.

"A Greenlander, without his fur coat, stood in the middle of the circle, and, beating on the drum, he began a song about the seal hunt; the chorus responded with 'Eia! Eia!' and hopped around and around in a circle, dressed in their garments of white fur. Their eyes and heads moved strangely, and the whole scene was like a polar bear's ball. Now judgment and sentencing began. Those who had come with a grievance stepped forward, and the injured person chanted forth, boldly and mockingly, the faults of his opponent in an extemporaneous song, accompanied by the drumbeats and dancing. Then the accused replied with equal shrewdness, while all the people laughed, and finally they pronounced sentence.

"From the mountains came a thunderous sound; the glaciers above had split into pieces, and the huge masses fell in showers of dust. It was a beautiful Greenland summer night.

"A sick man lay a hundred yards away, beneath an open tent of skins. There was still life in his warm blood, but he must die, for he believed that, and all the others believed it, too. Already his wife was sewing the skin covering tightly around his limbs, so that afterward she would not have to touch the dead body. 'Do you want to be buried on the mountain in the firm snow?' she asked him. 'I will cover your grave with your kayak and your arrows, and the angakok will dance over it. Or would you rather be buried in the sea?'

"'In the sea,' the sick man whispered, and nodded with a sad smile.

"'The sea is a pleasant summer pavilion!' said his wife. 'Thousands of seals play there, the walrus sleeps at your feet, and the hunt is safe and merry.'

"And then his crying children tore the stretched skin away from the window hole, so that the dying man could be carried out to sea, to the swelling ocean, which in his life had given him food and now in death was to give him rest. The floating icebergs, passing back and forth by day and night, became his tombstone. The seal slumbers on the icebergs while the storm bird flies over them."

TENTH EVENING

"I once knew an old maid," said the Moon. "Every winter, she wore a coat of yellow satin trimmed with fur, which always seemed new, and was always her only fashion. Every summer, she wore the same straw hat, and, I believe, the same gray-blue gown. She left her home only to visit an old lady friend who lived across the street; but in later years, even these visits ceased, for the friend was dead. In her solitude, my old maid used to putter about before her window, where all summer long a row of pretty flowers stood, and in winter a fine crop of cress grew on the top of a felt hat.

"During the last month, she no longer sat at the window; but I knew she was still alive, for I had not yet seen her set out on that great journey that the old lady and her friend had so often discussed. 'Yes,' she would say, 'one day, when I die, I shall make a longer journey than I have made in my whole lifetime. The family vault is six miles from here, and that is where they will carry me, that I may sleep with the rest of my family.'

"Last night, a hearse drove up before the house; a coffin was carried out, and then I knew that she had died. They packed straw and matting around the casket, and drove off. Now the quiet old maid, who in the last few years of her life had never left her house, slept quietly. And the hearse rolled swiftly out of town, as if this were a pleasure trip. On the highway, it traveled even faster. From time to time, the driver looked around nervously; I believe he feared seeing her seated behind him on the coffin, in her yellow satin and fur coat; therefore, he lashed the horses recklessly while still holding in the reins as tightly as he could, until the poor horses were covered with foam. The horses were young and high-spirited, and when a hare darted across the road, they became unmanageable and ran away. The quiet old maid, who year in and year out had only moved about slowly and noiselessly in a circle, was now a lifeless corpse, rushed and bumped along the highway over stick and stone. The coffin, with its covering of straw, fell off, and lay on the road, while horses, hearse, and driver dashed wildly off.

"A lark rose from the field, twittering its morning hymn over the coffin, and then alighted on it, pecking with its beak at the straw matting, as if it wanted to pull it to pieces. The lark, singing happily, flew into the air, and I withdrew behind the reddening clouds of dawn."

ELEVENTH EVENING

"It was a wedding celebration," related the Moon. "Songs were sung and toasts proposed; everything was rich and splendid. It was past midnight before the guests departed. The mothers kissed the bride and groom; then they were alone. I saw them through the window, although the curtains were almost drawn; a lamp lighted the cozy room.

"'Thank heaven they have left!' he said, and kissed her hands and lips. She smiled and cried, resting her head on his chest as happily as the lotus flower rests on the flowing water. And they spoke soft and blissful words.

"'Sleep sweetly!' he exclaimed, as she drew the window curtains aside.

"'How beautifully the Moon is shining!' she said; 'see how quiet and how clear it is.' And she put out the lamp; it became dark in the cozy room, but my light then shone, as brightly as his eyes shone.

"Femininity, kiss thou the poet's harp when he sings of the mysteries of life!"

TWELFTH EVENING

"I shall give you a picture of Pompeii," said the Moon. "I was outside the city, in the Street of the Tombs, as they call the place where happy youths, with wreaths of roses on their heads, once danced with the fair sisters of Lais. Now the silence of death reigns there.

"German soldiers in the service of Naples kept guard, and played cards and diced. A group of strangers from beyond the mountains walked into the city, conducted by a guard. They had come to see, in the full clear rays of my light, the city arisen from the grave. I showed them the ruts of the chariot wheels in the streets paved with great slabs of lava. I showed them the names upon the doors and the signs still hanging before the houses. In the narrow courts, they saw the fountain basins ornamented with shells, but the waters no longer spouted forth. No longer were songs heard from the richly painted chambers, where the bronze dogs kept watch before the doors. It was the City of the Dead. Vesuvius alone still thundered his eternal hymn, and each stanza of it men call a new eruption. We visited the Temple of Venus, built of pure white marble, with its high altar in front of its broad steps; the weeping willow has sprung up between the columns. The air here was transparent and blue, and in the background loomed Vesuvius, black as coal, its flames rising straight as the trunk of a pine tree. The glowing smoke cloud lay in the still calm of the night like the crown of the pine tree, but red as blood.

"Among the group was a lady singer, a truly great artiste; I have seen the honor done her in the first cities of Europe. They approached the amphitheater, and there they all seated themselves on the stone steps; thus a small space was filled, whereas thousands of years ago, the entire place had been. The stage was still there, as in the olden days, with its brick side walls and the two arches in the background, through which the same scenery was visible as in times of old, and Nature herself spread out before us the hills between Sorrento and Amalfi.

"In jest, the lady walked up onto the ancient stage and sang. The place inspired her, and I could not but think of a wild Arabian horse, snorting, its mane standing erect, as it dashes off in its wild course; here were the same ease and confidence. I had to think, too, of the suffering mother beneath the Cross of Golgotha, so deep was the feeling, the pain expressed. Round about sounded shouts of delight and applause, as they had thousands of years before here. 'What a heavenly gift!' they all exclaimed.

"Three minutes later, the scene was deserted; everyone was gone, and not a sound was heard, for the group had wandered off. But the ruin stood unchanged, as it will stand for centuries yet to come. The momentary applause is forgotten, as are the singer's notes and smiles, forgotten, gone. Even to me, this hour will be but a fleeting memory."

THIRTEENTH EVENING

"I looked in through the window of a newspaper editor," said the Moon. "It was somewhere in Germany. It was a handsomely furnished room, with many books and a chaos of newspapers. There were several young men present. The editor himself stood beside his desk; two little books, both by unknown authors, were to be reviewed.

"'This one has been sent to me,' he said. 'I haven't read it yet, but it's well put together. What do you think about its contents?'

"'Oh,' said one of the young men, who was a poet, 'it is very good—a bit drawn out, but then, good Lord! He's only a young man. It's true the verses might be improved. The thoughts are sound enough; it's only a pity they're so commonplace. But what can you expect? We can't always get something new. You might praise him a little, though in my opinion, it's clear he'll never be anything great as a poet. Still, he has read a good deal; he's an excellent Oriental scholar, and he has rather sound judgment. It was he who wrote the splendid review of my *Reflections on Domestic Life*. After all, we must be lenient toward a young man.'

"'But he's a complete ass!' said another gentleman in the room. 'There's nothing worse in poetry than mediocrity, and he certainly will never get any higher!'

"'Poor fellow,' said a third. 'And yet his aunt is so proud of him. She's the lady, Mr. Editor, who got together that large list of subscribers for your last volume of translations.'

"'Ah, the good woman! Well, I've just given the book a brief notice. Unquestionable talent—a welcome gift! A flower in the garden of poetry, well put together, and so forth. But now, about this other book—I suppose the author expects me to buy it. I have heard it praised; the author has genius, they say. Don't you think so?'

"'Yes, so they all say,' said the poet. 'But it's rather wild. The punctuation, however, is indicative of genius! It'll do him good to be treated roughly, to be pulled to pieces; otherwise, he will have far too good an opinion of himself.'

"'But that would be unfair,' said a fourth. 'Don't let's pick at little faults, but rather find pleasure in what is good; and there is much here worth praising. He writes better than all the rest of them.'

"'Heaven help us! If he's such a great genius, he can take some sharp criticism! There are enough people to praise him in private; let us not drive him mad with flattery!'

"'Decided talent,' wrote the editor. 'The usual carelessness here and there; that he can write bad verses may be seen on page twenty-five, where there are two hiatuses. We recommend that he study the classics, etc.'

"I passed on," the Moon continued, "and peeped through the window of the aunt's house. There sat the praised poet, the tame one, receiving homage from all the guests, and he was happy.

"I sought out the other poet, the wild one. He also was in a large gathering, at one of his patron's. The subject of the conversation was his rival's book.

"'Sometime or other I'll read your poems,' said the patron, 'but to tell the truth— and you know I always say what I think—I don't expect much from them. In my opinion, you're too wild for me, too fantastic. But I must admit that as a man you are highly respectable!'

"A young girl sat in a corner, reading a book:

> *In the dust are trodden genius and its glory,*
> *While everyday talent wins high acclaim.*
> *It is, alas, a very old story;*
> *It'll never be new, but ever the same.*"

FOURTEENTH EVENING

The Moon spoke. "Near the forest path are two farmhouses. The doors are low and the windows placed irregularly; white thorn bushes and barberry ramble around them. Their mossy roofs are overgrown with yellow flowers and houseleek. Only green cabbage and potatoes grow in the little garden, but by the hedge grows a willow tree; and beneath it sat a little girl, her eyes fixed on the old oak tree between the farmhouses. Its tall and withered trunk had been sawed off at the top, and upon it, a stork had built his nest. He stood above it now, rattling his bill. A little boy came out and stood beside the girl; they were brother and sister.

"'What are you looking at?' he asked.

"'At the stork,' she said. 'The neighbor woman told me he'll bring us a little brother or sister tonight, and I'm watching so I can see it when it comes.'

"'The stork doesn't bring anything,' said the boy. 'The neighbor woman, believe me, told me that too, but she laughed when she said it, so I asked her if she dared say "on my honor." No, she didn't dare do that. I know perfectly well that what they say about the stork is only a story they tell to children.'

"'But then where does the baby come from?' asked the girl.

"'Our Lord brings it,' said the boy. 'God has it under his mantle, but no one can see God, so we can't *see* him bring it.'

"Just then, a breeze stirred in the branches of the willow tree. The children folded their hands and looked at each other. Surely this was God, who had brought the little baby! Then they clasped each other's hands. The door of the house opened, and the neighbor woman appeared.

"'Come in now,' she said, 'and see what the stork has brought you; it is a little brother.'

"And the children nodded, for they already knew the baby had come."

FIFTEENTH EVENING

"I sailed over Lüneburg Heath," the Moon said. "A lonely hut stood there by the roadside. Around it grew a few withered bushes where a nightingale, which had lost its way, was singing. It would surely die during that cold night; it was its swan's song that I heard.

"Morning dawned, and along came a group of emigrant peasant families who wanted to go to Bremen or Hamburg to take a ship for America, where they hoped to see their dreams of good fortune come true. The youngest children were carried on the backs of the women, while the bigger ones skipped along beside them. A wretched horse was dragging a cart that bore the few household effects they possessed.

"The cold wind blew, causing a little girl to nestle more closely to her mother, who looked up at my round, decreasing orb and thought of the cruel hardships she had suffered in her home, of the heavy taxes they had not been able to pay. Her thoughts were those of the whole group. Hence, the rosy glimmer of the rising dawn seemed to them like a ray of promise, the forerunner of the sun of happiness that would rise again. They heard the song of the dying nightingale, and to them it seemed no false prophet, but the herald of good fortune.

"The wind whistled, but they could not understand its song: 'Sail over the ocean! You have paid for the long passage with all your possessions. Poor and helpless shall you set foot on the promised land. You may sell yourselves, your wives, and your children. Yet you shall not suffer long, for behind the broad, fragrant leaf sits the angel of death. Her welcome kiss breathes the deadly fever into your blood! Sail on, sail on over the swelling waves!'

"And the group listened happily to the song of the nightingale, for it surely seemed to promise good fortune.

"The day broke through the light clouds. The peasants were crossing the heath on their way to church. In their black gowns, and with the strip of white linen bound closely around their heads, the women looked as if they had stepped out of the old paintings in the church. Around them lay a vast, dead scene—the withered, brown heath, dark, scorched plains between white sand dunes. The women were carrying their prayer books as they made their way to the church. Oh pray! Pray for those who go forth to their graves, beyond the swelling waves!"

SIXTEENTH EVENING

"I know a punchinello," the Moon said. "The audience rejoices whenever he appears. Every movement he makes is so comical that it brings roars of laughter in the house, and yet there is nothing remarkable in his work to account for this—it is more his peculiarity. Even when he was only a boy, playing about with the other boys, he was a punchinello. Nature had shaped him for the character by putting a hump on his back and another on his chest; but the mind and soul hidden under the deformities were, on the contrary, richly endowed. No one possessed a deeper feeling, a stronger spiritual feeling, than he. The theater was his ideal world; if he had been tall and handsome, he might have become a great tragedian on any stage. His soul was filled with all that was heroic and great; still, it was his fate to be a punchinello. His very sadness, his melancholy, heightened the dry wit of his sharply drawn face, and aroused the laughter of a vast audience, which lustily applauded its favorite.

"The lovely Columbine was gentle and kind to him; yet she preferred to marry Harlequin. It would indeed have been too funny if in reality 'Beauty and the Beast' had married. Whenever Punchinello was dejected, she was the only one who could bring a smile to his lips; yes, she could even make him laugh loudly. At first, she was as melancholy as he, then somewhat calmer, and at last overflowing with gaiety.

"'I know well enough what's the matter with you,' she said. 'You are in love!'

"And then he couldn't help laughing. 'Love and I!' he cried. 'That would be funny indeed; how the public would applaud!'

"'It's love!' she continued, and added with comical pathos, 'it is I you love!'

"Yes, one may speak this way when one thinks there is no love in the other's heart. Punchinello laughed heartily and jumped high into the air, and his melancholy was forgotten. And yet she had spoken the truth; he did love her, loved her deeply, as he loved all that was great and noble in art.

"On her wedding day, he seemed the merriest of the merry, but that night, he wept. If people had seen his tormented face, they would have applauded him more than ever.

"A few days ago, Columbine died. On the day of her burial, Harlequin had permission not to appear on the stage, for he was a grief-stricken widower. The manager had to present something very gay, so that the public would not miss the pretty Columbine and the graceful Harlequin. Therefore, the nimble Punchinello had to be doubly merry; with grief in his heart, he danced and skipped about, and all applauded and cried, 'Bravo! Bravissimo!' Punchinello was called back again and again. Oh, he was priceless!

"After the performance last night, the poor little man strolled out of the town to the lonely churchyard. The wreath of flowers on Columbine's grave had already faded. There he sat—and what a study for a painter!—with his chin on his hand and his eyes turned toward me; he looked like a grotesque monument—a Punchinello on the grave, strange and comical. If the public had seen their favorite, how they would have applauded and cried, 'Bravo, Punchinello! Bravo! Bravissimo!'"

SEVENTEENTH EVENING

Listen to what the Moon told me: "I have seen a cadet become an officer and dress himself in his handsome uniform for the first time. I have seen a young maiden in her ball gown, and the happiness of a prince's pretty young bride in her wedding dress. But no joy can be compared to that which I saw last evening in a child, a little girl four years old. She had received a new blue dress and a new rose-colored bonnet. She was already dressed in her finery, and everyone called for candles, as my beams were too faint through the window, and more light was needed. The little girl stood as stiff as a doll, her arms carefully stretched away from the frock, the fingers spread wide apart from one another. Oh, how her eyes and every feature beamed with joy!

"'Tomorrow you shall go for a walk,' said her mother. The little girl looked up at her bonnet and down at her dress, and smiled happily. 'Mother,' she said, 'what will the dogs think when they see me in these beautiful things!'"

EIGHTEENTH EVENING

"I have told you about Pompeii," the Moon said, "that corpse of a city that is now once more listed among living cities. I know another, an even stranger one; it is not a corpse, but rather the phantom of a city. Whenever water splashes from fountains into marble basins, I seem to hear the tale of the floating city. Yes, the spouting water can tell about it. The waves of the sea sing about it.

"Over the face of the ocean there often hangs a mist—her widow's veil, for the bridegroom of the ocean is dead; his city and his palace are now but a mausoleum. Do you know this city? Never was the rattle of carriages or the clatter of horses' hoofs heard in its streets; only fish swim there, while the black gondola glides ghostlike over the green waters.

"I will show you the largest square in the city, the Piazza," continued the Moon, "and you will imagine yourself in fairyland. The grass grows up between the broad flagstones, and in the early dawn, thousands of tame pigeons flutter about the tall, isolated tower. There are archways about you on three sides, and beneath one of them sit the motionless Turk, with his long pipe, and the handsome young Greek, leaning against a pillar, gazing up at the trophies aloft, at the tall masts, monuments of a lost power. The flags hang down like mourning crepe. A girl is resting there; she has set down her heavy pails of water, though the yoke by which she carries them is still across her shoulders; she is leaning against the Mast of Victory.

"The building you see before you is not a fairy castle, but a church. The gilded domes and the golden balls around it glitter in my rays. Those magnificent bronze horses up there have traveled like the bronze horse in the fairy tale; they have journeyed to distant lands and returned. Can you see the brilliant colors on the walls and window panes? It is as if, at a child's plea, a fairy had decorated this strange temple. Can you see the winged lion upon that column? He still glitters with gold, but his wings are bound; the lion is dead, for the king of the ocean is dead. The great halls are empty, and where gorgeous pictures once hung there are now bare walls. Beggars sleep beneath the archways, whereas once only great nobles were permitted to tread the pavement there. A sigh sounds from the deep dungeons, or is from the leaden chambers near the Bridge of Sighs, where once were heard the tambourines in the gay gondolas, just as they were when the wedding ring was cast from the glorious *Bucentaur* into the Adriatic, the Queen of the Ocean. Wrap yourself in your mists, O Adriatic! Cover yourself with the widow's veil, and let it enwrap your bridegroom's mausoleum—marble, ghostlike Venice!"

NINETEENTH EVENING

"I looked down into a large theater," said the Moon. "The audience filled the house, for a new actor was making his first appearance. My rays glided through a small window in the wall, and I saw a painted face with the forehead pressed against the pane—it was the hero of the evening. The knightly beard curled around his chin, but there were tears in his eyes, for he had been hissed from the stage, and for a good reason. Poor fellow! But incompetence cannot be tolerated in the world of art. He had deep feeling, and loved his art with a fervor, but art did not love him.

"The prompter's bell tinkled. In his part was written, 'Boldly and valiantly the hero advances'—and he had to appear before an audience which ridiculed him.

"When the play was ended, I saw a man, muffled in a cloak, sneak down the stairs; it was he, the crushed hero of the evening. The stagehands whispered to each other. I followed the poor fellow to his room. Hanging oneself is an unsightly death, and poison is not always at hand. I know he was thinking of both.

"I saw him look at his pale face in the mirror and peep through half-closed eyes to decide whether he would look well as a corpse. A man may be very unhappy and at the same time very affected. He thought of death, of suicide, and I believe he pitied himself. He wept bitterly, and when a man has wept until no more tears can come, he no longer thinks of suicide.

"A year had passed since then, and again a play was produced, but in a little theater, by a company of poor wandering players. I again saw that familiar face with the curled beard, the painted cheeks. Again he looked up at me and smiled—and yet he had again been hissed from the stage, only a minute before, hissed from a miserable stage, hissed by a miserable audience!

"That same evening, a shabby hearse drove out of the gate of the town, with no one following. It was a suicide—our painted and hissed hero. The only attendant was the driver of the hearse, and none but the Moon followed it. The suicide lies buried in a corner by the churchyard wall. Nettles will soon grow over his grave, and the gravedigger will fling over it the weeds and thorns he roots from the other graves."

TWENTIETH EVENING

"I come from Rome," the Moon said. "There on one of the seven hills in the middle of the city are the ruins of the emperor's palace. The wild fig tree grows in the breaches of the wall and covers its bareness with broad, gray-green leaves. The donkey treads on the green laurels and enjoys the barren thistle among heaps of rubbish. To this spot, from which the Roman eagles once flew out over the world, and came, saw, and conquered, an entrance now leads through a humble little house, built of clay and wedged between two broken marble columns. Vine tendrils hang down like a mourning wreath over the crooked window.

"An old woman lives there with her little granddaughter. They are now the rulers of the emperor's palace, and show the place to tourists. A bare wall is all that remains of the magnificent throne hall, and the long shadow of a dark cypress points to the spot where the throne once stood. There is earth a yard high on the broken floor. The little girl, now the daughter of the emperor's palace, often sits there on her stool while the evening bells ring. Through the keyhole of a nearby door, which she calls her balcony window, she can overlook half of Rome, as far as the mighty dome of St. Peter's.

"The evening, as always, was still, and down below, the little girl was walking in my full clear light. Carrying an antique earthen pitcher of water on her head, she was barefooted, and her short skirt and little sleeves were torn. I kissed the child's finely rounded shoulders, her black eyes, and her dark, shining hair. She mounted the steps up to the house, which were steep and formed of broken bits of masonry and a crumbled column. Spotted lizards ran frightened past her feet, but she was not afraid of them. Her hand was raised to ring the doorbell—a rabbit's foot suspended from a string was now the bell handle at the emperor's palace—but she paused for a moment. What was she thinking of? Perhaps of the beautiful image of the infant Jesus, clad in silver and gold, in the chapel below, where the silver lamps burned and where her little friends sang the hymn she knew so well. I do not know. She moved, and stumbled. The earthen pitcher fell from her head and crashed on the marble step! She burst into tears; the beautiful daughter of the emperor's palace wept over a cheap, broken clay pitcher. She stood there barefooted and wept, and dared not pull the string, the bell rope at the emperor's palace."

TWENTY-FIRST EVENING

The Moon hadn't shone for more than two weeks, and then at last I saw him again, round and clear above the slowly rising mass of clouds. Listen to what the Moon told me.

"I followed a caravan out of one of the towns of Fezzan. The group halted near the sandy desert, on a salt plain, which glittered like an ice field, and was covered to but a small extent with the light drift-sand. The oldest man in the caravan, at whose girdle hung the water flask and on whose head was a sack of unleavened bread, drew a square figure on the ground with his staff and wrote inside it a few words from the Koran. Then the whole caravan passed over the consecrated spot. A young merchant, a son of the East, as I could see from his sparkling eyes and his handsome figure, rode thoughtfully on his white, snorting horse. Was he perhaps thinking of his pretty young wife at home? Only two days before, a camel covered with costly furs and splendid shawls had carried her, the lovely bride, around the walls of the city. Drums and bagpipes had sounded, and the women had sung, while all around the camel there had been rejoicing and gunshots, the greatest number of which the bridegroom had fired.

"And now—now he was journeying with the caravan far away into the desert. I followed them on their way for many nights and saw them rest beside the wells, under the palm trees. They plunged a knife into the breast of a camel that had fallen, and roasted the meat at the fire. My rays cooled the glowing sands and showed them the black rocks, dead islands in the immense ocean of sand. They met no hostile tribes on their pathless route; no storms arose; no wave of sand whirled destruction over the caravan.

"At home, the lovely young wife prayed for her husband and her father. 'Are they dead?' she asked my golden horn. 'Are they dead?' she asked my brilliant orb.

"Now the desert lies behind them. This evening, they are camped beneath tall palm trees, with the crane flying about them on long wings and the pelican watching them from the branches of mimosa. The luxuriant underbrush is trodden by the heavy feet of elephants.

A troop of Negroes is returning from a market in the interior; the women, with indigo-blue skirts and their black hair decked with brass buttons, are driving heavily laden oxen, on which the naked black children are lying asleep. A Negro is leading, by a rope, a lion cub that he has bought. They approach the caravan.

"The young merchant sits silent and motionless, thinking of his beautiful wife; in this land of the blacks, he is dreaming of his white and fragrant flower, far away across the desert; he raises his head...."

A cloud, and then another cloud, passed across the face of the Moon. I heard nothing more from him that evening.

TWENTY-SECOND EVENING

"I saw a little girl weeping," the Moon said, "weeping over the wickedness of the world. She had received the loveliest doll as a gift. Oh, what a doll that was, so pretty and delicate, and surely it could not have been made to experience hardship! But the little girl's brothers, who were tall boys, had placed the doll in a high tree in the garden, and had then run away. The little girl couldn't reach the doll and had no way of helping it down, and that was why she was crying. The doll undoubtedly wept too, for it stretched out its arms through the green branches and looked very sad indeed.

"Yes, this was one of the hardships of the world, of which Mamma spoke so often. Oh, that poor doll! The evening twilight was already coming on, and night would soon be here. Did it have to sit alone in the tree out here all night long? No, the little girl didn't have the heart to let it do that. 'I'll stay with you!' she said, although she really was not very brave. She already imagined she could see the little goblins, in their tall pointed caps, peeping out from the bushes, and tall ghosts dancing in the dark walk, coming closer and closer, stretching out their hands toward the tree where the doll sat, and laughingly pointing their fingers at it. Oh, how frightened the little girl was! 'But if we haven't done anything sinful,' she thought, 'the evil spirits can't hurt us. I wonder if I have done something wrong!' She thought for a moment. 'Oh, yes!' she said. 'I laughed at the poor little duck that had a red rag around its leg. It's so funny when it limps, and that's why I laughed at it! But I know it's wrong to laugh at animals.' Then she looked up at her doll. 'Have *you* ever laughed at animals?' she asked. And it seemed as if the doll shook its head."

TWENTY-THIRD EVENING

"I looked down on Tyrol," said the Moon, "and my rays caused the dark pine trees to cast heavy shadows across the rocks. I looked at the figures of St. Christopher with the infant Jesus on his shoulder that are painted on the walls of the houses, enormous figures that extend from the ground to the gables, pictures of St. Florian pouring water on the burning house, and of Christ on the great roadside crosses. To the present generation they are very old pictures, whereas I saw them being put up, one after the other.

"High up, on the slope of the mountain, is a lonely nunnery, wedged in between the rocks like a swallow's nest. Two of the sisters were in the tower above, tolling the bell; they were both young, and therefore they looked out over the mountains into the wide world beyond. A traveling coach rolled by on the highway below, and the postilion's horn sounded. The poor nuns looked after the carriage for a moment with a mournful glance, and a tear gleamed in the eye of the younger one. The horn sounded more and more faintly, until at last the convent bell silenced its dying sound."

TWENTY-FOURTH EVENING

Now listen to what the Moon told me.

"Several years ago, here in Copenhagen, I looked in through the window of a poor furnished room. The father and mother slept, but their little son was not asleep. I saw the flowered cotton bed curtain move and the child peep out from behind it. At first, I thought he was looking at the great Bornholm clock, which was brightly painted in red and green, with a cuckoo atop it, and heavy lead weights hanging below; the pendulum, with its glittering brass plate, swung to and fro—tick, tock! But it wasn't the clock that the little fellow looked at. No, it was his mother's spinning wheel, which stood just beneath the clock. To him, this was the most precious thing in the entire house; yet, he never dared touch it, unless he wished to have his fingers slapped. For hours, he would sit beside his mother while she spun, looking at the humming spindle and the circling wheel; and at those moments, he always had his own thoughts. Ah, if he only dared to turn the spinning wheel by himself!

"His father and mother still slept; he looked at them first, then at the spinning wheel. Presently, a little bare foot stuck out of bed, then another bare foot, and soon two small legs appeared. And—bumps!—then he was standing on the floor. Once more, he turned around to see if his father and mother slept; yes, they did; and then, dressed only in his short little shirt, he stole very, very softly to the spinning wheel and began to spin. The thread flew off, but the wheel only turned the more quickly. I kissed his yellow hair and his light blue eyes; it was a pretty picture.

"Suddenly, his mother awoke. The bed curtains moved; she peeped out, and instantly thought of goblins or other little sprites. 'In Jesus' name!' she said, and in her fright, she nudged her husband. He opened his eyes, rubbed them with his hand, and looked at the busy little fellow. 'Why,' he said, 'that is Bertel!'

"My eye turned from the humble room—I have so many things to see, you know—and in the same instant, I was looking down into the halls of the Vatican, where stand the marble statues of the gods. I lighted up the Laocoön group, and the stone seemed to sigh. I pressed my silent kiss on the breasts of the Muses, and they seemed to come to life. But my rays rested longest on the Nile group—on the colossal figure of the god. There he lay leaning on the Sphinx, dreaming, thoughtful, as if he were thinking of the years gone by. Around him, the little cupids played with the crocodiles. A tiny little cupid sat in the horn of plenty, his arms crossed, and gazed at the stern and mighty river god—a true picture of the little boy at the spinning wheel, with the very same features. Here, lifelike and charming, stood the little marble child; and yet the wheel of time has revolved more than a thousand times since it was cut out of the stone. And it would have to revolve again—as many times as the boy turned the spinning wheel in the humble room—before the world would once more produce marble figures like these.

"Many years have since passed," the Moon continued. "Only yesterday, I looked down on a bay on the eastern coast of Zealand, surrounded with high banks and beautiful forests. There is an old manor house there, with red walls and swans on the waters of the moat, while nearby is a pretty little country town, with its church situated among apple orchards.

"A great many boats, lighted with torches, glided over the calm surface of the water. The torches had not been lighted for catching eel; no, this was a festival. Music sounded, and a song was sung. In one of the boats stood the man who was the object of this homage, a tall, powerful figure, wrapped in a great cloak, a man with blue eyes and long white locks. I knew him, and I thought of the Nile group, and the marble statues of the gods in the Vatican. And I thought of that humble little room—I believe it was in Grönne Street—where little Bertel, in his short little shirt, sat and spun. The wheel of time has turned, and new gods have been carved in marble.... From the boats arose shouts, 'Hurrah! Hurrah for Bertel Thorvaldsen!'"

TWENTY-FIFTH EVENING

"I'll give you a picture from Frankfort," said the Moon. "I noticed one building in particular there. It was not the birthplace of Goethe, nor was it the old town hall, through whose grated windows one may still see the horned skulls of oxen that were roasted and given to the people at the coronation of the emperors. The building was a burgher's type of house, plain and painted green, and stood at the corner of the narrow Jew's Alley. It was the house of Rothschild.

"I looked in at the open door. The staircase was brightly lighted; servants in livery, with wax tapers in massive silver candlesticks, bowed low before an aged woman who was being carried down the stairs in a chair. The master of the house stood by, bareheaded, and pressed a respectful kiss on the old lady's hand. She was his mother; she nodded kindly to him and to the servants, who then carried her through the dark, narrow street, and into a little house. Here she lived, and here she had borne all her children. From this spot, their great fortunes had blossomed forth. Were she now to leave the miserable street and the little house, perhaps fortune would abandon them; that was her belief."

The Moon told no more; his visit to me that evening was all too short. But I thought about the old lady in the narrow, miserable street. A single word from her, and she could have had a magnificent house on the bank of the Thames; one word from her, and she could have had a villa on the Bay of Naples. "If I should desert the humble house from which the fortunes of my sons have sprung, then perhaps fortune might desert them!" This was a superstition, but one that, to those who know the story and have seen the picture, two words of postscript will give full meaning—*a mother*.

TWENTY-SIXTH EVENING

"It was yesterday morning at dawn"—these are the Moon's own words—"and I was looking at the chimneys of a large city, from which as yet no smoke arose. Suddenly, a little head popped up from one of them; then half the body followed, and both arms rested on the edge of the chimney. 'Hurrah!' It was a little chimney sweep, who for the first time in his life had climbed to the very top of a chimney and stuck his head out. 'Hurrah!'

"Yes, this was indeed very different from creeping about in the narrow flues and little chimneys. The air was so fresh, and he could look out over the whole city to the green woods. The sun was rising; it shone round and large into his face, which beamed with joy and was prettily blacked with soot. 'The whole city can see me now!' he said. 'The Moon can see me, and the Sun, too!' Hurrah!' And then he waved his broom above his head."

TWENTY-SEVENTH EVENING

"Last night I looked down on a city in China," said the Moon. "My beams shone on the long bare walls that formed its streets; here and there was a door, of course, but it was always shut, for what has a Chinese to do with the world outside? Tight blinds concealed the windows behind the walls; only from within the temple was there light, which shone faintly through its windows.

"I looked in and observed its colorful grandeur. From floor to ceiling the walls are painted with many pictures, in vivid colors and rich gilt, representing the actions of the gods on earth. In every niche is the statue of a deity, almost entirely concealed by colored draperies and hanging banners. Before each of the gods—they are all made of tin—is a little altar, with flowers, holy water, and burning candles. But foremost in the temple was Fu, the principal deity, clad in a silken robe of the sacred color, yellow.

"At the foot of his altar sat a living figure, a young priest, seemingly lost in prayer; but in the midst of his prayers, he seemed to fall into a deep reverie, and he must have had some sinful thought on his conscience, for his cheeks burned, and his head was bent to the ground. Poor Soui-houng! Could he perhaps be dreaming of working in his little bed of flowers, one such as separates every Chinese house from the long street wall? And was that work more agreeable to him than sweeping the temple and snuffing wax tapers? Or did he long to be seated at the richly laden table, wiping his lips with silver paper between courses? Or was his sin so great that, if he dared confess it, the Celestial Empire would punish him with death? Or were his thoughts bold enough to follow the barbarian's ships to their home in distant England? No, his thoughts did not wander so far, and yet they were as sinful as the hot passions of youth could make them—doubly sinful in the temple here, in the presence of Fu and the other holy gods. I know where his thoughts were.

"In the outskirts of the city, upon a flat, flagged roof, where the railing seemed to be of porcelain, and where there were beautiful vases with large white bellflowers, sat the beautiful Pe, with her small roguish eyes, full lips, and the tiniest feet. The shoes pained her feet, but in her there was a still greater pain. And the satin rustled as she raised her delicate, round arms. Before her was a glass globe with four goldfish. With a many-colored, varnished stick, she stirred the water, oh, so slowly, for she was lost in thought. Perhaps she was thinking how richly clothed in gold the fish were, how safely they lived in the glass bowl, how generously they were supplied with food, and yet how much happier they would have been free. Her thoughts roamed far away from her home; her thoughts wandered to the temple, but it was not with homage for the gods. Poor Pe! Poor Soui-houng! Their earthly thoughts met, but my cold beam lay between them like the sword of an angel!"

TWENTY-EIGHTH EVENING

"The ocean was calm," said the Moon. "The water was as transparent as the clear air through which I sailed. Deep down beneath the surface of the waves, I could see the strange plants that stretched up their long stalks like great forest trees, while the fishes played above the tops of them.

"High in the air flew a flock of wild swans. One of them, whose wings were exhausted, sank lower and lower, while its eyes followed the aerial caravan disappearing in the distance. It kept its wings spread wide, and sank as a soap bubble sinks in the still air, until at last it touched the surface of the water. Its head bent backwards between its wings, and it lay there motionless, like the white lotus flower on the peaceful lake.

"A breeze arose, fanning the quiet surface of the water, which gleamed and rippled until it curled up in large whitecapped waves. Then the swan raised its head, and the shiny water splashed, like blue fire, over its breast and back. The dawn of day touched the clouds with red. With new strength, the swan arose and flew toward the rising sun, toward the bluish coast, the way the aerial caravan had gone before, but the swan flew alone, with longing in its breast. In loneliness it flew over the blue, the swelling waves."

TWENTY-NINTH EVENING

"I'll give you another picture from Sweden," said the Moon. "Between dark pine forests, near the dreary banks of Lake Roxen, is the old convent church of Vreta. My rays penetrated through the grating in the wall into the spacious vault where the kings sleep in huge stone coffins. A kingly crown, symbol of earthly pomp, shines on the moldering wall above; but it is made of wood, painted and gilded, and hung on a wooden peg driven into the wall. The worm has eaten into the gilded wood, while the spider has spun its web from the crown to the coffin like a mourning veil, and it is as frail as sorrow for the departed often is.

"How peacefully they sleep! I can remember them quite well. I can still see the proud smiles on their lips, from which came mighty and decisive pronouncements that brought joy or sorrow.

"When the steamboat winds its course among the mountains like a magic bark, a stranger frequently makes a pilgrimage to that church and visits the burial vault. He asks the names of the kings, but they sound unfamiliar and empty to him. He smiles at the worm-eaten crowns, and if he happens to be of a pious nature, there is a sadness reflected in is smile. Slumber on, ye dead! The Moon still remembers you and by night sends his cold rays into your silent kingdom, where the pinewood crown hangs."

THIRTIETH EVENING

"Close by the highway," said the Moon, "stands an inn, and opposite it is a large wagon shed, the roof of which was being thatched. I looked down between the rafters and through the open loft shutters into the dismal shed. The turkey cock was asleep on a beam, and a saddle lay in the empty manger.

"In the middle of the shed stood a traveling coach, in which the travelers were napping in easy security, while the horses were being watered and the coachman was stretching his legs; I well know that he had spent more than half the journey sleeping comfortably. The door to the servant's room was open; the bed was all topsy-turvy, and on the floor stood a candle that had burned deep down into the socket of the candlestick. The wind blew coldly through the shed. The time was closer to dawn than to midnight. In one of the side stalls slept a family of poor wandering musicians. The father and mother were probably dreaming of the burning drops left in their bottle, while the pale little girl was dreaming of the burning tears in her eyes. At their head lay their harp, and at their feet their dog."

THIRTY-FIRST EVENING

"It occurred in a little provincial town," said the Moon; "it was last year that I saw it, but that doesn't matter, for I saw it very clearly. Tonight, I read about it in the newspaper, but there it was not nearly so clearly told. The owner of a dancing bear was tied up behind the woodpile in the yard—the poor bear that looked so fierce, but did nobody any harm. Up in the attic room, three small children were playing by the light of my rays; the oldest was perhaps six, the youngest not more than two. Tramp, tramp! There was somebody coming up the stairs; who could it be? The floor flew open—it was the bear! the huge, shaggy bear. He had tired of waiting so long out in the yard and had found his way up the stairs. I saw it all," said the Moon.

"The children were terribly frightened of the great, shaggy animal, and each ran to hide himself in a corner. The bear found all three of them and put his snuffling muzzle up to them, but didn't harm them. 'This must be a big dog,' thought the children, and then began to pet him. The bear stretched out at full length on the floor. The youngest boy rolled over him, and putting his curly head in the beast's shaggy black fur, began to play hide and seek. Then the eldest boy brought his drum and thumped away on it with might and main; whereupon the bear promptly stood erect on his hind legs and began to dance. What a charming sight! Each boy shouldered a musket, and of course the bear had to have one too, which he held onto firmly. What a playmate they had found! And away they marched—one, two, one, two!

"Suddenly the door opened, and the children's mother appeared. You should have seen her, speechless with horror, her face white as a sheet, her mouth half open, her eyes glassy with terror. But the smallest boy nodded to her with a look of great delight, and cried out childishly, 'Mamma, we're only playing soldier!'

"And then the bear's owner appeared."

THIRTY-SECOND EVENING

The wind was stormy and cold; the clouds flew swiftly by. Only for a moment at a time could I see the Moon.

"I looked down through the silent sky at the drifting clouds," he said. "I see the great shadows chase across the earth."

Recently, I looked down on a prison, outside of which stood a closed carriage waiting to take a prisoner away. My rays went in through the barred window to the wall where the prisoner was scratching lines as a parting memento. He was not writing words, but a melody, the outpourings of his heart, on his last night in this prison. Then the door opened, and he was led outside; he looked up at my round face. Clouds drifted between us, as if he should not see my face, nor I his. He entered the carriage; the door was closed, the whip cracked, and the horses galloped off into the deep forest, where my rays could not follow him. But as I glanced again through the barred window, my rays fell on the melody scratched on the wall—his last farewell. Where words fail, often music can speak. My beams could light up only a few of the notes, so that most of what was written there will be forever dark to me. Was it a song of death that he wrote? Or were these notes of joy? Was he driving away to meet his death, or to the embrace of his beloved? The rays of the Moon do not read all that mortals write.

"I look down through the great, silent sky at the drifting clouds. I see the great shadows chase across the earth."

THIRTY-THIRD EVENING

"I am very fond of children," said the Moon, "especially the little ones, who are so amusing. When they are not thinking of me at all, I peep into the room, between the curtain and the window frame. I like to watch them dressing and undressing. First the round, naked little shoulder comes creeping out of the frock, and then the arm slides out; or else I watch the stocking being drawn off, and a sweet little leg, so white and firm, appears, with a little white foot that's fit to be kissed—and I kiss it too!"

"This evening—and this I must tell you!—this evening, I looked through a window where there was no curtain drawn, for nobody lived opposite. I saw a whole flock of youngsters, brothers and sisters. Among them was a little girl; she is only four years old, but she can say the Lord's Prayer as well as any of the others, and every evening, the mother sits beside her bed and listens to her pray; then she gets a kiss, and the mother remains there until the child falls asleep, which happens as soon as she closes her little eyes.

"This evening the two elder children were a bit wild. One of them danced about on one leg in his long white nightgown, while the other stood on a chair where all the children's clothes were and announced he was posing for Greek statues. The third and fourth put their toys carefully away in a drawer, for that has to be done. Then the mother sat by the bed of the youngest and ordered all the rest to be quiet, for their little sister was going to say the Lord's Prayer.

"I peeped in over the lamp," said the Moon. "The four-year-old girl lay in her bed, between the neat white linen, her small hands folded, and her little face was very serious. She was saying the Lord's Prayer aloud.

"'Why is it,' said her mother, interrupting her in the middle of the prayer, 'that when you've said, "Give us this day our daily bread," you always add something else that I can't quite understand? What is it? You must tell me!'

"'Mother dear, please don't be angry. I only said, "with plenty of butter on it!"'"

THE WICKED PRINCE (1840)

Once upon a time, there was a proud and wicked prince who thought only about how he might conquer all the nations of the Earth and make his name a terror to all mankind. He plunged forth with fire and sword; his soldiers trampled down the grain in the fields, and put the torch to the peasant's cottage so that the red flames licked the very leaves from the trees and the fruit hung roasted from black and charred limbs. Many a poor mother caught up her naked baby and tried to hide behind the smoking walls, but the soldiers followed her, and if they found her and the child, then began their devilish pleasure. Evil spirits could do no worse, but the prince rejoiced in it all.

Day by day, his power increased; his name was feared by all, and fortune followed him in all his deeds. From the conquered cities, he carried away gold and precious treasures, until he had amassed in his capital riches such as were unequaled in any other place. Then he built superb palaces and temples and arches, and whoever saw his magnificence said, "What a great prince!" Never did they think of the misery he had brought upon other lands; never did they listen to the groans and lamentations from cities laid waste by fire.

The prince gazed upon his gold, looked at his superb buildings, and thought like the crowd, "What a great prince! But I must have more, much more! There is no power that can equal—much less surpass—mine!" And so he warred with his neighbors until all were defeated. The conquered kings were chained to his chariot with chains of gold when he drove through the streets; and when he sat at table, they lay at the feet of the prince and his courtiers, eating such scraps as might be thrown to them.

Now the prince had his own statue set up in the marketplaces and the palaces; yes, he would even have set it in the churches, on the altars, but to this, the priests said, "Prince, you are great, but God is greater! We dare not obey your orders!"

"Well," said the evil prince, "then I shall conquer God too!" In the pride and folly of his heart he had built a splendidly constructed ship in which he could sail through the air. It was as colorful as a peacock's tail, and seemed decorated with a thousand eyes, but each eye was the barrel of a cannon. The prince could sit in the center of the ship, and, upon his touching a certain button, a thousand bullets would stream forth, and the guns would at once be reloaded. Hundreds of strong eagles were harnessed to the ship, and so it flew away, up and up toward the sun.

Far beneath lay Earth. At first, its mountains and forests appeared like a plowed field, with a tuft of green peeping out here and there from the sod; then it seemed like an unrolled map, and finally it was wholly hidden in mists and clouds, as the eagles flew higher and higher.

Then God sent forth a single one of his countless angels, and immediately the prince let fly a thousand bullets at him, but they fell back like hail from the angel's shining wings. Then one drop of blood—just one—fell from one of the angel's white wing feathers onto the ship of the prince. There it burned itself into it, and its weight of a thousand hundredweights of lead hurled the ship back down with terrible speed to Earth. The mighty wings of the eagles were broken, the winds roared about the head of the prince, and the clouds on every side, sprung from the smoke of burned cities, formed themselves into menacing shapes. Some were like mile-long crabs stretching out their huge claws toward him; others were like tumbling boulders or fire-breathing dragons. The prince lay half dead in his ship, until it was finally caught in the tangled branches of a dense forest.

"I *will* conquer God!" he said. "I have sworn it; my will shall be done!" Then for seven years he built other magnificent ships in which to sail through the air, and had lightning beams forged from the hardest of steels to batter down the battlements of

Heaven itself. From all the conquered countries he assembled vast armies that, when formed in battle array, covered mile after mile of ground.

They embarked in the magnificent ships, but as the prince approached his own, God sent forth a swarm of gnats—just one little swarm—that buzzed about the prince and stung his face and hands. In rage, he drew his sword, but he could cut only the empty air; he could not strike the gnats. Then he ordered that he be brought costly cloths, which were to be wrapped around him so that no gnat could reach him with its sting. His orders were carried out; but one little gnat had concealed itself in the innermost covering, and now it crept into the prince's ear and stung him. It smarted like fire, and the poison rushed into his brain; he tore the clothes loose and flung them far away from him, rent his garments into rags, and danced naked before the rugged and savage soldiers. Now they could only mock at the mad prince who had started out to conquer God and had been himself conquered by a single little gnat!

THE BUCKWHEAT (1841)

When after a thunderstorm you pass by a field in which buckwheat is growing, you will very often notice that the buckwheat appears quite blackened and singed as if a fire had swept over it. The farmer will tell you, "It got that from lightning." But why and how did it happen?

I'll tell you the story as the sparrow told it to me, and he heard it from an old willow tree that stands beside a buckwheat field. And who could possibly know better than that old willow tree, for he still stands there? He is such a respectable and dignified tree, but is old and crippled, with grass and brambles growing out of a cleft in his middle. He bends forward, with his branches hanging down to the ground as if they were long green hair.

In the fields around the tree, corn was growing, and rye and barley, and oats—oh, very fine oats, which when ripe looked like a whole flock of little yellow canary birds sitting on sprays. The corn stood so prosperous in its field, and the fuller an ear was, the deeper it bent in pious humility.

But just opposite the old willow tree there was also a field of buckwheat. And the buckwheat didn't bend like the rest of the grain, but strutted very proudly and stiffly. "I'm as rich as any old corn," he said. "And besides, I'm lots handsomer; my flowers are as beautiful as the apple blossoms; it's a pleasure to look at me and my family. Do you know anybody more splendid than we are, you old willow tree?"

And the willow tree nodded his head, just as if he were saying, "Yes, certainly I do."

But the buckwheat puffed himself up with foolish pride and said, "That stupid tree's so old he has grass growing out of his stomach!"

Suddenly, a terrible storm broke out, and all the field flowers folded their petals and bowed their delicate heads while the storm passed over them, but the buckwheat strutted with arrogance.

"Bend your head down the way we do!" cried the flowers.

"I don't need to!" replied the buckwheat.

"Bend your head!" the other crops all cried. "The Angel of Storm is flying down on us! He has wings that reach from the clouds right down to earth, and he'll break you in two before you can cry for mercy!"

"Yes, but I certainly won't bend," replied the buckwheat defiantly. "Shut up your flowers and bend your leaves," the old willow tree called. "And whatever you do, don't look up at the lightning when the cloud bursts! Even human beings don't dare do that, for in the lightning, one can look into God's Heaven itself, and that sight will strike even human beings blind! So if we, who are so much less worthy than they, dared to do it, what would happen to us!"

"Now I'll certainly look straight up into Heaven itself!" And he did so with pride and haughtiness. So vivid was the lightning that it seemed as if the whole world were on fire.

When the storm finally passed, the flowers and crops stood again in the clear, sweet air, refreshed by the rain; but the buckwheat was blasted coal-black by the lightning, and he was now a dead, useless weed on the field. Then the willow tree waved his branches in the breeze, and great drops of water fell from his green leaves just as if he was crying. "Why are you weeping?" the sparrows asked him. "Everything is so wonderful here. Look how the sun shines, see how the clouds sail across the sky. Can't you smell the fragrance of the flowers and the bushes? Why do you weep, old willow tree?"

Then the willow tree told them of the pride and the haughtiness of the buckwheat, and of the punishment that he had to suffer.

And I who tell you this story have heard it from the sparrows. One evening when I asked them for a tale, they told it to me.

OLE LUKOIE (1841)

There's no one on Earth who knows so many stories as Ole Lukoie—he certainly can tell them!

When night comes on and children still sit in good order around the table or on their little stools, Ole Lukoie arrives. He comes upstairs quietly, for he walks in his socks. Softly he opens the door, and *flick!* He sprinkles sweet milk in the children's eyes—just a tiny bit, but always enough to keep their eyes closed so they won't see him. He tiptoes behind them and breathes softly on their necks, and this makes their heads hang heavy. Oh yes! But it doesn't hurt them, for Ole Lukoie loves children and only wants them to be quiet, and that they are only when they have been put to bed. He wants them to be quiet so that he can tell them stories.

As soon as the children fall asleep, Ole Lukoie sits down on the bed beside them. He is well dressed. His coat is made of silk, but it would be impossible to say what color it is because it gleams red, or green, or blue, as he turns about. Under each arm, he carries an umbrella. One has pictures on it, and that one he opens up over good children. Then they dream the most beautiful stories all night long. The other is just a plain umbrella with nothing on it at all, and that one he opens over naughty children. Then they sleep restlessly, and when they wake up in the morning, they have had no dreams at all.

Now you shall hear how for a whole week, Lukoie came every evening to a little boy named Hjalmar, and what he told him. There are seven of these stories, because there are seven days to a week.

MONDAY

"Now listen," Ole Lukoie said, as soon as he got Hjalmar to bed that evening. "First, let's put things to rights."

Then all the flowers in the flower pots grew to be big trees, arching their long branches under the ceiling and along the walls until the room became a beautiful bower. The limbs were loaded with flowers, each more lovely than any rose, and their fragrance was so sweet that if you wanted to eat it—it was sweeter than jam. The fruit gleamed like gold, and besides, there were dumplings bursting with currants. It was all so splendid!

Suddenly, a dreadful howl came from the table drawer where Hjalmar kept his schoolbooks.

"What can the matter be?" said Ole Lukoie, as he went to the table and opened the drawer. It was the slate, which was throwing a fit and was ready to fall to pieces because there was a mistake in the sum that had been worked on it. The slate pencil tugged and jumped at the end of its string as if it were a little dog. It wanted to correct the sum, but it could not.

Another lamentation came from Hjalmar's copybook. Oh, it was dreadful to listen to. On each page, the capital letters stood one under the other, each with its little letter beside it. This was the copy. Next to these were the letters which Hjalmar had written. Though they thought they looked just like the first ones, they tumbled all over the lines on which they were supposed to stand.

"See, this is how you should hold yourselves," said the copy. "Look, slanting like this, with a bold stroke."

"Oh, how glad we would be to do that!" Hjalmar's letters replied, "but we can't. We are so weak."

"Then you must take medicine," Ole Lukoie told them.

"Oh, no!" they cried, and stood up so straight that it was a pleasure to see them.

"Now we can't tell any stories," said Ole Lukoie. "I must give them their exercises. One, two! One, two!" He put the letters through their paces until they stood straight, more graceful than any copy could stand. But when Ole Lukoie left, and Hjalmar looked at them in the morning, they were just as miserable as ever.

TUESDAY

As soon as Hjalmar was in bed, Ole Lukoie touched all the furniture in the room with his little magic sprinkler, and immediately everything began to talk. Everything talked about itself except the spittoon, which kept silent. It was annoyed that they should be so conceited as to talk only about themselves and think only about themselves, without paying the least attention to it, sitting so humbly in the corner and letting everyone spit at it.

Over the chest of drawers hung a large painting in a gilt frame. It was a landscape in which one could see tall old trees, flowers in the grass, and a large lake from which a river flowed away through the woods, past many castles, far out to the open sea. Ole Lukoie touched the painting with his magic sprinkler, and the birds in it began to sing, the branches stirred on the trees, and the clouds billowed along. You could see their shadows sweep across the landscape.

Then Ole Lukoie lifted little Hjalmar up to the frame and put the boy's feet into the picture, right in the tall grass, and there he stood. The sun shone down on him through the branches of the trees as he ran to the water and got into a little boat that was there. It was painted red and white, and its sails shone like silver. Six swans, each with a golden crown around its neck and a bright blue star upon its forehead, drew the boat through the deep woods, where the trees whispered of robbers and witches, and the flowers spoke about the dainty little elves, and about all that the butterflies had told them.

Splendid fish with scales like gold and silver swam after the boat. Sometimes they gave a leap—so that it said "splash" in the water. Birds red and blue, large and small, flew after the boat in two long lines. The gnats danced, and the cockchafers went *boom, boom!* They all wanted to go with Hjalmar, and every one of them had a story to tell.

What a magnificent voyage that was! Sometimes the forest was deep and dark, and sometimes like the loveliest garden full of sun and flowers. There were palaces of marble and glass, and on the balconies stood princesses. Hjalmar knew them well. They were all little girls with whom he had played. Each of them stretched out her hand, and each held out the prettiest sugar pig that ever a cake woman sold. Hjalmar grasped each sugar pig as he went by, and the princess held fast, so that each got a piece of it. The princess got the smaller piece, and Hjalmar got the larger one. Little princes stood guard at each palace. They saluted with their swords and caused raisins and tin soldiers to shower down. You could tell that they were princes indeed.

Sometimes Hjalmar sailed through the forests, sometimes through great halls, or straight through a town. He also came through the town where his nurse lived, she who had carried him in her arms when he was a very small boy and had always been fond of him. She bowed and waved, and sang the pretty song which she had made up herself and sent to Hjalmar:

> *I think of you as often,*
> *Hjalmar, my little dear,*
> *As I've kissed your lips so soft, and*
> *Your cheeks and your eyes so clear.*
> *I heard your first laughter and weeping,*
> *And too soon I heard your good-byes.*
> *May God have you in his keeping,*
> *My angel from the skies.*

All the birds sang too, and the flowers danced on their stalks, and the old trees nodded, just as if Ole Lukoie were telling stories to *them*.

WEDNESDAY

How the rain came down outdoors! Hjalmar could hear it in his sleep, and when Ole Lukoie opened the window, the water had risen up to the window sill. There was a real lake outside, and a fine ship lay close to the house.

"If you will sail with me, little Hjalmar," said Ole Lukoie, "you can voyage to distant lands tonight and be back again by morning."

Immediately, Hjalmar stood in his Sunday clothes aboard this splendid ship. And immediately, the weather turned glorious as they sailed through the streets and rounded the church. Now everything was a great wild sea. They sailed until land was far out of sight, and they saw a flock of storks who also came from home and wanted to travel to warmer climes. These storks flew in line, one behind the other, and they had already flown a long, long way. One of them was so weary that his wings could scarcely carry him on. He was the very last in the line, and soon he was left a long way behind the others. Finally, he sank with outstretched wings, lower and lower. He made a few more feeble strokes with his wings, but it was no use. Now he touched the ship's rigging with his feet, slid down the sail, and landed, *bang!* upon the deck.

The cabin boy caught him and put him in the chicken coop with the hens, ducks, and turkeys. The poor stork stood among them most dejected.

"Funny looking fellow!" said all the hens. The turkey gobbler puffed himself as big as ever he could, and asked the stork who he was. The ducks backed off and told each other, "He's a quack! He's a quack!"

Now the stork tried to tell them about the heat of Africa; about the pyramids; and about the ostrich, how it runs across the desert like a wild horse. But the ducks did not understand him. They said to each other, "Don't we all agree that he's a fool?"

"Yes, to be sure, he's a fool," the turkey gobbler gobbled, as the stork kept silent and thought of his Africa.

"What beautiful thin legs you've got," said the turkey gobbler. "What do they cost a yard?"

"Quack, quack, quack!" The ducks all laughed, but the stork pretended not to hear them.

"You can laugh too," the gobbler told him, "for that was a mighty witty remark, or was it too deep for you? No indeed, he isn't very bright, so let's keep on being clever ourselves."

The hens cackled, the ducks went, "Quick, quack! quick, quack!" and it was dreadful to see how they made fun of him among themselves. But Hjalmar opened the back door of the chicken coop and called to the stork. He hopped out on the deck. He was rested now, and he seemed to nod to Hjalmar to thank him. Then he spread his wings and flew away to the warm countries. But the hens clucked, and the ducks quacked, and the turkey gobbler's face turned fiery red.

"Tomorrow, we'll make soup out of you," said Hjalmar. With these words, he woke up in his own little bed. It was a marvelous journey that Ole Lukoie had taken him on during the night.

THURSDAY

"I tell you what," Ole Lukoie said. "Don't be afraid if I show you a little mouse." He held out a hand with the quaint little creature in it. "It has come to ask you to a wedding. There are two little mice here who are to enter into the state of marriage this very night. They live under the floor of your mother's pantry, which is supposed to be the most charming quarters."

"How can I get through that little mouse hole in the floor?" Hjalmar asked.

"Leave that to me," said Ole Lukoie. "I'll make you small enough." Then he touched Hjalmar with his magic sprinkler. He immediately became shorter and shorter, until at last he was only as tall as your finger. "Now you may borrow the tin soldier's uniform. I think it will just fit you, and uniforms always look well when one is at a party."

"Oh, don't they!" said Hjalmar. Instantly he was dressed like the finest tin soldier.

"If you will be so kind as to sit in your mother's thimble," the mouse said, "I shall consider it an honor to pull you along."

"Will you really go to all that trouble, young lady?" Hjalmar cried.

And in this fashion, off they drove to the mouse's wedding. First, they went down a long passage under the floor boards. It was just high enough for them to drive through in the thimble, and the whole passage was lighted with touchwood.

"Doesn't it smell delightful here?" said the mouse. "This whole road has been greased with bacon rinds, and there's nothing better than that."

Now they came to the wedding hall. On the right stood all the little lady mice, whispering and giggling as if they were making fun of each other. On the left stood all the gentlemen mice, twirling their mustaches with their forepaws. The bridegroom and his bride stood in a hollow cheese rind in the center of the floor, and kissed like mad, in plain view of all the guests. But of course, they were engaged, and were to be married immediately.

More and more guests kept crowding in. The mice were nearly trampling each other to death, and the bridal couple had posted themselves in the doorway, so no one could come or leave. Like the passage, this whole hall had been greased with bacon rind, and that was the complete banquet. However, for the dessert, a pea was brought in, on which a little mouse of the family had bitten the name of the bridal couple, that is to say, the first letter of the name. This was a most unusual touch.

All the mice said it was a charming wedding and that the conversation was perfect. And then Hjalmar drove home again. He had been in very high society, for all that he had been obliged to make himself very small to fit in the tin soldier's uniform.

FRIDAY

"It's astonishing how many older people are anxious to get hold of me," said Ole Lukoie. "Especially those whose consciences are bothering them. 'Good little Ole,' they say to me, 'we can't close our eyes. We lie awake all night, facing our wicked deeds that sit on the edge of our beds like ugly little fiends and soak us in hot perspiration. Won't you come and turn them out so that we can have a good night's sleep?' At that, they sigh very deeply. 'We will be glad to pay you for it. Good night, Ole. The money lies on the window sill.' But I don't do things for pay," said Ole Lukoie.

"What are we going to have tonight?" little Hjalmar asked.

"I don't know whether you'd like to go to a wedding again tonight, but it's quite different from the one last night. Your sister's big doll, who looks like a man and is named Herman, is to be married to the doll called Bertha. It's Bertha's birthday, too, so there'll be no end to the presents."

"Yes, I know," Hjalmar told him. "Whenever the dolls need new clothes, my sister either lets them have a birthday or hold a wedding. It must have happened a hundred times already."

"Yes, but tonight is the hundred and first wedding, and, with one hundred and one, things come to an end. That's why it's to be so splendid. Oh, look!"

Hjalmar looked over at the table. There he saw a little pasteboard house with the windows alight, and all the tin soldiers presenting arms in front of it. The bridal couple sat on the floor and leaned against the table leg. They looked thoughtful, and with good reason. Ole Lukoie, rigged out in grandmother's black petticoat, married them off. When the ceremony was over, all the furniture in the room sang the following fine song, which the pencil had written. It went to the tune of the soldier's tattoo:

> Let us lift up our voices as high as the sun,
> In honor of those who today are made one.
> Although neither knows quite what they've done,
> And neither one quite knows who's been won,
> Oh, wood and leather go well together,
> So let's lift up our voices as high as the sun.

Then they were given presents, but they had refused to take any food at all, because they planned to live on love.

"Shall we go to a summer resort, or take a voyage?" the bridegroom asked. They consulted the swallow, who was such a traveler, and the old setting hen who had raised five broods of chicks. The swallow told them about the lovely warm countries where grapes hang in great ripe bunches, where the air is soft, and where the mountains have wonderful colors that they don't have here.

"But they haven't got our green cabbage," the hen said. "I was in the country with all my chickens one summer, and there was a sand pit in which we could scratch all day. We also had access to a garden where cabbages grew. Oh, how green they were! I can't imagine anything lovelier."

"But one cabbage looks just like another," said the swallow, "and then we so often have bad weather. It is cold here—it freezes."

"That's good for the cabbage," said the hen. "Besides, it's quite warm at times. Didn't we have a hot summer four years ago? For five whole weeks, it was so hot that one could scarcely breathe. Then too, we don't have all those poisonous creatures that infest the warm countries, and we don't have robbers. Anyone who doesn't think ours is the most beautiful country is a rascal. Why, he doesn't deserve to live here!" The hen burst into tears. "I have done my share of traveling. I once made a twelve-mile trip in a coop, and there's no pleasure at all in traveling."

"Isn't the hen a sensible woman!" said Bertha, the doll. "I don't fancy traveling in the mountains because first you go up, and then you go down. No, we will move out by the sand pit and take our walks in the cabbage patch."

That settled the matter.

SATURDAY

"Shall we have some stories?" little Hjalmar asked, as soon as Ole Lukoie had put him to bed.

"There's no time for any tonight," Ole told him, as he spread his best umbrella over the boy. "Just look at these Chinamen."

The whole umbrella looked like a large Chinese bowl, with blue trees and arched bridges on which little Chinamen stood nodding their heads.

"We must have all the world spruced up by tomorrow morning," said Ole. "It's a holiday because it is Sunday. I must go to church steeples to see that the little church goblins are polishing the bells so that they will sound their best. I must go out into the fields to see whether the wind is blowing the dust off of the leaves and grass, and my biggest job of all will be to take down all the stars and shine them. I put them in my apron, but first, each star must be numbered and the hole from which it comes must be numbered the same, so that they go back in their proper places, or they wouldn't stick. Then we would have too many falling stars, for one after another would come tumbling down."

"Oh, I say, Mr Lukoie," said an old portrait that hung on the wall of Hjalmar's bedroom. "I am Hjalmar's great-grandfather. I thank you for telling the boy your stories, but you mustn't put wrong ideas in his head. The stars can't be taken down and polished. The stars are worlds too, just like Earth, and that's the beauty of them."

"My thanks, you old great-grandfather," said Ole Lukoie. "I thank you, indeed! You are the head of the family, you are the oldest of the ancestors, but I am older than you are. I am an old heathen. The Greeks and the Romans called me their god of dreams. I have been to the nobles' homes, and still go there. I know how to behave with all people, great and small. Now you may tell stories yourself." Ole Lukoie tucked his umbrella under his arm and took himself off.

"Well! It seems one can't even express an opinion these days," the old portrait grumbled. And Hjalmar woke up.

SUNDAY

"Good evening," said Ole Lukoie.

Hjalmar nodded, and ran to turn his great-grandfather's portrait to the wall so that it wouldn't interrupt them, as it had the night before.

"Now," he said, "you must tell stories; about the five peas who lived in a pod, about the rooster's foot-track that courted the hen's foot-track, and about the darning needle who gave herself such airs because she thought she was a sewing needle."

"That would be too much of a good thing," said Ole Lukoie. "You know that I would rather show you things. I shall show you my own brother. He too is named Ole Lukoie, but he comes only once to anyone. When he comes, he takes people for a ride on his horse and tells them stories. He only knows two. One is more beautiful than anyone on Earth can imagine, and the other is horrible beyond description." Then Ole Lukoie lifted little Hjalmar up to the window. "There," he said, "you can see my brother, the other Ole Lukoie. He is also called Death. You can see that he doesn't look nearly as bad as they make him out to be in the picture books, where he is only bones and knuckles. No, his coat is embroidered with silver. It is the magnificent uniform of a hussar, and a cloak of black velvet floats behind him and billows over his horse. See how he gallops along."

And Hjalmar saw how the other Ole Lukoie rode off on his horse with young folk as well as old people. He took some up before him, and some behind, but first, he always asked them:

"What conduct is marked on your report card?" They all said, "Good," but he said, "Indeed. Let me see for myself." Then they had to show him the card. All those who were marked "very good" or "excellent," he put on his horse in front of him, and told them a lovely story. But those who were marked "below average" or "bad" had to ride behind him, and he told them a frightful tale. They shivered and wept, and tried to jump down off the horse. But this they couldn't do. They had immediately grown fast to it.

"Why, Death is the most beautiful Ole Lukoie," Hjalmar exclaimed. "I'm not afraid of him."

"You needn't be," Ole Lukoie told him, "only be sure that you have a good report card."

"There now, that's instructive," great-grandfather's portrait muttered. "It certainly helps to speak one's mind." He was completely satisfied.

You see, that's the story of Ole Lukoie. Tonight, he himself can tell you some more.

THE SWINEHERD (1841)

Once there was a poor prince. He had a kingdom; it was very tiny. Still, it was large enough to marry upon, and on marriage his heart was set.

Now it was certainly rather bold of him to say, "Will you have me?" to the emperor's own daughter. But he did, for his name was famous, and far and near there were hundreds of princesses who would have said, "Yes!" and "Thank you!" too. But what did the emperor's daughter say? Well, we'll soon find out.

A rose tree grew over the grave of the prince's father. It was such a beautiful tree. It bloomed only once in five long years, and then it bore but a single flower. Oh, that was a rose indeed! The fragrance of it would make a man forget all of his sorrows and his cares. The prince had a nightingale, too. It sang as if all the sweet songs of the world were in its little throat. The nightingale and the rose were to be gifts to the princess. So they were sent to her in two large silver cases.

The emperor ordered the cases carried before him to the great hall where the princess was playing at "visitors," with her maids-in-waiting. They seldom did anything else. As soon as the princess saw that the large cases contained presents, she clapped her hands in glee. "Oh," she said, "I do hope I get a little pussycat." She opened a casket, and there was the splendid rose.

"Oh, how pretty it is," said all the maids-in-waiting.

"It's more than pretty," said the emperor. "It's superb."

But the princess poked it with her finger, and she almost started to cry. "Oh, fie! Papa," she said, "it isn't artificial. It is natural."

"Oh, fie," said all her maids-in-waiting, "it's only natural."

"Well," said the emperor, "before we fret and pout, let's see what's in the other case." He opened it, and out came the nightingale, which sang so sweetly that for a little while no one could think of a single thing to say against it.

"*Superbe!*" "*Charmant!*" said the maids-in-waiting with their smattering of French, each one speaking it worse than the next.

"How the bird does remind me of our lamented empress' music box," said one old courtier. "It has just the same tone, and the very same way of trilling."

The emperor wept like a child. "Ah, me," he said.

"Bird?" said the princess. "You mean to say it's real?"

"A real live bird," the men who had brought it assured her.

"Then let it fly and begone," said the princess, who refused to hear a word about the prince, much less to see him.

But it was not so easy to discourage him. He darkened his face both brown and black, pulled his hat down over his eyes, and knocked at the door.

"Hello, Emperor," he said. "How do you do? Can you give me some work about the palace?"

"Well," said the emperor, "people are always looking for jobs, but let me see. I do need somebody to tend the pigs, because we've got so many of them."

So the prince was appointed "Imperial Pig Tender." He was given a wretched little room down by the pigsties, and there he had to live. All day long, he sat and worked, as busy as could be, and by evening, he had made a neat little kettle with bells all around the brim of it. When the kettle boiled, the bells would tinkle and play the old tune:

> *Oh, dear Augustin,*
> *All is lost, lost, lost.*

But that was the least of it. If anyone put his finger in the steam from this kettle, he could immediately smell whatever there was for dinner in any cooking pot in town. No rose was ever like this!

Now the princess happened to be passing by with all of her maids-in-waiting. When she heard the tune, she stopped and looked pleased, for she too knew how to play "Oh, dear Augustin." It was the only tune she did know, and she played it with one finger.

"Why, that's the very same tune I play. Isn't the swineherd highly accomplished? I say," she ordered, "go and ask him the price of the instrument."

So one of the maids had to go in among the pigsties, but she put on her overshoes first.

"What will you take for the kettle?" she asked.

"I'll take ten kisses from the princess," said the swineherd.

"Oo, for goodness' sakes!" said the maid.

"And I won't take less," said the swineherd.

"Well, what does he say?" the princess wanted to know.

"I can't tell you," said the maid. "He's too horrible."

"Then whisper it close to my ear." She listened to what the maid had to whisper. "Oo, isn't he naughty!" said the princess and walked right away from there. But she had not gone very far when she heard the pretty bells play again:

> *Oh, dear Augustin,*
> *All is lost, lost, lost.*

"I say," the princess ordered, "ask him if he will take his ten kisses from my maids-in-waiting."

"No, I thank you," said the swineherd. "Ten kisses from the princess, or I keep my kettle."

"Now isn't that disgusting!" said the princess. "At least stand around me so that no one can see."

So her maids stood around her and spread their skirts wide, while the swineherd took his ten kisses. Then the kettle was hers.

And then the fun started. Never was a kettle kept so busy. They boiled it from morning till night. From the chamberlain's banquet to the cobbler's breakfast, they knew all that was cooked in town. The maids-in-waiting danced about and clapped their hands.

"We know who's having sweet soup and pancakes. We know who's having porridge and cutlets. Isn't it interesting?"

"Most interesting," said the head lady of the bedchamber.

"Now, after all, I'm the emperor's daughter," the princess reminded them. "Don't you tell how I got it."

"Goodness gracious, no!" said they all.

But the swineherd—that's the prince, for nobody knew he wasn't a real swineherd—was busy as he could be. This time, he made a rattle. Swing it around, and it would play all the waltzes, jigs, and dance tunes that have been heard since the beginning of time.

"Why it's *superbe!*" said the princess as she came by. "I never did hear better music. I say, go and ask him the price of that instrument. But mind you—no more kissing!"

"He wants a hundred kisses from the princess," said the maid-in-waiting who had been in to ask him.

"I believe he's out of his mind," said the princess, and she walked right away from there. But she had not gone very far when she said, "After all, I'm the emperor's daughter, and it's my duty to encourage the arts. Tell him he can have ten kisses, as he did yesterday, but he must collect the rest from my maids-in-waiting."

"Oh, but we wouldn't like that," said the maids.

"Fiddlesticks," said the princess, "If he can kiss me, he certainly can kiss you. Remember, I'm the one who gives you board and wages." So the maid had to go back to the swineherd.

"A hundred kisses from the princess," the swineherd told her, "or let each keep his own."

"Stand around me," said the princess, and all her maids-in-waiting stood in a circle to hide her while the swineherd began to collect.

"What can have drawn such a crowd near the pigsties?" the emperor wondered, as he looked down from his balcony. He rubbed his eyes, and he put on his spectacles. "Bless my soul if those maids-in-waiting aren't up to mischief again. I'd better go see what they are up to now."

He pulled his easy slippers up over his heels, though ordinarily he just shoved his feet in them and let them flap. Then, my! How much faster he went. As soon as he came near the pens, he took very soft steps. The maids-in-waiting were so busy counting kisses, to see that everything went fair and that he didn't get too many or too few, that they didn't notice the emperor behind them. He stood on his tiptoes.

"Such naughtiness!" he said when he saw them kissing, and he boxed their ears with his slipper just as the swineherd was taking his eighty-sixth kiss.

"Be off with you!" the emperor said in a rage. And both the princess and the swineherd were turned out of his empire. And there she stood crying. The swineherd scolded, and the rain came down in torrents.

"Poor little me," said the princess. "If only I had married the famous prince! Oh, how unlucky I am!"

The swineherd slipped behind a tree, wiped the brown and black off his face, threw off his ragged clothes, and showed himself in such princely garments that the princess could not keep from curtsying.

"I have only contempt for you," he told her. "You turned down a prince's honest offer, and you didn't appreciate the rose or the nightingale, but you were all too ready to kiss a swineherd for a tinkling toy to amuse you. You are properly punished."

Then the prince went home to his kingdom, and shut and barred the door. The princess could stay outside and sing to her heart's content:

> Oh, dear Augustin,
> All is lost, lost, lost.

THE METAL PIG (1842)

In the city of Florence, not far from the Piazza del Granduca, there is a little cross street that I think is called Porta Rossa. In front of a sort of market in this street, where vegetables are sold, stands an artificial but beautifully fashioned metal pig. A fountain of fresh, clear water gushes out of the animal's mouth. Age has turned it dark green; only its snout shines as if it had been polished, and so it has by the many hundreds of children and poor people who take hold of it with their hands when they put their mouths to its mouth to drink the water. It is an interesting picture to see the perfectly formed animal embraced by a handsome, half-naked boy putting his young lips to its snout.

Everyone who goes to Florence surely finds the place; you only have to ask the first beggar you see about the metal pig, and he will find it for you.

Late one winter evening, the mountains were covered with snow, but it was moonlight, and in Italy, the moon gives as bright a light as on a dark winter's day in the north. Yes, it is even brighter, for the clear air seems to shine and to lift us above Earth, while in the north, the cold, gray leaden roof presses us to the ground, the same cold, wet ground that one day will press on our coffins.

In the duke's palace garden, a little ragged boy had been sitting all day under the stone pines, where thousands of roses bloom in the winter, a boy who might have stood for a picture of Italy, so pretty, so laughing, and yet so suffering. Although hungry and thirsty, he got a penny from no one, and when it grew dark and time to close the gardens, the porter drove him away. For a long time, he stood dreaming on the bridge over the River Arno, looking at the reflections of the glittering stars in the water beneath the stately marble bridge. Then he made his way to the metal pig, knelt before it, threw his arms around its neck, put his little mouth to its shining snout, and drank great draughts of fresh water. Nearby lay a few salad leaves and a couple of chestnuts, and these formed his supper. There was no living soul in the street; he was all alone; he climbed onto the metal pig's back, leaned forward so that his little curly head rested on the animal's head, and before he knew what was happening, he had fallen fast asleep.

It was midnight. The metal pig moved. The boy heard it say quite plainly, "Hold fast, little boy, for now I'm going to run off!" And away it ran with him!

It was a strange ride. First, they reached the Piazza del Granduca, and the bronze horse on which the Duke's statue was mounted neighed loudly to them. The colored coats of arms on the old Town Hall glowed like transparent pictures, and Michelangelo's *David* hurled his sling; it was a curious form of life that moved about. The bronze groups of *Perseus* and the *Rape of the Sabine Women* were only too much alive; their death shrieks resounded through the stately deserted piazza. The metal pig stopped by the Uffizi Palace, under the arcade where the nobles assembled for the carnival celebration during Lent.

"Hold fast," said the animal. "Hold fast now, for I'm going up the stairs!"

The little fellow hadn't yet said a word; he was half frightened, half delighted. They entered a long gallery, which he knew well, for he had been there before. The walls were covered with pictures, and the statues and busts all stood in a light as bright as if it were day; but the most splendid sight of all was when the door to one of the adjoining rooms opened. Yes, the splendor here the little boy remembered, but tonight, everything was especially magnificent.

Here stood the statue of a nude woman, as beautiful as only nature and the greatest marble sculptor could make her; she moved her lovely limbs, dolphins sprang to life at her feet, and immortality shone from her eyes. She is known to the world as the *Venus de' Medici*. Marble statues of superb men were grouped around her; one of them, the *Grinder*, was sharpening his sword; the next group was the *Wrestling Gladiators*. The sword was whetted, and the athletes wrestled for the goddess of beauty.

The boy was dazzled by the magnificence; the walls were radiant with color, and everything there had life and movement. The picture of Venus, the earthly Venus, impassioned and glowing life, as Titian saw her, shone in redoubled splendor. Near her were the portraits of two lovely women reclining on soft cushions, with beautiful, unveiled limbs, heaving bosoms, and luxuriant locks falling over rounded shoulders, while their dark eyes betrayed passionate thoughts. But none of these pictures dared to step forth from their frames. The goddess of beauty herself, the *Gladiators*, and the *Grinder* remained on their pedestals, subdued by the halo around the Madonna, with the infants Jesus and St. John. The holy pictures were no longer just pictures; they were the saints themselves.

What brilliance and beauty as they passed from gallery to gallery! And the little boy saw everything, for the metal pig went step by step past all this glory and magnitude. Each sight crowded out the previous one; only one picture really took hold of his thoughts, and that was chiefly because of the happy children in it; once during the daytime, the little boy had nodded to them.

Many probably pass this picture unnoticing, yet it contains the essence of poetry. It is Christ descending to hell, but he is not surrounded by souls in torment; no, these are heathen. The painting is by the Florentine Agnolo Bronzino. The expression of the children's faces is most beautiful in their certainty that they are going to Heaven. Two little ones are already embracing each other; one stretches a hand out to a companion below, and points to himself as if to say, "I am going to Heaven!" All the older people stand around doubting, or hoping, or humbly bowing in prayer to the Lord Jesus.

The boy gazed longer at this picture than at any of the others; and as the metal pig rested quietly before it, a gentle sigh was heard. Did it come from the picture, or from the breast of the animal? The boy stretched out his own hand toward the smiling children; and then the animal galloped off with him, galloped away through the long gallery.

"Thank you, and bless you, you beautiful animal!" said the little boy, patting the pig as it went bump, bump, bump down the stairs with him.

"Thank you, and blessings to you, too!" said the metal pig. "I've helped you, but you've helped me, because I only have the strength to run when I'm carrying an innocent child on my back! You see, now I even dare step under the rays of the lamp before the Madonna picture. I can carry you anywhere except into a church, but as long as you're with me, I can stand outside and look in through the open door. Don't get down off my back! If you do, I shall be dead, just as you see me every day in the Porta Rossa!"

"I'll stay with you, my blessed animal," said the little boy, and then they rushed at a dizzy pace through the streets of Florence to the church of Santa Croce in the piazza. The great folding door swung open, and the altar lights streamed through the church and out into the deserted piazza.

A strange light blazed from a sculptured tomb in the left aisle; thousands of twinkling stars formed a sort a halo around it. The tomb was surmounted by a coat of arms, a red ladder on blue ground, gleaming like fire. This was the tomb of Galileo. It is a simple monument; but the red ladder on the blue ground is a symbol of art, meaning that the pathway to fame is always upward on a flaming ladder. All genius soars to Heaven like the prophet Elijah.

Every statue on the costly sarcophagus in the right aisle of the church seemed endowed with life. Here were Michelangelo and Dante, with the laurel wreath on his brow; Alfieri and Macchiavelli rested here side by side—the pride of Italy. It is a very beautiful church, far more beautiful than, although not as large as, the marble Cathedral of Florence.

It seemed as if the marble raiment moved, as if those great figures once more raised their heads in the night, mid song and music, and gazed toward the altar glowing with many lights, where the white-robed altar boys swung the golden censers, while the fragrance of incense filled the church and streamed out into the open square.

The boy stretched his hands toward the lights, but at that moment, the metal pig galloped on again, and he had to hold tightly. The wind whistled in his ears, and he heard the church door creak on its hinges as it closed. But immediately, he seemed to lose consciousness, and felt an icy coldness—and then opened his eyes.

It was morning, and he had half slipped from the metal pig, which stood in its usual place in the Porta Rossa. Fright and terror seized the boy as he thought of the woman he called mother. Yesterday, she had sent him out to get money, and he had none; he was hungry and thirsty. Once more, he flung his arms around the metal pig's neck, kissed its snout, nodded to it, and walked off to one of the narrowest streets, which was only wide enough for a heavily laden ass. A big iron-studded door stood half open; he entered it and mounted a brick staircase, with dirty walls and a greasy rope for a handrail, until he reached an open gallery hung with rags. A flight of steps led into a courtyard with a fountain, from which water was drawn up to the different floors by means of a thick iron wire, with buckets hung side by side. Sometimes the pulley jerked, and the buckets danced in the air and splashed water all over the courtyard. Another dilapidated brick staircase led still higher, and two sailors, who were Russians, ran merrily down and almost upset the poor boy. A strongly built woman with thick black hair, though no longer young, followed them.

"What have you brought home?" she said to the boy.

"Don't be angry!" he begged, catching hold of her dress as if to kiss it. "I haven't got anything at all! Nothing at all!"

They passed on into an inner room. We need not describe it, but will only say that in it was an earthen pot, with handles for holding charcoal, called a *"marito."* She hung this on her arm to warm her fingers, and pushed the boy away from her with her elbow. "Of course you have some money!" she said.

The child began to sob, and she kicked him with her foot, making him cry more loudly. "Will you be quiet, or I'll break your yelling head!" she said, and swung the pot which she held in her hand. The boy ducked to the ground and screamed.

Then a neighbor woman came in, also with her *marito* on her arm. "Felicita!" she said. "What are you doing to that child?"

"The child is mine!" replied Felicita. "And I can murder him if I want to, and you too, Giannina!"

And she swung her fire pot again. The other woman raised hers to parry the blow, and the two pots clashed together, smashing to bits and scattering fire and ashes all over the room.

But the boy by that time was out of the door, across the courtyard, and out of the house. The poor child ran until he had no breath left. At last, he stopped before the church of Santa Croce, whose great door had opened to him last night, and he went inside. Everything there was bright. He knelt by the first tomb, the sepulcher of Michelangelo, and began to cry loudly. People passed to and fro; Mass was celebrated; yet, nobody paid attention to the boy except one elderly citizen, who paused and looked at him for a moment, then passed on like the rest. The poor child became faint and ill, overcome with hunger and thirst. At last, he crept into a corner behind the marble monument and fell asleep.

Toward evening he was awakened by someone shaking him, and when he started up he saw the same elderly citizen standing before him. "Are you ill? Where is your home? Have you been here all day?" were some of the questions the old man asked him.

He answered them, and the old man took him with him to a little house in a nearby side street. It was a glovemaker's shop they entered, and there they found a woman sitting busily sewing. A little white poodle, so closely clipped that one could see her pink skin, jumped on the table and bounced toward the little boy.

"The innocent souls soon make friends with each other!" said the woman, patting both the boy and dog.

These good people gave the boy something to eat and drink and told him he could spend the night there. Next morning, Father Giuseppe would go to speak to his mother. He had only a homely little bed that night, but it was a royal couch to the boy who had so often slept on hard stone floors, and he slept soundly and dreamed about the splendid pictures and the metal pig.

The next morning, Father Giuseppe went out, and the poor boy was sorry to see him go, for he knew that he had gone to his mother, and that the boy himself might have to return home. He wept and kissed the lively little dog, while the woman nodded at them both.

And what message did Father Giuseppe bring back? He talked to his wife for a long time, and she nodded and caressed the boy.

"He's a beautiful child," she said, "and he'll be a clever glovemaker, just like you. Look at his fingers, so delicate and flexible! Madonna intended him to be a glovemaker!"

And so the little boy stayed in that house, and the woman taught him to sew; he had plenty to eat and got plenty of sleep. He became quite gay, and one day he began to tease Bellissima, as the little dog was called. This angered the woman; she scolded him and shook her finger at him, and the boy took it to heart. He sat thoughtful in his little room, which faced the street, with thick iron bars outside its windows, for the skins were hung up there to dry. That night, he couldn't sleep, for his head was full of the metal pig. Suddenly he heard a "scramble, scramble!" outside; yes, that must be the metal pig. He rushed to the window, but there was nothing to see.

"Help the *signor* carry his color box," said the mistress next morning when their young neighbor, the painter, came down carrying his color box and a huge roll of canvas. The child at once took up the box and followed the artist.

They made their way to the picture gallery and climbed the stairs that he could remember so well from the night he rode the metal pig. He remembered all the statues, the beautiful marble Venus, and the painted pictures, too. Again he gazed at the Madonna, with St. John and the infant Jesus. They stopped before the Bronzino picture of Christ standing in the underworld with the children around Him, smiling in their sweet certainty of heaven. The poor boy smiled too, for he was in his own heaven.

"Now you may go home," the painter said to him when the child still remained after his easel was set up.

"Can't I stay to watch the *signor* paint?" said the boy. "Can't I see you put the picture on the white canvas?"

"I'm not painting just yet," answered the artist as he took out a piece of charcoal. His hand moved swiftly as his eye rapidly measured the great picture; though he made only a few light strokes, the figure of Christ stood there, just as in the colored painting.

"You must go now," said the painter.

Then the boy wandered quietly home, sat down on the table, and resumed learning to sew gloves. But all day, his thoughts were in the gallery, so he was awkward and pricked his fingers; but he didn't tease Bellissima. When evening came, he found the house door open, and crept out; it was cold, but bright starlight, beautiful and clear. He wandered through the streets, where everything was quiet, until he found himself at the metal pig; then he bent over it, kissed its shining snout, and seated himself on its back.

"You blessed creature!" he said. "How I've longed for you! We must have another ride tonight!"

But the pig remained lifeless; only the fresh water spouted from its mouth. The little boy was still sitting astride it when he felt something tug at his trouser leg. He looked down and saw the clipped, naked, little Bellissima! The dog had crept out of the house and followed the boy without his noticing. Bellissima barked, as if trying to say, "What are you sitting up there for? Can't you see I'm with you?"

A fire-breathing dragon couldn't have frightened the boy more than the little dog at that spot. "Bellissima out in the streets and not dressed!" As the old lady would say, "What will come of that?"

For the dog never went out in the winter without a little sheepskin coat, especially cut and sewed for it. The skin could be fastened around the neck and body with a red ribbon and decorated with little red bows and jingling bells. When the dog went out in the winter, tripping along behind its mistress, it looked almost like a little kid. Now, here it was out in the cold without the coat—what would be the consequences? All his fancies quickly fled, yet he did stop to kiss the pig before climbing down and taking Bellissima in his arms. The dog shivered with cold, so the boy ran as fast as he could.

"What are you running away with there?" demanded two gendarmes who stopped him, while Bellissima barked. "Where did you steal that beautiful dog?" they asked, as they took it away from him.

"Oh, please give her back to me!" cried the boy.

"If you didn't steal it, you can tell your people at home that they can get it at the police station." They gave him the address, and off they went with Bellissima.

This was a terrible state of affairs! He couldn't decide whether to jump into the Arno or go home and confess everything. They would surely kill him, he thought. "But I would gladly be killed; I will die, and then go to Jesus and the Madonna!" So he hurried home, almost hoping to be killed.

The door was locked; he couldn't reach the knocker, and there was no one in the street to help him. But a loose stone lay next to him, and picking it up, he hammered on the door with it. "Who's that?" said a voice from inside.

"It's I!" he said. "And Bellissima is lost! Let me in, and then kill me!"

This was frightening indeed, especially to his mistress, who was so fond of Bellissima. She quickly looked at the wall to see if the dog's coat hung in its place, and there the little sheepskin was.

"Bellissima at the police station!" she cried loudly. "You wicked child! Why did you take her out? She'll die of cold! That delicate little animal among all those big rough soldiers."

And Father Giuseppe had to rush off at once. His wife wailed, and the boy wept. Everyone in the house came to see what was going on, including the painter. He took the boy on his knee and questioned him, and gradually he learned the whole story of the metal pig and the picture gallery. It wasn't easy to understand, but the painter comforted the child and calmed the woman, though she wasn't happy until Giuseppe returned with Bellissima, who had been among the soldiers. Then there was great rejoicing, and the painter patted the poor boy on the head and gave him some pictures.

Oh, these were splendid. There were comical heads, but most important of all, the metal pig himself! Nothing could have been more wonderful! It was sketched in only a few strokes, but even the house behind it appeared clearly.

"Oh, if I could only draw and paint! I'd have the whole world before me!"

The next day, in the first lonely moment he had, the little boy found a pencil, and, on the white side of one of the pictures, tried to copy the drawing of the metal pig, and he succeeded! It was a little crooked, a little one-sided, with one leg thick and the other thin, but it was recognizable, and it delighted him. The pencil wouldn't go as straight as it should, he realized. Next day, another pig stood beside the first one, and this was a hundred times better; and the third one was so good anyone could tell what it represented.

But the glovemaking went badly, and he ran errands slowly; for he had learned from the metal pig that any picture may be put on paper, and the city of Florence is a complete picture book, if you only turn the leaves.

In the Piazza della Trinità stands a slender column, and on top of it stands the blindfolded Goddess of Justice with the scales in her hand. Soon she also stood on paper, and it was the little apprentice glovemaker who put her there. His collection grew, though they were still only copies of inanimate objects; but one day, Bellissima came bouncing toward him. "Stand still!" he said. "I'll make a beautiful portrait of you to have among my pictures!"

But Bellissima wouldn't stand still, so he had to tie her up. He tied her head and tail, and Bellissima barked and jumped about, straining at the cord. Then the *signora* came in.

"You wicked boy! That poor animal!" was all she had time to say. She flung the boy aside, kicked him, called him the most ungrateful, worthless, and wicked child, and turned him out of the house; and crying, she kissed the little half-strangled Bellissima.

At that moment, the painter came up the stairs and—but this is the turning point of the story.

In 1834, there was an exhibition in the Academy of Arts in Florence. Two paintings hung side by side, attracted much attention from the public. The smaller of them showed a happy little boy sitting at a table drawing; his model was a closely clipped little white poodle that was tied with string by the head and tail because it wouldn't stand still. The painting was so animated and true to life that it couldn't fail to interest all the spectators. The painter was, it was said, a young Florentine who had been found in the streets when a little child, had been raised by an old glovemaker, and had taught himself to draw. A now-famous artist had discovered his talent just as he was about to be turned out of the house for having tied up his mistress' beloved little poodle to be his model. The glover's boy had become a great painter, as the picture clearly showed. But the larger picture was a still greater proof of his genius. There was just a single figure in it, a handsome ragged boy leaning, fast asleep, against the metal pig of the Via Porta Rossa. All the spectators knew that spot very well. The child's arm rested on the pig's head, and he slept sweetly, with the lamp before the nearby Madonna throwing a strong light on his pale, handsome face. It was a beautiful picture. A large gilt frame surrounded it, and a wreath of laurel was fastened to one corner of it; but a black ribbon was entwined in the green leaves, and long, black streamers hung down from it. The young painter had just died!

THE BOND OF FRIENDSHIP (1842)

We've recently made a little journey, and already we want to make a longer one. Where? To Sparta, or Mycenae, or Delphi? There are hundreds of places whose names make the heart pound with the love of travel. On horseback, we climb mountain paths, through shrubs and brush. A single traveler looks like a whole caravan. He rides in front with his guide; a pack horse carries luggage, tent, and provisions; a couple of soldiers guard the rear for his protection. No inn with soft beds awaits him at the end of a tiring day's journey; often the tent is his roof in nature's great wilderness, and the guide cooks him his supper—a pilau of rice, fowl, and curry. Thousands of gnats swarm around the little tent. It is a miserable night, and tomorrow, the route will head across swollen streams. Sit tight on your horse lest you are washed away!

What reward is there for these hardships? The greatest! The richest! Nature reveals herself here in all her glory; every spot is history; eye and mind alike are delighted. The poet can sing of it, the painter portray it in splendid pictures; but neither can reproduce the air of reality that sinks deep into the soul of the spectator and remains there.

The lonely herdsman up on the hills could, perhaps, by the simple story of an event in his life, open your eyes and with a few words let you behold the land of the Hellenes better than any travel book could do. Let him speak, then! About a custom, a beautiful, peculiar custom. The shepherd in the mountains will tell about it. He calls it the bond of friendship, and relates:

Our house was built of clay, but the doorposts were fluted marble pillars found on the spot where the house was built. The roof almost reached the ground. Now it was black-brown and ugly; but when it was new, it was covered with blooming oleander and fresh laurel branches fetched from beyond the mountains. The walks around our house were narrow. Walls of rock rose steeply up, bare and black in color. On top of them, clouds often hung like white living beings. I never heard a bird sing here, and never did the men dance here to the sound of the bagpipe; but the place was sacred from olden times. Its very name reminded of that, for it was called Delphi. The dark, solemn mountains were all covered with snow. The brightest, which gleamed in the red evening sun the longest, was Parnassus. The brook close by our house rushed down from it, and was also sacred, long ago. Now the donkey makes it muddy with its feet, but the current rolls on and becomes clear again.

How well I remember every spot and its deep sacred solitude!

In the middle of the hut a fire was lit, and when the hot ashes lay high and glowing, the bread was baked in it. If the snow was piled up high round our hut and almost covered it, then my mother seemed to be her brightest. She would hold my head between her hands, kiss my forehead, and sing the songs she never sang at other times, for our masters, the Turks, did not like them. And she sang: "On the summit of Olympus, in the fir tree forest lived an old stag; its eyes were heavy with tears. It wept red, yes, and even green and light-blue tears. Then a roebuck came by and said, 'What ails you, that you cry so, that you weep red, green, yes, even light-blue, tears?' The stag replied, 'The Turk has entered our city. He has fierce dogs for the hunt, a goodly pack.' 'I will drive them away across the islands,' said the young roebuck. 'I will drive them away across the islands into the deep sea!' But before evening, the roebuck was slain, and before nightfall, the stag was hunted and killed."

When my mother sang this her eyes became moist, and a tear hung on the long lashes. But she concealed it, and turned our black bread in the ashes. Then I would clench my fists and say, "We'll kill the Turks!"

But she repeated the words of the song, "'I will drive them across the islands into the deep sea!' But before evening, the roebuck was slain, and before nightfall, the stag was hunted and killed."

For several days and nights, we had been alone in our hut, and then my father came home. I knew he would bring me sea shells from the Gulf of Lepanto, or maybe even a sharp gleaming knife. But this time, he brought us a child, a naked little girl whom he had carried under his sheepskin coat. She was wrapped in a fur, but when this was taken off and she lay in my mother's lap, all that she possessed was three silver coins fastened in her dark hair. And father explained to us that the Turks had killed her parents, and told us so much about it that I dreamed about it all night. Father himself had been wounded, and my mother dressed his arm. His wound was deep, and the thick sheepskin was stiff with blood.

The little girl was to be my sister! She was so beautiful, with clear, shining eyes; even my mother's eyes were not gentler than hers. Yes, Anastasia, as they called her, was to be my sister, for her father was united to mine, united in accordance with an old custom we still keep. They had sworn brotherhood in their youth, and had chosen the most beautiful and virtuous girl in the whole country to consecrate their bond of friendship. I had often heard of the queer and beautiful custom.

So now the little girl was my sister. She sat in my lap; I brought her flowers and feathers of the field birds. We drank together of the waters of Parnassus and slept head to head beneath the laurel roof of the hut, while many a winter my mother sang of the red, the green, and the light-blue tears. But still I didn't understand it was my own countrymen whose thousandfold sorrows were reflected in those tears.

One day, three Frankish men came, dressed differently than we were. They had their tents and beds packed on horses; and more than twenty Turks, armed with swords and muskets, accompanied them, for they were friends of the pasha and carried letters from him. They only came to view our mountains, to climb Parnassus through snow and clouds, and to see the strange, steep black rocks surrounding our hut. There was no room for them inside our home, nor could they stand the smoke rolling along the ceiling and out at the low door; so they pitched their tents in the narrow clearing outside our house, roasted lambs and birds, and drank strong, sweet wine, which the Turks did not dare to drink.

When they left, I went with them for some distance, and my little sister hung in a goatskin on my back. One of the Frankish gentlemen had me stand before a rock and sketched me and her, so lifelike as we stood there, so that we looked like one being—I had never thought of it before, but Anastasia and I were really one person. She was always sitting in my lap or hanging on my back in the goatskin, and when I dreamed, she appeared in my dreams.

Two nights later, other men came to our hut, armed with knives and muskets. They were Albanians, brave men, said my mother. They stayed only a short while, wrapping tobacco in strips of paper and smoking it. My sister Anastasia sat on the knees of one of them, and when he was gone, she had only two silver coins in her hair instead of three. The oldest of the men talked about which route they should take; he was not sure.

"If I spit upward," he said, "it will fall in my face; if I spit downward, it will fall in my beard!"

But they had to make a choice, so they went, and my father followed them. And soon afterward we heard the sound of shots! The firing increased; then soldiers rushed into our hut and took my mother, myself, and Anastasia prisoners. The robbers, they said, had stayed with us, and my father had gone with them; therefore, we had to be taken away. Soon I saw the robbers' corpses, and I saw my father's corpse too, and I cried myself to sleep. When I awoke, we were in prison, but the cell was no worse than the room in our hut. And they gave me onions to eat and musty wine poured from a tarred sack, but ours at home was no better.

I don't know how long we were held prisoners, but many days and nights went by. It was our holy Eastertime when we were released. I carried Anastasia on my back, for my mother was ill and could only walk slowly, and it was a long way down to the sea, to the Gulf of Lepanto. We entered a church magnificent with pictures on a golden background. They were pictures of angels, oh, so beautiful! but I thought our little Anastasia was just as beautiful. In the center of the floor was a coffin filled with roses. "The Lord Christ is symbolized there as a beautiful rose," said my mother; and then the priest chanted, "Christ is risen!" Everybody kissed each other. All the people had lighted tapers in their hands; I received one, and so did little Anastasia. The bagpipes played, men danced hand in hand from the church, and the women outside were roasting the Easter lamb. We were invited to share it, and when I sat by the fire, a boy older than I put his arms around my neck, kissed me, and cried, "Christ is risen!" Thus we met for the first time, Aphtanides and I.

My mother could make fishing nets, which gave her a good income here in the bay, so for a long time, we lived beside the sea—the beautiful sea that tasted like tears, and whose colors reminded me of the song of the weeping stag, for its waters were sometimes red, sometimes green, and then again light-blue.

Aphtanides knew how to guide a boat, and I often sat in it with Anastasia while it glided through the water, like a cloud over the sky. Then, as the sun set and the mountains turned a deeper and deeper blue, one range seemed to rise behind the other, and behind all of them was Parnassus, covered with snow. Its summit gleamed in the evening rays like glowing iron, and it seemed as though the light shone from within it; for long after the sun had set, the mountaintop still glittered in the clear, blue shimmering air. The white sea birds touched the water's surface with their wings, and indeed everything here was as calm as among the black rocks at Delphi.

I was lying on my back in the boat while Anastasia leaned against my chest, and the stars above shone more brightly than our church lamps. They were the same stars, and they were in exactly the same position above me, as when I had sat outside our hut at Delphi, and at last I imagined I was still there. Then there was a splash in the water, and the boat rocked violently! I cried out loud, for Anastasia had fallen overboard, but just as quickly Aphtanides had leaped in after her, and soon he lifted her up to me. We undressed her, wrung the water out of her clothes, and then dressed her again. Aphtanides did the same for himself. We remained on the water until their clothes were dry; and no one knew about our fright over the little adopted sister in whose life Aphtanides also now had a part.

Then it was summer! The sun blazed so fiercely that the leaves on the trees withered. I thought of our cool mountains and their freshwater streams, and my mother longed for them too; so one evening, we journeyed home. How quiet it was and how peaceful! We walked on through the high thyme, still fragrant though the sun had dried its leaves. Not a shepherd did we meet; not a single hut did we pass. Everything was quiet and deserted; only a shooting star told us that in heaven there still was life. I do not know if the clear blue air glowed with its own light, or if the rays came from the stars, but we could plainly make out the outlines of the mountains. My mother lit a fire and roasted the onions she had brought with her; then my sister and I slept among the thyme, with no fear of the wolf or the jackal, not to mention fear of the ugly, fire-breathing *smidraki*, for my mother sat beside us, and this I believed was enough.

When we reached our old home, we found the hut a heap of ruins and had to build a new one. A couple of women helped my mother, and in a few days, the walls were raised and covered with a new roof of oleander. My mother braided many bottle holsters of bark and skins; I tended the priests' little flock, and Anastasia and the little tortoises were my playmates.

One day, we had a visit from our dear Aphtanides, who said how much he had longed to see us; he stayed with us for two whole days.

A month later, he came again, to tell us he was taking a ship for Corfu and Patras but had to bid us good-bye first; he had brought our mother a large fish. He talked a great deal, not only about the fishermen out in the Gulf of Lepanto, but also of the kings and heroes who had once ruled Greece, just as the Turks rule it now.

I have seen a bud on a rosebush develop through the days and weeks into a full, blooming flower before I was even aware how large, beautiful, and blushing it had become; and now I saw the same thing in Anastasia. She was now a beautiful, full-grown girl, and I was a strong youth. I myself had taken from the wolves that fell before my musket the skins that covered my mother's and Anastasia's beds. Years had passed.

Then one evening, Aphtanides returned, strong, brown, and slender as a reed. He kissed us all, and had many stories to tell of the great ocean, the fortifications of Malta, and the strange tombs of Egypt. It all sounded wonderful, like a priestly legend, and I looked at him with a kind of awe.

"How much you know!" I said. "How well you can tell about it!"

"But after all, you once told me about the most wonderful thing," he said. "You told me something that has never been out of my thoughts—the grand old custom of the bond of friendship, a custom I want very much to follow. Brother, let us go to church, as your and Anastasia's fathers did before us. Your sister is the most beautiful and innocent of girls; she shall consecrate us! No nation has such beautiful old customs as we Greeks."

Anastasia blushed like a fresh rose, and my mother kissed Aphtanides.

An hour's walk from our house, where loose earth lies on the rocks and a few scattered trees give shade, stood the little church, a silver lamp hanging before its altar.

I wore my best clothes. The white fustanella fell in rich folds over my hips, the red jacket fitted tight and snug, the tassel on my fez was silver, and in my girdle gleamed my knife and pistols. Aphtanides wore the blue costume of the Greek sailors; on his chest hung a silver medallion with a figure of the Virgin Mary, and his scarf was as costly as those worn by rich men. Everyone could see that we two were going to some ceremony.

We entered the little empty church, where the evening sunlight, streaming through the door, gleamed on the burning lamp and the colored pictures on the golden background. We knelt on the altar steps, and Anastasia stood before us. A long white garment hung loosely and lightly over her graceful figure; on her white neck and bosom a chain of old and new coins formed a large collar. Her black hair was fastened in a single knot and held together by a small cap fashioned of gold and silver coins that had been found in the old temples. No Greek girl had more beautiful ornaments than she. Her face beamed, and her eyes were bright as two stars.

The three of us prayed silently, and then she asked us, "Will you be friends in life and in death?"

"Yes," we replied.

"Will each of you, whatever may happen, remember: My brother is a part of me! My secrets are his secrets; my happiness is his happiness! Self-sacrifice, patience, every virtue in me, belongs to him as well as to me!"

Then she placed our hands together and kissed each of us on the forehead, and again we prayed silently. Then the priest came through the door behind the altar and blessed the three of us; the singing voices of other holy men sounded from behind the altar screen. The bond of eternal friendship was completed. When we arose, I saw that my mother standing by the church door was weeping tenderly.

How cheerful it was now in our little hut by the springs of Delphi! The evening before his departure, Aphtanides sat with me on the mountainside, his arm around my waist, mine around his neck. We spoke of the suffering of Greece, and of the men the country could trust. Every thought of our souls was clear to each of us, and I took his hand. "One thing more you must know, one thing that till this moment only God and I have known! My whole soul is filled with a love—a love stronger than the love I feel for my mother and for you!"

"And whom do you love?" asked Aphtanides, his face and neck turning red.

"I love Anastasia," I said—and then his hand trembled in mine, and he turned pale as a corpse. I saw it and understood, and I also believe *my* hand trembled. I bent toward him, kissed his brow, and whispered, "I have never told her this. Maybe she doesn't love me. Consider this, brother. I've seen her daily; she has grown up by my side, grown into my soul!"

"And she shall be yours!" he said. "Yours! I cannot lie to you, nor will I. I love her too, but tomorrow, I go. In a year we shall meet again, and then you will be married, won't you? I have some money of my own; it is yours. You must, and shall, take it!"

Silently we wandered across the mountain. It was late in the evening when we stood at my mother's door. She was not there, but as we entered, Anastasia held the lamp up, gazing at Aphtanides with a sad and beautiful look. "Tomorrow, you're leaving us," she said. "How it saddens me!"

"Saddens you?" he said, and I thought that in his voice there was a grief as great as my own. I couldn't speak, but he took her hand and said, "Our brother there loves you; is he dear to you? His silence is the best proof of his love."

Anastasia trembled and burst into tears. Then I could see no one but her, think of no one but her; I threw my arms around her and said, "Yes, I love you!" She pressed her lips to mine, and her arms slipped around my neck; the lamp had fallen to the ground, and all about us was dark—dark as in the heart of poor, dear Aphtenides.

Before daybreak, he got up, kissed us all good-bye, and departed. He had given my mother all his money for us. Anastasia was my betrothed, and a few days later she became my wife.

A ROSE FROM HOMER'S GRAVE (1842)

Through all the songs of the east, the eternal theme is the nightingale's love for the rose. In the silent, starlit nights, the winged songster sings his serenade to his beautiful scented flower.

Under stately plantain trees, not far from Smyrna, where the merchant drives his heavily loaded camels, proudly raising their long necks and clumsily walking over the hallowed ground, I saw a hedge of blooming roses. Wild doves fluttered among the branches of the tall trees, and when the sunbeams floated on their wings, they shone like mother-of-pearl. In that rose hedge, one flower was more beautiful than all the rest, and to this the nightingale poured out its song of grief. But the rose was silent; no dewdrop lay like a tear of pity on her petals, and with the branch on which she grew, she bent down toward a heap of large stones.

"Here lies the sweetest singer the world has ever heard," said the rose proudly. "I will scent his grave, and when the storms tear off my petals, they shall fall on him. For the singer of the *Iliad* returned to this good earth whence I sprang! I, a rose from Homer's grave, am too sacred a bloom for a poor mere nightingale!"

And the nightingale sang himself to death.

Then came the bearded camel driver with his laden camels and his black slaves. His little boy found the dead bird, and in pity buried it in the grave of the great Homer while the rose trembled slightly in the wind.

The evening came, and the rose folded her petals tightly and dreamed. It dreamed that it was a beautiful sunny day and that a caravan of foreign Frankish men had come on a pilgrimage to the grave of Homer. And among the strangers was a singer from the north, from the land of drifting mists and crackling northern lights. He broke off the rose, and pressed it between the leaves of a book, and so carried it off with him to his own country, in that far part of the world. Tightly pressed in the narrow book, the rose withered away in grief until, in his own home, a poet opened the book and said, "Here is a rose from Homer's grave!"

This the flower dreamed, and in the morning, the rose woke up shivering in the wind; a dewdrop fell gently from her petals upon the grave of the poet. Then the sun rose, and the day was hot, and the rose bloomed in greater beauty than ever; it was still in her warm Asia.

Then the rose heard footsteps. The strange Franks she had seen in her dream came by, and among them was the poet of the north.

He did indeed break off the rose and press a kiss upon her fresh mouth, and carry her off with him to his distant home of mists and northern lights. The rose rests now like a mummy between the leaves of his *Iliad*, and as in her dream, she hears him say as he opens the book, "Here is a rose from Homer's grave!"

THE ANGEL (1843)

Every time a good child dies, an angel of God comes down to earth. He takes the child in his arms, spreads out his great white wings, and flies with it all over the places the child loved on earth. The angel plucks a large handful of flowers, and they carry it with them up to God, where the flowers bloom more brightly than they ever did on earth. And God presses all the flowers to His bosom, but the flower that He loves the best of all He kisses. And then that flower receives a voice and can join in the glorious everlasting hymn of praise.

You see, all this one of God's angels said as he was carrying a dead child to Heaven, and the child heard it as if in a dream. As they passed over the places where the child used to play, they came through gardens with lovely flowers. "Which flowers shall we take with us to plant in Heaven?" asked the angel.

And there stood a slender beautiful rosebush. A wicked hand had broken the stem, and the branches with their large, half-opened blossoms hung down withering.

"That poor bush!" cried the child. "Let's take it so that it may bloom again up there in God's garden."

So the angel plucked it, then kissed the child for its tender thought, and the little child half opened his eyes. They took others of the rich flowers, and even some of the despised marigolds and wild pansies.

"Now we have enough flowers," said the child, and the angel nodded. But they did not yet fly upward to God.

It was night, and it was very quiet. They remained in the great city and hovered over one of the narrowest streets, which was cluttered with straw, ashes, and refuse of all kinds. It was just after moving day, and broken plates, rags, old hats, and bits of plaster, all things that didn't look so well, lay scattered in the street.

In the rubbish the angel pointed to the pieces of a broken flowerpot and to a lump of earth that had fallen out of it. It was held together by the roots of a large withered field flower. No one could have had anymore use for it; hence, it had been thrown out in the street.

"We shall take that with us," said the angel. "As we fly onward, I will tell you about it." And as they flew, the angel told the story.

"Down in that narrow alley, in a dark cellar, there once lived a poor sick boy who had been bedridden since childhood. The most he could ever do, when he was feeling his best, was hobble once or twice across the little room on crutches. For only a few days in midsummer, the sunbeams could steal into his cellar for about half an hour or so. Then the little boy could warm himself and see the red blood in his thin, almost transparent fingers as he held them before his face. Then people would say, the boy has been out in the sunshine today.

"All he knew of the forests in the fresh breath of spring was when the neighbor's son would bring him home the first beech branch. He would hold this up over his head, and pretend he was sitting in the beech woods where the sun was shining and the birds were singing.

"One spring day, the neighbor's boy brought him also some field flowers, and by chance, one of them had a root to it! So it was planted in a flowerpot and placed in the window beside the little boy's bed. And tended by a loving hand, it grew, put out new shoots, and bore lovely flowers each year. It was a beautiful garden to the little sick boy—his one treasure on earth. He watered it and tended it and saw that it received every sunbeam, down to the very last that managed to struggle through the dingy cellar window.

"The flower wove itself into his dreams; for him it flowered; it spread its fragrance, and cheered his eyes, and toward it he turned his face for a last look when his Heavenly Father called him.

"He has been with God now for a year, and for a year the flower stood withered and forgotten in the window until on moving day it was thrown out on the rubbish heap in the street. That is the flower—the poor withered flower—we have added to our bouquet, for it has given more happiness than the richest flower in the queen's garden."

The child looked up at the angel who was carrying him. "But how do you know all this?" he asked.

"I know it," said the angel, "because I myself was the sick little boy who hobbled on crutches. I know my own flower very well."

Then the child opened his eyes wide and looked up into the angel's beautiful happy face, and at that moment, they found themselves in God's Heaven, where there was everlasting joy and happiness. And God pressed the child to His bosom, and he received glorious white wings like the angel's, so they flew together, hand in hand. Then God pressed all the flowers to His heart, but the poor withered field flower He kissed, and it received a voice and joined the choir of the angels who floated about God's throne. Some were near, some farther out in great circles that swept to infinity, but all were supremely happy. And they all sang, the great and the small, the good blessed child and the withered field flower that had lain so long in the rubbish heap in the dark narrow alley.

THE NIGHTINGALE (1843)

The emperor of China is a Chinaman, as you most likely know, and everyone around him is a Chinaman, too. It's been a great many years since this story happened in China, but that's all the more reason for telling it before it gets forgotten.

The emperor's palace was the wonder of the world. It was made entirely of fine porcelain, extremely expensive but so delicate that you could touch it only with the greatest of care. In the garden, the rarest flowers bloomed, and to the prettiest ones were tied little silver bells that tinkled so that no one could pass by without noticing them. Yes, all things were arranged according to plan in the emperor's garden, though how far and wide it extended not even the gardener knew. If you walked on and on, you came to a fine forest where the trees were tall and the lakes were deep. The forest ran down to the deep blue sea, so close that tall ships could sail under the branches of the trees. In these trees a nightingale lived. His song was so ravishing that even the poor fisherman, who had much else to do, stopped to listen on the nights when he went out to cast his nets, and heard the nightingale.

"How beautiful that is," he said, but he had his work to attend to, and he would forget the bird's song. But the next night, when he heard the song he would again say, "How beautiful."

From all the countries in the world, travelers came to the city of the emperor. They admired the city. They admired the palace and its garden, but when they heard the nightingale, they said, "That is the best of all."

And the travelers told of it when they came home, and men of learning wrote many books about the town, about the palace, and about the garden. But they did not forget the nightingale. They praised him highest of all, and those who were poets wrote magnificent poems about the nightingale who lived in the forest by the deep sea.

These books went all the world over, and some of them came even to the emperor of China. He sat in his golden chair and read, nodding his head in delight over such glowing descriptions of his city, and palace, and garden. *But the nightingale is the best of all.* He read it in print.

"What's this?" the emperor exclaimed. "I don't know of any nightingale. Can there be such a bird in my empire—in my own garden—and I not know it? To think that I should have to learn of it out of a book."

Thereupon, he called his lord-in-waiting, who was so exalted that when anyone of lower rank dared speak to him, or ask him a question, he only answered, "P," which means nothing at all.

"They say there's a most remarkable bird called the nightingale," said the emperor. "They say it's the best thing in all my empire. Why haven't I been told about it?"

"I've never heard the name mentioned," said the lord-in-waiting. "He hasn't been presented at court."

"I command that he appear before me this evening, and sing," said the emperor. "The whole world knows my possessions better than I do!"

"I never heard of him before," said the lord-in-waiting. "But I shall look for him. I'll find him."

But where? The Lord-in-Waiting ran upstairs and downstairs, through all the rooms and corridors, but no one he met with had ever heard tell of the nightingale. So the lord-in-waiting ran back to the emperor, and said it must be a story invented by those who write books. "Your Imperial Majesty would scarcely believe how much of what is written is fiction, if not downright black art."

"But the book I read was sent me by the mighty Emperor of Japan," said the emperor. "Therefore, it can't be a pack of lies. I must hear this nightingale. I insist upon his being here this evening. He has my high imperial favor, and if he is not forthcoming I will have the whole court punched in the stomach, directly after supper."

"Tsing-pe!" said the lord-in-waiting, and off he scurried up the stairs, through all the rooms and corridors. And half the court ran with him, for no one wanted to be punched in the stomach after supper.

There was much questioning as to the whereabouts of this remarkable nightingale, who was so well known everywhere in the world except at home. At last, they found a poor little kitchen girl, who said:

"The nightingale? I know him well. Yes, indeed, he can sing. Every evening, I get leave to carry scraps from table to my sick mother. She lives down by the shore. When I start back, I am tired, and rest in the woods. Then I hear the nightingale sing. It brings tears to my eyes. It's as if my mother were kissing me."

"Little kitchen girl," said the lord-in-waiting, "I'll have you appointed scullion for life. I'll even get permission for you to watch the emperor dine, if you'll take us to the nightingale who is commanded to appear at court this evening."

So they went into the forest where the nightingale usually sang. Half the court went along. On the way to the forest, a cow began to moo.

"Oh," cried a courtier, "that must be it. What a powerful voice for a creature so small. I'm sure I've heard her sing before."

"No, that's the cow," said the little kitchen girl. "We still have a long way to go."

Then the frogs in the marsh began to croak.

"Glorious!" said the Chinese court person. "Now I hear it—like church bells ringing."

"No, that's the frogs," said the little kitchen girl. "But I think we shall hear him soon." Then the nightingale sang.

"That's it," said the little kitchen girl. "Listen, listen! And yonder he sits." She pointed to a little gray bird high up in the branches.

"Is it possible?" cried the lord-in-waiting. "Well, I never would have thought he looked like that, so unassuming. But he has probably turned pale at seeing so many important people around him."

"Little nightingale," the kitchen girl called to him, "our gracious emperor wants to hear you sing."

"With the greatest of pleasure," answered the nightingale, and burst into song.

"Very similar to the sound of glass bells," said the lord-in-waiting. "Just see his little throat, how busily it throbs. I'm astounded that we have never heard him before. I'm sure he'll be a great success at court."

"Shall I sing to the emperor again?" asked the nightingale, for he thought that the emperor was present.

"My good little nightingale," said the lord-in-waiting, "I have the honor to command your presence at a court function this evening, where you'll delight His Majesty the Emperor with your charming song."

"My song sounds best in the woods," said the nightingale, but he went with them willingly when he heard it was the emperor's wish.

The palace had been especially polished for the occasion. The porcelain walls and floors shone in the rays of many gold lamps. The flowers with tinkling bells on them had been brought into the halls, and there was such a commotion of coming and going that all the bells chimed away until you could scarcely hear yourself talk.

In the middle of the great throne room, where the emperor sat, there was a golden perch for the nightingale. The whole court was there, and they let the little kitchen girl stand behind the door, now that she had been appointed "Imperial Pot-Walloper." Everyone was dressed in his best, and all stared at the little gray bird to which the emperor graciously nodded.

And the nightingale sang so sweetly that tears came into the emperor's eyes and rolled down his cheeks. Then the nightingale sang still more sweetly, and it was the emperor's heart that melted. The emperor was so touched that he wanted his own golden slipper hung round the nightingale's neck, but the nightingale declined it with thanks. He had already been amply rewarded.

"I have seen tears in the emperor's eyes," he said. "Nothing could surpass that. An emperor's tears are strangely powerful. I have my reward." And he sang again, gloriously.

"It's the most charming coquetry we ever heard," said the ladies-in-waiting. And they took water in their mouths so they could gurgle when anyone spoke to them, hoping to rival the nightingale. Even the lackeys and chambermaids said they were satisfied, which was saying a great deal, for they were the hardest to please. Unquestionably, the nightingale was a success. He was to stay at court and have his own cage. He had permission to go for a walk twice a day, and once a night. Twelve footmen attended him, each one holding tight to a ribbon tied to the bird's leg. There wasn't much fun in such outings.

The whole town talked about the marvelous bird, and if two people met, one could scarcely say "night" before the other said "gale," and then they would sigh in unison, with no need for words. Eleven pork-butchers' children were named "nightingale," but not one could sing.

One day, the emperor received a large package labeled "The Nightingale."

"This must be another book about my celebrated bird," he said. But it was not a book. In the box was a work of art, an artificial nightingale most like the real one except that it was encrusted with diamonds, rubies, and sapphires. When it was wound, the artificial bird could sing one of the nightingale's songs while it wagged its glittering gold and silver tail. Round its neck hung a ribbon inscribed: "The Emperor of Japan's nightingale is a poor thing compared with that of the Emperor of China."

"Isn't that nice?" everyone said, and the man who had brought the contraption was immediately promoted to be "Imperial-Nightingale-Fetcher-in-Chief."

"Now let's have them sing together. What a duet that will be," said the courtiers.

So they had to sing together, but it didn't turn out so well, for the real nightingale sang whatever came into his head while the imitation bird sang by rote.

"That's not the newcomer's fault," said the music master. "He keeps perfect time, just as I have taught him."

Then they had the imitation bird sing by itself. It met with the same success as the real nightingale, and besides, it was much prettier to see, all sparkling like bracelets and breastpins. Three and thirty times it sang the selfsame song without tiring. The courtiers would gladly have heard it again, but the emperor said the real nightingale should now have his turn. Where was he? No one had noticed him flying out the open window, back to his home in the green forest.

"But what made him do that?" said the emperor.

All the courtiers slandered the nightingale, whom they called a most ungrateful wretch. "Luckily, we have the best bird," they said, and made the imitation one sing again. That was the thirty-fourth time they had heard the same tune, but they didn't quite know it by heart because it was a difficult piece. And the music master praised the artificial bird beyond measure. Yes, he said that the contraption was much better than the real nightingale, not only in its dress and its many beautiful diamonds, but also in its mechanical interior.

"You see, ladies and gentlemen, and above all Your Imperial Majesty, with a real nightingale, one never knows what to expect, but with this artificial bird, everything goes according to plan. Nothing is left to chance. I can explain it and take it to pieces, and show how the mechanical wheels are arranged, how they go around, and how one follows after another."

"Those are our sentiments exactly," said they all, and the music master was commanded to have the bird give a public concert next Sunday. The emperor said that his people should hear it. And hear it they did, with as much pleasure as if they had all gotten tipsy on tea, Chinese fashion. Everyone said, "Oh," and held up the finger we call "lickpot," and nodded his head. But the poor fishermen who had heard the real nightingale said, "This is very pretty, very nearly the real thing, but not quite. I can't imagine what's lacking."

The real nightingale had been banished from the land. In its place, the artificial bird sat on a cushion beside the emperor's bed. All its gold and jeweled presents lay about it, and its title was now "Grand Imperial Singer-of-the-Emperor-to-Sleep." In rank, it stood first from the left, for the emperor gave preeminence to the left side because of the heart. Even an emperor's heart is on the left.

The music master wrote a twenty-five-volume book about the artificial bird. It was learned, long-winded, and full of hard Chinese words, yet everybody said they read and understood it, lest they show themselves stupid and would then have been punched in their stomachs.

After a year the emperor, his court, and all the other Chinamen knew every twitter of the artificial song by heart. They liked it all the better now that they could sing it themselves. Which they did. The street urchins sang, "Zizizi! kluk, kluk, kluk," and the emperor sang it, too. That's how popular it was.

But one night, while the artificial bird was singing his best by the emperor's bed, something inside the bird broke with a twang. *Whir-r-r,* all the wheels ran down, and the music stopped. Out of bed jumped the emperor and sent for his own physician, but what could he do? Then he sent for a watchmaker, who conferred, and investigated, and patched up the bird after a fashion. But the watchmaker said that the bird must be spared too much exertion, for the cogs were badly worn, and if he replaced them, it would spoil the tune. This was terrible. Only once a year could they let the bird sing, and that was almost too much for it. But the music master made a little speech full of hard Chinese words that meant that the bird was as good as it ever was. So that made it as good as ever.

Five years passed by, and a real sorrow befell the whole country. The Chinamen loved their emperor, and now he fell ill. Ill unto death, it was said. A new emperor was chosen in readiness. People stood in the palace street and asked the lord-in-waiting how it went with their emperor.

"P," said he, and shook his head.

Cold and pale lay the emperor in his great magnificent bed. All the courtiers thought he was dead, and went to do homage to the new emperor. The lackeys went off to trade gossip, and the chambermaids gave a coffee party because it was such a special occasion. Deep mats were laid in all the rooms and passageways to muffle each footstep. It was quiet in the palace, dead quiet. But the emperor was not yet dead. Stiff and pale he lay, in his magnificent bed with the long velvet curtains and the heavy gold tassels. High in the wall was an open window, through which moonlight fell on the emperor and his artificial bird.

The poor emperor could hardly breathe. It was as if something were sitting on his chest. Opening his eyes he saw it was Death who sat there, wearing the emperor's crown, handling the emperor's gold sword, and carrying the emperor's silk banner. Among the folds of the great velvet curtains there were strangely familiar faces. Some were horrible, others gentle and kind. They were the emperor's deeds, good and bad, who came back to him now that Death sat on his heart.

"Don't you remember—?" they whispered one after the other. "Don't you remember—?" And they told him of things that made the cold sweat run on his forehead.

"No, I will not remember!" said the emperor. "Music, music, sound the great drum of China, lest I hear what they say!" But they went on whispering, and Death nodded, Chinese fashion, at every word.

"Music, music!" the emperor called. "Sing, my precious little golden bird, sing! I have given you gold and precious presents. I have hung my golden slipper around your neck. Sing, I pray you, sing!"

But the bird stood silent. There was no one to wind it, nothing to make it sing. Death kept staring through his great hollow eyes, and it was quiet, deadly quiet.

Suddenly, through the window came a burst of song. It was the little live nightingale who sat outside on a spray. He had heard of the emperor's plight and had come to sing of comfort and hope. As he sang, the phantoms grew pale, and still more pale, and the blood flowed quicker and quicker through the emperor's feeble body. Even Death listened, and said, "Go on, little nightingale, go on!"

"But," said the little nightingale, "will you give back that sword, that banner, that emperor's crown?"

And Death gave back these treasures for a song. The nightingale sang on. It sang of the quiet churchyard where white roses grow, where the elder flowers make the air sweet, and where the grass is always green, wet with the tears of those who are still alive. Death longed for his garden. Out through the windows drifted a cold gray mist, as Death departed.

"Thank you, thank you!" the emperor said. "Little bird from Heaven, I know you of old. I banished you once from my land, and yet you have sung away the evil faces from my bed, and Death from my heart. How can I repay you?"

"You have already rewarded me," said the nightingale. "I brought tears to your eyes when first I sang for you. To the heart of a singer, those are more precious than any precious stone. But sleep now, and grow fresh and strong while I sing." He sang on until the emperor fell into a sound, refreshing sleep, a sweet and soothing slumber.

The sun was shining in his window when the emperor awoke, restored and well. Not one of his servants had returned to him, for they thought him dead, but the nightingale still sang.

"You must stay with me always," said the emperor. "Sing to me only when you please. I shall break the artificial bird into a thousand pieces."

"No," said the nightingale. "It did its best. Keep it near you. I cannot build my nest here, or live in a palace, so let me come as I will. Then I shall sit on the spray by your window, and sing things that will make you happy and thoughtful too. I'll sing about those who are gay, and those who are sorrowful. My songs will tell you of all the good and evil that you do not see. A little singing bird flies far and wide, to the fisherman's hut, to the farmer's home, and to many other places a long way off from you and your court. I love your heart better than I do your crown, and yet the crown has been blessed too. I will come and sing to you, if you will promise me one thing."

"All that I have is yours," cried the emperor, who stood in his imperial robes, which he had put on himself, and held his heavy gold sword to his heart.

"One thing only," the nightingale asked. "You must not let anyone know that you have a little bird who tells you everything; then all will go even better." And away he flew.

The servants came in to look after their dead emperor—and there they stood. And the emperor said, "Good morning."

THE UGLY DUCKLING (1843)

It was so beautiful out on the country, it was summer—the wheat fields were golden, the oats were green, and down among the green meadows, the hay was stacked. There the stork minced about on his red legs, clacking away in Egyptian, which was the language his mother had taught him. Round about the field and meadowlands rose vast forests in which deep lakes lay hidden. Yes, it was indeed lovely out there in the country.

In the midst of the sunshine, there stood an old manor house that had a deep moat around it. From the walls of the manor right down to the water's edge great burdock leaves grew, and there were some so tall that little children could stand upright beneath the biggest of them. In this wilderness of leaves, which was as dense as the forests itself, a duck sat on her nest, hatching her ducklings. She was becoming somewhat weary, because sitting is such a dull business and scarcely anyone came to see her. The other ducks would much rather swim in the moat than waddle out and squat under the burdock leaf to gossip with her.

But at last, the eggshells began to crack, one after another. "Peep, peep!" said the little things, as they came to life and poked out their heads.

"Quack, quack!" said the duck, and quick as quick can be they all waddled out to have a look at the green world under the leaves. Their mother let them look as much as they pleased, because green is good for the eyes.

"How wide the world is," said all the young ducks, for they certainly had much more room now than they had when they were in their eggshells.

"Do you think this is the whole world?" their mother asked. "Why, it extends on and on, clear across to the other side of the garden and right on into the parson's field, though that is further than I have ever been. I do hope you are all hatched," she said as she got up. "No, not quite all. The biggest egg still lies here. How much longer is this going to take? I am really rather tired of it all," she said, but she settled back on her nest.

"Well, how goes it?" asked an old duck who came to pay her a call.

"It takes a long time with that one egg," said the duck on the nest. "It won't crack, but look at the others. They are the cutest little ducklings I've ever seen. They look exactly like their father, the wretch! He hasn't come to see me at all."

"Let's have a look at the egg that won't crack," the old duck said. "It's a turkey egg, and you can take my word for it. I was fooled like that once myself. What trouble and care I had with those turkey children, for I may as well tell you, they are afraid of the water. I simply could not get them into it. I quacked and snapped at them, but it wasn't a bit of use. Let me see the egg. Certainly, it's a turkey egg. Let it lie, and go teach your other children to swim."

"Oh, I'll sit a little longer. I've been at it so long already that I may as well sit here half the summer."

"Suit yourself," said the old duck, and away she waddled.

At last, the big egg did crack. "Peep," said the young one, and out he tumbled, but he was so big and ugly.

The duck took a look at him. "That's a frightfully big duckling," she said. "He doesn't look the least like the others. Can he really be a turkey baby? Well, well! I'll soon find out. Into the water he shall go, even if I have to shove him in myself."

Next day, the weather was perfectly splendid, and the sun shone down on all the green burdock leaves. The mother duck led her whole family down to the moat. Splash! She took to the water. "Quack, quack," said she, and one duckling after another plunged in. The water went over their heads, but they came up in a flash, and floated to perfection. Their legs worked automatically, and they were all there in the water. Even the big, ugly gray one was swimming along.

"Why, that's no turkey," she said. "See how nicely he uses his legs, and how straight he holds himself. He's my very own son after all, and quite good-looking if you look at him properly. Quack, quack come with me. I'll lead you out into the world and introduce you to the duck yard. But keep close to me so that you won't get stepped on, and watch out for the cat!"

Thus they sallied into the duck yard, where all was in an uproar because two families were fighting over the head of an eel. But the cat got it, after all.

"You see, that's the way of the world." The mother duck licked her bill because she wanted the eel's head for herself. "Stir your legs. Bustle about, and mind that you bend your necks to that old duck over there. She's the noblest of us all, and has Spanish blood in her. That's why she's so fat. See that red rag around her leg? That's a wonderful thing, and the highest distinction a duck can get. It shows that they don't want to lose her, and that she's to have special attention from man and beast. Shake yourselves! Don't turn your toes in. A well-bred duckling turns his toes way out, just as his father and mother do—this way. So then! Now duck your necks and say quack!"

They did as she told them, but the other ducks around them looked on and said right out loud, "See here! Must we have this brood too, just as if there weren't enough of us already? And—fie! what an ugly-looking fellow that duckling is! We won't stand for him." One duck charged up and bit his neck.

"Let him alone," his mother said. "He isn't doing any harm."

"Possibly not," said the duck who bit him, "but he's too big and strange, and therefore he needs a good whacking."

"What nice-looking children you have, Mother," said the old duck with the rag around her leg. "They are all pretty except that one. He didn't come out so well. It's a pity you can't hatch him again."

"That can't be managed, your ladyship," said the mother. "He isn't so handsome, but he's as good as can be, and he swims just as well as the rest, or, I should say, even a little better than they do. I hope his looks will improve with age, and after a while, he won't seem so big. He took too long in the egg, and that's why his figure isn't all that it should be." She pinched his neck and preened his feathers. "Moreover, he's a drake, so it won't matter so much. I think he will be quite strong, and I'm sure he will amount to something."

"The other ducklings are pretty enough," said the old duck. "Now make yourselves right at home, and if you find an eel's head, you may bring it to me."

So they felt quite at home. But the poor duckling who had been the last one out of his egg, and who looked so ugly, was pecked and pushed about and made fun of by the ducks and the chickens as well. "He's too big," said they all. The turkey gobbler, who thought himself an emperor because he was born wearing spurs, puffed up like a ship under full sail and bore down upon him, gobbling and gobbling until he was red in the face. The poor duckling did not know where he dared stand or where he dared walk. He was so sad because he was so desperately ugly, and because he was the laughing stock of the whole barnyard.

So it went on the first day, and after that, things went from bad to worse. The poor duckling was chased and buffeted about by everyone. Even his own brothers and sisters abused him. "Oh," they would always say, "how we wish the cat would catch you, you ugly thing." And his mother said, "How I do wish you were miles away." The ducks nipped him, and the hens pecked him, and the girl who fed them kicked him with her foot.

So he ran away and he flew over the fence. The little birds in the bushes darted up in a fright. "That's because I'm so ugly," he thought, and closed his eyes, but he ran on just the same until he reached the great marsh where the wild ducks lived. There he lay all night long, weary and disheartened.

When morning came, the wild ducks flew up to have a look at their new companion. "What sort of creature are you?" they asked, as the duckling turned in all directions, bowing his best to them all. "You are terribly ugly," they told him, "but that's nothing to us so long as you don't marry into our family."

Poor duckling! Marriage certainly had never entered his mind. All he wanted was for them to let him lie among the reeds and drink a little water from the marsh.

There he stayed for two whole days. Then he met two wild geese, or rather wild ganders—for they were males. They had not been out of the shell very long, and that's what made them so sure of themselves.

"Say there, comrade," they said, "you're so ugly that we have taken a fancy to you. Come with us and be a bird of passage. In another marsh nearby, there are some fetching wild geese, all nice young ladies who know how to quack. You are so ugly that you'll completely turn their heads."

Bing! Bang! Shots rang in the air, and these two ganders fell dead among the reeds. The water was red with their blood. *Bing! Bang!* the shots rang, and as whole flocks of wild geese flew up from the reeds, another volley crashed. A great hunt was in progress. The hunters lay under cover all around the marsh, and some even perched on branches of trees that overhung the reeds. Blue smoke rose like clouds from the shade of the trees and drifted far out over the water.

The bird dogs came *splash, splash!* through the swamp, bending down the reeds and the rushes on every side. This gave the poor duckling such a fright that he twisted his head about to hide it under his wing. But at that very moment, a fearfully big dog appeared right beside him. His tongue lolled out of his mouth, and his wicked eyes glared horribly. He opened his wide jaws, flashed his sharp teeth, and—*splash, splash*—on he went without touching the duckling.

"Thank heavens," he sighed, "I'm so ugly that the dog won't even bother to bite me."

He lay perfectly still while the bullets splattered through the reeds as shot after shot was fired. It was late in the day before things became quiet again, and even then, the poor duckling didn't dare move. He waited several hours before he ventured to look about him, and then he scurried away from that marsh as fast as he could go. He ran across field and meadows. The wind was so strong that he had to struggle to keep his feet.

Late in the evening, he came to a miserable little hovel, so ramshackle that it did not know which way to tumble, and that was the only reason it still stood. The wind struck the duckling so hard that the poor little fellow had to sit down on his tail to withstand it. The storm blew stronger and stronger, but the duckling noticed that one hinge had come loose and the door hung so crooked that he could squeeze through the crack into the room, and that's just what he did.

Here lived an old woman with her cat and her hen. The cat, whom she called "Sonny," could arch his back, purr, and even make sparks, though for that you had to stroke his fur the wrong way. The hen had short little legs, so she was called "Chickey Shortleg." She laid good eggs, and the old woman loved her as if she had been her own child.

In the morning, they were quick to notice the strange duckling. The cat began to purr, and the hen began to cluck.

"What on earth!" The old woman looked around, but she was shortsighted, and she mistook the duckling for a fat duck that had lost its way. "That was a good catch," she said. "Now I shall have duck eggs—unless it's a drake. We must try it out." So the duckling was tried out for three weeks, but not one egg did he lay.

In this house, the cat was master and the hen was mistress. They always said, "We and the world," for they thought themselves half of the world, and much the better half at that. The duckling thought that there might be more than one way of thinking, but the hen would not hear of it.

"Can you lay eggs?" she asked.

"No."

"Then be so good as to hold your tongue."

The cat asked, "Can you arch your back, purr, or make sparks?"

"No."

"Then keep your opinion to yourself when sensible people are talking."

The duckling sat in a corner, feeling most despondent. Then he remembered the fresh air and the sunlight. Such a desire to go swimming on the water possessed him that he could not help telling the hen about it.

"What on Earth has come over you?" the hen cried. "You haven't a thing to do, and that's why you get such silly notions. Lay us an egg, or learn to purr, and you'll get over it."

"But it's so refreshing to float on the water," said the duckling, "so refreshing to feel it rise over your head as you dive to the bottom."

"Yes, it must be a great pleasure!" said the hen. "I think you must have gone crazy.

Ask the cat, who's the wisest fellow I know, whether he likes to swim or dive down in the water. Of myself, I say nothing. But ask the old woman, our mistress. There's no one on Earth wiser than she is. Do you imagine she wants to go swimming and feel the water rise over her head?"

"You don't understand me," said the duckling.

"Well, if we don't, who would? Surely you don't think you are cleverer than the cat and the old woman—to say nothing of myself. Don't be so conceited, child. Just thank your Maker for all the kindness we have shown you. Didn't you get into this snug room, and fall in with people who can tell you what's what? But you are such a numbskull that it's no pleasure to have you around. Believe me, I tell you this for your own good. I say unpleasant truths, but that's the only way you can know who are your friends. Be sure now that you lay some eggs. See to it that you learn to purr or to make sparks."

"I think I'd better go out into the wide world," said the duckling.

"Suit yourself," said the hen.

So off went the duckling. He swam on the water, and dived down in it, but still he was slighted by every living creature because of his ugliness.

Autumn came on. The leaves in the forest turned yellow and brown. The wind took them and whirled them about. The heavens looked cold as the low clouds hung heavy with snow and hail. Perched on the fence, the raven screamed, "Caw, caw!" and trembled with cold. It made one shiver to think of it. Pity the poor little duckling!

One evening, just as the sun was setting in splendor, a great flock of large, handsome birds appeared out of the reeds. The duckling had never seen birds so beautiful. They were dazzling white, with long graceful necks. They were swans. They uttered a very strange cry as they unfurled their magnificent wings to fly from this cold land, away to warmer countries and to open waters. They went up so high, so very high, that the ugly little duckling felt a strange uneasiness come over him as he watched them. He went around and round in the water, like a wheel. He craned his neck to follow their course, and gave a cry so shrill and strange that he frightened himself. Oh! He could not forget them—those splendid, happy birds. When he could no longer see them he dived to the very bottom and when he came up again, he was quite beside himself. He did not know what birds they were or whither they were bound, yet he loved them more than anything he had ever loved before. It was not that he envied them, for how could he ever dare dream of wanting their marvelous beauty for himself? He would have been grateful if only the ducks would have tolerated him—the poor ugly creature.

The winter grew cold—so bitterly cold that the duckling had to swim to and fro in the water to keep it from freezing over. But every night, the hole in which he swam kept getting smaller and smaller. Then it froze so hard that the duckling had to paddle continuously to keep the crackling ice from closing in upon him. At last, too tired to move, he was frozen fast in the ice.

Early that morning a farmer came by, and when he saw how things were, he went out on the pond, broke away the ice with his wooden shoe, and carried the duckling home to his wife. There the duckling revived, but when the children wished to play with him, he thought they meant to hurt him. Terrified, he fluttered into the milk pail, splashing the whole room with milk. The woman shrieked and threw up her hands as he flew into the butter tub, and then in and out of the meal barrel. Imagine what he looked like now! The woman screamed and lashed out at him with the fire tongs. The children tumbled over each other as they tried to catch him, and they laughed and they shouted. Luckily the door was open, and the duckling escaped through it into the bushes, where he lay down in the newly fallen snow, as if in a daze.

But it would be too sad to tell of all the hardships and wretchedness he had to endure during this cruel winter. When the warm sun shone once more, the duckling was still alive among the reeds of the marsh. The larks began to sing again. It was beautiful springtime.

Then, quite suddenly, he lifted his wings. They swept through the air much more strongly than before, and their powerful strokes carried him far. Before he quite knew what was happening, he found himself in a great garden where apple trees bloomed. The lilacs filled the air with sweet scent and hung in clusters from long, green branches that bent over a winding stream. Oh, but it was lovely here in the freshness of spring!

From the thicket before him came three lovely white swans. They ruffled their feathers and swam lightly in the stream. The duckling recognized these noble creatures, and a strange feeling of sadness came upon him.

"I shall fly near these royal birds, and they will peck me to bits because I, who am so very ugly, dare to go near them. But I don't care. Better be killed by them than to be nipped by the ducks, pecked by the hens, kicked about by the hen-yard girl, or suffer such misery in winter."

So he flew into the water and swam toward the splendid swans. They saw him and swept down upon him with their rustling feathers raised. "Kill me!" said the poor creature, and he bowed his head down over the water to wait for death. But what did he see there, mirrored in the clear stream? He beheld his own image, and it was no longer the reflection of a clumsy, dirty, gray bird, ugly and offensive. He himself was a swan! Being born in a duck yard does not matter, if only you are hatched from a swan's egg.

He felt quite glad that he had come through so much trouble and misfortune, for now he had a fuller understanding of his own good fortune and of beauty when he met with it. The great swans swam all around him and stroked him with their bills.

Several little children came into the garden to throw grain and bits of bread upon the water. The smallest child cried, "Here's a new one," and the others rejoiced, "Yes, a new one has come." They clapped their hands, danced around, and ran to bring their father and mother.

And they threw bread and cake upon the water, while they all agreed, "The new one is the most handsome of all. He's so young and so good-looking." The old swans bowed in his honor.

Then he felt very bashful, and tucked his head under his wing. He did not know what this was all about. He felt so very happy, but he wasn't at all proud, for a good heart never grows proud. He thought about how he had been persecuted and scorned, and now he heard them all call him the most beautiful of all beautiful birds. The lilacs dipped their clusters into the stream before him, and the sun shone so warm and so heartening. He rustled his feathers and held his slender neck high, as he cried out with a full heart: "I never dreamed there could be so much happiness, when I was the ugly duckling."

THE SWEETHEARTS; OR, THE TOP AND THE BALL (1843)

A top and a ball were lying together in a drawer among a lot of other toys. The top said to the ball, "Since we live in the same drawer, we ought to be sweethearts."

But the ball, which was covered with a morocco leather and thought as much of itself as any fine lady, would not even answer such a proposal.

The next day, the little boy to whom the top belonged took it out, painted it red and yellow, and drove a brass nail into it; so that the top looked very elegant when it was spinning around.

"Look at me!" it said to the ball. "What do you think? Shall we be sweethearts now? We are just made for each other! You bounce, and I dance. None could be happier than we two."

"That's what you think!" said the ball. "You evidently don't realize that my father and my mother were a pair of morocco slippers, and that I have a cork in my body!"

"Yes, but I am made of mahogany!" said the top. "The mayor himself turned me on his own lathe and had a lot of fun doing it."

"Am I supposed to believe that?" said the ball.

"May I never be whipped again if I'm lying!" answered the top.

"You speak very well for yourself, but I'm afraid it's impossible. I'm almost engaged to a swallow. Whenever I bounce up in the air, it puts its head out of its nest and says, 'Will you be mine? Will you be mine?' And to myself, I've always said 'Yes.' But I promise I shall never forget you."

"That will do me a lot of good," said the top, and that ended their conversation right then and there!

The next day, the ball was taken out, and the top saw her flying high up into the air, just like a bird, so high that you could hardly see her. And every time she came back, she bounced up again, as soon as she touched the ground. That was either because she was longing for the swallow or because she had cork in her body. At the ninth bounce, the ball disappeared; the boy looked and looked, but it was gone. The top sighed "I know where she is: She's in the swallow's nest and has married the swallow."

The more the top thought of this, the more infatuated he became with the ball. Just because he couldn't have her, his love for her increased, but, alas! She was in love with somebody else. The top danced and spun, and in his thoughts, the ball became more and more beautiful.

Many years went by—it was now an old love affair. The top was no longer young. But one day, he was gilded all over; never had he looked so beautiful. He was now a golden top, and he leaped and spun till he hummed. This certainly was something. But suddenly he jumped too high, and disappeared! They looked and looked, even down in the cellar, but he was not to be found. Where was he? He had jumped into the dustbin, where all sorts of rubbish was lying—old cabbage stalks, dust, dirt, and gravel that had fallen down through the gutter.

"What a place to land in! Here my gilding will soon disappear. And what kind of riffraff am I with?" he mumbled, as he glared at a long, scrawny-looking cabbage stalk and at a strange round thing that looked like an apple. But it wasn't an apple—it was an old ball that for years had been lying in the roof gutter and was soaked through with water.

"Thank goodness! At last I have an equal to talk to!" said the ball, looking at the golden top. "I want you to know that I am made of morocco leather, sewn by maiden hands, and that I have a cork in my body; but no one will think so now! I almost married a swallow, but I landed in the roof gutter instead, and there I have been for the last five years, soaked! That's a long time, believe me, for a young lady."

But the top said nothing. He thought of his old sweetheart, and the more he listened, the more certain he felt it was she. Just then the housemaid came to throw some rubbish in the dustbin.

"Why," she cried, "here's the golden top!"

And the top was carried back into the living room and admired by everybody. But the ball was never heard of again. The top never spoke a word about his old sweetheart, for love vanishes when one's sweetheart has been soaking in a roof gutter for five years. Yes, you don't even recognize her when you meet her in a dustbin.

THE FIR TREE (1844)

Out in the woods stood such a pretty little fir tree. It grew in a good place, where it had plenty of sun and plenty of fresh air. Around it stood many tall comrades, both fir trees and pines.

The little fir tree was in a headlong hurry to grow up. It didn't care a thing for the warm sunshine, or the fresh air, and it took no interest in the peasant children who ran about chattering when they came to pick strawberries or raspberries. Often when the children had picked their pails full, or had gathered long strings of berries threaded on straws, they would sit down to rest near the little fir. "Oh, isn't it a nice little tree?" they would say. "It's the baby of the woods." The little tree didn't like their remarks at all.

Next year, it shot up a long joint of new growth, and the following year, another joint, still longer. You can always tell how old a fir tree is by counting the number of joints it has.

"I wish I were a grown-up tree, like my comrades," the little tree sighed. "Then I could stretch out my branches and see from my top what the world is like. The birds would make me their nesting place, and when the wind blew, I could bow back and forth with all the great trees."

It took no pleasure in the sunshine, nor in the birds. The glowing clouds that sailed overhead at sunrise and sunset meant nothing to it.

In winter, when the snow lay sparkling on the ground, a hare would often come hopping along and jump right over the little tree. Oh, how irritating that was! That happened for two winters, but when the third winter came, the tree was so tall that the hare had to turn aside and hop around it.

"Oh, to grow, grow! To get older and taller," the little tree thought. "That is the most wonderful thing in this world."

In the autumn, woodcutters came and cut down a few of the largest trees. This happened every year. The young fir was no longer a baby tree, and it trembled to see how those stately great trees crashed to the ground, how their limbs were lopped off, and how lean they looked as the naked trunks were loaded into carts. It could hardly recognize the trees it had known when the horses pulled them out of the woods.

Where were they going? What would become of them?

In the springtime, when swallows and storks came back, the tree asked them, "Do you know where the other trees went? Have you met them?"

The swallows knew nothing about it, but the stork looked thoughtful and nodded his head. "Yes, I think I met them," he said. "On my way from Egypt, I met many new ships, and some had tall, stately masts. They may well have been the trees you mean, for I remember the smell of fir. They wanted to be remembered to you."

"Oh, I wish I were old enough to travel on the sea. Please tell me what it really is, and how it looks."

"That would take too long to tell," said the stork, and off he strode.

"Rejoice in your youth," said the sunbeams. "Take pride in your growing strength and in the stir of life within you."

And the wind kissed the tree, and the dew wept over it, for the tree was young and without understanding.

When Christmas came near, many young trees were cut down. Some were not even as old or as tall as this fir tree of ours, who was in such a hurry and fret to go traveling. These young trees, which were always the handsomest ones, had their branches left on them when they were loaded on carts and the horses drew them out of the woods.

"Where can they be going?" the fir tree wondered. "They are no taller than I am. One was really much smaller than I am. And why are they allowed to keep all their branches? "Where can they be going?"

"We know! We know!" the sparrows chirped. "We have been to town and peeped in the windows. We know where they are going. The greatest splendor and glory you can imagine awaits them. We've peeped through windows. We've seen them planted right in the middle of a warm room and decked out with the most splendid things— gold apples, good gingerbread, gay toys, and many hundreds of candles."

"And then?" asked the fir tree, trembling in every twig. "And then? What happens then?"

"We saw nothing more. And never have we seen anything that could match it."

"I wonder if I was created for such a glorious future?" The fir tree rejoiced. "Why, that is better than to cross the sea. I'm tormented with longing. Oh, if Christmas would only come! I'm just as tall and grown-up as the trees they chose last year. How I wish I were already in the cart, on my way to the warm room where there's so much splendor and glory. Then—then something even better, something still more important is bound to happen, or why should they deck me so fine? Yes, there must be something still grander! But what? Oh, how I long: I don't know what's the matter with me."

"Enjoy us while you may," the air and sunlight told him. "Rejoice in the days of your youth, out here in the open."

But the tree did not rejoice at all. It just grew. It grew and was green both winter and summer—dark evergreen. People who passed it said, "There's a beautiful tree!" And when Christmas time came again, they cut it down first. The ax struck deep into its marrow. The tree sighed as it fell to the ground. It felt faint with pain. Instead of the happiness it had expected, the tree was sorry to leave the home where it had grown up. It knew that never again would it see its dear old comrades, the little bushes and the flowers about it—and perhaps not even the birds. The departure was anything but pleasant.

The tree did not get over it until all the trees were unloaded in the yard, and it heard a man say, "That's a splendid one. That's the tree for us." Then two servants came in fine livery, and carried the fir tree into a big splendid drawing room. Portraits were hung all around the walls. On either side of the white porcelain stove stood great Chinese vases with lions on their lids. There were easy chairs, silk-covered sofas, and long tables strewn with picture books and with toys that were worth a mint of money, or so the children said.

The fir tree was planted in a large tub filled with sand, but no one could see that it was a tub because it was wrapped in a gay green cloth and set on a many-colored carpet. How the tree quivered! What would come next? The servants and even the young ladies helped it on with its fine decorations. From its branches, they hung little nets cut out of colored paper, and each net was filled with candies. Gilded apples and walnuts hung in clusters as if they grew there, and a hundred little white, blue, and even red candles were fastened to its twigs. Among its green branches swayed dolls that it took to be real living people, for the tree had never seen their like before. And up at its very top was set a large gold tinsel star. It was splendid, I tell you, splendid beyond all words!

"Tonight," they all said, "ah, tonight how the tree will shine!"

"Oh," thought the tree, "if tonight would only come! If only the candles were lit! And after that, what happens then? Will the trees come trooping out of the woods to see me? Will the sparrows flock to the windows? Shall I take root here, and stand in fine ornaments all winter and summer long?"

That was how much it knew about it. All its longing had gone to its bark and set it to arching, which is as bad for a tree as a headache is for us.

Now the candles were lighted. What dazzling splendor! What a blaze of light! The tree quivered, so in every bough a candle set one of its twigs ablaze. It hurt terribly.

"Mercy me!" cried every young lady, and the fire was quickly put out. The tree no longer dared rustle a twig—it was awful! Wouldn't it be terrible if it were to drop one of its ornaments? Its own brilliance dazzled it.

Suddenly, the folding doors were thrown back, and a whole flock of children burst in as if they would overturn the tree completely. Their elders marched in after them, more sedately. For a moment, but only for a moment, the young ones were stricken speechless. Then they shouted till the rafters rang. They danced about the tree and plucked off one present after another.

"What are they up to?" the tree wondered. "What will happen next?"

As the candles burned down to the bark, they were snuffed out, one by one, and then the children had permission to plunder the tree. They went about it in such earnest that the branches crackled, and, if the tree had not been tied to the ceiling by the gold star at top, it would have tumbled headlong.

The children danced about with their splendid playthings. No one looked at the tree now, except an old nurse who peered in among the branches, but this was only to make sure that not an apple or fig had been overlooked.

"Tell us a story! Tell us a story!" the children clamored, as they towed a fat little man to the tree. He sat down beneath it and said, "Here we are in the woods, and it will do the tree a lot of good to listen to our story. Mind you, I'll tell only one. Which will you have, the story of Ivedy-Avedy, or the one about Humpty-Dumpty who tumbled downstairs, yet ascended the throne and married the princess?"

"Ivedy-Avedy," cried some. "Humpty-Dumpty," cried the others. And there was a great hullabaloo. Only the fir tree held its peace, though it thought to itself, "Am I to be left out of this? Isn't there anything I can do?" For all the fun of the evening had centered upon it, and it had played its part well.

The fat little man told them all about Humpty-Dumpty, who tumbled downstairs, yet ascended the throne and married the princess. And the children clapped and shouted, "Tell us another one! Tell us another one!" For they wanted to hear about Ivedy-Avedy too, but after Humpty-Dumpty, the storytelling stopped. The fir tree stood very still as it pondered how the birds in the woods had never told it a story to equal this.

"Humpty-Dumpty tumbled downstairs, yet he married the princess. Imagine! That must be how things happen in the world. You never can tell. Maybe I'll tumble downstairs and marry a princess too," thought the fir tree, who believed every word of the story because such a nice man had told it.

The tree looked forward to the following day, when they would deck it again with fruit and toys, candles and gold. "Tomorrow I shall not quiver," it decided. "I'll enjoy my splendor to the full. Tomorrow I shall hear about Humpty-Dumpty again, and perhaps about Ivedy-Avedy too." All night long, the tree stood silent as it dreamed its dreams, and next morning, the butler and the maid came in with their dusters.

"Now my splendor will be renewed," the fir tree thought. But they dragged it upstairs to the garret, and there they left it in a dark corner where no daylight ever came. "What's the meaning of this?" the tree wondered. "What am I going to do here? What stories shall I hear?" It leaned against the wall, lost in dreams. It had plenty of time for dreaming, as the days and the nights went by. Nobody came to the garret. And when at last someone did come, it was only to put many big boxes away in the corner. The tree was quite hidden. One might think it had been entirely forgotten.

"It's still winter outside," the tree thought. "The earth is too hard and covered with snow for them to plant me now. I must have been put here for shelter until springtime comes. How thoughtful of them! How good people are! Only, I wish it weren't so dark here, and so very, very lonely. There's not even a little hare. It was so friendly out in the woods when the snow was on the ground and the hare came hopping along. Yes, he was friendly even when he jumped right over me, though I did not think so then. Here it's all so terribly lonely."

"Squeak, squeak!" said a little mouse just then. He crept across the floor, and another one followed him. They sniffed the fir tree and rustled in and out among its branches.

"It is fearfully cold," one of them said. "Except for that, it would be very nice here, wouldn't it, you old fir tree?"

"I'm not at all old," said the fir tree. "Many trees are much older than I am."

"Where did you come from?" the mice asked him. "And what do you know?" They were most inquisitive creatures.

"Tell us about the most beautiful place in the world. Have you been there? Were you ever in the larder, where there are cheeses on shelves and hams that hang from the rafters? It's the place where you can dance upon tallow candles—where you can dart in thin and squeeze out fat."

"I know nothing of that place," said the tree. "But I know the woods where the sun shines and the little birds sing." Then it told them about its youth. The little mice had never heard the like of it. They listened very intently, and said, "My! How much you have seen! And how happy it must have made you."

"I?" the fir tree thought about it. "Yes, those days were rather amusing." And it went on to tell them about Christmas Eve, when it was decked out with candies and candles.

"Oh," said the little mice, "how lucky you have been, you old fir tree!"

"I am not at all old," it insisted. "I came out of the woods just this winter, and I'm really in the prime of life, though at the moment, my growth is suspended."

"How nicely you tell things," said the mice. The next night they came with four other mice to hear what the tree had to say. The more it talked, the more clearly it recalled things, and it thought, "Those were happy times. But they may still come back—they may come back again. Humpty-Dumpty fell downstairs, and yet he married the princess. Maybe the same thing will happen to me." It thought about a charming little birch tree that grew out in the woods. To the fir tree, she was a real and lovely princess.

"Who is Humpty-Dumpty?" the mice asked it. So the fir tree told them the whole story, for it could remember it word by word. The little mice were ready to jump to the top of the tree for joy. The next night, many more mice came to see the fir tree, and on Sunday, two rats paid it a call, but they said that the story was not very amusing. This made the little mice so sad that they began to find it not so very interesting either.

"Is that the only story you know?" the rats asked.

"Only that one," the tree answered. "I heard it on the happiest evening of my life, but I did not know then how happy I was."

"It's a very silly story. Don't you know one that tells about bacon and candles? Can't you tell us a good larder story?"

"No," said the tree.

"Then good-bye, and we won't be back," the rats said, and went away.

At last, the little mice took to staying away, too. The tree sighed, "Oh, wasn't it pleasant when those gay little mice sat around and listened to all that I had to say? Now that, too, is past and gone. But I will take good care to enjoy myself, once they let me out of here."

When would that be? Well, it came to pass on a morning when people came up to clean out the garret. The boxes were moved, the tree was pulled out and thrown— thrown hard—on the floor. But a servant dragged it at once to the stairway, where there was daylight again.

"Now my life will start all over," the tree thought. It felt the fresh air and the first sunbeam strike it as if it came out into the courtyard. This all happened so quickly, and there was so much going around it, that the tree forgot to give even a glance at itself. The courtyard adjoined a garden, where flowers were blooming. Great masses of fragrant roses hung over the picket fence. The linden trees were in blossom, and between them, the swallows skimmed past, calling, "Tilira-lira-lee, my love's come back to me." But it was not the fir tree of whom they spoke.

"Now I shall live again," it rejoiced, and tried to stretch out its branches. Alas, they were withered, and brown, and brittle. It was tossed into a corner, among weeds and nettles. But the gold star that was still tied to its top sparkled bravely in the sunlight.

Several of the merry children, who had danced around the tree and taken such pleasure in it at Christmas, were playing in the courtyard. One of the youngest seized upon it and tore off the tinsel star.

"Look what is still hanging on that ugly old Christmas tree," the child said, and stamped upon the branches until they cracked beneath his shoes.

The tree saw the beautiful flowers blooming freshly in the garden. It saw itself, and wished that they had left it in the darkest corner of the garret. It thought of its own young days in the deep woods, and of the merry Christmas Eve, and of the little mice who had been so pleased when it told them the story of Humpty-Dumpty.

"My days are over and past," said the poor tree. "Why didn't I enjoy them while I could? Now they are gone—all gone."

A servant came and chopped the tree into little pieces. These heaped together quite high. The wood blazed beautifully under the big copper kettle, and the fir tree moaned so deeply that each groan sounded like a muffled shot. That's why the children who were playing nearby ran to make a circle around the flames, staring into the fire and crying, "Pif! Paf!" But as each groans burst from it, the tree thought of a bright summer day in the woods, or a starlit winter night. It thought of Christmas Eve and thought of Humpty-Dumpty, which was the only story it ever heard and knew how to tell. And so the tree was burned completely away.

The children played on in the courtyard. The youngest child wore on his breast the gold star that had topped the tree on its happiest night of all. But that was no more, and the tree was no more, and there's no more to my story. No more, nothing more. All stories come to an end.

THE SNOW QUEEN (1844)

A TALE IN SEVEN STORIES

FIRST STORY
WHICH HAS TO DO WITH A MIRROR AND ITS FRAGMENTS

Now then! We will begin. When the story is done, you shall know a great deal more than you do know.

He was a terribly bad hobgoblin, a goblin of the very wickedest sort, and, in fact, he was the devil himself. One day, the devil was in a very good humor because he had just finished a mirror that had this peculiar power: Everything good and beautiful that was reflected in it seemed to dwindle to almost nothing at all, while everything that was worthless and ugly became most conspicuous and even uglier than ever. In this mirror, the loveliest landscapes looked like boiled spinach, and the very best people became hideous, or stood on their heads and had no stomachs. Their faces were distorted beyond any recognition, and if a person had a freckle, it was sure to spread until it covered both nose and mouth.

"That's very funny!" said the devil. If a good, pious thought passed through anyone's mind, it showed in the mirror as a carnal grin, and the devil laughed aloud at his ingenious invention.

All those who went to the hobgoblin's school—for he had a school of his own—told everyone that a miracle had come to pass. Now, they asserted, for the very first time you could see how the world and its people really looked. They scurried about with the mirror until there was not a person alive nor a land on Earth that had not been distorted.

Then they wanted to fly up to Heaven itself, to scoff at the angels and our Lord. The higher they flew with the mirror, the wider it grinned. They could hardly manage to hold it. Higher they flew, and higher still, nearer to Heaven and the angels. Then the grinning mirror trembled with such violence that it slipped from their hands and fell to the earth, where it shattered into hundreds of millions of billions of bits, or perhaps even more. And now it caused more trouble than it did before it was broken, because some of the fragments were smaller than a grain of sand, and these went flying throughout the wide world. Once they got in people's eyes, they would stay there. These bits of glass distorted everything the people saw and made them see only the bad side of things, for every little bit of glass kept the same power that the whole mirror had possessed.

A few people even got a glass splinter in their hearts, and that was a terrible thing, for it turned their hearts into lumps of ice. Some of the fragments were so large that they were used as window panes—but not the kind of window through which you should look at your friends. Other pieces were made into spectacles, and evil things came to pass when people put them on to see clearly and to see justice done. The fiend was so tickled by it all that he laughed till his sides were sore. But fine bits of the glass are still flying through the air, and now you shall hear what happened.

SECOND STORY
A LITTLE BOY AND A LITTLE GIRL

In the big city, it was so crowded with houses and people that few found room for even a small garden, and most people had to be content with a flowerpot, but two poor children who lived there managed to have a garden that was a little bigger than a flowerpot. These children were not brother and sister, but they loved each other just as much as if they had been. Their parents lived close to one another in the garrets of two adjoining houses. Where the roofs met and where the rain gutter ran between the two houses, their two small windows faced each other. One had only to step across the rain gutter to go from window to window.

In these windows, the parents had a large box in which they planted vegetables for their use, and a little rosebush too. Each box had a bush, which thrived to perfection. Then it occurred to the parents to put these boxes across the gutter, where they very nearly reached from one window to the other and looked exactly like two walls of flowers. The pea plants hung down over the boxes, and the rosebushes threw out long sprays that framed the windows and bent over toward each other. It was almost like a little triumphal arch of greenery and flowers. The boxes were very high, and the children knew that they were not to climb about on them, but they were often allowed to take their little stools out on the roof under the roses, where they had a wonderful time playing together.

Winter, of course, put an end to this pleasure. The windows often frosted over completely. But they would heat copper pennies on the stove and press these hot coins against the frost-coated glass. Then they had the finest of peepholes, as round as a ring, and behind them appeared a bright, friendly eye, one at each window—it was the little boy and the little girl who peeped out. His name was Kay and hers was Gerda. With one skip, they could join each other in summer, but to visit together in the wintertime, they had to go all the way downstairs in one house and climb all the way upstairs in the other. Outside, the snow was whirling.

"See the white bees swarming," the old grandmother said.

"Do they have a queen bee, too?" the little boy asked, for he knew that real bees have one.

"Yes, indeed they do," the grandmother said. "She flies in the thick of the swarm. She is the biggest bee of all, and can never stay quietly on the earth, but goes back again to the dark clouds. Many a wintry night, she flies through the streets and peers in through the windows. Then they freeze over in a strange fashion, as if they were covered with flowers."

"Oh yes, we've seen that," both the children said, and so they knew it was true.

"Can the Snow Queen come in here?" the little girl asked.

"Well, let her come!" cried the boy. "I would put her on the hot stove and melt her."

But Grandmother stroked his head, and told them other stories.

That evening when little Kay was at home and half ready for bed, he climbed on the chair by the window and looked out through the little peephole. A few snowflakes were falling, and the largest flake of all alighted on the edge of one of the flower boxes. This flake grew bigger and bigger, until at last it turned into a woman who was dressed in the finest white gauze that looked as if it had been made from millions of star-shaped flakes. She was beautiful and she was graceful, but she was ice—shining, glittering ice. She was alive, for all that, and her eyes sparkled like two bright stars, but in them there was neither rest nor peace. She nodded toward the window and beckoned with her hand. The little boy was frightened, and as he jumped down from the chair, it seemed to him that a huge bird flew past the window.

The next day was clear and cold. Then the snow thawed, and springtime came. The sun shone, the green grass sprouted, swallows made their nests, windows were thrown open, and once again the children played in their little roof garden, high up in the rain gutter on top of the house.

That summer, the roses bloomed their splendid best. The little girl had learned a hymn in which there was a line about roses that reminded her of their own flowers. She sang it to the little boy, and he sang it with her:

Where roses bloom so sweetly in the vale,
There shall you find the Christ Child, without fail.

The children held each other by the hand, kissed the roses, looked up at the Lord's clear sunshine, and spoke to it as if the Christ Child were there. What glorious summer days those were, and how beautiful it was out under those fragrant rosebushes that seemed as if they would never stop blooming.

Kay and Gerda were looking at a picture book of birds and beasts one day, and it was then—just as the clock in the church tower was striking five—that Kay cried:

"Oh! Something hurt my heart. And now I've got something in my eye."

The little girl put her arm around his neck, and he blinked his eye. No, she couldn't see anything in it.

"I think it's gone," he said. But it was not gone. It was one of those splinters of glass from the magic mirror. You remember that goblin's mirror—the one that made everything great and good that was reflected in it appear small and ugly, but that magnified all evil things until each blemish loomed large. Poor Kay! A fragment had pierced his heart as well, and soon it would turn into a lump of ice. The pain had stopped, but the glass was still there.

"Why should you be crying?" he asked. "It makes you look so ugly. There's nothing the matter with me." And suddenly, he took it into his head to say:

"Ugh! That rose is all worm-eaten. And look, this one is crooked. And these roses, they are just as ugly as they can be. They look like the boxes they grow in." He gave the boxes a kick and broke off both of the roses.

"Kay! What are you doing?" the little girl cried. When he saw how it upset her, he broke off another rose and then leaped home through his own window, leaving dear little Gerda all alone.

Afterwards, when she brought out her picture book, he said it was fit only for babes in the cradle. And whenever Grandmother told stories, he always broke in with a "but—." If he could manage it, he would steal behind her, perch a pair of spectacles on his nose, and imitate her. He did this so cleverly that it made everybody laugh, and before long, he could mimic the walk and the talk of everyone who lived on that street. Everything that was odd or ugly about them, Kay could mimic so well that people said, "That boy has surely got a good head on him!" But it was the glass in his eye and the glass in his heart that made him tease even little Gerda, who loved him with all her soul.

Now his games were very different from what they used to be. They became more sensible. When the snow was flying about one wintry day, he brought a large magnifying glass out of doors and spread the tail of his blue coat to let the snowflakes fall on it.

"Now look through the glass," he told Gerda. Each snowflake seemed much larger and looked like a magnificent flower or a ten-pointed star. It was marvelous to look at.

"Look, how artistic!" said Kay. "They are much more interesting to look at than real flowers, for they are absolutely perfect. There isn't a flaw in them, until they start melting."

A little while later, Kay came down with his big gloves on his hands and his sled on his back. Right in Gerda's ear he bawled out, "I've been given permission to play in the big square where the other boys are!" and away he ran.

In the square, some of the more adventuresome boys would tie their little sleds on behind the farmer's carts, to be pulled along for quite a distance. It was wonderful sport. While the fun was at its height, a big sleigh drove up. It was painted entirely white, and the driver wore a white, shaggy fur cloak and a white, shaggy cap. As the sleigh drove twice around the square, Kay quickly hooked his little sled behind it, and down the street they went, faster and faster. The driver turned around in a friendly fashion and nodded to Kay, just as if they were old acquaintances. Every time Kay started to unfasten his little sleigh, its driver nodded again, and Kay held on, even when they drove right out through the town gate.

Then the snow began to fall so fast that the boy could not see his hands in front of him as they sped on. He suddenly let go the slack of the rope in his hands in order to get loose from the big sleigh, but it did no good. His little sled was tied on securely, and they went like the wind. He gave a loud shout, but nobody heard him. The snow whirled, and the sleigh flew along. Every now and then it gave a jump, as if it were clearing hedges and ditches. The boy was terror-stricken. He tried to say his prayers, but all he could remember was his multiplication tables.

The snowflakes got bigger and bigger, until they looked like big white hens. All of a sudden, the curtain of snow parted, and the big sleigh stopped, and the driver stood up. The fur coat and the cap were made of snow, and it was a woman, tall and slender and blinding white—she was the Snow Queen herself.

"We have made good time," she said. "Is it possible that you tremble from cold? Crawl under my bear coat." She took him up in the sleigh beside her, and as she wrapped the fur about him, he felt as if he were sinking into a snowdrift.

"Are you still cold?" she asked, and kissed him on the forehead. *Brr-r-r*. That kiss was colder than ice. He felt it right down to his heart, half of which was already an icy lump. He felt as if he were dying, but only for a moment. Then he felt quite comfortable and no longer noticed the cold.

"My sled! Don't forget my sled!" It was the only thing he thought of. They tied it to one of the white hens, which flew along after them with the sled on its back. The Snow

Queen kissed Kay once more, and then he forgot little Gerda, and Grandmother, and all the others at home.

"You won't get any more kisses now," she said, "or else I should kiss you to death." Kay looked at her. She was so beautiful! A cleverer and prettier face he could not imagine. She no longer seemed to be made of ice, as she had seemed when she sat outside his window and beckoned to him. In his eyes, she was perfect, and she was not at all afraid. He told her how he could do mental arithmetic even with fractions, and that he knew the size and population of all the countries. She kept on smiling, and he began to be afraid that he did not know as much as he thought he did. He looked up at the great big space overhead, as she flew with him high up on the black clouds, while the storm whistled and roared as if it were singing old ballads.

They flew over forests and lakes, over many a land and sea. Below them, the wind blew cold, wolves howled, and black crows screamed as they skimmed across the glittering snow. But up above, the moon shone bright and large, and on it Kay fixed his eyes throughout that long, long winter night. By day, he slept at the feet of the Snow Queen.

THIRD STORY
THE FLOWER GARDEN OF THE WOMAN SKILLED IN MAGIC

How did little Gerda get along when Kay did not come back? Where could he be? Nobody knew. Nobody could give them any news of him. All that the boys could say was that they had seen him hitch his little sled to a fine big sleigh, which had driven down the street and out through the town gate. Nobody knew what had become of Kay. Many tears were shed, and little Gerda sobbed hardest of all. People said that he was dead—that he must have been drowned in the river not far from town. Ah, how gloomy those long winter days were!

But spring and its warm sunshine came at last.

"Kay is dead and gone," little Gerda said.

"I don't believe it," said the sunshine.

"He's dead and gone," she said to the swallows.

"We don't believe it," they sang. Finally, little Gerda began to disbelieve it too. One morning, she said to herself:

"I'll put on my new red shoes, the ones Kay has never seen, and I'll go down by the river to ask about him."

It was very early in the morning. She kissed her old grandmother, who was still asleep, put on her red shoes, and all by herself, she hurried out through the town gate and down to the river.

"Is it true that you have taken my own little playmate? I'll give you my red shoes if you will bring him back to me."

It seemed to her that the waves nodded very strangely. So she took off her red shoes, which were her dearest possession, and threw them into the river. But they fell near the shore, and the little waves washed them right back to her. It seemed that the river could not take her dearest possession, because it did not have little Kay. However, she was afraid that she had not thrown them far enough, so she clambered into a boat that lay among the reeds, walked to the end of it, and threw her shoes out into the water again. But the boat was not tied, and her movements made it drift away from the bank. She realized this and tried to get ashore, but by the time she reached the other end of the boat, it was already more than a yard from the bank, and was fast gaining speed.

Little Gerda was so frightened that she began to cry, and no one was there to hear her except the sparrows. They could not carry her to land, but they flew along the shore twittering, "We are here! Here we are!" as if to comfort her. The boat drifted swiftly down the stream, and Gerda sat there quite still, in her stocking feet. Her little red shoes floated along behind, but they could not catch up with her because the boat was gathering headway. It was very pretty on both sides of the river, where the flowers were lovely, the trees were old, and the hillsides afforded pasture for cattle and sheep. But not one single person did Gerda see.

"Perhaps the river will take me to little Kay," she thought, and that made her feel more cheerful. She stood up and watched the lovely green banks for hour after hour.

Then she came to a large cherry orchard, in which there was a little house with strange red and blue windows. It had a thatched roof, and outside it stood two wooden soldiers, who presented arms to everyone who sailed past.

Gerda thought they were alive, and called out to them, but of course, they did not answer her. She drifted quite close to them as the current drove the boat toward the bank. Gerda called even louder, and an old, old woman came out of the house. She leaned on a crooked stick; she had on a big sun hat, and on it were painted the most glorious flowers.

"You poor little child!" the old woman exclaimed. "However did you get lost on this big swift river, and however did you drift so far into the great wide world?" The old woman waded right into the water, caught hold of the boat with her crooked stick, pulled it in to shore, and lifted little Gerda out of it.

Gerda was very glad to be on dry land again, but she felt a little afraid of this strange old woman, who said to her:

"Come and tell me who you are, and how you got here." Gerda told her all about it. The woman shook her head and said, "Hmm, hmm!" And when Gerda had told her everything and asked if she hadn't seen little Kay, the woman said he had not yet come by, but that he might be along any day now. And she told Gerda not to take it so to heart, but to taste her cherries and to look at her flowers. These were more beautiful than any picture book, and each one had a story to tell. Then she led Gerda by the hand into her little house, and the old woman locked the door.

The windows were placed high up on the walls, and through their red, blue, and yellow panes, the sunlight streamed in a strange mixture of all the colors there are. But on the table were the most delicious cherries, and Gerda, who was no longer afraid, ate as many as she liked. While she was eating them, the old woman combed her hair with a golden comb. Gerda's pretty hair fell in shining yellow ringlets on either side of a friendly little face that was as round and blooming as a rose.

"I've so often wished for a dear little girl like you," the old woman told her. "Now you'll see how well the two of us will get along." While her hair was being combed, Gerda gradually forgot all about Kay, for the old woman was skilled in magic. But she was not a wicked witch. She only dabbled in magic to amuse herself, but she wanted very much to keep little Gerda. So she went out into her garden and pointed her crooked stick at all the rosebushes. In the full bloom of their beauty, all of them sank down into the black earth, without leaving a single trace behind. The old woman was afraid that if Gerda saw them they would remind her so strongly of her own roses, and of little Kay, that she would run away again.

Then Gerda was led into the flower garden. How fragrant and lovely it was! Every known flower of every season was there in full bloom. No picture book was ever so pretty and gay. Gerda jumped for joy, and played in the garden until the sun went down behind the tall cherry trees. Then she was tucked into a beautiful bed, under a red silk coverlet quilted with blue violets. There she slept, and there she dreamed as gloriously as any queen on her wedding day.

The next morning, she again went out into the warm sunshine to play with the flowers—and this she did for many a day. Gerda knew every flower by heart, and, plentiful though they were, she always felt that there was one missing, but which one she didn't quite know. One day, she sat looking at the old woman's sun hat, and the prettiest of all the flowers painted on it was a rose. The old woman had forgotten this rose on her hat when she made the real roses disappear in the earth. But that's just the sort of thing that happens when one doesn't stop to think.

"Why aren't there any roses here?" said Gerda. She rushed out among the flower beds, and she looked and she looked, but there wasn't a rose to be seen. Then she sat down and cried. But her hot tears fell on the very spot where a rosebush had sunk into the ground, and when her warm tears moistened the earth, the bush sprang up again, as full of blossoms as when it disappeared. Gerda hugged it, and kissed the roses. She remembered her own pretty roses, and thought of little Kay.

"Oh, how long I have been delayed," the little girl said. "I should have been looking for Kay. Don't you know where he is?" she asked the roses. "Do you think that he is dead and gone?"

"He isn't dead," the roses told her. "We have been down in the earth where the dead people are, but Kay is not there."

"Thank you," said little Gerda, who went to all the other flowers, put her lips near them, and asked, "Do you know where little Kay is?"

But every flower stood in the sun and dreamed its own fairy tale, or its story. Though Gerda listened to many, many of them, not one of the flowers knew anything about Kay.

What did the tiger lily say?

"Do you hear the drum? *Boom, boom!* It was only two notes, always *boom, boom!* Hear the women wail. Hear the priests chant. The Hindu woman in her long red robe stands on the funeral pyre. The flames rise around her and her dead husband, but the Hindu woman is thinking of that living man in the crowd around them. She is thinking of him whose eyes are burning hotter than the flames—of him whose fiery glances have pierced her heart more deeply than these flames that soon will burn her body to ashes. Can the flame of the heart die in the flame of the funeral pyre?"

"I don't understand that at all," little Gerda said.

"That's my fairy tale," said the lily.

What did the trumpet flower say?

"An ancient castle rises high from a narrow path in the mountains. The thick ivy grows leaf upon leaf where it climbs to the balcony. There stands a beautiful maiden. She leans out over the balustrade to look down the path. No rose on its stem is as graceful as she, nor is any apple blossom in the breeze so light. Hear the rustle of her silk gown, sighing, 'Will he never come?'"

"Do you mean Kay?" little Gerda asked.

"I am talking about my story, my own dream," the trumpet flower replied.

What did the little snowdrop say?

"Between the trees, a board hangs by two ropes. It is a swing. Two pretty little girls, with frocks as white as snow and long green ribbons fluttering from their hats, are swinging. Their brother, who is bigger than they are, stands behind them on the swing, with his arms around the ropes to hold himself. In one hand, he has a little cup, and in the other, a clay pipe. He is blowing soap bubbles, and as the swing flies, the bubbles float off in all their changing colors. The last bubble is still clinging to the bowl of his pipe and fluttering in the air as the swing sweeps to and fro. A little black dog, light as a bubble, is standing on his hind legs and trying to get up in the swing. But it does not stop. High and low the swing flies, until the dog loses his balance, barks, and loses his temper. They tease him, and the bubble bursts. A swinging board pictured in a bubble before it broke—that is my story."

"It may be a very pretty story, but you told it very sadly, and you didn't mention Kay at all."

What did the hyacinths say?

"There were three sisters, quite transparent and very fair. One wore a red dress, the second wore a blue one, and the third went all in white. Hand in hand, they danced in the clear moonlight, beside a calm lake. They were not elfin folk. They were human beings. The air was sweet, and the sisters disappeared into the forest. The fragrance of the air grew sweeter. Three coffins, in which lie the three sisters, glide out of the forest and across the lake. The fireflies hover about them like little flickering lights. Are the dancing sisters sleeping, or are they dead? The fragrance of the flowers says they are dead, and the evening bell tolls for their funeral."

"You are making me very unhappy," little Gerda said. "Your fragrance is so strong that I cannot help thinking of those dead sisters. Oh, could little Kay really be dead? The roses have been down under the ground, and they say no."

"Ding, dong," tolled the hyacinth bells. "We do not toll for little Kay. We do not know him. We are simply singing our song—the only song we know."

And Gerda went on to the buttercup that shone among its glossy green leaves.

"You are like a bright little sun," said Gerda. "Tell me, do you know where I can find my playmate?"

And the buttercup shone brightly as it looked up at Gerda. But what sort of song would a buttercup sing? It certainly wouldn't be about Kay.

"In a small courtyard, God's Sun was shining brightly on the very first day of spring. Its beams glanced along the white wall of the house next door, and close by grew the first yellow flowers of spring, shining like gold in the warm sunlight. An old grandmother was sitting outside in her chair. Her granddaughter, a poor but very pretty maidservant, had just come home for a little visit. She kissed her grandmother, and there was gold, a heart full of gold, in that kiss. Gold on her lips, gold in her dreams, and gold above in the morning beams. There, I've told you my little story," said the buttercup.

"Oh, my poor old grandmother," said Gerda. "She will miss me so. She must be grieving for me as much as she did for little Kay. But I'll soon go home again, and I'll bring Kay with me. There's no use asking the flowers about him. They don't know anything except their own songs, and they haven't any news for me."

Then she tucked up her little skirts so that she could run away faster, but the narcissus tapped against her leg as she was jumping over it. So she stopped and leaned over the tall flower.

"Perhaps you have something to tell me," she said.

What did the narcissus say?

"I can see myself! I can see myself! Oh, how sweet is my own fragrance! Up in the narrow garret, there is a little dancer, half dressed. First she stands on one leg. Then she stands on both, and kicks her heels at the whole world. She is an illusion of the stage. She pours water from the teapot over a piece of cloth she is holding—it is her bodice. Cleanliness is such a virtue! Her white dress hangs from a hook. It too has been washed in the teapot, and dried on the roof. She puts it on and ties a saffron scarf around her neck to make the dress seem whiter. Point your toes! See how straight she balances on that single stem. I can see myself! I can see myself!"

"I'm not interested," said Gerda. "What a thing to tell me about!"

She ran to the end of the garden, and though the gate was fastened, she worked the rusty latch until it gave way and the gate flew open. Little Gerda scampered out into the wide world in her bare feet. She looked back three times, but nobody came after her. At last, she could run no farther, and she sat down to rest on a big stone, and when she looked up, she saw that summer had gone by and it was late in the fall. She could never have guessed it inside the beautiful garden where the sun was always shining and the flowers of every season were always in full bloom.

"Gracious! How long I've dallied," Gerda said. "Fall is already here. I can't rest any longer."

She got up to run on, but how footsore and tired she was! And how cold and bleak everything around her looked! The long leaves of the willow tree had turned quite yellow, and damp puffs of mist dropped from them like drops of water. One leaf after another fell to the ground. Only the blackthorn still bore fruit, and its fruit was so sour that it set your teeth on edge.

Oh, how dreary and gray the wide world looked.

FOURTH STORY
THE PRINCE AND THE PRINCESS

The next time that Gerda was forced to rest, a big crow came hopping across the snow in front of her. For a long time, he had been watching her and cocking his head to one side, and now he said, "Caw, caw! Good caw day!" He could not say it any better, but he felt kindly inclined toward the little girl, and asked her where she was going in the great wide world, all alone. Gerda understood him when he said "alone," and she knew its meaning all too well. She told the crow the whole story of her life, and asked if he hadn't seen Kay. The crow gravely nodded his head and cawed, "Maybe I have, maybe I have!"

"What! do you really think you have?" the little girl cried, and almost hugged the crow to death as she kissed him.

"Gently, gently!" said the crow. "I think that it may have been little Kay that I saw, but if it was, then he has forgotten you for the princess."

"Does he live with a princess?" Gerda asked.

"Yes. Listen!" said the crow. "But it is so hard for me to speak your language. If you understand crow talk, I can tell you much more easily."

"I don't know that language," said Gerda. "My grandmother knows it just as well as she knows baby talk, and I do wish I had learned it."

"No matter," said the crow. "I'll tell you as well as I can, though that won't be any too good." And he told her all that he knew.

"In the kingdom where we are now, there is a princess who is uncommonly clever, and no wonder. She has read all the newspapers in the world and forgotten them again—that's how clever she is. Well, not long ago she was sitting on her throne. That's by no means as much fun as people suppose, so she fell to humming an old tune, and the refrain of it happened to run:

Why, oh, why, shouldn't I get married?

"'Why, that's an idea!' said she. And she made up her mind to marry as soon as she could find the sort of husband who could give a good answer when anyone spoke to him, instead of one of those fellows who merely stand around looking impressive, for that is so tiresome. She had the drums drubbed to call together all her ladies-in-waiting, and when they heard what she had in mind, they were delighted.

"'Oh, we like that!' they said. 'We were just thinking the very same thing.'

"Believe me," said the crow, "every word I tell you is true. I have a tame ladylove who has the run of the palace, and I had the whole story straight from her." Of course his ladylove was also a crow, for birds of a feather will flock together.

"The newspapers immediately came out with a border of hearts and the initials of the princess, and you could read an announcement that any presentable young man might go to the palace and talk with her. The one who spoke best and who seemed most at home in the palace would be chosen by the princess as her husband.

"Yes, yes," said the crow, "believe me, that's as true as it is that here I sit. Men flocked to the palace, and there was much crowding and crushing, but on neither the first nor the second day was anyone chosen. Out in the street, they were all glib talkers, but after they entered the palace gate where the guardsmen were stationed in their silver-braided uniforms, and after they climbed up the staircase lined with footmen in gold-embroidered livery, they arrived in the brilliantly lighted reception halls without a word to say. And when they stood in front of the princess on her throne, the best they could do was to echo the last word of her remarks, and she didn't care to hear it repeated.

"It was just as if everyone in the throne room had his stomach filled with snuff and had fallen asleep; for as soon as they were back in the streets, there was no stopping their talk.

"The line of candidates extended all the way from the town gates to the palace. I saw them myself," said the crow. "They got hungry and they got thirsty, but from the palace they got nothing—not even a glass of lukewarm water. To be sure, some of the clever candidates had brought sandwiches with them, but they did not share them with their neighbors. Each man thought, 'Just let him look hungry, then the princess won't take him!'"

"But Kay, little Kay," Gerda interrupted, "when did he come? Was he among those people?"

"Give me time, give me time! We are just coming to him. On the third day, a little person, with neither horse nor carriage, strode boldly up to the palace. His eyes sparkled the way yours do, and he had handsome long hair, but his clothes were poor."

"Oh, that was Kay!" Gerda said, and clapped her hands in glee. "Now I've found him."

"He had a little knapsack on his back," the crow told her.

"No, that must have been his sled," said Gerda. "He was carrying it when he went away."

"Maybe so," the crow said. "I didn't look at it carefully. But my tame ladylove told me that when he went through the palace gates and saw the guardsmen in silver, and on the staircase the footmen in gold, he wasn't at all taken aback. He nodded and he said to them:

"'It must be very tiresome to stand on the stairs. I'd rather go inside.'

"The halls were brilliantly lighted. Ministers of state and privy councillors were walking about barefooted, carrying golden trays in front of them. It was enough to make anyone feel solemn, and his boots creaked dreadfully, but he wasn't a bit afraid."

"That certainly must have been Kay," said Gerda. "I know he was wearing new boots. I heard them creaking in Grandmother's room."

"Oh, they creaked all right," said the crow. "But it was little enough he cared as he walked straight to the princess, who was sitting on a pearl as big as a spinning wheel. All the ladies-in-waiting with their attendants and their attendants' attendants, and all the lords-in-waiting with their gentlemen and their gentlemen's men, each of whom had his page with him, were standing there, and the nearer they stood to the door, the more arrogant they looked. The gentlemen's men's pages, who always wore slippers, were almost too arrogant to look, as they stood at the threshold."

"That must have been terrible!" little Gerda exclaimed. "And yet Kay won the princess?"

"If I weren't a crow, I would have married her myself, for all that I'm engaged to another. They say he spoke as well as I do when I speak my crow language. Or so my tame ladylove tells me. He was dashing and handsome, and he was not there to court the princess but to hear her wisdom. This he liked, and she liked him."

"Of course it was Kay," said Gerda. "He was so clever that he could do mental arithmetic even with fractions. Oh, please take me to the palace."

"That's easy enough to say," said the crow, "but how can we manage it? I'll talk it over with my tame ladylove, and she may be able to suggest something, but I must warn you that a little girl like you will never be admitted."

"Oh, yes, I shall," said Gerda. "When Kay hears about me, he will come out to fetch me at once."

"Wait for me beside that stile," the crow said. He wagged his head, and off he flew. Darkness had set in when he got back.

"Caw, caw!" he said. "My ladylove sends you her best wishes, and here's a little loaf of bread for you. She found it in the kitchen, where they have all the bread they need, and you must be hungry. You simply can't get into the palace with those bare feet. The guardsmen in silver and the footmen in gold would never permit it. But don't you cry. We'll find a way. My ladylove knows of a little back staircase that leads up to the bedroom, and she knows where they keep the key to it."

Then they went into the garden and down the wide promenade where the leaves were falling one by one. When one by one the lights went out in the palace, the crow led little Gerda to the back door, which stood ajar.

Oh, how her heart did beat with fear and longing. It was just as if she were about to do something wrong, yet she only wanted to make sure that this really was little Kay. Yes, truly it must be Kay, she thought, as she recalled his sparkling eyes and his long hair. She remembered exactly how he looked when he used to smile at her as they sat under the roses at home. Wouldn't he be glad to see her! Wouldn't he be interested in hearing how far she had come to find him and how sad they had all been when he didn't come home. She was so frightened, and yet so happy.

Now they were on the stairway. A little lamp was burning on a cupboard, and there stood the tame crow, cocking her head to look at Gerda, who made the curtsy that her grandmother had taught her.

"My fiancé has told me many charming things about you, dear young lady," she said. "Your biography, as one might say, is very touching. Kindly take the lamp, and I shall lead the way. We shall keep straight ahead, where we aren't apt to run into anyone."

"It seems to me that someone is on the stairs behind us," said Gerda. Things brushed past, and from the shadows on the wall, they seemed to be horses with spindly legs and waving manes. And there were shadows of huntsmen, ladies and gentlemen, on horseback.

"Those are only dreams," said the crow. "They come to take the thoughts of their royal masters off to the chase. That's just as well, for it will give you a good opportunity to see them while they sleep. But I trust that when you rise to high position and power, you will show a grateful heart."

"Tut tut! You've no need to say that," said the forest crow.

Now they entered the first room. It was hung with rose-colored satin, embroidered with flowers. The dream shadows were flitting by so fast that Gerda could not see the lords and ladies. Hall after magnificent hall quite bewildered her, until at last they reached the royal bedroom.

The ceiling of it was like the top of a huge palm tree, with leaves of glass, costly glass. In the middle of the room two beds hung from a massive stem of gold. Each of them looked like a lily. One bed was white, and there lay the princess. The other was red, and there Gerda hoped to find little Kay. She bent one of the scarlet petals and saw the nape of a little brown neck. Surely this must be Kay. She called his name aloud and held the lamp near him. The dreams on horseback pranced into the room again, as he awoke—and turned his head—and it was not little Kay at all.

The prince only resembled Kay about the neck, but he was young and handsome. The princess peeked out of her lily-white bed and asked what had happened. Little Gerda cried and told them all about herself and about all that the crows had done for her.

"Poor little thing," the prince and the princess said. They praised the crows and said they weren't the least bit angry with them, but not to do it again. Furthermore, they should have a reward.

"Would you rather fly about without any responsibilities," said the princess, "or would you care to be appointed court crows for life, with rights to all scraps from the kitchen?"

Both the crows bowed low and begged for permanent office, for they thought of their future and said it was better to provide for their "old age," as they called it.

The prince got up and let Gerda have his bed. It was the utmost that he could do. She clasped her little hands and thought, "How nice the people and the birds are." She closed her eyes, fell peacefully asleep, and all the dreams came flying back again. They looked like angels, and they drew a little sled on which Kay sat. He nodded to her, but this was only in a dream, so it all disappeared when she woke up.

The next day, she was dressed from her head to her heels in silk and in velvet, too. They asked her to stay at the palace and have a nice time there, but instead, she begged them to let her have a little carriage, a little horse, and a pair of little boots, so that she could drive out into the wide world to find Kay.

They gave her a pair of boots and also a muff. They dressed her as nicely as could be, and when she was ready to go, there at the gate stood a brand new carriage of pure gold. On it the coat of arms of the prince and the princess glistened like a star.

The coachman, the footman, and the postilions—for postilions there were—all wore golden crowns. The prince and the princess themselves helped her into the carriage and wished her Godspeed. The forest crow, who was now a married man, accompanied her for the first three miles, and sat beside Gerda, for it upset him to ride backward. The other crow stood beside the gate and waved her wings. She did not accompany them because she was suffering from a headache, brought on by eating too much in her new position. Inside, the carriage was lined with sugared cookies, and the seats were filled with fruit and gingerbread.

"Fare you well, fare you well," called the prince and princess. Little Gerda cried and the crow cried too, for the first few miles. Then the crow said good-bye, and that was the saddest leave-taking of all. He flew up into a tree and waved his big black wings as long as he could see the carriage, which flashed as brightly as the sun.

FIFTH STORY
THE LITTLE ROBBER GIRL

The carriage rolled on into a dark forest. Like a blazing torch, it shone in the eyes of some robbers. They could not bear it.

"That's gold! That's gold!" they cried. They sprang forward, seized the horses, killed the little postilions, the coachman, and the footman, and dragged little Gerda out of the carriage.

"How plump and how tender she looks, just as if she'd been fattened on nuts!" cried the old robber woman, who had a long bristly beard and long eyebrows that hung down over her eyes. "She looks like a fat little lamb. What a dainty dish she will be!" As she said this, she drew out her knife, a dreadful, flashing thing.

"Ouch!" the old woman howled. At just that moment, her own little daughter had bitten her ear. The little girl, whom she carried on her back, was a wild and reckless creature. "You beasty brat!" her mother exclaimed, but it kept her from using that knife on Gerda.

"She shall play with me," said the little robber girl. "She must give me her muff and that pretty dress she wears, and sleep with me in my bed." And she again gave her mother such a bite that the woman hopped and whirled around in pain. All the robbers laughed, and shouted:

"See how she dances with her brat."

"I want to ride in the carriage," the little robber girl said, and ride she did, for she was too spoiled and headstrong for words. She and Gerda climbed into the carriage, and away they drove over stumps and stones, into the depths of the forest. The little robber girl was no taller than Gerda, but she was stronger and much broader in the shoulders. Her skin was brown and her eyes coal-black—almost sad in their expression. She put her arms around Gerda, and said:

"They shan't kill you unless I get angry with you. I think you must be a princess."

"No, I'm not," said little Gerda. And she told about all that had happened to her, and how much she cared for little Kay. The robber girl looked at her gravely, gave a little nod of approval, and told her:

"Even if I should get angry with you, they shan't kill you, because I'll do it myself!" Then she dried Gerda's eyes, and stuck her own hands into Gerda's soft, warm muff.

The carriage stopped at last, in the courtyard of a robber's castle. The walls of it were cracked from bottom to top. Crows and ravens flew out of every loophole, and bulldogs huge enough to devour a man jumped high in the air. But they did not bark, for that was forbidden.

In the middle of the stone-paved, smoky old hall, a big fire was burning. The smoke of it drifted up to the ceiling, where it had to find its own way out. Soup was boiling in a big caldron, and hares and rabbits were roasting on the spit.

"Tonight, you shall sleep with me and all my little animals," the robber girl said. After they had something to eat and drink, they went over to a corner that was strewn with rugs and straw. On sticks and perches around the bedding roosted nearly a hundred pigeons. They seemed to be asleep, but they stirred just a little when the two little girls came near them.

"They are all mine," said the little robber girl. She seized the one that was nearest to her, held it by the legs, and shook it until it flapped its wings. "Kiss it," she cried, and thrust the bird in Gerda's face. "Those two are the wild rascals," she said, pointing high up the wall to a hole barred with wooden sticks. "Rascals of the woods they are, and they would fly away in a minute if they were not locked up."

"And here is my old sweetheart, Bae," she said, pulling at the horns of a reindeer that was tethered by a shiny copper ring around his neck. "We have to keep a sharp eye on him, or he would run away from us, too. Every single night, I tickle his neck with my knife blade, for he is afraid of that." From a hole in the wall, she pulled a long knife and rubbed it against the reindeer's neck. After the poor animal had kicked up its heels, the robber girl laughed and pulled Gerda down into the bed with her.

"Are you going to keep that knife in bed with you?" Gerda asked, and looked at it, a little frightened.

"I always sleep with my knife," the little robber girl said. "You never can tell what may happen. But let's hear again what you told me before about little Kay, and about why you are wandering through the wide world."

Gerda told the story all over again, while the wild pigeons cooed in their cage overhead and the tame pigeons slept. The little robber girl clasped one arm around Gerda's neck, gripped her knife in the other hand, fell asleep, and snored so that one could hear her. But Gerda could not close her eyes at all. She did not know whether she was to live or whether she was to die. The robbers sat around their fire, singing and drinking, and the old robber woman was turning somersaults. It was a terrible sight for a little girl to see.

Then the wood pigeons said, "Coo, coo. We have seen little Kay. A white hen was carrying his sled, and Kay sat in the Snow Queen's sleigh. They swooped low, over the trees where we lay in our nest. The Snow Queen blew upon us, and all the young pigeons died except us. Coo, coo."

"What is that you are saying up there?" cried Gerda. "Where was the Snow Queen going? Do you know anything about it?"

"She was probably bound for Lapland, where they always have snow and ice. Why don't you ask the reindeer who is tethered beside you?"

"Yes, there is ice and snow in that glorious land," the reindeer told her. "You can prance about freely across those great, glittering fields. The Snow Queen has her summer tent there, but her stronghold is a castle up nearer the North Pole, on the island called Spitzbergen."

"Oh, Kay, little Kay," Gerda sighed.

"Lie still," said the robber girl, "or I'll stick my knife in your stomach."

In the morning, Gerda told her all that the wood pigeons had said. The little robber girl looked quite thoughtful. She nodded her head and exclaimed, "Leave it to me! Leave it to me.

"Do you know where Lapland is?" she asked the reindeer.

"Who knows it better than I?" the reindeer said, and his eyes sparkled. "There I was born, there I was bred, and there I kicked my heels in freedom, across the fields of snow."

"Listen!" the robber girl said to Gerda. "As you see, all the men are away. Mother is still here, and here she'll stay, but before the morning is over, she will drink out of that big bottle, and then she usually dozes off for a nap. As soon as that happens, I will do you a good turn."

She jumped out of bed, rushed over and threw her arms around her mother's neck, pulled at her beard bristles, and said, "Good morning, my dear nanny goat." Her mother thumped her nose until it was red and blue, but all that was done out of pure love.

As soon as the mother had tipped up the bottle and dozed off to sleep, the little robber girl ran to the reindeer and said, "I have a good notion to keep you here and tickle you with my sharp knife. You are so funny when I do, but never mind that. I'll untie your rope and help you find your way outside, so that you can run back to Lapland. But you must put your best leg forward and carry this little girl to the Snow Queen's palace, where her playmate is. I suppose you heard what she told me, for she spoke so loud, and you were eavesdropping."

The reindeer was so happy that he bounded into the air. The robber girl hoisted little Gerda on his back, carefully tied her in place, and even gave her a little pillow to sit on. "I don't do things half way," she said. "Here, take back your fur boots, for it's going to be bitter cold. I'll keep your muff, because it's such a pretty one. But your fingers mustn't get cold. Here are my mother's big mittens, which will come right up to your elbows. Pull them on. Now your hands look just like my ugly mother's big paws."

And Gerda shed happy tears.

"I don't care to see you blubbering," said the little robber girl. "You ought to look pleased now. Here, take these two loaves of bread and this ham along, so that you won't starve."

When these provisions were tied on the back of the reindeer, the little robber girl opened the door and called in all the big dogs. Then she cut the tether with her knife and said to the reindeer, "Now run, but see that you take good care of the little girl."

Gerda waved her big mittens to the little robber girl and said good-bye. Then the reindeer bounded away, over stumps and stones, straight through the great forest, over swamps and across the plains, as fast as he could run. The wolves howled, the ravens shrieked, and *ker-shew, ker-shew!* The red streaks of light ripped through the heavens, with a noise that sounded like sneezing.

"Those are my old northern lights," said the reindeer. "See how they flash." And on he ran, faster than ever, by night and day. The loaves were eaten and the whole ham was eaten—and there they were in Lapland.

SIXTH STORY
THE LAPP WOMAN AND THE FINN WOMAN

They stopped in front of the little hut, and a makeshift dwelling it was. The roof of it almost touched the ground, and the doorway was so low that the family had to lie on their stomachs to crawl in it or out of it. No one was at home except an old Lapp woman, who was cooking fish over a whale-oil lamp. The reindeer told her Gerda's whole story, but first he told his own, which he thought was much more important. Besides, Gerda was so cold that she couldn't say a thing.

"Oh, you poor creatures," the Lapp woman said, "you've still got such a long way to go. Why, you will have to travel hundreds of miles into the Finmark. For it's there that the Snow Queen is taking a country vacation and burning her blue fireworks every evening. I'll jot down a message on a dried codfish, for I haven't any paper. I want you to take it to the Finn woman who lives up there. She will be able to tell you more about it than I can."

As soon as Gerda had thawed out and had had something to eat and drink, the Lapp woman wrote a few words on a dried codfish, told Gerda to take good care of it, and tied her again on the back of the reindeer. Off he ran, and all night long, the skies crackled and swished as the most beautiful northern lights flashed over their heads. At last, they came to the Finmark and knocked at the Finn woman's chimney, for she hadn't a sign of a door. It was so hot inside that the Finn woman went about almost naked. She was small and terribly dowdy, but she at once helped little Gerda off with her mittens and boots and loosened her clothes. Otherwise the heat would have wilted her. Then the woman put a piece of ice on the reindeer's head and read what was written on the codfish. She read it three times and when she knew it by heart, she put the fish into the kettle of soup, for they might as well eat it. She never wasted anything.

The reindeer told her his own story first, and then little Gerda's. The Finn woman winked a knowing eye, but she didn't say anything.

"You are such a wise woman," said the reindeer, "I know that you can tie all the winds of the world together with a bit of cotton thread. If the sailor unties one knot, he gets a favorable wind. If he unties another, he gets a stiff gale, while if he unties the third and fourth knots, such a tempest rages that it flattens the trees in the forest. Won't you give this little girl something to drink that will make her as strong as twelve men, so that she may overpower the Snow Queen?"

"Twelve strong men," the Finn woman sniffed. "Much good that would be."

She went to the shelf, took down a big rolled-up skin, and unrolled it. On this skin strange characters were written, and the Finn woman read them until the sweat rolled down her forehead.

The reindeer again begged her to help Gerda, and little Gerda looked at her with such tearful, imploring eyes that the woman began winking again. She took the reindeer aside in a corner, and while she was putting another piece of ice on his head, she whispered to him:

"Little Kay is indeed with the Snow Queen, and everything there just suits him fine. He thinks it is the best place in all the world, but that's because he has a splinter of glass in his heart and a small piece of it in his eye. Unless these can be gotten out, he will never be human again, and the Snow Queen will hold him in her power."

"But can't you fix little Gerda something to drink that will give her more power than all those things?"

"No power that I could give could be as great as that which she already has. Don't you see how men and beasts are compelled to serve her, and how far she has come in the wide world since she started out in her naked feet? We mustn't tell her about this power. Strength lies in her heart, because she is such a sweet, innocent child. If she herself cannot reach the Snow Queen and rid little Kay of those pieces of glass, then there's no help that we can give her. The Snow Queen's garden lies about eight miles from here. You may carry the little girl there and put her down by the big bush covered with red berries that grows on the snow. Then don't you stand there gossiping, but hurry to get back here."

The Finn woman lifted little Gerda onto the reindeer, and he galloped away as fast as he could.

"Oh!" cried Gerda, "I forgot my boots and I forgot my mittens." She soon felt the need of them in that knifelike cold, but the reindeer did not dare to stop. He galloped on until they came to the big bush that was covered with red berries. Here he set Gerda down and kissed her on the mouth, while big shining tears ran down his face. Then he ran back as fast as he could. Little Gerda stood there without boots and without mittens, right in the middle of icy Finmark.

She ran as fast as ever she could. A whole regiment of snowflakes swirled toward her, but they did not fall from the sky, for there was not a cloud up there, and the northern lights were ablaze.

The flakes skirmished along the ground, and the nearer they came, the larger they grew. Gerda remembered how large and strange they had appeared when she looked at them under the magnifying glass. But here, they were much more monstrous and terrifying. They were alive. They were the Snow Queen's advance guard, and their shapes were most strange. Some looked like ugly, overgrown porcupines. Some were like a knot of snakes that stuck out their heads in every direction, and others were like fat little bears with every hair abristle. All of them were glistening white, for all were living snowflakes.

It was so cold that as little Gerda said the Lord's Prayer, she could see her breath freezing in front of her mouth, like a cloud of smoke. It grew thicker and thicker, and took the shape of little angels that grew bigger and bigger the moment they touched the ground. All of them had helmets on their heads, and they carried shields and lances in their hands. Rank upon rank, they increased, and when Gerda had finished her prayer, she was surrounded by a legion of angels. They struck the dread snowflakes with their lances and shivered them into a thousand pieces. Little Gerda walked on, unmolested and cheerful. The angels rubbed her hands and feet to make them warmer, and she trotted briskly along to the Snow Queen's palace.

But now, let us see how little Kay was getting on. Little Gerda was furthest from his mind, and he hadn't the slightest idea that she was just outside the palace.

SEVENTH STORY
WHAT HAPPENED IN THE SNOW QUEEN'S PALACE
AND WHAT CAME OF IT

The walls of the palace were driven snow. The windows and doors were the knife-edged wind. There were more than a hundred halls, shaped as the snow had drifted, and the largest of these extended for many a mile. All were lighted by the flare of the northern lights. All of the halls were so immense and so empty, so brilliant and so glacial! There was never a touch of gaiety in them; never so much as a little dance for the polar bears, at which the storm blast could have served for music, and the polar bears could have waddled about on their hind legs to show off their best manners. There was never a little party with such games as blind-bear's buff or hide the paw-kerchief for the cubs, nor even a little afternoon coffee over which the white fox vixens could gossip. Empty, vast, and frigid were the Snow Queen's halls. The northern lights flared with such regularity that you could time exactly when they would be at the highest and lowest. In the middle of the vast, empty hall of snow was a frozen lake. It was cracked into a thousand pieces, but each piece was shaped so exactly like the others that it seemed a work of wonderful craftsmanship. The Snow Queen sat in the exact center of it when she was at home, and she spoke of this as sitting on her "Mirror of Reason." She said this mirror was the only one of its kind, and the best thing in all the world.

Little Kay was blue, yes, almost black, with the cold. But he did not feel it, because the Snow Queen had kissed away his icy tremblings, and his heart itself had almost turned to ice.

He was shifting some sharp, flat pieces of ice to and fro, trying to fit them into every possible pattern, for he wanted to make something with them. It was like the Chinese puzzle game that we play at home, juggling little flat pieces of wood about into special designs. Kay was cleverly arranging his pieces in the game of ice-cold reason. To him, the patterns were highly remarkable and of the utmost importance, for the chip of glass in his eye made him see them that way. He arranged his pieces to spell out many words; but he could never find the way to make the one word he was so eager to form. The word was "Eternity." The Snow Queen had said to him, "If you can puzzle that out, you shall be your own master, and I'll give you the whole world and a new pair of skates." But he could not puzzle it out.

"Now I am going to make a flying trip to the warm countries," the Snow Queen told him. "I want to go and take a look into the black caldrons." She meant the volcanos of Etna and Vesuvius. "I must whiten them up a bit. They need it, and it will be such a relief after all those yellow lemons and purple grapes."

And away she flew. Kay sat all alone in that endless, empty, frigid hall and puzzled over the pieces of ice until he almost cracked his skull. He sat so stiff and still that one might have thought he was frozen to death.

All of a sudden, little Gerda walked up to the palace through the great gate that was a knife-edged wind. But Gerda said her evening prayer. The wind was lulled to rest, and the little girl came on into the vast, cold, empty hall. Then she saw Kay. She recognized him at once, and ran to throw her arms around him. She held him close and cried, "Kay, dearest little Kay! I've found you at last!"

But he sat still, and stiff, and cold. Gerda shed hot tears, and when they fell upon him, they went straight to his heart. They melted the lump of ice and burned away the splinter of glass in it. He looked up at her, and she sang:

> *Where roses bloom so sweetly in the vale,*
> *There shall you find the Christ Child, without fail.*

Kay burst into tears. He cried so freely that the little piece of glass in his eye was washed right out. "Gerda!" He knew her, and cried out in his happiness, "My sweet little Gerda, where have you been so long? And where have I been?" He looked around him and said, "How cold it is here! How enormous and empty!" He held fast to Gerda, who laughed until happy tears rolled down her cheeks. Their bliss was so heavenly that even the bits of glass danced about them and shared in their happiness. When the pieces grew tired, they dropped into a pattern that made the very word that the Snow Queen had told Kay he must find before he became his own master and received the whole world and a new pair of skates.

Gerda kissed his cheeks, and they turned pink again. She kissed his eyes, and they sparkled like hers. She kissed his hands and feet, and he became strong and well. The Snow Queen might come home now whenever she pleased, for there stood the order for Kay's release, written in letters of shining ice.

Hand in hand, Kay and Gerda strolled out of that enormous palace. They talked about Grandmother, and about the roses on their roof. Wherever they went, the wind died down and the sun shone out. When they came to the bush that was covered with red berries, the reindeer was waiting to meet them. He had brought along a young reindeer mate who had warm milk for the children to drink, and who kissed them on the mouth. Then these reindeer carried Gerda and Kay first to the Finn woman. They warmed themselves in her hot room, and when she had given them directions for their journey home, they rode on to the Lapp woman. She had made them new clothes, and was ready to take them along in her sleigh.

Side by side, the reindeer ran with them to the limits of the north country, where the first green buds were to be seen. Here they said good-bye to the two reindeer and to the Lapp woman. "Farewell," they all said.

Now the first little birds began to chirp, and there were green buds all around them in the forest. Through the woods came riding a young girl on a magnificent horse that Gerda recognized, for it had once been harnessed to the golden carriage. The girl wore a bright red cap on her head and a pair of pistols in her belt. She was the little robber girl, who had grown tired of staying at home and who was setting out on a journey to the north country. If she didn't like it there, why, the world was wide, and there were many other places where she could go. She recognized Gerda at once, and Gerda knew her too. It was a happy meeting.

"You're a fine one for gadding about," she told little Kay. "I'd just like to know whether you deserve to have someone running to the end of the Earth for your sake."

But Gerda patted her cheek and asked her about the prince and the princess.

"They are traveling in foreign lands," the girl told her.

"And the crow?"

"Oh, the crow is dead," she answered. "His tame ladylove is now a widow, and she wears a bit of black wool wrapped around her leg. She takes great pity on herself, but that's all stuff and nonsense. Now tell me what has happened to you and how you caught up with Kay."

Gerda and Kay told her their story.

"*Snip snap snurre, basse lurre,*" said the robber girl. "So everything came out all right." She shook them by the hand and promised that if ever she passed through their town, she would come to see them. And then she rode away.

Kay and Gerda held each other by the hand. And as they walked along, they had wonderful spring weather. The land was green and strewn with flowers, church bells rang, and they saw the high steeples of a big town. It was the one where they used to live. They walked straight to Grandmother's house, and up the stairs, and into the room, where everything was just as it was when they left it. And the clock said *tick-tock,* and its hands were telling the time. But the moment they came in the door, they noticed one change. They were grown-up now.

The roses on the roof looked in at the open window, and their two little stools were still out there. Kay and Gerda sat down on them, and held each other by the hand. Both of them had forgotten the icy, empty splendor of the Snow Queen's palace as completely as if it were some bad dream. Grandmother sat in God's good sunshine, reading to them from her Bible:

"Except ye become as little children, ye shall not enter into the Kingdom of Heaven."

Kay and Gerda looked into each other's eyes, and at last they understood the meaning of their old hymn:

> Where roses bloom so sweetly in the vale,
> There shall you find the Christ Child, without fail.

And they sat there, grown-up, but children—still children at heart. And it was summer—warm, glorious summer.

THE ELDER-TREE MOTHER (1844)

Once there was a little boy who went out and got his feet wet and caught cold. Nobody could understand how it had happened, because the weather was very dry.

His mother undressed him, put him to bed, and had the tea urn brought in to make him a good cup of elder tea, for that keeps one warm.

At the same time, there came in the door the funny old man who lived all alone on the top floor of the house. He had no wife or children of his own, but he was very fond of all children, and knew so many wonderful stories and tales that it was fun to listen to him.

"Now drink your tea," said the little boy's mother, "and then perhaps there'll be a story for you."

"Yes," nodded the old man kindly, "if I could only think of a new one! But tell me, how did the young man get his feet wet?" he asked.

"Yes, where did he?" said the mother. "Nobody can imagine how."

"Will you tell me a fairy tale?" the little boy asked.

"Yes, but I must know something first. Can you tell me as nearly as possible how deep the gutter is in the little street where you go to school?"

"Just halfway up to my top boots," answered the little boy. "That is," he added, "if I stand in the deep hole."

"That's how we got our feet wet," said the old man. "Now, I certainly ought to tell you a story, but I don't know any more."

"You can make one up right away," the little boy said. "Mother says that everything you look at can be turned into a story, and that you can make a tale of everything you touch."

"Yes, but those stories and tales aren't worth anything. No, the real ones come all by themselves. They come knocking at my forehead and say, 'Here I am!'"

"Will there be a knock soon?" the little boy asked. His mother laughed as she put the elder tea in the pot and poured hot water over it.

"Tell me a story! Tell me a story!"

"I would if a story would come of itself. But that kind of thing is very particular. It only comes when it feels like it. Wait!" he said suddenly. "There is one! Look! There's one in the teapot now!"

And the little boy looked toward the teapot. He saw the lid slowly raise itself and fresh white elder flowers come forth from it. They shot long branches even out of the spout and spread them abroad in all directions, and they grew bigger and bigger until there was the most glorious elder bush—really, a big tree! The branches even stretched to the little boy's bed and thrust the curtains aside—how fragrant its blossoms were! And right in the middle of the tree there sat a sweet-looking old woman in a very strange dress. It was green, as green as the leaves of the elder tree, and it was trimmed with big white elder blossoms; at first, one couldn't tell if this dress was cloth or the living green and flowers of the tree.

"What is this woman's name?" asked the little boy.

"Well, the Romans and the Greeks," said the old man, "used to call her a 'Dryad,' but we don't understand that word. Out in New Town, where the sailors live, they have a better name for her. There she is called 'Elder Tree Mother,' and you must pay attention to her; listen to her, and look at that glorious elder tree!"

"A great blooming tree just exactly like that stands in New Town. It grows in the corner of a poor little yard; and under that tree, two old people sat one afternoon in the bright sunshine. It was an old sailor and his very old wife; they had great-grandchildren and were soon going to celebrate their golden wedding anniversary, but they weren't quite sure of the date. The Elder Tree Mother sat in the tree and looked pleased, just as she does here. 'I know perfectly well when the golden wedding day is,' she said, but they didn't hear it—they were talking of olden times.

"'Yes, do you remember,' said the old sailor, 'when we were very little, how we ran about and played together? It was in this very same yard where we are now, and we put little twigs in the earth and made a garden.'

"'Yes,' replied the old woman. 'That I remember well; one of those twigs was an elder, and when we watered them, it took root and shot out other green twigs, and now it has become this great tree under which we old people are sitting.'

"'That's right,' said he. 'And there used to be a tub of water over in the corner, where I sailed the little boat I had made myself. How it could sail! But pretty soon I had to sail in a different way myself.'

"'Yes, but first we went to school and learned something,' said she, 'and then we were confirmed. Remember how we both cried? But in the afternoon we went together to the Round Tower, and looked out at the wide world over Copenhagen and across the water. And then we went to Frederiksborg, where the king and queen were sailing on the canal in their beautiful boat!'

"'But I had to sail in a different way myself,' said the old man. 'And for many years, far away on long voyages.'

"'I often cried over you,' she said. 'I thought you were dead and gone, and lying down in the deep ocean, with the waves rocking you. Many a night I got up to see if the weathercock was turning. Yes, it turned all right, but still you didn't come.

"'I remember so clearly how the rain poured down one day. The garbage man came to the place where I worked. I took the dustbin down to him and stood in the doorway. What dreadful weather it was! And while I was standing there, the postman came up and gave me a letter—a letter from you! My, how that letter had traveled about! I tore it open quickly and read it, and I was so happy that I laughed and cried at the same time. You had written me that you were in the warm countries where the coffee beans grow. What a wonderful country that must be! You wrote me all about it, and I read it there by the dustbin with the rain streaming down. Then somebody came and clasped me around the waist!'

"'And you gave him a good smack on the ear,' he said. 'One that could be heard!'

"'Yes, but I didn't know it was you! You had come just as quickly as your letter. And you were so handsome—but you still are, of course! I remember you had a long yellow silk handkerchief in your pocket and a shiny hat on your head. You looked so well! But what awful weather it was, and how the street looked!'

"'Then we were married, remember?' said he. 'And then out first little boy came, and then Marie, and Niels, and Peter, and Hans Christian?'

"'Yes, indeed,' she nodded. 'And how they've grown up to be useful people. Everyone likes them.'

"'And their children have had little ones in their turn,' said the old sailor. 'Yes, they are our great-grandchildren; they're fine children. If I'm not mistaken, it was at this very time of the year that we were married.'

"'Yes. This is the very day of your golden wedding anniversary!' said the Elder Tree Mother, stretching her head down between the two old people. They thought it was the neighbor woman nodding to them, and they looked at each other and took hold of each other's hands.

"Then the children and the grandchildren came; they knew very well that this was the old people's golden wedding day—they had already brought their congratulations that morning. But the old people had forgotten that, although they remembered everything that had happened years and years ago.

"And the elder tree smelled so fragrant, and the setting sun shone right in the faces of the old people so that their cheeks looked quite red and young; and the littlest of the grandchildren danced around them, and cried out happily that there was to be a grand feast that evening with hot potatoes! And the Elder Mother nodded in the tree and called out 'Hurrah!' with all the others."

"But that wasn't a fairy tale," said the little boy, who had been listening to the story.

"Yes, it was, if you could understand it," said the old man. "But let's ask the Elder Mother about it."

"No," the Elder Mother said, "that wasn't a story. But now the story is coming. For the strangest fairy tales come from real life; otherwise, my beautiful elder bush couldn't have sprouted out of the teapot."

Then she took the little boy out of his bed and laid him against her breast, and the blossoming elder branches wound close around them so that it was as if they were sitting in a thick arbor, and this arbor flew with them through the air! How very wonderful it was! Elder Mother all at once changed into a pretty young girl, but the dress was still green with the white blossoms trimming it, such as the Elder Tree Mother had worn. In her bosom, she had a real elder blossom, and a wreath of the flowers was about her yellow, curly hair. Her eyes were so large and so blue, and, oh, she was so beautiful to look at! She and the little boy were of the same age now, and they kissed each other and were happy together.

Hand in hand they went out of the arbor, and now they were standing in the beautiful flower garden at home. Near the green lawn, the walking stick of the little boy's father was tied to a post, and for the little children, there was magical life in that stick. When they seated themselves upon it, the polished head turned into the head of a noble neighing horse with a long, black flowing mane. Four slender, strong legs shot out; the animal was strong and spirited; and they galloped around the grass plot!

"Now we'll ride for miles!" said the boy. "We'll ride to that nobleman's estate, where we went last year!"

So they rode round and round the grass plot, and the little girl, who you must remember was the Elder Mother, kept crying, "Now we're in the country! See the farmhouse, with the big baking oven standing out of the wall like an enormous egg beside the road! The elder tree is spreading its branches over the house, and the cock is walking around, scratching for his hens. Look at him strut! Now we're near the church; it's high up on the hill, among the great oak trees. See how one of them is half dead! Now we're at the forge; the fire is burning, and the half-clad men are beating with the hammers. Look at the sparks flying all around! We're off! We're off to the nobleman's beautiful estate!"

They were only riding around and around the grass plot, yet the little boy seemed to see everything that the little maiden mentioned as she sat behind him on the magic stick. Then they played on the sidewalk, and marked out a little garden in the earth; and she took the elder flower out of her hair and planted it, and it grew just like the ones that the old people had planted in New Town, when they were little, as I have already told you. They walked hand in hand, the same way the old people did in their childhood, but they didn't go to the Round Tower or the Frederiksborg Garden. No, the little girl took the little boy around the waist, and they flew through the country of Denmark.

And it was spring and it became summer, and it was autumn and it became winter, and there were thousands of pictures in the boy's mind and heart, as the little girl sang to him, "You will never forget this."

And throughout their whole journey, the elder tree smelled sweet and fragrant. He noticed the roses and fresh beech trees, but the elder tree smelled the sweetest, for its flowers hung over the little girl's heart, and he often leaned his head against them as they flew onward.

"How beautiful it is here in the spring!" said the little girl.

Then they were standing in the new-leaved beech wood, where the fragrant green woodruff lay spread at their feet and the pale pink anemones looked glorious against the vivid green.

"Oh, if it could only always be spring in the fragrant beech woods of Denmark!"

"How beautiful it is here in the summer!" she said.

Then they were passing by knightly castles of olden times, where the red walls and pointed gables were mirrored in the canals and where swans swam about and peered down the shady old avenues. In the fields, the corn waved, as if it were a sea;

in the ditches were yellow and red flowers, and wild hops and blooming convolvulus were growing in the hedges. In the evening, the moon rose round and full, and the haystacks in the meadows smelled fragrant.

"One can never forget it. How beautiful it is here in the autumn!" said the little girl.

And the sky seemed twice as high and twice as blue as ever before, and the forest was brilliant with gorgeous tints of red and yellow and green. The hunting dog raced across the meadows; long lines of wild ducks flew shrieking above the ancient grave mounds, on which the bramble twined over the old stones. The ocean was a dark blue, dotted with white-sailed ships. In the barns, old women and girls and children picked hops into a large tub, while the young people sang ballads, and the older ones told fairy tales of elves and goblins. It could not be finer anywhere.

"How beautiful it is here in the winter!" said the little girl.

Then all the trees were covered with hoarfrost, until they looked like trees of white coral. The snow crackled crisply underfoot, as if you were always walking in new boots, and one shooting star after another fell from the sky. In the room, the Christmas tree was lighted, and there were presents and happiness. In the farmer's cottage, the violin sounded and games were played for apple dumplings, and even the poorest child cried, "It's beautiful in winter!"

Yes, it was beautiful, and the little girl showed the boy everything.

The blossoming elder tree always smelled fragrant, and the red flag with the white cross always waved, the same flag under which the old seaman in New Town had sailed away.

And the boy became a young man, and he too had to sail far away to warmer countries, where the coffee grows. But when they departed, the little girl took an elder blossom from her breast and gave it to him as a keepsake. He laid it away in his hymnal, and whenever he took out the book in foreign countries, it always came open by itself at the spot where lay the flower of memory. And the more he looked at the flower, the fresher and sweeter it became, so that he seemed to be breathing the air of the Danish forests, and he could plainly see the little girl looking up at him with her clear blue eyes from between the petals of the flower, and could hear her whispering, "How beautiful it is here in spring, summer, autumn, and winter!" And hundreds of pictures drifted through his thoughts.

Many years passed by, and now he was an old man, sitting with his old wife under a blossoming tree; they were holding hands, just as Great-grandfather and Great-grandmother out in New Town had done before. And like them, they talked of olden times and of their golden wedding anniversary.

Now the little maiden with the blue eyes and the elder blossoms in her hair sat up in the tree and nodded to them both and said, "Today is your golden wedding anniversary!" Then from her hair she took two flowers, and kissed them so that they gleamed, first like silver, and then like gold. And when she laid them on the heads of the old couple, each became a golden crown. There they both sat, a king and a queen, under the fragrant tree that looked just exactly like an elder bush, and he told his old wife the story of the Elder Tree Mother, just as it had been told to him when he was a little boy. They both thought that much of the story resembled their own, and that part they liked best.

"Yes, that's the way it is," said the little girl in the tree. "Some people call me Elder Tree Mother, and some call me the Dryad, but my real name is Memory. It is I who sit up in the tree that grows on and on, and I can remember and I can tell stories. Let me see if you still have your flower."

Then the old man opened his hymnal, and there lay the elder blossom, as fresh as if it had just been placed there. Then Memory nodded, and the two old people with the golden crowns sat in the red twilight, and they closed their eyes gently and—and—and that was the end of the story.

The little boy was lying in his bed, and he didn't know whether he had been dreaming or had heard a story. The teapot was standing beside him on the table, but there was no elder bush growing out of it now, and the old man was just going out of the door, which he did.

"That was so beautiful!" said the little boy. "Mother, I have been in the warm countries!"

"Yes, I believe you have," said his mother. "If one drinks two full cups of hot elder tea, one usually gets into the warm countries!" Then she tucked the bedclothes carefully around him so that he wouldn't take cold. "You've had a nice nap while I was arguing with him as to whether that was a story or a fairy tale."

"And where is the Elder Tree Mother?" asked the boy.

"She's in the teapot," said the mother. "And there she can remain!"

THE ELF MOUND (1845)

Several lizards darted briskly in and out of the cracks of a hollow tree. They understood each other perfectly, for they all spoke lizard language.

"My! How it rumbles and buzzes in the old elf mound," said one lizard. "It rumbles and bumbles so that I haven't had a wink of sleep for the past two nights. I might as well have a toothache, for that also prevents me from sleeping."

"There's something afoot," said another lizard. "Until the cock crowed for dawn, they had the mound propped up on four red poles to give it a thoroughgoing airing. And the elf maidens are learning to stamp out some new dances. Something is surely afoot."

"Yes, I was just talking about it with an earthworm I know," said a third lizard. "He came straight from the mound, where he has been nosing around night and day. He overheard a good deal. For he can't see, poor thing, but he knows his way around and makes an uncommonly good eavesdropper. They expect company in the elf mound, distinguished visitors, but the earthworm wouldn't say who they are. Or maybe he didn't know. All the will-o'-the-wisps have been told to parade with their torches, as they are called, and all of the flat silver and gold plate with which the hill is well stocked is being polished and put out in the moonlight."

"Who *can* the visitors be?" the lizards all wanted to know. "What in the world is going on? Listen to the hustle! Listen to the bustle!"

Just at that moment, the elf mound opened, and an old-maid elf minced out of it. The woman had no back, but otherwise she was quite properly dressed, with her amber jewelry in the shape of a heart. She kept house for her distant cousin, the old king of the elves, and she was very spry in the legs. *Trip, trot,* away she went. How she hurried and scurried off to see the night raven down in the marsh.

"You are hereby invited to the elf mound, this very night," she told him. "But may I ask you to do us a great favor first? Please deliver the other invitations for us. As you have no place of your own where you can entertain, you must make yourself generally useful. We shall have some very distinguished visitors—goblins of rank, let me tell you. So the old elf king wants to make the best impression he can."

"Who is being invited?" the night raven asked.

"Oh, everybody may come to the big ball—even ordinary mortals if they talk in their sleep or can do anything else that we can do. But at the banquet, the company must be strictly select. Only the very best people are invited to it. I've threshed that out thoroughly with the elf king, because I insist we should not even invite ghosts. First of all, we must invite the old man of the sea and his daughters. I suppose they won't like to venture out on dry land, but we can at least give them a comfortable wet stone to sit on, or something better, and I don't think they'll refuse this time. Then we must have all the old trolls of the first degree, with tails. We must ask the old man of the stream, and the brownies, and I believe we should ask the grave-pig, the bone-horse, and the church dwarf, though they live under churches and, properly speaking, belong to the clergy, who are not our sort of people at all. Still, that is their vocation, and they are closely related to us, and often come to call."

"Cra!" said the night raven as he flew to summon the guests.

On their mound, the elf maidens had already begun to dance, and they danced with long scarves made of mist and moonlight. To those who care for scarf dancing, it was most attractive.

The large central hall of the elf mound had been especially prepared for this great night. The floor was washed with moonlight, and the walls were polished with witch wax, which made them glisten like the petals of a tulip. The kitchen abounded with skewered frogs, snakeskins stuffed with small children's fingers, fungus salad made of mushroom seed, wet mouse noses, and hemlock. There was beer of the swamp witch's brewing and sparkling salpeter champagne from graveyard vaults. All very substantial! Rusty nails and ground glass from church windows were among the delicacies.

The old elf king had his gold crown polished with powdered slate pencil. It was a prize pupil's slate pencil, and a prize pupil's slate pencil is not so easy for an elf king to obtain. The curtains in the bedroom were freshly starched with snail slime. Oh, how they did hustle and bustle.

"Now we shall burn horsehair and pig's bristles for incense, and my duty is done," said the housekeeper.

"Dear papa elf," said his youngest daughter, "will you tell me now who the guests of honor are to be?"

"Well," he said, "it's high time that I told you. I have made a match for two of my daughters. Two of you must be ready to get married without fail. The venerable goblin chief of Norway, who lives in the old Dovrefjeld Mountains, and possesses a gold mine and crag castles and strongholds much better than people can imagine, is on his way here with his two sons, and each son wants a wife. The old goblin chief is a real Norwegian, honest and true, straightforward and merry. I have known him for many a year, and we drank to our lasting friendship when he came here to get his wife. She's dead now, but she was the daughter of the king of the chalk cliffs at Möen. I used to tell him that he got married on the chalk, as if he had bought his wife on credit. How I look forward to seeing him again. His sons, they say, are rough and rowdy. But they'll improve when they get older. It's up to you to polish them."

"How soon will they come?" one of his daughters asked.

"That depends on the wind and the weather," he said. "They are thrifty travelers— they will come by ship when they have a chance. I wanted them to travel overland by way of Sweden, but the old gentleman wouldn't hear of it. He doesn't keep up with the times, and I don't like that."

Just then, two will-o'-the-wisps came tumbling in, one faster than the other, and therefore he got there first. Both of them were shouting:

"Here they come, here they come!"

"Hand me my crown. Let me stand where the moon shines most brightly," the elf king said.

His daughters lifted their long scarves and curtsied low to the ground.

There came the venerable goblin chief from the Dovrefjeld, crowned with sparkling icicles and polished fir cones, muffled in his bearskin coat, and wearing his sledge boots. His sons dressed quite differently, with their throats uncovered and without suspenders. They were husky fellows.

"Is that a hill?" The smallest of the two brothers pointed his finger at the elf mound. In Norway, we would call it a hole."

"Son!" cried the old goblin chief. "Hills come up, and holes go down. Have you no eyes in your head?"

The only thing that amazed them, they said, was the language that people spoke here. Why, they could actually understand it.

"Don't make such tomfools of yourselves," said their father, "or people will think you ignoramuses."

They entered the elf mound, where all the best people were gathered, though they assembled so fast that they seemed swept in by the wind. Nevertheless, the arrangements were delightfully convenient for everybody. The Old Man of the Sea and his daughters were seated at the table in large casks of water, which they said made them feel right at home. Everybody had good table manners except the two young Norwegian goblins, who put their feet on the table as if anything they did were all right.

"Take your feet out of your plates," said the old goblin chief, and they obeyed, but not right away. They had brought fir cones in their pockets to tickle the ladies sitting next to them. To make themselves comfortable, they pulled off their boots and gave them to the ladies to hold. However, their father, the old Dovre goblin, conducted himself quite differently. He talked well of the proud crags of Norway, and of waterfalls rushing down in a cloud of spray, with a roar like thunder and the sound of an organ. He told how the salmon leap up through the waterfall when they hear the nixies twang away on golden harps. He described bracing winter nights on which the sleigh bells chime and boys with flaming torches skim over polished ice so clear that one can see the startled fish swish away underfoot. Yes, he had a way of talking that made you both hear and see the sawmill sawing and the boys and girls as they sang and danced the Norwegian Hallinge dance. Hurrah! In the wink of an eye, the goblin chief gave the old maid elf such a kiss that it smacked, though they weren't in the least related.

Then the elf maidens must do their dances, first the ordinary dances and then the dance where they stamped their feet, which set them off to perfection. Then they did a really complicated one called, "A Dance to End Dancing." Keep us and save us, how light they were on their feet. Whose leg was whose? Which were arms and which were legs? They whipped through the air like shavings at a planing mill. The girls twirled so fast that it made the bone-horse's head spin, and he staggered away from the table.

"Whir-r-r," said the goblin chief. "The girls are lively enough, but what can they do besides dancing like mad, spinning like tops, and making the bone-horse dizzy?"

"I'll show you what they can do," the elf king boasted. He called his youngest daughter. She was as thin and fair as moonlight. She was the most dainty of all the sisters, and when she took a white wand in her mouth, it vanished away. That was what she could do. But the goblin chief said this was an art he wouldn't like his wife to possess, and he didn't think his sons would either.

The second daughter could walk alongside herself as if she had a shadow, which is something that trolls don't possess. The third was a very different sort of girl. She had studied brewing with the swamp witch, and she was a good hand at seasoning alder stumps with glowworms.

"Now this one would make a good housewife," said the goblin chief, winking instead of drinking to her, for he wanted to keep his wits clear.

The fourth daughter played upon a tall, golden harp. As soon as she fingered the first string, everyone kicked up his left leg, for all of the troll tribe are left-legged. And as soon as she fingered the second string, everyone had to do just as she said.

"What a dangerous woman," said the goblin chief. His sons were very bored, and they strolled out of the elf mound as their father asked, "What can the next daughter do?"

"I have learned to like Norwegians," she told him. "I'll never marry unless I can live in Norway."

But her youngest sister whispered in the old goblin's ear, "She only says that because of the old Norwegian saying that even though the world should fall, the rocks of Norway would still stand tall; that's why she wants to go there. She's afraid to die."

"Hee, hee," said the goblin, "somebody let the cat out of the bag. Now for the seventh and last."

"The sixth comes before the seventh," said the elf king, who was more careful with his arithmetic. But the sixth daughter would not come forward.

"I can only tell the truth," she said, "so nobody likes me, and I have enough to do to sew upon my shroud."

Now came the seventh and last daughter. What could she do? She could tell tales, as many as ever she pleased.

"Here are my five fingers," said the old goblin. "Tell me a story for each of them."

The elf maiden took him by the wrist, and he chuckled till he almost choked. When she came to the fourth finger, which wore a gold ring just as if it knew that weddings were in the air, the old goblin said, "Hold it fast, for I give you my hand. I'll take you to wife myself."

The elf maiden said that the stories of Guldbrand, the fourth finger, and of little Peter Playfellow, the fifth finger, remained to be told.

"Ah, we shall save those until winter," said the old goblin chief. "Then you shall tell me about the fir tree and the birch, of the ghost presents and of the creaking frost. You will be our teller of tales, for none of us has the knack of it. We shall sit in my great stone castle where the pine logs blaze, and we shall drink our mead out of the golden horns of old Norwegian kings. I have two that water goblin washed into my hand. And while we sit there side by side, Sir Garbo will come to call, and he will sing you the mountain maidens' song. How merry we then shall be! The salmon will leap in the waterfall and beat against our stone walls, but he'll never get in to where we sit so snug. Ah, I tell you, it is good to live in glorious old Norway. But where have the boys gone?"

Where indeed? They were charging through the fields, blowing out the will-o'-the-wisps who were coming so modestly for their torchlight parade.

"Is that a way to behave?" said the goblin chief. "I have chosen a stepmother for you, so come and choose wives of your own."

But his sons said they preferred speeches and drink to matrimony. So they made speeches, and they drank healths, and turned their glasses bottom side up to show how empty they were. Then they took off their coats, and lay down on the table to sleep, for they had no manners. But the old goblin danced around the room with his young bride, and changed his boots for hers, which was much more fashionable than merely exchanging rings.

"There's that cock crowing!" the old maid housekeeper of the elves warned them. "Now we must close the shutters to keep the sun from burning us."

So they closed the mound. But outside, the lizards darted around the hollow tree, and one said to the other: "Oh, how we liked that old Norwegian goblin chief!"

"I preferred his jolly sons," said the earthworm, but then he had no eyes in his head, poor thing.

THE RED SHOES (1845)

There was once a little girl, very nice and very pretty, but so poor that she had to go barefooted all summer. And in winter, she had to wear thick wooden shoes that chafed her ankles until they were red, oh, as red as could be.

In the middle of the village lived Old Mother Shoemaker. She took some old scraps of red cloth and did her best to make them into a little pair of shoes. They were a bit clumsy, but well meant, for she intended to give them to the little girl. Karen was the little girl's name.

The first time Karen wore her new red shoes was on the very day when her mother was buried. Of course, they were not right for mourning, but they were all she had, so she put them on and walked barelegged after the plain wicker coffin.

Just then a large old carriage came by, with a large old lady inside it. She looked at the little girl and took pity upon her. And she went to the parson and said: "Give the little girl to me, and I shall take good care of her."

Karen was sure that this happened because she wore red shoes, but the old lady said the shoes were hideous, and ordered them burned. Karen was given proper new clothes. She was taught to read, and she was taught to sew. People said she was pretty, but her mirror told her, "You are more than pretty. You are beautiful."

It happened that the queen came traveling through the country with her little daughter, who was a princess. Karen went with all the people who flocked to see them at the castle. The little princess, all dressed in white, came to the window to let them admire her. She didn't wear a train, and she didn't wear a gold crown, but she did wear a pair of splendid red morocco shoes. Of course, they were much nicer than the ones Old Mother Shoemaker had put together for little Karen, but there's nothing in the world like a pair of red shoes!

When Karen was old enough to be confirmed, new clothes were made for her, and she was to have new shoes. They went to the house of a thriving shoemaker to have him take the measure of her little feet. In his shop were big glass cases, filled with the prettiest shoes and the shiniest boots. They looked most attractive, but, as the old lady did not see very well, they did not attract her. Among the shoes there was a pair of red leather ones that were just like those the princess had worn. How perfect they were! The shoemaker said he had made them for the daughter of a count, but that they did not quite fit her.

"They must be patent leather to shine so," said the old lady.

"Yes, indeed they shine," said Karen. As the shoes fitted Karen, the old lady bought them, but she had no idea they were red. If she had known that, she would never have let Karen wear them to confirmation, which is just what Karen did.

Every eye was turned toward her feet. When she walked up the aisle to the chancel of the church, it seemed to her as if even those portraits of bygone ministers and their wives, in starched ruffs and long black gowns—even they fixed their eyes upon her red shoes. She could think of nothing else, even when the pastor laid his hands upon her head and spoke of her holy baptism, and her covenant with God, and her duty as a Christian. The solemn organ rolled, the children sang sweetly, and the old choir leader sang too, but Karen thought of nothing except her red shoes.

Before the afternoon was over, the old lady had heard from everyone in the parish that the shoes were red. She told Karen it was naughty to wear red shoes to church. Highly improper! In the future, she was always to wear black shoes to church, even though they were her old ones.

Next Sunday, there was holy communion. Karen looked at her black shoes. She looked at her red ones. She kept looking at her red ones until she put them on.

It was a fair, sunny day. Karen and the old lady took the path through the cornfield, where it was rather dusty. At the church door, they met an old soldier, who stood with a crutch and wore a long, curious beard. It was more reddish than white. In fact, it was quite red. He bowed down to the ground and asked the old lady if he might dust her shoes. Karen put out her little foot too.

"Oh, what beautiful shoes for dancing," the soldier said. "Never come off when you dance," he told the shoes, as he tapped the sole of each of them with his hand.

The old lady gave the soldier a penny, and went on into the church with Karen. All the people there stared at Karen's red shoes, and all the portraits stared, too. When Karen knelt at the altar rail, and even when the chalice came to her lips, she could think only of her red shoes. It was as if they kept floating around in the chalice, and she forgot to sing the psalm. She forgot to say the Lord's Prayer.

Then church was over, and the old lady got into her carriage. Karen was lifting her foot to step in after her when the old soldier said, "Oh, what beautiful shoes for dancing!"

Karen couldn't resist taking a few dancing steps, and once she began, her feet kept on dancing. It was as if the shoes controlled her. She danced round the corner of the church—she simply could not help it. The coachman had to run after her, catch her, and lift her into the carriage. But even there, her feet went on dancing so that she gave the good old lady a terrible kicking. Only when she took her shoes off did her legs quiet down. When they got home the shoes were put away in a cupboard, but Karen would still go and look at them.

Shortly afterward the old lady was taken ill, and it was said she could not recover. She required constant care and faithful nursing, and for this she depended on Karen. But a great ball was being given in the town, and Karen was invited. She looked at the old lady, who could not live in any case. She looked at the red shoes, for she thought there was no harm in looking. She put them on, for she thought there was no harm in that either. But then she went to the ball and began dancing. When she tried to turn to the right, the shoes turned to the left. When she wanted to dance up the ballroom, her shoes danced down. They danced down the stairs, into the street, and out through the gate of the town. Dance she did, and dance she must, straight into the dark woods.

Suddenly, something shone through the trees, and she thought it was the Moon, but it turned out to be the red-bearded soldier. He nodded and said, "Oh, what beautiful shoes for dancing."

She was terribly frightened, and tried to take off her shoes. She tore off her stockings, but the shoes had grown fast to her feet. And dance she did, for dance she must, over fields and valleys, in the rain and in the sun, by day and night. It was most dreadful by night. She danced over an unfenced graveyard, but the dead did not join her dance. They had better things to do. She tried to sit on a pauper's grave, where the bitter fennel grew, but there was no rest or peace for her there. And when she danced toward the open doors of the church, she saw it guarded by an angel with long white robes and wings that reached from his shoulders down to the ground. His face was grave and stern, and in his hand he held a broad, shining sword.

"Dance you shall!" he told her. "Dance in your red shoes until you are pale and cold, and your flesh shrivels down to the skeleton. Dance you shall from door to door, and wherever there are children proud and vain, you must knock at the door till they hear you, and are afraid of you. Dance you shall. Dance always."

"Have mercy upon me!" screamed Karen. But she did not hear the angel answer.

Her shoes swept her out through the gate, and across the fields, along highways and byways, forever and always dancing.

One morning, she danced by a door she knew well. There was the sound of a hymn, and a coffin was carried out covered with flowers. Then she knew the old lady was dead. She was all alone in the world now, and cursed by the angel of God.

Dance she did and dance she must, through the dark night. Her shoes took her through thorn and briar that scratched her until she bled. She danced across the wastelands until she came to a lonely little house. She knew that this was where the executioner lived, and she tapped with her finger on his window pane.

"Come out!" she called. "Come out! I can't come in, for I am dancing."

The executioner said, "You don't seem to know who I am. I strike off the heads of bad people, and I feel my ax beginning to quiver."

"Don't strike off my head, for then I could not repent of my sins," said Karen. "But strike off my feet with the red shoes on them."

She confessed her sin, and the executioner struck off her feet with the red shoes on them. The shoes danced away with her little feet, over the fields into the deep forest. But he made wooden feet and a pair of crutches for her. He taught her a hymn that prisoners sing when they are sorry for what they have done. She kissed his hand that held the ax, and went back across the wasteland.

"Now I have suffered enough for those red shoes," she said. "I shall go and be seen again in the church." She hobbled to church as fast as she could, but when she got there, the red shoes danced in front of her, and she was frightened and turned back.

All week long she was sorry, and cried many bitter tears. But when Sunday came again, she said, "Now I have suffered and cried enough. I think I must be as good as many who sit in church and hold their heads high." She started out unafraid, but the moment she came to the church gate, she saw her red shoes dancing before her. More frightened than ever, she turned away, and with all her heart, she really repented.

She went to the pastor's house and begged him to give her work as a servant. She promised to work hard, and do all that she could. Wages did not matter, if only she could have a roof over her head and be with good people. The pastor's wife took pity on her, and gave her work at the parsonage. Karen was faithful and serious. She sat quietly in the evening and listened to every word when the pastor read the Bible aloud. The children were devoted to her, but when they spoke of frills and furbelows and of being as beautiful as a queen, she would shake her head.

When they went to church next Sunday, they asked her to go too, but with tears in her eyes, she looked at her crutches, and shook her head. The others went to hear the word of God, but she went to her lonely little room, which was just big enough to hold her bed and one chair. She sat with her hymnal in her hands, and as she read it with a contrite heart, she heard the organ roll. The wind carried the sound from the church to her window. Her face was wet with tears as she lifted it up, and said, "Help me, O Lord!"

Then the sun shone bright, and the white-robed angel stood before her. He was the same angel she had seen that night at the door of the church. But he no longer held a sharp sword. In his hand was a green branch, covered with roses. He touched the ceiling with it. There was a golden star where it touched, and the ceiling rose high. He touched the walls, and they opened wide. She saw the deep-toned organ. She saw the portraits of ministers and their wives. She saw the congregation sit in flower-decked pews and sing from their hymnals. Either the church had come to the poor girl in her narrow little room, or it was she who had been brought to the church. She sat in the pew with the pastor's family. When they had finished the hymn, they looked up and nodded to her.

"It was right for you to come, little Karen," they said.

"It was God's own mercy," she told them.

The organ sounded, and the children in the choir sang, softly and beautifully. Clear sunlight streamed warm through the window, right down to the pew where Karen sat. She was so filled with the light of it, and with joy and with peace, that her heart broke. Her soul traveled along the shaft of sunlight to heaven, where no one questioned her about the red shoes.

THE JUMPERS (1845)

Once upon a time, a flea, a grasshopper, and a jumping goose wanted to see which one could jump the highest, so they invited the whole world, and even a few others, to come to a festival to watch the test. They were three famous jumpers indeed, and they all met together in a big room.

"I'll give my daughter to the one who jumps the highest," said the king. "It seems so stingy to have these fellows jump for nothing."

The flea was the first to be introduced. He had such beautiful manners and bowed right and left, for he had noble blood in him, and besides, he was accustomed to move in human society, and that makes a great difference.

The grasshopper was next. He was certainly heavier than the flea, but he was equally well mannered, and wore a green uniform, which was his by right of birth. He explained that he belonged to a very ancient Egyptian family and that everyone thought a great deal of him in the country where he was then living. They had brought him in out of the fields and put him in a three-storied card house, all made of picture cards with the colored side inwards.

The doors and windows were cut out of the body of the Queen of Hearts.

"I sing so extremely well," he explained, "that sixteen native grasshoppers who have been singing since childhood and still haven't any house of cards to live in grew even thinner with jealousy than they were before when they heard about me."

So both the flea and the grasshopper had now explained who they were, and they felt sure they were quite good enough to marry the princess.

The jumping goose didn't say anything, but the company decided that meant he was thinking a great deal, and when the court dog sniffed at him, he reported that the jumping goose was certainly of good family. The old councillor, who had received three decorations to keep him quiet, declared that he knew that the jumping goose was gifted with magic power; you could tell by his back if the winter would be severe or mild, and that was more than you could say even for the man who writes the almanac.

"I'm not saying anything," the king remarked, "but I have my opinion of these things."

Now it was time for the trial. The flea jumped first, and he went so high that nobody could see him. So they all said he hadn't jumped at all, but had only been pretending. And that was a cheap thing to do.

The grasshopper only jumped half as high as the flea, but he jumped right into the king's face! And the king said it was disgusting.

The jumping goose stood still for a long time, lost in thought, and people began to wonder if he could jump at all.

"I hope he isn't sick," said the court dog, and gave him another sniff. Then suddenly, plop! The jumping goose jumped sideways right into the lap of the princess, who was sitting on a little golden stool nearby.

At once the king said, "To jump up to my daughter is the highest jump that can be made. But it takes brains to get an idea like that, and the jumping goose has shown that he does have brains. He is a pretty clever fellow."

And that's how the jumping goose won the princess.

"I don't care a bit," said the flea. "I jumped the highest. She can have that old goosebone, with his stick and his wax. In this world, real merit is very seldom rewarded. A fine physique is what people look at nowadays."

So the flea went away to fight in foreign service, and it is said that he was killed.

The grasshopper settled down in a ditch and pondered over the way of the world, and he too said, "Yes, a good physique is everything. A good physique is everything." Then he chirped his own sad little song, from which I've taken this story. The story may just possibly not be true, even if it is printed here in black and white.

THE SHEPHERDESS AND THE CHIMNEY SWEEP (1845)

Have you ever seen a very old chest, black with age and covered with outlandish carved ornaments and curling leaves? Well, in a certain parlor, there was just such a chest, handed down from some great-grandmother. Carved all up and down it ran tulips and roses—odd-looking flourishes—and from fanciful thickets, little stags stuck out their antlered heads.

Right in the middle of the chest, a whole man was carved. He made you laugh to look at him grinning away, though one couldn't call his grinning laughing. He had hind legs like a goat's, a little horn on his forehead, and a long beard. All his children called him "General Headquarters-Hindquarters-Gives-Orders-Front-and-Rear-Sergeant-Billygoat-Legs." It was a difficult name to pronounce, and not many people get to be called by it, but he must have been very important, or why should anyone have taken trouble to carve him at all?

However, there he stood, forever eyeing a delightful little china shepherdess on the tabletop under the mirror. The little shepherdess wore golden shoes and looped up her gown fetchingly with a red rose. Her hat was gold, and even her crook was gold. She was simply charming!

Close by her stood a little chimney sweep, as black as coal, but made of porcelain, too. He was as clean and tidy as anyone can be, because you see he was only an ornamental chimney sweep. If the china makers had wanted to, they could just as easily have turned him out as a prince, for he had a jaunty way of holding his ladder, and his cheeks were as pink as a girl's. That was a mistake, don't you think? He should have been dabbed with a pinch or two of soot.

He and the shepherdess stood quite close together. They had both been put on the table where they stood, and, having been placed there, they had become engaged because they suited each other exactly. Both were young, both were made of the same porcelain, and neither could stand a shock.

Near them stood another figure, three times as big as they were. It was an old Chinaman who could nod his head. He too was made of porcelain, and he said he was the little shepherdess's grandfather. But he couldn't prove it. Nevertheless, he claimed that this gave him authority over her, and when General Headquarters-Hindquarters-Gives-Orders-Front-and-Rear-Sergeant-Billygoat-Legs asked for her hand in marriage, the old Chinaman had nodded consent.

"There's a husband for you!" the old Chinaman told the shepherdess. "A husband who, I am inclined to believe, is made of mahogany. He can make you Mrs. General Headquarters-Hindquarters-Gives-Orders-Front-and-Rear-Sergeant-Billygoat-Legs. He has the whole chest full of silver, and who knows what else he's got hidden away in his secret drawers?"

"But I don't want to go and live in the dark chest," said the little shepherdess. "I have heard people say he's got eleven china wives in there already."

"Then you will make twelve," said the Chinaman. "Tonight, as soon as the old chest commences to creak, I'll marry you off to him, as sure as I'm a Chinaman." Then he nodded off to sleep. The little shepherdess cried and looked at her true love, the porcelain chimney sweep.

"Please let's run away into the big, wide world," she begged him, "for we can't stay here."

"I'll do just what you want me to," the little chimney sweep told her. "Let's run away right now. I feel sure I can support you by chimney sweeping."

"I wish we were safely down off this table," she said. "I'll never be happy until we are out in the big, wide world."

He told her not to worry, and showed her how to drop her little feet over the table edge and how to step from one gilded leaf to another down the carved leg of the table. He set up his ladder to help her, and down they came safely to the floor. But when they glanced at the old chest, they saw a great commotion. All the carved stags were craning their necks, tossing their antlers, and turning their heads. General Headquarters-Hindquarters-Gives-Orders-Front-and-Rear-Sergeant-Billygoat-Legs jumped high in the air and shouted to the old Chinaman, "They're running away! They're running away!"

This frightened them so that they jumped quickly into a drawer of the window seat. Here they found three or four decks of cards, not quite complete, and a little puppet theater, which was set up as well as it was possible to do. A play was in progress, and all the diamond queens, heart queens, club queens, and spade queens sat in front row and fanned themselves with the tulips they held in their hands. Behind them the knaves lined up, showing that they had heads both at the top and at the bottom, as face cards do have. The play was all about two people who were not allowed to marry, and it made the shepherdess cry because it was so like her own story.

"I can't bear to see any more," she said. "I must get out of this drawer at once." But when they got back to the floor and looked up at the table, they saw the old Chinaman was wide awake now. Not only his head, but his whole body rocked forward. The lower part of his body was one solid piece, you see.

"The old Chinaman's coming!" cried the little shepherdess, who was so upset that she fell down on her porcelain knees.

"I have an idea," said the chimney sweeper. "We'll hide in the potpourri vase in the corner. There we can rest upon rose petals and lavender, and when he finds us, we can throw salt in his eyes."

"It's no use," she said. "Besides, I know the potpourri vase was once the old Chainman's sweetheart, and where there used to be love, a little affection is sure to remain. No, there's nothing for us to do but to run away into the big wide world."

"Are you really so brave that you'd go into the wide world with me?" asked the chimney sweep. "Have you thought about how big it is, and that we can never come back here?"

"I have," she said.

The chimney sweep looked her straight in the face and said, "My way lies up through the chimney. Are you really so brave that you'll come with me into the stove, and crawl through the stovepipe? It will take us to the chimney. Once we get there, I'll know what to do. We shall climb so high that they'll never catch us, and at the very top, there's an opening into the big wide world."

He led her to the stove door.

"It looks very black in there," she said. But she let him lead her through the stove and through the stovepipe, where it was pitch-black night.

"Now we've come to the chimney," he said. "And see! See how the bright star shines over our heads."

A real star, high up in the heavens, shone down as if it wished to show them the way. They clambered and scuffled, for it was hard climbing and terribly steep—way, way up high! But he lifted her up, held her safe, and found the best places for her little porcelain feet. At last, they reached the top of the chimney, where they sat down. For they were so tired, and no wonder!

Overhead was the starry sky, and spread before them were all the housetops in the town. They looked out on the big wide world. The poor shepherdess had never thought it would be like that. She flung her little head against the chimney sweep and sobbed so many tears that the gilt washed off her sash.

"This is too much," she said. "I can't bear it. The wide world is too big. Oh! If I only were back on my table under the mirror. I'll never be happy until I stand there again, just as before. I followed you faithfully out into the world, and if you love me the least bit you'll take me right home."

The chimney sweep tried to persuade her that it wasn't sensible to go back. He talked to her about the old Chinaman, and of General Headquarters-Hindquarters-Gives-Orders-Front-and-Rear-Sergeant-Billygoat-Legs, but she sobbed so hard and kissed her chimney sweep so much that he had to do as she said, though he thought it was the wrong thing to do.

So back down the chimney they climbed with great difficulty, and they crawled through the wretched stovepipe into the dark stove. Here they listened behind the door to find out what was happening in the room. Everything seemed quiet, so they opened the door and—oh, what a pity! There on the floor lay the Chinaman, in three pieces. When he had come running after them, he tumbled off the table and smashed. His whole back had come off in one piece, and his head had rolled into the corner. General Headquarters-Hindquarters-Gives-Orders-Front-and-Rear-Sergeant-Billygoat-Legs was standing where he always stood, looking thoughtful.

"Oh, dear," said the little shepherdess, "poor old Grandfather is all broken up, and it's entirely our fault. I shall never live through it." She wrung her delicate hands.

"He can be patched," said the chimney sweep. "He can be riveted. Don't be so upset about him. A little glue for his back and a strong rivet in his neck, and he will be just as good as new, and just as disagreeable as he was before."

"Will he, really?" she asked, as they climbed back to their old place on the table.

"Here we are," said the chimney sweep. "Back where we started from. We could have saved ourselves a lot of trouble."

"Now if only old Grandfather were mended," said the little shepherdess. "Is mending terribly expensive?"

He was mended well enough. The family had his back glued together, and a strong rivet put through his neck. That made him as good as new, except that never again could he nod his head.

"It seems to me that you have grown haughty since your fall, though I don't see why you should be proud of it," General Headquarters-Hindquarters-Gives-Orders-Front-and-Rear-Sergeant-Billygoat-Legs complained. "Am I to have her, or am I not?"

The chimney sweep and the little shepherdess looked so pleadingly at the old Chinaman, for they were deathly afraid he would nod. But he didn't. He couldn't. And neither did he care to tell anyone that, forever and a day, he'd have to wear a rivet in his neck.

So the little porcelain people remained together. They thanked goodness for the rivet in Grandfather's neck, and they kept on loving each other until the day they broke.

HOLGER DANSKE (1845)

In Denmark, there is an old castle named Kronborg. It lies on the coast of the Öresund, where hundreds of great ships pass through every day—English, Russian, German, and many others. And they salute the old castle with their cannons—"Boom!" And the castle returns their salute with cannons—"Boom!" For that's the way cannons say "Good day" and "Many thanks." In the wintertime, no ships sail there, for then the sea is frozen over right to the Swedish coast, and it appears exactly like a regular highway.

There wave the flags of Denmark and the flags of Sweden, and Danish and Swedish people meet on the ice and say "Good day" and "Many thanks," but not with cannons; no, with a firm shake of the hand, and each one comes to buy white bread and cakes from the other—for strange food always tastes best.

But the most beautiful sight of all is old Kronborg, and in a deep, dark cellar beneath it, where no one ever goes, sleeps Holger Danske. He is clad in iron and steel and rests his head on his strange arms; his long beard hangs down over the marble table and has grown through it. He sleeps and dreams, and in his dreams, he sees all that happens here in Denmark. Every Christmas Eve, one of God's angels comes to him and tells him that what he had dreamed is true; he may sleep again, for no real peril threatens Denmark. But should real danger come, old Holger Danske will rise in his fury, and the table itself will burst as he wrenches his beard from it, and the mighty blows he strikes for Denmark will be heard throughout the world.

An old grandfather was telling his little grandson all this about Holger Danske, and the little boy knew that what his grandfather said was true. And while the old man told his tale, he sat carving a large wooden figure, intended to represent Holger Danske and to be used as the figurehead of a ship. For the old grandfather was a wood-carver. You see, a wood-carver is a man who carves the figures that are to be fastened to the front of every ship, and from which the ship is named. Here he had fastened Holger Danske, standing erect and proud with his long beard; in one hand, he held his broad battle sword, while the other rested on a shield with the arms of Denmark.

And the old man told many stories about the strange Danish men and women, until the little boy felt he must know as much about them as Holger Danske himself, who could only dream. And when the youngster went to bed, he thought so much about all he had heard that he pressed his chin hard against the quilt, until he fancied that he had a long beard that had grown through it.

The old man sat at his work until he had finished the last carving, the Danish coat of arms on the shield. Then, as he looked at his carving, he thought of all he had read and heard and of what he had told the little boy that night. He nodded and wiped his spectacles, put them on again, and said, "Well, I don't suppose Holger Danske will ever come in my day, but the little boy there in bed may see him and may help to defend Denmark when there is really need."

And the grandfather nodded again, and the more he looked at his figurehead, the better he knew that his work was good. It almost seemed to him that color came into it; the armor seemed to gleam like steel and iron; in the coat of arms, the hearts became redder, and the lions with the golden crowns on their heads were leaping.

"It's the most beautiful coat of arms in the world!" he said proudly. "The lions mean strength, and the hearts mean gentleness and love."

He looked at the uppermost lion and thought of the old King Canute, who had bound mighty England to the throne of Denmark; he looked at the second lion and thought of Valdemar, who had conquered the Wendish lands and united Denmark; he looked at the third lion and thought of Margaret, who had joined together Denmark, Sweden, and Norway. But when he looked at the red hearts, they seemed to shine even more than before; they became leaping flames of fire, and in his own thoughts, he followed each of them.

The first flame led him into a dark, narrow dungeon cell, and there he could see the prisoner, a beautiful woman—Eleonora Ulfeld, daughter of King Christian IV. The flame became a rose that blossomed on her breast and became one with the heart of that noblest and best of all Danish women. "Yes, that is indeed a heart in Denmark's arms!" said the old grandfather.

And his thoughts followed the second flame far out to sea, where cannons thundered and the ships were shrouded in smoke, and the flame like a ribbon of honor fastened itself to the breast of Hvitfeldt, who blew up himself and his ship to save the fleet.

The third flame led him to the miserable huts of Greenland, where the preacher Hans Egede labored with loving words and deeds; that flame became a star on his breast, another heart in the arms of Denmark.

And the thoughts of the old grandfather hastened on before the leaping flame, for he knew where it wanted to go. In the humble little room of the peasant woman stood Frederick VI, and wrote his name with chalk on the beam. The flame trembled on his breast and in his heart, and in the peasant's room, that kingly heart became a heart in the arms of Denmark. The old grandfather wiped a tear from his eyes, for he had known and lived for King Frederick of the silvery locks and the honest blue eyes, and he sat in silence with folded hands.

Just then his daughter-in-law came and said it was late, and that he ought to rest; besides, the supper table was spread.

"But what a beautiful figure you have made, grandfather!" she cried. "Holger Danske and our old coat of arms! But wait! It is almost as if I've seen that face before!"

"No, I'm sure you haven't," said the old grandfather. "But I've seen it, and I've tried to carve it in wood just as I remembered it. It was long ago, when the English fleet lay in front of Copenhagen, on that Danish second of April, when we proved we were all good old Danes. On board the *Denmark*, where I fought in Steen Bile's squadron, there was a man beside me—why, the bullets themselves seemed to be afraid of him! Joyfully he sang the grand old ballads as he fought and struggled, and it seemed as if he was something more than a man like me! I can remember his face still, but where he came from, or what became of him, I don't know. Nobody knows. I have often wondered if it could have been old Holger Danske himself who had swum out from the Kronborg to help us in that terrible hour. That was in my mind, and there stands his portrait!"

The great shadow of the figurehead spread up the wall and even over the ceiling, and it looked as if the real Holger Danske was standing there. As they watched it, the shadow seemed to move, but perhaps that was just because the candle flame was flickering.

Then the daughter-in-law kissed the old man and led him to the great armchair at the head of the table, and she and her husband, who was the old grandfather's son, and father to the little boy in bed, ate their supper with him. And the old grandfather told them of the Danish lions and Danish hearts, of strength and gentleness.

Then he very plainly explained to them that there is another strength beside the strength of the sword. He pointed to his bookshelf filled with old books. There stood the comedies of Holberg, which we so often read, for they are so very amusing that in them, one seems to recognize those people of bygone days. "He knew how to strike, too. For in his plays, he ridiculed the foolishness and prejudice around him as much as he dared."

The old grandfather nodded toward the mirror, where hung the calendar with a picture of the Round Tower. "Tycho Brahe was another who could use the sword, not to cut at men's flesh and bones, but to carve a plainer path among the stars of Heaven. And then there was Bertel Thorvaldsen, whose father was a wood-carver like me. We have seen him ourselves, with his silvery locks falling to his broad shoulders. His name is known throughout the world; he was a sculptor—I am only a carver. Yes, Holger Danske can appear in many shapes, so that every country in the world knows of Denmark's strength! Let's drink now to the health of Bertel Thorvaldsen!"

But the little boy in bed saw plainly the ancient Kronborg by the Öresund and the real Holger Danske who was sitting deep below, with his beard growing through the marble table, dreaming of all that happens above. Holger Danske dreamed, too, of the humble little room where the wood-carver sat at supper, and in his sleep, he nodded and said, "Aye, remember me, you people of Denmark! Remember me! In your hour of darkest need, I shall come!"

And outside Kronborg, it was bright daylight, and the wind bore the notes of the huntsman's horn from the opposite shore of the neighboring country. The ships sailed past and saluted, "Boom! Boom!" and Kronborg spoke back, "Boom! Boom!" But Holger Danske did not awaken, however loudly the cannons roared, for they were only saying "Good day" and "Many thanks." There must be a very different kind of shooting to awaken him; but he will awake, for there is still strength and courage in Holger Danske.

THE BELL (1845)

In the narrow streets of the big town, toward evening when the sun was setting and the clouds shone like gold on the chimney tops, people would hear a strange sound like that of a church bell. But they heard it only for a few moments before it was lost in the rumble of city carriages and the voices of the multitudes, for such noises are very distracting. "Now the evening bell is ringing," people used to say. "The sun is setting."

People who were outside the town, where the houses were more scattered, with little gardens or fields between them, could see the evening sky in even more splendor and hear the bell more distinctly. It was as if the tones came from some church, buried in the silent and fragrant depths of the forest, and people looked solemnly in that direction.

A long time passed, and people began to say to each other, "I wonder if there really is a church out there in the woods? That bell has a mysterious, sweet tone. Let's go out there and see what it looks like."

So the rich people drove out, and the poor people walked out, but to all of them, it seemed a very long way. When they reached a grove of willows on the outskirts of the woods, they sat down and looked up into the branches and imagined they were really in the heart of the forest. The town confectioner came out and set up his tent there, and then another confectioner came, and he hung a bell right above his tent; but the bell had no clapper and was all tarred over as a protection against the rain.

When the people went home again, they said it had all been very romantic, much more fun than a tea party. Three people even said that they had gone right through the forest to the far side and had still heard the strange sound of the bell, only then it seemed to be coming from the direction of town.

One of these even wrote a poem about the bell and compared its tones to those of a mother singing to a beloved child—no melody could be sweeter than the tones of that bell.

The emperor of the country heard about the bell and issued a solemn proclamation promising that whoever discovered the source of the lovely sounds would receive the title of "Bell Ringer to the World," even if there were not really a bell there at all.

Of course, a great many people went to the woods now to try to gain that fine title, but only one of them came back with some kind of an explanation. No one had been deep enough into the forest—neither had he, for that matter—but just the same, he said the sound was made by a very large owl in an old hollow tree, a wise owl that continually knocked its head against the trunk of the tree. He wasn't quite sure whether the sound came from the bird's head or from the hollow trunk, but still, he was appointed "Public Bell Ringer Number One," and every year, he wrote a little treatise about the remarkable old owl. No one was much the wiser for it.

Now on a certain confirmation day, the minister had preached a very beautiful and moving sermon; the children who were confirmed were deeply touched by it. It was a tremendously important day in their lives, for on this day, they were leaving childhood behind and becoming grown-up persons. Their infant souls would take wing into the bodies of adults. It was a glorious, sunny day, and after the confirmation the children walked together out of the town, and from the depths of the woods, the strange tolling of the bell came with a mysterious clear sweetness.

At once, all the children decided to go into the woods and find the bell. All except three, that is to say. The first of these three just had to go home and try on a new ball dress for that forthcoming ball was the very reason she had been confirmed at this time; otherwise, she would have had to wait until next year's ceremony. The second was a poor boy who had borrowed his confirmation coat and boots from the landlord's son and had to give them back by a certain hour. And the third said he never went to a strange place without his parents; he had always been a dutiful child and would continue to be good, even though he was confirmed now. The others made fun of him for this, which was very wrong of them indeed.

So these three dropped out while the others started off into the woods. The sun shone, the birds sang, and the children sang, too, walking along hand in hand. They had not yet received any responsibilities or high position in life—all were equal in the eyes of God on that confirmation day.

But soon two of the smallest grew tired and returned to town; two other little girls sat down to make wreaths and so did not go any farther. The rest went on until they reached the willows where the confectioner had his tent, and then they said, "Well, here we are! You see, the bell doesn't really exist at all; it's just something people imagine!"

And then suddenly, the sound of the bell came from the depths of the woods, so sweet and solemn that four or five of the young people decided to follow it still farther. The underbrush was so thick and close that their advance was most difficult. Woodruff and anemone grew almost too high; convolvuluses and blackberry brambles hung in long garlands from tree to tree, where the nightingale sang and the sunbeams played through the leaves. It was so lovely and peaceful, but it was a bad place for the girls, because they would get their dresses torn on the brambles.

There were large boulders overgrown with many-colored mosses, and a fresh spring bubbled forth among them with a strange little gurgling sound. "Cluck, cluck," it said.

"I wonder if that can be the bell," one of the children thought, lying down to listen to it. "I'd better look into this." So he remained there, and the others went on without him.

They came to a little hut, all made of branches and tree bark. Its roof was covered with roses, and over it a wild apple tree was bending as if it would shower its blessings down on the little house. The long sprays of the apple tree clustered around the gable, and on that there hung a little bell!

Could that be the one they had heard? Yes, they all—except for one boy—agreed it must be. This one boy said it was much too small and delicate to be heard so far away, and besides, its tones were very different from those that moved human hearts so strangely. The boy who spoke was a king's son, so the other children said, "Of course he thinks he knows a lot more than anybody else."

So the king's son went on alone, and as he proceeded deeper into the woods, his heart was filled more and more with the solitude of the forest. He could still hear the little bell that had satisfied the others, and when the wind was from the right direction, he could even hear the voices of the people around the confectioner's tent, singing while they were having their tea.

But above all rose the peeling of that mysterious bell. Now it sounded as if an organ were being played with it, and the tones came from the left-hand side, where the heart is.

Suddenly there was a rustling in the bushes, and a little boy stood before the king's son. He was wearing wooden shoes and such a short jacket that the sleeves did not cover his long wrists. They knew each other at once, for this was the poor boy who had had to go back to return the coat and boots to the landlord's son. This done, he had changed again into his shabby clothes and wooden shoes and come into the woods, for the bell sounded so loudly and so deeply that he had to follow its call.

"Then let's go on together," suggested the king's son.

But the poor boy in his wooden shoes was very shy, pulled at his short sleeves, and said he was afraid he could not walk as fast as the king's son; besides, he was sure the sound of the bell came from the right, because that side looked much more beautiful.

"Then I guess we can't go together," said the king's son, nodding his head to the poor boy, who went in the direction he thought best, which took him into the thickest and darkest part of the forest. The thorns tore his shabby clothes and scratched his face, hands, and feet until they bled.

The king's son received some scratches too, but the sun shone on his path. And he is the one we will follow, for he was a bright young lad.

"I will and must find that bell," he said, "even if I have to go to the end of the world!"

High in the trees above him, ugly monkeys sat and grinned and showed their teeth. "Let's throw things at him!" they said to each other. "Let's thrash him, 'cause he's the son of a king."

But he went on unwearied, and went farther and farther into the woods, where the most wonderful flowers were growing. There were lilies white as stars, with blood-red stamens; there were light-blue tulips that gleamed in the breeze, and apple trees with their fruit shining like big soap bubbles. Imagine how those trees sparkled in the sunlight! Around the beautiful rolling green meadows where the deer played grew massive oaks and beeches; and wherever one of the trees had a crack in the bark, mosses and long tendrils were growing out of it. In some of the meadows were quiet lakes, where beautiful white swans swam and beat the air gently with their wings. The king's son often stopped to listen, for the tones of the bell sometimes seemed to come from the depths of these lakes; then again, he felt sure that the notes were coming from farther away in the forest.

Slowly the sun set, and the clouds turned a fiery red; a stillness, a deep stillness, settled over the forest. The boy fell on his knees, sang his evening hymn, and said to himself, "I'll never find what I'm seeking now. The sun is setting, and the night is coming—the dark night. But perhaps I can catch one more glimpse of the round red sun before it disappears below the horizon. I'll climb up on those rocks; they rise up as high as the tallest trees!" Seizing the roots and creepers, he slowly made his way up the slippery stones, where the water snakes writhed and the toads and frogs seemed to be barking at him. Yet he reached the summit just as the sun was going down. Oh, what a wonderful sight!

The sea, the great, the beautiful sea, rolling its long waves against the shore, lay stretched out before him, and the sun stood like a large shining altar, where ocean and heaven met; the whole world seemed to melt together in glowing colors. The forest sang, the sea sang, and the heart of the boy sang, too. Nature was a vast, holy church, where the trees and drifting clouds were the pillars; flowers and grass made the velvet carpet, and Heaven itself was the great dome. Up there, the red colors faded as the sun sank into the ocean, but then millions of stars sprang out, like millions of diamond lamps, and the king's son spread out his arms in joy toward the heavens, the sun, and the forest.

At that moment, from the right-hand path, there appeared the poor boy with the short sleeves and the wooden shoes. He had come there as quickly and by following his own path. Joyfully they ran toward each other, and held each other by the hand in the great tabernacle of Nature and Poetry, while above them sounded the invisible, holy bell. The blessed spirits floated around them and lifted up their voices in a joyful hallelujah.

GRANDMOTHER (1845)

Grandmother is so very old; she has so many wrinkles, and her hair is completely white, but her eyes shine just like two stars; yes, yet they are much more beautiful; they are so gentle, so wonderful to look into. And then, she knows the most delightful stories, and she has a gown of heavy, rustling silk, with great big flowers in it. Grandmother knows a great deal, for she was alive long before father and mother—that much is certain! She has a hymnbook with heavy clasps of silver, and often reads from it. In the middle of the book is a rose, which is very flat and dry, and not nearly so lovely as the roses she has in the vase, yet she smiles at it the most sweetly of all, and the tears even come into her eyes. Why is it that Grandmother looks that way at the withered flower in the old book? Do you know? Why, every time her tears fall upon the rose, its colors become fresh again; the rose swells and fills the whole room with its perfume; the walls sink as if they were made of mist, and all about her is the green, beautiful wood, with the summer sunlight streaming through the leaves of the trees. And Grandmother—why, she's young again, a lovely girl with yellow curls and round red cheeks, pretty, graceful, fresher than any rose. But the eyes, the mild, blessed eyes, they are still Grandmother's eyes. Beside her is a man, so young, strong, and handsome; he hands her a rose, and she smiles. Grandmother cannot smile like that now. Yes, the smile is coming back now! He has gone, and with him many other thoughts and forms of the past; the handsome man has gone, and only the rose lies in the hymnbook, and Grandmother—yes, she still sits there, an old woman, glancing down at the withered rose in her book.

Now Grandmother is dead. She was sitting in her armchair, telling a long, long lovely story. "And now the story is finished," she said. "I am very tired. Let me sleep a little." And then she leaned back, breathed gently, and slept. But it became quieter and quieter, as her face became full of happiness and peace. It was as if the sunshine spread over her features; and then they said she was dead.

She was laid in the black coffin, and lay shrouded in folds of white linen, looking so beautiful, though her eyes were closed. All the wrinkles were gone, and there was a smile on her lips; her hair was so silvery and so venerable, and one wasn't at all afraid to look at the corpse, for it was sweet, dear, good Grandmother. The hymnbook was placed under her head, as she had wished, and the rose was still in the old book; and then they buried Grandmother.

They planted a rose tree on the grave beside the churchyard wall. It was full of roses, and the nightingale sang over it; and in the church, the organ pealed forth the finest psalms, psalms that were written in the book under the dead one's head. And the moon shone down on the grave, but the dead one wasn't there. Any child could venture safely, even at night, and pluck a rose there beside the churchyard wall. A dead person knows more than all we living ones know. The dead know what terror would sweep over us if the strange thing were to happen that they should return among us. The dead are better than we; and they return no more. Dust has been piled over the coffin; dust is inside it; the leaves of the hymnbook are dust; and the rose, with all its memories, is asleep. But above bloom fresh roses, the nightingale sings, the organ peals, and we think of the old grandmother with the gentle, eternally young eyes. Eyes can never die. Ours will some time behold Grandmother again, as young and beautiful as when for the first time she kissed the fresh red rose that is now dust in her grave.

THE DARNING NEEDLE (1845)

O nce upon a time, there was a darning needle who imagined she was so fine that she really was a sewing needle.

"Be careful and hold me tightly!" she warned the fingers that picked her up. "Don't drop me! If I fall on the floor, you may never find me again; that's how fine I am!"

"That's what you think!" replied the fingers, and squeezed her around the waist.

"Look, here I come with my train!" said the darning needle, and she drew a long thread behind her, but there was no knot in the thread.

The fingers aimed the needle straight at the cook's slipper, where the upper leather had burst and had to be sewed together.

"My! What vulgar work!" sniffed the darning needle. "I'll never get through! Look out! I'm breaking! I'm breaking in two." And just then, she did break. "I told you so," she said. "I'm much too delicate!"

"Well, she's no good now," thought the fingers, but they had to hold onto her all the same. For the cook dropped a little sealing wax on the end of the needle to make a head, and then she pinned her kerchief together with it in front.

"Look! Now I'm a breastpin," said the needle. "I knew perfectly well I'd be honored. If you are something, you always amount to something."

Then she laughed, but it was inwardly, because no one can ever really see a darning needle laugh. There she sat on the cook's bosom, proud as if she were in a state coach, and looked all around her.

"May I be permitted to inquire if you're made of gold?" she very politely asked a little pin near her. "You look pretty, and you have a head of your own, but it's rather small. You must be careful to grow bigger. Not everyone can have sealing wax on one end like me!"

Then the darning needle drew herself up so proudly that she fell right out of the kerchief into the sink, at the very moment the cook was rinsing it out.

"Looks now as if we are off on a journey," she said to herself. "Let's hope I don't get lost." But she really was lost down the drain.

"I'm too fine for this world," she observed calmly as she lay in the gutter outside. "But I know who I am, and that's always a satisfaction." So the darning needle was still proud, and she never lost her good humor. She watched the many strange things floating above her—chips and straws and pieces of old newspapers.

"Look at them sail!" she said to herself. "They don't know what's down below them! Here I sit! I can sting! Look at that stick go, thinking of nothing in the world but himself—a stick! And that's exactly what he is! And there's a straw floating by; look at him twist and look how he turns! You'd better not think so much about yourself up there! You'll run into the curb! There goes a newspaper. Everybody has forgotten what was written on it, but still it spreads itself out, while I sit quietly down here below. I know who I am, and I shall never forget it!"

One day, the darning needle saw something beside her that glittered splendidly in the sunbeams. It was only a bit of broken bottle, but because the darning needle was quite sure it was something valuable like a diamond, she spoke to it, introducing herself as a breastpin.

"I suppose you're a diamond?" she asked.

"Yes, something like that," was the reply.

Then, since each thought the other was very important, they began talking about the world and how conceited everyone was.

"I used to live in a lady's case," said the darning needle. "And this lady was a cook. On each hand, she had five fingers, and you never saw anything so conceited as those five fingers! And yet they were only there so that they could hold me, take me out of my case, and put me back into it."

"Did they shine?" asked the bit of bottle glass.

"Shine? Not at all," said the darning needle. "They were arrogant. There were five brothers, all belonging to the Finger family, and they kept close together, although they were all of different lengths. The one on the outside, Thumbling, who walked out in front of the others, was short and fat and had only one joint in his back, so he could only make a single bow. But he insisted that if he were cut off a person's hand, that person could not be a soldier. Lickpot, the second one, pushed himself into sweet and sour, and pointed at the sun and the moon, and it was he who pressed on the pen when they wrote. Longman, the third, looked over the heads of the others. Guldbrand was the fourth—he always wore a golden belt around his waist. And little Peter Playfellow didn't do anything at all, and was very proud of it. They did nothing but brag all the time; that's why I went down the sink."

"And now we just sit here and glitter," said the bit of broken bottle. But just then, a flood of water came rushing down the gutter so that it overflowed and swept the bottle glass away.

"See now! He's been promoted," remarked the darning needle, "but I'm still here. I'm too fine for that sort of thing. But that's my pride, and that is very commendable!" So she sat up straight, lost in many big thoughts. "I almost think I was born a sunbeam, I'm so fine; besides, the sunbeams always seem to be trying to get to me, under the water. I'm so fine that even my mother can't find me. If I had my old eye, the one that broke off, I think I might cry about that. But no! I think I wouldn't cry anyway; it's not at all refined to cry."

One day, some street boys were grubbing in the gutter, looking for coins and things of that sort. It was filthy work, but they were having a wonderful time.

"Ouch!" one cried as he pricked himself on the darning needle. "You're a pretty sharp fellow!"

"I'm not a fellow; I'm a young lady," replied the darning needle. But of course, they couldn't hear her.

Her sealing wax had come off, and she had turned black; but black always makes you look more slender, and she was sure she was even finer than before.

"Look!" cried the boys. "Here comes an eggshell sailing along," And they stuck the darning needle fast into the shell.

"White walls, and I am black myself!" cried the darning needle. "That's very becoming! People can really see me now! I only hope I'm not seasick; that would surely break me!" But she wasn't seasick, and she did not break. "It's a very good protection against seasickness to have a steel stomach and to remember that one is a little finer than ordinary human beings. Oh, yes! I'm all right. The finer you are, the more you can bear."

"Crack!" went the eggshell at that moment, for a heavily loaded wagon ran over it.

"Goodness, I'm being crushed!" cried the darning needle. "I'm going to get really seasick now! I'm breaking! I'm breaking!" But she didn't break, though the wagon went over her; she lay at full length along the cobblestones, and there we'll leave her.

THE LITTLE MATCH GIRL (1845)

It was so terribly cold. Snow was falling, and it was almost dark. Evening came on, the last evening of the year. In the cold and gloom, a poor little girl, bareheaded and barefoot, was walking through the streets. Of course, when she had left her house she'd had slippers on, but what good had they been? They were very big slippers, way too big for her, for they belonged to her mother. The little girl had lost them running across the road, where two carriages had rattled by terribly fast. One slipper she'd not been able to find again, and a boy had run off with the other, saying he could use it very well as a cradle someday when he had children of his own. And so the little girl walked on her naked feet, which were quite red and blue with the cold. In an old apron, she carried several packages of matches, and she held a box of them in her hand. No one had bought any from her all day long, and no one had given her a cent.

Shivering with cold and hunger, she crept along, a picture of misery, poor little girl! The snowflakes fell on her long fair hair, which hung in pretty curls over her neck. In all the windows, lights were shining, and there was a wonderful smell of roast goose, for it was New Year's Eve. Yes, she thought of that!

In a corner formed by two houses, one of which projected farther out into the street than the other, she sat down and drew up her little feet under her. She was getting colder and colder, but did not dare to go home, for she had sold no matches, nor earned a single cent, and her father would surely beat her. Besides, it was cold at home, for they had nothing over them but a roof through which the wind whistled even though the biggest cracks had been stuffed with straw and rags.

Her hands were almost dead with cold. Oh, how much one little match might warm her! If she could only take one from the box and rub it against the wall and warm her hands. She drew one out. *R-r-ratch!* How it sputtered and burned! It made a warm, bright flame, like a little candle, as she held her hands over it; but it gave a strange light! It really seemed to the little girl as if she were sitting before a great iron stove with shining brass knobs and a brass cover. How wonderfully the fire burned! How comfortable it was! The youngster stretched out her feet to warm them too; then the little flame went out, the stove vanished, and she had only the remains of the burnt match in her hand.

She struck another match against the wall. It burned brightly, and when the light fell upon the wall, it became transparent like a thin veil, and she could see through it into a room. On the table a snow-white cloth was spread, and on it stood a shining dinner service. The roast goose steamed gloriously, stuffed with apples and prunes. And what was still better, the goose jumped down from the dish and waddled along the floor with a knife and fork in its breast, right over to the little girl. Then the match went out, and she could see only the thick, cold wall. She lighted another match. Then she was sitting under the most beautiful Christmas tree. It was much larger and much more beautiful than the one she had seen last Christmas through the glass door at the rich merchant's home. Thousands of candles burned on the green branches, and colored pictures like those in the printshops looked down at her. The little girl reached both her hands toward them. Then the match went out. But the Christmas lights mounted higher. She saw them now as bright stars in the sky. One of them fell down, forming a long line of fire.

"Now someone is dying," thought the little girl, for her old grandmother, the only person who had loved her and who was now dead, had told her that when a star fell down, a soul went up to God.

She rubbed another match against the wall. It became bright again, and in the glow, the old grandmother stood clear and shining, kind and lovely.

"Grandmother!" cried the child. "Oh, take me with you! I know you will disappear when the match is burned out. You will vanish like the warm stove, the wonderful roast goose, and the beautiful big Christmas tree!"

And she quickly struck the whole bundle of matches, for she wished to keep her grandmother with her. And the matches burned with such a glow that it became brighter than daylight. Grandmother had never been so grand and beautiful. She took the little girl in her arms, and both of them flew in brightness and joy above Earth, very, very high, and up there was neither cold, nor hunger, nor fear—they were with God.

But in the corner, leaning against the wall, sat the little girl with red cheeks and smiling mouth, frozen to death on the last evening of the old year. The New Year's sun rose upon a little pathetic figure. The child sat there, stiff and cold, holding the matches, of which one bundle was almost burned.

"She wanted to warm herself," the people said. No one imagined what beautiful things she had seen, and how happily she had gone with her old grandmother into the bright New Year.

A PICTURE FROM THE RAMPARTS (1846)

It is autumn, and we are standing on the ramparts of the citadel, gazing at the ships on the sound and the distant coast of Sweden rising beyond, bright in the evening sunlight. Behind us, the ramparts drop abruptly; growing below us are stately trees whose golden leaves are falling from their branches. Down below them are dark and gloomy buildings with wooden palisades, and inside, where the sentry paces back and forth, it is dreary and dark. But behind the grated windows, it is still darker and drearier, for here are confined the most hardened criminals, the convict slaves.

A sunbeam from the setting sun creeps into the bare dungeon, for the sun shines on good and evil alike. A sullen, savage prisoner glares bitterly at the cold sunbeam. Then a tiny bird flutters against his grated window, for the bird too sings for the evil as well as for the good. For a moment, it twitters softly, "Qvivit," then remains perched on the grating, fluttering its wings, plucking a feather from its breast, and ruffling up its plumage.

As the chained criminal gazes at it, a milder expression steals softly over his ugly face. A feeling that he scarcely realizes slowly enters his heart—a feeling that is somehow akin to the sunbeam that has strayed through the grating and the scent of violets that in the spring bloom so abundantly outside his prison.

Now there sound the clear, strong, and lively notes of the huntsman's horn. Away from the grating flies the startled bird; the sunbeam fades; all is again dark in the cell and in the heart of the wicked man. But for one brief moment, the sun has shone therein, and the little song of the bird has been heard.

Keep on, sweet tones of the huntsman's horn! For the evening is mild, and the sea as calm and smooth as a mirror.

A VIEW FROM VARTOU'S WINDOW (1846)

Near the green ramparts that run around Copenhagen is a large red house with many windows. These are garnished with balsams and green leaves, but the rooms within are bare and rude, for poor old folk live there. This place is called Vartou.

Look there! An old maid is leaning out of a window, plucking the withered leaves from her balsam and looking over the green rampart where happy children are playing. What is she thinking about? A whole life drama unfolds before her mind's eye.

The poor children, how gaily they play! What bright eyes and what red cheeks! But they have neither shoes nor stockings. And they are dancing and playing on the green rampart, on that very spot where, as the old story goes, the ground always sank in until an innocent child was lured with flowers and toys into its open grave, which was walled up even while the child played. Then the ramparts were firm and were soon covered with a garment of beautiful green turf. But the children have never heard that old legend, or else they would hear the poor little one still weeping beneath the mound, and the dew on the grass would seem to them the pearls of her tears.

Nor have they heard the story of that ancient king of Denmark who, when the enemy lay encamped around the city, rode past this very spot and swore he would die at his post; or how the women and men together poured boiling water down on the white-clad foemen as they crawled up through the snow on the outer side of the ramparts.

Play on, little ones!

Yes, play, little girl, for years pass quickly! Yes, the blessed years! Soon enough will come that solemn confirmation time, when the candidates walk together hand in hand, and you among them, in a white dress that your mother, with much time and labor, has fashioned from her own confirmation dress of long years ago. You will get a red shawl, too; it is far too big for you, but at least everyone can see how large it is, much too large. You think about your attire and about the kind Father above. And it is wonderful indeed to walk on the green ramparts after the services.

Then the years roll on; dark days come, but youth is ever hopeful. You have a new friend, you know not how you met. You walk together on the rampart in the early spring, when all the church bells toll out on the solemn prayer day. No violets are yet in blossom, but just outside Rosenborg Castle, you pause beside a tree decked with the first green buds of spring. There you both pause. Each year, that tree puts forth fresh green shoots; but the human heart does not, and the clouds that pass over the mind of man are heavier and darker than ever the northern skies have known.

Poor child! Your bridegroom's bridal chamber shall be a coffin, and you shall live on, an old maid; from Vartou, you shall peer through the balsam blossoms, watch the children at play, and see your own history repeated.

This is indeed the life drama that unfolds before the eyes of the old maid who looks out on the ramparts, where the sun shines, and the merry red-cheeked children sing and play in their bare feet, carefree as the birds of the air themselves.

THE OLD STREET LAMP (1847)

Have you ever heard the story of the old Street Lamp? It's really not very amusing, but you might listen to it for once.

It was such an honest lamp that had done its duty for many, many years and that was now going to be discarded. It was the last evening it hung on its post and gave light to the street beneath it. The Lamp felt like an old ballet dancer who is performing for the last time and who knows that tomorrow she will be in a cold garret. The Lamp dreaded the morrow, for then it was to appear in the town hall and be inspected by the thirty-six council members, to see whether or not it was fit for further service.

It would be decided whether in the future the Lamp was to give light for the inhabitants of some suburb, or perhaps for some manufacturing plant in the country. But it might go at once to be melted down in an iron foundry! In that case, it might become anything, but the Lamp was terribly troubled, wondering whether, in some new state, it would remember it had once been a Street Lamp. In any case, the Lamp would be separated from the watchman and his wife, whom it had come to consider part of its family. It became a Lamp at the same time that he became a watchman.

In those days, the watchman's wife was a little haughty. She would glance at the Lamp only when she passed under it in the evening—never in the daytime. However, in later years, when those three, the watchman, his wife, and the Lamp, had grown old together, the wife helped tend the Lamp, clean it, and poured oil into it. The old couple were thoroughly honest; never had they cheated the Lamp of a single drop of oil.

Now it was the Lamp's last night in the street, and tomorrow, it would go to the town hall. Those were two dark thoughts indeed, and it's no wonder the old Lamp didn't burn very brightly. But other thoughts too passed through its mind. How many events it had lighted, how much it had seen of life! Perhaps as much as the thirty-six councilmen put together. But it didn't really say anything, for it was a good, honest old Lamp, and wouldn't willingly insult anyone—least of all those in authority. It remembered so much, and now and then its flame flashed up, as if the Lamp had the feeling: "Yes, I will also be remembered."

"There was that handsome young man—my, it was a long time ago! He came with a letter, written on pink paper, so fine and gilt-edged, so prettily written by a lady's hand. Twice he read it, and kissed it, and as he looked up to me, his eyes said, 'I'm the happiest person in the world!' Yes, only he and I knew what was written in that first letter from his beloved.

"I also remember another pair of eyes—it's strange how my thoughts are rambling! Here in this street was a magnificent funeral procession, a beautiful young maiden lying in a coffin on the velvet-covered hearse. There were many wreaths and flowers, and the many torches quite overpowered my light. The sidewalk was filled with people who all followed the procession. But after the torches had passed me, and I looked around, I could see one single person, leaning against my post and weeping. I shall never forget the eyes that looked up at me then!"

Many thoughts flitted through the mind of the old Street Lamp, for tonight, it shone for the last time.

The sentry who is relieved of his post at least knows his successor, and may say a few words to him; but the Lamp did not know who would succeed it. It could have given one or two useful hints about rain and mist, how far the rays of the moon lit up the pavement, and from what direction the wind blew.

On the gutter plank stood three individuals who had introduced themselves to the Lamp, because they thought it was the Lamp that could choose its successor. One of them was a herring's head, and because it could gleam in the darkness, it was sure there would be a real saving in oil if they would put him up on the lamppost. The second was a piece of touchwood, which also glowed, and certainly better than a herring's head, at least so it said. Furthermore, it was the last descendant of an old stem, once the pride of the forest. And the third was a glowworm. Where that had come from the Lamp couldn't imagine; but there it was, and it could give light, too. But the herring's head and the touchwood swore it could do so only at certain times, and therefore could not be taken into account.

The old Lamp said that not one of them gave enough light to fulfill the duties of a street lamp; but they wouldn't believe it. And when they heard that the Lamp had nothing to do with appointing its successor, they were much relieved and said the Lamp was much too decrepit to make a choice.

Just then, the Wind came tearing around the street corner, and whistled through the air holes of the Lamp, and said to it: "What's this I hear? Are you going away tomorrow? Is this the last evening I'll see you here? Then I'm certainly going to give you a farewell present. I'll blow into your brain box so that in the future, you'll be able not only to remember everything you've seen and heard, but you'll also have such a light within you that you can see all that is read or spoken in your presence."

"Oh, that's way too much!" said the old Lamp. "Thank you very much! I only hope I'm not going to be melted down!"

"That won't happen right away," said the Wind. "Now I'll blow a memory into you; if you receive several presents like this, you'll have a happy old age."

"If only I'm not melted down!" said the Lamp. "Or can you guarantee my memory even in that case?"

"Don't be silly, old Lamp!" said the Wind, and then it blew. At that moment, the Moon came out.

"What are you going to give?" asked the Wind.

"Nothing at all," replied the Moon. "I'm on the wane, and besides, the lamps have never lighted me. On the contrary, I've often given light for the lamps." Whereupon it slid behind the clouds again, for it didn't want to be pestered.

Now a drop fell on the Lamp. It seemed to come from the roof, but it explained that the gray clouds sent it as a present—perhaps the best possible present. "I'll penetrate you so completely that you'll be able, if you wish, to turn into rust in one night, and then crumble into dust."

But the Lamp thought this was a poor present, and so did the Wind.

"Isn't someone going to give something better?" it blew as loudly as it could.

Just then, a bright shooting star fell, blazing down in a long bright stripe.

"What was that?" cried the herring's head. "Wasn't that a falling star? Why, I think it went right into the Lamp! Well, if such a highborn personage as that is trying for his position, we'd better quit and go home!" And so it did, and the others, too. But the old Lamp shone more marvelously than ever.

"That was a wonderful present!" it said. "The bright stars that I've always admired and that shine far more brightly than I ever have been able to, despite my ambition and efforts, have actually noticed me, a poor old lamp, and have sent me a present! They have granted that everything I remember and see as clearly as if it stood before me shall also be seen by those I love! And in that lies true happiness; for if we cannot share happiness with others, it can only be half enjoyed."

"Those are very honorable thoughts," said the Wind. "But for that, you need wax lights. Without a wax candle lit up in you, your rare faculties will be of no use to others. The stars didn't think of that! They think everything that shines has at least one wax light in it always. But now I am tired! I am going to lie down." And then the Wind lay down.

The next day—well, we'd better pass over the next day. But the next evening, the Lamp was resting in a big easy chair. And where? In the old watchman's house!

The old man had begged as a favor of the thirty-six councilmen that he be allowed to keep the Lamp as a reward for his long and faithful service to the city. They laughed at him when he asked for it, but finally gave it to him.

Now the Lamp lay in the big armchair close to the warm stove, and it seemed to be much larger. It almost filled the whole chair. As the old couple sat at supper, they looked fondly at the old Lamp and would gladly have given it a place at their table.

It is true that their home was only a cellar two yards below the sidewalk, and that one had to walk through a stone-paved front room to get into their room, but inside, it was very comfortable. There were strips of list on the door, and everything looked clean and neat, with curtains around the bed and over the little windows. On the window sill stood two strange flowerpots. Sailor Christian had brought them home from the East or West Indies. They were made of clay and represented two elephants, with their backs cut off. From the earth in one of the elephants there grew the most excellent chives, and that was the old people's vegetable garden; in the other was a great blooming geranium, and that was the flower garden. On the wall hung a large colored print of the Congress of Vienna; there you could see all the kings and emperors at once. There was a Bornholm clock with heavy lead weights that went "tick! tock!" It was always a little fast, but that was much better than having it a little slow, said the old people.

They were eating their supper, and the Street Lamp lay, as you know, in the big armchair close to the warm stove. It seemed to the Lamp as if the whole world were turned upside down. But when the old watchman looked at it, and talked of all they had gone through together in rain and in mist, in the short bright summer nights, and when the snow beat down and he longed for his home in the cellar, then the old Lamp felt all right again. It could see everything as clearly as if it were happening then; yes, the Wind had certainly given it a splendid light.

The old people were always active and industrious; not a single hour was wasted in idleness. Sunday afternoons, the old man would bring out some book or other—generally a volume of travels. And he would read aloud about Africa, about great jungles, with elephants running about wild, and the old woman would listen closely and peer at the clay-elephant flowerpots. "I can almost visualize it myself," she would say.

Then the Lamp would wish most particularly that a wax candle had been lighted inside it, for then, the old woman would have been able to see everything in detail, just as the Lamp saw it—the tall trees with their great branches all entwined, the naked, black men riding horseback, and big herds of elephants, crushing the reeds and bushes with their huge feet.

"What good are all my faculties if I can't get a wax light?" sighed the Lamp. "They have only oil and tallow candle here, and they won't do."

One day, the old man brought a number of wax-candle ends down into the cellar. The larger pieces were burned, and the smaller ones were used by the old woman for waxing her thread when she was sewing. There were plenty of wax candles then, but no one thought of putting a little piece into the Lamp.

"Here I am, with all my rare faculties!" said the Lamp. "I have everything within me, but I can't share it with those I love. They don't know that I can cover these white walls with the most gorgeous tapestry, or change them into noble forests, or show them anything they could wish to see! They don't know that!"

The Lamp stood neat and scoured in a corner, where it always caught the eyes of visitors, and although people considered it a piece of rubbish, the old couple didn't care; they loved the Lamp.

One day—it was the old watchman's birthday—the old woman went to the Lamp, smiling a little to herself. "I'll light it today, in his honor," she said.

Then the Lamp rattled its metal cover, for it thought, "At last they have a fine idea!" But it was only oil, and no wax candle. The Lamp burned throughout that whole evening, but now it understood at last that the gift the stars had given it, the best of all gifts, would be a lost treasure for all its life.

That night, the Lamp had a dream, for with such faculties, it is easy enough to dream. It seemed as if the old people were dead and the Lamp itself sent to the iron foundry to be melted down. It was as frightened as on that dreadful day when it appeared in the council hall to be inspected by the thirty-six council members.

But though it had the power to crumble into rust and dust at will, it did not use that faculty. It was put into a furnace, and cast into as beautiful an iron candlestick as you could wish—and it was a candlestick for wax lights! It was in the form of an angel holding a bouquet; and the wax candle was to be placed right in the middle of the bouquet.

The candlestick had a place of its own on a green writing table. And the room was very cozy, its walls lined with many books and hung with beautiful pictures—the room of a poet. Everything that the poet wrote about appeared near him. The room became thick dark forests, beautiful meadows where storks strutted, and then the deck of a ship sailing high on the foaming ocean.

"What powers are hidden in me!" said the old Lamp, as it awoke from its dream. "I could almost wish to be melted down! But no, that must not happen so long as the old people live. They love me for myself. I am their child, and they have cleaned me and given me oil. I'm as happy now as the whole Congress of Vienna, and that it something really elegant."

And from that day on, it enjoyed more inner peace, and that the modest old Lamp well deserved.

THE NEIGHBORING FAMILIES (1847)

One would certainly think that something quite unusual had happened in the duck pond to cause such a commotion, but nothing really had happened.

All the ducks that had been floating gracefully on the water, some standing on their heads, for they knew how to do that, now abruptly rushed straight onto land. Leaving their footprints in the wet clay, they shrieked so that one could hear them far away. The water was agitated. It had been smooth as a mirror, reflecting calmly and clearly everything around it; every tree and bush, the old peasant's cottage with holes in its gable, the swallow's nest, and especially the large rose tree whose branches and flowers covered the wall and hung almost into the water. All these had been painted on the clear surface like a picture, only upside down. But now that the water was troubled, everything ran together, and the whole picture was ruined. Two feathers that had fallen from the ducks were tossed to and fro, and suddenly took flight as though carried away by the wind, yet there was no wind. And soon the feathers lay still, and the water became smooth as a mirror again, reflecting as before the peasant's cottage, the swallow's nest, and the rose tree. Each rose could see itself in the pond;

all were beautiful, but they didn't know it—no one had told them so. The sun shone through their delicate petals, which were so full of fragrance, and each rose felt the way we do when we are happy in our thoughts.

"How delightful it is to live!" said each rose. "The only thing I'd wish for is to kiss the sun, because it's so warm and bright. Yes, and those lovely roses down in the water! I'd like to kiss them, too; they're just like us. And I'd like to kiss those dear baby birds in the nest down there; yes, there are also some above us. They pop out their heads and twitter so softly, and they haven't any feathers like their father and mother! We certainly have pleasant neighbors, above and below. Oh, how wonderful it is to be alive!" Now the young birds up above—yes, those down below were just their reflection in the water—were sparrows. Father and Mother Sparrow had taken possession of the empty swallow's nest the year before, and it was now their home.

"Are those the ducklings swimming down there?" asked the young sparrows when they saw the two feathers drifting on the water.

"Ask sensible questions if you ask any," said the mother.

"Don't you see that they are feathers—live clothes, such as I wear, and you will have someday? Only ours are finer! But I wish we had those feathers up here; they'd make our nest warm and comfortable. I'd like to know what frightened the ducks just now! Must have been something in the water. I'm sure it wasn't I, even if I did say 'twit!' rather loudly. Those thick-headed roses ought to know, but they don't know anything; they only look at themselves and scent the air. I'm completely sick of these neighbors of ours!"

"Listen to the sweet little birds up there!" said the roses. "They're really trying to sing; of course, they can't yet, but they will in time. What a great pleasure that must be! It's such fun to have such happy neighbors!"

Just then, there came galloping up to the pond two big horses, to be watered. A peasant boy was on one of them, and he had taken off all his clothes except his black hat, which was large and broad-brimmed. The boy whistled as if he himself were a little bird, as he rode through the deepest part of the pond. When he came to the rose tree, he broke off one of the roses and stuck it in his hat; then, considering himself properly decorated, he rode off with it. The other roses looked after their lost sister, and asked each other, "Where has she gone to?" But none of them knew.

"I think I would like to go out in the world," said one of the roses to another, "but still, it's nice here at home in our own green branches. The sun is so warm all day long, and at night the sky shines still more beautifully; then we can see through the many little holes that are in the sky."

It was the stars that they thought were holes, for the roses didn't know any better.

"We make it lively around the house!" said the mother sparrow. "People say that a swallow's nest brings luck, so they're glad to have us. But our neighbors here—a great rosebush like that against the wall only makes the place damp. I think they'll dig it up soon, and then perhaps corn will grow there. Roses are only to look at and smell, or at the most to stick in hats. Every year, I know from my mother, they fall to pieces; the peasant's wife collects them and sprinkles salt on them; they're given some French name that I can't pronounce, and don't care to, and then they're thrown into the fire to make a nice smell. You see, that's their life; they live only to please the ears and nose. Now you know!"

As it became evening and the gnats danced in the warm air, where the clouds glowed so red, the nightingale came and sang to the roses. He sang that beauty was like the sunshine of the world, and that the beautiful lives forever. But the roses imagined that the nightingale was singing about himself, and indeed that may have been true. They never would have thought that the song might have been addressed to them, but it pleased them, and they wondered if the young sparrows might also become nightingales.

"I understood quite well what that bird was singing about," said the young sparrow. "There was only one word I didn't understand. What is 'the beautiful'?"

"That's nothing," said their mother. "It's just an appearance. Up at the manor house, the doves have a house of their own, and peas and grains of corn are spread out for them every day in the yard. I've dined with them, and you shall too sometime. 'Tell me who you go with, and I'll tell you who you are.' Well, up there at the manor house, they have two birds with green necks and crests on their heads; the tail of each can spread out as though it were a large wheel and has so many colors that it hurts your eyes to look at it. Peacocks, they are called, and they are 'the beautiful.' They should be stripped of their feathers; then they wouldn't look any differently than we others. I'd have plucked them myself, if they hadn't been so large."

"I'll pluck them!" said the smallest sparrow, who had no feathers of his own yet.

In the farmhouse lived two young married people who were very devoted to each other; they were industrious and healthy, and everything was very neat in their house. Sunday morning, the young wife went out and gathered a handful of the loveliest roses, put them in a glass of water, and set it on the cupboard.

"Now I see it is Sunday," said the husband. He kissed his pretty little wife, and they sat down and read a psalm, holding hands, while the morning sun shone brightly through the window on the fresh roses and the young couple.

"I'm so tired of looking at this!" said the mother of the sparrows as she looked down into the room; and then she flew away.

She did the same thing the following Sunday, for every Sunday, fresh roses were placed in the glass, but the rose tree still blossomed just as much. The young sparrows, who now had feathers of their own, wanted to fly with their mother. But she said, "You stay!" And so they stayed.

She flew off; but, whatever the reason, she suddenly was caught in a horsehair net that some boys had fastened to a bough! The horsehair bound about her leg so tightly she thought it was cut in half. How it pained and terrified her! The boys sprang forward and seized the bird with a cruelly hard grasp.

"It's nothing but a sparrow!" they said, but they wouldn't let her go. They took her home, and every time she cried, they hit her on the beak.

In the farmhouse, there was an old man who knew how to make soap for shaving and washing hands, soap in balls and pieces. He was a wandering, merry old fellow. When he saw the sparrow that the boys brought, and which they said they didn't care about, he said to them, "Shall we make it beautiful?"

The sparrow mother shivered with fear as he said this. Out of his box of the brightest colors he took a lot of shining gold leaf; then he sent the boys for an egg, smeared its white all over the sparrow, and laid the gold upon it. Thus the sparrow mother was gilt, but she didn't think about this pomp; her limbs shook with terror. Then the old soap maker tore a piece of red cloth from his jacket, cut it into the shape of a cock's comb, and glued it on the bird's head.

"Now you shall see the golden bird fly!" he said, and let the sparrow loose. In deadly horror, she flew away in the bright sunshine. My, how she glittered! All the sparrows, even a large crow, who was no youngster, were quite frightened at the sight. But they flew after her, for they wanted to know what this unusual bird was.

"Where from! Where from!" screamed the crow.

"Wait a bit! Wait a bit!" said the sparrows. But she would not wait; in terror and pain, she flew on toward home. She was ready to sink to the earth, and the crowd of birds, small and large, increased every moment, and some even flew in to peck at her. "Such a one! Such a one!" they all cried.

"Such a one! Such a one!" squeaked the young sparrows as she approached the nest. "That is surely a young peacock, for there are the colors that hurt your eyes, as Mother said. Twit! That is 'the beautiful.'" And then they attacked her with their little beaks, so that it wasn't possible for her to enter the nest; and she was so overcome with fright that she could no longer even say "twit," much less say, "I am your mother." The other birds all joined in pecking at her until every one of her feathers was gone; and, bleeding, the sparrow mother sank down into the rosebush.

"The poor animal!" said the roses. "Come, we will hide you. Rest your little head upon us!"

Once more, the sparrow mother spread her wings, but then folded them close to her body again, and died among her neighbors, the fresh, beautiful roses.

"Twit!" said the young sparrows in the nest.

"What's become of Mother! I can't understand it. Could this be a trick of hers to teach us to look out for ourselves? She has left us the house for an inheritance, but which of us is to have it alone when we get families?"

"Yes, I can't have you others here when I have a wife and children!" said the smallest.

"I'll have more wives and children than you!" said another.

"But I'm the oldest!" said a third. Then they all got into a fight; they flapped their wings and pecked at each other, and—bumps!—one after another popped out of the nest! There they lay, full of anger; they held their heads to one side and blinked their upturned eyes; that was their way of sulking.

They could fly a little, and so they practiced some more. And finally, they agreed that in order to recognize each other when they met in the world, they would say "twit!" and scrape three times with the left leg.

The youngest sparrow, who remained in the nest, puffed himself up as big as he could, for he was now the owner, but that did not last long. During the night, fire gleamed through the windows of the farmhouse; the flames burst forth from under the roof, and the dry straw went up in a blaze. The whole house burned, and with it the little sparrow and his nest; however, the young couple luckily escaped.

When the sun was up next morning, and everything seemed so refreshed, as after a night's gentle sleep, there was nothing left of the farmhouse except some black, charred beams leaning against the chimney that was its own master now. The smoke still rose from the ground, but the whole rose tree stood fresh and blooming, with every bough mirrored in the calm water.

"My, how pretty those roses are there in front of the burnt-down house!" said a man, who came by. "It's the most charming little picture! I must have it!" And the man took from his pocket a little book with white leaves and a pencil, for he was an artist, and he sketched the smoking ground, the charred beams, and the chimney that leaned more and more to one side; but first of all, the big, blooming rose tree, which was certainly beautiful, and was, of course, the reason the picture was drawn.

Later that day, two of the sparrows who had been born there came by. "Where is the house?" they said. "Where is the nest? Twit! It's all burnt, and our strong brother is burnt, too! That's what he got for keeping the nest. Those roses escaped well! They're still standing there with red, red cheeks. They don't mourn over their neighbors' misfortunes. I won't speak to them; and it's ugly here—that's my opinion!" So they flew away.

When autumn came, there was a beautiful sunshiny day; one would have thought it was in the middle of the summer. It was so dry and clean in the courtyard before the great steps at the manor house, and there walked the doves, both black and white, and violet, glistening in the sunshine. The old dove mothers waddled about and said to their children, "Stand in groups! Stand in groups!" For that made them look better.

"What are those little gray birds that run about among us?" asked an old dove who had red and green in her eyes. "Little gray ones! Little gray ones!" she repeated.

"Those are sparrows, modest creatures. We have always been known to be good-natured, so we let them pick up a little of our corn. They don't talk to us, and they scrape so politely with their legs."

Yes, they scraped, three times with the left leg, and then said "twit!" and thus they recognized each other; they were three of the sparrows from the burnt house. "It is very good to eat here," said the sparrows.

The doves walked about among themselves, carrying themselves proudly, and had private opinions to exchange. "See that crop pigeon?" said one about another. "Do you see her and how she devours the peas? She gets too many! She gets the best! Coo, coo! See how bald she's getting in her crest! See that ugly, wicked creature! Coo, coo!" And then the eyes of them all gleamed red with malice. "Stand in groups, stand in groups! Little gray birds! Little gray ones! Coo! Coo! Coo!" So it went on unceasingly, and so will it still be in a thousand years.

The sparrows ate well, and they heard well. Yes, and they even stood in groups with the others, but that didn't suit them. They were full, so they left the doves and exchanged opinions about them. Then they wriggled under the garden fence, and, since the door to the garden room was open, one of them hopped upon the threshold. He was filled to satiety, and therefore courageous. "Twit!" he said. "I dare do this!"

"Twit!" said another. "I also dare do that, and more too!" And then he hopped into the room.

There were no people there; the third saw this, and then he flew even farther into the room, and said, "All the way in, or not at all! What a funny human nest this is! And what have they put up there? Why, what is that!"

Right in front of the sparrows bloomed the roses; they were mirrored in the pond, and the charred beams rested against the ready-to-fall chimney! Well, what was this? How did all this get in the manor parlor? All three sparrows tried to fly over the roses and the chimney, but it was a flat wall that they flew against; it was all a painting, a large, beautiful piece of work that the artist had made from his little sketch.

"Twit!" said the sparrows. "It's nothing! It's only a likeness! Twit! That is 'the beautiful.' Can you understand it? For I can't!" And then they flew out, because people came into the room.

Now days and years went by; many times had the doves cooed, and quarreled too, the wicked birds! The sparrows had nearly frozen in winter, and lived luxuriously in summer; they were all engaged or married, or whatever one wants to call it, and those with young ones naturally thought his own were the handsomest and cleverest. One flew here and another there, and whenever they met, they recognized each other by a "twit!" and three scrapes of the left leg.

The eldest of them, who was now such an old one, had no nest or young ones. She wanted so much to visit a large city, so she flew to Copenhagen.

A big house of many colors stood by the palace and the canal, where there were vessels laden with apples and pottery. Its windows were wider at the bottom than at the top; the sparrow peered inside, and each room, she thought, looked like the inside of a tulip, with all sorts of colors and decorations. In the middle of the tulip stood white people; they were of marble and some of plaster, but to a sparrow, they all looked the same.

On top of the house stood a metal car, with metal horses, and the Goddess of Victory, also of metal, driving them. This was Thorvaldsen's Museum!

"How it shines! How it shines!" said the sparrow. "This must be 'the beautiful'! Twit! But here it's larger than a peacock!" She still remembered from when she was little what the most beautiful thing was that her mother knew.

Then she flew down into the courtyard, and this was also lovely. There were palms and green foliage painted on the walls, and in the middle of the courtyard stood a big, blooming rose tree that spread its fresh green branches, with their many flowers, over a grave. She flew to it, for she saw several other sparrows there. "Twit!" she said, and scraped three times with her left leg. She had practiced that greeting many times in past days and years, but no one had understood it, for those who are once parted don't meet every day; the greeting had become hardly more than a habit. But today, there were two old sparrows and one young one who said, "twit!" in return and scraped with their left legs.

"Ah, good day, good day!" It was a couple of the sparrows from the old nest, and a little one of the family. "That we should meet here!" They said, "This is a very fine place, but there isn't much to eat. It's 'the beautiful.' Twit!"

And then many people came into the courtyard from one of the rooms where the beautiful marble figures stood, and they went to the grave that held the remains of the great master who had created those figures. All stood with their eyes on Thorvaldsen's grave, and some gathered scattered rose petals to save. There were people from faraway places; they had come from mighty England, from Germany, and France; and the fairest lady took one of the roses and placed it near her heart.

The sparrows then thought that the roses reigned there, that the whole house had been built for them. This seemed to them to be really a little too much, but since the people all showed such regard for the roses, they would do the same. "Twit!" they said, and swept the ground with their tails, with one eye on the roses. They did not look at them long before they were convinced that they were their old neighbors, and so they really were. The artist who had sketched the rosebush near the charred ruins of the house had later obtained permission to transplant it, and had then given it to the architect of the museum, for lovelier roses could not be found; and the architect had planted it on Thorvalsden's grave, where, as a living symbol of the beautiful, it blossomed and gave its red, fragrant petals to be carried as remembrances to foreign lands.

"Have you got an establishment in town now?" asked the sparrows. And the roses nodded; they recognized their gray neighbors, and were so glad to see them.

"How wonderful it is to live and blossom here, and to see old friends and kind faces every day! It is as if every day were a big holiday!"

"Twit!" said the sparrows. "Yes, they are our old neighbors. We remember them from the duck pond! Twit! How they have been honored! But then, some people are while they're asleep. And what there is so wonderful in a red lump like that, I don't know! Ah, there's a withered leaf, for that I can see!"

So they pecked at the leaf until it fell off, but it only made the rose tree look fresher and greener. And the roses bloomed fragrantly in the sunshine on the grave of Thorvaldsen, with whose immortal name their beauty thus became linked.

LITTLE TUCK (1847)

Yes, that was little Tuck. As a matter of fact, his name wasn't really Tuck, but before he could speak plainly, he called himself "Tuck." That was supposed to mean "Carl," but "Tuck" does just as well if one only knows it.

Now he had to learn his lessons and at the same time take care of his sister Gustava, who was much smaller than he; and it was pretty hard to manage the two things at once. So the poor boy sat with his little sister on his lap and sang to her all the songs he knew, at the same time glancing into his geography book, which was open before him. By the next morning, he was supposed to know all the towns in the counties of Seeland by heart and everything there was to know about them.

Then his mother returned, for she had been away, and took little Gustava herself. Tuck ran quickly to the window and studied until he almost read his eyes out, for it was getting darker and darker, and his poor mother could not afford candles.

Suddenly, his mother looked out of the window. "There goes the old washerwoman from down the lane," she said. "She can hardly drag herself along, and she has to carry a pail of water from the well, too! Be a good boy, Tuck, and run over and help the old woman."

And little Tuck jumped up and ran to help the old woman, but when he got home again, it was quite dark. Nothing was said about candles, so all he could do was go to bed—and his bed was an old folding bench. He lay there thinking about Seeland, and his geography lesson, and everything the teacher had said. He should certainly have studied that lesson some more, but of course he couldn't do that now.

So he put his geography book under his pillow, because he had heard that this helps a great deal when you want to learn a lesson. But you can't depend on that!

There he lay, thinking and thinking, then all of a sudden it seemed as if someone kissed his eyes and lips. He slept and yet he didn't sleep, and he felt as if the old washerwoman was looking at him out of the kind eyes and saying, "It would be a great shame if you didn't know your lesson tomorrow. You helped me, and now I'll help you; and our Lord will help us both."

Then all at once, the book under his pillow began to wriggle and squirm around!

"Kekelikee! Cluck, cluck!" It was a hen that came crawling out—and she was from Kjöge. "I'm a Kjöge hen," she said. And then she told him all about her town, and how many people there were in it, and about a battle that had taken place there once, though that wasn't really worth mentioning.

"Krible, kragle, bang!" Something dropped down. And a wooden bird appeared; it was the parrot from the shooting match at Praestö. The bird told the little boy very proudly that there were just as many inhabitants in its town as there were nails in its body. "Thorvaldsen used to live around the corner from me! Bang! Here I lie comfortably!"

But little Tuck was no longer lying in bed—all of a sudden, he was on horseback! Gallopy, gallopy, it went! He was sitting in front of a splendidly dressed knight with shining helmet and nodding plume. On through the woods they galloped to the old town of Vordingborg, and that was a big and lively town. High towers rose above the royal castle, and radiant lights streamed from its windows; inside there was singing and dancing, and King Valdemar led the lovely court ladies in the dance. But soon morning came, and as the sun rose, the town seemed to melt away, and the king's castle sank down, one tower after another, until at last only one tower was left standing on the hill where the castle had been, and the town had become very small and very poor. The schoolboys came along with their books under their arms, and said, "Two thousand inhabitants," but that wasn't true. There were not so many as that.

And still little Tuck lay in his bed, as if he were dreaming and not dreaming at the same time, but there seemed to be someone standing close beside him.

"Little Tuck, little Tuck!" someone said. It was a sailor, a very little fellow, small enough to have been a midshipman, although he wasn't a midshipman. "I bring you many greetings from Korsör, that's a growing town, a lively flourishing town with steamboats and mail coaches. In olden times, people used to call it ugly, but that's not true anymore.

"'I lie by the seashore,' Korsör says to you. 'I have high roads and beautiful parks, and I once gave birth to a poet who was very witty. That's more than can be said for all of them. I wanted to send a ship around the world, but I didn't. But I could have done it. Anyway, I smell deliciously, because close by my gates, the most beautiful roses bloom!'"

Little Tuck saw them, and everything was green and red before his eyes, but when the confusion of colors was over, they changed to wooden heights, sloping down to the sparkling waters of a fjord. A stately old twin-spired church towered above the waters. From out of the cliffside, springs of water rushed down in bubbling streams, and nearby sat an old king with a golden crown on his long hair. It was King Hroar of the Springs, and the place is now the town of Roskilde (Hroar's Springs). Up the hill and into the old church the kings and queens of Denmark walked hand in hand, all with their golden crowns, and the organ was playing, and the springs rippled.

"Don't forget the towns of the kingdom!" said King Hroar.

Then all at once, everything vanished—and where had it all gone? It was like turning a leaf in a book.

Now an old peasant woman stood before little Tuck; she was a weeding woman from Sorö, where grass grows in the marketplace. She had thrown her gray linen apron over her head and down her back, and it was soaking wet—it must have been raining.

"Yes, it certainly has been," she said. She knew many of the comic parts from Holberg's comedies, and all about Valdemar and Absolon.

But all at once, she squatted down and wagged her head, just as if she were about to leap. "Ko-ax," she said. "It's wet! It's wet! It's quiet as a grave in Sorö!" Suddenly, she was a frog, "Ko-ax!" and then she became an old woman again. "You should always dress according to the weather!" she explained. "It's wet! Very wet! My town is just like a bottle—you go in with the cork, and you have to come out the same way. In the old days, I used to have beautiful fish there, and now I have red-cheeked little boys down in the bottom of the bottle. They learn a lot of wisdom there—Greek! Greek! Hebrew! Hebrew! Ko-ax!" It sounded like the croaking of frogs, or the creaking of big boots as you walk across the moor; always the same sound—so monotonous—so tiresome—yes, so tiresome that little Tuck fell into a deep sleep, which was the best thing in the world for him.

But even in this sleep, he had a dream or something like that. It seemed that his little sister, Gustava, with her blue eyes and golden curly hair, had suddenly become a grown-up beautiful lady, and she could fly without wings. Together they flew over the green forests and the deep blue waters of Seeland.

"Do you hear the cock crowing, little Tuck? Cock-a-doodle-do! The hens are flying up out of Kjöge. You'll have a big, big chicken yard; you'll never suffer want or hunger; yes, you shall shoot the parrot, as the saying goes; you shall be a rich and happy man. Your manor shall rise up like King Valdemar's towers, and it shall be richly adorned with marble statues, like those in Praestö! Can you understand me? The fame of your name shall travel around the world, like this ship that was to sail from Korsör!" And from Roskilde town came the voice of King Hroar, "Remember the towns of the kingdom!"

"There you shall speak wisely and well, little Tuck. And when you are in your grave, you shall sleep as peacefully as—"

"As if I were in Sorö!" cried little Tuck, and then he woke up.

It was broad daylight, and he couldn't remember the smallest part of his dream. And he wasn't supposed to either, for we shouldn't know things that are going to happen in the future.

Now he sprang quickly out of bed and read his geography book, and at once he knew the whole lesson!

And the old washerwoman put her head in the door and nodded good morning to him.

"Many thanks for your help yesterday, dear child," she said. "May the Lord make all your dreams come true!"

Little Tuck didn't know anything that he had dreamed, but you see—our Lord knew it!

THE SHADOW (1847)

It is in the hot countries that the sun burns down in earnest, turning the people there a deep mahogany-brown. In the hottest countries of all, they are seared into negroes, but it was not quite that hot in this country to which a man of learning had come from the colder north. He expected to go about there just as he had at home, but he soon discovered that this was a mistake. He and other sensible souls had to stay inside. The shutters were drawn, and the doors were closed all day long. It looked just as if everyone were asleep or away from home. The narrow street of high houses where he lived was so situated that from morning till night the sun beat down on it—unbearably!

To this young and clever scholar from the colder north, it felt as if he were sitting in a blazing hot oven. It exhausted him so that he became very thin, and even his shadow shrank much smaller than it had been at home. Only in the evenings, after sundown, did the man and his shadow begin to recover.

This was really a joy to see. As soon as a candle was brought into the room, the shadow had to stretch itself to get its strength back. It stretched up to the wall, yes, even along the ceiling, so tall did it grow. To stretch himself, the scholar went out on the balcony. As soon as the stars came out in the beautifully clear sky, he felt as if he had come back to life.

In warm countries, each window has a balcony, and on all the balconies up and down the street, people came out to breathe the fresh air that one needs, even if one is already a fine mahogany-brown. Both up above and down below, things became lively. Tailors, shoemakers—everybody—moved out in the street. Chairs and tables were brought out, and candles were lighted, yes, candles by the thousand. One man talked, another sang, people strolled about, carriages drove by, and donkeys trotted along, *ting-a-ling-a-ling*, for their harness had bells on it. There were church bells ringing, hymn singing, and funeral processions. There were boys in the street firing off Roman candles. Oh yes, it was lively as lively can be down in that street.

Only one house was quiet—the one directly across from where the scholarly stranger lived. Yet someone lived there, for flowers on the balcony grew and thrived under that hot sun, which they could not have done unless they were watered. So someone must be watering them, and there must be people in the house. Along in the evening, as a matter of fact, the door across the street was opened. But it was dark inside, at least in the front room. From somewhere in the house, farther back, came the sound of music. The scholarly stranger thought the music was marvelous, but it is quite possible that he only imagined this, for out there in the warm countries, he thought everything was marvelous—except the sun. The stranger's landlord said that he didn't know who had rented the house across the street. No one was ever to be seen over there, and as for the music, he found it extremely tiresome. He said:

"It's just as if somebody sits there practicing a piece that's beyond him—always the selfsame piece. 'I'll play it right yet,' he probably says, but he doesn't, no matter how long he tries."

One night, the stranger woke up. He slept with the windows to his balcony open, and as the breeze blew his curtain aside, he fancied that a marvelous radiance came from the balcony across the street. The colors of all the flowers were as brilliant as flames. In their midst stood a maiden, slender and lovely. It seemed as if a radiance came from her, too. It actually hurt his eyes, but that was because he had opened them too wide in his sudden awakening.

One leap, and he was out of bed. Without a sound, he looked out through his curtains, but the maiden was gone. The flowers were no longer radiant, though they bloomed as fresh and fair as usual. The door was ajar, and through it came music so lovely and soft that one could really feel very romantic about it. It was like magic. But who lived there? What entrance did they use? Facing the street, the lower floor of the house was a row of shops, and people couldn't run through them all the time.

On another evening, the stranger sat out on his balcony. The candle burned in the room behind him, so naturally, his shadow was cast on the wall across the street. Yes, there it sat among the flowers, and when the stranger moved, it moved with him.

"I believe my shadow is the only living thing to be seen over there," the scholar thought to himself. "See how he makes himself at home among the flowers. The door stands ajar, and if my shadow were clever, he'd step in, have a look around, and come back to tell me what he had seen."

"Yes," he said as a joke, "you ought to make yourself useful. Kindly step inside. Well, aren't you going?" He nodded to the shadow, and the shadow nodded back. "Run along now, but be sure to come back."

The stranger rose, and his shadow across the street rose with him. The stranger turned around, and his shadow turned, too. If anyone had been watching closely, he would have seen the shadow enter the half-open balcony door in the house across the way at the same instant that the stranger returned to his room and the curtain fell behind him.

Next morning, when the scholar went out to take his coffee and read the newspapers, he said, "What's this?" as he came out in the sunshine. "I haven't any shadow! So it really did go away last night, and it stayed away. Isn't that annoying?"

What annoyed him most was not so much the loss of his shadow, but the knowledge that there was already a story about a man without a shadow. All the people at home knew that story. If he went back and told them his story, they would say he was just imitating the old one. He did not care to be called unoriginal, so he decided to say nothing about it, which was the most sensible thing to do.

That evening, he again went out on the balcony. He had placed the candle directly behind him, because he knew that a shadow always likes to use its master as a screen, but he could not coax it forth. He made himself short and he made himself tall, but there was no shadow. It didn't come forth. He hemmed and he hawed, but it was no use.

This was very vexing, but in the hot countries, everything grows most rapidly, and in a week or so, he noticed with great satisfaction that when he went out in the sunshine, a new shadow was growing at his feet. The root must have been left with him. In three weeks' time, he had a very presentable shadow, and as he started north again, it grew longer and longer, until it got so long and large that half of it would have been quite sufficient.

The learned man went home and wrote books about those things in the world that are true, that are good, and that are beautiful.

The days went by, and the years went past, many, many years, in fact. Then one evening when he was sitting in his room, he heard a soft tapping at his door. "Come in," said he, but no one came in. He opened the door and was confronted by a man so extremely thin that it gave him a strange feeling. However, the man was faultlessly dressed and looked like a person of distinction.

"With whom do I have the honor of speaking?" the scholar asked.

"Ah," said the distinguished visitor, "I thought you wouldn't recognize me, now that I've put real flesh on my body and wear clothes. I don't suppose you ever expected to see me in such fine condition. Don't you know your old shadow? You must have thought I'd never come back. Things have gone remarkably well with me since I was last with you. I've thrived in every way, and if I have to buy my freedom, I can." He rattled a bunch of valuable charms that hung from his watch, and fingered the massive gold chain he wore around his neck. Ho! How his fingers flashed with diamond rings—and all this jewelry was real.

"No, I can't get over it!" said the scholar. "What *does* it all mean?"

"Nothing ordinary, you may be sure," said the shadow. "But you are no ordinary person, and I, as you know, have followed in your footsteps from childhood. As soon as you thought me sufficiently experienced to strike out in the world for myself, I went my way. I have been immeasurably successful. But I felt a sort of longing to see you again before you die, as I suppose you must, and I wanted to see this country again. You know how one loves his native land. I know that you have got hold of another shadow. Do I owe anything to either of you? Be kind enough to let me know."

"Well! Is it really you?" said the scholar. "Why, this is most extraordinary! I would never have imagined that one's own shadow could come back in human form."

"Just tell me what I owe," said the shadow, "because I don't like to be in debt to anyone."

"How can you talk that way?" said the student. "What debt could there be? Feel perfectly free. I am tremendously pleased to hear of your good luck! Sit down, my old friend, and tell me a bit about how it all happened, and about what you saw in that house across the street from us in the warm country."

"Yes, I'll tell you all about it," the shadow said, as he sat down. "But you must promise that if you meet me anywhere, you won't tell a soul in town about my having been your shadow. I intend to become engaged, for I can easily support a family."

"Don't you worry," said the scholar. "I won't tell anyone who you really are. I give you my hand on it. I promise, and a man is as good as his word."

"And a word is as good as its—shadow," the shadow said, for he couldn't put it any other way.

It was really remarkable how much of a man he had become, dressed all in black, with the finest cloth, patent-leather shoes, and an opera hat that could be pressed perfectly flat until it was only brim and top, not to mention those things we already know about—those seals, that gold chain, and the diamond rings. The shadow was well dressed indeed, and it was just this that made him appear human.

"Now I'll tell you," said the shadow, grinding his patent-leather shoes on the arm of the scholar's new shadow, which lay at his feet like a poodle dog. This was arrogance, perhaps, or possibly he was trying to make the new shadow stick to his own feet. The shadow on the floor lay quiet and still, and listened its best, so that it might learn how to get free and work its way up to be its own master.

"Do you know who lived in the house across the street from us?" the old shadow asked. "She was the most lovely of all creatures—she was Poetry herself. I lived there for three weeks, and it was as if I had lived there three thousand years, reading all that has ever been written. That's what I said, and it's the truth! I have seen it all, and I know everything."

"Poetry!" the scholar cried. "Yes, to be sure, she often lives as a hermit in the large cities. Poetry! Yes, I saw her myself, for one brief moment, but my eyes were heavy with sleep. She stood on the balcony, as radiant as the northern lights. Tell me! Tell me! You were on the balcony. You went through the doorway, and then—"

"Then I was in the anteroom," said the shadow. "It was the room you were always staring at from across the way. There were no candles there, and the room was in twilight. But door upon door stood open in a whole series of brilliantly lit halls and reception rooms. That blaze of lights would have struck me dead had I gone as far as the room where the maiden was, but I was careful—I took my time, as one should."

"And then what did you see, my old friend?" the scholar asked.

"I saw everything, and I shall tell everything to you, but—it's not that I'm proud—but as I am a free man and well educated, not to mention my high standing and my considerable fortune, I do wish you wouldn't call me your old friend."

"I beg your pardon!" said the scholar. "It's an old habit, and hard to change. You are perfectly right, my dear sir, and I'll remember it. But now, my dear sir, tell me of all that you saw."

"All?" said the shadow, "for I saw it all, and I know everything."

"How did the innermost rooms look?" the scholar asked. "Was it like a green forest? Was it like a holy temple? Were the rooms like the starry skies seen from some high mountain?"

"Everything was there," said the shadow. "I didn't quite go inside. I stayed in the dark anteroom, but my place there was perfect. I saw everything, and I know everything. I have been in the antechamber at the court of Poetry."

"But what did you see? Did the gods of old march through the halls? Did the old heroes fight there? Did fair children play there and tell their dreams?"

"I was there, I tell you, so you must understand that I saw all that there was to be seen. Had you come over, it would not have made a man of you, as it did of me. Also, I learned to understand my inner self, what is born in me, and the relationship between me and Poetry. Yes, when I was with you, I did not think of such things, but you must remember how wonderfully I always expanded at sunrise and sunset. And in the moonlight, I almost seemed more real than you. Then I did not understand myself, but in that anteroom, I came to know my true nature. I was a man! I came out completely changed. But you were no longer in the warm country. Being a man, I was ashamed to be seen as I was. I lacked shoes, clothes, and all the surface veneer that makes a man.

"I went into hiding—this is confidential, and you must not write it in any of your books. I went into hiding under the skirts of the cake-woman. Little she knew of what she concealed. Not until evening did I venture out. I ran through the streets in the moonlight and stretched myself tall against the walls. It's such a pleasant way of scratching one's back. Up I ran and down I ran, peeping into the highest windows, into drawing rooms, and into garrets. I peered in where no one else could peer. I saw what no one else could see, or should see. Taken all in all, it's a wicked world. I would not care to be a man if it were not considered the fashionable thing to be. I saw the most incredible behavior among men and women, fathers and mothers, and among those 'perfectly darling' children. I saw what nobody knows but everybody would like to know, and that is what wickedness goes on next door. If I had written it in a newspaper, oh, how widely it would have been read! But instead, I wrote to the people directly concerned, and there was the most terrible consternation in every town to which I came. They were so afraid of me, and yet so remarkably fond of me. The professors appointed me a professor, and the tailor made me new clothes—my wardrobe is most complete. The master of the mint coined new money for me, the women called me such a handsome man; and so I became the man I am. Now I must bid you good-bye. Here's my card. I live on the sunny side of the street, and I am always at home on rainy days." The shadow took his leave.

"How extraordinary," said the scholar.

The days passed. The years went by. And the shadow called again. "How goes it?" he asked.

"Alack," said the scholar, "I still write about the true, the good, and the beautiful, but nobody cares to read about such things. I feel quite despondent, for I take it deeply to heart."

"I don't," said the shadow. "I am getting fat, as one should. You don't know the ways of the world, and that's why your health suffers. You ought to travel. I'm taking a trip this summer. Will you come with me? I'd like to have a traveling companion. Will you come along as my shadow? It would be a great pleasure to have you along, and I'll pay all the expenses."

"No, that's a bit too much," said the scholar.

"It depends on how you look at it," said the shadow. "It will do you a lot of good to travel. Will you be my shadow? The trip won't cost you a thing."

"This has gone much too far!" said the scholar.

"Well, that's the way the world goes," the shadow told him, "and that's the way it will keep on going." And away he went.

The learned man was not at all well. Sorrow and trouble pursued him, and what he had to say about the good, the true, and the beautiful appealed to most people about as much as roses appeal to a cow. Finally, he grew quite ill.

"You really look like a shadow," people told him, and he trembled at the thought.

"You must visit a watering place," said the shadow, who came to see him again. "There's no question about it. I'll take you with me, for old friendship's sake. I'll pay for the trip, and you can write about it, as well as doing your best to amuse me along the way. I need to go to a watering place too, because my beard isn't growing as it should. That's a sort of disease too, and one can't get along without a beard. Now do be reasonable and accept my proposal. We shall travel just like friends!"

So off they started. The shadow was master now, and the master was the shadow. They drove together, rode together, and walked together, side by side, before or behind each other, according to the way the sun fell. The shadow was careful to take the place of the master, and the scholar didn't much care, for he had an innocent heart, besides being most affable and friendly.

One day, he said to the shadow, "As we are now fellow-travelers and have grown up together, shall we not call each other by our first names, the way good companions should? It is much more intimate."

"That's a splendid idea!" said the shadow, who was now the real master. "What you say is most open-hearted and friendly. I shall be just as friendly and open-hearted with you. As a scholar, you are perfectly well aware how strange is man's nature. Some men cannot bear the touch of gray paper. It sickens them. Others quail if they hear a nail scratched across a pane of glass. For my part, I am affected in just that way when I hear you call me by my first name. I feel myself ground down to the earth, as I was in my first position with you. You understand. It's a matter of sensitivity, not pride. I cannot let you call me by my first name, but I shall be glad to call you by yours, as a compromise." So thereafter, the shadow called his one-time master by his first name.

"It has gone too far," the scholar thought, "when I must call him by his last name while he calls me by my first!" But he had to put up with it.

At last, they came to the watering place. Among the many people was a lovely princess. Her malady was that she saw things too clearly, which can be most upsetting. For instance, she immediately saw that the newcomer was a very different sort of person from all the others.

"He has come here to make his beard grow, they say. But I see the real reason. He can't cast a shadow."

Her curiosity was aroused, and on the promenade she addressed this stranger directly. Being a king's daughter, she did not have to stand upon ceremony, so she said to him straight:

"Your trouble is that you can't cast a shadow."

"Your Royal Highness must have improved considerably," the shadow replied. "I know your malady is that you see too clearly, but you are improving. As it happens, I do have a most unusual shadow. Don't you see that figure who always accompanies me? Other people have a common shadow, but I do not care for what is common to all. Just as we often allow our servants better fabrics for their liveries than we wear ourselves, so I have had my shadow decked out as a man. Why, you see, I have even outfitted him with a shadow of his own. It is expensive, I grant you, but I like to have something uncommon."

"My!" the princess thought. "Can I really be cured? This is the foremost watering place in the world, and in these days, water has come to have wonderful medicinal powers. But I shan't leave just as the place is becoming amusing. I have taken a liking to this stranger. I only hope his beard won't grow, for then he would leave us."

That evening, the princess and the shadow danced together in the great ballroom. She was light, but he was lighter still. Never had she danced with such a partner. She told him what country she came from, and he knew it well. He had been there, but it was during her absence. He had looked through every window, high or low. He had seen this, and he had seen that. So he could answer the princess and suggest things that astounded her. She was convinced that he must be the wisest man in all the world. His knowledge impressed her so deeply that while they were dancing, she fell in love with him. The shadow could tell, for her eyes transfixed him, through and through. They danced again, and she came very near telling him she loved him, but it wouldn't do to be rash. She had to think of her country, and her throne, and the many people over whom she would reign.

"He is a clever man," she said to herself, "and that is a good thing. He dances charmingly, and that is good too. But is his knowledge more than superficial? That's just as important, so I must examine him."

Tactfully, she began asking him the most difficult questions, which she herself could not have answered. The shadow made a wry face.

"You can't answer me?" said the princess.

"I knew all that in my childhood," said the shadow. "Why, I believe that my shadow over there by the door can answer you."

"Your shadow!" said the princess. "That would be remarkable indeed!"

"I can't say for certain," said the shadow, "but I'm inclined to think so, because he has followed me about and listened to me for so many years. Yes, I am inclined to believe so. But your Royal Highness must permit me to tell you that he is quite proud of being able to pass for a man, so if he is to be in the right frame of mind to answer your questions he must be treated just as if he were human."

"I like that!" said the princess.

So she went to the scholar in the doorway and spoke with him about the Sun and the Moon, and about people, what they are inside, and what they seem to be on the surface. He answered her wisely and well.

"What a man that must be, to have such a wise shadow!" she thought. "It will be a godsend to my people and to my country if I choose him for my consort. That's just what I'll do!"

The princess and the shadow came to an understanding, but no one was to know about it until she returned to her own kingdom.

"No one. Not even my shadow!" said the shadow. And he had his own private reason for this.

Finally they came to the country that the princess ruled when she was at home.

"Listen, my good friend," the shadow said the scholar, "I am now as happy and strong as one can be, so I'll do something very special for you. You shall live with me in my palace, drive with me in my royal carriage, and have a hundred thousand dollars a year. However, you must let yourself be called a shadow by everybody. You must not ever say that you have been a man, and once a year, while I sit on the balcony in the sunshine, you must lie at my feet as shadows do. For I tell you I am going to marry the princess, and the wedding is to take place this very evening."

"No! That's going too far," said the scholar. "I will *not*. I won't do it. That would be betraying the whole country and the princess too. I'll tell them everything—that I am the man, and you are the shadow merely dressed as a man."

"No one would believe it," said the shadow. "Be reasonable, or I'll call the sentry."

"I'll go straight to the princess," said the scholar.

"But I will go first," said the shadow, "and you shall go to prison."

And to prison he went, for the sentries obeyed the one who, they knew, was to marry the princess.

"Why, you're trembling," the princess said, as the shadow entered her room. "What has happened? You mustn't fall ill this evening, just as we are about to be married."

"I have been through the most dreadful experience that could happen to anyone," said the shadow. "Just imagine! Of course a poor shadow's head can't stand very much. But imagine! My shadow has gone mad. He takes himself for a man, and— imagine it! He takes *me* for his shadow."

"How terrible!" said the princess. "He's locked up, I hope!"

"Oh, of course. I'm afraid he will never recover."

"Poor shadow," said the princess. "He is very unhappy. It would really be a charitable act to relieve him of the little bit of life he has left. And, after thinking it over carefully, my opinion is that it will be necessary to put him out of the way."

"That's certainly hard, for he was a faithful servant," said the shadow. He managed to sigh.

"You have a noble soul," the princess told him.

The whole city was brilliantly lit that evening. The cannons boomed, and the soldiers presented arms. That was the sort of wedding it was! The princess and the shadow stepped out on the balcony to show themselves and be cheered, again and again.

The scholar heard nothing of all this, for they had already done away with him.

THE OLD HOUSE (1847)

S omewhere in the street stood an old, old house; it was almost 300 years old, as you could tell from the date cut into the great beam. Tulips and hopbines and also whole verses of poetry were carved into the wood as people used to do in those days, and over every window, a mocking face was cut into the beam. The second story hung way out over the ground floor, and right under the eaves was a leaden spout with a dragon's head. Rain water was supposed to run out of the dragon's mouth, but it came from his belly instead, for there was a hole in it.

All of the other houses in the street were so neat and modern, with large windowpanes and smooth walls, that you could easily tell they would have nothing to do with the old house. They evidently thought, "How long do you suppose that decrepit old thing is going to stand there, making an eyesore of our street? And that bay window stands so far out we can't see from our windows what's happening in that direction. Those front steps are as broad as those of a palace, and as high as those that go up to a church tower! The iron railings—they look like the door to an old family vault! And those dreadful brass rails on them! It makes one feel ashamed!"

Across the street were other neat and modern houses, and they thought the same way. But at the window in the house directly opposite sat a little boy with bright shining eyes and fresh rosy cheeks. And he liked the old house best of all those on the street, whether by sunshine or by moonlight.

When he looked across at the wall where the mortar had fallen out, he could imagine the strangest pictures. He could see the street as it was in the old days; he could see soldiers with halberds, and the houses with their steps and projecting windows and pointed gables, and rainspouts in the shapes of dragons and serpents. Yes, to him, that was indeed a house worth looking at!

An old man lived over there—an old man who wore old-fashioned plush breeches and a coat with big brass buttons, and a wig that you could plainly tell was a real one. Every morning, an old male servant came to put the rooms in order and do the marketing, but aside from that, the old man in the plush breeches lived all alone in his old house. Sometimes he came to the window and looked out, and the little boy waved to him, and the old man waved back, and so they became acquaintances and then friends. Of course, they had never spoken to each other, but that really made no difference.

One day, the little boy heard his parents say, "The old man over there is very well-to-do, but he's terribly lonely!"

Next Sunday, the little boy wrapped a small object in a piece of paper, went downstairs to his doorway, and, when the old servant who did the marketing came by, said to him, "Look, sir, will you please give this to the old gentleman across the way? I have two tin soldiers; this is one of them, and I want him to have it 'cause I know he's terribly lonely."

The old servant looked very pleased as he nodded, and took the tin soldier across to the house. And later, he brought back a message inviting the little boy to come over and pay a visit. Happily, the little boy asked his parents' permission, then went across to the old house.

The brass knobs on the railings shone brighter than ever—one would think they had been especially polished in honor of his visit. And the little trumpeters carved in tulips on the doorway seemed to puff out their cheeks and blow with all their might, "Tratteratra! The boy approaches! Tratteratra!" Then the door opened.

The whole hallway was hung with old portraits of knights in armor and ladies in silken gowns, and the armor seemed to rattle and the silken gowns rustle! Then there was a flight of stairs that went a long way up and a little way down, and then the little boy came out on a balcony. It was very dilapidated, with grass and leaves growing out of holes and long crevices, for the whole balcony outside, the yard, and the walls were so overgrown that it looked like a garden. But still, it was just a balcony. There were old flowerpots with faces and donkey's ears, and flowers growing out of them just as they pleased. One of the pots was almost brimming over with carnations—that is, with the green part; shoot grew by shoot, and each seemed to say quite distinctly,

"The air has blessed me, and the sun has kissed me and promised me a little flower on Sunday! A little flower on Sunday!"

Now the little boy entered a room where the walls were covered with pigskin and printed with golden flowers.

Gilding fades fast;
But pigskin will last,

said the walls.

There were heavily carved easy chairs there, with high backs and arms on both sides. "Sit down! Sit down!" they cried. "Oh, how I creak! I know I'll get the gout, like the old cupboard! Oh!"

And at last, the little boy came into the room where the bay window was, and there sat the old man.

"I thank you for the tin soldier, my young friend," he said. "And I thank you again because you came over to see me."

"Thanks! Thanks!" or perhaps "Creak! Creak!" sounded from all the furniture. And there was so much of it in the room that the pieces seemed to crowd in each other's way, trying to get a look at the little boy.

In the middle of the wall hung a painting of a beautiful lady, young and happy, but dressed as in olden times, with clothes that stood out stiffly and with powdered hair. She neither said, "Thanks!" nor "Creak!" but just looked with mild eyes at the little boy. He promptly asked, "Where did she come from?"

"From the secondhand dealer down the street," said the old man, "where there are so many pictures. No one knows or cares anything about them, for all the people are buried. That lady has been dead and gone these fifty years, but I knew her in the old days."

In a glass frame beneath the portrait there hung a bouquet of withered flowers; they, too, must have been fifty years old—at least they looked it.

The pendulum of the great clock slowly swung to and fro, and the hands slowly turned, and everything in the room slowly became still older, but they didn't notice it.

"My mother and daddy say," said the little boy, "that you're terribly lonely."

"Oh," he answered, "the old thoughts, with what they may bring with them, come to see me, and now you come, too! I'm really very happy."

Then he took a picture book down from the shelf. There were long processions and strange coaches such as one never sees nowadays, soldiers who looked like the Knave of Clubs, and tradesmen with waving banners. The tailors had a banner that showed a pair of shears held by two lions; and the shoemakers had on theirs not a boot, but an eagle with two heads, for shoemakers must have everything in pairs. What a wonderful picture book that was!

And the old man went into the next room to fetch jam, apples, and nuts. Yes, the old house was a wonderful place. "I can't bear this any longer," cried the tin soldier, who was sitting on a chest of drawers. "It's so lonely and sad here! Anyone who has been in a family circle as I have can't get used to this sort of life. I can't bear it any longer! The days are so long, and the evenings are still longer! Things here aren't the way they were over at your house, where your father and mother spoke so pleasantly, and you and the other nice children made such delightful, happy noises. How lonely this old man is! Do you think he ever gets a kiss? Do you think he ever gets a kindly look or a Christmas tree? He'll get nothing but a funeral—I simply can't stand it any longer!"

"You mustn't let it make you so sad," said the little boy. "I think it's fun here, and then all the old memories, with what they may bring with them, come to visit here."

"Yes," said the tin soldier, "but I can't see them, because I don't know them. I tell you, I can't stand it!"

"But you must!" replied the little boy firmly.

Then the old man came back with his face all smiling, and with the most delicious jam and apples and nuts! So the little boy forgot about the tin soldier.

He went home, happy and pleased, and days and weeks passed, while nods and waves were exchanged to the old house and from the old house. Then he went over to call again.

Again the carved trumpeters seemed to blow, "Tratteratra! The little boy approaches! Tratteratra!" And the swords and armor on the knight paintings rattled, and the silken gowns rustled; the pigskin spoke, and the old chairs had rheumatism in their backs—"Ouch!" It was just like the first time, for in that house, one day or hour was just like another.

"I can't bear it!" wailed the tin soldier. "I've been shedding tin tears—it's too sad here! I'd rather go to the wars, and lose arms and legs; at least that would be a change! I just can't stand it! Now I know what it's like to have a visit from one's old memories and what they may bring with them. One of mine came to see me, and let me tell you, that isn't a very pleasant experience! I nearly jumped down from this chest!

"Because I saw you all over there so clearly, as if you really were right here! It was again that Sunday morning that you surely remember; all you children stood before the table and sang your hymns, just as you do every Sunday. You looked so devout, with your hands folded together; and your father and mother were just as pious. Then the door was opened, and little Sister Mary was put in the room. She really shouldn't have been there because she's less than two years old, and always tries to dance when she hears any kind of music or singing. She began to dance then, but she couldn't keep time—the music was too slow. First she stood on one leg and bent her head forward, and then she stood on the other leg and bent her head again—but it wouldn't do. You all stood together and looked very serious, although it was difficult to keep from laughing, but I did laugh to myself so hard I fell off the table and got a bump that I still have! It was very wrong of me to laugh. But it all comes back to me now in thought, and everything that I've seen all my life; these are the old memories, and what they may bring with them!

"Tell me, do you still sing on Sundays? Tell me about little Mary! And how is my comrade, the other tin soldier, doing? I imagine he's happy enough! Oh, I can't stand it anymore!"

"You were given away as a present," said the little boy firmly. "And you must stay here! Can't you understand that?"

Now the old man brought in a drawer in which there were many treasures—balm boxes and coin boxes and large, gilded, old playing cards, such as one never sees anymore. Several drawers were opened, and then the piano was opened; landscapes were painted on the inside of its lid, and it was so squeaky when the old man played it! Then he hummed a little song.

"She used to sing that," he said softly as he nodded up at the portrait he had bought from the secondhand dealer. And the old man's eyes shone brightly.

"I'm going to the wars! I tell you, I'm going to the wars!" the tin soldier shouted as loudly as he could; then, he threw himself off the chest right down to the floor.

What had become of him? The old man searched, and the little boy searched, but he was gone; they couldn't find him.

"I'll find him," said the old man, but he never did; the flooring was open and full of holes, and the tin soldier had fallen into one of the many cracks in the floor and lay there as if in an open grave.

And that day passed, and the little boy went home. A week passed, and several more weeks passed.

The windows of his home were frosted over, and the little boy had to breathe hard on one to make a peephole over to the old house. Then he saw that the snow had drifted into all the carving and inscriptions and up over the steps, just as if there were no one there. And there wasn't, really. For the old man was dead!

That evening, a hearse drove up before the door, and the old man's coffin was borne into it; he was going out into the country now, to lie in his grave. And so he was driven away, but there was no one to follow him, for all the old man's friends were dead. There was only the little boy who blew a kiss to the coffin as it was driven away.

A few days later, the old house was sold at auction, and from his window, the little boy watched them carry away the old knights and their ladies, and the long-eared flowerpots, the old chairs, and the old cupboards; some pieces landed here, and others landed there; the portrait that had come from the secondhand dealer went back to the secondhand dealer again, and there it hung, for no one knew the lady anymore, and no one cared about the old picture.

In the spring, the house was torn down, for everybody said it was nothing but a ruin. One could see from the street right into the room with the pigskin hangings, which were slashed and torn; and the green foliage about the balcony hung wild among the falling beams. The site was cleared.

"Good riddance," said the neighboring houses.

Then a fine house was built there, with large windows and smooth white walls; but in front of it, where the old house used to stand, a little garden was laid out, with a wild grapevine running up the wall of the neighboring house. Before the garden was a large railing with an iron gate; it looked quite splendid, and many people stopped to peer in. Scores of sparrows fluttered in the vines and chattered away to each other as fast as they could, but they didn't talk about the old house, for they couldn't remember it. So many years had passed.

Yes, many years had passed, and the little boy had grown up now to be a fine man; yes, an able man, and a great joy to his old parents. He had just been married, and, with his pretty little wife, came to live in the new house where the garden was.

He was standing beside her in the garden while she planted a wild flower she was so fond of. She bedded it in the ground with her little hand and pressed the earth around it with her fingers. Ouch, what was that! She had pricked herself. There was something there, pointed straight up in the soft dirt.

Yes, it was—just imagine, the little tin soldier! The same one that had been lost in the old man's room. He had tumbled and tossed about among the gravel and the timber and at last had lain for years in the ground.

The young wife wiped the dirt off the soldier, first with a green leaf and then with her delicate handkerchief, which had such a delightful scent that it woke the soldier up from his trance.

"Let me see him," said the young man. Then he laughed and shook his head. "No, it couldn't be he, but he certainly reminds me of a tin soldier I had when I was a little boy." Then he told her all about the old house and the old man and the tin soldier that had been sent over to keep him company because he was so terribly lonely. He told it just as it had happened, and the tears came into the eyes of his young wife—tears of pity for the old house and the old man.

"It might just possibly be the same tin soldier," she said gently. "I'll keep it, and remember everything you've told me. But you must show me the old man's grave."

"But I don't know where it is," he replied. "Nobody knows. All his friends were dead, and there was no one to take care of it. I was then just a little boy."

"How terribly lonely he must have been!" she murmured.

"Terribly lonely!" repeated the tin soldier. "But it's wonderful not to be forgotten!"

"Wonderful!" cried something else close by, but only the tin soldier saw that it was a scrap of the pigskin hanging. It had lost all of its gilding and looked like a piece of wet clay, but it still had its opinion, and gave it:

> Gilding fades fast;
> But pigskin will last!

But the tin soldier didn't really believe it.

THE DROP OF WATER (1847)

Of course, you must know what a microscope is, that round magnifying glass that makes everything look hundreds of times larger than it really is. If you take it and hold it close to your eye and look at a single drop of ditchwater, you'll see thousands of strange little creatures, such as you couldn't imagine living in a drop of water. But they are really there. They look almost like a plateful of shrimp, all jumping and crowding against each other, and they are so ferocious, they tear off each other's arm and legs; yet in their own way, they are happy and merry.

Now, once there was an old man whom his neighbors called Krible-Krable, for that was his name. He always tried to make the best of everything, and if he couldn't do it any other way, he would try magic.

One day, he sat with his eye glued to his microscope, peering at a drop of water taken from a puddle in the ditch. My! How it crawled and squirmed! All those thousands of little imps leaping and springing about, devouring each other, or pulling each other to pieces.

"This is too hideous for words!" said the old Krible-Krable. "There must be some way to make them live in peace and quiet and each mind his own business." But though he thought and thought, he couldn't find the answer. So he decided to use magic. "At least I can give them a color," he said, "so I can see them better." And then he let fall into the water a tiny drop of something that looked like red wine, but was really witches' blood, the very finest kind, and worth two pennies. Instantly, the strange little creatures became red all over, and the drop of water now looked like a whole town full of naked wild men.

"What have you got there?" asked another old magician, who had no name at all, which made him very distinguished.

"If you can guess what it is," replied Krible-Krable, "I'll give it to you. But it's not very easy to find out if one doesn't know."

So the nameless magician peered down through the microscope. The scene before his eyes really resembled a town where all the inhabitants ran about without clothing. What a terrible sight it was! But it was still more horrible to see them kick and cuff, and struggle and fight, and pull and bite at each other. All those on the bottom were struggling to get to the top, and those on the top were being pushed to the bottom. "Look! Look!" the creatures seemed to be crying. "His leg is longer than mine! Bah! Off with it! And here's one with a little lump behind his ear! An innocent little lump, but it hurts him, and it'll hurt him more!" And they hacked at it and tore at him and devoured him, all because of the little lump.

But one sat very quiet and still, all by itself, like a modest maiden, wishing for nothing but peace and quiet. But the others couldn't stand for that—they pulled her out, beat her, cut her, and ate her.

"This is extremely amusing!" said the magician.

"Yes, but what do you think it is?" asked Krible-Krable. "Can you find out?"

"Why, that's easy to see," answered the magician. "Of course, it is Copenhagen, or some other large city. I can't tell which, for they all look alike. But it's certainly some large city."

"It's a drop of ditchwater!" said Krible-Krable.

THE HAPPY FAMILY (1847)

The biggest leaf we have in this country is certainly the burdock leaf. If you hold one in front of your little stomach, it's just like a real apron; and in rainy weather, if you lay it on your head, it does almost as well as an umbrella. It's really amazingly large. Now, a burdock never grows alone; no, when you see one, you'll always see others around it. It's a splendid sight; and all this splendor is nothing more than food for snails—the big white snails that the fine people in olden days used to have made into fricassees. When they had eaten them, they would smack their lips and say, "My! How good that is!" For somehow, they had the idea that the snails tasted delicious. You see, these snails lived on the burdock leaves, and that's why the burdock was first grown.

There was a certain old manor house where the people didn't eat snails anymore. The snails had almost died out, but the burdock hadn't. These grew and grew on all the walks and flower beds—they couldn't be stopped—until the whole place was a forest of burdocks. Here and there stood an apple or a plum tree, but except for that, people wouldn't have thought there had ever been a garden there. Everywhere was burdock, and among the burdocks lived the last two incredibly old snails!

They themselves didn't know how old they were, but they could remember very clearly that once there had been a great many more of them, that they had descended from a prominent foreign family, and they knew perfectly well that the whole forest had been planted just for them and their family.

They had never been away from home, but they did know that somewhere there was something called a manor house, and that there you were boiled until you turned black, and were laid on a silver dish; but what happened afterwards they hadn't the least idea. Furthermore, they couldn't imagine what it would be like to be boiled and laid on a silver dish, but everyone said it must be very wonderful and a great distinction. Neither the cockchafer nor the toad nor the earthworm, whom they asked about it, could give them any information. None of their families had ever been boiled or laid on silver dishes.

So the old white snails knew they were by far the most important people in the world. The forest was there just for their sake, and the manor house existed just so that they could be boiled and laid on silver dishes!

The two old snails led a quiet and happy life, and since they were childless, they had adopted a little orphan snail, which they were bringing up as their own child. He wouldn't grow very large, for he was only a common snail; but the two old snails— and especially the mother snail—thought it was easy to see how well he was growing. And she begged the father snail to touch the little snail's shell, if he couldn't see it, and so he felt it and found that she was right.

One day, it rained very hard.

"Just listen to it drum on the burdock leaves!" cried Father Snail. "Rum-dum-dum! Rum-dum-dum!"

"Drops are also coming down here!" said the mother. "It's coming straight down the stalks, and it'll be wet down here before you know it. I'm certainly glad we have our own good houses and the little one has his own. We're better off than any other creatures; it's quite plain that we're the most important people in the world. We have our own houses from our very birth, and the burdock forest has been planted just for us. I wonder how far it extends, and what lies beyond it."

"There can't be anything beyond," said Father Snail, "that's any better than we have here. I have nothing in the world to wish for."

"Well, I have," said the mother. "I'd like to be taken to the manor house and boiled and laid on a silver dish. All our ancestors had that done to them, and, believe me, it must be something quite uncommon!"

"Maybe the manor house has fallen to pieces," suggested Father Snail. "Or perhaps the burdock forest has grown over it, so that the people can't get out at all. Don't be in such a hurry—but then you're always hurrying so. And the little one is beginning to do the same thing. Why, he's been creeping up that stalk for three days. It really makes my head dizzy to watch him go!"

"Don't scold him," said Mother Snail. "He crawls very carefully. He'll bring us much joy, and we old folk don't have anything else to live for. But have you ever thought where we can find a wife for him? Don't you think there might be some more of our kind of people farther back in the burdock woods?"

"I suppose there may be black snails back there," said the old man.

"Black snails without houses! Much too vulgar! And they're conceited, anyway. But let's ask the ants to find out for us; they're always running around as if they had important business. They're sure to know of a wife for our little snail."

"Certainly, I know a very beautiful bride," said one of the ants. "But I don't think she'd do, because she's a queen!"

"That doesn't matter," said Mother Snail emphatically. "Does she have a house?"

"She has a castle!" replied the ant. "The most beautiful ant's castle, with seven hundred corridors!"

"Thank you very much," said Mother Snail, "but our boy shall not go into an anthill! If you don't know of anything better, we'll ask the white gnats to find out for us. They flit around in the rain and sunshine, and they know this forest inside and out."

"We have just the wife for him," said the gnats. "A hundred man-steps from here, a little snail with a house is sitting on a gooseberry bush. She is all alone in the world, and quite old enough to marry. It's only a hundred man-steps from here!"

"Fine, but she must come to him," said the old couple. "Our child has a whole burdock forest, and she has only a bush."

And so the gnats had the little maiden snail come over. It took her eight days to get there, but that was the wonderful part of it—for it showed she had the right sort of dignity.

And then they had a fine wedding! Six glowworms lit up the place as well as they could, but aside from that, it was a very quiet ceremony, for the old people did not care for feasting or merriment. A charming speech was made by Mother Snail, but Father Snail couldn't say a word; he was too deeply moved. And so she gave the young couple the whole burdock forest for a dowry, and repeated what she had always said—that it was the finest place in the world, and that the young people, if they lived honorably and had many children, would someday be taken with their young ones to the manor house, to be boiled black and laid on a silver dish. And when Mother Snail's speech was finished, the old people crept into their houses and never came out again, for they went to sleep.

Now the young couple ruled the forest and did have many children. But since none of them were ever boiled and laid in silver dishes, they decided that the manor house must have fallen into ruins and that all the people in the world had died out. And since nobody contradicted them, I think they must have been right. So the rain beat on the burdock leaves, to play the drum for them, and the sun shone, to color the forest for them; and they were very happy. The whole family was happy—extremely happy, indeed they were.

THE STORY OF A MOTHER (1847)

A mother sat by her little child. She was so sad, so afraid he would die. The child's face was pallid. His little eyes were shut. His breath came faintly now, and then heavily as if he were sighing, and the mother looked more sadly at the dear little soul.

There came a knocking at the door, and a poor old man hobbled into the house. He was wrapped in a thick horseblanket. It kept him warm, and he needed it to keep out the wintry cold, for outside the world was covered with snow and ice, and the wind cut like a knife.

As the child was resting quietly for a moment, and the old man was shivering from the cold, the mother put a little mug of beer to warm on the stove for him. The old man rocked the cradle, and the mother sat down near it to watch her sick child, who labored to draw each breath. She lifted his little hand, and asked:

"You don't think I shall lose him, do you? Would the good Lord take him from me?"

The old man was Death himself. He jerked his head strangely, in a way that might mean yes or might mean no. The mother bowed her head and tears ran down her cheeks. Her head was heavy.

For three days and three nights, she had not closed her eyes. Now she dozed off to sleep, but only a moment. Something startled her and she awoke, shuddering in the cold.

"What was that?" she said, looking everywhere about the room. But the old man had gone and her little child had gone. Death had taken the child away. The old clock in the corner whirred and whirred. Its heavy lead weight dropped down to the floor with a thud. *Bong!* The clock stopped. The poor mother rushed wildly out of the house, calling for her child.

Out there in the snow sat a woman, dressed in long black garments. "Death," she said, "has been in your house. I just saw him hurrying away with your child in his arms. He goes faster than the wind. And he never brings back what he has taken away."

"Tell me which way he went," said the mother. "Only tell me the way, and I will find him."

"I know the way," said the woman in black, "but before I tell you, you must sing to me all those songs you used to sing to your child. I am Night. I love lullabies, and I hear them often. When you sang them, I saw your tears."

"I shall sing them again—you shall hear them all," said the mother, "but do not stop me now. I must catch him. I must hurry to find my child."

Night kept silent and still, while the mother wrung her hands, and sang, and wept. She sang many songs, but the tears that she shed were many, many more. At last Night said to her, "Go to the right. Go into the dark pine woods. I saw Death go there with your child."

Deep into the woods, the mother came to a crossroad, where she was at a loss which way to go. At the crossroad grew a blackthorn bush, without leaf or flower, for it was wintertime and its branches were glazed with ice.

"Did you see Death go by with my little child?"

"Yes," said the blackthorn bush. "But I shall not tell you which way he went unless you warm me against your heart. I am freezing to death. I am stiff with ice."

She pressed the blackthorn bush against her heart to warm it, and the thorns stabbed so deep into her flesh that great drops of red blood flowed. So warm was the mother's heart that the blackthorn bush blossomed and put forth green leaves on that dark winter's night. And it told her the way to go.

Then she came to a large lake, where there was neither sailboat nor rowboat. The ice on the lake was too thin to hold her weight, and yet not open or shallow enough for her to wade. But across the lake she must go if ever she was to find her child. She stooped down to drink the lake dry, and that of course was impossible for any human being, but the poor woman thought that maybe a miracle would happen.

"No, that would never do," the lake objected. "Let us make a bargain between us. I collect pearls, and your two eyes are the clearest I've ever seen. If you will cry them out for me, I shall carry you over to the great greenhouse where Death lives and tends his trees and flowers. Each one of them is a human life."

"Oh, what would I not give for my child," said the crying mother, and she wept till her eyes dropped down to the bottom of the lake and became two precious pearls. The lake took her up as if in a swing and swept her to the farther shore.

Here stood the strangest house that ever was. It rambled for many a mile. One wouldn't know whether it was a cavernous, forested mountain, or whether it was made of wood. But the poor mother could not see this, for she had cried out her eyes.

"Where shall I find Death, who took my child from me?" she cried.

"He has not come back yet," said the old woman who took care of the great greenhouse while Death was away. "How did you find your way here? Who helped you?"

"The Lord helped me," she said. "He is merciful, and so must you be. Where can I find my child?"

"I don't know him," said the old woman, "and you can't see to find him. But many flowers and trees have withered away in the night, and Death will be along soon to transplant them. Every human being, you know, has his tree or his flower of life, depending on what sort of person he is. These look like other plants, but they have a heart that beats. A child's heart beats, too. You know the beat of your own child's heart. Listen and you may hear it. But what will you give me if I tell you what else you must do?"

"I have nothing left," the poor mother said, "but I will go to the ends of the Earth for you."

"I have nothing to do there," said the old woman, "but you can give me your long black hair. You know how beautiful it is, and I like it. I'll give you my white hair for it. White hair is better than none."

"Is that all you ask?" said the mother. "I will gladly give it to you." And she gave her beautiful long black tresses in exchange for the old woman's white hair.

Then they went into Death's great greenhouse, where flowers and trees were strangely intertwined. In one place, delicate hyacinths were kept under glass bells, and around them, great hardy peonies flourished. There were water plants too, some thriving where the stalks of others were choked by twisting water snakes or gnawed away by black crayfish. Tall palm trees grew there, and plane trees, and oaks. There grew parsley and sweet-smelling thyme. Every tree or flower went by the name of one particular person, for each was the life of someone still living in China, in Greenland, or in some other part of the world. There were big trees stunted by the small pots that their roots filled to bursting, and elsewhere grew languid little flowers that came to nothing, for all the care that was lavished upon them and for all the rich earth and the mossy carpet where they grew. The sad, blind mother bent over the tiniest plants and listened to the beat of their human hearts, and among so many millions, she knew her own child's heartbeat.

"This is it," she cried, groping for a little blue crocus, which had wilted and dropped to one side.

"Don't touch that flower," the old woman said. "Stay here. Death will be along any minute now, and you may keep him from pulling it up. Threaten him that, if he does, you will pull up other plants. That will frighten him, for he has to account for them to the Lord. Not one may be uprooted until God says so."

Suddenly an icy wind blew through the place, and the blind mother felt Death come near.

"How did you find your way here?" he asked her. "How did you ever get here before me?"

"I am a mother," she said.

Then Death stretched out his long hand toward the wilted little flower, but she held her hands tightly around it, in terror lest he touch a single leaf. Death breathed upon her hands, and his breath was colder than the coldest wind. Her hands fell, powerless.

"You have no power to resist me," Death told her.

"But our Lord has," she said.

"I only do his will," said Death, "I am his gardener. I take his flowers and trees and plant them again in the great Paradise gardens, in the unknown land. But how they thrive, and of their life there, I dare not speak."

"Give me back my child," the mother wept and implored him. Suddenly, she grasped a beautiful flower in each hand, and as she clutched them, she called to Death: "I shall tear out your flowers by the roots, for I am desperate."

"Do not touch them!" Death told her. "You say you are desperate, yet you would drive another mother to the same despair."

"Another mother!" The blind woman's hands let go the flowers.

"Behold," said Death, "you have your eyes again. I saw them shining as I crossed the lake, and fished them up, but I did not know they were yours. They are clearer than before. Take them and look deep into this well. I shall tell you the names of the flowers you were about to uproot, and you shall see the whole future of those human lives that you would have destroyed and disturbed."

She looked into the well, and it made her glad to see how one life became a blessing to the world, for it was so kind and happy. Then she saw the other life, which held only sorrow, poverty, fear, and woe.

"Both are the will of God," said Death.

"Which one is condemned to misery, and which is the happy one?" she asked.

"That I shall not tell you," Death said. "But I tell you this. One of the flowers belongs to your own child. One life that you saw was your child's fate, your own child's future."

Then the mother shrieked in terror, "Which was my child? Tell me! Save my innocent child. Spare him such wretchedness. Better that he be taken from me. Take him to God's kingdom. Forget my tears. Forget the prayers I have said and the things I have done."

"I do not understand," Death said. "Will you take your own child back, or shall I take him off to a land unknown to you?"

Then the mother wrung her hands, fell on her knees, and prayed to God:

"Do not hear me when I pray against your will. It is best. Do not listen, do not listen!" And she bowed her head, as Death took her child to the unknown land.

THE SHIRT COLLAR (1847)

There was once a perfect gentleman whose whole household goods consisted of one bootjack and a comb. But he also had one of the most remarkable shirt collars in the world. I'll tell you a story about it.

When the shirt collar had passed his prime, he turned his thoughts to marriage. In the fullness of time, he went to the wash, and there he met with a garter.

"My!" said the collar, "Anyone so slender, so tender, so neat and nice as you are, I never did see. May I know your name?"

"No," said the garter. "I won't tell you."

"Then at least tell me where you live?" asked the collar.

But the garter was so modest that she couldn't bring herself to answer such an embarrassing question.

"I believe you are a girdle," said the collar. "A sort of underneath girdle. And I dare say you're as useful as you are beautiful, my pretty little dear."

"I forbid you to speak to me," said the garter. "I'm sure I haven't given you the slightest encouragement."

"Your beauty is every encouragement," said the collar.

"Kindly keep away from me," said the garter. "You look too masculine."

"Oh, I'm a perfect gentleman," said the collar. "I've a bootjack and a comb to prove it."

This wasn't true at all, for they belonged to his master, but he liked to boast.

"Please don't come so close," said the garter. "I'm not used to such behavior."

"Prude!" the collar called her as they took him from the washtub. They starched him, hung him over a chair back in the sun, and then stretched him out on an ironing board. There he met with a sadiron.

"My dear lady," said the collar, "you adorable widow woman, the closer you come, the warmer I feel. I'm a changed collar since I met you, without a wrinkle left in me. You burn clear through me. Oh, won't you be mine?"

"Rag!" said the sadiron, as she flattened him out, for she went her way like a railway engine pulling cars down a track. "Rag!" was what she said.

The collar was the worse for wear at the edges, so the scissors were called to trim him.

"Oh," said the collar, "you must be a ballet dancer. How straight you stretch your legs out. Such a graceful performance! No one can do that like you."

"I'm well aware of it," said the scissors.

"You deserve to be no less than a countess," said the collar. "All I have to offer is my perfect gentleman, bootjack and comb. Oh, if only I had an earldom."

"I do believe he's daring to propose," said the scissors. She cut him so furiously that he never recovered.

"Now I shall have to ask the comb," said the collar. "My dear, how remarkably well you've kept your teeth. Have you ever thought of getting engaged?"

"Why, of course," said the comb. "I am engaged—to the bootjack."

"Engaged!" the collar exclaimed. Now that there was no one left for him to court, the collar pretended that he had never meant to marry.

Time passed, and the collar went his way to the bin in a paper mill, where the rags kept company according to rank, the fine rags in one bin, the coarse in another, just as it is in the world. They all gossiped aplenty, but the collar chattered the most, for he was an awful braggart.

"I've had sweethearts by the dozen," he told them. "Ladies never would leave me alone, and you can't blame them; for I was such a perfect gentleman, stiff with starch, and with a bootjack and comb to spare. You should have seen me then. You should have seen me unbend.

"I'll never forget my first love—such a charming little girdle, so slender and tender. She threw herself into a tub of water, all for the love of me. Then there was the widow, glowing to get me, but I jilted her and let her cool off. And there was the ballet dancer, whose mark I bear to this day. What a fiery creature she was! And even my comb fell so hard in love with me that she lost all her teeth when I left her. Yes, indeed, I have plenty on my conscience. But the garter—I mean the girdle—who drowned herself in the wash tub, is the one I feel most badly about. Oh, I have a black record, and it's high time I turned into spotless white paper."

And that's exactly what happened. All the rags were made into paper, and the collar became the page you see, the very paper on which this story is printed. That was because he boasted so outrageously about things that never had happened. So let's be careful to behave we better than he did, for you never can tell. Someday we may end up in the ragbag and be made into white paper on which the whole story of our life is printed in full detail. Then we'd have to turn tattletale on ourselves, just as the shirt collar has done.

THE FLAX (1848)

The flax was in full bloom. It had such pretty blue blossoms, as soft as the wings of a moth and even more delicate. And the sun shone down on the flax, and the rain clouds watered it, and that was as good for it as it is for little children to be bathed and kissed by their mothers—it makes them look so much prettier, and so it did the flax.

"People say that I stand exceedingly well," said the flax, "and that I am growing so charmingly tall that I'll make a grand piece of linen. Oh, how happy I am! No one could possibly be happier! How well off I am! And I'm sure I'll be put to some good use, too. The sunshine makes me so cheerful, and the rain tastes so fresh! I'm exceedingly happy; yes, I'm sure I'm the happiest being in the world!"

"Oh, yes," jeered the hedge stakes. "But you don't know the world the way we do. There are knots in us." And then they creaked out dolefully:

> *Snip, snap, snurre,*
> *Basse lurre!*
> *The ballad is over!*

"No, it's not," said the flax. "The sun will shine tomorrow, and the rain is so good for me, I can hear myself grow; I can feel that I'm in blossom. Who could ever be as happy as I?"

But one day, people came, grabbed the flax by the top, and pulled it up by the roots. Oh, how that hurt! Then it was thrown into the water as if to be drowned, and after that laid on the fire as if to be roasted. It was terrible!

"You can't always have what you want," said the flax. "It's good to suffer sometimes; it gives you experience."

But there was still worse to come. The flax was broken and cracked, hackled and scalded—it didn't even know what the operations were called—and finally put on the wheel—snurre, snurre! It was impossible to think clearly.

"I have been very happy in the past," it thought in all its pain. "You should always be thankful for the happiness you've enjoyed. Thankful, oh, yes!" And the flax clung to that thought as it was taken to the loom. And there it was woven into a large, beautiful piece of linen. All the flax from one field was made into one piece of cloth.

"But this is amazing!" cried the flax. "I never should have expected it! How lucky I am! What nonsense the hedge stakes used to talk with their

> *Snip, snap, snurre,*
> *Basse lurre!*

"Why, the ballad is by no means over! No, it is just beginning! This is wonderful! I've suffered, yes, but I've been made into something through suffering. I'm happier than anyone could be. How strong and yet soft I am, how white and long! This is much better than just being a plant; even if you bear flowers, nobody attends to you, and you only get watered when it rains. Now I get attention! The maid turns me over every morning, and gives me a shower bath in the washtub every evening. Why, the parson's wife herself came and looked at me, and said I was the finest piece of linen in the whole parish! Who could be any happier than I am now!"

Now the linen was taken into the house and cut up by the scissors. How they clipped and how they cut, and how it was pierced through with needles! Yes, that's what they did, and it was all very unpleasant. But at last, it was made up into twelve garments—garments that are unmentionable, but that people cannot do without. Twelve of them.

"Well, look at that! Now I am really useful!" cried the linen. "So this is my destiny! What a blessing! Now I am useful. And nothing brings such happiness as to be useful in the world! Now we're twelve pieces, but we're still one and the same. We are one dozen. What a stroke of luck!"

The years passed, and at last the linen pieces wouldn't hold together any longer.

"Everything must come to an end," said each piece. "I should like to have lasted a little longer, but you shouldn't wish for things like that."

Now the pieces were torn into rags and fragments, and they were sure it was going to be the end of them. They were hacked and mashed and boiled—yes, they didn't know what else was done to them—but finally, they became beautiful white paper!

"Well, if this isn't a surprise!" said the paper. "And a wonderful surprise! Why, I'm finer than ever! And people will write on me now. What wonderful stories they'll write! I certainly am lucky!"

And beautiful stories were written on the paper, and people read them and said they were very fine and would make mankind wiser and better. The words written on that paper would bring great blessings to the world.

"This is more than I could ever have dreamed of when I was a tiny blue flower in the field. How could I have expected to spread wisdom and joy to mankind? I can't yet understand it, but that's what has happened. Our Lord knows that I've really never done anything myself, but just tried to live as well as I could, yet He carries me one honor to another. Every time I think, 'Now surely the ballad is over,' I am moved up to something better. Now I suppose people will send me around the world, so everybody can read me. That's most likely. For every blue flower I used to have, I will now carry a beautiful thought! How could anyone be happier!"

But the paper did not travel around the world—instead it went to the printer, and there everything that was written on it was printed in a book, yes, in hundreds of books. In that way, a great many more people could get pleasure and benefit from the writings than if the one paper on which it was written had been sent out into the world and been worn out before it had gone very far.

"Yes, this is the most sensible way," thought the paper. "I didn't think of it. I'll stay at home, and be held in great honor, like an old grandfather. Because the book was written on me first; every word came down from the author's pen right onto me. But it is much better for the printed books to go out into the world and do good; I couldn't have wandered as far as they can go. My, how happy I am, and how lucky!"

Then the paper was bundled up and put away on a shelf. "It's good to rest a little after working," said the paper. "It gives you a chance to collect your thoughts and figure out what's inside of you. Now! I really know all that is written on me, and that means true progress. I wonder what's going to happen to me now! At any rate, I know I'll go forward again; I'm always going forward."

At last, the paper was taken out to the stove—it was to be burnt, for everybody said it wouldn't be proper to sell that paper to the huckster for wrapping butter and powdered sugar. And all the children in the house flocked around, for they wanted to see the blaze and count the many tiny red sparks as they died out, one after another. They call these sparks "the children going out of school," and the last spark of all is the "schoolmaster." Sometimes they think he has gone, but then comes another—the schoolmaster always come a little behind the rest.

So the big bundle of paper was laid on the fire. "Oh!" it cried, as it suddenly burst into flame. It rose higher into the air than the flax had ever been able to send its little blue blossoms, and it shone more brilliantly than the linen had ever been able to shine. Instantly the letters written on it became fiery red, and the words and thoughts of the writer vanished in the flame.

"I'm going straight up to the Sun!" said a voice in the flame. It was as if a thousand voices cried this together, as the flames burst through the chimney and out at the top. And brighter than the flames, but still invisible to mortal eyes, little tiny beings hovered, just as many as there had been blossoms on the flax long ago. They were lighter even than the flame that gave them birth, and when that flame had died away and nothing was left of the paper but black ashes, they danced over the embers again. Wherever their feet touched, their footprints, the tiny red sparks, could be seen. Thus the children came out of school, and the schoolmaster came last. It was a pleasure to watch, and the children of the house sang over the dead ashes:

> *Snip, snap, snurre,*
> *Basse lurre!*
> *The ballad is over!*

But the tiny invisible beings cried, "The ballad is never over! That is the best of all! We know that, and therefore none are so happy as we!"

But the children couldn't hear or understand that. And perhaps that's just as well; children shouldn't know everything.

THE PHOENIX BIRD (1850)

Beneath the Tree of Knowledge in the Garden of Paradise stood a rosebush. And here, in the first rose, a bird was born. His plumage was beautiful, his song glorious, and his flight was like the flashing of light. But when Eve plucked the fruit of the Tree of Knowledge, and she and Adam were driven from Paradise, a spark fell from the flaming sword of the angel into the nest of the bird and set it afire. The bird perished in the flames, but from the red egg in the nest there flew a new bird, the only one of its kind, the one solitary phoenix bird. The legend tells us how he lives in Arabia and how every century he burns himself to death in his nest, but each time, a new phoenix, the only one in the world, flies out from the red egg.

The bird darts about as swift as light, beautiful in color, glorious in song. When a mother sits beside her infant's cradle, he settles on the pillow and forms a glory with his wings about the head of the child. He flies through the room of contentment and brings sunshine into it, and he makes the violets on the humble cupboard smell sweet.

But the phoenix is not a bird of Arabia alone. In the glimmer of the northern lights, he flies over the plains of Lapland and hops amid the yellow flowers in the short Greenland summer. Deep beneath the copper mountains of Falun, and in England's coal mines, he flies in the form of a powdered moth over the hymnbook resting in the hands of the pious miner. He floats down the sacred waters of the Ganges on a lotus leaf, and the eye of the Hindu maid brightens when she beholds him.

Phoenix bird! Don't you know him? The bird of Paradise, the holy swan of song? He sat on the car of Thespis, like a chattering raven, flapping his black gutter-stained wings; the swan's red, sounding beak swept over the singing harp of Iceland; he sat on Shakespeare's shoulder, disguised as Odin's raven, and whispered, "Immortality!" into his ear; and at the minstrels' feast, he fluttered through the halls of the Wartburg.

Phoenix bird! Don't you know him? He sang the "Marseillaise" to you, and you kissed the feather that fell from his wing; he came in the glory of Paradise, and perhaps you turned away from him toward the sparrow that sat with gold tinsel on its wings.

The bird of Paradise—renewed each century—born in flame, dying in flame! Your portrait in a frame of gold hangs in the halls of the rich, but you yourself often fly around lonely and misunderstood—a myth only: "The phoenix bird of Arabia."

When you were born in the Garden of Paradise, in its first rose, beneath the tree of knowledge, our Lord kissed you and gave you your true name—poetry!

A STORY (1851)

All the apple trees in the garden were blooming. They had hastened to cover themselves with blossoms before their green leaves were fully unfolded. All the ducklings were in the farmyard, and so was the cat; it basked in the sun and tried to lick the sunshine from its own paws.

And to look across the fields was a pleasing sight; there stood the corn, so beautifully green, while all the small birds chirped and twittered as happily as if they were having a great holiday.

And, indeed, people could rightly think of this as a holiday, for it was Sunday. The bells were chiming while people in their best clothes were walking to church and looking so cheerful. It was such a bright, warm day that one might well say: "How good God is to grant us so many blessings!"

But inside the church, the preacher in the pulpit spoke in a loud and angry tone; he said that all humans were wicked and that God would certainly punish them by sending them to the eternal torments of hell when they died. He said that they would never find peace or rest in hell, for their consciences would never die nor would the fires ever be extinguished.

This was terrible to hear, but still he went on as if the subject he was explaining were really true. He described hell to them as a stagnant cave, where all the impure and sinful of the world would be; there would be no air, only the hot sulphur flames, and no bottom there, and the wicked would sink deeper and deeper into eternal silence forever!

It was horrible to hear this, but the preacher spoke from his heart, and all the people in the church were terrified.

But the birds outside the church sang joyously, and the sun was shining warmly; it was as if each little bird were saying, "Nothing is so great as the loving-kindness of the Almighty!"

Yes, outside the church, it was not at all like the preacher's sermon.

Before the preacher went to bed that evening, he noticed that his wife sat silent and thoughtful. "What's the matter with you?" he said to her.

"Why," she replied, "the matter with me is that I can't quite bring myself to agree with what you said today in your sermon. It doesn't seem right to say that so many sinners will be condemned to everlasting fire forever. Forever! Ah, how long! I'm only a poor sinful creature myself, but I can't believe in my heart that even the vilest sinner will be condemned to burn in torment forever! We know the mercy of the Almighty is as great as His power; He knows how people are tempted from without and within by their own evil natures. No, I do not believe it, even if you said so."

It was autumn, the trees scattering their leaves on the ground, and the severe but earnest preacher sat beside the bed of a dying person. A faithful soul closed her eyes forever; it was the preacher's wife.

"If anyone can find peace and rest in the grave, through God's mercy, it is you!" sighed the preacher, as he folded her hands and read a psalm over the dead woman.

She was laid in her grave. Two large tears rolled down the cheeks of the sincere man, and in the parsonage, everything seemed so empty and still. The sunshine of his home had vanished, for *she* had gone.

It was night, and a cold wind blew over the head of the preacher. He opened his eyes, and it seemed to him that the moon was shining into the room, but there was no moonlight. A figure stood beside his bed, and the spirit of his deceased wife shone upon him. Earnestly and sadly, she looked at him, as if she had something on her mind that she wanted to say to him.

He half raised himself in bed, stretched out his arms to her, and cried, "Then even *you* aren't permitted to rest in peace forever? Must you suffer, too? You, the best, the most pious!"

The dead bowed her head as if to say "yes," and laid her hand on her heart.

"And can I give you peace in the grave?" he asked.

"Yes," was the distinct reply.

"And how?"

"Bring me a hair, just one single hair, from the head of just one sinner whom God will condemn to eternal torture in hell."

"Yes, you should be freed that easily, you pure, you pious woman!" he said.

"Then follow me," said the dead. "It has been granted us that you can fly through the air by my side, wherever your thoughts are directed. To mortals, we shall be invisible and able to pass unseen through the closed and bolted doors of inner rooms. But you must be *certain* that the man you point out to me as eternally damned is really one whom God will condemn to the torments of hellfire forever, and he must be found before the cock crows."

And quickly, as if carried by the wings of thoughts, they arrived at the great city. On the walls of the houses, letters of living flame gave the names of the deadly sins: Arrogance, Greed, Drunkenness, Wantonness—in fact, the whole seven-colored bow of sin.

"Yes, in these houses, as I thought, as I knew," said the preacher, "live those who will be punished forever."

And then they stood before a brilliantly lighted gate. The broad steps were covered with flowers and carpets, while from the festive rooms came the sounds of music and dancing.

A footman dressed in velvet and silk, with a large silver-handled stick in his hand, stood erect near the door.

"Our ball is as splendid as those at the palace of the king," said he, and turned toward the people outside. From tip to toe, his thoughts were evident: "Poor beggars who stare in at the gate; compared to me, you people are only cattle!"

"Arrogance," said the dead wife. "Do you see him?"

"Him!" replied the preacher. "Yes, but this man is only a fool and a simpleton. He'll not be condemned to everlasting fire or eternal torment."

"Only a fool!" echoed through the whole house of Arrogance; they were all fools there.

Then they flew within the four bare walls of a miser's room where, skinny, shivering with cold, hungry and thirsty, an old, old man clung desperately with all his thoughts to his gold. They saw how he, as in a fever, sprang from his miserable bed and took a loose stone out of the wall. There lay a stocking crammed full of gold pieces. The man kept fumbling in his ragged pockets, where he had sewn more gold, and his clammy fingers trembled.

"He is ill; it is insanity, a dreadful insanity. Haunted by terrors and evil dreams!"

Swiftly they left the miser's room, and stood before a dormitory of a jail, where the prisoners slept close together in long rows. Suddenly, one of them started up in his sleep and uttered the terrible cry of a wild beast! With his pointed elbow, he gave his companion a ferocious blow, and the latter turned around sleepily: "Shut up, you beast, and go to sleep! You go on like this every night!"

"Every night!" the man repeated. "Yes, every night *he* howls and torments me like this. I have committed many wrongs because of the passionate temper with which I was born. Twice my wicked temper has brought me here, but if I have done wrong, I am certainly being punished for it.

"There is only one thing I have not confessed. The last time I went out from here and passed by my master's farm, evil thoughts rose within me. I struck a match against the wall; it came a bit too close to the thatched roof. The heat seized onto the straw, as it often seizes onto me, and everything was burned. I helped to rescue the house property and the animals; no living creature perished, except a flock of pigeons that flew right into the fire, and also the yard dog, which was chained up. I had not thought of him. One could hear him howl, and that howl I can still hear when I want to sleep, and when I do fall asleep, the dog comes also. He is very large, with thick, shaggy fur, and he lies on me and howls and squeezes me until I am nearly choked. Now listen to what I tell you! You all can sleep and snore the whole night, but I can sleep for only a short quarter of an hour." And the blood rose to the head of the tormented; he threw himself upon his comrade and struck him in the face with his clenched fist.

"The madman is raging again!" everyone cried. Then the other criminals threw themselves on him, wrestled with him, bent his body down until his head was forced between his legs, and then bound him so tightly that the blood seemed about to burst from his eyes and his pores.

"You're killing him!" cried the preacher, and stretched his protecting hand over the sinner who had already suffered severely.

Then the scene changed. Unseen, they glided through rich homes, as well as through the huts of the poor. Wantonness and envy, and all the deadly sins, passed before them.

An angel from the judgment seat appeared to read to each of them their sins and their excuses. These excuses meant little to God, for He reads the hearts; He knows every hidden sin that dwells there; He knows the temptations that are before us in the outer world as well as in our own hearts, and knows when to show mercy and pitying love.

The preacher's hand trembled, and now he dared not stretch it out to pluck a single hair from the head of any sinner. Tears streamed from his eyes as he thought of the fountain of mercy and love, which can quench even the everlasting fire of hell.

And then the cock crowed!

"All-merciful God, I pray Thee grant her that peace in the grave that I have not been able to produce for her!"

"I have it now," said the dead wife. "It was your hard words and your gloomy belief in God and His creatures that drove me to you. Learn to know mankind. Even the soul of the wicked is a part of God Himself, a part that will conquer and extinguish even hellfire forever."

The preacher felt a kiss upon his lips, and a light streamed about him. God's bright sunshine shone into the room, and his living wife stood beside him, tender and loving. She had awakened him from a dream sent him by God.

THE PUPPET-SHOW MAN (1851)

On board the steamer was an elderly man with such a joyful face that if it didn't belie him, he must have been the happiest person on earth. In fact, he said he was the happiest; I heard it from his own mouth. He was a Dane, a countryman of mine, and a traveling theatrical producer. His whole company was with him and lay in a large box, for he was the proprietor of a puppet show. He said that his natural cheerfulness had been enlightened by a polytechnic student, and the experiment had left him completely happy. At first, I didn't understand what he meant, but later he explained the whole thing to me, and here is the story.

"In the town of Slagelse," he said, "I gave a performance in the post office courtyard before a brilliant audience, all juvenile except for two old matrons. Suddenly, a person in black, looking like a student, entered the hall and sat down; he laughed at the right places and applauded appropriately. He was an unusual spectator. I was anxious to know who he was, and I learned that he was a student from the Polytechnic Institute of Copenhagen who had been sent out to teach the people in the provinces. My performance ended promptly at eight o'clock, for children must go to bed early, and a manager must consider the convenience of his public. At nine o'clock, the student began his lecture and experiments, and now I was one of his spectators. It was all extraordinary to hear and see. Most of it went over my head and into the parson's, as one says, but it made me think that if we mortals can learn so much, we must surely be intended to last longer than the little span we're here on earth. What he performed were miracles, and though only small ones, everything was done as easily as a foot fits into a stocking, as naturally as nature functions. In the days of Moses and the prophets, such a man would have been counted among the wise men of the land; in the Middle Ages, he would have been burned at the stake. I didn't sleep that whole night. And the next evening, when I gave another performance and the student was again present, I was in an exuberantly good humor. I once heard from an actor that when he played the part of a lover, he always thought of one particular lady in the audience; he played only to her and forgot the rest of the house. Now the polytechnic student was my 'she,' my only spectator, for whom alone I performed.

"After the performance, when the puppets had taken their curtain calls, the polytechnic student invited me into his room to have a glass of wine; he spoke of my plays, and I spoke of his science, and I think we were equally pleased. But I had the better of it, for there was much of what he did that he couldn't explain to me. For instance, a piece of iron that falls through a spiral becomes magnetic. Now why does that happen? The spirit enters it, but where does it come from? It is just as it is with the humans in our world, I think; our Lord lets them fall through the spiral line of time; the spirit enters them, and there then stands a Napoleon, a Luther, or some such person. 'The whole world is a series of miracles,' said the student, 'but we're so used to them that we call them everyday things.' And he continued talking and explaining until finally my skull seemed lifted from my brain, and I honestly confessed that if I weren't already an old fellow, I would at once attend the Polytechnic Institute and learn to examine the world more closely, even though I was one of the happiest of men.

"'One of the happiest!' said the student, and seemed to be quite thoughtful about it. 'Are you really happy?' he asked me.

"'Yes,' I said, 'I am happy. All the towns welcome me whenever I come with my company. But I do, to be sure, have *one* wish, which sometimes haunts me like a goblin—a nightmare that rides on my good nature. I should like to be a real theatrical manager, director of a troupe of real men and women!'

"'You wish your puppets would come to life; you wish they would become real actors,' he said, 'and you would be their director; and then would you be completely happy, you think?' He didn't believe it, but I believed it, and we talked back and forth about it, without coming any nearer a solution; still, we clinked glasses together, and the wine was excellent. There must have been some magic in it, for otherwise, the story would have been that I got drunk. That didn't happen, though; I kept my clear viewpoint. Somehow there was sunlight in the room, and it shone from the face of the polytechnic student. It made me think of the old tales of the gods in their eternal youth, when they wandered on earth. I told him that, and he smiled. I could have sworn that he was one of the old gods in disguise, or at least that he belonged to their family! And he certainly must have been something of that sort, for my greatest wish was to be fulfilled; the puppets would come to life, and I would be the director of real people. We drank to that.

"He packed all my puppets into a wooden box, strapped it on my back, and then let me fall through a spiral. I can still hear how I tumbled; and then I was lying on the floor—this is positively true—and the whole company sprang from the box! The spirit had come upon all of them; all the puppets had become great artists—at least, so they said—and I was their director. Everything was ready for the first performance. But the whole company wanted to speak to me, and the public, too.

"The prima ballerina said that the 'house' was going to 'fall' if she didn't stand on one leg in the show; she was mistress of the whole company, and insisted on being treated as such. The lady who played the empress wanted to be treated as an empress off stage, or else she would get out of practice. The man who had only to deliver a letter made himself as important as the leading man, for the little parts were just as important as the big ones, and all were of equal consequence in making up an artistic whole, he said. The hero would play only parts composed of nothing but exit lines, because those brought him the applause. The prima donna would only play act in a red light, for that suited her best; she refused to appear in a blue one. They were like a troupe of flies in a bottle, and I was in the middle of the bottle with them, for I was the director. My breath stopped, and my head was dizzy; I was as miserable as a man can be. It was quite a new kind of people among whom I found myself now. I only wished I had them all back in their box and that I had never been a director at all. I told them straight out that they were all nothing but puppets—and so they killed me!

"I found myself lying on my bed in my room; how I got there, or how I got away from the polytechnic student, he may know—I don't. The moon shone in on the floor where the box lay overturned, and all the dolls, great and small, were scattered about in confusion; but I wasn't idle. I jumped out of bed and popped them all back into the box, some on their heads and some on their feet; then I slammed down the lid, and seated myself on the box. It was a picture worth painting! Can't you just see it? I can! 'Now you'll just have to stay in there,' I said. 'And I'll never again wish that you have flesh and blood!' I was in such a relieved frame of mind, I was the happiest of men. The polytechnic student had entirely purified me. I sat there in a state of utter contentment and fell asleep on the box.

"The next morning—it was really noon, for I slept wonderfully late that day—I was still sitting there, lighthearted, and conscious that my one former wish had been foolish. I asked for the polytechnic student, but he was gone, like the gods of Greece and Rome; and since that time, I have been the happiest of men. I am a happy director; my company never grumbles, or my public either—they're amused to their hearts' content. I can put my plays together just as I like, taking out of other plays anything that pleases me, and no one is annoyed at it. Plays that nowadays are disdained in the big theaters, but that the public ran to see, and wept over, thirty years ago—those plays I now put on. I perform them for the little ones, and the little ones weep just as Papa and Mamma did. I give them *Johanne Montsaucon* and *Dyveke*, but in abbreviated versions, for the youngsters don't want long-winded love stories; what they want is something sad but short.

"I have traveled through Denmark from one end to the other; I know everyone there, and everyone knows me. Now I'm on my way to Sweden, and if I'm successful there and make good money, I'll be a man of Scandinavia; otherwise I won't. I tell you this because you are my countryman."

And I, as his countryman, in turn naturally tell it—just for the sake of telling it.

THE SILENT BOOK (1851)

On the highroad in the forest, there stood a lonely farmhouse; the road passed right through its courtyard.

All the windows were open to the warm sun; within the house, there was bustling life, but out in the yard, under an arbor of blooming lilacs, there rested an open coffin. The dead man had been carried to it, and this morning, he was to be buried. There was no one to stand by the coffin and look down in sorrow at the dead, no one to shed a tear over him.

A white cloth covered his face, and under his head lay a great thick book, its leaves formed of whole sheets of gray paper. And between each leaf there lay withered flowers, kept close and hidden, so that the book was really a complete herbarium, gathered in many different places. His request had been that the book be buried with him, for each flower had formed a chapter of his life.

"Who is the dead man?" we asked; and the answer was:

"The old student of Upsala. They say he was once a brilliant man who knew foreign languages and could sing and write songs, too. But it was also said that something went wrong with him, and he wasted his thoughts and himself in drinking. Finally, when his health was gone, he came out here to the country, where some kindly person paid his board and lodging. He was as gentle as a child, but when his dark moods came on him, he became as strong as a giant and ran about the forest like a hunted beast. But if we could manage to get him home and persuade him to open the book with the withered flowers, he would sit quietly all day long, looking at one flower after another, and often the tears rolled down his cheeks. God only knows what thoughts those flowers brought back to him. But he begged that the book be laid in the coffin with him, so there it is. In a little while, we'll nail the lid down, and then he will have his sweet rest in the grave."

We lifted up the cloth; there was a peaceful look on the face of the dead man; a ray of sunshine flickered across it. A swallow darted swiftly into the arbor and wheeled rapidly, twittering above the dead man's head.

Surely we all know that strange feeling when we take out old letters of our youth and read them. All the hopes and sorrows of our life seem to rise up before us again. How many of those whom we then knew and were on intimate terms with are dead to us now! Yet they are still alive, although for a long time they have not been in our thoughts—those whom we once thought we should cling to forever and share their joys and sorrows.

The faded oak leaf in that silent book is the memento of a friend, the school friend who was to remain a friend for life. He himself had fastened that leaf in the student's cap in the green forest long ago, when that lifelong bond of friendship was made. Where is that friend now? The leaf is kept; the bond—broken.

Here is a foreign hothouse plant, far too tender for the gardens of the north; its fresh odor seems to cling to it still. The daughter of a noble house gave it to him out of her own garden.

Here is a water lily that he himself plucked and watered with his bitter tears, a water lily of sweet waters. And what do the leaves of this nettle tell us? What were his thoughts when he plucked it and laid it away?

Here are lilies of the valley from the dark solitudes of the forest, honeysuckle from the taproom flowerpot, and here the sharp, bare grass blade.

Gently, the blooming lilac bends its fresh and fragrant clusters over the dead man's head; the swallow darts by again—"Quivit! Quivit!" Now the men come with nails and hammer; the lid is laid over the dead, who rests his head silently on the silent book.

Hidden—forgotten!

THERE IS A DIFFERENCE (1851)

It was in the month of May. The wind was still cold, but spring had come, said the trees and the bushes, the fields and the meadows. Everywhere, flowers were budding into blossom; even the hedges were alive with them. Here spring spoke about herself; it spoke from a little apple tree, from which hung a single branch so fresh and blooming, and fairly weighed down by a glorious mass of rosy buds just ready to open.

Now this branch knew how lovely it was, for that knowledge lies in the leaf as well as in the flesh, so it wasn't a bit surprised when one day a grand carriage stopped in the road beside it, and the young countess in the carriage said that this apple branch was the most beautiful she had ever seen—it was spring itself in its loveliest form. So she broke off the apple branch and carried it in her own dainty hand, shading it from the sun with her silk parasol, as they drove on to her castle, in which there were lofty halls and beautifully decorated rooms. Fleecy-white curtains fluttered at its open windows, and there were many shining, transparent vases full of beautiful flowers. In one of these vases, which looked as if it were carved of new-fallen snow, she placed the apple branch, among fresh green beech leaves—a lovely sight indeed.

And so it happened that the apple branch grew proud, and that's quite human.

All sorts of people passed through the rooms, and, according to their rank, expressed their admiration in different ways; some said too much, some said too little, and some said nothing at all. And the apple branch began to realize that there were differences in people as well as in plants.

"Some are used for nourishment, some are for ornament, and some you could very well do without," thought the apple branch.

From its position at the open window, the apple branch could look down over the gardens and meadows below, and consider the differences among the flowers and plants beneath. Some were rich, some were poor, and some were very poor.

"Miserable, rejected plants," said the apple branch. "There is a difference, indeed! It's quite proper and just that distinctions should be made. Yet how unhappy they must feel, if indeed a creature like that is capable of feeling anything, as I and my equals do. But it must be that way; otherwise, everybody would be treated as though they were just alike."

And the apple branch looked down with especial pity on one kind of flower that grew everywhere in meadows and ditches. They were much too common ever to be gathered into bouquets; they could be found between the paving stones; they shot up like the rankest and most worthless of weeds. They were dandelions, but people have given them the ugly name, "the devil's milk pails."

"Poor wretched outcasts," said the apple branch. "I suppose you can't help being as common as you are, and having such a vulgar name! It's the same with plants as with men—there must be a difference."

"A difference?" repeated the sunbeam, as it kissed the apple branch; but it kissed the golden "devil's milk pails," too. And all the other sunbeams did the same, kissing all the flowers equally, poor as well as rich.

The apple branch had never thought about our Lord's infinite love for everything that lives and moves in Him, had never thought how much that is good and beautiful can lie hidden but still not be forgotten; and that, too, was human.

But the sunbeam, the ray of light, knew better. "You don't see very clearly; you are not very farsighted. Who are these outcast flowers that you pity so much?"

"Those devil's milk pails down there," replied the apple branch. "Nobody ever ties them up in bouquets; they're trodden under foot, because there are too many of them. And when they go to seed, they fly about along the road like little bits of wool and hang on people's clothes. They're just weeds! I suppose there must be weeds, too, but I'm certainly happy and grateful that I'm not like one of them!"

Now a whole flock of children ran out into the meadow to play. The youngest of them was so tiny that he had to be carried by the others. When they set him down in the grass among the golden blossoms, he laughed and gurgled with joy, kicked his little legs, rolled over and over, and plucked only the yellow dandelions. These he kissed in innocent delight.

The bigger children broke off the flowers of the dandelions and joined the hollow stalks link by link into chains. First, they would make one for a necklace, then a longer one to hang across the shoulders and around the waist, and finally one to go around their heads; it was a beautiful wreath of splendid green links and chains.

But the biggest of the children carefully gathered the stalks that had gone to seed, those loose, aerial, woolly blossoms, those wonderfully perfect balls of dainty white plumes, and held them to their lips, trying to blow away all the white feathers with one breath. Granny had told them that whoever could do that would receive new clothes before the year was out. The poor, despised dandelion was considered quite a prophet on such occasions.

"Now do you see?" asked the sunbeam. "Do you see its beauty and power?"

"Oh, it's all right—for children," replied the apple branch.

Now an old woman came into the meadow. She stooped and dug up the roots of the dandelion with a blunt knife that had lost its handle. Some of the roots she would roast instead of coffee berries; others she would sell to the apothecary to be used as drugs.

"Beauty is something higher than this," said the apple branch. "Only the chosen few can really be allowed into the kingdom of the beautiful; there's as much difference between plants as between men."

Then the sunbeam spoke of the infinite love of the Creator for all his creatures, for everything that has life, and of the equal distribution of all things in time and eternity.

"That's just your opinion," replied the apple branch.

Now some people came into the room, and among them was the young countess who had placed the apple branch in the transparent vase. She was carrying a flower— or whatever it was—that was protected by three or four large leaves around it like a cap, so that no breath of air or gust of wind could injure it. She carried it more carefully and tenderly than she had the apple branch when she had brought it to the castle. Very gently, she removed the leaves, and then the apple branch could see what she carried. It was a delicate, feathery crown of starry seeds borne by the despised dandelion!

This was what she had plucked so carefully and carried so tenderly, so that no single one of the loose, dainty, feathered arrows that rounded out its downy form should be blown away. There it was, whole and perfect. With delight, she admired the beautiful form, the airy lightness, the marvelous mechanism of a thing that was destined so soon to be scattered by the wind.

"Look how wonderfully beautiful our Lord made this!" she cried. "I'll paint it, together with the apple branch. Everybody thinks it is so extremely beautiful, but this poor flower is lovely, too; it has received as much from our Lord in another way. They are very different, yet both are children in the kingdom of the beautiful!"

The sunbeam kissed the poor dandelion, and then kissed the blooming apple branch, whose petals seemed to blush a deeper red.

THE WORLD'S FAIREST ROSE (1851)

There was once a mighty queen, in whose gardens were found the most glorious flowers at all seasons of the year and from all countries of the world. But best of all she loved roses, and therefore she had all possible varieties of this flower, from the wild dog rose, with its apple-scented green leaves, to the most splendid roses of Provence. They grew along the walls of the castle, wound around pillars and window frames, and spread into the passages and along the ceilings of all the halls; and the roses were varied in fragrance, form, and color.

But there were sorrow and mourning in those halls now, for the queen lay upon a sickbed, and the doctors declared she must die.

"Yet there is still one thing that can save her," said the wisest of the doctors. "Bring her the world's fairest rose, the one that is the expression of the brightest and purest love. If that can be brought before her eyes before they close, she will not die!"

Now, young and old came from everywhere with roses, the fairest from each garden. But none was the right sort. The flower had to come out of the Garden of Love, but which was the rose there that expressed the brightest and purest love?

And the poets sang of the world's fairest rose; each one named his own. And word was sent throughout the land to every age, every station in life, every heart that beat with love.

"No one has yet named the flower," said the wise old man. "No one has pointed out the spot where it bloomed in its glory. It is not the rose from the coffin of Romeo and Juliet, or from the grave of Valborg, though these shall ever be fragrant in song and tales. It is not the rose that bloomed forth from Winkelried's bloodstained lance, or from the sacred blood that flows from the breast of the hero who dies for his country, though no death is sweeter than that, and no rose redder than that blood. Nor is it that magic flower in the pursuit of which men in their quiet chambers devote many long and sleepless nights and much of their fresh life—the magic flower of science."

"I know where it blooms," said a happy mother, who came with her tender child to the queen's bedside. "I know where the world's fairest rose is found! The rose that is the expression of the brightest and purest love blooms on the cheeks of my sweet child when it opens its eyes after a refreshing sleep and smiles at me with all its love!"

"Fair indeed is that rose, but there is still a fairer," said the wise man.

"Yes, one much more beautiful," said another of the women. "I have seen it; a brighter, more sacred rose does not bloom, but it was pale as the petals of the tea rose. I saw it on the cheeks of the queen herself! She had laid aside her royal crown, and through the long, dreary night, she carried her sick child in her arms. She wept, kissed him, and said a prayer to God for him as only a mother prays in the hour of her anguish!"

"Holy and wonderful in its might is the white rose of a mother's grief, but it is still not the right one."

"No, the world's fairest rose I saw at the altar of the Lord," said the pious old bishop. "I saw it shine like the face of an angel. The young maidens went to the Lord's altar to renew the promises of their baptism, and roses were blushing and shining on their fresh cheeks. A young girl stood there; with all the purity and love of her young spirit, she looked up to God. That was the expression of the highest and purest love!"

"May her love be blessed!" said the wise old man. "But not one of you has yet named to me the world's fairest rose."

There came into the room a child, the queen's little son. Tears were in his eyes and on this cheeks, and he carried a great open book; its binding was of velvet, held with huge silver clasps.

"Mother!" said the little one. "Oh, hear what I have read!"

And the child sat beside the bed and read from the book of him who had suffered death on the Cross to save mankind, even those not yet born.

"Greater love there is not!"

And a roseate color spread over the queen's cheeks, and her eyes again became big and clear, for she saw the loveliest rose rise from the leaves of the book, the image of the rose that sprang from the blood of Christ shed on the Cross.

"I see it!" she said. "He who sees this, the world's fairest rose, shall never die!"

THE PIGS (1851)

Dear Charles Dickens once told us the story of the pig, and since that time it has put us in a good humor just to hear one grunt. Saint Anthony took the pig under his protection; and when we think of "the prodigal son," our thoughts promptly carry us into the midst of a pigsty.

And it was, as a matter of fact, in front of a pigsty that our carriage stopped, over in Sweden. Out near the highway, close beside the house, the farmer had put his pigsty, and another like it could scarcely have been found in the world. It had been an old state carriage; the seats had been removed and the wheels taken off so that the body of the old coach stood on its stomach. And four pigs were shut up inside it. Whether these were the first that had ever been in there, one couldn't ascertain; but that this had been born to be a state coach, there was every evidence of, even to the damask rag that hung down from the roof and that indeed bore witness of having seen better days. This is true, every blessed word.

"Oink! Oink!" was said inside. And the coach creaked and groaned; it was indeed having a mournful end. "The beautiful has gone," it sighed and said, or at least that's what it might have said.

We came back in the autumn and the coach was still there, but the pigs were gone. They were now lords in the forest. Rain and storm reigned, the wind blowing all the leaves from the trees, and gave them neither peace nor rest. The birds of passage had flown.

"The beautiful has gone," said the carriage. And all through nature the same sentiment was sighed, and even from the heart of man it sounded: "The beautiful has gone. The glorious greenwood, the warm sunshine, and the song of the birds are gone! Gone!"

So it was said, and it creaked in the trunks of the lofty trees. And a sigh, a very deep sigh, was heard right from the heart of the wild rose tree and from him who sat there—the Rose King. Do you know him? He is all beard, the finest reddish-green beard, and he is good to know. Go to the wild rosebushes, and when all the flowers have faded from them in autumn and only the red hips remain, you will often find among them a large red-green moss flower; that's the Rose King. A little green leaf grows out of the top of his head; that's his feather. He is the only man of his kind on the rosebush; and it was he who sighed.

"Gone! Gone! The beautiful is gone! The roses have gone, and the leaves have fallen from the trees. It's wet here; it's rough here. The birds who sang are silent. The pigs go hunting acorns; the pigs are the lords of the forest."

The nights were cold and the days were gray, but the raven sat on the branch and sang nevertheless, "Caw! Caw!" Both raven and crow sat on the high bough; they had a large family, and all of them said, "Caw! Caw!"—and, of course, the majority is always right.

In the hollow beneath the high trees was a great puddle, and here lay a herd of pigs, large and small ones. They found the place incomparably lovely. "*Oui! Oui!*" they said. This was the only French they knew, but even that was something. They were so clever, and so fat.

The old ones lay still, for they were thinking; the young ones, on the other hand, were very busy and had no time for rest. One little piglet had a curl in his tail that was his mother's pride and joy. She thought that all the other pigs were looking at the curl and thinking only of the curl, but they weren't; they were thinking of themselves, and what was useful to them, and of what the forest was for. They had always heard that the acorns they ate grew at the roots of trees, and therefore they had always dug up the ground. But now there was a little pig—it's always the young ones who come out with new ideas—who insisted that the acorns dropped from the branches; one had fallen on his head, and that had given him the idea; he had then made observations, and now he was quite sure of it. The older ones put their heads together.

"Oink!" said the pigs. "Oink! All the beauty is gone. The twittering of the birds is ended. We want fruit. Anything that's good to eat is good, and we eat everything."

"*Oui*! *Oui*!" they all said together.

But now the mother sow looked at her little piglet with the curl in his tail. "One mustn't forget the beautiful," she said.

"Caw! Caw!" cried the crow, and flew down from the tree to try to get appointed as a nightingale; one was needed, and so the crow was promptly appointed.

"Gone! Gone!" sighed the Rose King. "All the beautiful is gone!"

It was wet; it was gray; it was cold and windy; and through the forest and over the fields the rain beat down in long, murky streaks. Where were the birds who sang; where were the flowers in the meadow, and the sweet berries of the wood? Gone! Gone!

Then a light shone from the house of the forester. It lighted up like a star and cast its long ray through the trees. A song sounded from within the house; beautiful children played there around the old grandfather. He sat with the Bible on his knee and read of God and the eternal life, and told them about the spring that would return, about the forest that would become green anew, the roses that would bloom, the nightingales that would sing, and the beautiful that again would sit upon the throne.

But the Rose King did not hear it; he sat in the cold, wet weather and sighed, "Gone! Gone!"

And the pigs were the lords of the forest; and Mother Sow looked at her little piglet and the curl in his tail.

"There's always somebody who has an appreciation of the beautiful!" said the Mother Sow.

THE OLD TOMBSTONE (1852)

In a small provincial town lived a man who owned his own house. There one evening he and his whole family were gathered together. It was the time of year when people say, "The evenings are growing longer," and it was still pleasant and warm; the lamp was lit, long curtains hung down before the windows—by which stood several flowerpots—and bright moonlight flooded the world outside.

But they were not talking about the moonlight; they were discussing a huge old stone that lay out in the yard, near the kitchen door, where the servants often placed their copper utensils, when they had been washed, to dry in the sun, and where the children usually played. As a matter of fact, it was an old tombstone.

"I believe," explained the master of the house, "that it came from the old ruined chapel of the convent. Pulpit and tombstones, with their epitaphs, were sold, and my departed father bought several of them. We broke up the others into paving stones, but we didn't use that one and left it lying in the yard."

"You can easily tell that it was a tombstone," said the eldest of the children. "You can still see an hourglass on it, and a piece of an angel, but the inscription is just about gone. You can make out the name 'Preben' and a capital 'S' just after it, and 'Martha' a little further down, but it is impossible to read any more. And you can see that only after it has been raining or we have washed the stone."

Now a very old man, who from his age might have been the grandfather of everybody in the room, spoke up. "Why, that must be the tombstone of Preben Svane and his wife," he said. "Yes, of course, that grand old couple were almost the last to be buried in the churchyard of the old convent. In my childhood days, I knew them as an honorable old couple. Everybody knew them and loved them; they were like a king and queen in this town. People said they had more than a barrelful of money, and yet they always dressed simply, in very coarse cloth—but their linen was always snowy white. Yes, they were a lovable old pair, Preben and Martha. When they sat on the bench at the top of the stone staircase, over which the old linden tree spread its branches, nodding friendly and gently to passersby, it made you glad to see them.

"They were so wonderfully kind to the poor people! They gave them food and clothing, but there was good sense and a true Christian spirit in all their charity.

"She died first. I can remember that day very well, though I was only a little boy. My father took me to see old Preben right after she passed away; the old man was so heartbroken, he cried like a child. The corpse of his wife lay in her bedroom, near where we were sitting. The old man told my father and a couple of his neighbors how lonely he would be now, how wonderful she had been, and how many years they had spent together, and how they had first met and come to love each other.

"As I told you, I was only a child and stood by listening, but it touched me deeply to hear the old man and see how he grew more animated as he talked; a faint color came into his cheeks as he told us of the days of their courtship, how pretty she had been, and how many little tricks he had played to get to meet her. And when he told us about his wedding day, his eyes really sparkled; he seemed to be living his happy hours again. Yet all the while she was lying dead near us in the bedroom, an old lady, and he was an old man who spoke of the days of hope! Yes, that's the way it goes! I was only a child then, and now I'm very, very old, as old as Preben Svane was.

"Yes, time and change come to all things. I can remember so clearly the day of the funeral, and Preben Svane following her coffin. A couple of years before, they had had their tombstone carved with names and inscriptions, just leaving the dates of their deaths blank; and that same evening, the stone was set in its place on the grave. And only a year later, the grave had to be reopened, for old Preben joined his wife again. It turned out that they were not so rich as people had thought, and the little they did leave went to distant relatives far away, to people who had never been heard of before.

The old wooden house, with the bench under the linden tree at the top of the high stone staircase, was pulled down by order of the town council, for it was much too ruined to stand any longer. And later, the same fate befell the chapel, and the cemetery was leveled. Preben's and Martha's old tombstone was sold, like the rest, to anybody who wanted to buy it. And so it happened that it wasn't broken in pieces, but that it is now lying out there in the yard for the children to play on, or to be used as a shelf for the servant maid's kitchen utensils. And the paved street now covers the resting place of old Preben and his wife; and nobody ever thinks about them any more."

Then the old man who had told them the story shook his head sadly. "Yes, forgotten! All things are forgotten!"

The rest began to speak of other things, but the youngest child, a little boy with large, grave eyes, climbed up on a chair and peered through the curtains into the yard. The moon shone down brightly on the huge stone, which previously had seemed to the little boy very flat and dull, but which now had become like a page from a wonderful storybook. For the stone seemed to contain within it all that the little boy had heard about Preben and his wife. He looked down at the stone, then up at the brilliant moon, which seemed like a divine face peering down on Earth through the pure still air.

"Forgotten! All things are forgotten!" The words were again repeated in the room; and at that moment, an invisible angel kissed him on the forehead and whispered softly, "Keep the seed carefully; cherish it until the time for ripening shall come. Through you, my child, shall the half-vanished inscription on the crumbling tombstone stand out in clear characters for generations yet to come. Through you shall the old couple once more walk arm in arm through the old streets and sit with smiling, rosy-cheeked faces on their bench under the linden tree, greeting rich and poor alike. From this moment on through the years, the seed shall ripen into a blooming poem. For the good and the beautiful perish never; they live eternally in story and song!"

THE SWAN'S NEST (1852)

Between the Baltic and the North Sea there lies an old swan's nest, and it is called Denmark. In it have been born, and will be born hereafter, swans whose names shall never die.

In the olden days, a flock of swans from that nest flew over the Alps to the green plains of Milan, for it was wonderful to live there. These swans were called Lombards.

Another flock, with brilliant shining plumage and clear, truthful eyes, alighted at Byzantium, nestled around the throne of the emperor, and spread out their broad white wings like shields to protect him. Then swans were known as Varangians.

From the coasts of France arose a cry of terror—terror at the bloody Swans who, with fire in their wings, flew down from the north! And the people prayed, "God save us from the wild Northmen!"

On the fresh turf of an English meadow, near the open shore, with the triple crown on his kingly head, his golden scepter stretching out over the land, stood another royal Swan.

And on the far shores of Pomerania, the heathens bent the knee, for thither too, with drawn swords and under the standard of the Cross, had flown the Danish Swans.

"But all that was in the ancient days!" you say.

But in times nearer our own have mighty Swans also been seen flying from the Nest. A flash of lightning cleft the air—lightning that blazed over every country in the world—for a Swan had flapped his great wings and scattered the twilight mist. Then the starry heavens became more visible and seemed nearer to Earth. That Swan's name was Tycho Brahe.

"Yes, that was years ago," you may say. "But what about now, in our own generation?"

Well, in our own generation, we have seen swans soaring together in glorious flight.

We saw one gently sweep his wings over the golden chords of the harp, and sweet music thrilled through the lands of the north. Then the wild mountains of Norway lifted their crests higher in the blazing sunlight of ancient times; the pine and the birch rustled their leaves; the gods of the north, the heroic men and noble women of Scandinavian history, came to life again against the background of deep dark forests.

We saw a swan strike his wing against the hard marble mountain till it broke in pieces, and new shapes of beauty that had been shut up in the stone stepped forward in the bright sunny day. Then the nations of the world raised their heads in wonder to gaze at the glorious statuary.

A third swan we have seen spinning threads of thoughts that spread from land to land around Earth, so that words fly with lightning speed throughout the world.

Yes, our Lord protects the old Swan's Nest between the Baltic and the North Sea. Let mighty birds speed through the air to tear it to pieces. It shall never be! We have seen even the unplumed young ones circle the edge of the Nest to fight with their beaks and their claws, their young breasts bleeding.

Centuries will pass, and the Swans will still fly forth from the Nest, and they shall be seen and heard in every part of the world. Long will it be before the time comes when in spirit and truth men say, "That was the last Swan! The last song from the Swan's Nest!"

THE STORY OF THE YEAR (1852)

It was in the latter part of January, and a heavy snowfall was driving down. It whirled through the streets and the lanes, and the outsides of the windowpanes seemed plastered with snow. It fell down in masses from the roofs of the houses. A sudden panic seized the people. They ran, they flew, and they fell into each other's arms and felt that at least for that little moment, they had a foothold. The coaches and horses seemed covered with sugar frosting, and the footmen stood with their backs to the carriages, to protect their faces from the wind.

The pedestrians kept in the shelter of the carriages, which could move only slowly through the deep snow. When the storm at last ceased, and a narrow path had been cleared near the houses, the people as they met would stand still in this path, for neither wanted to take the first step into the deep snow to let the other pass. So they would stand motionless, until by silent consent each would sacrifice one leg and, stepping aside, bury it in the snowdrift.

By evening, it had grown calm. The sky looked as if it had been swept and had become very lofty and transparent. The stars seemed quite new, and some of them were wonderfully blue and bright. It was freezing so hard that the snow creaked, and the upper crust of it was strong enough by morning to support the sparrows. These little birds were hopping up and down where the paths had been cleared, but they found very little to eat and were shivering with cold.

"Peep," said one to another. "They call this the new year, but it's much worse than the old one! We might just as well have kept the other year. I'm completely dissatisfied, and I have a right to be, too!"

"Yes," agreed a little shivering sparrow. "The people ran about firing off shots to celebrate the new year. And they banged pans and pots against the doors, and were quite noisy with joy because the old year was over. I was glad too, because I thought that meant we would have warm days, but nothing like that has happened yet. Everything has frozen much harder than before! People must have made a mistake in figuring their time!"

"They certainly have," a third added—an old sparrow with a white topknot. "They have a thing they call a calendar, something they invented themselves, and everything has to be arranged according to that, but it doesn't work. The year really begins when the spring comes; that's the way of nature, and that's the way I reckon it."

"But when will spring come?" the others wailed.

"It will come when the stork comes back! But his plans are very uncertain; here in town, they don't know anything about them. People out in the country are better informed. Let's fly out there and wait. At least we'll be that much closer to spring."

Now, one of the sparrows who had been hopping about for a long time, chirping, without saying anything very important, spoke up. "That's all very well, but I've found some comforts here in town that I'm afraid I'd miss in the country. In a courtyard quite near here, a family of people have had the very sensible idea of placing three or four flowerpots against the wall, with their open ends all turned inward and bottoms pointing out. In each pot, they've cut a hole, big enough for me to fly in and out. My husband and I have built a nest in one of those pots, and we have raised all our young ones there.

"Of course, the people just did it to have the fun of watching us; otherwise, they surely wouldn't have done it; and to please themselves further, they put out crumbs of bread. That gives us food, and thus we are provided for. So I think my husband and I will stay here—though we're very dissatisfied, mind you. Yes, I guess we'll stay."

"But we'll fly out into the country, to see if spring isn't coming," cried the others. And away they flew.

Now, in the country, the winter was still a little harder, and the temperature a few degrees lower, than in town. Sharp winds swept across snow-covered fields. The farmer, his hands muffled in warm mittens, sat in his sleigh with his whip on his knees and beat his arms across his chest to keep himself warm. The lean horses ran until steamy smoke seemed to rise from them. The snow creaked with the cold, and the sparrows hopped around in the ruts and shivered. "Peep! When will spring come? It's taking a very long time about it!"

"Very long," sounded a deep voice from the highest snow-covered hill, far across the field. Perhaps it was an echo, or perhaps the words had been spoken by a strange old man who was sitting, in spite of wind and weather, on the top of a high drift of snow. He was all white, with long hair, a pale face, and big clear eyes, dressed like a peasant in a coarse white coat of frieze.

"Who is that old fellow over there?" demanded the sparrows.

"I know who he is," said an old raven sitting on a fence rail. Now, this raven was wise enough to know that we are all like little birds in the sight of the Lord, so he wasn't above speaking to the sparrows and answering their question.

"Yes, I know who the old man is. He's Winter, the old man of last year. He isn't dead, as the calendar says; no, he is guardian to little Prince Spring, who is coming. Yes, Winter rules here now. Ugh! The cold makes you shiver, doesn't it, you small creatures?"

"Yes," replied the smallest sparrow. "Didn't I tell you? The calendar is only a stupid invention of men, and isn't arranged according to nature. They ought to leave that sort of thing to us; we're born much more sensitive than they are."

So one week passed away; yes, almost two weeks went by. The forest was black, and the frozen lake still lay hard and stiff, looking like a sheet of lead. The clouds, like damp cold mists, lay brooding over the land, while the great black crows flew in long silent lines. It was as if nature were sleeping.

Then a sunbeam glided over the surface of the lake, and it shone like melted tin. The snowy blanket over field and hill did not glitter quite so coldly. But still the white form of King Winter sat, his gaze fixed unswervingly toward the south. He did not notice that the snowy carpet seemed to sink very slowly into the earth itself and that here and there little grass-green patches were appearing. But the sparrows crowded into these patches, chirping, "Peep! Peep! Is spring coming now?"

"Spring!" It resounded over the field and meadow and through the dark-brown woods, where the green moss was shining on the tree trunks. And through the air, from far away in the south, the first two storks came flying swiftly, carrying on their backs two lovely children, a little boy and a little girl. They greeted the earth with a kiss, and wherever they set their little feet, tiny white flowers pushed up from beneath the snow. Then the children ran hand in hand to the old man of ice, Winter, greeted and embraced him. At that moment, they and he and all the field around them were hidden in a thick, damp mist that closed down like a dark, heavy veil. Then the wind rose gradually until it was roaring and drove away the mist with its heavy blast, so that the sun shone warmly, and Winter had vanished, while the beautiful children of spring on the throne of the year.

"That's what I call a new year!" cried the sparrows. "Now we'll again get our rights back and make up for the hard winter!"

Wherever the two children turned, bushes and trees put forth new green buds, the grass shot upward, and the cornfields turned green and became more and more lovely. And the little maiden strewed flowers all around. She carried them in her apron up before her, and it was always full of them; indeed, they seemed to grow there, for her lap was always full, however wantonly she tossed the flowers about. In her eagerness, she scattered a drifting snow of blossoms over the apple trees and peach trees, so that they burst forth in full beauty before their green leaves had fully shown themselves.

Then she clapped her hands, and the boy clapped his, and great flocks of birds came flying—nobody knew where they came from—and all sang, "Spring has come!"

It was beautiful to behold. Many an aged grandmother came out of her doorway into the bright sunshine, gleefully gazing at the bright yellow flowers that dotted the fields just as they used to do when she was young. The world seemed young again to her, and she said, "It is a blessing to be out here today."

The forest still wore its dress of brown-green buds, but the fresh and fragrant bokar was already there. There were violets in abundance; anemones and primroses sprang up; and sap and strength were in each blade of grass. That grass was a marvelous carpet, on which no one could resist sitting, so the young spring couple sat hand in hand, and sang and smiled, and grew taller.

A mild rain fell down on them from heaven, but they scarcely noticed it, for the raindrops were mingled with their own tears of happiness. The bride and bridegroom kissed each other, and at that moment, all the verdure of the woods was unfolded, and when the sun rose, all the forest was green.

Hand in hand, the betrothed pair wandered under the fresh, hanging canopy of leaves, where the rays of the sun flickered through in lovely, ever-changing green shadows. What virgin purity, what refreshing balm there was in those delicate leaves! Clearly and quickly, the brooks and streams rippled over the colored pebbles and among the velvety green rushes. All nature seemed to cry, "There is abundance, and there shall always be abundance!" And the lark caroled and the cuckoo sang; it was beautiful spring. But the willows kept woolly gloves over their blossoms; they were desperately careful of their tender buds, and that is too bad!

So the days and weeks went by, and the heat seemed to whirl down. The corn became more and more yellow as hot waves of air swirled through it. The great white water lily of the north spread its huge green leaves on the mirror surface of the lakes, and the fishes lingered in the shady spots beneath them. At the sheltered edge of the wood, where the sun beat down on the walls of the farmhouse, warming the blooming roses and the cherry trees laden with juicy black berries, which were almost hot from the fierce beams, there sat the lovely woman of summer. She it is whom we have seen as a child and as a bride.

Her gaze was fixed on the rising blue-black, heavy clouds that, in wavy outlines, were piling themselves up like mountains, higher and higher. Growing like a petrified, reversed ocean, they came from three sides, swooping toward the forest where all sounds had been silenced as if by magic. Every breath of air was stilled; every bird was mute. A grave suspense hung over all nature; and in the highways and lanes, people, on foot or horseback or in carriages, hurried toward shelter.

Suddenly there was a flash of light, as if the sun itself had burst forth in a blinding, burning, all-devouring flame! Then darkness again, and a rolling crash of thunder! The rain poured down in sheets. Darkness and flaming light alternated; silence and deafening thunder followed one another. The young, feathery reeds on the moor whipped to and fro in long waves; the branches of the trees were hidden behind a wall of water; and still darkness and light, silence and thunder, alternated. The grass and corn were beaten down by the rain and lay as if they could never rise again.

And just as suddenly, the rain died away to a few gentle drops, and the sun shone again. The droplets hung from the leaves like glittering pearls, and the birds sang; the fishes leaped from the surface of the lakes, and the gnats danced. And there on the rock in the warm sunshine, strengthened by the refreshing rain, sat Summer himself—a strong man with sturdy limbs and long, dripping hair. All nature seemed renewed; everything was luxuriant and beautiful. It was summer, warm, lovely summer.

A pleasant and sweet fragrance streamed up from the rich clover field, where the bees buzzed around the old ruined meeting place. The altar stone, newly washed by the rain, glittered in the sunshine, and the bramble wound its tendrils around it. Thither the queen bee led her swarm, and they busily made their wax and honey. Only Summer saw them, Summer and his lovely wife. For them, the altar table was covered with the gifts of nature.

The evening sky shone with more brilliant gold than any church dome can boast; and between the evening and the morning, there was moonlight. It was summer.

So the days and weeks went by. The flashing scythes of the reapers glittered in the cornfields, and the branches of the apple trees bent down, heavy with red and yellow fruit. The sweet-smelling hops hung in large clusters, and under the hazel bushes with their great bunches of nuts, there rested a man and a woman—Summer and his quiet wife.

"What wealth!" she cried. "There is a blessing all around us; everything looks homelike and good. And yet—I don't know why—I find I am longing for peace and rest—I scarcely know how to express it. Already the people are plowing the fields again, always trying to gain more and more. Look there, the storks are flocking together and following a little behind the plow. They are the birds of Egypt that brought us through the air. Do you remember how we both came as children to this land of the north? We brought flowers with us, and pleasant sunshine, and new green to the woods. The wind has been rough with those trees; they're dark and brown now like the trees of the south, but they do not bear golden fruit like them."

"Do you wish to see the golden fruit?" said Summer. "Then look and rejoice!"

He stretched out his arms, and the leaves of the forest were splendid in red and gold, while beautiful tints spread over the woodland. The rosebush glowed scarlet; the elder branches hung down with great heavy bunches of black-brown berries; the wild chestnuts were ripe in their dark-green husks; and deep in the forest, the violets bloomed again.

But the queen was becoming more and more silent and pale.

"It is growing cold," she said, "and the nights bring damp mists. I am longing for the land of my childhood."

Then she watched the storks fly away, one after the other; and in longing, she stretched forth her arms toward them. She looked up at the nests. They were empty. The long-stalked cornflower was growing in one of them; in another was a yellow mustard seed, looking as if the whole nest were there solely for its protection. And the sparrows flew up into the storks' nests, to take possession.

"Peep! What happened to the stork family?" one of them asked. "I suppose they can't bear it when the wind blows on them, so they've left the country. I wish them a happy journey!"

Gradually, the forest leaves became more and more yellow, and leaf after leaf drifted down to earth; and the stormy winds of autumn howled; harvesttime was over. The queen lay on the fallen yellow leaves and looked with lovely mild eyes at the glittering stars above, while her husband stood beside her. Suddenly, a gust of wind whirled through the leaves, a shower of them fell again, and the queen was gone! Only a butterfly, the last of the season, fluttered through the chilly air.

The wet fogs came, the icy winds blew, and the nights became darker and longer. Now the Ruler of the year stood there with snow-white hair, but he was not aware of it. He thought it was the snowflakes that were falling from the sky.

A thin layer of snow covered the green field, and then the church bells rang for the glad Christmas season.

"The birthday bells are ringing," said the Ruler of the year slowly. "Soon the new king and queen will be born, and I shall go to my rest as my wife has done; my rest in the gleaming star."

And in the green fir wood, where the white snow lay, there stood the Angel of Christmas, and consecrated the young trees that would adorn the feast.

In a few weeks, the Ruler of the year had become a very old man, white as snow. "May there be joy in the room and under the green branches," he said. "My time for rest draws nigh, and the young pair of the new year shall receive my crown and scepter."

"But you are still in power," said the Angel of Christmas, "and not yet shall you be granted rest. Let the snow lie close and warm upon the young seed. Learn to endure that another receive homage while you are still the Ruler. Learn to be forgotten and yet to live. The hour of your release shall come when spring appears!"

"And when will spring come?" said Winter.

"It will come when the stork returns!"

With white locks and snowy beard, cold, bent, and old, but still strong as the winter storm and firm as the glittering ice, old Winter sat high up on the snowdrift on the hill, his gaze fixed toward the south, just as the Winter before him had. The ice and snow creaked with the cold; the skaters skimmed over the smooth lakes; the black ravens and crows looked fine against the white ground; no breath of wind stirred. In that quiet air, old Winter clenched his fists, and the ice was fathoms thick between land and land. Then the sparrows flew out again from town, and demanded, "Who is that old man over there?"

And the raven sat on the fence rail again—perhaps a son of the other one, which amounts to the same thing—and answered them. "It is Winter, the old Ruler of last year. He isn't dead as the calendar says, but he's the guardian of spring, which is coming."

"When will spring come?" asked the sparrows. "Then we'll have good times and a better year. The old one was no good at all!"

Winter nodded in silent thought at the leafless black forest, where every tree showed the graceful form and bend of its branches; and during the winter night, icy mists came down from the clouds, and the Ruler dreamed of his childhood and young manhood; and toward the morning dawn, the whole wood was clothed in glittering hoarfrost. That was the summer dream of winter, and soon the sun scattered the frost from the branches.

"When will spring come?" asked the sparrows again.

"Spring!" Again that word echoed back from the snow-covered hills. Now the sun shone more warmly, and the snow melted, and the birds sang, "Spring is coming!"

And high through the air came the first stork, with the second close behind him. A lovely child rode on the back of each, and they alighted in an open field and kissed the earth. Then they embraced the silent old man, and, like Moses on the mount, he disappeared, wrapped in cloudy mists. And so the story of the year was ended.

"That's all very well," said the sparrows. "And it's beautiful, too, but it's not according to the calendar, so it must be all wrong!"

IT'S QUITE TRUE! (1852)

It's a dreadful story!" said a hen, and she said it in a part of town, too, where it had not taken place. "It's a dreadful story to happen in a henhouse. I'm afraid to sleep alone tonight; it's a good thing there are many of us on the perch!" And then she told a story that made the feathers of the other hens stand on end and the rooster's comb fall. It's quite true!

But we will begin at the beginning and tell what had happened in a henhouse at the other end of town.

The sun went down, and the hens flew up. One of them was a white-feathered and short-limbed hen who laid her eggs according to the regulations and who was a respectable hen in every way. As she settled herself on the perch, she plucked herself with her beak, and a tiny feather came out.

"There it goes," she said. "No doubt the more I pluck, the more beautiful I will get." But she said it only in fun, for she was considered the jolliest among the hens, although, as we've said before, most respectable. Then she fell asleep.

There was darkness all around, and the hens sat closely together. But the hen that sat closest to the white hen was not asleep; she had heard and had not heard, as one should do in this world, if one wishes to live in peace. But still, she couldn't resist telling it to her nearest neighbor.

"Did you hear what was said? Well, I don't want to mention any names, but there is a hen here who intends to pluck out all her feathers just to make herself look well. If I were a rooster, I would despise her."

Right above the hens lived a mother owl with a father owl and all her little owls. They had sharp ears in that family, and they all heard every word that their neighbor hen had said. They all rolled their eyes, and the mother owl flapped her wings and said; "Don't listen to it. But I suppose you all heard what was said. I heard it with my own ears, and one must hear a great deal before they fall off. One of the hens has so completely forgotten what is becoming conduct to a hen that she plucks out all her feathers, while the rooster watches her."

"Little pitchers have long ears," said the father owl. "Children shouldn't hear such talk."

"I must tell it to the owl across the road," said the mother owl. "She is such a respectable owl!" And away flew Mamma.

"Hoo-whoo! Hoo-whoo!" they both hooted to the pigeons in the pigeon house across the road. "Have you heard it? Have you heard it? Hoo-whoo! There is a hen who has plucked out all her feathers just to please the rooster. She must be freezing to death; that is, if she isn't dead already. Hoo-whoo! Hoo-whoo!"

"Where? Where?" cooed the pigeons.

"In the yard across the way. I have as good as seen it myself. It is almost not a proper story to tell, but it's quite true!"

"True, true, every word of it," said the pigeons, and cooed down into their poultry yard. "There is a hen, and some say there are two hens, who have plucked out all their feathers in order to look different from the rest and to attract the attention of the rooster."

"Wake up! Wake up!" crowed the rooster, and flew up on the fence. He was still half asleep, but he crowed just the same. "Three hens have died of a broken heart, all for the sake of a rooster, and they have plucked all their feathers out! It's a dreadful story, but I will not keep it to myself. Tell it everywhere!"

"Tell it everywhere!" shrieked the bats; and the hens clucked and the roosters crowed. "Tell it everywhere!"

And so the story traveled from henhouse to henhouse until at last it was carried back to the very same place from where it had really started.

"There are five hens," now ran the tale, "who all have plucked out all their feathers to show which of them had lost the most weight through unhappy love for their rooster. And then they pecked at each other till they bled and all five dropped dead, to the shame and disgrace of their families, and to the great loss of their owner."

And the hen who had lost the little loose feather naturally didn't recognize her own story; and as she was a respectable hen, she said, "I despise such hens, but there are many of that kind! Such stories should not be hushed up, and I'll do my best to get the story into the newspapers. Then it will be known all over the country; that will serve those hens right, and their families, too." And it got to the newspapers, and it was printed. And it is quite true. One little feather may grow till it becomes five hens.

A GOOD HUMOR (1852)

From my father I have inherited that most worthy of bequests—a cheerful temper. And who was my father? Well, that really has nothing to do with a good humor. He was thrifty and lively, fat and round; in fact, his exterior and interior were both at variance with his office.

And what was his office, his position in the community? Why, if the answer to that question were written and printed at the very beginning of a book, most people would lay the book down as soon as they opened it, saying, "There is something dismal about it. I don't want anything like this."

And yet my father was neither a hangman nor a headsman. On the contrary, his office often brought him into contact with the most honorable men of the state, and he was certainly entitled to be there; he had to be ahead of them, even ahead of bishops and princes of the royal blood, for, to tell the truth, he was the driver of a hearse!

Now you know it! But I must add that when one saw my father sitting high up on the carriage of death, dressed in his long black mantle and crepe-bordered, three-cornered hat, his face as round and smiling as the sun, one could not think of sorrow and graves, for that face said, "Never mind, it's going to be much better than you think."

You see, then, that from him I have my good humor and also the habit of frequently visiting the churchyard; and that is rather amusing, if one goes there in a cheerful temper. Oh, yes, I also subscribe to the *Advertiser,* just as he used to do.

I am not exactly young, and I have neither wife, nor children, nor library to divert me. But, as I have told you, I read the *Advertiser*—that's all I need; it was my father's favorite newspaper, and it's mine, too. It is a most useful paper, and contains everything a person ought to know.

From it I learn who is preaching in the churches and who preaches in the new books; I know where I may obtain houses, servants, clothes, and food; I know who is selling out and who is buying up. Then, too, I learn of so many deeds of charity, and I read so many innocent verses, which are quite free of any offense, and of marriages desired. Yes, it is all so natural and simple. One can live very happily, and be happily buried, if one reads the *Advertiser*—and then when death comes about, one has such a lot of paper that one can rest softly on it, if one doesn't care to rest on wood shavings. The churchyard and the *Advertiser* were as always the things that most elevated my mind.

Everyone is free, of course, to read the *Advertiser,* but if anybody would like to share my walks in the churchyard, let him join my someday when the sun is shining and the trees are green.

Then let us ramble together among the old graves; each one is like a closed book with the cover toward you, so you can read the title that tells you what the book contains and yet says nothing at all. But from my father, and through my own experiences, I know all about it. I have written it all in a book for my own especial benefit and instruction; there is something written about most of them.

Now we are in the churchyard.

Behind this white-painted trellis, where once grew a rosebush—it is dead now, but a stray bit of evergreen from the next grave stretches a long green finger across the sod, as if to make up for the loss—there rests a man who was singularly unhappy. Yet you would not have called him unfortunate; he had sufficient income and never suffered any great calamity. His unhappiness was of his own making; as we say it, he took everything, especially his "art," too much to heart. Thus, if he spent an evening at the theater, he nearly went out of his mind if the machinist had put too strong a light into each cheek of the moon, or if canvases representing the sky were hanging in front of the scene instead of behind, or if a palm tree appeared in a local landscape, cacti on the Tyrolean plains, or beech trees in the high mountains of Norway. What does it matter; who cares! It is only a play intended for amusement. The audience was sure to be wrong, sometimes applauding too much and sometimes too little. "Look, that is wet wood tonight," he said. "It won't burn!" And when he turned around to see what kind of people were there, he found them laughing in the wrong places. All this annoyed and pained him. He was a miserable man, and now he is in his grave.

Here rests, on the other hand, a very fortunate man—I mean to say he was a man of extremely noble birth. In fact, that constituted his good fortune, for had he not been highborn he would never have amounted to anything. But, then, everything is so wisely arranged, and that is a pleasure to know. His coats were embroidered in front and in back, very much like a fine, embroidered bellpull in a room, for behind the handsome, gaudy bellpull is always a good, strong, plain cord that really does all the work. And this man had his good, stout cord behind him, which now does the work behind a new embroidered bellpull. That's the way it is; everything is so wisely arranged that it is very easy to keep one's good humor.

Over here there rests—now, this is really sad!—a man who for sixty-seven years worried and wracked his brains to hit upon a great idea. For the sake of this idea he lived alone all his days, and when at last he had convinced himself that he had succeeded, he was so overcome that he died of joy at having found it—before he even had time to announce it to the world—so nobody ever heard about his great idea. I can almost fancy that he has no rest in his grave, because of that great idea which no one but himself has enjoyed or ever can enjoy. For suppose this was an idea that could be explained successfully only at breakfast time; and everyone knows that ghosts can walk only at midnight. And if this ghost should appear among his friends at that appointed hour, his idea would be an utter failure. No one would laugh, for jesting comes unseasonably at midnight, and so the unhappy ghost would return to the grave with his great idea. It is really very sad.

Here lies a lady who was a miser. During her lifetime she often arose at night and mewed, so that the neighbors would imagine she kept a cat, which she was too stingy to do.

And here is a young lady of good family. She always insisted upon singing in society, and when she sang, "*Mi manca la voce!*" that was the only truth she ever spoke.

Here rests another young girl, of a very different nature. Alas! When the bird of the heart begins to sing, too often will Reason stop up her ears. Lovely maiden, she was to be married; but that's an everyday story—may she rest in peace!

Here lies a widow who had the sweetness of the swan on her lips and the gall of the owl in her heart. She went from one family to another, feeding upon the faults of her neighbors.

Now, this is a family vault; every member of that family lived in the sublime faith that whatever the world and the newspapers said must indeed be true. If the young son of that house came home from school and announced, "This is how I heard it—," his news, whatever it might be, was received without question, because he belonged to the family. And certain it is that if the cock of that family had decided to crow at midnight, the whole family would have insisted that morning had dawned, even if the watchman and all the clocks of the town announced it was midnight.

The great Goethe concluded his *Faust* with the words, "It may be continued"; and thus will I conclude our walk in the churchyard.

I go there often, for whenever one of my friends or unfriends, gives me to understand that he wishes to be as one dead to me, I go there, find a spot of green turf, and dedicate it to him or her, whomever I wish to bury. In this way I have buried many of my acquaintances. There they lie, powerless to harm me, until the time when they may return to life, better and wiser than before. I write down in my book their life and history, as seen from my point of view. Everybody ought to do so!

You shouldn't be upset if your friends do something foolish; bury them at once, keep your good humor, and read the *Advertiser,* for this paper is written by the people, although their pens are sometimes wrongly guided.

When at last I myself and the story of my life are to be bound in the grave, then write upon it the epitaph:

A GOOD HUMOR!

This is my story.

ON JUDGMENT DAY (1852)

The most solemn of all the days of our life is the day we die. It is judgment day, the great sacred day of transfiguration. Have you really seriously given a fleeting thought to that grave and mighty last hour we shall spend on earth?

There was once a man, a stanch upholder of truth, as he was called, to whom the word of his God was law, a zealous servant of his zealous God. With a stern but heavenly look, the Angel of Death stood at his bedside.

"The hour has come; you shall follow me!" said Death, and touched the man's feet with ice-cold fingers, and his feet became like ice. Then Death touched his forehead, and lastly his heart, and when it burst, the soul was free to follow the Angel of Death.

But during those brief seconds while the icy touch shivered through feet and head and heart, there passed through the mind of the dying man, like great ocean waves, the recollection of all he had wrought and felt throughout his life. So does one terrified glance into a whirlpool reveal in thought as swift as lightning the whole unfathomable depth of it; so with one fleeting glance at the countless stars of heaven can one conceive the infinite multitude of worlds and spheres in the great universe.

In such a moment the terrified sinner shrinks into himself and has nothing to cling to, and he feels himself shrinking further into infinite emptiness. And at such times the devout soul bows its head to the Almighty and yields itself up to Him in childlike trust, praying, "Thy will be done with me!"

But this dying man had not the mind of a child, nor was he a terrified sinner; his thoughts were of self-praise. He knew that he had abided by religious traditions. Millions, he knew, would have to face judgment. But he believed most confidently that his path would lead straight heavenward, and that mercy, promised to all men, would open the gates to him.

And the soul followed the Angel of Death, casting only one wistful glance back at the bed where, in its white shroud, lay the lifeless image of clay, still bearing the print of the soul's individuality.

Now they hovered through the air, now glided along the ground. Were they passing through a vast, decorated hall, or perchance a forest? It was hard to tell. Nature appeared formally set out for show, as in the stately, artificial, old French gardens, and through its strange, carefully arranged scenes there passed many men and women, all clad as if for a masquerade.

"Such is human life!" spoke the Angel of Death.

It seemed as if the figures tried to disguise themselves; those who flaunted the glories of velvet and gold were not always the noblest and the richest, neither were all those who wore the garb of poverty the most wretched and vulgar. A strange masquerade indeed! And most strange of all was to see how each one carefully concealed under his clothing something he would not have the others discover. Each was determined to learn his neighbor' secret, and they tore at one another until here and there the heads of different animals were bared. One was that of a grinning ape, another the head of a goat, still others a clammy snake and a feeble fish.

In all was some token of the animal which is fast rooted in human nature, and which here was struggling and jumping to burst forth. And however closely a person might hold his garment over it to hide it, the others would never rest until they had torn aside the veil, and all kept crying out, "Look here! See! It is he! It is she!" and everyone mockingly laid bare his fellow's shame.

"Then what was the animal in me?" inquired the soul.

The Angel of Death silently pointed to a haughty form around whose head spread a bright glory of rays, with shining colors, but in whose heart could be seen lurking, half hidden, the feet of a peacock.

The spreading glory above was merely the speckled tail of the peacock.

As they passed on, huge birds shrieked horribly at them from the boughs of trees. In voices harsh but clear, intelligible, and human, they cried, "You who walk with Death, do you remember me?" All the evil thoughts and lusts that had lurked within the man from birth to death now called after him in forbidding tones, "Do you remember me?"

For a moment the soul shuddered, for it recognized the voices; it could not deny knowledge of the evil thoughts and desires that were now rising as witnesses against it.

"In our flesh, in our evil nature, nothing good lives!" said the soul. "But, at least with me, thoughts never turned into action; the world has not seen their evil fruit!"

The soul rushed on to escape the ugly screams, but the huge black birds swept in circles, screaming out their vicious words louder and louder, as though they wished to be heard to the ends of the world. The soul fled like a hunted stag, and at every step stumbled against sharp flint stones, painfully cutting his feet on them. "How came these sharp stones here? They seem like mere withered leaves lying on the ground."

"Each stone is some careless word you have spoken, which wounded your neighbor's heart far more deeply than these sharp flints that now hurt your feet."

"I never thought of that!" cried the soul.

"Judge not, that ye be not judged!" rang through the air.

In a moment the soul recovered from its self-abasement. "We have all sinned. But I have kept the Law and the Gospel. I have done what I could do; I am not like the others."

And then he stood at the gates of Heaven itself, and the Angel who guarded the entrance asked, "Who are you? Tell me your faith, and show it to me in your works."

"I have faithfully kept all the Commandments," replied the soul proudly. "I have humbled myself in the eyes of the world. I have hated and persecuted evil and those who practice it, and I would do so still, with fire and sword, had I yet the power."

"Then you are a follower of Mohammed?" said the Angel.

"I? Never!"

"'He who strikes with the sword shall perish by the sword,' thus spoke the Son. His religion you do not have. Are you then perchance one of the children of Israel, who with Moses said: 'An eye for an eye, and a tooth for a tooth?'"

"I am a Christian."

"I see it neither in your faith nor in your actions! The teaching of Christ is forgiveness, love, and mercy!"

"Mercy!" The echo of this rang through infinite space, the gates of Heaven opened, and the soul hovered toward the realms of eternal bliss.

But the flood of light that streamed forth from within was so dazzling, so penetrating, that the soul shrank back as from a double-edged sword. And the sound of music was so soft and touching that no mortal tongue could describe it. The soul trembled and prostrated itself lower and lower, and the celestial light cut through it until it felt, as it had never felt before, the weight of its own pride and cruelty and sin.

"Whatever good I have done in the world, I did because I could not do otherwise; but the evil that I did—that was of myself!"

And more and more the soul was dazzled and overwhelmed by the pure light of Heaven; it seemed falling into a bottomless abyss—the abyss of its own nakedness and unworthiness. Shrunk into itself, humbled, cast out, unfit for the Kingdom of Heaven, trembling at the thought of the just and holy God, hardly dared it to gasp, "Mercy!"

And the Angel of Mercy came to him—the mercy he had not expected; and in the infinite space of Heaven, God's everlasting love filled the soul.

"Holy, loving, glorious forever shalt thou be, O erring human spirit!" sang the chorus of angels. And as this soul did, so shall we all, on our last day on earth, humbly tremble in the glorious sight of the Kingdom of Heaven. But the infinite love and mercy of our Heavenly Father will carry us through other spheres, so that, purified and strengthened, we may ascend into God's eternal light.

HEARTACHE (1852)

The story we have for you here is really divided into two parts. The first part could be omitted, but it gives us some preliminary information which is useful.

We were staying at a manor house in the country, and it happened that the owner was absent for a day or so. Meanwhile a lady with a pug dog arrived from the next town; come, she explained, to dispose of the shares in her tannery. She had her certificates with her, and we advised her to seal them in an envelope and to write on it the address of the proprietor of the estate, "General War Commissary, Knight," etc.

She listened to us, took up the pen, then hesitated, and begged us to repeat the address slowly. We complied and she wrote, but in the middle of the "General War—" she stopped, sighed, and said, "I'm only a woman!" While she wrote, she had placed her Puggie on the floor, and he was growling, for the dog had come with her for pleasure and health's sake, and a visitor shouldn't be placed on the floor. He was characterized outwardly by a snub nose and a fleshy back.

"He doesn't bite," said the woman. "He hasn't any teeth. He's like one of the family, faithful and grouchy; but the latter is the fault of my grandchildren for teasing him. They play wedding, and want to make him the bridesmaid, and that's too strenuous for the poor old fellow."

Then she delivered her certificates and took Puggie up in her arms. And that's the first part of the story, which could have been omitted.

Puggie died! That's the second part.

About a week later we arrived in the town and put up at the inn. Our windows looked out into the tannery yard, which was divided into two parts by a wooden fence; in one section were hides and skin caps, raw and tanned. Here was all the equipment for carrying on a tanning business, and it belonged to the widow. Puggie had died that morning and was to be buried in this section of the yard. The widow's grandchildren (that is, the tanner's widow's, for Puggie had never married) covered the grave—a grave so beautiful it must have been quite pleasant to lie there.

The grave was bordered with broken flowerpots and strewn over with sand; at its head they had stuck up a small beer bottle with the neck upward, and that wasn't at all symbolic.

The children danced around the grave, and then the oldest of the boys, a practical youngster of seven, proposed that there should be an exhibition of Puggie's grave for everybody living in the street. The price of admission would be one trouser button; that was something every boy would be sure to have and which he also could give to the little girls. This suggestion was adopted by acclamation.

And all the children from the street, and even from the little lane behind, came, and each gave a button. Many were seen that afternoon going about with one suspender, but then they had seen Puggie's grave, and that sight was worth it.

But outside the tannery yard, close to the entrance, stood a ragged little girl, very beautiful, with the prettiest curly hair, and eyes so clear and blue that it was a pleasure to look into them. She didn't say a word, nor did she cry, but every time the gate was opened she looked into the yard as long as she could. She had no button, as she knew very well, so she had to stand sorrowfully outside, until all the others had seen the grave and everyone had left. Then she sat down, put her little brown hands before her eyes, and burst into tears, for she alone hadn't seen Puggie's grave. It was a heartache as great as any grown-up can experience.

We saw this from above—and seen from above, this, like many of our own and others' griefs could, made us smile! That's the story, and anyone who doesn't understand it can go and buy a share in the widow's tannery.

EVERYTHING IN ITS PROPER PLACE (1852)

It was over a hundred years ago. By the great lake behind the wood there stood an old mansion. Round about it circled a deep ditch, with bulrushes, reeds, and grasses growing in it. Close by the bridge, near the entrance gate, an old willow tree bent over the reeds.

From the narrow lane came the sound of horns and the trampling of horses, and therefore the little girl who tended the geese hastened to drive her charges away from the bridge before the hunting party came galloping up. They approached with such speed that she was obliged to climb up onto one of the high cornerstones of the bridge, to avoid being run down. She was still little more than a child, pretty and slender, with a gentle expression in her face and lovely bright eyes. But the baron took no note of this; as he galloped past her, he reversed the whip in his hand, and in rough play gave her such a blow in the chest with the butt end that she fell backward into the ditch.

"Everything in its proper place!" he cried. "Into the mud with you!" And he laughed loudly, for this was intended to be funny, and the rest of the company joined in his mirth. They shouted and clamored, while the hunting dogs barked even more loudly than before. It was indeed: "Rich birds come rushing."

But goodness knows how rich he was. The poor goose girl, in falling, managed to seize one of the drooping branches of the willow tree and hang from it over the muddy water. As soon as the company and the dogs had disappeared through the castle gate, she tried to climb up again, but the branch broke off at the top, and she would have fallen into the reeds if, at that moment, a strong hand had not caught her from above. It was a peddler who from a little distance away had seen what had happened and had hurried up to give aid.

"Everything in its proper place," he said, mocking the baron, and pulled her up to the dry ground. He put the tree branch back to the place from which it had broken, but "everything in its place" cannot always be managed, and so he thrust it into the soft ground. "Grow if you can, until you can furnish a good flute for them up yonder," he said. It would have given him great pleasure to see the baron and his companions well thrashed.

And then the peddler made his way to the mansion, but did not go into the main hall; he was much too humble for that! He went instead to the servants' quarters, and the men and maids looked over his stock of goods and bargained with him. From above, where the guests were at table, was heard a sound of roaring and screaming that was intended for song; that was the best they could do! There was loud laughter, mingled with the barking and yapping of dogs, for there was riotous feasting up there. Wine and strong old ale foamed in jugs and glasses, and the dogs ate with their masters, and some of them, after having their snouts wiped with their ears, were kissed by them.

The peddler was told to come upstairs with his wares, but it was only to make fun of him. The wine had mounted into their heads and the sense had flown out. They insisted that the peddler drink with them, but, so that he would have to drink quickly, they poured his beer into a stocking. This was considered a great joke and caused more gales of laughter. And then entire farms, complete with oxen and peasants, were staked on a single card, and lost and won.

"Everything in its proper place," said the peddler thankfully when he had finally escaped from what he called "the Sodom and Gomorrah up there." "The open road is my proper place," he said. "I didn't feel at all happy up there."

And the little goose girl nodded kindly to him as he walked by the pasture gate.

Days passed and weeks passed; and the willow branch that the peddler had thrust into the ground beside the water ditch remained fresh and green and even put forth new shoots. The little goose girl saw that it must have taken root, and she was very happy about it; this was her tree, she thought.

Yes, the tree flourished, but everything else at the mansion went to seed, what with feasting and gambling. For these two are like wheels, upon which no man can stand securely.

Scarcely six years had passed before the baron left the mansion, a beggar, with bag and stick in hand; and the mansion itself was bought by a rich merchant. And the purchaser was the very peddler who had once been mocked at in the great hall and forced to drink beer from a stocking! Honesty and industry are good winds to speed a vessel, and now the peddler was the master of the mansion. But from that moment card playing was not permitted there any more.

"That is bad reading," he said. "When the Devil saw a Bible for the first time, he wanted something to counteract it, and so he invented card playing."

The new owner took himself a wife, and who do you suppose she was but the pretty little goose girl, who had always been so faithful and good! In her new clothes she looked as beautiful and fine as if she had been of high birth. How did all this happen? Well, that is too long a story to tell you in these busy times, but it really did happen, and the most important part of the story is still to come.

It was pleasant and cheerful to live in the old mansion. The mother managed the household affairs, and the father superintended the estate, and blessings seemed to rain down on the home. For where there is rectitude, prosperity is sure to follow. The old house was cleaned and repainted; ditches were cleared, and new fruit trees were planted. The floors were as polished as a draughtboard, and everything wore a bright cheerful look.

In the large hall the lady sat in the winter evenings, with all her maids spinning woolen and linen yarn, and every Sunday evening there was a reading from the Bible by the Councillor of Justice himself. In his old age the peddler had achieved this title. There were children, and as they grew up they received the best possible education, although all were not equally gifted—just as it is in all families.

But the willow branch outside had grown to be a big splendid tree, which stood free and undisturbed. "That is our family tree," the old people said. And they explained to all the children, even those who were not very bright, that the tree was to be honored and respected.

So a hundred years rolled by.

Now it was our own time. The lake had grown into a marsh, and the old mansion had almost disappeared. A long narrow pool of water near the remains of a stone wall was all that was left of the deep ditch; yet here still stood a magnificent old willow tree with drooping branches. It was the family tree, and it showed how beautiful a tree may be if left to itself. To be sure, the main trunk was split from root to crown, and storms had given it a little twist, but it still stood firmly. From every cleft and crack into which the winds had carried soil, grasses and flowers had sprung forth, especially near the top, where the great branches separated. There a sort of a small hanging garden had been formed of wild raspberries and chickweed, and even a little serviceberry tree had taken root and stood slender and graceful in the midst of the old tree, which reflected itself in the dark water when the wind had driven all the duckweed into a corner of the pool. A narrow path, which led across the fields, passed close by the old tree.

High on the hill near the forest, with a splendid view in every direction, stood the new mansion, large and magnificent, the glass of its windows so clear and transparent that there seemed to be no panes there at all. The stately flight of steps that led up to the entrance looked like a bower covered with roses and broad-leaved plants. The lawn was as freshly and vividly green as if each separate blade of grass were washed mornings and evenings. In the great hall hung valuable pictures; there were silken chairs and sofas so airy and graceful that they seemed almost ready to walk on their own legs; there were tables with polished marble tops, and books bound in rich morocco and gold. Yes, they were really wealthy people who lived here; they were people of position; here lived the baron and his family.

Everything here fitted with everything else. The motto of the house was still "Everything in its proper place." So all the pictures that at one time had hung with honor and glory in the former mansion were now relegated to the passage that led to the servants' hall, for they were considered nothing but old junk; especially two old portraits, one of a man in a pink coat and a wig, the other of a lady with powdered, high-dressed hair and a rose held in her hand, and each surrounded by a large wreath of willow branches. These two old pictures were marred by many holes, for the baron's children were fond of using the two old people as targets for their crossbows. They were the portraits of the Councillor of Justice and his lady, from whom the whole family descended.

"But they didn't really belong to our family," said one of the young barons. "He was a peddler, and she was a goose girl! They weren't like Papa and Mamma!"

The pictures were judged to be worthless junk, and as the motto was "Everything in its proper place," Great-grandmother and Great-grandfather were hung in the passage that led to the servants' hall.

Now, the son of the village pastor was the tutor at the mansion. One day he was out walking with his pupils, the young barons and their older sister, who had just been confirmed. They followed the path toward the old willow, and as they strolled along, the young girl gathered some field flowers and bound them together—"Everything in its proper place"—and the flowers became a beautiful bouquet. At the same time she heard every word that was spoken, for she liked to listen to the clergyman's son talk of the power of nature and the great men and women of history. She had a good, sweet temper, with true nobility of soul and mind, and a heart that appreciated all that God had created.

They stopped at the old willow tree, where the youngster boy insisted on having a flute made for him, as had been cut for him from other willow branches before; and the pastor's son therefore broke off a branch.

"Oh, don't," cried the young baroness, but it was already too late. "That is our famous old tree," she explained, "and I love it dearly. They laugh at me at home for it, but I don't care. There's an old tale attached to this tree."

Then she told them all the story about the tree, about the old mansion, and the peddler and the goose girl who had met for the first time on this very spot and had afterward founded the noble family to which these young people belonged.

"They didn't want to be knighted, the grand old people!" she said. "They kept their motto, 'Everything in its proper place,' and so they thought it would be out of place for them to buy a title. It was their son—my grandfather—who was made a baron. They say he was very learned, a great favorite with princes and princesses, and was present at all their festivals. The others at home love him the best, but I don't know—there seems to be something about that first pair that draws my heart to them. How comfortable and patriarchal it must have been in the old mansion then, with the mistress sitting at her spinning wheel among all her maids, and the old master reading aloud from the Bible!"

"They must have been wonderful people, sensible people," said the pastor's son.

Then the conversation turned naturally toward noblemen and commoners. The young man hardly seemed to belong to the lower classes, so well did he understand and speak of the purpose and meaning of nobility.

"It is good fortune," he said, "to belong to a family that has distinguished itself. In your own blood there is then, so to speak, a spur that urges you on to make progress in everything that is good. It's gratifying to bear the name of a family that is a card of admission to the highest circles. Nobility means something great and noble; it is a gold coin that has been stamped to show its worth. It is a modern belief, and many poets, of course, agree with it, that all of nobility must be bad and stupid, and that the lower you go among poor people, the more wisdom and virtue do you find. But that isn't my opinion, for I think it's entirely foolish, entirely false. There are many beautiful and kindly traits found in the upper classes. I could give you many examples; here's one my mother told me once.

"She was visiting a noble family in town, where I think my grandmother had nursed the lady of the house. The old nobleman and my mother were together in his apartments when he noticed an old woman come limping into the courtyard on crutches. She used to come there every Sunday, to receive a little gift.

"'Ah! There is the poor old lady!' said the nobleman. 'Walking is so hard for her!' And before my mother understood what he meant, the seventy-year-old excellency was out of the room and down the stairs, carrying his gift to the old woman, to spare her the difficult walk.

"Now that was only a little thing, but like the widow's mite it has a sound that echoes to the depths of the human heart. Those are the things that poets ought to sing about, especially in these times, for it does good; it soothes and reconciles mankind. But when a person, just because he is of noble birth and has a pedigree, stands on his hind legs and neighs in the street like an Arabian horse, and, when a commoner has been in the rooms, sneers, 'Something out of the street has been in here!'—that is nobility in decay and just a mask—a mask such as Thespis created. People are glad to see one like that satirized."

That was the way the pastor's son spoke. It was a rather long speech, but while talking he had finished carving the flute.

That night there was a great party at the mansion, with many guests from about the neighborhood and from the capital. The main hall was full of people; some of the ladies were dressed tastefully, while others showed no taste at all. The clergymen of the neighborhood remained gathered respectfully in a corner, looking as if they were conducting a burial service there. But it was a party of pleasure; only the pleasure hadn't begun yet.

There was to be a great concert, so the little baron brought in his new willow flute. But neither he nor his father could get a note from it, so they decided it was worthless. There were chamber music and song, both of the sort that pleases the performers most—yet quite charming.

Suddenly a certain cavalier—his father's son and nothing else—spoke to the tutor. "Are you a musician?" he demanded. "You play the flute and make it, too! That's genius! That should command, and receive, the place of honor! Heaven knows, I try to follow the times. You have to do that, you know. Come, you will enchant us all with the little instrument, won't you?"

Then he handed the tutor the flute made from the old willow down by the pool and announced loudly that the tutor was about to favor them with a solo on that instrument.

Now, it was easy to tell that they only wanted to make fun of him, so the tutor refused, though he could really play well. But they crowded around him and insisted so strongly that at last he put the flute to his lips.

That was a strange flute! A tone was heard, as sustained as the whistle of a steam engine, yes, and much stronger; it echoed over the courtyard, garden, and wood, and miles away into the country. And with that note there came a rushing wind that seemed to roar, "Everything in its proper place!"

And then Papa flew, as if carried by the wind, straight out of the great hall and into the shepherd's cottage, while the shepherd was blown—not into the main hall, for there he could not come—no, up into the servants' room, among the haughty lackeys strutting in their silk stockings. The proud servants were almost paralyzed at the very thought that such a common person would dare to sit at table with them!

But in the great hall the young baroness flew to the upper end of the table, where she was worthy to sit; the pastor's son found himself next to her, and there they both sat as if they were a newly married couple. A gentle old count of one of the most ancient families in the country remained unmoved in his honorable place, for the flute was just, as everyone ought to be. But the witty cavalier who was nothing more than the son of his father, and who had caused the flute playing, flew head over heels into the poultry house—and he was not alone.

For a whole mile around the countryside the sound of the flute could be heard, and remarkable things happened. The family of a rich merchant, driving along in their coach and four, was blown completely out of the carriage and could not even find a place on the back of it. Two wealthy peasants who in our times had grown too high for their own cornfields were tumbled back into the ditch.

Yes, that was indeed a dangerous flute. But luckily it burst after that first note, and that was a fortunate thing for everybody, for then it was put back into the owner's pocket. "Everything in its proper place."

The next day no one spoke of what had happened; and that is where we get the expression, "To pocket the flute." Everything was back in its former state, except for the two old portraits of the merchant and the goose girl. They had been blown up onto the wall of the drawing room; and when one of the well-known experts said they had been painted by an old master, they were left there, and carefully restored. Nobody knew before that they were worth anything, and how could they have known? Now they hung in the place of honor. "Everything in its proper place."

And it will come to that. Eternity is long—even longer than this story.

THE GOBLIN AND THE GROCER (1852)

There was a student, who lived in the garret and didn't own anything. There was also a grocer, who kept shop on the ground floor and owned the whole house. The household goblin stuck to the grocer, because every Christmas Eve it was the grocer who could afford him a bowl of porridge with a big pat of butter in it. So the goblin stayed in the grocery shop, and that was very educational.

One evening the student came in by the back door to buy some candles and cheese. He had no one to send, and that's why he came himself. He got what he came for, paid for it, and the grocer and his wife nodded, "Good evening." There was a woman who could do more than just nod, for she had an unusual gift of speech. The student nodded too, but while he was reading something on the piece of paper which was wrapped around his cheese, he suddenly stopped. It was a page torn out of an old book that ought never to have been put to this purpose, an old book full of poetry.

"There's more of it," the grocer told him. "I gave an old woman a few coffee beans for it. If you will give me eight pennies, you shall have the rest."

"If you please," said the student, "let me have the book instead of the cheese. There's no harm in my having plain bread and butter for supper, but it would be sinful to tear the book to pieces. You're a fine man, a practical man, but you know no more about poetry than that tub does."

Now this was a rude way to talk, especially to the tub. The grocer laughed and the student laughed. After all, it was said only as a joke, but the goblin was angry that anyone should dare say such a thing to a grocer, a man who owned the whole house, a man who sold the best butter.

That night, when the shop was shut and everyone in bed except the student, the goblin borrowed the long tongue of the grocer's wife, who had no use for it while she slept. And any object on which he laid this tongue became as glib a chatterbox as the grocer's wife herself. Only one object could use the tongue at a time, and that was a blessing, for otherwise they would all have spoken at once. First the goblin laid the tongue on the tub in which old newspapers were kept.

"Is it really true," asked the goblin, "that you don't know anything about poetry?"

"Of course, I know all about poetry," said the tub. "It's the stuff they stick at the end of a newspaper column when they've nothing better to print, and which is sometimes cut out. I dare say I've got more poetry in me than the student has, and I'm only a small tub compared to the grocer."

Then the goblin put the tongue on the coffee mill—how it did chatter away. He put it on the butter cask and on the cashbox, he put it on everything around the shop, until it was back upon the tub again. To the same question everyone gave the same answer as the tub, and the opinion of the majority must be respected.

"Oh, won't I light into that student," said the goblin, as he tiptoed up the back stairs to the garret where the student lived. A candle still burned there, and by peeping through the keyhole the goblin could see that the student was reading the tattered old book he had brought upstairs with him.

But how bright the room was! From the book a clear shaft of light rose, expanding into a stem and a tremendous tree which spread its branching rays above the student. Each leaf on the tree was evergreen, and every flower was the face of a fair lady, some with dark and sparkling eyes, some with eyes of the clearest blue. Every fruit on the tree shone like a star, and the room was filled with song.

Never before had the little goblin imagined such splendor. Never before had he seen or heard anything like it. He stood there on tiptoe, peeping and peering till the light went out. But even after the student blew out his lamp and went to bed, the little fellow stayed to listen outside the door. For the song went on, soft but still more splendid, a beautiful cradle song lulling the student to sleep.

"No place can compare with this," the goblin exclaimed. "I never expected it. I've a good notion to come and live with the student." But he stopped to think, and he reasoned, and he weighed it, and he sighed, "The student has no porridge to give me."

So he tiptoed away, back to the shop, and high time too. The tub had almost worn out the tongue of the grocer's wife. All that was right-side-up in the tub had been said, and it was just turning over to say all the rest that was in it, when the goblin got back and returned the tongue to its rightful owner. But forever afterward the whole shop, from the cashbox right down to the kindling wood, took all their ideas from the tub. Their respect for it was so great and their confidence so complete that, whenever the grocer read the art and theatrical reviews in the evening paper, they all thought the opinions came out of the tub.

But the little goblin was no longer content to sit listening to all the knowledge and wisdom down there. No! As soon as the light shone again in the garret, he felt as if a great anchor rope drew him up there to peep through the keyhole. And he felt the great feeling that we feel when watching the ever-rolling ocean as a storm passes over it. And he started to cry, for no reason that he knew, but these were tears that left him strong and glad. How glorious it would be to sit with the student under the tree of light! He couldn't do that. He was content with the keyhole. There he stood on the cold landing, with wintry blasts blowing full upon him from the trapdoor to the roof. It was cold, so cold, but the little fellow didn't feel it until the light went out and the song gave way to the whistle of the wind. Ugh! He shivered and shook as he crept down to his own corner, where it was warm and snug. And when Christmas came round—when he saw that bowl of porridge and the big pat of butter in it—why then it was the grocer whose goblin he was.

But one midnight, the goblin was awakened by a hullabaloo of banging on the shutters. People outside knocked their hardest on the windows, and the watchman blasted away on his horn, for there was a house on fire. The whole street was red in the light of it. Was it the grocer's house? Was it the next house? Where? Everybody was terrified! The grocer's wife was so panicky that she took off her gold earrings and put them in her pocket to save them. The grocer ran to get his stocks and bonds, and the servant for the silk mantilla she had scrimped so hard to buy. Everyone wanted to rescue what he treasured most, and so did the little goblin. With a leap and a bound he was upstairs and into the garret. The student stood calmly at his window, watching the fire, which was in the neighbor's house. The goblin snatched the wonderful book from the table, tucked it in his red cap, and held it high in both hands. The treasure of the house was saved! Off to the roof he ran. Up to the top of the chimney he jumped. There he sat, in the light of the burning house across the street, clutching with both hands the cap which held his treasure.

Now he knew for certain to which master his heart belonged. But when they put the fire out, and he had time to think about it, he wasn't so sure.

"I'll simply have to divide myself between them," he decided. "I can't give up the grocer, because of my porridge."

And this was all quite human. Off to the grocer all of us go for our porridge.

UNDER THE WILLOW TREE (1852)

The country around the town of Kjöge is very bare. The town itself lies by the seashore, which is always beautiful, although it might be more beautiful than it is, because all around are flat fields, and a forest a long way off. But one always finds something beautiful in the spot that is one's own home, something for which one longs, even when one is in the most wonderful spot in the world.

And we must admit that the outer edge of Kjöge, where small, humble gardens line the little stream that flows into the sea, could be very pretty in the summertime. This was the opinion of the two small children, Knud and Johanne, who were playing there, crawling under the gooseberry bushes to reach each other.

In one of the gardens there stood an elder tree, in the other an old willow, and under the latter the children were especially fond of playing. Although the tree stood close beside the stream and they might easily have fallen into the water, they were allowed to play there, for the eye of God watches over little ones. Otherwise they would be very badly off indeed. Besides, these two were careful about the water; in fact, the boy was so afraid of it that in the summer he could not be lured into the sea, where the other children were fond of splashing about. As a result, he had to bear the teasing of the others as best he could.

But once Johanne, the little girl, dreamed she was out in a boat, and Knud waded out to join her, with the water rising until it closed over his head. And from the moment little Knud heard of this dream he could no longer bear to be called a coward. He might really go into the water now, he said, since Johanne had dreamed it. He never carried that idea into practice, but for all that the dream remained his great pride.

Their poor parents often came together, while Knud and Johanne played in the gardens or on the high road, where a long row of willows had been planted along the ditch. These trees with their polled tops certainly did not look very beautiful, but they were there for use rather than for ornament. The old willow tree in the garden was much lovelier, which was why the children took most delight in sitting under it.

In Kjöge itself was a great marketplace, and at fair time this plaza was gay with whole streets of tents filled with silk ribbons, boots, and everything a person might desire. There were great crowds then, and generally the weather was rainy. One could easily smell the odor of peasants' clothes, but this could not destroy the fragrance that streamed from a booth full of honey cakes. And best of all, the man who kept this particular booth came every year during fair time to lodge in the house of little Knud's parents. Consequently, every now and then, there was a present of a bit of honey cake, and of course Johanne always received her share.

But the best thing of all was that this gingerbread dealer knew all sorts of charming stories and could even tell tales about his own gingerbread cakes. One evening he told a story about them which made such a deep impression on the two children that they never forgot it. For that reason perhaps we should hear it, too, especially since it is not very long.

"On the shop counter," he said, "there once lay two gingerbread cakes. One was in the shape of a man with a hat on, the other of a maiden with no bonnet but with a blot of yellow on top of her head. Both their faces were on the upper side, for that was the side that was supposed to be looked at, and not the other. Indeed, most people have one side from which they should be viewed. On his left side the man wore a bitter almond for a heart; but the maiden, on the other hand, was honey cake all through. They were placed on the counter as samples, so they remained there for a long time, until at last they fell in love with each other. But neither told the other, which they should have done if they had expected anything to come of it.

"'He is a man, so he must speak first,' thought the maiden. But she was quite contented, for she knew in her heart that her love was returned. His thoughts were far more extravagant, which is just like a man. He dreamed that he was a street urchin, and that he had four pennies all his own, and that he bought the maiden and ate her up.

"So they lay on the counter for days and weeks, and grew dry, but the thoughts of the maiden remained still gentle and womanly.

"'It's enough for me that I have lived on the same table with him, 'thought the maiden, and then she broke in two.

"'If only she had known of my love she would have held together a little longer,' thought he.

"So that's the story, and here they are, both of them," said the baker. "They're remarkable for their strange history and for their silent love, which never came to anything. And now they're both for you!" With that he gave Johanne the man, who was still in one piece, and Knud got the broken maiden; but the children had been so touched by the story that they couldn't be so bold as to eat up the lovers.

Next day they took them out to the Kjöge churchyard, where, winter and summer, lovely ivy covers the church wall like a rich carpet. They stood the two cake figures up among the green leaves in the bright sunshine and told a group of other children the story of the silent love that was useless; that is to say, the love was, for the story was charming, they all found.

But when they looked again at the gingerbread couple they found that a mischievous big boy had eaten up the broken maiden. The children cried about that and later— probably so that the poor lover might not be left alone in the world—they ate him up, too. But they never forgot the story. The two children were always together by the elder tree or under the willow, and little Johanne sang the most beautiful songs in a voice as clear as a silver bell. Knud had not a note of music in him, but at least he knew the words of the songs, and that was something. But the people of Kjöge, even the wife of the hardware merchant, stopped and listened when Johanne sang. "She has a very sweet voice, that little girl," she said.

Those were glorious days; but glorious days do not last forever, and finally the neighbors separated. Johanne's mother died, and her father planned to marry again in Copenhagen, where he had been promised a position as messenger, a job supposed to be very profitable. While the neighbors parted with regrets, the children wept bitterly, but the parents promised to write to each other at least once a year.

And Knud was made apprentice to a shoemaker, for such a big boy was too old to run around wild any longer; and, furthermore, he was confirmed.

Oh, how he would have liked to see little Johanne in Copenhagen on that day of celebration! But he didn't go; and he had never been there, although Kjöge is only five Danish miles away. On a clear day Knud could see the distant towers of the city across the bay, and on the day of his confirmation he could even see the golden cross on the tower of the Church of Our Lady glitter in the sun.

Ah, how often his thoughts turned toward Johanne! And did she remember him? Yes! At Christmastime a letter came from her father to Knud's parents, saying that they were doing very well in Copenhagen, and Johanne could look forward to a brilliant career on the strength of her lovely voice. She already had a position in the opera house and was already earning a little money, out of which she sent her dear neighbors of Kjöge a dollar for a merry Christmas Eve. Johanne herself added a postscript, asking them to drink to her health, and in the same postscript was also written, "Friendly greetings to Knud!"

They all wept; but this was all very pleasant, for they were tears of joy that they shed. Knud's thoughts had been with Johanne every day, and now he knew that she also thought of him. The nearer came the end of his apprenticeship, the more clearly did he realize that he was in love with Johanne and that she must be his little wife.

When he thought of this a smile brightened his face, and he drew the thread faster than before and pressed his foot against the knee strap. He didn't even pay any attention when he ran the awl deep into one of his fingers. He was determined that he would not play the silent lover, like the two gingerbread cakes. The story had taught him a lesson.

Now he was a journeyman, and his knapsack was packed ready for his trip. At last, for the first time in his life, he was to go to Copenhagen, where a master was already expecting him. How surprised and happy Johanne would be to see him! She was just seventeen now, and he nineteen.

He wanted to buy a gold ring for her before he left Kjöge, but then decided he could get a much nicer one in Copenhagen. And so he took leave of his parents, and on a rainy, windy day in autumn set forth on foot from the town of his birth. The damp leaves were dropping from the trees, and he was wet to the skin when he arrived at his new master's home in the big city of Copenhagen. The following Sunday he would pay a visit to Johanne's father!

So, on Sunday he put on the new journeyman's clothes, and the new hat from Kjöge that became him very well, for till then he had only worn a cap. He easily found the house he was seeking, and mounted flight after flight of stairs until he became almost dizzy. It seemed terrible to him for people to live piled up on top of each other in this intricate city.

Everything in the parlor looked prosperous, and Johanne's father received him in kindly friendship. Knud was a stranger to the new wife, but she too shook hands with him and gave him a cup of coffee.

"Johanne will be glad to see you," said the father. "You've grown into a nice-looking young man. Yes, wait till you see her. There is a girl who rejoices my heart, and please God she will rejoice it still more. She has her own room now and pays us rent regularly for it!"

Then he knocked quite politely at his daughter's door, as if he were a stranger, and they went in.

Oh, how pretty it was! He was certain there wasn't such a lovely room in all Kjöge; the queen herself could not be more charmingly lodged. There were carpets, and window curtains that hung quite to the floor, and flowers and pictures, and a velvet chair, and even a mirror as large as a door and so clear there was a danger of walking into it.

A glance showed all this to Knud, and yet he could look at nothing but Johanne. She was a full-grown maiden now, quite different from Knud's memories of her, and much more beautiful. There wasn't a girl in Kjöge like her. How graceful she was, and with what a strange, unsure gaze she looked at Knud! But that was only for a moment, and then she rushed toward him as if to kiss him. She did not actually do so, but she very nearly did.

Yes, she was really happy to see her childhood friend again! There were tears in Johanne's eyes; she had so much to say, and so many questions to ask about everything, from Knud's parents to the elder tree and the willow, which she called Elder Mother and Willow Father, just as if they had been human beings; and indeed they might be called so, just as much as the gingerbread cakes. She spoke of them too, and their silent love, and how they had lain on the shop counter and broken in two—and at this she laughed heartily, while the blood rushed to Knud's cheeks and his heart beat faster and faster. No, she had not grown haughty at all.

And Knud noticed quite well that it was because of her that her parents invited him to spend the evening. With her own hands she poured out the tea and gave him a cup; and afterward she read aloud to them from a book, and it seemed to Knud that what she read was all about himself and his love, for it matched with his thoughts. Then she sang a simple little song, but her singing made it a real story that seemed to be the outpouring of her very heart.

Yes, Knud knew she cared for him. He could not keep tears of joy from rolling down his cheeks, nor could he speak a single word—he seemed struck dumb. But she pressed his hand and murmured, "You have a good heart, Knud. Stay always the way you are now!"

That was a magnificent evening; it was impossible to sleep afterward, and accordingly, Knud did not sleep.

When he had left, Johanne's father had said, "Now, don't forget us altogether. Don't let the whole winter go by before you come to us again!" Knud felt that gave him permission to repeat the call the following Sunday, and determined to do so.

But every evening after work—and the working hours lasted until candlelight there—Knud went out into the town. He returned to the street in which Johanne lived and looked up at her window. It was almost always lighted, and one evening he could even see the shadow of her face quite plainly on the curtain. That was an evening he would never forget. His master's wife did not like his "gallivanting abroad every evening," as she put it, and shook her head ruefully over him; but the master only smiled.

"He's just a young fellow," he said.

"On Sunday we shall see each other," Knud thought, "and I shall tell her how she is always in my thoughts and that she must be my little wife. I know I'm only a poor journeyman shoemaker, but I can become a master, and I'll work and save—yes, I'll tell her that! No good comes from a silent love; I've learned that much from the gingerbread!"

Sunday came at last, and Knud set out, but to his great disappointment they had to tell him they were all invited out that evening. But as he left Johanne pressed his hand and said, "Have you ever been to the theater? You must go there sometime. I shall be singing on Wednesday, and if you have time that evening, I'll send you a ticket. My father knows where you are living."

How kind it was of her! And at noon on Wednesday he received a sealed envelope. There were no words inside, but the ticket was there, and that evening Knud went to the theater for the first time in his life. And what did he see? He saw Johanne, looking more charming and beautiful than he ever could have believed possible! To be sure, she was married to a stranger, but that was just in the play; it was only make-believe, as Knud understood very well. If it had been true, he thought, she would never have had the heart to send him a ticket so that he could go and see it. And everybody shouted and applauded, and Knud cried out, "Hurrah!"

Even the king was there, smiling at Johanne, and he seemed to delight in her loveliness. How small Knud felt then! Still he loved her dearly, and felt that she loved him, too; but he knew it was up to the man to speak the first word, as the gingerbread maiden in the story had taught him. Indeed, there was a great deal of truth in that story.

So, as soon as Sunday came, he went to see her again, feeling as solemn as if he were going into a church. Johanne was at home alone; it could not have happened more fortunately.

"I'm glad you came," she said. "I almost sent Father after you, but I felt in my heart that you would be here this evening. I have to tell you that I am leaving for France on Friday; I must study there if I am to become a great artiste!"

At those words it seemed to Knud as if the whole room were whirling round and round with him. He felt as if his heart would break; there were no tears in his eyes, but Johanne could not fail to see how stricken he was .

"You honest, faithful soul!" she said.

And her tenderness loosened his tongue. He told her how much he loved her and begged her to become his little wife. Then he saw Johanne turn pale as she dropped his hand and said seriously and sadly, "Dear Knud, don't make us both unhappy. I shall always be a loving sister to you, one in whom you may trust, but I shall never be anything more."

Gently she placed her soft hand on his hot forehead. "God gives us the strength for much," she said, "if only we try to do our best." At that moment her stepmother entered the room, and Johanne said, "Knud is quite heartbroken because I'm going away! Come, be a man," and she laid her hand on his shoulder; it seemed as if they had been talking only of her journey. "You're a child," she laughed, "but now you must be good and reasonable, as you used to be under the willow tree when we were both children!"

Knud felt as if the whole world were out of joint, and his thoughts were like a loose thread fluttering in the wind. He remained for tea, though he hardly knew if they had asked him to; and they were kind and gentle, and Johanne poured out his tea and sang to him. Her voice did not have its old tone, but still it was wonderfully beautiful and nearly broke his heart. And then they parted. Knud could not bear to offer his hand, but she took it and said, "Surely you'll shake hands with your sister at parting, old playmate!"

She smiled through the tears that were in her own eyes, and repeated the word "brother." Yes, that was supposed to be a great consolation! Such was their parting.

She sailed for France, and Knud wandered about the muddy streets of Copenhagen. His comrades in the workshop asked why he was so gloomy and urged him to join them and amuse himself, for he was still a young fellow.

So they took him to a dance hall. He saw many pretty girls there, but there was not one to compare with Johanne; here, where he had hoped to forget her, she was more vivid than ever before the eyes of his soul. "God gives us the strength for much," she had said, "if only we try to do our best." Then a devotion came to his mind, and he folded his hands quietly. The violins played, and the girls danced gaily, and suddenly it seemed to him that he should never have brought Johanne into a place like this—for she was there with him, in his heart.

Knud ran out and wandered aimlessly through the streets. He passed by the house where she had lived; it was dark there—everywhere were darkness and emptiness and loneliness. The world went in its way, and Knud went his.

Winter set in, and the waters froze over; it was as if everything were preparing itself for burial. But when spring returned, and the first steamer was to start, an intense longing seized him to go away, far into the world, anywhere—but not too close to France. So he packed his knapsack and wandered deep into Germany, from town to town, finding rest and peace nowhere. It was not until he came to the glorious old city of Nuremberg that he could quiet his restless spirit, and there he decided to stay.

Nuremberg is a strange old city, looking as if it had been cut out of an old-fashioned picture book. The streets seem to wander along just as they please. The houses did not like to stand in regular rows. Gables with little towers, arabesques, and pillars lean out over the walks, and from the queer peaked roofs waterspouts, shaped like dragons or long, slim dogs, push out far over the streets.

There in the Nuremberg marketplace stood Knud, his knapsack, on his back. He was beside one of the old fountains, where splendid bronze figures, scriptural and historical, rose up between the gushing jets of water. A pretty little servant girl was just filling her pails, and she gave Knud a refreshing drink; and as her hand was full of roses she gave him one of them, too, and he accepted that as a good sign.

From the church nearby came the strains of an organ; they rang as familiar to him as the tones of the organ at home in Kjöge church, and he entered the great cathedral. The sunlight streamed in through the high stained-glass windows and down between the lofty, slender pillars. His spirit found rest.

And Knud found a good master in Nuremberg, and he lived in his house, and there learned to speak German.

The old moat around the town of Nuremberg has been converted into little kitchen gardens, but the high walls with their heavy towers are standing yet. The ropemaker twists his cords on a wooden gallery along the inside of the town wall, where elder bushes grow out of the cracks and clefts, spreading their green branches over the small, lowly houses below. In one of these houses Knud lived with his master; and over the little garret window where he slept the elder tree waved its branches.

Here he lived for a summer and winter. But when spring returned he could bear it no longer, for the elder was blooming and the fragrance of its blossoms carried him back to home and the garden at Kjöge. So Knud left that master and found another farther in town, over whose house no elder bush blossomed.

His new workshop was close to one of the old stone bridges, by an ever-foaming, low water mill. The stream roared past it, hemmed in by the houses, whose decayed old balconies looked about to topple into the water. No elder grew here—there was not even a little green plant in a flowerpot—but just opposite stood a grand old willow tree that seemed to cling fast to the house, as if it feared being carried away by the stream. It stretched its branches out over the river, just as the willow at Kjöge spread its arms across the stream by the gardens of home.

Yes, Knud had gone from the Elder Mother to the Willow Father. This tree had something, especially on moonlit evenings, that went straight to his heart, and that something was not of the moonlight but of the old willow tree itself.

He could not remain there. Why not? Ask the willow tree; ask the blossoming elder! And so he bade farewell to his kind master and to Nuremberg and traveled on further.

To no one did he speak of Johanne, but hid his sorrow in his innermost heart; and he thought of the deep meaning of the old story of the gingerbread. Now he understood why the man had a bitter almond for a heart—he himself had felt the bitterness of it. And Johanne, who was always so gentle and smiling, she was only like the honey cake.

The strap of Knud's knapsack seemed so tight across his chest that he could scarcely breathe, but even when he loosened it he was not relieved. He saw only half the world around him; the other half he carried within him. That's how it was!

Not until he was in sight of the high mountains did the world appear freer to him; now his thoughts were turned outward again, and the tears came into his eyes.

The Alps seemed to him like the folded wings of Earth; what if they were to unfold themselves and display their varied pictures of black woods, foaming waters, clouds, and great masses of snow! On the last day, he thought, the world will lift up its mighty wings and mount upward to God, to burst like a soap bubble before the glance of the Highest.

"Ah," he sighed, "that that last day were here now!"

Silently he wandered through a country that seemed to him like an orchard covered with soft turf. From the wooden balconies of the houses girls, busy with their lace making, nodded down at him. The summits of the mountains glowed in the red evening sun; and when he saw the blue lakes gleaming through the dark trees, he thought of the seacoast near Kjöge, and there was a sadness in his heart—but it was pain no longer.

There where the Rhine rolls onward like a great wave and then bursts into snow-white, gleaming, cloudlike masses, as if clouds were being created there, with the rainbow fluttering like a loose band above them—it was there that he thought of the mill at Kjöge, with its rushing, foaming stream.

He would have been glad to have remained in the quiet Rhenish town, but here also there were too many elder trees and too many willows, so he traveled on, over the mighty, towering mountains, through shattered walls of rock, and on roads that clung to the mountainsides like the nests of swallows. The waters foamed in the depths, the clouds themselves were below him, and he strode on in the warm summer sun over shiny thistles, Alpine roses, and snow. Thus he said farewell to the lands of the north and journeyed on under the shade of blooming chestnut trees, and through vineyards and fields of maize. Now the mountains were a wall between him and all his memories; that was how he wished it to be.

At last he reached that great, glorious city called Milan, and here he found a German master who gave him work. The master and his wife, in whose workshop he labored now, were a pious old couple. And they became quite fond of the quiet journeyman, who said little but worked all the harder and led a devout Christian life. And to Knud also it seemed that God had lifted the heavy burden from his heart.

His favorite relaxation was to climb from time to time to the mighty marble church, which seemed to him to have been built of the snow of his native Northland, formed into images, pointed towers, and decorated open halls; from every corner and every niche the white statues smiled down upon him. Above him was the blue sky; below him were the city and the wide-spreading green plains of Lombardy, and toward the north the high mountains capped with perpetual snow. Then he thought of the church at Kjöge, with its red ivy-colored walls, but he did not long to go there again. Here, beyond the mountains, he would be buried.

He had lived there a year, and three years had passed since he had left his home, when one day his master took him into the city—not to the circus with its daring riders; no, to the great opera, where was an auditorium well worth seeing. There were seven tiers of boxes, and from each, beautiful silken curtains hung, while from the ground to the dizzy heights of the roof there sat the most elegant ladies, with corsages in their hands as if they were at a ball, and gentlemen in full dress, many of them with decorations of gold and silver. It was as bright there as in the noonday sunshine, and the music rolled gloriously and beautifully; everything was much more splendid than in the theater at Copenhagen, but then Johanne had been in Copenhagen, and here—

Yes! It was like magic—Johanne was here also! The curtain rose, and she appeared, clad in silk and gold, with a gold crown upon her head. She sang as none but an angel could sing, and came far forward to the front of the stage, and smiled as only Johanne could smile, and looked straight down at Knud! The poor boy seized his master's arm and called out aloud, "Johanne!" The loud music sounded above everything, but no one heard but the master, who nodded his head.

"Yes," he said, "her name is Johanne!" Then he drew forth his program and showed Knud her name—for the full name was printed there.

No, it was not a dream! The great audience applauded and threw wreaths and flowers to Johanne, and every time she went away they called her back on stage, so that she was always going and coming.

In the street outside afterward the people crowded about her carriage and drew it away in triumph. Knud was in the first row and shouted as joyfully as any; and when the carriage halted before her brightly lighted house he was standing close beside the door. It opened, and she stepped out; the light fell upon her beloved face, and she smiled, thanked them graciously, and appeared deeply touched. Knud looked straight into her eyes, and she into his, but she never knew him. A gentleman with a decoration glittering on his breast gave her his arm—people said they were betrothed.

Then Knud went home and packed his knapsack. He had decided to return to his own home, to the elder and willow trees—ah, beneath the willow tree!

The old couple begged him to remain, but no words could change his mind. It was in vain that they pointed out to him that winter was coming and the snow had already fallen in the mountains. He replied that he could march, with his knapsack on his back, and supported by his cane, in the wake of a slow-moving carriage, for which a path would have to be cleared.

So Knud left for the mountains and climbed up them and down them. His strength grew less, but still he saw no village or house; always he plodded onward toward the North. High above him the stars gleamed; his feet stumbled, and his head grew dizzy with the heights. Stars seemed to shine deep in the valley, too, as if there were another sky below him. He felt ill. More and more stars became visible below him; they glowed brighter and brighter and moved to and fro. Then he realized it was the lights of a little town that were shining down there. When he was sure of that, he put forth the last of his strength and finally reached the shelter of a humble inn.

He remained there that night and the whole of the next day, for his body was in desperate need of rest and refreshment. The ice was beginning to thaw, and there was rain in the valley. But on the second morning a man with a hand organ came to the inn and played a Danish melody—and now Knud could not remain.

He resumed his journey northward, tramping on for many days, hurrying as though he were trying to reach home before all were dead there. But to no man did he speak of his longing, for no one would have believed in the sorrow of his spirit, the deepest a human heart can feel. Such grief is not for the world, for it is not amusing; nor is it for friends. And this man had no friends; a stranger, he wandered through strange lands toward his home in the North. He had received only one letter from home, and it was now years since his parents had written. "You are not really Danish as we here at home. We love our country, but you love only a strange country." Thus his parents had written him—yes, they thought they knew him!

Now it was evening. He was tramping along the public highway. The frost had settled down, and the country had become flatter, with fields and meadows on all sides. And near the road there grew a great willow tree! The whole outlook reminded Knud strongly of home; it looked so Danish, and with a deep sigh he sat down under the tree. He was very tired, his head began to nod, and his eyes closed in slumber, but still he seemed to see the tree stretching its arms above him, and in his wandering fancy the tree seemed to be a mighty old man—the Willow Father himself—carrying his tired son in his arms back to his Danish home, to the bare, bleak shore of Kjöge and the garden of his childhood.

Yes, he dreamed that this was the willow tree of Kjöge that had traveled out into the world in search of him, and at last had found him, and had carried him back into the little garden beside the stream. And there stood Johanne, in all her splendor, with the golden crown on her head, just as he had seen her last, and she called out "Welcome!" to him.

And before him stood two remarkable figures, looking much more human than he remembered them from his childhood. They had changed, too, but they were still the two gingerbread cakes, the man and the maiden, that turned their right sides toward him and looked very handsome.

"We thank you!" both said to Knud. "You have loosened our tongues and taught us that thoughts should be spoken freely or nothing will come of them. And now something has come of them—we are betrothed!"

Then they walked hand in hand through the streets of Kjöge, and looked very respectable even on the wrong side; no one could have found any fault with them. On they went, straight toward Kjöge Church, and Knud and Johanne followed them— they, too, walked hand in hand. The church stood there as it had always stood, with the beautiful green ivy growing on its red walls, and the great door of the church swung open, and the organ pealed, and the gingerbread couple walked up the aisle.

"Our master first," said the cake pair, and made room for Johanne and Knud to kneel before the altar. And she bent her head over him, and the tears fell from her eyes, but they were icy cold, for it was the ice around her heart that was melting, softened by his strong love.

The tears fell upon his burning cheeks, and then he awoke—and he was sitting under the old willow tree in a foreign land on that cold winter evening; an icy hail from the clouds was beating on his face.

"That was the most wonderful hour of my life!" he cried. "And it was just a dream. Oh, God, let me dream again!"

Then he closed his eyes once more and dreamed again.

Toward morning there was a great snowstorm, and the wind blew it in drifts over him, and when the villagers came forth to go to church they found a journeyman sitting by the roadside. He was dead—frozen to death beneath the willow tree!

FIVE PEAS FROM A POD (1852)

There were five peas in one pod; the peas were green and the pod was green, and so they believed that the whole world was green—and that was absolutely right! The pod grew and the peas grew; they adjusted themselves to their surroundings, sitting straight in a row. The sun shone outside and warmed the pod; the rain made it clear and clean. It was nice and cozy inside, bright in the daytime and dark at night, just as it should be; and the peas became larger, and more and more thoughtful, as they sat there, for surely there was something they must do.

"Shall I always remain sitting here?" said one. "If only I don't become hard from sitting so long. It seems to me there must be something outside; I have a feeling about it."

And weeks went by; the peas became yellow and the pod became yellow. "The whole world's becoming yellow," they said, and that they had a right to say.

Then they felt a jerk at the pod. It was torn off, came into human hands, and then was put down into the pocket of a jacket, along with other full pods.

"Now it will soon be opened up!" they said, and they waited for that.

"Now I'd like to know which of us will get the farthest," said the smallest pea. "Yes, now we'll soon find that out."

"Let happen what may!" said the biggest.

"Crack!" the pod burst open, and all five peas rolled out into the bright sunshine. They were lying in a child's hand; a little boy held them, and said that they were suitable peas for his peashooter, and immediately one was put in and shot out.

"I'm flying out into the wide world! Catch me if you can!" And then it was gone.

"I'm going to fly right into the sun!" said the second. "That's a perfect pod, and very well suited to me!" Away it went.

"We'll go to sleep wherever we come to," said two of the others, "but we'll roll on, anyway." And they rolled about on the ground before being put into the shooter, but they went into it all the same.

"We'll go the farthest!"

"Let happen what may!" said the last one as it was shot into the air. And it flew up against the old board under the garret window, right into a crack, where there was moss and soft soil; and the moss closed around the pea. There it lay hidden, but not forgotten by our Lord.

"Let happen what may!" it said.

Inside the little garret lived a poor woman who went out by the day to polish stoves; yes, even to chop up wood and do other hard work, for she had strength and she was industrious; but still she remained poor. And at home in the little room lay her half-grown, only daughter, who was so very frail and thin. For a whole year the girl had been bedridden, and it seemed as if she could neither live nor die.

"She will go to her little sister," the woman said. "I had the two children, and it was hard for me to care for both, but then our Lord divided with me and took the one home to himself. I want to keep the one I have left, but probably he doesn't want them to be separated, and she will go up to her little sister."

But the sick girl stayed; she lay patient and quiet the day long, while her mother went out to earn money.

It was springtime, and early one morning, just as the mother was about to go to work, the sun shone beautifully through the little window, across the floor. The sick girl looked over at the lowest windowpane.

"What is that green thing that's peeping in the window? It's moving in the wind."

And the mother went over to the window and opened it a little. "Why," she said, "it is a little pea that has sprouted out here with green leaves! How did it ever get here in the crack? You now have a little garden to look at!"

And the sick girl's bed was moved closer to the window, where she could see the growing pea vine, and the mother went to her work.

"Mother, I think I am going to get well!" said the little girl in the evening.

"The sun today shone so warmly in on me. The little pea is prospering so well, and I will also prosper and get up and out into the sunshine!"

"Oh, I hope so!" said the mother, but she didn't believe it would happen; yet she was careful to strengthen with a little stick the green plant that had given her daughter such happy thoughts about life, so that it wouldn't be broken by the wind. She tied a piece of string to the window sill and to the upper part of the frame, so that the vine could have something to wind around as it shot up. And this it did. You could see every day that it was growing.

"Look, it has a blossom!" said the woman one morning; and now she had not only the hope, but also the belief, that the little sick girl would get well. She recalled that lately the child had talked more cheerfully and that the last few mornings she had risen up in bed by herself and had sat there and looked with sparkling eyes at the little pea garden with its one single plant. The following week the sick child for the first time sat up for over an hour. Joyous, she sat there in the warm sunshine; the window was opened, and outside stood a fully blown pink pea blossom. The little girl bent her head down and gently kissed the delicate leaves. This was just like a festival day.

"Our Lord himself planted the pea and made it thrive to bring hope and joy to you, my blessed child, and to me, too!" said the happy mother, and smiled at the flower, as if to a good angel from God.

But now the other peas! Well, the one that flew out into the wide world crying, "Catch me if you can!" fell into the gutter of the roof and landed in a pigeon's crop, where it lay like Jonah in the whale. The two lazy ones got just that far, for they also were eaten by pigeons, and that's being of real use. But the fourth pea, who wanted to shoot up to the sun, fell into a gutter and lay for days and weeks in the dirty water, where it swelled up amazingly.

"I'm becoming so beautifully fat!" said the pea. "I'm going to burst, and I don't think any pea can, or ever did, go farther than that. I am the most remarkable of the five from that pod!"

And the gutter agreed with it.

But at the garret window stood the young girl with sparkling eyes and the rosy hue of health on her cheeks, and she folded her delicate hands over the pea blossom and thanked our Lord for it.

"I still stand up for my pea!" said the gutter.

SHE WAS GOOD FOR NOTHING (1852)

The mayor was standing at his open window; he was wearing a dress shirt with a dainty breastpin in its frill. He was very well shaven, self-done, though he had cut himself slightly and had stuck a small bit of newspaper over the cut.

"Listen, youngster!" he boomed.

The youngster was none other than the washerwoman's son, who respectfully took off his cap as he passed. This cap was broken at the rim, so that he could put it into his pocket. In his poor but clean and very neatly mended clothes and his heavy wooden shoes, the boy stood as respectfully as if he were before the king.

"You're a good boy, a well-behaved lad!" said the Mayor. "I suppose your mother is washing down at the river, and no doubt you are going to bring her what you have in your pocket. That's an awful thing with your mother! How much have you there?"

"A half pint," said the boy in a low, trembling voice.

"And this morning she had the same?" continued the Mayor.

"No, it was yesterday!" answered the boy.

"Two halves make a whole! She is no good! It is sad there are such people. Tell your mother she ought to be ashamed of herself. Don't you become a drunkard—but I suppose you will! Poor child! Run along now."

And the boy went, still holding his cap in his hand, while the wind rippled the waves of his yellow hair. He went down the street and through an alley to the river, where his mother stood at her washing stool in the water, beating the heavy linen with a wooden beater. The current was strong, for the mill's sluices were open; the bed sheet was dragged along by the stream and nearly swept away her washing stool, and the woman had all she could do to stand up against it.

"I was almost carried away," she said. "It's a good thing you've come, for I need something to strengthen me. It's so cold in the water; I've been standing here for six hours. Have you brought me anything?"

The boy drew forth a flask, and his mother put it to her lips and drank a little.

"Oh, that does me good! How it warms me! It's just as good as hot food, and it isn't as expensive! Drink, my boy! You look so pale, and you're freezing in your thin clothes. Remember, it is autumn. Ooh, the water is cold! If only I don't get ill! But I won't. Give me a little more, and drink some yourself, but only a little drop, for you mustn't get used to it, my poor dear child!"

And she walked out of the water and up onto the bridge where the boy stood. The water dripped from the straw mat that she had tied around her waist and from her petticoat.

"I work and slave till the blood runs out at my fingernails, but I do it gladly if I can bring you up honestly, my sweet child!"

Just then came an elderly woman, poorly clad, lame in one leg, and with an enormously large, false curl hanging down over one of her eyes, which was blind. This curl was supposed to hide the eye, but it only made the defect the more conspicuous. The neighbors called her "limping Maren with the curl," and she was an old friend of the washerwoman's.

"You poor thing," she cried, "slaving and toiling in the cold water! You certainly need something to warm you a little, and yet the gossips cry about the few drops you take!" And soon all that the Mayor had said to the boy was repeated to his mother, for Maren had overheard it, and it had angered her to hear him talk so to the child about his own mother and the few drops she took, because on that same day the Mayor was having a big dinner party with many bottles of wine.

"Good wine, strong wine! Many will drink more than they should, but *they* don't call that drinking. *They* are all right, but you are good for nothing!"

"What! Did the Mayor really say that, child?" asked the laundress, her lips quivering. "So you have a mother who is good for nothing! Perhaps he's right, though he shouldn't say so to a child. But I mustn't complain; good things have come to me from that house."

"Why, yes, you were in service there, when the Mayor's parents were alive. That was many years ago. Many bushels of salt have been eaten since then, so people may well be thirsty!" laughed Maren. "The big dinner today at the Mayor's would have been postponed if everything hadn't been prepared. I heard the news from the porter. A letter came, an hour ago, telling them that the Mayor's younger brother, in Copenhagen, is dead."

"Dead!" cried the laundress, turning as white as a ghost.

"What does it matter to you" said Maren. "Of course, you must have known him, since you worked in the house."

"Is he really dead? He was the best and kindest of men-indeed, there aren't many like him!" Tears were rolling down her cheeks. "Oh, my God! Everything is going around! That's because I emptied the bottle. I couldn't stand so much. I feel so ill!" And she leaned against the fence for support.

"Good heavens, you are ill, indeed!" said Maren. "Try to get over it! No, you really are sick! I'd better get you home!"

"But the washing there!"

"I'll take care of that. Here, give me your arm. The boy can stay here and watch it till I come back and wash what's left. It's only a few pieces."

The poor laundress' legs were trembling under her. "I've stood too long in the cold water, with no food since yesterday! I have a burning fever. Oh, dear Lord Jesus, help me to get home! Oh, my poor child!" And she wept.

The boy cried too, as he sat alone beside the river, guarding the wet linen. The two women made their way slowly, the washerwoman dragging her shaky limbs up the little alley and through the street where the Mayor lived. Just as she reached the front of his house, she sank down on the cobblestones. A crowd gathered around her.

Limping Maren ran into his yard for help. The Mayor and his guests came to the windows.

"It's the washerwoman!" he said. "She's had a bit too much to drink; she's no good! It's a pity for that handsome boy of hers, I really like that child, but his mother is good for nothing."

And the washerwoman was brought to her own humble room, where she was put to bed. Kindly Maren hastened to prepare a cup of warm ale with butter and sugar—she could think of no better medicine in such a case—and then returned to the river, where, although she meant well, she did a very poor job with the washing; she only pulled the wet clothes out of the water and put them into a basket.

That evening, she appeared again in the washerwoman's miserable room. She had begged from the Mayor's cook a couple of roasted potatoes and a fine fat piece of ham for the sick woman. Maren and the boy feasted on these, but the patient was satisfied with the smell, "For that was very nourishing," she said.

The boy was put to bed, in the same one in which his mother slept, lying crosswise at his mother's feet, with a blanket of old blue and red carpet ends sewed together.

The laundress felt a little better now; the warm ale had given her strength, and the smell of the good food had been nourishing.

"Thank you, my kind friend," she said to Maren, "I'll tell you all about it, while the boy is asleep. He's sleeping already; see how sweet he looks with his eyes closed. He doesn't think of his mother's sufferings; may our Lord never let him feel their equal! Well, I was in service at the Councillor's, the Mayor' parents, when their youngest son came home from his studies. I was a carefree young girl then, but honest—I must say that before Heaven. And the student was so pleasant and jolly; every drop of blood in his veins was honest and true; a better young man never lived. He was a son of the house, and I was only a servant, but we became sweethearts—all honorably; a kiss is no sin, after all, if people really love each other. And he told his mother that he loved me. She was an angel in his eyes, wise and kind and loving. And when he went away again he put his gold ring on my finger.

"After he had gone my mistress called me in to speak to me; she looked so grave and yet so kind, and spoke as wisely as an angel indeed. She pointed out to me the gulf of difference, both mentally and materially, that lay between her son and me. 'Now he is attracted by your good looks, but that will fade in time. You haven't received his education; intellectually you can never rise to his level. I honor the poor,' she continued, 'and I know that there is many a poor man who will sit in a higher seat in the Kingdom of Heaven than many a rich man; but that is no reason for crossing the barrier in this world. Left to yourselves, you two would drive your carriage full tilt against obstacles, until it toppled over with you both. Now I know that Erik, the glovemaker, a good, honest craftsman, wants to marry you; he is a well-to-do widower with no children. Think it over!'

"Every word my mistress spoke went through my heart like a knife, but I knew she was right, and that weighed heavily upon me. I kissed her hand, and my bitter tears fell upon it. But still bitterer tears fell when I lay upon my bed in my own room. Oh, the long, dreary night that followed—our Lord alone knows how I suffered!

"Not until I went to church on Sunday did peace of mind come after my pain. It seemed the working of Providence that as I left the church I met Erik himself. There were no doubts in my mind now; we were suited to each other, both in rank and in means; he was even a well-to-do man. So I went straight up to him, took his hand, and asked, 'Do you still think of me?'

"'Yes, always and forever,' he said.

"'Do you want to marry a girl who likes and respects you, but does not love you?'

"'I believe love will come,' he said, and then we joined hands.

"I went home to my mistress. The gold ring that her son had given me I had been wearing every day next to my heart, and every night on my finger in bed, but now I drew it out. I kissed it until my lips bled, then gave it to my mistress and told her that next week the banns would be read for me and the glovemaker.

"My mistress took me in her arms and kissed me; she didn't say I was good for nothing, but at that time I was perhaps better than I am now, for I had not yet known the misfortunes of the world. The wedding was at Candlemas, and for our first year we were quite happy. My husband had a workman and an apprentice with him, and you, Maren, were our servant."

"Oh, and such a good mistress you were!" said Maren. "I shall never forget how kind you and your husband were to me!"

"Ah, but you were with us during our good times! We had no children then. I never saw the student again. Oh, yes, I saw him once, but he didn't see me. He came to his mother's funeral, and I saw him standing by her grave, looking so sad and pale—but that was all for his mother's sake. When his father died later he was abroad and didn't come to that funeral. He didn't come here again; he became a lawyer, and he never married, I know. But he thought no more of me, and if he had seen me he would certainly have never recognized me, ugly as I am now. And it is all for the best!"

Then she went on to tell of the bitter days of hardship, when misfortune had fallen upon them. They had saved five hundred dollars, and since in their neighborhood a house could be bought for two hundred, they considered it a good investment to buy one, tear it down, and build again. So the house was bought, and the bricklayers and carpenters estimated that the new house would cost a thousand and twenty dollars. Erik had credit and borrowed that sum in Copenhagen, but the captain who was to have brought the money was shipwrecked and the money lost.

"It was just then that my darling boy, who lies sleeping there, was born. Then his father had a long and severe illness, and for nine months I even had to dress and undress him every day. We kept on going backward. We had to borrow more and more; one by one all our possessions were sold; and at last Erik died. Since then I have worked and slaved for the boy's sake, have gone out scrubbing floors and washing linen, done coarse work or fine, whatever I could get. But I was not to be better off; it is the Lord's will! He will take me away and find better provisions for my child." Then she fell asleep.

In the morning she seemed better and decided she was strong enough to return to her work. But the moment she felt the cold water a shivering seized her; she grasped about convulsively with her hands, took one step forward, and fell. Her head lay on the dry bank, but her feet were in the water of the river; her wooden shoes, in each of which there was a handful of straw, were carried away by the current.

And here she was found by Maren, when she came to bring her some coffee.

A message had come to her lodging that the Mayor wanted to see her, for he had something to say to her. It was too late. A doctor was summoned; the poor washerwoman was dead.

"She has drunk herself to death," said the Mayor.

The letter that had brought the Mayor the news of his brother's death also gave a summary of his will, and among other bequests he had left six hundred dollars to the glovemaker's widow, who had formerly served his parents! The money was to be paid at discretion in large or small sums to her and her child.

"There was some nonsense about love between my brother and her," said the Mayor. "It's just as well she's out of the way. Now it will all come to the boy, and I'll place him with some honest people who will make him a good workman." And on these words our Lord laid his blessings.

And the Mayor sent for the boy, promised to take care of him, and told him it was a lucky thing his mother was dead; she was good for nothing.

They carried her to the churchyard, to a pauper's grave. Maren planted a little rose tree on her grave, while the boy stood beside her.

"My darling mother," he said as the tears started from his eyes. "Is it true that she was good for nothing?"

"No, it is not true!" said the old woman, looking up to heaven. "I have known it for many years and especially since the night before she died. I tell you she was a good and fine woman, and our Lord in Heaven will say so, too, so let the world say: 'She was good for nothing!' "

THOUSANDS OF YEARS FROM NOW (1853)

Yes, thousands of years from now, men will fly on wings of steam through the air, across the ocean. The young inhabitants of America will visit old Europe. They will come to see the monuments and the great cities, which will then lie in ruins, just as we in our time make pilgrimages to the ruined splendors of southern Asia. Thousands of years from now they will come!

The Thames, the Danube, and the Rhine still roll in their valleys, Mont Blanc still stands firm with its snowy summit, the northern lights still glitter over the lands of the North, but generation after generation has become dust. Mighty names of today are forgotten—as forgotten as those who already slumber under the hill where the rich corn merchant sits and gazes out across his flat and waving cornfields.

"To Europe!" cry the young sons of America. "To the land of our ancestors, that glorious land of memory and legends! To Europe!"

The ship of the air comes. It is crowded with passengers, for this is a much faster crossing than by sea. The electromagnetic wire under the ocean has already cabled the number of the aerial travelers. Already Europe is in sight—the coast of Ireland. But the passengers are still asleep and will not be called until they are over England. It is there that they still take their first step onto the soil of Europe, in the land of Shakespeare, as the intellectual call it, or the land of politics and land of machines, as it is called by others.

Here they stay a whole day! That is all the time this busy generation can give to the whole of England and Scotland. Then they rush on, through the tunnel under the English Channel, to France, the country of Charlemagne and Napoleon. The learned among them speak of Molière and the classic and romantic school of remote antiquity; others applaud the names of heroes, poets, and scientists whom our time does not yet know, but who will in afterdays be born in that crater of Europe, Paris.

Now the steamboat of the air crosses the country whence Columbus set sail, where Cortez was born, and where Calderón sang his dramas in resounding verse. Beautiful, black-eyed women still live in those blooming valleys, and the ancient songs tell of the Cid and the Alhambra.

Then through the air, across the sea, to Italy, where once stood old, eternal Rome. It has vanished! The Campagna is a desert; a solitary ruined wall is shown as the remains of St. Peter's, and there is even doubt that this ruin is authentic.

On to Greece, to spend a night in the hotel at the top of Mount Olympus, just so they can say that they have been there. Then to the Bosporus, for a few hours' rest and to see the spot where Byzantium stood; and where legends tell of the harems of the Turks, poor fishermen are now spreading their nets.

Over the ruins of the mighty cities of the Danube, cities that we in our days know not yet; and on the rich sites of some of those that time shall yet bring forth, the air travelers sometimes descend, only to depart again quickly.

Down below lies Germany, which was once covered with a massive network of railways and canals. Germany, where Luther spoke, and Goethe sang, and Mozart once held the scepter of music! Great names of science and art now shine there— names still unknown to us. One day's stopover for Germany, and one for the other— the country of Oersted and Linnaeus, and for Norway, land of old heroes and young Norwegians. Iceland is visited on the journey home; the geysers burst forth no more, the volcano Hecla is extinct, but that great island is still fixed in the foaming sea, mighty monument of legend and poetry.

"There is really a great deal to be seen in Europe," says the young American proudly. "And we've seen it in eight days; and it is quite possible, as the great traveler" (and here he names one of his contemporaries) "tells us in his famous book, *How to See All Europe in Eight Days.*"

THE LAST PEARL (1853)

There was a rich and happy house. All those in it—the owners, and servants, and friends, too—were happy and cheerful, for on this day, a son and heir had been born, and mother and child were doing well.

The lamp in the cozy bedroom had been partly covered, and heavy curtains of costly silken material had been drawn tightly together before the windows. The carpet was as thick and soft as moss. Everything here invited rest and sleep; it was a delightful place for repose. And the nurse found it so, too; she slept, and indeed she might, for all was well and blessed here.

The Guardian Spirit of the house stood by the head of the bed; and over the child, at the mother's breast, it spread itself like a net of shining stars, stars of great richness; each was a pearl of good fortune. Life's good fairies had brought their gifts to the newborn child; here sparkled health, wealth, happiness, love—everything that man can desire on Earth.

"Everything has been brought and bestowed here," said the Guardian Spirit.

"No," said a voice nearby; it was the voice of the child's good Angel. "One fairy has not yet brought her gift, but she will bring it; she'll bring it in time, even if years should pass first. The *last pearl* is yet lacking."

"Lacking! Nothing must be lacking here! If that actually is the case, let us go and seek the powerful fairy; let us go to her!"

"She will come! She will come someday! Her pearl must be given to bind the wreath together!"

"Where does she live? Where is her home? Tell me that, and I'll go fetch the pearl!"

"You do want to, then," said the child's good Angel. "I will guide you to her, or to where she is to be sought. She has no permanent place; she visits the palace of the emperor and the cottage of the poorest peasant. She passes no one by without leaving a trace of herself; to all she brings her gift, be it a world or a toy. And this child, also, she will come to. You think that while the time to come will be equally long one way or the other, it will not be equally profitable if you await her; well, then, we will go and fetch the pearl, the last pearl in this wealth of gifts."

And so, hand in hand, they flew to the place which at the moment was the fairy's home.

It was a large house, with dark halls and empty rooms, all strangely still. A row of windows stood open, so the fresh air could flow in, and the long white curtains rustled in the breeze.

In the middle of the floor stood an open coffin, and within it lay the corpse of a woman still in the prime of life. The loveliest fresh roses lay upon her, leaving visible only the folded, delicate hands and the noble face, beautiful in death, with the exalted solemnity of one initiated into God's service.

By the coffin stood her husband and children, a whole flock of them, the smallest of whom was held in his father's arm. They had come to bid a last farewell, and the husband kissed her hand, that which, now like a withered leaf, had once clasped theirs with strength and love. Bitter tears of sorrow fell in heavy drops upon the floor, but not a word was spoken. Silence expressed a world of grief. And silent and sobbing, they left the room.

A lighted candle stood there, the flame struggling against the wind as it shot up its long red tongue. Strangers entered the room, closed the lid of the coffin, and hammered in the nails. The hammer strokes clanged sharply through the halls and rooms of the house, resounding in the hearts that bled there.

"Where do you take me?" inquired the Guardian Spirit. "Here could live no fairy whose pearl belong among life's best gifts."

"She dwells in this very place, now at this holy hour," said the Angel, pointing to a corner.

And there, where the mother had sat in life amid flowers and pictures, and had been like the good fairy of the house, where she had affectionately greeted husband, children, and friends, and, like rays of sunshine, had spread happiness, love, and harmony, and had been the very heart of everything, there now sat a strange woman clad in long, heavy robes. It was Sorrow, and she now ruled here in the mother's place. A hot tear rolled down her cheek, into her lap, where it became a pearl, sparkling with all the hues of the rainbow, and as the Angel caught it up it shone with the sevenfold luster of a star.

"The Pearl of Sorrow, the last pearl, which must never be lacking! Through it the light and splendor of all other gifts are enhanced. Behold in it a reflection of the rainbow, which unites Earth with Heaven itself! In the place of each of our beloved ones taken from us by death, we gain one friend more to look forward to being with in Heaven. In the night we look up beyond the stars, toward the end of all things. Reflect, then, upon the Pearl of Sorrow, for within it lie the wings of Psyche, which carry us away from here."

TWO MAIDENS (1853)

Have you ever seen "a maiden"? I am referring to what road pavers call a "maiden," a thing used for ramming down the paving stones. "She" is made entirely of wood, broad at the bottom, with iron hoops around it, and a stick run through it at the upper, narrower end, which gives the maiden arms.

Two maidens like this were once standing in the yard shed, among shovels, measuring tapes, and wheelbarrows. Now, there was a rumor going around that they were no longer to be called "maidens," but "stamps" or "hand rammers"; and this is the newest and only correct term in road pavers' language for what we all in olden times called "a maiden."

There are among us human beings certain individuals we call "emancipated women," such as institution superintendents, midwives, ballet dancers, milliners, and nurses; and with this group of "emancipated," the two "maidens" in the yard shed associated themselves. They were known as "maidens" among the road pavers and would under no circumstances give up their good old name and let themselves be called "stamps" or "hand rammers."

"Maiden is a human name," they said, "but a 'stamp' or a 'hand rammer' is a thing, and we certainly do not want to be called things; that's insulting us!"

"My betrothed is liable to break off our engagement," said the younger of the two, who was engaged to a ramming block, a large machine used to drive stakes into the ground. In fact, he did on a larger scale the same sort of work that she did on a smaller. "He'll take me as a 'maiden,' but I'm sure he won't have me as a 'stamp' or 'hand rammer,' and so I'll not permit them to change my name."

"As for me, I'd just as soon have both my arms broken off!" said the elder.

But the wheelbarrow had a different idea, and the wheelbarrow was really somebody! He considered himself a quarter of a carriage because he went about on one wheel. "I must, however, tell you that it's common enough to be called 'maidens'; that isn't nearly so distinctive a name as 'stamp,' because that belongs under the category of 'seals.' Just think of the 'royal signet' and the 'seal of the state.' If I were you I would give up the name 'maiden.'"

"Never!" said the elder. "I'm much too old for that!"

"You don't seem to understand what is called the European necessity," said the honest old measuring tape. "People have to adapt themselves to circumstances, limit themselves, give in to the needs of the times. And if there is a law that the 'maidens' are to be called 'stamps' or 'hand rammers,' then by that new name she must be called. There is a measuring tape for everything."

"Well, if there must be a change," said the younger, "I'd rather be called 'miss,' for 'miss' reminds one a little of 'maiden.'"

"But I'd rather be chopped up for firewood than change at all," said the old "maiden."

Now it was time for work. The "maidens" rode; they were put in the wheelbarrow, which was respectful treatment, but they were now called "stamps."

"Maid——!" they cried as they stamped on the paving stones. "Maid——!" They almost said the whole word "maiden," but they didn't finish; they had decided not to say any more about it. But among themselves they always spoke of each other as "maidens," and praised the good old days when things were called by their proper names and those who were "maidens" were called "maidens."

And "maidens" they both remained, for the ramming block, the big machine I told you about, did break off his engagement with the younger; he would have nothing to do with a "stamp" or "hand rammer"!

A LEAF FROM HEAVEN (1853)

High up in the thin, clear air there flew an angel bearing a flower from the Garden of Heaven. As he kissed it, a tiny leaf drifted down into the muddy soil in the middle of the wood; it very soon took root there, and sprouted, and sent up shoots among the other plants.

"That's a funny kind of slip," said the plants.

And neither the thistle nor the stinging nettle would have anything to do with the stranger. "It must be some low kind of garden plant," they said, grinning and making fun at it. But it grew and grew, and like no other plant its long branches spread far about.

"Where do you think you're going?" said the tall thistles, who have thorns on each of their leaves. "You're taking a good deal of space. That's a lot of nonsense—we can't stand here and support you!"

When winter came, the snow covered the plant, but from it the blanket of snow received a glow as if the sun were shining from below. Then the spring returned, and the plant was in glorious bloom, more beautiful than any other in the forest.

And now there came to the forest a professor of botany, who could show what he was with many degrees. He carefully inspected the plant and tested it, but decided it was not included in his system of botany; he could not possibly learn to what class it did belong.

"This must be some unimportant variety," he said. "I certainly don't know it. It's not included in any system."

"Not included in any system!" said the thistles and the nettles.

The big trees which grew around it heard what was said, and they also saw the tree was not one of their kind, but they said nothing, good or bad. And that is much the wisest course for stupid people to take.

Then a poor, innocent girl came through the forest. Her heart was pure, and her understanding was glorious with faith. Her only inheritance was an old Bible, but from its pages the voice of God spoke to her: "If people wish to do you evil, remember the story of Joseph. They had evil in their hearts, but God turned it to good. If you suffer wrong, if you are despised and misunderstood, then you must remember the words of him who was purity and goodness itself, and who prayed for those who struck him and nailed him to the cross. 'Father, forgive them; for they know not what they do!'"

She stopped before the wondrous plant, whose great leaves gave forth sweet and refreshing fragrance and whose flowers glowed in the sun like a wonderful firework of color. And from each flower there came a sound as though it held concealed within itself a deep well of melody that thousands of years would not empty. With devout gratitude the girl gazed on this exquisite work of the Creator, and bent down one of the branches, that she might examine the flower and breathe in its sweetness; and a lovely light burned in her soul. It seemed to uplift her heart, and she wanted to pluck a flower, but she had not the heart to break one off, for she knew it would soon fade if she did. So she took only a single green leaf, carried it home, and there she pressed it in between the pages of her Bible; and it lay there quite fresh, always green, and never fading.

It was kept in the pages of that Bible, and with that Bible it was placed under the girl's head when, some weeks thereafter, she lay in her coffin. On her gentle face was the solemn peace of death, as if the earthly remains carried the imprint of the truth that she now was in the presence of her Creator.

But the marvelous plant still bloomed in the forest. It looked almost like a great tree now, and all the birds of passage, especially the storks and the swallows, bowed down before it.

"That thing is taking on foreign airs now," said the thistles and the burdocks. "We never act like that here in this country!"

And the black forest snails spat at the plant.

Then the swineherd came, collecting thistles and other shrubs, to burn them for their ashes. He tore up the heavenly plant by the roots and crammed it into his bag.

"I can use that, too," he said, and no sooner said than done.

But for years the king of that country had been troubled by a deep melancholy of spirit. He kept busy and laborious always, but it seemed to do him no good. They read books to him—deep and learned tomes, or the lightest and most trifling they could find; but nothing did any good. Then one of the world's wisest men, to whom they had applied for help, sent a messenger to explain to the king that there was but one sure remedy that would relieve and cure him.

"In a forest in the king's own country there grows a plant of heavenly origin. Its appearance cannot be mistaken." And then the messenger brought out a drawing of the plant; it would be easy to recognize it. "Its leaves are green winter and summer, so every evening put a fresh leaf on the king's forehead. His thoughts will then clear, and a beautiful dream will refresh and strengthen him."

"I think I took it up in my bundle and burned it to ashes a long time ago," said the swineherd. "I just didn't know any better."

"You did not know any better!" they all said. "Ignorance, oh, ignorance! How great you are!"

And those words the swineherd might well take to heart, for they were meant for him and no one else.

Not a single leaf of that plant could be found; no one knew about the one leaf that lay in the coffin of the dead girl.

And the king himself, in his terrible depression, wandered out to the spot in the woods. "This is where the plant grew," he said. "It shall be a sacred place." Then he had it surrounded by a golden railing, and a sentry was posted there, by day and by night.

The professor of botany wrote a thesis on the heavenly plant. As a reward, he was gilded all over, and that gilding suited him and his family very well indeed. As a matter of fact, that was the pleasantest part of the whole story, for the plant had disappeared.

The king remained as melancholy and sad as before; but then, he had always been that way—said the sentry.

AT THE UTTERMOST PARTS
OF THE SEA (1854)

A couple of large ships were sent up toward the North Pole to discover the boundaries of land and sea and how far it would be possible for the human race to penetrate in that direction.

A year and a day had already passed, and with great difficulty they had traveled high up amid mist and ice. Now winter had set in again; the sun was gone, and one long night would last for many, many weeks. All around them was a vast, unbroken plain of ice, and ships were moored fast to the ice itself. The snow was piled high, and huts were made of it in shape of beehives, some as big as our barrows, others just large enough to give shelter for two or four men. However, it wasn't dark, for the northern lights flashed red and blue—it was like everlasting, splendid fireworks—and the snow glittered brightly; here the night was one long, blazing twilight.

At the time when it was brightest, troops of natives came, strange-looking figures, dressed in hairy skins and dragging sleighs made from ice blocks. They brought skins in large bundles, which served as warm rugs for the snow huts and were used as beds and bed blankets, upon which the sailors could rest, while outside the cold was more intense than we ever experience even in our severest winters.

And the sailors remembered that at home it was still autumn, and they thought of the warm sunbeams and the glorious crimson and gold of the leaves still clinging to the trees. The clock showed it was evening and time for going to bed, and in one of the snow huts two sailors had already lain down to rest.

The younger of these two had with him his most treasured possession from home, the Bible that his grandmother had given him at parting. From childhood he had known what was written in it; every night it was under his pillow, and every day he read a portion; and often as he lay on his couch he remembered those words of holy comfort, "If I take the wings of the morning and dwell in the uttermost parts of the sea; even there shall thy hand lead me, and thy right hand shall hold me."

Under the influence of those sublime words of faith, he closed his eyes. Sleep came to him, and dreams came with sleep. He dreamed that, although the body may sleep, the soul must ever be awake. He felt this life, and he seemed to hear the old well-known songs so dear to him; a gentle summer breeze seemed to breathe upon him, and a light shone down upon his couch, as though the snowy dome above had become transparent. He lifted his head and lo! The dazzling white light did not come from the walls or the ceiling; it was the light of the great wings of an angel, into whose gentle, shining face he looked.

Rising up from out of the pages of the Bible, as from the mouth of a lily blossom, the angel extended its arms way out, and the walls of the snow hut sank back as if they were a light airy veil of fog. The green meadows and hills of his home lay about him, with the red-brown woods bathed in the gentle sunshine of a beautiful autumn day. The storks' nest was empty now, but the apples still clung to the wild apple trees; though leaves had fallen, the red hips glistened and the blackbird whistled in the little green cage over the window of the little farmhouse—his old home. The blackbird was whistling a tune that he himself had taught him, and the old grandmother twined chickweed about the bars of the cage, just as her grandson had always done.

The pretty young daughter of the blacksmith was standing at the well, drawing water, and as she waved to the grandmother, the latter beckoned to her and showed her a letter that had come that morning from the frigid lands of the North, far, far away, from the North Pole itself, where her grandson now was—safe beneath the protecting hand of God. They laughed and they cried; and all the while that young sailor whose body slept amid the ice and snow while his spirit roamed the world of dreams, under the angel's wings, saw and heard everything and laughed and cried with them.

Then from the letter they must read aloud these words from the Bible, "Even at the uttermost parts of the sea His right hand shall hold me fast"; and a beautiful psalm song sounded about him, and the angel folded its wings. Like a soft, protecting veil they fell close over the sleeper.

The dream was ended, and all was darkness in the snow hut; but the Bible lay beneath the sailor's head, while faith and hope dwelt in his heart. God was with him and his home was with him, "even at the uttermost parts of the sea."

THE MONEY PIG (1854)

There were so many toys in the nursery. On the top of the cabinet stood the penny bank, made of clay in the shape of a little pig. Of course, he had a slit in his back, which had been enlarged with a knife so that silver dollars also could be put in; and two such dollars had been slipped into the box, along with a great number of pennies. The Money Pig was stuffed so full he could no longer rattle, which is the highest honor a Money Pig can attain. There he stood, high up on the shelf, looking down on everything else in the room. He knew very well that with what he had in his stomach he could buy all the other toys, and that's what we call having self-confidence.

The others thought the same, but they didn't speak of it, because there were so many other things to talk about. The cabinet drawer was half open, and a large doll appeared; she was somewhat old, and her neck had been riveted. She peeped out and said, "Now let's play human beings; that's always something!"

Now there was a great commotion, and even the pictures on the walls turned around to show they also had a backside; but that didn't mean they objected.

It was the middle of the night; the moon shone in through the windows and gave free lighting. They were ready to begin the game now, and all of them, even the children's Go-cart, which certainly belonged to the coarser, out-of-door-toys, were invited to join the fun.

"Everyone has his own particular value," said the Go-cart. "We can't all be noblemen. There must be some to do the work, as they say."

The Money Pig was the only one to receive a written invitation; he stood so high they all thought that he could not hear a verbal message. He didn't answer to say if he would come or not; but if he was to take part they would have to arrange it so that he could enjoy the game from his own home; they would have to make their plans accordingly, and this they did.

The little toy theater was at once set up in such a way that the Money Pig could look straight into it. They planned to start with a comedy, and afterward have tea and a discussion for mental exercise, and they began with this latter part immediately. The Rocking Horse talked about training and thoroughbreds, and the Go-cart spoke about railways and steam power, all of which were subjects belonging to their own professions, so it was proper they should speak on them. The Clock talked about politics—tick, tock!—and knew the time of day, though it was said that it didn't run very well. The Bamboo Cane just stood there, for he was very proud of his brass ferule and his silver top, for he was mounted above and below. And on the sofa lay two embroidered cushions, very pretty and very stupid. And now the play began.

Everybody sat and watched, and the audience had been asked to applaud, crack, and stamp as they were pleased. But the Riding Whip said he never cracked for old folks, only for young ones who weren't yet married.

"I crack for everybody," said the Cracker.

"One must, of course, be in the proper place!" thought the Spittoon. And such were their thoughts as the play went on.

The play was worthless, but it was well performed. All of the characters turned their painted sides to the audience, for they were made to be looked at only from that side, not the other. All of them acted splendidly, coming out far beyond the footlights, because the wires were too long, but this made them all the easier to see. The mended Doll was quite overcome with excitement, so deeply moved that the rivets in her neck got loose. And in his own way, the Money Pig was so enchanted that he resolved to do something for one of the actors, to remember him in his will as the one who should be publicly buried with him when the proper time came.

It was such enjoyment for them that they gave up having tea and went on with their mental exercises. That's what they called playing men and women, and there was no harm in that, because they were only playing. Each one thought of himself and what the Money Pig might think about him, but the Money Pig's thoughts went farthest, for he was thinking about his will and his burial. And when would it be time for this?

Certainly far sooner than you expect. Crash! He fell down from the cabinet, and there he lay on the floor, smashed into bits and pieces, while the pennies hopped and danced about. The smallest spun like tops, and the bigger ones rolled away, particularly one big silver dollar who wanted to go out and see the world. And so he did, and so did all the rest.

The pieces of the Money Pig were swept into the dustbin, but the next day there was a new Money Pig standing on the cabinet. It didn't yet have a penny in it, so it couldn't rattle, and in that much at least it was just like the old one.

But that was a beginning—and it's a good place for us to come to an end.

CLUMSY HANS (1855)

Out in the country there was an old mansion where an old squire lived with his two sons, who were so witty that they thought themselves too clever for words. They decided to go out and propose to the king's daughter, which they were at liberty to do, for she had announced publicly that she would take for a husband the man who had the most to say for himself.

The two brothers made their preparations for eight days beforehand. That was all the time they had, but it was enough, for they had many accomplishments, and everyone knows how useful they can be. One of them knew the whole Latin dictionary by heart and the town's newspaper for three years—so well that he could repeat it backward or forward. The other had learned all the articles of law and knew what every alderman must know; consequently, he was sure he could talk of governmental affairs, and besides this he could embroider suspenders, for he was very gentle and also clever with his fingers.

"I shall win the princess!" they both said, as their father gave each one of them a beautiful horse. The one who had memorized the dictionary and the newspapers had a coal-black horse, while the one who knew all about governmental affairs and could embroider had a milk-white one. Then they smeared the corners of their mouths with cod-liver oil, to make them more glib.

All the servants assembled in the courtyard to watch them mount their horses, but just then the third brother came up; for there were really three, although nobody paid much attention to the third, because he was not so learned as the other two. In fact, everybody called him "Clumsy Hans."

"Where are you going in all your Sunday clothes?" he asked.

"To the king's court, to woo the princess. Haven't you heard what the king's drummer is proclaiming all over the country?" Then they told him about it.

"Gracious," said Clumsy Hans, "I guess I'll go, too!" But his brothers only burst out laughing at him as they rode away.

"Father," shouted Clumsy Hans, "Let me have a horse. I feel like getting married, too. If she takes me, she takes me; and if she doesn't take me, I'll take her, anyway."

"That's a lot of nonsense!" replied his father. "You'll get no horse from me. Why, you don't know how to talk properly. Now, your brothers are intelligent men."

"If I can't have a horse I'll take the billy goat," said Clumsy Hans. "He belongs to me, and he can carry me very well." So he mounted the billy goat, dug his heels into its sides, and galloped off down the highway.

"Alley-oop! What a ride! Here I come!" shouted Clumsy Hans, singing so loud that his voice was heard far away.

But his two brothers rode quietly on ahead of him. They were not speaking a word to each other, for they were thinking about all the clever speeches they would have to make, and of course these had to be carefully prepared and memorized beforehand.

"Halloo!" cried Clumsy Hans. "Here I come! Look what I found on the road!" Then he showed them a dead crow he had picked up.

"Clumsy!" said the brothers. "What are you going to do with that?"

"Why, I am going to give it to the princess!"

"Yes, you do that," they said as they rode on laughing.

"Halloo, here I come again! Just look what I've found this time! You don't find things like this in the road every day!" So the brothers turned around to see what it was this time.

"Clumsy!" they said. "That's just an old wooden shoe, and the upper part's broken off, anyway. Is the princess going to have that, too?"

"She certainly is," replied Hans, and the brothers again laughed and rode on far in advance of him.

"Halloo! Here I am again," shouted Clumsy Hans. "Now this is getting better and better! This is really something!"

"Well, what have you found this time?" asked the brothers.

"Oh, I can't really tell you," Clumsy Hans said. "How pleased the princess will be!"

"Uh!" said the brothers. "Why, it's nothing but mud out of the ditch!"

"Yes, of course," said Clumsy Hans, "but the very finest sort of mud. Look, it runs right through your fingers." Then he filled his pockets with it.

But his brothers galloped on ahead as fast as they could, and so they arrived at the town gate a full hour ahead of Hans. At the gate each suitor was given a numbered ticket, and as fast as they arrived they were arranged in rows, six to a row, packed together so tightly that they could not even move their arms. That was a wise plan, for otherwise they could have cut each other's backs to pieces, just because one stood in front of another. All the inhabitants of the town stood around the castle, peering in through the windows to watch the princess receive her suitors; but as each young man came into the room, he became tongue-tied.

"No good!" said the princess. "Take him away!"

Now came the brother who had memorized the dictionary, but he had completely forgotten it while standing in line. The floor creaked under his footsteps, and the ceiling was made of mirrors so that he could see himself standing on his head; and at each window stood three clerks and an alderman, writing down every word that was spoken, so that it immediately could be printed in the newspapers and sold for two pennies on the street corners.

It was a terrible ordeal, and besides there were such fires in the stoves that the pipe was red-hot.

"It's terribly hot in here," said the suitor.

"That's because my father is roasting chickens today," said the princess.

"Baa!" There he stood. He was not ready for a speech of this kind and hadn't a word to say, just when he wanted to say something extremely witty. "Baa!"

"No good!" said the princess. "Take him away!" And consequently he had to leave.

Now the second brother approached.

"It's dreadfully warm here," he said.

"Yes, we're roasting chickens today," replied the princess.

"What—what did you—uh—what?" he stammered, and all the clerks carefully wrote down, "What—what did you—uh—what?"

"No good," said the princess again. "Out with him!"

Now it was Clumsy Hans' turn, and he rode his billy goat right into the hall.

"Terribly hot in here," he said.

"I'm roasting young chickens," replied the Princess.

"Why, that's fine!" said Clumsy Hans. "Then I suppose I can get my crow roasted?"

"That you can," said the princess. "But have you anything to roast it in? I haven't any pots or pans."

"But I have," replied Clumsy Hans. "Here's a cooking pot with a tin handle!" Then he pulled out the old wooden shoe and put the crow right into it.

"Why, that's enough for a whole meal!" said the princess. "But where do we get the sauce from?"

"I have that in my pocket," replied Clumsy Hans. "In fact, I have so much I can afford to spill some of it." Then he poured a little of the mud from his pocket.

"I like that!" said the princess. "You have an answer for everything, and you know how to speak. I'll take you for my husband. But do you know that everything we've said and are saying is written down and will be published in the paper tomorrow? Look over there, and you'll see in each window three clerks and an old alderman, and that alderman is the worst of all; he doesn't understand anything!"

She said this only to frighten him, but all the clerks chuckled with delight and spurted blots of ink on the floor.

"Oh, so these are the gentlemen!" said Clumsy Hans. "Then I must give the alderman the best thing I have." Then he turned out his pockets and threw the wet mud in the face of the alderman.

"Cleverly done!" said the princess. "I could never have done that, but I'll learn in time!"

So Clumsy Hans was made a king, with a wife and a crown, and sat on a throne. And we had this story straight from the alderman's newspaper—but that is one you can't always depend upon.

IB AND LITTLE CHRISTINE (1855)

Near the river Gudenaa in the forest of Silkeborg, a great ridge of land rises. This ridge is called Aasen, and it resembles a large ball. Below it, on the western side, stands a little farmhouse surrounded by very poor land; in fact, the sand of the soil can be seen through the sparse rye and wheat that grow there.

We are speaking of a time some years ago, when the people who lived there cultivated the fields, and kept three sheep, a pig, and two oxen. To put it briefly, they supported themselves very well, with enough to live on if they took things in their stride; yes, and they were even well enough off to have kept a couple of horses, but, like the neighboring farmers, they said, "A horse eats itself up"—it eats as much as it earns. In summer Jeppe-Jens cultivated his small field, and in the winter he made wooden shoes; and at that time he had a journeyman assistant who, like him, knew how to make the wooden shoes strong, light, and fashionable. Their carved shoes and spoons brought in good money, and therefore no one could call the Jeppe-Jenses poor people.

Little Ib, a boy seven years old, was the only child of the family. He loved to sit by, watching the workmen, whittling at a stick, and sometimes whittling his finger. But one day he was so successful with two little pieces of wood that they really looked like tiny wooden shoes, and he decided to give them to little Christine.

She was the boatman's little daughter, as graceful and pretty as a child of a noble family; if she had been dressed differently, no one would have believed that she came from the hut with the peat-covered roof in the neighboring hamlet of Seishede. Her father, a widower, lived there and supported himself by transporting boatloads of firewood from the forest down to the eel pond and weir at Silkeborg, and sometimes even all the way up to the town of Randers. Since there was no one at home to take care of little Christine, who was just a year younger than Ib, she nearly always went with him in his boat, or played among the heath plants and barberry bushes of the forest. But sometimes, when he had to go all the way up to Randers he would leave little Christine at the Jeppe-Jenses'.

Ib and Christine got along very well together in every way. They shared their food and they played together; they dug in the ground together; they walked, they crept, they ran together. One day they even climbed up the high ridge, far into the forest; once they found some snipe's eggs, and that was a great event.

Ib had never been at Seishede, where Christine's father lived, nor had he ever sailed down the Gudenaa. But at last this happened; Christine's father invited him to accompany them, and on the evening before the trip he went home with the boatman.

Early next morning, the two children were perched high on the big pile of faggots in the boat, eating bread and raspberries, while the boatman and his helper pushed them on with long poles. The current was with them, and they glided swiftly down the stream, through the lakes formed in its course. Sometimes they seemed shut in by woods and water reeds, but there was always just room for them to pass, though the old trees leaned out over the water and the oaks bent down their peeling branches as if they had rolled up their sleeves to show their knotted, naked arms. Ancient elder trees, washed away from the bank by the stream, clung with their roots to the bottom, looking like little wooded islets. Water lilies rocked placidly on the surface of the stream. It was a wonderful trip.

At last, they reached the great eel weir, where the water rushed through the floodgates; and to Ib and Christine, this was a beautiful sight.

In those days, there was no manufacturing plant there, or even a town; there was only the old farmhouse, with a few servants and a few head of cattle. The roar of the water through the sluices and the cry of wild ducks were then the only lively sounds there.

After the firewood had been unloaded, Christine's father bought a big bundle of eels and a slaughtered suckling pig and packed them all in a basket in the stern of the boat. Then they started back again. They were going upstream now, but the wind was favorable, and with the sails hoisted, they went as well as if two horses had been harnessed to the boat.

When they reached that point in the stream near which the assistant boatman lived, the boat was moored, and the two men went ashore, after ordering the children to be quiet and careful. But this they could not do, at least not for very long. They had to be peeping into the basket at the eels and the pig; they had to pull the pig out and hold it in their hands and turn it over and over. Then, when they both tried to hold it at the same time, they lost it and it slipped right into the water, and the pig drifted away down the stream. That was a terrible catastrophe!

Ib quickly jumped ashore and began running along the bank, while Christine leaped after him, shouting, "Take me with you!"

Soon the children disappeared in the bushes and could no longer see either the boat or the river. They ran on still farther, and then Christine fell down and began to cry. Ib picked her up.

"Come on!" he said. "The house is over that way!"

But the house was not over that way. On and on they walked, over dry, dead leaves and over fallen branches that crackled under their small feet. All of a sudden they heard a loud scream. They stopped and listened, and again the scream of an eagle sounded through the woods. It was an ugly cry, and it frightened them, but they soon forgot it when they saw before them, in the thick wood, the most beautiful blueberries growing in unbelievably large numbers. They were so inviting that the children could not help stopping; and they stayed there, eating the blueberries until they had blue mouths and cheeks. And again they heard the eagle's cry.

"We'll get a beating on account of that pig," said Christine.

"Come on, let's go home," said Ib. "Our house is here in the woods somewhere."

So they went on until they came to a road, but it still did not lead them home; then darkness settled down, and both grew afraid. The strange stillness around was broken now and then by the shrill cries of the great horned owl or other birds strange to them. And at last, they were completely lost among some bushes. Then Christine cried, and Ib cried too, and after they had cried for some time, they lay down on the dry leaves and fell fast asleep.

The sun was high in the heavens when the children awoke. They were cold, but on the hill near their resting place, the sun shone down through the trees, and they could warm themselves. Besides, Ib hoped that from there he would be able to see his parents' house.

But they were really far from that house, in an entirely different part of the forest.

They climbed to the top of the hill and found themselves on the edge of a clear, transparent lake. They could see innumerable fish sparkling in the rays of the sun. This view was a sudden and lovely surprise.

Near them, they found a bush full of the finest nuts, and now they picked them and cracked them and ate the delicate young kernels, which had only just become ripe. But there was still another frightening surprise in store for them.

Out of the bushes there stepped a tall old woman whose face was very brown and whose hair was shining black. The whites of her eyes glistened like a mulatto's; on her back she carried a knapsack, and in her hand a knotted stick. She was a gypsy.

At first, the children couldn't understand her. Then she took three large nuts from her pocket and explained that these were wishing nuts and that in them the most wonderful things were hidden.

When Ib looked at her she seemed so friendly that he found courage to ask her to give him the nuts. The woman handed them to him, and then she gathered a whole pocketful more for herself from the nut bush.

Ib and Christine looked at the wishing nuts with wondering eyes. "Is there a carriage and horses in this nut?" he asked.

"There is a carriage of gold with golden horses," said the woman.

"Then give me that one!" said little Christine.

So Ib gave it to her, and the woman tied it in the little girl's neckerchief for her.

"And in this one is there a pretty little neckerchief like the one Christine is wearing around her neck?" asked Ib.

"There are ten neckerchiefs in it," replied the woman. "There are beautiful dresses, too, and stockings, and a hat."

"Then I want that one, too," said Christine.

So little Ib gave her the second nut also. The third was a little black one.

"You can keep that one," said Christine. "And it's a very pretty one, too."

"What's in it?" asked Ib.

"The best of all things for you," said the old gypsy.

So Ib held onto that nut very tightly. The woman promised to start them on the right way to their homes; and then they went, but certainly in an entirely different direction than they should go. Yet we have no reason to suspect the gypsy woman of wanting to steal the children.

In a wild part of the wood they met Chraen, the game warden; he knew Ib, and with his help Ib and little Christine finally arrived home, where everybody had been very anxious about them. They were forgiven, although they both really had earned a good beating—first, for letting the pig fall into the water, and, second, for running away.

Christine went home with her father on the heath, and Ib remained in the little farmhouse. The first thing he did that evening was take from his pocket the black nut in which "the best of all things" was supposed to be enclosed. He placed it carefully between the door and the doorpost, then shut the door sharply. The nut cracked all right, but there was no kernel in it. It was what we call worm-eaten, looking as if it were filled with snuff or rich, black earth.

"That's what I thought," opined Ib. "How could there be room for the best of all things in this little nut? And Christine won't get any more out of her two nuts either, no fine clothes or golden carriage."

So winter came on, and the new year began.

Several years passed, and Ib was to be confirmed. To prepare for it he studied with the clergyman far off in the next village. It was at this time that the boatman came one day to visit Ib's parents and told them that little Christine was going to work as a servant girl and that she had been really fortunate in getting an unusually good position with very worthy people, for, just imagine, she was going to the rich innkeeper's at Herning, west of there. There she was to help the housekeeper, and later, if she did well and was confirmed there, the people would adopt her as their own daughter.

So Ib and Christine parted. People were calling them "the sweethearts," and before she left she showed Ib that she still had the two nuts he had given her during their adventure in the forest so long ago, and she told him that in her chest drawer she still kept the little wooden shoes he had carved as a present for her when he was a boy. And that was their parting.

After Ib was confirmed, he remained in his mother's house, for he had become a clever shoemaker, and in the summer he took care of the little field. He worked alone, for his father had died, and his mother kept no farm hand.

It was only seldom that he heard of Christine from some passing rider or eel fisherman. But he knew she was doing very well at the rich innkeeper's; and after her confirmation she wrote to her father and sent greetings to Ib and his mother. In the letter Christine wrote of six new linen garments and a lovely new dress that her employer and his wife had given her as a present. That was certainly good news.

One beautiful day, the following spring, there was a knock on Ib's and his mother's door, and there stood the boatman with Christine. She had come over for a day's visit in the next village, and she had taken the opportunity of seeing her friends again. She looked as lovely as a fine lady, and she wore a pretty dress that had been carefully sewn expressly for her. There she stood, in grand array, and Ib was in his working clothes. He could not stammer a word; he seized her hand and in his delight held it fast in his own, but he could not make his tongue obey him. But Christine was not embarrassed; she talked and talked, and kissed Ib right on his mouth.

"Didn't you know me again, Ib?" she said.

Even later, when they were left by themselves, and he was still holding her hand in his, he could only say, "You look like a real lady, and I'm so rough and clumsy! How often I have thought of you, Christine, and the old times!"

Arm in arm, they wandered up the ridge and gazed across the Gudenaa toward Seishede with its great hills rich with heather. Ib didn't speak, but by the time they parted, it was clear to him that Christine must become his wife. Had they not, even in their childhood, been called "sweethearts"? To him, they were really engaged to each other, though neither had spoken a word on that subject.

They had only a few more hours together before Christine had to return to the next village, whence the carriage would start early the next morning for home. Her father and Ib went with her through the clear moonlit evening as far as the village. When they reached it, Ib still held the girl's hand in his own, for he could not bear to let her go. His eyes were bright, but the words came haltingly from his lips. Yet every word came from the depths of his heart.

"If you haven't become too grand, Christine, and if you can make up your mind to live in my mother's house as my wife, we can be married someday! But we can wait awhile yet."

"Yes, let's wait for a little while, Ib," she said as she squeezed his hand; and he kissed her mouth. "I trust you, Ib," said Christine, "and I believe I care for you, but let me sleep on it."

And so they parted. On the way home Ib told Christine's father that they were as good as engaged, and the boatman declared he had always expected that would happen. He went home with Ib and remained that night in the young man's house, but nothing further was said about the engagement.

A year passed by, during which two letters were exchanged between Ib and Christine. The signature was prefaced by the words, "Faithful till death." But one day the boatman came to Ib's house, bringing him a greeting from Christine. He found it difficult to deliver the rest of his message, but it was to the effect that Christine was doing very well, that she had become a pretty girl, respected and well liked. And the innkeeper's son, who was employed in the office of a large business in Copenhagen, had been home on a visit; he was much attracted to Christine, and she liked him. His parents were ready to give their consent, but Christine was very anxious to keep Ib's good opinion, "and so she has thought of refusing this good fortune," the boatman concluded.

Ib turned as white as a sheet, and at first said nothing, but shook his head slightly. At last he said. "Christine mustn't refuse this good fortune."

"Then write a few words to her yourself," said her father.

Ib sat down to write, but he couldn't put the words together the way he wanted to. He crossed out and tore up one letter after another—not until next morning was a letter ready to be sent to Christine, and here it is:

> I read the letter you sent your father, and understand from it that you are prospering in every way and that there is a chance of still higher fortune for you. Ask your heart, Christine, and think carefully about your future. If you marry me, I have very little to give you. Do not think of me or my future; think of what is best for you. You are bound to me by no promise, but if in your heart you think you have given me one, I release you from it. May all the treasures of happiness be yours, little Christine. Our Lord will comfort my heart.
>
> Always your sincere friend,
>
> Ib

And the letter was sent, and Christine received it.

That November her banns were published in the church on the heath, as well as in Copenhagen, where her bridegroom lived. Since various business affairs prevented the bridegroom from making the journey into Jutland, she went to Copenhagen, escorted by her future mother-in-law. On the way she met her father in the little village of Funder, which was close to her father's home and which she had to pass through, and there they took leave of each other.

Word of this came back to Ib, but he made no mention of it; his mother noticed that he had grown very silent of late. Indeed, he had become very thoughtful, and there came into his mind again the thought of the three nuts that the gypsy woman had given him when he was a child, two of which he had given to Christine. Yes, it all seemed to be coming out that way—they were indeed wishing nuts, and in one of them was a golden carriage with two horses, and in the other beautiful clothes. These luxuries would now be Christine's in Copenhagen, so her part had come true. But his own nut had offered only black earth. The gypsy had said this was "the best thing of all for him." And that was right, too; that also was coming true. The black earth was indeed the best for him. At last he understood clearly the old woman's meaning. In the black earth, in the dark grave, would be the only happiness for him.

Again the years rolled by—not many, but they seemed long years to Ib. The old innkeeper and his wife died, one shortly after the other, and their entire property, amounting to many thousands of dollars, came to their son. Yes, now Christine could have the golden carriage and beautiful clothes.

For the next long two years there was no letter from Christine, and when her father finally heard from her she was not writing in prosperity or joy, by any means. Poor Christine! Neither she nor her husband had known how to hold onto their wealth; since they had not worked for it, it seemed to bring no blessing with it.

Again the heather bloomed and faded. For many winters the snow had swept across Seishede and over the ridge beneath which Ib lived, sheltered from the winds.

When the spring sun shone again Ib guided his plow across the field, and one day it struck against something that seemed to be a firestone. A piece like a big black wood shaving came out of the ground, but when Ib examined it he found it was a piece of metal. And where the plow blade had cut into it, the stone gleamed brightly with ore. He had found a big, heavy, golden bracelet of ancient workmanship. For he had disturbed a Viking's grave and discovered the costly treasure that had been buried in it. Ib showed his find to the clergyman, who explained to him how valuable it was and sent him to the District Judge. The latter in turn reported the discovery to the curator of the museum in Copenhagen and recommended that Ib take the treasure there in person.

"You have found in the earth the best thing you could have found!" said the District Judge.

"The best thing," thought Ib. "The very best thing for me—and in the earth! Then, if that is the best, the gypsy woman was right."

So Ib took the ferryboat from Aarhus to Copenhagen; it was like an ocean voyage to him, for he had only sailed over the Gudenaa before this.

In Copenhagen he received the value of the gold he had found, and it was a large sum—six hundred dollars. And then Ib of the heath near Seishede wandered about in the great and intricate capital.

On the evening before the day when he was to return with the captain to Aarhus, Ib got lost in the streets, went in quite a different direction than he intended to go, and then found himself in Christianshavn instead of Vesterport. There was not a human being to be seen on the street.

At last a very little girl emerged from one of the wretched houses. When Ib inquired of her the way to the street he was seeking, she only looked shyly at him, then began to cry bitterly. He asked her what was the matter, but could not understand her reply. But as they went along the street together they passed beneath a lamp, and when the light fell on the child's face he felt a strange emotion come over him, for it was exactly as if little Christine stood before him, just as he remembered her from the days when they both were children!

He followed the little girl into the wretched house and climbed the narrow, tumbledown staircase, which led to a tiny attic room high up under the roof. The air in this room was heavy and almost suffocating; no light burned; but from one corner came a heavy sighing and moaning. Ib struck a match. On a miserable bed lay the child's mother.

"Can I help you in any way?" said Ib. "This little girl has brought me up here, but I'm a stranger in the city. Haven't you any neighbors or friends I could call in to help you?" Then he raised her head.

It was Christine from Seishede!

For years her name had not been mentioned there, for it would have disturbed Ib's peace of mind, and the rumors and the truth about her had all been unhappy. All the money her husband had inherited from his parents had made him proud and arrogant. He had given up his good position, had traveled for half a year in foreign lands, and on his return had gone heavily into debt and still lived in an expensive manner. The coach had leaned over more and more, so to speak, until at last it turned over completely. The many merry companions he had entertained declared it served him right, for he had kept his house like a madman. And so one morning his corpse was found in a canal.

The icy hand of death was already on Christine. Her youngest child, expected in prosperity but born in misery only a few weeks ago, was already in its grave, and

Christine was close to it herself. She lay forsaken, sick unto death, in a miserable room, amid poverty which she might have endured in her younger days at Seishede, but which now, accustomed as she had been to better things, she felt most painfully. It was her eldest child, also a little Christine, and sharing her hunger and poverty, whom Ib had now brought home.

"I am tormented at the thought of dying and leaving the poor child alone!" she sighed. "Ah, what is to become of the poor little thing!" And not a word more could she speak.

Ib took another match and lit a piece of candle he found in the room, and the flame illuminated the pitiful dwelling. Then he looked at the little girl and remembered how Christine had looked when she was that age, and he felt that for her sake he would love this child, which was still a stranger to him. The dying woman gazed at him, and her eyes opened wider and wider; did she recognize him? He was never to know, for no further word passed her lips.

In the forest by the Gudenaa, near Seishede, the air was thick and dark, and there were no blossoms on the heath plant. The autumn winds whirled the yellow leaves from the wood into the stream or out over the heath toward the boatman's hut, where strangers lived now. But beneath the ridge, safe beneath the protection of the large trees, stood the little farmhouse, neatly painted and whitewashed, and within it the turf blazed up cheerfully in the chimney. Inside was sunlight, the beaming sunlight of a child's two bright eyes; and the singing of the larks sounded in the words that came from the little Christine's rosy, laughing lips. She sat on Ib's knee, and Ib was both father and mother to her, for her own parents were dead and had vanished from her mind as a dream vanishes alike from the mind of a child or a grown man. Ib lived in the neat, pretty house, for he was a prosperous man now, while the little girl's mother rested in the churchyard for the poor in Copenhagen.

Ib had money, said people, gold from out of the black earth, and he had his little Christine, too.

THE THORNY ROAD OF HONOR (1855)

There is an old fairy tale: "The Thorny Road of Honor was trodden by a marksman named Bryde, to whom came great honor and dignity, but not until after manifold adversities and peril of life." More than one of us had heard that tale in childhood, and perhaps read it in later years, and thought of his own unsung "thorny road" and "manifold adversities." Romance and reality are very nearly alike, but romance has its harmonious ending here on earth, while reality more often delays it and leads us to time and eternity.

The history of the world is a magic lantern, showing us picture slides against the dark backgrounds of the ages, of how the benefactors of mankind, the martyrs of progress, have trodden their Thorny Roads of Honor.

From all times, from all lands, these pictures of splendor come to us; each picture lasts a moment only, yet it is a whole lifetime of struggles and triumphs. Let us glance at a few in the ranks of the martyrs, those ranks which will never be filled until Earth itself shall pass a way.

We see a crowded theater! The *Clouds* of Aristophanes is sending forth to the audience a river of mirth and mockery; the stage of Athens is ridiculing, in both body and mind, her most remarkable man, who was the shield and defense of the people against the Thirty Tyrants. Socrates, who in the heat of battle rescued Alcibiades and Xenophon, whose spirit soared above the deities of the ancient world, is here in person. He has risen from the spectators' bench and has stepped forward, so that the mocking Athenians may decide whether he and the stage caricature resemble each other. There he stands erect before them, and in high spirit he is high above them.

You green, juicy, poisonous hemlock, be you, and not the olive tree, the shadowy symbol of this Athens!

Seven cities claimed to be the birthplace of Homer—that is, after he was dead. But look at him in his lifetime! Through these same cities he wanders, reciting his verses for a pittance. Care for the morrow turns his hair gray. He, mightiest of seers, is blind and alone; and the sharp thorns tear the mantle of the king of poesy.

His songs yet live, and in them alone live still the gods and heroes of olden times.

Picture after picture leaps forth from the morning land and the evening land, far separated by time and space, yet all with the same thorny path, where the thistle never bears blossoms till it adorns the grave.

Under the palm trees walk swaying camels, laden with indigo and other precious gifts, sent by the ruler of the land to him whose songs are the people's delight and the country's pride. He whom spite and slander drove into exile is found again, for the caravan draws near the little town where he has taken refuge. But a poor corpse is being carried out of the gate, and the caravan is stopped. The dead is the very man they seek, Firdausi; ended is his Thorny Road of Honor.

There sits an African Negro, with blunt features, thick lips, and black kinky hair, begging on the marble steps of the palace in Portugal's capital; he is the faithful slave of Camöens. If it were not for him and the coppers that he begs, his master, the singer of *The Lusiad*, would have starved to death. Now an expensive monument rises over the grave of Camöens.

Still another picture. Behind iron bars a man appears, ghostly white, with a long and matted beard. "I have made an invention!" he cries. "The greatest in centuries; and for more than twenty years they have kept me caged up here!"

"Who is he?"

"A lunatic," replies the keeper. "What crazy ideas a man may get! He thinks people could move along by steam power!" It is Salomon de Caus, inventor of the steam engine. His prophetic words have not been clear enough for a Richelieu, and he dies imprisoned in a madhouse.

Here stands Columbus, whom once street boys pursued and mocked at, because he would discover a new world. He has discovered it! The bells of jubilation ring at his triumphant return; but soon the bells of envy sound more loudly still. The world discoverer, who raised the American land of gold from the ocean and gave it to his king, is rewarded with chains of iron. He asks that they be laid in his coffin, to show the world how a man is valued in his own age.

Picture rushes after picture, for rich is the Thorny Road of Honor.

Here in dismal gloom sits he who measured the heights of the Moon mountains, who forced his way out among the planets and stars of space—mighty Galileo, who could see and hear Earth itself turning beneath him. Blind and deaf he sits now in his old age, suffering wracking pain and neglect, hardly able to lift his foot—that foot which once, when the words of truth were blotted out, he stamped on the earth in mental agony, crying out, "Yet it moves!"

Here stands a woman with the heart of a child, with inspiration and faith. She bears her banner before the fighting army and brings victory and freedom to her motherland. There is shouting—and the fire burns high; Joan of Arc, the witch, is burned at the stake. Yes, the coming age will spit upon the white lily; Voltaire, wit's own satyr, will sing of *La Pucelle*.

At the Viborg-Thing the nobles of Denmark are burning the king's laws; they burst into flames that light up both age and lawmaker and send a flash of glory into a dark dungeon tower. There he sits, gray-haired, bent, digging at the stone table with his fingers. Once he ruled over three kingdoms, the popular leader, friend of townfolk and peasant alike, Christian II—he of the hard will in a hard age. Enemies wrote his story. Twenty-seven long years of prison, let us remember, when we think of his blood guilt.

There sails a ship from Denmark, and a man stands beside the tall mast; for the last time, he looks upon Hveen. Tycho Brahe, who lifted Denmark's name to the stars themselves and was repaid with scorn and mockery, is setting forth to a foreign land. "Heaven is everywhere; what more do I want?" Those are his words as he sails away, our most famous man, sure in foreign lands of being honored and free.

"Yes, free! Ah, if only free from the intolerable pains of this body!" sighs a voice to us from across the centuries. What a picture! Griffenfeld, the Danish Prometheus, chained to Munkholm's rocky isle.

Now we are in America, beside a large river. A great crowd has gathered there, for it is said that a ship is to sail against wind and tide, to be itself a power against the elements. Robert Fulton is the name of the man who thinks he can do this strange thing. The ship begins its trip, but suddenly, it stops. The crowd laughs, whistles, and mocks; his own father mocks with them. "Conceit! Madness! He has got what was coming to him! Put the crackbrain under lock and key!" Then a small nail rattles loose—for a moment it had stopped the machinery—the engines turn the paddle wheels again and cut through the opposition of the waves—the ship moves!

The weaver shuttle of steam turns hours into minutes between all the lands of the world.

Mankind, can you realize the happiness of that moment of assurance when the soul understands its mission? That moment when the sorest wounds from the Thorny Road of Honor, even if caused by one's own fault, are healed and forgotten in spiritual health and strength and freedom. When all discords melt into harmony, and men perceive a revelation of God's grace, granted to one alone, and by him made known to all!

Then the Thorny Road of Honor shines like a path of glory around Earth. Happy is he who is chosen to be a pilgrim on that road and, through no merit of his own, is made one of the master builders of the bridge between God and man.

The Genius of History wings his mighty way down through the ages and gives us comfort and good cheer and thoughtful peace of mind by showing us, in brilliant pictures against nightdark backgrounds, the Thorny Road of Honor—not a path that ends, like a fairy tale, in gladness and triumph here on Earth, but one that leads onward and upward, far into time and eternity.

THE JEWISH GIRL (1855)

Among the other children in the charity school was a little Jewish girl, clever and good—in fact, the brightest of them all. But there was one class she could not attend, the one where religion was taught, for she was in a Christian school.

During the hour of this class, she had her geography book before her to study, or did her arithmetic, but the lessons were quickly learned, and then, though the book might still be open before her, she did not read from it; she listened. And the teacher soon noticed that she listened more intently than any of the rest.

"Study your book," said the teacher, gently yet earnestly. But she looked back at him with her black, eager eyes, and when he put his questions to her as well as the rest he found she knew more than all the others. She had listened, understood, and kept his words.

Her father was a poor but honest man, and when he first brought her to the school he had given instructions that she should not be taught the Christian faith. But to send her from the room during the Scripture lesson might have given offense and raised various thoughts in the minds of the other children in the class, and so she remained. But this could not go on any longer.

So the teacher went to her father and explained that he must either take his daughter away from the school or consent to her becoming a Christian.

"I cannot bear to see those burning eyes, that sincere yearning thirst of the soul, so to speak, after the words of the Gospel," he said.

Then her father burst into tears. "I know very little myself of our own faith," he replied, "but her mother was a daughter of Israel, strong and steadfast in her faith, and on her deathbed I promised her that our child should never receive Christian baptism. That promise I must keep, for to me it is like a pact with God."

So the little Jewish girl was taken away from the Christian school.

Years had passed.

In a humble household, in one of the smallest provincial towns of Jutland there was a maidservant, a poor girl of the Jewish faith; this was Sarah. Her hair was as black as ebony, and her eyes were dark yet full of brilliant light, such eyes as you see among the daughters of the East. And the expression in the face of the grown-up girl was still that of the child who sat on the schoolroom bench, listening with eager and wistful eyes.

Every Sunday the sound of the organ and the singing of the congregation sounded from the church, and the tones floated across the street and into the house where the Jewish girl attended diligently and faithfully to her work. "Remember the Sabbath day, to keep it holy," was her law; but her Sabbath was a day of labor to Christians, and only in her heart could she keep it holy. And that she believed was not enough.

But then the thought came to her soul, "What do days and hours matter in the sight of God?" and on the Sunday of the Christians she had her own undisturbed hour of devotion. Then if the sound of the organ and the singing came across to her as she stood behind the sink in the kitchen, even this became a quiet and consecrated spot. Then she would read the treasure and property of her own people, the Old Testament, and that alone; for she kept deep in her heart what her father had told the teacher and herself when she was taken from the school—the promise he had made to her dying mother, "that Sarah should not be baptized, nor forsake the faith of her fathers." The New Testament was, and would forever remain, a sealed book to her; and yet she knew much of it, for it shone through the memories of her childhood.

One evening she was sitting in a corner of the living room while her master read aloud. She allowed herself to listen, for this was not the Gospel; no, he was reading from an old storybook, so she could remain. The master read to them of a Hungarian knight who was taken captive by a Turkish pasha and yoked with oxen to the plow. He was driven with lashes of the whip and suffered pain and thirst almost beyond endurance.

But at home his wife sold her jewels and mortgaged their castle and lands, while friends contributed large sums to help raise the almost unbelievable amount of money that was demanded as ransom. This finally was collected, and he was delivered from slavery and disgrace. Sick and suffering, he returned home.

But soon there resounded over the countryside the summons to a crusade against the foe of Christianity. The sick man heard the call and could have neither peace nor rest any longer; they had to lift him on his war horse. Then the blood rushed again to his cheeks, his strength seemed to return, and he rode forth to victory. The very pasha who had made him suffer pain and humiliation yoked to the plow became his captive. He was taken home to the castle dungeon, but before he had been there an hour the knight came to him and asked his prisoner, "What do you think now awaits you?"

"I know," replied the Turk. "Retribution."

"Yes, the retribution of a Christian," said the knight. "The teachings of Christ tell us to forgive our enemies and love our fellow men. God is love! Go in peace to your home and loved ones, and be gentle and good to all who suffer."

Then the prisoner burst into tears. "How could I have believed such a thing possible?" he cried. "I was certain I would have to suffer shame and torture, hence I took poison, and within a few hours I shall die. There is no remedy. But before I die, teach me the faith which is so full of such love and mercy; it is great and divine! In that faith let me die; let me die a Christian!" And his request was granted him.

That was the legend, the story that was read to them. All listened to it with close attention, but it sank deepest into the heart of her who sat in the corner, the maidservant, Sarah, the Jewess. Large tears stood in her sparkling coal-black eyes while she sat there, as years ago on the school bench, and felt the greatness of the Gospel. The tears rolled down her cheeks.

"Let not my child become a Christian!" Her mother's dying words rang through her soul with those of the law, "Honor thy father and thy mother!"

"Still I have not been baptized! They call me 'the Jewess'; the boys of the neighborhood mocked me last Sunday as I stood outside the church door and looked in at the burning altar lights and the singing congregation. Ever since my school days, up to this very hour, the power of Christianity, which is like a sunbeam, and which, no matter how much I close my eyes, penetrates into my heart. But, my mother, I will not bring you sorrow in your grave! I will not betray the promise my father made to you; I will not read the Christian's Bible! Have I not the God of my fathers? On him let me rest my head!"

And the years rolled by.

The husband died, and the wife was left in difficult circumstances. The servant girl had to be dismissed, but Sarah would not leave the widow. She became her help in time of trouble and kept the little household together; she worked late every night, and by the labor of her own hands got bread for the house. There were no close relatives to help a family where the widow grew weaker each day, lingering for months on a sickbed. Gentle and good Sarah watched and nursed and labored and was the blessing of the poverty-stricken home.

"There is the Bible," said the sick woman one evening. "Read a little to me; the evening is so long, and I sadly need to hear the word of God."

Sarah bowed her head, picked up the Bible and folded her hands around it, opened it, and read aloud to the sick woman. Often the tears came into her eyes, but they shone more clearly, and the darkness lifted from her soul. "Mother, your child shall not receive the baptism of the Christians, shall not be named in their communion. You have wished it, and I shall honor your wish. In this we are united here on Earth, but above this is—is a greater union in God. He leads and guides us beyond Death. 'I will pour water upon him that is thirsty, and floods upon the dry ground.' Oh, I understand now! I do not know myself how I came to it! Through him it was—in him—Christ!"

And she trembled as she spoke the holy name; a baptism of fire streamed through her, stronger than her feeble frame could bear, and she sank down, more exhausted even than the sick woman whom she nursed.

"Poor Sarah!" people said. "She is worn out with labor and nursing!"

They took her to the charity hospital, and there she died, and thence she was carried to her grave. It was not to the graveyard of the Christians—that was not the place for a Jewish girl; no, outside by the wall they dug a grave for her.

But God's sun, which shines upon the graves of the Christians, shines as well upon that of the Jewish girl; and the hymns which are sung beside the Christian graves sound also beside her grave outside the wall. And out there, too, reaches the promise: "There is resurrection in Christ, in him, the Savior, who said to his Disciples, 'John truly baptized with water; but ye shall be baptized with the Holy Ghost!'"

A STRING OF PEARLS (1856)

The railroad in Denmark still extends only from Copenhagen to Korsör; it is a string of pearls. Europe has a wealth of these pearls; its most costly are named Paris, London, Vienna, Naples. And yet many a man will point out as his favorite pearl not one of these great cities but rather some little country town that is still the home of homes to him, the home of those dearest to him. Yes, often it is not a town at all, but a single homestead, a little house, hidden among green hedges, a place hardly visible as the train speeds by.

How many pearls are there on the line from Copenhagen to Korsör? We will consider just six, which most people must notice; old memories and poetry itself give a luster to these pearls, so that they shine in our thoughts.

Near the hill where stands the palace of Frederick VI, the home of Oehlenschläger's childhood, one of these pearls glistens, sheltered by Söndermarken's woody ground. It used to be called "The Cottage of Philemon and Baucis." Here lived Rahbek and his wife, Camma; here, under their hospitable roof, assembled many of the generation's finest intellects from busy Copenhagen; it was the festival home of the intellectual. Now, don't say, "Ah, what a change!" No, it is still the home of the intellect, a conservatory for sick plants, for buds which do not have the strength to unfold their true beauty of color and form or show the blossoming and fruit-bearing which is hidden within them. The insane asylum, surrounded by human love, is truly a spot of holiness, a hospital for the sick plants that shall someday be transplanted to bloom in the Paradise of God. The weakest minds are assembled now here, where once the strongest and keenest met to exchange thoughts and ideas, but still the flame of generosity mounts heavenward from "The Cottage of Philemon and Baucis."

Ancient Roskilde, the burial town of kings, by Hroar's Spring, now lies before us. The slender towers of the church lift up above the low town and mirror themselves in Issefjord. Only one grave shall we seek here; it is not that of the mighty Queen Margrethe; no within the white-walled churchyard which we speed close by is the grave, and over it lays a small, plain stone. The master of the organ, the reviver of the old Danish romances, rests here. We recall, "The Clear Waves Rolled" and "There Dwelt a King in Leire." Roskilde, burial place of kings—in your pearl we see the insignificant gravestone whereon is cut a lyre and the name Weyse.

Now we reach Sigersted, near the town of Ringsted. The bed of the river is low here; yellow corn waves over the spot where Hagbarth's boat lay at anchor, not far from Signe's maiden bower. Who does not know the legend of Hagbarth, who was hanged on the oak tree while the bower of Signe burst into flames? Who can forget that legend of immortal love?

"Beautiful Sorö, encircled by woods!" Your quiet old cloistered town peeps out through its mossy trees; the keen eyes of youth from the academy can look across the lake toward the world's highway and hear the roar of the locomotive's dragon as it speeds through the woods. Sorö, pearl of poetry, you are guarding the dust of Holberg! Your palace of learning stands beside the deep woodland lake like a great white swan, and nearby, like the bright starflower of the woods, there gleams a tiny cottage, whence pious hymns echo throughout the land; words are spoken within, and the peasant listens and learns of Denmark's bygone days. As the song of the bird is to the greenwood, so is Ingemann to Sorö.

On to the town of Slagelse! What is mirrored here in this pearl's luster? Gone forever is the cloister of Antvorskov; vanished are the rich halls of the castle, even the last remaining wing; yet one relic of olden times still lingers here, the wooden cross on the hill. It has been repaired again and again, for it marks the spot where, legend tells us, Saint Anders, holy priest of Slagelse, awoke, after having been brought there from Jerusalem in a single night.

Korsör, birthplace of Baggesen, master of words and wit! The ruined old ramparts of the fallen fortress are now the last visible witness of your childhood home; their lengthening sunset shadows point to the spot where stood the house in which you were born. From these hills, you looked toward Sprogö and sang in undying verse.

Nowhere have roses so red a hue
And nowhere are feathers so light and so blue,
Nowhere the thorns so daintily grown,
As those to childhood innocence known.

Humorous, charming singer! We shall weave for thee a garland of woodbine and fling it into the lake, so that the current may bear it to the coast of Kielerfjord, where your ashes rest. The tide shall bring you a greeting from the new generation, a greeting from your birthplace Korsör—where I drop my string of pearls.

"That's quite right! A string of pearls does stretch from Copenhagen to Korsör," said Grandmother when she had heard this read aloud. "It's a string of pearls for me now, as it was more than forty years ago. We had no railroad then; we spent days on a trip that can now be made in as many hours. That was in 1815, and I was twenty-one; that is a charming age! Although to be up in the sixties, that is also a wonderful age! In my young days it was a much rarer event than it is now to come to Copenhagen, which we considered the town of all towns! My parents hadn't visited it for twenty years, but at last they were going, and I was going with them. We had talked about that journey for years before, and now it was actually coming true; it seemed as though a new life were beginning for me, and really, in a way, a new life did begin for me.

"There was such a bustle of sewing and packing; and when at last we were ready to start, such a crowd of friends came to bid us farewell! It was a long journey we had ahead of us. Shortly before noon we drove out of Odense in my parents' Holstein carriage, and our friends waved to us from the windows all the way down the street, till we passed through St. Jörgen's Gate. The weather was beautiful; the birds sang, and everything was joyful; we forgot what a long and tiresome road it was to Nyborg. We reached it toward evening; but the little sailing vessel had to wait for the mail, which didn't arrive until night. Then we got on board, and as far as we could see the wide, smooth waters lay before us. We lay down and went to sleep in our clothes. When I awoke and came on deck next morning, I could see nothing at all; a heavy fog covered everything. When I heard the cocks crowing, I knew it must be sunrise; bells were ringing, but I didn't know where; then the mist lifted, and we found we were still lying very close to Nyborg. Later in the day a wind came up, but it was against us; we tacked back and forth, and at last were lucky enough to reach Korsör by a little past eleven that night, having spent twenty-two hours to go sixteen miles!

"It was good to get ashore, but it was dark; the lamps were weak, and it all seemed very strange to me, who had never been in any other town but Odense.

"'Look!' said my father. 'Baggesen was born there! And Birckner lived in that house!' When I heard that, somehow the dark old town with its narrow little streets seemed to grow larger and brighter. And we were so glad to feel solid earth under our feet! There was no sleep for me that night, for I was so excited over all that I had seen and heard since I had left home the day before.

"Next morning, we had to leave early; there was a terrible road ahead of us, with great bumps and holes as far as Slagelse, and not much better from there on, and we wanted to get to the Crab Inn early, so that on the same day we could reach Sorö and visit the Möllers' Emil, as we called him then; yes, he was your grandfather, my late husband, the dean. He was a student at Sorö then, and had just passed his second examination.

"That afternoon, we reached the Crab Inn, which was a gallant place at that time, the very best inn on the whole trip, with the prettiest country around it. Yes, but you must all admit that it still is. Madame Plambek was an industrious hostess, and everything in her house was as smoothly scoured as a larding board. On the wall they had, framed under glass, Baggesen's letter to her; it was indeed worth seeing, and I greatly enjoyed looking at it. Then he went to Sorö and found Emil there. You can imagine how glad we were to see him, and he to see us. He was so thoughtful and charming; he took us to see the church, and the graves of Absalon and Holberg; he inspected the old monkish inscriptions with us, and sailed with us across the lake to Parnasset. It was the most wonderful evening I remember! I was thinking that to become a poet one had only to come to Sorö and meditate among those lovely, peaceful scenes. By moonlight, we followed the 'Philosopher's Walk,' as it's called, the wonderful and lonely little path beside the lake that joins the highway near the Crab Inn. Emil stayed for supper with us, and my father and my mother declared he had grown so sensible and looked so well. It was almost Whitsuntide, and he promised that in a few days he would be in Copenhagen to join us and his family. Ah, those few hours in Sorö and at the Crab Inn I count among the choicest pearls of my life!

"Next morning, we again started very early, for we had a long trip to Roskilde, where we wanted to see the church and Father wanted to visit an old school friend that evening. We spent that night in Roskilde and reached Copenhagen by noon the next day. So we had spent about three days on a journey that can now be made in three hours—Korsör to Copenhagen. The pearls on that way have not grown more costly—that could never be—but the string is new and wonderful.

"I stayed with my parents in Copenhagen for three weeks. Emil was with us for eighteen whole days, and when we returned to Fünen he went with us as far as Korsör. There, before we parted, we were betrothed. So it is no wonder I should call the road from Copenhagen to Korsör a string of pearls.

"Afterwards, when Emil received his post at Assens, we were married. We often talked about that journey to Copenhagen, and intended doing it again, but then your mother came along, and after her came her brothers and sisters, and with all of them there was so much to do and take care of! Then your grandfather was promoted and made a dean; yes, everything was happiness and joy, but we never got to Copenhagen again. No, I have never been there since, though we often thought and talked about it. Now I'm much too old to travel by rail, but still I'm right glad there is a railway; it's a real blessing, because it brings you young ones to me more quickly!

"Nowadays, Odense is hardly farther from Copenhagen than in my youth it was from Nyborg; you can speed to Italy in the time it took us to reach Copenhagen! Yes, that is certainly something! It doesn't matter that I just sit here always; let the others travel, so long as they sometimes travel to me.

"And you needn't laugh at me, you young people, for sitting so still here, day after day! I have really a wonderful journey ahead of me; I shall soon have to travel at a speed far greater than the railway's. For when our Lord calls me, I shall go to join your grandfather; and when you have completed your work on this dear earth, you too will join us; and then, if we talk over the days of our mortal life, believe me, dear children, I shall say then as I do now, 'From Copenhagen to Korsör is a perfect string of pearls!'"

THE BELL DEEP (1856)

Ding-dong! Ding-dong!" rings out from the Bell Deep in the Odense River. And what sort of river is that? Why, every child in Odense Town knows it well. It flows around the foot of the gardens, from the locks to the water mill, under the wooden bridges. Yellow water lilies grow in the river, and brown, featherlike reeds, and the black, velvety bulrushes, so high and so thick. Decayed old willow trees, bent and gnarled, hang far over the water beside the monks' marsh and the pale meadows; but a little above are the many gardens, each very different from the next. Some have beautiful flowers and arbors as clean and neat as dolls' houses, while some have only cabbages, and in others no attempts at formal gardens can be seen at all, only great elder trees stretching out and overhanging the running water, which in places is deeper that an oar can measure.

The deepest part is right opposite the old nunnery. It is called the Bell Deep, and it is there that the Merman lives. By day, when the sun shines through the water, he sleeps, but on clear, starry, or moonlit nights he comes forth. He is very old; Grandmother has heard of him from her grandmother, she says; and he lives a lonely life, with hardly anyone to speak to except the big old church bell. It used to hang up in the steeple of the church, but now no trace is left either of the steeple or of the church itself, which used to be called St. Alban's.

"Ding-dong! Ding-dong!" rang the Bell when it hung in the steeple. But one evening, just as the sun was setting and the Bell was in full swing, it tore loose and flew through the air, its shining metal glowing in the red beams of the sunset. "Ding-dong! Ding-dong! Now I'm going to bed!" sang the Bell, and it flew into the deepest spot of the Odense River, which is why that spot is now called the Bell Deep. But it found neither sleep nor rest there, for it still rings and clangs down at the Merman's;

often it can be heard up above, through the water, and many people say that it rings to foretell the death of someone—but that is not the reason; no, it really rings to talk to the Merman, who then is no longer alone.

And what stories does the Bell tell? It is so very old; it was cast before Grandmother's grandmother was born, yet it was scarcely more than a child compared with the Merman. He is a quiet, odd-looking old fellow, with pants of eelskin, a scaly coat decorated with yellow water lilies, bulrushes in his hair, and duckweeds in his beard. He isn't exactly handsome to look at.

It would take years and days to repeat everything the Bell has said; it tells the same stories again and again, in great detail, sometimes lengthening them, sometimes shortening them, according to its mood. It tells of the olden times, those hard and gloomy times.

Up to the tower of St. Alban's Church, where the Bell hung, there once ascended a monk, young and handsome, but deeply thoughtful. He gazed through the loophole out over the Odense River. In those days its bed was broad, and the marsh was a lake. He looked across it, and over the green rampart called "The Nun's Hill," to the cloister beyond, where a light shone from a nun's cell. He had known her well, and he recalled that, and his heart beat rapidly at the thought.

"Ding-dong! Ding-dong!" Yes, such are the stories the Bell tells.

"One day the Bishop's silly manservant came up to the tower; and when I, the Bell, cast as I am from hard and heavy metal, swung to and fro and rang I almost crushed his head, for he sat down right under me and played with two sticks, exactly as if they formed a musical instrument. He sang to them, 'Here I may dare to sing aloud what elsewhere I dare not whisper—sing of all that is hidden behind locks and bolts. It is cold and damp there. The rats eat people up alive! No one knows of this; no one hears of it; even now, for the Bell is ringing so loudly, ding-dong! Ding-dong!'

"Then there was a king called Knud. He bowed low before bishops and monks, but when he unjustly oppressed the people of Vendelbo with heavy taxes and hard words, they armed themselves with weapons and drove him away as if he had been a wild beast. He sought refuge in this church and bolted fast the gate and doors. I have heard tell how the furious mob surrounded the sacred building, until the crows and ravens, and even the jackdaws became alarmed by the tumult. They flew up in and out of the tower and peered down on the multitude below; they gazed in at the church windows and shrieked out what they saw.

"King Knud knelt and prayed before the altar while his brothers, Erik and Benedict, stood guarding him with drawn swords. But the king's servant, the false Blake, betrayed his master, and when those outside knew where he could be hit, one of them hurled a stone in through the windows, and the king lay dead! Then there were shouts and screams from the angry mob, and cries, too, from the flocks of terrified birds, and I joined them all. I rang and sang, 'Ding-dong! Ding-dong!'

"The Church Bell hangs high and can see far around; it is visited by the birds and understands their language. The Wind whispers to it through the wickets and loopholes and every little crack, and the Wind knows all things. He hears it from the Air, for the Air surrounds all living creatures, even enters the lungs of humans, and hears every word and sigh. Yes, the Air knows all, the Wind tells all, and the

Church Bell understands all and peals it forth to the whole world, 'Ding-dong! Ding-dong!'

"But all this became too much for me to hear and know; I was no longer able to ring it all out. I became so tired and so heavy that at last the beam from which I hung broke, and so I flew through the glowing air down to the deepest spot of the river, where the Merman lives in solitude and loneliness. And year in and year out, I tell him all I have seen and all I have heard. Ding-dong! Ding-dong!"

Thus it sounds from the Bell Deep in the Odense River—at least, so my grandmother has told me.

But our schoolmaster says there's no bell ringing down there, for there couldn't be; and there's no Merman down there, for there aren't any Mermen. And when all the church bells are ringing loudly, he says it's not the bells, but that it is really the air that makes the sound! And my grandmother told me that the Bell said the same thing; so, since they both agree on it, it must be true. The air knows everything. It is around us and in us; it tells of our thoughts and our actions, and it voices them longer and farther than the Bell down in the Odense River hollow where the Merman lives; it voices them into the great vault of Heaven itself, so far, far away, forever and ever, until the bells of Heaven ring out, "Ding-dong! Ding-dong!"

THE BOTTLE NECK (1857)

In the narrow, crooked street, among several shabby dwellings, stood a very tall and very narrow house, the framework of which had given so that it was out of joint in every direction. Only poor people lived here, and poorest of all were those who lived in the attic. Outside the small attic window, an old, bent bird cage hung in the sunshine; it didn't even have a real bird glass, but had only a bottle neck, upside down, with a cork in its mouth, and filled with water. At the open window stood an old maid who had just been decking the cage with chickweed; the little canary in it hopped from perch to perch and sang with all his might.

"Yes, you may well sing!" said the Bottle Neck. Of course, it didn't say it audibly, as we're able to, for a bottle neck cannot speak, but it thought it, just as when we humans speak inwardly. "Yes, you may well sing—you, with your limbs whole! But what if you had lost your lower half as I have, and had only a neck and a mouth left, and then had a cork stuffed into you! You certainly wouldn't sing then! But it's good that somebody is pleased. I have no reason to sing, and I can't anyway; I could once, when I was a whole bottle, and someone rubbed me with a cork; they used to call me a real lark then, 'the grand lark.' Didn't I sing that day in the woods when the furrier's daughter became engaged? I can remember it as though it were yesterday. When I come to think of it, I've lived through many things; I've been through fire and water—down in the black earth, and higher up than most people. And now I hang here on the outside of the cage in the air and sunshine. It might be worth while to hear my story, but I'm not going to tell it aloud, because I can't!"

And so it inwardly told, or thought, its story, which was a strange one, and in the meantime the little bird sang merrily, and people rode or walked through the streets down below. Each thought of his own story or didn't think at all; but, at any rate, the Bottle Neck was engrossed in thought.

It remembered the flaming furnace in the manufacturing plant, where it had been blown into existence. It still remembered how warm it was at first, how it looked into that roaring furnace, its birthplace, and longed to leap back into it. But then as it gradually cooled, it found itself well off where it was, standing in a long row with a whole regiment of brothers and sisters. All had been born from the same furnace, but some had been blown into champagne bottles, some into beer bottles, and that makes a difference. To be sure, as things happen in the world, a beer bottle may hold the costliest Lachryma Christi wine, while a champagne bottle may be filled with black ink; but what each one was born for may still be clearly seen in its form; nobility remains nobility, even with black ink inside.

All the bottles were soon packed up, our Bottle among them. Little did it think then that it would end as a bottle neck, serving as a bird glass, and yet that is an honorable existence—it's at least something. It did not see daylight again until it was unpacked, together with its comrades, in the cellar of a wine merchant; and then for the first time it was rinsed out—that was an odd sensation. It then lay empty and corkless, and felt strangely dull, as if it lacked something, though it didn't know what. But then it was filled with good, glorious wine received a cork, and was sealed up; a label was pasted on it, "Best Quality," and it felt as if it had been awarded the highest rating as the result of its examination—though it had to be admitted that the wine was good, as well as the Bottle.

When one is young, one is a lyric poet! The Bottle was singing inwardly of things it knew nothing about—green, sunlit mountains, where the vineyards grow, and where merry maidens and happy youths sing and kiss. Yes, it is wonderful to be alive! Indeed, the Bottle inwardly sang of all this, as do young poets, who frequently also know nothing about the things of which they sing.

One morning it was bought. The furrier's boy had been sent to fetch a bottle of the best wine; and then it was packed into a large basket, together with ham, cheese, sausages, the best butter, and the finest bread. The furrier's daughter herself packed the basket. She was so young, so pretty; her brown eyes laughed, and there was a smile on her lips, which seemed as expressive as her eyes. Her hands were small, soft, and white, but not so white as her forehead and throat. You could see at once that she was one of the prettiest girls in the village, and still she was not yet betrothed.

When the party drove out into the woods, the basket lay in her lap. The neck of the Bottle peeped out from the folds of the white tablecloth; the red sealing wax on the cork looked right in the face of the young girl and looked also at the young sailor who sat beside her. He had been her friend since childhood, and was a portrait painter's son. He had recently passed his examination for the navel service with high honors, and on the next day he was to sail away, far away, to foreign lands. This had been spoken of during the packing of the basket, and it hadn't been quite so pleasant to look at the eyes and lips of the furrier's pretty daughter while there'd been talk of that.

The two young people went for a walk in the green forest, talking—and what did they talk about? The Bottle couldn't hear that, for it was left in the basket. A long time passed before the basket was unpacked, but when it was, it was apparent that some pleasant thing had happened in the meantime, for all eyes were filled with happiness, particularly those of the furrier's daughter, though she said less than the others, and her cheeks blushed like two red roses.

The father unwrapped the Bottle and took up the corkscrew. Yes, it was a strange sensation that the Bottle felt when, for the first time, the cork was drawn! The Bottleneck could never forget that solemn moment; it said "pop!" as the cork was pulled out, and then the wine gurgled when it flowed into the glasses.

"A toast to the betrothed!" said the father, and every glass was emptied, and then the young man kissed his pretty fiancée. "Good luck and blessings," said the old couple. And the young man then refilled the glasses, exclaiming, "To my homecoming and our wedding, a year from today!" When the glasses had been emptied; he raised the Bottle in the air, saying, "You have been a part of the happiest day of my life. You shall never serve anyone else!"

Then he flung it high into the air. Little did the furrier's daughter think that she would ever see the Bottle again—and yet she would. The Bottle fell down among the thick reeds fringing the little woodland lake. The Bottle neck could remember clearly how it lay there, thinking, "I gave them wine, and they gave me swamp water—but they meant well." It could no longer see the happy betrothed and their pleased parents, but it could hear them talking and singing in the distance. Then after a while two peasant boys came along, found the Bottle among the reeds, and took it away. Now it had someone to take care of it.

At the woodland hut where the boys lived, they and their elder brother, who was a sailor, had parted the day before, when he had come home to say good-bye prior to leaving on a long voyage. Now their mother was packing a few things that their father was going to take to him in the town that evening; this would give him an opportunity to see his son once more before his departure and to bring him greetings from his mother and himself. A little flask of spiced brandy was placed in the package. But then the boys came home with the bottle they had found; it was larger and stronger and would hold more than the little flask; it was just right for a good-sized schnapps for a stomach in need of such. So it was filled, not with red wine as before, but with brandy containing herbs that are good for the stomach. The newly found Bottle, rather than the little one, would go on the trip.

And so the Bottle continued on its travels. It went with Peter Jensen on board the very same ship as this young officer who had been betrothed. He hadn't yet seen the Bottle again, and if he had, he wouldn't have recognized it, or thought, "This is the bottle from which the toasts to our betrothal and my homecoming were drunk!"

Now, of course, it no longer contained red wine, but there was something just as good in it. Whenever Peter Jensen brought it out, his shipmates always called it "the apothecary"; it provided good medicine for the stomach, they agreed, and indeed it helped them as long as there was a drop left in it. Those were happy times, and the Bottle sang when it was rubbed with the cork, and thus it came to be called "the grand lark," and "Peter Jensen's lark."

A long time had passed; the Bottle stood empty in a corner, and it did not know whether it was on the voyage out or bound for home, for it hadn't been ashore. Then a mighty storm arose. Huge, heavy, black waves rose up and hurled the vessel about. The mast crashed overboard; a mighty wave smashed in a plank, and the pumps were useless. The ship was sinking, but in the last minute the young officer wrote on a piece of paper, "Lord Jesus have mercy on us—we perish!" He wrote his fiancée's name, his own, and that of the ship, put the note into an empty bottle he found nearby, pressed the cork in tightly, and then flung the bottle out into the stormy sea. Never did he realize that this was the Bottle that had provided wine for toasts to his and her happiness and the fulfillment of their hopes. It now tossed on the surging billows, carrying its tidings of death, its greeting to the living.

The ship sank, and the crew with it. The Bottle was like a bird in flight, the way it was tossed above the waves—and, what's more, it had a heart within it, in the form of a lover's message. The sun rose, and the sun set—and that reminded the Bottle of the time of its birth, in the red, glowing furnace; it longed to fly back into the heat.

It went through calm seas and more storms; it was neither dashed against rocks nor swallowed by a shark. For more than a year and a day it drifted, now north, now south, as it was carried by the currents. To be sure it was its own master, but one gets tired of that.

The note, that last farewell from the young officer to his betrothed, would bring only sorrow if it ever should fall into the proper hands. But where were those hands, the hands that had gleamed so white while spreading the tablecloth over the fresh grass on the betrothal day?

Where was the furrier's daughter? Yes, and where was land? What land lay nearest? The Bottle had no idea. It drifted on and on and finally became very weary of drifting—for which it had never been intended, anyway—but still it drifted on, until at last it was cast ashore on a foreign land. It couldn't understand a word that was spoken here; this was not the language it had always heard before, and one misses a great deal when in a country where one cannot understand the language.

The Bottle was picked up and examined; the note inside it was noticed, taken out, turned around, and turned over, but the people could not understand what was written on it. They realized, of course, that the bottle had been thrown overboard and that there was something about that written on the paper, but what it said was a mystery. And so the note was put back into the Bottle, and the Bottle itself placed in a large cabinet in a large room in a large house. Whenever strangers came to the house the note was brought forth, turned around and over, and viewed from every angle, until the writing—which was only pencil, to begin with—became more and more illegible, and at last the letters could hardly be made out at all. For a year the Bottle remained in the cabinet; then it was sent up to the attic, where it was smothered with dust and spider webs. Up there it thought of its better days, when it had provided the red wine in the fresh woods, and when it had been rocked by the billows, and had had a secret, a letter, a sigh of farewell, entrusted to its care.

For twenty years it was left in the attic, and it might have remained there still longer if the house had not been rebuilt. The roof was torn down; the Bottle was found, and remarks were made about it, but it still couldn't understand the language; one doesn't learn a language by standing in an attic, even in twenty years. "If only I had stayed in the parlor downstairs," it thought, "I would have learned it!"

It now was washed and rinsed out, and it needed cleaning badly. It felt itself once more quite clear and transparent; it felt young in its old age. But the note it had carried had been destroyed in the washing. Now it was filled with seed corn—what sort, it didn't know—was well packed, and corked up tightly; it could see neither lamp nor candle, not to mention sun or moon. "One should be able to see something when one goes on a journey," thought the Bottle. But while it saw nothing, it did something— and that is of far greater importance. It traveled, and at last came to its destination, where it was unpacked.

"What a lot of trouble those foreigners have gone to with that!" it was said. "And yet it's probably cracked!" But the Bottle wasn't cracked. It understood all that was said here, for every word was spoken in the language it had heard on coming out of the furnace at the factory, and at the wine merchant's, and in the woods, and aboard the ship—the only language that was right, the good, old language that one could understand. The Bottle had come home to its own country; to hear the language was a welcome greeting in itself, and in its joy it nearly jumped from the hands that held it! It was barely aware that its cork was pulled out and that it was emptied of its contents and sent down to the cellar—there to be kept and forgotten; however, there is no place like home, even in the cellar! It never gave thought to how long a time it lay there, for it lay in comfort; it was there for many years. Then, finally, one day people came down and took the bottles away, ours among them.

The garden of the house was magnificently decorated; colorfully lighted lamps were hung in garlands, and paper lanterns glowed festively, resembling big, seemingly transparent tulips. It was a beautiful evening, too; the air was calm and mild; the stars twinkled brightly, and there was a new moon; people with sharp eyes could see the whole round moon, which looked like a blue-gray globe half encircled with gold.

There was some illumination along the outlying walks, too—at least enough to enable one to find his way along them. Rows of bottles, each with a candle in it, had been set up along the hedges. Among these stood the Bottle we know— that which was to end as a bottle neck, a bird glass—and it found everything here completely delightful; it was again out among the greenery; again it heard the sounds of gladness and festivity, song and music, the buzz and chatter of many people, especially from the section of the garden where the lamps were burning and the paper lanterns showed their bright colors. Though the Bottle stood along an out-of-the-way walk, even that gave it food for thought; in standing here and bearing its light, it was being both useful and enjoyable to others, and such was its rightful purpose. In an hour like that one can forget twenty years in an attic—and that is a good thing to forget.

A couple passed close by, arm in arm, like the betrothed pair out in the woods—the naval officer and the furrier's daughter; it seemed to the Bottle that it was living its life over again. Guests strolled to and fro in the garden; there were also passersby who had ventured here for a glimpse of the guests and the festivities, and among them was an old maid who had no relatives or family but was not friendless. She was thinking of the same thing that the Bottle was; she thought of the green woods and the young betrothed couple of so long ago. That indeed concerned her, because she had been a part of it—she was one of the two lovers! That had been the happiest time of her life, a time never to be forgotten, however old an old maid may be. But she did not recognize the Bottle, nor did it recognize her; and thus it is that we pass one another by in this world—though sooner or later we are sure to meet again, as did these two, who were now residents of the same town.

From the garden the Bottle went back to the wine merchant's; there it was once more filled with wine and then sold to an aeronaut, whose next balloon ascension was to be on the following Sunday. A crowd of people came to see the event; there was military music, and many elaborate preparations had been made for the occasion. The Bottle saw it all from a basket, where it lay with a live rabbit, who was very disheartened because he knew he was going up only to come down again by parachute. The Bottle knew nothing about going up or coming down, but it saw how the balloon swelled out larger and larger, and that when it could grow no larger it began to raise itself, higher and higher, and rolled uneasily; then the ropes that held it down were cut, and it floated up with the aeronaut, the basket, the rabbit, and the bottle. The band played, and all the people cried, "Hurrah!"

"It's funny to go up in the air like this!" thought the Bottle. "It must be a new kind of sailing; you can't run onto rocks up here!"

Many thousands of people looked up at the balloon, and the old maid watched it, too. She was standing at the open attic window, beside the cage with the little canary, who at that time didn't have a glass for his water but had to get along with an old cup. In the window was a flowering myrtle, which the old woman had moved aside so it wouldn't fall out when she leaned forward to see the proceedings. She could see the aeronaut in the balloon basket; he let the rabbit fall by parachute, then drank a toast to all the spectators and flung the Bottle high into the air. She naturally had no thought of having seen the same bottle fly through the air on that happy day in the green woods, in her youth.

The Bottle didn't have time to think at all, so suddenly did it reach the highest point of its life. Far below lay the towers and roofs of the town; people were so tiny that they were hardly visible at all.

Now it fell, but it was a quite different fall from the rabbit's. The Bottle turned somersaults in the air, and felt itself so young, so wild! It was half full of wine, but not for long. What a voyage! The sun glittered on the Bottle, and all eyes followed it; the balloon itself was already a considerable distance aloft, and soon the Bottle was out of view. It fell on a roof, and broke in two, but there was such spirit in the pieces that they couldn't remain still! They leaped and rolled, downward, downward until they reached the courtyard, where they broke into still smaller pieces. Only the neck of the Bottle was left whole; it looked as if it had been cut off cleanly with a diamond.

"It can be used as a bird glass," said the man who lived in the cellar. But he himself had neither bird nor cage, and it would hardly have been worth while to get them just because he had a bottle neck that might be used as a bird glass. He knew, however, that the old maid up in the attic could use it. So the Bottle Neck was taken upstairs, a cork was put in, and the part that had always been the top was now at the bottom—as often happens in life's changes; it was filled with fresh water, and was hung on the cage for the little bird who sang so merrily.

"Yes, you may well sing," said the Bottle Neck. And it was indeed a remarkable bottle neck, for it had been up in a balloon; this, however, was all that was known of its story. Now, in hanging here as a bird glass, it could hear the hum and buzz of people in the street below and the voice of the old maid in her chamber. She had a visitor just now, a friend of her own age, and they were talking—not about the bird glass, but about the myrtle at the window.

"You certainly shan't waste two dollars for a bridal bouquet for your daughter!" said the old maid. "You shall have a charming one from me, full of flowers! See how lovely my myrtle is! Yes, it's an offshoot from the myrtle you gave me, the day after my betrothal. I was going to have my own bridal bouquet made of it, when the year was up, but that day never came. Those eyes that were to have been my light and joy throughout life were closed; at the bottom of the sea he sleeps sweetly, the angel. The myrtle grew until it was like an old tree, but I aged even more; and when it withered I took the last fresh shoot and set it into the ground, and now that shoot is like a tree, and at last it shall serve at a wedding, as a bridal bouquet for your daughter!"

And there were tears in the old maid's eyes; she spoke again of the friend of her youth and of their betrothal in the woods; she thought of the toasts that had been drunk, thought of his first kiss—but she said nothing about that; she was an old maid now.

She thought of so many things, but little did she think that just outside her window was a remembrance of that time, the neck of that very Bottle which had said "pop!" when its cork had been pulled out for the drinking of the toasts. The old Bottle didn't know her either, for it hadn't listened to what she had said, partly—in fact, chiefly—because it thought only of itself.

SOUP FROM A SAUSAGE PEG (1858)

I. SOUP FROM A SAUSAGE PEG

That was a perfectly delightful dinner yesterday," one old female mouse told another, who had not attended the feast. "I sat number twenty-one from the old mouse king, which wasn't at all bad. Would you like to hear the menu? The courses were exceedingly well arranged—mouldy bread, bacon rind, tallow candle, and sausage, and then the same dishes all over again, from start to finish, so it was as good as two banquets. There was such a pleasant atmosphere, and such good humor, that it was like a family gathering. Not a scrap was left except the pegs at the ends of the sausages.

"The conversation turned to these wooden pegs, and the expression 'soup from a sausage peg,' came up. Everybody had heard it, but nobody had ever tasted such a soup, much less knew how to make it. We drank a fine toast to the health of whoever invented the soup, and we said he deserved to be appointed manager of the poorhouse. Wasn't that witty? And the old mouse king rose and promised that the young maiden mouse who could make this soup should be his queen. He gave them a year and a day to learn how."

"That wasn't so bad, after all," said the other mouse. "But how do you make this soup?"

"Yes, how do you make it? That's exactly what all the female mice are asking—the young ones and the old maids, too. Every last one of them wants to be the queen, but they don't want to bestir themselves and go out in the wide world to learn how to make soup, as they certainly would have to do. Not everyone has the courage to leave her family and her own snug corner. Out in the world one doesn't come upon cheese parings or smell bacon every day. No indeed. One must endure hunger, yes, and perhaps be eaten alive by the cat."

Very likely this was what frightened most of them from venturing out in the wide world to find the secret of the soup. Only four mice declared themselves ready to go. They were young and willing, but poor. Each would go to one of the four corners of the world, and then let fortune decide among them. All four took sausage pegs with them as a reminder of their purpose. These were to be their pilgrim staffs.

It was the beginning of May when they set out, and they did not return until May of the following year. But only three of them returned. The fourth did not report, and there was no news about her, though the day for the contest had come.

"Yes, something always goes wrong on even the most pleasant occasions," the mouse king observed. But he commanded that all the mice for many miles around should be invited.

They gathered in the kitchen, and the three travelers lined up in a row by themselves. For the fourth, who was missing, they placed a sausage peg-shrouded in crepe. No one dared to express an opinion until the three travelers had made their reports, and the mouse king had rendered his decision. Now we shall hear.

II. WHAT THE FIRST LITTLE MOUSE HAD SEEN AND HEARD ON HER TRAVELS

"When I went out into the wide world," the little mouse said, "I thought, as many others do when they are my age, that I knew everything. But such was not the case. It takes days and years to know everything. I immediately set out to sea. I went on a northbound ship, for I had heard that ships' cooks must know how to manage. But it isn't so hard to manage at sea when you have an abundance of bacon, and whole barrels of salt meat and mouldy flour. You live like a lord, but you don't learn to make soup from a sausage peg. We sailed many days and we sailed many nights. The boat rolled dreadfylly, and we got many a drenching. When we reached port at last, I left the ship. That was far up in the north country.

"It's a strange thing to leave one's chimney corner, sail away in a ship which is a sort of corner too, and then suddenly find oneself in a foreign land, hundreds of miles away. There were vast and trackless forests of birch and pine. They smelled so strong that I didn't like it! The fragrance of the wild herbs was so spiced it made me sneeze and think of sausages.

"There, too, were broad lakes of water which was perfectly clear when you came close to it, though from a distance it looked as black as ink. White swans rested on the lakes, and they were so still that at first I thought they were flecks of foam. But when

I saw them fly, and I saw them walk, I knew at once that they were members of the duck family—I could tell by the way they waddled. One can't disown his relatives! I kept to my own kind. I went with the field and forest mice, although they knew little enough of anything, and nothing at all of cookery, which was the very thing, I had traveled so far to find out about. That it was possible to think soup could be made from a sausage peg startled them so that the information was immediately bandied throughout the vast forest. But that there could be any solution to such a problem they thought was utterly impossible, and little did I expect that there, before the night was over, I should be initiated into the making of it.

"It was midsummer. The mice said that this was why the woods and the herbs were redolent, and the waters so clear and yet so dark blue in contrast with the whiteness of the swans. At the edge of the forest, between three or four houses they had raised a pole as high as a ship's mainmast. Garlands and ribbons fluttered from the peak of it. It was a maypole. Young men and maidens danced around it and sang at the top of their voices, while the fiddler played them a tune. They were merry in the sunset and merry in the moonlight, but I had no part in it, for what would a little mouse be doing at a forest dance? So I sat in the soft moss, and held tight to my sausage peg. The moonlight fell particularly bright on one spot, where there was a tree. This spot was carpeted with moss so soft that I dare say it was as fine as the mouse king's fur, but its color was green and it was a blessing to the eyes.

"All of a sudden there appeared a few of the most enchanting little folk, no taller than my knee. They resembled human beings, except that they were better proportioned. 'Elves' was what they called themselves. They went dressed very fine, in clothes made of flower petals trimmed with the wings of flies and gnats. It wasn't at all bad looking. They seemed in search of something, but I didn't know what it could be until a couple of them came up to me. Then their leader pointed to my sausage peg and said:

"'That's just what we need. It's pointed. It's perfect!' The more he looked at my sausage peg, the happier it made him.

"'You can borrow it,' I told him, 'but not keep it.'

"'Not keep it,' all of them promised, as they took the sausage peg that I gave them and danced away with it to the place where the soft moss grew. They wanted to have a maypole of their own, and mine seemed made to order for them. Then they decorated it. Yes, what a sight it was!

"Small spiders spun gold thread around it. They draped it with streamers and banners so fine and bleached so snowy white in the moonlight that they dazzled my eyes. They took the color from a butterfly's wing and splashed it about on my sausage peg until it seemed blooming with flowers and sparkling with diamonds. I scarcely knew it, for in all the world there is no match to the maypole they had made of it.

"Now the real party of elves appeared, in great numbers. Not a stitch did they wear, yet it couldn't have been more refined. I was invited to look on, but from a distance, because I was too big for them.

"Then the music struck up, and such music! It seemed as if a thousand bells of glass were ringing. It was so rich and full that I thought it was the swans who were singing. Yes, I even thought I heard the cuckoos, and blackbirds, until it was as if the whole forest had joined in the chorus. Children's voices, bell tones, and birds' songs, all seemed to keep tune in the loveliest melody, yet it all came from the elves' maypole. It was a whole chime of bells—yet it was my sausage peg. I would never have imagined so much could have been done with it, but that depends altogether upon who gets hold of it. I was deeply touched. From sheer pleasure, I wept as much as a little mouse can weep.

"The night was all too short, but the nights in the far north are not any longer at that time of the year. As dawn broke, and the morning breeze rippled the mirrored surface of the lake, the fine-spun streamers and banners were blown away. The billowing garlands of spider web, the suspension bridges from leaf to leaf, the balustrades and whatever else they are called, blew away like nothing at all. Six elves brought back my sausage peg, and asked if I wished for anything they could give me. So I begged them to tell me how to make soup from a sausage peg.

"The chief elf smiled, and said, 'How do we do it? Why, you have just seen it. I'm sure you scarcely knew your sausage peg.'

"'To you, it's only a trick of speech,' I said. I told him honestly what I traveled in search of, and what importance was attached to it here at home. 'What good,' said I, 'does it do our mouse king or our great kingdom for me to witness all this merrymaking? I can't just wave my sausage peg and say, "See the peg. Here comes the soup." This sort of dish is good only after all the guests at the table have had their fill.'

"Then the chief elf dipped his little finger in the blue cup of a violet, and told me:

"'Watch this. I shall anoint your pilgrim's staff. When you come home again to the mouse king's palace, you need only touch his warm heart with it, and the staff will immediately be covered with violets, even in the coldest wintertime. So I should say I have given you something to take home with you, and a little more for good measure.'"

Before the little mouse said what this "little more" was, she held out her stick to the king's heart. Really and truly, it became covered with the most beautiful bouquet of flowers, and their fragrance was so strong that the mouse king ordered the mice who stood nearest the fire to singe their tails. He wanted a smell of something burning to overcome the scent of violets, which was not the kind of perfume that he liked.

"What was that 'little more for good measure'?" he asked.

"Oh yes," said the little mouse. "I think it is what they call an effect." She turned the stick around and, behold! there was not a flower to be seen on the bare sausage peg in her hand. She flourished it like a music baton. "'Violets are to see, and smell, and touch,' the elf told me. So something must be done for us to hear and taste."

The little mouse began to beat time, and music was heard. It was not the elfin music of the forest. No, it was such as can be heard in the kitchen. There was the bubbling sound of boiling and stewing. It came all at once, as though the wind rushed through every chimney funnel and every pot and kettle boiled over. The fire shovel clanged upon the copper kettle, and then all at once the sound died down. One heard the whisper of the teakettle's song, so sweet to hear and so low they could scarcely tell when it began or left off. The little pot simmered and the big pot boiled, and neither kept time with the other. It was as if there were no reason left in the pots. And the little mouse flourished her baton even more fiercely. The pots seethed, bubbled, and boiled over. The wind whistled and roared down the chimney. *Puff!* It rose so tremendously that the little mouse at length lost hold of her stick.

"That was thick soup," said the mouse king. "Is it ready to be served?"

"That's all there is to it." The little mouse curtsied.

"All?" said the mouse king. "Then we had better hear what the next has to tell us."

III. WHAT THE SECOND LITTLE MOUSE HAD TO TELL

"I was born in the palace library," said the second mouse. "I and other members of my family have never known the luxury of visiting a dining room, much less a pantry. Only on my journey and here today have I seen a kitchen. In the library, we often went hungry indeed, but we got a great deal of knowledge. The news of the royal reward offered for making soup from a sausage peg finally reached us. It was my grandmother who promptly ferreted out a manuscript, which of course she could not read, but from which she has heard the following passage read: 'If one is a poet, one can make soup out of a sausage peg.'

"She asked me if I were a poet. I told her I was entirely innocent in such matters, but she insisted that I must go forth and manage to be one. I asked how to do it, for that was as hard for me to learn as it was to find out how to make the soup. But my grandmother had heard a good many books read, and she told me that three things were essential: 'Understanding, imagination, and feeling—if you can manage to get these into you, you'll be a poet, and this business of the sausage peg will come to you by nature.'

"So off I went, marching westward, out into the wide world to become a poet.

"I knew that understanding comes first in everything, because the other two virtues aren't half as well thought of, so I set off in search of understanding at once. Yes, but where does it live? 'Go to the ant and be wise,' said the great King of the Jews. I learned that in the library. So I did not rest until I came to a big ant hill. There I posted myself on watch, to learn wisdom.

"The ants are a very respectable race. They understand things thoroughly. With them everything is like a well-worked problem in arithmetic that comes out right. Work and lay eggs, they say, for you must both live your life and provide for the future. So that is just what they do. They are divided into clean ants and those who do the dirty work. Each one is numbered according to his rank, and the ant queen is number *one*. What she thinks is the only right way to think, for she contains all wisdom, and it was most important for me to learn this from her. But she talked so cleverly that it seemed like nonsense to me.

"She asserted that her ant hill was the highest thing in all the world, though quite close to it grew a tree which was obviously higher. It was so very much higher that there was no denying it, and consequently, it was never mentioned. One evening, an ant got lost in the tree. She climbed up the trunk, not to the very top but higher than any ant had climbed before. When she came home and told of finding something even more lofty than the ant hill, the other ants considered that she had insulted the whole community. She was muzzled and comdemned to solitary confinement for life. Shortly afterward, another ant climbed the tree, making the same journey and the same discovery. But this ant reported it with suitable caution and diffidence, as they say. Besides, she was one of the upper-class ants—one of the clean ones. So they believed her, and when she died, they gave her an eggshell momument, to show their love of science."

The little mouse went on to say, "I saw the ants continually running to and fro with eggs on their backs. One of them dropped hers, and tried to pick it up again, but she couldn't manage it. Two others came to help her with all their power. But when they came near dropping their own eggs in the attempt, they at once stopped helping, for each must first think of himself. The queen ant said that they had displayed both heart and understanding.

"'These two virtues,' she said, 'raise ants above all other creatures of reason. Understanding must and shall always come first, and I have more of it than anyone else.' With this, she reared up on her hind legs so that all could be sure who she was. I was sure who she was, and I ate her. 'Go to the ant and be wise'—and I had swallowed the queen.

"I now went over to the tree I mentioned. It was an oak, with a mighty trunk and far-flung branches, for it was very old. I knew that a living spirit must live in it, a dryad, as she is called, who is born when the tree is born and dies when it dies. I had heard of this in the library, and now I saw such a tree with such an oak maiden. She shrieked frightfully when she saw me so near her, for like other women, she is terribly afraid of mice. But she had more reason to fear me than the others have, because I might have gnawed through the bark of the tree on which her life depended. I spoke to her in a cordial, friendly fashion, and told her she had nothing to fear.

"She took me up in her slender hand, and when I told her why I had come out into the wide world she promised that perhaps that very evening I should find one of the two virtues for which I still searched. She told me that Fantasy was her very good friend, that he was as beautiful as the god of love, and that he often rested under the leafy boughs of the tree, which would then rustle even more softly over these two. He called her his dryad, she said, and the tree his tree, for the magnificent gnarled oak just suited him. He liked its roots which went down so deep and steadfast in the earth, and the trunk which rose so high in the clear air that it felt the pelting snow, the driving wind, and the warm sun as they ought to be felt.

"'Yes,' the dryad talked on, 'the birds up aloft there sing and tell of distant lands. On the single dead branch the stork has built a nest which is very picturesque, and he tells me about the land where the pyramids are. Fantasy loves to hear all this, but it is not enough for him. I too must tell him of my life in the forest, from the time when I was small and the tree so tiny that a nettle could shade it, until now when the tree is so tall and strong. Sit down under the sweet thyme, and watch closely. When Fantasy comes I shall manage to pinch his wings and pull out a little feather. Take it. A poet can get no better gift—and it will be all you need.'

"When Fantasy came, the feather was plucked and I took it," said the little mouse. "I soaked it in water until it was soft. Still it was hard to swallow, but I nibbled it down at last. It's no easy matter to become a poet, with all the things one must cram inside oneself.

"Now I had both understanding and imagination, and they taught me that the third virtue was to be found in the library. For a great man once said and wrote that there are romances whose only purpose is to relieve people of their superfluous tears, and that these romances are like sponges, sopping up the emotions. I remembered that a few of these old books had always looked especially tasty. They had been thumbed quite greasy. They must have absorbed an enormous lot of tears.

"I returned to the library and devoured a whole novel—that is to say, the soft and the essential part; but the crust—that is, the binding, I left. When I had digested this, and another one too, I felt fluttery inside. I ate still a third and there I was, a poet. That is what I told myself, and that is what I told everyone else. I had headache, stomach aches—I can't remember all the different aches.

"Now I began to recall all the stories that could be made to apply to a sausage peg. Many pegs came to mind—the ant queen must have had magnificent understanding. I remembered the story about a man who would take a white peg out of his mouth to make both himself and the peg invisible. I thought of old beer with a peg stuck in it, of peg legs, and 'round pegs in square holes,' and 'the peg to one's coffin.' All my thoughts ran on pegs. When one is a poet—as I am, for I have worked like mad to become one—one can turn all of these subjects into poems. So every day, I shall be able to entertain your majesty with another peg, another story—yes that's my soup."

"Let's hear what the third one has to say," the king commanded.

"Squeak, squeak!" they heard at the kitchen door, and the fourth little mouse—the one they had given up for dead—whizzed in like an arrow and upset the crepe-covered sausage peg. She had been running night and day, and when she saw her chance, she had traveled by rail on the freight train. Even so, she was almost too late. She pushed forward, looking the worse for wear. She had lost her sausage peg but not her tongue, for she immediately took over the conservation as if everybody had been waiting to hear her, and her alone, and as if nothing else mattered in the world. She spoke at once, and she spoke in full. She appeared so suddenly that no one had time to check her or her speech until she was through. So let's hear her.

IV. WHAT THE FOURTH MOUSE, WHO SPOKE BEFORE THE THIRD, HAD TO SAY

"I went at once to the largest town," she said. "I don't recall the name of it. I have such a bad memory for names. From the railway station I was carried with some confiscated goods to the courthouse, and from there I ran to see the jailor. He was talking about his prisoners, and especially about one who had spoken rashly. One word led to another. About these words, other words had been spoken, read and recorded.

"'The whole business is soup from a sausage peg,' said the jailor, 'but it is a soup that may cost him his head.'

"This gave me such an interest in the prisoner," the little mouse went on to say, "that I watched my chance, and darted into his cell. For there is always some mouse hole behind every locked door. The prisoner looked pale. He had a big beard and big, brilliant eyes. His lamp smoked up the cell, but the walls were so black that they couldn't get any blacker, and the prisoner whiled away the time by scratching drawings and verses in white on this black background. I didn't read them, but I believe he found it dull there, for I was a welcome guest. He tempted me out with crumbs, and whistling, and pet words. He was glad to see me, won my confidence, and we became fast friends. We shared his bread and water, and he treated me to cheese and sausage, so I lived well. However, I would say that it was chiefly for his good company that I stayed with him. He let me run up his hand and arm into his sleeve, and climb in his beard. He called me his little friend, and I really liked him, for friendship is a two-sided thing. I forgot my mission in the wide world and I forgot my sausage peg. It is lying there still in a crack in the floor. I wanted to stay with him, for if I had gone away the poor prisoner wouldn't have had a friend in the world. That would not be right, so I stayed. But he did not stay. He spoke to me sadly for the last time, gave me a double ration of bread and cheese, and blew me a parting kiss. Then he went away and he never came back. I don't know what became of him.

"'Soup from a sausage peg,' the jailor had said, so I went to see him. But he was not to be trusted. He took me up in his hand, right enough, but he popped me into a cage, a treadmill, a terrible machine in which you run around and around without going anywhere. And, besides, people laugh at you.

"The jailor's grandchild was a charming little girl, with curls that shone like gold, such sparkling eyes, and such merry lips.

"'Why, you poor little mouse,' she said, as she peeped into my ugly old cage. She drew back the iron bolt, and out I jumped to the window sill, and from there to the rain spout. I was free, free! That was all I thought of, and not of the purpose of my journey.

"It was almost dark. Night was coming on when I established myself in an old tower already inhabited by a watchman and an owl. I didn't trust either of them, and the owl least of all. It is like the cat, and has the unforgivable vice of eating mice. But one can be mistaken, as I was, for this old owl was most worthy and knowing. She knew more than the watchman, and as much as I did. The young owls were always making a fuss about everything. 'Don't try to make soup out of a sausage peg,' she told them, and she had such tender affection for her own family that those were the hardest word she would say.

"Her behavior gave me such confidence in her that from the crevice where I hid, I called out, 'Squeak!' My trust in her pleased her so that she promised to take me under her protection. No animal would be allowed to molest me, and she would save me for the wintertime when food ran short.

"She was wise in every way. The watchman, she told me, can only hoot with the horn that hangs by his side. 'He is vastly puffed up about it,' she declared, 'and thinks he's an owl in a tower. It sounds so big, but it is very little—all soup from a sausage peg.'

"I begged her to give me the recipe for this soup, but she explained to me that, '"Soup from a sausage peg" is only a human expression. It means different things, and everybody thinks his meaning is the right one, but the real meaning is nothing at all.'

"'Nothing at all?' I squeaked. That was a blow! Truth isn't always pleasant, but 'Truth above all else.' The old owl said so, too. Now that I thought about it, I clearly saw that if I brought back what was 'above all else,' I would be bringing something much better than soup from a sausage peg. So I hurried back, to be home in time and to bring back the best thing of all, something above everything else, which is the *truth*.

We mice are an enlightened people, and the mouse king is the most enlightened of us all. He is capable of making me his queen for the sake of truth."

"Your truth is false!" said the mouse who had not yet had her say. "I can make the soup, and I intend to do so."

V. HOW THE SOUP WAS MADE

"I didn't go traveling," the third mouse informed them. "I stayed at home, and that's the right thing to do. There's no need to travel. One can get everything just as well here, so I stayed at home. I have not learned what I know from fabulous creatures, or swallowed it whole, or taken an owl's word for it. I found it out from my own meditation. Kindly put a kettle brimful of water on the fire! Now stir up the fire until the water boils up and boils over. Now throw the peg in! And now will the mouse king kindly dip his tail in the scalding water, to stir it. The longer he stirs it, the stronger the soup will be. There's no expense—it needs no other ingredients. Just stir it around."

"Can't someone else stir it?" the mouse king asked.

"No," she told him. "The necessary touch can be given only by the mouse king's tail."

The water bubbled and boiled as the mouse king stood close to the kettle. It was almost dangerous. He held out his tail, as mice do in a dairy when they skim a pan of milk and lick the cream from their tails. But no sooner did the hot steam strike his tail than away he jumped.

"Naturally, you are my queen," he declared. "The soup can wait until our golden anniversary. That will give the poor people among my subjects something to which they can look forward, with pleasure—and a long pleasure."

And then the wedding was held. But as the mice returned home, some of them said that it could scarcely be called soup from a sausage peg. Soup from a mouse tail was more like it. This or that of what had been told was quite good, they admitted, but the whole thing could have been done very differently.

"Now I would have said this, and that, and the other thing." So said the critics, who are so wise after a thing is done. But the story was told around the world. Various opinions were held of it but they didn't do the story itself any harm. So it's well to remember that for all things great and small, as well as in regard to soup from a sausage peg, don't expect any thanks.

THE NIGHTCAP OF THE
"PEBERSVEND" (1858)

There is a street in Copenhagen that bears the odd name of Hysken Street. Why is it called that? And what does "Hysken" mean? It is supposed to be German, but that is an injustice to the German word *Häuschen*, which means "small houses." Many years ago, when it was named, the houses in this street were not much more than wooden booths, almost like those we nowadays see set up in the markets—yes, a little larger, and with windows, but the panes were made only of horn or stretched bladder, for in those days, glass windows were too expensive to be used in all houses. But then the time we are referring to was so long ago that when my great-grandfather's grandfather spoke of it, he called it "the olden days." It was several hundred years ago.

The rich merchants of Bremen and Lübeck traded in Copenhagen in those days; they did not go there personally, but sent their clerks, who lived in the wooden booths in the Street of Small Houses, and sold their beers and spices there. The German beers were indeed excellent, and there were many different kinds, including Bremen, Prysing, and Emser beer—yes, and Brunswick ale, too—all sorts of spices, such as saffron, anise, ginger, and especially pepper. Yes, pepper was the most important of these, and consequently the German traders in Denmark came to be called *pebersvende* (pepper sellers). It was part of the contract they made before leaving home that they should not marry in Denmark. Many of them remained there until they were very old, and they had to look out for themselves, live alone, and light and put out their own fires, if they had any. Some of them became odd old fellows, with eccentric ideas and habits. From them, the name of *pebersvende* has come to be given to all bachelors who have reached a certain age. All this one must know in order to understand the story. People make light of the *pebersvend*, the bachelor; they tell him to put on his nightcap, pull it down over his eyes, and go to bed.

> *Saw, saw the wood!*
> *His bed feels so good!*
> *The pebersvend wears a nightcap on his head,*
> *And must himself light the candle by his bed.*

Yes, they sing this about the *pebersvend* and thus make fun of him and his nightcap—only because they know so little about either. Ah, but such a nightcap one must never wish for! And why not? Just listen!

In the olden times, there was no pavement in the Street of Small Houses; people stumbled into one hole after another, for it was like a dug-up street. And it was so narrow, and the booths were so near each other, that in the summertime, a canvas was often stretched across the street from one booth to another, and then the aroma of pepper, saffron, and ginger was very strong there.

Behind the counters stood not many young men; no, most of the clerks were old fellows, and not dressed as we might think, with wigs or nightcaps, knee breeches, or with vests and coats buttoned up to their chins; no, it was our great-grandfather's grandfather who went about dressed like that and who appears in such attire in his portrait. The *pebersvende* couldn't afford to have their portraits painted, and that is a pity, for it would be well worth while now to have a picture of any one of them, just as he stood behind his counter, or walked to church on Sundays. The hat used was broad brimmed and high crowned, and often one of the younger clerks would stick a feather in his; the woolen shirt worn was partly covered by a turndown linen collar; the jacket was tightly buttoned, with a cape hanging loosely over it, and the breeches extended down to square-toed shoes; stockings were not worn. In the belt were fastened a spoon and a knife for eating and also a larger knife for self-defense, which was often necessary in those days.

This was the dress, on festival days, of old Anton, one of the oldest *pebersvende* of the Street of Small Houses, except that instead of the high-crowned hat, he wore a low bonnet and, under it, a knitted cap, a regular nightcap. He was so used to it that he was never without it; in fact, he had two exactly alike. He would have been just the right model for a painter, for he was as thin as a lath, wrinkled about the lips and eyes, and had gray, bushy eyebrows and long, bony fingers. Over his left eye hung a big tuft of hair, which certainly wasn't good-looking, but it made him a man easily recognized. He was known to have come from Bremen, though that was not his native town; his master lived there, but he himself had come from the town of Eisenach, in Thuringia, just below Wartburg Castle. Old Anton did not say much about these places, but he thought a good deal of them.

The old fellows of the street seldom gathered together; each remained in his own booth, which was shut up early every evening and then looked dark indeed, with only a faint ray of light showing through the little horn windowpane on the roof. Inside, the old clerk would be sitting on his bed, chanting the evening psalm from his German hymnbook, or he would be mulling over his household matters until far into the night; it was not a very pleasant life, by any means. The lot of a stranger in a strange land is a hard one; nobody pays any attention to one, unless he happens to get in the way.

When in the darkness of night, rain and sleet engulfed the street, this was a very gloomy and deserted place. There were no lamps here then, except a very small one that hung under the picture of the Blessed Virgin that was painted on the wall at one end of the street. Water could be heard rolling and splashing against the wharf by the castle, which the other end of the street faced. Such evenings are long and lonely and would be even more so if people had nothing to do. To unpack and pack, to polish one's scales, or to make paper bags is not necessary every day, and so one tries to find something else to do.

And that old Anton did; he sewed his own clothes and repaired his shoes. And when finally he went to bed, yes, he always kept his nightcap on, and drew it a little further down over his face, but then usually he soon pulled it up to enable him to see if his light was properly extinguished. He felt about it and pressed down the wick, then turned on the other side and lay down again. But often when he had done so, he had the thought, "I wonder if every coal in the little fire pan was really burned out; one little spark may be left; it could make the fire burn anew and cause trouble." And then he invariably got out of bed, crept down the stepladder—it could not be called a staircase—and yet when he got to the fire pan, there was never a single spark to be seen, and so he could go back to bed, feeling relieved. But he frequently got only halfway back and then began to wonder if he had drawn the iron bolt of the door and if the shutters were fastened; yes, then his skinny legs had to carry him down the steps again. He shivered and his teeth chattered when he crawled back into bed, for one often feels the cold more on going from it into a warm place. He always drew the blanket tighter and the nightcap closer over his eyes and then turned his thoughts away from the trade and troubles of the day, but this was not always pleasant. For then, old memories came and drew their curtains around him, and memories sometimes have sharp needles in them that pierce us until we cry "Oh!" They pierce the flesh and burn and bring tears to our eyes!

And so it was with old Anton; often hot tears, like the brightest pearls, came to his eyes and rolled down across the blanket or onto the floor; it was as if one of his heartstrings had broken; they seemed to smolder and then blaze forth in flames, illuminating pictures of his life that never faded from his heart. He always dried his eyes with his nightcap, wiping away the tears and pictures, though the source of these was still within him, deep in his heart. Whenever these pictures appeared before him, they didn't follow one another in the order of the actual happenings; the most painful ones came the oftenest, but the happier ones came quite frequently too, though these cast the deepest shadows.

"How beautiful the beech woods of Denmark are!" people often said. But far more beautiful to old Anton were the beech woods near Wartburg; mightier and more venerable than any Danish trees were the old oaks up by the proud, stately castle, where the ivy crept over the hard blocks of stone; the scent of the apple blossoms there was sweeter than any fragrance in the land of Denmark. He could remember it all very vividly.

A tear, big and bright, rolled down Anton's cheek. In this tear, he clearly saw two children playing, a little boy and a little girl. The boy had red cheeks, curly yellow hair, and honest blue eyes; he was little Anton, the son of the rich trader—himself, in fact. The little girl had brown eyes and black hair, and looked bright and clever; she was the burgomaster's daughter, Molly. The two children were playing with an apple, shaking it, and listening to the seeds rattle inside. Then they cut it in two and, between them, ate all but one seed, which the little girl suggested they plant in the ground.

"Then you'll see what will come of it! Something you would never expect; a whole apple tree will come out, but not right away!"

So they planted it in a flowerpot, both very excited over their work, the boy digging a hole in the earth with his fingers, the little girl dropping the seed into it, then both smoothing the earth over it.

"You mustn't dig it up again tomorrow to see if it has taken root," she said. "You must never do that! I did that with my flowers, but only twice. I just wanted to see if they were growing; I didn't know any better then, and the flowers died."

The flowerpot was left with Anton, and he looked at it every morning all winter long, but still saw nothing but the black earth. Then when spring came, and the sun shone warmly, two tiny green leaves peeped through.

"That's me and Molly! said Anton to himself. "That's beautiful! That's perfect!"

But soon there appeared a third leaf—now whom did that represent? Then another followed, and another; every day, every week, the plant grew bigger and bigger, until it became a tree.

And all this seemed to be reflected in that one big, bright tear that followed and then vanished so soon; but more such tears were quite likely to come forth from the fountain that was old Anton's heart.

Near Eisenach, there is a chain of rocky mountains, and one of them is curiously rounded and completely bare of trees, shrubbery, or grass. This is called Mount Venus, for within it dwells the Lady Venus, a goddess of old pagan times. Every child in Eisenach knows that Lady Venus—or Lady Holle, as she is sometimes called—lives here, and that once long ago, she lured into her home that noble knight, Tannhäuser, a minnesinger from the Wartburg circle of singers.

Anton and little Molly often walked near this mountain, and once she said to him, "Anton, do you dare knock at the mountain and say, 'Lady Venus, Lady Venus, open! Tannhäuser is here!'?" Anton did not dare do it, but Molly did. She spoke out loudly and clearly, but only the first words, "Lady Venus, Lady Venus!" The rest seemed to die away on her lips. Anton was sure she hadn't really said anything out loud. She kept her bold look, just as she did when sometimes she and the other little girls would meet him in the garden and try to kiss him simply because they knew he didn't like to be kissed and would push them away. She alone dared to. "I can kiss him!" she would say vainly, and put her arms around him. Anton never objected to anything she wanted to do. How pretty she was, and how clever!

Lady Venus in the mountain was said to be beautiful, too, but that was an evil spirit's alluring beauty; it was a very different beauty from that of the holy Elisabeth, patron saint of the country, the pious princess of Thuringia, whose good deeds were immortalized through stories and legends. Her picture hung in the chapel, lighted by lamps of silver; but she was not at all like Molly.

Year after year, the apple tree that the children had planted grew larger, until it had to be transplanted into the garden out in the fresh air; there the dew watered it and the sun shone warmly upon it and gave it strength to endure the long winter. And when the severity of winter was past, it seemed to put forth its blossoms purely from joy that the cold weather was gone. And that autumn it bore two apples, one for Molly and one for Anton; it could not very well do less.

Molly grew up quickly, like the apple tree itself, and she was as fresh as an apple blossom, but Anton could not much longer enjoy the sight of this flower. All things change! Molly's father left his old home, and Molly went with him, far away. In our day, the journey from Eisenach to the town that is still called Weimar takes only a few hours by railway, but then it took more than a whole day and a night. And Molly wept and Anton wept, but their tears united when they parted, and Molly told him that she loved him better than all the splendors of Weimar.

A year passed—two, three years passed—and during those three years only two letters came from her. One was brought by the regular carrier, and the second by a traveler; the route was long and hard, with many twistings, and through many different towns and villages.

Often Anton and Molly had listened to the sad old story of Tristan and Isolde, and whenever he had heard it, Anton had always imagined himself and Molly in their circumstances. But the name of Tristan, "one born in sorrow," did not fit him, he thought, nor would he ever be like Tristan in imagining that she whom he loved had forgotten him. That was so unjust! For Isolde never did really forget Tristan, and when both were dead, and buried on opposite sides of the church, the lime trees that grew from their graves met over the roof of the church and there their blossoms intermingled. Anton thought that story so lovely and yet so sad—but his and Molly's story should never be sad; and then he would gaily whistle a song by Walther von der Vogelweide, the minnesinger. "Under the lime tree on the heath," it began, and its chorus was so pretty:

Out in the wood, in the quiet dale,
Tandarai!
Sang so sweetly the nightingale!

This song was continually on his lips. He sang and whistled it all through one bright moonlit night as he rode along the deep defile, on the road to Weimar, to visit Molly. He wanted to arrive unexpectedly, and so he did.

He was welcomed warmly, with goblets full of wine, friendly company, a comfortable room, and a good bed, and yet it wasn't as he had imagined it. He did not understand himself or the others, but we can easily understand it. One can so often stay in a home with a family without taking root in any way; one talks as people talk in a carriage; one knows the people as people know each other in a carriage; mutual annoyances become irritations, until one wishes either oneself or one's neighbor were far away. It was something like this that Anton felt.

"I am an honest girl," Molly finally said to him, "and I want to tell you the truth. Much has changed since we were together as children; things are different, both inside and outside us. Habit and will have no control over our hearts. Anton, I don't want you to hate me, but soon I shall be far away from here. Believe me, I shall always think kindly of you, but love you—the way I know now I can love someone else—that I can't do. I never have loved you that way. You must reconcile yourself to this. Farewell, Anton!"

And Anton bade her farewell; he shed no tears, even though he felt he was no longer Molly's friend. The red-hot bar of iron and the frozen bar of iron will both tear the skin from our lips if we kiss them; Anton was as wild with hatred now as he had been with love before.

It didn't take Anton nearly the usual twenty-four hours to ride home to Eisenach, but his poor horse was ruined by his speed. "What does it matter?" he said. "I'm ruined, and I'll ruin everything that reminds me of her—Lady Venus, the false heathen! I shall cut down and smash the apple tree and tear up its roots; never shall it bloom or bear fruit again!"

But the apple tree was not felled; he himself was felled by a fever and brought to his bed. What could help him to rise again? A medicine was brought to him, the bitterest to be found, but with power to strengthen the sick body and the diseased mind.

Anton's father was no longer a rich merchant; dark days of trial were waiting at the door; misfortune, like a flood, poured in and streamed over the once rich house. The father had become a poor man, shattered by sadness and anxiety, and Anton had other things to occupy his mind besides his love grief and anger against Molly. He had to be both father and mother in that house; he had to keep things in order, to help in every way, really to pitch in and work; he even had to go out into the world and earn his bread.

He traveled to Bremen. There he experienced many a day of poverty and hardship, and these either strengthen or weaken the heart. How very different the world of real men and women was from the imaginary world of his childhood! What were the songs of the minnesingers to him now? Just so many empty words! Sometimes he felt that way, but then sometimes the old songs would sound in his soul again, and he would become pious in his attitude.

"God's will is best," he would then say. "It was good that our Lord did not let the heart of Molly cling to me, for how would it have ended, now that fortune has turned against me? She gave me up before she knew of this misfortune. Our Lord has been merciful toward me; all has been for the best, all things are ordered wisely. And she could not help herself; it was wrong of me to feel so bitter and angry!"

And years passed: Anton's father was dead, and now strangers lived in the old house. Yet Anton was to see his old home once more, for his wealthy master sent him on a journey that took him through his native town, Eisenach. Old Wartburg stood unchanged on the mountain, with its "Monk and Nun" carved in stone; the mighty oak trees lent the same majestic splendor to it all as they had in the time of his childhood; the Mountain of Venus still gleamed gray in its barrenness. He would gladly have said, "Lady Venus, Lady Venus! Open your mountain and take me in! Then, at least, I shall remain in my own country!" But that was a sinful thought, and so he crossed himself. A little bird was singing at a nearby bush, and this turned Anton's thoughts to the old minnesong.

> Out in the wood, in the quiet dale,
> Tandarai!
> How sweetly sang the nightingale!

He recalled so many things as he stood here and saw once again the home of his childhood; he was looking at it through a veil of tears. The house stood exactly as before, but the garden had been laid out anew; a road now crossed a corner of it, and the apple tree, which he had never destroyed, now was on the other side of the road. The sun shone on it, and the dew fell on it as before; the weight of its rich fruit bowed its branches almost to the earth. "It thrives," he said, "and that is good." However, one of the large branches of the tree had been broken off, the victim of cruel hands— but then, of course, the tree now stood close to the road.

"People tear off its blossoms without a word of thanks. They steal the fruit and break off the branches; one could say, speaking of a tree, as we do of a human, that at the tree's cradle no song was sung about what would be its fate. Its story began so delightfully, and what has happened to it? It's forsaken and forgotten, an orchard tree standing by a ditch along a highway! There it stands without protection—plucked at and broken! It won't die of that, but every year there will be fewer blossoms, and soon there will be no fruit at all—and, yes, then its story will be ended." Thus thought Anton under the old apple tree.

And these later were his thoughts on many a night in the lonely little room in the Street of Small Houses in Copenhagen. His wealthy master, a merchant of Bremen, had sent him there with the understanding that he would not marry. "Marry, indeed! Ha! Ha!" and Anton had laughed a strange and bitter laugh.

Winter had come early, and it was freezing cold. There was a snowstorm, so everyone not compelled to go out remained indoors. Thus it happened that Anton's neighbors didn't notice that his booth was not open for two whole days. Nor did he show himself, for who would go out in such weather if he didn't have to? These were gray, gloomy days. In the booth, where, of course, the windows were not made of glass, it appeared to be either twilight or dark night. During these two days, old

Anton never left his bed, for the bitter cold had sapped his strength and numbed his limbs. The old bachelor, the *pebersvend*, lay forsaken and unable to do more for himself than reach the water pitcher beside his bed, and now the last drop was gone. It was not a fever, not an illness; it was simply old age that had laid him low. There was almost continuous night about him where he lay. A tiny spider, which he couldn't see, contentedly and diligently spun its web above him, as if preparing some fine new crepe for mourning, in case his old eyes should close in death.

Long and dull were the hours; he had no tears, and he felt no pain. Molly was far from his thoughts now; it seemed that he no longer was a part of the world and its tumult, that he lay somewhere beyond it, with no one to remember him. For a moment, he felt hunger and thirst—yes, that was painful!—but no one came to help him, and no one was going to come.

His thoughts turned to others who had suffered; he remembered that the holy Elisabeth, the patron saint of his homeland, the magnanimous sovereign of Thuringia, had visited the humblest cottages and administered comfort and nourishment to the sick and needy. His thoughts brightened as he reflected upon her good deeds; he recalled the pious words of hope and trust in God which she had spoken to those poor sufferers, how she had bound up their wounds and brought food to the hungry, although her cruel husband had forbidden it. He remembered the legend about her— how, as she passed along with a basket packed with food and wine, her husband, who had been following her, suddenly rushed forward and asked her angrily what it was she carried in her basket. Terrified, she replied, "These are only roses I have picked in the garden." Whereupon he tore back the cloth from the basket—and, lo, a miracle had been performed for the pious woman—the bread, the wine, and all else in the basket had been changed into the loveliest roses!

Thus lived the gentle saint in the thoughts of old Anton, and thus she stood vividly before his failing eyes, beside his bed in the wretched wooden booth in the land of Denmark. He uncovered his head and looked up into her kindly eyes; brightness surrounded him, and sweet, fragrant roses sprang up all about him! Then a different fragrance, that of apple blossoms, reached him; he saw a flowering apple tree, and it was spreading its branches over him; it was the tree that had grown from the little seed he and Molly had planted.

And the tree sprinkled its fragrant petals upon him, and they cooled his hot forehead; they fell upon his parched lips and seemed to strengthen him like wine and bread; they fell upon his breast, and now he felt so relieved, so protected, and wanted to sleep.

"Now I'll sleep," he whispered softly. "Sleep will be good for me; tomorrow I shall be up again, well and strong. Beautiful, beautiful! The apple tree planted in love! I can see it now in glory!" And then he slept.

The next day—the third after his booth had been closed—the snow ceased, and old Anton's neighbor from across the way came to see what had happened to him. There he lay, dead, holding between his clasped hands his old nightcap. He did not wear this one when he lay in his coffin; he had another, clean and white, on then.

Where were now the tears he had shed? What had become of the pearls of his memories? They were left in his nightcap, and in the cap they remained, for the genuine ones are never lost in the washing. The old thoughts, the old dreams, all were left in the nightcap of the *pebersvend*. Don't wish for that nightcap for yourself! It will make your forehead too hot, your pulse race too fast, and will bring dreams as vivid as reality.

This was experienced by the first man who wore the cap after Anton, though this was half a century later. He was the burgomaster himself, a very prosperous man, with a wife and eleven children; but he promptly dreamed of unhappy love, bankruptcy, and hard times.

"Oh, how hot this nightcap makes you!" he said, tearing it off, as one pearl after another trickled down and glittered before his eyes. "It must be the gout!" said the burgomaster. "Something glitters before my eyes!"

What he saw were tears shed half a hundred years before—shed by old Anton of Eisenach.

Everyone who later wore the nightcap had visions and dreams. The life of each became like Anton's. This grew to be quite a story—in fact, many stories—but we shall leave it to others to tell these. We have told the first of them, and we conclude with these words—don't ever wish for the nightcap of the *pebersvend*.

SOMETHING (1858)

I'm going to be Something!" said the eldest of five brothers. "I'm going to be useful in the world, however humble a position I hold; if that which I'm doing is useful, that will be Something. I'll make bricks; people can't do without bricks, so at least I'll do Something."

"But Something very unimportant," said the second brother. "What you'd be doing would be as good as nothing! That's a laborer's job and can be done by a machine. No, you'd better become a mason; that's really Something, and that's what I'm going to be. That is a position! Then you belong to a guild and become a citizen, have a banner of your own and your own quarters at the inn. Yes, and if things come out well, I may get to be a master, and have workmen under me, and my wife will be known as the master's wife. That will be Something!"

"That's nothing at all," said the third. "Just think how many different classes there are in a town far above a master mason. You may be an honest man, but even as a master, you'll only be what is called 'common.' No, I know Something better than that. I'll be an architect, will live among the thinkers, the artists; I'll raise myself up to the intellectual aristocracy. Of course, I may have to begin at the bottom; yes, I might as well say it—I will have to start as a carpenter's boy, wearing a cap, though I'm used to wearing a silk hat, and to fetch beer and spirits for the simple workmen, and listen to their insults. Of course, that's irritating, but I'll try to pretend it's only a masquerade. 'Tomorrow,' I'll say, 'when I'm a journeyman, I'll be on my own course, and I'll have nothing to do with the others.' Yes, I'll go to the academy, learn to draw, and get to be an architect. That is Something! That's a whole lot! I may even get a title—yes, have one placed before or after my name; and I shall build and build, as others have done before me. Yes, that's Something one can rely on; it's Something wholly worthwhile."

"But Something that I care nothing about," said the fourth. "I shouldn't care to travel on and on in the beaten track, to be only a copyist. I want to be a genius, cleverer than all of you put together. I want to create a new style, provide the idea for a building suitable to the climate and materials of our country, our national character, and the development of our age; besides, I want to build an extra floor for my own genius!"

"But suppose the climate and materials aren't good," said the fifth. "That will be very unfortunate, since they are of vital importance. As for our national character, to represent that in architecture would be sheer affectation, while the requirements of modern times may cause you to run wild, as youth frequently does. I can see that none of you will ever amount to anything, however much you yourselves think you will. But do as you like; I won't be like you. I shall consider what you do; there's something ridiculous in everything; I'll discover it, and it will be my business to expose it—that will be Something!"

He did as he promised; and people said of this fifth brother, "There's Something in him, certainly; he has plenty of brains, but he doesn't do anything!" But it was just that which made him Something.

This is only a little story, and yet as long as the world exists, it will have no end.

But, then, did nothing more become of the five brothers? Listen further now, and you will hear the whole story.

The eldest brother, the brickmaker, found that every brick he made brought him in a small copper coin. It was only copper, but enough of these small copper coins added together could be changed into a bright dollar, and wherever he knocked with this— at the butcher's, the baker's, or the tailor's, yes, everywhere—the door flew open, and he was given what he wanted.

That was the virtue of his bricks. Of course, some of them crumbled or broke in two, but a use was found even for them. You see, old Mother Margaret wanted so much to build herself a little house up by the dike, so all the broken bricks were given to her, and even a few whole ones too, for though he was only a brickmaker, the eldest brother had a generous heart. The poor woman built her house with her own hands; it was very narrow; its one window was all lopsided; the door was too low, and the thatching might have been laid on the roof more skillfully, but it gave her shelter and a home and could be seen from far out at sea. The sea in all its power sometimes broke over the dike and sprinkled a salty shower over the little house, which still stood there years after he who made its bricks was dead and gone.

As for the second brother—yes, he could now build in a different fashion, as he had decided to learn. When he had served his apprenticeship, he buckled on his knapsack and started out on his travels, singing as he went. When he came back to his hometown, he became a master mason there and built house after house, a whole street of houses. There they stood, looking very handsome and giving an air of dignity to the town; and these houses soon built him a little house for himself. But how can houses build a house? If you ask the houses they will give you no answer, but the people will reply, "Why, of course, the street built him his house!" It was not very large, and had only a clay floor, but when he and his young bride danced over it, that floor became as smooth as if it had been polished, and from every stone in the wall sprung a flower, gay as the costliest tapestry. It was a charming house, and they were indeed a happily married couple. The banner of the Masons' Guild waved gaily outside, and workmen and apprentices shouted, "Hurray!" Yes indeed, that was Something! And at last he died—and that was Something, too!

Next comes the third brother, the architect. He had begun as a carpenter's apprentice, wearing a cap and running errands all over town; but from the academy, he had steadily risen to become a builder. If the street of houses had built a house for his brother the mason, the street took its very name from the architect; his was the handsomest house in the whole street—that was Something, and he was Something, with a long title before and after his name. His children could boast of their "birth"; and when he died his widow was a lady of standing—that is Something—and his name was on the corner of the street as well as on everybody's lips—that is Something indeed!

Then comes the fourth brother, the genius who had wanted to invent something new and original and have an extra floor on top of that. But that floor gave way once beneath his feet, so that he fell and broke his neck. However, he had a splendid funeral, with music and banners, and flowery obituaries in the newspapers. Three eulogies were spoken over him, one longer than the other, and that would have pleased him, for he had so loved being talked about. Then a monument was erected over his grave— only one story high, but still that is Something!

So now he was dead, along with his three elder brothers. The youngest one, the critic, outlived them all, and that was quite proper, for it gave him the last word, which to him was a matter of great importance. "He has a good head on him," people said. But at last his hour came, too; he died, and his soul went to the gates of Heaven. Souls always enter in couples, so there he stood beside another soul, old Mother Margaret from the house by the dike.

"I suppose it is for the sake of contrast that I and this miserable soul should come here at the same time," said the critic. "Well, now, my good woman," he asked, "who are you? Do you also want to go in there?"

The old woman curtsied as well as she could, thinking it was Saint Peter himself who spoke to her. "I am just a poor old soul with no family. Just old Margaret from the house near the dike."

"I see. And what have you done down below?"

"I have done really nothing in the world, nothing at all to warrant my being admitted here. It will be God's mercy, indeed, if I am allowed to pass through this gate."

It bored the critic to stand there waiting, so he felt he must talk about something. "And how did you leave the world?" he asked carelessly.

"How did I leave it? Well, I hardly know how; I was sick and miserable indeed in the last few years, and could hardly bear to creep out of bed at all in the cold and frosty weather. It has been a hard winter, but that's all past now. For a few days, as your reverence must know, the wind was quite still, but it was bitterly cold; the ice covered the water as far as you could see. Everybody in town was out on the ice, where there was what they called ski racing, and dancing, I think, with music, and entertainment. I could hear it where I lay in my poor room. And along toward evening, the moon came up, but it still wasn't very bright. From my bed, I looked through the window and saw a strange white cloud rising up over the sea. I lay there and watched it, watched the black spot in it grow bigger and bigger, and then I knew what it meant; you don't see that sign very often, but I was old and experienced. I knew it, and horror crept over me. Just twice before in my life had I seen that sign, and I knew it meant there would be a terrible storm and a flash flood; it would burst over the poor people who were drinking and dancing and making merry, out there on the ice. Young and old, the whole town was there; who could warn them if no one saw the cloud or could recognize it as I could? I felt so terrified that it gave me more strength than I'd had in many years. I felt alive all over. I got out of bed and managed to get over to the window; I couldn't drag myself any farther, but I did get the window open; I could see the people dancing on the ice and the gaily colored flags, I could hear the boys shouting and the young men and women singing; all were so merry. But that white cloud with its black spot rose higher and higher. I screamed as loudly as I could, but they were all too far away to hear me. Soon the storm would break loose; the ice would be smashed into pieces, and all the people would be drowned! They could not hear me; I wasn't able to get out to them; how could I get them onto land? Then our Lord sent me the idea of setting fire to my bed; it would be better for my house to be burned to the ground than for so many people to meet a miserable death. So I made a light, and saw the red flame leap up! Somehow, I got out of the door, but then I fell and lay there, for I could not rise again. But the flames burst out through the window and the roof; the people down below saw it and all ran as fast as they could to help me, the poor old woman they were afraid would be burned; there was not one who didn't come to my aid. I heard them come, but then, too, I heard a sudden roaring in the air, and then a thundering like the shots of heavy cannons; the flood was breaking up the ice, and it was all crumbling to pieces. However, the people had all come off the ice to the trenches, where the sparks were flying about me; I had saved all of them. But I couldn't stand the cold and the fright, and so I came up here to the gates of Heaven. Do you think they can be opened to such a wretched old creature as I? I have no little house now by the dike, though I guess that fact will not gain me admission here."

Then the heavenly gates opened, and the Angel bade poor old Margaret to enter. As she crossed the threshold, she dropped a straw, one of the straws from the bed she had set afire to save the people on the ice, and lo! It changed into the purest gold—gold that grew and twisted itself into the most beautiful shapes!

"See, this was brought by the poor woman," said the Angel. "Now what do you bring? Yes, I know full well that you have made nothing, not even bricks. If only you could go back and return here with at least one brick, not that it would be good for anything when you had made it, but because anything, the very last thing, if done with a kindly heart, is Something. But you cannot return, and I can do nothing for you."

Then the poor soul, the old woman from the hut by the dike, spoke up for him. "His brother gave me all the bricks and broken pieces I used to build my miserable shack—that was great generosity to a poor old soul like me. Cannot all those bits and pieces, put together, be considered one brick for him? It would be an act of mercy; he needs mercy, and this is the very home of mercy."

"Your brother, he whom you called the humblest," said the Angel, "he whose honest labor seemed to you the lowliest, sends you this heavenly gift. You shall not be turned away, but shall be permitted to stand here outside and consider your manner of life below. But you shall not enter, not before you have done a good deed and thereby accomplished—Something!"

"I could have said that much better," thought the critic, but he didn't say it out loud. And for him that was already—Something!

THE OLD OAK TREE'S LAST DREAM (1858)

In the woods, on a high bank near the open seashore, there stood such a very old oak tree. It was exactly 365 years old, but this long span of years seemed to the tree scarcely longer than as many days do to people like us. A tree's life is not the same as a man's. We are awake during the day, and sleep at night, and we have our dreams.

It is different with a tree; it is awake throughout three seasons, and not until winter comes does it go to sleep. Winter is its time for sleeping; that is its night after the long day which we call spring, summer, and autumn.

Many a warm summer day the mayflies danced around its crown, lived happily and felt fortunate as they flitted about; and if one of the tiny creatures rested from its blissful play for a moment on a large oak leaf, the tree always said, "Poor little insect! Your whole life is but one day long! How sad!"

"Sad?" the little mayfly always answered. "What do you mean by that? Everything is so bright and warm and beautiful, and I am so happy!"

"But only for one day, and then all is over."

"Over?" said the mayfly. "What does over mean? Is it also over for you?"

"No, I shall live perhaps thousands of your days, and a day for me lasts a whole year. That is something so long you can't even figure it out."

"No, I don't understand you at all. You have thousands of my days to live, but I have thousands of moments in which to be happy and joyous. Will all the beauty of this world die when you die?"

"No," said the tree. "It will probably last longer, infinitely longer, than I am able to imagine."

"Well, then, we each have an equally long lifetime, only we figure differently."

And so the mayfly danced and glided in the air, with its fine, artistic wings of veil and velvet, rejoicing in the warm air that was so perfumed with delicious scents from the clover field and the wild roses, elders, and honeysuckles of the hedges, not ot speak of the bluebells, cowslip, and wild thyme; the fragrance was so strong that the tiny insect felt a little intoxicated from it. The day was long and beautiful, full of happiness and sweet experiences, and by sunset, the little May fly was pleasantly weary from all the excitement. Its dainty wings would no longer support it; very gently it glided down onto the cool, rocking blades of grass, nodded its head as a mayfly can, and fell into a very peaceful slumber; it was dead.

"Poor little mayfly," said the Oak; "that was really too short a life!"

And every summer day was repeated the same dance, the same question, the same answer, and the same peaceful falling asleep; it happened through many generations of mayflies, and all of them were lighthearted and happy.

The Oak stood wide awake through its spring morning, its summer noon, and autumn evening; soon now it would be sleeping time, the tree's night, for winter was coming. Already the winds were singing, "Good night! Good night! There falls a leaf; there falls a leaf! We plucked it, we plucked it! See that you go to sleep! We will sing you to sleep, we will rock you to sleep! Surely it will do your old limbs good. They crackle from pure contentment. Sleep sweetly, sleeep sweetly! This is your 365th night, but you are really only a yearling! Sleep sweetly! The skies are sprinkling snow; it will spread a warm coverlet over your feet. Sleep sweetly and have pleasant dreams!"

And now the great Oak stood stripped of its foliage, ready to rest throughout the long winter, and in its sleep to dream of something that had happened to it, just as men dream.

The tree had once been very small; yes, an acorn had been its cradle. According to human calculation, it was now in its fourth century; it was the tallest and mightiest tree in the forest; its crown towered high above all the other trees and could be seen far out at sea, where it served as a landmark to ships. The Oak had never thought of how many eyes sought it out from the watery distance. High up in its green crown, the wood doves had built their nests, and there the cuckoo made its voice heard; and in the autumn, when its leaves looked like hammered-out copper plates, the birds of passage rested awhile there before flying on across the seas. But now it was winter; the tree was leafless, and the bowed and gnarled branches showed their dark outlines; crows and jackdaws came to gossip about the hard times that were beginning and how difficult it was to find food in the winter.

It was just at the holy Christmastime that the Oak dreamed its most beautiful dream—and this we shall hear.

The tree had a distinct feeling that it was a holiday season. It seemed to hear all the church bells ringing round about, and at that the day was mild and warm, like a lovely summer day. The Oak spread its mighty crown; sunbeams flickered among the leaves and branches, and the air was filled with the fragrance of herbs and blossoms. Colored butterflies played tag, and the mayflies danced, which was the only way they could show their happiness. All that the tree had encountered and witnessed through the many years passed by as if in a holiday procession.

Knights and ladies of bygone days, with feathers in their caps and hawks on their wrists, rode gaily through the forest; dogs barked, and the hunting horn sounded. The tree saw hostile soldiers, in shining armor and gaily colored garments, with spears and halberds, pitching their tents and then striking them again; the watchfire blazed, and they sang and then slept under the tree's protecting boughs. It saw lovers meet in quiet happiness there in the moonlight and carve their names, or their initials, on the gray-green bark. At one time, many years before, a guitar and an Aeolian harp had been hung up in the Oak's boughs by carefree traveling youths; now they hung there again, and now once more their lovely music sounded. The wood doves cooed, as if they were trying to express what the tree felt, and the cuckoo announced many more summer days it had to live.

Then it seemed that a new and stronger current of life flowed through the Oak, down into its smallest roots, up into its highest twigs, even out into the leaves! The tree felt that it was stretching; it could feel how life and warmth stirred down in the earth about its roots; it felt the strength increase and that it was growing taller and taller. The trunk shot up; there was no rest for the tree; it grew more and more; its crown became fuller; it spread and towered. And as the tree grew, its strength grew also, as did its ardent yearning to reach higher and higher toward the bright, warm sun.

Already it was high above the clouds, which drifted far below it, like a troop of dark migratory birds or like flocks of white swans.

And every leaf of the tree could see as if it had eyes; the stars became visible to them by daylight, large and bright, all shining, like very clear, mild eyes. They reminded the Oak of dear, kindly eyes it had known, the eyes of children, the eyes of lovers, who had met beneath the tree.

It was a blessed moment, so full of joy! And yet in all its joy, the Oak felt a longing, a great desire that all the other trees below, all the bushes, plants, and flowers of the forest, might be lifted up with it to share in its glory and gladness. Amid all its dream of splendor, the mighty Oak could not be fully happy without all the others, small and great, sharing in it, and this yearning thrilled through boughs and leaves as fervently, as strongly, as it would within a human heart.

The crown of the tree bowed and looked back, as if it sought someting it had missed. Then it felt the thyme and soon the still stronger scent of honeysuckle and violet, and imagined it could hear the cuckoo talking to itself.

Yes, and now the green tops of the forest peeped up through the clouds. The Oak saw that the other trees below were growing and lifting themselves up as it had; bushes and plants rose high into the air, some even tearing themselves loose from their roots, to soar up all the faster. The birch grew the most rapidly; like a white flash of lightning its slender stem shot up, its boughs waving like green gauze and banners. The whole forest, even the feathery brown reeds, grew high into the sky; the birds followed and sang, and on the grass that waved to and fro like long, green silken ribbons, the grasshopper sat, and drummed with his wings against his lean legs. The cockchafers hummed and the bees buzzed and every bird sang to the best of its ability; song and happiness were everywhere, right up into Heaven.

"But the little red flower by the water—that should come along!" said the Oak tree. "And the bluebell flower, and the little daisy!" Yes, the Oak wanted to have them all with it.

"We are here! We are with you!" they sang and rang out.

"But the pretty anemones of last summer—and the mass of lilies of the valley of the year before that—and the wild crabapple tree that bloomed so beautifully—and all the beauties of the forest, throughout the many years—if only they had lived on and remained till now, then they also could have been with us!"

"We are here! We are with you!" they sang and rang out, even higher up; it seemed that they had ascended before the others.

"No, this is too wonderful to be true!" rejoiced the Oak. "I have them all with me; small and great, not one is forgotten! How can all this blessedness be conceivable and possible?"

"In the kingdom of God, all things are conceivable and possible," came the mighty answer.

And the tree, which continued to grow, felt its very roots loosening themselves from the earth. "This is the best of all," it said. "Now no bonds shall hold me; I can soar upward to the heights of glory and light! And my loved ones are all with me, small and great—all with me!"

"All!"

That was the dream of the Oak tree, and while it dreamed on that holy Christmas Eve, a mighty storm was sweeping over land and sea. The ocean piled its heavy billows onto the shore; the tree cracked, groaned, and was torn up by the roots, at the very moment when it was dreaming that its roots were freeing themselves from the earth. It fell. Its 365 years were now as a day is to the mayfly.

Christmas morning, when the sun rose, the storm was past. All the church bells rang, while from every chimney, even the smallest one, on the peasant's hut, the blue smoke curled upward, like sacrificial steam rising from the altars of the ancient Druids. The sea became more and more calm, and aboard a big vessel that had weathered the storm of the night before, all flags were hoisted now in greeting to the Yuletide. "The tree is gone—the old oak tree that was our landmark!" said the sailors. "It must have fallen during the storm last night. What can ever replace it? Nothing!"

That was the tree's eulogy, brief but sincere. There it lay, stretched out on the carpet of snow near the shore, while over it sounded the hymn sung on the ship, sung in thanksgiving for the joy of Christmas, for the bliss of the human soul's salvation through Christ, for the gift of eternal life:

> Sing loud, sweet angel, on Christmas morn.
> Hallelujah! Christ the Savior is born.
> In joy receive His blessing.
> Hallelujah! Hallelujah!

Thus sounded the old hymn, and everyone aboard the ship felt himself lifted heavenward by the hymn, and by prayer, even as the old tree had lifted itself in its last, most beautiful dream that Christmas Eve.

THE MARSH KING'S DAUGHTER (1858)

The storks tell many, many stories to their young ones, all about the bogs and marshes. In general, each story is suited to the age and sense of the little storks. While the youngest ones are satisfied with, "Kribble-krabble, plurry-murry," and think it a very fine story, the older ones demand something with more sense to it, or at least something about the family.

Of the two oldest stories which have been handed down among the storks, we all know the one about Moses, who was put by his mother on the banks of the Nile, where a king's daughter found him. How well she brought him up, how he became a great man, and how no one knows where he lies buried, are things that we all have heard.

The other tale is not widely known, perhaps because it is almost a family story. This tale has been handed down from one mother stork to another for a thousand years, and each succeding storyteller has told it better and better, and now we shall tell it best of all.

The first pair of storks who told this tale and who themselves played a part in it, had their summer home on the roof of the Viking's wooden castle up by the Wild Marsh in Vendsyssel. If we must be precise about our knowledge, this is in the country of Hjorring, high up near Skagen in Jutland. There is still a big marsh there, which we can read about in the official reports of that district. It is said that the place once lay under the sea, but the land has risen somewhat and is now a wilderness extending for many a mile. One is surrounded on all sides by marshy meadows, quagmires, and peat bogs, overgrown by cloud berries and stunted trees. Dank mists almost always hang over the place, and about seventy years ago, wolves still made their homes there. Well may it be called the Wild Marsh. Think how desolate it was, and how much swamp and water there must have been among all those marshes and ponds a thousand years ago! Yet in most matters, it must have looked then as it looks now. The reeds grew just as high, and had the same long leaves and feathery tips of a purplish-brown tint that they have now. Birch trees grew there with the same white bark and the same airily dangling leaves. As for the living creatures, the flies have not changed the cut of their gauzy apparel, and the favorite colors of the storks were white trimmed with black, and long red stockings.

However, people dressed very differently from the fashion of today. But if any of them—thrall or huntsman, it mattered not—set foot in the quagmire, they fared the same a thousand years ago as they would fare today. In they would fall, and down they would sink to him whom they call the Marsh King, who rules below throughout the entire marsh land. They also call him King of the Quicksands, but we like the name Marsh King better, and that was what the storks called him. Little or nothing is known about his rule, but perhaps that is just as well.

Near the marsh and close to the Liim Fjord, lay wooden castle of the Vikings, three stories high from its watertight stone cellars to the tower on its roof. The storks had built their nest on this roof, and there the mother stork sat hatching her eggs. She was certain they would be hatched.

One evening, the father stork stayed out rather late, and when he got home, he looked ruffled and flurried.

"I have something simply dreadful to tell you," he said to the mother stork.

"Then you had better keep it to yourself," she told him. "Remember, I am hatching eggs! If you frighten me, it might have a very bad effect on them."

"But I must tell you," he insisted. "The daughter of our Egyptian host has come here. She has ventured to take this long journey, and—she's lost!"

"She who comes of fairy stock? Speak up. You know that I must not be kept in suspense while I'm on my eggs."

"It's this way, Mother. Just as you told me, she must have believed the doctor's advice. She believed that the swamp flowers up here would cure her sick father, and she has flown here in the guise of a swan, together with two other princesses who put on swan plumage and fly north every year, to take the baths that keep them young. She has come, and she is lost."

"You make your story too long-winded," the mother stork protested. "My eggs are apt to catch cold. I can't bear such suspense at a time like this."

"I have been keeping my eyes open," said the father stork, "and this evening I went among the reeds where the quagmire will barely support me. There I saw three swans flying my way. There was something about their flight that warned me, 'See here! These are not real swans. These creatures are merely disguised in swan feathers!' You know as well as I do, Mother, that one feels instinctively whether a thing is true or false."

"To be sure, I do," said she. "But tell me about the princess. I am tired of hearing about swan feathers."

"Well," the father stork said, "as you know, in the middle of the marsh, there is a sort of pool. You can catch a glimpse of it from here if you will rise up a trifle. There, between the reeds and the green scum of the pool, a large alder stump juts up. On it the three swans alighted, flapped their wings and looked about them. One of them threw off her swan plumage and immediately I could see that she was the princess from our home in Egypt. There she sat with no other cloak than her own long hair. I heard her ask the others to take good care of her swan feathers, while she dived down in the water to pluck the swamp flower which she fancied she saw there. They nodded, and held their heads high as they picked up her empty plumage.

"'What are they going to do with it?' I wondered, and she must have wondered, too. Our answer came soon enough, for they flew up in the air with her feather garment.

"'Dive away,' they cried. 'Never more shall you fly about as a swan. Never more shall you see the land of Egypt. You may have your swamp forever.' They tore her swan guise into a hundred pieces, so that feathers whirled around like a flurry of snow. Then away they flew, those two deceitful princesses."

"Why, that's dreadful," the mother stork said. "I can't bear to listen. Tell me what happened next."

"The princess sobbed and lamented. Her tears sprinkled down on the alder stump, and the stump moved, for it was the Marsh King himself, who lives under the quagmire. I saw the stump turn, and this was no longer a tree stump that stretched out its two muddy, branchlike arms toward the poor girl. She was so frightened that she jumped out on the green scum which cannot bear my weight, much less hers. She was instantly swallowed up, and it was the alder stump, which plunged in after her, that dragged her down. Big black bubbles rose, and these were the last traces of them. She is now buried in the Wild Marsh, and never will she get back home to Egypt with the flowers she came to find. Mother, you could not have endured the sights I saw."

"You ought not to tell me such a tale at a time like this. Our eggs may be the worse for it. The princess can look out for herself. Someone will surely help her. Now if it had been I, or you, or any of our family, it would have been all over with us."

"I shall look out for her, every day," said the father stork, and he did so.

A long time went by, but one day, he saw a green stalk shooting up from the bottom of the pool. When it came to the surface, it grew a leaf, which got broader and broader, and then a bud appeared. As the stork was flying by one morning, the bud opened in the strong sunbeams, and in the center of it lay a beautiful child, a baby girl who looked as fresh as if she had just come from her bath. So closely did the baby resemble the princess from Egypt that the stork thought it was she, who had become a child again. But when he considered the matter, he decided that this child who lay in the cup of a water lily must be the daughter of the princess and the Marsh King.

"She cannot remain there," the stork said to himself, "yet my nest is already overcrowded. But I have an idea. The Viking's wife hasn't any children, although she is always wishing for a little one. I'm often held responsible for bringing children, and this time I shall really bring one. I shall fly with this baby to the Viking's wife. What joy there will be."

The stork picked up the little girl, flew with her to the log castle, pecked a hole with his beak in the piece of bladder that served as a window pane, and laid the baby in the arms of the Viking woman. Then he flew home to his wife and told her all about it. The baby storks listened attentively, for they were old enough now to be curious.

"Just think! The princess is not dead," he told them. "She sent her little one up to me, and I have found a good home for it."

"I told you to start with that it would come out all right," said the mother stork. "Turn your thoughts now to your own children. It is almost time for us to start on our long journey. I am beginning to tingle under my wings. The cuckoo and the nightingale have flown already, and I heard the quail saying that we shall soon have a favorable wind. Our young ones will do us credit on the flight, or I don't know my own children."

How pleased the Viking's wife was when she awoke in the morning and found the lovely child in her arms. She kissed it and caressed it, but it screamed frightfully and thrashed about with its little arms and legs. There was no pleasing it until at last it cried itself to sleep, and as it lay there, it was one of the loveliest little creatures that anyone ever saw. The Viking's wife was so overjoyed that she felt light-headed as well as light-hearted. She turned quite hopeful about everything, and felt sure that her husband and all his men might return as unexpectedly as the little one had come to her. So she set herself and her entire household to work, in order to have everything in readiness. The long, colored tapestry on which she and her handmaidens had embroidered figures of their gods—Odin, Thor, and Freya, as they were called— were hung in place. The thralls were set to scouring and polishing the old shields that decorated the walls; cushions were laid on the benches; and dry logs were stacked on the fireplace in the middle of the hall, so that the pile might be lighted at a moment's notice. The Viking's wife worked so hard that she was tired out, and slept soundly when evening came.

Along toward morning she awoke, and was greatly alarmed to find no trace of her little child. She sprang up, lighted a splinter of pine wood, and searched the room. To her astonishment, she found at the foot of her bed not the beautiful child, but a big, ugly frog. She was so appalled that she took up a heavy stick to kill the creature, but it looked at her with such strange, sad eyes that she could not strike. As she renewed her search, the frog gave a faint, pitiful croak. She sprang from the bed to the window, and threw open the shutter. The light of the rising sun streamed in and fell upon that big frog on the bed. It seemed as if the creature's wide mouth contracted into small, red lips. The frog legs unbent as the most exquisitely shaped limbs, and it was her lovely little child that lay there, and not that ugly frog.

"What's all this?" she exclaimed. "Have I had a nightmare? This is my pretty little elf lying here." She kissed it and pressed it affectionately to her heart, but it struggled and tried to bite, like the kitten of a wild cat.

Neither that day nor the next did her Viking husband come home. Though he was on his way, the winds were against him. They were blowing southward to speed the storks. A fair wind for one is a foul wind for another.

In the course of a few days and nights, it became plain to the Viking's wife how things were with the little child. It was under the influence of some terrible spell of sorcery. By day it was as lovely as a fairy child, but it had a wicked temper. At night, on the contrary, it was an ugly frog, quiet and pathetic, with sorrowful eyes. Here were two natures that changed about both inwardly and outwardly. This was because the little girl whom the stork had brought had by day her mother's appearance, together with her father's temper. But at night, she showed her kinship with him in her outward form, while her mother's mind and heart inwardly became hers. Who would be able to release her from this powerful spell of sorcery that lay upon her? The Viking's wife felt most anxious and distressed about it, yet her heart went out to the poor little thing.

She knew that when her husband came home she would not dare tell him of this strange state of affairs, for he would certainly follow the custom of those times and expose the poor child on the high road, to let anyone take it who would. The Viking's good-natured wife had not the heart to do this, so she determined that he should only see the child in the daytime.

At daybreak one morning, the wings of storks were heard beating over the roof. During the night, more than a hundred pairs of storks had rested there, and now they flew up to make their way to the south.

"Every man ready," was their watchword. "Let the wives and children make ready, too."

"How light we feel!" clacked the little storks. "We tingle and itch right down to our toes, as if we were full of live frogs. How fine it feels to be traveling to far-off lands."

"Keep close in one flock," cried their father and mother. "Don't clack your beaks so much, it's bad for your chest."

And away they went.

At that very instant, the blast of a horn rang over the heath, to give notice that the Viking had landed with all of his men. They came home with rich booty from the Gaelic coast, where, as in Britain, the terrified people sang, "Deliver us from the wild Northmen."

What a lively bustle now struck this Viking's castle near the Wild Marsh! A cask of mead was rolled out into the hall, the pile of wood was lighted, and horses were slaughtered. What a feast they were going to have! Priests sprinkled the horses' warm blood over the thralls as a blood offering. The fires crackled, the smoke rolled up to the roof, and soot dropped down from the beams, but they were used to that. Guests were invited and were given handsome presents. Old grudges and double-dealings were forgotten. They all drank deep and threw the gnawed bones in each other's faces, but that was a sign of good humor. The skald, a sort of minstrel but at the same time a fighting man who had been with them and knew what he sang about, trolled them a song, in which he told of all their valiant deeds in battle, and all their wonderful adventures. After each verse came the same refrain:

> *Fortunes perish, friends die, one dies oneself,*
> *But a glorious name never dies!*

Then they all banged their shields, and rattled on the table with their knives or the knucklebones, making a terrific noise.

The Viking's wife sat on the bench that ran across this public banquet hall. She wore a silken dress with gold bracelets and big amber beads. She was in her finest attire, and the skald included her in his song. He spoke of the golden treasure which she had brought her rich husband. This husband of hers rejoiced in the lovely child whom he had seen only by day, in all its charming beauty. The savage temper that went with her daytime beauty rather pleased him, and he said that she might grow up to be a stalwart soldier maid, able to hold her own—the sort who would not flinch if a skilled hand, in fun, took a sharp sword and cut off her eyebrows for practice.

The mead cask was emptied, a full one was rolled in, and it too was drunk dry. These were folk who could hold a great deal. They were familiar with the old proverb to the effect that, "The cattle know when to quit their pasture, but a fool never knows the measure of his stomach."

Yes, they all knew it quite well, but people often know the right thing and do the wrong thing. They also knew that, "One wears out his welcome when he sits too long in another man's house," but they stayed on, for all that. Meat and mead are such good things, and they were a jovial crew. That night the thralls slept on the warm ashes, dipped their fingers into the fat drippings, and licked them. Oh yes, those were glorious days.

The Vikings ventured forth on one more raid that year, though the storms of autumn were beginning to blow. The Viking and his men went to the coast of Britain—"just across the water," he said—and his wife stayed at home with her little girl. It soon came about that the foster mother cared more for the poor frog with its sad eyes and pathetic croaking, than for the little beauty who scratched and bit everyone who came near her.

The raw, dank mist of fall invaded the woods and thickets. "Gnaw-worms," they called it, for it gnawed the leaves from the trees. "Pluck-feathers," as they called the snow, fell in flurry upon flurry, for winter was closing in. Sparrows took over the stork nest and gossiped about the absent owners, as tenants will. The two storks and all their young ones—where were they now?

The storks were now in the land of Egypt, where the sun shone as warm as it does upon us on a fine summer day. Tamarind and acacia trees bloomed in profusion, and the glittering crescent of Mohammed topped the domes of all the mosques. On the slender minarets many a pair of storks rested after their long journey. Whole flocks of them nested together on the columns of ancient temples and the ruined arches of forgotten cities. The date palm lifted its high screen of branches, like a parasol in the sun. The gray-white pyramids were sharply outlined against the clear air of the desert, where the ostrich knew he could use his legs and the lion crouched to gaze with big solemn eyes at the marble sphinx half buried in the sand. The waters of the Nile had receded, and the delta was alive with frogs. The storks considered this the finest sight in all the land, and the young storks found it hard to believe their own eyes. Yes, everything was wonderful.

"See! It is always like this in our southern home," their mother told them. And their little bellies tingled at the spectacle.

"Do we see any more?" they asked. "Shall we travel on into the country?"

"There is nothing else worth seeing," their mother said. "Beyond this fertile delta lie the deep forests, where the trees are so interwoven by thorny creepers that only the elephant can trample a path through them with his huge, heavy feet. The snakes there are too big for us to eat, and the lizards too nimble for us to catch. And, if you go out in the desert, the slightest breeze will blow your eyes full of sand, while a storm would bury you under the dunes. No, it is best here, where there are plenty of frogs and locusts. Here I stop, and here you stay."

So they stayed. In nests atop the slender minarets the old storks rested, yet kept quite busy smoothing their feathers and sharpening their bills against their red stockings. From time to time, they would stretch their necks, bow very solemnly, and hold up their heads with such high foreheads, fine feathers, and wise brown eyes. The young maiden storks strolled solemnly through the wet reeds, making eyes at the other young storks and scraping acquaintances. At every third step they would gulp down a frog, or pause to dangle a small snake in their bills. They were under the impression that this became them immensely and besides, it tasted so good.

The young bachelor storks picked many a squabble, buffeted each other with their wings, and even stabbed at each other with their sharp bills till blood was shed. Yes, and then this young stork would get engaged, and that young stork would get engaged. Maidens and bachelors would pair off, for that was their only object in life. They built nests of their own and squabbled anew, for in the hot countries everyone is hotheaded. But it was very pleasant there, particularly so for the old storks, who thought that their children could do no wrong. The sun shone every day, there was plenty to eat, and they had nothing to do but enjoy themselves.

However, in the splendid palace of their Egyptian host, as they called him, there was no enjoyment. This wealthy and powerful lord lay on his couch, as stiff and stark as a mummy. In the great hall, which was as colorful as the inside of a tulip, he was surrounded by his kinsmen and servants. Though he was not quite dead, he could hardly be said to be alive. The healing flower from the northern marshes, which she who had loved him best had gone to seek, would never reach him. His lovely young daughter, who had flown over land and sea in the guise of a swan, would never come home from the far North.

"She is dead and gone," the two other swan princesses reported, when they returned. They concocted the following yarn, which they told:

"We three were flying together through the air, when a huntsman shot an arrow at us, and it struck our companion, our young friend. Like a dying swan, she sang her farewell song as she slowly dropped down to a lake in the forest. There on the shore we buried her, under a drooping birch tree. But we avenged her. We bound coals of fire to the wings of a swallow that nested under the thatched eaves of the huntsman's cottage. The roof blazed up, the cottage burst into flames, and the huntsman was burned to death. The flames were reflected across the lake, under the drooping birch tree where she lies, earth of this Earth. Never, alas! shall she return to the land of Egypt."

They both wept. But when the father stork heard their tale he rattled his bill, and said, "All lies and invention! I should dearly love to drive my bill right through their breasts."

"And most likely break it," said the mother stork. "A nice sight you'd be then. Think first of yourself, and then of your family. Never mind about outsiders."

"Nevertheless, I shall perch on the open cupola tomorrow, when all the wise and learned folk come to confer about the sick man. Perhaps they will hit upon something nearer the truth."

The wise men assembled and talked loud and long, but neither could the stork make sense out of what they had to say, nor did any good come of it to the sick man or to his daughter in the Wild Marsh. Yet we may as well hear what they had to say, for we have to listen to a lot in this world.

Perhaps it will be well to hear what had gone on before down there in Egypt. Then we shall know the whole story, or at least as much of it as the father stork knew.

"Love brings life. The greatest love brings the greatest life. Only through love may life be brought back to him." This doctrine the learned men had stated before, and they now said they had stated it wisely and well.

"It is a beautiful thought," the father stork quickly agreed.

"I don't quite understand it," said the mother stork. "That's its fault though, not mine. But no matter. I have other things to think about."

The learned men talked on about all the different kinds of love: the love of sweethearts, the love between parents and their children, plants' love of the light, and the love that makes seeds grow when the sun's rays kiss the earth. Their talk was so elaborate and learned that the father stork found it impossible to follow, much less repeat. However, their discussion made him quite thoughtful. All the next day he stood on one leg, with his eyes half closed, and thought, and thought. So much learning lay heavy upon him.

But one thing he understood clearly. Both the people of high degree and the humble folk had said from the bottom of their hearts that for this man to be sick, without hope of recovery, was a disaster to thousands, yes, to the whole nation, and that it would bring joy and happiness to everyone if he recovered.

"But where does the flower grow that can heal him?" they asked. For the answer they looked to their scholarly manuscripts, to the twinkling stars, to the wind, and to the weather. They searched through all the bypaths of knowledge, but all their wisdom and knowledge resolved down to the doctrine: "Love brings life—it can bring back a father's life," and although they said rather more than they understood, they accepted it, and wrote it down as a prescription. "Love brings life." Well and good, but how was this precept to be applied? That was their stumbling block.

However, they had at last agreed that help must come from the princess, who loved her father with all her heart. And they had devised a way in which she could help him.

It was more than a year ago that they had sent the princess into the desert, just when the new moon was setting, to visit the marble sphinx. At the base of the sphinx she had to scrape away the sand from a doorway and follow a long passage which led to the middle of a great pyramid where one of the mightiest kings of old lay wrapped as a mummy in the midst of his glory and treasure. There she leaned over the corpse to have it revealed to her where she might find life and health for her father. When she had done all this, she had a dream in which she learned that in the Danes' land there was a deep marsh—the very spot was described to her. Here, beneath the water, she would feel a lotus flower touch her breast, and when that flower was brought home to her father it would cure him. So, in the guise of a swan she had flown from the land of Egypt to the Wild Marsh.

All this was known to the father and mother stork, and now we too are better informed. Furthermore, we know that the Marsh King dragged her down, and that those at home thought her dead and gone. Only the wisest among them said, as the stork mother had put it, "She can look out for herself." They waited to see what would come to pass, for they knew nothing better they could do.

"I believe I shall make off with those swan feathers of the faithless princesses," said the father stork. "Then they will fly no more to do mischief in the Wild Marsh. I'll hide the two sets of feathers up North, until we find a use for them."

"Where would you keep them?" the mother stork asked.

"In our nest by the Wild Marsh," he said. "I and our sons will take turns carrying them when we go back. If they prove too much of a burden, there are many places along the way where we can hide them until our next flight. One set of swan feathers would be enough for the princess, but two will be better. In that northern land it's well to have plenty of wraps."

"You will get no thanks for it," she told him, "but please yourself. You are the master, and except at hatching time, I have nothing to say."

Meanwhile, in the Viking's castle near the Wild Marsh, toward which the storks came flying, now that it was spring, the little girl had been given a name. She was called Helga, but this name was too mild for the violent temper that this lovely girl possessed. Month by month her temper grew worse. As the years went by and the storks traveled to and fro, to the banks of the Nile in the fall, and back to the Wild Marsh in the springtime, the child grew to be a big girl. Before anyone would have thought it, she was a lovely young lady of sixteen. The shell was fair to see but the kernel was rough and harsh—harsher than most, even in that wild and cruel age.

She took delight in splashing her hands about in the blood of horses slaughtered as an offering to the gods. In savage sport, she would bite off the head of the black cock that the priest was about to sacrifice, and in dead earnest she said to her foster father:

"If your foe were to come with ropes and pull down the roof over your head, I would not wake you if I could. I would not even hear the house fall, for my ears still tingle from that time you boxed them, years ago—yes, you! I'll never forget it."

But the Viking did not believe she was serious. Like everyone else, he was beguiled by her beauty, and he did not know the change that came over Helga's body and soul.

She would ride an unsaddled horse at full gallop, as though she were part of her steed, nor would she dismount even though he fought with his teeth against the other wild horses. And many a time she would dive off the cliff into the sea, with all of her clothes on, and swim out to meet the Viking as his boat neared home. To string her bow, she cut off the longest lock of her beautiful hair, and plaited it into a string. "Self-made is well made," said she.

The Viking's wife had a strong and determined will, in keeping with the age, but with her daughter she was weak and fearful, for she knew that an evil spell lay on that dreadful child.

Out of sheer malice, as it seemed, when Helga saw her foster mother stand on the balcony or come into the courtyard, she would sit on the edge of the well, throw up her hands, and let herself tumble into that deep, narrow hole. Froglike, she would dive in and clamber out. Like a wet cat, she would run to the main hall, dripping such a stream of water that the green leaves strewn on the floor were floating in it.

However, there was one thing that held Helga in check—and that was evening. As she came on, she grew quiet and thoughtful. She would obey and accept advice. Some inner force seemed to make her more like her real mother. When the sun went down and the usual change took place in her appearance and character, she sat quiet and sad, shriveled up in the shape of a frog. Now that she had grown so much larger than a frog, the change was still more hideous. She looked like a miserable dwarf, with the head and webbed fingers of a frog. There was something so very pitiful in her eyes, and she had no voice. All she could utter was a hollow croak, like a child who sobs in her dreams. The Viking's wife would take this creature on her lap. Forgetting the ugly form as she looked into those sad eyes, she would often say, "I almost wish that you would never change from being my poor dumb-stricken frog child. For you are more frightful when I see you cloaked in beauty."

Then she would write out runes against illness and witchcraft and throw them over the wretched girl, but it was little good they did.

"One can hardly believe that she was once so tiny that she lay in the cup of a water lily," said the father stork. "She has grown up and is the living image of her Egyptian mother, whom we'll never see again. She did not look out for herself as well as you and those wise men predicted she would. Year in, year out, I've flown to and fro across the Wild Marsh, but never a sign have I seen of her. Yes, I may as well tell you that year after year, when I flew on ahead to make our nest ready and put things in order, I spent whole nights flying over the pool as if I were an owl or a bat, but to no avail. Nor have we found a use for the two sets of swan feathers, which I and our sons took so much trouble to bring all the way from the banks of the Nile. It took us three trips to get them here. For years now they have lain at the bottom of our nest. If perchance a fire broke out and this wooden castle burned down, they would be gone."

"And our good nest would be gone too," the mother stork reminded him. "But you care less for that than you do for your swan feathers and your swamp princess. Sometime you ought to go down in the mire with her and stay there for good. You are a poor father to your children, just as I've been telling you ever since I hatched our first brood. All I hope is that neither we nor our young ones get an arrow shot under our wings by that wild Viking brat. She doesn't know what she is doing. I wish she would realize that this has been our home much longer than it has been hers. We have always been punctilious about paying our rent every year with a feather, an egg, and a young one, according to custom. But do you think that, when she is around, I dare venture down into the yard, as I used to, and as I still do in Egypt, where I am everyone's crony and they let me peer into every pot and kettle? No, I sit up here vexing myself about her—the wench!—and about you, too. You should have left her in the water lily, and that would have been the end of her."

"You aren't as hardhearted as you sound," said the father stork. "I know you better than you know yourself." Up he hopped, twice he beat with his wings, and stretching his legs behind him, off he flew, sailing away without moving his wings until he had gone some distance. Then he took a powerful stroke. The sunlight gleamed on his white feathers. His neck and head were stretched forward. There were speed and swing in his flight.

"After all, he's the handsomest fellow of all," said the mother stork, "but you won't catch me telling him so."

Early that fall the Viking came home with his booty and captives. Among the prisoners was a young Christian priest, one of those who preached against the northern gods. Of late there had been much talk in hall and bower about the new faith that was spreading up from the south, and for which St. Ansgarius had won converts as far north as Hedeby on the Slie. Even young Helga had heard of this faith in the White Christ, who so loved mankind that he had given his life to save them. But as far as she was concerned, as the saying goes, such talk had come in one ear and gone out the other. Love was a meaningless word to her except during those hours when, behind closed doors, she sat shriveled up as a frog. But the Viking's wife had heard the talk, and she felt strangely moved by the stories that were told about the son of the one true God.

Back from their raid, the Vikings told about glorious temples of costly hewn stone, raised in honor of him whose message is one of love. They had brought home with them two massive vessels, artistically wrought in gold, and from these came the scent of strange spices. They were censers, which the Christian priests swung before altars where blood never flowed, but instead the bread and wine were changed into the body and blood of him who had given himself for generations yet unborn.

Bound hand and foot with strips of bark, the young priest was cast into the deep cellars of the Viking's castle. The Viking's wife said that he was as beautiful as the god Balder, and she was sorry for him, but young Helga proposed to have a cord drawn through his feet and tied to the tails of wild oxen.

"Then," she exclaimed, "I would loose the dogs on him. Ho, for the chase through mud and mire! That would be fun to see, and it would be even more fun to chase him."

But this was not the death that the Viking had in mind for this enemy and mocker of the high gods. Instead, he planned to sacrifice the priest on the blood stone in their grove. It would be the first human sacrifice that had ever been offered there.

Young Helga begged her father to let her sprinkle the blood of the victim upon the idols and over the people. When one of the many large, ferocious dogs that hung about the house came within reach while she was sharpening her gleaming knife, she buried the blade in his side, "Just to test its edge," she said.

The Viking's wife looked in distress at this savage, ill-natured girl, and when night came and the beauty of body and soul changed places in the daughter, the mother spoke of the deep sorrow that lay in her heart. The ugly frog with the body of a monster gazed up at her with its sad brown eyes. It seemed to listen, and to understand her as a human being would.

"Never once, even to my husband, have I let fall a word of the two-edged misery you have brought upon me," said the Viking's wife. "My heart is filled with more sorrow for you than I would have thought it could hold, so great is a mother's love. But love never entered into your feelings. Your heart is like a lump of mud, dank and cold. From whence came you into my house?"

The miserable form trembled strangely, as if these words had touched some hidden connection between its soul and it hideous body. Great tears came into those eyes.

"Your time of disaster will come," said the Viking's wife, "and it will be a disastrous time for me, too. Better would it have been to have exposed you beside the highway when you were young, and to have let the cold of the night lull you into the sleep of death." The Viking's wife wept bitter tears. In anger and distress, she passed between the curtains of hides that hung from a beam and divided the chamber.

The shriveled-up frog crouched in a corner. The dead quiet was broken at intervals by her half-stifled sighs. It was as if in pain a new life had been born in her heart. She took a step forward, listened, stepped forward again, and took hold of the heavy bar of the door with her awkward hands. Softly she unbarred the door. Silently she lifted the latch. She picked up the lamp that flickered in the hall outside, and it seemed that some great purpose had given her strength. She drew back the iron bolt from the well-secured cellar door, and stole down to the prisoner. He was sleeping as she touched him with her cold, clammy hand. When he awoke and saw the hideous monster beside him, he shuddered as if he had seen an evil specter. She drew her knife, severed his bonds, and beckoned for him to follow her.

He uttered holy names and made the sign of the Cross. As the creature remained unchanged, he said, in the words of the Bible:

"'Blessed is he that considereth the poor. The Lord will deliver him in time of trouble.' Who are you, that in guise of an animal are so gentle and merciful?"

The frog beckoned for him to follow her. She led him behind sheltering curtains and down a long passage to the stable, where she pointed to a horse. When he mounted it, she jumped up in front ot him, clinging fast to the horse's mane. The prisoner understood her, and speedily they rode out on the open heath by a path he could never have found.

He ignored her ugly shape, for he knew that the grace and kindness of God could take strange forms. When he prayed and sang hymns, she trembled. Was it the power of song and prayer that affected her, or was she shivering at the chill approach of dawn? What had come over her? She rose up, trying to stop the horse so that she could dismount, but the Christian priest held her with all his might, and chanted a psalm in the hope that it might have power to break the spell which held her in the shape of a hideous frog.

The horse dashed on, more wildly than ever. The skies turned red, and the first ray of the sun broke through the clouds. In that first flash of sunlight she changed. She became the lovely maiden with the cruel, fiendish temper. The priest was alarmed to find himself holding a fair maid in his arms. He checked the horse, and sprang off it, thinking he faced some new trick of the devil. Young Helga sprang down too, and the child's smock that she wore was so short that it came only to her knee. From the belt of it she snatched her sharp knife, and attacked the startled priest.

"Let me get at you," she screamed. "Let me get at you and plunge my knife in your heart. You are as pale as straw, you beardless slave!"

She closed with him, and fiercely they struggled together, but an unseen power seemed to strengthen the Christian priest. He held her fast, and the old oak tree under which they stood helped him, for it entangled her feet in its projecting roots. With clear water from a nearby spring, the priest sprinkled her neck and face, commanding the unclean spirit to leave her, and blessing her with the sign of the Cross in Christian fashion. But the waters of baptism have no power unless faith wells from within.

Even so, against the evil that struggled within her, he had opposed a power more mighty than his own human strength. Her arms dropped to her sides, as she gazed in pale-faced astonishment at this man whom she took for a mighty magician, skilled in sorcery and in the secret arts. Those were magic runes he had repeated, and mystic signs he had traced in the air. She would not have flinched had he shaken a keen knife or a sharp ax in her face, but she flinched now as he made the sign of the Cross over her head and heart. She sat like a tame bird, with her head drooped upon her breast.

Gently he spoke to her of the great kindness she had shown him during the night, when she had come in the guise of a hideous frog to sever his bonds and to lead him out into light and life again. He said she was bound by stronger bonds than those which had bound him, but that he would lead her out of darkness to eternal life. He would take her to the holy Ansgarius at Hedeby, and there in the Christian city, the spell that had power over her would be broken. But he would not let her sit before him on the horse, even though she wished it. He dared not.

"You must sit behind me on the horse, not in front of me," he said, "for your enchanted beauty has a power that comes of evil, and I fear it. Yet, with the help of the Lord, I shall win through to victory."

He knelt and prayed devoutly and sincerely. It seemed as if the quiet wood became a church, consecrated by his prayers. The birds began to sing as if they belonged to the new congregation. The wild mint smelled sweet, as if to replace incense and ambergris, and the young priest recited these words from the Bible:

"To give light to them that sit in darkness, and in the shadow of death; to guide our feet into the ways of peace."

While he spoke of the life everlasting, the horse that had carried them in wild career stood quietly by and pulled at the tall bramble bushes until the ripe juicy berries fell into Helga's hand, offering themselves for her refreshment.

Patiently, she let herself be lifted on horseback, and sat there like one in a trance, neither quite awake nor quite asleep. The priest tied two green branches in the shape of a cross, and held it high as they rode through the woods. The shrubs grew thicker and thicker, until at last they rode along in a pathless wilderness.

Bushes of the wild sloe blocked their way so that they had to ride around these thickets. The springs flowed no longer into little streams but into standing ponds, and they had to ride around these, too. But the cool breezes of the forest refreshed and strengthened them, and there was no less strength in the words of faith and Christian love that the young priest found to say, because of his great desire to lead this poor lost soul back to light and life.

They say that raindrops will wear a hollow in the hardest stone, and that the waves of the sea will in time wear the roughest stones smooth and round. Thus did the dew of mercy, which fell on Helga, soften that which was hard, and smooth that which was rough in her nature. Not that any change could yet be seen, or that she knew she was changing, any more than the seed in the ground is aware that the rain and the warm sun will cause it to grow and burst into flower.

When a mother's song unconsciously impresses itself on her child's memory, he babbles the words after her without understanding, but in time, they assume order in his mind and become meaningful to him. Even so, God's healing word began to impress itself on Helga's heart.

They rode out of the wilderness, crossed a heath, and rode on through another pathless forest. There, toward evening, they met with a robber band.

"Where did you kidnap this beautiful wench?" the robbers shouted. They stopped the horse and dragged the two riders from its back.

The priest was surrounded, and he was unarmed except for the knife he had taken from Helga, but with this he now tried to defend her. As one of the robbers swung his ax, the priest sprang aside to avoid the blow, which fell instead on the neck of the horse. Blood spurted forth, and the animal fell to the ground. Startled out of the deep trance in which she had ridden all day, Helga sprang forward and threw herself over the dying horse. The priest stood by to shield and defend her, but one of the robbers raised his iron hammer and brought it down on the priest's head so hard that he bashed it in. Brains and blood spattered about as the priest fell down dead.

The robbers seized little Helga by her white arms, but it was sundown, and as the sun's last beam vanished, she turned back into a frog. The greenish white mouth took up half her face, her arms turned spindly and slimy, and her hands turned into broad, webbed fans. In terror and amazement, the robbers let go of this hideous creature. Froglike she hopped as high as her head and bounded into the thicket. The robbers felt sure this was one of Loki's evil tricks, or some such secret black magic, so they fled from the place in terror.

The full moon rose. It shone in all its splendor as poor frog-shaped Helga crept out of the thicket and crouched beside the slain priest and the slaughtered horse. She stared at them with eyes that seemed to weep, and she gave a sob like the sound of a child about to burst into tears. She threw herself on first one and then the other. She fetched them water in her large hands, which could hold a great deal because of the webbed skin, and poured it over them, but dead they were and dead they would remain. At last, she realized this. Wild animals would come soon and devour their bodies. But no, that must not be!

She dug into the ground as well as she could, trying to make for them a grave as deep as possible. But she had nothing to dig with except the branch of her tree and her own two hands. The webs between her fingers were torn by her labors until they bled, and she made so little headway that she saw the task was beyond her. Then she brought clear water to wash the dead man's face, which she covered with fresh green leaves. She brought large branches to cover him, and scattered dry leaves between them. Then she brought the heaviest stones she could carry, piled them over the body, and filled in the cracks with moss. Now she thought the mound would be strong and safe, but the difficult task had taken her all night long. The sun came up, and there stood young Helga in all her beauty, with blood on her hands and for the first time maidenly tears on her flushed cheeks.

During this transformation, it seemed as if two natures were contending within her. She trembled, and looked about her as if she had just awakened from a nightmare. She took hold of the slender branch of a tree for support. Presently she climbed like a cat to the topmost branches of this tree, and clung there. Like a frightened squirrel, she stayed there the whole day through, in the deep solitude of the forest where all is dead still, as they say.

Dead still! Why, butterflies fluttered all about in play or strife. At the ant hills nearby, hundreds of busy little workmen hurried in and out. The air was filled with countless dancing gnats, swarms of buzzing flies, ladybugs, dragonflies with golden wings, and other winged creatures. Earthworms crawled up from the moist earth, and moles came out. Oh, except for all these, the people might be right when they call the forest "dead still."

No one paid any attention to little Helga except the jays that flew screeching to the tree top where she perched. Bold and curious, they hopped about her in the branches, but there was a look in her eyes that soon put them to flight. They could not make her out, any more than she could understand herself. When evening came on, the setting sun gave warning that it was time for her to change, and it aroused her to activity again. She had no sooner climbed down than the last beam of the sun faded out, and once more she sat there, a shriveled frog with the torn webbed skin covering her hands.

But now her eyes shone with a new beauty that in her lovely form they had not possessed. They were gentle, tender, maidenly eyes. And though they looked out through the mask of a frog, they reflected the deep feelings of a human heart. They brimmed over with tears—precious drops that lightened her heart.

Beside the grave mound lay the Cross of green boughs that had been tied together with bark string, the last work of him who lay buried there. Helga picked it up, and the thought came to her to plant it between the stones that covered the man and the horse. Memory of the priest brought fresh tears to her eyes, and with a full heart she made cross marks in the earth around the grave, as a fence that would guard it well. When with both hands she made the sign of the Cross, the webbed membrane fell from her fingers like a torn glove. She washed her hands at the forest spring, and gazed in amazement at their delicate whiteness. Again, in the air she made the holy sign between herself and the dead man. Her lips trembled, her tongue moved and the name she had heard the priest mention so often during their ride through the woods rose to her lips. She uttered the name of the savior.

The frog's skin fell from her. Once more she was a lovely maiden. But her head hung heavy. She was much in need of rest, and she fell asleep.

However, she did not sleep for long. She awoke at midnight and saw before her the dead horse, prancing and full of life. A shining light came from his eyes and from the wound in his neck. Beside him stood the martyred Christian priest, "more beautiful than Balder," the Viking woman had truly said, for he stood in a flash of flame.

There was such an air of gravity and of righteous justice in the penetrating glance of his great, kind eyes that she felt as if he were looking into every corner of her heart. Little Helga trembled under his gaze, and her memories stirred within her as though this were Judgment Day. Every kindness that had been done her and each loving word spoken to her, were fresh in her mind. Now she understood how it had been love that sustained her through those days of trial, during which all creatures made of dust and spirit, soul and clay, must wrestle and strive. She realized that she had only obeyed the impulse of her inclinations. She had not saved herself. Everything had been given to her, and Providence had guided her. Now, in humility and shame, she bent before him who could read every thought in her heart, and at that moment she felt the pure light of the Holy Spirit enter her soul.

"Daughter of the marsh," the priest said, "out of the earth and the marsh you came, and from this earth you shall rise again. The light in you that is not of the sun but of God, shall return to its source, remembering the body in which it has lain. No soul shall be lost. Things temporal are full of emptiness, but things eternal are the source of life. I come from the land of the dead. Someday, you too shall pass through the deep valley to the shining mountain tops, where compassion and perfection dwell. I cannot lead you to receive Christian baptism at Hedeby, for you must first break the watery veil that covers the deep marsh and bring out of its depths the living source of your birth and your being. You must perform a blessed act before you may be blessed."

He lifted her on the horse and put in her hand a golden censer, like the ones she had seen in the Viking's castle. From it rose a sweet incense, and the wound in the martyr's forehead shone like a diadem. He took the cross from the grave and raised it high as they rose swiftly through the air, over the rustling woods and over the mounds where the heroes of old are buried, each astride his dead war horse. These mighty warriors rose and rode up to the top of the mounds. Golden crowns shone on their foreheads in the moonlight, and their cloaks billowed behind them in the night wind. The dragon on guard over his treasure also lifted his head and watched them pass. Goblins peered up from their hills and hollows, where they swarmed to and fro with red, blue, and green lights as numerous as the sparks of burning paper.

Away over the forest and heath, river and swamp, they hastened until they circled over the Wild Marsh. The priest held aloft the cross, which shone like gold. From his lips fell holy prayers. Little Helga joined in the hymns that he sang, as a child follows its mother's song. She swung the censer, and it gave forth a churchly incense so miraculously fragrant that the reeds and sedges burst into bloom, every seed in the depths sent forth stalks, and all things flourished that had a spark of life within them. Water lilies spread over the surface of the pool like a carpet patterned with flowers, and on this carpet a young and beautiful woman lay asleep. Helga thought this was her own reflection, mirrored in the unruffled water. But what she saw was her mother, the princess from the land of the Nile, who had become the Marsh King's wife.

The martyred priest commanded that the sleeper be lifted up on horseback. Under this new burden, the horse sank down as though his body were an empty, wind-blown shroud. But the sign of the Cross lent strength to the spectral horse, and he carried all three riders back to solid earth.

Then crowed the cock in the Viking's castle, and the spectral figures became a part of the mist that drove before the wind. But the Egyptian princess and her daughter were left there, face to face.

"Is this myself I see, reflected in the deep waters?" cried the mother.

"Is this myself I see, mirrored on the bright surface?" the daughter exclaimed. As they approached one another and met in a heart-to-heart embrace, the mother's heart beat faster, and it was the mother who understood.

"My child! My heart's own flower, my lotus from beneath the waters." She threw her arms about the child and wept. For little Helga, these tears were a fresh baptism of life and love.

"I flew hither in the guise of a swan," Helga's mother told her. "Here I stripped off that plumage and fell into the quagmire. The deep morass closed over me like a wall, and I felt a strong current—a strange power—drag me deeper and deeper. I felt sleep weigh down my eyelids. I slumbered and dreamed. I dreamed that I stood again in the Egyptian pyramid, yet the swaying alder stump that had frightened me so on the surface of the morass stood ever before me. As I watched the check marks in its bark, they took on bright colors and turned into hieroglyphics. I was looking at the casket of a mummy. It burst open, and from it stepped that monarch of a thousand years ago. His mummy was pitch black, a shining, slimy black, like the wood snail or like the mud of the swamp. Whether it was the Marsh King or that mummy of the pyramid, I know not. He threw his arms around me, and I felt that I would die. When I came back to consciousness, I felt something warm over my heart, and there nestled a little bird, twittering and fluttering its wings. From my heart it flew into the heavy darkness overhead, but a long, green strand still bound it to me. I heard and understood its plaintive song, 'To freedom, to the sunlight, to our Father!' Then I remembered my own father, in the sunflooded land of my birth, my life, and my love. I loosed the strand and let the little bird fly home to my father. From that moment, I have known no other dreams. I have slept, long and deep, until this hour when wondrous sounds and incense woke me and set me free."

What had become of that green strand between the mother's heart and the heart and the bird's wing? Where did it flutter now? What had become of it? Only the stork had ever seen it. That strand was the green stalk, and the bow at the end of it was the bright flower that had cradled the child, who was grown in beauty and now rested once more on her mother's heart.

As they stood there in each other's arms, the stork circled over their heads. Away he flew to his nest for the two sets of swan feathers that he had stored there for so many years. He dropped these sets of feathers upon the mother and daughter, and, once the plumage had covered them, they rose from the ground as two white swans.

"Let's have a chat," said the father stork, "for now we can understand one another, even though different birds have different beaks. It's the luckiest thing in the world that I found you tonight. Tomorrow we shall be on our way, Mother, the young ones, and I, all flying south. Yes, you well may stare. I am your old friend from the banks of the Nile, and Mother is too. Her heart is softer than her beak. She always did say the princess could look out for herself, but I and our sons brought these sets of swan feathers up here. Why, how happy this makes me, and how lucky it is that I am still here. At daybreak we shall set out, with a great company of storks. We shall fly in the vanguard, and if you follow us closely you can't miss your way. The young ones and I will keep an eye on you, too."

"And the lotus flower which I was to fetch," said the Egyptian princess, "now flies beside me in the guise of a swan. I bring with me the flower that touched my heart, and the riddle has been solved. Home we go!"

But Helga said she could not leave the land of the Danes until she had once more seen her good foster mother, the Viking's wife. Helga vividly recalled every fond moment spent with her, every kind word, and even every tear she had caused the foster mother to shed. At that moment she almost felt that she loved her foster mother best of all.

"Yes, we must go to the Viking's castle," said the father stork. "Mother and the young ones are waiting for me there. How their eyes will pop and their beaks will rattle! Mother is no great one for talking. She's a bit curt and dry, but she means very well. Now I must make a great to-do so that they will know we are coming."

So the father stork rattled his beak as he and the swans flew home to the Viking's castle.

Everyone there lay sound asleep. The Viking's wife had gone to bed late that night because she was so worried about Helga, who had been missing ever since the Christian priest disappeared three days ago. She must have helped him escape, for it was her horse that was gone from the stable. But what power could have brought this about? The Viking's wife thought of all the miracles she had heard were performed by the White Christ and by those who had the faith to follow Him. Her troubled thoughts gave way to dreams. She dreamed that she lay there, on her bed, still awake, still lost in thought while darkness reigned outside. A storm blew up. To the east and to the west she heard the high seas roll—waves of the North Sea and waves of the Kattegat. The great snake, which in the depth of the ocean coils around Earth, was in convulsions of terror. It was the twilight of the gods, Ragnarok, as the heathens called Judgment Day, when all would perish, even their highest gods. The war horn sounded, and over the rainbow bridge the gods rode, clad in steel, to fight their last great fight. The winged Valkyries charged on before them, and dead heroes marched behind. The whole firmament blazed with the northern lights, yet darkness conquered in the end. It was an awful hour.

Beside the terror-stricken dreamer, little Helga seemed to crouch on the floor, in the ugly frog's shape. She shuddered, and crept close to her foster mother, who took the creature up in her lap and, hideous though it was, lovingly caressed it. The air resounded with the clashing of swords and clubs, and the rattle of arrows like a hailstorm upon the roof. The hour had come when Heaven and Earth would perish, the stars would fall, and everything be swallowed up by Surtur's sea of fire. Yet she knew there would be a new Heaven and a new Earth. The grain would grow in waving fields where the sea now rolled over the golden sands.

Then the god whose name could not yet be spoken would reign at last, and to him would come Balder, so mild and loving, raised up from the kingdom of the dead. He came, and the Viking's wife saw him clearly. She knew his face, which was that of the captive Christian priest. "The White Christ," she cried aloud, and as she spoke that name she kissed the ugly brow of her frog child. Off fell the frog skin, and it was

Helga who stood before her in radiant beauty, gentle as she had never been before, and with beaming eyes. She kissed her foster mother's hands, and blessed her for all the loving kindness that had been lavished upon her in those days of bitter trials and sorrow. She thanked the Viking's wife for the thoughts she had nurtured in her, and for calling upon the name which she repeated—the White Christ. And little Helga arose in the shape of a white, mighty swan. With the rushing sound of a flock of birds of passage taking flight, she spread her powerful wings.

The Viking's wife awakened to hear this very same noise overhead. She knew it was about time for the storks to fly south, and that they must be what she heard. She wanted to see them once more and bid them good luck for their journey, so she got up and went out on her balcony. There, on the roofs of all the outbuildings she saw stork upon stork, and all round the castle bands of storks whirled in widening circles above the high trees. Directly in front of her, beside the well where Helga had so often sat and frightened her with wild behavior, two white swans were sitting. They looked up at her with such expressive eyes that it recalled her dream, which still seemed to her almost real. She thought of Helga in the guise of a swan. She thought of the Christian priest, and suddenly her heart felt glad. The swans waved their wings and bowed their necks to her as if in greeting. The Viking's wife held out her arms as if she understood, and thinking of many things, she smiled at them through her tears.

Then, with a great clattering of beaks and flapping of wings, the storks all started south.

"We won't wait for those swans," said the mother stork. "If they want to go with us they had better come now. We can't dillydally here until the plovers start. It is nicer to travel as we do in a family group, instead of like the finches and partridges, among whom the males and females fly in separate flocks. I call that downright scandalous. And what kind of strokes do those swans call those that they are making?"

"Oh, everyone has his own way of flying," the father stork said. "Swans fly in a slantwise line, cranes in a triangle, and the plovers in snakelike curves."

"Don't talk about snakes while we are flying up here," said the mother stork. "It will put greedy thoughts in the young ones' heads at a time when they can't be appeased."

"Are those the high mountains of which I have heard?" Helga asked as she flew along in the swan plumage.

"There are thunder clouds, billowing below us," her mother told her.

"And what are the white clouds that rise to such heights?" Helga asked.

"Those heights that you see are the mountains that are always capped with snow," her mother said, as they flew over the Alps, out over the blue Mediterranean.

"African sands! Egyptian strands!" In the upper air through which her swan wings soared, the daughter of the Nile rejoiced when she spied once more the yellow wave-washed coast of her native country. The storks spied it too, and they quickened their flight.

"I can sniff the Nile mud and the juicy frogs," the mother stork cried. "What an appetizing feeling! Yes, there you shall have fine eating and things to see—marabou storks, ibises, and cranes. They are all cousins of ours, but not nearly so handsome as we. They are vain creatures, especially the ibises. The Egyptians stuff them with spices and make mummies of them, and this has quite turned their heads. As for me, I would rather be stuffed with live frogs, and so would you, and so you shall be. Better to have your mouth well stuffed when you are alive than have such a to-do made over you when you are dead. That's the only way I feel about it, and I am always right."

"The storks have come back," said the people in the magnificent home on the banks of the Nile where, on a leopard skin spread over soft cushions in the lofty hall, the master lay between life and death, waiting and hoping for the lotus flower from the deep marshes in the far north. His kinsmen and servants were standing beside his couch, when into the room flew two magnificent white swans who had come with the storks. They doffed their glistening swan feathers, and there stood two lovely women who resembled each other as closely as two drops of water. They bent over the pale, feeble old man, and threw back their long hair. When little Helga leaned above her grandfather, the color returned to his cheeks, light to his eyes, and life to his stiffened limbs. Hale and hearty, the old man rose. His daughter and granddaughter threw their arms around him, as if they were joyously greeting him on the morning after a long and trying dream.

Great was the rejoicing in that house, and in the stork's nest, too, though the storks rejoiced chiefly because of the good food and the abundance of frogs. While the learned men sketchily scribbled down the story of the two princesses, and of the healing flower that had brought such a blessing to that household and throughout all the land, in their own way the parent storks told the story to their children, but not until all of them were full, or they would have had better things to do than listen to stories.

"Now you will become a somebody at last," the mother stork whispered. "It's the least we can expect."

"Oh, what would I become?" said the father stork. "What have I done? Nothing much."

"You have done more than all the others put together. Except for you and our young ones, the two princesses would never have seen Egypt again, nor would the old man have been healed. You will assuredly become a somebody. At the very least, they will give you the title of doctor, and our young ones will inherit it, and their little ones after them. Why, at least to my eyes, you already have the look of an Egyptian doctor."

The wise and learned men propounded the basic principle, as they called it, on which the whole matter rested. "Love brings life," was their doctrine, and this they explained in different ways. "The warm sunbeam was the Egyptian princess. She descended unto the Marsh King, and from their meeting, the flower arose."

"I can't quite repeat the exact words," said the father stork, who had been listening on the roof and wanted to tell his family all about it. "What they said was so incomprehensibly wise that they were given titles and presents too. Even the chief cook was rewarded, no doubt for his soup."

"And what was your reward?" the mother stork wanted to know. "It was not right for them to pass over the most important one in the whole affair, which is just what you are. The learned men did nought but wag their tongues. However, I have no doubt that your turn will come."

Late that night, when the happy household lay peacefully asleep, there was one person left awake. This was not the father stork, who, like a drowsy sentry, stood in his nest on one leg. No, this wide-awake person was little Helga. She leaned over the rail of her balcony and looked up through the clear air at the great shining stars. They were larger and more lustrous than she had ever seen them in the North, but they were the same stars. She thought of the Viking's wife near the Wild Marsh, of her gentle eyes, and of the tears which she had shed over her poor frog child, who now was standing in the splendor of the clear starlight and the wonderful spring air by the waters of the Nile. She thought of the love that filled the heathen woman's heart, the love she had shown that wretched creature who was hateful in her human form and dreadful to see or touch in her animal shape. She looked at the shining stars and was reminded of the glory that had gleamed on the brow of the martyred priest when he flew with her over moor and forest. She recalled the tone of his voice. She recalled those words he had said, when they rode together and she sat like an evil spirit—those words that had to do with that high source of the greatest love that encompasses all mankind throughout all the generations.

Yes, what had she not received, won, gained! Night and day, Helga was absorbed in contemplating her happiness. She regarded it like a child who turns so quickly from the giver to all those wonderful gifts. Her happy thoughts ran on to the even greater happiness that could lie ahead, and would lie ahead. On and on she thought, until she so lost herself in dreams of future bliss that she forgot the giver of all good things. It was the wanton pride of her youth that led her on into the pitfall. Her eyes were bright with pride when a sudden noise in the yard below recalled her straying thoughts. She saw two large ostriches rushing about in narrow circles, and never before had she seen this animal, this huge, fat, and awkward bird. The wings looked as if they had been roughly handled. When she asked why this was, for the first time she heard the legend that Egyptians tell about the ostrich.

Once, they said, the ostriches were a race of glorious and beautiful birds with wings both wide and strong. One evening the other large birds of the forest said to the ostrich, "Brother, shall we fly to the river tomorrow, God willing, and quench our thirst?"

"Yes," the ostrich answered, "so I will." At dawn, away they flew. First they flew aloft toward the sun, which is the eye of God. Higher and higher the ostrich flew, far ahead of all the other birds. In his pride he flew straight toward the light, vaunting his own strength and paying no heed to him from whom strength comes. "God willing," he did not say.

Then, suddenly the avenging angel drew aside the veil from the flaming seas of the sun, and in an instant the wings of that proud bird was burned away, and he wretchedly tumbled to earth. Never since that day has the ostrich or any of his family been able to rise in the air. He can only flee timidly along the ground and run about in circles. He is a warning to us that in all human thoughts and deeds we should say, "God willing."

Helga bowed her head in thoughts. As the ostrich rushed about, she observed how timorous he was and what vain pride he took in the size of the shadow he cast on the white, sunlit wall.

She devoted herself to more serious thoughts. A happy life had been given her, but what was to come of it? Great things, "God willing."

When, in the early spring, the storks made ready to fly north again, Helga took the golden bracelet from her arm and scratched her name upon it. She beckoned to the father stork, slipped the golden band around his neck, and told him to take it to the Viking's wife, as a sign that her adopted daughter was alive, and happy, and had not forgotten her.

"It's a heavy thing to carry," the father stork thought, as he wore it around his neck. "But gold and honor are not to be tossed away on the highroad. The people up there will indeed be saying that the stork brings luck."

"You lay gold and I lay eggs," the mother stork told him, "although you lay only once, while I lay every year. Neither of us gets any thanks for it, which is most discouraging."

"One knows when he's done his duty," the father stork said.

"But you can't hang such knowledge up for all to admire," she said. "Neither will it bring you a favorable wind nor a full meal." Then away they flew.

The little nightingale who sang in the tamarind tree would also be flying north soon. Helga had often heard him singing up near the Wild Marsh. She decided to use him as a messenger, for she had learned the language of the birds when she flew in the guise of a swan, and as she had often talked with the storks and swallows she knew the little nightingale would understand her. She begged him to fly to the beech forest in Jutland, where she had built the tomb of stone and branches. She begged him to tell all the little birds there to guard the grave, and to sing there often. The nightingale flew away—and time went flying by.

That fall, the eagle that perched on the pyramid saw a magnificent caravan of camels, richly laden and accompanied by armed men. These men were splendidly robed and were mounted on prancing Arab horses as white as shining silver, with quivering pink nostrils and big flowing manes that swept down to their slender legs. A royal prince of Arabia, handsome as a prince should be, came as an honored guest to the palace where the storks' nest now stood empty. The nest-owners had been away in the far North, but they would soon return. They did return, on the very evening when the festive celebration was at its height.

It was the wedding that was being celebrated, and the bride was lovely Helga, jeweled and robed in silk. The bridegroom was the young Arabian prince. They sat at the head of the table, between Helga's mother and grandfather. But Helga was not watching the bridegroom's handsome bronzed face, round which his black beard curled. Nor was she looking into the dark, fiery eyes that he fixed upon her. She was staring out at a bright, glistening star that shone down from the sky.

Then there was a rush of wings through the air, and the storks came back. Tired though they were, and badly as they needed rest after their journey, the two old parent storks flew straight to the veranda railing. They knew of the marriage feast, and at the frontier they had already heard news that Helga had commanded their pictures to be painted on the walls, for truly they were a part of her life story.

"That certainly was very nice and thoughtful," said the father stork.

"It was little enough," the mother stork told him. "She could hardly do less."

When Helga saw them, she rose from the table and went out on the veranda to stroke their backs. The old storks bowed their heads, while the youngest of their children looked on and appreciated the honor bestowed on them.

Helga looked up at the bright star, which grew yet more brilliant and clear. Between her and the star hovered a form even purer than the air, and therefore visible through it. As it floated down quite near her, she saw that it was the martyred priest. He too came to her wedding feast—came from the Kingdom of Heaven.

"The splendor and happiness up there," he said, "surpass all that is known on earth."

More humbly and fervently than she had ever yet prayed, Helga asked that for one brief moment she might be allowed to go there and cast a single glance into the bright Kingdom of Heaven. Then he raised her up in splendor and glory, through a stream of melody and thoughts. The sound and the brightness were not only around her but within her soul as well. They lay beyond all words.

"We must go back, or you will be missed," the martyred priest said to her.

"Only one more glance," she begged. "Only one brief moment more."

"We must go back to Earth, for all your guests are leaving."

"Only one more look! The last!"

Then Helga stood again on the veranda, but all the torches had been extinguished, and the banquet hall was dark. The storks were gone. No guests were to be seen, and no bridegroom. All had vanished in those three brief moments.

A great fear fell upon her. She wandered through the huge, empty hall into the next room, where foreign soldiers lay asleep. She opened the side door that led into her own bedroom. When she thought she had entered it, she found herself in the garden, but it wasn't the garden she knew. Red gleamed the sky, for it was the break of day. Only three moments in Heaven, and a long time had passed on Earth.

She saw the storks and called to them in their own language. The father stork turned his head, listened and came down to her.

"You speak our language," he admitted. "What is your wish, strange woman, and why do you come here?"

"But it is I—Helga. Do you not know me? Only three moments ago we were talking together over there on the veranda."

"You are mistaken," the stork said. "You must have dreamed it."

"No, no!" she said, and reminded him of the Viking's castle, of the Wild Marsh, and of the journey hither.

Then the father stork blinked his eyes. "Why, that is a very old story that my great-great-grandmother told me," he said. "Truly, there once was a princess in Egypt who came from the land of the Danes. But she disappeared on the night of her wedding, hundreds of years ago, and never was seen again. You may read about it yourself, there on the monument in the garden. Swans and storks are carved upon it, and at the top is your own figure, sculptured in white marble."

And this was true. Little Helga saw it, understood it, and dropped upon her knees.

The sun shone brightly in all its splendor. As in the old days when at the first touch of sunlight the frog's skin fell away to reveal a beautiful maiden, so now, in that baptism by the sun a form of heavenly beauty, clearer and purer than the air itself, rose as a bright beam to join the Father. The body crumbled to dust, and only a wilted lotus flower lay where she had knelt.

"Well," said the father stork. "That's a new ending to the story. I hadn't expected it, but I liked it quite well."

"How will the young ones like it?" the mother stork wondered.

"Ah," said the father stork, "that certainly is the most important thing, after all."

THE RACERS (1858)

A prize was offered—or rather two prizes, a large one and a small one—for the greatest speed shown, not in just one race, but by one who had been racing for the whole year.

"I won the first prize," said the Hare. "Of course, one can expect justice when one's own family and good friends are members of the jury; but for the Snail to have received the second prize I consider almost an insult to me!"

"No," assured the Fence Rail, who had been witness to the distribution of prizes. "You have to consider diligence and good will. Several very worthy persons made that remark to me, and I quite agree with it. Of course, the Snail took a whole six months to cross the threshold, but he broke his thighbone in his haste, for haste it was for him. He devoted himself entirely to this race; and he even ran with his house on his back. All this is very commendable, and so he was awarded second prize."

"I think my claims ought to have received consideration," said the Swallow. I believe no one has shown himself swifter than I, in flight and motion. And where haven't I been? Far, far away!"

"That's just your trouble," said the Fence Rail. "You don't settle down enough. You're always going somewhere, leaving the country when it begins to freeze here. You haven't any love for your fatherland, so you can't claim any consideration in it."

"But suppose I slept the whole winter through on the moor," asked the Swallow, "slept my whole time away. Then would I deserve to be considered?

"Get an affidavit from the old woman of the marsh that you slept a half year in your fatherland, and then your claims will be given consideration."

"I really deserved the first prize instead of the second," said the Snail. "I know perfectly well that the Hare ran only because he was afraid, whenever he thought danger was near. On the other hand, I made the trial the task of my life, and I have crippled myself through my efforts. If anyone had a right to the first prize it was I; but I'm not making a fuss; I despise fusses!" And then he spat.

"I can give you my word of honor," said the old Signpost who had been one of the judges, "that each prize, at least as far as my influence went, was awarded with strict justice. I always proceed according to order, reflection, and calculation. Seven times before now I have had the honor of helping in giving out the prize, but not until today have I been able to do it in my own way. At each distribution I have always had something specific in mind. For the first prize I have always started from the first letter of the alphabet, and for the second I've started from the last. If you'll give me your attention for a moment I'll explain it to you. The eighth letter of the alphabet from *A* is *H*. That stands for *Hare*, so I voted the first prize to go to the Hare. And the eighth letter from the end is *S*, so I voted the second prize to the *Snail*. Next time the letter *I* will get the first prize and *R* the second. There should always be proper order in everything. One must have certain rules to go by."

"Well, I should certainly have voted for myself, if I hadn't been one of the judges," said the Mule, who was also a juryman. "People must consider not only how quickly you run, but other conditions that are pertinent, such as how much you are able to pull. But I wouldn't have laid stress on this point this time, nor about the shrewdness of the Hare's flight—how cleverly he sprang suddenly to one side, in order to lead people into a wrong track and away from his hiding place. No, there is still another thing of great importance to many people that should be considered. It is called 'the beautiful.' I saw it in the Hare's handsome, well-made ears; it's really a pleasure to see how long they are. I thought I was seeing myself when I was small; that's why I voted for him."

"Oh, hush!" said the Fly. "As for me, I won't make a speech; I just want to say one word. I know for certain that I've outrun more than one hare. The other day I broke the hind legs of a young one. I was sitting on the railway engine at the front of the train. I often do that; you can see your own speed so well there. For a long time a young hare ran in front of the engine—he had no idea I was there. At last, just as he was going to turn off the tracks, the locomotive ran over his hind legs and broke them, because I was sitting on it. He remained lying there, but I passed on. That was certainly outrunning him; but I don't need the prize."

"It seems to me," thought the Wild Rose, although she didn't speak it out loud—it was not her nature to express her ideas openly, though it might have been a good thing to do—"it seems to me that the Sunbeam should have had the first prize, and the second, too. It crosses in a moment the limitless space from the sun to us and brings such power that all nature is awakened by it. And under its beauty we roses blush and become fragrant. These high and mighty judges don't seem to have noticed it at all. If I were a Sunbeam I'd give them each a sunstroke! But then, it would only make them crazy, and they'll probably be that, anyway. No, I won't say anything," thought the Wild Rose. It's peaceful here in the woods; it's delightful to bloom, to shed fragrant perfume everywhere, to live in story and in song! But the Sunbeams will outlive all of us."

"What's the first prize?" asked the Earthworm, who had overslept and just now arrived.

"Free entrance to a kitchen garden," said the Mule. "I suggested that prize. The Hare must and should have it; as a clear-thinking and rational member of the committee, this seemed to me a sensible way of looking at it. I was determined that he should have it, so now the Hare is provided for. The Snail has permission to sit on the stone fence and enjoy the moss and sunshine; and in addition to this, he has been appointed one of the head judges of the next race. It is sensible to have one who has practical knowledge of the business at hand sitting on a committee, as the humans calls it. I must say I expect a great deal from the future—we have already made such a sound beginning!"

THE STONE OF THE WISE MAN (1858)

You know the story of Holger Danske, so we won't repeat it, but will ask you if you remember how "Holger Danske conquered the great land of India, eastward at the end of the world, to the tree called 'the Tree of the Sun,'" as Christen Pedersen says. Do you know Christen Pedersen? It makes no difference if you don't.

Holger Danske gave Prester John his power and rule over India. Have you heard about Prester John? Yes? Well, it makes no difference if you haven't, because he doesn't come into our story. You are going to hear about the Tree of the Sun "in India, eastward at the end of the world," as people believed it to be then, for they hadn't studied their geography the way we have—but that makes no difference, either!

The Tree of the Sun was a magnificent tree, such as we have never seen and most likely never will see. Its crown stretched out for miles around; it was really an entire wood, for each of its smallest branches formed, in turn, a whole tree. Palms, beech pines, plane trees, yes, and many other kinds of trees grew here, trees that are to be found all over the world; they sprang forth, as small branches, from the great branches, and these, with their knots and windings, were like hills and valleys, carpeted with soft, velvety green and covered with thousands of flowers. Each branch was like a great blooming meadow or the most beautiful garden. The blessed Sun shone down upon it, for, remember, it was the Tree of the Sun.

Here the birds from all over the world gathered together, birds from the primeval forests of America, the rose gardens of Damascus, or the wild woods of Africa, where the elephant and the lion imagine that they alone reign. Polar birds came here, and the stork and swallow naturally did, too. But the birds were not the only living creatures here; the stag, the squirrel, the antelope, and hundreds of other beautiful and light-footed animals were at home in this place. The crown of the tree was a spreading, fragrant garden, and in the very center of it, where the great branches rose up into a green hill, there stood a castle of crystal, with a view toward every country in the world. Each tower rose up in the form of a lily, and one could ascend through the stem, for inside there were winding stairs. One could step out onto the leaves—these were the balconies; and up in the cup of the flower was a beautiful, brilliant round hall, with no roof above it, only the blue sky, with either the sun or the stars.

Down below, in the wide halls of the castle, there was just as much splendor, though of a different sort. Here the whole world was reflected on the walls. One could see everything that happened, so there was no need to read newspapers; there were no newspapers here, anyway. Everything could be seen in living pictures, if one wanted to or was able to see it all; for too much is too much, even for the wisest man. And the wisest of all men lived here.

His name is too difficult for you to pronounce, and it makes no difference, anyway. He knew everything that a man on Earth can know or hope to know; he knew every invention that had been made or was yet to be made; but he knew nothing more than that, for everything in the world has its limits. Wise old King Solomon was only half as wise as this man, and yet he was very wise indeed, and governed the forces of nature and ruled over mighty spirits; even Death itself was forced to report every morning with a list of those who were to die during the day. But King Solomon himself had to die, too, and this was the thought that often occupied the mind of the learned, mighty ruler of the castle on the Tree of the Sun. However high he might rise above men in wisdom, he also must die someday. He knew that he and his children, too, must fade like the leaves of the forest and become dust. He could see the human race fade away like leaves on the trees and new men come forth to take their places. But the leaves that fell never lived again; they became dust about other plants.

What happened to man when the Angel of Death came to him? What could Death be? The body became decayed. And the soul? Yes, what was the soul? What became of it? Where did it go? "To the life eternal," the comforting voice of religion said. But what was the transition? Where did one dwell, and how? "In Heaven above," said the pious people, "it is there we go." "Above?" repeated the Wise Man, and gazed up at the Moon and stars. "Up there?"

From the earthly globe, he saw that "above" and "below" could be one and the same, depending upon where one stood on the revolving earth. And if he ascended as high as Earth's loftiest mountains rear their peaks, there in the air that we below call clear and transparent—"the pure heaven"—would be a black darkness, spread over all like a cloth, and the sun would have a coppery glow without giving forth rays, and our Earth would lie wrapped in an orange mist. How narrow were the limits of the mortal eye, and how little could be seen by the eye of the soul! Even the wisest knew little of that which is the most important of all to us.

In the most secret chamber of that castle lay Earth's greatest treasure—the Book of Truth. Page after page, the Wise Man had read it through. Every man may read in this book, but only parts of it; to many an eye the letters seem to fade, so that the words cannot even be spelled; on some pages, the writing is so pale that they seem like blank leaves. But the wiser a man becomes, the more he can read; and the wisest men read the most. The Wise Man knew how to unite the sunlight and the starlight with the light of reason and the hidden powers of his soul, and under this dazzling light, many things stood out clearly on the pages before him. But in the chapter of the book entitled "Life After Death" there was not so much as one single letter to see. That grieved him. Could he not somewhere on Earth obtain a light by which everything written in the Book of Truth would become clear to him?

Like wise King Solomon, he understood the language of the animals and could interpret their talk and their songs. But that made him none the wiser. He had learned the powers of plants and metals, powers that could be used for the cure of diseases or for delaying death, but none that could destroy death. In all created things that he could reach, he sought the light that would shine upon the certainty of eternal life, but he did not find it. Blank leaves still appeared in the Book of Truth before him. Christianity gave him words of promise of an eternal life in the Bible, but he wanted to read it in *his* book; and there he could see nothing about it.

The Wise Man had five children, four sons, educated as well as the sons of the wisest of fathers should be, and a daughter, lovely, gentle, and clever, but blind. Yet this affliction was no deprivation to her, for her father and brothers were mortal eyes to her, and her own keen perception gave her clear mental vision.

The sons had never ventured farther from the castle than the extent of the branches of the tree, nor had the sister ever left the home. They were happy children in the home of their childhood—the beautiful, fragrant Tree of the Sun. Like all children, they were happy to have stories told them, and their father told them many things that other children would never have understood, but these children were as clever as most of our old people are. He explained to them the pictures of life that they saw on the castle walls—the labors of men and the march of events in all the lands of Earth. Often the sons wished that they could go into the world and take part in the great deeds of other men, and then their father explained to them that it was hard and wearisome out in the world, that the world was not as they saw it from their beautiful home.

He told them of the good, the true, and the beautiful, and explained that these three clung together in the world, and that under the pressure they endured they hardened into a precious stone, purer than the water of a diamond—a splendid jewel of value to God Himself, whose brightness outshone all things; this was called the "Stone of the Wise Man." He told them that, just as man could gain knowledge of the existence of God by seeking it, so was it within the power of man to gain proof that such a jewel as the Stone of the Wise Man existed. This explanation would have been beyond the understanding of other children, but these children could grasp it, and in time other children, too, will learn to understand its meaning.

They asked their father about the true, the beautiful, and the good, and he told them many things—how when God made man from the dust of the earth, he gave to his work five kisses—fiery kisses, heart kisses—which we now call the five senses. Through these, that which is the true, the beautiful, and the good is seen, felt, and understood; through them, it is valued, protected, and augmented. Five senses have been given, physically and mentally, inwardly and outwardly, to body and soul.

By day and by night, the children thought deeply about all these things. Then the eldest of the brothers had a wonderful dream; and, strangely enough, the second brother had the same dream, and the third did, too, and the fourth—all of them dreamed exactly the same thing. They dreamed that each went out into the world and found the "Stone of the Wise Man," which gleamed like a radiant light on his forehead when, in the morning dawn, he rode his swift horse back over the velvety green meadows of home to the castle of his father. Then the jewel threw such a divine light and brilliance upon the pages of the book that everything written there on the life beyond the grave was illuminated. But the sister dreamed nothing about venturing out into the world, for it had never entered her mind. Her world was her father's castle.

"I shall ride out into the wide world," said the eldest brother. "I must find what life is like there, and mix with people. I shall do only what is good and true, and with these I shall protect the beautiful. Many things shall change for the better when I am there."

Yes, his thoughts were bold and big, as our thoughts always are at home, before we have gone out into the world and have met with wind and rain, thorns and thistles.

Now in all of these brothers the five senses were highly developed, both inwardly and outwardly; but in each of them *one* sense had reached a keenness surpassing the other four. In the case of the eldest, this outstanding sense was sight. This was to be of special benefit to him. He had eyes for all times, he said, and eyes for all nations, eyes that could look into the very depths of the earth, where treasures lie hidden, or into the depths of people's hearts, as though only a clear pane of glass were before them;

in other words, he saw more than we could in the cheek that blushes or turns pale, in the eye that cries or laughs.

Stags and antelopes escorted him to the western boundaries of his home, and there the wild swans received him and led him on into the northwest. And now he was far out into the world, far from the land of his father, which extended eastward to the ends of Earth.

How widely his eyes opened in amazement! There were many things to be seen here; and things appear very different when a man look at them with his own eyes instead of merely at a picture, as he had done in his father's house, however good the picture may be, and those in his father's house were unusually good. At first he nearly lost his eyes in astonishment at all the rubbish, all the carnival-like decorations that were supposed to represent the beautiful; but he did not quite lose them, and soon found full use for them. He wished to work thoroughly and honestly to understand the beautiful, the true, and the good. But how were these represented in the world? He saw that often the praise which by right belonged to the beautiful was given to the ugly; that the good was often overlooked, and mediocrity was applauded when it should have been hissed. People looked at the dress and not at the wearer, asked for a name instead of a value, and were guided more by reputation than by worth. It was the same everywhere.

"I must attack these things," he thought, and he did so.

But while he was seeking the truth there came the Devil, who is the father of all lies. Gladly would he have plucked out the eyes of this seer, but that would have been too blunt, for the Devil works in a more cunning way. He let him continue to seek and see the true and the good; but while the young man was doing so, the Devil blew a mote into his eye, into both eyes, one mote after another; this, of course, would harm even the clearest sight. Then the fiend blew upon the motes until they became beams, and the eyes were destroyed. There the Seer stood like a blind man in the great world and had no faith in it, for he had lost his good opinion of it and of himself. And when a man loses confidence in the world and himself, it is all over with him.

"All over!" sang the wild swans, flying across the sea toward the east. "All over!" repeated the swallows, also flying eastward toward the Tree of the Sun. It was not good news that they were carrying to the young man's home.

"The *Seer* must have done badly," said the second brother, "but the *Hearer* may have better luck." For in this son the sense of hearing was developed to a very high degree; so keen was it that he could hear the very grass grow.

He lovingly bade farewell and rode away from home, full of sound abilities and good intentions. The swallows followed him, and he followed the swans, until he was far from his home, far out in the wide world.

Then he discovered that one may have too much of a good things. For his hearing was *too* fine. Not only could he hear the grass grow, but he could hear every man's heart beat, whether in sorrow or in joy. To him the whole world was like the great workshop of a clockmaker, with all the clocks going "Tick, tock," and all the tower clocks striking "Ding, dong." The noise was unbearable. For a long time his ears held out, but at last all the noise, the shrieking, became too much for one man. Then "street boys" of some sixty years of age—for years alone don't make men—raised a tumult, at which the Hearer would have laughed, except for the slanderous talk that followed and echoed through every house and street; it was heard even in the country lanes. Falsehood pushed itself forward and pretended to be the master; bells on the fools' caps jangled and insisted they were church bells, until the noise became too much for the Hearer and he thrust his fingers into his ears. But still he could hear false singing and evil sounds, gossip and idle words, scandal and slander, groaning and moaning, on all sides—none of it worth listening to. Heaven help us! It was impossible to endure; it was all too mad! He thrust his fingers deeper and deeper into his ears, until at last his eardrums burst. Now he heard nothing at all; he could not hear the true, the beautiful, and the good; his hearing was to have been the bridge by which he would have crossed to it. He became morose and suspicious, at last trusting no one, not even himself, and that was most unfortunate. He would not be able to discover and bring home the divine jewel, and so he gave up; he even gave himself up, and that was the worst of all. The birds that flew eastward brought the tidings of this also to the father's castle in the Tree of the Sun; no letters arrived there, for there was no mail service.

"Now I'll try," said the third brother. "I have a sharp *nose.*"

It wasn't a very good practice for him to boast like that, but that was his way, and we must take him as he was. He had a happy disposition and was a poet, a great poet; he could sing many things that he could not speak, and ideas came to him far more quickly than they did to others.

"I can smell a rat!" he said. And it was his highly developed sense of smell to which he attributed his great range of knowledge about the realm of the beautiful.

"Every fragrant spot in the realm of the beautiful has its denizens," he said. "Some like the smell of apple blossoms; some like the smell of a stable. One man is at home in the atmosphere of the tavern, among the smoking tallow candles, where the smell of spirits mingles with the fumes of cheap tobacco. Another prefers to be near the heavy scent of jasmine, or to scent himself with strong oil of cloves. Some seek the fresh sea breezes, while others climb the highest mountain to look down on the bustling little life beneath."

Yes, thus he spoke. It seemed to him as if he had already been out in the wide world and known people from close association with them. But this conviction arose from within himself; it was the poet within him, the gift Heaven had bestowed on him in his cradle.

He bade farewell to his ancestral home in the Tree of the Sun and went on foot through the pleasant countryside. When he arrived at the boundaries of his home, he mounted an ostrich, which runs faster than a horse, and when he later met the wild swans, he swung himself onto the strongest of them, for he loved variety. Away he flew across the sea to distant lands of great forests, deep lakes, towering mountains, and proud cities. And wherever he appeared it seemed as if sunlight traveled with him across the countryside, for every flower and bush gave forth a new fragrance, conscious that nearby was a friend and protector who understood them and knew their value. Then the crippled rosebush stretched out its branches, opened its leaves, and gave bloom to the most beautiful roses; even the black, slimy wood snail saw its beauty.

"I will put my mark on the flower," said the snail. "Now I have spit on it, and there is nothing more I can do for it."

"Thus the beautiful always fares in this world!" said the Poet.

Then he sang a song about it in his own way, but nobody listened. So he gave a drummer two pennies and peacock's feather, and then arranged the song for the drum, and had it drummed throughout the town, in all the streets and lanes. When the people heard it they said that they understood it—it was very profound!

And so the Poet sang other songs about the beautiful, the good, and the true, and people listened to them among the smoking tavern candles, listened in the fresh meadows, in the forests, and on the high seas. It seemed as if this brother was going to have better luck than the other two.

But that angered the Devil, and so he promptly set to work with all the incense powder and smoke to be found, the very strongest, which can stifle anyone, and which he can prepare artfully enough to even confuse an angel—and surely, therefore, a poor poet! The Devil knows how to take hold of a man like that! He surrounded the Poet so completely with incense that the poor man lost his head, forgot his mission, his home, everything—even himself; he then vanished in smoke.

When the little birds heard about this they were sad, and for three days they didn't sing. The black wood snail became blacker still, not from grief but from envy.

"They should have burned incense for me," he said, "for it was I who gave him the idea for the most famous of his songs, the drum song about the way of the world. It was I who spat at the rose! I can bring witnesses to prove that!"

But no news of this reached the Poet's home in India, for all the little birds were mourning and silent for three days; and when their time of mourning was over, their grief had been so profound that they had forgotten for whom they wept. That's the way it goes.

"Now I'll have to go into the world and stay away like the others," said the fourth brother.

He had as good a humor as the third, though he was no poet, which was a fine reason for him to have a good humor. Those two had filled the castle with gaiety, and now the last of that gaiety was leaving. Men have always considered sight and hearing the two most important senses, those that it is most desirable to strengthen and sharpen; the other three senses are generally looked upon as subordinate. But that was not the belief of this son, for he had especially cultivated his *taste* in every way possible, and taste is very powerful indeed. It governs what goes into the mouth and into the mind; hence this brother tasted everything there was in pots and pans, in bottles and barrels, explaining that this was the uncouth side of his function. To him every man was a vessel with something cooking within, and every country was an enormous kitchen, a kitchen of the mind—this he considered fine indeed, and he wanted to go out into the world and taste of it.

"Perhaps I'll have better luck than my brothers. I shall be on my way—but how shall I travel? Are balloons invented yet?" he asked his father, who knew about all inventions that had been made or would be in the future. But men had not yet invented balloons, or steamships, or railways. "Then I'll go by balloon," he said. "My father knows how they're made and steered, and that I can learn. They aren't invented yet, so people will think it's some spirit of the air. When I have finished with the balloon I'll burn it, and for that you must give me some pieces of another invention to come— matches."

When he had received what he wanted, he flew away. The birds flew much farther along with him than they had with his brothers. They were curious to know how the flight would come out, for they thought it was some new kind of bird. More and more came sweeping up until the air was black with birds; they came on like the cloud of locusts over the land of Egypt. And so now he, the last brother, was out in the wide world.

"The East Wind is a good friend and helper to me," he said.

"You mean the East Wind and the West Wind!" said the winds. "You couldn't have flown northwest if we both hadn't helped you."

But he didn't hear what the wind said, and that makes no difference. The birds tired of flying along with the balloon. Too much had been made of that thing, said a pair of them. It had become conceited! "It isn't worth flying with; it's nothing!" And then they withdrew; they all withdrew, for indeed too much had been made of nothing.

The balloon descended over one of the greatest cities, and the aeronaut landed on the highest point, the church steeple. The balloon rose into the air again, which it shouldn't have done; we don't know where it went, but that doesn't matter, for it was not yet invented. There the young man sat on the church steeple, the birds no longer hovering around him; he had grown as tired of them as they had of him.

All the chimneys of the town smoked fragrantly.

"Those are altars erected in your honor," said the Wind, which thought it ought to say something pleasant.

He sat up there boldly and gazed down at the people in the streets. One person was prancing along, proud of his purse; another was proud of the key that hung at his girdle, though he had nothing for it to unlock; one was proud of his moth-eaten coat, another of his worm-eaten body.

"Vanity!" he said. "I must go down, dip my fingers into that pot, and taste it. But I'll sit here a little longer, for the wind is blowing very pleasantly against my back; I'll take a little rest. 'It is good to sleep long in the mornings, when one has much to do,' the lazy man says. Laziness is the root of all evil, but there is no evil in our family. I'll stay here as long as the wind blows, for it feels good."

So he sat there; but since he was sitting on the weathercock of the steeple, which turned round and round with him, he had the false idea that the same wind was still blowing, so he remained seated there; he might as well stay a long while and have a good taste.

Back in India, in the castle of the Tree of the Sun, it had become empty and quiet after the brothers, one after another, had gone away.

"Things are going badly with them," said the father. "Never will they bring home the gleaming jewel; it is not for me. They are all dead and gone!" And then he bent over the Book of Truth and gazed at the page that should have told him of life after death, but there was nothing for him to see or learn from it.

Now his blind daughter was his sole joy and consolation; she clung to him with deep affection, and for the sake of his happiness and peace of mind she wished the precious jewel might be discovered and brought home. With sorrow and longing she thought of her brothers. Where were they? Where could they be living? With all her heart she wished she might dream of them, but strangely enough, not even in her dreams could she reach them.

At last one night she dreamed that their voices sounded across to her, calling to her from out in the wide world, and she could not hold back, but traveled far, far away; and yet she seemed still to be in her father's house. She never met her brothers, but in her dream she felt a sort of fire burning in her hand that did not pain her—it was the shining jewel she was bringing to her father.

When she awoke she thought for a moment that she still held the stone in her hand, but it was the knob of her distaff that she was grasping. Through that long night she had spun incessantly, and on the distaff was a thread finer than the finest spider's web; human eyes could not distinguish the separate threads in it, so fine were they. She had moistened it with her tears, and it was as strong as a rope. She arose; her decision was made—the dream must become a reality.

It was still night, and her father was sleeping. She pressed a kiss on his hand, and then, taking her distaff, fastened the end of the thread to her father's castle. But for this, in her blindness she would never have been able to find her way home; she must hold fast to that thread and trust neither to herself nor to others. From the Tree of the Sun she broke off four leaves; these she would entrust to the winds to bring to her brothers as letters of greeting in case she should not meet them out there in the wide world.

How could she fare, that poor blind child? She could hold fast to her invisible thread. She possessed one gift that all the others lacked—sensibility—and by virtue of this she seemed to have eyes in the very tips of her fingers and ears in her heart.

Then she went forth quietly into the noisy, whirling, strange world, and wherever she went the sky became so bright with sunshine that she could feel the warm rays; and the rainbow spread itself through the blue air where there had been dark clouds. She heard the birds sing, and smelled the scent of orange groves and apple orchards so strongly that she seemed to taste the fruit. Soft tones and delightful sounds reached her ears, but with them came howlings and roarings; manifold thoughts and opinions strangely contradicted each other. The echoes of human thoughts and feelings penetrated into the depths of her heart. One chorus sounded mournfully,

> *Our earthly life is filled with mist and rain;*
> *And in the dark of night we cry with pain!*

But then she heard a brighter strain,

> *Our earthly life is like a rosebush, so bright;*
> *It is filled with sunshine and true delight!*

And if one chorus sounded bitterly,

> *Each person thinks of himself alone;*
> *This truth to us is often shown.*

from the other side came the answer,

> *Throughout our life a Fairy of Love*
> *Guides our steps from Heaven above.*

She could hear the words,

> *There's pettiness here, far and wide;*
> *Everything has its wrong side.*

But then she heard,

> *So much good is done here*
> *That never reaches man's ear.*

And if sometimes the mocking words sounded to her,

> *Make fun of everything, laugh in jest,*
> *Laugh along with all the rest!*

a stronger voice came from the Blind Girl's heart,

> *Trust in God and thyself; pray then*
> *His will be done forever; amen.*

Whenever the Blind Girl entered the circle of humanity and appeared among people, young or old, knowledge of the true, the good, and the beautiful was radiant in their hearts. Wherever she went, whether she entered the studio of the artist, or the hall decorated for the feast, or the crowded factory with its whirring wheels, it seemed as though a sunbeam were entering, as though the string of a lute sounded, or a flower exhaled its perfume, or a refreshing dewdrop fell upon a withering leaf.

But the Devil could not put up with this. With more cunning than that of ten thousand men, he devised a way to bring about his purpose. From the marsh he collected little bubbles of stagnant water and muttered over them a sevenfold echo of untrue words, to give them strength. Then he blended bought heroic poems and lying epitaphs, as many as he could find, boiled them in the tears of envy, colored them with grease paint he had scraped from the faded cheeks of an old lady, and from all this he fashioned a maiden with the appearance and carriage of the Blind Girl, the blessed angel of sensibility. Then the Devil's plot was consummated, for the world knew not which of the two was the true one, and indeed how could the world know?

> *Trust in God and thyself; pray then*
> *His will be done, forever; amen.*

sang the Blind Girl in complete faith. Then she entrusted to the winds the four green leaves from the Tree of the Sun as letters of greeting to her brothers, and she was quite sure that they would reach their destinations and the jewel be found, the jewel that dims all the glories of the world. From the forehead of humanity it would gleam even to the house of her father.

"Even to the house of my father," she repeated. "Yes, the place of the jewel is on this earth, and I shall bring with me more than the promise of it. I can feel its glow; in my closed hand it swells larger and larger. Every grain of truth, however fine it was, which the wind whirled toward me, I caught up and treasured; I let penetrate into it the fragrance of the beautiful, of which there is so much in the world, even for the blind. To the first I added the sound of the beating heart, doing good. I bring only dust with me, but still it is the dust of the jewel we sought, and it is in ample quantity. I have my whole hand full of it!"

Then she stretched forth her hand toward her father. She was home. She had traveled there with the swiftness of thoughts in flight, having never let go of the invisible thread leading to home.

With the fury of a hurricane, the evil powers swept over the Tree of the Sun, and their wind blasts rushed through the open doorway, into the sanctuary of the Book of Truth.

"It will be blown away by the wind!" cried the father, and he seized the hand she had opened.

"Never!" she replied with calm assurance. "It cannot be blown away; I can feel the rays warming my very soul."

And the father became aware of a dazzling flame, right where the shining dust poured from her hand onto the Book of Truth, that would grant the certainty of an everlasting life. Now on the white page there glowed one shining word—one word only—

BELIEVE

And once more the four brothers were with their father and sister. When the green leaf had fallen upon the bosom of each, a great longing for home had taken hold of them and led them back; the birds of passage had followed them, as had the stag, the antelope, and all the wild creatures of the forest, for all wished to share in their joys— and why shouldn't they when they could?

We have often seen how a column of dust whirls around where a sunbeam bursts through a crack in a door into a dusty room. But this was not common, insignificant dust; even the colors of the rainbow are lifeless compared with the beauty that showed itself here. From the page of the book, from the glowing word *Believe*, arose each grain of truth, decked with the loveliness of the beautiful and the good, flaming more brightly than the mighty pillar of fire that led Moses and the children of Israel to the land of Canaan. And from the word *Believe* arose the bridge of *Hope*, extending to the eternal love in the realm of the Infinite.

THE A-B-C BOOK (1858)

Once there was a man who had written some new rhymes for the A-B-C Book—two lines for each letter, just as in the old A-B-C Book. He believed the old rhymes were too antiquated, that something new was needed, and he thought well indeed of his own rhymes.

His new A-B-C Book was still only in handwriting, and already it had been placed beside the old printed one in the great bookcase where there stood many books, both of knowledge and for amusement. But the old A-B-C Book didn't want to be a neighbor to the new one, and therefore had sprung down from the shelf and at the same time had given the new one a push, so that it, as well as the old one, now lay on the floor, with all its loose leaves scattered about.

The old A-B-C Book lay open at the first page—and that is the most important page, for there all the letters, large and small, are displayed. That one page contains on it the essence of all the books that ever were written; it contains the alphabet, that wonderful army of signs which rules the world; truly a marvelous power they have! Everything depends on the order in which they are commanded to stand; they have the power to give life or to kill, to gladden and to sadden. Separately they mean nothing, but marshaled and ranked in word formations, what can they not accomplish! Yes, when God put them into man's thoughts, human strength became inferior to that which lay in the alphabet, and we yielded with a deep bow.

There, then, they lay now, facing upward, and the Cock which was pictured at the big A of the alphabet gleamed with feathers of red, blue, and green. Proudly he puffed himself up and ruffled his plumage, for he knew how important the letters were and that he was the only living thing among them.

When he found the old A-B-C Book had fallen open on the floor, he flapped his wings, flew out, and perched himself on a corner of the bookcase. There he preened himself with his beak and crowed loudly and long. Every single book in the case, all of which would stand day and night, as if in a trance when nobody was reading them, was roused by his trumpet call. Then the Cock spoke out loudly and clearly about the way the worthy old A-B-C Book had been insulted.

"Everything has to be new and different nowadays," he said. "Everything has to be advanced. Children are so wise that they can read before they have even learned the alphabet. 'They should have something new!' said the man who wrote those new verses sprawling there on the floor. I know them all by heart; he admires them so much that I have heard him read them aloud more than ten times over. No, I prefer my own, the good old rhymes with Xanthus for X, and with the pictures that belong to them! I'll fight for them and crow for them! Every book in the case here knows them very well. Now I'll read aloud these new rhymes. I'll try to read them patiently, and I know we'll all agree they're worthless."

A—Adam
Had Adam obeyed, he'd not have had to leave
The Garden where first dwelt he and Eve.
B—Bank; Bee

The Bank is a place where you put your money;
The Bee is an insect that gathers honey.

"Now that verse I find profoundly insipid!" said the Cock. "But I'll read on.

C—Columbus
Columbus sailed the ocean to the distant shore,
And then the Earth became twice as big as before.
D—Denmark
About the kingdom of Denmark, there's a saying which goes
God's hand protects it, as every Dane knows.

"That many people will consider beautiful," said the Cock. "But I don't. I see nothing beautiful about it. But I'll go on.

E—Elephant
The Elephant has a heavy step,
Though young in heart and full of pep.
F—Face
The Moon above feels at its best
When an eclipse gives its Face a rest.
G—Goat
It is easier to sail a boat
Than to teach manners to a Goat!
H—Hurrah
Hurrah is a word we often hear;
How often does the deed merit such cheer?

"How will a child understand that!" said the Cock. "I suppose they'll put on the title page, 'A-B-C Book for Big People and Little People'; but the big people have something else to do besides read the rhymes in A-B-C Books, and the little people won't be able to understand them. There is a limit to everything. But to continue:

J—Job
We have a Job to do on Earth
Till Earth becomes our final berth.

"Now, that's crude!" said the Cock.

K—Kitten
When Kittens grow up we call them cats
And hope they'll catch our mice and rats.
L—Lion
The savage Lion has much more sense
Than the arty critic's stinging offense!

"How are you going to explain that one to children?" said the Cock.

M—Morning Sun
The golden Morning sun arose,

But not because of the cock's crows.

"Now he's getting personal!" said the Cock. "But then I'm in excellent company. I'm in company with the sun. Let's go on.

> N—Negro
> Black is a Negro, black as Night,
> And we cannot wash him white!
> O—Olive Leaf
> The best of leaves—you know its name?
> The dove's Olive leaf—of Bible fame.
> P—Peace
> That Peace may ever reign, far and near,
> Is indeed a hope we all hold dear.
> Q—Queen; Quack
> A Queen is a lady of royal position.
> A Quack is a fake and not a physician.
> R—Round
> One may be Round and well extended,
> But that doesn't mean one is well descended!
> S—Swine
> Be not a braggart; be honest and true,
> Though many Swine in the forest belong to you!

"Will you permit me to crow!" said the Cock. "It tries your strength, reading so much; I must catch my breath." And then he crowed, shrill as a trumpet of brass, and it was a great pleasure to listen to—for the Cock. "I'll go on.

> T—Teakettle; Tea Urn
> The Teakettle in the kitchen will always belong,
> And yet to the Tea urn it gives its song.
> U—Universe
> Our Universe will always be,
> Through ages to eternity.

"Now that is meant to be deep!" said the Cock. "It's so deep I can't get to the bottom of it!

> W—Washerwoman
> A Washerwoman will wash and scrub
> Until there's nothing left but the tub!

"Now, it's certainly impossible that he can have found anything new for X.

> X—Xantippe
> In the sea of marriage are rocks of strife,
> As Socrates found with Xantippe, his wife.

"He would have to take Xantippe! Xanthus is much better.

Y—Ygdrasil
Under Ygdrasil tree the gods sat every day;
But the tree is dead and the gods have gone away.

"Now we are almost through," said the Cock. "That's a relief. I'll continue on.

Z—Zephyr
Zephyr, in Danish, is a west wind so cold
It penetrates fur and skin, we're told.

"That's that. But that's not the end of it. Now it will be printed and then it will be read. It will be offered in place of the noble old rhymes in my book. What says this assembly—learned and not so learned, single volumes and collected works? What says the alphabet? I have spoken; now let the others act."

The books stood still, and the bookcase stood still; but the Cock flew back to his place at the capital A in the old A-B-C Book and looked proudly around. "I have spoken well, and I have crowed well. The new A-B-C Book can't do anything like that. It will certainly die; in fact, it's dead already, for it has no Cock!"

THE WIND TELLS ABOUT VALDEMAR DAAE AND HIS DAUGHTERS (1859)

When the wind sweeps over the grass, the blades of grass ripple like the water of a lake; and when it sweeps over the cornfield, the ears of corn curl into waves like those on a lake; this is the dance of the Wind. But listen to him tell the story; he sings it out; and how different his song among the trees of the forest is from his shriek through the cracks, crannies, and crevices of old walls. Watch him chase the white, fleecy clouds across the sky like a flock of sheep; notice how he howls through the open gate, as if he were the watchman blowing his horn. Strangely he whistles through the chimney until the fire on the hearth beneath blazes up, and it is pleasant and comfortable to sit in the chamber warmed by its glow and listen to stories. Let only the Wind himself be the storyteller! He knows more wonderful tales than all the rest of us put together. Hear now how he tells the story: "Whew, whew, whew! On, on, on!" That is the theme of his song.

"Near the Great Belt there stands an old mansion with thick red walls," says the Wind. "I know every stone of those walls; I knew them in the olden days when they were part of Marsk Stig's castle on the promontory. They were torn down from there, but then they were built up again to form a new wall and a new mansion; this was Borreby Mansion, which stands to this day. I have seen and known all the noble men and women of many different families who have lived there. Now I shall tell you of Valdemar Daae and his daughters.

"He was a very proud man, for he was of royal blood. He knew more than how to hunt the stag or empty the jug. 'Everything will come out right,' he used to say.

"His highborn wife walked daintily in her golden-cloth garment over floors of polished mosaic. Magnificent tapestries and costly, beautifully carved furniture surrounded her; she had brought both silver and gold into the house; there was German beer in the cellar; proud black horses neighed in the stables; ah, Borreby Mansion was then the home of wealth. And there were children; three fair daughters—I can still remember their names—Ide, Johanne, and Anna Dorothea. These were rich folk, noble folk, born and reared in luxury. Whew, whew, whew! On, on, on!" sang the Wind, and then continued his tale.

"Here I never saw, as in other old houses, the noble mistress turning the spinning wheel among her maidens in the great hall. She played upon the lute and sang, though not always the old Danish songs, but songs in foreign languages. There were life and gaiety here; guests of distinction came from far and near; the sounds of music and the clinking of glasses were so loud that even I could not drown them. There was pride here, with boasting and bragging, and talk of domination, but not the blessings of our Lord!

"Then there was one May Day even," said the Wind, "when I came upon it from the west. I had seen ships wrecked on the coast of West Jutland, had hunted over the heath and the green-wooded shore to Fünen, and now I came over the Great Belt, blowing and roaring. I lay down for a rest on the coast of Zeeland, quite near Borreby Mansion, where the beautiful forest of oaks still grew. The young lads of the neighborhood came out to the forest to collect the biggest and driest branches and twigs they could find; they carried them into the town, laid them in piles, set fire to them, then the young men and girls sang as they danced around them.

"I lay still," said the Wind, "but then gently I just touched one of the branches that had been brought by the handsomest lad of them all, and immediately his pile of wood blazed up the highest. That meant he became the leader among them, with the privilege of choosing first one of the young girls to be his own May lamb. There was a joy, a merriment, such as I had never found in the rich Borreby Mansion.

"Then there came driving toward the mansion, in a gilded carriage drawn by six horses, the noble lady herself with her three daughters—so young and so fair—three sweet blossoms, a rose, a lily, and a pale hyacinth. Their mother was like a proud, splendid tulip; no word of greeting did she have for the peasants, who stopped their game and bowed and scraped to her; stiff as a tulip she held herself. Yes, rose, lily, and pale hyacinth, I saw all three; whose May lambs would they become one day, I wondered. Surely their young men would be proud knights, perhaps even princes! Whew, whew, whew! On, on, on!

"So the carriage rattled past, and the peasants returned to their dance. Summer was being celebrated from one town to another, in Borreby, Tjaereby, and all the towns around.

"But when I rose up that same night, the highborn lady had laid herself down, never to rise again. That had come to her which comes to all men; that is nothing new. Grave and thoughtful stood Valdemar Daae; he seemed to be saying, 'The proudest tree may be bowed, but not broken.' The daughters wept, and all eyes in the mansion had to be dried. Lady Daae had passed on—and I then passed on! Whew, whew, whew!

"I came again, as I often came across Fünen and the waters of the Belt, and rested near Borreby in the shelter of the beautiful oak forest. Here ospreys, wood pigeons, blue ravens, and even the black storks build their nests; it was the spring of the year, and some had eggs while others had even young ones. How they flew! How they cried! The sound of the ax could be heard, stroke after stroke; the trees were to be felled. Valdemar Daae had decided to build a ship, a great warship with three decks, which the king would surely buy, and for this the trees must fall and the birds lose their homes. The hawk flew away in terror as his nest was destroyed; the osprey and all the other birds flew around in terrified anger, screaming of their wrath and agony; I could understand them well enough. The crows and jackdaws shrieked in scorn, 'Caw, caw! From the nests!'

"And in the middle of the forest, with the workmen, stood Valdemar Daae and his three daughters, and they all laughed at the wild protests of the birds—all but the youngest, Anna Dorothea. She was a tenderhearted child, and when an old half-dead tree, on whose bare branches a black stork had built his nest, was to be cut down, it saddened her so to see the helpless young ones thrusting their heads out in the terror that she begged with tears in her eyes that this one tree be spared. So the tree with the black stork's nest was left standing.

"There was much hammering and sawing as the three-deck ship was being built. The master shipbuilder was a fine-looking young fellow, though of lowly birth, his eyes sparkling with life and his brow thoughtful. Valdemar Daae liked to hear him talk, and so did little Ide, his eldest daughter, who was now fifteen years old. And while he built the ship for her father, he built many a castle in the air besides, and saw himself and little Ide sitting there as man and wife. That might actually have come to pass if the castle had been of walled stone, with ramparts and moat, forest and gardens. But with all his skill, the builder was only a common bird, and what business did a sparrow have among a flock of cranes? Whew, whew, whew! I flew away and he flew away, and little Ide forgot it, as forget she must.

"In the stable the beautiful black horses neighed. They were worth looking at, and they *were* looked at. The admiral was sent by the king himself to inspect the new warship and to discuss buying it. He was loud in admiration for the splendid horses. I heard him well," said the Wind. "I followed the gentlemen through the open stable door and scattered about their feet wisps of straw, yellow as gold. Gold! That was what Valdemar Daae wanted, and the admiral wanted the black horses he admired so greatly, but all their discussion came to nothing. The horses weren't bought, and neither was the ship! It was left on the shore with planks over it, a Noah's ark that was never to float on water. Whew, whew, whew! It was a pity!

"In the winter, when the fields were covered with snow and ice floes choked the Belt," said the Wind, "flocks of black ravens and crows came and perched on the lifeless, solitary ship as it stood on the shore. The frantic old birds and the homeless young ones screamed hoarse tales about the oak forest that had been ravished and the many wonderful nests that had been destroyed, all for the sake of this great piece of useless lumber, the proud vessel that was never to sail the seas. And I tossed and whirled the snow about until it lay thickly over the ship; I made it listen to my voice and taught it all that a storm has to say; I certainly did my part in teaching it all a ship should know of life. Whew, whew, whew! On, on, on!

"And winter passed away, winter and summer passed, as they always pass, as I pass, as the snow melts, as the leaf drifts downward, as the apple blossom fades, away, away, away! And as people pass away!

"But the daughters were still young. Little Ide was still as blooming a rose as when the shipbuilder had seen her. Often I caught hold of her long brown hair when she stood thoughtfully beside the apple tree in the garden, and she didn't notice that I shook petals down on her hair, loosening it, as she gazed at the crimson sunset and the streak of golden sky through the dark bushes and trees. Her sister Johanne was still like a lily, bright and slender, straight and tall, as stiff upon her stalk as her mother had been. She loved to linger in the great hall where the portraits of their ancestors hung; the ladies were painted wearing velvets and silk, with tiny, pearl-embroidered hats set on their braids; they were beautiful ladies, indeed; the men were shown in steel armor, or in stiff white ruffs and rich mantles lined with squirrel fur, their swords belted to their sides, not around their waists. Johanne often wondered how her own portrait would look on those same walls, and what her husband would look like. Yes, she thought about that, and talked about it to herself. I heard it as I whipped through the long gallery into the hall and whirled around again.

"Anna Dorothea, the pale hyacinth, was still a very quiet child of fourteen, with large, thoughtful blue eyes, and the smile of childhood still lingering on her lips. Even if I could have I would never have blown that smile away. I met her in the garden, in the narrow lane, or in the fields, gathering herbs and flowers for her father to use in the wondrous potions and mixtures he used to prepare.

"Valdemar Daae, though haughty and conceited, was also a man of skill and great knowledge. People knew that and spoke about it. Fire burned in summer as well as winter in the fireplace in his study; his chamber door was always locked; night and day he worked, yet he seldom spoke of his labors. He knew that the secrets of nature must be wooed secretly, and he was seeking the best secret of all—how to produce pure red gold!

"The smoke therefore rose out of the chimney continuously, and the fire crackled as it burned. I was there!" sang the Wind. "I whistled up the chimney. 'Stop it! Stop it!' I sang through the chimney. 'It will all end in smoke, dust, embers, and ashes! You will burn yourself up! Whew, whew! Stop it!' But Valdemar Daae did not stop.

"Those superb horses in the stable—what became of them? And the fine old gold and silver in cupboards and chests, the cattle in the meadows, the mansion and all its riches? Yes, they were all melted down in the gold-making crucible, and yet no gold came of it. Barn and granary, cellar and pantry, all were empty now; the house sheltered fewer folk and more mice. One windowpane was broken, another cracked," said the Wind, "and now I had no need to go around to the door to get in. The chimney still smoked, to be sure, not for cooking dinner, but for cooking the red gold.

"I blew through the courtyard gates, like the watchman blowing his horn, but there was no watchman here," said the Wind. "I whirled the weathercock round and round, and it creaked like the snoring of the watchman, but there was no watchman; only rats and mice were there; poverty loaded the table and stuffed wardrobe and larder; the doors sagged from their hinges; there were chinks and cracks in plenty, so that I could go in and out at will.

"In the smoke and ashes, beset by sorrow and sleepless nights, Valdemar's hair and beard turned gray; his skin grew coarse and yellowish; his eyes still looked greedily for gold—the long hoped-for gold!

"I blew ashes and smoke into his face and beard. I whistled through the broken panes and open cracks and blew into the daughters' chest of drawers, where they kept their clothes, which now were faded and threadbare from constant use, but which had to last them. The poor dears never had such a song as this sung at their cradles; but none, save I, sang any song at all in the great hall now. The life of abundance had turned into one of poverty," said the Wind. "I snowed them in, and it is said that snow puts one in a good humor. They had no firewood, for the forest was destroyed. There came a sharp frost, and while I sprang through holes and passages and over walls and roofs to keep myself warm, the highborn daughters huddled in bed against the cold, and their father crept beneath a covering of rude skins. Nothing to eat, nothing to burn!

"It was a hard lesson they had to learn!

"Whew, whew, whew! But Valdemar Daae couldn't learn. 'After winter comes the spring,' he said, 'and after troubles come the good times; we have only to wait, wait! Now the mansion is mortgaged! Now it is high time indeed—and so we shall have gold! By Easter!' And then I saw him watching a spider at work, and heard him mutter, 'Good, industrious little weaver, you teach me to persevere! Your web may be broken, but you only begin it again; again it may be torn asunder, but all undismayed you return again and again to your work, and you are rewarded at last!'

"Then Easter morning came, and the bells rang and the sun shone in the heavens. He had awakened in a feverish heat; he had boiled and seethed and distilled and compounded. I heard him sigh like a lost soul and I heard him pray; I felt that he was holding his breath. The lamp had gone out, but he did not notice it. I blew on the coals until a flame shone on his chalk-white face and lighted up those staring eyes. But then those eyes became larger and larger—until they seemed about to burst.

"Behold the alchemistic glass! It glittered, glowing, pure and heavy; he lifted it with faltering hand; he cried with stumbling tongue, 'Gold! Gold!' He staggered, dizzy, and I could have blown him down as he stood," said the Wind, "but I only blew on the live coals, then followed him through the door to where his daughters sat, shivering. Ashes sprinkled his beard, clung to his dress, and lay in his matted hair. He stood erect and lifted high his treasure in its fragile glass. 'I've found it! I've won!' he cried. 'Gold!' The glass flashed in the sunbeams as he held it high—and then, lo! his hand trembled so that the alchemistic glass fell to the floor and shivered into a thousand fragments! His last bubble had burst! Whew, whew, whew! On, on, on! And I went on, away from the alchemist's home.

"Toward the end of that year, during the short days when the mist flings wet drops on the red berries and leafless branches, I came back in happy spirits, swept the heavens clean, and broke off the dead branches; that is not very hard work, to be sure, but it has to be done. And at the same time there was a different sort of sweeping and cleaning out at Borreby Mansion. Valdemar Daae's old enemy, Ove Ramel of Basnaes, was there with the mortgage on the mansion and all its contents. I drummed on the broken panes, beat against the ruined doors, and whistled through the cracks and chinks; Master Ove shouldn't find it pleasant to stay there. Ide and Anna Dorothea wept quietly; Johanne stood pale and stately and bit her thumb till it bled; but all that did no good.

"Ove Ramel generously offered to allow Mr. Daae to remain at the mansion during his lifetime, but he got no thanks for the gesture. I listened, and noticed how the homeless old nobleman held his head more proudly than ever. I rushed against the mansion and the old lime trees, so that the thickest branch broke off—and it wasn't a rotten one, either. There it lay at the gate, like a broom for sweeping out—and there was sweeping out there, you may be sure! But I had expected it.

"Oh, that was a day of bitterness—a sorrowful day! But with a stiff neck and a stout back the proud man bore his burden bravely.

"They had nothing left except the clothes they wore, and the new alchemistic glass, filled with the brittle treasure that had promised so much—the fool's gold scraped up from the floor; this Valdemar Daae hid in his breast. He took his cane in his hand, and with his three daughters the once rich nobleman walked out of Borreby Mansion. I blew cold upon his flaming cheeks and stroked his gray beard and long white hair to and fro as I sang, as loudly as I could, "Whew, whew, whew! This was the end of his glory!

"Ide and Anne Dorothea walked on each side of him, but as Johanne crossed the threshold she turned back. Perhaps, as he gazed so wistfully at the red stones that had once made up Marsk Stig's castle, she remembered the old ballad about Marsk Stig's daughters:

> *The elder took the younger by the hand,*
> *And forth they went to a distant land.*

"Was she thinking of this song? Here were three daughters, and their father was with them. They turned off from the highway, where they had used to drive in their carriage, and made their way to Smidstrup Field, to a little shack of mud they had rented for ten marks a year. These bare walls and empty chambers were their new 'mansion.' Crows and jackdaws circled above their heads, screaming, as if in mockery, 'Turned out of the nest! Caw, Caw!' just as they had screamed in Borreby Wood when the oaks were being cut down. Mr. Daae and his daughters must have understood the cries; they were not pleasant to listen to, so I did my best to drown them out by blowing about their ears.

"Thus they passed into the shack of mud on Smidstrup Field, and I passed away over field and moor, through bare hedges and leafless woods, away over open waters, to other lands—whew, whew! On, on! Year after year!"

What happened to Valdemar Daae; what happened to his daughters? The Wind will tell us:

"The last time I went to see them I found only Anna Dorothea, the pale hyacinth. She was then old and bent; it was half a hundred years later. She had lived the longest; she knew the whole story.

"Across the heath, near the town of Viborg, there stood the dean's beautiful new house, with red stones and pointed gables and chimneys always smoking busily. The gentle lady and her beautiful daughters sat on the balcony and looked out over the hanging buckthorn in the garden, out to the brown heath; what did they look at there? They looked at the stork's nest on that dilapidated cottage out there. Houseleek and moss made up most of the roof, if one could call it a roof; the stork's nest covered the greater part of it, and that alone was in good condition, for the stork kept it that way.

"It was a house to look at but not to touch," said the Wind. "I had to pass by it very gently. The hut was left there only for the sake of the stork's nest, for it was a certainly no credit to the heath. The dean didn't want to drive the stork away, so the poor old woman who had lived in the hut had permission to stay there and shelter herself as well as he could. For that she owed thanks to the queer Egyptian bird; or was it because, so many years ago, she had pleaded for the nest of his wild black brother in Borreby Wood? Then she, the poor woman, was a happy child, a delicate, pale hyacinth in the garden of her ancestral home. She remembered it now; Anna Dorothea forgot nothing.

"'Oh!' she sighed—yes, humans can sigh almost like the Wind himself does among the reeds and rushes. 'Oh!—there were no bells to ring at your funeral, Valdemar Daae! No groups of poor schoolboys sang psalms when Borreby's former master was laid to rest! Oh, but everything comes to an end—misery as well as happiness! It grieved my father worst of all that my sister Ide should become the wife of a peasant, a miserable peasant whom he could have punished by making him ride a hard plank. But he is at peace in the grave now, and you are with him, Ide! Oh, yes, ah, me—I am still here. I am old and poor. Deliver me, kind Christ!'"

Such was the prayer of Anna Dorothea in the miserable mud hut that was allowed to stand only for the sake of the stork.

"The boldest and most resolute of the three sisters I carried off myself," said the Wind. "She cut her clothes like a man's, disguised herself as a poor lad, and went into service as a sailor. She was sparing of speech, cross-looking, but quick at her work, although she couldn't climb the mast. So one night I blew her overboard, before anyone found out she was a woman; and I think that was the right thing to do.

"It was another Easter morning, bright as that morning when Valdemar Daae thought he had found the gold. Among those tumbledown walls beneath the stork's nest I could hear a faint voice chanting a psalm. It was Anna Dorothea's last hymn.

"There was no window with glass, only a hole in the wall; but the sun set itself there like a lump of gold, and as she gazed on its glory her heart broke and her eyes grew fixed. The stork had given her shelter to the day of her death. I sang at her funeral," said the Wind, "as I had sung at her father's; I know where his grave is, and her grave, but no one else knows.

"Now there are new times, changed times. The old highway is lost in the fields, old cemeteries have been made into new roads, and soon the steam engine, with its row of cars, will come to rush over the forgotten graves of unknown ancestors. Whew, whew, whew! On, on!

"And that's the story of Valdemar Daae and his daughters; tell it better, you people, if you think you can," said the Wind, then veered around.

He was gone.

THE GIRL WHO TROD ON THE LOAF (1859)

You have quite likely heard of the girl who trod on a loaf so as not to soil her pretty shoes, and what misfortunes this brought upon her. The story has been written and printed, too.

She was a poor child, but proud and arrogant, and people said she had a bad disposition. When but a very little child, she found pleasure in catching flies, to pull off their wings and make creeping insects of them. And she used to stick May bugs and beetles on a pin, then put a green leaf or piece of paper close to their feet, so that the poor animals clung to it, and turned and twisted as they tried to get off the pin.

"The May bug is reading now," little Inger would say. "See how it turns the leaves!"

As she grew older she became even worse instead of better; but she was very pretty, and that was probably her misfortune. Because otherwise she would have been disciplined more than she was.

"You'll bring misfortune down upon you," said her own mother to her. "As a little child you often used to trample on my aprons; and when you're older I fear you'll trample on my heart."

And she really did.

Then she was sent into the country to be in the service of people of distinction. They treated her as kindly as if she had been their own child and dressed her so well that she looked extremely beautiful and became even more arrogant.

When she had been in their service for about a year, her mistress said to her, "You ought to go back and visit your parents, little Inger."

So she went, but only because she wanted to show them how fine she had become. But when she reached the village, and saw the young men and girls gossiping around the pond, and her mother sat resting herself on a stone nearby, with a bundle of firewood she had gathered in the forest, Inger turned away; she was ashamed that one dressed as smartly as she should have for a mother such a poor, ragged woman who gathered sticks for burning. It was without reluctance that she turned away; she was only annoyed.

Another half year went by.

"You must go home someday and visit your old parents, little Inger," said her mistress. "Here's a large loaf of white bread to take them. They'll be happy to see you again."

So Inger put on her best dress and her fine new shoes and lifted her skirt high and walked very carefully, so that her shoes would stay clean and neat, and for that no one could blame her. But when she came to where the path crossed over marshy ground, and there was a stretch of water and mud before her, she threw the bread into the mud, so that she could use it as a steppingstone and get across with dry shoes. But just as she placed one foot on the bread and lifted the other up, the loaf sank in deeper and deeper, carrying her down until she disappeared entirely, and nothing could be seen but a black, bubbling pool! That's the story.

But what became of her? She went down to the Marsh Woman, who brews down there. The Marsh Woman is an aunt of the elf maidens, who are very well known. There have been poems written about them and pictures painted of them, but nobody knows much about the Marsh Woman, except that when the meadows begin to reek in the summer the old woman is at her brewing down below. Little Inger sank into this brewery, and no one could stand it very long there. A cesspool is a wonderful palace compared with the Marsh Woman's brewery. Every vessel is reeking with horrible smells that would turn a human being faint, and they are packed closely together; but even if there were enough space between them to creep through, it would be impossible because of the slimy toads and the fat snakes that are creeping and slithering along. Into this place little Inger sank, and all the horrible, creeping mess was so icy cold that she shivered in every limb. She became more and more stiff, and the bread stuck fast to her, drawing her as an amber bead draws a slender thread.

The Marsh Woman was at home, for the brewery was being visited that day by the Devil and his great-grandmother, the latter a very poisonous old creature who was never idle. She never goes out without taking some needlework with her, and she had brought some this time. She was sewing bits of leather to put in people's shoes, so that they should have no rest. She embroidered lies, and worked up into mischief and slander thoughtless words that would otherwise have fallen harmlessly to the ground. Yes, she could sew, embroider, and weave, that old great-grandmother!

She saw Inger, then put on her spectacles and looked again at her. "That girl has talent," she said. "Let me have her as a souvenir of my visit here; she will make a suitable statue in my great-grandchildren's antechamber." And she was given to her!

Thus little Inger went to hell! People don't always go directly down there; they can go by a roundabout way, when they have the necessary talent.

It was an endless antechamber. It made one dizzy to look forward and dizzy to look backward, and there was a crowd of anxious, exhausted people waiting for the gates of mercy to be opened for them. They would have long to wait. Huge, hideous, fat spiders spun cobwebs, of thousands of years' lasting, over their feet, webs like foot screws or manacles, which held them like copper chains; besides this, every soul was filled with everlasting unrest, an unrest of torment and pain. The miser stood there, lamenting that he had forgotten the key to his money box. Yes, it would take too long to repeat all the tortures and troubles of that place.

Inger was tortured by standing like a statue; it was as if she were fastened to the ground by the loaf of bread.

"This is what comes of trying to have clean feet," she said to herself. "Look at them stare at me!"

Yes, they all stared at her, with evil passions glaring from their eyes, and spoke without a sound coming from their mouths. They were frightful to look at!

"It must be a pleasure to look at me," thought little Inger. "I have a pretty face and nice clothes." And then she turned her eyes; her neck was too stiff to move. My, how soiled she had become in the Marsh Woman's brewery! Her dress was covered with clots of nasty slime; a snake had wound itself in her hair and dangled over her neck; and from every fold of her dress an ugly toad peeped out, barking like an asthmatic lap dog. It was most disagreeable. "But all the others down here look horrible, too," was the only way she could console herself.

Worst of all was the dreadful hunger she felt. Could she stoop down and break off a bit of the bread on which she was standing? No, her back had stiffened, her arms and hands had stiffened, her whole body was like a statue of stone. She could only roll her eyes, but these she could turn entirely around, so she could see behind her, and that was a horrid sight. Then the flies came and crept to and fro across her eyeballs. She blinked her eyes, but the flies did not fly away, for they could not; their wings had been pulled off, and they had become creeping insects. That was another torment added to the hunger, and at last it seemed to her as if part of her insides were eating itself up; she was so empty, so terribly empty.

"If this keeps up much longer, I won't be able to stand it!" she said.

But she had to stand it; her sufferings only increased.

Then a hot tear fell upon her forehead. It trickled over her face and neck, down to the bread at her feet. Then another tear fell, and many more followed. Who could be weeping for little Inger? Had she not a mother up there on Earth? A mother's tears of grief for her erring child always reach it, but they do not redeem; they only burn, and they make the pain greater. And this terrible hunger, and being unable to snatch a mouthful of the bread she trod underfoot! She finally had a feeling that everything inside her must have eaten itself up. She became like a thin, hollow reed, taking in every sound.

She could hear distinctly everything that was said about her on Earth above, and what she heard was harsh and evil. Though her mother wept sorrowfully, she still said, "Pride goes before a fall. It was your own ruin, Inger. How you have grieved your mother!" Her mother and everyone else up there knew about her sin, that she had trod upon the bread and had sunk and stayed down; the cowherd who had seen it all from the brow of the hill told them.

"How you have grieved your mother, Inger!" said the mother. "Yes, I expected this!"

"I wish I had never been born!" thought Inger. "I would have been much better off. My mother's tears cannot help me now."

She heard how her employers, the good people who had been like parents to her, spoke. "She was a sinful child," they said. "She did not value the gifts of our Lord, but trampled them underfoot. It will be hard for her to have the gates of mercy opened to let her in."

"They ought to have brought me up better," Inger thought. "They should have beaten the nonsense out of me, if I had any."

She heard that a song had been written about her, "the haughty girl who stepped on a loaf to keep her shoes clean," and was being sung from one end of the country to the other.

"Why should I have to suffer and be punished so severely for such a little thing?" she thought. "The others certainly should be punished for their sins, too! But then, of course, there would be many to punish. Oh, how I am suffering!"

Then her mind became even harder than her shell-like form.

"No one can ever improve in this company! And I don't want to be any better. Look at them glare at me!"

Her heart became harder and full of hatred for all mankind.

"Now they have something to talk about up there. Oh, how I am suffering!"

When she listened she could hear them telling her story to children as a warning, and the little ones called her "the wicked Inger." "She was so very nasty," they said, "so nasty that she deserved to be punished." The children had nothing but harsh words to speak of her.

But one day, when hunger and misery were gnawing at her hollow body, she heard her name mentioned and her story told to an innocent little girl, who burst into tears of pity for the haughty, clothes-loving Inger.

"But won't she ever come up again?" the child asked.

"She will never come up again," they answered her.

"But if she would ask forgiveness and promise never to be bad again?"

"But she will not ask forgiveness," they said.

"Oh, how I wish she would!" the little girl said in great distress. "I'd give my doll's house if she could come up! It's so dreadful for poor Inger!"

These words reached right down to Inger's heart and seemed almost to make her good. For this was the first time anyone had said, "Poor Inger," and not added anything about her faults. An innocent little child had wept and prayed for her, and she was so touched by it that she wanted to weep herself, but the tears would not come, and that was also a torture.

The years passed up there, but down below there was no change. Inger heard fewer words from above; there was less talk about her. At last one day she heard a deep sigh, and the cry, "Inger, Inger, how miserable you have made me! I knew that you would!" Those were the dying words of her mother.

She heard her name mentioned now and then by her former mistress, and it was in the mildest way that she spoke: "I wonder if I will ever see you again, Inger! One never knows where one is to go!" But Inger knew that her kindly mistress would never descend to the place where *she* was.

Again a long time passed, slowly and bitterly. Then Inger heard her name again, and she beheld above her what seemed to be two bright stars shining down on her. They were two mild eyes that were closing on earth. So many years had passed since a little girl had wept over "Poor Inger" that that child had become an old woman, now being called by the Lord to himself. At that last hour, when the thoughts and deeds of a lifetime pass in review, she remembered very clearly how, as a tiny child, she had wept over the sad story of Inger. That time and that sorrow were so intensely in the old woman's mind at the moment of death that she cried with all her heart, "My Lord, have I not often, like poor Inger, trampled underfoot your blessed gifts and counted them of no value? Have I not often been guilty of the sin of pride and vanity in my inmost heart? But in your mercy you did not let me sink into the abyss, but did sustain me! Oh, forsake me not in my final hour!"

Then the old woman's eyes closed, but the eyes of her soul were opened to things formerly hidden; and as Inger had been so vividly present in her last thoughts she could see the poor girl, see how deeply she had sunk. And at that dreadful sight the gentle soul burst into tears; in the Kingdom of Heaven itself she stood like a child and wept for the fate of the unhappy Inger. Her tears and prayers came like an echo down to the hollow, empty shape that held the imprisoned, tortured soul. And that soul was overwhelmed by all that unexpected love from above. One of God's angels wept for her! Why was this granted her?

The tormented soul gathered into one thought all the deeds of its earthly life, and trembled with tears, such tears as Inger had never wept before. Grief filled her whole being. And as in deepest humility she thought that for her the gates of mercy would never be opened, a brilliant ray penetrated down into the abyss to her; it was a ray more powerful than the sunbeams that melt the snowmen that boys make in their yards. And under this ray, more swiftly than the snowflake falling upon a child's warm lips melts into a drop of water, the petrified figure of Inger evaporated; then a tiny bird arose and followed the zigzag path of the ray up to the world of mankind.

But it seemed terrified and shy of all about it; as if ashamed and wishing to avoid all living creatures, it hastily concealed itself in a dark hole in a crumbling wall. There it sat trembling all over, and could utter no sound, for it had no voice. It sat for a long time before it dared to peer out and gaze at the beauty about; yes, there was beauty indeed. The air was so fresh and soft; the moon shone so clearly; the trees and flowers were so fragrant; and the bird sat in such comfort, with feathers clean and dainty. How all creation spoke of love and beauty! The bird wanted to sing out the thoughts that filled its breast, but it could not; gladly would it have sung like the nightingale or the cuckoo in the springtime. Our Lord, who hears the voiceless hymn of praise even from a worm, understood the psalm of thanksgiving that swelled in the heart of the bird, as the psalm echoed in the heart of David before it took shape in words.

For weeks these mute feelings of gratitude increased. Someday surely they would find a voice, perhaps with the first stroke of the wing performing some good deed. Could not this happen?

Now came the feast of holy Christmas. Close by the wall a farmer set up a pole and tied an unthreshed bundle of oats on it, that the fowls of the air might also have a merry Christmas, and a joyous meal in this, the day of our Savior.

Brightly the sun rose that Christmas morning and shone down upon the oats and all the chirping birds that gathered around the pole. Then from the wall there came a faint "tweet, tweet." The swelling thoughts had at last found a voice, and the tiny sound was a whole song of joy as the bird flew forth from its hiding place; in the realm of Heaven they well knew who this bird was.

The winter was unusually severe. The ponds were frozen over thickly; the birds and wild creatures of the forest had very little food. The tiny bird flew about the country roads, and whenever it chanced to find a few grains of corn fallen in the ruts made by the sleds, it would eat but a single grain itself, while calling the other hungry birds, that they might have some food. Then it would fly into the towns and search closely, and wherever kindly hands had strewed bread crumbs outside the windows for the birds, it would eat only a single crumb and give all the rest away.

By the end of the winter the bird had found and given away so many crumbs of bread that they would have equaled in weight the loaf upon which little Inger had stepped to keep her fine shoes from being soiled; and when it had found and given away the last crumb, the gray wings of the bird suddenly became white and expanded.

"Look, there flies a sea swallow over the sea!" the children said as they saw the white bird. Now it seemed to dip into the water; now it rose into the bright sunshine; it gleamed in the air; it was not possible to see what became of it; they said that it flew straight into the sun.

OLE, THE TOWER KEEPER (1859)

"In this world things go up and down and down and up!" said Ole, the tower keeper. "Now I can't get any higher! Up and down and down and up; that's the fate of most of us; in fact, we all become tower keepers at last; we look at life and things from above."

Thus spoke my friend Ole, in his tower—a chatty, jolly fellow who seemed to say whatever came into his head yet had so many serious thoughts concealed deep in his heart. He came from a good family; there were some who said that he was a conference councillor's son, or might have been. He had a good education, had been the assistant to a schoolmaster, the deputy of a parish clerk, but what help could that have been! When he lived with the parish clerk it was agreed that he should have free use of everything in the house. He was then young and a bit of a dandy as we call it, and he wanted shoe polish to brush and shine his boots with; but the parish clerk would only allow him grease, and so they had a quarrel. One spoke of stinginess, the other of vanity; the shoe polish became the black cause of their strife, and so they separated.

But what he wanted from the parish clerk he wanted of the world generally—the very best polish, and he always got its substitute, grease, so he turned his back on everybody and finally became a hermit. But in a big city, hermitage with a livelihood is to be found only in the church tower, so up it he went, and there he would smoke his pipe and pace up and down on his lonely walks, looking upward and downward, and talking in his own way about what he saw or didn't see, what he read in books or in himself.

I often lent him books to read, good books, for by the company one keeps shall he be known. He didn't care for the English-governess type of novel, he said, nor for the French ones, either, which he called a brew of empty wind and rose stalks; no, he liked biographies and books about the wonders of nature. I visited him at least once a year, generally soon after the new year; he always had something to tell which the change of year suggested to his thoughts.

I shall tell about two visits, and use his own words as far as I can.

FIRST VISIT

Among the books I had recently lent Ole was one about pebbles, which had greatly pleased him.

"They are truly veterans from olden times, those pebbles," he said, "yet people pass them by without thinking, and trample them down in fields or on beaches, those fragments of antiquity. I have done so myself. From now on I shall hold every paving stone in high respect! Thank you for the book; it has driven cobwebby old thoughts and ideas out of my head and made me eager to read more of the same type.

"The romance of the Earth is truly the most fascinating of all romances. It's a shame we can't read the first parts of it; but they're written in a language we haven't learned yet; we have to dig away among strata and rocks, puzzling out bits here and there from the early acts of earth's drama. The acting persons of the drama, old Mr.

Adam and Mrs. Eve, don't make their entrance before the sixth act; that's far too late for many impatient readers, who want them to come on stage right away, but it's all the same to me. It is indeed a most marvelous romance, and here we are all in it. We creep and crawl about, but always stay where we are, while all the while the globe keeps turning around, but never splashing its ocean spray over us. The crust on which we move remains solid so that we never fall through, and so it is a story of millions of years, with steady progress.

"Many thanks for your book on pebbles; those old fellows could tell us so much if only they could talk. Isn't it funny to be a nobody once in a while, like me, and then remember that we all, whether we have the best shoe blacking or not, are just like tiny ants on the anthill of the world, even though some of us ants have stars and decorations, honors and offices? And it makes you feel so ridiculously young, compared with the millions of years of these venerable stones! I read your book on New Year's Eve and became so lost in it that I entirely forgot my usual New Year's Eve entertainment— watching the wild hunt to Amager; but you don't know what that is.

"The witches' flight to the Blocksberg on Midsummer Eve is, of course, well known, but we also have a wild mob, in this land and in our time, which speeds to Amager on New Year's Eve. All the bad poets, poetesses, newspaper hack writers, musicians, and artistic lions who are not worth anything else ride through the air to Amager on New Year's Eve. They sit astride their pencils or quill pens—for steel pens are too stiff for riding. I watch them every New Year's Eve—I could name most of them, but it isn't worthwhile—they don't imagine that anybody knows of their trip through the air on the quill pens. There is a sort of a niece of mine who is a fisherwoman and writes scandal and slander for three respectable papers; she says she has been out there as an invited guest, and they carried her, for since she cannot herself use a pen she couldn't ride on one. She has described the whole affair. Half of what she told me is probably a lie, but the other half is enough.

"When she was well underway they all broke into song; each of the guests had written his own song, and each sang his own composition, because, of course, he thought it was the best. They were all very much alike; and all sung to the same melody. Then, in little groups, up marched those who occupy themselves only as chatterboxes. They were now singing bells that sang alternately. Then came the small drummers, who drummed in family groups. Those who write anonymously were introduced—those, let me say here, whose grease is used for shoe polishing. There was the executioner, and his helper, and the helper was the worst, for otherwise no one would have paid any attention to him. There was the street sweeper with his cart, who turns over his dustbin and calls it "good, very good, remarkably good." During all this merriment, such as it was, there would shoot forth from holes scattered about now a gaunt stalk, now a leafless tree, a huge flower, or a large mushroom, and finally a roof that bore upon itself everything this honorable assembly had given to the world during the preceding year. Bright sparks could be seen glittering among them—there were the borrowed thoughts they had used, which now cut themselves loose and flew up like fireworks.

"A game called 'the stick burns' was played; and the younger poets played 'heartburns.' The jesters told their jokes, and the jokes rang out like empty pots being thrown against doors. My niece said it was most amusing; she told me a good deal more, too malicious to mention, but very funny. So you see, since I know so much about this midnight festival, it's only natural I should be interested in watching for it every New Year's Eve.

"But this year I forgot all about it. I was rolling through millions of years with my rocks, watching them break loose up in the North, drift along on icebergs ages before the building of Noah's ark, sink to the bottom of the sea, then mount again on a reef, and at last peer up through the water and say, 'This shall be Zealand!' I saw them become the homes of many different birds whose species we don't know, and the homes of savage chieftains we don't know either, until the ax hewed out in runic letters the names of a few that can thus take a place in our histories. I had gone beyond all lapse of time and had become a nonentity.

"Then three or four beautiful shooting stars fell; they shone brightly, and started my thoughts off in an entirely different direction. Does anybody know what a shooting star really is? The learned do not know! But I have my own idea about them, and this is it:

"How often is it that not a single word of thanks or blessing is given for a generous action or beautiful work that rejoices all who witness it! Yes, often that gratitude is voiceless, but still it doesn't fall wasted to the ground. I can fancy it is caught up by the sunshine, and eventually the sunbeams carry it away and shower it over the head of the benefactor. Sometimes the thanks of a whole nation are thus due; they may come late, but at last they do come like a bouquet, when a shooting stars falls over the grave of some hero or statesman. Thus it's a great thrill to me when I see a shooting star, especially on New Year's Eve, and try to guess for whom that bouquet of gratitude can be meant. A short time ago a radiant shooting star fell in the southwest—now for whom could that have been intended? I am sure it fell right over the bank by the Flensborg Fjord, where the white-crossed flag of Denmark floats over the graves of Schleppegrell, Laessoe, and their comrades. Another one fell in the heart of Zealand, fell upon Sorö; I'm sure that was a bouquet for Holberg's grave, a thanksgiving from the multitude who during years past have laughed over his delightful plays.

"It is a great thought, a happy thought, to know that a shooting star like that will fall upon our own graves! Well, none will ever fall on mine; no sunbeam will bring me thanks, for I haven't done anything to be thanked for. I don't even merit polish for my boots," said Ole. "My lot in life has been only to get grease."

SECOND VISIT

On another New Year's Day I went to the tower, and this time Ole talked about the "Skaal" toasts that had been drunk with the change of the old year to the new. Then he gave his story of the glasses, and there was sense in what he said.

"On New Year's Eve when the clock strikes twelve, people rise from the table with freshly filled glasses and drink a toast to the new year. So people begin the new year with a glass in their hands, and that's fine for people who like to drink; others start the year by going to bed, and that's first rate for lazybones! But then, sleep is sure to play a leading part in the coming year, and so is the glass.

"Do you know what lives in the glasses?" he asked. "Why, health, happiness, and joy live there! Misfortune and bitter misery dwell there! When I count up the glasses I can tell the gradations of the different people.

"You see, the first glass is the glass of health. In it grows the health herb. Stick that into your beam, and by the end of the year you may sit in the arbor of health.

"Now take the second glass. Ah, yes, out of it there flies a little bird, singing with such innocent happiness that men listen to it and perhaps sing with it, 'Life is beautiful! We will not hang our heads! Put cheer and courage forth!'

"From the third glass a tiny winged imp darts out. You can't call him a little angel, for he has the blood and soul of a goblin, all for jest and mischief. He lurks behind our ear and whispers some queer drollery; he creeps into our heart and warms it until one becomes frolicsome, becomes the great wit in a party of wits.

"In the fourth glass there is neither herb, nor bird, nor fairy. That glass is the boundary line of sense, beyond which you should never, never pass.

"Do you take the fifth glass? Then will you weep over yourself, or laugh with a fierce shout. For out of this glass will spring riotous Prince Carnival, flippant and wild as an elf. He will overcome you, until you forget your dignity, if you ever had any, and forget things you ought not to forget. All is dance and song and revelry; the masks carry you away with them, and the daughters of evil, in silk and flowers, come with flowing hair and alluring charms. Tear yourself loose if you can!

"And the sixth glass! Yes, in that sits Satan himself, a little, well-dressed charming man who never contradicts you, tells you that you are always right. He comes with a lantern to guide you home! What sort of home, and what sorts of spirits live there? There's an old legend about a saint who was ordered to choose one of the seven deadly sins, and chose what he thought was the least—drunkenness. But in it he committed all the other six. Man and the Devil mixed with blood—that is the sixth glass; and all the evil seeds within us thrive on it, and each of them sprouts with a force like the grain of mustard, in the Bible, and grows into a mighty tree, spreading out over the whole world.

"Most have nothing before them but to be put into the smelting oven and be cast in a new mold.

"This is the story of the glasses," said Ole, the tower keeper, "and it can be told both with shoe polish and grease! I give it to you with both."

That was my second visit to Ole. If you want to hear more, we will have to pay him another visit.

ANNE LISBETH (1859)

Anne Lisbeth's complexion was like peaches and cream; her eyes were bright, her teeth shiny white; she was young, gay, and beautiful to look upon; her steps were light and her mind was even lighter. What would come of all this? "That awful brat," people said about her baby; and indeed he wasn't pretty, so he was left with the ditchdigger's wife.

Anne Lisbeth went into service in the count's castle. There she sat in a magnificent room, dressed in silk and velvet; not a breath of wind was allowed to blow on her nor anyone to speak a harsh word to her. She was nurse to the count's child, who was as beloved as a prince, beautiful as an angel. How she loved him!

Her own child was provided for in the ditchdigger's house, where his wife's temper boiled over more often than her pot. Sometimes the child was left alone all day long, and cried; but what nobody hears doesn't bother anyone! He cried himself to sleep, and in sleep there is neither hunger nor thirst; sleep is such a good invention!

"Ill weeds grow fast," says the proverb, and Anne Lisbeth's boy did indeed shoot up rapidly. It was as if he had taken root in the ditchdigger's household; his mother had paid for his upbringing and considered herself well rid of him. She was a city lady now, was well provided for, and whenever she went out she was beautifully dressed; but she never went to see her son at the ditchdigger's; that was too far from the city, and there was no reason for her to go there, anyway; the boy was theirs, and now, they decided, it was time for him to earn his keep; so he found work tending Mads Jensen's red cow.

The watchdog at Blegdam Manor sits proudly on top of its house in the sunshine, barking at passersby, but in rainy weather it lies, warm and dry, inside its kennel. Anne Lisbeth's boy sat at the edge of a ditch in the sunshine, whittling sticks or watching three blossoming strawberry plants; he hoped they would soon turn into berries— that was his happiest thought—but the berries never ripened. Through sunshine or showers he sat there; he was often soaked to the skin, but the cold wind soon dried his clothes on his body. Whenever he went to the farmyard he received only kicks and cuffs and was called "stupid and ugly"; he was used to that—nobody loved him.

How did Anne Lisbeth's boy get along? How could he under such circumstances? It was his fate never to be loved.

At last he was literally pushed off the earth and sent to sea in a wretched little sailing vessel. Here he took the helm while the skipper drank—a frostbitten, shabby-looking little boy, and always hungry! One would think he never had enough to eat, and that really was the case.

It was late in the autumn, wet, raw, stormy weather, with a wind that cut through the warmest clothing, especially out at sea. A miserable little vessel with one sail drove on before the wind; it had a crew of two men, or rather a man and a half— the skipper and his boy. All day the light had been no brighter than twilight; now it grew still darker and it was bitterly cold. The skipper brought forth a bottle and a glass and took a swallow to warm himself up; the top of the glass was whole, but its foot had been broken off, so instead it had a little piece of wood, painted blue, to stand on. A drink is a great comfort, and two are even better. The boy was at the helm, holding it with rough, tarred hands, a wretched, shrinking form with unkempt hair; it was the ditchdigger's boy, registered in the parish records as the son of Anne Lisbeth.

The wind drove the ship hard before it; the sail bellied out before the power of the wind; it was rough and wet everywhere, and it might soon be even worse. Stop! What was that? What crashed? What sprang up? What grasped the little vessel? The boat whirled around. Was it a waterspout or a tidal wave? The boy at the helm screamed, "Lord Jesus, save us!" The vessel had struck on a great rock, and it sank like a waterlogged old shoe in a duckpond; sank with "man and mouse," as the saying goes; there were mice on board, but only a man and a half—the skipper and the ditchdigger's boy. No one saw it, save the screaming gulls above and the darting fishes beneath, and these hardly saw it clearly, for they fled in terror when the water poured into the doomed vessel. There it lay, scarcely a fathom below the water, and the two were drowned and forgotten. Only the glass was left, for the blue wooden block kept it afloat, and it drifted onto the shore. Where and when? That is of no consequence. That old broken glass had been useful, and had been loved, too, in a way; which Anne Lisbeth's son had never been. However, in the Kingdom of Heaven no soul shall ever have cause to sigh, "Never loved!"

Anne Lisbeth meanwhile had been living for several years in a large town; she was addressed as "madam" and always held herself very proudly when she spoke of olden times, of the times when she rode in a carriage and talked with countesses and baronesses. And she talked of her foster child, that sweetest of little angels, and how he had loved her and she had loved him, how they had kissed and caressed each other, for he was her pride and joy. Now he was tall, fourteen years old, a bright, beautiful boy. She hadn't seen him since the time she carried him in her arms; for many years she had not been at the count's castle, which was a long journey away.

"But I must find a way to get there someday," said Anne Lisbeth. "I must see my sweet young count again. He must be missing me, and loving me as he did when his angelic little arms clung around my neck and he said, 'Ann-Lis,' as sweet as a violin. Ah, yes, I must make short work of it and see him again!"

So she made the long trip, partly on foot and partly by wagon. The castle was as magnificent and the gardens as lovely as ever, but the servants were all new to her, and not one of them knew Anne Lisbeth or what she had once meant there. But the countess would tell them, she thought, and her own boy; how she longed for him!

Now Anne Lisbeth was finally here, but they kept her waiting a long time. At last, just before the household went to dinner, she was called in. The countess spoke to her very courteously and promised that after dinner she should see her beloved boy. So she had to wait for another summons.

How tall, thin, and lanky he had grown, but he still had his beautiful eyes and angelic mouth; and he looked straight at her without a word. Certainly he had no recollection of her. He turned to go, but she caught his hand and pressed it to her lips. "All right," he said, "that's enough," and then he left the room.

The ungrateful young nobleman, whom she had loved above all on Earth and had made the pride of her life!

So Anne Lisbeth left the castle and made her way homeward along the highway. She was very sorrowful; he had been so cold and strange to her, without a word or thought for her, he whom she had once carried in her arms night and day and always had carried in her heart.

Then a huge black raven flew down and alighted on the road just in front of her and croaked again and again. "Oh, what bird of ill omen are you?" she said.

As she passed the ditchdigger's house, his wife was standing in the doorway, and they spoke to one another.

"How robust you look!" said the ditchdigger's wife. "You are plump and stout! Everything must be going well with you."

"Pretty well," replied Anne Lisbeth.

"The boat went down with them," said the ditchdigger's wife. "Skipper Lars and your boy were both drowned. So that ends that. But I hoped that the boy would have lived to help me out from time to time with a little money; he hasn't cost you anything for a long while, you know, Anne Lisbeth."

"Drowned, are they?" repeated Anne Lisbeth, and then said nothing more on that subject.

Anne Lisbeth was heartsick because the young count wouldn't speak to her, she who loved him so and had taken that long trip to see him; the journey had also been expensive. The pleasure it had brought her was little indeed. But she didn't say a word about it; she wouldn't lighten her mind by talking about it to the ditchdigger's wife, who might think she was no longer welcome at the count's castle. While they were talking, the raven again flew screaming over her head. "That ugly black thing!" said Anne Lisbeth. "That's the second time it's frightened me today!"

She had brought some coffee beans and chicory with her; it would be a kindness to the ditchdigger's wife to give these to her and share a cup with her. While the old woman went to make the coffee Anne Lisbeth sat down and soon fell asleep.

Strangely enough, she dreamed of one whom she had never seen in her dreams before—her own child, who in that very house had hungered and wept, who had been kicked about in heat and cold, and who now lay deep below the sea, the good Lord only knew where. She dreamed that even as she sat there waiting for the coffee and smelling the fragrance drifting in to her from the kitchen, a shining little angel, beautiful as the young count, stood in the doorway and spoke to her.

"The end of the world is come," said the little angel. "Hold fast to me, for you are still my mother! You have an angel in Paradise. Hold fast to me!" Then he took hold of her, and at that very moment there came a tremendous crash, as though the whole world were bursting into pieces, and as the angel rose in the air, holding her tightly by her sleeves, she felt herself lifted from the ground. But then something heavy clung to her feet and dragged her down; it was as if a hundred other women were holding tightly to her, screaming, "If you are to be saved, we must be saved, too! Hold fast! Hold fast!" And then they all clung to her. The weight was too heavy; ritsch, ratsch!— her sleeves were split, and she fell down in terror—and awoke.

Her head was so dizzy she nearly fell off the chair where she was sitting. She could not understand her dream clearly, but she felt it foretold evil for her.

They had their coffee and talked for a while. Then Anne Lisbeth walked on to the nearest village, where she was to meet the carrier and drive home with him that evening. But when she got there, the carrier told her he couldn't start until the following evening. She thought it over—what it would cost her to stay there, the length of the distance home, and realized that if she went along the seashore instead of by road, it would be nearly two miles shorter; it was clear weather and the moon was at the full. And so Anne Lisbeth decided to go at once; she could be home the next day.

The sun had set, the vesper bells were still ringing—no, it was not the bells, but Peter Oxe's frogs croaking in their pond. Soon they, too, were silent, and then all was still; no bird raised its voice, for all were at rest; and it seemed the owl was not at home.

The hush of death settled over forest and shore. She could hear her own footsteps in the sand. No wave disturbed the sea, the deep waters were at peace; everywhere was silence, silence among the living and the dead.

Anne Lisbeth walked on, not thinking of anything in particular, as we say. Yet, though she was not conscious of it, her thoughts were busy within her, as they always are within all of us. They lie asleep inside us, thoughts that have already shaped themselves into action and thoughts that have never yet stirred—there they lie still, and someday they will come forth. It is written: "The labor of righteousness is peace;" and again it is written: "The wages of sin are death!" Much has been said and written that one does not know—or, as it was with Anne Lisbeth, does not remember—but such things can appear before one's subconscious self, can come to mind, though one is unaware of it.

The germs of vices and virtues are alive deep in our hearts—in yours and mine; they lurk like tiny invisible seeds. There comes a ray of sunshine or the touch of an evil hand; you turn to the right or to the left, and the little seed quivers into life, puts forth shoots, and pours its life throughout all the veins. Walking in a daydream, one may be unconscious of many painful thoughts, but they have their being within us all the same; thus Anne Lisbeth walked as if in a daydream, but her thoughts lived within her.

From Candlemas to Candlemas the heart has much written upon it, even the record of the whole year. Many sins are forgotten, sins in word or thought, sins against God or our neighbor or our own conscience; we think not of them, nor did Anne Lisbeth. She had broken no laws of the land; she knew that she was popular, esteemed, even respected.

Now, as she walked along the shore, suddenly something made her start and stand still! What was it? Only an old man's hat. Where could that have been washed overboard? She drew closer and looked down at it.

Oh! What was that lying over there? She became very frightened, and yet it was nothing but a heap of tangled seaweed, but to her fancy it had seemed for a moment the body of a man. As she continued on her way she remembered many stories she had heard as a child about the old superstitious belief in the "sea ghost"—the ghost of a drowned body that lay still unburied, washed by the tides on the wild seashore. The lifeless body itself could harm no one, but the "sea ghost" would follow a solitary wanderer, clinging fast to him and demanding to be carried to the churchyard and buried in consecrated ground. "Hold on! Hold on!" it would cry; and as Anne Lisbeth thought of these words, all at once there came back to her most vividly her dream— how the mothers had clung to her, screaming, "Hold fast! Hold on!" how the world had split beneath her, how her sleeves had been torn apart and she had fallen from the grasp of her child, who had tried to hold her up in the hour of doom. Her child, her own flesh and blood, whom she had never loved and scarcely ever thought of, was now lying at the bottom of the sea; any day his body might be washed ashore, and his ghost might follow her, wailing, "Hold on! Hold on! Bury me in Christian earth!"

Panic-stricken by this horrible thought, she ran faster and faster. Terror touched her heart with a cold, clammy finger; she was ready to faint. And as she looked upon the sea, the air grew thicker and thicker, a heavy mist fell over the scene, veiling tree and bush in strange disguises. She turned to seek for the Moon behind her—and it was only a pale disk without rays. Then something heavy seemed to drag at her limbs; "Hold on! Hold on!" she thought. And when she again turned toward the Moon its white face seemed close beside her, and the mist hung like a shroud over her shoulders. "Hold on! Bury me in Christian earth!"—she could almost hear those words. And then she did hear a sound, so hollow, so hoarse—not the voices of the frogs in the pond nor the tones of the raven, for neither was nearby, but clearly she heard the dreadful words, "Bury me! Bury me!" Yes! It was, it must be, the ghost of her own child, who could find no rest for his soul until his body was carried to the churchyard and laid in a Christian grave.

To the churchyard she would hurry; that very hour she would dig the grave; and as she turned toward the church her burden seemed to grow lighter, until it disappeared altogether. As soon as she felt that, she started back to follow the short cut to her home, but once more her limbs sank beneath her, and again the terrible words rang in her ears, "Hold on! Hold on!" It sounded like the croaking of a frog and like a wailing bird.

"Bury me! Bury me!"

Cold and clammy was the mist, but still colder and clammier were her hands and face under the touch of fear! A heavy weight again clung to her and seemed to drag her down; her heart quaked with thoughts and feelings that had never stirred within her before this moment.

In our northern countries a single spring night is often enough to dress the beech wood, and in the morning sunlight it appears in its young, bright foliage.

In one second the seed of sin within us may be lifted to the light and unfolded into thoughts, words, and deeds; and thus it is when conscience is awakened. And our Lord awakens it when we lest expect it; when there is no way to excuse ourselves, the deed stands open to view, bearing witness against us; thoughts spring into words, and words ring clearly throughout the world. Then we are horrified to find what we have carried within us, that we have not overcome the evil we have sown in thoughtlessness and pride. The heart hides within itself all vices and virtues, and they grow even in the shallowest ground.

Anne Lisbeth, overwhelmed with the realization of her sin, sank to the ground and crept along for some distance. "Bury me! Bury me!" still rang in her ears, and gladly would she have buried herself, if the grave could have brought eternal forgetfulness. It was her hour of awakening, and she was full of anguish and horror; superstition made her blood run hot and cold. Many things of which she had feared to speak came into her mind. There passed before her, silently as a shadowy cloud in the clear moonlight, a vision she had heard of before. It was a glowing chariot of fire, drawn by four snorting horses, with fire blazing from their eyes and nostrils; and inside sat a wicked nobleman who more than a century ago had ruled here. Every midnight, he rode into his courtyard and right out again. He was not pale, like other ghosts; no, his face was as black as burnt coal. As he passed Anne Lisbeth he nodded and beckoned to her, "Hold on! Hold on! You may ride in a count's carriage once more and forget your child."

She pulled herself together and hastened to the churchyard, but the black crosses and the black ravens mingled before her eyes; the ravens screamed as they had done that morning, but now she could understand what they were saying. "I am Mother Raven! I am Mother Raven!" said each of them, and Anne Lisbeth knew the name fitted herself well; maybe she would be changed into a huge black bird like these, and have to cry as they cried, if she did not dig the grave.

Then she flung herself on the ground and began frantically digging with her hands in the hard earth; she dug till the blood ran from her fingers.

"Bury me! Bury me!" Still she heard those words, and every moment she dreaded to hear the cock crow and see the first streak of dawn in the east. For if her task were not completed before daylight she knew she would be lost.

And the cock did crow, and the light appeared in the east—and the grave was only half dug, and behold! An icy hand slid over her head and face, down to her heart. A voice seemed to sigh, "Only half the grave!" and a shadowy form drifted past her and down to the bottom of the ocean. Yes, it was indeed the "sea ghost," and Anne Lisbeth fell fainting to the earth, exhausted and overpowered, and her senses left her.

When she came to, it was bright daylight, and two men were lifting her up. She was lying not in the churchyard, but down on the seashore, where she had been digging a deep hole in the sand, and had cut her fingers on a broken glass, the stem of which was stuck in a wooden block painted blue.

Anne Lisbeth was ill; her conscience had spoken loudly to her that night, and superstitious terror had mingled its voice with the voice of conscience. She had no power to distinguish between them; she was now convinced that she had but half a soul, while the other half had been borne away by her child, away to the bottom of the ocean; and never could she hope for the mercy of God until she again possessed the half soul that was imprisoned in those deep waters.

Anne Lisbeth went home, but she was no longer the same. Her thoughts were like tangled yarn; there was only one thread that she could clearly grasp; just one idea possessed her, that she must carry the "sea ghost" to the churchyard and there dig a grave for it. Many a night they missed her from her home and always found her down by the shore, waiting for the "sea ghost." So a whole year passed, and then one night she disappeared and this time was sought in vain. All of the following day was spent in searching for her.

Toward evening, when the parish clerk entered the church to ring the bell for vespers, he found Anne Lisbeth lying before the altar. She had been here ever since dawn; her strength was nearly gone, but her eyes were bright and a faint rosy hue lighted her face; the last sunbeams shone down upon her, streamed over the altar, and glowed on the bright silver clasps of the Bible, open at this text from the Prophet Joel; "Rend your heart and not your garments, and turn unto the Lord your God." This was just by chance, said people, as so many things happen by chance.

In Anne Lisbeth's face, as the setting sun shone upon it, were peace and grace. Now she was so happy, she said. Now she had won back her soul! During the past night the spirit of her own child had been with her and had said, "You dug but half a grave for me, but now for a year and a day you have entombed me in your own heart, and that is the only proper resting place a mother can provide for her child!" And then he had returned to her lost half soul and guided her to the church!

"Now I am in God's house!" she said. "And only there can one be happy!"

When the sun had set, the soul of Anne Lisbeth had gone way up from this Earth to where there are no fears nor the troubles that we have here, even such as those of Anne Lisbeth.

CHILDREN'S PRATTLE (1859)

There was a large party for children at the house of the merchant; rich people's children and important people's children were all there. Their host, the merchant, was a learned man; his father had insisted that he have a college education. You see, his father had been only a cattle dealer, but he had always been honest and thrifty. This business had brought him a fortune, and his son, the merchant, had later managed to increase this fortune. Clever as he was, he also had a kind heart, but there was less talk about his heart than about his money. His house was always full of guests; some who had "blue blood," as it is called, and some who had mind; some who had both, and some who had neither. But this time it was a children's party, with children's prattle; and children say what they mean. Among the guests was a pretty little girl, most absurdly proud that her father was a groom of the bedchamber. The servants had taught her this arrogance, not her parents; they were much too sensible.

"I'm a child of the chamber," she said. She might as well have been a child of the cellar, for no one can help his birth. Then she explained to the other children that she had "birth," and insisted that anyone who didn't have "birth" from the beginning couldn't in any way get it; it did no good to study or be ever so industrious if you didn't have "birth." And as for people whose names ended with "sen," she declared, "They'll never amount to anything. You must put your arms out at the side and keep them, these 'sen' people, at a distance, like this!" And with this she stretched her delicate little arms with the elbows turned out to show what she meant—and the little arms were very pretty. Sweet child!

But the little daughter of the merchant was very angry, for her father's name was Madsen, and of course she knew that ended with "sen," so she answered, as proudly as she could: "My father can buy a hundred dollars' worth of sugar candy and just throw it away; can your father afford to do that?"

"Yes, but my father," said the little daughter of a writer, "can put your father and her father and everybody else's father into a newspaper! My mother says everybody is afraid of him because he owns the paper!" And then she strutted as though she were a real little princess who knows how to strut!

Meanwhile a poor boy stood right outside the half-open door, peeping through the crack. This youngster was so humble that he wasn't even allowed into the room; he had been helping the cook by turning the spit, and now he had permission to peep through the door at the beautifully dressed children who were enjoying themselves inside, and that meant a lot to him.

"Wish I were one of them," he thought, and then he heard what they said, and that was enough to make him very sad. His parents had not saved a penny; they couldn't afford to buy a newspaper, much less write for one. Worst of all, his father's name, and hence his own, ended with "sen." He could never amount to anything in this world! That was sad, indeed. But still it seemed to him he had been "born." Yes, just like everybody else—it couldn't possibly be otherwise.

So much for that evening.

Many years had passed, and in that time children grow up. Now there stood in the city a handsome house, full of beautiful treasures, and everybody wanted to see it, even people who lived outside the city came to see it. And which of the children we have told you about owned this house? Yes, that's very easy for you to guess. No, it's not so very easy after all! That house belonged to the poor little boy! He had amounted to something, in spite of the "sen" at the end of his name—Thorvaldsen!

And the three other children—the children of blue blood, money, and intellectual pride? Well, one had nothing to reproach the other with. They were all equal as children, and they turned into charming and pleasant people, for they were really good at heart; what they had thought and said that evening had just been children's prattle.

THE CHILD IN THE GRAVE (1859)

There was sorrow in the house; there was sorrow in every heart, for the youngest child, a four-year-old boy, the joy and future hope of his parents, was dead. They had two older daughters, the eldest of whom was to be confirmed that year; sweet, good girls, they both were; but the child one has lost is always the most precious, and this was not only the youngest but the only son. It was indeed a heavy affliction. The sisters grieved as the young grieve, awed by the sorrow of their parents; the father's head bowed in grief; but most of all the mother suffered.

Night and day she had cared for the sick child, nursed it, carried it with her, guarded it constantly until it was a part of herself. She could not conceive that he was dead, that he should be laid in a coffin and rest in a dark grave. God would never take her child from her, she thought; when it happened, however, and was a certainty, she cried aloud in her agony, "God had known nothing of this! He has heartless servants here upon earth; they do as they like and pay no heed to the prayers of a mother!"

In her grief she turned from God, and then came dark thoughts, thoughts of death, everlasting death—that human beings became earth in the Earth and that all was over.

Her words were bitter, for her heart was black with despair. There were hours when she could not even find solace of tears; she had no thought for her young daughters; she never looked up at her husband when his tears fell on her hot forehead; her thoughts were all with her dead child; her mind could recall only cherished memories of him—his winning ways, his innocent, childish prattle.

The day of the funeral came. For several nights she had not closed her eyes; but early in the morning of this day, overcome at last by weariness, she fell asleep. And during her sleep the coffin was carried into a distant room and there the lid was nailed down, so that she would not hear the sound of the hammering.

When she awoke she demanded to see her child, but her husband replied through his tears, "We have closed the coffin; it had to be done."

"When God deals cruelly with me," she cried, "why should people treat me better!" And then she was overcome with bitter tears.

The coffin was carried to the grave; the inconsolable mother sat with her young daughters, but she looked at them without seeing them, for her thoughts had nothing more to do with her home. She resigned herself to sorrow, and it tossed her to and fro as the sea tosses the rudderless ship. Thus passed the day of the funeral, and several days followed, all dark with the same heavy monotony of sorrow. Her family watched her with moist eyes and sorrowful glances; she did not heed their words of comfort. What comfort could they offer when they themselves were grieving?

It seemed to her as though she would never sleep again, yet sleep could be her best friend; it could strengthen her body and bring rest to her embittered soul. They persuaded her to lie down, and she would lie in her bed as quietly as though she were actually sleeping.

One night her husband listened to her steady breathing and really thought that at last she had found repose. With folded hands he thanked God, and soon fell into a sound, deep sleep. So he was not aware that his wife rose, dressed herself, and went quietly out of the house, to seek the spot where her thoughts were night and day, the grave that hid her child. She walked through the garden and into the field beyond, where a footpath led to the churchyard. Nobody saw her, and she saw no one.

It was a beautiful, starry night in early September; the air was mild. She entered the churchyard, and when she reached the little grave it was like one huge bouquet of fragrant flowers. She sat there and bowed her head over the grave, as if she could see through the thick covering of earth the dear child whose smile she so well remembered, that adoring look in the sweet eyes as she bent over his sickbed and lifted the tiny hand he had no strength to raise. And as then she sat beside his bed, now she sat beside his grave, but here her tears flowed freely and fell upon the grave.

"You wish to go down to your child!" said a voice close to her, a voice so clear, so profound, it resounded in her heart. She looked up, and there standing beside her was a figure shrouded in a heavy black mourning cloak. Over the head spread a hood, yet she could see the face beneath it, and that stern face inspired trust; those grave eyes sparkled with the light of youth.

"Down to my child!" she repeated in a sad, pleading tone, like a despairing prayer.

"Do you dare to follow me?" asked the figure. "I am Death!"

And she bowed her head in silent assent. Suddenly each of the millions of stars above shone with the brightness of the full moon; she beheld the richly colored splendor of the flowers on the grave, while the earth covering it yielded gently and softly like a waving cloth. She sank, and the black mantle of Death was spread over her, and all was darkness; she sank deeper than the spade of the gravedigger can reach, until the churchyard lay like a roof above her head.

The black folds of the mantle fell aside, and she was standing in a mighty hall that was as friendly as it was big; there was a twilight all around. Before her appeared her child, and in the same moment she held him close to her heart. He smiled at her and looked more beautiful than ever before; she uttered a cry, which, however, was inaudible, for just then the hall was filled with music, now swelling high and triumphant, now dying away into tones faint but clear. Such blessed sounds had never before reached her ears; they seemed to come from beyond the heavy black curtain that divided the hall from the great land of eternity.

"My sweet mother! My own mother!" she heard her child say. It was the familiar, beloved voice; and kiss followed kiss in boundless happiness. Then the child pointed to the black curtain. "Look, Mother! There is nothing as beautiful as this on earth! Do you see, Mother? Do you see them all? This is happiness!"

But the mother could see nothing where the child pointed, nothing but the blackness of night; she gazed with earthly eyes and could not see as could the child whom God had called to himself. So it was with the music; she could hear the sounds, the tones, but not the words, the words in which she was to believe.

"I can fly now, Mother!" said the child. "Fly, with all the other happy children, straight into God's Paradise! Oh, I love that, but when you cry as you are crying now it calls me back, and I can no longer fly, and I want so much to. Will you not let me? You will join me here in only a little time, dearest Mother!"

"Oh, stay, stay!" she begged. "Only for a moment longer! Let me look at you once more, kiss you again, hold you fast in my arms!"

And she kissed him, holding him tightly. Suddenly she heard her name called from far overhead, called in a sad, imploring tone! What could it mean?

"Don't you hear?" said the child. "It is Father calling you!"

And a few seconds later she heard deep sighs, which sounded as if they came from weeping children. "They are my sisters!" said the child. "Oh, Mother, surely you have not forgotten them!"

And now she remembered the beloved ones she had left in her home, and a great fear swept over her. She looked around her and saw the different forms that were continually gliding past, to disappear behind the black curtain. She imagined she recognized some of them; could her husband or her little girls be among them? No, their cries, their sighs, had come from far above her; she had nearly forgotten them for the dead.

"Mother," said the child, "the bells of Paradise are ringing! The sun is rising!"

Then an overpowering light streamed out on her—and the child was gone, and she herself was carried upward. Then all was cold around her, and when she lifted her head she found herself lying on her child's grave in the churchyard. But in her dream the Lord had become a rest for her foot, a light for her understanding. She sank to her knees and prayed, "O my Lord, forgive me that I wished to keep an immortal spirit from its flight into eternity and could forget my duties toward the living ones you have given me here!"

And with that prayer it seemed as if her heart at last found relief.

The sun came out, a little bird sang above her, and the church bells began to ring for the morning service. Light was all about her; light was once more in her heart; she felt the goodness of God and remembered her duties as, longing, she hurried to her home. There she bent over her husband, and her warm, tender kiss awakened him, and they could speak together of their loss. Now she was strong and calm, as a wife should be, and from her lips came words of trust and confidence. "God's will is always best."

"Where did you so suddenly gain this strength," her husband asked her, "this comfort?"

Then she kissed him and kissed her daughters. "It came to me from God, by the grave of my child!"

TWO BROTHERS (1859)

On one of the Danish islands, where old thingsteads, the judgment seats of our forefathers, loom up in the cornfields and mighty trees raise their heads above the beech forests, there lies a little town of low houses with red roofs. In one of these houses strange things were being prepared on the open stove, over the coals and embers. There was boiling in test tubes, mixing and distilling, and pounding of drugs in mortars. An elderly man was in charge of everything.

"One must be careful and do the right thing," he said. "Yes, the right, the correct thing; the truth in each created thing, we must recognize and keep hold of."

In the living room sat the mother with her two sons—still young, with mature thoughts. Their mother had always taught them about right and reason and to hold fast to truth, which she said is the face of God in this world.

The elder of the boys looked bright and alert; he liked to read about the forces of nature, of suns and stars—no fairy tale could give him greater joy. Oh, how wonderful to be able to go on voyages of discovery, or to discover how to imitate birds' wings and fly! Yes, these were the great things to find! Father was right and Mother was right; truth holds the world together.

The younger brother was more quiet and lived entirely in his books. If he read of Jacob, and how he clad himself in sheepskins to resemble Esau and thus cheat him of his birthright, the boy would clench his tiny fists in anger against the deceiver. If he read of tyrants and of all the injustice and wickedness that reigned in the world, tears would come into his eyes. Thoughts of the right, the truth that should and someday would triumph, moved him profoundly.

One evening, the little boy was already in bed, but the curtains were not drawn about him and the light shone in on him. He lay there with his book, eager to finish reading the history of Solon.

Then his thoughts lifted him and carried him strangely on, as if his bed had changed into a vessel under sail—was he dreaming? Or what else could it mean? He was gliding over rolling waves, across the great ocean of time; and he heard the voice of Solon, proclaiming in his foreign tongue, which the boy could still understand, the motto of Denmark—"By law the land is built!"

Then the Genius of the human race stood in that humble room, bent down over the bed, and kissed the boy on his forehead. "Be strong in fame and strong in the battle of life! With truth in your heart fly toward the land of truth!"

The older brother was not yet in bed; he stood at the window, gazing out at mists arising from the meadow. They were not elf maidens dancing out there, as an honest old servant had told him; he knew much more about it. They were vapors, warmer than the air, and that is why they rose. A shooting star lit up the sky, and the boy's thoughts went instantly from the vapors of the earth way up into the regions of the shining meteor.

The stars of Heaven twinkled; it was as if long threads of gold were floating from them down on our Earth.

"Fly with me!" it sang and rang in the boy's heart. The mighty Genius of mankind carried him up, far swifter than bird or arrow or any flying thing of Earth, out into space, where ray after ray from star to star bound all the globes together; Earth was spinning in the thin air and cities seemed to lie close to each other. Through the spheres it sounded: "What is near and what is far, while the mighty genius of thought lifts you on high?"

And again the boy was at the window, gazing out, while the younger brother lay abed; and their mother called them by their names, "Anders and Hans Christian!"

Denmark knows both those two brothers—the world knows them—Oersted!

PEN AND INKSTAND (1859)

In a poet's study, somebody made a remark as he looked at the inkstand that was standing on the table: "It's strange what can come out of that inkstand! I wonder what the next thing will be. Yes, it's strange!"

"That it is!" said the Inkstand. "It's unbelievable, that's what I have always said." The Inkstand was speaking to the Pen and to everything else on the table that could hear it. "It's really amazing what comes out of me! Almost incredible! I actually don't know myself what will come next when that person starts to dip into me. One drop from me is enough for half a piece of paper, and what may not be on it then? I am something quite remarkable. All the works of this poet come from me. These living characters, whom people think they recognize, these deep emotions, that gay humor, the charming descriptions of nature—I don't understand those myself, because I don't know anything about nature—all of that is in me. From me have come out, and still come out, that host of lovely maidens and brave knights on snorting steeds. The fact is, I assure you, I don't know anything about them myself."

"You are right about that," said the Pen. "You have very few ideas, and don't bother about thinking much at all. If you did take the trouble to think, you would understand that nothing comes out of you except a liquid. You just supply me with the means of putting down on paper what I have in me; that's what I write with. It's the pen that does the writing. Nobody doubts that, and most people know as much about poetry as an old inkstand!"

"You haven't had much experience," retorted the Inkstand. "You've hardly been in service a week, and already you're half worn out. Do you imagine you're the poet? Why, you're only a servant; I have had a great many like you before you came, some from the goose family and some of English make. I'm familiar with both quill pens and steel pens. Yes, I've had a great many in my service, and I'll have many more when the man who goes through the motions for me comes to write down what he gets from me. I'd be much interested in knowing what will be the next thing he gets from me."

"Inkpot!" cried the Pen.

Late that evening the Poet came home. He had been at a concert, had heard a splendid violinist, and was quite thrilled with his marvelous performance. From his instrument he had drawn a golden river of melody. Sometimes it had sounded like the gentle murmur of rippling water drops, wonderful pearl-like tones, sometimes like a chorus of twittering birds, sometimes like a tempest tearing through mighty forests of pine. The Poet had fancied he heard his own heart weep, but in tones as sweet as the gentle voice of a woman. It seemed as if the music came not only from the strings of the violin, but from its sounding board, its pegs, its very bridge. It was amazing! The selection had been extremely difficult, but it had seemed as if the bow were wandering over the strings merely in play. The performance was so easy that an ignorant listener might have thought he could do it himself. The violin seemed to sound, and the bow to play, of their own accord, and one forgot the master who directed them, giving them life and soul. Yes, the master was forgotten, but the Poet remembered him. He repeated his name and wrote down his thoughts.

"How foolish it would be for the violin and bow to boast of their achievements! And yet we human beings often do so. Poets, artists, scientists, generals—we are all proud of ourselves, and yet we're only instruments in the hands of our Lord! To him alone be the glory! We have nothing to be arrogant about."

Yes, that is what the Poet wrote down, and he titled his essay "The Master and the Instruments."

"That ought to hold you, madam," said the Pen, when the two were alone again. "Did you hear him read aloud what I had written?"

"Yes, I heard what I gave you to write," said the Inkstand. "It was meant for you and your conceit. It's strange that you can't tell when anyone is making fun of you. I gave you a pretty sharp cut there; surely I must know my own satire!"

"Inkpot!" said the Pen.

"Scribble-stick!" said the Inkstand.

They were both satisfied with their answers, and it is a great comfort to feel that one has made a witty reply—one sleeps better afterward. So they both went to sleep.

But the Poet didn't sleep. His thoughts rushed forth like the violin's tones, falling like pearls, sweeping on like a storm through the forest. He understood the sentiments of his own heart; he caught a ray of the light from the everlasting Master.

To him alone be the glory!

THE FARMYARD COCK AND THE WEATHERCOCK (1859)

Once there were two cocks, one on a dunghill and one on the roof, both of them conceited; but which of the two did the most? Tell us what you think—we'll keep our own opinion, anyway.

The chicken yard was separated by a board fence from another yard, where there lay a manure heap, and on this grew a great cucumber, which was fully aware of being a forcing—bed plant.

"That's a privilege of birth," said the Cucumber to herself. "Not everyone can be born a cucumber; there must be other living things, too. The fowls, the ducks, and the cattle in the next yard are creatures, too, I suppose. I now look up to the Farmyard Cock on the fence. He certainly is much more important than the Weathercock way up there, who can't even creak, much less crow, who has no hens or chickens, who thinks only about himself and perspires rust. No, the Farmyard Cock—he's a real cock! His walk is like a dance, to hear him crow is like music, and whenever he comes around people can hear what a trumpeter he is! If he would only come over here! Even if he should eat me up, stalk and all, it would be a happy death!" said the Cucumber.

That night the weather turned very bad. The hens and chickens and even the Cock himself sought shelter. The wind blew down the fence between the two yards with a terrific crash; tiles fell from the roof, but the Weathercock sat firm. He didn't even turn around, because he couldn't. Although he was young and just cast he was very steady and sedate. He had been "born old," and wasn't a bit like the sparrows and swallows that fly through the vault of heaven. He despised them: "Ordinary piping birds of no importance!" he called them. He admitted that the pigeons were big and glossy, and gleamed like mother-of-pearl, and almost looked like some kind of weathercock, but then they were fat and stupid, and all they could think of was stuff themselves with food.

"Besides, they're such terrible bores to associate with," said the Weathercock.

The migratory birds had also visited the Weathercock and told him tales of foreign lands—of caravans in the sky and fierce robber stories of encounters with birds of prey—and that was new and interesting the first time, but the Weathercock knew that afterward they kept repeating themselves, and that became monotonous.

"They're boring, and everything is dull. Nobody's fit to associate with; all of them are tiresome and dull. The world is no good!" he said. "The whole thing is a bore!"

The Weathercock was what you might call blasé, and that would certainly have made him interesting to the Cucumber if she had known about it; but she had eyes only for the Farmyard Cock, who had now come into her own yard.

The wind had blown down the fence, but the lightning and the thunder were over.

"How's *that* for crowing? the Farmyard Cock said to his hens and chicks. "It was a little rough perhaps—not elegant enough."

And the hens and chickens picked at the manure heap, while the Cock strutted to and fro on it like a knight.

"Garden plant!" he said to the Cucumber; and with that word she understood his great importance and forgot that he was pecking at her and eating her up—a happy death!

Then the hens came and the chickens came, for when one of them runs somewhere the rest run, too; they clucked and chirped and gazed at the Cock and were proud that he belonged to them.

"Cock-a-doodle-doo!" he crowed. "The chickens will immediately grow up to be fine large fowls if I make a noise like that in the chicken yard of the world!"

And the hens and chickens answered him with their clucking and their chirping. And then the Cock told them a great piece of news. "A cock can lay an egg, and do you know what that egg has inside it? In that egg there's a basilisk. But no one can stand the sight of a basilisk. People know that, and now you know it, too—you know what's in me, and what a wonderful fellow I am!"

With that the Farmyard Cock flapped his wings, swelled up his comb, and crowed again. All the hens shivered, and the little chickens shivered, but they were tremendously proud that one of their kind should be such a cock of the world. They clucked and they chirped until the Weathercock could hear it; he heard it, but he never moved.

"It's all stupid nonsense!" said a voice within the Weathercock. "The Farmyard Cock never lays eggs, and I'm too lazy to do it. If I wanted to I could lay a wind egg; but the world isn't worth a wind egg. It's all stupid nonsense. And now I don't even want to sit here any longer."

With that the Weathercock broke off; but he didn't fall on the Farmyard Cock and kill him, "although he intended to!" said the hens. And what's the moral of this? "It is better to crow than to be 'stuck-up' and break off!"

"BEAUTIFUL" (1859)

Alfred the sculptor—yes, you know him, don't you? We all know him; he was awarded the gold medal, traveled to Italy, and came home again. He was young then; in fact, he is still young, though he is ten years older than he was at that time.

After he returned home, he visited one of the little provincial towns on the island of Zealand. The whole village knew who the stranger was, and in his honor one of the richest families gave a party. Everyone of any importance or owning any property was invited. It was quite an event, and all the village knew about it without its being announced by the town crier. Apprentice boys and the children of poor people, and even some of their parents, stood outside the house, looking at the lighted windows with their drawn curtains; and the watchman could imagine that *he* was giving the party, there were so many people in his street. There was an air of festivity everywhere, and inside the house, too, for Mr. Alfred the sculptor was there.

He talked and told stories, and everybody listened to him with pleasure and enthusiasm, but none more so than the elderly widow of a state official. As far as Mr. Alfred was concerned, she was like a blank sheet of gray blotting paper, absorbing everything that was said and demanding more. She was highly susceptible and unbelievably ignorant—a sort of female Kaspar Hauser.

"I should love to see Rome!" she said. "It must be a wonderful city, with all the many strangers continually arriving there. Now, do tell us what Rome is like. How does the city look when you come in by the gate?"

"It is not easy to describe it," said the young sculptor. "There's a great open place, and in the middle of it there is an obelisk that is four thousand years old."

"An *organist!*" cried the lady, who had never heard the word "obelisk."

Some of the guests could hardly keep from laughing, among them the sculptor, but the smile that rose to his lips quickly faded away, for he saw, close by the lady, a pair of dark-blue eyes; they belonged to the daughter of the lady who had been talking, and anyone with such a daughter could not really be silly! The mother was like a fountain of questions, and the daughter, who listened silently, might pass for the naiad of the fountain. How beautiful she was! She was something for a sculptor to look at, but not to speak with, for indeed she talked but very little.

"Has the Pope a large family?" asked the lady.

And the young man answered considerately, as if the question had been put differently, "No, he doesn't come of a very great family."

"That's not what I mean," said the lady. "I mean, does he have a wife and children?"

"The Pope isn't allowed to marry," he replied.

"I don't approve of that," said the lady.

She might well have talked and questioned him more intelligently, but if she hadn't said and asked what she did, would her daughter have leaned so gracefully on her shoulder, looking straight before her with an almost melancholy smile on her lips?

And Mr. Alfred told them of the glorious colors of Italy, the purple of the mountains, the blue of the Mediterranean, the blue of the southern skies, a beauty that could only be surpassed in the north by the deep-blue eyes of a maiden. This he said with peculiar meaning, but she who should have understood it looked quite unconscious, and that, too, was charming!

"Ah, Italy!" sighed some of the guests.

"Traveling!" sighed others.

"Charming, charming!"

"Well," said the widow, "if I win fifty thousand dollars in the lottery, we'll travel! My daughter and I. You Mr. Alfred, must be our guide. We'll all three go, with just one or two good friends with us." Then she smiled in such a friendly manner at the company that each of them could imagine he was the person who would accompany them to Italy. "Yes, we'll go to Italy! But not to the parts where the robbers are; we'll stay in Rome and only travel by the great highways where we'll be safe."

And the daughter sighed very gently. And how much may lie in one little sigh or be read into it! The young man read a great deal into it. Those two blue eyes, bright that evening in his honor, must conceal treasures of heart and mind rarer than all the glories of Rome! When he left the party, he had lost his heart—lost it completely—to the young lady.

Now, the widow's house was where Mr. Alfred the sculptor could most frequently be found. It was understood that his calls were not for the lady herself, though he and she did all the talking; he really came for the sake of the daughter. They called her Kala. Her real name was Karen Malene, but the two names had been contracted into the single name Kala. She was extremely beautiful, but some people said she was rather dull and probably slept late in the mornings.

"She has been accustomed to that since childhood," said her mother. "She is as beautiful as Venus, and a beauty always tires easily. She does sleep rather late, but that's what makes her eyes so bright."

What a power there was in these clear eyes, these deep blue eyes! "Still waters run deep." The young man felt the truth of that proverb, and his heart sank into the depths. He spoke of his adventures, and Mamma always asked the same naïve and pertinent questions she had asked at their first meeting.

It was a delight to hear Mr. Alfred speak. He told them of Naples, of trips to Mount Vesuvius, and showed them colored prints of some of the eruptions. The widow had never heard of such things before, much less taken time to think about them.

"Mercy save us!" she said. "So that's a burning mountain! But isn't it dangerous for the people who live there?"

"Entire cities have been destroyed," he answered. "For example, Pompeii and Herculaneum."

"Oh, the poor people! And you saw all that yourself?"

"Well, no, I didn't see any of the eruptions shown in these pictures, but I'll show you a drawing I made of an eruption I did see."

He laid a pencil sketch on the table, and when Mamma, who had been studying the highly colored prints, glanced at the black-and-white drawing, she cried in amazement, "When you saw it did it throw up white fire?"

For a moment Alfred's respect for Kala's mamma nearly vanished; but then, dazzled by the light from Kala, he decided it was natural for the old lady to have no eye for color. After all, it didn't matter, for Kala's mamma had the most wonderful thing of all—she had Kala herself.

And Alfred and Kala were engaged, which was inevitable, and the engagement was announced in the town newspaper. Mamma brought thirty copies of the paper, so she could cut out the announcement and send it to her friends. The betrothed couple were happy, and the mamma-in-law-to-be was happy, too; she said it seemed like being related to Thorvaldsen himself.

"At any rate, you are his successor," she told Alfred.

And it seemed to Alfred that Mamma had this time really said something clever. Kala said nothing, but her eyes sparkled; her every gesture was graceful. Yes, she was beautiful; that cannot be repeated too often.

Alfred made busts of Kala and his future mamma-in-law; they sat for him and watched how he molded and smoothed the soft clay between his fingers.

"I suppose it's only for us that you do this common work," said Mamma-in-law-to-be, "and don't have your servant do all that dabbing together."

"No, I have to mold the clay myself," he explained.

"Oh, yes, you're always so exceedingly polite," said Mamma, while Kala silently pressed his hand, still soiled by the clay.

Then he unfolded to both of them the loveliness of nature in creation, explaining how the living stood higher in the scale than the dead, how the plant was above the mineral, the animal above the plant, and man above the animal, how mind and beauty are united in outward form, and how it was the task of the sculptor to seize that beauty and imprison it in his works.

Kala sat silent and nodded approval of the thought, while Mamma-in-law confessed, "It's hard to follow all that. But my thoughts manage to hobble slowly along after you; they whirl around, but I try to hold them fast."

And the power of Kala's beauty held Alfred fast, seizing him and mastering him and filling his whole soul. There was beauty in Kala's every feature; it sparkled in her eyes, lurked in the corners of her mouth and even in each movement of her fingers. The sculptor saw this; he spoke only of her, thought only of her, until the two became one. Thus it might be said that she also spoke often, for he was always talking of her, and they two were one.

Such was the betrothal; and now came the wedding day, with bridesmaids and presents, all duly mentioned in the wedding speech.

Mamma-in-law had set up a bust of Thorvaldsen, attired in a dressing gown, at one end of the table, for it was her whim that he was to be a guest. There were songs and toasts, for it was a gay wedding and they were a handsome pair. "Pygmalion gets his Galatea," one of the songs said.

"That is something from mythology!" said Mamma-in-law.

Next day the young couple left for Copenhagen, where they were to live. Mamma-in-law went with them, "to give them a helping hand," she explained—which meant to take charge of the house. Kala was to live in a doll's house. Everything was so bright, new, and fine. There the three of them sat, and as for Alfred, to use a proverb that describes his circumstances, he sat like the bishop in the goose yard.

The magic of form had fascinated him. He had regarded the case and had no interest in learning what the case contained, and that is unfortunate, very unfortunate, in married life! If the case breaks and the gilding rubs off, the purchaser may repent of his bargain. It is very embarrassing to discover in a large party that one's suspender buttons are coming off and that one has no belt to fall back on; but it is still worse to realize at a great party that one's wife and mother-in-law are talking nonsense and that one cannot think of a clever piece of wit to cover up the stupidity of it.

The young couple often sat hand in hand, he speaking and she letting drop a word now and then—with always the same melody, like a clock striking the same two or three notes constantly. It was really a mental relief when one of her friends, Sophie, came to visit them.

Sophie wasn't pretty. To be sure, she was not deformed; Kala always said she was a little crooked, but no one but a female friend would have noticed that. She was a very level-headed girl and had no idea that she might ever become dangerous here. Her visits brought a fresh breath of air into the doll's house, air that they all agreed was certainly needed there. But they felt they needed more airing, so they came out into the air, and Mamma-in-law and the young couple traveled to Italy.

"Thank Heaven we are back in our own home again!" said both mother and daughter when they and Alfred returned home a year later.

"Traveling is no fun," said Mamma-in-law. "On the contrary, it's very tiring; pardon me for saying so. I found the time dragged, even though I had my children with me; and it is expensive, very expensive, to travel. All those galleries you have to see, and all the things you have to look at! You must do it for self-protection, because when you get back people are sure to ask you about them; and then they're sure to tell you that you've missed the most worthwhile things. I got so tired at last of those everlasting Madonnas; I thought I would turn into a Madonna myself!"

"And the food one gets!" said Kala.

"Yes," agreed Mamma. "Not even a dish of honest meat soup! It is awful the way they cook!"

And Kala had become tired from traveling; she was always tired; that was the trouble. Sophie came to live with them, and her presence was a real help.

Mamma-in-law had to admit that Sophie understood both housekeeping and art, though you would hardly have expected a knowledge of the last from a person of her modest background. Moreover, she was honest and loyal; she showed that clearly when Kala lay sick, fading away.

If the case is everything, that case should be strong, or it is all over. And it *was* all over with the case—Kala died.

"She was so beautiful," said Mamma. "She was very different from the antiques, because they're all so damaged. Kala was completely perfect, just as a beauty should be."

Alfred wept and the mother wept, and both went into mourning. The black dresses became Mamma very well, so she wore her mourning the longer. Moreover, she soon experienced another grief, when she saw Alfred marry again. And he married Sophie, who had no looks at all!

"He has gone from one extreme to the other!" said Mamma-in-law. "Gone from the most beautiful to the ugliest! How could he forget his first wife! Men have no constancy. Now, my husband was entirely different, and he died before I did."

"Pygmalion got his Galatea," said Alfred. "Yes, that's what the wedding song said. I really fell in love with a beautiful statue, which came to life in my arms, but the soulmate that Heaven sends down to us, one of its angels who can comfort and sympathize with and uplift us, I have not found or won till now. You came to me, Sophie, not in the glory of superficial beauty—but fair enough, prettier than was necessary. The most important thing is still the most important. You came to teach a sculptor that his work is only clay and dust, only the outward form in a fabric that passes away, and that we must seek the spirit within. Poor Kala! Ours was but a wayfarer's life. In the next world, where we shall come together through sympathy, we shall probably be half strangers to each other."

"That was not spoken kindly," said Sophie, "not like a true Christian. In the next world, where there is no marriage, but where, as you say, souls find each other through sympathy, where everything beautiful is developed and elevated, her soul may attain such completeness that it may resound far more melodiously than mine. Then you will again utter the first exciting cry of your love, 'Beautiful, beautiful!'"

A STORY FROM THE SAND DUNES (1859)

This is a story of the sand dunes of Jutland, but it doesn't begin there; no, it begins far away to the south, in Spain. The ocean is the highway between the two countries. So now let your thoughts journey to Spain!

It is warm there, and it is beautiful. The fiery red pomegranate blossoms grow among the dark laurels; a refreshing wind from the mountains breathes over the orange gardens and the graceful Moorish palaces with golden cupolas and colored walls. Children walk in procession through the streets, carrying torches and waving banners, while high above them stars sparkle in the clear arching vault of heaven.

Song and castanets can be heard; young men and girls dance under the blossoming acacias, while the beggar lies on a carved marble block, quenches his thirst with a juicy watermelon, and dozes his life away. It is all like a beautiful dream; give yourself up to it. Yes, as did the young married couple to whom had been granted all the choicest of earthly blessings—health, beauty, good nature, riches, and honor.

"We are as happy as anyone could ever be!" they said, with full conviction in their hearts. Yet they had one step higher to go to attain complete happiness, and that would be reached when God would give them a child, a son in their own image, body and soul. That blessed child would be welcomed with jubilance, cared for with the utmost love and tenderness, and be surrounded by all the luxuries that riches and an influential family can provide.

Meanwhile the days glided past, each like a holiday.

"Life is a precious gift of love, almost too great to understand," said the wife. "And just to think that this fullness of bliss shall still increase and grow, in another life, throughout eternity. I can hardly conceive of it!"

"And it certainly also shows the arrogance of people," said her husband. "It really shows a terrible conceit when people persuade themselves to think they'll live forever—become as God! Were these not the words of the serpent, the master of lies?"

"You surely don't doubt that there is a life after this, do you?" asked his young wife, and it was as if a shadow passed through their sunlit thoughts for the first time.

"Faith promises it, I know, and the priests tell us it is so," said the young man. "But, happy as I am now, I feel and know that it is only pride, an arrogant thought that demands another life after this—an extension of this happiness. Haven't we been granted enough in this life, so that we could and should be satisfied?"

"Yes, that has been given us," said the young wife, "but how many thousands find this life a heavy trail! How many have been thrown into this world only to find poverty, shame, sickness, and misfortune! No, if there were no afterlife, the blessings on this Earth would be too unequally divided—our God would not be a God of justice!"

"The beggar down on the street has pleasures just as dear to him as the king enjoys in his splendid palace," said the young man. "And what about the poor beast of burden that is beaten and starved and works itself to death? Doesn't it sense the bitterness of its miserable life? Why shouldn't it too demand an afterlife, and call it unfair that it wasn't granted the advantages of a higher creation?"

"Christ told us, 'In my Father's house are many mansions,'" answered the young wife. "The Kingdom of Heaven is as infinite as God's love. The animal is His creation too, and I don't believe that any single life will be lost, but that each will be granted the greatest share of happiness it is capable of receiving."

"But this world is good enough for me now," said the young man, as he slipped his arm around his lovely, amiable wife and smoked a cigarette on the open balcony, where the cool air was heavy with the fragrance of orange blossoms and carnations. Songs and the clicking of castanets came from the street, while the stars glittered high above, and two eyes full of love—his wife's eyes—gazed on him with the expression of eternal love. "A moment like this," he said, "makes being born well worthwhile—just to experience such a moment—and then vanish," he said smiling, while his wife shook her finger reprovingly. And the cloud soon passed; they were much too happy.

Everything that happened seemed only to add to their happiness and well-being. A change came, but it was only a change of place, not a change that diminished their happiness and enjoyment of life. The young man was appointed by the king to be ambassador to the court of imperial Russia, a post of great honor, such as his birth and ability well fitted him to occupy. He had a great fortune of his own, and his young wife's wealth was equal to his, for she was the daughter of the richest and most respected merchant. And since one of her father's largest and finest ships would sail this year to Stockholm, it was arranged that the dear children, the daughter and the son-in-law, would travel on it to St. Petersburg. Everything was royally fitted out for the voyage, with soft carpets underfoot and silken splendor everywhere.

There is an old heroic ballad familiar to all Danes, called "The King of England's Son." He also goes to sea in a splendid ship, with its anchor inlaid with pure gold and every rope woven of silk. The ship of the Spanish merchant might have reminded one of this vessel, for the magnificence was similar, and the farewell thoughts were very much the same:

> *God grant that we meet with joy again!*

The parting was brief, for a fair wind blew briskly off the Spanish coast. They hoped to reach their destination in a few weeks. But as soon as they were well out at sea the wind died down to rest. The ocean grew smooth, and the waters reflected the glittering light of the stars of heaven. There were festive evenings in their richly appointed cabin.

At last they wished the wind would rise again, to speed them on their voyage. But every wind that arose came from the wrong direction. Weeks went by; two whole months passed, in fact, before the wind blew in their favor, from the southwest.

They were somewhere between Scotland and Jutland when the west wind burst forth, just as in the old ballad, "The King of England's Son":

> *While the sky was dark and the wind blew,*
> *And there was neither port nor land in view,*
> *They cast their anchor, but to no avail;*
> *They were blown to Denmark by a west wind gale.*

This occurred a long time ago. King Christian VII, still a young man, then sat on the throne of Denmark. Much has happened since then; there have been many changes and innovations. Lakes and swamps have become green meadows, while heaths have been plowed into useful land. And in the shelter of the West Jutlander's house there now grow apple trees and roses, but you must seek these out, for they hide from the sharp west wind.

Still, it is easy to imagine yourself back in times more remote than even the reign of Christian VII, for now, as then, the brown heath of Jutland stretches for miles with its barrows, its mirages, its winding, rough, sandy roads. To the west, where broad streams of water flow into the fjords, there are marshes and meadows, encircled by the high sand hills which rise up toward the sea like an Alpine chain with jagged summits, broken only by high banks of clay. From these the waves eat off giant mouthfuls year after year, so that the edges and summits topple down as though shaken by an earthquake. That's how it looks today, and that's how it looked many years ago, when the happy couple sailed past it in their splendid ship.

It was a bright, sunshiny Sunday in late September; the peals of the church bells extended to one another all along the Nissum Fjord. The churches there are like immense stones, each like a piece of rock mountain; the North Sea itself might wash over them, and they would still stand firm. Most of them have no towers, their bells hanging out in the open air between two wooden beams.

The services had ended, and the congregation emerged from the house of God into the churchyard where then, as now, there grew neither tree nor shrub. No plants, flowers, or wreaths adorned the graves; only rough hillocks showed where the dead had been buried, while sharp grass, beaten flat by the wind, covered the whole cemetery. Here and there a single grave still has a tombstone, perhaps a moldering log, cut in the shape of a coffin. These are pieces of driftwood from the forests of West Jutland. The wild sea provides the shore dwellers with many hewn planks, cast upon the coast. But the wind and salt sea spray soon wear away these monuments.

One of these blocks had been placed on the grave of child, to which a young woman came from the church. She stopped and gazed down at the rotted wood; shortly her husband joined her. They spoke no word; presently he took her hand, and together they walked away from the grave, on over the brown heath and over the moor toward the sand dunes. For a long time they walked in silence.

"That was a good sermon today," said the man. "If we didn't have our Lord we would have nothing."

"Yes," replied his wife, "He sends us happiness and sorrow. He has a right to. Our little boy would have been five years old tomorrow if we had been allowed to keep him."

"It does no good to grieve," said the man. "He is much better off there than here; he is where we pray to go."

They said no more, but passed on silently toward their home among the sand dunes. Suddenly, from one of these, where there was no grass to hold the sand down, it looked as if a column of heavy smoke were rising; it was really a gust of wind boring into the bank and whirling the fine particles of sand into the air. A second gust followed, so strong that the strings of fish hung on the line rattled against the walls of the house; but it lasted for only a moment; then all was quiet again, and the sun shone warmly.

The man and his wife went into their house, quickly changed from their Sunday clothes, and then hurried across the dunes, which looked like enormous waves of sand suddenly frozen in motion. The sea reed and the bluish green of the sharp dune grass alone relieved the monotony of the white sand. A couple of neighbors appeared, and all helped in pulling the boats higher up on the sandy shore, while the wind steadily strengthened and blew bitingly cold. When they returned across the dunes the waves were lifting their whitecaps; sand and sharp pebbles were beating into their faces, and the wind cut off the top ridges of some of the dunes, breaking them into sand showers.

Evening came, and a swelling sound filled the air; there was a howling and wailing like a host of despairing spirits, and even though the fisherman's hut lay near the shore, the noise of the wind drowned the roar of the sea. The sand drifted against the windowpanes, and every now and then there came a violent gust of wind that seemed to shake the house to its very foundation. It was a dark evening; the moon would not rise until nearly midnight.

The air cleared a little, but the storm was now raging with all its fury over the deep, black ocean. The fisherman and his wife had long since gone to bed, but in such weather it was impossible to close an eye.

Suddenly there was a tap at the window; the door was pushed open, and someone said, "A large ship is stranded on the outer reef!" In a moment the man and his wife were out of bed and dressing themselves hurriedly.

The Moon was up now, and it would have been light enough to see had it not been for the flying sand which forced eyes to squint. Only with great difficulty, waiting for each lull and creeping a little farther between gusts, could they make their way across the sand dunes. And now, like swansdown in the air, salty white foam flew in from the sea as it hurled its waves against the coast in boiling fury.

Only a long-experienced eye could have distinguished the ship way out there; it was a splendid two-master. At that very instant it was lifted over the reef, three or four cables' lengths off the usual channel; it drove on toward land, struck against the second reef, and there stuck fast.

It was impossible to send any help, for the sea was far too tumultuous; waves broke over the entire vessel. They imagined hearing screams of terror, the cries of death agony; they could see the aimless rushing to and fro on board; it was all hopeless, helpless. Now a wave like a thundering avalanche crashed down on the bowsprit, and then it disappeared. The stern rose high above the water, and two people could be seen leaping from it into the sea; they disappeared—a moment more—and a tremendous wave thundering toward the dunes flung a body on the shore. It was a woman, and surely she was dead! A couple of women who quickly gathered around her believed she showed signs of life, and carried her over the dunes to the fisherman's cottage. How beautiful and dainty she was!—no doubt a lady of rank.

They laid her in the fisherman's humble bed; there was no linen to wrap her in, only a woolen blanket; but at least this was warm and comfortable. She breathed, but she was in a high fever. She had no idea where she was or what had happened; perhaps this was just as well, for all that was dear to her now lay at the bottom of the ocean; they had met the same fate as those sung of in the ballad about "The King of England's Son":

> *A sorrowful sight it was to all;*
> *The ship was broken into pieces small!*

Many bits of the wreck were driven ashore, but the lady alone survived of all the voyagers. Still the wind howled and wailed along the coast.

For a few minutes she seemed to rest, but then came screams of pain and fear. Her beautiful eyes opened, and she spoke a few words, but no one could understand her. At last, after hours of suffering and struggles, there nestled in her arms a tiny, newborn child.

That child was to have rested under silken curtains in a beautiful home, was to have been welcomed to a life full of this world's riches; but our Lord had willed that he should be born in this humble hut; and not so much as one kiss was he to receive from the lips of his mother!

The fisherman's wife placed the baby against its mother's heart, a heart that beat no longer—she was dead. And the child who was to have been brought up in luxury and pleasure had been hurled headlong into life, tossed by the sea among the sand dunes, there to experience the lot of a poor man, and weary and dark days.

And always the old song comes to our mind:

> On the king's son's cheek there was a tear
> "Pray, Christ, I reach Bovbjerg; then I shan't fear!
> If only I had come to Herr Bugge's Strand;
> Then no knight nor squire of any band
> Would have dared against me lift a hand."

The ship had been wrecked a little to the south of the Nissum Fjord, on the very shore that Herr Bugge had once called his own. The hard, cruel times of the ballad, when the dwellers on the western coast treated castaways so inhumanly, had long passed. The shipwrecked were now treated with love and kindness, as they are in our own time. The dying mother and the unfortunate child would have been treated with the utmost care and tenderness, wherever the storm had driven them; but nowhere could they have received more sincere kindness than in the hut of that poor fisherwoman who, only yesterday, had stood with a sorrowful heart beside the grave of her child who, if God had allowed him to live, would today have completed his fifth year.

No one knew the identity of the dead woman or from where she had come. The broken fragments of the wrecked ship brought no explanation.

No letter or news of the daughter and son-in-law was ever received at the rich merchant's house in Spain. They could not have reached their destination, considering the violent storms that had raged for the last few weeks. For months they waited before admitting to themselves the sad truth: "All lost! All perished!"

But in the hut of the fisherman near the sand dunes of Hunsby there was now a tiny infant.

Where God provides food for two there is sure to be enough for a third; and near the sea there is always at least a plate of fish for hungry mouths. They christened the little one Jörgen.

"Surely he must be a Jewish child," people said; "his skin is so dark." "He may just as easily be Italian or Spanish," said the clergyman. To the fisherman's wife all three races seemed very much the same, but it was a great comfort to her to know that at least the child was really a baptized Christian.

The boy thrived, his noble blood sustaining warmth and gaining strength from the poor fare as he grew in that humble hut; the Danish language, as spoken in West Jutland, became his own language. The pomegranate seed from Spain had become a sea-grass plant on Jutland's western coast, and in this home, so foreign to his inheritance, he took root for the rest of his life. He was to experience hunger and cold, a poor man's wants and troubles, but also he was to know a poor man's pleasures.

For everyone childhood has its highlights, and the memories of these sparkle throughout one's whole life. What a full share of play and pleasure he had! All the miles of shore were strewn with playthings for him; it was a mosaic of pebbles, red as coral, yellow as amber, or white and round as birds' eggs, all bright with colors and smooth and polished by the sea. Even the dried-out skeleton of a fish, the water plants, dried by the wind, or the shiny, white seaweed, long and narrow like strings fluttering among the rocks, were a delight to eye and heart. The boy was a wide-awake child, full of ability. How he could remember all the old stories or songs he had ever heard! And how clever he was with his fingers! He could make sailing ships out of stones and shells or draw pictures that were quite an ornament to the room. He could "carve his thoughts out of a stick," as his foster mother said, when he was still only a little boy, and his voice was so sweet and caught the strain of a melody so quickly! That little heart was attuned to many fine harmonies which might have rung throughout the world if he had been placed in a less narrow home than the fisherman's hut near the North Sea.

One day a box of rare flower bulbs drifted ashore after a shipwreck. Some were taken out and made into soup, with the idea that they might be good to eat; others were just left to rot in the sand and never fulfilled their destiny, never unfolded the glorious beauty of form and color that lay hidden within them. Would such be the case with Jörgen? Life was soon over for the flower bulbs, but he still had many years to live and struggle.

It never occurred either to him or his foster parents that their lives were lonely and monotonous; days went by, and there was plenty to do and hear and see. The ocean itself was a great book of lessons; every day it seemed to turn over a new page, storm or calm. A shipwreck was an exciting event. The visit to the church was a festive event. Twice a year the fisherman's hut had a visitor, and a very welcome one. This was the eel seller from Fjaltring, up near Bovbjerg, who was the brother of Jörgen's foster mother. He came with a red wagon full of eels; it was shut up like a box and had blue and white tulips painted on it. It was drawn by two black oxen, and Jörgen was permitted to drive them.

The eel man had a good head on him. He was a jolly guest; he always brought a little keg of schnapps, and everyone had a drink of it, sometimes from a coffee cup, if there were not enough glasses. Even Jörgen, little as he was, had a thimbleful; that was so he could digest the fat eels, said the eel man. Then he would tell them his old story, and whenever he heard people laugh at it, he always repeated it at once, to the very same people, as all talkative folks do. And as Jörgen used phrases from this story throughout his youth and later in life, we had better listen to it.

"The eels played out in the river, and Mother Eel said to her daughters, when they had begged for permission to explore a little way up the stream, 'Don't go too far! The wicked man with his spear will come and catch you all!' But they did go too far, and of the eight of them only three returned to their mother and wailed out their story, 'We had only gone a little distance beyond the door when the ugly man with the spear came and stabbed our five sisters to death!'

"'They'll come back,' said the eel mother.

"'No,' said the daughters. 'For he skinned them and cut them into bits and fried them.'

"'They'll surely come back,' said the eel mother.

"'Yes, but he ate them!'

"'Still they'll come back,' said the eel mother.

"'But he drank schnapps afterwards!' said the daughters.

"'Oh, my! Oh my!' howled the eel mother. 'Then they'll never return! For schnapps drowns eels!'

"And for that very reason people should always take a little schnapps after eating them," finished the eel spearer.

And this story ran like a thread of gold tinsel—his most humorous recollection—through the web of Jörgen's life. He too wanted to go past the threshold, "a little way up the river," or rather out into the wide world in a ship; but his foster mother objected, just as Mother Eel had objected, "There are so many wicked men with spears." He longed to go a little past the sand dunes into the heath. And at last he did for four pleasant days, the brightest of his whole childhood; and he saw all of Jutland's happy, homelike beauty and sunshine. He went to a party; it was a funeral party.

A wealthy relative of the fisherman had died; his farm was far inland, "to the east, a bit northerly," as the saying goes. Jörgen's foster parents had to go, and they took him with them. They passed from the dunes over heath and swamp to the green pastures where the Skjaerum River hollows out its bed—that brook full of eels, where lived Mother Eel and her daughters whom the wicked people speared and cut in pieces. And hadn't men often acted just as cruelly toward their fellow men? The good knight, Sir Bugge, whose name lives in the old song, was murdered by wicked men; and, though he himself was called "good," he is said to have come very close to slaying the architect who built his castle, with its tower and thick walls, on the slope where the brook Skjaerum falls into the Nissum Fjord, just where Jörgen now stood with his foster parents. The ramparts and the red crumbling fragments of the walls could still be seen.

It was here that Sir Bugge, after the architect had left, ordered one of his men to follow him. "Say to him, 'Master, the tower leans to one side.' And if he turns and looks to find out, you must slay him and take from him the money I have paid him; but if he turns not, let him depart in peace." The man obeyed, but the architect did not turn; rather did he answer clearly and boldly. "The tower does not lean, for I have built it well; but one day a man shall come from the west in a blue cloak, and he shall make it lean." And a hundred years later this came to pass, for the North Sea broke in and the tower collapsed; but Predbjörn Gyldenstjerne, who owned the castle at that time, built a new mansion on the slope higher up; this is still standing, and is called Nörre Vosborg.

Jörgen and his foster parents had to pass this place, so now he saw this and other spots that he had heard stories about in the long winter evenings. He saw the castle, with its double moats choked with trees and bushes and its rampart overhung with bracken. But the loveliest sight to him were the tall lime trees that reached right up to the roof and filled the air with fragrance. In the northwest corner of the garden stood a large bush bearing flowers as white as snow—they seemed strange to him among the green leaves of summer. It was an elder bush, the first he had seen blooming; that bush and the lime trees were stored safely away throughout the years in a corner of his mind, a bit of the fragrance and beauty of Denmark, "kept to delight the old man."

The journey continued and became still more pleasant, for outside Nörre Vosborg, where they had found the flowering elder bush, they met other people who were also going to the funeral, and drove on with them. Of course, all three of them had to sit on a little wooden chest with iron trimmings at the rear of the carriage, but they decided even that was better than walking. The carriage rolled away over the rough hillocks of the heath, and the oxen that drew it stopped to graze whenever a patch of fresh grass appeared among the heather. The sun shone warmly, and they saw the strange sight of rising smoke in the distance, as transparent as though beams of light were rolling and dancing over the heath. "That is Loki driving his flock," people said, and that was enough explanation for Jörgen. He felt as though he were driving right into fairyland—and yet everything was real! And how still it all was about them!

The heath spread out before them, a wide, rich carpet, with the heather in blossom. Mingled with the dark green juniper and fresh oak shoots, it studded the ground as if with bouquets. This was an inviting place to throw oneself down, if it were not for the many poisonous snakes people said were there. And people spoke too of the wolves that used to be found there so often that the district was known as Ulvborg Herred. The old man who was driving the wagon told them how, in his father's day, the horses often had fierce battles with wild beasts since exterminated, and how one morning he found a horse trampling on a wolf he had slain, while his own legs were quite bare of flesh which had been gnawed off in the struggle.

The wagon rolled too quickly over the rough heath and through the deep sand. They reached the house of mourning, where they found many strangers inside and outside; many wagons stood side by side, with their horses or oxen turned out to seek meager pasture; from the back of the house great sand dunes, like those at home near the sea, extended far and wide. How could they be here? It was twelve miles into the country, yet they were as tall and large as those by the shore. The wind had lifted them up and blown them here; they too had a history.

Psalms were sung, and a few of the older people wept, but aside from this, everything was very pleasant, Jörgen thought. There was plenty to eat and drink; the finest fat eels, with schnapps afterwards "to settle the eels," as the eel seller had said. And his words were certainly carried out at this gathering.

Jörgen went in and out of the house, and by the third day he was as thoroughly at home there as in the fisherman's hut among his own sand dunes, where he had spent all his life. But the heath here was far more beautiful, with its myriads of brilliant blossoms and luscious sweet bilberries, growing so thickly that if one stepped on them, the ground became stained with their red juice. Here lay an old Viking grave, and near it lay another. When the mysterious columns of mist curled upward through the calm air, they said, "The heath is on fire." It shone brightest toward evening.

But the fourth day came at last and brought the end of the wake; it was time to return from the inland sand dunes to the coastal sand dunes.

"Ours are the real ones after all," said the father. "These have no strength."

Then they talked about the sand dunes and how they came to be here, and this was very interesting. The peasants found a corpse on the shore and buried it in the churchyard; then the sand began to fly about, and the sea broke in with violence. A wise man of the parish advised that the grave be opened, for if the stranger were found sucking his thumb, they could then be sure that he whom they had buried was a merman and that the sea would not rest till it had fetched him back. So they opened the grave, and sure enough, the dead man lay with his thumb between his lips. He was quickly laid on a cart drawn by two oxen, and as though stung by hornets they rushed with him over heath and moor to the sea. That stopped the shower of flying sand, but the dunes that it formed are still there.

That was what Jörgen learned and carried away with him from the happiest days of his childhood—those four days at the funeral party.

How wonderful it was, he thought, to go out into the world and see new places and new people! And he was to go still farther away. Before he had finished his fourteenth year—he was still a child—he did actually go out to look at he world, through the eyes of a cabin boy. Now he had to endure bad weather, rough seas, and evil men; scanty fare, cold nights, the rope's end, and blows from a hard fist—yes, such were his experiences. There was something in his noble Spanish blood that continually boiled over and brought hot words to his lips. He soon learned it was wisest to restrain them, but in doing so, he felt somewhat as the eel must feel when it is skinned, cut up, and tossed into the frying pan. "I shall return again!" said a voice within him.

Now the ship touched at the Spanish coast, the home of Jörgen's parents, in fact at the very town where they used to live in splendor and happiness. But he knew nothing of his homeland or his relatives, and even less did his family know of him. The shabby cabin boy was not even permitted to go ashore while the others went; but on the last day it happened that some provisions had been bought, and Jörgen was told to carry them on board.

There stood Jörgen in his wretched clothes that looked as if they had been washed in a ditch and dried in a chimney; this was the first time that he, the dweller of the sand dunes, had ever seen a great city. How tall the houses were, how narrow the streets, swarming with human beings constantly rushing to and fro, a regular whirlpool of townspeople and farmers, monks and soldiers—a clamor, a screaming, a jangling of bells from asses and mules, a clanging of bigger bells from the churches—song and musical instruments—knocking and hammering, for every tradesman seemed to have his shop either on his threshold or on the sidewalk. And all the while the hot sun burned down, and the air was heavy. It was as if one had entered a bake oven full of beetles, cockchafers, bees, and flies, all humming and buzzing with all their might; Jörgen hardly knew if he were walking or standing still.

Suddenly he saw before him the mighty portals of a cathedral, with lights streaming out through the twilight of the colonnades and the fragrance of incense saluting him. Even the poorest beggar in rags could venture to climb those stairs and enter. The sailor who had taken Jörgen ashore went into the church; Jörgen followed, and soon he stood in the sanctuary. Colored pictures glowed out from golden backgrounds; amid flowers and candles at the altar he beheld the Blessed Virgin holding the Holy Child; priests in their vestments were chanting, while pretty choirboys swung silver censers. What magnificence he saw there! All this glory and beauty, streaming into Jörgen's soul, nearly overpowered him. The church and the faith of his fathers surrounded him and awakened a chord in his soul, causing tears to come to his eyes.

From the cathedral they proceeded to the market. A heavy load of provisions was piled upon him. It was a long way back, and when he grew tired he wanted to rest in front of a large and splendid palace decorated with statues and marble pillars, with broad steps. But as he rested his burden against the wall a porter dressed in gold lace bustled out, waving a silver-headed cane, and drove him away—him, the grandson of that house! But no one knew it, himself least of all.

And so he returned to the ship and accepted, as before, his share of cuffs, broken slumbers, and hard work. Such was his first experience in life! "It is good for a man to bear the yoke in his youth," they say: "Yes, if he makes up for it in old age."

When the term of his signing on was ended and the ship was anchored in the Ringkjöbing Fjord, he went home to the Hunsby sand dunes. But his foster mother was dead—she had died during his voyage.

A hard winter followed, with snowstorms raging over sea and land. It was difficult to get from one place to another. How differently are things divided in this life. Here were icy cold and driving snowstorms, while in Spain the sun burned too fiercely. And yet one clear frosty day, while Jörgen watched the swans flying from the ocean across the Nissum Fjord toward Nörre Vosborg, he felt that here, in the northern land, he could breathe more freely. And Denmark had its beauty of summer too; he imagined he could see the heath with its flowers and ripe, juicy berries, while the lime trees and elder bush of Nörre Vosborg stood blooming before him. He must go back there again.

It was toward spring, and the fishing began. Jörgen helped, for he had grown during the last year; he was quick and alert at his work, and there was no lack of spirit in him. He could swim and tread water, turn over and tumble in the water. They often warned him to beware of the mackerel shoals, which, it is said, seize the best swimmer, drag him down into the water, and eat him—that would be the end of him. But that never happened to Jörgen.

Among his neighbors on the sand dunes was boy named Morten. He and Jörgen had become good friends, and now they shipped out together on a vessel bound for Norway. Afterwards, they went to Holland together. They had never quarreled, but when one is hot-blooded by nature, one can easily start something; and that Jörgen did one day, over nothing. They were sitting together, behind the cabin door, eating off the same clay dish, when Jörgen, who held his pocket knife in his hand, raised it toward Morten with a threatening gesture, his cheeks deadly pale and his eyes blazing with fury. But Morten only said, "So you're the sort who uses a knife!" At those words Jörgen's hand was lowered; he said no word, but finished his dinner and went off to work Morten and said, "Hit me in the face! I deserve it. There's something in me that's always boiling over."

"Oh, forget it," said Morten, and they became better friends than ever.

When they had returned home to the sand dunes and people heard the story of this quarrel, they said that Jörgen was like a pot that easily boiled over, but that he was an honest pot, anyway.

"But he's no Jutlander. No one can call him a Jutland pot," was Morten's witty answer.

They were both young and healthy, well built, and with strong limbs. Jörgen was the more active.

Up in Norway the peasants go into the mountains and take their cattle there to find pasture. On the western coast of Jutland, the fisherman build huts among the sand dunes. They build them with planks from shipwrecks and cover them over with heath and turf; here the fishermen live and sleep during the early spring. Each fisherman has a girl as a servant—she is called his *aesepige;* she supplies the bait for the hooks, must be ready on the wharf with warm ale to refresh him, and cooks his food when he returns to his hut, tired and hungry. The girls carry the fish up from the boat, cut it up, and, in short, have plenty to do.

Jörgen, his foster father, a few other fishermen, and their girls had a hut together; Morten lived in the next hut.

One of the girls, named Elsa, had known Jörgen ever since they were both little children; they were quite fond of each other and always happy to be together. They were much alike in disposition, but quite different in appearance, for Jörgen was very dark-complexioned, while her skin was white, her hair as yellow as flax, and her eyes as blue as the sea on a sunny day.

One day Elsa and Jörgen were walking together, and Jörgen was holding her hand in a warm, fervent grasp, when she said to him, "Jörgen, I want to unburden my heart to you. Let me be your *aesepige,* instead of Morten's. I know he has hired me, but you're like a brother to me, and Morten—he and I are sweethearts. But now, don't go and tell everybody else about it!"

Jörgen felt as if the sand dunes were whirling beneath him. He didn't say a word; he only nodded—and that was the same as saying, "Yes." This was all that was necessary to make him feel a bitter hatred in his heart for Morten. The more he thought about it, the clearer he realized that Morten had robbed him of the only creature he loved. Never before had he understood his own feelings toward Elsa, and now all hope of winning her for himself was gone.

When the fishermen are returning home over a fairly rough sea, it is interesting to see how the boats pass over the sand reefs. One man stands upright while the rest watch him, sitting with their oars ready to use the moment he signals that a great wave is coming which will lift the boat over the reef. It comes, and the vessel is tossed up so that its very keel can be seen from the shore; in another moment the entire boat vanishes from sight and neither boat, men, nor mast can be seen—you might imagine the ocean has swallowed everything up; another moment, and the boat reappears, crawling up the wave like a mighty sea monster, its oars moving like the creature's legs. The second and third reefs are crossed in the same way, and then the fisherman spring into shallow water and drag their boat ashore. Every wave helps them, until finally they have it beyond the reach of the breakers. But the slightest mistake in the signal when passing those reefs, the delay of a moment, and they would be shipwrecked.

"It would soon be all over with me and Morten too, if that happened," came into

Jörgen's mind out at sea. They were approaching the outer reef when his foster father suddenly became seriously ill; the fever had seized him. Jörgen jumped up and stood in the bow. "Father, let me take your place!" he said; and his eyes moved from Morten to the sea, and from the sea back to Morten, as the oars swung on with the steady strokes, and the great wave rolled toward them. Then suddenly his look fell on the pale face of his foster father, and he could not obey his wicked impulse. The boat crossed the reefs in safety, and in safety they came ashore. But that evil thought still lurked in Jörgen's heart and roused every little fiber of bitterness that he remembered from his childhood days; but he could not weave the fibers together, so he dismissed it all from his mind.

He felt that Morten had robbed him, and that was reason enough to hate him. Some of the fishermen noticed the change in Jörgen, but Morten himself saw nothing; he was just the same as ever, ready to help and eager to talk—in fact, a little too much of the latter.

Jörgen's foster father took to his bed; it became his death bed, for a week later he was dead. Jörgen was his heir, now master of the cottage behind the sand dunes. It was a poor enough hut, but still it was something; and Morten didn't have so much.

"I suppose you won't go to sea again, Jörgen," said one of the old fishermen. "You'll always stay with us now."

But that was by no means Jörgen's thought; on the contrary, he thought about seeing some more of the world. The eel seller up at Fjaltring had a cousin up at Old Skagen, also a fisherman, but wealthy, and a shipowner too; they said he was a kindly old man with whom it would be very pleasant to take service. Old Skagen lies way up at the northern part of Jutland, as far away from the Hunsby sand dunes as one can go; that part of the idea pleased Jörgen best; he had no intention of attending the wedding of Elsa and Morten, which was to take place in a couple of weeks.

It was foolish for Jörgen to go away, said the old fisherman; now that he had a house of his own Elsa would very likely prefer him to Morten. Jörgen's reply was so abrupt that it wasn't easy to make out his meaning. The old man brought Elsa to him; she didn't say much, but she did say: "You have a house; that must be considered."

And Jörgen did consider many things. The ocean has its heavy waves, but the waves of the human heart are even heavier; many thoughts, strong and weak, passed through Jörgen's heart and head before he asked Elsa, "Suppose Morten had a house as good as mine; which of us would you rather have?"

"But Morten doesn't have one, and never will have one."

"But suppose he did have one."

"Why then I'd take Morten, of course; for that's the way I feel about him! But one must have something to live on."

All night Jörgen thought over this answer. There was something within him, he found, something he himself couldn't figure out; it was stronger even than his love for Elsa.

He went to Morten, and what he said and did had been well considered; he offered to sell his house to him on the lowest possible terms, explaining that it would please him better to go to sea again. When Elsa heard about it, she thanked him with a kiss, for she really did love Morten better.

Jörgen was going to leave early next morning. Late the evening before, he had a sudden desire to go to see Morten once more. On his way among the sand dunes he met the old fisherman, who greatly disapproved of his leaving and who declared Morten must carry a charm sewn up in his pocket to make the young girls fall in love with him. Jörgen brushed aside such talk and bade him farewell. Then he proceeded to Morten's hut where he heard loud voices; evidently Morten was not alone. For a moment Jörgen stood irresolute; least of all did he want to meet Elsa there, and now that he thought it over, he would prefer not having Morten thank him all over again. So he turned back without entering.

Next morning, before daylight, he tied up his bundle, gathered his provisions, and started through the sand dunes to the shore. It was easier walking by the sea than along the heavy, sandy road, and besides it was shorter, for he was going first to Fjaltring, near Bovbjerg, where lived the eel seller, whom he had promised to visit.

The ocean was smooth and blue, and as he walked he crushed under his feet the shells and pebbles, the playthings of his childhood. As he was walking his nose began to bleed, and a couple of large drops fell on his sleeve; it seemed a trivial enough matter, but a trivial matter can sometimes be of importance. He soon stopped the bleeding, wiped his sleeve, and walked on. It seemed as if this had cleared both his heart and head. When he found sea kale growing in the sand, he broke off a branch and stuck it in his hat, determined to be joyful and happy; wasn't he going out into the world "a little way up the river," as the young eels had so longed to do? "But beware of wicked people, who will spear you, skin you, cut you in pieces, and lay you in dishes!" he repeated to himself. "I'll slip through the world whole-skinned. Courage is a strong weapon."

The sun was already high when he reached the narrow inlet between the North Sea and the Nissum Fjord; then he looked back and made out in the distance two men on horseback with others following them, all riding at great speed. This did not concern him.

The ferryboat was on the opposite side of the bay, but Jörgen shouted till it came across for him. He sprang on board, but before the ferry was halfway across, the men who had followed him on horseback arrived on the shore, and with threatening gestures called for him to return in the name of the law. Jörgen couldn't imagine what it meant, but thought it would be best to return; so he took the oar himself, and rowed back. In an instant the men had leaped into the boat and before he was aware of it, they had bound his hands together with a rope. "It's well you're caught!" they said. "Your crime will cost you your life!"

He was accused of nothing less than murder! Morten had been found stabbed in the neck with a knife; late, the evening before, one of the fishermen had met Jörgen on his way to Morten's house, and it was remembered that it wasn't the first time Jörgen had threatened Morten with a knife; there seemed no doubt that he was the murderer.

Now the question was where to confine him. Ringkjöbing was the proper place, but it was a long way off, and the wind was against them. In less than half an hour they had crossed Skjaerum Fjord, and now they were only a quarter of a mile from Nörre Vosborg, which was a strong mansion with moats and ramparts. One of the men in the boat was the brother of the keeper of this mansion; he suggested that they might get permission to confine Jörgen, for the time being, in the dungeon where Long Margrethe, the gypsy, had been imprisoned until her execution.

No one listened to Jörgen's denials, and those few drops of blood on his shirt were silent witnesses against him. Conscious of his innocence and of the fact that there was no chance of his being cleared, he calmly resigned himself to his fate.

They landed near the old rampart, where the castle of Sir Bugge had stood—it was the very same spot that Jörgen's feet had trodden years before when he had gone with his foster parents to the funeral party, where he had spent those four happy days on the heath. By the very same path they now led him up to Nörre Vosborg; and here, as then, the elder bush was in full bloom, and the tall lime trees wafted their fragrance to him—he might have imagined it was only yesterday that he had been here last.

Under the grand staircase in the western wing of the building a passage leads into a low-roofed vaulted cell; it was from here that Long Margrethe was led to her execution. She had confessed to having devoured the hearts of five children and believed that, could she have eaten two more, she would have been able to make herself invisible and fly away. In the cell was a tiny, narrow airhole in the wall; but the lime trees outside sent none of their refreshing fragrance within; all was cold, damp, and moldy. There was only a rough bench in the cell; but a good conscience makes an easy pillow, so Jörgen could really lie comfortably.

The thick wooden door was closed and the iron bolts were shot, but superstition can creep through the keyhole of a mansion as well as a fisherman's hut; and as Jörgen lay in the silence and darkness he could not help thinking of Long Margrethe and her horrible crimes. Her last thoughts had filled that narrow dungeon the night before her execution. Nor could he help remembering the black arts that had been practiced by the owner of this mansion, Herr Swanwedel, when he lived there many years ago, and how the watchdog that guarded the bridge had every morning been found hung in his chains across the railing. Such thoughts came to Jörgen's mind and made him shiver; but a sunbeam, a refreshing thought from without, also came to his mind, the remembrance of the blossoming elder and lime trees.

He was not left here long, but was removed to Ringkjöbing; but there his imprisonment was none the less rigorous. For Jörgen's times were not like ours; they were hard times for poor men; peasant farms and peasant settlements were still being converted into new knights' estates. The coachman or valet of a nobleman was often appointed village judge, with power to condemn the peasant to a severe flogging or the loss of all his property for some trifling offense. And thus, in Jutland, far from "The King's Copenhagen" and the wise and just rulers of state, the law took its course with little regard for justice. Jörgen could expect that his case would be delayed.

His wretched cell was bitterly cold; when would this misery end? Innocent, he had been thrown into misfortune and sorrow; that was his lot! He had plenty of time to think over the hard dealing that this world had given him and to wonder why this fate had been allotted him. Still, all would correct itself in that "second life" which assuredly awaits us. In the poor fisherman's cottage that faith had taken firm root in his soul; the light that, even amid the sunshine and plenty of Spain, could not pierce the darkness of his father's mind was sent to him to comfort him in poverty and distress, a sign of the mercy of God, which never disappoints.

Now the spring storms settled in. The roaring of the North Sea can be heard for miles inland, and when the tempests abate there is a thundering as of hundreds of heavy wagons rolling over a hard tunneled road. In his dungeon Jörgen heard this sound, and it was a relief to him; no old melodies could so move him as the music of the rolling ocean—the boundless ocean that had carried him throughout the world with the speed of winds—the ocean over which men pass, carrying their own house with them like the snails carry theirs, always standing on their own native ground, even in foreign lands. How he listened to that deep thunder! How his thoughts surged into a turmoil within him! Free, free! How wonderful to be free—even if with a patched shirt and shoes without soles! Sometimes his soul burned with indignant anger, and he pounded the wall with his clenched fist.

Weeks, months, a whole year passed, and then the gypsy Niels Tyv, the horse dealer, as he was called, was picked up, and then better times came; it was established that Jörgen was innocent.

The evening before Jörgen's departure—the night of the murder—Morten and Niels Tyv had met at a little tavern north of Ringkjöbing Fjord. A couple of glasses were emptied, not enough to get drunk on, but enough to loosen Morten's tongue; he began to boast of having bought a house and of getting married, and when Niels asked from where he was getting the money, Morten proudly slapped his hand to his pocket.

"The money's here, right where it ought to be," he said. This boast cost him his life, for when he rose to go Niels followed him and stabbed him in the back with a knife—all for the sake of money that was not in his pocket at all.

There was a great deal of talk about the affair, but for us it is enough to know that Jörgen was released. But what compensation did he receive for the long, weary days he spent in the cold and loneliness, and for being despised by his fellowman? Why, he was told it was lucky for him he was innocent; now he could go. To be sure, the mayor gave him ten marks for traveling expenses, and several citizens of Ringkjöbing offered him beer and good food, for there are a few kind hearts in the world; not all men "spear, skin, and devour" their fellows.

But the best thing of all was that a merchant from Skagen named Brönne—the same man with whom Jörgen had intended to take service before his imprisonment—had come to Ringkjöbing on business at just that time and heard the whole story. He was kindhearted and sympathized with Jörgen's sufferings; now he would do him a little kindness and prove to him that there are some good people in the world.

Out of prison, not only to freedom, but to a paradise of love and kindness! But it is no man's fate to drain a cup of unmixed bitterness. If even man could not endure to offer such to his fellow man, how could the all-loving God?

"Let the past be dead and buried," said Merchant Brönne. "We'll draw a heavy black line over the last year and burn the calendar, and in two days we'll be off together for Skagen—happy, friendly, peaceful Skagen! People call it the out-of-the -way corner of the country; it's a blessed chimney corner, with windows opening out to the whole wide world!"

What a journey! To breathe the fresh air again; to emerge from the cold damp prison air into the warm sunshine! The heath was gay with blooming heather; the shepherd boy perched on a warrior's grave mound, shrilling his flute made from sheep bones; Fata Morgana, the beautiful mirage of the desert, flaunted her hanging gardens and floating woods; and the wonderful transparent phenomenon called "Loki driving his flock" could be seen.

They traveled up toward the Lime Fjord, toward Skagen, through the land of the Vends, whence the men with the long beards—which had earned them the name of Lombards—had emigrated when, in the days of the famine under King Snio, it was decreed that all the children and old people should be put to death. But Gambaruk, a noble woman of great wealth, had proposed instead that all the young should leave the country.

Jörgen was learned enough to know all this, and although he had never seen the land of the Lombards beyond the Alps, he could easily picture it to himself, for had he not in his boyhood seen the south, Spain? He could remember clearly the piled heaps of fruit, the scarlet pomegranate blossoms, the noise and din and ringing of bells in that great beehive of a city. But he still loved best the land of his home, and Jörgen's home was Denmark.

At last they reached "Vendilskaga," as Skagen is called in the old Norse and Icelandic sagas. Even then old Skagen, with its Easter and Westertown, stretched for miles with sand dunes and farmland as far as the lighthouse near Grenen. Houses and farms were strewn among the shifting sand dunes—it is a wild land where the wind plays constantly in the loose sand, and where the screams of sea gulls, sea swallows, and wild swans cut sharply through the eardrum.

A few miles southwest of Grenen is High or Old Skagen; here Merchant Brönne lived, and here Jörgen would now live. The house was tarred; each of the little outhouses had an inverted boat for a roof, and driftwood joined together formed the pigsty. There was no enclosure, for there was nothing to enclose; but on ropes, strung in long rows one above another, hung countless fishes drying in the wind. The whole shore was strewn with dead herring; in fact, the nets could hardly be thrown into the sea before they would be filled with them. Great loads of herring were caught and taken inland. They were so plentiful that many were often thrown back into the sea or left to rot on the sand.

The merchant's wife and daughter, and even the servants, rushed out in delight to greet the father when they arrived home. There was such handshaking, so much noise, so much to talk about! And the daughter had such a sweet face and lovely eyes!

The house was cozy and roomy inside; the table was set with plates of fish, flounder fit for a king, and wine from Skagen's own vineyard, the great ocean, from which the grapes drifted ashore already pressed, both in barrels and bottles.

When mother and daughter had heard who Jörgen was, and learned how cruelly he, an innocent man, had been treated, they looked upon him with kindness, and the beautiful Miss Clara's bright eyes sparkled more warmly than before.

Jörgen found a blessed home in Old Skagen; it did his heart good; it had suffered so much cruelty, even the bitterness of love, which either softens or hardens the heart. But Jörgen was still young, his heart still soft, and there was a vacant place in it. For that reason it was perhaps just as well that in three weeks Clara was to sail for Christiansand, in Norway, to spend the winter with an aunt.

THE COMPLETE FAIRY TALES

The Sunday before her departure, all were to go together to Holy Communion. The church was large and stately, built by the Dutch and Scotch many centuries before, and quite a distance from where the town is now situated. The church was somewhat dilapidated now, and the way through the deep sand made hard walking, but people did not mind these difficulties to get to the house of God to sing psalms, and to hear the sermon. The sand was piled up outside the wall around the cemetery, but the graves had still been kept free of it.

It was the largest church north of the Lime Fjord. The Virgin Mary, with a golden crown on her head and the infant Savior in her arms, was painted in bright colors above the altar; the holy apostles were ranged around the choir, and high on the wall there hung portraits of Skagen's old burgomasters and councilmen, with their insignia of office. The pulpit was carved. The sun shone brightly into the church, lighting up the polished brass chandelier and the little vessel that hung down from the roof. Jörgen was overwhelmed by the same pure, childlike feeling of devotion that had thrilled his soul when, a boy, he had stood in the rich Spanish cathedral. But here the feeling was different, for in this place he felt that he was one of the congregation.

After the sermon came the communion, and when Jörgen knelt with the others to receive the consecrated bread and wine, he found that he was kneeling next to Miss Clara. But his thoughts were so raised to God and the holy sacrament that not until they rose did he realize that she had been his neighbor. Then he saw the salt tears rolling down her cheeks.

Two days later she sailed for Norway, and Jörgen went out to help on the farm and with the fishing; there were more fish to be caught there in those days than there are now. Shoals of mackerel shone brightly in the darkness of the night, thus betraying the course they were following. The sea robins snarled, and the crabs gave pitiful cries when they were caught; fish are not as voiceless as people say. Jörgen was more quiet than they; he kept his secret—and yet someday it would perhaps burst forth.

Every Sunday when he sat in church and his eyes rested on the picture of the Virgin Mother, they also paused a moment on the spot where Miss Clara had knelt beside him, and he thought of her and her kindness to him.

The autumn brought its rain and sleet. The water rose up in the town of Skagen, for the sand could not absorb it all; people had to wade through it, and sometimes even sail through the streets in boats. Snowstorms and sandstorms followed; ship after ship was wrecked on those fatal reefs; the sand whirled about and buried the houses until the occupants had to creep out through the chimneys. But that was not an unusual occurrence there. Indoors were comfort and warmth; the blazing and crackling fires were fed with peat or with dried wood from the wrecks, and Merchant Brönne read aloud from an old chronicle. He read about Prince Hamlet of Denmark and of how he landed from England and fought a great battle near Bovbjerg; his grave was at Ramme, only a few miles from the eel seller's home, where the heath was like an immense cemetery, studded with hundreds of Viking grave mounds. Merchant Brönne had visited Hamlet's grave. There was more talk of the olden days and of their English and Scottish neighbors, and then Jörgen sang the old ballad about "The King of England's Son," about the stately ship, and how it was decked out:

The blessed words of our dear Lord
Were written in gold on panels aboard.
On the prow, in colors rare,
The king's son clasped his maiden fair.

Jörgen sang this verse with especial sincerity, while his eyes, luminous and black from his birth, sparkled with more fire than ever.

Thus the evenings passed pleasantly, with song and reading; all were happy in that house, even the very animals. The tin shelves gleamed with clean plates; hams and sausages hung under the ceiling and they had winter supplies in abundance. Many rich farmhouses like this are still to be found in West Jutland, abundant as this one in good comfort, good cheer, good sense, and good humor, and like the tent of an Arab for hospitality.

Jörgen had never spent so happy a time, at least since the four days of the funeral, when he was a child. And still Miss Clara was absent; but she was never absent from their thoughts or conversation. In April a vessel was to be sent out to Norway to bring her home, and Jörgen was to go with it.

He had become so joyous and hearty, Mother Brönne said that it was a pleasure to look at him.

"And so it is to look at you!" said the old merchant. "Jörgen has put new life in our winter evenings, and in Mother, too. Why, you have grown younger this year! You were once the prettiest girl in Viborg, and that's saying a lot, for I've always considered the girls of Viborg to be the prettiest."

Jörgen said nothing in reply, but he couldn't help thinking of one Skagen girl, the one he was to bring home.

One morning Merchant Brönne went out to the lighthouse, which stands quite some distance from old Skagen, but not far from Grenen. The signal lights had been extinguished for quite some time, for the sun was already high when he climbed the tower. Four miles from the extreme point of land the sand reefs stretched under water. Many ships could be seen that day, and among them, with the help of his telescope, he believed he could distinguish the *Karen Brönne*; that was the name of his vessel. Yes, there she was, sailing home with Clara and Jörgen on board! Clara sat on the deck and saw the sand dunes slowly appear in the distance. If the wind held, they would be home in an hour. So near were they to home and its happiness, so near to death and its terrors.

Suddenly a plank gave way in the ship, and the water poured in! They tried to plug the leak; the pumps worked furiously; the sails came down, and the distress flag was hoisted. They were still four miles out at sea, and the fishing boats that they could see were too far off. The wind carried them landward; the tide was in their favor; but they were not strong enough. When the ship began to sink, Jörgen threw his right arm about Clara.

What a look she gave him as, crying on the holy name of our Lord, he leaped with her into the ocean! She shrieked in terror, but she knew he would never let go his hold.

On the prow, in colors rare,
The king's son clasped his maiden fair.

Jörgen acted out the old words in this moment of terror and peril; how fortunate that he was an excellent swimmer! He made his way with his feet and one free hand, the other clasped tightly around the girl. Now he floated; now he trod water with his feet, using every trick he knew to husband his strength so that it might last till he reached shore. When he heard the girl sigh, and felt a shuddering thrill pass through her body, he only held her closer. Now a wave rolled over them, but the current still carried them on; the water was so deep and clear that for a moment he fancied he saw shoals of mackerel flashing beneath them—or was it Leviathan, waiting to devour them? Shadows of the clouds swept over the water, to be followed by dazzling sunshine; flocks of birds flew screaming overhead while wild ducks, heavily and sleepily drifting on the surface of the water, started into the air in panic at the sight of the swimmer. Jörgen felt his strength going fast when he was only a few cables' lengths from shore. But help was coming—a boat was drawing near! Just then he distinctly saw a white figure in the water. A wave lifted him up; the figure came nearer; he felt a stunning shock, and everything became dark around him.

There on the sand reef lay the wreck of a ship with the sea partly covering it; the white figurehead leaned against an anchor, and only the sharp iron edge projected above the water. Driven on by the fatal force of the current, Jörgen had struck against this figurehead; in a daze he sank with his burden, but the next wave lifted him and the young girl.

The fisherman got them both into his boat; blood was streaming over Jörgen's face, and he looked as if he were dead; but he still held the girl so tightly they had to tear her from his arm. They placed Clara, pale and lifeless, in the boat and rowed toward Grenen. All methods of restoring her were tried, but in vain—she was dead. For some time Jörgen must have been carrying a corpse, struggling and wrestling for the life of one who was already dead.

Jörgen still breathed, and they carried him to the nearest cottage in the sand dunes. A sort of army surgeon—he was also a smith and a trader—who happened to be on the spot bound up his wound, and the next day a physician was sent for from Hjörring.

But his brain was affected; he lay raving and uttering wild cries until the third day, when he fell into a sort of trance. It seemed his life hung by a thread, and for this thread to give way, the doctor said, was the best wish they could have for him. "Let us pray for our Lord to take him; he will never be a man again."

But life did not leave him; the thread did not break, though memory and all other faculties of the mind were injured. It was horrible! Only a living body was left, a body that soon regained health and strength.

Jörgen remained in Merchant Brönne's home. "He lost his mind trying to save our child," said the old man. "He is now our son!"

"Crazy": that was what they called Jörgen now, but it was hardly the right word; he was like a musical instrument with loosened strings that have lost the power of sound.

Very rarely, and only for a few moments, would the old power seem to return; then they would give old melodies, or a few chords would be played. Sometimes pictures of the past would seem to rise before his mind, but then they would fade away into the mist, and once more he would sit with a blank, motionless, thoughtless face. We can only hope that he did not suffer. His dark eyes had lost their brightness and looked like black clouded glass.

"Poor crazy Jörgen," people said. And this was he who before he was born, was destined to have such a rich, earthly fortune and such happiness that it would be arrogance, terrible vanity, even to wish for or believe in an afterlife. Were all the fine qualities of his soul wasted? Only cruel days, anguish, and broken hopes had been his lot. He was like a precious root which is torn from its rich soil and flung out to rot in the sand. Could this really be the destiny of a soul created in the image of God—a mere game, battered by the chances of this world? No! The God of love will compensate him in another life for all that he lost and suffered in this. "The Lord is loving unto every man, and his mercy is over all His works." The pious old wife of Merchant Brönne repeated these words from the Psalms of David in faith and comfort, and she prayed that our Lord would soon end Jörgen's life of sorrow and take him to enjoy "God's gift of grace," the life everlasting.

Clara lay buried in the churchyard, where the sand drifted over the walls, but Jörgen did not seem to know this. It never penetrated the narrow world of his thoughts, which lived only in fragments from the past. Every Sunday he accompanied the family to church, and sat quietly with a blank face. Once, during the psalm singing, he sighed deeply, and his eyes took on life. He was gazing at the altar, at the very spot where, over a year ago, he had knelt beside his dead friend; his face turned white, his lips murmured her name, and the tears rolled down his cheeks.

They gently led him from the church, but he told them that he was well, and that he had no recollection of what had happened. Poor soul, tried indeed, but not rejected by our Lord! For who dares doubt that God, our Creator, is all-wise and all-loving? Our hearts and our minds give us this truth, and the Bible confirms it. "His mercy is over all His works."

In Spain, where gilded Moorish cupolas are fanned by the warm breezes amid laurels and orange trees, and where song and castanets are heard, a childless old man, the rich merchant, sat in his beautiful palace, sadly watching a procession of pretty children passing through the street with torches and waving banners. How much of his wealth would he not give to have such children himself! He thought of his daughter and her child who perhaps had never seen the light of this world, hence would never attain the glory of Paradise. "Poor child!"

Yes, "Poor child!" indeed—a child still, though past thirty years old; for Jörgen had lived thus for many years in Old Skagen.

The flying sand had drifted over the graves in the churchyard up to the very walls of the church; here among those who had gone before them, among relatives and friends, the dead were still being buried. Merchant Brönne and his wife now rested here under the white sand, among their children.

It was early in the year, the time of storms; the sand curled up like smoke from the sand dunes; the ocean tossed huge waves; large flocks of birds, like storm clouds, flew screaming overhead; and ship after ship was wrecked on those fatal reefs that stretched along the coast from Skagen to the Hunsby sand dunes.

One afternoon, as Jörgen sat alone in his room, a sudden light broke in his mind; it was the same restless feeling that had often in his younger years driven him out over the sand dunes or the heath.

"Home! Home!" he said. No one heard him. He left the house, and sand and pebbles whirled around him and beat into his face. He went toward the church, where the sand lay drifted up against the wall and half covered the windows. The church door was unlocked and easy to open; Jörgen went in.

The wind raged and howled over the town of Skagen; such a hurricane had not been known within the memory of man. It was awful weather! But Jörgen was sheltered within the house of God, and while black night reigned outside, within him everything grew bright—bright with the light of the immortal soul. He felt as if the heavy stone in his head had burst with a clang! He imagined that the organ was playing, but it was only the storm and the roaring of the ocean that he heard. As he sat down in one of the pews he thought the candles were being lighted, one by one, until there was a blaze of light such as he had only seen in the land of the Spaniards. Then all the portraits of the old councillors and burgomasters came to life; they stepped down from the walls where they had hung for so many years and seated themselves in the choir. Then the gates and doors of the church swung open, and all the dead entered, festively dressed, as was customary in the olden days; sweet music was played as they walked in and seated themselves in the pews. The psalm singing swelled like the rolling of the ocean. Jörgen's old foster parents from the Hunsby sand dunes were there, and the good Merchant Brönne and his wife, and beside them, next to Jörgen, sat their gentle, loving daughter. She gave her hand to Jörgen, and together they went up to the altar where they had knelt once before, and the pastor joined their hands and consecrated them to a life of love. Then the sound of the trumpet burst forth, marvelously like the voice of child, full of longing and expectation; it swelled into the sound of an organ, full of rich, glorious tones, blessed to hear and yet mighty enough to burst the tombstones on the graves.

The ship hanging in the choir sank downward, in front of them, and grew vast and splendid with silken sails and golden masts, with anchors of red gold and ropes of silken twine, like the ship in the old ballad. The bridal couple stepped on board, and all the congregation followed; there were room and enjoyment for all. Then the arches and walls of the church blossomed like the elder and the fragrant lime trees; joyfully they waved their green branches, and bowed, and parted. The ship was lifted up and sailed with them through the ocean, through the air. Every candle in the church became a tiny star; the winds sang a hymn, and all joined in:

"In love, to glory! No life shall be lost! Supreme happiness forever! Hallelujah!"

And these were Jörgen's last words in this mortal world, for the thread that held the immortal spirit snapped; only a lifeless corpse lay in the dark church, while the storm howled and covered it with drifting sand.

The next morning was Sunday, and the pastor and congregation set out for church. The road, buried in sand, was almost impassable. When they reached the church they found an enormous sand heap completely covering the door. Then the pastor prayed briefly and said that as God had now closed the door to this his house, they must go forth and raise Him a new one elsewhere. So they sang a psalm and returned home.

In vain Jörgen was sought throughout the town of Skagen and the sand dunes; it was supposed that the rolling waves of sand had buried him beneath them.

But his body was entombed in a vast sarcophagus, in the very church itself. During the storm our Lord cast earth over his coffin; the great heaps of sand lay above and around it, and they cover it to this day. The drifting sand lies piled above those mighty arches; thorns and wild roses now twine over the church, where the visitor struggles on toward its tower still showing above the sand. His tombstone may be seen for miles; no king ever had a more magnificent one. And no one will ever disturb the repose of the dead, for none until now has ever known his resting place; for this story was sung to me by the storm among the sand dunes.

MOVING DAY (1860)

You surely remember Ole, the tower watchman. I have told you about two visits I paid him, and now I'll tell you of a third, although it won't be the last one.

I have gone up to see him generally on New Year's Day, but this time it was Moving Day, when everything down in the city streets is very unpleasant, for they are littered with heaps of rubbish and crockery and all kinds of sweepings, not to mention musty old straw that you have to trample about in. Well, there I was, and in the middle of this rubbish from attic and dustbin I saw a couple of children playing going to bed; they thought it looked so inviting there for that game. Yes, they snuggled down in the straw and drew a ragged old scrap of a curtain over them for a quilt. "That was wonderful!" they said. It was too much for me, so I hurried off to see Ole.

"It's Moving Day," he said. "Streets and alleys are dustbins, dustbins in the grand style; but one cartload is enough for me. I can always find something to pick out of it, and I did that, soon after Christmas. I was walking down the street, a damp, raw, and dirty street, and just the right kind of weather for catching cold. The rubbish man had drawn up his cart there; it was loaded and looked like a sample of Copenhagen streets on Moving Day. In the back of the cart was a fir tree still quite green and with tinsel still hanging on its twigs. It had been the centerpiece of a Christmas display, but now it was thrown out into the street and the rubbish man had stuck it up behind on his pile; a sight to laugh at or weep at—yes, you might even go so far as that—it all depends on your turn of mind. And I thought about it, and so did some of the odds and ends in the cart. At least they may have thought, which is just about the same. Here was a worn lady's glove; what was it thinking about? Shall I tell you? It lay there pointing its little finger straight at the fir tree. 'That fir tree touches me,' it thought. 'I have been to a party, too, among the lighted chandeliers. My life was just a night at a ball. A squeeze of the hand, and I burst; that's all I remember, so now I have nothing more to live for.' That's the way the glove thought, or it may have thought like that. 'That's a tasteless thing for that fir tree to do!' said the potsherds. But you see, broken crockery finds everything tasteless. 'When you come to the rubbish cart,' they said, 'it's time to give up your fine airs and your tinsel. As for ourselves, we've been of some use in the world—far more use than an old green stick like that!' You see, that was another point of view on the same subject, and many people have it. But still the fir tree looked pretty well, and it was a bit of poetry on the rubbish heap; there are many like that to be found in the streets on Moving Day. But the streets down there were crowded and tiresome, and I longed to get back up to my tower and stay there; so here I sit and look down on them from above, and that's very amusing.

"Down below the good people are changing houses; they work hard packing up and then go off with their movables, and the house goblin sits on the tail of the cart and moves with them. Household quarrels, family arguments, sorrows, and cares move from the old to the new houses, and so what do they and we get out of it all? Yes, that was told us already long ago, in the good old verse in the newspaper columns:

Remember Death's Great Moving Day!

"It is a serious thought, but I hope it is not disagreeable to you to hear about it. Death is the most faithful administrator after all, in spite of his many petty duties. Have you ever thought about them?

"Death is a bus conductor; he is a passport writer; he signs his name to our references; and he is the director of life's great savings bank. Do you understand that? All our earthly deeds, great and small, are deposited in that savings bank. Then, when Death comes with his Moving Day bus and we have to get in to be driven to eternity, he gives us our references on the frontier as a passport. For our expense money on the journey he draws from the savings bank one of our deeds, whichever of them most distinctly characterizes our conduct; this may be very pleasant to us, or it may be very horrible!

"Nobody has ever escaped that omnibus journey. They tell stories, indeed, of one man who was not allowed to enter—they call him the Wandering Jew; he still has to run along behind it. If he had managed to get in, he would have escaped the treatment he received from the poets.

"Let's take an imaginary look into that big Moving Day omnibus. What a mixed group! Side by side sit kings and beggars, the genius and the idiot. On they must go, without goods or wealth, with only their references and their expense money from life's savings bank. But of each man's deeds, which one has been found and given to him? Perhaps only a very small one, no bigger than a pea, yet a great blooming vine may grow from it.

"The poor beggar, who sat on a low stool in the corner and received blows and hard words, perhaps is given the battered stool to take, as a token and as expense money. That stool will become the cart to bear him into eternity, and there it will grow into a throne, gleaming with gold and blooming like an arbor.

"He who was always drinking from the bubbling cup of pleasure, and thus forgetting the wrong things he had done here, receives a wooden keg as his lot. On the journey he has to drink from it; and that pure and cleansing drink will clear his thoughts and awaken his better and nobler nature, so that he sees and feels what before he could not or would not see. Thus he bears within himself his own punishment, the gnawing worm that never dies. If on his wineglass was inscribed *Forgetfulness*, the inscription on the keg is *Memory*.

"Whenever I read a good historical book, I cannot help picturing to myself the person of whom I am reading at the final moment of all, when he begins to enter Death's omnibus. I cannot help wondering which of his deeds Death has given him from the savings bank, and what sort of expense money he will take with him to eternity.

"Once upon a time there was a French king—his name I have forgotten, for the names of good people can sometimes be forgotten by you and me, but it will surely come to light again, because in the time of famine this king became the savior of his people. In his honor they raised a monument of snow with the inscription, 'More quickly than this melts did you help us!' I think, remembering that monument, that Death must have given him one single snowflake that would never melt but flew like a white butterfly above his royal head, on into the land of eternity.

"Then there was Louis XI—yes, I remember his name; one always remembers what is wicked—a sample of his doings often comes to mind; I wish I could say the story is untrue.

"He had his lord high chancellor beheaded, and that he had a right to do, justly or unjustly; but on the same scaffold he set up the chancellor's innocent children, the one eight and the other seven, so that they would be spattered with their father's warm blood. Then they were taken to the Bastille and set in an iron cage, without even a blanket to cover them. Every eighth day the king sent the executioner to them, to pull a tooth from each of them, so that they might suffer even more. The elder said, 'My mother would die of sorrow if she knew how my little brother suffered. Pray, pull out two of my teeth, and spare him! There were tears in the hangman's eyes when he heard this, but the king's will was stronger than the tears. Every eighth day a silver dish, with two children's teeth on it, was brought to the king; as he had demanded them, so he had them. And I think it was two teeth that Death drew out of life's savings bank for Louis XI to take with him on his journey to the great land of eternity. They flew before him like two fireflies; they glowed and burned and stung him, the teeth of those innocent children."

"Yes, a serious drive it is, that bus drive on the great Moving Day. And when does our turn come?"

"That's why it's so very serious; any day, any hour, any minute the bus may come for us. Which of our deeds will Death draw from the savings bank and give us for the journey? Yes, think that over! That Moving Day will not be found on the calendar!"

THE BUTTERFLY (1860)

The Butterfly wanted a sweetheart, and naturally he wanted one of the prettiest of the dear little flowers. He looked at each of them; there they all sat on their stalks as quiet and modest as little maidens ought to sit before they are engaged; but there were so many to choose from that it would be quite difficult to decide. So the Butterfly flew down to the Daisy, whom the French call "Marguerite." They know she can tell fortunes. This is the way it's done: the lovers pluck off the little petals one by one, asking questions about each other, "Does he love me from the heart? A little? A lot? Or loves he not at all?"—or something like that; everyone asks in his own language. So the Butterfly also came to ask, but he wouldn't bite off the leaves; instead he kissed each one in turn, thinking that kindness is the best policy.

"Sweet Miss Marguerite Daisy," he said, "you're the wisest woman of all the flowers—you can tell fortunes! Tell me, should I choose this one or that one? Which one am I to have? When you have told me, I can fly straight to her and propose."

But Marguerite answered not a word. She resented his calling her "a woman," for she was unmarried and quite young. He put his question a second time, and then a third time, and when he still couldn't get a word out of her, he gave up and flew away to begin his wooing.

It was early spring; the snowdrops and crocuses were growing in abundance. "They're really very charming," said the Butterfly. "Neat little schoolgirls, but a bit too sweet." For, like all very young men, he preferred older girls. So he flew to the anemones, but they were a bit too bitter for his taste. The violets were a little too sentimental, the tulips much too gay, the lilies too middle class, the linden blossoms too small, and, besides, there were too many in their family. He admitted the apple blossoms looked like roses, but if they opened one day and the wind blew they fell to pieces the very next; surely such a marriage would be far too brief. He liked the sweet pea best of all; she was red and white, dainty and delicate, and belonged to that class of domestic girl who is pretty yet useful in the kitchen. He was about to propose to her when he noticed a pea pod hanging nearby, with a withered flower clinging to it. "Who's that?" he asked.

"It's my sister," said the pea flower.

"Oh, so that's how you'll look later on!" This frightened the Butterfly, and away he flew.

Honeysuckles hung over the hedges; there were plenty of those girls, long-faced and with yellow complexions. No, he didn't like that kind at all. Yes, but what *did* he like? You ask him!

Spring passed and summer passed; then autumn came, and he was still no nearer making up his mind. Now the flowers wore beautiful, colorful dresses, but what good did that do? The fresh, fragrant youth had passed, and it is fragrance the heart needs as one grows older; and of course dahlias and hollysocks have no particular fragrance. So the Butterfly went to see the mint.

"It's not exactly a flower—or rather it's all flower, fragrant from root to top, with sweet scent in every leaf. Yes, she's the one I want!" So at last he proposed to her.

But the mint stood stiff and silent, and at last said, "Friendship, if you like, but nothing else. I'm old, and you're old, too. It would be all right to live for each other, but marriage—no! Don't let's make fools of ourselves in our old age!"

And so the Butterfly did not find a sweetheart at all. He had hesitated too long, and one shouldn't do that! The Butterfly became an old bachelor, as we call it.

Now it was a windy and wet late autumn; the wind blew cold down the backs of the poor trembling old willows. And that made them creak all over. When the weather is like that it isn't pleasant to fly about in summer clothing, outside. But the Butterfly was not flying out-of-doors; he had happened to fly into a room where there was a fire in the stove and the air was as warm as summer. Here he could at least keep alive. "But just to keep alive isn't enough," he said. "To live you must have sunshine and freedom and a little flower to love!"

And he flew against the windowpane, was noticed by people, admired, and set on a needle to be stored in a butterfly collection. This was the most they could do for him.

"Now I'm sitting on a stalk, just like the flowers," said the Butterfly. "It isn't very much fun; it's just like being married, you're bound up so tightly!" He comforted himself with this reflection.

"A poor consolation, after all," said the pot plants in the room.

"But you can't take the opinion of pot plants," thought the Butterfly. "They converse too much with human beings!"

THE BISHOP OF BÖRGLUM AND HIS MEN (1861)

We are up in Jutland, near the wild marsh. We can hear the North Sea, hear it tossing about, for it is quite close by. Before us there rises a great sand dune; we have been looking at it for a long while, and we've been, and still are, driving toward it, very slowly, through the deep sand. On the top of this sand dune is an old, rambling building, the Börglum Monastery, the largest wing of which is the church. We arrive there in the late evening, but the air is clear and the night is bright, so we can enjoy an expansive view over meadow and moor as far as the Aalborg Fjord, over field and heath, out over the dark-blue sea.

Now that we are up there, we drive on through barn and shed, then turn through the gates and on into the old castle court, where the linden trees stand in a row along the walls; sheltered from wind and weather, they thrive here, and their leafy branches almost hide the windows.

We climb up the winding stone staircase; we then walk through the long corridors, beneath raftered ceilings. The wind whistles so strangely here, whether outside or inside; one doesn't quite know where the sounds come from. And then one tells stories. Yes, a person tells and sees so many things when he is frightened or wants to frighten others. The old dead monks, one says, glide silently past us and into the church, where the wind rushes through and seems to us to be singing Mass for their souls; this brings strange thoughts to one, thoughts that carry us back into the olden times.

There is a stranded ship on the coast, and the bishop's men are active there on the beach. While the ocean has spared some of the voyagers, these men spare none; the water will wash away all trace of crimson blood that has flowed from broken skulls. The stranded goods—and there are many—all belong to the bishop. The waves have washed up the anchor and barrels filled with fine wines for the cellar of the monks, where there is already a full supply of ale and mead; there is also a plenitude of poultry, sausages, and ham in their kitchen, and in the ponds outside are fat bass and delicious carp. The Bishop of Börglum is a man of power; he owns much land and yet he wants to acquire more; all must bow before him, Oluf Glob. A wealthy kinsman of his, at Thy, has just died; the widow will find Oluf Glob neither kin nor kind to her. Her late husband ruled the whole district, with the exception of the church properties; her son is in a foreign land, having been sent away, at his own wish, when no more than a boy, to learn foreign customs. For years no word has come from him; he may be in his grave and may never return home to take over the rule that now his mother must assume.

"What! Shall a woman rule?" says the bishop. He summons her into the courts, but for what gain? She has broken no law; right and justice are on her side.

Bishop Oluf of Börglum, what are you pondering over? What are you writing on that white parchment? What is it that you now conceal under band and seal and then give to a knight and his servant, who ride off with it, out of the country, far away to the city of the pope?

The time of the falling leaves, the season of storms and wrecks, is past, and now icy winter comes. Twice it has come with no tidings from abroad, but now finally with its return the knight and his servant ride back from Rome, bearing a papal ban against the widow who dared oppose the pious bishop.

"A curse upon her and all that is hers! Cast out is she from church and congregation. None shall dare lend her a helping hand; friends and kinfolk alike must shun her as a plague and pestilence! What will not bend must break," said the bishop.

The people all forsake her; yet she is steadfast in her trust in God, who alone will be her strength and bulwark. Only one servant, an elderly maid, remains faithful to her; together they guide the plow over fields where the corn flourishes, though the land has been cursed.

"You child of hell, I shall yet carry out my purpose!" says the Bishop of Börglum. "Now I summon you before the tribunal that will condemn you!"

Then the widow harnesses her last two oxen to her carriage, and she and her faithful servant drive away across the heath, out of the land of Denmark. Now she is a stranger among strangers, where a strange tongue is spoken, and where foreign customs prevail, far away, where the green hills rise into mountains, and where the vineyards grow. Traveling peddlers pass her, carefully guarding their loaded wagons, in deadly fear of attack from robber barons. But the two poor women, in their humble cart drawn by the black oxen, may pass in safety along the dangerous roads and through the dense forests. Now they are in France, and they meet a gallant knight followed by twelve men-at-arms. The knight pauses and looks at the strange wagon and then asks the younger of the women what country they have come from and what their journey's destination is. She explains that they are from Thy, in Denmark, tells of her cares and misery, but these all seem to come to an end; our Lord has guided them together—the stranger knight is her son! He holds out his arms and embraces her, and the poor mother weeps, which she has not been able to do for many years, but rather has bitten her lips until blood has come forth.

It is the time of the falling leaves, the season of wrecks. The ocean washes ashore filled wine casks for the bishop's cellars; in his kitchen the wild venison is roasting; it is pleasant and warm within doors, though winter freezes without. But news is brought;

Jens Glob has returned to Thy with his mother. Jens Glob summons the bishop into court to demand their lands and rights.

"Much good that will do him!" said the bishop. "Spare your efforts, Sir Jens!"

Another year passes; again the time of the falling leaves returns, the season of wrecks; icy winter follows, and the white bees swarm about and sting one's face until they melt. It is sharp weather today, say people who have ventured out into it. Jens Glob stands close to his fire, lost in thought; he singes his mantle, burns a hole in it unawares. "I will master you yet, Bishop of Börglum! You are safe from the law, sheltered by the mantle of the Pope, but not safe from Jens Glob!" He writes to his brother-in-law, Sir Oluf Hase of Salling, bidding him meet him Christmas Eve at Mass in Hvidberg Church; the bishop must leave Börglum and come to Thyland, to read the Mass there; this Jens Glob knows.

Meadow and moorland are buried beneath ice and snow, and across them speeds a cavalcade of horse and riders—the bishop, his clerks, his squires. They take the short cut among the waving reeds, where the wind sings its melancholy song. Blow your brazen trumpet, you trumpeter dressed in foxskin! It sounds sharply in the clear air! They ride on over heath and moorland, where in the warm summertime Fata Morgana decks her magic bowers; on they ride, to the south, toward Hvidberg Church.

The wind blows *his* trumpet, too, blows it louder and louder, creating a storm, a terrible storm, that continues to grow in force. On, on through the storm, toward the church, they ride. The house of God stands firm, but the storm drives on over field and moorland, over fjord and ocean. The bishop reaches the church. But Sir Oluf Hase can scarcely do so, however hard he rides. He reaches the opposite side of the fjord with his men, whom Jens Glob has summoned to aid him in calling the bishop to account. The church is the courthouse; the altar is the counsel table. The candles in the heavy brass candlesticks are all burning. Outside the storm screams out the accusation and the sentence. The wind rushes through the air, over moorland and heath, over the rolling billows; no ferryboat can cross the fjord in such weather.

Oluf Hase is held at Ottesund; he dismisses his men, bids them keep his horse and armor and take his farewell to his wife, for alone will he risk his life in the roaring waters. They will be his witnesses that it is not his fault if Jens Glob stands alone in Hvidberg Church. But his faithful warriors will not leave him; they will follow him even into the raging waters. Ten of them are swept away by the torrent; Oluf Hase and the two youngest reach the opposite shore in safety and have still four miles to ride.

It is past midnight, Christmas Eve. The wind has died down; the church is lighted up, the light shining from the windows over meadow and heath. The service is ended, and the house of God is so still that the wax can be heard dripping from the candles to the stone floor. Now at last Oluf Hase arrives.

Jens Glob meets him in the forecourt, saying, "Good day. The bishop and I are reconciled now!"

"Are you, indeed!" says Oluf. "Then neither you nor the bishop shall leave this church alive!" His sword flashes from its scabbard and splits in two the wooden door of the church, which Jens has closed between them. "Hold back, dear brother-in-law! First see what sort of reconciliation this is! I have slain the bishop and all his men! Not one of them will do evil again, and we need say nothing more of the wrongs done my mother!"

The altar lights burn red, but redder is the stain that shines from the church door; there, lying in blood, is the bishop, with a cloven skull, and lying dead around him are his men. It is quiet and calm on the holy eve of Christmas.

The third evening after Christmas, funeral bells in Börglum Convent. The murdered bishop and his slain men lie in state beneath a black canopy, lighted by candelabras swathed in crepe. The once mighty lord is a corpse, robed in a silver-bordered mantle, with the crosier in his powerless hand. Incense fills the air as the monks chant a funeral dirge; it sounds like a sentence of wrath and condemnation, and may be heard over the whole countryside as it is carried along and wailed by the wind. Sometimes the accusing voice sinks to rest for a while, but it never dies out completely; it always rises again, carrying its dismal strains late into our own century, singing of the cruel Bishop of Börglum and his wicked men. On many a dark night the terrified peasant, driving along the heavy sandy road past Börglum Convent, hears it; and the sleepless listener within Börglum's thick walls hears it, too. The church entrance has long been walled up, but superstitious eyes still see the door there, opening before them; the candles in the church brass crowns shine, and the church is revealed in its former splendor, rich with the smoke of incense, while the monks still sing the funeral Mass for the murdered bishop. He lies there in his silver-bordered robe, the crosier in his powerless hand, the bloody wound shining as red as fire from his pale, proud forehead. There are the worldly mind and evil passions that burned.

Sink into the grave, into the night of oblivion, you dismal memories of the olden days!

Listen to the voice of the wind, sweeping over the rolling sea! Out there a storm is raging and will take many lives, for the sea has not changed its nature because the times have changed. Tonight it is all mouths to devour; tomorrow perhaps it will be as clear as a mirror, just as it was in the olden times we have now buried. Sleep calmly if you can!

Now it is morning; the new day brings sunshine into the room. But the wind still blows, and there is news of a wreck, as in the olden times. Last night, down by Lökken, the little red-roofed fishing village visible from our windows, a ship was wrecked. But by the use of a rocket apparatus a line was cast ashore and a bridge made between the wreck and the mainland; all on board were saved and brought to land, and beds were found for them. Today they are going to Börglum Convent. There they will find warm hospitality, be sheltered in comfortable rooms, see friendly eyes, and hear kindly voices speaking their own language. The piano will sound for them with melodies of their native land, and before these have died away, a chord of another sort will be struck; soundless and yet full of sound and certainty, the telegraph wire will reach the homes of the shipwrecked in a foreign land and tell of their safety. Then with their minds at ease, they will join in the dancing at the feast given in the hall at Börglum. Waltzes and folk dances will be danced, and songs will be sung about Denmark and her valiant soldier in our time.

Blessed be you, our new age! Let a fresh and pure summer breeze sweep through the towns! Send your sunrays into our hearts and minds! Let them erase the dark traditions of the cruel days of old!

TWELVE BY THE MAIL (1861)

It was very frosty, starry clear weather, quiet and calm.

Bump! A pot was thrown against a door. Bang! Fireworks were shot off to welcome the new year, for it was New Year's Eve; and now the clock struck twelve!

Trateratra! There came the mail. The big mail coach stopped outside the gate to the town. It carried twelve people and couldn't hold more, for all the seats were taken.

"Hurrah! Hurrah!" rang out in the houses, where people were celebrating New Year's Eve. They arose with full glasses and drank a toast to the new year.

"Health and good wishes for the new year!" they said. "A pretty little wife! Lots of money! An end to nonsense!"

Yes, these were their wishes for one another, and glasses were struck together, while the mail coach stopped in front of the town gate with the unknown guests, the twelve travelers.

What kind of people were they? They had passports and luggage with them; yes, even presents for you and me and for all the people in the town. Who were these strangers? What did they want, and what did they bring?

"Good morning!" they said to the sentry at the town gate.

"Good morning!" said he, as the clock had struck twelve. "Your name? Your profession?" asked the sentry when the first of them stepped out of the carriage.

"Look in the passport!" said the man. "I am myself!" And a splendid-looking fellow he was, too, dressed in a bearskin and fur boots. "I am the man on whom many people pin their hopes. Come to see me tomorrow, and I'll give you a real new year! I throw dollars and cents about, give presents, and, yes, I even give balls, thirty-one of them; that's all the nights I have to spare. My ships are frozen tight, but in my office it is warm. I am a merchant, and my name is *January*. I have only bills!"

Then came the second. He was a comedian, a theatrical director, the manager of masked balls, and all the amusements you could think of. His luggage consisted of a great barrel.

"We'll beat the cat out of the barrel at carnival time!" he said. "I'll amuse others, and myself, too, for I have the shortest time to live of the whole family; I get to be only twenty-eight days old. Yes, sometimes they throw in an extra day, but that doesn't make much difference. Hurrah!"

"You must not shout so loud!" said the sentry.

"Yes, I may!" said the man. "I am Prince Carnival, and traveling under the name of *February!*"

Now came the third. He looked very much like Fasting itself, but strutted proudly, for he was related to the Forty Knights, and was a weather prophet. But that is hardly fattening employment, and for that reason he approved of Fasting. He had a cluster of violets in his buttonhole, but they were very small.

"March, March!" shouted the fourth, and pushed the third. "March, March! Into the guardroom; there's punch there! I can smell it!"

But it wasn't true; he only wanted to make an *April* fool of him; thus the fourth began his career in the town. He looked very jolly, did little work, and had lots of holidays.

"Good humor one day and bad the next!" he said. "Rain and sunshine. Moving out and moving in. I am also moving-day commissioner; I am an undertaker. I can both laugh and cry. I have summer clothes in my trunk, but it would.be very foolish to use them now. Here I am! When I dress up I wear silk stockings and carry a muff!"

Now a lady came out of the carriage. "Miss *May,*" she called herself, and wore summer clothes and overshoes. She had on a beech-tree-green silk dress, and anemones in her hair, and she was so scented with wild thyme that the sentry had to sneeze.

"God bless you!" she said, and that was her greeting.

She was beautiful. And she was a singer; not of the theater, but a singer of the woodlands; not at county fairs; no, she roamed through the fresh green forest and sang there for her own entertainment. In her handbag she had a copy of Christian Winther's *Woodcuts*, which were like the beech-tree forest itself, and also *Little Poems* by Richardt, which were like the wild thyme.

"Now comes the mistress, the young mistress!" shouted those inside the carriage.

And then out came the lady, young and delicate, proud and pretty. You could easily see that she was born to be a lady of leisure. She gave a great feast on the longest day of the year, so that her guests might have time to eat the many dishes of food at her table. She could afford to ride in a carriage of her own, but still she traveled in the mail coach like the others, for she wanted to show she wasn't too proud. But she didn't travel alone; with her was her elder brother, *July.*

He was a well-fed fellow, in attire, and with a Panama hat. He had but little baggage with him, because it was a nuisance in the heat. He had brought only his bathing cap and swimming trunks; that isn't much.

Now came the mother, Madam *August,* a wholesale fruit dealer, proprietor of many fish tanks, and landowner, wearing a great crinoline. She was fat and hot, and took an active part in everything; she herself even carried beer out to the workmen in the fields.

"In the sweat of thy face shalt thou eat bread," she said. "That is written in the Bible. Afterward we can have the picnics and dances in the woods and the harvest festivals."

Such was the mother.

Now again came a man, a painter by profession, a master of colors, as the forest soon learned. The leaves had to change their colors—but how beautifully—whenever he wished it; soon the wood glowed with red, yellow, and brown. The painter whistled like the black starling bird and was a brisk worker. He wound the brown-green hop plants around his beer jug, which decorated it beautifully; indeed, he had an eye for decorating. There he stood with his color pot, and that was all the luggage he had.

Now followed a land proprietor, who was thinking of the grain month, of the plowing and preparing of the land, and, yes, also a little of the pleasures of field sports. He had his dog and his gun, and he had nuts in his game bag. Crack, crack! He had an awful lot of baggage with him, and even an English plow. And he talked about farming, but you couldn't hear much of what he said, because of the coughing and gasping.

It was *November* coming. He had a cold, such a violent cold that he used a bed sheet instead of a handkerchief; and yet he had to accompany the servant girls and initiate them into their winter service, he said; but his cold would go when he went out woodcutting, which he had to do, because he was master sawyer for the firewood guild. His evenings he spent cutting soles for skates, knowing that in a few weeks there would be good use for these amusing shoes.

Now came the last passenger, a little old mother, with her firepot. She was cold, but her eyes sparkled like two bright stars. She carried a flowerpot with a little fir tree growing in it.

"I shall guard and nurse this tree, so that it may grow large by Christmas Eve and reach from the ground right up to the ceiling, and be covered with lighted candles, golden apples, and little cutout paper decorations. This fire-kettle warms like a stove. I take the storybook from my pocket and read aloud, so that all the children in the room become quiet. But the dolls on the tree come to life, and the little wax angel on top of the tree shakes its golden tinsel wings, flies down from the green top, and kisses in the room, yes, the poor children, too, who stand outside and sing the Christmas carol about the star of Bethlehem."

"And now the coach can drive again," said the sentry. "We have the twelve. Let another coach drive up!"

"First let the twelve come inside," said the Captain of the Guard, "one at a time. I'll keep the passports. Each is good for a month; when that has passed, I'll write a report of their behavior on each passport. Be so good, Mr. January; please step inside."

And in he went.

When a year has passed, I shall be able to tell you what the twelve have brought you, me, and all of us. I don't know it now, and they probably don't know it themselves, for these are strange times we live in.

THE BEETLE (1861)

The emperor's horse was shod with gold—a golden shoe on each of its feet.

And why was he getting golden shoes?

He was a magnificent-looking animal, with slender legs, intelligent eyes, and a mane that hung down his neck like a soft veil of silk. He had carried his master through the smoke and flame of battle and heard the bullets sing and whistle around him; he had kicked and bitten those about him and done his share of the fighting whenever the enemy advanced; he had leaped, carrying his master on his back, over the enemy's fallen horse and had saved the emperor's red-gold crown, saved the life of the emperor, which was much more valuable than the red gold; and that's why the emperor's horse had golden shoes, a golden shoe on each of his feet.

And the Beetle came creeping out.

"First the big ones," he said, "and then the little ones; but size isn't the only thing that does it." Then he stretched out his thin legs.

"And what do you want?" demanded the Blacksmith.

"Golden shoes," replied the Beetle.

"Why, you must be crazy!" said the Blacksmith. "Do you want golden shoes, too?"

"Golden shoes," said the Beetle. "I'm just as good as that great creature that is waited on, currycombed, and brushed, and served with food and drink. Don't I belong to the imperial stable, too?"

"But *why* does the horse have golden shoes?" asked the Blacksmith. "Don't you understand that?"

"Understand? I understand that it is a personal insult to me," said the Beetle. "It's just done to annoy me, so I'm going out into the world."

"Get out of here!" said the Blacksmith.

"What a rude person!" said the Beetle as he left the stable. He flew a little way and presently found himself in a beautiful flower garden, all fragrant with roses and lavender.

"Isn't it lovely here?" asked one of the little Ladybirds that were flying about, with black spots on their red shieldlike wings. "How sweet it smells here and how beautiful it is!"

"I'm used to much better things," said the Beetle. "Do you call *this* beautiful? Why, there isn't so much as a manure pile here!"

Then he went on and got into the shadow of a large Gillyflower. A Caterpillar was crawling along on it.

"How beautiful the world is!" said the Caterpillar. "The sun is so warm, and everything is so pleasant! And when my time comes and I must die, as people call it, I'll wake up again, and I'll be a butterfly!"

"What conceit!" said the Beetle. "*You* fly about like a butterfly, indeed! I'm from the stable of the emperor, and no one there, not even the emperor's favorite horse— who wears my castoff golden shoes—has any idea like that! Get wings! Fly! Why, I can fly already!" and then the Beetle flew away. "I don't really want to be annoyed, and yet I am annoyed."

Soon afterward he settled on a large lawn. Here he lay quietly for a while, and then he fell asleep.

My goodness! The rain came down in buckets! The noise woke up the Beetle, and he wanted to get down into the earth at once, but he couldn't. He tumbled over; sometimes he was swimming on his stomach, sometimes on his back, and it was out of the question to try to fly; would he ever escape from there with his life? So he just lay where he was and remained lying there.

When the rain had let up a little, and the Beetle had blinked the water from his eyes, he saw something gleaming white. It was linen that had been put out there to bleach; he managed to make his way to it and creep into a fold of the damp cloth. Certainly this place wasn't as comfortable as the warm stable, but there was nothing better, and so he stayed there for a whole day and a whole night, while the rain stayed, too. The next morning he crept out, very much annoyed with the weather.

Two frogs were sitting on the linen, their bright eyes shining with pleasure.

"What wonderful weather this is!" one of them said. "How refreshing! And this linen holds the water together so perfectly! My hind legs are tickling as if I were going to swim."

"I'd like to know," said the other frog, "whether the swallow, who flies so far in her many trips to foreign countries, ever finds a better climate than ours. Such a storm, and such a downpour! You really might think you were lying in a wet ditch. Anybody that doesn't enjoy this weather certainly doesn't love his native country!"

"Have you ever been in the emperor's stable?" asked the Beetle. "The dampness there is both warm and refreshing. That's what I am used to; that's the climate for me; but one can't take it along on a journey. Isn't there a nice hotbed here in the garden, where persons of rank, like me, can find a place to live and make himself at home?"

But the frogs either didn't or wouldn't understand him.

"I never ask a question twice," said the Beetle, after he had already asked three times without getting any answer.

He went on a little farther and bumped against a piece of broken pottery. It certainly shouldn't have been lying there, but since it was it gave good shelter. Several families of Earwigs lived here, and they didn't need very much room; but they liked company. The females were full of the most devoted mother love, and so each one considered her own child the most beautiful and clever of all.

"Our son has become engaged!" said one mother. "The sweet, innocent baby! His greatest ambition is to creep someday into a clergyman's ear! He's such a lovely boy. And being engaged will keep him out of mischief. What joy for a mother!"

"Our son," said another mother, "had hardly crept from the egg before he got into mischief. He's so full of life and spirits he'll run his horns off! What joy that is for a mother! Isn't that true, Mr. Beetle?" for she had recognized the stranger by his shape.

"You're both quite right," said the Beetle; so they invited him to walk in—that is, to come as far as he could under the broken flowerpot.

"Now you ought to see *my* little earwig!" observed a third mother, and a fourth. "They're such lovely children, and so amusing! They never behave badly, except when they have a stomachache, but that happens pretty often at their age."

Then each mother spoke of her own youngster, and the youngsters joined in the conversation, and used the little forks in their tails to pull the Beetle's mustache.

"The little scamps, they're always up to something!" said the mothers, beaming with maternal love. But the Beetle was bored by all this, and so he asked how far it was to the nearest hotbed.

"Oh, that's way out in the world, on the other side of the ditch," said an Earwig. "I hope none of my children ever goes that far—it would be the death of me."

"Just the same *I'll* try to go that far," said the Beetle, and then he went off without taking any formal leave, for that's considered the politest thing to do. And by the ditch he met several of his kind—all Beetles.

"We live here," they said. "And we're very cozy here, too. May we invite you to step down into this rich soil? The journey must have tired you out."

"Indeed it has," said the Beetle. "I've been lying on linen out in the rain, and cleanliness tires me very much. I also have rheumatism in my wing joints, from standing in a draft under a broken flowerpot. It's really very relaxing to be among one's own kind again."

"Perhaps you come from the hotbed?" asked the oldest of them.

"Oh, I come from a much higher place," said the Beetle. "I come from the emperor's stable, where I was born with golden shoes on! I'm traveling on a secret mission. You mustn't ask me any questions, for I won't tell you anything."

And so the Beetle stepped down into the rich soil. There sat three young lady Beetles, and they tittered because they didn't know what to say.

"They are not engaged yet," said their mother, and then the young lady Beetles tittered again, this time from embarrassment.

"I have never seen greater beauties even in the emperor's stables!" said the traveling Beetle.

"Now don't you spoil my daughters," said the mother, "and please don't speak to them unless you have serious intentions. But of course your intentions are honorable, and so I give you my blessing!"

"Hurrah!" cried all the other Beetles at once, and so the Beetle was engaged. First the engagement, then the wedding; there was nothing to wait for.

The following day passed pleasantly, and the next was fair enough, but by the third day it was time to think of food for the wife and perhaps for children.

"I've let them put something over on me," he said, "and now the only thing to do is put something over on them in return."

And that he did. Away he went, away all day, and away all night, while his wife was left a widow.

The other Beetles said that they had taken nothing more than a complete tramp into the family and now his wife was left a burden on their hands.

"Well, then, she shall be unmarried again," said her mother, "and sit here among my unmarried daughters. Shame on that disgusting rascal who deserted her!"

Meanwhile the Beetle had been traveling on and had sailed across the ditch on a cabbage leaf. That morning two persons came by, and when they saw the Beetle they picked him up, turned him over and over, and both looked very learned—especially one of them, a boy.

"Allah sees the black beetle in the black stone and in the black mountain," he said. "Isn't that in the Koran?" Then he translated the Beetle's name into Latin and discoursed upon its nature and family history. The older scholar was opposed to carrying him home, saying they had just as good a specimen there. This, the Beetle thought, was a very rude thing to say; consequently he suddenly flew out of the speaker's hand. As his wings were dry now, he flew a considerable distance and reached a greenhouse, where he found a sash of the glass roof partly open, so, with the greatest of ease, he slipped in and buried himself in the manure.

"It's very comfortable here," he remarked.

Soon he feel asleep and dreamed that the emperor's horse had fallen down and that Mr. Beetle had been given its golden shoes, with the promise that he should have two more.

It was all very charming. And when the Beetle woke up he crept out and looked around him. What splendor there was in the greenhouse! Great palm trees were growing high, and the sun made them look transparent. And beneath them what a riot of green, and blooming flowers, red as fire, yellow as amber, or white as freshly fallen snow!

"What magnificent plants! How delicious they'll taste when they're nice and decayed!" said the Beetle. "This is a splendid larder! I am sure some of my relatives live here; I'll just see if I can find anyone fit to associate with. I'm proud, and I'm proud of being that way."

So he thought of the dream he had had about the dying horse and the golden shoes he had won. But suddenly a hand seized the Beetle and squeezed him and turned him over and over.

The gardener's little son and his playmate had come to the greenhouse and, seeing the Beetle, had decided to have some fun with him. First he was wrapped in a vine leaf and then shoved down into a warm trousers pocket. He squirmed and wriggled, but he got a good squeezing from the boy's hand. The boy went rapidly toward the great lake at the bottom of the garden. Here they put the Beetle in an old broken wooden shoe, with the top part missing. A little stick was placed upright for a mast, and to this the Beetle was bound with a woolen thread. Now he was a skipper and had to sail away.

The lake was very large, and to the Beetle it seemed a vast ocean; he was so amazed at its size that he fell over on his back and kicked out with all his legs.

The wooden shoe sailed away. The current bore it along, but whenever it went too far from shore one of the boys would roll up his trousers, go in after it, and bring it back. However, just as it sailed merrily out to sea again, the boys were called away, and quite sharply, too, so that they ran away from the lake, leaving the wooden shoe to its fate. It drifted away from the shore, farther and farther out; it was a terrible situation for the Beetle; he couldn't fly, for he was bound tightly to the mast.

Then a Fly paid him a visit.

"What beautiful weather we're having!" said the Fly. "I'll rest here; I can take a sun bath here. You're certainly having a nice time of it!"

"You don't know what you're talking about," replied the Beetle. "Can't you see I'm tied up?"

"I'm not a prisoner," said the Fly, and promptly flew away.

"Well, now I guess I know the world," the Beetle said. "And it's a mean place. I'm the only honest person in it. First, they won't give me my golden shoes, then I have to lie on wet linen and stand in a draft, and as a climax they hitch a wife to me. Then, when I made a quick move out into the world, and found out how people live, and how I ought to live, one of these human puppies comes and ties me up and leaves me to the mercy of the wild ocean, while the emperor's horse prances about proudly in golden shoes. That's what annoys me more than anything else! But you mustn't expect sympathy in this world! My career has been very interesting, but what's the good of that, if nobody knows about it? The world doesn't deserve to know about it, for it should have given me golden shoes when the emperor's horse was shod and I stretched out my feet to be shod, too. If they'd given me golden shoes I'd have been an honor to the stable. Now the stable has lost me, and the world has lost me! It's all over!"

But it wasn't all over yet. Some young girls came rowing up in a boat.

"There's an old wooden shoe sailing along over there!" said one of them.

"And there's a little animal tied fast in it!" said another.

Their boat came quite close to the wooden shoe, and they fished him out of the water. One of the girls took out a tiny pair of scissors and cut the woolen thread without hurting the Beetle; and when she stepped on shore she placed him down on the grass.

"Crawl, crawl, fly, fly away if you can!" she said. "Freedom is a precious thing!"

And the Beetle flew straight through the open window of a large building, and there he sank down, tired and exhausted, in the long, fine, soft mane of the emperor's favorite horse, which was standing in the stable where he and the Beetle lived. He clung fast to the mane and sat there a little while until he had collected himself.

"Here I am sitting on the emperor's favorite horse! Yes, sitting on him as his rider! But what am I saying? Oh, yes, now it's clear to me; yes, it's a good idea and quite right. Why did the horse get golden shoes, the blacksmith asked me. Now I know the answer. They were given to the horse on *my* account!"

That put the Beetle in good spirits again.

"Traveling broadens the mind," he said.

The sun's rays streamed in on him and shone very brightly.

"On the whole, the world isn't so bad, after all!" said the Beetle. "But you must know how to take it!"

The world was wonderful, because the emperor's favorite horse had golden shoes and because the Beetle was its rider.

"Now I am going down to the other beetles and tell them about all the pleasures I have enjoyed on my trip abroad, and I am going to say that now I'm going to stay at home until the horse has worn out his golden shoes."

WHAT THE OLD MAN DOES IS ALWAYS RIGHT (1861)

Now I'm going to tell you a story that I heard when I was a little fellow and that I like better and better the more I think of it. For it's the same with stories as with many people; the older they grow, the nicer they grow, and that is delightful.

You have been out in the country, of course. There you must have seen a really old farmhouse with a thatched roof, where moss and weeds have planted themselves; a stork's nest decorates the chimney (you can never do without the stork); the walls are slanting; the windows are low (in fact, only one of them was made to open); the baking oven sticks out like a fat little stomach; and an elder bush leans over the gate, where you can see a tiny pond with a duck or ducklings under a gnarled willow tree. Yes, and then, of course, there's a watchdog which barks at everybody and everything.

Well, there was a farmhouse just like that out in the country, and in it there lived two people, a farmer and his wife. They had few enough possessions, but still there was one they could do without, and that was a horse, which grazed along the ditch beside the highway. The old farmer used it to ride to town and lent it to his neighbors, receiving some slight services from them in return, but still it would be much more profitable to sell the horse, or at least exchange it for something that would be more useful to them.

But which should they do, sell or trade?

"You'll know what's best, Father," said the wife. "It's market day. Come on, ride off to town, and get money for the horse, or make a good bargain with it. Whatever you do is always right; so be off for the market!"

So she tied on his neckerchief—for that was something she understood much better than he—tied it with a double bow, and made him look quite dashing. She brushed his hat with the palm of her hand, and she kissed him on the mouth, and then off he went, riding the horse that was to be either sold or bartered. Of course, he would know the right thing to do.

The sun was scorching, and there was not a cloud in the sky. The road was dusty and crowded with people on their way to market, some in wagons, some on horseback, and some on their own two legs. Yes, it was a fierce sun, with no shade all the way.

Now a man came along, driving a cow, as pretty a cow as you could wish to see. "I'm sure she must give grand milk," thought the peasant. "It would be a pretty good bargain if I got her. Hey, you with the cow!" he said. "Let's have a little talk. Look here, I believe a horse costs more than a cow, but it doesn't matter to me, since I have more use for a cow. Shall we make a swap?"

"Fair enough," said the man with the cow; and so they swapped.

Now the farmer might just as well have turned home again, for he had finished his business. But he had planned to go to market, so to market he would go, if only to look on; hence, with his cow, he continued on his way. He walked fast, and so did the cow, and pretty soon they overtook a man who was leading a sheep; it was a fine-looking sheep, in good condition and well clothed with wool.

"I certainly would like to have that," thought the peasant. "It would find plenty of grazing beside our ditch, and in the winter we could keep it in our own room. It would really be much more sensible for us to be keeping a sheep rather than a cow. Shall we trade?"

Yes, the sheep's owner was quite willing, so the exchange was made, and now the farmer went on along the highway with his sheep. Near a road gate he met a man with a big goose under his arm.

"Well, you've got a fine heavy fellow there!" said the farmer. "It's got plenty of feathers and fat! How nice it would be to have it tied up near our little pond, and, besides, it would be something for Mother to save the scraps for. She has often said, 'If we only had a goose.' Now she can have one—and she shall, too! Will you swap? I'll give you my sheep for your goose, and my thanks, too."

The other had no objection, so they swapped, and the farmer got the goose. By now he was close to the town; the road was getting more and more crowded, people and cattle pushing past him, thronging in the road, in the ditch, and right up to the toll keeper's potato patch, where his one hen was tied up, in case it should lose its head in a panic and get lost. It was a bobtailed hen that winked with one eye and looked in good condition.

"Cluck, cluck," it said; what it meant by that, I wouldn't know; but what the peasant thought when he saw it was this, "She's the prettiest hen I've ever seen—much prettier than any of our parson's brood hens. I would certainly like to have her. A hen can always find a grain of corn, and she can almost provide for herself. I almost think it would be a good idea to take her instead of the goose. Shall we trade?" he asked.

"Trade?" said the other. "Well, not a bad idea!" And so they traded. The toll keeper got the goose, and the farmer got the hen.

He had completed a good deal of business since he started for town; it was hot, and he was tired. What he needed was a drink and a bite to eat.

He had reached an inn and was ready to enter, when the innkeeper's helper met him in the doorway, carrying a sackful of something.

"What have you got there?" asked the farmer.

"Rotten apples," was the answer. "A whole sackful for the pigs."

"What a lot! Wouldn't Mother like to see so many! Why, last year we had only one single apple on the old tree by the peat shed. That apple was to be kept, and it stood on the chest of drawers till it burst. 'That is always a sign of prosperity,' Mother said. Here she could see plenty of prosperity! Yes, I only wish she could have it!"

"Well, what'll you give me for them?" asked the innkeeper's helper.

"Give for them? Why, I'll give you my hen!" So he turned over the hen, took the apples, and went into the inn, straight up to the bar; he set his sack upright against the stove, without noticing that there was a fire in it. There were a number of strangers present, horse dealers, cattle dealers, and two Englishmen so rich that their pockets were bursting with gold coins. They were fond of making bets, as Englishmen in stories always are.

"Suss! Suss! Suss!" What was that noise at the stove? It was the apples beginning to roast!

"What's that?" everybody said, and they soon found out. They were hearing the whole story of the horse that had been traded first for a cow and finally for a sack of rotten apples.

"Well, you'll get a good beating from your old woman when you go home!" said the Englishmen. "You're in for a rough time."

"I'll get kisses, not cuffs," said the farmer. "Mother will say, 'Whatever the old man does is right.'"

"Shall we bet on it?" said the Englishmen. "We have gold by the barrel! A hundred pounds sterling to a hundred-pound weight?"

"Let's say a bushelful," replied the peasant. "I can only bet my bushel of apples, and throw in myself and the old woman, but I think that'll be more than full measure."

"That's a bet!" the Englishmen cried, and the bet was made! So the innkeeper's cart was brought out, the Englishmen got into it, the farmer got into it, the rotten apples got into it, and away they went to the old man's cottage.

"Good evening, Mother."

"Same to you, Father."

"Well, I've made the bargain."

"Yes, you know how to do business," said the wife, and gave him a big hug, forgetting both the sack and the strangers.

"I traded the horse for a cow."

"Thank God for the milk!" said the wife. "Now we can have milk, butter, and cheese on our table! What a splendid swap!"

"Yes, but I swapped the cow for a sheep."

"That's still better!" cried the wife. "You're always so thoughtful. We have plenty of grass for a sheep. But now we'll have sheep's milk, and sheep's cheese, and woolen stockings, yes, and a woolen nightgown, too. A cow couldn't give us that; she loses all her hairs. But you're always such a thoughtful husband."

"But then I exchanged the sheep for a goose."

"What! Will we really have goose for Michaelmas this year, dear Father? You always think of what would please me, and that was a beautiful thought! We can tie up the goose, and it'll grow even fatter for Michaelmas Day."

"But I traded the goose for a hen," continued the peasant.

"A hen? Well, that was a fine trade!" replied his wife. "A hen will lay eggs and sit on them and we'll have chickens. Imagine, a chicken yard! Just the thing I've always wanted most!"

"Yes, but I exchanged the hen for a sack of rotten apples."

"Then I must certainly give you a kiss!" said the wife. "Thank you, my own husband. And now I have something to tell you. When you had gone I decided I'd get a fine dinner ready for you—omelet with chives. Now I had the eggs all right, but no chives. So I went over to the schoolmaster's, because I know they have chives; but that sweet woman is so stingy she wanted something in return. What could I give her? Nothing grows in our garden, not even a rotten apple; I didn't even have that for her. But now I can give her ten or even a whole sackful! Isn't it funny, Father!" she said, and kissed him right on his mouth.

"I like that!" cried both the Englishmen. "Always downhill, but always happy. That alone is worth the money!" So they were quite content to pay the bushelful of gold pieces to the peasant, who had got kisses instead of cuffs for his bargains.

Yes, it always pays when the wife believes and admits that her husband is the wisest man in the world and that whatever he does is right.

Well, this is the story. I heard it when I was a youngster, and now you've heard it, too, so you know that what the old man does is always right.

THE SNOW MAN (1861)

I t's so bitterly cold that my whole body crackles!" said the Snow Man. "This wind can really blow life into you! And how that glaring thing up there glares at me!" He meant the sun; it was just setting. "She won't make *me* blink; I'll hold onto the pieces."

"The pieces" were two large triangular pieces of tile, which he had for eyes. His mouth was part of an old rake, hence he had teeth. He had been born amid the triumphant shouts of the boys and welcomed by the jingling of sleigh bells and the cracking of whips from the passing sleighs.

The sun went down, and the full moon rose, big and round, bright and beautiful, in the clear blue sky.

"Here she comes again from the other side," said the Snow Man, for he thought it was the sun showing itself again. "Ah, I've cured her of staring, all right. Now let her hang up there and shine so that I can see myself. If I only knew how to move from this place—I'd like so much to move! If I could, I'd slide along there on the ice, the way I see the boys slide, but I don't know how to run."

"Away! Away!" barked the old Watchdog. He was quite hoarse from the time when he was a house dog lying under the stove. "The sun will teach you how to run. I saw your predecessor last winter, and before that *his* predecessor. Away! Away! And away they all go!"

"I don't understand you, friend," said the Snow Man. "Is that thing up there going to teach me to run?" He meant the Moon. "Why, she was running the last time I saw her a little while ago, and now she comes sneaking back from the other side."

"You don't know anything at all," replied the Watchdog. "But then, of course, you've just been put together. The one you are looking at now is called the Moon, and the one who went away was the Sun. She will come again tomorrow, and she will teach you to run down into the ditch. We're going to have a change of weather soon; I can feel it in my left hind leg; I have a pain in it. The weather's going to change."

"I don't understand him," said the Snow Man to himself, "but I have a feeling he's talking about something unpleasant. The one that stared at me and went away, whom he called the Sun, is no friend of mine either, I can feel that."

"Away! Away!" barked the Watchdog, and then he walked around three times and crept into his kennel to sleep.

The weather really did change. Early next morning a thick, damp mist lay over the whole countryside. At dawn a wind rose; it was icy cold. The frost set in hard, but when the sun rose, what a beautiful sight it was! The trees and bushes were covered with hoarfrost and looked like a forest of white coral, while every twig seemed smothered with glittering white flowers. The enormously many delicate branches that are concealed by the leaves in summer now appeared, every single one of them, and made a gleaming white lacework, so snowy white that a white radiance seemed to spring from every bough. The birch waved in the wind as if it had life, like the rest of the trees in the summer. It was all wonderfully beautiful. And when the sun came out, how it all glittered and sparkled, as if everything had been strewn with diamond dust, and big diamonds had been sprinkled on the snowy carpet of the earth; or one could also imagine that countless little lights were gleaming, brighter even than the snow itself.

"It's wonderfully beautiful!" said a young girl, who had come out into the garden with a young man. They stopped near the Snow Man and gazed at the flashing trees. "Summer can't show us a lovelier sight!" she said, and her eyes sparkled with delight.

"And we can't have a fellow like this in the summertime, either," the young man agreed, as he pointed to the Snow Man. "He's splendid."

The young girl laughed, nodded to the Snow Man, and then danced over the snow with her friend—over snow that crackled under their feet as though they were walking on starch.

"Who were those two?" asked the Snow Man of the Watchdog. "You've been around this yard longer than I have. Do you know them?"

"Of course I know them," said the Watchdog. "She pets me, and he once threw me a meat bone. I don't bite those two."

"But what are they supposed to be?" asked the Snow Man. "Sweethearts!" replied the Watchdog. "They'll go to move into the same kennel someday and gnaw the same bone together. Away! Away!"

"But are they as important as you and I?" asked the Snow Man.

"Why, they are members of the master's family," said the Watchdog. "People certainly don't know very much if they were only born yesterday; I can tell that from you. Now I have age and knowledge. I know everybody here in the house, and I know a time when I didn't have to stand out here in the cold, fastened to a chain. Away! Away!"

"The cold is lovely," said the Snow Man. "But tell me, tell me. Only don't rattle that chain; it makes me shiver inside when you do that."

"Away! Away!" barked the Watchdog. "They used to tell me I was a pretty little puppy, when I lay in a velvet-covered chair up in the master's house, or sat in the mistress' lap. They used to kiss me on the nose and wipe my paws with an embroidered handkerchief.

"They called me 'the handsomest' and 'little puppsy-wuppsy.' But then I grew too big for them to keep, so they gave me away to the housekeeper. That's how I came to live down in the basement. You can look down into it from where you're standing; you can look right into the room where I was master, for that was what I was to the housekeeper. Of course, the place was inferior to that upstairs, but I was more comfortable there and wasn't constantly grabbed and pulled about by the children as I had been upstairs. I had just as good food as ever, and much more of it. I had my own cushion, and then there was a stove, which is the finest thing in the world at this time of year. I crept right in under it, so that I was out of the way. Ah, I still dream of that stove sometimes. Away! Away!"

"Does a stove look so beautiful?" asked the Snow Man. "Does it look like me?"

"It's just the opposite of you. It's as black as coal and has a long neck and a brass stomach. It eats firewood, so that fire spurts from its mouth. You must keep beside it or underneath it; it's very comfortable there. You must be able to see it through the window from where you're standing."

Then the Snow Man looked, and he really saw a brightly polished thing with a brass stomach and fire glowing from the lower part of it. A very strange feeling swept over the Snow Man; he didn't know what it meant, and couldn't understand it, but all people who aren't snowmen know that feeling.

"Why did you leave her?" asked the Snow Man, for it seemed to him that the stove must be a female. "How could you leave a place like that?"

"I was compelled to," replied the Watchdog. "They turned me outside and chained me up here. You see, I had bitten the youngest of the master's children in the leg, because he had kicked away a bone I was gnawing. 'A bone for a bone,' I always say. They didn't like that at all, and from that time I've been chained out here and have lost my voice. Don't you hear how hoarse I am? Away! Away! And that was the end of that!"

But the Snow Man wasn't listening to him any longer. He kept peering in at the housekeeper's basement room, where the stove stood on its four iron legs, just about the same size as the Snow Man himself.

"What a strange crackling there is inside me!" he cried. "I wonder if I'll ever get in there. That's an innocent wish, and our innocent wishes are sure to be fulfilled. It is my only wish, my biggest wish; it would almost be unfair if it wasn't granted. I must get in and lean against her, even if I have to break a window."

"You'll never get in there," said the Watchdog. "And if you go near that stove you'll melt away! Away!"

"I'm as good as gone, anyway," replied the Snow Man. "I think I'm breaking up."

All day long the Snow Man stood looking in through the window. At twilight the room grew still more inviting; a mild glow came from the stove, not like the Moon or the Sun either, but just like the glow of a stove when it has been well filled. Every time the room door was opened, the flames leaped out of the stove's mouth; this was a habit it had. The flame fell distinctly on the white face of the Snow Man and glowed ruddy on his breast.

"I can't stand it any longer!" he cried. "How beautiful she looks when she sticks out her tongue!"

The night was very long, but it didn't seem long to the Snow Man; he stood lost in his own pleasant thoughts, and they froze until they crackled.

In the morning the windowpanes of the basement room were covered with ice. They showed the most beautiful ice flowers that any Snow Man could desire, but they hid the stove. The windowpanes wouldn't thaw, so he couldn't see the stove. It creaked, and it crackled.

It was just the sort of weather a Snow Man should most thoroughly enjoy. But he didn't enjoy it; indeed, how could he enjoy anything when he was so stove-sick?

"That's a terrible sickness for a Snow Man," said the Watchdog. "I've also suffered from it myself, but I got over it. Away! Away! There's going to be a change in the weather."

And there was a change in the weather; it began to thaw! The thaw increased, and the Snow Man decreased. He never complained, and that's an infallible sign.

One morning he collapsed. And behold! Where he had stood there was something like a broomstick sticking up from the ground.

It was the pole the boys had built him up around.

"Now I can understand why he had such an intense longing for the stove," said the Watchdog. "The Snow Man has had a stove rake in his body; that's what moved inside him. Now he has gotten over that, too. Away! Away!"

And soon the winter was over, too.

"Away! Away!" barked the Watchdog. But the little girls in the house sang:

> Oh, woodruff, spring up, fresh and proud, round about!
> And, willow tree, hang your woolen mitts out!
> Come, cuckoo and lark, come and sing!
> At February's close we already have spring.
> Tweet-tweet, cuckoo! I am singing with you.
> Come out, dear sun! Come often, skies of blue!

And nobody thought any more about the Snow Man.

IN THE DUCK YARD (1861)

A duck arrived from Portugal. Some people said she came from Spain, but that doesn't really matter. She was called the Portuguese; she laid eggs and was killed and dressed and cooked; that's the story of her life. But all the ducklings that were hatched from her eggs were also called Portuguese, and there's some distinction in that. At last there was only one left of her whole family in the duck yard—a yard to which the hens also had access, and where the cock strutted about with endless arrogance.

"His loud crowing annoys me," said the Portuguese Duck. "But there's no denying he's a handsome bird, even if he isn't a drake. Of course, he should moderate his voice, but that's an art that comes from higher education, such as the little songbirds over in our neighbors lime trees have. How sweetly they sing; there's something so touching over their melodies; I call it Portugal. If I only had a little songbird like that I'd be a kind and good mother to him, for that's in my blood—my Portuguese blood!"

While she was speaking, suddenly a little songbird fell head over heels from the roof into the yard. The cat had been chasing him, but the bird escaped with a broken wing and fell down into the duck yard.

"That's just like the cat, that monster!" said the Portuguese Duck. "I remember his tricks from when I had ducklings of my own. That such a creature should be permitted to live and roam about on the roofs! I'm sure such things could not happen in Portugal!"

She pitied the little Songbird, and even the other ducks who weren't Portuguese felt pity for him, too.

"Poor little fellow," they said, and then one after another came up to look at him. "Of course, we can't sing," they said, "but we have an inner understanding of song, or something like that. We can feel it, even if we don't talk about it."

"Then I will talk about it," said the Portuguese. "And I'll do something for this little fellow; it's only my duty." And then she stepped into the water trough and thrashed her wings about the water so vigorously that the little Songbird was almost drowned by the shower he got, but he knew the Duck meant well. "There, that's a good deed," she said. "The others may observe it and profit by my example."

"Peep!" said the little Bird; one of his wings was broken, and he was finding it difficult to shake himself, but he quite understood that the bath was meant kindly. "You're very kindhearted, madam," he said, hoping she wouldn't give him another shower.

"I never thought much about my heart," said the Portuguese. "But I know this much—I love all my fellow creatures except the cat; nobody could expect me to love him, for he ate up two of my ducklings. Now make yourself at home, for you can be quite comfortable here. I myself am a foreigner, as you can tell from my bearing and my feather dress. My drake is a native of this country; he doesn't have my blood, but still I'm not proud. If anyone in this yard can understand you, I may safely say it is I."

"Her beak is full of portulaca," said a common little Duck, who was considered very witty. All the other common ducks decided the word *portulaca* was very funny, for it sounded like *Portugal*. They poked each other and said, "Quack!" He was really so witty! And now all the other ducks began to pay attention to the little Songbird.

"The Portuguese certainly has a great command of language," they said. "For our part, we haven't room in our beaks for such big words, but we have just as much sympathy, anyway. Even if we don't actually do anything for you, at least we will go about quietly with you; and that we think is the nicest thing we can do."

"You have a lovely voice," said one of the older Ducks. "It must be a great satisfaction to you to give so many as much pleasure as you do. I don't really understand singing, so I keep my beak shut; that's better than chattering nonsense to you the way the others do."

"Don't bother him," said the Portuguese. "He needs rest and care. My little Songbird, do you want me to give you another shower bath?"

"Oh, no, please let me stay dry!" he begged.

"The water cure is the only that does me any good when I'm sick," said the Portuguese. "But amusement helps, too. The neighboring hens will soon be coming to visit us; there are two Chinese hens among them. They wear breeches, are well educated, and have been imported, so they stand higher than the others in my esteem."

And the hens came, and the Cock came with them; today he was polite enough not to be rude.

"You're a true songbird," he said, "and you do all you possibly can with such a small voice as yours. But you should have a little steam power, so everyone would hear that you are a male."

The two Chinese were enraptured at the appearance of the Songbird. He was still very much rumpled up after his bath, so he looked to them like a little China chicken.

"He's charming!" they cried, and then engaged themselves in conversation with him; they talked in whispers and with a *p*-sound, in elegant Chinese. "We belong to your race.

"The Ducks, even the Portuguese one, are swimming birds, as you must have noticed. You don't know us yet; not very many people take the trouble to know us—not even any of the hens, though we were born to occupy a higher perch than most of the others. But that doesn't bother us; we go our way quietly among the others, whose ideals are quite different from ours. We look only at the bright side of things and mention only what's good, though it's sometimes difficult to find something like that when there isn't anything. Besides us two and the Cock, there is no one in the whole hen yard who is talented. And honesty does not exist among the inhabitants of this duck yard.

"We warn you, little Songbird, don't trust that one over there with the short feathers in her tail—she's tricky. The spotted one there, with the crooked stripes on her wings, is always looking for an argument and won't let anybody have the last word, though she's always in the wrong. The fat Duck over there never has a good thing to say about anybody, and that is contrary to our nature; if we haven't something good to say, we keep our beaks shut. The Portuguese is the only one who has a little education and whom one can associate with, but she's hot-tempered and talks too much about Portugal."

"How those two Chinese are always whispering!" said one of the Ducks. "They annoy me; I have never spoken to them."

Now the Drake came up; and he thought the little Songbird was a sparrow.

"Well, I don't see any difference," he said. "It's all the same, anyway. He's just a plaything, and if you have one, why, you have one."

"Don't pay any attention to what he says," the Portuguese whispered. "He is a very respectable businessman, and with him business always comes first. But now I'm going to lie down for a rest. You owe that to yourself, so you'll be nice and fat when the time comes to be embalmed with apples and plums."

And then she lay down in the sun and blinked one eye; she lay so comfortably and felt so well, and so she slept very comfortably.

The little Songbird busied himself with his broken wing, but finally he too lay down, pressed close beside his patroness; the sun was bright and warm; it was a good place to be.

The neighbor's hens scurried about, scratching up the earth, for, to tell the truth, they had come visiting solely for the sake of getting something to eat. The Chinese were the first to leave the duck yard, and the other hens soon followed them.

The witty little Duck was talking about the Portuguese and said the old lady was on the brink of "Duckdom's dotage." At this the other Ducks chuckled. "Duckdom's dotage!" they cackled. "That's unusually witty!" Then they repeated the other joke about portulaca—that was very amusing to them—and then they lay down.

They had been sleeping for some time when suddenly some food was thrown in for them. It landed with such a thump that the whole flock started up from sleep and flapped their wings. The Portuguese woke up, too, and rolled over on the other side, squeezing the little Songbird very hard as she did so.

"Peep!" he said. "You stepped so hard on me, madam."

"Well, why do you lie in the way?" she said. "You mustn't be so touchy. I have nerves, too, but I have never yet said, 'Peep!'"

"Please don't be angry," said the little Bird. "The 'Peep' slipped off my beak before I knew it."

The Portuguese didn't listen to him, but began gobbling as fast as she could, until she had made a good meal. When she had finished, she lay down again, and the little Bird came up and tried to please her by singing:

> *Tillee-lilly-lee,*
> *Of your heart with glee*
> *I shall sing with love*
> *When I fly above!*

"I need to rest after my meal," said the Portuguese. "While you're here you must follow the house rules. I want to take a nap now."

The little Songbird was quite bewildered, for he had only tried to please her. When she awoke later he stood before her with a grain of corn he had found and laid it in front of her; but as she hadn't slept well she was in a very bad humor.

"You can give that to a chicken!" she said. "And don't stand and hang over me!"

"Why are you angry with me?" he asked. "What have I done?"

"Done?" said the Portuguese. "Your manner of expression isn't very refined; I must call your attention to that."

"Yesterday it was all sunshine here," said the little Bird. "But today it's dark and cloudy. It makes me very sad."

"You don't know much about weather, I guess," said the Portuguese. "The day isn't over yet. Don't just stand there looking stupid."

"But you're looking at me just as those two wicked eyes did when I fell into the yard!"

"Impudent!" said the Portuguese. "Comparing me with the cat—a beast of prey! There's not a drop of wicked blood in me! I've stood up for you, and I'll have to teach you good manners." And with that she bit off the Songbird's head, and he lay there dead.

"Now what does this mean?" she said. "Couldn't he even stand that? Then he certainly wasn't intended for this world. I know I've been like a mother to him, because I have such a good heart."

And then the neighbor's Cock stuck his head into the yard and crowed like a steam engine.

"Your crowing will kill me!" she cried. "It's all your fault! He's lost his head, and I've nearly lost mine."

"There isn't much left of him," said the Cock.

"You speak of him with respect," said the Portuguese, "because he had a voice and a fine education. He was tender and soft, and that's as good in animals as in so-called human beings."

And all the Ducks gathered around the little dead Songbird. Ducks have strong passions, whether they feel envy or pity, and since there was no one here to envy, they all felt pity, and so did even the two Chinese hens.

"We'll never find such a songbird again; he was almost a Chinese," and they both wept with a great clucking noise. All the other chickens clucked, too, but the Ducks walked around with the reddest eyes.

"We have hearts," they said. "Nobody can deny that."

"Hearts!" said the Portuguese. "Yes, that we have; they're almost as tender as in Portugal."

"Let us now think about getting something in our stomachs," said the Drake. "That's the most important thing. If one of our playthings is broken, why, we have plenty more of them!"

THE ICE MAIDEN (1861)

Let us visit Switzerland. Let us take a look at that magnificent land of mountains, where the forests creep up the sides of the steep rocky walls; let us climb to the dazzling snowfields above, and descend again to the green valleys below, where the rivers and streams rush along as if afraid they will be too late to reach the ocean and disappear. The burning rays of the sun shine in the deep dales and also on the heavy masses of snow above, so that the ice blocks which have been piling for years melt and turn to thundering avalanches or heaped-up glaciers.

Two such glaciers lie in the broad ravines under the Schreckhorn and the Wetterhorn, near the little mountain town of Grindelwald. They are strange to look at, and for that reason, in summertime many travelers come here from all parts of the world. They cross the lofty, snow-capped hills, and they come through the deep valleys; then they have to climb for several hours, and as they ascend, the valleys seem to become deeper and deeper, until they look as if they are being viewed from a balloon. Often the clouds hang around the towering peaks like thick curtains of smoke, while down in the valley dotted with brown wooden houses, a ray of the sun may be shining brightly, throwing into sharp relief a brilliant patch of green, until it seems transparent. The water foams and roars and rushes along below, but up above the water murmurs and tinkles; it looks as if silver ribbons were streaming down over the rocks.

On both sides of the ascending road are wooden houses. Each house has its little potato garden, and this is a real necessity; for within those doors are many hungry mouths—there are many children, and children are often wasteful with food. From all the cottages they swarm out and besiege travelers, whether these be on foot or in carriages. All the children are little merchants; they offer for sale charming toy wooden houses, replicas of those that are built here in the mountains.

Some twenty years ago there often stood here, but always somewhat apart from the other children, a little boy who was also eager to do some business. He would stand there with an earnest, grave expression, holding his chip-box tightly with both hands, as if afraid of losing it; but it was this seriousness and the fact that he was so small that caused him to be noticed and called forward, so that he often sold more than all the others—he didn't exactly know why himself.

His grandfather lived high up on the mountain, where he carved out the neat, pretty little houses. In a room up there he had an old chest full of all sorts of carved things—nutcrackers, knives, forks, boxes with cleverly carved scrollwork, and leaping chamois—everything that would please a child's eye. But little Rudy, as he was called, gazed with greater interest and longing at the old gun that hung under the beams of the roof. "He shall have it someday," his grandfather had said, "but not until he's big and strong enough to use it."

Small as the boy was, he took care of the goats. If knowing how to climb along with the goats meant that he was a good goatherd, then Rudy certainly was an excellent goatherd; he could even go higher than the goats, for he loved to search for birds' nests high up in the tops of the trees. He was bold and daring. No one ever saw him smile, except when he stood near the roaring waterfall or heard the rolling of an avalanche.

He never played with the other children; in fact, he never went near them except when his grandfather sent him down to sell the things he had carved. And Rudy didn't care much for that; he would much rather climb about in the mountains or sit home with his grandfather and hear him tell stories of ancient times and of the people at nearby Meiringen, where he was born. This race, he said, had not always lived there; they were wanderers from other lands; they had come from the far north, where their people still lived, and were called "Swedes." This was a good deal for Rudy to learn, but he learned still more from other teachers—the animals that lived in the house. There was a big dog, Ajola, which had belonged to Rudy's father, and there was a tomcat. Rudy had much to thank the tomcat for—the Cat had taught him to climb.

"Come on out on the roof with me!" the Cat had said one day, very distinctly and intelligibly, too. For to a little child who can hardly speak, the language of hens and ducks, cats and dogs, is almost as easily understood as that of fathers and mothers.

But you must be very young indeed then; those are the days when Grandpa's stick neighs and turns into a horse, with head, legs, and tail.

Some children keep these thoughts longer than others, and people say that these are exceedingly backward and remain children too long. But people say so much!

"Come on out on the roof with me, little Rudy!" was one of the first things the Cat said, and Rudy could understand him.

"It's all imagination to think you'll fall; you won't fall unless you're afraid! Come on! Put one of your paws here, and another there, and then feel your way with your forepaws. Use your eyes and be very active in your limbs. If there's a hole, jump over it the way I do."

And that's what little Rudy did. Very often he sat on the sloping roof of the house with the Cat, and often in the tops of the trees, and even high up among the towering rocks, where the Cat never went.

"Higher! Higher!" the trees and bushes said. "Can't you see how we climb—how high we go, and how tightly we hold on, even on the narrowest ledge of rock?"

And often Rudy reached the top of the hill even before the sun; there he took his morning draught of fresh, strengthening mountain air, that drink which only our Lord can prepare, and which human beings call the early fragrance from the mountain herbs and the wild thyme and mint in the valley. Everything that is heavy in the air is absorbed by the overhanging clouds and carried by the winds over the pine woods, while the essence of fragrance becomes light and fresh air—and this was Rudy's morning draught.

Sunbeams, daughters of the sun who bring his blessings with them, kissed his cheeks. Dizziness stood nearby watching, but dared not approach him. The swallows from his grandfather's house below (there were at least seven nests) flew up toward him and the goats, singing, "We and you, and you and we!" They brought greetings from his home, even from the two hens, who were the only birds in the house; however, Rudy had never been very intimate with them.

Young as he was he had traveled, and quite a good deal for such a little fellow. He was born in Canton Valais and brought from there over the hills. He had recently traveled on foot to the nearby Staubbach, that seems to flutter like a silver veil before the snow-clad, glittering white Jungfrau. And he had been to the great glaciers near Grindelwald, but there was a sad story connected with that trip; his mother had met her death there, and it was there, as his grandfather used to say, that "little Rudy had lost all his childish happiness." When he was less than a year old he laughed more than he cried, as his mother had written; but from the time he fell into the crevasse his whole nature had changed. His grandfather didn't talk about this very much, but it was known all over the mountain.

Rudy's father had been a coach driver, and the big dog that now shared the boy's home had always gone with him on his journeys over the Simplon down to Lake Geneva. Rudy's relatives on his father's side lived in the Rhone valley, in Canton Valais, where his uncle was a celebrated chamois hunter and a famous Alpine guide. Rudy was only a year old when he lost his father and his mother decided to return with the child to her own family in the Berner Oberland. Her father lived a few hours' journey from Grindelwald; he was a woodcarver, and his trade enabled him to live comfortably.

With her infant in her arms she set out toward home in June, accompanied by two chamois hunters, over the Gemmi toward Grindelwald. They had made the greater part of the journey, had climbed the highest ridges to the snowfields and could already see her native valley with the familiar scattered cottages; they now had only to cross the upper part of one great glacier. The newly fallen snow concealed a crevasse, not deep enough to reach the abyss below where the water rushed along, but deeper than a man's height.

As she was carrying her child the young woman suddenly slipped, sank down, and instantly disappeared. Not a shriek or groan was heard, only the wailing of a little child. It was over an hour before her two companions could obtain ropes and poles from the nearest house to pull her out; and after tremendous labor they brought from the crevasse what they thought were two dead bodies. Every means of restoring life was tried, and at last they managed to save the child, but not the mother. Thus the old grandfather received in his house not a daughter, but a daughter's son, the little one who laughed more than he cried. But a change seemed to have come over him since his terrible experience in the glacier crevasse—that cold, strange ice world, where the Swiss peasant believes the souls of the damned are imprisoned till doomsday.

The glacier lies like a rushing stream, frozen and pressed into blocks of green crystal, one huge mass of ice balanced on another; the swelling stream of ice and snow tears along in the depths beneath, while within it yawn deep hollows, immense crevasses. It is a wondrous palace of crystal, and in its dwells the Ice Maiden, queen of the glaciers. She, the slayer, the crusher, is half the mighty ruler of the rivers, half a child of the air. Thus it is that she can soar to the loftiest haunts of the chamois, to the towering summits of the snow-covered hills, where the boldest mountaineer has to cut footrests for himself in the ice; she sails on a light pine twig over the foaming river below and leaps lightly from one rock to another, with her long, snow-white hair fluttering about her and her blue-green robe glistening like the water in the deep Swiss lakes.

"To crush! To hold fast! That is my power!" she says. "And yet a beautiful boy was snatched from me—one whom I had kissed, but not yet kissed to death! He is again among human beings—he tends his goats on the mountain peaks; he is always climbing higher and still higher, far, far from other humans, but never from me! He is mine! I will fetch him!"

So she commanded Dizziness to undertake the mission; it was in the summertime and too hot for the Ice Maiden in the valley where the green mint grew; so Dizziness mounted and dived. Now Dizziness has a flock of sisters—first one came, then three of them—and the Ice Maiden selected the strongest of those who wield their power indoors and out. They perch on the banisters of steep staircases and the guard rails of lofty towers; they run like squirrels along the mountain ridges and, leaping away from them, tread the air as a swimmer treads water, luring a victim onward to the abyss beneath.

Dizziness and the Ice Maiden both reach out for mankind, as the polypus reaches after whatever comes near it. The mission of Dizziness was to seize Rudy.

"Seize him, you say!" said Dizziness. "I can't do it. That wretched Cat has taught him its skill. That human child has a power within himself that keeps me away. I can't touch the little fellow when he hangs from branches out over the abyss, or I'd be glad to tickle his feet and send him flying down through the air. I can't do it!"

"We can seize him!" said the Ice Maiden. "Either you or I! I will! I will!"

"No! No!" A whisper, a song, broke upon the air like the echo of church bells pealing; it was the harmonious tones of a chorus of other spirits of Nature, the mild, soft, and loving daughters of the rays of the sun. Every evening they encircle the mountain peaks and spread their rosy wings, which, as the sun sinks, become redder and redder until the lofty Alps seem blazing. Mountaineers call this the Alpine glow. When the sun has set, they retire into the white snow on the peaks and sleep there until they appear again at sunrise. Greatly do they love flowers and butterflies and mankind, and they had taken a great fancy to little Rudy.

"You shall not catch him! You shall not have him!" they sang.

"I have caught greater and stronger ones than he!" said the Ice Maiden.

Then the daughters of the sun sang of the traveler whose cap was torn from his head by the whirlwind and carried away in stormy flight. The wind had power to take his cap, but not the man himself. "You can seize him, but you cannot hold him, you children of strength. The human race is stronger and more divine even than we are; they alone can mount higher than our mother the sun. They know the magic words that can compel the wind and waves to obey and serve them. Once the heavy, dragging weight of the body is loosened, it soars upward."

Thus sounded the glorious bell-like chorus.

And every morning the sun's rays shone on the sleeping child through the one tiny window of the old man's house. The daughters of the sun kissed the boy; they tried to thaw, to wipe out the ice kiss given him by the queen of the glaciers when, in his dead mother's arms, he lay in the deep ice crevasse from which he had only been rescued as if by a miracle.

THE JOURNEY TO THE NEW HOME

Now Rudy was eight years old. His uncle, who lived in the Rhone valley on the other side of the mountain, wanted to take the boy, so that he could have a better education and be taught to take care of himself. The grandfather thought this would be better for the boy, so agreed to part with him.

As the time for Rudy's departure drew near, there were many others besides Grandfather to take leave of. First there was Ajola, the old dog.

"Your father was the coachman, and I was the coachman's dog," said Ajola. "We often traveled back and forth, and I know both dogs and men on the other side of the mountains. I never had the habit of speaking very much, but now that we have so little time to talk to each other, I'll say a little more than I usually do and tell you a story that I've been thinking about for a long time. I can't understand it, and you can't either, but that doesn't matter. I have learned this: the good things of this world aren't dealt out equally either to dogs or to men; not everyone is born to lie in someone's lap or to drink milk. I've never been accustomed to such luxury. But I've often seen a puppy dog traveling inside a post carriage, taking up a human being's seat, while the lady to whom he belonged, or rather who belonged to him, carried a bottle of milk from which she fed him. She also offered him sweet candy, but he wouldn't bother to eat it; he just sniffed at it, so she ate it herself. I was running in the mud beside the carriage, about as hungry as a dog could be, but I had only my own bitter thoughts to chew on. Things weren't quite as they ought to be, but then there is much that is not! I hope you get to ride inside carriages, and ride softly, but you can't make all that happen by yourself. I never could either by barking or yawning."

That was Ajola's lecture, and Rudy threw his arms around the dog's neck and kissed his wet nose. Then he took the Cat in his arms, but he struggled to be free, and cried, "You're getting much too strong for me, but I won't use my claws against you. Climb away over the mountains—I've taught you how to climb. Never think about falling, but hold tightly; don't be afraid, and you'll be safe enough."

Then the Cat ran off, for he didn't want Rudy to see how sorry he was.

The hens were hopping about the floor. One of them had lost its tail, for a traveler, who thought himself a sportsman, had shot it off, mistaking the poor hen for a game bird.

"Rudy is going over the mountains," said one of the hens.

"He's in a hurry," said the other, "and I don't like farewells." So they both hopped away.

And the goats also said their farewells. "Maeh! Maeh!" they bleated; it sounded so sad.

Just at that time there happened to be two experienced guides about to cross the mountains; they planned to descend the other side of the Gemmi, and Rudy would go with them on foot. It was a hard trip for such a little fellow, but he had considerable strength, and was untiring and courageous.

The swallows accompanied him a little way, and sang to him, "We and you, and you and we."

The travelers' route led across the foaming Lütschine, which falls in many small rivulets from the dark clefts of the Grindelwald glaciers. Fallen tree trunks made bridges, and pieces of rock served here as steppingstones. Soon they had passed the alder thicket and began to climb the mountain near where the glaciers had loosened themselves from the cliff. They went around the glacier and over the blocks of ice.

Rudy crept and walked. His eyes sparkled with joy as he firmly placed his iron-tipped mountain shoes; it seemed as if he wished to leave behind him an impression of each footstep. The patches of black earth, tossed onto the glacier by the mountain torrents, gave it a burned look, but still the blue-green, glassy ice shone through. They had to circle the little pools that seemed dammed up by detached masses of ice. On this route they approached a huge stone which was balanced on the edge of an ice crevasse. Suddenly the rock lost its balance and toppled into the crevasse; the echo of its thunderous fall resounded faintly from the deep abyss of the glacier, far, far below.

Upward, always upward, they climbed; the glacier stretched up like a solid stream of masses of ice piled in wild confusion, wedged between bare and rugged rocks. For a moment Rudy remembered what had been told him, how he had lain in his mother's arms, buried in one of these terrible crevasses. But he soon threw off such gloomy thoughts, and considered the tale as only one of the many stories he had heard. Occasionally, when the guides thought the way was too difficult for a such a little boy, they held out their hands to help him; but he didn't tire, and he crossed the glacier as sure-footedly as a chamois itself.

From time to time they reached rocky ground; they walked between mossless stones, and sometimes between low pine trees or out on the green pastures—always changing, always new. About them towered the lofty, snow-capped peaks, which every child in the country knows by name—the Jungfrau, the Eiger, and the Mönch.

Rudy had never before been up so high, had never before walked on the wide ocean of snow with its frozen billows of ice, from which the wind occasionally swept little clouds of powdery snow as it sweeps the whitecaps from the waves of the sea. Glacier stretched beside glacier, almost as if they were holding hands; and each is a crystal palace of the Ice Maiden, whose joy and in whose power it is to seize and imprison her victims.

The sun shone warmly, and the snow dazzled the eye as if it were covered with the flashing sparks of pale blue diamonds. Countless insects, especially butterflies and bees, lay dead in heaps on the snow; they had winged their way too high, or perhaps the wind had carried them up to the cold regions that to them meant death. Around the Wetterhorn there hung a threatening cloud, like a large mass of very fine dark wool; it sank, bulging with what was concealed within—a foehn, the Alpine south wind that foretells a storm, fearfully violent in its power when it should break loose.

This whole journey—the stops for the nights high up in the mountains, the wild route, the deep crevasses where the water, during countless ages of time, had cut through the solid stone—made an unforgettable impression on little Rudy's mind.

A deserted stone hut, beyond the snowfields, gave them shelter and comfort for the night. Here they found charcoal and pine branches, and a fire was soon kindled. Sleeping quarters were arranged as well as possible, and the men settled near the blazing fire; they smoked their tobacco and drank some of the warm, spiced beverage they had prepared—and they didn't forget to give Rudy some.

The talk turned to the mysterious creatures who haunt the high Alps: the huge, strange snakes in the deep lakes—the night riders—the spectral host that carry sleepers through the air to the wonderful, floating city of Venice—the wild herdsman, who drives his black sheep over the green pastures: these had never been seen, although men had heard the sound of their bells and the frightful noise of the phantom herd.

Rudy listened to these superstitious tales with intense interest, but with no fear, for that he had never known; yet while he listened he imagined he could hear the roar of that wild, spectral herd. Yes! It became more and more distinct, until the men heard it too. They stopped their talking and listened to it, and then they told Rudy that he must not fall asleep.

It was a foehn that had risen—that violent tempest which whirls down from the mountains into the valley below, and in its fury snaps large trees like reeds, and tosses the wooden houses from one bank of a river to the other, as easily as we would move chessmen.

After an hour they told Rudy the wind had died down and he might go to sleep safely; and, weary from his long walk, he followed their instructions and slept.

Early next morning, they set off again. That day the sun shone for Rudy on new mountains, new glaciers, and new snowfields. They had entered Canton Valais, on the other side of the ridge of mountains visible from Grindelwald; but they still had a long way to go to his new home.

More mountain clefts, pastures, woods, and new paths unfolded themselves; then Rudy saw other houses and other people. But what kind of human beings were these? They were misshapen, with frightful, disgusting, fat, yellowish faces, the hideous flesh of their necks hanging down like bags. They were the cretins—miserable, diseased wretches, who dragged themselves along and stared with stupid, dead eyes at the strangers who crossed their path; the women were even more disgusting than the men. Were these the sort of people who lived in his new home?

THE UNCLE

When Rudy arrived in his uncle's house he thanked God to see people such as he was accustomed to. There was only one cretin, a poor imbecile boy, one of those unfortunate beings who, in their poverty, which amounts to utter destitution, always travel about in Canton Valais, visiting different families in turn and staying a month or two in each house. Poor Saperli happened to be living in the house of Rudy's uncle when the boy arrived.

This uncle was a bold hunter and a cooper by trade, while his wife was a lively little person, with a face somewhat like a bird's, eyes like an eagle's, and a long, skinny, fuzz-covered neck.

Everything was strange and new to Rudy—dress, customs, employment, even the language, though his young ear would soon learn to understand that. A comparison between his grandfather's little home and his uncle's domicile greatly favored the latter. The room they lived in was larger; the walls were decorated with chamois heads and brightly polished guns; a painting of the Virgin Mary hung over the door, with fresh Alpine roses and a constantly burning lamp before it.

As you have learned, his uncle was one of the most famous chamois hunters of the canton, and also the most experienced and best guide.

Rudy became the pet of the house, but there was another pet too—a blind, lazy old dog, of not much use any more. But he had been useful once, and his value in former years was remembered, so he now lived as one of the family, with every comfort. Rudy patted him, but the dog didn't like strangers and still considered Rudy one. But the boy did not long remain so, for soon he won his way into everyone's heart.

"Things are not so bad here in Canton Valais," said his uncle. "We have plenty of chamois; they don't die off as fast as the wild goats. Things are much better now than in the old days, however much we praise the olden times. A hole has been burst in the bag, so now we have a little fresh air in our cramped valley. When you do away with out-of-date things you always get something better," he said.

When the uncle became really talkative, he would tell the boy about his own and his father's childhood. "In those days Valais was," he called it, "just a closed bag full of too many sick people—miserable cretins. But the French soldiers came, and they made excellent doctors—they soon killed the disease, and the patients too. They knew how to strike—yes, to strike in many different ways; even their girls knew how to strike!" Then he winked at his wife, who was French by birth, and laughed. "The French knew how to split solid stones if they wanted to. It was they who cut out of solid rock the road over the Simplon Pass—yes, and made such a road that I could tell a three-year-old child to go to Italy! You just have to keep on the highway, and there you are!" Then the uncle sang a French song, and ended by shouting "hurrah!" for Napoleon Bonaparte.

It was the first time Rudy had ever heard of France or of Lyons, that great city on the Rhone which his uncle had visited.

In a few years Rudy would become an expert chamois hunter, for he showed quite a flair for it, said the uncle. He taught the boy to hold, load, and fire a gun; in the hunting season he took him up into the hills and made him drink warm chamois blood to ward off hunter's giddiness; he taught him to know the times when, on different slopes of the mountains, avalanches were likely to fall, in the morning or evening, whenever the sun's rays had the greatest effect. He taught him to observe the movements of the chamois and copy their leaps, so that he might light firmly on his feet. He told him that if there was no footing in the rock crevices, he must support himself by the pressure of his elbows and the muscles, of his thighs and calves; if necessary even the neck could be used.

The chamois is cunning and places sentinels on guard, so the hunter must be still more cunning and scent them out. Sometimes he could cheat them by arranging his hat and coat on his alpine staff, so that the chamois would mistake the dummy for the man. The uncle played this trick one day when he was out hunting with Rudy.

It was a narrow mountain path—indeed, scarcely a path at all; it was nothing more than a slight ledge close to the yawning abyss. The snow there was half thawed, and the rock crumbled away under the pressure of a boot, so that uncle lay down at full length and inched his way forward. Every fragment of rock that crumbled off fell, knocking and bouncing from one side of the wall to the other, until it came to rest in the depths far below. Rudy stood on the edge of the last point of solid rock, about a hundred paces behind his uncle, and from there he suddenly saw, wheeling through the air and hovering just above his uncle, an enormous vulture, which, with one stroke of its tremendous wings, could easily have hurled the creeping form into the abyss beneath, and there feed on his carcass.

The uncle had eyes for nothing but the chamois, which had appeared with its young kid on the other side of the crevasse. But Rudy kept watching the bird, with his hand on his gun to fire the instant it became necessary, for he understood its intention. Suddenly the chamois leaped upward; the uncle fired, and the animal was hit by the deadly bullet; but the kid escaped as skillfully as if it had had a lifelong experience of danger and flight. The huge bird, frightened by the report, wheeled off in another direction; and the uncle was saved from a danger of which he knew nothing until Rudy told him about it later.

As they were making their way homeward in high good humor, the uncle humming an air he remembered from his childhood, they heard a strange noise very close to them. They looked all around, and then upward; and there, on the slope of the mountain high above, the heavy snow covering was lifted up and heaving as a stretched linen sheet heaves when the wind creeps under it. Then the great mass cracked like a marble slab, broke, and changed into a foaming cataract, rushing down on them with a rumbling noise like distant thunder. An avalanche was coming, not directly toward Rudy and his uncle, but close to them—much too close!

"Hang on, Rudy!" he cried. "Hang on with all your might!"

Rudy threw his arms around the trunk of a nearby tree, while his uncle climbed higher and clung to the branches of the tree. The avalanche roared past a little distance away, but the gale of wind that swept behind it, the tail of a hurricane, snapped trees and bushes all around them as if they had been dry rushes and hurled them about in wild confusion. Rudy was flung to the ground, for the trunk of his tree looked as if it had been sawed in two, and the upper part was tossed a great distance. And there, among the shattered branches, Rudy found his poor uncle, with a fractured skull! His hands were still warm, but his face was unrecognizable. Rudy turned pale and trembled, for this was the first real shock of his life, the first terror he had ever experienced.

Late that evening he brought the fatal news to his home—his home, which was now to be the home of grief. The wife stood like a statue, uttering no word, shedding no tear; it was not until the corpse was brought home that her sorrow found utterance. The poor cretin crept into his bed, and was not seen throughout the whole next day. But the following evening he came to Rudy.

"Write a letter for me please!" he said. "Saperli can't write. Saperli can only take letter to post office."

"A letter for you?" Rudy asked. "To whom?"

"To our Lord Christ!"

"What do you mean?"

And the half-wit, as he was called, looked at Rudy with a touching expression, clasped his hands, and said solemnly and reverently, "Jesus Christ! Saperli would send him a letter to pray him that Saperli lie dead, and not the master of the house here."

And Rudy pressed his hand. "That letter wouldn't reach up there. That letter wouldn't restore him to us."

He found it very difficult to convince Saperli how impossible his request was.

"Now you must be the support of the house," said his aunt. And Rudy became just that.

BABETTE

"Who is the best hunter in Canton Valais?" The chamois knew well. "Beware of Rudy!" they might have said to each other. And, "Who is the handsomest hunter?" "Oh, it's Rudy!" the girls said. But they didn't add, "Beware of Rudy!" And their serious mothers didn't say so either, for he bowed as politely to them as to the young girls.

He was so brave and happy; his cheeks were so brown, his teeth so white, his dark eyes so sparkling! He was a handsome fellow, just twenty years old. The most icy water never seemed too cold for him to go swimming; in fact, he was like a fish in water. He could outclimb anyone else; he could cling as tightly as a snail to the cliffs. There were steel muscles and sinews in him; that was clear whenever he jumped. He had learned how to leap, first from the Cat, and later from the chamois. Rudy was considered the best mountain guide, and he could have made a great deal of money in that vocation. His uncle had also taught him the trade of a cooper, but he had no inclination for that. He was interested in nothing but chamois hunting; that was his greatest pleasure, and it also brought in good money. Everybody said Rudy would be an excellent match, if only he didn't set his sights too high. He was the kind of graceful dancer that the girls dreamed about; and more than one carried him in her thoughts while she was awake.

"He kissed me while we were dancing!" the schoolmaster's daughter, Annette, told her dearest friend; but she shouldn't have told it, even to her dearest friend. Such secrets are seldom kept; they ooze out, like sand from a bag that has holes in it. Consequently, however well-behaved and good Rudy was, the rumor soon spread about that he kissed his dancing partners. And yet he had never kissed the one he really wanted to kiss.

"Watch him!" said an old hunter. "He has kissed Annette. He has begun with A, and he's going to kiss his way through the whole alphabet!"

A kiss in the dance was all the gossips so far could find to bring against Rudy; but he certainly had kissed Annette, and yet she wasn't the real flower of his heart.

Down at Bex, among the great walnut trees near a small rushing mountain stream, there lived a rich miller. His home was a large house, three stories high, with small turrets; it was made of wood and covered with tin plates, which shone both in sunshine and moonlight. On the highest turret was a weather vane, a shining arrow piercing an apple—an allusion to William Tell's famous arrow shot. The mill was prominent and prosperous looking and allowed itself to be sketched and written about, but the miller's daughter did not permit herself to be described in painting or writing, at least so Rudy would have said. Yet her image was engraved on his heart; her eyes sparkled in it so that it was quite on fire. This fire had, like most fires, begun suddenly. The strangest part of it was that the miller's daughter, the lovely Babette, had no suspicion of it, for she and Rudy had never spoken so much as two words to each other.

The miller was rich, and because of his wealth Babette was rather high to hope for. "But nothing is so high," Rudy told himself, "that one may not reach it. You must climb on, and if you have confidence you won't fall." This was how he had been taught as a child.

Now it so happened that Rudy had some business in Bex. It was quite a journey, for in those days there was no railroad. From the Rhone glaciers, at the very foot of the Simplon, the broad valley of Canton Valais stretches among many and often-shifting mountain peaks, with its mighty Rhone River, whose rising waters often overflow its banks, covering fields and roads, destroying everything. Between the towns of Sion and St. Maurice the valley bends sharply like an elbow, and below St. Maurice it narrows until there is room only for the bed of the river and the narrow carriage road. Canton Valais ends here, and an old tower stands on the side of the mountain like the guardian of the canton, commanding a view across the stone bridge to the customhouse on the other side, where Canton Vaud commences. And the closest of the nearby towns is Bex. Fruitfulness and abundance increase here with every step forward; one enters, so to speak, a grove of chestnut and walnut trees. Here and there cypresses and pomegranates peep out; it is as warm here as if one were in Italy.

Rudy reached Bex, and after finishing his business he took a walk about town; but he saw no one belonging to the mill, not even Babette. And that wasn't what he wanted.

Evening came on; the air was heavy with the fragrance of the wild thyme and the blossoming lime trees; a shining veil of sky blue seemed to lie over the wooded green hills; and a stillness was everywhere. It was not the stillness of sleep or of death—no, it was as if nature were holding her breath, as of posing for her image to be photographed on the blue surface of the heavens above. Here and there among the trees in the green field stood poles that carried the telegraph wires through the silent valley. Against one of them there leaned an object, so motionless that it might have been the dead trunk of a tree; it was Rudy, standing there as still as the world around him at that moment. He wasn't sleeping, nor was he dead; but just as great events of the world, or matters of the highest importance to individuals often are transmitted through the telegraph wires without those wires betraying them by the slightest movement or the faintest sound, so there passed through Rudy's mind the one, mighty, overwhelming thought that now constantly occupied him—the thought of his life's happiness. His eyes were fixed on a single point before him—a light that glimmered through the foliage from the parlor of the miller's house, where Babette lived. Rudy stood as still as if he were taking aim at a chamois; but at that moment he was like the chamois itself, which could stand as if chiseled from rock, and in the next instant, if only a stone rolled past, would spring into life and leave the hunter far behind. And so it was with Rudy, for a thought passed through his mind.

"Never give up!" he said. "Visit the mill; say good evening to the miller, and good day to Babette. You won't fall unless you're afraid of falling. If I'm going to be Babette's husband, she'll have to see me sooner or later!"

Then Rudy laughed, and in good spirits, he went to the mill. He knew what he wanted; he wanted Babette!

The river with its yellowish-white water was rolling along, overhung with willows and lime trees. Rudy went along the path, and, as the old nursery rhyme says,

> *Found to the miller's house his way;*
> *But no one was at home*
> *Except a pussycat at play!*

The cat, which was standing on the steps, arched its back and mewed, but Rudy was not inclined to pay my attention to it. He knocked at the door, but no one heard him; no one opened the door. "Meow!" said the cat. If Rudy had still been a little boy, he would have understood the cat's language, and known that it said, "No one is home!" But now he had to go over to the mill to find out; and there he was told that the miller had gone on a long journey to Interlaken—"Inter Lacus, among the lakes," as the highly learned schoolmaster, Annette's father, had explained the name. There was going to be a great shooting match held there, to begin the next morning and last for eight days. The Swiss from all the German cantons were assembling there, and the miller and Babette had gone, too.

"Poor Rudy," we may well say. It wasn't a lucky time for him to have come to Bex. He could only go home again, which he did, taking the road over St. Maurice and Sion to his own valley, his own mountains. But he wasn't disheartened. The next morning when the sun rose he was in good spirits, for they had never been really depressed.

"Babette is in Interlaken, a good many days' journey from here," he said to himself. "It's a long way if you follow the highway, but not so far if you cut across the mountain, and that's the best way for a chamois hunter. I've traveled that route before; over there is my first home, where I lived with my grandfather when I was a little boy. And there are shooting matches at Interlaken; I'll show I'm the best one there, and I'll be with Babette there too, after I've made her acquaintance."

With his musket and gamebag and his light knapsack packed with his Sunday best, Rudy went up the mountain; it was the shortest way, though still fairly long. But the shooting matches would only begin that day, and were to last more than a week. During all that time, he had been told, the miller and Babette would be staying with their relatives at Interlaken. So Rudy crossed the Gemmi; he planned to descend near Grindelwald.

Happily and in good health he walked along, enjoying the fresh, pure, invigorating mountain air. The valley sank below him; the horizon widened, showing here one snow-capped summit, there another, until the whole of the bright shining Alpine range was visible. Rudy well knew every snow-covered mountain peak. He was now approaching the Schreckhorn, which pointed its white, powdered stone finger high toward the blue vault above.

At last he had crossed the highest mountain ridge. Now the pasture lands sloped down to the valley that was his old home. The air was light, and his thoughts were light; mountain and valley were blooming with flowers and foliage, and his heart was blooming with the bright dreams of youth. He felt as if old age and death would never approach him; life, power, and enjoyment would be before him always. Free as a bird, light as a bird was Rudy; and as the swallows flew past him they sang as in the days of his childhood, "We and you, and you and we!" Everything was light and happy.

Down below lay the green-velvet meadows, dotted with brown wooden houses; and the river Lütschine murmured and rolled along. He could see the glacier, with its edges like green glass bordering the dirty snow, and looking down into the deep crevasses, he saw both the upper and lower glacier. The pealing of the church bells came to his ears, as if they were welcoming him to his old home. His heart beat faster, and so many old memories filled his mind that for a moment he almost forgot Babette.

He was again passing along the same road where, as a little boy, he had stood with the other children to sell the carved wooden toy houses. His grandfather's house still stood over above the pine trees, but strangers lived there now. As in the olden days, the children came running to sell their wares. One of them offered him an Alpine rose, and Rudy took it as a good omen, thinking of Babette. Soon he came to the bridge where the two Lütschines unite; here the foliage was heavier and the walnut trees gave grateful shade. Then he could make out waving flags, the white cross on the red ground—the standard of Switzerland as of Denmark—and before him lay Interlaken.

To Rudy it certainly seemed like a wonderful town—a Swiss town in its Sunday dress. Unlike other market towns, it was not a heap of heavy stone buildings, stiff, cold, foreign looking. No, it looked as if the wooden chalets from the hills above had moved down into the green valley below, with its clear stream rushing swiftly as an arrow, and had ranged themselves in rows, somewhat unevenly, to be sure, to form a street. And most beautiful of all, the streets, which had been built since Rudy had last been there as a child, seemed to be made up of all the prettiest wooden houses his grandfather had carved and that had filled the cupboard at home. They seemed to have transplanted themselves down here and to have grown very much in size, as the old chestnut trees had done.

Every house was a so-called hotel, with carved wooden grillwork around the windows and balconies and with projecting roofs; they were very neat and dainty. Between each house and the wide, hard-surfaced highway was a flower garden. Near these houses, though on only one side of the road, there stood other houses; if they had formed a double row, they would have cut off from view the fresh green meadows where cattle grazed, their bells jingling as in the high Alpine pastures. The valley was surrounded by high mountains, with a little break on one side that revealed the glittering, snow-white Jungfrau, in form the most beautiful of all the Swiss mountains.

What a multitude of gayly dressed ladies and gentlemen from foreign countries! What crowds of country people from the nearby cantons! The marksmen carried the number of their posts in a garland round their hats. There were shouting and racket and music of all kinds, from singing to hand organs and wind instruments. The houses and bridges were decorated with flags and verses. Banners waved, and shot after shot was being fired; to Rudy's ears that was the best music. In all this excitement he almost forgot Babette, though it was for her sake alone that he had gone there.

The marksmen were crowding around the targets. Rudy quickly joined them, and he was the best shot of them all, for he always made a bull's-eye.

"Who's that strange fellow, that very young marksman?" people asked. "He speaks the French of Canton Valais; but he can also express himself fluently in our German," said some.

"He is supposed to have lived in the valley, near Grindelwald, when he was a child," someone explained.

The lad was full of life; his eyes sparkled; his aim and his arm were steady, so his shots were always perfect. Good luck brings courage, and Rudy always had courage. Soon a whole circle of admirers was around him; they showed him their esteem and honored him. Babette had almost disappeared from his thoughts. But suddenly a heavy hand was laid on his shoulder, and a deep voice spoke to him in French.

"You're from Canton Valais?"

Rudy turned and saw a fat man with a jolly face. It was the rich miller from Bex, his broad body hiding the slender, lovely Babette; however, she soon came forward, her dark eyes sparkling brightly. The rich miller was very proud that it was a marksman from his own canton who proved to be the best shot and was so much admired and praised. Rudy was truly the child of good fortune; that which he had traveled so far to find, but had nearly forgotten since his arrival, now sought him out.

When in a far land one meets people from his own part of the country, it is easy to make friends, and people speak as if they were well acquainted. Rudy was the foremost at the shooting matches, as the miller was foremost at Bex, because of his money and his fine mill. So, though they had never met before, the two men shook hands warmly. Babette, too, gave the young man her hand frankly, and he pressed it and gazed at her in such a way that it made her blush.

The miller spoke of the long trip they had made and of the many large towns they had seen; it had been quite a journey, for they had traveled partly by railroad and partly by post.

"I came the shorter way," said Rudy. "I came over the mountains. There's no road so high that you can't try it."

"But you can also break your neck," said the miller. "And you look as if you probably *will* break your neck someday; you're so daring."

"One never falls so long as one doesn't think of it," said Rudy.

The miller's relatives at Interlaken, with whom he and Babette were staying, invited Rudy to visit them, since he came from the same canton as their kinfolk. It was a wonderful invitation for Rudy. Luck was running with him, as it always does with those who are self-reliant and remember that "Our Lord gives nuts to us, but he does not crack them for us!"

And Rudy sat with the miller's relatives, almost like one of the family. They drank a toast in honor of the best marksman; Babette clinked glasses with Rudy too, and he in return thanked them for the toast.

In the evening the whole party walked on the lovely avenue, past the gay-looking hotels under the walnut trees, and there was such a large crowd that Rudy had to give Babette his arm. He explained to her how happy he was to have met people from Canton Vaud, for Vaud and Valais were good neighbors. He expressed himself so cordially about this that Babette could not keep from squeezing his hand. As they walked there, they seemed almost like old friends, and she was such a lively, pretty little person. Rudy was greatly amused at her remarks about the absurd affectations in the dress of some of the foreign ladies and the airs they put on; but she really didn't mean to make fun of them, because there must be some nice people among them—yes, some sweet and lovely people, she was sure, for her godmother was a very superior English lady. Eighteen years before, when Babette was christened, that lady had lived in Bex and had given Babette the valuable brooch she was wearing. Her godmother had written her twice, and this year they were to have met her here at Interlaken, where she was bringing her daughters; they were old maids, almost thirty, said Babette—she herself was just eighteen.

Her pretty little mouth was not still for an instant, and everything she said appeared to Rudy to be of the greatest importance, and he in turn told her all he had to tell, how he had been to Bex, and how well he knew the mill, and how often he had seen her, though, of course, she had never noticed him. He told her he had been too disappointed for words when he found she and her father were far away; but still it wasn't far enough to keep him from climbing the wall that made the road so long.

Yes, he said all this, and a great deal more, too. He told her how fond he was of her, and how it was for her sake, and not because of the shooting matches, that he had come to Interlaken.

Babette became very silent now; all this that he confided to her was almost too much to listen to.

As they walked on, the sun set behind the mighty peaks, and the Jungfrau stood in all her glory, encircled by the dark green woods of the surrounding mountains. The big crowd stopped to gaze at it; even Rudy and Babette enjoyed the magnificent scene.

"Nowhere is it more beautiful than it is here!" said Babette.

"Nowhere!" agreed Rudy, with his eyes fixed on Babette.

"Tomorrow I must leave," he said a little later.

"Come and visit us at Bex," Babette whispered. "My father will be very pleased!"

ON THE WAY HOME

Oh, what a load Rudy had to carry the next day, when he started his return home over the mountains! He had two handsome guns, three silver cups, and a silver coffeepot—this last would be useful when he set up his own home. But these valuable prizes were not the heaviest burden he had to bear; a still weightier load he had to carry—or did it carry him?—across the high mountains.

The weather was dismal, gloomy, and rainy; the clouds hung like a mourning veil over the mountain summits and shrouded the shining peaks. The last stroke of the axe had resounded from the woods, and down the side of the mountain rolled the great tree trunks. From the vast heights above they looked like matchsticks, but were nevertheless as big as masts of ships. The Lütschine River murmured its monotonous song; the wind whistled, and the clouds sailed swiftly by.

Suddenly there appeared next to Rudy a young girl; he had not noticed her until she was quite near him. She also was planning to cross the mountain. Her eyes had a peculiar power that compelled one to look into them; they were so clear and deep—bottomless.

"Do you have a sweetheart?" asked Rudy, whose thoughts were filled with love.

"I have none," she laughed, but it seemed as if she were not speaking the truth. "Let us not take the long way around; let us keep to the left—it is shorter."

"Yes, and easier to fall into some crevasse," said Rudy. "You ought to know the route better if you're going to be the guide."

"I know the way very well," she said, "and I have my thoughts collected. Your thoughts are down there in the valley; but up here you should think of the Ice Maiden. People say she is not friendly to the human race."

"I'm not a bit afraid of her," said Rudy. "She couldn't keep me when I was a child, and she won't catch me now that I'm a grown-up man."

Now it became very dark. First rain fell, then snow, and its whiteness was quite blinding.

"Give me your hand, and I shall help you climb," said the girl, touching him with her icy fingers.

"*You* help me?" said Rudy. "I don't yet need a woman's help in climbing!"

Then he walked on away from her quickly. The falling snow thickened about him like a curtain, the wind moaned, and behind him he could hear the girl laughing and singing. It sounded very strange. Surely it must be a specter in the service of the Ice Maiden; Rudy had heard of these things when, as a little boy, he had spent that night on the mountain, during his trip across the mountains.

The snow no longer fell so thickly, and the clouds lay far below him. He looked back, but there was no one to be seen; he could only hear laughing and jeering that did not seem to come from a human being.

When at last he reached the highest part of the mountain, where the path led down into the Rhone valley, he saw in the clear blue heaven, toward Chamonix, two glittering stars. They shone brightly; and he thought of Babette, of himself, and of his good fortune. And these thoughts made him warm.

THE VISIT TO THE MILL

"What grand prizes you have brought home," said his old foster mother. And her strange, birdlike eyes sparkled, as she twisted her thin, wrinkled neck even more strangely and faster than usual. "You carry good luck with you, Rudy. I must kiss you, my dear boy!"

Rudy allowed himself to be kissed, but one could read in his face that he did not enjoy this affectionate greeting.

"How handsome you are, Rudy!" said the old woman.

"Oh, stop your flattery," Rudy laughed; but still the compliment pleased him.

"I repeat it," said the old woman. "And fortune smiles on you."

"Yes, I think you're right there," he said, thinking of Babette. Never before had he longed so for the deep valley.

"They must have come home by now," he told himself. "It's more than two days past the day they intended to return. I must go to Bex!"

So to Bex he went, and the miller and his daughter were home. He was received in friendly fashion, and many messages of remembrance were given him from the family at Interlaken. Babette spoke very little; she had become quite silent, but her eyes spoke, and that was enough for Rudy. The miller, who usually had plenty to say, and was accustomed to making jokes and having them laughed at, for he was "the rich miller," seemed to prefer listening to Rudy's adventures—hearing him tell of the hardships and risks that the chamois hunters had to undergo on the mountain heights, how they had to crawl along the treacherous snowy cornices on the edges of cliffs, attached to the rocks only by the force of wind and weather, and cross the frail bridges cast by the snowstorms over deep ravines.

Rudy looked very handsome, and his eyes flashed as he described the life of a hunter, the cunning of the chamois and the wonderful leaps they made, the powerful foehn, and the rolling avalanche. He noticed that every new description held the miller's interest more and more, and that he was particularly fascinated by the youth's account of the vulture and the great royal eagle.

Not far from there, in Canton Valais, there was an eagle's nest, built cleverly under a projecting platform of rock, in the face of a cliff; and in it there was an eaglet, but it was impossible to get at it.

A few days before an Englishman had offered Rudy a whole handful of gold if he would bring him the eaglet alive.

"But there is a limit to everything," said Rudy. "You can't get at that eaglet up there; it would be madness to try."

As the wine flowed freely and the conversation flowed just as freely, Rudy thought the evening was much too short, although it was past midnight when he left the miller's house after this, his first visit.

For a little while the lights shone through the windows and through the green branches of the trees, while out from the open skylight on the roof crept the Parlor Cat, and along the drainpipe the Kitchen Cat came to meet her.

"Is there any news at the mill?" said the Parlor Cat. "There's some secret lovemaking in this house! The father doesn't know anything about it yet. Rudy and Babette have been stepping on each other's paws under the table all evening. They trod on me twice, but I didn't mew; that would have aroused suspicion."

"Well, *I* would have mewed," said the Kitchen Cat.

"What would go in the kitchen wouldn't do in the parlor," said the Parlor Cat. "I certainly would like to know what the miller will say when he hears about this engagement."

Yes, what would the miller say? That Rudy also was most anxious to know; and he couldn't make himself wait very long. Before many days had passed, when the omnibus crossed the bridge between Cantons Valais and Vaud, Rudy sat in it, with his usual self-confidence and happy thoughts of the favorable answer he would hear that evening.

And later that evening, when the omnibus was driving back along the same road, Rudy was sitting in it again, going home, while the Parlor Cat was running over to the mill with the news.

"Look here, you kitchen fellow, the miller knows everything now. The affair has come to a fine end. Rudy came here toward evening, and he and Babette found a great deal to whisper about, as they stood in the hallway outside the miller's room. I lay at their feet, but they had neither eyes nor thoughts for me.

"'I'll go straight to your father,' said Rudy. 'My proposal is perfectly honorable.'

"'Do you want me to go with you?' said Babette, 'to give you courage?'

"'I have enough courage,' said Rudy, 'but if you're with me, he'll have to be friendly, whether he likes it or not.'

"So they went in. Rudy stepped hard on my tail—he's awfully clumsy. I mewed, but neither he nor Babette had any ears for me. They opened the door, and went in together, and I, too. I jumped up on the back of a chair, for I didn't know if Rudy would kick me. But it was the miller who kicked—and what a kick! Out of the door and back up to the mountains and the chamois! Rudy could take care of them, but not of our little Babette!"

"But what was said?" asked the Kitchen Cat.

"Said? Oh, they said everything that people say when they're wooing! 'I love her, and she loves me; and if there's milk in the can for one, there's milk in the can for two.'

"'But she's much above you,' said the miller. 'She sits on heaps of grain, golden grain—as you know. You can't reach up to her!'

"'There's nothing so high that one can't reach it, if one has the will to do it!' said Rudy, for he is a determined fellow.

"'But you said a little while ago that you couldn't reach the eaglet in its nest! Babette is still higher than that.'

"'I'll take them both,' said Rudy.

"'Yes,' said the miller. 'I'll give her to you when you bring me the eaglet alive!'"

Then he laughed until the tears stood in his eyes. 'But now, thank you for your visit, Rudy. Come again tomorrow; then you'll find nobody home! Good-bye, Rudy!'

"Then Babette said farewell too, as meekly as a little kitten that can't see its mother.

"'A promise is a promise, and a man's a man!' said Rudy. 'Don't cry, Babette. I'll bring the eaglet.'

"'I hope you break your neck!' said the miller. 'And then we'll be spared your visits here!' That's what I call kicking him out! Now Rudy's gone, and Babette just sits and cries; but the miller sings German songs he learned in his travels. I'm not going to worry myself about the matter; it wouldn't do any good."

"But it would look better if you pretended," said the Kitchen Cat.

THE EAGLE'S NEST

From the mountain path there sounded lively yodeling that meant good humor and gay courage. The yodeler was Rudy; he was going to see his friend Vesinand.

"You must help me," he said. "We'll take Ragli with us. I have to capture the eaglet up there on the top of the cliff!"

"Better try to capture the Moon first. That would be about as easy a job," said Vesinand. "I see you're in good spirits."

"Yes; I'm thinking about marrying. But now, seriously, you must know how things stand with me."

And soon Vesinand and Ragli knew what Rudy wanted.

"You're a daring fellow," they said. "But you won't make it. You'll break your neck."

"One doesn't fall, so long as one doesn't think of it!" said Rudy.

They set out about midnight, with poles, ladders, and ropes. The road led through brushwood and over loose stones, up, always up, up through the dark night. The water roared below, and the water trickled down from above; damp clouds swept heavily along. At last the hunters reached the edge of the precipice, where it was even darker, for the rock walls almost met, and the sky could only be seen through the narrow opening above. Close by was a deep abyss, with the hoarsely roaring water far beneath them.

All three sat quite still. They had to await daybreak, for when the parent eagle flew out, they would have to shoot it if they were to have any hopes of capturing the young one. Rudy was as still as if he were a part of the rock on which he was sitting. He held his gun ready; his eyes were fixed steadily on the highest part of the cleft, where the eagle's nest was hidden under the projecting rock. The three hunters had a long time to wait.

But at last they suddenly heard high above them a crashing, whirring sound, and the air was darkened by a huge object. Two guns took aim at the enormous eagle the moment it left the nest. A shot blazed out; for an instant the outspread wings fluttered, and then the bird slowly began to sink. It seemed that with its tremendous size and wingspread it would fill the whole chasm, and in its fall drag the hunters down with it. The eagle disappeared in the abyss below; the hunters could hear the crashing of trees and bushes, crushed by the fall of the bird.

And now the men began to get busy. Three of the longest ladders were tied tightly together. They were supposed to reach the last stepping place on the margin of the abyss, but they did not reach far enough; and the perpendicular rock side was smooth as a brick wall on up to where the nest was hidden under the highest projecting rock overhang. After some discussion they agreed that the only thing to do was to tie two more ladders together, let them down into the chasm from above, and attach these to the three already raised. With immense difficulty they dragged the two ladders up, binding them with ropes to the top; they were then let out over the rock and hung there swaying in the air over the bottomless abyss. Rudy was already seated on the lowest rung. It was an icy-cold morning, and the mist was rising heavily from the dark chasm below. Rudy was like a fly sitting on some bit of a straw that a bird, while building its nest, might have dropped on the edge of a tall factory chimney; but the insect could fly if the straw gave way, while Rudy could only break his neck. The wind howled about him, while far below in the abyss the gushing water roared out from the melting glacier—the palace of the Ice Maiden.

He then made the ladder swing to and fro, like the spider swings its body when it wants to catch anything in its slender thread; and when he, for the fourth time touched the top of the ladders set up from below, he got a good hold on them, and bound them together with sure and skillful hands, though they swayed as if they hung on worn-out hinges.

The five long ladders, which now reached the nest, seemed like a swaying reed knocking against the perpendicular cliff. And now the most dangerous part of the job was to be done, for he had to climb as a cat climbs. But Rudy could do that, for a cat had taught him. He never noticed the presence of Dizziness, who floated in the air behind him and stretched forth her embracing arms toward him. At last he reached the last step of the highest ladder, and then he found that he was still not high enough even to see into the nest. He would have to use his hands to raise himself up to it; he tried the lowest part of the thick, interwoven branches, forming the base of the nest, to learn if it was sufficiently strong; then having secured a firm hold on a heavy, strong branch, he swung himself up from the ladder until his head and chest were level with the nest. Then there swept over him a horrible stench of carrion, for putrefied lambs, chamois, and birds littered the nest.

Dizziness, who had little power over him, blew the poisonous odor into his face to make him faint, while down below, on the dank, foaming waters of the yawning ravine, sat the Ice Maiden herself, with her long pale-green hair, staring at him with eyes as deadly as two gun barrels. "Now I will catch you!"

In a corner of the nest Rudy could see the eaglet sitting—a big powerful bird, even though it could not yet fly. Staring straight at it, Rudy somehow held on with one hand, while with the other he cast a noose around the bird. Thus it was captured alive; its legs were held by the tightened cord, and Rudy flung the noose over his shoulder, so that the bird hung a good distance below him. Then he held onto a rope, flung out to help him, until his toes at last touched the highest rung of the ladder.

"Hold tightly; don't be afraid of falling and you won't fall!" That was his early training, and Rudy acted on it. He held tightly, climbed down, and believing he couldn't fall, he didn't fall.

Then there arose loud and joyous yodeling. He stood safely on the firm rocky ledge, with his eaglet.

WHAT NEWS THE PARLOR CAT HAD TO TELL

"Here's what you asked for!" said Rudy, as he entered the miller's house at Bex and placed a large basket on the floor. When he took the lid off two yellow eyes surrounded by dark rings glared out, eyes so flashing, so fierce, that they looked as though they would burn or blast anything they saw. The neck was red and downy; the short strong beak opened to bite.

"The eaglet!" cried the miller. Babette screamed and sprang back, but could not tear her eyes from Rudy and the eaglet.

"Nothing frightens you!" said the miller to Rudy.

"And you always keep your word," said Rudy. "Everyone has his principles."

"But how did it happen that you didn't break your neck?" asked the miller.

"Because I held tightly," said Rudy. "And so I'm doing now—holding tightly to Babette."

"Better wait till you get her!" laughed the miller; and Babette knew that was a good sign.

"Let's take the eaglet out of the basket; it's horrible to see its eyes glaring. How did you manage to capture it?"

And Rudy had to describe his adventure. As he talked the miller's eyes opened wider and wider.

"With your courage and good luck you could take care of three wives!" said the miller.

"Thank you! Thank you!" cried Rudy.

"But you won't get Babette just yet!" said the miller, slapping the young hunter good-humoredly on the shoulder.

"Do you know the latest news at the mill?" said the Parlor Cat to the Kitchen Cat. "Rudy has brought us the eaglet and takes Babette in exchange. They have actually kissed each other, and her father saw it! That's as good as an engagement! The old man didn't make any fuss at all; he kept his claws pulled in, took his afternoon nap, and left the two of them to sit and spoon. They have so much to tell each other that they won't have finished until Christmas!"

And they hadn't finished by Christmas, either. The wind shook down the yellow leaves; the snow drifted up in the valleys as well as on the high mountains; the Ice Maiden sat in her stately palace, which grew larger during the winter. The cliffs were covered with sleet, and icicles, big and heavy as elephants, hung down. Where in summer the mountain streams poured down, there were now enormous masses of icy tapestry; fantastic garlands of crystal ice hung over the snow-covered pine trees. Over the deepest valleys the Ice Maiden rode the howling wind. The carpet of snow spread down as far as Bex, so she could go there and see Rudy in the house where he spent so much time with Babette. The wedding was to take place the following summer; and their ears often tingled, for their friends often talked about it.

Then everything was sunny, and the most beautiful Alpine rose bloomed. The lovely, laughing Babette was as charming as the early spring itself—the spring which makes all the birds sing of the summertime and weddings.

"How those two do sit and drool over each other!" said the Parlor Cat. "I'm tired of their mewing now!"

THE ICE MAIDEN

Spring has unfolded her fresh green garlands of walnut and chestnut trees which burst into bloom, especially in the country extending from the bridge at St. Maurice to Lake Geneva and along the banks of the Rhone. With wild speed the river rushes from its sources beneath the green glaciers—the Ice Palace, home of the Ice Maiden, from where she allows herself to be carried on the biting wind up to the highest fields of snow, there to recline on their drifting masses in the warm sunshine. Here she sat and gazed down into the deep valleys below, where she could see human beings busily bustling about, like ants on a sunlit stone.

"'Mental giants,' the children of the sun call you," said the Ice Maiden. "You are only vermin! One rolling snowball, and your houses and villages are crushed, wiped out!" Then she raised her proud head still higher and stared with death-threatening eyes about and below her. Then from the valley there arose a strange sound; it was the blasting of rocks—the labors of men—the building of roadbeds and tunnels for the coming of the railroad.

"They work like moles," she said, "digging passages in the rocks, and therefore are heard these sounds like the reports of guns. If I move my palaces, the noise is stronger than the roar of thunder itself."

Then up from the valley there arose thick smoke—moving forward like a fluttering veil, a waving plume—from the locomotive which on the new railway was drawing a train, carriage linked to carriage, looking like a winding serpent. It shot past with the speed of an arrow.

"They think they're the masters down there, these 'mental giants!'" said the Ice Maiden. "But the powers of nature are still the real rulers!"

And she laughed and sang, and it made the valley tremble.

"It's an avalanche!" the people down there said.

But the children of the sun sang still more loudly of the power of mankind's thought. It commands all, it yokes the wide ocean, levels mountains, fills valleys; the power of thought makes mankind lord over the powers of nature.

At that moment a party of climbers crossed the snowfield where the Ice Maiden sat; they had roped themselves together, to form one large body on the slippery ice, near the deep abyss.

"Vermin!" she said. "*You* the lords of the powers of nature!" And she turned from them and gazed scornfully into the deep valley, where the railway train was rushing along.

"There they sit, those thoughts! But they are in the power of nature's force. I see every one of them! One sits alone like a king, others sit in a group, and half of them are asleep! And when the steam dragon stops, they climb out and go their way. Then the thoughts go out into the world!" And she laughed.

"There's another avalanche!" said the people in the valley.

"It won't reach us!" said two who sat together in the train—"two minds with but a single thought," as we say. They were Rudy and Babette, and the miller was going with them.

"Like baggage," he said. "I'm along with them as sort of extra baggage!"

"There sit those two!" said the Ice Maiden. "Many a chamois have I crushed, millions of Alpine flowers have I snapped and broken, leaving no root behind—I destroy them all! Thoughts! 'Mental giants,' indeed!" Again she laughed.

"That's another avalanche!" said those down in the valley.

THE GODMOTHER

At Montreux, one of the nearby towns which, with Clarens, Bernex, and Crin, encircle the northeast shore of Lake Geneva, lived Babette's godmother, the highborn English lady, with her daughters and a young relative. They had been there only a short while, but the miller had already visited them, announced Babette's engagement, and told them about Rudy and the visit to Interlaken and the young eagle—in short, the whole story. It had pleased them greatly, and they felt very kindly toward Rudy and Babette, and even the miller himself. They insisted upon all three of them coming to Montreux, and that's why they went. Babette wanted to see her godmother, and her godmother wanted to see her.

At the little village of Villeneuve, at the end of Lake Geneva, lay the steamboat which, in a voyage of half an hour, went from there to Bernex, a little below Montreux. That coast has often been celebrated by poets in song and story. There, under the walnut trees, beside the deep, blue-green lake, Byron sat and wrote his melodious verses about the prisoner in the dark, mountain Castle of Chillon. There, where Clarens is reflected amid weeping willows in the clear water, Rousseau wandered, dreaming of his Héloïse. The Rhone River glides beneath the lofty, snow-capped hills of Savoy, and near its mouth there is a small island, so tiny that from the shore it looks as if it were a ship floating in the water. It is just a patch of rocky ground, which a century before a lady had walled around and covered with earth, where three acacia trees were planted that now overshadowed the whole island. Babette was enchanted with this little spot; to her it was the loveliest place to be seen on the whole trip. She said they ought to land there—they must land there—it would be so charming under those beautiful trees. But the steamer passed by and did not stop until it reached Vernex.

The little party passed up among the white sunlit walls that surrounded the vineyards before the little mountain town of Montreux, where the peasants' cottages are shaded by fig trees and laurels and cypresses grow in the gardens. Halfway up the mountain was the hotel where the godmother lived.

The meeting was very cordial. The godmother was a stout, pleasant-looking woman with a smiling, round face. As a child she must certainly have resembled one of Raphael's cherubs; it was still an angel's head, but older, with silver-white hair. The daughters were tall and slender, well dressed and elegant looking. The young cousin with them, who had enough golden hair and golden whiskers for three gentlemen, was dressed in white from head to foot, and promptly began to pay devoted attention to little Babette.

Beautifully bound books and music and drawings were on the large table. The balcony door was open, and from the balcony, there was a lovely view of the calm lake, so bright and clear that the villages, woods, and snow-peaks of Savoy were reflected in it.

Rudy, who was generally so lively and gay, found himself very ill at ease. He moved about as if he were walking on peas over a slippery floor. How slowly the time passed—it was like being in a treadmill! And now they had to go out for a walk! And that was just as tiresome. Rudy had to take two steps forward and one back to keep abreast of the others. They went down to Chillon, the gloomy old castle on the island, to look at dungeons and instruments of torture, rusty chains hanging from rocky walls, stone benches for those condemned to death, trap doors through which the doomed were hurled down onto iron spikes amid the surge. They called it a pleasure to look at these things! It was a dreadful place of execution, elevated by Byron's verse into the world of poetry—but to Rudy still only a place of execution. He leaned out of one of the great windows and gazed down into the blue-green water, and over to the lonely little island with the three acacias. How he longed to be there, free from the whole chattering party!

But Babette was very happy. She had had a wonderful time, she said later; and the cousin she thought was perfect!

"Yes, perfectly flippant!" said Rudy; and that was the first time he had ever said anything to her that did not please her.

The Englishman had given her a little book as s souvenir of Chillon; it was Byron's poem, *The Prisoner of Chillon*, translated into French so that she could read it.

"The book may be all right," said Rudy, "but the finely combed fellow who gave it to you didn't make a hit with me."

"He looks like a flour sack without any flour!" said the miller, laughing at his own wit.

Rudy laughed too, and said that he was exactly right.

THE COUSIN

When Rudy went to visit the mill a couple of days later, he found the young Englishman there. Babette had just set a plate of boiled trout before him, which she herself had decorated with parsley, to make it look appetizing, no doubt. Rudy thought that was entirely unnecessary. What did he want there? What was his business? To be served and pampered by Babette? Rudy was jealous, and that pleased Babette. It amused her to see revealed all the feelings of his heart—the weak as well as the strong.

Love was still an amusement to her, and she played with Rudy's heart; but it must be said that he was still the center of all her thoughts, the dearest and most cherished in the world. Still, the gloomier he looked the more merrily she laughed at him with her eyes. She would even have kissed the blond Englishman with the golden whiskers if it would have made Rudy rush out in a fury, for it would have shown her how much he loved her.

This was not the fair nor the wise thing for little Babette to do, but she was only nineteen. She had no intention of being unkind to Rudy; still less did she think how her conduct would appear to the young Englishman, or how light and improper it was for the miller's modest, newly betrothed daughter.

Where the road from Bex passes beneath the snow-clad peaks, which in the language of the country are called *diablerets*, the mill stood, near a rushing, grayish-white mountain stream that looked as if it were covered with soapsuds. It wasn't that stream that turned the mill wheel, but a smaller one which came tumbling down the rocks on the other side of river. It ran through a reservoir dammed up by stones in the road beneath, and forced itself up with violence and speed into an enclosed wooden basin formed by a wide dam across the rushing river, where it turned the large mill wheel. When the water had piled up behind the dam it overflowed and made the path so wet and slippery that it was difficult for anyone who wanted to take this short cut to the mill to do so without falling into the water. However, the young Englishman thought he would try it.

Dressed in white like a mill worker, he was climbing the path one evening, following the light that shone from Babette's window. He had never learned to climb, and so almost went head first into the stream, but escaped with wet arms and spattered trousers. Soaking wet and covered with mud, he arrived beneath Babette's window, climbed the old linden tree, and there began to make a noise like an owl, which was the only bird he could even try to imitate. Babette heard it and peeped out through the thin curtains, but when she saw the man in white and realized who he was, her little heart pounded with fright, but also with anger. Quickly she put out her light, made sure the window was securely fastened, and then left him to his hooting and howling.

How terrible it would be, she thought, if Rudy were now at the mill! But Rudy wasn't at the mill—no, it was much worse—he was standing right under the tree. Loud words were spoken—angry words—they might come to blows, or even murder!

Babette hurried to open her window and called down to Rudy to go away, adding that she couldn't let him stay there.

"You won't let me stay here!" he cried. "Then this is an appointment! You're expecting some good friend—someone you'd rather see than me! Shame on you, Babette!"

"You are very nasty!" said Babette, and started to cry. "I hate you! Go away! Go away!"

"I haven't deserved anything like this," said Rudy as he went away, his cheeks burning, his heart on fire.

Babette threw herself on her bed and cried. "And you can think that of me, Rudy, of me who loves you so!"

She was angry, very angry, and that was good for her, for otherwise she would have been deeply hurt. As it was, she could fall asleep and enjoy youth's refreshing slumber.

EVIL POWERS

Rudy left Bex and started homeward, following the mountain path, with its cold fresh air, and where the snow is deep and the Ice Maiden reigns. The trees with their thick foliage were so far below him that they looked like potato tops; the pines and bushes became smaller; the Alpine roses were blanketed with snow, which lay in isolated patches like linen put out to be bleached. A single blue gentian stood in his path, and he crushed it with the butt of his gun. Higher up two chamois became visible, and Rudy's eyes sparkled as his thoughts turned into another course, but he wasn't near enough for a good shot. Still higher he climbed, to where only a few blades of grass grew between the rocks. The chamois passed calmly over the snowfields as Rudy pressed on.

The thick mists enshrouded him, and suddenly he found himself on the brink of a steep rock precipice. Then the rain began to fall in torrents. He felt a burning thirst; his head was hot, and his limbs were cold. He reached for his hunting flask, but found it was empty; he had not given it a thought when he rushed away, up the mountain. He had never been sick in his life, but now he suddenly felt that he was ill. He felt exhausted, and wanted only to lie down and sleep; but the rain was streaming down around him. He tried to pull himself out of it, but every object seemed to dance strangely before his eyes.

Suddenly he became aware of something he had never before seen in that place—a small, newly built hut leaning against the rock; and in the doorway stood a young girl. First he thought she was the schoolmaster's daughter, Annette, whom he had once kissed while dancing with her; but she wasn't Annette. But he was sure he had seen her before, perhaps near Grindelwald the evening he went home from the Interlaken shooting matches.

"How did you get here?" he asked.

"I'm home," she said. "Watching my flocks."

"Your flocks! Where do they find grass? There's nothing here but snow and rocks!"

"You know a lot about it!" she said and laughed. "A little way down behind here is a very nice pasture, where my goats go. I take good care of them, and never lose one. What's mine is mine!"

"You're very brave," said Rudy.

"And so are you," she answered.

"If you have any milk, please give me some; I have a terrible thirst."

"I have something much better than milk," she replied, "and you may have some. Yesterday some travelers came here with guides and left half a flask of wine behind them, such wine as you have never tasted. They won't come back for it, and I don't drink it, so you may have it."

She brought the wine, poured some into a wooden goblet, and gave it to Rudy.

"That's fine!" he said. "I have never tasted a wine so warming and reviving!" His eyes sparkled with life; a glowing thrill of happiness swept over him, as if every sorrow and vexation had vanished from his mind; a carefree feeling awoke in him.

"But surely you are Annette, the schoolmaster's daughter!" he exclaimed. "Give me a kiss!"

"Yes, but first give me that pretty ring you're wearing on your finger!"

"My engagement ring?"

"Yes, just that ring," said the girl, then refilling the goblet, she held it to his lips, and he drank again. A feeling of joy seemed to flow through his blood. The whole world was his, he seemed to think, so why torture himself! Everything is created for our pleasure and enjoyment. The stream of life is the stream of happiness; let yourself be carried away on it—that is joy. He looked at the young girl. She was Annette, and yet *not* Annette; but still less was she the magical phantom, as he had called the one he had met near Grindelwald. This girl on the mountain was fresh as newly fallen snow, as blooming as an Alpine rose, as lively as a young lamb; yet still she was formed from Adam's rib, a human being like Rudy himself.

He flung his arms about her and gazed into her marvelously clear eyes. It was only for a second, but how can that second be expressed or described in words? Was it the life of the soul or the life of death that took possessions of his being? Was he carried up high, or did he sink down into the deep and deathly icy crevasse, deeper, always deeper? He beheld the ice walls shining like blue-green glass; bottomless crevasses yawned about him; the waters dripped, sounding like the chimes of bells, and were as clear as a pearl glowing with pale blue flames. Then the Ice Maiden kissed him—a kiss that sent an icy shiver through his whole body. He gave a cry of pain, tore himself away from her, stumbled, and fell; all went dark before his eyes, but he opened them again. The powers of evil had played their game.

The Alpine girl was gone, and the sheltering hut was gone; water streamed down on the bare rocks, and snow lay everywhere. Rudy was shivering with cold, soaked through to the skin, and his ring was gone—the engagement ring Babette had given him. His gun lay on the snow beside him, but when he took it up and tried to fire it as a signal, it misfired. Damp clouds filled the chasm like thick masses of snow. Dizziness sat there, glaring at her helpless prey, while there rang through the deep crevasse beneath her a sound as if a mass of rock had fallen and was crushing and carrying away everything that obstructed its course.

Back at the miller's Babette sat and wept. It was six days since Rudy had been there—Rudy, who had been in the wrong, and should ask her pardon, for she loved him with all her heart.

AT THE MILLER'S HOUSE

"It's lot of nonsense with those people!" said the Parlor Cat to the Kitchen Cat. "It's all off now between Babette and Rudy. She just sits and cries, and he doesn't think about her any more."

"I don't like that," said the Kitchen Cat.

"I don't either," said the Parlor Cat. "But I'm not going to mourn about it. Babette can take golden whiskers for her sweetheart. He hasn't been here since the night he tried to climb onto the roof!"

The powers of evil carry out their purposes around us and within us. Rudy understood this, and thought about it. What was it that had gone on about him and inside him up there on the mountain? Was it sin or just a feverish dream? He had never known illness or fever before. While he blamed Babette, he also searched his own heart. He remembered the wild tornado, the hot whirlwind that had broken loose in there. Could he confess everything to Babette—every thought which in that hour of temptation almost brought about his action? He had lost her ring, and by that very loss she had won him back. Would she be able to confess to him? When his thoughts turned to her, so many memories crowded his mind that he felt that his heart was breaking. He saw her as a laughing, happy child, full of life; the many loving words she had addressed to him from the fullness of her heart gladdened his soul like a ray of light, and soon there was only sunshine there for Babette.

However, she would have to confess to him, and he would see that she did so.

So he went to the mill, and there was a confession; it began with a kiss, and ended with Rudy's being the sinner. His great fault was that he could have doubted for one moment Babette's faithfulness—*that* was very wicked of him! Such distrust, such violence, might bring misery to both of them. Yes, that was very true! Babette preached him a little sermon, which pleased her greatly and which was very becoming to her. But Rudy was right about one thing—the godmother's nephew was a babbler. She'd burn the book he had given her, and wouldn't keep the slightest thing that would remind her of him.

"Now that's all over with," said the Parlor Cat. "Rudy's back again, and they've made up; and they say that's the greatest of happiness."

"Last night," said the Kitchen Cat, "I heard the rats saying that their greatest happiness was to eat candle grease and have plenty of tainted bacon. Which of them should we believe, the lovers or the rats?"

"Neither of them," said the Parlor Cat. "That's always the safest."

Rudy's and Babette's greatest happiness was drawing near, the most beautiful day, as they call it, was coming—their wedding day!

But the wedding was not to take place in the church at Bex, nor in the miller's house; the godmother had asked that the party be held at her house, and that the ceremony be performed in the pretty little church at Montreux. And the miller was very insistent that they should agree to this arrangement, for he alone knew what the godmother intended giving the young couple—her wedding gift would be well worth such a small concession to her wishes. The day was agreed upon. They would go to Villeneuve the evening before, then proceed to Montreux by boat the next morning, so that the godmother's daughters would have time to dress the bride.

"I suppose there'll be a second ceremony in this house," said the Parlor Cat. "Or else I know I wouldn't give a mew for the whole business."

"There's going to be a feast here, too," said the Kitchen Cat. "The ducks have been killed, the pigeons plucked, and a whole deer is hanging on the wall. My mouth waters when I look at all the food. Tomorrow they start their journey."

Yes, tomorrow! That evening Rudy and Babette sat in the miller's house for the last time as an engaged couple. Outside, the evening glow was on the Alps; the vesper bells were chiming; and the daughters of the sun sang, "That which is best shall come to pass!"

VISIONS IN THE NIGHT

The sun had gone down, and the clouds lay low in the valley of the Rhone between the tall mountains; the wind blew from the south, an African wind; it suddenly sprang up over the high summits like a foehn, which swept the clouds away; and when the wind had fallen everything for a moment was perfectly still. The scattered clouds hung in fantastic shapes between the wooded hills skirting the rushing Rhone; they hung in the shapes of sea monsters of the prehistoric world, of eagles hovering in the air, of frogs leaping in a marsh; they settled down on the swift river and seemed to sail on it, yet they were floating in the air. The current swept along an uprooted pine tree, with the water making circles around it. It was Dizziness and some of her sisters dancing in circles on the foaming stream. The moon lighted up the snow-covered mountain peaks, the dark woods, and the strange white clouds—those visions of the night that seemed to be the powers of nature. The mountain peasant saw them through his window; they sailed past in great numbers before the Ice Maiden, who had come from her glacier palace. She was sitting on a frail boat, the uprooted pine, as the waters from the glacier carried her down the river to the open lake.

"The wedding guests are coming!" was sung and murmured in the air and in the water.

There were visions outside and visions inside. And Babette had a very strange dream.

It seemed to her that she had been married to Rudy for many years. He had gone chamois hunting, leaving her at home; and the young Englishman with the golden whiskers was sitting beside her. His eyes were passionate—his words seemed to have a magic power in them. He held out his hand to her, and she was obliged to follow him; they walked away from her home, always downward. And Babette felt a weight in her heart that became heavier every moment. She was committing a sin against Rudy—a sin against God Himself. And suddenly she found herself alone; her dress had been torn to pieces by thorns, and her hair had turned gray. In deep grief she looked upward, and saw Rudy on the edge of a mountainous ridge. She stretched up her arms to him, but dared neither pray nor call out to him; and neither would have been of any avail, for she soon discovered it was not Rudy, but only his cap and shooting jacket hanging on an alpenstock, as hunters often place them to deceive the chamois. In miserable grief Babette cried, "Oh, if I had only died on my wedding day—the happiest day of my life! Oh, Lord, my God, that would have been a blessing! That would have been the best thing that could have happened for me and Rudy. No one knows his future!" Then in godless despair she hurled herself down into the deep chasm. A thread seemed to break, and the echo of sorrowful tones was heard.

Babette awoke; the dream was ended, and although partly forgotten she knew it had been a frightful one and that she had dreamed about the young Englishman whom she had not seen or thought of for several months. She wondered if he still was at Montreux, and if she would see him at the wedding. A faint shadow passed over Babette's pretty mouth—her brows knitted; but soon there came a smile, and the sparkle returned to her eye. The sun was shining brightly outside, and tomorrow was her and Rudy's wedding day!

When she came down he was already in the parlor, and soon they set off for Villeneuve. They were both so happy, and so was the miller. He laughed and joked, and was in excellent humor, for he was a kind father and an honest soul.

"Now we are the masters of the house," said the Parlor Cat.

THE CONCLUSION

It was not yet evening when the three happy people reached Villeneuve and sat down to dinner. The miller settled himself in a comfortable armchair with his pipe and had a little nap. The young bridal couple went out of the town arm in arm, along the highway, under the wooded hills by the side of the deep blue-green lake. The clear water reflected the gray walls and heavy towers of gloomy-looking Chillon. The little island with its three acacias seemed quite close, looking like a bouquet lying on the lake.

"How lovely it must be over there!" said Babette, who again felt a great desire to go to the island; and her desire could be satisfied at once, for a boat was lying near the bank, and it was easy to undo the rope securing it. There was no one around of whom they could ask permission, so they got into the boat anyway.

Rudy knew how to use the oars. Like the fins of a fish, the oars divided the water, so pliant and yet so powerful, with a back for carrying and a mouth for swallowing—gentle, smiling, calmness itself, yet terrible and mighty in destruction. Foamy wake stretched out behind the boat, and in a few minutes they arrived at the little island, where they landed. There was just room for the two of them to dance.

Rudy whirled Babette around two or three times. Then they sat on the little bench under the drooping acacia and held each other's hands and looked deep into each other's eyes, while the last rays of the setting sun streamed about them. The pine forests on the mountains took on a purplish-red tint like that of blooming heather, and where the trees stopped and the bare rocks began, they glowed as if the mountain itself were transparent. The clouds in the sky glowed a brilliant crimson; the whole lake was like a fresh, blushing rose petal. As the shades of evening gathered, the snow-capped mountains of Savoy turned a dark blue, but the highest summits still shone like red lava and for a moment reflected their light on the mountains before the vast masses were lost in darkness. It was the Alpine glow, and Rudy and Babette thought they had never before seen so magnificent a sight. The snow-covered Dent du Midi glistened like the disk of the full moon when it rises above the horizon.

"Oh, what beauty! What happiness!" both of them said.

"Earth can give me no more," said Rudy. "An evening like this is like a whole life. How often have I realized my good fortune, as I realize it now, and thought that if everything ended for me at once now I have still had a happy life! What a blessed world this is! One day passes, and a new one, even more beautiful than the other, begins. Our Lord is infinitely good, Babette!"

"I'm so happy!" she said.

"Earth can give me no more," exclaimed Rudy. Then the vesper bells sounded from the Savoy mountains and the mountains of Switzerland. The dark-blue Jura stood up in golden splendor in the west.

"God give you all that is brightest and best!" exclaimed Babette.

"He will," said Rudy. "Tomorrow I shall have that wish. Tomorrow you'll be wholly mine—my own lovely, little wife!"

"The boat!" Babette suddenly cried.

For the boat that was to take them back had broken loose and was drifting away from the island.

"I'll get it!" said Rudy, and he stripped off his coat and boots, plunged into the lake, and swam with vigorous strokes after the boat.

The clear blue-green water from the mountain glacier was icy and deep. Rudy looked down into the depths; he took only a single glance, and yet, he thought he saw a gold ring trembling, glittering, wavering there! He thought of his lost engagement ring, and the ring became larger and spread out into a glittering circle, within which appeared the clear glacier. Endless deep chasms yawned about it, and the dropping water tinkled like the sound of bells and glowed with pale blue flames. In a second he beheld what will take us many long words to describe!

Young hunters and young girls, men and women who had once fallen into the glacier's crevasses, stood there as in life, with open eyes and smiling lips, while far below them arose from buried villages the chimes of church bells. The congregation knelt beneath the church roofs; icicles made the organ pipes, and the mountain torrents furnished the music. And the Ice Maiden sat on the clear, transparent ground. She stretched herself up toward Rudy and kissed his feet, and there shot through his limbs a deadly chill like an electric shock—ice and fire, one could not be distinguished from the other in that brief touch.

"Mine! Mine!" sounded around him and within him. "I kissed you when you were little—kissed you on the mouth! Now I kiss you on your toes and your heels—now you belong to me!"

And he disappeared in the clear blue water.

All was still. The church bells had ceased their ringing; their last tones had died away with the glow on the red clouds above.

"You are mine!" sounded from the depths below. "You are mine!" resounded from beyond the heights—from infinity itself!

How wonderful to pass from love to love, from Earth to Heaven!

A thread seemed to break, and sorrowful tones echoed around. The icy kiss of death had conquered what was mortal; the prelude to the drama of life had ended before the play itself had begun. And discord had resolved itself into harmony.

Do you call this a sad story?

Poor Babette! For her it was the hour of anguish. The boat drifted farther and farther away. No one on the mainland knew that the bridal couple had crossed over to the little island. Evening came on, the clouds gathered, and darkness settled down. Alone, despairing and crying, she stood there. A storm broke out; lightning flashed over the Jura mountains and over the peaks of Savoy and Switzerland; from all sides came flash after flash, while one peal of thunder followed the other for minutes at a time. One instant the lightning was so vivid that the surroundings were bright as day—every single vine stem was as distinct as at high noon—and in the next instant everything was plunged back into the blackest darkness. The lightning formed circles and zigzagged, then darted into the lake; and the increasing noise of the rolling thunder echoed from the surrounding mountains. On the mainland the boats had been drawn far up the beach, while all living things sought shelter. And now the rain poured down in torrents.

"Where can Rudy and Babette be in this terrible storm?" said the miller.

Babette sat with folded hands, her head in her lap, utterly worn out by grief, tears, and screams for help.

"In the deep water," she said to herself, "far down there as if under a glacier, *he* lies!"

Then she thought of what Rudy had told her about his mother's death, and of his escape, how he was lifted up out of the cleft of the glacier almost dead. "The Ice Maiden has him again!"

Then there came a flash of lightning as dazzling as the rays of the sun on white snow. Babette jumped up; at that moment the lake rose like a shining glacier; there stood the Ice Maiden, majestic, bluish, pale, glittering, with Rudy's corpse at her feet.

"Mine!" she said, and again everything was darkness and torrential rain.

"Horrible!" groaned Babette. "Ah, why should he die when our day of happiness was so near? Dear God, make me understand; shed light into my heart! I cannot understand the ways of your almighty power and wisdom!"

And God enlightened her heart. A memory—a ray of mercy—her dream of the night before—all rushed vividly through her mind. She remembered the words she had spoken, the wish for the best for herself and Rudy.

"Pity me! Was it the seed of sin in my heart? Was my dream, a glimpse into the future, whose course had to be violently changed to save me from guilt? How miserable I am!"

In the pitch-black night she sat weeping. And now in the deep stillness around her she seemed to hear the last words he had spoken here, "Earth can give me no more." They had been spoken in the fullest of joy; they echoed in the depths of great sorrow.

A few years have passed since that night. The lake smiles; its shores are smiling; the vines yield luscious grapes; steamboats with waving pennants glide swiftly by; pleasure boats with their two sails unfurled skim like white butterflies over the mirrored water; the railway beyond Chillon is open now, leading far into the valley of the Rhone. At every station strangers get out, studying in their little red guidebooks what sights they should see. They visit Chillon, see the little island with the three acacias, and read in their books about a bridal couple who in 1856 rowed over to it one evening—how not until the next morning could the bride's despairing cries be heard on the mainland.

But the guidebooks tell nothing about Babette's quiet life in her father's house—not at the mill, for strangers live there now—in the pretty house near the railway station, where many an evening she gazes from her window beyond the chestnut trees to the snowy mountains over which Rudy had loved to range. In the evening hours she can see the Alpine glow—up there where the daughters of the sun settle down, and sing again their song about the traveler whose coat the whirlwind snatched off, taking it, but not the man himself.

There is a rosy glow upon the mountain's snowfields; there is a rosy tint in every heart in which lives the thought, "God wills what is best for us!" But it is not always revealed to us as it was revealed to Babette in her dream.

THE PSYCHE (1861)

A t dawn, when the clouds are red, a great star shines, the beautiful morning star. Her beams tremble on the white wall, as if she would like to write there the story of all she has seen during the thousands of years she has watched our revolving earth.

Listen to one of her stories.

A little while ago—a few centuries ago, which, though a long time to you men, is just a little while to me—my beams watched a young artist. He lived in the papal state, in one of the world's great cities, Rome. Many things there have changed since those days, but they haven't changed as quickly as the human being changes from childhood to old age. The eternal city was then, as it is now, a city of ruins. The fig tree and the laurel tree grew among the overturned marble columns and over the destroyed baths, their walls still inlaid with gold. The Coliseum was a ruin. Church bells rang, and fragrant incense filled the air, while processions with magnificent canopies and lighted candles passed through the streets. It was a beautiful church service honoring the great and inspired arts. The world's greatest painter, Raphael, and the greatest sculptor of his time, Michelangelo, lived in Rome then. The Pope himself admired them both and honored them with his visits. Indeed, art was acknowledged, honored, and rewarded; but not all great and noble things were known and seen in those days, any more than they are now.

In a little, narrow street stood an old house that had formerly been a temple, and here lived a young artist; he was poor, and he was unknown. Of course, he had plenty of friends, other artists, young in mind and thought, who kept telling him he was blessed with ability and talent and that he was a fool for having no more self-confidence. Anything he formed out of clay he always broke into pieces; he was never satisfied with what he did; nor did he ever finish anything, which, of course, one must do to become known, acclaimed, and to earn money.

"You're a dreamer!" his friends said. "And that's your misfortune. That is because you haven't enjoyed life the way life should be enjoyed. Youth and life go hand in hand. Look at the great master Raphael, whom the Pope honors—does he live the way you do?"

Yes, they had much to say, all of them, aroused by their youth and outlook. They wanted the young artist to join them in riotous pleasures, and sometimes he would succumb to a moment of desire; his blood would become warm; he would join in the lively talk and laugh loudly with the others. But the thought of the "life that Raphael lived," as they called it, disappeared like morning dew when he saw that master's great pictures before him and felt the power of God's holy and divine gift. And when he stood in the Vatican among the noble and beautiful figures that great masters had shaped from marble so very long ago, his breast would heave with joy and longing. He could feel some power stirring within him, great, good, holy, and uplifting, and he longed to create such forms, to carve them out of marble. He wanted to create an image of what he felt in his heart—but how, and in what shape? The soft clay molded easily under his fingers, but the next day he would always break his work to pieces.

One day he happened to pass by one of the rich palaces, of which Rome has so many; he paused at the large open gates and inside saw colonnades adorned with statues, surrounding a little garden that was filled with the loveliest roses. Large calla lilies with rich green leaves grew about a fountain in a marble basin, where clear water splashed. A young girl, daughter of that princely house, glided through the garden and past the fountain. How beautiful, how graceful and delicate she was! He had never seen such a beautiful woman before. Yes, once! He had seen one painted by Raphael, painted as Psyche, in one of Rome's palaces. Yes, her portrait was there—and here she was alive!

He carried her image away in his heart and thoughts; and when he had returned to his humble room he molded a Psyche in clay. The figure was the rich, noble young daughter of Rome, and for the first time he was satisfied with his work. It had expression and feeling; no longer was his ideal vague and shadowy. And when his friends saw his work they were delighted. Here was the work of a true genius, they knew, and the world would acknowledge.

Clay is lifelike, but it has not the whiteness or durability of marble; Psyche must receive her life from the precious block. This would not be too costly for the young artist, since a large block had been lying in the yard for many years; it had belonged to his parents. Broken glass, stalks of cabbage, and pieces of artichoke had been flung over it, soiling its purity; but inside it was still as white as the mountain snow. From this block Psyche would lift her wings.

Now, it happened one day—the morning star didn't tell me this, for she never saw it, but I know it, anyway—that a party of Roman nobles visited the narrow, humble street. The carriage stopped a little way off, and the visitors came to inspect the young artist's work, having heard of it by accident. And who were these distinguished strangers? Poor young man! Or should we say happy young man? The young maiden herself stood in his room, and how she smiled when her father said, "Why, it's you, to the life!" That smile, that strange look she gave the young artist! It cannot be described; it was a look that uplifted, ennobled, but at the same time crushed him!

"Psyche must be completed in marble," said the rich gentleman. These were words of life for the heavy marble block, and in a sense for the dead clay, just as they were words of life for the young man. "When you have finished it I shall buy it," added the noble gentleman.

Now a new life began in that humble studio. Life and happiness shone there, and the hustle and bustle of business kept them company. The twinkling morning star watched the progress of the work. It seemed that the clay had taken on life while *she* had been there and bent in loveliness over her image with its familiar features. "Now I know what life is!" beamed the artist. "It's love! It is being lifted above yourself, the rapture of losing yourself in beauty! What my friends call life and pleasure is unreal and as fleeting as a bubble; they know nothing of the pure, heavenly altar wine that initiates us into life!"

The marble block was placed, and the chisel cut away large pieces. Careful measurements were made, and the work proceeded. Little by little, the stone was transformed into a figure of beauty, Psyche, as beautiful and perfect as God's own image in the young girl. That weighty stone was changed into a light, dancing, aerial form, a charming Psyche, with the smile of divine innocence that had captured the young sculptor's heart.

The morning star saw it and understood all that was stirring in the young man's mind, understood the changing color of his cheeks, the look in his eyes, while he strove to utilize the gift God had granted him.

"You are a master like those in the time of the Greeks," said his friends. "Soon the whole world will be admiring your Psyche!"

"My Psyche!" he repeated. "Mine! Yes, she must be mine! I am an artist like the mighty ones of olden times! God has given me this gift in order to raise me to the level of the nobility!" He fell upon his knees and cried in gratitude to God; but he soon forgot him and thought only of her and her image in marble, his Psyche who stood there as though carved from snow, blushing in the morning sunlight.

He went to see the living, moving Psyche, whose words were like music; he could bring her the news that the marble Psyche was completed at last. He walked through the courtyard, with its fountain trickling through dolphin shapes into the marble basin, where the calla lilies and fresh roses bloomed, and into a great, lofty antechamber, its walls splendid with tapestries and coats of arms. Handsomely dressed servants, haughty, and strutting like sleigh horses with their bells, passed to and fro; some were even stretched out lazily and overbearingly on the carved wooden benches, as much at their ease as if they were the masters of the house.

He explained his errand and was led up the carpeted marble staircase. Statues lined either side. He passed through splendid aparments hung with magnificent pictures and paved with shining mosaic; the wealth and show about him left him almost breathless. But his courage soon returned when he was kindly, almost cordially, received by the dignified, courteous old prince who, after a brief talk, bade him visit the young *signorina*, his daughter, who wished to see him. Again he was conducted by servants through beautiful halls and chambers, until he was ushered into a room whereof she herself was the pomp and splendor.

She spoke to him, and no solemn, churchly music could have greater power to melt the heart and raise the soul. He took her hand and pressed it to his lips; no rose could be so soft, but that light touch seemed to overpower him with a strong, magical spell. Words he never thought to speak rushed from his lips. He did not know what he was saying; is the volcano conscious when the burning lava flows from it? He told her of his love.

She drew herself up before him, astounded, offended, and haughty; then an expression of disgust, as though she had accidentally touched a wet, slimy frog, passed over her features; her cheeks flushed, and her lips grew pale; her eyes flashed and yet were as dark as the night.

"Maniac!" she said. "Away! Out of my sight!" And as she turned her back on him, her lovely face had the look of that legendary beauty with the stony face and the snakes in her hair.

Like a sleepwalker, he made his way downstairs, into the streets, and at last reached his home. Then a fit of wild rage and pain swept over him; he seized his hammer and, raising it on high, was about to smash his beautiful marble image into a thousand pieces. But in his madness he had not noticed that his friend Angelo stood right behind him. With a strong grip he caught his arm, crying, "Are you crazy? What's the matter?" They wrestled, but Angelo was the stronger. Breathing heavily, the young sculptor flung himself into a chair.

"What has happened?" asked Angelo. "Pull yourself together! Tell me!"

But what could he tell him? What could he say? And since Angelo was unable to make him talk, he gave him one of his usual lectures.

"Why don't you stop your eternal dreaming! Be a man like your friends. Don't be an idealist; if you do you'll have a breakdown. Get a little tipsy; then you'll sleep well. Let a beautiful girl be your doctor. The girl from the Campagna is as beautiful as your princess in the marble castle. They are both daughters of Eve, and you can't tell them apart. You follow your Angelo—your angel and me, your angel of life! The time will come when you're old; your body will crumble, and some sunny day when everyone is laughing and gay, you'll lie like a withered straw. I don't believe what the ministers tell us about life beyond the grave; that's a beautiful imagination, a fairy tale for children, and pleasant enough if you can make yourself believe it. I do not live in imagination; I live in reality. Come along! Be a man!"

And he was able to drag him along, for at that moment the young artist felt a desire to tear himself loose from his old self; there was fire in his blood, a change in his soul. And so he followed Angelo.

In the outskirts of Rome there was a tavern frequented by artists. It was built in the ruins of an old Roman bath chamber. Large yellow lemons hung down among dark, shining leaves, partly covering the old red-yellow walls. The tavern was in the form of a deep vault, almost like a cave in the ruins. A lamp burned inside before a picture of the Madonna. A large fire blazed in the fireplace, and food was being fried, cooked, and roasted. Outside, under the lemon and laurel trees, stood two tables, all prepared.

The two young men were happily, gaily received by their friends. They all had a little to eat but a lot to drink. They sang and played the guitar, and then the dancing started. A couple of young girls from Rome, who worked for the artists as models, joined in the dancing and festivities—two charming girls, not so lovely as Psyche, not fine, beautiful roses, but fresh and colorful carnations.

How warm the weather was, even at sunset! There was fire in the blood, fire in the air, fire in every look! The air was swimming with gold and roses; life was gold and roses!

"Come now, enjoy yourself, now that you have finally joined our company."

"I've never felt so happy!" said the young artist. "You're right—you're all right—I have been a fool, a dreamer. Man belongs to reality, not to fantasy."

To the accompaniment of singing and the playing of guitars, the young artists left the tavern and then walked through the narrow streets in the clear, starlit evening. The two girls, the colorful carnations, were with them.

In Angelo's room, their voices became quieter but no less fiery.

"Apollo! Jupiter! Into your heaven and glory I am carried! The flower of life has blossomed forth in my heart this very moment!"

Yes, it blossomed—broke, withered, and a nauseating fume whirled from it, blinding his sight; his thoughts went blank as the firework of truth burned out, and everything was dark.

He reached home and flung himself down on his cot. "Shame!" This came from his own mouth, right from the bottom of his heart. "Away! Out of my sight!" These, his living Psyche's words, resounded in his heart as they came from his lips. Overcome with fatigue, he buried his face in the pillow and slept.

Next morning when he arose he tried to collect his thoughts. What had happened? Had it all been a dream—her repulse, his visit to the tavern, and the evening spent with his friends and their girls? No, it had all happened; facts hitherto unknown to him were now revealed. The bright morning star shone through the purple-colored air onto the marble Psyche. He felt unworthy to look upon the symbol of immortality and drew a curtain over the statue; he could no longer look at his own work.

He was silent, gloomy, lost in reverie, the entire day. He never knew what might be going on outside, and no one knew what stirred within that human heart.

Days passed and weeks passed, and the nights were endless. At last one morning the twinkling star saw him rise from his bed, pale, and, trembling with fever, go to his marble statue, lift the veiling curtain, gaze on his work with one last, sad, yearning look, and then, staggering under its weight, drag the statue down into the garden. Here was a ruined, dried-up well or hole, and he lowered his Psyche into it, threw dirt over it, then scattered a lot of dry sticks and nettles over the spot, so that no one could tell the earth had been disturbed. "Away! Out of my sight!" The was his brief burial service.

The morning star looked down through the rose-colored sky, and her beams quivered on two big tears on the young man's pale cheeks. Fever-striken, deathly ill, he lay on his bed.

From a nearby convent, Brother Ignatius came to see him daily as physician, nurse, and friend. He brought to the sick man the consolation of religion, spoke about the peace and happiness of the church, spoke of man's sin and the peace and blessings of God. And his words were like warm sunbeams falling on the wet, fermented ground. They lifted the mist and showed him life in all its reality, with its missteps and disappointments. The Goddess of Art is a witch who carries us toward vanity, toward earthly pleasures. We are untrue to ourselves, to our friends, and to God. "Taste and ye shall be as gods," the serpent always says within us.

Everything was clear to him now; he had found the road to truth and peace. In church, God's light and wisdom were ever present, and in the monastery he would find the peace where the tree of humanity could grow through all eternity.

His mind was made up, and Brother Ignatius supported him in his decision. The young artist became a servant of God. How kindly, how cordially, he was received by the brethren; how festive it was when he took his vows! And when he stood in his little cell at sunset that evening, and looked through his open window over old Rome with its ruined temples and its wonderful but dead Coliseum, and saw the spring blossoms of the acacias, the fresh shoots of the evergreen, the multitude of roses, the shiny citron and orange trees, and the fanlike palms, he was thrilled with a calm happiness he had never felt before. The wide, still campagna stretched as far as the bluish, snow-capped mountains, which seemed painted on the sky; the whole landscape in its quiet beauty seemed a floating dream.

Yes, life in a cloister is a life of long, monotonous years. He realized that temptation came from within rather than from without. Why did worldly thoughts always come over him? He punished his body for it, but that was of no avail.

One day, after many years had passed, he met Angelo, who recognized him.

"Man!" he said. "Yes, it *is* you! Are you happy now? Why, you have sinned against God and thrown away His divine gift, wasted your wonderful talent! What have you gained? What have you found? Are you not living a dream, a religion that's simply in your head? Why, it is all a dream, a fantasy, only beautiful thoughts!"

"Get thee behind me, Satan!" said the monk, and walked away from Angelo.

"He is a devil, a devil in flesh and blood!" mumbled the monk. "Once I gave him my little finger, and he grabbed my whole hand! But," he sighed, "the evil is within me as it is within him."

Torn and conscience-stricken, he cried out, "Oh, Lord, Lord! Be merciful and restore in me my faith!"

His weary eyes grew dim. The church bells tolled for him—the dead. He was buried in earth brought from Jerusalem, his dust mingling with the dust of pious pilgrims.

Many years later the bones were disinterred, a rosary was placed in the fleshless hands, and the skeleton was set up in a niche, with other similar ghastly forms, to make room for newcomers, as is the custom in convent graveyards. And the sun shone down on the grisly sight, while inside Mass was read and incense burned.

With the passing of years, the bones of the skeletons crumbled. And in time the skulls were gathered and placed along the outside church wall. There they stood, his among them, in the burning sunlight. Nobody knew his or their names. And look! Something alive was moving in the eye socket of his skull! What was it? A spotted lizard slipped in and out of the hollow skull, back and forth through the big empty eyeholes. It was now the only thing alive where once great thoughts, happy dreams, and love for the arts had been, and where hope for eternity had lived. The lizard played, then disappeared. The skull crumbled to dust.

Centuries passed, but the bright morning star still shone, big and clear, as it had for thousands of years, and the dawn clouds were still as fresh as roses, as red as blood.

A stately convent now occupied the site of the ruined temple on the little narrow street. It happened that a young nun, one of the inmates of this convent, died, and at early dawn her grave was dug in the garden. Suddenly the spade struck against what seemed to be a stone, and a dazzling whiteness gleamed through the dirt—it was white marble rounded into the perfect form of a shoulder. The spade was guided with tender care, until the head of a woman was uncovered, then butterfly wings. From the grave in which the young nun was to be buried there was lifted into the rosy light of dawn the form of lovely Psyche, chiseled from white marble. "How beautiful, how perfect it is!" people cried. "It is the work of some great master!" But whose work could it have been? No one could say; no one knew anything about it save the morning star that had twinkled for so many thousands of years; it alone had witnessed the sculptor's earthly life, his sufferings, and his weakness.

The sculptor's body had long since returned to dust, but the work in which God's gracious gift to him had found expression—the masterpiece on which he had lavished the treasures of heart and soul—remained, lived still, to be known, admired, and loved by people who never heard his name.

And in the rose-colored sky the bright morning star twinkled down upon Psyche, upon the innocent smile parting her lips, and upon the admiring eyes of the crowd gathered around to gaze on that glorious symbol of the immortal soul.

What is earthly will crumble and be forgotten; only the eternal star will remember it. What is heavenly will shine through ages to come. And so will Psyche.

THE SNAIL AND THE ROSEBUSH (1861)

Around the garden ran a hedge of hazelnut bushes, and beyond it lay fields and meadows with cows and sheep; but in the middle of the garden stood a blooming Rosebush, and under it sat a Snail, who had a lot inside his shell—namely, himself.

"Wait till my time comes," it said. "I'll do a great deal more than grow roses; more than bear nuts; or give milk, like cows and the sheep!"

"I expect a great deal from you," said the Rosebush. "May I dare ask when this is going to happen?"

"I'll take my time," said the Snail. "You're always in such a hurry! That does not arouse expectations!"

Next year the Snail lay in almost the same spot, in the sunshine beneath the Rose Tree, which was budding and bearing roses as fresh and as new as ever. And the Snail crept halfway out of its shell, stretched out its horns and drew them back in again.

"Everything looks just as it did last year. No progress at all; the Rose Tree sticks to its roses, and that's as far as it gets."

The summer passed; the autumn came. The Rose Tree still bore buds and roses till the snow fell. The weather became raw and wet, and the Rose Tree bent down toward the ground. The Snail crept into the ground.

Then a new year began, and the roses came out again, and the Snail did, too.

"You're an old Rosebush now," the Snail said. "You must hurry up and die, because you've given the world all that's in you. Whether it has meant anything is a question that I haven't had time to think about, but this much is clear enough—you've done nothing at all for your inner development, or you would certainly have produced something else. How can you answer that? You'll soon be nothing but a stick. Can you understand what I'm saying?"

"You frighten me!" said the Rosebush. "I never thought about that at all."

"No, you have never taken the trouble to think of anything. Have you ever considered yourself, why you bloomed, and how it happens, why just in that way and in no other?"

"No," said the Rosebush. "I was just happy to blossom because I couldn't do anything else. The sun was warm and the air so refreshing. I drank of the clear dew and the strong rain; I breathed, I lived. A power rose in me from out of the earth; a strength came down from up above; I felt an increasing happiness, always new, always great, so I had to blossom over and over again. That was my life; I couldn't do anything else."

"You have led a very easy life," said the Snail.

"Certainly. Everything was given to me," said the Rosebush. "But still more was granted to you. You're one of those with a deep, thoughtful nature, one of those highly gifted minds that will astonish the world."

"I've no intention of doing anything of the sort!" said the Snail. "The world means nothing to me. What do I have to do with the world? I have enough to do with myself and within myself."

"But shouldn't all of us on Earth give the best we have to others and offer whatever is in our power? Yes, I've only been able to give roses. But you? You who are so richly gifted—what have you given to the world? What do you intend to give?"

"What have I given? What do I intend to give? I spit at the world. It's no good! It has nothing to do with me. Keep giving your roses; that's all you can do! Let the hazel bush bear nuts, let the cows and sheep give milk. They each have their public; but I have mine inside myself. I retire within myself, and there I shall stay. The world means nothing to me." And so the Snail withdrew into his house and closed up the entrance behind him.

"That's so sad," said the Rose Tree. "I can't creep into myself, no matter how much I want to; I must go on bearing roses. Their petals fall off and are blown away by the wind, although once I saw one of the roses laid in a mother's hymnbook, and one of my own roses was placed on the breast of a lovely young girl, and another was kissed by a child in the first happiness of life. It did me good; it was a true blessing. Those are my recollections—my life!"

So the Rose Tree bloomed on in innocence, and the Snail loafed in his house—the world meant nothing to him.

And years rolled by.

The Snail had turned to earth in the earth, and the Rose Tree had turned to earth in the earth. Even the rose of memory in the hymnbook was withered, but in the garden new rosebushes bloomed, and new snails crept into their houses and spat at the world, for it meant nothing to them.

Shall we read this story all over again? It'll never be different.

THE OLD CHURCH BELL (1861)

In the German country of Württemberg, where the beautiful acacia trees bloom beside the highways and the apple and pear trees bend down in autumn under the weight of their ripe blessings, there lies the little town of Marbach. It belongs to the class of quite unimportant towns, but it is located in a beautiful spot near the Neckar, the river that flows swiftly past towns and green vineyards and old knights' castles, to join its waters with those of the proud Rhine.

It was late one year; the vines had red leaves; showers fell, and the cold winds increased. This was not a happy time for the poor people. The days were dark, but it was darker still within the cramped old houses. One of these stood with its gabled end toward the street, with low windows, poor and humble in appearance; and poor indeed was the family that lived there, yet courageous and diligent, with the love and fear of God within their hearts.

God was soon to give them one more child. The hour of its birth had come; the mother lay in pain and need. From the church tower came the sound of chiming bells, so deep, so festive. It was a holiday, and the solemn ringing of the bells filled the heart of the praying woman with faith and devotion; she lifted her soul to God in fervent prayer, and at that moment her little son was born; and she was happy beyond words. The bell from the church tower seemed to send forth her joy over town and country. Two bright baby eyes gazed up at her, and the little one's hair shone as if it were gilded. On that gloomy November day the child had been welcomed into the world by the chiming bells; the mother and father kissed it and wrote in their Bible, "The tenth of November, 1759, God gave us a son," adding later that he had received at his baptism the names, "Johann Christoph Friedrich."

What became of the little fellow, the poor boy from the humble town of Marbach?

At that time nobody knew, not even the old church bell high in its belfry, though it had first rung and sung for him, that he should one day sing that most beautiful song about "The Bell."

And the little boy grew, and the world grew larger about him; the parents moved to another town, but some dear friends of theirs still remained in Marbach; and thus it happened that mother and son returned there one day for a visit. The boy was still only six years old, but already he knew parts of the Bible and the pious old hymns; many an evening while seated on his little cane stool, he had heard his father read Gellert's *Fables* and the poem about the Messiah; hot tears had come into the boy's eyes, and his sister had cried at hearing of him who had suffered death on the Cross of Golgotha, that he might save us.

At the time of their first visit to Marbach the town had not changed very much—in fact, it was not very long since they had left it. The houses stood exactly as before, with their pointed gables, sloping walls, and low windows; but there were new graves in the churchyard; and there, down in the grass, close by the wall, lay the old church bell, fallen from its high position. It had developed a flaw and could ring no longer, and a new one had been put up in its place.

The mother and son had entered the churchyard and stood still before the old bell, while she told the little boy how this bell had performed its duty for centuries; it had pealed at baptisms, and joyful weddings, and funerals. Its tones had told of joy and of the horrors of fire; yes, the bell had sung of the most important moments in human life.

And never did the child forget what his mother told him that day; it sounded within his breast until, when he was grown to be a man, he could pour it out in song. And the mother told him how this old bell had pealed comfort and joy to her in her hour of fear, had rung and sung when her little boy was given to her. The child looked almost with awe at the grand old bell; he stooped over and kissed it as it lay there, old and broken and cast aside among grass and nettles.

And it lingered in the memory of that little boy, as he grew up in poverty, tall and thin, with reddish hair and a freckled face.

Yes, that's what he looked like, but his eyes were as clear and blue as the deep water. And how did he get on? Well, he had been lucky, enviably lucky. He had been received graciously into the military school, and even into the section where the children of the rich people were. This was an honor, a piece of rare good fortune; and he wore top boots, a stiff collar, and a powdered wig. He was taught under the system of "March! Halt! Front!" This was likely to result in something!

The old church bell would probably someday go into the smelting furnace, and what would become of it next? Well, nobody could tell that, and nobody could tell, either, what would come from the bell in the breast of the young man. There was a turmoil within him; it rang and echoed and strained to sound forth into the wide world. The more cramped the space within the school walls, the more deafening the commands of "March! Halt! Front!" the more strongly it rang within the youth's breast. What he felt he sang to his comrades, and it was heard beyond the boundaries of the country; but it was not for this that he had received a scholarship, clothing, and food. He already had the number of the screw he was to be in the great watchwork that we all belong to. How little we understand ourselves, and how then shall others, even the best of them, understand us? But it is the pressure that forms the precious gem. The pressure was here; would the world in the course of time be able to recognize the precious gem?

There was a great festival in the capital of the country. Thousands of lamps glittered, and rockets flamed; people still remember that splendor, remember it because of him who in tears and sorrow tried then to escape unnoticed to foreign soil. He must leave his native land, his mother, and all his loved ones far behind, or perish in the stream of commonplace life.

But the old bell was well off; it lay hidden in the shelter of the church wall of Marbach. As the wind swept over it, it could have told of him at whose birth the bell had rung; it could have told how coldly it had blown upon him as, weary and exhausted, he sank down in the forest of a neighboring country, with all his treasures, all his hopes for the future, in some written pages of *Fiesco*. The wind could have told how, when he read it aloud, his only patrons, artists all of them, stole away and amused themselves by playing ninepins. The wind could have told of the pale fugitive who lived for weeks and months in the miserable inn, where the landlord was noisy and drank, and where vulgar merriment took place while he sang of the Ideal. Hard days, dark days! The heart itself must suffer and understand what it would sing to the world.

Dark days and cold nights passed over the old bell, and it did not feel them; but the bell within the human breast is sensitive to these miseries. What happened to the young man? What happened to the old bell? Well, the bell went far away, farther than its sound could ever be heard even from its high tower; the young man—ah, yes, the bell within his breast sounded farther into distant lands than ever his foot would ever tread or his eyes ever see; it sounded and resounded across the ocean and around Earth.

But first you must hear about the church bell. It was taken away from Marbach and sold for old copper, and now it was to go into a smelting furnace in Bavaria. How did it come there, and when? Well, this the bell itself may tell you, if it can—it's of no great importance; but it is certain that it came to the capital of Bavaria. Many years had passed since it fell from the tower; and now it was to be melted down, to become part of the casting of a great monument, a statue in honor of one of the German people's great men. Now listen to how it all came about. Strange and beautiful things do happen in this world!

Up in Denmark, on one of the green islands where the beech tree grows and there are many ancient Viking graves, there once lived a very poor little boy who wore wooden shoes and used to carry the meals, wrapped up in an old piece of cloth, to his father who worked on the wharves, carving figureheads for ships. This poor child had become his country's pride; he carved out of marble such wonderful things that they amazed the whole world, and to him the noble task was given to shape from clay a majestic and beautiful figure that would be cast in bronze, a statue of him whose name his father wrote in the Bible, Johann Christoph Friedrich.

And the bronze flowed glowing into the mold. Nobody thought of where the old church bell had come from, or of its sounds that had died away—the bell, too, flowed into the mold and became the head and breast of the statue that now stands unveiled before the old palace in Stuttgart. There it stands, on the spot where he whom it represents walked in life, amid strife and struggles, oppressed by the world around him—he, the boy from Marbach, the pupil from the military school, the fugitive, the immortal poet of Germany, who sang of the liberator of Switzerland and the Heaven-inspired Maid of France.

It was a beautiful sunny day, and flags waved from the towers and roofs of the royal town of Stuttgart. The church bells chimed in holiday joy; only one bell was silent, but it shone in the bright sunlight, shone from the breast and face of that noble statue. It was just a hundred years since that day when, in Marbach's church tower, it had pealed joy and comfort to the suffering mother when in that lowly house she gave birth to her child—who would one day be a rich man, whose treasures the world blesses, the heart-thrilling poet of noble women, the great and glorious singer—Johann Christoph Friedrich Schiller.

THE SILVER SHILLING (1861)

There was once a shilling; it came out bright and shiny from the mint, and sprang up, shouting, "Hurrah! Now I'm going out into the wide world!" And into the wide world he went. The child held it with soft, tender hands; the miser clutched it with cold, clammy fingers; the old man turned it over many times before letting it go; while the youth immediately passed it along. The Shilling was of silver, with very little copper in it; already it had been in the world for a whole year now—that is, in the country where it was made. But one day it started to travel to foreign lands; it was the last native coin in the purse that the traveling gentleman had with him. He himself didn't know he had this coin until it happened to come between his fingers.

"Why, here's a shilling from home I still have," he said. "It can make the trip with me."

And the Shilling rattled and jumped for joy as it was put back into the purse. So here it lay among foreign companions, who came and went, each making a place for the next one. Only the Shilling from home always stayed in the purse, which was a mark of distinction.

Several weeks passed, and the Shilling was far out in the world, without knowing exactly where it was, although it did hear that the other coins were French or Italian. One said they were in a certain town, another reported that they had reached another place, but the Shilling hadn't any idea about it. Anyone who keeps his head in a bag can't see a thing; and that was the case with the Shilling.

But as it lay there one day it noticed that the purse was not completely shut, so it sneaked forward to the opening to take a peek. It shouldn't have done that, but it was full of curiosity, and people often have to pay for that. It slipped out into the trouser pocket, and when the purse was taken out that night the Shilling remained behind and was taken with the clothes to the hall closet. There it dropped on the floor; no one heard it, and no one saw it.

Next morning the clothes were returned to the room; the gentleman put them on, and started on his journey again, but the Shilling was left behind. It was found, required to do service again, and was sent out with three other coins.

"It's an interesting thing to look about you in the world," thought the Shilling, "and to get to know different people and customs."

"What kind of coin is that?" said someone at that very moment. "That's not a genuine coin! It's a fake! It's no good!"

Yes, now began the real history of the Shilling, as told by itself.

"'False! No good!' Those words really hurt me," said the Shilling. "I knew I was made of good silver, had a good ring and a genuine stamp on me. People were certainly mistaken; they couldn't mean me! But they did mean me; I was the one they called false and no good! 'I must get rid of that fellow in the dark!' said the man I belonged to. So I was passed on at night, and then again chided in broad daylight. 'False—no good! We must hurry up and get rid of it!'"

And the Shilling trembled in its master's fingers each time it was to be passed on as a native coin.

"What a wretched shilling I am! What good is my silver to me, or my value, or my stamp, if all these things are considered worthless? The world gives you only such value as it chooses. It must be really dreadful to have a bad conscience, and to sneak about in the path of evil, if I, who am quite innocent, can feel so wretched just because I have my looks against me!

"Each time they brought me out I shuddered at the thought of the eyes that would glare at me, because I knew I would be rejected and flung back on the counter like a liar and a fraud.

"One time I came into the hands of a poor old woman, who received me as wages for a hard day's toil and labor, and she couldn't get rid of me at all. Nobody would accept me, and I was a real worry to the old woman.

"'I shall certainly have to fool somebody with this shilling,' she said, 'for I can't afford to keep a false shilling. I'll pass him on to the rich baker; he'll be able to stand the loss better than I can; but still it is an injustice I will be doing.'

"What a weight I must be on that woman's conscience, too," sighed the Shilling. "Am I really changed so much in my old age? And the woman went to the rich baker, but he knew the current shillings too well to accept me; I was thrown back in the woman's face, and she got no bread for me. And I felt grieved that I should be the cause of trouble to others—I, who in my young days had been so proud of my value and the soundness of my coinage. I was as melancholy as a poor shilling can be whom no one will accept; but the woman took me home, looked at me earnestly, with kindly, friendly eyes, and said, 'No, I won't deceive anyone with you. I'll bore a hole through you, so everyone can see you're false. And yet—a thought just occurs to me—perhaps you are a lucky shilling; yes, I believe you are; I have such a strong feeling about it! I'll make a hole through the coin, pass a string through it, and then give it to the neighbor's little child to hang around her neck as a good-luck shilling.'

"And she drilled a hole right through me. It certainly isn't very pleasant to have a hole bored through you, but you can stand many things when you know the intentions are good. A thread was passed through the hole, and I was hung around the child's neck like a kind of medal. The child smiled at me and kissed me, and all that night I slept on its warm, innocent breast.

"Next morning the child's mother took me up and looked at me and had another idea about me—I could feel that immediately. She brought out a pair of scissors and cut the string.

"'A lucky shilling!' she cried. 'Well, we'll see about that!'

"Then she soaked me in vinegar, until I turned quite green, puttied up the hole, rubbed me a little, and that evening took me to the lottery collector, to buy a lottery ticket that would make her fortune.

'How utterly unhappy I felt! There was a stinging inside me as if I were going to break in half. I knew that I should be called false and thrown away, and before a crowd of other coins, too, who lay there proud of their inscriptions and faces. But I escaped that time, for there were many people in the collector's office—he was very busy, so I rattled into the box with the other coins. I don't know if my ticket won anything or not, but I do know that the very next morning I was recognized as a bad coin and sent out to deceive again and again. That is a very trying thing to endure when you have a good character, and this I cannot deny that I have.

"For years and days I wandered this way from house to house, from hand to hand, always rebuked, always unwelcome; nobody believed me, and finally I lost confidence in the world and myself; those were hard times. One day a traveler arrived, and naturally I was passed on to him, and he was courteous enough to accept me as good. But when he tried to pass me on again, I heard once more the cry, 'That coin's no good! It's false!'"

"'I accepted it as genuine,' said the man, and looked closely at me. Then he smiled all over his face; never before had a face looked like that after a close examination of me. 'Why, what's this?' he said. 'That's a coin from my own country, a good honest shilling from home, that someone has bored a hole through and called false. Now, that's a strange coincidence. I'll just keep it and take it home with me.'

"A thrilling glow of joy shot through me when I heard him call me a honest shilling; now I would go home, where each and everyone would know me and realize that I was of good silver and bore a genuine stamp. I felt like throwing out sparks of happiness, but after all it isn't my nature to throw out sparks; that's something for steel to do, not silver.

"I was wrapped up in a clean white piece of paper, so that I wouldn't be mixed up with the other coins and be lost; and only on special occasions when people from my own country got together was I shown around, and they said nice things about me. They thought I was interesting—and it's surprising how interesting you can be without saying a single word.

"So at last I was home again. All my troubles were over, and I was happy again, for I was made of good silver and had the genuine stamp. I had no more misery to endure, even though a hole had been bored through me as if I were false; that doesn't matter if you're not really false. Just wait for the end, and everything will come out all right. That is my firm belief," said the Shilling.

THE NEW CENTURY'S GODDESS (1861)

The New Century's Goddess—whom our great-grandchildren or perhaps a still later generation will know, but we shall not—when and how does she reveal herself? What does she look like? What is the theme of her song? Whose heartstrings will she touch? To what heights will she lift her century?

Why so many questions, in a busy day like ours, when poetry is very nearly superfluous, when it is agreed that the many "immortal" productions of today's poets will, in the future, perhaps exist only in the form of charcoal tracings on a prison wall, seen and read only by a few curiosity seekers?

Poesy is required to serve in the ranks—at least to accept the challenge in party wars, whether it be blood or ink that flows.

But this is only one-sided talk, many will say; poesy has not been entirely forgotten in our time.

No, there are still people who, when they are not busy, are conscious of a desire for poetry, and no sooner do they feel that spiritual rumbling in their respective nobler parts than they promptly go to a bookstore and buy four shillings' worth of poetry of the most approved styles. Others take much pleasure from whatever they can get at a bargain; they are contended with reading the scrap that is on the grocer's wrapping paper; it is much cheaper, and in our busy time we must take notice of that. There is demand for whatever is supplied, and that is enough! The poetry of the future, as well as the poetry of music, is reckoned with the Don Quixotiana; to speak of it is much like speaking of a voyage of discovery to Uranus.

Time is too short and precious for the mere plays of fantasy, and, to speak seriously for once, what is poetry? These resonant outpourings of feeling and thought, they are only the offspring of nervous vibrations. Enthusiasm, joy, pain, all the movements of the organism, the wise men tell us, are but nerve vibrations. Each of us is but a string instrument.

But who touches the strings? Who causes them to vibrate into sound? The Spirit, the unseen Heavenly Spirit, who echoes in them His emotion, His feelings; and these are understood by other string instruments, which respond in melting harmonies or clashing dissonances. So it was, and so it will be, in mankind's mighty onward march in the consciousness of freedom.

Each century, each thousand years, one might even say, has its chief expression in its poetry. Born in the passing era, it comes forth and reigns in the new, succeeding era.

Thus she is already born, this Goddess of the New Century, amid the roar of today's machinery. We send her our greetings! May she hear this, or sometime read it, perhaps among the charcoal tracings we just mentioned.

The rocker of her cradle extended from the farthest point reached by the foot of man on polar voyages, as far as the living eye can gaze into the jet depth of the polar sky. We would never hear the rocking for the clatter of engines, the screams of locomotives, the thunder of quarry blasts, and the bursting of the Spirit's old bonds.

She is born in the vast factory of the present, where steam sets in action its power, and where Master Bloodless and his crew toil night and day.

She bears the womanly heart of love, the vestal's flame, and the furnace of passion. Hers is the lightning ray of intellect, in all its endless, shifting, prismatic hues of the ages. Fantasy's vast, swanfeathered tunic is her strength and pride; science wove it; the "elemental forces" gave it power of wing.

On her father's side, she is a child of the people, sound in sense and heart, with an earnest eye, and with humor on her lips. Her mother is the highborn, academy-trained emigrant's daughter, with gilded rococo reminiscences. The Goddess of the New Century has in her the blood and soul of both.

Upon her cradle were laid splendid birthday gifts. Plentiful as bonbons, the occult riddles of nature, with their solutions, are strewn there. The diver's bell gives mystic souvenirs from the deep. The map of the heavens, that high-hung Pacific Ocean with its countless isles, each a world in itself, is embroidered on the cradle cloth. The sun paints her pictures; photography has given her toys to play with.

The nurse has sung to her of Eivind Skalde-spiller and Firdausi, of the minnesingers, and what Heine, bold as a boy, sang from his poetic soul. Much, far too much, has the nurse told her; she knows the Edda, the old great-grandmother's frightful tales, where horrors sweep the air with bloody wings. The whole of the Oriental Thousand and One Nights she heard in the quarter part of an hour.

The Goddess of the New Century is still a child, but she has sprung forth from her cradle and is governed by will, though she still doesn't know what she wants.

She is still at play in her vast nursery packed with treasures of art and the rococo. Greek tragedy and Roman comedy are carved there in marble. The folk songs of the nations cover the walls like withered vines; a kiss from her, and they blossom forth with freshness and sweet vapor. The mighty tones and thoughts of Beethoven, Mozart, Glück, and the other great masters surround her with eternal chords. On her bookshelves are many laid to rest who in their day were immortal; and there is yet room for many another whose name we hear clicking from the telegraph of immortality but who dies with the telegram.

She has read an awful lot, far too much, for is she not born in our time? And all too much must again be forgotten; but the Goddess will know how to forget.

She doesn't think of her song, which will flourish in thousands of years to come, beside the legends of Moses and Bidpai's golden fable about the craft and luck of the fox. She doesn't think of her mission or of her melodious future; she is still playing, while the struggles of nations shake the air and sound figures of pen and cannon rush to and fro—runes of mystic reading.

She wears a Garibaldi hat, and when she reads her Shakespeare she stops for a moment to think; he can still be played when I am grown! Calderón rests in the tomb of his works, beneath the tablet of his glory. The Goddess is cosmopolitan, for she has bound together Holberg with Molière, Plautus, and Aristophanes; but most she reads her Molière.

She is free from the turbulence that drives the goats of the Alps, but still her soul yearns for the salt of life, as the goats pant for the mountain salt. There is calm in her heart as in the ancient Hebrew songs the voice of the nomad drifts over green pastures beneath starry skies; and yet in song her heart swells mightier than the heart of the inspired warrior from the Thessalonian mountains in the old days of Greece.

How goes it with her Christendom? She has learned the ins and outs of philosophy; the elements broke one of her milk teeth, but a new one grew. While yet in the cradle she ate of the fruit of knowledge and grew wise, so that Immortality flashed forth before her as mankind's happiest thought.

When begins the New Age of Poesy? When will the Goddess be known? When will she be heard?

On a wonderful spring morning she will come on the locomotive dragon, thundering over bridges and through dark tunnels; or on the back of the puffing dolphin across the calm but surging sea; or high in the air, carried by Montgolfier's bird, Roc, descending in the land where first her God-given voice shall greet the race of man. When? Will she come from the newfound land of Columbus, the land of freedom, where the native is hunted and the African is a beast of burden, the land from where we heard The Song of Hiawatha? Or from the antipodes, that golden nugget in the southern sea, the land of opposites, where our nighttime is their daytime, and where the black swans sing in mossy forests? Or maybe from the land where Memnon's pillar rings but we never understood the song of the Sphinx in the desert from the isle of the coalpit, where, since the age of the great Elizabeth, Shakespeare has reigned? Or from Tycho Brahe's home, where he wasn't wanted; or from California's fairyland, where the redwood holds high its crown as king of the earth's forests?

When shall the star be lit, the star on the brow of the Goddess, the flower on whose petals is inscribed the century's ideal of beauty in form, color, and fragrance?

"What is the Goddess' new platform?" inquires the skillful politician of the day. "What does she stand for?"

Better ask what she does not stand for!

She will not appear as a ghost of bygone times! She will not fashion her dramas from the discarded splendor of the stage, nor cover the lack of dramatic architecture with the dazzling colors of lyric drapery! Her flight forth among us will be as from the car of Thespis to the marble arena. She will not shatter normal human speech to fragments, to be clinked together for an artificial music box with tones from troubadour tournaments. Nor will she separate patrician Verse and plain plebeian Prose—twins are they in voice, quality, and power! Nor will she carve from the saga blocks of Iceland and ancient gods, for they are dead; no sympathy or fellowship awaits them in our day! Nor will she command her generation to occupy their thoughts with the fabric of a French novel; nor will she dull them with the chloroform of everyday history! She will bring the elixir of life; her song, whether in verse or prose, will be brief, clear, and rich. The nations' heartbeats are but letters in the endless alphabet of mankind's growth; she grasps each letter with equal lovingness, and ranges all in words, and weaves her words into rhythms for her Age's Hymn.

And when shall the hour come?

It will be long to us who are still here; brief to those who have flown ahead.

The Chinese Wall will soon fall. The railways of Europe open old Asia's tightly sealed culture archives, and the opposing streams of human culture meet, mayhap with a thunderous crash. The oldsters of our days will tremble at that sound and hear in it a judgment, the fall of ancient gods, forgetting that times and peoples must pass from the earth, and only a tiny image, sealed in a word casket, remain of each, floating like a lotus flower on the stream of eternity, and telling us that all were flesh of our flesh, dressed in different attire. The Jewish image shines radiant from the Bible; the Greek from the Iliad and the Odyssey; and ours? Ask it of the coming Goddess, at judgment time, when the new heaven is lifted to light and sight at the judgment day.

All the power of steam and all the pressure of modern times were levers! Master Bloodless and his busy crew, who seem the all-powerful rulers of our day, are but its servants, black slaves to adorn the festive hall, open its treasures, set its tables, for the great feast day when the Goddess, a child of innocence, a maid of inspiration, a matron of calm wisdom, shall lift on high the wonderful Lamp of Poetry, that rich, full human heart flaming with the fire of God.

Greetings, you Goddess of Poetry's coming age! May our salutation be heard as is heard the worm's hymn of thanksgiving—the worm that is cut to pieces beneath the plow, while a new springtime is dawning and the plowman draws his furrow among us worms, crushing us, that your blessings may be bestowed upon the coming generation.

Greetings, you Goddess of the New Century!

THE SNOWDROP (1862)

It was wintertime; the air was cold, the wind sharp, but indoors all was snug and well. Indoors lay the flower; it lay in its bulb, under earth and snow.

One day the rain fell; the drops trickled down through the snow blanket, down into the earth, and stirred against the bulb, telling it of the world of light up above. Soon a sunbeam, so slender and penetrating, bored through the snow, down to the bulb, and tapped on it.

"Come in," said the Flower.

"That I can't do," said the Sunbeam. "I'm not strong enough to open you up. I shall be very strong by summer."

"When will it be summer?" asked the Flower, and repeated this every time a new sunbeam came down to it. But summer was far off; snow remained on the earth, and ice formed on the water in the streams every blessed night.

"How long this lasts! How long this lasts!" said the Flower. "I feel a tingling and tickling. I must stretch myself; I must extend myself. I must open up; I must come out and wave good morning to the summer; that will be a wonderful time!"

And the Flower stretched itself and extended itself against the thin shell that had been softened by the rain water, warmed by the blanket of earth and snow, and tapped upon by the Sunbeam. It burst forth beneath the snow, with a white and green bud on its green stalk, with narrow, thick leaves, curled around it as if for protection. The snow was cold, but light radiated down into it, making it quite easy to break through; and here now the Sunbeam streamed down with greater strength than before.

"Welcome! Welcome!" sang and rang out every sunbeam as the Flower rose above the snow, out into the world of light. The Sunbeams caressed and kissed it, so that it opened itself fully, white as snow and adorned with green stripes. It bowed its head in happiness and humility.

"Beautiful flower!" sang the Sunbeams. "How fresh and pure you are! You are the first; you are the only one! You are our love! You ring out the call of summer, lovely summer, over town and country! All the snow shall melt, the cold winds be driven away! We shall reign! Everything shall grow green! And then you shall have company, the lilacs and laburnums and finally the roses. But you are the first, so tender and pure!"

This was a great delight to the Flower. It was as if the air itself were ringing and singing, as if the Sunbeams were all penetrating the leaves and stem of the Flower. There it stood, so fine and fragile, and yet so strong, in all its youthful beauty, in its white kirtle with the green bands, praising the summer. But summertime was far off; clouds shrouded the sun; sharp winds blew on the Flower.

"You have come a little too early!" said Wind and Weather. "We still have power, and this you shall feel and have to comply with! You should have remained indoors instead of rushing out here to display your finery! It is not the time for that yet!"

It was bitingly cold, and the days that followed didn't bring a sunbeam. It was weather to freeze such a delicate little flower to bits. But there was more strength in it than even it realized. That strength was in its happy faith that summer must come, and this had been imparted by its own deep desire and confirmed by the warm sunlight. And so with patient hope it stood there in its white dress, in the white snow, bowing its head when the snowflakes fell thick and heavy or while the icy winds swept over it.

"You'll break!" they said. "Wither, freeze! What did you want out here? Why did you let yourself be enticed? The Sunbeam has hoaxed you! Now make the best of it, you snowdrop, summer fool!"

"Snowdrop, summer fool!" repeated the Flower there in the cold morning.

"Snowdrop!" rejoiced some children who came into the garden. "There stands one, so sweet, so beautiful—the first, the only one!"

And these words made the Flower feel so well; they were like the warm Sunbeams. In its gladness it never noticed that it was being plucked. Then it lay in a child's hand, was kissed by a child's lips, brought into a warm room, gazed upon by kindly eyes, and set in water—so strengthening, so exhilarating. The Flower thought that it had all of a sudden come into midsummer.

The daughter of the house was a lovely little girl who had just been confirmed. And she had a dear boy friend; he also had been confirmed and was studying to equip himself for earning a living. "He shall be my snowdrop!" she told herself. Then she took the lovely Flower and laid it on a scented piece of paper that had a verse written on it, a verse about the Flower, beginning with "snowdrop" and ending with "snowdrop." "Little sweetheart, be my snowdrop, my winter fool!"—thus she had playfully mocked him with the summer. Yes, that was written in the verses. And it was then folded up like a letter, with the Flower placed inside; it was dark in there where it lay, as dark as when it had been in the bulb. The Flower was sent on a journey; it lay in a mail sack, was pressed and squeezed, and that was not at all pleasant, but finally this came to an end.

When the journey was over, the letter was opened and read by her dear friend. He was so delighted that he kissed the Flower. And then it was locked up, with the poem around it, in a drawer where there lay many charming letters, though none had a flower in it. Here, too, it was the first, the only one, as the Sunbeams had called it, and that was pleasant to think about.

It had a long period of leisure in which to think about it; it thought while the summer passed, and the long winter passed, and then when it was summer again, it was brought forth from the drawer. But this time the young man was not at all happy. He seized up the letters very harshly, and flung away the poem, so that the Flower fell onto the floor. It had become flattened and withered, but that was no reason to throw it onto the floor, though it was better off lying there than in the fire, where poems and letters were blazing. What had happened? What so often happens. The Flower had mocked him, and that was a joke; the girl had mocked him, but that was no joke; she had chosen another boyfriend this midsummer.

In the morning the sun shone in on the little flattened Snowdrop, which looked as if it were painted on the floor. The maid who swept the room picked it up and placed it in one of the books on the table, for she thought it had fallen out when she was clearing up and putting things in order. And so once again the Flower lay between verses, printed verses this time, which are grander than the written ones—at least they cost more.

Years passed, throughout which the book stood on its shelf. But now at last it was taken down, opened, and read. It was a good book—the songs and poems of the Danish poet, Ambrosius Stub, who is well worth your knowing. The man who was reading the book turned a page.

"Ah, here is a flower!" he said. "A snowdrop! It is with significance indeed that it lies here. Poor Ambrosius Stub! He was a snowdrop, too, a poet-snowdrop. He was before his time, and therefore he had to face sharp winds and sleet as he passed among the gentlemen of Funen; he was like a flower in a water glass, a flower in a valentine; a summer fool, winter fool, full of fun and drollery. And yet he was the first, the only youthfully fresh Danish poet. Yes, lie there as a marker in this book, little Snowdrop. You are laid here with meaning!"

And then the Snowdrop again was placed in the book, and felt both honored and delighted to know that it was a marker in the beautiful book of poetry, and that he who had first written and sung about the flower had also been a snowdrop and been mocked in the winter. Now the Flower understood this in its own way, just as we understand things in our way.

That is the fairy story of the Snowdrop.

THE TEAPOT (1863)

There was a proud Teapot, proud of being made of porcelain, proud of its long spout and its broad handle. It had something in front of it and behind it; the spout was in front, and the handle behind, and that was what it talked about. But it didn't mention its lid, for it was cracked and it was riveted and full of defects, and we don't talk about our defects—other people do that. The cups, the cream pitcher, the sugar bowl—in fact, the whole tea service—thought much more about the defects in the lid and talked more about it than about the sound handle and the distinguished spout. The Teapot knew this.

"I know them," it told itself. "And I also know my imperfections, and I realize that in that very knowledge is my humility and my modesty. We all have many defects, but then we also have virtues. The cups have a handle, the sugar bowl has a lid, but of course I have both, and one thing more, one thing they can never have; I have a spout, and that makes me the queen of the tea table. The sugar bowl and the cream pitcher are permitted to be serving maids of delicacies, but I am the one who gives forth, the adviser. I spread blessings abroad among thirsty mankind. Inside of me the Chinese leaves give flavor to boiling, tasteless water."

This was the way the Teapot talked in its fresh young life. It stood on the table that was prepared for tea and it was lifted up by the most delicate hand. But that most delicate hand was very awkward. The Teapot was dropped; the spout broke off, and the handle broke off; the lid is not worth talking about; enough has been said about that. The Teapot lay in a faint on the floor, while the boiling water ran out of it. It was a great shock it got, but the worst thing of all was that the others laughed at it—and not at the awkward hand.

"I'll never be able to forget that!" said the Teapot, when later on it talked to itself about its past life. "They called me an invalid, and stood me in a corner, and the next day gave me to a woman who was begging for food. I fell into poverty, and was speechless both outside and inside, but as I stood there my better life began. One is one thing and then becomes quite another. They put earth in me, and for a Teapot that's the same as being buried, but in that earth they planted a flower bulb. Who put it there and gave it to me, I don't know; but it was planted there, a substitution for the Chinese leaves and the boiling water, the broken handle and spout. And the bulb lay in the earth, inside of me, and it became my heart, my living heart, a thing I never had before. There was life in me; there were power and might; my pulse beat. The bulb put out sprouts; thoughts and feeling sprang up and burst forth into flower. I saw it, I bore it, and I forgot myself in its beauty. It is a blessing to forget oneself in others!

"It didn't thank me, it didn't even think of me—everybody admired it and praised it. It made me very happy; how much more happy it must have made it!

"One day I heard them say it deserved a better pot. They broke me in two—that really hurt—and the flower was put into a better pot; then they threw me out into the yard, where I lie as an old potsherd. But I have my memory; that I can never lose!"

THE BIRD OF FOLKLORE (1864)

It is wintertime, and the earth is covered with a layer of snow, as smooth as if it were marble cut from a mountain. The sky is high and clear, and the wind as sharp as an elfin-forged sword; the trees stand like white coral or resemble blooming almond branches, and the air is as fresh as it is in the high Alps. The night is beautiful with streaming northern lights and countless twinkling stars.

Storms are coming; the clouds rise and scatter swan feathers; the snowflakes drift down, covering the hollow lane, the houses, the open fields, and the quiet streets. But we are sitting in a cozy room, before a glowing fire, and tales of olden days are being told. We hear a legend.

"By the open sea there lay a Viking's grave, and on it at midnight sat the ghost of that buried hero. He had been a king, the golden crown encircling his brow. His hair fluttered in the wind, and he was clad in iron and steel. He bowed his head sorrowfully and sighed in deep grief, like an unblessed spirit.

"Then a ship came near. The men cast anchor and went on land. Among them was a scald, and he stepped forth toward the kingly form and asked, 'Why do you grieve and suffer?'

"Thereupon the dead man answered, 'No man has sung of my deeds; they are dead and gone. Song has never carried them over the lands and into the hearts of men; therefore I have no rest, no peace.'

"And he told of his work and his mighty deeds; the men of his time had known them, but not sung of them, for then there were no scalds.

"Then the old scald plucked the strings of his harp and sang of the hero—of his daring as a youth, his strength in manhood, and his great and noble deeds. At that the dead one's face brightened, like the edge of a cloud touched with moonlight; happy and blessed, the form arose in beams of glory and vanished like a trail of the northern lights. Only the green mound of turf with the stone devoid of runes remained to be seen; but over it, at the last sound of the chords, and as if it had come from the harp itself, there flew a tiny bird. It was a most beautiful songbird, with the tuneful melodies of the thrush, the throbbing melodies of the human heart, songs of home, as the bird of passage hears them. The bird flew over hill, over valley, and over forest and meadow. It was the Bird of Folklore, which never dies."

We hear the song; we hear it now here in our room, in the winter evening, while the white bees swarm outside and the tempest tightens its strong grip. The Bird sings not only heroic songs; it sings soft, sweet love songs, rich and many; it sings of faithfulness in the north; it gives us fairy tales in melodies and words; it has proverbs and a language in song, and thereby, as if runes were laid on a dead man's tongue, it can speak to us of ancient times, and thus we know the homeland of the Bird of Folklore.

In ancient heathen days, in the times of the Vikings, its nest was in the harp of the bard. In the days of knighthood, when iron fists held the scales of justice and only might was right, when the peasant and the dog were of equal value, where then did the Bird find shelter? Brutality and narrow-mindedness alike had no thought for it. But over the balcony of the castle, where the lady sat before her parchment and wrote down the old records in song and story; in the humble green-turf hut, where the wandering peddler sat on the bench beside the good woman, telling her tales—there, above them, fluttered and flew, twittered and sang, the Bird that never dies so long as earth is green under the foot of man—the Bird of Folklore.

Now it sings for us in here. Outside are the snowstorm and the night. The Bird lays runes on our tongue; we know again our homeland, as God speaks to us in our mother tongue in the melodies of the Bird of Folklore, and the old memories rise within us; faded colors are bright again; song and tale give the joy of a blessed drink, lifting mind and soul until the evening seems like a Christmas festivity. The snow is drifting, and the ice is crackling; the storm reigns; it has great power; it is the lord, but not *our* Lord!

It is wintertime, the wind still as sharp as an elfin-forged sword; the snow is drifting—it has been drifting, it seems to us, for days and weeks—and it lies like a monstrous snow mountain over the big town; it is like a weighty dream in the winter night. All beneath it is hidden and seemingly nonexistent; only the golden cross on the church, the symbol of faith, rises above the snow grave and glitters against the blue sky in the clear sunshine.

And away over the snow-covered town fly the birds of heaven, the large and the small; they chirp and they sing, each in its own tongue.

First is the flock of sparrows; they chirp about all the little things in street and lane, in nest and house; they know tales of the kitchen and the parlor. "We know that buried town," they say. "Every living soul there has cheep, cheep, cheep!"

Then the black ravens and crows fly over the white snow. "Dig! Dig!" they scream. "There's still something to get down there, something for the belly—that's the most important thing. That's the opinion of most people down below there, and that opinion is caw, caw, caw!"

The wild swans come with whizzing wings and sing of the greatness and glory that still live in the thoughts and hearts of the men in the snow-covered slumber of the town. It is not the sleep of death, for evidence of life comes forth; we hear it in tones of music; they swell and sound as if they are coming from the church organ, they are gripping as a strain from an elfin mound, as Ossianic songs, as the winged rush of the Valkyries. What harmony! It speaks to our inmost heart, uplifts our thoughts; we hear the Bird of Folklore! And now the warm breath of God breathes down from above; the snow mountain breaks open, and the sun shines in through it. The spring is coming, and the birds are coming, a new generation, with the same familiar tones. Hearken to the drama of the year—the mighty snowstorm—the weighty dream of a winter night! All fetters shall be broken here, and everything shall rise again at the beautiful song of the Bird of Folklore—the Bird that never dies.

THE WILL-O'-THE-WISPS
ARE IN TOWN (1865)

There was a man who once had known a great many new fairy tales, but he had forgotten them, he said. The fairy tale that used to come to visit him of its own accord no longer came and knocked at his door; and why didn't it come any more? It's true that for a year and a day the man hadn't thought of it, hadn't really expected it to come and knock; and it certainly wouldn't have come anyway, for outside there was war and, inside, the misery and sorrow that war brings with it.

The stork and the swallow returned from their long journey, for they had no thought of danger. But when they arrived they found the nests burned, people's houses burned, the fences smashed, yes, and some even completely gone, and horses of the enemy were trampling down the old grave mounds. Those were hard, cruel times; but they always come to an end.

And now those times were past, people said; but still no fairy tale came to knock at the door or gave any sign of its presence.

"It may well be dead and gone, like so many other things," said the man. But then the fairy tale never dies!

More than a year passed, and he longed so for the fairy tale.

"I wonder if it will ever come back and knock again." And he remembered so vividly all the various forms in which it had come to him—sometimes as young and charming as spring itself, as a beautiful maiden with a thyme wreath in her hair and a beechen branch in her hand, her eyes shining as clear as the deep woodland lakes in the bright sunshine; and sometimes it had come to him in the likeness of a peddler and had opened its pack and let the silver ribbons inscribed with old verses and mottoes flutter out. But it had been best of all when it had come as an old grandmother, with silvery hair and such large and kindly eyes. She knew so well the tales of the old, old times, of even long before the princesses spun with golden spindles, and the dragons, the serpents, lay outside, guarding them. She told her tales so vividly that black spots would dance before the eyes of her listeners and the floor become black with human blood; it was terrible to see and to hear, and yet very entertaining, since it had all happened so long ago.

"Will she ever knock at my door again?" said the man, and gazed at the door until black spots appeared before his eyes and on the floor, and he didn't know if it was blood or mourning crepe from the dark and dismal days of yore.

As he sat there, the thought came to him that perhaps the fairy tale had hidden itself, like the princess in the very old tale, and if he should now go in search of it and find it, it would shine in new splendor, lovelier than ever. "Who knows? Perhaps it is hidden in the discarded straw lying near the edge of the well. Careful, careful! Perhaps it's hidden in a faded flower, shut up in one of the big books on the shelf!"

So the man went to one of the newest books and opened it to find out, but there was no flower there. It was a book about Holger Danske, and the man read how the whole story had been invented and put together by a French monk, that it was only a romance, "translated and printed in the Danish language," and that since Holger Danske had never really lived he could never come again, as we have sung and wanted to believe. As with Holger Danske, so it was with William Tell; both were only popular legends, nothing we could depend on. Here it was all written down in a very learned manner.

"Yes, but I shall believe my own beliefs," said the man. "No road grows where no foot has trod!"

So he closed the book, put it back on the shelf, and walked over to the fresh flowers on the window sill; perhaps the fairy tale had hidden itself in the red tulips with the golden-yellow edges, or in the fresh roses, or in the brilliantly colored camellias. But only sunshine lay among the flowers—no fairy tale.

"The flowers which grew here in the days of misery were much more beautiful; but one after another was cut off, woven into wreaths, and laid in coffins, with the flag placed over them. Perhaps the fairy tale was buried with them; but then the flowers would have known of it, and the coffin would have heard of it, and every little blade of grass that shot up would have told of it. The fairy tale never dies!

"Perhaps it was here and knocked, but who at that time had ears for it or would have thought of it? Then people looked darkly, gloomily, almost angrily, at the spring sunshine, the singing birds, and all the cheerful greenery; yes, and their tongues wouldn't even repeat the merry old folk songs, and they were laid in the coffin with so much else that our heart cherished. The fairy tale may well have knocked but not been heard, and with no one to bid it welcome, it may have departed.

"I shall go out and seek it! In the country—in the woods—on the open beaches."

Out in the country stands an old manor house with red walls, pointed gables, and a flag waving from the tower. The nightingale sings under the fringed beech leaves while it gazes at the blooming apple trees in the garden and thinks they are rose trees. Here the bees labor busily in the summertime, hovering around their queen with humming song. Here the autumn storm tells much of the wild chase, of the falling leaves, and of the generations of men that pass away. At Christmastime the wild swans sing on the open water, while in the old manor house the guests beside the fire are happy to hear the ancient songs and legends.

Down into the old part of the garden, where the great avenue of old chestnut trees invites the wanderer to pause in their shade, went the man who was seeking the fairy tale. Here the wind had once told him of "Valdemar Daae and His Daughters"; here the dryad in the tree—the fairy-tale mother herself—had told him "The Old Oak Tree's Last Dream." In our grandmother's time clipped hedges stood here; now there grow only ferns and stinging nettles, hiding the broken fragments of old figures sculptured in stone; moss grows in their very eyes, but still they can see as well as ever, which the man seeking the fairy tale couldn't, for he didn't see it. Where could it be?

Hundreds of crows flew over him and the old trees, crying, "Caw! Caw!"

Then he left the garden and crossed the rampart surrounding the manor, into the alder grove. There a little six-sided house stands, with a poultry yard and a duck yard. In the midst of the living room in the house sat the old woman who managed everything and who knew exactly when every egg would be laid and when each chicken would creep out of its egg. But she wasn't the fairy tale the man was seeking; she could prove that with the certificates of Christian baptism and vaccination that she kept in her chest of drawers.

Outside, not far from the house, there is a hill covered with red thorn and broom; here lies an old gravestone, brought here many years ago from the churchyard of the nearby town in memory of one of the most honored councilmen of the neighborhood. Carved in stone, his wife and five daughters, all with folded hands and stiff ruffs, stand about him. If you looked at them for a long time it would affect your thoughts, which in turn would react on the stone, so that it would seem to tell of olden times. At least that was the way it had been with the man who was searching for the fairy tale.

As he approached, he noticed a living butterfly sitting right on the forehead of the sculptured councilman. The insect flapped its wings, flew a little bit away, then returned to sit close by the gravestone, as if to call attention to what was growing there. Four-leaved clovers grew there, seven in all, side by side. When good luck comes, it comes in bunches. The man plucked all the clovers and put them into his pocket. "Good luck is as good as ready cash," thought the man, "though a new, beautiful fairy tale would be better still." But he could find none here.

The sun went down, big and red, and vapor rose from the meadow; the Woman of the Marsh was at her brewing.

That evening the man stood alone in his room, gazing out upon the sea, over the meadow, moor, and beach. The Moon shone brightly; the mist over the meadow made it look like a great lake; indeed, legend tells us it once was a lake, and in the moonlight the eye can understand these myths.

Then the man thought of how he had been reading that Holger Danske and William Tell never really lived; yet they do live in the faith of the people, just like the lake out there, living evidence of the myth. Yes, Holger Danske will return again!

As he stood thinking, something struck heavily against the window. Was it a bird, an owl, or a bat? We don't let those creatures in even when they knock. But the window burst open by itself, and an old woman looked in on the man.

"What is this?" he said. "What do you want? Who are you? Why, she's looking in at the second-floor window! Is she standing on a ladder?"

"You have a four-leaved clover in your pocket," she replied. "Or rather you have seven, but one of them has six leaves."

"Who are you?" asked the man.

"The Woman of the Marsh," she said, "the Woman of the Marsh, who brews. I was busy at my brewing. The tap was in the cask, but one of those mischievous little marsh imps pulled it out and threw it over here, where it hit your window. Now the beer's running out of the barrel, and nobody can make money that way!"

"Please tell me—" said the man.

"Yes, but wait a little," said the Woman of the Marsh. "I have something else to do right now." Then she was gone.

But as the man was about to close the window, the Woman stood before him again.

"Now it's fixed," she said, "but I'll have to brew half the beer over again tomorrow— that is, if it's good weather. Well, what did you want to know? I came back, for I always keep my word, and besides, you have seven four-leaved clovers in your pocket, one of which has six leaves; that demands respect, for that type grows beside the roadside, and not many people find them. What did you want to ask me? Don't stand there looking foolish; I have to go back to my tap and my barrel very quickly."

Then the man asked her about the fairy tale, and if she had met it in her journeys. "For the love of my big brewing vat!" said the Woman. "Haven't you told enough fairy tales? I certainly think most people have had enough of them. There are plenty of other things for you to do and take care of. Even the children have outgrown fairy tales! Give the small boys a cigar, and the little girls a new dress; they'll like that much better. But listen to fairy tales! No, indeed, there are certainly other things to attend to, more important things to do!"

"What do you mean?" the man asked. "And what do you know about the world? You never see anything but frogs and will-o'-the-wisps!"

"Beware of the will-o'-the-wisps!" said the Woman. "They're out—they're on the loose! That's what we should talk about! Come to me at the marsh, for I must go there now; there I'll tell you about it. But you must hurry and come while your seven four-leaved clovers, one of them with six leaves, are still fresh and the moon is still high!"

And the Woman of the Marsh was gone.

The town clock struck twelve, and before the last stroke had died away the man had left the house, crossed the garden, and stood in the meadow. The mist had cleared away; the Woman of the Marsh had finished her brewing. "You took your time getting here!" said the Woman of the Marsh. "Witches move much faster than men; I'm glad I'm a witch."

"What do you have to tell me now?" asked the man. "Anything about the fairy tale?"

"Is that all you can ever ask about?" said the Woman.

"Is it something about the poetry of the future that you can tell me?"

"Don't become impatient," said the Woman, "and I'll answer you. You now think only of poetry. You ask about the fairy tale as if she were the mistress of everything. She's the oldest all right, but she always passes for the youngest; I know her very well. I was young once, and that's no children's disease! Once I was quite a pretty little elf maiden, and I danced with the others in the moonlight, listened to the nightingale, went into the forest, and met the fairy-tale maiden there, where she was always running about. Sometimes she spent the night in a half-opened tulip or in some field flower; sometimes she would slip into the church and wrap herself in the mourning crepe that hung down from the altar candles."

"You seem to know all about it," said the man.

"I should at least know as much as *you* do," said the Woman of the Marsh. "Fairy tales and poetry—yes, they're like two pieces of the same material. They can go and lie where they wish. One can brew all their talk and goings-on and have it better and cheaper. I'll give it to you for nothing; I have a whole cabinet full of bottles of poetry, the essences, the best of it—both sweet and bitter herbs. I have all the poetry people might want, bottled up, and on holidays I put a little on my handkerchief to smell."

"Why, these are wonderful things you're telling me!" said the man. "You actually have poetry in bottles?"

"More than you can stand," said the Woman. "I suppose you know the story of 'The Girl Who Trod on the Loaf,' so that she would not soil her shoes. That has been written down and printed, too."

"I told that one myself," said the man.

"Yes, then you know it, and you know, too, that the girl sank right into the earth, to the Woman of the Marsh, just as the Devil's grandmother was there on a visit to inspect the brewery. She saw the girl come down and asked to have her as a souvenir of her visit, and she got her, too. I received a present from her which is of no good to me—a regular traveling drugstore, a whole cabinet full of bottled poetry. The grandmother told me where to put the cabinet, and it's still there. Now look here! You have your seven four-leaved clovers in your pocket, one of which has six leaves, so you should be able to see it!"

Sure enough, in the middle of the marsh was what looked like a great gnarled alder block, and that was the grandmother's cabinet. She explained that it was open to her and to everyone else in the world at any time, if they just knew where it was. It could be opened in front or at the back and at every side and corner; it was a real work of art and yet appeared to be only an alder stump. Poets of all countries, and especially of our own land, had been reproduced here; the essence of each had been extracted, refined, criticized, distilled, and then put into bottles. With great skill—as it's called, if one doesn't want to call it genius—the grandmother had taken a little of this poet and a little of that, added a touch of deviltry, and then corked up the bottles for the use of future ages.

"Please let me see," said the man.

"All right, but there are much more important things to listen to," said the Woman of the Marsh.

"But we're right here at the cabinet," said the man, as he looked inside it. "Why, here are bottles of all sizes. What's in this one, and what's in that one over there?"

"This is what they call May dew," said the Woman. "I haven't tried it myself, but I know that if you spill only a little drop of it on the floor, you will see before you a lovely forest lake with water lilies, flowering rushes, and wild mint. You need pour only two drops on an old exercise book, even one from the lowest class in school, and the book becomes a complete, fragrant play that is good enough to be performed and to fall asleep over, so strong is its smell. It must be as a compliment to me that they labeled the bottle 'The Brew of the Woman of the Marsh.'

"Here stands the bottle of scandal. It looks as if there is only dirty water in it, and, of course, it *is* dirty water, but with sparkling powder, three ounces of lies, and two grains of truth, stirred with a birch twig, not taken from a stalk pickled in salt and used on the bleeding backs of sinners, nor a piece of the schoolmaster's switch—no, but taken right from the broom that had been used to sweep the gutter.

"Here stands the bottle with the pious poetry set to psalm music. Every drop has a sound like the slamming of hell's gates and has been made from the blood and sweat of punishment. Some say it's only the gall of a dove; but doves are the gentlest of animals; they have no gall, say people who don't know their natural history."

"Here stood the bottle of all bottles; it took up half of the cabinet. It was the bottle with 'Stories of Everyday Life,' and it was covered with both hogskin and bladder so that it couldn't lose any of its strength. Every nation could get its own soup here; what would come forth would depend upon how you'd turn and tip the bottle. Here was an old German blood soup with robber dumplings, and there was also thin peasant soup, with genuine court officials, who lay like vegetables on the bottom, while fat, philosophical eyes floated on the top. There was English-governess soup, and French *potage à la coq*, made from chicken legs and sparrow eggs and, in Danish, called 'cancan soup.' But the best of all soups was Copenhagen soup; the whole family said so."

Here stood "Tragedy," in a champagne bottle; it could make a popping noise, and that was as it should be. "Comedy" looked like fine sand to throw into people's eyes—

that is, the more refined comedy; the broader kind was also bottled, but consisted only of future playbills; there were some excellent comedy titles, such as *Dare You Spit in the Machinery?*, *One on the Jaw*, *The Sweet Ass*, and *She Is Dead Drunk!*

While the man was completely lost in his thoughts, the Woman of the Marsh thought ahead; she wanted to put an end to this.

"By now you must have seen enough of the hodgepodge chest," she said. "You know what it is now. But I haven't told you the important thing you must know. The will-o'-the-wisps are in town! That's much more important than poetry or fairy tales. I really should keep my mouth shut about it, but it seems that a compulsion—a force—something has come over me, and it sticks in my throat and wants to come out. The will-o'-the-wisps are in town! They are on the loose! Take care, you mortals!"

"I don't understand a word you're saying!" said the man.

"Please sit down on the cabinet," she said, "but be careful not to fall through and break the bottles—you know what's inside them. I'll tell you about the great event. It happened only yesterday; yet it has happened before. And now it has 364 days to go. I suppose you know how many days there are in a year?"

And this was the story of the Woman of the Marsh:

"There was much excitement yesterday out here in the marsh! There was a christening party! A little will-o'-the-wisp was born here; in face, twelve of them were born all at once. And they have permission to go out among men, if they want to, and move around and command, just as if they were human beings! That was a great event in the marsh, and for that reason all the lady and gentlemen will-o'-the-wisps danced across the marsh and the meadow like little lights. Some of them are of the canine species, but they aren't worth talking about. I sat right there on my cabinet and held all the twelve little newborn will-o'-the-wisps on my lap. They glittered like glowworms; already they had begun to hop, and they grew bigger every minute, and after a quarter of an hour each of them was as big as his father or uncle. Now it's an old, established law that when the moon stands just where it did yesterday, and the wind blows just the way it blew yesterday, it is granted to all will-o'-the-wisps born at that hour and at that minute that they may become human beings and each of them exercise their power for a whole year.

"The will-o'-the-wisp can go about in the country, or anywhere in the world, as long as it is not afraid of falling into the sea or being blown away by a great storm. It can go right into a person, and speak for him, and perform any action it wants. The will-o'-the-wisp can take any form it likes, man or woman, and act in his or her spirit, and so go to the extreme in doing what it wishes. But in the course of that year it must succeed in leading 365 people into bad paths, and in grand style, too; it must lead them away from the right and truth, and then it will receive the highest honor a will-o'-the-wisp can, that of being a runner before the Devil's stagecoach; it can then wear a fiery yellow uniform and breathe flames from its mouth. That's enough to make a simple will-o'-the-wisp lick his lips in desire. But there's danger, too, and a lot of work for an ambitious will-o'-the-wisp who wants to reach that height. If the eyes of the person are opened and he realizes what is happening and can blow the will-o'-the-wisp away, it is done for and has to come back to the marsh. Or if, before the year is over, the will-o'-the-wisp is overcome with longing for its home and family and so gives up and comes back, then it is also done for; it can't burn clearly any longer, and soon goes out, and can't be lighted again. And if, at the end of the year, it hasn't led 365 people away from the truth and all that's fine and noble, it is condemned to lie in a rotten stump and shine without being able to move. That's the worst punishment of all for a lively will-o'-the-wisp.

"Now, I know all about this, and I told it all to the twelve little ones that I held on my lap, and they were quite wild with joy. I warned them that the safest and easiest way would be to give up the honor and just do nothing at all, but the little flames wouldn't listen to that; already they could imagine themselves dressed in fiery yellow uniforms, breathing flames from their mouths.

"'Stay here with us!' said some of the older ones.

"'Go and have your fun with the human beings!' others said.

"'Yes, they are draining our meadows and drying them up! What will become of our descendants?'

"'We want to flame with flames!' said the newborn will-o'-the-wisps, and that settled it.

"Then presently began the minute ball, which couldn't have been any shorter. The elf maidens whirled around three times with all the others, so as not appear proud, but they always preferred dancing with each other. Then the godparents' gifts were given—'throwing pebbles,' it's called. The 'pebbles' were flung over the marsh water. Each of the elf maidens gave a little piece of her veil.

"'Take that,' they said, 'and you'll be able to do the highest dance, the most difficult turns and twists—that is, if you should ever need to. You'll have the best manners, so you can show yourselves in the highest of society.'

"The night raven taught the young will-o'-the-wisps to say, 'Bra-bra-brave!' and to say it at the right times; and that's a great gift that brings its own reward.

"The owl and the stork dropped their gifts. But they said these weren't worth mentioning, and so we won't talk about it.

"The wild hunt of King Valdemar was just then rushing across the marsh, and when the nobles heard of the celebration they sent as a present a couple of handsome dogs which could hunt with the speed of the wind and carry a will-o'-the-wisp, or three, on their backs. A couple of old witches who make a living riding broomsticks were at the party, and they taught the young will-o'-the-wisps how to slip through any keyhole as if the door stood open to them. These witches offered to carry the young ones to the town, which they knew quite well. They usually rode through the air on their own back hair fastened into a knot, for they prefer a hard seat. But now they sat on the hunting dogs and took on their laps the young will-o'-the-wisps, who were ready to go into town to start misleading and bewildering human beings. Whiz! And they were gone!

"That's what happened last night. Today the will-o'-the-wisps are in town and have started to work—but how, and where? Can you tell me that? Still, I have a telegraph wire in my big toe, and that always tells me something."

"That's a whole fairy tale!" said the man.

"Why, it's just the beginning of one," said the Woman. "Can you tell me how the will-o'-the-wisps are behaving themselves and what they're doing, in what shapes they're appearing and leading people astray?"

"I believe," said the man, "that a whole novel could be written about the will-o'-the-wisps, in twelve parts; or better still, a complete comedy-drama could be written about them."

"You should write it," said the Woman. "Or perhaps you'd better leave it undone."

"Yes, that's easier, and more pleasant," said the man. "Then we'll not be condemned by the newspapers, which is just as bad as it is for a will-o'-the-wisp to be shut in a rotten stump, shining, and afraid to say anything."

"It doesn't matter to me what you do," said the Woman. "Let the others write, if they can, or even if they can't. I'll give you an old tap from my cask; that will open the cabinet where I keep the poetry in bottles, and you can take anything you want. But you, my good man, seem to have stained your fingers enough with ink, and at the age and stability you have reached, you don't have to be running around every year looking for fairy tales, especially as there are much more important things to be done. Have you understood what's happening?"

"The will-o'-the-wisps are in town," said the man. "I heard you, and I understand. But what do you think I ought to do about it? I'd be locked up if I were to go up to people and say, 'Look! There goes a will-o'-the-wisp in honest clothes!'"

"Sometimes they wear skirts!" said the Woman. "The will-o'-the-wisp can take on any form and appear anywhere. It goes into the church, not for the sake of our Lord, but perhaps so that it can enter the minister. It speaks on election day, not for the good of state or country, but only for itself. It is an artist with the paint pot, and in the theater, but when it gets complete power, then the pot's empty! Here I go, chattering on, but what's sticking in my throat must come out, even if it hurts my own family. But now I must be the woman to save a lot of people. But, truthfully, I'm not doing it with good intentions or for the sake of any medal. I do the most insane thing I possibly can; I tell a poet about it, and soon everybody in town gets to know about it."

"The town won't take it to heart," said the man. "It won't disturb a single person. They'll all think I'm only telling them a fairy tale if I say, 'The will-o'-the-wisps are in town, said the Woman of the Marsh! Beware!'"

THE WINDMILL (1865)

On the hill there stood a windmill stately to look at and very proud of itself.

"But I'm not proud at all," it said, "though I'm much enlightened, outside and inside. On the outside I have the sun and moon, and for inward use, too; and I also have wax candles, oil lamps, and tallow candles. Yes, I daresay I'm enlightened. I'm a thinking individual and so well built that I'm a pleasure to look at. I have a good windpipe in my chest, and I have four wings placed upon my head, just under my hat. Even the birds have only two wings and have to carry them on their backs. I'm a Dutchman by birth—you can tell that from my figure—a Flying Dutchman! People call them supernatural beings, I know, and yet I'm quite natural. There's a gallery round my stomach, and a dwelling place underneath it; that's where my thoughts live. My strongest thought, who rules and governs, is called by the other thoughts: 'The

Millers.' He knows what he wants, and rules over the flour and the oats; but he has a mate, too, who calls herself 'Mother.' She is my real heart. She doesn't run around awkwardly; she knows what she wants and what she can do. She's as gentle as the wind and as strong as a tempest; she knows how to lead up to a thing carefully but get her own way. She is my softer side, and the father is my harder; they are two and yet one; and each calls the other 'My better half.'

"These two have youngsters, little thoughts that will grow up, and these little ones make a lot of noise.

"The other day I wisely let the father and his helpers examine my throat and the hole in my chest. I wanted to know what was wrong, for something was wrong, and when you're out of order it's well to look into yourself. The youngsters made a tremendous racket, which was very annoying to me; for, remember, on the top hill where I stand I am in the limelight, and one is judged accordingly. The youngest one jumped up into my hat and shouted so up there that it tickled me. Yes, I know those little thoughts will grow up. Out in the world thoughts come, too, but they're not my sort; as far as I can see, I cannot make out anything like me. Those wingless houses that can't make a noise in their throats, have thoughts, too, and these sometimes come to my thoughts, and make love to them, as people call it. Yes, it's very strange, but there are many strange things. Some change has come over me, or inside me something is different in the working of the mill. It seems as if the one half, the father, has altered and got an even gentler and more affectionate mate—young and good as before, but more tender and gentle through the course of time. The bitter has somehow passed away, and everything is much more pleasant.

"The days pass, and the days come, always forward to brightness and happiness, until the day comes when it will be all over with me and yet not entirely over. I'll have to be torn down so that I can be built up again, new and better; I shall cease, but I'll still live! Become a different being, and yet be the same! Enlightened as I am with sun, moon, wax, oil, and tallow, I still find that difficult to understand. My old timbers and brickwork will rise again from the dust!

"I hope I'll be able to keep my old thoughts, the Miller, the mother, the great ones and little ones—the family, as I call all that great and little company of thoughts; because I cannot do without them.

"And I must also remain *myself*, with my throat in my chest, wings on my head, and the balcony around my waist; otherwise I wouldn't know myself, and other people wouldn't know me and say, 'There's the Mill on the hill, a proud sight to see, and yet not proud at all!'"

That's what the Mill said. It said a great many more things, too, but that's the most important part of it.

And the days came and the days passed, and yesterday was the last day. Then the Mill caught fire. The flames shot up: they whipped in; they whipped out; they licked beams and planks and ate them up. The Mill disappeared, and only a heap of ashes remained. The smoke rose from the embers until the wind carried it away.

Whatever had been alive in the Mill still remained; nothing happened to any of them; indeed, they gained by it.

The Miller's family—one soul, may thoughts, and yet only one thought—got a new, a beautiful mill, a mill they could be very proud of. It looked exactly like the old one, and people said, "Why, there's the Mill on the hill, a proud sight to see!"

But this Mill was better arranged, much more up to date than the other one, for there is always some progress. The old timber, which had become damp and worm-eaten, now was dust and ashes. The body of the Mill did not actually rise out of the dust, as it had believed it would do; it had taken the thought literally, and not everything is supposed to be taken literally.

IN THE CHILDREN'S ROOM (1865)

Father and mother and all the brothers and sisters had gone to the theater; only little Anna and her grandfather were left at home.

"We'll put on a play, too," he said, "and it can start right away."

"But we don't have any theater!" said little Anna. "And we haven't anybody to do the acting. My old doll can't, because she looks dreadful, and my new one mustn't, because she'd rumple her new dress."

"You can always find actors if you use what you have," said Grandfather. "Now let's build the theater. We'll set up a book here, and another there, and one more over there, in a slanting row. Now three on the other side; so, now we have the side wings. The old box lying over there can be the backdrop, and we'll turn the bottom out. The stage represents a room; everyone can see that. Now we need the actors. Let's see what we can find in your toy drawer. First the characters, and then we'll prepare the play; one holds the other together. This is going to be splendid! Here's a pipe head, and there an odd glove; they'll do very well for father and daughter."

"But that's only two characters," said little Anna. "Here's my brother's old waistcoat—couldn't that play a part, too?"

"It's certainly big enough," said Grandfather. "We'll make it the lover. There's nothing in its pockets, and that's very interesting, for that's why the course of true love doesn't run smoothly! And here we have the nutcracker's boot, with spurs on it. Potz, blitz, mazurka! Look how he can dance and strut! He'll be the unwelcome suitor, whom the lady doesn't care for. Now what kind of play do you want? A tragedy? Or a domestic drama?"

"A domestic drama," said little Anna. "The others like that sort of play. Do you know one?"

"I know a hundred!" said Grandfather. "The most popular ones are from the French, but they're not good for little girls. Instead, we'll take one of the prettiest; they're all about the same inside. Now I'll shake my bag! Kukkelrum! Brand-new! And now here's the play, all brand-new! Now listen to the program."

Then Grandpapa took up a newspaper, and pretended to be reading from it:

THE PIPE HEAD AND THE GOOD HEAD

A Family Drama in One Act

CHARACTERS

MR. PIPE HEAD, *a father*	MR. WAISTCOAT, *a lover*
MISS GLOVE, *a daughter*	MR. BOOT, *a suitor*

"Now we're ready to start. The curtain rises! But we don't have any curtain, so it's up already. All the characters are on the stage, so we see them immediately. Now I speak as Father Pipe Head; he's angry today. You can see that he's a colored meerschaum.

"'Chitchat! Muttering! Poppycock! I'm master of this house! I'm my daughter's father! Listen to what I have to say! Mr. Boot is a person in whom you can see your face; his upper part is made of morocco, and he has spurs at the bottom. Prattle! Chitchat! He shall have my daughter!'

"Now listen to what the Waistcoat says, little Anna," said Grandfather. "He's speaking now. The Waistcoat has a laydown collar, is very modest, but knows his own value and has a right to speak his mind. 'I haven't a spot on me!' he says. 'Good material ought to be taken into consideration; I'm made of real silk, and have strings on me.'

"'On the wedding day, but not after that. You don't keep your color in the wash!' This is Mr. Pipe Head speaking. 'But Mr. Boot is watertight, made of strong leather, and yet very delicate. He can creak and clank his spurs, and looks Italian!'"

"But they ought to speak in poetry," said little Anna. "I've heard that's the nicest way."

"Oh, they can do that, too," said Grandfather. "And if the public wants it, they'll do it. Just look at little Miss Glove, pointing her fingers!

> "'A glove without a mate;
> That's forever my fate!
> Ah!
> I can't get over it!
> I think my skin will split!'
> 'Bah!'

"It was Father Pipe Head who said, 'Bah!' And now Mr. Waistcoat speaks:

> "'Oh, beautiful Glove,
> You must be my love,
> Though you're from Spain
> And I'm Holger the Dane!'

"When Mr. Boot hears this he kicks up his heels, jingles his spurs, and knocks down three of our side wings."

"This is such wonderful fun!" said little Anna.

"Quiet, quiet!" said Grandfather. "Silent approval will show that you belong to the educated public in the front rows. Now Miss Glove sings her great aria with a break in her voice:

> *"'I have no voice;*
> *I can crow, but that's all;*
> *Caw, caw—in the lofty hall!'*

"Now comes the really exciting part, little Anna. This is the most important scene in the whole play. Mr. Waistcoat unbuttons himself and addresses his speech to you out front, so that you will applaud. But don't do it; it's more refined not to. Hear how his silk cloth rustles.

"'I am driven to extremities! Take care of yourself! Here's my plot! You are the pipe head, and I am the good head. Zip! and away you go!'

"Did you see that, little Anna!" said Grandfather. "That's a most delightful comic scene; Mr. Waistcoat seized the old Pipe Head and put him into his pocket! There he lies, and Mr. Waistcoat speaks:

"'Aha, you are in my pocket now, in my deepest pocket! You will never come out unless you promise to unite me to your daughter, Miss Left-hand Glove. I hold out my right hand!'"

"My, that's awfully pretty!" said little Anna.

"And now old Pipe Head replies:

> *"'I'm getting so awfully dizzy!*
> *Unlike before, I'm not busy.*
> *Gone is my humor, I fear.*
> *Never have I felt so queer.*
> *Without my stem here I feel so frail.*
> *Take me from your pocket without fail,*
> *And you shall have my daughter here,*
> *To marry and to hold dear.'*"

"Is the play over already?" said little Anna.

"Certainly not," said Grandfather. "It's just all over with Mr. Boot. Now the lovers kneel and one of them sings:

> *"'Father!'*

"and the other:

> *"'Mr. Pipe Head, do as you oughter,*
> *Bless your son and daughter!'*

"They receive his blessing and celebrate their wedding, and all the furniture sings in chorus:

> *"'Clinks and clanks,*
> *A thousand thanks,*
> *And now our play is over!'*

"And now we can applaud," said Grandfather. "We'll bring them all out for a curtain call, and the pieces of furniture, too, for they're made of mahogany."

"And isn't our play just as good as the ones you see in a real theater?"

"Our play is much better!" said Grandfather. "It's shorter; the admission was free; and it has passed away the time before our tea!"

GOLDEN TREASURE (1865)

The drummer's wife went to church and saw the new altar with painted pictures and carved angels. The angels were very beautiful, both those painted on cloth, in all their colors and glory, and those carved in wood, painted and gilded. Their hair shone like gold and sunshine and was beautiful to look at. But God's sunshine was still more beautiful; it glowed bright and red between the dark trees as the sun was setting. And as the woman gazed on the descending sun, her innermost thoughts were about the little child the stork was bringing her. She was radiantly happy as she gazed, and she wished most fervently that her child might be as bright as a sunbeam, or at least look like one of the shining angels on the altarpiece.

And when she actually lifted up her child in her arms to show her husband, it seemed to her that the infant really did resemble one of the angels in the church; at least it had golden hair, hair that had caught the reflection of that setting sun.

"My Golden Treasure, my wealth, my sunshine!" said the mother as she kissed the bright locks; and this sounded like music and song in the drummer's home; there was joy, and lots of life, and celebrating. The drummer beat a whirlwind on his drum, a whirlwind of happiness; the drum, the fire drum shouted, "Red hair! The young one has red hair! Listen, believe the drum and not the mother! Dr-rum-a-lum! Dr-rum-a-lum!"

And all the town agreed with what the fire drum said.

The boy was taken to church and was christened. There was nothing unusual about the name given him; he was called Peter. Everybody in town called him "Peter, the drummer's red-haired boy," but his mother kissed that red hair and called him "Golden Treasure."

In the clayey embankment along the hollow road, many people had scratched their names to be remembered. "Fame," said the drummer. "That's always important." So he, too, scratched his name there and that of his little son. And in the spring the swallows came; in their long travels they had seen many characters cut into rock cliffs and on the temple walls of India, telling of the great deeds of mighty kings, immortal names so old that no one could even read them now. Name value! Fame! The swallows built their nests in the hollow road, in holes in the embankment. Rain crumbled it and washed away all the names, the drummer's and his little son's with them. "However, Peter's name stayed there for a year and a half," said the father.

"Fool!" thought the fire drum, but it only said, "Dr-rum, dr-rum, dr-rum! Dr-rum-a-lum!"

"The drummer's son with the red hair" was a lively and high-spirited boy. He had a lovely voice; he could sing, and sing he did, as does the bird in the forest: all melody and no tune. "He ought to be a choirboy," said his mother, "and sing in the church, standing under the pretty gilded angels whom he looks like."

"Fire cat!" said the town wits. The drum heard it from the neighbors.

"Don't go home, Peter," cried the street boys. "If they make you sleep in the attic your hair will set the thatch on fire, and that will start the fire drum."

"Look out for the drumsticks!" retorted Peter; although he was only a little fellow, he was courageous, and threw his fist right into the stomach of the boy nearest him, knocking his legs from under him; and the others took to their legs—their own legs!

The state musician was proud and haughty; he was the son of a royal servant. He liked Peter and took him home with him for hours at a time, gave him a violin and taught him to play; it seemed to show in the boy's fingers that he would become more than a drummer, that he would become a state musician.

"I want to be a soldier," said Peter, for he was still a very small fellow and thought it would be the finest thing in the world to shoulder a gun and to march—"One, two! One, two!"—and to wear a uniform and carry a saber.

"You'll learn to obey the drum! Dr-rum-a-lum! Come, come!" said the drum.

"Yes, you may march ahead to become a general," said the father, "but only if there is a war."

"God save us from that!" said the mother.

"We have nothing to lose!" said the drummer.

"Yes, we have my boy!" said she.

"But when he could come home a general!" said the father.

"Without any arms or legs!" said the mother. "No, thank you, I'd rather keep my Golden Treasure whole!"

"Dr-rum! Dr-rum! Dr-rum!" beat the fire drum, and all the drums joined in. War really did come; the soldiers marched out, and the drummer's boy marched with them. "Red-top!" "Golden Treasure!" The mother wept; the father imagined him coming home famous; the state musician thought he would have been better off staying home and studying music.

"Red-top!" the soldiers said, and Peter laughed, but when some of them called him "Foxy," his mouth tightened and he looked straight ahead, as if that name did not concern him. The boy was smart, carefree, and good-humored, and that made him a favorite with his older comrades. Many nights he had to sleep under the open sky, in rain and mist, wet to the skin; but his good humor never failed. His drumsticks beat, "Dr-rum-a-lum! Everybody up!" Yes, he was certainly a born drummer boy.

It was a day of battle; the sun was not yet up, but it was morning; the air was cold and the fight was hot; the morning was foggy, but there was a still heavier fog from gunpowder. Bullets and grenades flew overhead and into heads, bodies, and limbs; still the command was "Forward!" One after another sank to his knees with bleeding temple and pale white face. The little drummer boy's color was still healthy; he wasn't hurt at all. With flashing eyes he watched the regimental dog running before him, and the animal was really happy, as if the whole thing were in fun and they were firing the bullets only to play with him.

"March! Forward, march!" was the command given the drummers; but sometimes orders have to be changed, with good reason, and now the word was, "Retreat!" But the little drummer boy still sounded, "March forward!" not understanding that the orders had been changed. The soldiers obeyed the drum, and it was lucky they did, for the mistake resulted in victory.

Lives and limbs were lost in the battle. The grenade tears away the flesh in bleeding fragments; the grenade sets fire to the straw heap where the poor wounded has dragged himself, to lie forsaken for many hours, forsaken perhaps until dead. It doesn't help to think about it, and yet people do think about it even far away in the peaceful town at home. There the drummer and his wife thought of it, for, of course, Peter was in the war.

It was the day of battle; the sun was not yet up, but it was morning. After a sleepless night spent in talking about their boy, the drummer and his wife had finally fallen asleep, for they knew that wherever he was God's hand was protecting him. And the father dreamed that the war was over, that the soldiers came home, and Peter was wearing a silver cross on his breast; but the mother dreamed that she walked into the church and looked at the painted pictures and the carved angels with the gilded hair and that her own dear boy, her heart's Golden Treasure, stood among the angels clad in white, and sang as sweetly as surely only the angels can sing, and was carried up into the sunshine with them, nodding tenderly to his mother.

"My Golden Treasure!" she cried, and awoke in the same instant. "Now I know that our Lord has taken him!" Then she folded her hands, leaned her head against the cotton bed curtain, and wept. "Where has he found rest? In the wide common grave they dig for so many of the brave dead, or in the deep waters of the marsh? No one will know his grave! No holy words will be read over it!" Silently the Lord's Prayer passed over her lips; her head drooped in fatigue, and she fell asleep.

Days pass by, in wakeful hours and in dreams.

It was toward evening, and a rainbow arched over the battlefield; it touched the edge of the wood and the deep marsh. There is an old saying that where the rainbow touches the earth a treasure lies buried, a golden treasure. And here was one. No one thought about the little drummer except his mother, and that's why she had dreamed of him. Not a hair of his head had been injured, not a single golden hair. "Dr-rum-a-lum, dr-rum-a-lum! There he is, there he is!" would the drum have said, and his mother would have sung, had she seen or dreamed this.

With song and hurrah, and wearing the green leaves of victory, the regiment marched home, when the war was over and peace had come. The regimental dog jumped and ran in wide circles, as though trying to make the journey three times longer.

Days passed and weeks passed, and at last Peter entered his parents' room; he was as brown as a hermit, his eyes bright, and his face as radiant as the sunshine. His mother held him in her arms and kissed his lips, his eyes, his red hair. She had her boy home again; he had no silver decoration on his breast, as his father had dreamed, but then he was unharmed, which his mother had not dreamed. And there was great joy; they laughed and they wept. And Peter embraced the old fire drum. "The old thing is still standing here!" he said. And his father beat a tattoo on it. "There's as much fuss as though there were a big fire in town!" said the drum to itself. "Fire in the roof, fire in the hearts! Golden Treasure! Dr-rum, dr-rum, dr-rum!"

And then? Yes, what then? Just ask the state musician. "Peter has outgrown the drum," he said. "He'll be a bigger man than I." And remember he was the son of a royal servant! But what had taken him a lifetime to learn, Peter had learned in half a year. There was something cheerful about him; his eyes sparkled, and his hair shone— that cannot be denied.

"He ought to dye his hair," said their next-door neighbor. "The policeman's daughter did, and look what it did for her; she was engaged at once!"

"Yes, but a little later her hair turned as green as duckweed, and she has to dye it again and again!"

"Well, she can afford to," said the neighbor woman, "and so can Peter. Doesn't he go into the best houses, even the mayor's, to teach Miss Lotte the harpsichord?"

Yes, play he could, play right out of his heart, the most charming pieces that had never been written down in notes. He played on moonlit nights and stormy ones as well. It was difficult to put up with, said the neighbors and the fire drum. He played until his thoughts soared strongly upward, and great plans for the future took shape before him. Fame!

The mayor's daughter, Lotte, sat at the harpsichord, and as her delicate fingers danced over the chords they vibrated in Peter's heart, until it seemed as if it were growing too big for his body. This happened not once, but many times, until one day he seized her delicate hand, kissed it, and gazed into her large brown eyes. Our Lord knows what he said; we others may guess it. Lotte blushed crimson, face and neck, and answered not a word, and just then they were interrupted by strangers, among them the councillor's son, with his high, smooth forehead. But Peter did not go, and Lotte's kindest glances were for him. At home that evening he talked of going abroad and of the golden treasure that his violin would bring him. Fame! "Dr-rum-a-lum! Dr-rum-a-lum! Dr-rum-a-lum!" said the fire drum. "Now something is surely wrong with Peter; I think the house must be on fire!"

The mother went to market the next day. "Have you heard the news, Peter?" she said, when she returned. "Such wonderful news! The mayor's daughter, Lotte, was betrothed to the councillor's son; it happened last evening!"

"No!" said Peter, and sprang up from his chair. But his mother said yes; she had learned it from the barber's wife, and the barber had it from the lips of the mayor himself. And Peter grew as pale as death and sat down again.

"Lord God! How do you feel?" said his mother.

"Fine, fine. Just let me alone!" he said, but the tears were rolling down his cheeks.

"My sweet child! My Golden Treasure!" said the mother, and cried. But the fire drum grumbled to itself, "Lotte is dead! Lotte is dead! Yes, that song is over now!"

The song was not over; it still had many unsung verses, long verses, the most beautiful, about a life's golden treasure. "What a fuss she makes!" said the next-door neighbor. The whole world has to read the letters she gets from her Golden Treasure, and hear what the newspapers say about him and his violin playing. He sends her money, too, for she needs that, now that she's a widow!"

"He plays before kings and emperors," said the state musician. "That was never my good luck, but at least he was my pupil, and he hasn't forgotten his old master."

"My husband dreamed," said his mother, "that Peter came home from the war with a silver cross on his chest. Well, he does wear a cross now, but it's not a decoration earned in the war; it's an order of knighthood. If his father had only lived to see it!"

"Famous!" said the fire drum, and everybody in his home town said the same. Peter, the red-haired boy of the drummer—Peter, whom they had seen wearing wooden shoes as a youngster, and seen as a drummer boy playing at dances—was now famous.

"He played to us before he played before the kings," said the mayor's wife. "Once upon a time he was crazy about our Lotte; he always aimed high! How my husband laughed when he learned that nonsense! Now Lotte is a councillor's wife."

Yes, there was a golden treasure hidden in the heart and soul of the poor child who as a little drummer boy had beaten "Forward!" to troops supposed to retreat; in his breast was a golden treasure indeed, the gift of music. It resounded from his violin as if an organ were inside, as if all the elves of Midsummer Eve danced along its strings, and one could hear the song of the throstle and the human voice together; his playing enraptured people's hearts, and carried his name throughout all lands, like a great fire, a fire of inspiration. "And he's so handsome, too!" said the young ladies and the old ones as well. Yes, the oldest lady bought herself an album for the locks of celebrities, just so she could beg for a tress from the young violinist's abundant and beautiful hair—a treasure, a golden treasure.

And the son returned to the drummer's humble dwelling, as handsome as a prince, happier than a king, his eyes bright, his face like sunshine. He held his mother in his arms, and she kissed his warm mouth and wept as happily as one can weep with joy. He greeted every old piece of furniture in the room, the chest of drawers with the teacups and flower vases on it and the little cot where he had slept as a child. But he dragged the old fire drum into the middle of the room and said, both to his mother and to the drum, "Father would have beaten a welcome on you today; now I must do it instead!"

So he thundered a regular tempest on the drum, and the old drum felt itself so honored that the skin of the drumhead burst.

"He certainly has a fine fist!" said the drum. "Now I'll always have a souvenir of him. I expect that his mother, too, will burst from joy over her Golden Treasure!"

That's the story of Golden Treasure.

THE STORM SHIFTS THE SIGNBOARDS (1865)

In olden days, when Grandfather was just a little boy and wore red trousers, a red jacket, a sash around his waist, and a feather in his cap—for that's the way little boys dressed in his childhood when they wore their best clothes—so many things were different from nowadays. There were often street pageants, which we don't see now, for they have been done away with, because they became old-fashioned; but it's fun to hear Grandfather tell about them.

It must have been quite a show to see the shoemakers move their signboard when they changed to a new guild hall. A big boot and a two-headed eagle were painted on their waving silken banner; the youngest journeymen carried the welcome cup and the guild chest, and had red and white ribbons dangling from their shirt sleeves; the older ones wore naked swords with lemons stuck on the points. They had a full band, and the best of their instruments was "The Bird," as Grandfather called the long pole with the half moon and all sorts of sounding dingle-dangle things on it—real Turkish music. It was lifted up and swung, and it was dazzling to the eyes when the sun shone on all that polished gold and silver and brass.

In front of the procession ran a Harlequin in clothes made of many-colored patches, with a black face and with bells on his head, like a sleigh horse. He struck the people with his wand, which made a noise without hurting, and the people pushed against each other to move back and forth; little boys and girls fell over their own feet right into the gutters; old women elbowed their way along, looking sour and scolding. Some people laughed and some people chatted; there were spectators on the steps and in the windows, and, yes, even on the roofs. The sun shone; a little rain fell on the people now and then, but that was a good thing for the farmers; and when finally they became wet through, that was a real blessing to the country.

Ah, what stories Grandfather could tell! When he was a little boy he had seen all that grand show at the height of its splendor. The oldest guild journeyman made a speech from the scaffold where the signboard was hung; it was in verse, just like poetry—which, indeed, it was. There had been three of them working on it, and before writing it they had drunk a whole bowl of punch, so that it would be really good. And the people cheered the speech, but still more they cheered the Harlequin when he appeared on the scaffold and mocked the speaker. The clown cut his capers so gaily, and drank punch out of schnapps glasses, which he then threw out among the people, who caught them in the air. Grandfather had one of them, which the plasterer had caught and presented to him. Yes, it was fun. And at last the signboard hung, decked with flowers and wreaths, on the new guild hall.

You never forget a sight like that, no matter how old you grow, Grandfather said. He himself never forgot it, though afterward he saw many things of pomp and splendor and could tell about them; but the funniest thing of all was when he told about the moving of the signboards in the big town.

Grandfather had gone there with his parents when he was a little boy, and that was the first time he had seen the largest town in the country.

There were so many people in the streets that he thought the signboards were going to be moved; and there were many signboards to move. If these signs had been hung up inside instead of out of doors they would have been filled up hundreds of rooms. There were all kinds of garments painted on the sign at the tailor's; he could change people from uncouth to genteel. There were signboards of tobacconists, with the most cunning little boys smoking cigars, just as in real life; there were signs with butter and salted herrings, minister's ruffs and coffins, and signboards that just carried inscriptions and announcements. Indeed, one could spend a whole day going up and down the streets and looking at the pictures, and at the same time you could learn what sort of people lived inside the houses, for they had hung their own signs outside. That is a very good thing, Grandfather said; in a large town it is instructive to know who lives in all the houses.

But then, something was about to happen to the signboards, just as Grandfather came to town; he has told me about it himself, and there wasn't then any twinkle in his eye, as Mother used to say there was when he was fooling me; he looked quite trustworthy.

That first night he came to the big town, the weather was worse than any we ever have read about in the papers, a storm such as there had never been within man's memory. All the air was full of roof tiles; old wooden fences were blown over; a wheelbarrow even ran for its life by itself along the street. The wind howled in the air; it whistled and it shook everything. It was indeed a terrible storm. The water in the canal ran over the banks, not knowing where it belonged. The storm swept over the town, carrying the chimneys with it; more than one old, proud church tower bent and has never been quite straight since.

A sentry box stood outside the house of the honest old fire chief, whose engine was always the last one at the fire; the storm begrudged him that little box and flung it down the steps and rolled it along the street until, strangely enough, it arose and remained upright before the house of the poor carpenter who had saved the lives of three people at the last fire. But the sentry box didn't give that a thought. The barber's signboard, a large brass dish, was torn off and carried across into the councillor's window. All the neighbors said this seemed almost like malice, for they, like the most intimate lady friends of the family, called the mistress "the Razor"—she was so sharp and knew more about people than they knew about themselves.

A sign with a dried codfish drawn on it flew over to the door of a newspaper writer. That was a pretty poor joke on the part of the storm; it probably didn't remember that a newspaper writer isn't the sort of person to be joked about; he is a king in his own paper and in his own opinions.

The weathercock flew over to the roof of the opposite house, and there it remained—a picture of the darkest wickedness, said the neighbors.

The cooper's barrel was hung just under the sign for "Ladies' Apparel."

The restaurant's menu, which hung in a heavy frame near the door, was placed by the storm just over the entrance to the theater, where nobody ever went. It was a comical program, "Horseradish Soup and Stuffed Cabbage," but it made people go in.

The furrier's foxskin, which was his respectable sign, was hung on the bellpull of the young man who always went to morning church services looking like a folded umbrella, strove for the truth, and was "a model young man," said his aunt.

The sign "Establishment for Higher Education" was moved to the pool hall, and the establishment itself received a board inscribed, "Babies Brought Up Here by the Bottle." This wasn't really witty, only naughty; but the storm did it, and we can't control a storm.

It was a terrible night; and by morning, just think, nearly every signboard in town had been moved! In some cases it was done with so much malice that Grandfather wouldn't talk about it, but he laughed inwardly; I could see that, and it is possible he was up to some mischief.

The poor inhabitants of the big town, especially those who were not familiar with it, were all mixed up figuring out who was who; they couldn't help it when they judged by the signboards. Some people who thought they were coming to a solemn meeting of the town elders, assembled to discuss highly important matters, found themselves instead in a school full of noisy boys just about to jump over their desks.

There were even some people who mistook the church for the theater; and that was really awful!

There has never been such a storm in our days; only Grandfather saw one, and that was when he was a very little boy. Such a storm may never come in our time, but it may in our grandchildren's, and then we must hope and pray that they will keep indoors while the storm shifts the signboards!

KEPT SECRET BUT NOT FORGOTTEN (1866)

There was once an old mansion with a moat and drawbridge. The drawbridge was more often up than down; not all visitors are good or welcome. Under the eaves were loopholes to shoot out through, and for throwing boiling water, yes, even molten lead, down on the enemy if he approached too closely. Indoors were high rafted ceilings, and this was good because of the space it provided for the large amount of smoke that rolled up from the hearth fires, where huge, damp logs burned. On the walls hung pictures of men in armor and proud ladies in heavy robes; the grandest of all the ladies was living here. She was named Mette Mogens, and she was the lady of the manor.

One evening robbers came; they killed three of her guards, along with the watchdog, and they bound Lady Mette with the dog chain in the kennel and then seated themselves in the great hall and drank the wine and all the good beer from her cellar.

Lady Mette stood chained like a dog and yet could not even bark at them.

Then the robbers' servant boy came to her; he had very quietly stolen away from them, knowing this must not be noticed, for if it were they would put him to death.

"Lady Mette Mogens," said the boy, "can you remember when my father rode the wooden horse in your husband's time? You prayed for him then, but it wasn't possible for you to help further toward freeing him; he was made to sit astride the block until he became a cripple. But you sneaked down to him, as I have done now, and you laid a little stone under each of his feet, to give him some relief. No one saw it, or perhaps they pretended not to see it, for you were the gracious young mistress of the manor. This my father has told me, and this I have kept secret but not forgotten. Now I will free you, Lady Mette Mogens!"

And then the two of them took horses from the stable and rode, through rain and wind, to get the help of friends.

"This was being well repaid for that small service to the old man," said Mette Mogens.

"Kept secret but not forgotten," said the boy.

The robbers were hanged.

There stood an old house; it still stands there, in fact—not the home of Lady Mette Mogens, but that of another noble family.

It is in our own time. The sun is shining on the gilded spires on the turrets; little wooded isles lie like bouquets on the lake, and around them swim wild swans. There are roses growing in the garden, but the lady of the house herself is the loveliest rose, bright with happiness, the happiness of good deeds, not done outwardly before the wide world, but within the hearts of people—and there kept secret but not forgotten.

Now she goes from the mansion to a little peasant cottage in the field. In it there lives a poor, paralyzed girl. A window in the little room faces the north, where the sun does not enter, and where her only view is a patch of meadow that is shut off by the high earth around a ditch. But today there is sunshine inside; God's warm, wonderful sun is there. It comes from the south through a new window where before there had been just a wall.

The paralyzed girl sits in the warm sunshine and looks out on wood and stream; her world has become so wide and so beautiful, and all at a single word from the kindly lady of the manor.

"That word was so easy, the deed so small," she says, "and the happiness it gave me was so unspeakably great and blessed."

And that is why she does so many good deeds and remembers all those in the poor homes about her and in the rich homes, too, where there also are afflicted people. Her deeds are done in secret, and kept secret, but they are not forgotten by our Lord.

There was an old house in the middle of the great, busy city. In it were halls and chambers, but we won't enter them; we'll remain in the kitchen. And here it is snug and bright; it is clean and neat. The copper utensils shine; the table is polished, and the sink is as spotless as a freshly scrubbed larding board. All this has been done by the maid-of-all-work, who has still found time to put on her own best dress, as if she were going to church. She has a bow on her cap, a black bow, which signifies mourning. Yet she has no one of her own to mourn, neither father nor mother, neither family nor lover. She is a poor, serving maid. Once she was engaged to a poor young man, and they loved each other dearly. One day he came to her.

"We two have nothing," he said, "and the rich widow across the way has expressed a warm interest in me. She wants to make me well-to-do, but you are in my heart. What would you advise me to do?"

"That which you think will be best for your happiness," said the girl. "Be kind and devoted to her; but remember that from the moment we part, we two must never see each other again."

A couple of years went by. Then she met him, her former friend and sweetheart, on the street. He looked ill and miserable. Then she could not keep from asking him, "How are you getting on?"

"Prosperously and well in every way," he said. "My wife is brave and good, but you are still in my heart. I have fought hard, and it will soon be over. Now we will not see each other again before we are with the Lord!"

A week has since passed. This morning it said in the newspaper that he has passed on; therefore the maid wears mourning. Her sweetheart has left a wife and three stepchildren, it said in the paper; that rings badly, and yet the metal is pure.

The black bow tells of mourning; the girl's face tells of it still more; in her heart it is kept secret but will never be forgotten.

Yes, as you see, there are three stories, three leaves on one stalk. Would you like to have more such clover leaves? There are many in the book of the heart, kept secret but not forgotten.

THE PORTER'S SON (1866)

The General's family lived on the first floor, and the Porter's family lived in the cellar. There was a vast distance between them—the whole first floor, as well as all the grades of society; but both families lived under the same roof, and their windows looked out in the same street and the same garden.

In this garden there was a blooming acacia—whenever it did bloom—and sometimes the smartly dressed nurse would sit under it with the still more smartly dressed child, the General's "Little Emilie."

The Porter's little son, with his dark hair and large brown eyes, used to dance barefoot before them; and the little girl would laugh and stretch her tiny hands out to him. And if the General saw this from his window he would nod down at them and say, *"Charmant!"* The General's wife, who was so young that she might almost have been her husband's daughter by an earlier marriage, never herself looked out into the yard; but she had given orders that the Porter's boy could play near her own child, but never touch it. And the nurse strictly carried out the lady's orders.

The sun shone in upon those who dwelt on the first floor and those who lived in the cellar. The acacia put out its blossoms, they fell away, and new ones came the next year. The tree bloomed, and the Porter's little son bloomed; he looked like a fresh tulip.

The General's little daughter grew to be a delicate child, as dainty as the rosy petal of the acacia blossom. Now she seldom sat under the tree, for she took the fresh air in a carriage, She went with her mother on drives, and always nodded to the Porter's son, George; yes, and even kissed her fingers toward him, till her mother told her she was now too grown-up for that.

One morning he had to bring the General some papers and mail that had been left in the Porter's room. He had mounted the staircase and was passing the door of the broom closet when he heard a peep from inside it. He thought perhaps it was a stray chicken chirping, but it was the General's little daughter, dressed in muslin and lace.

"Don't tell Papa and Mamma, for they would be angry!"

"What's the matter, little lady?" asked George.

"It's all burning everywhere!" she said. "It's in full blaze!"

George flung open the door to the little nursery, where the window curtain was nearly all burned; the curtain rod had caught fire and was flaming! Quickly he sprang forward, pulled it down, and called for help: without him the whole house would have caught fire.

The General and his wife questioned Little Emilie.

"I just took only one single match," she said, "and that lighted up and then the whole curtain lighted up! I spit to put out the fire; I spit all I could, but I didn't have enough spit, so I came out and hid, 'cause I knew Papa and Mamma would be angry!"

"Spit!" said the General. "What sort of word is that? When did you ever hear your papa or your mamma talk of spitting? You must have learned that word downstairs!"

But little George received a penny. It didn't go to the candy store, but into his savings bank, and there were soon so many pennies there that he could buy himself a paintbox and color his drawings.

He had many of these drawings, for they seemed to come out of his very pencil and finger tips. He presented the first colored pictures to Little Emilie.

"Charmant!" said the General.

The General's wife admitted that it was quite clear what the little one meant in his pictures.

"There's genius in him!"

Those were the words the Porter's wife brought back down into the cellar.

The General and his lady were of the nobility; they had two coats of arms on their carriage, one for each of them. The lady had a crest worked on every piece of clothing, inside and outside, in her nightcap, and even on her night cover. This, her own coat of arms, was an expensive one, bought by her father for bright dollars, for he hadn't been born with it, and neither had she.

She had come into the world seven years before the crest, a fact that was remembered by most people, though forgotten by the family. The General's coat of arms was old and large; one's back might well creak with dignity of this one alone, to say nothing of the two of them. And there was indeed a creaking in the lady's back when she drove stiff and stately to the court balls.

The General was old and gray, but he knew how to sit on a horse, and rode out every day, with a groom at a respectful distance behind him. When he arrived at a party it was as if he had ridden into the room on his high horse, and he wore so many decorations that it was almost unbelievable, but that was by no means his fault. When a very young man he had performed military duties by taking part in the great autumnal war games that used to be held in times of peace. He always told an anecdote of those days—his only one. The officer under him cut off and captured one of the princes; and the prince and his little troop, all prisoners like himself, had to ride back to towns behind the General. It was an event never to be forgotten, and the General told it again and again, year after year, always ending with the remarkable words he had spoken when he returned the prince's sword to him: "Only my subaltern officer could have made your Royal Highness a prisoner; I—never!" Whereupon the prince had answered, "You are incomparable!"

The General had never seen active service, for when war came to his native land he went on diplomatic missions, through three foreign countries. He spoke French until he had almost forgotten his own language; he danced beautifully, and he rode well; decorations blossomed on his blouse in indescribable abundance; sentinels presented arms to him; one of the prettiest of the girls presented herself to him—and became his wife. And they had a lovely little girl, so pretty that she seemed to have fallen from Heaven; and the Porter's son danced in the garden before her as soon as she was old enough to take notice, and gave her all his colored drawings; and she looked at them and was so delighted with them that she tore them to pieces. She was so beautiful and charming.

"My rose petal!" said the General's wife. "You were born to be the bride of a prince!"

The prince was already standing outside the door, but no one knew it. People can't see much farther than the doorstep.

"The other day our boy shared his bread and butter with her," said the Porter's wife. "There was neither cheese nor meat with it, but she enjoyed it every bit as much as roast beef. There'd have been a fine hullabaloo if the General and his wife had seen that little party, but they didn't!"

George had shared his bread and butter with Little Emilie, and gladly would he have shared his very heart with her, if only it would have pleased her. He was a good boy, wide-awake and intelligent, and now he was studying drawing at the evening school at the academy. Little Emilie, too, was advancing in learning; she talked French and had a dancing master.

"George is going to be confirmed at Easter," said the Porter's wife. That was how far George was advanced.

"It would be very sensible to have him serve an apprenticeship," said the father; "in some good profession, of course; and then we would have him out of the house!"

"But he could come home at nights to sleep," said the mother.

"It wouldn't be easy to find a master who had a spare room. And we'd have to give him clothes, too; the little food he eats now we can easily afford to give him; he is happy with a couple of boiled potatoes; then he has his teaching free. Just let him go on the way he is, and he'll turn out a blessing to us, you may be sure! Didn't the professor say so?"

The confirmation clothes were ready. Mother did the sewing herself, but the cloth had been cut by the tailor, and he knew how to cut it. The Porter's wife said that if he had only been better placed, and could have opened a shop with apprentices, he could have become court tailor.

Yes, the clothes were ready, and the candidate was ready. On confirmation day George received a great pocket watch from his godfather, the flax dealer's old clerk, the wealthiest of George's godfathers. The watch was old and honored; it was always a little fast, but that's better than being too slow. It was a precious present. And from the General's there came a hymnbook bound in leather, sent by the little lady to whom George had given his pictures. On the flyleaf were written his name and her name as "his gracious well-wisher." This was written according to the dictation of the General's wife, and the General himself had read it through and said, *"Charmant!"*

"That was really a great courtesy from a family of such rank," said the Porter's wife. And George would have to go upstairs, in his confirmation clothes and carrying his hymnbook, to thank them.

The General's wife had a number of compresses on her head, for she had one of her bad headaches, which always came when she was bored. She looked very kindly at George and wished him the best of luck and none of her headaches.

The General was wearing his dressing gown, with a tasseled cap and red-legged Russian boots. He paced up and down the floor three times, engrossed in his own thoughts and memories. Then he stood still and said, "So now little George is a Christian man! Let him be also an honest man, paying due respect to his government! Someday, when you are old, you can say the General taught you that sentence." That was a much longer speech than the General usually made; and he returned to his inner thoughts and looked impressive.

But George heard and saw little of all that up there; nothing remained fixed in his memory so firmly as little Miss Emilie. How lovely she was, and how gentle; how she flitted about, and how delicate she was! If one should draw her portrait it would have to be in a soap bubble. There was a fragrance about her clothing and her curly blonde hair as if she were a rosebush that had just burst into bloom. And he had once shared his bread and butter with her, and she had eaten it with a huge appetite and smiled at him with every second mouthful. Could she possibly still remember it? Surely she did; it was in memory of this that she had given him the beautiful hymnbook.

And so, on New Year's Day, just as the new moon of the new year rose, he went out of doors with a loaf and a shilling and opened the book at random to see what hymn should appear. It was a song of praise and thanksgiving. Then he opened it again to see what should come forth for Little Emilie. He tried very hard not to dip into the part of the book containing the funeral hymns, but in spite of his care he *did* dip in between death and the grave. You couldn't believe in that sort of thing—not in the least! And yet he was terribly frightened when soon afterward the dainty little girl was laid up with sickness and the doctor's carriage came to the street door daily.

"They won't be able to keep her," said the Porter's wife. "Our Lord knows very well whom He wants."

But they kept her, and George sent her pictures he drew. He drew the Czar's palace, the ancient Kremlin in Moscow, exactly as it was, with turrets and cupolas; in George's drawing they looked like big green and gilt cucumbers. Little Emilie was so pleased that during the week George sent her several more pictures, all of buildings, because that would give her plenty to think about, wondering what went on inside the doors and windows.

He drew a Chinese house, with bells hanging on all the sixteen stories. He drew two Greek temples, with steps around slender marble pillars. He drew a Norwegian church; you could see it was made entirely of timbers, deeply carved and curiously put together; every story looked as if it had rockers. But the most beautiful design of all was a castle, which he called "Little Emilie's." This was to be her own home, so George had made it all up from his imagination and selected for it whatever seemed prettiest in each of the other buildings. It had the carved beams of the Norwegian church, the marble pillars of the Greek temples, bells on every story, and green and gilded cupolas on the top, like those on the Czar's Kremlin. It was a true child's castle! And under every window was written what took place in that hall or that room: "Here Emilie sleeps": "Here Emilie dances"; and "Here she is to play 'visitors coming.'" It was amusing to look at, and you may be sure it was looked at. "*Charmant!*" said the General.

But the old Count—for there was an old count, of even greater distinction than the General, with a castle and a mansion of his own—said nothing. They had told him that all this had been imagined and drawn by the little son of the Porter. Not that the boy was so very little now; indeed, he had been confirmed. The old Count looked carefully at the pictures and had his own long, quiet thoughts about them.

One gray, damp, and dismal morning proved one of the brightest and best days for little George. The professor at the art academy sent for him.

"Listen, my friend," he said. "Let's have a little talk together. Our Lord has favored you with good talent; now He's favoring you with good friends. The old Count in the corner house has spoken to me about you. I have seen your pictures, too; frankly, those we can cross out, for there would be too much to correct in them. From now on you may come twice a week to my drawing school, and so in time you'll learn to do better. I believe there is more of the architect in you than of the painter. You will have time to think about this, but now go up right away to the old Count on the corner and thank the good Lord for such a friend."

It was a great mansion, that corner house! Carved figures of elephants and camels of the olden days were around the windows, but the Count was fonder of modern times, and anything good they brought, whether from drawing room, cellar, or garret.

"I believe," said the Porter's wife, "that the grander folks really are the less stuck-up they are. How kind and plain the old Count is! And he can talk just like you and me! You won't find that at the General's. There was George yesterday, head over heels with delight, because the Count treated him so graciously; and I'm much the same way today, after talking with that great man. Wasn't it lucky now that we didn't have George serve an apprenticeship? That boy has talent."

"But he must have outside help," said the father.

"Well, he's got that help now," said the mother. "The Count spoke right out, plain and honest."

"But it was at the General's that it was all started," said the father. "We must thank them, too."

"We can do that, too," said the mother, "though there's not much to thank them for, in my opinion. I'll thank our Lord first of all, and thank Him all the more now that Little Emilie is getting better again."

Emilie kept getting better, and George kept getting better; inside of a year he won the small silver medal, and later the large one.

"It would have been better, after all, if he had learned a trade!" said the Porter's wife, and cried. "We would have kept him here then. Why does he have to go off to Rome? I shall never see him any more, even if he comes home again, and that he'll never do, the sweet child!"

"But it's to his good fortune and glory," said the father.

"Ah, it's all very well to talk that way, my friend!" said the mother. "You talk, but you don't mean a word of it. You're just as heartbroken as I am!"

And it was all true, both about the sorrow and the departure. It was, however, a great piece of luck for the young man, said everyone.

And then there was a round of farewells, also at the General's. His wife did not appear, for she had one of her bad headaches. At parting the General related his only anecdote—what he had said to the prince, and how the prince had replied to him, "You are incomparable!" Then he gave George his hand, a flabby old hand.

Emilie gave George her hand, too, and looked almost sad; but George was the saddest.

Time passes when one is busy, but it also passes when one is idle. The time is equally long, though not equally profitable. It was profitable to George, and never seemed long, except when he thought of those at home and how they were getting along, in the drawing room and in the cellar. Yes, he had news of them, and a great deal may be folded up in a letter—bright sunshine and dark, heavy days. One letter told that his father had died, and so his mother was alone now. Emilie had been an angel of comfort at the time, having come down to her, wrote his mother. And as for herself, she added, she had received permission to keep her husband's job.

The General's wife kept a diary; in it were entered every ball, every party she had attended, every visit she had paid or received. The diary was illustrated with the cards of diplomats and other noblemen. She was very proud of her diary; it increased in size season after season, through many great headaches, but also through many bright evenings—that is, court balls.

Emilie went to her first court ball. Her mother wore pink, with black Spanish lace, while Emilie's dress was white, so fine and pure! Green ribbons fluttered like leaves in her curly blonde locks, and she was crowned with a wreath of white water lilies. Her eyes were so blue and clear, her mouth so beautiful and red; she looked like a little mermaid, as beautiful as you could imagine. Three princes danced with her; that is, one after the other. Her mother had no headache for a week.

But the first ball wasn't the last of the season. The pace became too much for Emilie, and so it was well that summer brought rest and a change of air. The family was invited to the old Count's castle.

The garden of this castle was worth seeing. A part of it was quite old-fashioned, with stiff green hedges, where one seemed to be walking between green screens pierced with peepholes. Box trees and yew trees were clipped into stars and pyramids; water sprang from fountains set with cockleshells; on all sides stood figures made of the heaviest stone, as one could plainly tell from both the clothes and the faces; each flower bed had its own device—a fish, a heraldic shield, or a monogram. This was the French part of the garden. From this section one seemed to emerge into the free, natural woods, where the trees could grow as they wished, and therefore, grew great and splendid. The grass was green and could be walked on; it was mowed, rolled, and well cared for. This was the English half of the garden.

"Old times and modern times," said the Count. "They meet here with loving embraces! In a couple of years the house itself will take on its proper importance. It will be a complete change into something handsomer and better. I'll show you the plans, and I'll even show you the architect; he is coming to dinner."

"*Charmant!*" said the General.

"This garden is paradise!" said the General's wife. "And over there you have a baronial castle!"

"Oh, that's my henhouse," replied the Count. "The pigeons live in the tower, and the turkeys on the first floor, but old Else reigns in the parlor. She has guest rooms all around her, one for the sitting hens, one for the hens and chickens, while the ducks have their own outlet to the water."

"*Charmant!*" repeated the General, and they all went to see this fine place.

Old Else stood in the middle of the parlor, and beside her stood the architect— George! After so many years, he and Little Emilie met again—in the henhouse! Yes, there he stood, and he was a handsome figure to look at, his face frank and firm, his hair black and shiny, and in the corners of his mouth a little smile that said, "There's a little imp behind my ear who knows all about you, outside and inside!" Old Else had taken off her wooden shoes and stood in her stocking feet, out of respect for her illustrious visitors. And the hens clucked, and the cock crowed, while the ducks waddled along, tap, tap, tap.

But the pale, slender girl, his childhood friend, the General's daughter, stood before George with her otherwise pallid cheeks now blushing like the rose, her eyes wide, and her lips speaking without uttering a syllable. Such was his greeting—the sweetest that any young man could hope for from a young lady, unless they were of the same family or had often danced together; she and the architect had never danced together.

The Count took his hand and presented him, saying, "He's not a perfect stranger, our young friend, Mr. George."

The General's wife curtsied; her daughter was about to offer her hand, but drew it back.

"Our little Mr. George!" said the General. "We're old housefriends; *charmant!*"

"You have become quite an Italian," said his wife, "and I presume you speak the language now like a native."

The General's wife could sing in Italian but not speak it, said the General.

At the dinner table George sat at Emilie's right side. The General had escorted her, while the Count had escorted the General's wife. George talked, and told anecdotes, which he could tell well. He was the life of the party, though the old Count could have been, too, had he wanted to be.

Emilie sat silently; her ears listened, her eyes sparkled—but she said nothing.

Then she and George stood among the flowers, behind a screen of roses on the veranda, and again it was left to him to begin speaking.

"Thank you for your kindness to my old mother," he said. "I know that on the night of my father's death you went down and stayed with her till his eyes had closed. Thank you!" Then he raised her hand and kissed it, as was proper on such an occasion. She blushed, becoming rosy red, but pressed his hand in return and gazed at him with tender blue eyes.

"Your mother was a loving soul, and she was so fond of you. She let me read all your letters, so I almost feel I know you. And I remember how kind you were to me when I was little. You gave me pictures—"

"Which you tore to pieces," said George.

"No, I still have my own castle left—I mean the drawing of it."

"And now I must really build it!" said George, and grew quite excited himself as he said it.

In their own rooms the General and his wife talked about the Porter's son. Why, he knew how to carry himself and to speak with knowledge and refinement. "He could be a tutor," said the General.

"Genius!" said the General's wife, and that was all she did say.

Often during those fine summer days George came to the castle of the Count. They missed him when he didn't come.

"How much more our Lord has given to you than to us ordinary beings!" Emilie said to him. "Are you grateful for it now?"

George was flattered that this beautiful young girl should look up to him. He found her very gifted.

And the General was more and more convinced that Mr. George could hardly have been a real child of the cellar. "However, his mother was a mighty fine woman," he said; "I owe her that sentence as an epitaph!"

Summer passed, winter came, and there was still more to tell about Mr. George. He had received attention and favor in the highest of all highest places. The General had met him at the court ball!

And now there was a ball planned at home for Little Emilie. Could Mr. George be invited?

"Whom the King invites, the General can invite!" said the General, drawing himself up a good inch higher.

So Mr. George was invited, and he came. And princes and counts came, and each danced better than the other. But Emilie danced only the first dance, for during that she strained her ankle, not seriously but painfully, so she had to stop dancing and watch the others. And there she sat, looking on, while the architect stood beside her.

"You're giving her the whole of St. Peter's Church at Rome!" said the General as he passed, smiling like good humor itself.

A few days later he received Mr. George with the same smile of good humor. The young man had come to thank him for the ball, of course, and had he anything else to say? Yes—and the most surprising, astonishing, insane words were uttered by him. The General could hardly believe his ears. A preposterous declamation, an unbelievable proposition! Mr. George actually asked for Emilie as his wife!

"Man!" said the General as he began to boil. "I cannot understand you! What are you saying? What do you want? I don't know you! Sir! Fellow! You come and break into my house! Am I to remain here or am I not?" And then he backed into his bedroom, turned the key, and let Mr George stand alone. He stood there for a few moments, then turned around and left.

In the hallway he met Emilie. "What did my father say?" she asked in a trembling voice.

George pressed her hand. "He ran away from me—a better time will come."

There were tears in Emilie's eyes, while in the young man's were courage and confidence; the sun shone in upon them both and blessed them.

In his bedroom the General sat boiling; yes, still boiling—and then he boiled over and spluttered, "Lunacy! Porter madness!"

Inside of an hour the General's wife had heard it all from the General himself, and she sent for Emilie, to be alone with her. "Poor girl," she said. "To think of his insulting you like that, insulting all of us! I see there are tears in yours eyes; they're quite becoming to you. You really look charming in tears; you remind me of myself on my wedding day. Go ahead, cry, Little Emilie."

"Yes, that I certainly shall," said Emilie, "unless you and Papa say 'yes'!"

"Child!" cried the General's wife. "You're ill! You're delirious, and I'm getting one of my dreadful headaches! Oh, the miseries that are descending upon our house! Don't let your mother die, Emilie, because then you'll have no mother!" And her eyes filled with tears; she couldn't bear to consider her own death.

Among the notices of appointments to be read in the news paper was the following: "Mr. George has been appointed Professor, 5th Class, No. 8."

"What a shame his father and mother are dead and can't read that!" said the new porters who now lived in the cellar under the General. They knew that the Professor had been born and brought up within those four walls.

"Now he'll have to pay the title tax!" said the man.

"Now, isn't that a lot for a poor child!" said the wife.

"Eighteen rix-dollars a year!" said the man. "Yes, that's a lot of money."

"No, I'm talking about the title!" said the wife. "You don't suppose having to pay the tax will worry him! He can earn that money many times over, and he'll probably marry a rich wife as well. If we had children, husband, a child of ours would also be an architect and a professor!"

Thus George was well spoken of in the cellar. He was well spoken of on the first floor, too; the old Count took good care of that.

It was the old drawings from his childhood days that presented an occasion for speaking about him. But how did these come to be mentioned? There was talk of Russia and Moscow, and so, of course, this brought one right to the Kremlin, of which little George had made that drawing for little Miss Emilie. How many pictures he used to draw! There was one the Count especially remembered—"Little Emilie's Castle," with signs showing where she slept, where she danced, and where she played "visitors coming." Yes, the Professor had great talent. He might someday become an old privy councillor—that wasn't at all unlikely—and build a real castle for the young lady before he died; why not?

"That was a strange form of gaiety," said the General's wife after the Count had gone. The General nodded thoughtfully and then went out riding, with the groom a respectful distance behind him, and he sat prouder than ever on his high horse.

Little Emilie's birthday brought cards and notes, books and flowers. The General kissed her on the brow, and his wife kissed her on the lips. They were loving parents, and both they and Emilie were honored with noble visitors—even two of the princes. Then there was much talk about balls and theaters, about diplomatic embassies, and the governments of kingdoms and empires. Then the talk turned on rising young men and native talent, and this brought the name of the young Professor into the conversation—Mr. Architect George.

"He is building for immortality," someone said. "And meanwhile he is building himself into one of the first families!"

"One of the first families!" repeated the General when he was alone with his wife. "Which one of our first families!"

"I can guess which was meant," said the General's wife. "But I won't speak of it or even think about it. God may have ordained it so, but I will be very surprised if he has!"

"Let me be surprised, too!" said the General. "I haven't an idea in my head!" Then he sank into a reverie, waiting for an idea to come.

There is a power, an unspeakable power, granted to a man by a few drops of grace from above—the grace of kings, the grace of God—and both of these were granted to little George.

But we are forgetting the birthday.

Emilie's room was fragrant with flowers from her friends and playmates. On her table lay fine presents, tokens of greeting and remembrance, but not one came from George. A gift from him would not have reached her, but it was not needed, for the whole house was a souvenir of him. A memorial flower peeped out from the broom closet under the stairs, where Emilie had peeped out when the curtain was burning and George had rushed up as first fireman. When she glanced from the window the acacia tree reminded her of childhood days. The blossoms and leaves were gone, but the tree stood shrouded in frost, like a great branch of coral, and the moon shone big and clear through the branches, unchanged though ever-changing, just as it was when George shared his bread and butter with Little Emilie.

From a drawer she took out the drawings of the Czar's Kremlin and her own castle remembrances from George. As she looked at them and mused over them, many thoughts arose in her mind. She remembered the day when, unnoticed by father or mother, she had stolen down to where the Porter's wife lay on her deathbed; she had sat by her side, held her hand, and heard her last words, "Blessings—George!" The mother's thoughts had been of her son. But now the words seemed to Emilie to carry a deeper meaning. In truth, George was with her on her birthday.

It so happened that the next day there was another birthday in the house, the General's, for he had been born the day after his daughter—naturally, many years earlier. Again there were presents, and among them a splendid—looking saddle, extremely comfortable and expensive; its only duplicate belonged to one of the princes. Who could have sent it? The General was in ecstasy. If the little card with it had said, "Thanks for yesterday," we could all guess where it came from, but the card said, "From one whom the General does not know."

"Who in the world is there I don't know?" said the General. "I know everybody!" And his thoughts went from one to another of the many people he knew; indeed, he knew everybody. "It is from my wife!" he said at last. "She's playing a trick on me! *Charmant!*"

But she wasn't playing a trick on him; that time was past.

Once more there was a party, but this one wasn't at the General's. It was a fancy-dress ball given by one of the princes; many of the guests wore masks.

The General went as Rubens, in a Spanish costume with a small ruff and a rapier, and carried himself well indeed. His wife was Madame Rubens, in black velvet with a high bodice that was terribly warm, and her neck in a millstone—that is to say, of course, a large ruff. She looked exactly like a Dutch painting of the General's, in which the hands were especially admired; they were an exact likeness of those of the General's wife. Emilie went as Psyche, in lace and muslin. She was a floating tuft of swansdown; she had no need of the wings and just wore them to show she was Psyche.

It was a scene of magnificent pomp and splendor, with lights and flowers and many riches, and all in good taste. There was so much to see that one hardly had a chance to take notice of Madame Rubens' beautiful hands.

Then a black domino, with an acacia flower in his hood, danced by with Psyche.

"Who's that?" asked the General's wife.

"His Royal Highness," said the General. "I'm quite sure of it. I knew him immediately by his handshake."

The Generals' wife was doubtful.

General Rubens wasn't doubtful. He drew the black domino aside and traced the royal initials in the palm of his hand. They were denied, but a hint was given—the motto of the saddle—"One whom the General does not know!"

"But then I do know you!" said the General. "It was you who sent me the saddle." The domino waved his hand and disappeared among the dancers.

"Who was that black domino you were dancing with, Emilie?" asked the General's wife.

"I didn't ask his name," she replied.

"Because you knew it! It's the Professor! Count," she continued, turning to the Count, who stood nearby, "your protégé is here; the black domino with the acacia flower."

"It's quite possible, your ladyship," he replied. "But still, one of the princes is wearing the same costume."

"I know that handshake," said the General. "I received the saddle from the prince! I'm so sure I'm right that I am going to ask him to dinner."

"Do so," said the Count. "If it's the prince, he'll be sure to come."

"And if it's the other he won't come," said the General, making his way to the black domino, who was standing talking to the king. The General offered a most respectful invitation, together with hopes of a better acquaintance. He smiled confidently, for he knew quite well whom he was inviting, and he spoke loudly and distinctly.

The domino lifted his mask, and it was George!

"Does the General repeat his invitation?" he asked.

The General drew himself up an inch, took on a stiffer bearing, took two steps backward and one step forward, as if he were dancing a minuet. All the gravity and sternness he could muster—in short, *all the General*—were in his patrician features.

"I never go back on my word—the Professor is invited!" And he bowed, with a sidelong glance at the king, who must certainly have heard everything.

And so the General gave a dinner, and his only guests were the old count and his protégé.

"Now that I've got my foot under the table," thought George, "the foundation stone is laid."

And indeed it was; it was laid with great solemnity by the General and his wife.

The young man had come and gone and as the General well knew, had spoken like a member of good society and been most interesting; the General had even found himself repeating his "*Charmant!*" many times. The General's wife spoke of her dinner, spoke of it to one of the highest and most important of the court ladies, and the latter asked for an invitation for herself the next time the Professor should come. So of course, he had to be invited again. And invited he was, and came, and again he was "*Charmant.*" He could even play chess!

"He doesn't come from the cellar," said the General. "Most certainly he is some scion of nobility; there are many such, and it isn't any fault of his!"

The Professor could enter the King's house, so he could very well enter the

General's; but as for taking root there—there was no talk of that—except by the whole town!

He did take root, and he grew. The dew of grace had fallen from above.

So no one was surprised that, when the Professor became State Councillor, Emilie became Madame State Councillor.

"Life is either tragedy or comedy," said the General. "In a tragedy people die; in a comedy they win each other."

And here they won each other. And they had three sturdy sons, though not all at once.

Whenever the sweet children came to see Grandfather or Grandmother, they galloped on sticks through rooms and halls. And the General rode on a stick behind them—"As a groom for the little State Councillors!" The General's wife sat on a sofa and smiled, even if she did have one of her bad headaches.

That's how far George got on in the world, and he got much farther, too; or else it wouldn't have been worth my while to tell you the story of "The Porter's Son."

AUNTY (1866)

You ought to have known Aunty; she was so lovely. And yet, to be more specific, she wasn't lovely in the usual sense of the word, but she was sweet and charming and funny in her own way—just the type to gossip about when one is in the mood to gossip and be facetious over someone. She should have been put in a play, just because she herself simply lived for the theater and everything that goes on in it. She was so very respectable, even if Agent Nob, whom Aunty called Snob, said she was stage-struck.

"The theater is my schoolroom," she said, "my fountain of knowledge. There I have brushed up on my old Biblical history. Take *Moses*, for instance, or *Joseph and His Brethren*—they're operas now. It is from the theater that I've gained my knowledge of world history, geography, and human nature. I've learned about Parisian life from French farces—it's naughty, but very interesting. How I have cried over *The Riquebourg Family*—to think that the husband had to drink himself to death just so his wife could get her young sweetheart! Ah, yes, many's the tear I've shed in the fifty years I've been going to the theater!"

Aunty knew every play, every piece of scenery, every actor who came on or ever had come on. She really only lived during the nine months of the theatrical season. A summer without a summer stock company was enough to age her, while an evening at the theater that lasted till past midnight prolonged her life. She didn't say, as people did, "Now we will have spring; the stork has come!" or, "There's an item in the paper about the early strawberries!" Instead, she announced the coming of autumn; "Have you seen that the box office is open? They'll begin the performances soon!"

She reckoned the value of a house and its location by its distance from the theater. She was heartbroken to have to leave the narrow alley behind the theater and move to a wide street a little farther away, and live in a house where there were no neighbors opposite her.

"At home my window must be my box at the theater. You can't sit by yourself without ever seeing people. But where I live now, it seems as if I've moved way out into the country. If I want to see people, I have to go into the kitchen and climb up onto the sink. That's the only way I can see my neighbors. Now, in that old alley of mine I could look right into the linen dealer's, and then I was only three steps from the theater; now I am three thousand steps away—a guardsman's steps, at that!"

Aunty might sometimes be ill, but however badly she happened to feel, she never missed the theater. One evening her doctor ordered her to put her feet in sourdough poultices; she did as he told her, but rode off to the theater and sat there with her feet in sourdough. If she had died there it would have pleased her. Thorvaldsen died in the theater; and she called that "a blessed death."

She could not imagine Heaven if there were no theater there; indeed, it was never promised to us, but it surely was conceivable that the many great actors and actresses who had gone on before would want to continue their work.

Aunty had her own private wire from the theater to her room; and the "telegram" came every Sunday for coffee. Her private wire was Mr. Sivertsen of the stage-setting department. It was he who gave the signal for the raising and lowering of the curtain, the setting or striking of the scenery.

From him she received a brief, expressive report of each of the plays. Shakespeare's *Tempest* he called "detestable stuff—there's so much to set up! Why, it begins with water down to the first side drop!" That is to say, the rolling billows extended far forward on the stage. On the other hand, if a play could go through five acts in one and the same set, he said it was sensible and well written; it was a play of rest that could play itself, without all that setting up to do.

In the earlier days, Aunty recalled, meaning some thirty-odd years back, when she and Mr. Sivertsen were indeed much younger, he was then already in the mechanical department, and, as she called him, her "benefactor." At that time it was customary at the town's big and only theater to admit spectators into the cockloft; every stage carpenter had one or two places to dispose of. It was often filled to capacity, and with a very select company; it was said the wives of generals and councilmen had been there, because it was so interesting to look down behind the scenes and see how the performers stood and moved when the curtain was down.

Aunty had been there several times, to tragedies and ballets, for the productions requiring the largest casts were the most interesting to watch from the loft. You sat up there in almost complete darkness, and most people brought their suppers with them. But once three apples and a package of sandwiches filled with sausage fell straight down into the prison where Ugolino was about to die of hunger! The sausage produced a tremendous effect. The audience laughed and cheered, and the sausage was one of the main reasons why the management decided to forbid admission to the cockloft.

"But still I've been there thirty-seven times," said Aunty. "And for that I shall always be grateful to Mr. Sivertsen."

On the last evening that the cockloft was open to the public, they were giving *The Judgment of Solomon*. Aunty could remember it so well, for from her benefactor, Mr. Sivertsen, she had obtained a ticket for Agent Nob. Not that he deserved it, for he always made fun of the theater and teased her about it, but still she had got him a seat in the cockloft. He wanted to look at the goings-on in the theater upside down. "Those were his very words, and just like him," said Aunty.

And so he saw *The Judgment of Solomon* from above, and fell asleep. One would surely have thought that he had come from a big dinner and had drunk many toasts. He slept until after the theater was locked up and had to spend the whole dark night up in the loft. He had a story to tell of his waking up, but Aunty didn't believe a word of it. *The Judgment of Solomon* was played out, the lights were out, and all the people were out, above and below; but then began the epilogue, the real comedy, the best thing of all, according to the agent. Then life came into the properties, and it wasn't *The Judgment of Solomon* that was given now; no, it was *Judgment Day at the Theater*. All this Agent Nob impudently tried to cram into Aunty; that was her thanks for getting him into the cockloft.

The story the agent told was amusing enough to hear, but there were mockery and spite behind it.

"It was very dark up there," said the agent, "but then the witchery began, the great spectacle, *Judgment Day at the Theater*. Ticket takers were at the doors, and every spectator had to show his spiritual testimonial, to decide whether he could enter free or handcuffed, and with or without a muzzle. Fine society people who came too late, after the performance had begun, and young fellows who wasted their time were hitched outside. There they were muzzled, and had felt soles put under their shoes, to walk in on in time for the beginning of the next scene. And then they began *Judgment Day at the Theater*."

"Purely wickedness," said Aunty, "which our Lord knows nothing about!"

Had the scene painter wanted to get into Heaven he would have had to climb up some stairs he had painted himself but which were too steep for anybody to use. That, of course, was because of his sin against perspective. The stage carpenter who had placed the plants and buildings in lands where they didn't belong had to move them into their proper places before cockcrowing time, if he expected to go to Heaven. Mr. Nob would have to watch his own chances of getting there! And to hear what he said about the actors, both in comedy and tragedy, or in song and dance—why, it was shameful of Mr. Nob! Mr. Nob! He never deserved his place in the cockloft! Aunty didn't believe a word of what he said. He had written it all out, he said—the snob!— and would have it printed, but not until he was dead and buried, since he had no wish to be skinned alive.

Only once had Aunty known terror and anguish in her own temple of happiness, the theater. It was one of those gray winter days when we have only two hours of foggy daylight; it was cold and snowing, but Aunty was bound for the theater. They were giving *Hermann von Unna*, besides a little opera and a grand ballet, with prologue and epilogue—it would last well into the night. Aunty had to be there; her lodger had lent her a pair of sleigh boots, shaggy both outside and inside, that reached all the way up her legs.

Aunty arrived at the theater and was seated in a box; the boots felt warm, so she kept them on. Suddenly there arose the cry of "Fire!" as smoke rolled from one of the wings and down from the cockloft! There was a fearful panic, and people stormed out.

Aunty was sitting farthest from the door—"second tier, left-hand side; from there the decorations look best," she said. "They always arrange them so they will look the prettiest from the king's side of the house." Now she wanted to get out of there, but the excited people in front of her thoughtlessly slammed and jammed the door shut. There was Aunty, with no way out and no way in, for the partitions between the boxes were too high. She called for help, but nobody heard her. When she looked over at the tier beneath, she saw it was empty; the balustrade was low; and the drop wasn't very far. Her fright made her feel young and active, so she prepared to jump. She got one foot on the seat and the other over the railing; there she sat astride, well draped in her flowered skirt, with one long leg dangling below, a leg in a huge sleigh boot. That was a sight to see! And it was seen, when finally her cries were heard; and then she was easily rescued, for the fire didn't amount to much.

That was the most memorable evening of her life, she said, and she was glad she hadn't seen herself, for she would have died of shame!

Her benefactor in the mechanical department, Mr. Sivertsen, came to see her regularly every Sunday. But it was a long time between Sundays. So in later years, in the middle of the week, a small child would come to her for the "leavings"; that is, to get her supper from the remains of Aunty's dinner.

This little child was a member of the ballet who really needed the food. She played the roles of a page or a fairy, but her hardest part was the hind legs of the lion in Mozart's *Magic Flute*. She eventually grew up to become the front legs, but for this she was paid only three marks, while as the hind legs she had received one rix-dollar. She had had to creep about as the hind legs, stooping, panting for fresh air. This was very interesting to know, thought Aunty.

Aunty deserved to have lived as long as the theater itself, but she couldn't hold out that long; nor did she die in the theater, but quietly and decently in her own bed. Her dying words were full of significance; she asked, "What are they playing tomorrow?"

She must have left about five hundred rix-dollars; we came to that conclusion from the yearly rental, which amounted to twenty rix-dollars. The money was left by Aunty as a legacy for some deserving old spinster who had no family. It was to be used for a seat in the second tier, left side, every Saturday, for that was when they gave the best plays. There was only one condition imposed on the legatee. As she sat in the theater every Saturday, she was to think of Aunty lying in her grave.

This was Aunty's religion.

THE TOAD (1866)

The well was deep, and therefore the rope was long; the wheel went around with difficulty when the water-filled bucket had to be pulled up over the side of the well. The sun could never mirror itself down in the water, no matter how brightly it shone; but as far down as its rays penetrated, green weeds were growing from between the stones.

There was a family of toads living down there. It was an immigrant family which, as a matter of fact, had come down there headlong in the person of the old toad mother, who was still living. The green frogs that swam in the water had made their homes there for a much longer time, but they acknowledged their cousins and called them "well guests." The latter, however, had no thoughts of ever leaving; they found it very comfortable here on the dry land, as they called the wet stones.

Mamma Frog had once traveled; she'd been in the bucket when it had gone up, but the light above had been too strong for her and given her a frightful pain in the eyes. Luckily she had managed to get out of the bucket. She'd fallen into the water with a tremendous splash and been laid up for three days with a backache. She didn't have much to tell about the world above, but she did know, and so did all the others, that the well wasn't the whole world. Mamma Toad, on the other hand, might have told them a few things about it, but she never answered when anyone inquired, so they stopped inquiring.

"Big and ugly, fat and loathsome, she is!" said the young green frogs. "And her brats are getting to be just like her!"

"Maybe so," said Mamma Toad, "but one of them has a jewel in its head, if I don't have it myself!"

And the green frogs listened and stared at her, and as they didn't like this news, they made faces at her and dived down to the bottom. But the young toads stretched out their hind legs proudly. Each of them thought it was the one which had the jewel, so they all kept their heads quite rigid, but at last they began to ask what it was they had to be proud of and just what a jewel was, anyway.

"It's something so glorious and precious," said Mamma Toad, "that I can't describe it. It's something you wear for your own pleasure and others become irritated over. But ask no more, for I won't answer."

"Well, I haven't got the jewel," said the smallest Toad, which was as ugly as it could be. "Why should I have anything so splendid? And if it irritates others, why, it wouldn't please me. No, all I want is to get up to the top of the well sometime and take one peep out! It must be wonderful up there!"

"Better stay where you are," said the old Toad. "You're at home here, and you know what it's like. Keep away from the bucket, or it may squash you! And even if you did get safely into it you might fall out. Not everyone can come down as luckily as I did and keep limbs and eggs all safe and sound."

"Croak!" said the little one; and that was the same as when we humans say, "Oh!"

It had such a great desire to get up to the top of the well and look out; it felt an intense longing for the green things up there. And next morning, when the bucket, filled with water, was being pulled up and happened to pause for an instant beside the stone where the Toad sat, the little creature quivered through and through and then jumped into the bucket. It sank to the bottom of the water, which soon was drawn up and emptied out.

"Phooie, what a nuisance!" said the man when he saw it. "That's the ugliest thing I've ever seen!" And then he kicked with his heavy wooden shoe at the Toad, which came close to being crippled, but managed to escape into the middle of some tall nettles. It saw stalk after stalk around it; it looked upward and saw the sun shining on the leaves, making them quite transparent.

For the Toad it was the same as it is for us when we come suddenly into a great forest, where the sun shines between leaves and branches.

"It's much prettier here than down in that well! You could stay here for your whole lifetime!" said the little Toad. It lay there for an hour; it lay there for two hours. "Now what could there be outside? Since I've come this far I might as well go farther." So it crept as fast as it could, until it came out into the road, where the sun shone on it; and then it was powdered with dust as it hopped across the road.

"Here one is really on dry land," said the Toad. "I'm getting almost too much of a good thing; it tickles right through me!"

Now it reached a ditch, where grew forget-me-nots and meadowsweet, while beyond it was a hedge of white thorn and elder bushes, with convolvulus creeping and hanging about it. What vivid colors there were to see here! And here flew a butterfly, too. The Toad thought it was a flower that had torn itself loose in order to get a better look at the world; that, of course, was very reasonable.

"If I could only move about like that!" said the Toad. "Croak! Oh! How glorious!"

For eight days and nights, it remained by the ditch and felt no want of food. Then on the ninth day it thought, "Oh, forward." But was there anything more beautiful to be found anywhere? Perhaps a little toad or some green frogs; there had been a sound in the wind the night before which had seemed to indicate there were cousins in the neighborhood.

"It's wonderful to be alive! To come up out of that well and lie in the bed of nettles, to creep along and hop across the dusty road and rest in the wet ditch! But on, further forward! I must find frogs or a little toad; one can't do without companions, after all. Nature alone isn't enough for one!" And so it started its wanderings again.

In a field, it came to a large pond with rushes around it, and it went exploring in there.

"It's too wet for you in here, isn't it?" said the frog inside. "But you're quite welcome. Are you a he or a she? Not that it matters; you're equally welcome in either case."

And so it was invited to a concert that evening, a family concert, with a lot of gaiety and feeble voices; we all know that sort of affair. There were no refreshments, except free drinks—the whole pond, if they could drink it.

"Now I'll be traveling on," said the little Toad, which was always craving for something better.

It saw the stars twinkling, so large and so clear; it saw the new moon shine, and it saw the sun rise higher and higher.

"I think I'm still in a well, but a bigger well. I must get higher up! I feel a restlessness, a longing!" And when the moon was full and round, the poor creature thought, "I wonder if that is the bucket that's let down, and which I must hop into if I want to get higher? Or is the sun the big bucket? How large that is, and how bright! Why, it could hold all of us at once! I must watch for my chance! What a brightness there is in my head! I don't believe the jewel could shine more brightly. But I don't have the jewel, and I shall not cry for it. No; still higher in brightness and happiness! I feel confidence and yet fear. It's a hard step to take, but I must take it. On, further forward! Right on down the road!"

Then it moved along in leaps, as indeed such a creature can, until it reached the highway where humans lived. Here were both flower gardens and vegetable gardens. It stopped to rest by a cabbage garden.

"How many different beings there are that I've never known of! And how great and blessed the world is! But you must keep looking about you, instead of always sitting in the same place." And so it hopped into the cabbage garden. "How green it is here! How pretty it is here!"

"That I well know," said the Caterpillar on a cabbage leaf. "My leaf is the largest one here; it covers half the world, and the rest of the world I can do without!"

"Cluck! Cluck!" said somebody, and hens came hopping into the garden.

The first Hen was farsighted; she spied the worm on the curly leaf and pecked at it so that it fell to the ground, where it lay twisting and turning. The Hen looked at it first with one eye and then with the other, for she couldn't figure out what would become of that wriggling.

"It isn't doing that of its own accord," thought the Hen, and she raised her head to strike again. Whereupon the Toad became so frightened that it bumped right into the Hen.

"So that thing has auxiliary troops to fight for it!" she said. "Just look at that vermin!" Then the Hen turned away. "I don't care about that little green mouthful; it would only tickle my throat!" The other hens agreed with her, and so away they went.

"I got away from her with my wriggling," said the Caterpillar. "It's good to keep your presence of mind, but the hardest job is ahead—to get back up onto my cabbage leaf. Where is it?"

Then the little Toad came forward to sympathize. It was happy that its own ugliness had frightened away the Hen.

"What makes you think that?" asked the Caterpillar. "I wriggled away from her myself. You're indeed very unpleasant to look at! Let me get back to my own place. Now I can smell cabbage; I'm near my own leaf! There's nothing so beautiful as one's own. But I must get up higher."

"Yes, higher!" said the little Toad. "Higher up! It feels just as I do, but it isn't in a good humor today, because of its fright. We all want to get up higher!" And it looked up as high as it could.

A stork sat in his nest on the roof of the farmhouse; he clattered and the stork mother clattered.

"How high up they live!" thought the Toad. "If only I could get up there!"

In the farmhouse lived two young students; one was a poet, the other a naturalist. The one sang and wrote with gladness of all that God had created, as it was mirrored in his heart; he sang of it in short, clear, and rich, imposing verses. The other took hold of the creation itself, yes, and took it apart when it needed analyzing. He treated our Lord's work like a great piece of arithmetic; subtracted, multiplied, wanted to know it outside and inside, and to talk of it with intelligence, with complete understanding; and yet he talked of it with gladness and with wisdom. They were good, happy people, both of them.

"Why, there is a good specimen of a toad," said the Naturalist. "I must have it to preserve in alcohol!"

"You have two already," said the Poet. "Let it stay there in peace and enjoy itself."

"But it's so beautifully ugly!" said the other.

"If we could find the jewel in its head," said the Poet, "then I myself would give you a hand at splitting it open."

"The jewel!" said the other. "How well you know your natural history!"

"But isn't there something very splendid about the old folk legend that the toad, the ugliest of creatures, often has hidden in its head the most precious of jewels? Isn't it much the same with people? Wasn't there a jewel like that hidden in Aesop, and Socrates, too?"

The Toad didn't hear any more and hadn't understood half of what it had heard. The two friends went on, and it escaped being preserved in alcohol.

"They were talking about that jewel, too," said the Toad. "It's good that I don't have it; otherwise I would have got into trouble."

Then there was a clattering on the farmer's roof. Father Stork was giving a lecture to his family, and they were all looking down askance at the two young men in the cabbage garden.

"A human being is the most conceited of creatures," said the Stork.

"Hear how they go on jabbering, and yet they can't even make as much noise as a rattle! They crow over their eloquence, their language! A fine language that is! It becomes more unintelligible even to them with each day's journey. We can speak our language the whole world over, in Denmark or in Egypt. As for flying, they can't do that at all. They crawl along by means of an invention they call a railway, but there they often get their necks broken. I get the shivers in my bill when I think of it! The world can exist without people. We could well do without them. May we only have frogs and earthworms!"

"My, that was a powerful speech!" thought the little Toad. "What a great man he is, and how high he sits up there! I never saw anyone that high before. And how well he can swim!" it exclaimed, for just then the Stork soared off into the air on outstretched wings.

And then Mother Stork talked in the nest. She told about the land of Egypt and the water of the Nile, and of all the wonderful mud there was to be found in foreign countries; it sounded entirely new and charming to the little Toad.

"I must get to Egypt!" it said. "If only the Stork would take me along, or if one of its youngsters would, I would do the little one some favor in turn, on his wedding day. Yes, I'll get to Egypt, because I'm lucky! All the longing and yearning I feel is surely better than having a jewel in one's head."

And still it had the true jewel! That eternal longing and desire to go upward, ever upward, was the jewel, and it shone within the little Toad, shone with gladness, shone brightly.

At that very moment the Stork came. He had seen the Toad in the grass, and now he swooped down and, not very gently, siezed the little creature. His bill pinched, and the wind whistled; this was anything but comfortable. But still the Toad was going upward, and off to Egypt, it knew; therefore its eyes brightened until it seemed as if a spark shot out from them.

"Croak! Oh!"

The body was dead; the little Toad had been killed. But the spark from its eyes—what became of that?

The sunbeam caught it up and bore away the jewel from the head of the Toad. Where?

You should not ask the Naturalist; rather ask the Poet. He'll tell it to you as a fairy tale; and the Caterpillar will be in it, and the Stork family will have a part in it. Just think—the Caterpillar will be changed into a beautiful butterfly. The Stork family will fly over mountains and seas to faraway Africa and yet find the shortest way home again to the land of Denmark, to the same village, to the same roof! Yes, it's all almost too much like a fairy tale, and still it is true! You may well ask the Naturalist about *that;* he'll have to admit it; and yet you know it yourself, for you've witnessed it.

But the jewel in the head of the Toad? Look for it in the sun; look *at* it if you can.

The brightness is too great. We have not yet eyes that can look directly at all the glories God has created, but someday we shall have them, and that will be the most beautiful fairy tale of all, for we ourselves shall have a part in it.

THE LITTLE GREEN ONES (1867)

A rose tree drooped in the window. Not so long ago it was green and blooming, but now it looked sickly—something was wrong with it. A regiment of invaders were eating it up; and by the way, it was a very decent and respectable regiment, dressed in green uniforms. I spoke to one of the invaders; he was only three days old but already a grandfather. Do you know what he said? Well, what he said is all true—he spoke of himself and the rest of the invaders. Listen!

"We're the strangest regiment of creatures in the world! Our young ones are born in the summertime, for the weather is pleasant then. We're engaged and have the wedding at once. When it gets cold we lay our eggs, and the little ones are snug and warm. The ant, that wisest of creatures (we have a great deal of respect for him!), studies us and appreciates us. He doesn't eat us up all at once; instead, he takes our eggs and lays them out on the ground floor of his and his family's anthill—stores layer after layer of them, all labeled and numbered, side by side, so that every day a new one may creep out of the egg. Then he keeps us in a stable, pinches our hind legs, and milks us, and then we die. It is really a great pleasure. The ants have the prettiest name for us—'little milk cow!'

"All creatures who have the common sense that the ant has call us that; it's only humans who don't, and that is an insult great enough to embitter all our lives. Couldn't you write us a protest against it? Couldn't you put those people in their right place? They look at us so stupidly, look at us with jealous eyes, just because we eat rose leaves, while they eat everything that's created, everything that is green or grows. Oh, they give us the most despicable, the most distasteful name: I won't even repeat it! Ugh! It turns my stomach; no, I won't repeat it—at least not when I'm wearing my uniform, and I am always wearing my uniform!

"I was born on a rose leaf. My whole regiment and I live off the rose tree; but then it lives again in us, who are of a higher order of beings. Humans detest us! They come and kill us with soapsuds—that's a horrible drink! I seem to smell it even now; it's dreadful to be washed when you're born not to be washed. Man, you who look at us with your stupid soapsud eyes, consider what our place in nature is; consider our artistic way of laying eggs and breeding children! We have been blessed to accomplish and multiply! We are born on the roses and we die in the roses—our whole life is a lovely poem. Don't call us by that name which you yourself think most despicable and ugly—the name I can't bear to speak or to repeat! Instead, call us the ants' milk cows, the rose-tree regiment, the little green ones!"

And I, the man, stood looking at the tree and at the little green ones—whose name I'll not mention, for I shouldn't like to hurt the feelings of a citizen of the rose tree, a large family with eggs and youngsters. And the soapsuds I was going to wash them in, for I had come with soap and water and evil intentions—I'll blow it to foam and use it for soap bubbles instead. Look at the splendor! Perhaps there's a fairy tale in each. And the bubble grows so large with radiant colors, looking as if there were a silver pearl lying inside it!

The bubble swayed, and drifted to the door, and burst; but the door sprung wide open, and there was Mother Fairy Tale herself! Yes, now she will tell you better than I can about—I won't say the name—the little green ones.

"Tree lice!" said Mother Fairy Tale. "You should call things by their right names; if you do not always dare to do so, you should at least be able to do it in a fairy tale!"

VÄNÖ AND GLÄNÖ (1867)

Near the coast of Zealand, off Holsteinborg castle, there once lay two wooded islands, Vänö and Glänö, on which were villages, churches, and farms. The islands were quite close to the coast and quite close to each other; now there is but one of these tracts remaining.

One night a fierce tempest broke loose. The ocean rose higher than ever before within man's memory. The storm increased; it was like doomsday weather, and it sounded as if the earth were splitting. The church bells began to swing and rang without the help of man.

That night Vänö vanished into the ocean depths; it was as if that island had never existed. But afterward on many a summer night, when the still, clear water was at low tide, and the fisherman was out on his boat to catch eel by the light of a torch, he could, on looking sharply, see Vänö, with its white church tower and high church wall, deep down below. He would recall the saying, "Vänö is waiting to take Glänö," as he saw the island, and he could hear the church bells ringing down there, but in that he was mistaken, for the sound came from the many wild swans which frequently rested on the water there, and whose clucking and complaining sounded like faraway church bells.

There was a time when there were still many old people on Glänö who well remembered that stormy night, and that they, when little, had ridden between the two islands at ebb tide, as we nowadays ride from the coast of Zealand over to Glänö, the water reaching up only to the middle of the wheels.

"Vänö is waiting to take Glänö," it was said, and this saying was accepted as a certainty. Many little boys and girls would lie in bed on stormy nights and think, "Tonight the hour will come when Vänö calls for Glänö." In fear, they said the Lord's Prayer, fell asleep, had sweet dreams—and the following morning Glänö was still there, with its woods and cornfields, its friendly farmhouses and hop gardens; the bird sang and the deer sprang; the gopher couldn't smell seawater, however far he could dig.

And still Glänö's days were numbered; we could not say just how many there were, but they were numbered, and one beautiful morning the island would no longer exist.

You were perhaps down there at the beach on a day prior to this and saw the wild swans resting on the water between Zealand and Glänö, while a sailboat in full sail glided by the wooded shore, and perhaps you, too, rode across at low tide, with the horses trampling in the water as it splashed over the wagon wheels.

You went away from there, perhaps traveled out into the wide world, and after a few years you have returned. You see the same woods, now surrounding a large, green meadow, where fragrant hay is stacked in front of pretty farmhouses. Where are you? Holsteinborg, with its golden tower spires, is still there, but not close to the bay; it now lies farther up in the country. You walk through the woods, across the field, down toward the beach. Where is Glänö? You don't see little wooded island before you; you see only the open water. Has Vänö finally taken Glänö, as it so long was expected to? On what stormy night did this happen, and when did an earthquake move old Holsteinborg so far inland?

There was no stormy night; it all happened on clear, sunny days. Human skill built a dam to hold back the ocean; human skill dried up the water and bound Glänö to the mainland. The bay has become a meadow with luxuriant grass; Glänö has become part of Zealand. And the old castle stands where it always stood. It was not Vänö that took Glänö; it was Zealand that, through mechanical skill, gained many new acres of land.

This is the truth; you can find it in the records. Glänö Island is no more.

THE GOBLIN AND THE WOMAN (1867)

You know the Goblin, but do you know the Woman—the Gardener's wife? She was very well read and knew poems by heart; yes, and she could write them, too, easily, except that the rhymes—"clinchings," as she called them—gave her a little trouble. She had the gift of writing and the gift of speech; she could very well have been a parson or at least a parson's wife.

"Earth is beautiful in her Sunday gown," she said, and this thought she had expanded and set down in poetic form, with "clinchings," making a poem that was so long and lovely.

The Assistant Schoolmaster, Mr. Kisserup (not that his name matters at all), was her nephew, and on a visit to the Gardener's he heard the poem. It did him good, he said, a lot of good. "You have soul, Madam," he said.

"Stuff and nonsense!" said the Gardener. "Don't be putting such ideas in her head! Soul! A wife should be a body, a good, plain, decent body, and watch the pot, to keep the porridge from burning."

"I can take the burnt taste out of the porridge with a bit of charcoal," said the Woman. "And I can take the burnt taste out of you with a little kiss. You pretend you don't think of anything but cabbage and potatoes, but you love the flowers, too." Then she kissed him. "Flowers are the soul!"

"Mind your pot!" he said, as he went off to the garden. That was his pot, and he minded it.

But the Assistant Schoolmaster stayed on, talking to the woman. Her lovely words, "Earth is beautiful," he made a whole sermon of, which was his habit.

"Earth is beautiful, and it shall be subject unto you! was said, and we became lords of the earth. One person rules with the mind, one with the body; one comes into the world like an exclamation mark of astonishment, another like a dash that denotes faltering thought, so that we pause and ask, why is he here? One man becomes a bishop, another just a poor assistant schoolmaster, but everything is for the best. Earth is beautiful and always in her Sunday gown. That was a thought-provoking poem, Madam, full of feeling and geography!"

"You have soul, Mr. Kisserup," said the Woman, "a great deal of soul, I assure you. After talking with you, one clearly understands oneself."

And so they talked on, equally well and beautifully. But out in the kitchen somebody else was talking, and that was the Goblin, the little gray-dressed Goblin with the red cap—you know the fellow. The Goblin was sitting in the kitchen, acting as pot watcher. He was talking, but nobody heard him except the big black Pussycat— "Cream Thief," the Woman called him.

The Goblin was mad at her because he had learned she didn't believe in his existence. Of course, she had never seen him, but with all her reading she ought to have realized he *did* exist and have paid him a little attention. On Christmas Eve she never thought of setting out so much as a spoonful of porridge for him, though all his ancestors had received that, and even from women who had no learning at all. Their porridge used to be so swimming with cream and butter that it made the Cat's mouth water to hear about it.

"She calls me just a notion!" said the Goblin. "And that's more than I can understand. In fact, she simply denies me! I've listened to her saying so before, and again just now in there, where she's driveling to that boy whipper, that Assistant Schoolmaster. I say with Pop, 'Mind the pot!' That she doesn't do, so now I am going to make it boil over!"

And the Goblin blew on the fire till it burned and blazed up. "Surre-rurre-rup!" And the pot boiled over.

"And now I'm going to pick holes in Pop's socks," said the Goblin. "I'll unravel a large piece, both in toe and heel, so she'll have something to darn; that is, if she is not too busy writing poetry. Madam Poetess, please darn Pop's stocking!"

The Cat sneezed; he had caught a cold, though he always wore a fur coat.

"I've opened the door to the larder," said the Goblin. "There's boiled cream in there as thick as paste. If you won't have a lick, *I* will."

"If I am going to get all the blame and the whipping for it, anyway," said the Cat, "I'll lick my share of the cream."

"First a lick, then a kick!" said the Goblin. "But now I'm off to the Assistant Schoolmaster's room, where I'll hang his suspenders on the mirror, put his socks into the water pitcher, and make him think the punch was too strong and has his brain in a whirl. Last night I sat on the woodpile by the kennel. I have a lot of fun teasing the watchdog; I let my legs dangle in front of him. The dog couldn't reach them, no matter how hard he jumped; that made him mad, he barked and barked, and I dingled and dangled; we made a lot of noise! The Assistant Schoolmaster woke up and jumped out of bed three times, but he couldn't see *me*, though he was wearing his spectacles. He always sleeps with his spectacles on."

"Say *mew* when you hear the Woman coming," said the Cat. "I'm a little deaf. I don't feel well today."

"You have the licking sickness," said the Goblin. "Lick away; lick your sickness away. But be sure to wipe your whiskers, so the cream won't show on it. I'm off to do a little eavesdropping."

So the Goblin stood behind the door, and the door stood ajar. There was nobody in the parlor except the Woman and the Assistant Schoolmaster. They were discussing things which, as the Assistant Schoolmaster so nobly observed, ought to rank in every household above pots and pans—the Gifts of the Soul.

"Mr. Kisserup," said the Woman, "since we are discussing this subject, I'll show you something along that line which I've never yet shown to a living soul—least of all a man. They're my smaller poems; however, some of them are rather long. I have called them 'Clinchings by a *Danneqvinde*.' You see, I am very fond of old Danish words!"

"Yes, we should hold onto them," said the Assistant Schoolmaster. "We should root the German out of our language."

"That I am doing, too!" said the Woman. "You'll never hear me speak of *Kleiner* or *Butterteig*; no, I call them fatty cakes and paste leaves."

Then she took a writing book, in a light green cover, with two blotches of ink on it, from her drawer.

"There is much in this book that is serious," she said. "My mind tends toward the melancholy. Here is my 'The Sign in the Night,' 'My Evening Red,' and 'When I Got Klemmensen'—my husband; that one you may skip over, though it has thought and feeling. 'The Housewife's Duties' is the best one—sorrowful, like all the rest; that's my best style. Only one piece is comical; it contains some lively thoughts—one must indulge in them occasionally—thoughts about—now, you mustn't laugh at me—thoughts about being a poetess! Up to now it has been a secret between me and my drawer; now you know it, too, Mr. Kisserup. I love poetry; it haunts me; it jeers, advises, and commands. That's what I mean by my title, 'The Little Goblin.' You know the old peasants' superstitions about the Goblin who is always playing tricks in the house. I myself am the house, and my poetical feelings are the Goblin, the spirit that possesses me. I have written about his power and strength in 'The Little Goblin'; but you must promise with your hands and lips never to give away my secret, either to my husband or to anyone else. Read it loud, so that I can tell if you understand the meaning."

And the Assistant Schoolmaster read, and the Woman listened, and so did the little Goblin. He was eavesdropping, you'll remember, and he came just in time to hear the title 'The Little Goblin.'

"That's about me!" he said. "What could she have been written about me? Oh, I'll pinch her! I'll chip her eggs, and pinch her chickens, and chase the fat off her fatted calf! Just watch me do it!"

And then he listened with pursed lips and long ears; but when he heard of the Goblin's power and glory, and his rule over the woman (she meant poetry, you know, but the Goblin took the name literally), the little fellow began grinnning more and more. His eyes brightened with delight; then the corners of his mouth set sternly in lines of dignity; he drew himself up on his toes a whole inch higher than usual; he was greatly pleased with what was written about the Little Goblin.

"I've done her wrong! The Woman has soul and fine breeding! How, I have done her wrong! She has put me into her 'Clinchings,' and they'll be printed and read. Now I won't allow the Cat to drink her cream; I'll do that myself! One drinks less than two, so that'll be a saving; and *that* I shall do, and pay honor and respect to the Woman!"

"He's a man all right, that Goblin," said the old Cat. "Just one sweet *mew* from the *Woman,* a mew about himself, and he immediately changes his mind! She is a sly one, the Woman!"

But the Woman wasn't sly; it was just that the Goblin was a man.

If you can't understand this story, ask somebody to explain it to you; but don't ask the Goblin or the Woman, either.

THE DRYAD (1868)

We're going to Paris to see the exposition!

Now we're there! It was a speedy journey, done completely without witchcraft—we went by steam, in a ship and on a railroad. Our time is indeed a time of fairy tales.

Now we are in a large hotel in the middle of Paris. The staircase is decorated with flowers, and soft carpets are spread over the steps. Our room is pleasant; the balcony door is open, and we can look out onto a large square. Down there is spring, which has come to Paris, having arrived at the same time we did, in the form of a big, young chestnut tree with delicate leaves beginning to open. How much more richly that tree is dressed in the beauty of spring than the other trees on the square! One of them has stepped out of the row of living trees and lies on the ground with its roots torn up. Where that tree stood the young chestnut will be planted, and there it will grow.

It is still standing high up on the heavy wagon that brought it to Paris this morning from many miles out in the country. For years it had stood out there, close to a mighty oak, under which the pious old pastor often used to sit and tell his stories to the listening children. Of course, the young chestnut tree had also listened.

The Dryad that lived in this tree was then but a child; she could remember way back when the chestnut tree was so small it could hardly peep over the tall grass blades and ferns. These were then as large as they ever would be; but the tree grew bigger every year, drinking in air and sunshine, dew and rain; the powerful winds shook it and bent it back and forth, which was an important part of its education.

The Dryad was pleased with her life and enjoyed living, was pleased with the sunshine and the songs of birds; but she liked best of all the human voice for she knew the language of people as well as that of the animals. Butterflies, cockchafers, and dragonflies—indeed, everything that could fly came to visit her, and everyone that came would gossip. They talked about the villages, the vineyards, the woods, and the old castle with its park, in which there were dikes and canals; down there in water also dwelt beings who in their own way could fly from place to place—beneath the water—beings with knowledge and imagination, but who said nothing, for they were too wise. The swallow, which often dived down deep into the water, told about the bright goldfish, the fat turbot, the sturdy perch, and the old moss-covered carp. The swallow gave very good descriptions, but it's always better to go and look for oneself, it said. But how could the Dryad ever see all these things? She had to be satisfied with the beautiful landscape and the buzz of human activity.

Everything was delightful, but most delightful when the old pastor stood there under the oak tree and talked about France and about the great deeds of men and women whose names are remembered through the ages with admiration. The Dryad heard of the shepherd maid, Joan of Arc, of Charlotte Corday; she learned of ancient times, and the times of Henry IV and Napoleon I, and she even heard of the genius and glory of our own times. She heard of names that were deep in the hearts of the people, and that France is the world's country, the world's gathering place of genius, with the cradle of liberty at its center.

The village children listened attentively, and the Dryad just as attentively; she became a schoolchild like the rest. In the shapes of the drifting clouds she could see many pictures of those things she had learned. The cloudy sky was her picture book.

She had thought she was very happy in this beautiful France, but she began to believe that the birds—in fact, all creatures that could fly—were much better off than she. Even the fly could look far beyond her horizon. France was so large and so beautiful, but she could see only a very small part of it. France was as broad as the world, with vineyards and forests and great cities, and of all these Paris was the greatest and most glorious! The birds could fly there, but she, never!

Among the village children there was a little girl so ragged and so poor, but very pretty to look upon. She was always singing and laughing, and often tied red flowers in her black hair.

"Don't go to Paris!" said the old pastor. "Poor child, if you go there it will be the ruin of you!"

And yet she went. The Dryad often thought of her, for they had both had the same desire and yearning to see the great city.

Spring came, and then summer; autumn came, and then winter. A couple of years went by.

The Dryad's tree was bearing its first chestnut blossoms, and the birds chirped around them in the bright sunlight. A noble lady came driving along the road in a grand carriage. She herself was driving the beautiful and spirited horses, with a smartly dressed little groom sitting behind her. The Dryad recognized her; the old pastor knew her. He shook his head and said sadly, "You did go there, and it proved your ruin, poor Marie!"

"She, poor?" thought the Dryad. "No! What a change! She's dressed like a duchess; that's what she got in the city of enchantment. Oh, if only I were there in all that light and splendor! When I look over there where I know the city is, I can see how it lights up the clouds in the night."

Indeed, she would look in that direction every evening, every night; there she could see the brightness along the horizon. On clear, moonlit nights she missed the bright cloudiness; she missed the drifting clouds that showed her pictures of the great city and its history.

The child clings to its picture book. The Dryad clings to her cloud book, her book of thoughts.

A balmy, cloudless sky was like a blank page to her, and it had now been several days since she had seen one like that. It was summertime, and the days were hot and sultry, without a cooling breeze; every flower and leaf was drowsy, and people were, too.

The clouds rose at that corner of the horizon where in the night the brightness announced, "Here is Paris!" All the clouds gathered and rose together, forming what appeared to be whole mountains; they pushed through the air and spread out over the entire countryside as far as the Dryad could see. They were heaped in mighty, rocklike, thundery-blue masses, layer on layer, high into the air. Then flashes of light shot out from them. "These are also the servants of God our Master," the old pastor had said. And then out flashed a bluish, blinding light, a blaze of lightning, which tried to rival the sun itself; it shattered the piled-up clouds.

The lightning struck down, down at the mighty old oak tree, splitting it to its very roots; the crown was shattered, the trunk torn apart. The tree crashed down and fell as if spreading itself out to receive the messenger of light. Not even the mightiest cannon could roar through the air and over the land at the birth of a king's son as did the thunder in saluting the passing of the old oak tree.

The rain streamed down. A refreshing breeze sprang up; the storm was over, and a holiday calm settled on the countryside. The villagers gathered around the fallen old oak tree; the old pastor spoke a few words in praise of it, and a painter made a sketch of the old tree as a lasting souvenir.

"Everything passes on," said the Dryad, "passes on as the clouds do, never to return."

Never again did the pastor come there. The roof of the schoolhouse had crashed in, and the pulpit was broken. No more did the children come. But autumn came, and winter came, and then spring. And during this time the Dryad's eyes were turned toward that corner on the distant horizon where every evening and night the lights of Paris shone like a belt of radiance. Out of Paris sped locomotive after locomotive, train after train, whistling and roaring, constantly. At every hour, in the evenings, at midnight, in the morning, and throughout the day, the trains arrived, and from these, and into these, people from all countries of the world pushed. A new wonder of the world drew them to Paris. How did this wonder show itself?

"A gorgeous flower of art and industry," people said, "has sprung up on the barren sands of the Champ de Mars. It's a gigantic sunflower, and from its leaves you can study geography or statistics, or become as wise as a councilman, or be inspired by art and poetry, or learn about the products and greatness of every country.

"It's a fairy-tale flower," others said, "a colored lotus, spreading its green leaves like a velvet carpet, the leaves that shot up in the early spring. Summer will see it in its greatest glory, and the storms of autumn will blow it away, leaving neither leaves nor roots."

Before the military school, the Champ de Mars lay stretched out in time of peace, a field without grass and straw, a piece of sandy desert cut from the African wilderness, where Fata Morgana shows her mysterious air castles and hanging gardens; they were more magnificent, more wondrous, now on the Champ de Mars, for they had been converted into reality by human skill.

"They have built the palace of the modern Aladdin," it was said. "Day after day, hour after hour, it unfolds more and more of its new splendors."

There was an endless array of halls in marble and many colors. The giant with bloodless veins moved his steel and iron limbs there in the great circular hall. Works of art in metal, in stone, in tapestry, loudly proclaimed the powerful genius that labored in all the lands of the world. There were picture galleries and flower shows. Everything that hand and brain could create was on exhibition in the workshop of the mechanic. Even relics from ancient castles and peat moors were to be found there. The overwhelmingly great, colorful show should have been reproduced in miniature and squeezed into the dimensions of a toy, to be seen and appreciated in its entirety.

There on the Champ de Mars stood, as on a huge Christmas table, Aladdin's castle of art and industry, and around it were knickknacks of greatness from every country; every nation found a memory of its home.

There was the royal palace of Egypt, and there a caravansery from the desert. The Bedouin from the land of the hot sun galloped past; and there were the Russian stables, with beautiful fiery horses from the steppes. Over there was the small thatched cottage of a Danish peasant, with Dannebrog, the flag of Denmark, next to Gustavus Vasa's beautifully carved wooden cottage from Dalarne. American log cabins, English cottages, French pavilions, mosques, churches, and theaters were all spread about in a wonderful manner. And in the middle of all this was the fresh green turf, with clear running water, flowering shrubs, rare trees, and glass houses where one might imagine oneself in a tropical forest. Complete rose gardens, brought from Damascus, bloomed in glory under glass roofs. What colors and fragrance! Artificial grottoes contained specimens of various fishes in fresh- and salt-water ponds—it was like standing at the bottom of the ocean there among the fishes and polyps.

Word spread that all these things were now being exhibited on the Champ de Mars, and an immense crowd of human beings crawled all over this richly decked feast table like a swarm of ants on a journey. Some went on foot or were drawn in wagons, for not everyone's legs can endure such tiresome traveling.

From early dawn until late at night they came there. Steamer after steamer, crowded with visitors, glided down the Seine. The mass of carriages was continually increasing, and the multitude of travelers on foot and horseback increased; streetcars and busses were jammed, packed, and spilling over with human beings. All these currents flowed toward one goal—the Paris Exposition!

Every entrance was bright with the flag of France, and around the bazaar of all nations waved the flags of the various countries. A burring and buzzing sounded from the hall of the machines, and chimes rang out from the towers, while the tones of the organs sounded from the churches, mingled with hoarse, nasal strains from Oriental coffeehouses. It was a Babel empire, a Babel language, a wonder of the world.

All this really happened—at least, according to reports. Who hasn't heard about it? The Dryad knew all about it; she knew everything that has been told here of the world's new wonder in the city of cities. "Hurry, all you birds, fly there and see it; then come back and tell me about it!" was the prayer of the Dryad.

Her longing grew until it became a great desire; it became the one thought of her life. And then…

In the silent, solemn night the full moon was shining, and from its face the Dryad saw a spark come forth, as bright as a falling star, and fall to the foot of the tree, whose branches shivered as if shaken by a tempest—and then a mighty, shining figure stood there. It spoke with a tender voice, and yet as powerfully as the judgment-day trumpet that kisses to life and calls to judgment.

"You shall go to the city of enchantments! There you shall take root and enjoy the air and the sunshine, but your life shall be shortened. The long procession of years that awaited you here in the open country will shrink to a small number. Poor Dryad, it will be your ruin! Your longing will grow and your great desire and craving will increase until the tree itself will be a prison to you. You will leave your shelter and change your nature; you will fly forth to mingle with human beings, and then your years will shrink to half of a mayfly's lifetime—to one night only! The flame of your life will be blown out. The leaves of the tree will wither and blow away, never to return."

So said the voice; thus it rang out. And then the shining being disappeared—but not the Dryad's longing and desire; she trembled in a violent fever of anticipated joy. Rejoicingly she said, "I shall go the city of cities. Life will begin for me—floating like the clouds, whither no one knows!"

The time of fulfillment came at early dawn, when the moon had grown pale and the skies had reddened; then the words of promise were to come true. Men came with spades and poles. They dug carefully around and deep under the roots of the tree. Then they lifted the tree out of the ground with its roots and the earth about them, and wound straw mats around the roots to make a warm foot bag. And then the tree was set on a wagon and tied securely. Now it was to go on a journey to Paris, and it was to remain and grow in the great metropolis of France, the city of cities.

The branches and leaves of the chestnut tree trembled as they began to move it. The Dryad trembled, too, but with the joy of expectation.

"Away! Away!" sounded every heartbeat. "Away! Away!" rang the trembling words of longing. The Dryad forgot to say "Farewell" to her old home, to the swaying blades of grass and the innocent daisies that had looked up to her as to a great lady in the garden of our Father, a young princess playing shepherdess in the country.

The chestnut tree on the wagon nodded "Farewell" or "Away!"—the Dryad didn't know which. Her thoughts and dreams were of the wonderful new and yet familiar life which would soon unfold itself. Neither the happy heart of an innocent child nor the heart filled with passion was ever more filled with thought than hers was on her journey to Paris.

Not "Farewell!"—but "Away! Away!" The wagon wheels turned round and round; the distance came near and then soon lay behind. The country changed, as the clouds above changed. New vineyards, woods, villages, villas, and gardens came into view, came closer, and then rolled past. The chestnut tree moved on, and the Dryad moved on with it. Locomotive after locomotive roared past. They blew clouds that took on the shapes of figures, which spoke of Paris, where they came from and where the Dryad was going.

Of course, everything around her knew where she was going. It seemed to her that every tree she passed stretched its branches toward her and begged, "Take me with you! Take me with you!" In every tree there lived a yearning dryad.

What a change! What a trip! The houses seemed to come springing right up out of the ground, more and more of them, closer and closer together. Chimneys appeared like flowerpots, placed side by side, one after another, on the roofs. Huge inscriptions, in letters a yard long, and colorfully painted figures covered the walls from ground to roofs, and shone brightly.

"Where does Paris begin, and when will I be there?" the Dryad asked herself.

There were increasing crowds of people; the tumult and noise grew louder. Carriage followed carriage; people were on foot and on horseback. There were shops on all sides, and music, song, talking, and screaming.

Now the Dryad, in her tree, was in the center of Paris.

The big, heavy wagon stopped in a little square where trees were planted and around which were high houses. Every window had its own balcony, and from these people looked down at that fresh, young chestnut tree which had been driven there to be planted in the place of the dead, uprooted tree that lay on the ground. People passing by stopped for a while to smile at that fresh green bit of early spring. The older trees, their leaves yet scarcely budding, greeted it with rustling branches: "Welcome! Welcome!" And the fountain, which spouted its water into the air so that it splashed into the basin, let the wind carry a few drops to the new arrival, to give it welcome drink.

The Dryad felt the tree being taken down from the wagon and then being put into its destined home. The roots were covered with earth, and fresh green turf was laid on top of that. Blooming shrubs were planted, and earthen pots with flowers in them were placed about. Thus a whole little garden appeared in the midst of the square.

The dead, uprooted tree, killed by gas fumes, hearth smoke, and all the stifling city air, was thrown upon the wagon and hauled away. The crowd watched; old people and children sat upon the bench in the little park, looking at the leaves of the newly planted tree. And we, who tell you about all this, stood on our balcony, gazing down on the young tree that had just come from the fresh air of the country and said what the old pastor would have said if he had been there: "Poor Dryad!"

"How happy I am, how happy!" said the Dryad. "And yet I can't quite understand it. I can't explain how I feel; it all seems to be the way I thought it would be, and yet it isn't quite what I expected!"

The houses were so high and so close. The sun shone upon only one wall; that was covered with posters and placards, and people crowded and thronged around it. Carriages rushed by, light ones and heavy ones. Busses, filled to overflowing, rattled by like moving houses. Carts and carriages squabbled over the right of way.

"Won't these overgrown houses standing so stiflingly close," thought the Dryad, "move away and make room for other shapes and forms, the way the clouds do in the sky? Why don't they move aside, so I can really see Paris and beyond Paris?" She felt she had to see Notre-Dame, the Vendôme Column, and the many wonderful works that had drawn and were still drawing so many people there.

But the houses didn't move from their places.

The lamps were lighted while it was still daylight, and the gaslight gleamed from all the shopwindows, lighting up the branches of the trees; it was almost like summer sunlight. But the stars above looked exactly the same as the Dryad had seen them back home. She thought she felt a clean and mild breeze come from there. She felt uplifted, strengthened, and could feel a new vigor flow through the tree from the very tips of the leaves to its roots. She then realized that she was in the world of living people and felt she was looked upon with kindly eyes; all around her were tumult and tones, colors and lights. The tones of wind instruments came to her from the side streets, hurdy-gurdies playing dance-provoking melodies. Yes, for dancing, for dancing! For pleasure and amusement, these were played. It was a music to make men and horses, even carriages trees, and houses, dance, if they could. All this fanned an intoxicating yearning for pleasure in the heart of the Dryad.

"How glorious! How beautiful all this is!" she cried rejoicingly. "I'm in Paris!"

The day that came, and the night that followed it, and then the following day brought the same display, the same uproar, the same life, changing and yet always the same.

"By now I know every tree and flower in this square; I know every house, balcony, and shop in this little corner where they've stuck me and where I can see nothing of the great and mighty city. Where is the Arc de Triomphe, and the boulevards, and that wonder of the world? I can't see anything of all this. I stand as if imprisoned in a cage here among these high houses, which I know by heart now, with all their inscriptions, posters, and placards—all the painted delicacies for which I have no more appetite. Where is that which I've heard so much about, which I have known and longed for, the reason I wanted to come here? What have I got—gained, found? I yearn as much as I did before. I know the life I want. I want to go out among the living people and mingle with them; I want to fly like the birds and see and feel and become like a human being! I would rather really live for half a day than spend a lifetime of years in daily idleness and languor, becoming sick, sinking, falling like dew in the meadow, and then disappearing! I want to sail like the clouds, bathe in the sun of life, look down on everything below as the clouds do, and then disappear as they do—where, no one knows!"

This was the sigh of the Dryad, going aloft as a prayer.

"Take from me all my years of life and grant me but half of a mayfly's life! Free me from my prison; give me human life and human happiness, though it be but for a fleeting moment, for only this one night, and then punish me, if you wish, for my longing for life! Free me, even if this dwelling of mine, this fresh young tree, wither, be cut down, turned to ashes, and blown away by the winds!"

There was a rustling among the boughs of the tree, and a strange sensation came over it. Every leaf shivered, and fiery sparks seemed to shoot forth from them. A gust of wind shook the crown of the tree. And then there came forth a feminine form— the Dryad herself! In the same instant she found herself beneath the green boughs, rich with leaves and lit by gaslight from all sides. She was as young and beautiful as poor Marie, to whom one had said, "The great city will be your ruin!"

The Dryad sat at the foot of the tree, which she had locked and whose key she had thrown away. So young, so lovely! The stars saw her, and they twinkled; the gas lamps saw her as they glittered, beckoning to her. How slender she was, and yet so strong, a child and yet a full-grown maiden! Her dress was as smooth as silk, as green as the freshly unfolded leaves of the crown of the tree. In her nut-brown hair was a half-opened chestnut blossom. She looked like the Goddess of Spring.

For a brief moment she sat there motionless, and then she bounded off around the corner like a gazelle. She ran and darted the way reflected sunbeams dart here and there from a mirror being moved in the sunshine. If one had looked closely and could have seen what was there to see, how wondrous this would have been to him! Whenever she rested a moment, the color of her dress and of her figure was changed, according to the nature of the place where she stood and the lights that fell on her.

She reached the boulevards, where there was an ocean of light from the gas flames in the street lamps, stores, and cafés. There were rows of young and slender trees, each of which shielded its dryad from the artificial sunlight. The whole vast sidewalk was like one large dining room, with tables of all sorts of refreshments, from champagne and chartreuse to coffee and beer. There were exhibits of flowers, pictures, statues, books, and colored materials.

From the crowd by the high houses she watched the roaring streams between the rows of trees; there was a surging river of rolling wagons, cabriolets, chariots, busses, coaches, men on horseback, and marching troops. Life and limb were endangered by any attempt to cross to the other side. Now a blue light shone the brightest, and then the gaslight was again the most brilliant; a rocket had suddenly shot up—from where, to where?

Surely this must be the greatest highway of the world's greatest city! There were charming Italian melodies and Spanish songs with castanet accompaniment. But the strains from Minutet's music box drowned all the other sounds—that exciting cancan music which Orpheus never knew and Helen never heard. Even the wheelbarrow would have danced on its one wheel if it could have. The Dryad did dance; she whirled and soared, and changed colors like a hummingbird in the sunshine, every house and its interior being reflected on her.

As the glorious lotus flower, torn from its roots, is carried away by the whirling river, so was the Dryad carried along, and whenever she stopped she changed into a new form; consequently, no one could follow her, recognize her, or even view her. Everything passed by her like cloud pictures—face after face—but she recognized none of them; she saw no familiar forms from home. Before her mind came two bright eyes, and she thought at once of Marie. Poor Marie, that ragged, gay child with the red flowers in her black hair. She was here in this worldly city—rich and charming, as when she had driven by the pastor's house, the Dryad's tree and the old oak. More than likely, she was somewhere in this deafening uproar; perhaps she had just alighted from that magnificent carriage waiting over there. Brilliant carriages, with richly liveried coachmen and footmen wearing silk stockings, were drawn up in a line, and the nobility alighting from them were all ladies, beautifully dressed. They passed through the open gates and ascended the broad, high steps that led into that stately building with the marble columns. Could this, perhaps, be the great wonder of the world? Surely Marie must be there!

"Sancta Maria!" was being sung within. The fragrance of incense rolled out under the high, painted and gilded arch, where it was always twilight. This was the Church of the Madeleine.

Dressed in the most costly black, fashioned after the finest and newest modes, the ladies of the aristocracy glided over the polished floor. Crests sparkled from the clasps of magnificent prayerbooks bound in velvet and were embroidered on perfumed handkerchiefs bordered with costly Brussels lace. A few of the women knelt in silent prayer before the high altar; others went to the confessionals. The Dryad felt an uneasiness, a fear, as if she were in a place where she should not be. It was a house of silence, a great hall of mystery and secrecy. Everything was said in whispers or in silent trust.

Now the Dryad realized that she was wrapped in silk and a lace veil, like the ladies of wealth and noble birth. Was every one of them a child of desire and longing like herself?

A deep, painful sigh was heard; did it come from the confessional or from the bosom of the Dryad? She drew the veil more closely about her. She was breathing in incense fumes and not the fresh air. This was not the place she had long for.

"Away, away! Take flight, without rest! The mayfly that lives but a day has no rest; her flight is her life!"

The Dryad was out again among the bright gas lamps and the magnificent fountains.

"Not all the water from the fountain can wash away the blood of the innocents slain here!"

Those words were spoken. Here stood many strangers who spoke in loud and lively tones, which no one had dared to do in the great hall of secrecy from which she had just come.

A big stone slab was turned and then raised—why, she did not understand. She saw an opening into the depths of Earth. The strangers stepped down, leaving the starlit sky, the brilliant gaslights, and all the life of the living.

"I'm afraid!" said one of the women who stood here. "I don't dare go down! I care little about seeing the wonders there. Stay here with me!"

"And go home?" said a man. "Leave Paris without having seen the most remarkable thing of all, the wonderwork of modern times, the result of one man's mind and skill?"

"I'll not go down there," was the reply.

"The wonderwork of modern times," it had been said. And the Dryad had heard this and understood. At last she was to reach the goal of her greatest longing, and here was the entrance—down to the vast depths beneath Paris. She had not expected this, but now she had heard about it and had seen the strangers descend, and she followed them.

The steps were of cast iron, spiral-shaped, broad and comfortable; a lamp was burning below, and deeper down there was another. She found herself in a labyrinth of endless passages and halls crossing each other. Every street and lane in Paris could be seen there, as if reflected in a mirror. Their names could be read, and every house above had its number here, and its root, which led down under the hard, lonely walk that squeezed its way along the wide canal with its onward-rolling drainage. Above this was the aqueduct of fresh running water, and still higher gas pipes and telegraph wire hung like a network. Lamps shone in the distance, as if they were reflected images from the worldly city above. Now and then a rumbling could be heard overhead; it came from the heavy wagons crossing the bridges. Where was the Dryad?

You have heard of the catacombs; they are nothing compared with this underground world, this wonder of our times, the sewers of Paris! That was where the Dryad was, and not at the World's Fair on the Champ de Mars.

On all sides were heard exclamations of astonishment, wonder, and approval.

"Out of the deep here," they said, "come health and long life for the thousands above. Our age is the age of progress, with all its blessings!"

That was the opinion of people, the talk of people, but not that of the scavengers who were born here and built their homes and lived here—the rats. From the cracks of an old stone wall the rats squeaked so loudly and distinctly that the Dryad could understand them. A big, old rat whose tail had been bitten off piped in a shrill voice of his feelings, his anguish, and the only idea in his mind; and his whole family approved of every word he said.

"I am disgusted by the meow, the human meow, the ignorant talk! Indeed, everything is very fine now, with gas and oil, but I don't eat such things. It has become so clean and light here that one is ashamed and doesn't know what one is ashamed of. I wish we lived in the good old days of the tallow candles; those times are not so far back—those romantic times, as people call them."

"What are you talking about?" asked the Dryad. "I've never seen you before. What are you talking about?"

"The wonderful old days," said the rat, "the days when Great-grandfather and Great-grandmother rat were young. At that time it was a great adventure to come down here. Those were the days for the rats of Paris! Mother Pest used to live down here then; she would kill human beings, but never rats. Robbers and smugglers could breathe freely down here. Then this was the asylum for the most fascinating characters I ever saw, such characters as one sees nowadays only in the melodramatic plays. Those romantic days have gone, even for us rats; we have fresh air now—and petroleum!"

Thus the rat squeaked, squeaked over the new times, and in honor of the good old days with Mother Pest.

Now they came to a carriage, a sort of open bus, drawn by two small, lively ponies. The group entered and drove along the Boulevard Sébastopol—that is, along the underground boulevard. Right above them, in Paris, was the real boulevard of that name, crowded with people.

The carriage disappeared in the twilight, and the Dryad disappeared, too, but she came to light again in the fresh, open air under the glare of the gas lamps. Here the wonder was to be found, and not in the damp atmosphere of the crossing and recrossing passages. Here she found the wonder of the world, which she had been seeking in her short lifetime. It burst forth in far richer glory than all the gaslights above, stronger than the Moon, which was now gliding by.

Yes, indeed, she saw it greet her; it winked and twinkled like Venus in the heavens.

She saw a brilliant gate open into a little garden gay with light and dance music. Colored gas lamps shone on small artificial lakes and ponds, where water plants, artistically made of bent and painted tinsel, were displayed, and these hurled jets of water high into the air from their chalices, the water sparkling under the brilliant lights. Graceful weeping willows—real, spring weeping willows—trailed their fresh green branches in curving waves, like a transparent and yet screening veil. A bowl of light among the shrubbery threw its red glow over half-lit bowers made of green foliage, while magic tones of music thrilled the ears, teasing and alluring and chasing the blood through the human limbs.

She saw beautiful young women in evening dress, with innocent smiles on their lips, and laughing with the carelessness of youth. There was a Marie with roses in her hair, but with no carriage or footmen. How they whirled about; how they swung in that wild dance, now up, now down! They laughed and smiled, and leaped as if smitten by the tarantella dance; they looked so joyous, so gay, as if ready to embrace the whole world through pure happiness!

The Dryad felt herself irresistibly drawn into the dance. Her small, delicate feet were shod in silken shoes as brown as the ribbon that fluttered from her hair onto her bare shoulders. The large folds of the green silk dress enveloped her, but could not hide the perfectly shaped legs and the dainty feet, which seemed to be trying to draw a magic circle in the air before her dancing cavalier's head. Was she in the enchanted garden of Armida? What was the name of this place? In bright gas flames outside shone the name "Mabille."

There were shouts and applause, rockets and running water, and the popping of champagne bottles. The dance was bacchanalian, wild. And above all this the Moon was sailing across the sky, its face sloping a bit. The sky was cloudless, clear and pure, and one thought of looking right into Heaven from Mabille.

A consuming intoxication seized the Dryad, like the aftereffect of opium. Her eyes spoke, and her lips spoke, but her words were drowned by the tones of flute and violin. Her cavalier whispered words in her ear with the rhythm of the cancan; she did not understand them, nor do we understand them. He stretched his arms out to her, around her—but embraced only the transparent, gas filled air! The Dryad was carried away by the wind like a rose petal; and high in the air she saw a flame ahead, a brilliant light at the top of a tower. This light came from the goal of her desires, from the red lighthouse of the Fata Morgana of the Champ de Mars. The spring breeze carried her to it. She circled around the tower, and the workmen thought it was a butterfly that had come too early in the spring and was fluttering down to die.

The Moon was shining, and so were the gaslights and lanterns in the great halls, and throughout the widespread buildings of all nations they shone on the green hills and on the rocks that human skill had created and over which waterfalls were precipitated by the power of the "bloodless giant."

The depths of the oceans and of bodies of fresh water—the realm of fishes—were displayed there. One could imagine oneself at the bottom of the sea—deep down in a diving bell, with the water pressing hard on all sides against the thick glass walls. Fathom-long polyps, flexible, bending like eels, trembling with living thorns, swayed to and fro and held fast to the bottom of the sea.

A large flounder lay close by in deep thought, spreading himself out comfortably. A crab, resembling an enormous spider, crawled over him, while the shrimps moved about swiftly and restlessly, as if they were the moths and butterflies of the ocean.

Many beautiful plants were growing in the fresh water. Goldfish had arranged themselves in rows like red cows in a pasture, with all their heads in one direction, so that the stream would flow into their mouths. Thick, fat tenches stared with dull eyes at the glass walls; they knew they were in the Paris Exposition; they knew they had completed a tiring journey in tubs filled with water, and had been on a railroad train, where they had become landsick as men become seasick on the ocean. They had also come to see the Exposition, and they saw it from their own salt- or freshwater "loges," gazing at the swarms of humans that passed by from morning to night. All the countries of the world had sent their specimens of humanity there, so that the old tenches and breams, the perch and moss-covered carps, might look at the creatures and give their opinions about the various tribes.

"Man is a scalefish," said a slimy little carp, "changing his scales two or three times a day. They make mouth noises—speaking, they call it. We don't change our scales, and we make ourselves understood much more easily, by the motions of the corners of our mouths and the look in our eyes. We have many advantages over men."

"But they've learned how to swim," said a small freshwater fish. "I come from the great inland lake, and in the hot days of summer people go into the water there, but first they strip off their scales and then they swim. The frogs have taught them how to do it; the hind legs push and the front legs row, but they can't do it very long. They think they can rival us, but they can't. Poor people!"

The fishes stared; they thought that the crowd of people there now was the same one they had seen in the bright daylight; yes, and they even believed those figures were the same ones that had beaten against their nerves of observation on the very first day.

A little perch with pretty, mottled skin and an enviably rounded back said he was sure that the same "human scum" was still there.

"I can see it, too, very plainly," said a golden tench. "I distinctly see a beautiful, well-shaped human, a 'long-legged lady,' or whatever it is they call her. She has mouth corners and staring eyes like us, two balloons in the back, a folded umbrella hanging down in front, and a lot of seaweed on her dingling and dangling. She ought to throw all that off and go about the way we do, in nature's gift, and then she would look like an honorable tench—that is, as much as a human can look like us."

"What's become of that laced one, that he-human?"

"He was riding around here in a wheel chair, sitting there with paper, ink, and a pen, and writing everything down. What was he doing? They called him a journalist."

"He is still riding around!" said a moss-covered, old-maid carp who had a bit of worldly temptation stuck in her throat, making her quite hoarse. She had once swallowed a fishhook and since then had been swimming about tolerantly with the hook in her throat. "Journalist," she said; "that's spoken like a fish. It really means a sort of octopus among men!"

Thus the fishes talked on in their own way. But amid this artificial grotto and its water-filled tanks there sounded hammer blows and the songs of workmen, who had to work at night in order to get everything completed. These songs resounded in the midsummer night's dream of the Dryad, who stood there herself, but was soon to fly again and disappear.

"These are goldfish," she said, and nodded to them. "I'm glad to have been able to see you. Yes, I know you and have known you for a long time! The swallow told me all about you in my own home. How pretty and shining and charming you are! I could kiss each and every one of you! I know the others, too. That must be a crucian, and this is a delicate bream, and there's an old moss-covered carp. I know you, but you don't know me."

The fishes just stared, unable to understand a word she said; they gazed through the dim twilight.

The Dryad was gone; she was in the open air again, where the world's "wonder flower" spread its fragrance from many lands—from the rye-bread land, the codfish seashore, the Russian-leather country, eau-de-cologne valley, and rose-oil Orient.

When we drive home half asleep in our carriage after a ball, the melodies we have heard continue to ring plainly in our ears, and we may sing each of them again. And as in the dead man's eye the last impression received in life remains photographed for some time, so the impression of the day's tumult and brilliance remained yet upon the eye of the night; it was neither absorbed nor quite blown away. The Dryad could see it and knew that it would persist even into the morrow.

Now the Dryad was among fragrant roses; she thought she recognized them as being from her own country, from the castle park and the garden of the pastor. She also saw a red pomegranate blossom; it was one like this that Marie had worn in her coal-black hair. The memory of her childhood home in the country rushed back into her thoughts; eagerly she drank in the sights around her, while a feverish desire seized her and carried her through the wondrous halls.

She was tired, and her fatigue increased. She felt a yearning to rest on the soft Oriental cushions and carpets, or to duck into the clear water as did the branches of the weeping willow. But the mayfly has no rest. In a few minutes the day would end. Her thoughts and her limbs trembled, and she sank in the grass beside the babbling stream.

"You spring from the earth with eternal life," she said. "Cool my tongue; give me a refreshing drink!"

"I am no living spring," answered the water. "I run by machinery!"

"Give me some of your freshness, you green grass!" begged the Dryad. "Give me one of the fragrant flowers!"

"We shall die if we are torn from our plants," answered grass blade and flower.

"Kiss me, you cooling breeze! Give me but a single kiss!"

"Soon the sun will kiss the clouds red," said the wind, "and then you will be among the dead, gone as all this glory will be gone before the year is out. And then I can once more play with the light, loose sand in this place and blow the dust over the earth and into the air. Dust! Nothing but dust!"

The Dryad felt a terror creep over her, like a woman who, bleeding to death in the bath from a severed artery, still wishes to live, while her strength gradually leaves her from loss of blood. She rose, staggered a few steps forward, and then sank again before a little church. The door was open; a light burned on the altar, and the organ sounded. What music! The Dryad never had heard such tones before, though she seemed to hear familiar voices; they came from the depths of the great heart of creation. She thought she heard the whistling of the old oak tree; she thought she heard the old pastor speaking of the great deeds of famous men and of what a creation of God could and might give to the coming ages and thus win himself eternal life. The tones of the organ swelled and rang out; they spoke in song:

"Your desire and longing tore your roots from the place God had given them. That became your ruin, poor Dryad!"

Then the tones from the organ grew soft and gentle; they sounded like weeping and then died away like a weeping whisper. The clouds in the sky began to redden with the dawn. The wind whispered, and sang, "Go away, you dead, for the sun is rising!" The first ray fell upon the Dryad; her figure was radiant with changing colors, like a soap bubble before it bursts, vanishes, and becomes a drop, a tear, which falls and disappears. Poor Dryad, a dewdrop, only a tear, wept, and swept away!

The sun shone down on the Champ de Mars' Fata Morgana, shone over mighty Paris, over the little square with its trees and its rippling fountain, and between the high houses, where the chestnut tree stood, its branches now drooping, its leaves withered, the tree that only yesterday had stood as erect and fresh as spring itself. It was dead now, said the people, for the Dryad had left it, had passed away like the clouds—where, no one knew. On the ground there lay a withered, crumpled chestnut blossom. All the holy water of the church could not recall it to life. Human feet soon stepped on it and crushed it into the dust.

All this has happened and been experienced. We ourselves have seen it, at the Paris Exposition in 1867, in our time, the great and wonderful time of fairy tales.

GODFATHER'S PICTURE BOOK (1868)

Godfather could tell stories, so many of them and such long ones, and he could cut out paper figures and draw pictures. When it was nearly Christmas he would bring out a scrapbook with clean white pages, and on these he pasted pictures cut out of books and newspapers; and if there weren't enough for the story he was going to tell, he drew them himself. When I was a little boy I got several of these picture books, but the prettiest of them all was the one from "that memorable year when gas replaced the old oil lamps in Copenhagen"—and that was the inscription written on the first page.

"We must take great care of this book," said Father and Mother, "and only bring it out on important occasions."

But Godfather had written on the cover:

If you should tear the book, that's not a great wrong;
Other little friends have done worse for ever so long.

Best of all were the times when Godfather himself showed the book, read the verses and other writings in it, and told many things besides; then the story would become a very real one.

On the first page was a picture from "The Flying Post," showing Copenhagen with its Round Tower and Our Lady's Church. On its left was pasted an old lantern, on which was written, "Train oil," and on the right was a chandelier, with "Gas" written on it.

"See, that's the title page," said Godfather. "That's the beginning of the story you're going to hear. It could also be given as an entire play, if one could perform it. *Train Oil and Gas; or, The Life and Times of Copenhagen.* That's a very good title! At the bottom of the page is still another little picture; it's quite hard to understand, so I'll explain it to you. That is a hell horse. He shouldn't have come until the end of the book, but he has run on ahead to say that neither the beginning, nor the middle, nor the end is any good; he could have done it much better—if he could have done it at all. The hell horse, you see, stands hitched all day in the newspaper, and walks on the columns, they say. But in the evening he slips out, stations himself outside the poet's door, and neighs, so that the man inside will instantly die; but he won't die if there's any real life in him."

The hell horse is usually a poor creature who can't understand himself and can't earn a living, and he gets his air and food by going around and neighing. I am certain that he doesn't like Godfather's picture book, but in spite of that, it may be worth at least the paper it's written on.

"Now that's the first page of the book; that's the title page.

"It was the very last evening on which the oil lamps were to be lighted; the town had gas, and it was so bright that the old street lamps seemed quite lost in it.

"I was in the street myself that evening," said Godfather. "The people were walking about, looking at the old and the new lighting. There were a great many people and twice as many legs as heads. The watchmen stood around sadly, for they didn't know how soon they would be dismissed, like the oil lamps. They could remember so far back, but dared not think forward. They had so many memories of quiet evenings and dark nights. I leaned up against a lamppost," continued Godfather, "and there was a great spluttering in the oil and the wick. I could hear what the lamp said, and you shall hear it, too.

"'We've done the best we could,' said the lamp. 'We were good enough for our time, and have lighted up joy and sorrow; we have lived through many wonderful things; you might say we have been the night eyes of Copenhagen. Now let new lights take our place and take over our duties; but how many years they'll shine, and what they will light up, remains to be seen! Indeed, they shine a little stronger than we old fellows, but that's nothing; when you're molded like a gas chandelier and have the connections they have, the one pours into the other. They have pipes going in all directions and can get strength from both inside the town and outside it. But each one of us oil lamps shines because of what he has in himself, and not because of any family connections. We and our ancestors have lighted Copenhagen from olden times, from immeasurably long ago. But since this is now the last evening that we'll stand and shine in the second row, so to speak, in the street here along with you, you shining comrades, we won't sulk or be envious. No, far from it; we'll be happy and good-natured. We are the old sentinels, being relieved by new guards in better uniforms than ours. We'll tell you what our family, way back to great-great-great-grandmother lantern, has seen and experienced—the whole history of Copenhagen. May you and your successors, right down to the last gas chandelier, experience and be able to relate such wonderful things as we can, when you get your discharge someday. And you'll get it!

'You may be sure of that! People are certain to find a better light than gas. I've heard a student say that there's a possibility they may someday burn seawater!' When the lamp said these words, the wick spluttered, as if it had water in it already."

Godfather had listened closely, thought it over, and decided it was an excellent idea of the old lantern, on this evening of the change from oil to gas, to tell and display the whole history of Copenhagen.

"You mustn't let a good idea slip," said Godfather. "I took it at once, went home, and made this picture book for you. It goes even farther back in time than the lamps could go. Here's the book, and here's the story!"

COPENHAGEN'S LIFE AND TIMES

"It begins in darkness, on a coal-black page—that's the Dark Ages.

"Now let's turn the page," said Godfather. "Do you see the picture? Only the wild sea and the swelling northeast wind, driving heavy ice floes before it. There's no one out sailing on them, only great stone blocks, which rolled down onto the ice from the mountains of Norway. The north wind blows the ice away; he wants to show the German mountains what rocks are found up in the north. The ice floes are already down in the sound, off the coast of Zealand, where Copenhagen now stands; but there was no Copenhagen there then. There were great sandbanks under the water, and the ice floes with the big boulders struck against one of these. Then the whole ice field stuck so fast that the northeast wind couldn't move it again, and so he became as furious as could be and pronounced a curse on the sandbank, the 'Thieves' ground,' as he called it. He swore that if ever it should rise above the surface of the sea, thieves and robbers would live there, and the gallows and wheel be raised on it.

"But while he cursed and swore this way, the sun came out, and those bright and gentle spirits, the children of light, swayed and swung in its beams; they danced over the ice floes until they melted, and the great boulders sank to the sandy bottom of the sea.

"'Sun scum!' said the northeast wind. 'Is that friendship and kinship? I'll remember and take revenge for that. Now I pronounce a curse!'

"'We pronounce a blessing!' sang the children of light. 'The sandbank will rise, and we shall guard it. Truth, goodness, and beauty shall dwell there!'

"'Stuff and nonsense!' said the northeast wind.

"You see, the lantern knew nothing of all this and therefore couldn't tell about it," said Godfather. "But I know it, and it's very important to the life and times of Copenhagen.

"Now we'll turn the page," said Godfather. "Years have passed, and the sandbank has lifted itself; a sea gull has settled on the biggest rock, which has jutted out of water. You can see it in the picture. Years and years have passed.

"The sea cast up dead fish onto the shore. Tough lyme grass sprang up, withered, rotted, and fertilized the soil; many different kinds of grasses and plants followed, until the bank became a green island. There the Vikings landed, for there was level ground for fighting and good anchorage beside the island off the coast of Zealand.

"I think the first oil lamp was lit to cook fish over, and there were plenty of fishes here. The herring swam through the sound in great shoals; it was hard to force a boat through them. They glittered in the water as if there were lightning down there, and shone in the depths like the northern lights. The sound had a wealth of fishes; therefore houses were built on the coast of Zealand, with walls of oak and roofs of bark—there were trees enough for that purpose. Ships anchored in the harbor, oil lamps hanging from swaying ropes, and the northeast wind blew and sang, 'O-out!' If a lantern glimmered on the island it was a thieves' lantern, for smugglers and thieves plied their trade on Thieves' Island.

"'I believe that all the evil I wished for is coming,' said the northeast wind. 'Soon the tree will come, from which I can shake the fruit.'

"And here is the tree," said Godfather. "Do you see the gallows on Thieves' Island? Robbers and murderers hang there in iron chains, exactly as they hung in those days. The wind blew until it rattled the long skeletons, but the moon shone down on them as serenely as it now shines on a country dance. The sun also shone down pleasantly, crumbling away the dangling skeletons, and from the sunbeams the children of light sang, 'We know it! We know it! Here it shall be beautiful in the days to come; here it shall be good and splendid!'

"'Chicken prattle!' said the northeast wind.

"Now we'll turn the page," said Godfather.

"The bells were ringing in the town of Roskilde, where Bishop Absalon lived. He could both read his Bible and wield his sword; he had power and will. He wished to protect from assault the busy fishermen at the harbor, whose town had grown until it was now a market town. He sprinkled the unhallowed ground with holy water; thus, Thieves' Island received the mark of honor. Masons and carpenters set to work on it; at the bishop's command, a building grew up, and the sunbeams kissed the red walls as they rose. There stood the house of Axel:

> *The castle, with its towers, so stately and high,*
> *Had balconies and stairs up to the sky*
> *Booo! Whooo!*
> *The northeast wind huffed and puffed,*
> *But the castle stood unyielding, unruffed.*

"And outside it lay 'The Haven,' the merchants' harbor:

Mermaid's bower amid seas of sheen,
Built beside groves of green.

"The foreigners came there and bought the wealth of fish, and built shops and houses with bladders for windowpanes, as glass was too expensive. Warehouses followed, with gables and windlasses. See the old fellows sitting there in the shops—they dare not marry; they trade in ginger and pepper, the *pebersvende*.

"The northeast wind whistled through the streets and lanes, sending the dust flying and tearing off a thatched roof. Cows and pigs wandered about in the street ditch.

"'I shall tame and subdue them!' said the northeast wind. 'I'll whistle around the houses and around Axel's house! I can't fail! They call it Gallows' Castle on Thieves' Island.'"

Then Godfather showed a picture of it, which he himself had drawn. On the wall were rows of stakes, and on every stake was the head of a captured pirate showing its teeth.

"That really happened," said Godfather. "And it's worth hearing and worth knowing about.

"Bishop Absalon was in his bath, and through the thin walls he heard the arrival of a ship of freebooters. He instantly sprang out of the bath and into his ship, blew his horn, and his crew assembled. The arrows shot into the backs of the robbers as they rowed desperately to escape. The arrows pierced into their hands, and there was no time to pull them out. Bishop Absalon caught everyone and cut their heads off, and every head was set up on the outer wall of the castle. The northeast wind blew with puffed-out cheeks—with bad weather in his jaw, as the sailors say.

"'I'll stretch myself,' said the wind. 'Here I'll lie down and look the whole matter over.'

"It rested for hours, then blew for days. Years went past.

"The watchman appeared on the castle tower; he looked to the east, the west, the north, and the south. You can see it there in the picture," said Godfather, pointing it out. "You can see him there, but I'll tell you what *he* saw.

"There is open water from the wall of Stejleborg right out to Kjöge Bay, and a broad channel over to the coast of Zealand. In front of Serritslev and Solberg Meadows, with their large villages, the new town, with its gabled timber houses, is growing up more and more. There are entire streets for shoemakers and tailors, for grocers and beer sellers; there is a marketplace and there is a guildhall, and near the shore, where there was once an island, stands the splendid Church of St. Nicolaus. It has an immensely high tower and spire; how it is reflected in the clear water! Near this is Our Lady's Church, where Masses are sung, where incense gives out its fragrance and wax candles burn. The 'merchants' haven' is now the bishop's town; the bishop of Roskilde rules and reigns there.

"Bishop Erlandsen sits in Axel's house. There is good cooking in the kitchen; ale and claret are served to the sound of fiddles and kettledrums. Burning candles and lamps make the castle shine as if it were a lantern for the whole country and kingdom. The northeast wind whistles around the tower and walls, but they stand firmly. The northeast wind swoops around the western fortification of the town—only an old wooden fence—but it holds up well. Christopher I, King of Denmark, stands outside it; the rebels have beaten him at Skelskör, so he seeks shelter in the bishop's town.

"The wind whistles, and says, like the bishop, 'Keep out! Keep out! The gate is shut to you!'

"It is a time of trouble, dismal days, when every man is his own master. The Holstein banner waves from the castle tower. There is want and woe, for it is the night of anguish. War and the black death stalk the land in the pitch-dark night—but then comes Valdemar Atterdag. Now the bishop's town is the king's town. It has gabled houses and narrow streets, watchmen and a town hall, and a permanent gallows by the west port. No man from out of town can be hanged on it; you must be a citizen to be allowed to dangle there, to get so high as to see Kjöge and the hens of Kjöge.

"'That's a lovely gallows,' says the northeast wind. 'The beautiful is growing!' And it whistles and whoops.

"And from Germany blew trouble and want.

"The Hanseatic merchants came," continued Godfather, "from warehouse and counter, the rich traders of Rostock, Lübeck, and Bremen. They wanted to seize more than the golden goose from Valdemar's Tower; they had more power in the town of the Danish king than the Danish king himself. They came in armed ships, and no one was prepared. And King Eric had no desire to fight with his German kinsfolk; they were too many and too strong. So King Eric and all his courtiers escaped through the west port to the town of Sorö, to the quiet lake and green forests, to the song of love and the clang of goblets.

"But there was one left behind in Copenhagen, a kingly heart and a kingly mind. Do you see this picture here, this young woman, so fine and tender, with sea-blue eyes and yellow hair? It is the Queen of Denmark, Philippa, the English princess. She stayed in the distracted city, where the townspeople swarmed in panic in the narrow lanes and streets with steep stairs, sheds, and shops of lath and plaster. With the courage of a man, she summoned townspeople and peasants, to inspire and encourage them. They fitted out the ships and garrisoned the blockhouses; they fired with their carbines; there were fire and smoke and lightness of spirit—our Lord will never forsake Denmark! The sun shone into all hearts, and in all eyes was the bright gladness of victory. Blessed be Philippa! Blessed she was in hut and in house; and blessed she was in the king's castle, where she nursed the wounded and the sick. I have clipped a wreath and laid it around this picture," said Godfather. "Blessed be Queen Philippa!"

"Now we spring forward for years," said Godfather, "and Copenhagen springs with us. King Christian I has been to Rome to receive the Pope's blessing and has been greeted with honor and homage on the long journey. Here at home he is building a hall of red brick; there shall be learning there, displaying itself in Latin. The poor man's children, from plow and workshop, can also come there, to live upon alms, to attain the long black gown, and sing before the doors of citizens.

"Near the hall of learning, where everything is in Latin, is a little house where Danish rules, in language and in customs. There is beer soup for early breakfast, and dinner is at ten o'clock in the morning. The sun shines through small panes onto cupboards and bookcases; on the shelves are written treasures—Master Mikkel's *Rosary* and *Godly Comedies*, Henrik Harpestreng's *Leech-book*, and *Denmark's Rhyming*

Chronicle by Brother Niels of Sorö. 'Every Danish man should know these,' says the master of the house, and he is the one to make them known. He is the Dutchman, Gotfred van Gehmen, Denmark's first printer, who practices the divine black art of printing.

"And the books enter the castle of the king and the houses of the citizens. Proverbs and songs are given immortality. Things that men dare not say either in sorrow or in joy are sung by the Bird of Folklore, allegorically and yet clearly. For it flies free and wide through the common man's room and the knightly castle; it sits and twitters like a falcon on the hand of the noble lady; it steals in like a tiny mouse and squeaks in the dungeon of the enslaved peasant.

"'Merely words—all of it!' says the sharp northeast wind.

"'It's the spring!' say the sunbeams. 'See how the green buds are peeping out!'

"Now we'll turn more pages in our picture book," said Godfather.

"How radiant Copenhagen is! There are tournaments and sports and splendid processions! Look at the gallant knights in armor and the noble ladies in silk and gold! King Hans gives his daughter, Elizabeth, to the Elector of Brandenburg. How young she is, and how happy she is! She is treading on velvet; there is a whole future in her thoughts—a future of domestic happiness. Close beside her is her royal brother, Prince Christian, with the melancholy eyes and the hot, passionate blood. He is beloved by the commoners, for he knows their burdens; in his thoughts, he has the poor man's future. God alone decides our fate!

"Now we'll turn another leaf in the picture book," said Godfather. "The wind blows sharply and sings of the sharp sword and this difficult time of trouble.

"It is an icy-cold day in mid-April. Why is the crowd gathering outside the castle and before the old customhouse, where the king's ship lies with its sails and banners? People are crowded in the windows and on the roofs. There are sorrow and trouble, expectation and anxiety. They look toward the castle, now so still and empty, but where formerly there were torch dances in the gilded halls; they look at the balcony from which King Christian so often gazed out over the 'court bridge' and down the narrow court-bridge street to his dovelet, the little Dutch girl he brought from the town of Bergen. The shutters are bolted. As the crowd gazed toward the castle, the gate is opened and the drawbridge is let down. There comes King Christian with his faithful wife, Elizabeth; she will not forsake her royal lord, now when he is so hard pressed.

"There is fire in his blood and fire in his thoughts; he has wished to break with the olden times, to strike off the peasants' yoke, to do good to the commoners, to clip the wings of the 'greedy hawks,' but they have been too much for him. He leaves his country and his kingdom, to win allies and friends for himself abroad. His wife and loyal men go with him. Every eye is moist in this hour of parting.

"Voices are blended in the song of time, against him and for him a three-part choir.

"Listen to the words of the nobles; they are written and printed: 'Woe to you, Christian the Wicked! The blood that poured out in the marketplace of Stockholm cries aloud and curses you!'

"And the monks' cry echoes the same refrain: 'Be you cast off by God and by us! You have called hither the Lutheran doctrine; you have given it church and pulpit and bid the tongue of the Devil speak out! Woe to you, Christian the Wicked!'

"But the peasants and commoners weep: 'Christian, beloved of the people! No longer may the peasant be sold like cattle or exchanged for a hunting hound! That law shall bear you witness!' But the words of the poor man are only chaff before the wind.

"Now the ship sails past the castle, and the commoners line the ramparts, so that they may once more see the royal galley sail.

"'The time is long; the time is hard. Trust neither in friends nor in kinsmen!'

"Uncle Frederick in the Castle of Kiel would like to be King of Denmark. King Frederick is before Copenhagen. See the picture here—'The Faithful Copenhagen.' Coal-black clouds are around it—in picture after picture; just look at each of them! It is all a resounding picture; it resounds still in song and story—those heavy, hard, and bitter times during the long procession of years.

"How did it go with that wandering bird, King Christian? The birds have sung about it, and they fly far over distant lands and seas.

"Early in the spring the stork came from the south, across the land of Germany; it had seen what I will tell you now.

"'I saw the fugitive King Christian crossing a heather-grown moor; he met a wretched cart drawn by only one horse. A woman sat in it, his sister, the Countess of Brandenburg. Faithful to the Lutheran religion, she had been exiled by her husband. And so on that dark heath, the exiled children of a king met. The time is hard; the time is long. Trust neither friend nor kinsman!'

"The swallow came from Sönderborg Castle with a sad song, 'King Christian is betrayed! He sits in the dungeon tower, deep as a well; his heavy steps wear tracks in the stone floor, and his fingers leave their marks in the hard marble.'

> Oh, what sorrow ever found such vent
> As that in the furrows of the stone?

"The fish eagle has come from the tossing sea, which is open and free. A ship flies over it, bearing the brave Sören Norby from Fyn. Fortune is with him—but fortune is as changeable as wind and weather.

"In Jutland and Fyn the crows and ravens scream, 'We seek spoil! It is grand! Caw, caw! Here lie the bodies of horses and of men, too!' It is a time of trouble; it is during the Count of Oldenburg's war. The peasant raises his club and the townsman his knife, and loudly they shout, 'We shall slay the wolves and leave no cub of them alive!' Clouds of smoke roll up from the burning towns.

"King Christian is a prisoner in Sönderborg Castle; he cannot escape or see the bitter distress of Copenhagen. On the North Common stands Christian III, where his father stood before him. Despair is in the city, and plague, and famine.

"A ragged, emaciated woman sits reclined against the church wall. She is a corpse; two living children lie on her lap and can suck only blood from the dead breast.

"Courage has collapsed; resistance collapses. Oh, you faithful Copenhagen!

"Fanfares are blown; hear the drums and trumpets! In rich garments of silk and velvet, with nodding plumes, the noble lords come on horses adorned with gold, riding to Old Market Square. Is there a customary festivity or tournament? Commoners and peasants in holiday attire flock in that direction. What is there to see? Is there a bonfire to burn popish images? Or is the hangman standing there, as he stood at the death fire of Slaghoek? The king, ruler of all the land, is a Lutheran, and this shall now be proclaimed with solemnity.

"Noble ladies and highborn maidens, with high collars and caps of pearls, sit behind the open windows and see all the splendor. Beneath a canopy near the king's throne, the councillors of state sit in antique dress on an outspread carpet. The king is silent, but his will, the will of the council of state, is proclaimed in the Danish tongue. Commoners and peasants are sternly rebuked for the opposition they have shown to the nobility. The commoner is humbled, and the peasant becomes a slave. Now condemning words are uttered against the bishops of the land. Their power is gone, and all the property of the church and cloisters is transferred to the king and the nobles.

"Pride and hatred are there, and pomp and misery, too.

> *The poor bird comes limping, drooping,*
> *Comes stooping.*
> *The rich bird comes huffing,*
> *Comes puffing.*

"The time of change brings heavy clouds, but sunshine, too; it then shines in the halls of learning and in the student's home. And names shine from it on down to our own days. There is Hans Tousen, the son of a poor smith of Fyn:

> *This was the little lad who came from Birkende town;*
> *His name flew over Denmark; widely spread his renown.*
> *A Danish Martin Luther, he drew the Gospel sword,*
> *And gained a mighty victory for truth and for the Lord.*

"There is also the immortal name of Petrus Palladius; that is the Latin, but in Danish, it is Peter Plade, Bishop of Roskilde, also the son of a poor smith of Jutland. And among noblemen shines the name of Hans Friis, chancellor of the kingdom. He would seat the students at his own table and see to their wants and those of the schoolboys as well. But one name above all others is greeted with cheers and song.

> *So long as there's a student to be found*
> *Near Axel's Haven, at work or play,*
> *Will King Christian's name loudly resound*
> *And with hurrahs be greeted every day!*

"Yes, there were sunbeams between the heavy clouds in the time of change.

"Now we turn the page.

"What is it that whistles and sings in the Great Belt under the coast of Samsö? A mermaid, with sea-green hair, rises from the sea; she reveals the future to the peasant. A prince shall be born who shall become a great and powerful king."

"He was born in the field, beneath the blossoming whitethorn. His name now lives in song and story, in the knightly halls and castles everywhere. The stock exchange came forth with tower and spire; Rosenborg Castle rose up and gazed far out over the ramparts; the students got their own house. And close by, where it still points to heaven, stood 'the Round Tower,' facing toward the island of Hveen, where Uranienborg once stood. Its golden domes glittered in the moonlight, and the mermaids sang of the man who lived there, whom kings and sages visited, the master sage of noble blood—Tycho Brahe. He raised the name of Denmark so high that it was known with the stars of Heaven in all the cultured lands of Earth. And Denmark turned him away.

"In his sorrow he sang for comfort:

> *Is not Heaven everywhere?*
> *What more do I require?*

"His song lives in the hearts of the people, like the mermaid's song about Christian IV.

"Now comes a page that you must look at carefully," said Godfather.

"There is picture after picture here, just as there is verse after verse in the old ballads. It is a song, so happy in its beginning, so sorrowful at its close.

"A king's child is dancing in the castle of the king. How lovely she is to look at! She is sitting on the lap of Christian IV—his beloved daughter, Eleonore. She grows in all the virtues and graces of a woman. The foremost among the nobles, Corfits Ulfeldt, is her betrothed. She is still only a child and is beaten by her stern governess; she complains of this to her sweetheart, and rightly, too. How clever and cultured and learned she is! She can speak Latin and Greek, sing in Italian to her lute, and talk about the Pope and Martin Luther.

"Now King Christian lies in the vault in Roskilde Cathedral, and Eleonore's brother is king. In the palace at Copenhagen there are pomp and show; there are beauty and wit—and foremost is the queen herself, Sophie Amalie of Lyneborg. Who can guide her horse as cleverly as she? Who dances with such grace? Who can talk with such wisdom and wit as the Queen of Denmark?

"'Eleonore Christine Ulfeldt!' These are the words of the French Ambassador. 'She surpasses all in beauty and wit!'

"Up from the polished floor of the palace ballroom has grown the burdock of envy; it has clung there, worked itself in, and twisted around—contempt and scorn. 'That illegitimate creature! Her carriage shall stop at the bridge of the castle! Where the queen drives, the commoner shall walk!' There is a storm of gossip, of lies and slander.

"Then Ulfeldt takes his wife by the hand in the still of the night. He has the keys to the town gates; he opens one of them, and horses wait outside. They ride to the shore and sail to Sweden.

"Now let's turn the page, just as fortune turned itself for those two.

"It is autumn. The days are short and the nights are long; it is gray and damp. The cold wind rises in its strength, and it whistles through the leaves of the trees on the ramparts. The leaves drop into Peter Oxe's courtyard, empty and forsaken of its owners. The wind sweeps over Christianshavn, around the mansion of Kai Lykke, which now is a penitentiary. He himself has been driven from home and honor; his escutcheon is smashed and his effigy hung on the highest gallows. Thus is he punished for his thoughtless, frivolous words about the powerful Queen of Denmark. The wind pipes loudly as it rushes over the open space where the mansion of the Lord High Steward once stood. Only one stone of it is now left. 'And that I drove down here as a boulder on the floating ice,' shrieks the wind. 'That stone stranded where since has grown Thieves' Island, under my curse, and so it became a part of the mansion of Lord Ulfeldt, where his lady sang to the sounding lute, and read Greek and Latin, and bore herself proudly. Now only the stone is here with its inscription:

The traitor Corfits Ulfeldt
In eternal scorn, shame, and disgrace.

"'But where is the stately lady now? Whoo-ee-oo!' blows the wind with a piercing shriek.

"For many years she has been shut up in the Blue Tower, behind the palace, where the sea water beats against the slimy walls. There is more smoke than warmth in the cell; its tiny window is high up under the ceiling. In what discomfort and misery sits the adored child of Christian IV, the daintiest of maids and matrons! Memory hangs curtains and tapestries on the smoke-blackened walls of her prison. She recalls the lovely days of her childhood, her father's gentle, beaming face; she recalls her splendid wedding, her days of pride, but also her days of misery in Holland, England, and Bornholm.

Nothing seems too hard for wedded love to bear,
And loyalty is not cause for shame or care.

"But he was with her in those days; now she is alone, alone forever. She does not know his grave; no one knows it.

Faithfulness to her husband was her only crime.

"For long and many years she sat there, while life went on outside. Life never pauses, but we will for a moment here, and think of her and the words of the song.

I keep my promise to my husband still,
In want and dire need, and always will.

"Now do you see this picture here?" said Godfather. "It's winter, and the frost has thrown a bridge of ice between Laaland and Fyn, a bridge for Carl Gustav, who pushes on unchecked. There are plundering and burning, fear and want, throughout the whole land.

"Now the Swedes are encamped before Copenhagen. It is bitterly cold and the snow is blinding, but, true to their king and themselves, men and women stand ready to fight. Every tradesman, shopman, student, and schoolmaster is on the ramparts, ready to guard and defend, with no fear of the red-hot cannon balls. King Frederick has sworn he will die in his nest. There he rides to and fro, and the queen is with him, and courage, patriotism, and discipline are there. Let the Swede don his white shroud and crawl forward in the white snow and try to storm the walls! Beams and stones are hurled down on him; even women come with steaming caldrons and pour boiling pitch and tar onto the storming enemy.

"That night, king and peasant are one united power. Then there is relief, and there is victory. Church bells ring, and songs of thanksgiving resound. Commoners, on this spot you won your knightly spurs!

"What comes next? Look at this picture. Bishop Svane's wife drives in a closed carriage, which only the high and mighty nobility dare do. The proud young men stop the carriage; the bishop's wife must walk to the bishop's house.

"Is that the whole story? Something much greater is stopped next—the power of pride.

"Burgomaster Hans Nansen and Bishop Svane clasp hands to work in the name of the Lord. Their wise and honest talk is heard in the church and the house of the commoner. One handclasp of fellowship, and the harbor is blocked, the gates are locked, and the alarm bell rings.

"Power is granted to the king alone, who remains in his nest in the hour of peril; he governs, and rules over great and small. It is the time of absolute monarchy.

"Now let's turn the page, and time with it.

"'Halloo, halloo, halloo!' The plow stands idle, and the heather grows wild, but the hunting is good. 'Halloo, halloo!' Listen to the sounding horn and the baying hounds! See the huntsmen, and look at the young and gay king himself, Christian V! There is merrymaking in palace and in town. In the halls are waxlights, in the courtyards torches, and in the streets of the town are new lamps. Everything is so new! Favors and gifts go to the barons and counts of the new nobility, brought in from Germany. Nothing is accepted now except titles and rank and the German language.

"But then there sounds a voice that is truly Danish, the voice of the weaver's son, who is now a bishop; it is the voice of Kingo, singing his beautiful psalms.

"There is another commoner's son, this time the son of a vintner, whose thoughts shine forth in law and justice. His book of laws has become gold-ground for the king's name, and will stand for ages to come. That commoner's son, the greatest man in the land, receives a coat of arms—and enemies as well, so that the sword of the executioner is raised over the head of Griffenfeld.

"But mercy is granted, with life imprisonment, and he is banished to a rocky islet off the coast of Trondhjem.

Munkholm—Denmark's St. Helena

"But the dance continues merrily in the palace hall; there are splendor and pomp there, and courtiers and ladies dance to lively music.

"Now these are the times of Frederick IV!

"See the proud ships with their flags of victory! See the tossing sea! It can tell of great deeds for the glory of Denmark. We remember the victorious Sehested and Gyldenlöve! We remember Hvitfeldt, who blew up his ship to save the Danish fleet, and flew to Heaven with Dannebrog. We think of the struggles of those ages, and of the hero who sprang to the defense of Denmark from the mountains of Norway—Peder Tordenskjold.

Across the surging sea his name thunders from country to country.

> *Lightning flashed through the powder dust;*
> *A thunderbolt roared through the whispering age.*
> *A tailor's boy jumped down from the tailor's table;*
> *From Norway's coast he sailed a little sloop.*

And over Northern seas there flew again
The Viking spirit, youthful, and clad in steel.

"Then a fresh breeze blew from the coast of Greenland, bringing a gentle fragrance, as if from the land of Bethlehem; it brought tidings of the gospel light kindled by Hans Egede and his wife.

"So this half page has a golden ground; but the other half, which means sorrow, is ashen gray with black specks, as from fire and disease and pestilence.

"The plague is raging in Copenhagen. The streets are empty. The doors are barred, and where crosses are chalked on them the plague is inside, but where the cross is black all within are dead.

"The bodies are carried away by night, with no tolling bell; the half dead in the streets are taken with them. Funeral wagons rumble, piled with corpses. But from the taverns sound the horrid songs and wild shrieks of the drunkards. They try to forget their bitter in drink; they want to forget, and end—end! Yes, everything comes to an end. The page ends here, with the second time of distress and trial for Copenhagen.

"King Frederick IV is still alive. The course of the years has turned his hair gray. From the window of his palace he looks out on the stormy weather of late winter.

"In a little house near the Westgate a boy is playing with his ball; it bounces up into the loft. The child takes a candle and goes up to seek it, but he sets fire to the little house—to the whole street. The fire leaps into the air so that the clouds themselves reflect it! See how the flames grow higher! There is food for the fire—hay and straw, bacon and tar, piles of firewood for winter—and it all burns. There is weeping, shrieking; there is great panic. The old king rides through the tumult, commanding and encouraging. There is blowing up with gunpowder, and the tearing down of houses. Now the fire has swept into the north quarter, and the churches are burning, St. Peter's and Our Lady's. Listen to the bells playing their last tune, 'Turn from Us Thy Wrath, O Lord God of Mercy!'

"Only the Round Tower and the castle are left standing, with smoking ruins about them. King Frederick is kind to the people; he is a friend to the homeless; he comforts and feeds them and is with them constantly. Blessed be Frederick IV!

"Now look at this page!

"See that gilded carriage with footmen around it and armed riders before and behind it, coming from the castle, where an iron chain is stretched to keep the people from coming too near! Every common man must cross the square with bare head; and therefore few are seen there; they avoid the place. There comes one now, with downcast eyes, and with hat in hand, and he is the one man of that time whom we can name with pride:

His voice like a cleansing storm wind rang.
To sunshine in the days which yet were to come!
Then smuggled-in tunes like grasshoppers sprang
In haste to return to where they were from.

"Witty and humorous—that is Ludvig Holberg. The Danish stage, the castle of his greatness, has been closed as if it were the dwelling place of shame. All merriment is banished; dance, song, and music are forbidden and gone. For the dark side of religion is now in power.

"'The Danish prince!' his mother used to call him. Now come his days of sunshine, with the song of birds, with gladness and true Danish gaiety. Frederick V is king, and the chain is taken from the square beside the castle; the Danish theater is reopened; there are laughter and pleasure and good cheer. And the peasants again hold their summer festivals, for it is a time of joy after the time of fasting and oppression. The beautiful lives again, blossoming and bearing fruit in sound, color, and creative art. Listen to Grétry's music! Watch Londemann's acting! And Denmark's queen loves all that is Danish. God in his Heaven bless you, beautiful and gentle Louise of England! The sunbeams sing in spirited chorus about the queens of Denmark—Philippa, Elizabeth, Louise!

"The earthly shells have long been buried, but the souls live, and the names live. England again sends a royal bride, Matilde, so young and so soon forsaken! In days to come poets will sing of your youthful heart and your hours of trail! And song has an indescribable power through all times and all peoples. See the burning of the castle of King Christian! They try to save the best they can find. Look at the men from the dockyard dragging away a basket of silverware and precious things—a great treasure! But suddenly through an open door, where the flames are brightest, they see a bronze bust of King Christian IV. Then they cast aside the treasure they are rescuing; his image means so much more to them that it must be saved, regardless of how heavy it may be to carry. They know him from the song of Ewald and the beautiful melody of Hartmann.

"Indeed, there is power in words and song, and someday it shall resound as strongly for the poor Queen Matilde.

"Now let's go further in our picture book.

"On Ulfeldt's Place stood the stone of shame, and where in the world is there one like it? By the Westgate a column was raised, and how many in the world are there like it?

"The sunbeams kissed the boulder foundation of the Column of Freedom. All church bells rang and the flags waved, and the people cheered for Crown Prince Frederick. The names of Bernstorff, Reventlow, Colbjörnsen were held in the hearts and were on the lips of old and young. With bright eyes and grateful hearts they read the blessed inscription on the column:

"'The king has decreed that serfdom shall cease, the agrarian laws be set in order and enforced, so that the free peasant may become brave and enlightened, diligent and good, a worthy and happy citizen!'

"What a sunny day! Summer is in town!

"The spirits of light sang, 'The good is growing! The beautiful is growing! Soon the stone on Ulfeldt's Place shall fall, but the Column of Freedom shall stand in the sunlight, blessed by God, king, and people.'

We have an ancient highway;
It goes to the ends of the earth.

"There in the open sea—open for friend and foe—was the foe! The mighty English fleet sailed up; a great power came against a little one. The battle was hard, but the people were valiant.

> *Each stood firm, untiring, held his place,*
> *Stood and fought until death's embrace.*

"They won the admiration of the enemy and inspired the poets of Denmark. The day of that battle is still commemorated with unfurled banners—Denmark's glorious Second of April, the Maundy Thursday battle at Copenhagen Harbor.

"Years passed. A fleet was seen in Öresund. Was it bound for Russia or for Denmark? No one knew, not even those on board the ships.

"There is a legend in the hearts of the people which tells that on that morning in Öresund, when the sealed orders were opened and the instructions to destroy the Danish fleet were read, a young captain stepped forward, a son of Britain, noble in word and deed. 'I swore,' he said, 'that I would fight for England's flag to my death, in open and honorable battle, but not overpower the weak!' And with that he jumped overboard!

> *The fleet sailed toward Copenhagen just the same;*
> *But far from the place where the battle was to be*
> *Lay he, the captain—and unknown is his name—*
> *An ice-cold corpse, in the dark-blue sea.*
> *Shoreward he drifted, until Swedish men,*
> *Fishing beneath the stars with their nets,*
> *Found him, bore him to shore, and then*
> *Cast dice to win his epaulets!*

"The enemy made for Copenhagen. The town was soon in flames. We lost our fleet, but not our courage and faith in God; He casteth down but He raiseth again. Our wounds healed, as those of the warriors in Valhalla. The history of Copenhagen is rich in consolation.

> *Our faith, from the beginning of time to the end,*
> *Is that Our Lord is Denmark's friend;*
> *If we hold firmly, He will hold, too,*
> *And tomorrow the sun will shine on you.*

"Soon the sun did shine on the rebuilt city, on the rich cornfields, and on the skill and art of our people. It was blessed summer day of peace, when poetry raised her Fata Morgana, so rich in color, through the words of Oehlenschläger.

"And a great discovery was made in science. It was a discovery far greater than the gold horn of ancient days, for a bridge of gold was found:

A bridge for thought to flash like lightning
At all times into other lands and nations.

"Hans Christian Örsted wrote his name on that bridge. And look! Beside the church by the castle, a building was raised to which the poorest man and woman gladly gave their pennies.

"You will remember that in the first part of our picture book," said Godfather, "the old stone blocks rolled down from the mountains of Norway and were carried here on the ice. They are raised up again from the sandy depths at the bidding of Thorvaldsen, in marble beauty, magnificent to look at!

"Remember all that I have shown you and all that I have told you! That sandbank in the sea raised itself up to become a breakwater in the harbor; it bore Axel's house, and the bishop's mansion, and the king's castle, and now it bears the temple of the beautiful. The words of the curse have vanished, but all that the children of sunlight sang in their gladness about the coming ages has been fulfilled. Many storms have passed; they will come again and pass again. The true and the good and the beautiful have the victory.

"And that finishes the picture book, but not the history of Copenhagen—far from it! Who knows what you may live to see! It has often looked black, and storms have raged, but the sunshine has never been blown away—it remains. And stronger yet than the brightest sunshine is God! Our Lord reigns over more than Copenhagen."

That is what Godfather said as he gave me the book. His eyes were shining; he was so certain of it all. And I took the book so gladly and proudly and carefully, just the way I carried my little sister for the first time.

And Godfather said, "You're quite welcome to show your picture book to people, and you may also tell them that I made it, pasted it, and drew the whole thing. But it's of great importance that they know at once where I got the idea for it. You know where, so tell them! The idea came from the old oil lamps, which, on the last evening they burned, showed the new gaslights, like a Fata Morgana, everything that had been seen from the time the first lamp was lit at the harbor until that evening when Copenhagen was lighted with both oil and gas.

"You may show the book to anybody you like; that is, to people with kindly eyes and friendly minds; but if a hell horse should come, then close Godfather's picture book."

THE RAGS (1868)

Outside the paper mill, masses of rags lay piled in high stacks; they had been gathered from far and wide. Every rag had a tale to tell, and told it, too; but we can't listen to all of them. Some of the rags were native; others came from foreign countries.

Now here lay a Danish rag beside a rag from Norway; one was decidedly Danish, the other decidedly Norse, and that was the amusing part about the two, as any good Dane or Norwegian could tell you. They could understand each other well enough, though the two languages were as different, according to the Norwegian, as French and Hebrew. "We go to the hills for our language, and there get it pure and firsthand, while the Dane cooks up some sort of a suckling-sweet lingo!"

So the rags talked—and a rag is a rag in every land the world over; they are considered of no value except in the rag heap.

"I am Norse!" said the Norwegian. "And when I've said I'm Norse I guess I've said enough. I'm firm of fiber, like the ancient granite rocks of old Norway. The land up there has a constitution, like the free United States. It makes my fibers tingle to think what I am and to sound out my thoughts in words of granite!"

"But we have literature," said the Danish rag. "Do you understand what that is?"

"Understand?" repeated the Norwegian. "Lowland creature! Shall I give him a shove uphill and show him a northern light, rag that he is? When the sun of Norway has thawed the ice, then Danish fruit barges come up to us with butter and cheese—an eatable cargo, I grant you—but by way of ballast they bring Danish literature, too! We don't need the stuff. You don't need stale beer where fresh springs spout, and up there is a natural well that has never been tapped or been made known to Europeans by the cackling of newspapers, jobbers, and traveling authors in foreign countries. I speak freely from the bottom of my lungs, and the Dane must get used to a free voice. And so he will someday, when as a fellow Scandinavian he wants to cling to our proud mountain country, the summit of the world!"

"Now a Danish rag could never talk like that—never!" said the Dane. "It's not in our nature. I know myself, and all the other rags are like me. We're too good-natured, too unassuming; we think too little of ourselves. Not that we gain much by our modesty, but I like it; I think it's quite charming. Incidentally, I'm perfectly aware of my own good values, I assure you, but I don't talk about them; nobody can ever accuse me of that. I'm soft and easygoing; bear everything patiently, envy nobody, and speak good of everybody—though there isn't much good to be said of most other people, but that's their business. I can afford to smile at them; I know I'm so gifted."

"Don't speak to me in that lowland, pasteboard language—it makes me sick!" said the Norwegian, as he caught a puff of wind and fluttered away from his own heap to another.

They both became paper; and, as it turned out, the Norwegian rag became a sheet on which a Norwegian wrote a love letter to a Danish girl, while the Danish rag became the manuscript for a Danish poem praising Norway's beauty and strength.

So something good may come even of rags when they have once come out of the rag heap and the change has been made into truth and beauty; they keep up understanding relations between us, and in that there is a blessing.

That is the story. It's rather amusing and offends no one—but the rags.

WHICH WAS THE HAPPIEST? (1868)

S uch lovely roses!" said the Sunshine. "And each bud will soon burst in bloom and be equally beautiful. These are my children. It is I who have kissed them to life."

"They are my children," said the Dew. "It is I who have nourished them with my tears."

"I should think I am their mother," the Rosebush said. "You and Sunshine are only their godmothers, who have made them presents in keeping with your means and your good will."

"My lovely Rose children!" they exclaimed, all three. They wished each flower to have the greatest happiness. But only one could be the happiest, and one must be the least happy. But which of them?

"I'll find out," said the Wind. "I roam far and wide. I find my way into the tiniest crevices. I know everything, inside and out."

Each rose in bloom heard his words, and each growing bud understood them.

Just then a sad devoted mother, in deep mourning, walked through the garden. She picked one of the roses; it was only half-blown but fresh and full. To her it seemed the loveliest of them all, and she took it to her quiet, silent room, where only a few days past her cheerful and lively young daughter had merrily tripped to and fro. Now she lay in the black coffin, as lifeless as a sleeping marble figure. The mother kissed her departed daughter. Then she kissed the half-blown rose and laid it on the young girl's breast, as if by its freshness and by the fond kiss of a mother, her beloved child's heart might again begin to beat.

The rose seemed to expand. Every petal trembled with joy. "What a lovely way has been set for me to go," it said. "Like a human child, I am given a mother's kiss and her blessing as I go to the blessed land unknown, dreaming upon the breast of Death's pale angel.

"Surely I am the happiest of all my sisters."

In the garden where the Rosebush grew walked an old woman whose business it was to weed the flower beds. She also looked at the beautiful bush, with especial interest in the largest full-blown rose. One more fall of dew, one more warm day, and its petals would shatter. When the old woman saw this she said that the rose had lived long enough for beauty, and that now she intended to put it to practical use. Then she picked it, wrapped it in old newspaper, and took it home, where she put it with other faded roses and those blue boys they call lavender, in a potpourri, embalmed in salt. Mind you, embalmed—an honor granted only to roses and kings.

"I will be the most highly honored," the rose declared, as the old weed puller took her. "I am the happiest one, for I am to be embalmed."

Then two young men came strolling through the garden. One was a painter; the other was a poet. Each plucked a rose most fair to see. The painter put upon canvas a likeness of the rose in bloom, a picture so perfect and so lovely that the rose itself supposed it must be looking into a mirror.

"In this way," said the painter, "it shall live on, for generations upon generations, while countless other roses fade and die."

"Ah!" said the rose, "after all, it is I who have been most highly favored. I had the best luck of all."

But the poet looked at his rose and wrote a poem about it to express the mystery of love. Yes, his book was a complete picture of love. It was a piece of immortal verse.

"This book has made me immortal," the rose said. "I am the most fortunate one."

In the midst of these splendid roses was one whom the others hid almost completely. By accident, and perhaps by good fortune, it had a slight defect. It sat slightly askew on its stem, and the leaves on one side of it did not match those on the other. Moreover, in the very heart of the flower grew a crippled leaf, small and green.

Such things happen, even to roses.

"Poor child," said the Wind, and kissed its cheek. The rose took this kiss for one of welcome and tribute. It had a feeling that it was made differently from the other roses, and that the green leaf growing in the heart of it was a mark of distinction. A butterfly fluttered down and kissed its petals. It was a suitor, but the rose let him fly away. Then a tremendously big grasshopper came, seated himself on a rose nearby, and rubbed his shins. Strangely enough, among grasshoppers, this is a token of affection.

The rose on which he perched did not understand it that way, but the one with the green crippled leaf did, for the big grasshopper looked at her with eyes that clearly meant, "I love you so much I could eat you." Surely this is as far as love can go, when one becomes part of another. But the rose was not taken in, and flatly refused to become one with this jumping fop. Then, in the starlit night a nightingale sang.

"He is singing just for me," said the rose with the blemish, or with the mark of distinction as she considered it. "Why am I so honored, above all my sisters? Why was I given this peculiarity—which makes me the luckiest one?"

Next to appear in the garden were two gentlemen, smoking their cigars. They spoke about roses and about tobacco. Roses, they say, are not supposed to stand tobacco smoke; it fades them and turns them green. This was to be tested, but the gentlemen would not take it upon themselves to try it out on the more perfect roses.

They tried it on the one with the defect.

"Ah ha! A new honor," the rose said. "I am lucky indeed—the luckiest of all." And she turned green with conceit and tobacco smoke.

One rose, little more than a bud but perhaps the loveliest one on the bush, was chosen by the gardener for the place of honor in an artistically tied bouquet. It was taken to the proud young heir of the household and rode beside him in his coach. Among other fragrant flowers and beautiful green leaves it sat in all its glory, sharing in the splendor of the festivities. Gentlemen and ladies, superbly dressed, sat there in the light of a thousand lamps as the music played. The theater was so brilliantly illuminated that it seemed a sea of light. Through it swept a storm of applause as a young dancer came upon the stage. One bouquet after another showered down, in a rain of flowers at her feet.

There fell the bouquet in which the lovely rose was set like a precious stone. The happiness it felt was complete, beyond any description. It felt all the honor and splendor around it, and as it touched the floor it fell to dancing too. The rose jumped for joy. It bounded across the stage at such a rate that it broke from its stem. The flower never came into the hands of the dancer. It rolled rapidly into the wings, where a stagehand picked it up. He saw how lovely and fragrant the rose was, but it had no stem. He pocketed it, and when he got home he put it in a wine glass filled with water. There the flower lay throughout the night, and early next morning it was placed beside his grandmother. Feeble and old, she sat in her easy chair and gazed at the lovely stemless rose that delighted her with its fragrance.

"You did not come to the fine table of a lady of fashion," she said.

"You came to a poor old woman. But to me you are like a whole rosebush. How lovely you are." Happy as a child, she gazed at the flower, and perhaps recalled the days of her own blooming youth that now had faded away.

"The window pane was cracked," said the Wind. "I got in without any trouble. I saw the old woman's eyes as bright as youth itself, and I saw the stemless but beautiful rose in the wine glass. Oh, it was the happiest of them all! I knew it! I could tell!"

Every rose on that bush in the garden had its own story. Each rose was convinced that it was the happiest one, and it is faith that makes us happy. But the last rose knew indeed that it was the happiest.

"I have outlasted them all," it said. "I am the last rose, the only one left, my mother's most cherished child!"

"And I am the mother of them all," the Rosebush said.

"No, *I* am," said the Sunshine.

"And *I*, " said the Dew.

"Each had a share in it," the Wind at last decided, "and each shall have a part of it." And then the Wind swept its leaves out over the hedge where the dew had fallen, and where the sun was shining.

"I have my share too," said the Wind. "I have the story of all the roses, and I shall spread it throughout the wide world. Tell me then, which was the happiest of them all? Yes, that you must tell, for I have said enough."

THE DAYS OF THE WEEK (1868)

The days of the week once wanted to be free to get together and have a party. But each of the seven days was so occupied, the year around, that they had no time to spare. They wanted a whole extra day; but then they had that every four years, the intercalary day that comes in February for the purpose of keeping order in chronology.

On the intercalary day they would get together for a party, and, as February is the month of carnivals, they would come in costumes of each one's taste and choice; they would eat well, drink well, make speeches, and be complimentary and disagreeable to one another in unrestrained comradeship. While the Vikings of olden times used to throw their gnawed-off bones at each other's heads during mealtime, the days of the week intended to throw jokes and sarcastic witticisms such as might be in keeping with the innocent carnival spirit.

So when it was intercalary day, they assembled.

Sunday, foreman of the days of the week, appeared in a black silk cloak; pious people thought he was dressed for church in a minister's gown, but the worldly minded saw that he was attired in a domino for merriment and that the flashing carnation he wore in his buttonhole was a little red theater lantern on which it said, "All sold out; see now that you enjoy yourselves!"

Monday, a young fellow related to Sunday, and very fond of pleasures, came next. He left his workshop, he said, whenever he heard the music of the parade of the guard.

"I must go out and listen to Offenbach's music; it doesn't go to my head or to my heart; it tickles my leg muscles; I must dance, have a few drinks, get a black eye, sleep it off, and then the next day go to work. I am the new part of the week!"

Tuesday is Tyr's day, the day of strength.

"Yes, that I am," said Tuesday. "I take a firm grip on my work; I fasten Mercury's wings onto the merchant's boots, see that the wheels in the factory are oiled and turning, that the tailor sits at his table, and that the street paver is by his paving stones; each attends to his business, for I keep my eye on all. Accordingly, I am here in a police uniform and call myself Tuesday, a well-used day! If this is a bad joke, then you others try to think of a better one!"

"Then I come," said Wednesday. "I'm in the middle of the week. The Germans call me Herr Mittwoch. I stand like a journeyman in a store and like a flower in the midst of the other esteemed days of the week! If we all march up in order, then I have three days before me and three days behind; they are like an honor guard, so I should think that I am the most prominent day in the week!"

Thursday appeared dressed as a coppersmith, with a hammer and a copper kettle, as a symbol of his noble descent.

"I am of the highest birth," he said, "paganish, godlike! In the northern countries I am named after Thor, and in the southern countries after Jupiter, who both knew how to thunder and lighten, and that has remained in the family!"

And then he beat his copper kettle, thereby proving his high birth.

Friday was dressed as a young girl and called herself Freia, also Venus for a change, depending upon the language of the country in which she appeared. She was of a quiet, cheerful character, she said, but today she felt gay and free, for this was intercalary day, which, according to an old custom, gives a woman the right to dare propose to a man and not have to wait for him to propose to her.

Saturday appeared as an old housekeeper with a broom and other cleaning articles. Her favorite dish was beer soup, though at this festive occasion she did not request that it be served for everyone, only that she get it, and she got it.

And so the days of the week had their party.

Here they are in print, all seven of them, ready for use as tableaux at family parties. There you can make them as funny as you wish; we give them here as a joke on February, the only month with an extra day.

PIETER, PETER, AND PEER (1868)

It is unbelievable all that children know nowadays; one can scarcely say what they don't know. They no longer believe the old story that the stork brought them to father and mother out of the well or the millpond when they were little, and yet it is really true.

But how did the little ones get down into the millpond or the well? Ah, not everyone knows that, but there are some who do. Have you ever gazed at the sky on a clear, starry night and watched the many shooting stars? It is as if the stars fall from and disappear into nowhere. Even the most learned persons can't explain what they don't know themselves; but one can explain this when he knows it. It is like a little Christmas-tree candle that falls from heaven and is blown out. It is a soul spark from our Lord that flies toward the earth, and when it reaches our thick, heavy air, it loses its brilliancy, becoming something that our eyes cannot see, something much finer than air itself; it is a little child from heaven, a little angel, but without wings, for it is to become a human child.

Softly it glides through the air, and the wind carries it into a flower, which may be an orchid, a dandelion, a rose, or a cowslip, and there it lies and rests itself. And so light and airy is it that a fly can carry it off, as, of course, a bee can, when they alternately come to seek the sweetness of the flower. If the little air child lies in their way, they do not brush it aside. That they wouldn't have the heart to do! They take it and lay it under the leaf of a water lily in the sunshine, and from there it crawls and creeps into the water, where it sleeps and grows until it is large enough for the stork to see and bring to a human family that has been longing for a sweet little child. But whether it becomes sweet or not depends on whether it has drunk pure clean water or has swallowed mud and duckweed the wrong way; that makes one so filthy!

The stork, always without preference, takes the first one he sees. One goes to kind and loving parents in a fine home; another comes to unpleasant people in such misery that it would have been much better for it to have remained in the millpond.

The little ones can never remember afterward what they dreamed while they were lying under the water-lily leaf, listening to the frogs in the evening singing, "Coax! Coax! Coax!" In human language that means, "Now you go to sleep and dream!" Nor can they remember the flower where they first lay, nor how it smelled; and yet there is always something inside them, even when they are grown people, which makes them say, "I like this flower the best." That's because it is the one in which they were placed when they were air children.

The stork lives to be a very old bird, and he always has interest in the little ones he has brought and watches how they get along in the world and how they behave themselves. Of course, he can't do much for them or change anything in their lives, for he has his own family to look after, but at least he never lets them get out of his thoughts.

I know a very worthy, honest old stork who has had a great deal of experience, and has brought many little ones out of the water, and knows their stories—in which there is always a little mud and duckweed from the millpond. I begged him to tell me the story of one of them, and he said I should have three instead of one, and all from the Pietersens' house.

The Pietersens were an extremely nice family; the father was one of the thirty-two members of the town council, and that was an honor; he was completely wrapped up in his work with the thirty-two councilmen. When the stork brought a little fellow to this home he was named Peiter; the next year the stork brought another, and they named him Peter, and when the third one came they called him Peer—for all three names—Peiter, Peter, and Peer—are parts of the name Pietersen. So there were three brothers here—three shooting stars—and each had been cradled in a flower, then laid under the water-lily leaf in the millpond, and brought from there by the stork to the Pietersen family, whose house is on the corner, as you surely know.

They grew in body and mind, and wanted to become something more than the thirty-two councilmen were. Peiter had decided he wanted to be a robber; he had just seen the play Fra Diavolo, and that had convinced him that a robber's life was the most delightful in the world. Peter wanted to be a trash collector. And Peer, who was such a sweet and good boy, round and plump, whose only fault was biting his nails, wanted to be "Papa." That was what each of them said he was going to be in life, whenever anybody asked them about it.

Then they went to school. One was at the head of the class, and one at the foot, and one in the middle, but in spite of that they could be equally good and clever, and they were, said their very clearsighted parents. The three went to children's parties; they smoked when nobody was watching. They gained knowledge and made acquaintances.

From the time he was quite small, Peiter was quarrelsome, just the way a robber ought to be. He was a very naughty boy, but his mother said that came from worms—naughty children always have worms—or from mud in the stomach. And one day his mother's new silk dress suffered from his obstinacy and naughtiness.

"Don't push the tea table, my good little lamb," she had said. "You might tip over the cream pitcher, and then I'd get spots on my new silk dress."

And so the "good little lamb" firmly took up the cream pitcher and firmly poured all the cream right into Mamma's lap. Mamma couldn't help saying, "Oh, lamb, lamb, that was careless of you, lamb!" But she had to admit that the child had a will of his own. A will means character, and that's very promising to a mother.

He might, of course, have become a robber, but he didn't, in the actual sense of the word; he only came to look like one, with his slouch hat, bare throat, and long, lank hair. He was supposed to be an artist, but he only got as far as the clothes. He looked like a hollyhock, and all the people he made drawings of looked like hollyhocks, so lanky were they. He was very fond of hollyhocks, and the stork said he had lain in that flower when he was an air child.

Peter must have lain in a buttercup. He looked buttery around the corners of his mouth, and his skin was so yellow that one would think that if his cheek were cut, butter would ooze out. He should have been a butter dealer, and could have been his own signboard; but on the inside he was a trash collector with a rattle. He was a musician of the Pietersen family—"musical enough for all of them," the neighbors said. He composed seventeen new polkas in one week, and then put them all together and made an opera out of them, with a trumpet and rattle accompaniment. Ugh! How delightful that was!

Peer was white and red, small and quite ordinary; he had lain in a daisy. He never hit back when the other boys beat him up; he said he was the most sensible, and the most sensible always gives way first.

He was a collector, first of slate pencils, and later of letter seals. Then he got a little cabinet of curiosities of natural history, in which were the skeleton of a stickleback, three blind baby rats preserved in alcohol, and a stuffed mole. Peer had a keen appreciation of science and an eye for the beauties of nature, and that was a comfort to his parents and to him, too. He preferred wandering in the woods to going to school, preferred nature to education.

Both his brothers were engaged to be married, but he could think of nothing but completing his collection of water-bird eggs. He knew much more about animals than he did about human beings; he even thought we could never reach the heights of the animals in the feeling we consider the loftiest of all—love. He saw that when the female nightingale was setting on the nest, Papa Nightingale would perch on a branch close by and sing to his little wife all night, "Kluk-kluk! Zi-Zi! Lo-lo-li!" Peer knew he could never do that or even think of doing such a thing. When Mamma Stork had her babies in the nest, Father Stork stood guard on the edge of the roof all night, on one leg. Peer couldn't have stood that way for an hour!

Then one day when he examined a spider's web, and saw what was in it, he gave up completely any idea of marriage. Mr. Spider weaves his web for catching thoughtless flies, old and young, fat and lean; he lives only to weave and to support his family. But Madam Spider lives only for him. Out of sheer love she eats him up; she eats his heart, his head, his stomach, until only his long thin legs are left in the web where he used to sit, anxious for the welfare of his family. Now that's the real truth, right out of the natural-history book! When Peer saw all this he grew very thoughtful; to be so dearly loved by a wife that she eats one up out of violent love? No! No human being could love like that, and would it be desirable, anyway?

Peer resolved never to marry, or even to give or take a kiss, for that might seem the first step toward marriage. But he did receive a kiss, anyway, the same kiss we all get someday, the great kiss of Death. When we have lived long enough, Death is given the order, "kiss him away," and so away the human goes. A ray of sunshine comes straight from our Lord, so bright that it almost blinds one. Then the soul that came from heaven as a shooting star goes back like a shooting star, but this time not to sleep in a flower or dream beneath the leaf of the water lily; it has more important things than that to do. It enters the great land of eternity; but what that is like and what it looks like there, no one can say. No one has looked into it, not even the stork, though he sees far and knows much.

The stork knew nothing more of Peer, whereas he could have told me lots more about Peiter and Peter. But I had heard enough of them, and I suppose you have, too, so I thanked him and bade him good-bye for this time. But now he demands three frogs and a little snake as payment for this simple little story—you see, he takes his pay in food. Will you pay him? I can't; I have neither frogs nor snakes.

THE COURT CARDS (1869)

Oh, so many dainty things can be cut out of pasteboard and pasted together! In this fashion there was cut and pasted a castle so large that it took up a whole tabletop, and it was painted so that it seemed to be built out of red brick. It had a shining copper roof; it had towers and a drawbridge; the water in the canals looked like plate glass, which is just what it was; and in the topmost tower there stood a watchman cut out of wood. He had a trumpet, but he didn't blow it.

All this belonged to a little boy named William. He raised and then lowered the drawbridge himself, and made his tin soldiers march over it. He opened the castle gate to peep into the spacious reception hall, where all the face cards from a pack—Hearts, Diamonds, Clubs and Spades—hung in frames upon the wall, like portraits in a real reception hall. The Kings each held a scepter and wore a crown. The Queens wore flowing veils over their shoulders, and in their hands each held a flower or a fan. The Knaves had halberds and nodding plumes.

One evening the little boy peered through the open gates of the castle to have a look at the Court Cards in the reception hall. It seemed to him that the Kings saluted him with their scepters, the Queen of Spades waved the golden tulip she held, the Queen of Hearts raised her fan, and all four Queens graciously took notice of him. As he came a little closer to get a better view, his head struck against the castle and shook it. Then the four Knaves, of Hearts, Diamonds, Clubs, and Spades, lifted their halberds to warn him not to try to press his way through.

The little boy understood, and gave them a friendly nod. He nodded again, and then he said: "Say something," but the Court Cards said not a word. However, when he nodded a third time to the Knave of Hearts, the Knave jumped out of his card and placed himself in the middle of the floor.

"What's your name?" he asked the youngster. "You have bright eyes and good teeth, but you don't wash your hands often enough." This was not a very polite way to talk.

"My name is William," said the youngster. "This castle is mine, and you are my Knave of Hearts."

"I'm my King's and my Queen's Knave, not yours," said the Knave of Hearts. "I can get off of the card and out of the frame too. So can my gracious King and Queen, even more easily than I. We can march right out into the wide world, but that's such a tiresome journey, and we have grown weary of it. It's more convenient, and more pleasant for us to be sitting in the cards, just being ourselves."

"Were all of you really human beings once?" asked the youngster.

"Human beings?" the Knave of Hearts said. "Yes, but we were not as good as we should have been. Now please light a little wax candle for me. I'd like a red one best, for red is the color of my King and Queen. Then I shall tell our whole story to the lord of the castle—I believe you said you were lord of the castle, didn't you? But don't interrupt me. If I speak, there must not be the slightest interruption.

"Do you see my King—the King of Hearts? Of these four Kings, he is the oldest, the first-born. He was born with a golden crown and a golden apple, and he began to rule immediately. His Queen was born with a golden fan. She still has it. They had a wonderful time, even in childhood. They did not have to go to school. They could amuse themselves all day long, building up castles and knocking them down, setting up tin soldiers, and playing with dolls. If they asked for a slice of bread and butter, their bread was buttered on both sides and nicely sprinkled with brown sugar too. This was in the good old days which were called the golden age, but they tired of it all, and so did I. Yes, those were the good old days!—and then the King of Diamonds took over the government."

The Knave didn't say any more. The little boy waited to hear something else, but not a syllable was spoken, so after a while he asked, "What then?"

The Knave of Hearts made him no answer. He stood erect and silent, with his eyes fixed on the burning wax candle. The youngster nodded, and nodded again, but he got not response. He then turned to the Knave of Diamonds, and when he had nodded to him three times the Knave leaped from the card to the center of the floor. He said only two words: "Wax candle!"

Understanding what he wanted, little William at once lighted a red candle and placed it before him. The Knave of Diamonds presented arms with his halberd, and said:

"Then the King of Diamonds came to the throne—a King with a pane of glass in his chest. The Queen also had a pane of glass in her chest, so people could look right inside them, though in all other respects they were shaped as normal human beings. They were so pleasant that a monument was raised in their honor. It stood without falling for seven whole years, but it was built to stand forever." The Knave of Diamonds presented arms and stared at the red wax candle.

Immediately, without any nod of encouragement from little William, the Knave of Clubs stepped down, as serious as the stork that strides with such dignity across the meadow. Like a bird, the black three-leafed clover in the corner of the card flew past the Knave and back again, to fit itself where it had fitted before. Without waiting for his wax candle—as the other knaves had done—the Knave of Clubs said:

"Not everyone gets his bread buttered on both sides and powdered with sugar. My King and Queen had none of that. They were compelled to go to school and learn what they had not learned before. They too had panes of glass in their chests, but nobody looked through the glass except to see if something was wrong with their works inside, and if possible to find out some reason for scolding them. I know it. I have served my King and Queen all my life long. I know all about them, and I obey all their orders. They commanded me to say nothing more tonight, so I keep silence and present arms."

But William lighted a candle for this Knave too—a candle, white as snow. Quickly—even more quickly than the candle was lighted—the Knave of Spades appeared in the center of the hall. He hurried along, yet he limped as if he had a lame leg. It creaked and cracked as if it had once been broken. Yes, he had met with many ups and downs in his life. Now he spoke:

"Yes, you have each got a candle, and I shall get one too. I know that. But if we Knaves are honored so highly, our Kings and Queens should have triple honors. And it is right that My King and Queen should have *four* candles each. Their story and trials are so sad and unhappy that they have good reason to dress in mourning and to wear a gravedigger's spade on their coat of arms. Poor Knave that I am, in one game of cards I have been nicknamed 'Black Peter.' Yes! but I have a name that isn't even fit to mention." So he whispered, "In another game I am nicknamed 'Dirty Mads'—I who was once first cavalier to the King of Spades. Now I am last! The history of my royal master and mistress I will not tell, for they do not wish me to do so. The little lord of the castle may imagine their story for himself if he will, but it is a most melancholy one. They have sunk pretty low, and their fate is not apt to change for the better until we all go riding on the red horse, higher than there are clouds."

And little William proceeded to light three candles apiece for the Kings, and three for the Queens. But for the King and Queen of Spades, he lighted four candles apiece, and the whole reception hall became as dazzlingly bright as the wealthiest emperor's palace. The four Kings and Queens made each other serene bows and gracious curtsies. The Queen of Hearts fluttered her golden fan, and the Queen of Spades twirled her golden tulip in a wheel of fire. The royal couples came down from their cards and frames to move in a graceful minuet across the floor. They were dancing in and out among the candle flames, and the Knaves were dancing too.

Suddenly the entire reception hall was ablaze. The fire roared up through the windows and the walls, and everything was a curtain of flames that crackled and hissed. The whole castle was wrapped in fire and smoke. William was frightened. He ran shouting to his father and mother, "Fire, fire! My castle's on fire!" It sparkled and blazed, but from the flames it sang:

"Now we are riding the red horse, higher than the clouds. This is the way it behooves Kings and Queens to go. And this is the way it behooves their Knaves to follow."

Yes! That was the end of William's castle, and of the Court Cards. William is still alive, and he washes his hands. It was not his fault that the castle burned.

LUCK MAY LIE IN A PIN (1869)

A STORY TOLD FOR MY YOUNG AMERICAN FRIENDS

I'll tell you a story about luck. All of us know what it is to be lucky. Some know good luck day in, day out; others only now and then in their lucky seasons; and there are some people who know it only once in a lifetime. But luck comes at some time or other to us all.

Now I needn't tell you what everyone knows, that it's God who puts little children in their mother's lap; maybe in a nobleman's castle, maybe in a workingman's home, or maybe in the open field where the cold wind blows. What you may not know, though it's just as true, is that when God leaves the child he always leaves it a lucky piece. He doesn't put this where the child is born, but tucks it away in some odd corner of the Earth where we least expect it. Yes, you can rest assured that it always turns up, sooner or later, and that is nice to know.

This lucky piece may turn out to be an apple. That was the case with one man, a scholar called Newton. The apple fell into his lap, and his luck came with it. If you don't know the story, get someone to tell it to you. I've a different story to tell, about a pear.

Once there was a man born poor, bred poor, and married without a penny. By the way, he was a turner by trade, but as he made nothing except umbrella handles and umbrella rings, he earned only enough money to live from hand to mouth.

"I'll never find my luck," he used to say.

Now this is a gospel true story. It really happened. I could name the man's county and his town, but that isn't important. Wild service berries, with their red, sour fruit, grew around his house and garden as if they were the richest ornament. However, in the garden was also a pear tree. It had never borne fruit; yet the man's luck lay hidden in the tree, in the shape of a pear not yet to be seen.

One night the wind blew in a terrible gale. In the next town men said that the great mail coach was lifted from one side of the road to the other as easily as a rag, so it was not to be wondered at that a large branch was torn from the pear tree. The branch was brought into the workshop and, just as a joke, the turner made from it wooden pears, big, little, and middle-sized.

"For once my tree has borne pears," he smiled, and gave them to his children for playthings.

Among the necessities of life are umbrellas, especially in lands where it rains a lot. But the turner's family had only one umbrella between them. When the wind blew hard, their umbrella would blow inside out. Sometimes it would break, and luckily the man knew how to mend it. However, with the button and loop that held the umbrella closed, things went from bad to worse. The button would always fly off just as they thought they had the umbrella neatly folded.

One day it popped off, and the turner hunted for it everywhere. In a crack of the floor he came across one of the smallest pears he had given his children for a toy.

"If I can't find the button," he said, "I'll make this do." He fitted a string through it, and the little pear buttoned up the umbrella to perfection. It was the best umbrella fastener that ever was seen.

The next time the turner sent umbrella handles and umbrella rings to the city, he added several of the small wooden pears. They were fitted to a few new umbrellas, and put with a thousand others on a ship bound for America. Americans catch on very quickly. They saw that the little pears held better than the other umbrella buttons, and the merchant gave orders that all the umbrellas sent to him henceforth should be fastened with little wooden pears.

There was work for you—thousands of pears to be made for all the umbrellas that went to America. The turner turned them out wholesale, until the whole pear tree was used up making little wooden pears. They brought pennies that grew into dollars. There was no end to the money he made.

"My luck was in that pear tree all along," the man said. Soon he had a great factory with plenty of workmen to help him. Now that he always had time for a joke he would say, "Good luck may lie in a pin."

And I who tell this story say so too, for it's a true proverb in Denmark that if you put a white pin in your mouth you'll be invisible. But it must be the right sort of pin, a lucky piece from God's own hand. I have one of them, and whenever I come to America, that new world so far away and yet so near me, I'll always carry that pin. Already my words have gone there. The ocean rolls toward America, and the wind blows that way. Any day I can be where my stories are read, and perhaps see the glitter of ringing gold—the gold that is best of all, which shines in children's eyes, or rings from their lips and the lips of their grown-ups. I am in all my friends' homes, even though they don't see me. I have the white pin in my mouth.

And luck may lie in a pin.

SUNSHINE STORIES (1869)

I'll tell you a story," said the Wind. "Kindly remember," said the Rain, "that it's my turn to talk. You've been howling around the corner at the top of your voice quite long enough."

"Is that the thanks I get for all of the favors I've done you?" the Wind blustered. "Many an umbrella I've turned inside out, or even blown to tatters, when people tried to avoid you."

"Be silent! It is I who shall speak," said the Sunshine, who spoke with such brilliance and warmth that the weary Wind fell flat on his back, and the Rain shook him and tried to rouse him, crying: "We won't stand for it. This Madam Sunshine is forever interrupting us. Don't let's listen to her. What she says is not worth hearing."

And the Sunshine began: "A beautiful swan flew over the rolling, tossing waves of the ocean. Each of its feathers shone like gold. One feather drifted down above a great merchant ship that sailed the sea with all its canvas spread. The feather came to rest upon the curly hair of a young overseer who looked after the goods aboard that ship—"supercargo," they called him. The bird of fortune's feather touched his forehead, became a quill pen in his hand, and brought him such luck that he soon became a merchant, a man of wealth, a man so rich that he could wear spurs of gold and change a golden dish into a nobleman's shield. I know—I have shone on it," said the Sunshine.

"The swan flew far away, over a green meadow where a little shepherd boy, not more than seven years old, lay in the shade of an old tree, the only tree in that meadow. As the swan flew past it, she brushed one leaf from the tree. This leaf fell into the boy's hands, where it turned into three leaves, ten leaves—yes, it turned into all the leaves of a book. In this book he read of the many wonderful things that are in nature, about his native language, about faith, and about knowledge. Before he went to sleep he laid the book under his pillow to keep from forgetting what he had learned during the day. The wonderful book led him first to school, and then far into the fields of learning. I have seen his name where they carve the names of great scholars," the Sunshine said.

"The swan flew over the forest, where it was lonely and quiet. She came to rest on a deep blue lake, where the water lilies grow, where wild apple trees flourish along the shore, and where the cuckoo and wild pigeon make their nests.

"A poor woman was in the forest, gathering fallen branches. She carried them on her back, and held a baby in her arms. She saw the golden swan, that bird of fortune, rise from the rush-covered shore. What was this glittering thing the swan had left? It was a golden egg, still warm. She put it in her bosom, and the warmth stayed in it. Truly there was life in that egg. Yes, she heard a tapping inside the shell, but it was so faint that she mistook it for the sound of her own heartbeat.

"When she came home to her own poor cottage, she took the egg out to look at it. 'Tick,' it said, 'tick,' as if it had been a costly gold watch. But it was no watch. It was an egg, just about to hatch. The shell cracked open, and a dear little baby swan looked out. It was fully feathered, all in gold, and around its neck were four gold rings. As the poor woman had four boys—three at home and the baby she had carried in her arms—she knew that one of the rings was meant for each of her sons. As soon as she realized this, the little golden bird flew away. She kissed all of the rings, and she made each son kiss one of them, touch it against his heart, and wear it on his finger. I saw all this," said the Sunshine, "and I saw what came of it.

"As one of the boys played in the bed of a stream, he picked up a handful of clay. He turned it, and twisted it, and he shaped it in his fingers until he had made a statue of Jason. Like Jason, the young sculptor had found the golden fleece he sought.

"The second boy ran across the meadow, where there were flowers of every hue. He gathered a handful, and squeezed them so tightly that the colored juices wet his ring and splashed in his eye. They stuck to his fingers and colored his thoughts. The days went by, and the years went past, until people in the big city came to speak of him as 'the great painter.'

"The third boy clenched his ring in his teeth so tightly that it echoed the song that lay deep in his heart. The things he thought and the things he felt were turned to music. The rose like singing swans, and like swans they plunged down as deep as the depths of the sea, 'the Deep Sea of Thoughts.' He became a great musician, a great composer of whom every land has the right to say: 'He belongs to me.'

"The fourth boy—the baby—was an outcast. They said he had the pip, and that like a sick little chicken he should be dosed with butter and pepper. They gave him pepper enough with his butter, but I gave him warmth and the kiss of the sun," said the Sunshine. "He got ten kisses for one that the other children received. He was a poet, who met with a blow and a kiss, all his life long. But he had something that no one could take from him. He had the ring of fame from the golden swan of fortune. There were golden wings to his thoughts. Up they flew and away they went, like golden butterflies, which are the symbol of things immortal."

"What an extremely long story," said the Wind.

"And so awfully dull," the Rain agreed. "Fan me, if you please, so I may revive a little."

The Wind blew again, and the Sunshine said: "The swan of fortune flew over the deep gulf, where fishermen spread their nets. The poorest of the fishermen thought of getting married, and marry he did. And to him the swan brought a lump of amber. Amber has the power to draw things to it, and it drew the hearts to the fisherman's home. Amber makes the most wonderful incense, and there came a fragrant air as from a church, like a balmy breeze from God's nature. So the fisherman and his bride were happy and thankful in their quiet home. They were content with what little they had, and their life became a complete sunshine story."

"I think," said the Wind, "that these stories should stop. The Sunshine has talked long enough, and I am very bored."

"So am I," said the Rain.

And what do we others who *knew* this story say?

We say: "Now it's out."

WHAT ONE CAN INVENT (1869)

There was once a young man who studied to become a poet. He wanted to be a poet by next Easter, so that he could marry and earn his living from poetry, which he knew was just a matter of making things up. But he had no imagination. He firmly believed he had been born too late. Every subject had been used up before he had a chance at it, and there was nothing in the world left to write about.

"How happy were the people born a thousand years ago," he sighed. "Then it was an easy thing to be immortal. Even those who were born a hundred years ago were lucky compared with me. They still had things left to make poems about. But now every subject is worn out, and it's no use for me to try my pen on such threadbare stuff."

He thought about it, and worried about it, until he grew very thin and woebegone, the poor fellow. No doctor could help him, but there was one person who would know just the remedy he needed to set him right. She was a little old lady, wonderfully wise, who lived in a tiny gatehouse in the turnpike. She opened and closed the toll gate for everyone who rode by, but she was learned in the ways of the world. She was a clever woman who could do more than open a gate, and she knew far more than the doctor who drives in his own carriage and pays taxes.

"I must go to her," the young man said. He found her house small and tidy, but most uninteresting. Not a tree, not a flower, grew anywhere near it. There was a beehive by her door—very useful; there was a potato patch—very useful; and over the ditch a blackthorn bush had flowered, and now bore fruit—very sour berries that puckered your mouth if you tasted them before they were ripened by frost.

The young man thought to himself, "What a perfect picture this is of the commonplace times we live in." But at least it had set him thinking. He had found the flash of an idea at the old lady's doorway.

"Write it down," she told him. "Crumbs are the same stuff that bread is made of. I know why you have come. You have no imagination, but you want to be a poet by Easter."

"Everything has been written before I was born," he sighed. "Our times are not like the old days."

"Indeed they aren't," the little old lady agreed. "In the old days women like me, who knew dark secrets and how to cure by the use of strange herbs, were burned alive. In the old days poets went about with empty stomachs, and their clothes ragged and patched. Ours are excellent times, the best times of all. But your lack of imagination comes from not using your eyes, and not using your ears, and not saying your prayers at night. There are things all around you to write about, if you only knew how. You can find poetry in the earth, where it grows and flourishes. Whether you dip into the water of a running stream or a stagnant pool, you will find poetry. But first you must understand how to find it. You must learn how to catch the sunlight as it falls. Just try on my spectacles, listen through my ear trumpet, say your prayers, and please, for once in your life, stop thinking about yourself."

That last request was asking almost too much of him. It was more than any woman, however wise and wonderful, should demand of a poet.

When he put on her spectacles and ear trumpet, she turned him out into the potato patch, where she gave him a large potato to hold in his hands.

What did the potato find to tell him about? It told about itself and its forefathers, about the coming of the potato to Europe; about how unjustly it was suspected and abused before anyone realized that potatoes were far more valuable than any lump of gold.

"By the king's own order, we were distributed from the town hall of each city and village. A manifesto was issued to proclaim our great value and merits, but nobody believed it. No one had the least notion of how to plant us. One man dug a hole and emptied his whole bushel of potatoes in it. Another stuck them in the ground, far apart from each other, and waited for the potatoes to grow into trees, so one could shake them off the branches. They saw us grow buds and flowers and watery fruit, but it all withered away. No one thought to look for our real fruit, the potatoes that lay out of sight in the ground. Ah yes, we suffered many abuses—at least our forefathers did—but it was all for the best. Now you know our story."

"That will do," the old lady said. "Come and look at the blackthorn bush."

"We, too," said the blackthorn, "have many relations in the land from which the potatoes came, further north than where they grew. A party of bold Norsemen steered westerly from Norway through fogs and storms, till they came to an unknown land. Here, buried under snow and ice, they found grass and shrubs, and a bush with dark blue berries like the grapes that grow on the vine. These were blackthorn berries that ripen in the frost, the same as ours, so the country was called 'Vineland,' or 'Greenland,' and sometimes 'Blackthorn Land.'"

"What a romantic story!" the young man said.

"Now follow me," the little old lady told him, and she led him to the beehive. It seethed with life. When he looked inside it he saw bees stationed in all the hallways, moving their wings like fans so that the air would be fresh in every part of this great honey mill. That was their business. Other bees came in from the sunshine and flowers. Those bees were born with baskets on their legs. They brought flower dust and emptied it out of their little leg-baskets, to be sorted and made into honey or wax. There was much going and coming. The queen of the hive wanted to try her wings, but when she flies all the other bees have to fly with her. Though the time for this swarming had not yet come, she was bent upon flight. So the bees bit off her majesty's wings to keep her from flying away, and she had to stay right where she belonged.

"Now climb to the top of the ditch, where you have a view of the high road," said the little old lady.

"My goodness! What swarms of people I see," said the young man. "What endless stories I seem to hear in all that buzzing, droning, and confusion. I feel dizzy! I shall fall!"

"Don't!" said the old lady. "Don't fall backward. Go straight forward, right in among the people. Have eyes for all you see, ears for all you hear, and above all throw your whole heart into it. Soon you will find that you do have imagination, and you'll have many thoughts to write down. But before you go, you must give back my spectacles and ear trumpet." She took them from him.

"Now I can't see anything," the young man said. "I can't even hear anything."

"In that case, you won't be a poet by Easter," the little old lady told him.

"Then when shall I be one?" he asked her.

"Neither by Easter, nor yet by Whitsuntide. You have no knack for imagination."

"But how then shall I ever make my living from poetry?"

"That you can do even before Lent. Write about those who write. To criticize their writing is to criticize them, but don't let that trouble you. The more critically you write, the more you'll earn, and you and your wife will eat cake every day."

"How she does imagine things," the young man thought, as he thanked her and said goodbye. But he did just as she told him. Since he could not be a poet himself—since he could not imagine—he took to writing criticism of all those who were poets. And he handled them with no light hand.

All this was told me by the little old lady who knows what one may imagine.

WHAT HAPPENED TO THE THISTLE *(1869)*

Adjoining the rich estate was a lovely and beautifully kept garden of rare trees and flowers. Guests at the estate enjoyed this fine garden and praised it. People from the countryside all round about and townspeople as well would come every Sunday and holiday to ask if they might see the garden. Even whole schools made excursions to it.

Just outside the fence that separated the garden from a country lane, there grew a very large thistle. It was so unusually big with such vigorous, full-foliaged branches rising from the root that it well deserved to be called a thistle bush. No one paid any attention to her except one old donkey that pulled the dairymaid's cart. He would stretch his old neck toward the thistle and say, "You're a beauty. I'd like to eat you!" But his tether was not long enough to let him reach the thistle and eat her.

There was a big party at the manor house. Among the guests were fine aristocratic relations from the capital—charming young girls, and among them was a young lady who had come from a foreign land, all the way from Scotland. Her family was old, and noble, and rich in lands and gold. She was a bride well worth winning, thought more than one young man, and their mothers thought so too.

The young people amused themselves on the lawn, where they played croquet. As they strolled about in the garden, each young lady plucked a flower and put in a young man's buttonhole. The young lady from Scotland looked all around her for a flower. But none of them suited her until she happened to look over the fence and saw the big, flourishing thistle bush, full of deep purple, healthy-looking flowers. When she saw them she smiled and asked the young heir of the household to pick one of them for her.

"That is Scotland's flower," she said. "It blooms on my country's coat of arms. That's the flower for me."

He plucked the best flower of the thistle, and pricked his finger in the process as much as if he had torn the blossom from the thorniest rosebush.

When she put it in his buttonhole, he considered it a great honor. Every other young man would gladly have given his lovely garden flower for any blossom from the slender fingers of the girl from Scotland. If the heir of the household felt himself highly honored, how much more so the thistle! She felt as full as if the sunshine and dew went through her.

"I must be more important than I thought," she said to herself. "I really belong inside, not outside the fence. One gets misplaced in the world, but I now have one of my offspring not only over the fence but actually in a buttonhole!"

To every one of her buds that bloomed, the thistle bush told what had happened. Not many days went by before she heard important news. She heard it not from passersby, nor from the chirping of little birds, but from the air itself, which collects sounds and carries them far and wide—from the shadiest walks of the garden and from the furthest rooms of the manor, where doors stood ajar and windows were left open. She heard that the young man who got the thistle flower from the slender fingers of the girl from Scotland now had won her heart and hand. They made a fine couple, and it was a good match.

"I brought that about," the thistle believed, thinking of how her flower had been chosen for the gentleman's buttonhole. Each new bud that opened was told of this wonderful happening.

"Undoubtedly I shall now be transplanted into the garden," thought the thistle. "Perhaps they will even pinch me into a flowerpot, which is the highest honor of all." She thought about this so long that at length she said with full and firm conviction, "I am to be planted in a flowerpot."

Every little thistle bud which opened was promised that it too would be put in a pot, perhaps even in a buttonhole, which was the highest it could hope to go. But not one of them reached a flowerpot, much less a buttonhole. They lived upon light and air. By day they drank sunshine, by night they drank dew, and were visited by bees and wasps who came in search of a dowry—the honey of the flower. And they took away the honey, but left the flowers behind.

"Such a gang of robbers!" said the thistle bush. "I'd like to stick a thorn through them, but I can't."

Her flowers faded and fell away, but new ones came in their place. "You have come as if you were called for," the thistle bush told them. "I expect to cross the fence any minute now."

A couple of innocent daisies and some tall, narrow-leaved canary grass listened with deepest admiration and believed everything that they heard. The old donkey, who had to pull the milk cart looked longingly at the blooming thistle bush and reached out for it, but his tether was too short.

The thistle thought so hard and so long about the Scotch thistle, whom she considered akin to her, that she began to believe that she herself had come from Scotland and that it was her own ancestors who had grown on the Scottish arms. This was toplofty thinking, but then tall thistles are apt to think tall thought.

"Sometimes one is of more illustrious ancestry than he ventures to suppose," said a nettle which grew nearby. It had a notion that it could be transformed into fine muslin if properly handled.

Summer went by, and fall went by, and the leaves fell from the trees. The flowers were more colorful, but less fragrant. On the other side of the fence the gardener's boy sang:

> Up the hill and down the hill,
> That's the way the world goes still.

And the young fir trees in the woods began to look forward to Christmas, though Christmas was a long time off.

"Here I still stay," said the thistle. "It is as if nobody thinks of me any more, yet it was I who made the match. They were engaged, and now they have been married. That was eight days ago. But I haven't progressed a single step—how can I?"

Several weeks went by. The thistle had one last, lonely flower. Large and full, it grew low, near the root. The cold wind blew over it, its color faded, its splendor departed. Only the thistle-shaped cup remained, as large as an artichoke blossom, and as silvery as a sunflower.

The young couple, who now were man and wife, came down the garden walk along the fence. The bride looked over the fence, and said, "Why, there still stands the big thistle, but it hasn't a flower left."

"Yes, there's the ghost of one—the very last one." Her husband pointed to the silvery shell of the flower—a flower itself.

"Isn't it lovely!" she said. "We must have one just like that carved around the frame of our picture."

Once again, the young man had to climb the fence and pluck the silvery shell of the thistle flower. It pricked his fingers well, because he had called it a ghost. Then it was brought into the garden, to the mansion, and to the parlor. There hung a large painting—*The Newly Married Couple*! In the groom's buttonhole, a thistle was painted. They spoke of that thistle flower, and they spoke of this thistle shell, this last silvered, shining flower of the thistle which they had brought in with them, and which was to be copied in the carving of the frame. The air carried their words about, far and wide.

"What strange things can happen to one," said the thistle. "My oldest child was put in a buttonhole, and my youngest in a picture frame. I wonder where I shall go."

The old donkey by the roadside looked long and lovingly at the thistle. "Come to me, my sweet," he said. "I cannot come to you because my tether is not long enough."

But the thistle did not answer. She grew more and more thoughtful, and she thought on right up to Christmastime, when this flower came of all her thinking:

"When one's children are safe inside, a mother may be content to stand outside the fence."

"That's a most honorable thought," said the sunbeam. "You too shall also have a good place."

"In a flowerpot or in a frame?" the thistle asked.

"In a fairy tale," said the sunbeam. And here it is.

CHICKEN GRETHE'S FAMILY (1869)

Chicken Grethe was the only human tenant of the fine new house that was built for the hens and ducks on the estate. It was built where the old baronial castle had stood with its tower, crow's-perch gable, moat, and drawbridge. Close by was a complete wilderness of trees and bushes. This had been the garden, running down to a big lake which was now a marsh. Rooks, crows, and jackdaws—a whole horde of screeching, cawing birds, hovered over the trees. The flock did not seem to diminish but rather to increase when one fired among them. They could be heard even inside the poultry house where Chicken Grethe sat with the ducklings waddling about her wooden shoes. She knew each chicken and every duck from the moment it hatched. She took pride in her chickens and her ducks, and in the fine house that had been built for them.

Her little room was clean and tidy. Her mistress, who owned the chicken house, insisted upon neatness, for she frequently brought distinguished visitors to see "the barracks of her hens and ducks," as she called the place.

She had a rocking chair, and a wardrobe, and even a chest of drawers, on which stood a highly polished brass plate with the name "Grubbe" engraved on it. This was the name of the old noble family that had lived there in the days when the castle was standing. The brass plate had been found while they were digging the ground and the parish clerk said that it had no value except as a relic. The clerk knew all about the place and the old days, for he was a scholar and his table drawer was filled with manuscripts. He knew much about the old days, but perhaps the oldest crow knew more and jabbered it out in his own language, but that was crow-talk, which the clerk did not understand, learned though he was.

Toward the end of a hot summer day, the mist would rise over the marsh until it looked as if there were a lake beyond the old trees where the rooks, crows, and jackdaws lived. This was how it had looked when old Sir Grubbe had lived there, and the castle with its massive red walls was still standing. In those days the dog's chain used to reach clear across the gateway. By way of the tower one came to the stone-flagged passage that led to the living quarters. The windows were narrow and the panes quite small, even in the great hall where they used to dance. But in the days of the last Grubbes, there had been no dancing for as far back as a man could remember, though an old kettledrum that had been used in the orchestra still remained in the hall. And there was also a curiously carved cupboard in which the rare flower bulbs were stored, for Lady Grubbe took pleasure in planting and in cultivating flowers and trees. Her husband preferred to hunt wild boars and wolves, and his little daughter, Marie, always rode with him. When she was no more than five years old, she sat proudly on horseback and gazed fearlessly about with her great dark eyes. She delighted in cracking her whip among the hounds, though her father would rather have seen her lash out among the peasant boys who came to stare at the gentry.

The peasant who lived in a clay hut near the castle had a son named Sören who was of the same age as the well-born little lady. He knew how to climb trees, and he had to bring bird nests down to her. The birds screamed as loud as they could scream, and one of the largest of them struck him so hard right above his eye that blood ran down, and they thought at first that he had lost an eye, but it had not been injured. Marie Grubbe called him "her Sören," a sign of high favor which once served to protect even his father, poor Jon. When he had done something wrong one day, Jon was condemned to ride the wooden horse. This contrivance stood in the yard, with four poles for legs, and for its back a single small rail which Jon had to straddle. Lest he ride it too comfortably, heavy bricks were tied to his feet. He made such agonized faces that little Sören wept and went down on his knees to beg Marie to have his father released. She instantly commanded that his father should be taken down. When she was not obeyed, Marie stamped her small feet on the flagstones and tugged at her father's coat sleeve until she tore it. She would have her way, and she got it. Sören's father was released.

Lady Grubbe came to her, stroked her hair, and looked at her daughter with mild, approving eyes. But Marie did not understand why. She would go with the hounds, not with her mother, who went down through the garden to the lake, where the water lilies bloomed, and where the bulrushes swayed among the reeds. "How charming," Lady Grubbe would say, as she admired this fresh, abundant growth. A then very rare tree, which she herself had planted, grew in her garden. A blood beech it was called, a sort of dark Moor among the other trees, so dark brown were its leaves. It needed plenty of sunlight, for in constant shade its leaves would turn green like those of other trees and thus lose their distinction. In her tall chestnut trees, in the shrubbery, and even the grass were many bird nests. The birds seemed to understand that they were safe here, where no one dared fire a gun.

But little Marie came here with Sören who, as we know, could climb, and she sent him to bring her down both the eggs and the downy little birds. The parent birds fluttered about in terror and anguish. Large and small—lapwings from the lawns, rooks, crows, and jackdaws from the tall trees—they screamed and shrieked just as their progeny shriek today.

"Children, what are you doing?" the gentlewoman cried. "What a wicked thing to do."

Sören looked ashamed and even the high-born young girl looked a little embarrassed, but then she said in an abrupt and sulky way: "My father lets me do this."

"Away, away!" the blackbirds shrieked, and away they flew, but they came back the next day because they lived there.

But the quiet gentlewoman did not live there much longer. The Lord called her away, and with him she was more at home than ever she was in this house. The church bells solemnly tolled as her body was carried to the church, and poor men's eyes grew dim, for she had shown them kindness. And now that she was gone no one looked after her plants, so the garden went to rack and ruin.

"Sir Grubbe is a hard man," people would say, "but young as she is, his daughter can handle him." He would laugh and let her have her will. She was twelve years old now, tall and well built. She looked right through people with her great dark eyes, rode her horse like a man, and shot her gun like an experienced hunter.

It came to pass that great men visited that district. They were as great as great can be—the young king with his half brother and crony, Lord Ulrick Frederick Gyldenlöve. They came to hunt wild boar, and they planned to stay overnight at Sir Grubbe's castle.

At the table, when Gyldenlöve sat beside Marie, he took her about the neck and gave her a kiss, just as if they had been related. But she gave him a slap in the face, and told him she could not stand him. This caused great laughter, as if it were a most pleasing sight.

And maybe it was, because five years later, when Marie was seventeen, Gyldenlöve sent a messenger with a letter asking for her hand in marriage. That was something!

"He is the highest and most gallant lord in the land," said Sir Grubbe. "You cannot refuse him."

"I don't like him much," Marie Grubbe said, but she did not turn down the highest lord in the land, who sat next to the king.

Her silver, woolens, and linens were sent by ship to Copenhagen. Marie made the trip overland in ten days, but the ship with the dowry met with contrary winds, or no wind at all. It took four months to reach Copenhagen, and when it did get there Lady Gyldenlöve had gone.

"I'd sooner lie on sacks than in his silken bed," she said. "I'd sooner walk barefoot than ride in a carriage with him."

Late on an evening in November, two women came riding into the town of Aarhus. They were Lady Gyldenlöve and her maid. They came from Veile, where they had arrived by ship from Copenhagen. They rode up to Sir Grubbe's town house. He was not at all pleased to see Marie. He gave her harsh words, but he did give her a bedroom. She got her beer broth for breakfast, but no good words to go with it. Her father's bad temper had turned against her, and she was not used to it. Her own temper was by no means mild. As one is spoken to, so one answers, and answer she did. Of her husband she spoke with bitterness and hatred. She declared that she could not live with him; she was too honorable and virtuous for that.

In this fashion a year went by, most unpleasantly. Bitter words passed between father and daughter. That should not be. Bitter words bear bitter fruit. What would be the outcome?

One day her father said, "We cannot live under the same roof. You must move to our old castle. I would rather you bit off your tongue than spoke lies."

So they parted. With her maid, she went to the old estate where she was born and bred, and where her mother, that pious gentlewoman, lay in the churchyard vault.

An old cowherd lived in the castle, and that was all. Cobwebs, heavy and black with dirt, draped every room. The garden was not taken care of. Wild hops and other climbing vines wove a tangled web between trees and shrubbery. Hemlock and nettles grew tall and rank. The blood beech had been outgrown, and in the deep shade, its leaves had turned as green as those of ordinary trees. Its glory was gone.

Rooks, crows, and jackdaws flew in enormous flocks above the tall chestnuts. They shrieked and cawed as if they had great news to tell each other. Here she was again, the girl who ordered their eggs and babies to be stolen from their nests. The real thief, the one who had actually stolen them, was now climbing a leafless tree. He clung to the tall ship's mast, and got his share of lashes with a rope's end if he didn't behave himself.

All this was told in our own time by the parish clerk. He had pieced it together from books and letters, and it lay with many another manuscript hidden away in his table drawer. "Up and down is the way the world goes," said he. "It's a curious story to hear." We want to hear how it went with Marie Grubbe, but we shall not lose track of Chicken Grethe who sat there in her fine hen house, in our own day. Marie Grubbe sat in this place in her day, but not so contentedly as old Chicken Grethe.

Winter went by. Spring and summer passed, and again came the stormy autumn with its cold and wet fog. It was a dull and dreary life there on the old estate. Marie Grubbe would snatch up her gun and go out on the heath to shoot hares or foxes and whatever birds she could find. More than once on these excursions she encountered a nobleman, Sir Palle Dyre from Nörrebaek, with his gun and his dogs. He was a big man who enjoyed boasting of his strength when he talked with her. He might have been a match for the departed Mr. Brockenhus of Egeskov, at Fyen, whom people still remember as a man of might. Like him, Palle Dyre had fastened a hunting horn to an iron chain over his gateway. When he came home he would catch hold of the chain, lift himself and his horse clear off the ground, and sound the horn.

"You must come to my castle and see that, Lady Marie," he said, "for we have fine fresh air at Nörrebaek." We have no record of when she went to Nörrebaek, but on the candlesticks at Nörrebaek church it is inscribed that they were given by Palle Dyre and Marie Grubbe of Nörrebaek Castle. Body and strength had Palle Dyre. He could drink like a sponge. He was like a cask that could never be filled. He snored enough for a whole pig pen, and he looked red and bloated.

"A cunning swine and a nagging fool he is," said Lady Palle Dyre, the daughter of Grubbe. She soon grew weary of the life there, which did not improve matters. At dinnertime one day, the food got cold on the table. Palle Dyre was off fox hunting, and Lady Dyre could not be found. Palle Dyre came home at midnight. Lady Dyre came home neither by midnight nor by morning. She turned her back upon Nörrebaek, and rode away without a word of farewell. The weather was cloudy and wet. The wind was sharp, and the flock of blackbirds that croaked over her head were not as homeless as she.

First she rode south, almost to Germany. She turned a couple of gold rings with precious stones into ready money. She went east and she went west, with no fixed goal. She was angry with everybody and even with the good Lord himself, so sick was her mind. And soon her body was sick, too. She could scarcely drag her feet along. The lapwing flew up from its tuft of grass when she stumbled upon it and fell. The bird screamed, as it always does, "You thief, you thief!" Yet she had never stolen her neighbors' goods, except for the birds' eggs and nestlings taken from the clumps of grass and the tall trees when she was a little girl. She thought of that now.

From where she lay, she could see the sand dunes along the beach. Fishermen lived there, but she was too ill to crawl so far. The great white sea gulls came screaming over her as the rooks, crows, and jackdaws screamed above the trees at home. The birds flew nearer and nearer, until at last she thought they were blackbirds. But then everything went black before her eyes.

When she opened her eyes again she was being carried in the arms of a tall, strapping fellow. She looked straight into his bearded face and saw that he had a scar over one eye that appeared to divide the eyebrow in two. Sick as she was, he carried her to his ship, where he was abused by the shipmaster for bringing such a burden.

The ship set sail next day. Marie Grubbe sailed with it—she was not put ashore. Didn't she ever come back? Yes, but when and how?

The parish clerk could tell about this, too. It was not a tale which he had pieced together. He had the whole strange story from a reliable book which we can get and read for ourselves.

The Danish author, Ludvig Holberg, who has written so many books worth reading and so many gay comedies by which we get to know his time and its people, mentions Marie Grubbe in his letters, which tell how and in what part of the world he found her. This is well worth hearing, but we shall not lose track of Chicken Grethe, who sits so happy and comfortable in her imposing chicken house.

The ship sailed off with Marie Grubbe. That was where we left off. Year upon year went by.

The plague was raging in Copenhagen. That was in the year of 1711. The Queen of Denmark went to her German home. The king left his capital, and everyone who could made haste to leave. The students, even those who had free board and lodging, scurried out of the city. One of them, the last student left at what they called Borch's College, near the students' headquarters, made ready to go. At two o'clock in the morning he started out, with his knapsack stuffed with more books and manuscripts than clothes. A raw, dank mist hung over the city. Not a soul was to be seen in the street through which he passed. All around him the gates and doors were marked with the crosses which showed that there people lay ill or had died of the plague. Even in broad and winding Meatmonger's street—as the street leading from the round tower to the king's palace was called then—there was not a man to be seen. Suddenly a large hearse came rumbling by. The driver cracked his whip to urge his horses into a gallop, for the wagon was crammed with corpses. The young student covered his face with his hands, and breathed the fumes of strong spirits which he carried in a brass-boxed sponge.

From a grog shop in one of the streets came the sound of songs and forced laughter. Men were drinking the night away in an effort to forget that Death stood at their door, beckoning to them to come with him and join the other dead men in the hearse. The student hurried on to Castle Bridge, where two small boats were moored. One of them was just about to cast off and quit the plague-ridden city.

"If the Lord spares our lives and the wind serves us, we shall sail to Grönsund, on Falster," the captain said, and he asked the name of this student who wanted to go with them.

"Ludvig Holberg," the student said, and at that time it sounded like any other name. Now it resounds as one of Denmark's proudest names, but he was then only a young student, and unknown.

The boat slipped past the castle, and before daybreak they came to the open sea.

A light breeze sprang up and the sails filled. The student sat down with the wind in his face and fell asleep. And that wasn't exactly an advisable thing to do! On the third morning the boat was already at Falster.

"Do you know of anyone in this place with whom I can live cheaply?" Holberg asked the captain.

"I believe you had best go to the ferryman's wife at Borrehouse," he said. "If you want to be polite, call her Mother Sören Sörensen Möller, but she may turn angry if you show her too much politeness. Her husband is under arrest for some crime or other, and she runs the ferry herself. What fists she has!"

The student shouldered his knapsack and went to the ferry house. The door was not locked, so he lifted the latch and entered a brick-floored room in which a large folding bed with a big furred cover was the most noticeable piece of furniture. A white hen, with her chickens around her, was tied to the bedstead. She had upset her drinking dish, and water ran across the floor. No one was there or in the next room, except a little child who lay in a cradle.

The ferryboat came back with only one person on board—whether man or woman was hard to say. This person was wrapped in a great cloak, with a hood that covered the head.

When the boat was docked, it was a woman who entered the room. She had an impressive air as she straightened up and looked at him. Two proud eyes were set under her dark brows. It was Mother Sören, the ferryman's wife, though rooks, crows, and jackdaws could scream out another name by which we would know her better.

Glum she looked, and little enough she cared for talk, but it was settled that the student would stay and board with her for an undetermined time, until things went well again in Copenhagen.

Now and then some honest fellows from the neighboring town dropped in at the ferryhouse. Among them were Frank, the cutler, and Sivert, the customs collector, who came to drink a mug of ale and to chat with the student. He was a thoughtful young man who knew what's what, as they said. He read Latin and Greek, and was well posted in many fields of knowledge.

"The less one knows, the lighter his burden," said Mother Sören.

One day when Holberg watched her wash clothes in strong lye, and chop up knotty stumps for firewood, he told her:

"You work too hard."

"That's my business," she said.

"Have you had to toil and slave this way ever since you were a child?"

"Read the answer in my hands," she said, and showed him her two hands, small but strong and hard, with broken nails. "You know how to read. Read them."

At Christmastime there was a heavy snowfall. The cold made itself at home, and the winds blew as bitterly as if they were dashing acid in people's faces. Mother Sören didn't care. She flung on her cloak, drew up the hood, and went about her business. When the house grew dark early in the afternoon, she would throw pine knots on the fire and sit by it to darn her stockings, for she had no one to do it for her. As evening came on she talked with the student more than she usually did. She spoke of her husband:

"By accident he killed a captain from Dragor, and for this they put him in chains and sentenced him to three years of hard labor on the King's Island. He is only an ordinary sailor, so the law must take its course, you know."

"The law applies to the upper classes too," Holberg said.

"Do you believe that?" Mother Sören stared into the fire, and then went on. "Do you know the story of Kay Lykke, who ordered one of his churches torn down? When Mads, the pastor, thundered from the pulpit against this, he had Mads clapped in irons and thrown in prison. Then he appointed himself judge, found Mads guilty, condemned him, and had his head struck off. That was no accident, yet Kay Lykke was never punished."

"He was within his right, according to the custom of his time," Holberg said. "We have come a long way since then."

"Try to make fools believe you." Mother Sören got up and went into the next room where Toesen, her little child, lay in the cradle. When she had tidied and aired the cradle, she made the student's bed. He had the big furred cover, for though he was born in Norway he felt the cold more than she did.

New Year's Day dawned clear and sunny. It was so cold that the snowdrifts were hard enough for one to walk across them. The bells in the village were ringing for church, as student Holberg wrapped himself in his heavy cloak to set off for town. Rooks flew screeching over Börrehouse, and so did the crows and jackdaws. They made such a racket that you could scarcely hear the bells. Mother Sören stood outside, filling a brass kettle with snow, to melt over the fire for drinking water. She gazed up at the dark swarm of birds and thought her own thoughts.

Student Holberg went to church and on his way back he passed the house of Sivert, the customs collector. Sivert invited him in to warm himself from a bowl of mulled ale, sweetened with syrup and ginger. They started to talk about Mother Sören, but the customs collector knew little about her. Indeed, there were few who did. "She is not a native of Falster," he said, "and she has probably seen better days. Her husband is a common sailor, with a violent temper. He killed a captain on Dragör, and, though he used to beat his wife, she always sticks up for him."

"I would never stand for that," said the customs collector's wife. "I too come of better stock. My father wove stockings for the king."

"So naturally you married one of the king's officers," Holberg said, with a bow to her husband.

Twelfth Night came, and Mother Sören lighted for Holberg a candle of the Three Kings—that is, three small tallow candles—which she herself had prepared.

"A candle for each man!" said Holberg.

"Each man?" she exclaimed, and looked at him hard.

"Each of the wise men from the east," Holberg said.

"Oh, that's how you meant it," she said, and sat in silence for a while. But on that evening of the Three Kings, he learned a great deal about her that he had not known.

"You are fond of the man you are wedded to," Holberg said, "yet people tell me he daily mistreated you."

"That concerns no one but me," Mother Sören declared. "The blows would have done me good had they fallen when I was a child. Now they probably fall for my sins. I only know the good he has done me." She stood up straight. "When I lay ill and weak among the sand dunes, and no one would come near me except perhaps the rooks, the crows, and the jackdaws, who came to pick at me, he carried me in his arms, and got hard words for bringing such a find on board his ship. I do not come of sickly stock, so I recovered. All of us have our faults, and Sören has his. One must not judge the horse by his halter. With him I have led a more pleasant life than I did with him whom they called the highest and most gallant one of all the king's men. I have been married to Governor Gyldenlöve, half brother to the king. Afterward I took Palle Dyre. Good or bad, each has his own way, and I have mine. That was a long story, and now you know it."

Mother Sören went out of the room.

So this was Marie Grubbe, so strangely does the ball of fortune turn. She did not live to see many more feasts of the Three Kings. Holberg wrote that she died in June, 1716, but he did not write, for he did not know, that when Mother Sören, as they called her, lay dead in Borrehouse, a flock of large black birds flew over the roof in silence. They did not scream, and it was as if they knew that at funerals one must be quiet. As soon as she was in her grave, the birds departed, but on that same evening the birds were seen in enormous numbers over her old estate in Jutland. Rooks, crows, and jackdaws, screamed to each other as if they had much to tell. Perhaps they croaked of him who robbed them of their eggs and young ones when he was a boy—the peasant boy who received an iron garter on the King's Island—and also of the highborn young lady who died a ferrywoman at Grönsund.

"Bra! Bra!" they croaked. And "Bra, Bra!" the whole tribe croaked when the old castle was torn down. "And this they cry still, though there is nothing left to croak about," said the parish clerk, when he told the story. "The family died out, the castle was torn down, and where it stood the new hen house now stands, with its gilded weathercock on the roof and Chicken Grethe inside. There she sits, well satisfied with her cosy residence, for if she had not come here she would have gone to the workhouse!" The pigeons cooed above her, the turkeys clucked, and the ducks quacked around her. "No one knew her," they said. "She had no relatives. By an act of charity she came here, and children she had none!"

Nevertheless, she had ancestors, though she did not know of them, nor did the parish clerk, for all the manuscripts he had in his table drawer. But one of the old crows knew, and he told about it. From its mother and its grandmother, it had heard tell of Chicken Grethe's mother and grandmother, whom we know too. We know how, as a child, she rode over the drawbridge and looked about proudly, as if the whole world and all the bird nests in it belonged to her. We also saw her on the sand dunes, and last at the ferryhouse. Her granddaughter, last of her line, had come home again where the old castle had stood and where the wild birds croaked. But she sat among her tame fowls, known by them and on friendly terms with them.

Chicken Grethe had nothing more to wish for. She was happy to die and old enough to die.

"Grave, grave!" the crows croaked.

And Chicken Grethe was buried in a good grave. No one knows where it lies except the old crow, if he isn't dead too.

Now we know the story of the old castle, and of all Chicken Grethe's family.

THE COMET (1869)

Now there came a comet with its shiny nucleus and its menacing tail. People from the great castles and people from the poor huts gazed at it. So did the crowd in the street, and so did the man who went his solitary way across the pathless heath. Everyone had his own thoughts. "Come and look at the omen from heaven. Come out and see this marvelous sight," they cried, and everyone hastened to look.

But a little boy and his mother still stayed inside their room. The tallow candle was burning and the mother thought she saw a bit of wood shaving in the light. The tallow formed a jagged edge around the candle, and then it curled. The mother believed these were signs that her son would soon die. The wood shaving was circling toward him. This was an old superstition, but she believed it. The little boy lived many more years on earth. Indeed he lived to see the comet return sixty years later.

The boy did not see the wood shaving in the candlelight, and his thoughts were not about the comet which then, for the first time in his life, shone brightly in the sky. He sat quietly with an earthenware bowl before him. The bowl was filled with soapy water, into which he dipped the head of a clay pipe. Then he put the pipe stem in his mouth, and blew soap bubbles, large and small. They quivered and spun in beautiful colors. They changed from yellow to red, and from red to purple or blue and then they turned bright green, like leaves when the sun shines through them.

The boy's mother said, "May God grant you many more years on Earth—as many years as the bubbles you are blowing."

"So many, so many!" he cried. "I can never blow all the soapy water into bubbles. There goes one year, there goes another one; see how they fly!" he exclaimed, as bubbles came loose from his pipe and floated away. A few of them blew into his eye, where they burned and smarted, and made his tears flow. In every bubble he saw a picture of the future, glimmering and glistening.

"This is the time to look at the comet," cried their neighbors. "Come outdoors. Don't sit in your room."

The mother took her boy by the hand. He had to put aside his clay pipe and stop playing with the soap bubbles, because there was a comet to see.

The boy saw the bright ball of fire, with its shining tail. Some said it was three yards long, while others insisted it was several million yards long—such a difference.

Most of the people who said these things were dead and buried when the comet came again. But the little boy, toward whom the wood shaving had circled and of whom his mother thought, "He will soon die," still lived on, though he had grown old and his hair was white. "White hairs are the flowers of age," the saying goes, and he had many such flowers. He was an old schoolmaster. The school children thought him very wise and learned, because he knew history, and geography, and all there is to be known about the heavens and the stars.

"Everything comes again," he said. "If you will pay attention to people and events, you will learn that they always come back. There may be a hundred years between, or many hundreds of years, but once again we shall see the same character, in another coat and in another country." And the schoolmaster then told them about William Tell, who was forced to shoot an apple from his son's head, but before he shot the arrow he hid another one in his shirt, to shoot into the heart of the wicked Gessler. This happened in Switzerland. But many years before, the same thing happened in Denmark to Palnatoke. He too was forced to shoot an apple from his son's head, and he too hid an arrow in his shirt to avenge the cruelty. And more than a thousand years before that, the same story was written in Egypt. It happened before and will happen again, just as sure as the comet returns. "Off it flies into space, and is gone for years, but still it comes back." He spoke of the comet that was expected, the same comet he had seen as a boy.

The schoolmaster knew what went on in the skies, and he thought much about it too, but he did not neglect history and geography. His garden was laid out in the shape of a map of Denmark. In it grew herbs and flowers which flourished in different parts of the land.

"Fetch me peas," he said, and they went to the garden bed that represented Laaland. "Fetch me buckwheat," he said, and they fetched it from Langeland. Lovely blue gentian was planted in Skagen, and the shining Christthorn in Silkeborg. Towns and cities were marked with small statues. Here was the dragon and St. Knud, who stood for Odense. Absalon with the bishop's staff stood for Sorö. The little boat with oars marked the site of Aarhus. In the schoolmaster's garden you could learn the geography of Denmark, but first you had to be instructed by him and that was a pleasure.

Now that the comet was expected again, he told about it, and he told what people had said in the old days when it last was seen. They had said that a comet year was a good year for wine, and that water could be mixed with this wine without being detected. Therefore the wine merchants thought well of a comet year.

For fourteen days and fourteen nights the sky was clouded over. They could not see the comet, and yet it was there. The old schoolmaster sat in his little chamber next to the schoolroom. The old Bornholm clock of his grandfather's time stood in the corner, though its heavy lead weights moved neither up nor down, nor did its pendulum ever swing. The little cuckoo that used to come out to call the passing hours had long ago stopped doing his duty. The clock neither struck nor ticked. The clock was decidedly out of order.

But the old clavichord at which he sat had been made in his parents' time, and it still had a tune or two left in it. The strings could still play. Tremulous though they were, they could play for him the melodies of a whole lifetime. As the old man heard them, he remembered many things, both pleasant and sad, that had happened in the long years which had gone by since he was a little boy and saw the comet. Now that the comet had come again, he remembered what his mother had said about the wood shaving circling toward him. He remembered the fine soap bubbles he had blown, one for every year of his life he had said as he looked at them glistening and gleaming in wonderful colors. He saw in them all his pleasures and sorrow—everything, both the good and the bad. He saw the child at his play and the youth with his fancies. His whole life, iridescent and bright, floated before his eyes. And in that splendor he saw his future too, in bubbles of time to come.

First, the old man heard from the strings of the clavichord the melodies of times past, and saw the bubbles of years gone by, colored with memories. He heard his grandmother's knitting song:

Surely no Amazon
The first stockings knit.

And then the strings played the songs his old nurse used to sing for him:

There were so many dangers
In this world to pass through
For people who were young
And only little knew.

Now the melodies of his first ball were playing, for the minuet and molinasky—soft melancholy tunes that brought tears to the old man's eyes. A roaring war march, then a psalm, then happy tunes. The years whirled past as if they were those bubbles he blew when he was a little boy.

His eyes were turned toward the window. A cloud billowed across the sky, and as it passed he saw the comet with its shining nucleus and its shining, misty veil. It seemed to him as though it were only yesterday evening when he had last seen that comet, yet a whole busy lifetime lay between that evening and this. Then he was a child, looking through bubbles into the future; now those bright bubbles were all behind him. Once more he had a child's outlook and a child's faith. His eyes sparkled, and his hands struck the keys. There was the sound of a breaking string.

"Come out and see," cried his neighbors. "The comet is here, and the sky is clear. Come out and look!"

The old schoolmaster did not answer. He had gone where he could see more clearly. His soul was on a journey far greater than the comet's, and the realm to which it went was far more spacious than that in which the comet moved.

Again the comet was seen from the high castle and from the lowly hut. The crowd in the street gazed up at it, and so did the man who went his solitary way across the pathless heath. But the schoolmaster's soul was seen by God, and by those dear ones who had gone before him, and whom he longed to see.

THE CANDLES (1870)

There was once a big wax candle who had the highest opinion of his merits.

"I," he said, "am made of the purest wax, cast in the best mold. I burn more brilliantly than any other candle, and I outlast them all. I belong in the high chandelier or the silver candlestick."

"What a delightful life you must lead," the tallow candle admitted. "I am only tallow. Just a tallow dip. But it's a comfort to think how much better off I am than the taper. He's only dipped twice, while I am dipped eight times to make a thick and respectable candle of me. I'm satisfied. To be sure it would be better to be born of wax than of tallow, and a lucky thing to be shaped in a mold, but one isn't asked how he wants to be born. Your place is in the big rooms with glass chandeliers. Mine is in the kitchen. But the kitchen is a good place too. All the food in the house comes from there."

"There are more important things in the world than food," the wax candle boasted. "There's the glitter of good society in which I shine. Why, I and all my family are invited to a ball that's being given here this very evening."

No sooner had he said this than all the wax candles were sent for. But the tallow candle was not left behind. The mistress of the house took it in her own hand and carried it to the kitchen, where a poor boy waited with his basket full of potatoes and a few apples that she had given him.

"And here's a candle for you too, my little friend," she told him. "Your mother can use it to work by when she sits up late at night."

The lady's small daughter stood close beside her mother, and when she heard the magic words "late at night," she forgot to be shy. "I'm going to stay up late tonight too!" she exclaimed. "We are to have a ball this evening, and I'm to wear my big red ribbon." No candle ever could shine like the eyes of a child.

"Happiness is a blessed thing to see," the tallow candle thought to himself. "I mustn't forget how it looks, for I certainly shan't see it again." They put him in the basket and closed the lid. Away the boy went with it.

"Where can he be taking me?" the candle wondered. "I may have to live with poor people who don't even own a brass candlestick, while the wax candle sits in silver and beams at all the best people. How fine it must be to shine in good company. But this is what I get for being tallow, not wax."

And the candle did come to live with poor people. They were a widow and her three children, who had a low-ceilinged room across the way from the well-to-do house.

"God bless our neighbor for all that she gave us," the widow said. "This good candle will burn far into the night."

She struck a match to it.

"Fut, fie," he sputtered. "What a vile smelling match she lights me with. Would anyone offer such a kitchen match to the wax candle in the well-to-do house across the way?"

There the candles were lighted too. They made the street bright as carriages came rumbling with guests dressed in their best for the ball. The music struck up.

"Now the ball's beginning." The tallow candle burned brighter as he remembered the happy little girl whose face was more shining than the light of all those wax candles. "I'll never see anything like that again."

The smallest of the poor children reached up, for she was very small, and put her arms around the necks of her brother and sister. What she had to tell them was so important that it had to be whispered. "Tonight we're going to have—just think of it—warm potatoes, this very night."

Her face beamed with happiness and the candle beamed right back at her. He saw happiness again, and a gladness as great as when the little girl in the well-to-do house said, "We're having a ball this evening, and I'm to wear my red ribbon."

"Is it such a treat to get warm potatoes?" the candle wondered. "Little children must manage to be happy here, too." He wept tallow tears of joy, and more than that a candle cannot do.

The table was spread and the potatoes were eaten. How good they tasted! It was a real feast. There was an apple for everyone, and the smallest child said grace:

Now thanks, dear Lord, I give to Thee
That Thou again hast filled me. Amen.

"And didn't I say it nicely?" the little girl asked.

"Don't say such things," her mother told her. "Just thank the good Lord for filling you up."

The children went to bed, were kissed good night, and fell fast asleep. Their mother sat up late and sewed to make a living for them and for herself. From the well-to-do house came light and music. But the stars overhead shone on all the houses, rich or poor, with the same light, clear and kind.

"This has been a wonderful evening," the tallow candle told himself. "Can the wax candle have had any better time of it in his silver candlestick? I'd like to know that before I'm burned out."

He remembered the two happy children, one face lighted up by the wax candle, the other shining in the tallow candle's light. One was happy as the other. Yes, that is the whole story!

THE MOST INCREDIBLE THING (1870)

Whosoever could do the most incredible thing was to have the king's daughter and half of his kingdom.

The young men, yes, and the old ones too, bent their heads, their muscles, and their hearts upon winning. To do what they thought was the most incredible thing, two ate themselves to death, and one died of overdrinking. Even the boys in the street practiced spitting on their own backs, which they supposed was the most incredible thing anyone could do.

On a certain day there was to be an exhibition of things most incredible and everyone showed his best work. Judges were appointed, ranging from children of three to old men of ninety. It was a grand exposition of things out of the ordinary, but everybody promptly agreed that most incredible of all was a great hall clock—an extraordinary contraption, outside and in.

When the clock struck, out came lifelike figures to tell the hour. There were twelve separate performances of these moving figures, with speaking and singing. People said that nothing so incredible had ever before been seen.

The clock struck *one*, and there stood Moses on the mountain, writing in the tablets of the law the first great commandment: "There is only one true God." The clock struck *two*, and there were Adam and Eve, just as they first met in the Garden of Eden. Were ever two people so lucky! They didn't own so much as a clothes closet, and they didn't need one. At the stroke of *three*, the three Holy Kings appeared. One was as black as a coal, but he couldn't help that. The sun had blackened him. These kings brought incense and precious gifts. When the stroke of *four* sounded, the seasons advanced in their order. Spring carried a budding bough of beech, on which a cuckoo sang. Summer had for her sign a grasshopper on a ripening ear of wheat. Autumn had only an empty stork's nest, for the birds had flown away. Winter's tame crow perched on the corner of the stove, and told old tales of bygone days. At *five* o'clock there was a procession of the five senses. Sight was represented by a man who made spectacles. Hearing was a noisy coppersmith. Smell was a flower girl with violets for sale. Taste came dressed as a cook. Feeling was a mourner with crepe down to his heels. As the clock struck *six,* there sat a gambler, throwing dice for the highest cast of all, and they fell with the sixes up. Then came the *seven* days of the week, or they might be the seven deadly sins. People could not be sure which they were, for they were not easy to distinguish. Next came a choir of monks to sing the *eight* o'clock evensong. At the stroke of *nine,* the nine muses appeared. One was an astronomer, one kept the books of history, and the others were connected with the theater. *Ten* o'clock struck, and Moses came forth again, this time with the tables on which were written all ten of God's commandments. When the clock struck again, boys and girls danced out. They played and sang this song:

> *All the way to Heaven*
> *The clock struck eleven.*

And *eleven* it struck. Then came the stroke of twelve. Out marched the night watchman, wearing his cap and carrying his morning star, which is a truncheon tipped with spikes. He sang the old watch song:

> *'Twas at the midnight hour*
> *Our Savior He was born——*

and as he sang, the roses about him unfolded into the heads of angels with rainbow-tinted wings.

It was good to hear. It was charming to see. The whole thing was a work of extraordinary craftsmanship, and everyone agreed that it was the most incredible thing. The artist who had made it was young, generous, and sincere, a true friend, and a great help to his poor father and mother. He was altogether worthy of the princess and of half the kingdom.

On the day that they were to proclaim who had won, the whole town was bedecked and be-draped. The princess sat on her throne. It had been newly stuffed with horsehair for the occasion, but it was still far from comfortable or pleasant. The judges winked knowingly at the man they had chosen, who stood there so happy and proud. His fortune was made, for had he not done the most incredible thing!

"No!" a tall, bony, powerful fellow bawled out. "Leave it to me; I am the man to do the most incredible thing," and then he swung his ax at the craftsman's clock. *Crack, crash, smash!* There lay the whole thing. Here rolled the wheels, and there flew the hairsprings. It was wrecked and ruined. "I did that," said the lout. "My work beat his, and bowled you over, all in one stroke. I have done the most incredible thing."

"To destroy such a work of art!" said the judges. "Why, it's the most incredible thing we've ever seen." And the people said so, too. So he was awarded the princess and half the kingdom, because a law is a law, even if it happens to be a most incredible one.

They blew trumpets from the ramparts and the city towers, and they announced, "The wedding will now take place." The princess was not especially happy about it, but she looked pretty and she wore her most expensive clothes. The church was at its best by candlelight, late in the evening. The ladies of the court sang in processions, and escorted the bride. The lords sang and accompanied the groom. From the way he strutted and swaggered along, you'd think that nothing could ever bowl him over.

Then the singing stopped. It was so still that you could have heard a pin fall in the street. But it was not quiet for long. *Crash! crash!* the great church doors flew open, and *boom! boom!* all the works of the clock came marching down the church aisle and halted between the bride and the groom.

Dead men cannot walk the earth. That's true, but a work of art does not die. Its shape may be shattered, but the spirit of art cannot be broken. The spirit of art jested, and *that* was no joke.

To all appearances it stood there as if it were whole and had never been wrecked. The clock struck one hour right after another, from one to twelve, and all the figures poured forth. First Moses came, shining as if bright flames issued from his forehead. He cast the heavy stone tablets of the law at the bridegroom's feet and tied them to the church floor. "I cannot lift them again," said Moses, "for you have broken my arms. Stand where you are!"

Then came Adam and Eve, the three Wise Men of the East, and the four Seasons. Each told him the disagreeable truth. "Shame on you!" But he was not ashamed.

All the figures of all the hours marched out of the clock, and they grew wondrous big. There was scarcely room for the living people. And at the stroke of twelve, out strode the watchman, with his cap and his many-spiked morning star. There was a strange commotion. The watchman went straight to the bridegroom, and smote him on the forehead with his morning star.

"Lie where you are," said the watchman. "A blow for a blow. We have taken out vengeance and the master's too, so now we will vanish."

And vanish they did, every cogwheel and figure. But the candles of the church flared up like flowers of fire, and the gilded stars under the roof cast down long clear shafts of light, and the organ sounded though no man had touched it. The people all said that they had lived to see the most incredible thing.

"Now," the princess commanded, "summon the right man, the craftsman who made the work of art. He shall be my husband and my lord."

He stood beside her in the church. All the people were in his train. Everyone was happy for him, everyone blessed him, and there was no one who was envious. And that was the most incredible thing.

DANISH POPULAR LEGENDS (1870)

Denmark is rich in old legends of heroes, of churches and manor houses, of hills and fields, and of the bottomless moorland. These stories date from the days of the great plague, from times of war, and from times of peace. They live on in books or on the tongues of people. They fly far about like a flock of birds, but they are as different, one from another, as the thrush is from the owl, and the wood pigeon from the gull. Listen to me, and I will tell you some of these legends.

I

In the olden days, when invaders were ravaging the Danish countryside, it happened that a pitched battle was fought, and the Danes won. That evening, many dead and many wounded men lay on the stricken field. One of these was an enemy, who had lost both his legs by a shot. Nearby a Danish soldier had just taken a flask filled with beer from his pocket and was about to put it to his mouth when the desperately wounded man begged him for a drink. As the soldier bent down to give the bottle to his enemy, the wounded man discharged his pistol at him, but he missed his aim. The soldier took his bottle back and drank half of it. As he handed the rest to his enemy, his only comment was, "You rascal, now you will get only half of it."

When the king was told of this, in memory of the deed he granted to the soldier and to his descendants a noble coat of arms on which was blazoned a bottle, half full.

II

There is a beautiful tradition worth telling of the church bell at Farum. Here the parsonage and the church stand side by side. It was a dark night, late in the fall. The minister was sitting at work upon his Sunday sermon when he heard the large church bell sound, very lightly and very strangely. No wind was blowing, and he could not account for the noise.

The minister took his keys and went to the church. As he entered it, the bell tone ceased, but he heard a faint sigh from the belfry.

"Who is there?" he asked in a loud voice. "Who is disturbing the peace of this church?" Footsteps pattered down the bell tower steps, and he saw a little boy coming toward him.

"Don't be angry," the boy said. "I slipped in here when the bell was rung for vespers. My mother is very ill—" Tears choked him, and he could not speak. The minister patted him on the cheek and encouraged the boy to tell his story frankly.

"They say that my mother—my sweet and good mother—is going to die. But I've heard tell that, when people are sick unto death, they may live to be well again if someone dares enter the church and at midnight scrape a little rust from the great church bell. That will keep death away, so I came here and hid myself till I heard the clock strike twelve. I was afraid. I thought of the dead people rising from their graves, and of their coming into the church, and I dared not look out in the churchyard. But I said the Lord's Prayer, and scraped the rust off of the bell."

"Come, my brave child," said the minister. "The good Lord will not forsake you or your mother." They went together to the poor cottage where the sick woman lay. She was in a sound and peaceful sleep.

God granted that she should live, and His blessings shone on her and her child.

III

This is a legend they tell about a poor young fellow, Paul Vendelbo, who came to be a great man, highly honored. He was born in Jutland. After he had struggled hard and studied so well that he got through his examination as a scholar, he felt a still greater ambition to be a soldier and to stroll about in faraway lands.

One day he was walking along the ramparts of Copenhagen with two young prosperous comrades. As he was telling them of his ambition, all of a sudden, he stopped and looked up at the window of a house where the young daughter of a professor was sitting. They all found her astonishingly pretty. When Paul's comrades saw how he blushed, they said as a joke:

"Paul, if you can get her to give you a kiss in front of the window where we can see it, we will give the money you need to travel. Then you can see if fortune favors you better abroad than at home."

Paul Vendelbo went into the house and knocked at the parlor door. "My father is not at home," the young girl told him.

"Don't be angry," he begged her, as the blood rushed up into his cheeks, "but it's not your father I want." Then he told her frankly of his wholehearted ambition to adventure out into the world and make an honorable name for himself. He told her of his two friends who were standing outside and how they had promised him his traveling expenses if, of her own free will, she would kiss him at the open window. He looked at her so bashfully, so honorably, and so frankly, that her anger died away.

"It is wrong for you to propose such a thing to a modest young girl," she told him. "But you look so honest that I won't stand in the way of your good fortune." She led him to the window and gave him a kiss.

His comrades kept their bargain and gave him the money. He went into the service of the Tsar of Russia, made a name for himself in the battle of Pultawa, and honors were heaped upon him. Afterward, when Denmark stood in need of him, he came home to become a man of might in the army and in the council of the king. *Lövenörn,* they called him, which means Lion-Eagle.

One day he again entered the professor's modest room. Again, it was not the professor he wanted, but the professor's daughter, Ingeborg Vinding—the girl who gave him the kiss with which his good fortune began. Fourteen days later Paul Vendelbo Lövenörn celebrated his wedding.

IV

The enemy once made a great attack on the Danish island of Fyen. Only one village was left standing, and this was soon to be sacked and burned.

Two poor people lived in a low-roofed house at the edge of the town. It was a dark winter's night, and the enemy were expected at any minute. The two poor, anxious people opened their psalm book to see if they could find anything in it to help or to comfort them. They opened their book and turned to the psalm, "A Mighty Fortress Is Our God."

Full of confidence, they sang the psalm, and their faith was renewed. They went to bed and slept well in the care of the Lord. In the morning, when they awoke, they found the room entirely dark. There was no glimmer of daylight, and the door would not open when they tried it. Then they climbed to the loft and opened a trapdoor in the roof, from which they saw that it was broad daylight. But a heavy snow had fallen in the night. It had drifted over their whole house and hidden it from the enemies who had pillaged and burned the town during the night. The two people clasped their hands in thankfulness, and again they sang, "A Mighty Fortress Is Our God," for he had shielded them and raised a rampart of snow around their home.

V

In North Seeland they tell of a dark mystery that challenges one's imagination. The church of Roervig lies far out among the sand dunes by the stormy Kattegat. One evening a great ship came to anchor off the shore. It seemed to be a Russian man-of-war. That night there was a knock at the parsonage door, and several people, armed and masked, demanded that the minister put on his robes and come with them, out to the church. They promised to pay him well, and they threatened him if he should refuse to go. He went.

He found the church lighted. Unknown people were gathered there, and all was in deep silence. A bride and groom waited in front of the altar. The magnificent clothes they wore suggested the highest rank, but the bride was deathly pale. When the marriage ceremony ended, a shot rang out, and the bride fell dead at the altar. The people took her corpse and went away with it. Next morning, the ship was gone, and to this day no one has been able to give any explanation of these happenings.

The minister who took part in it wrote the whole story down in his Bible, which his family has kept to this day. The old church still stands between the sand dunes, near the tossing waters of the Kattegat, and the story still lives in memory and in writing.

VI

I must tell you one more church legend. On the island of Falster, which is part of Denmark, there lived a lady of rank and wealth. She had no children, and her family was about to die out. So she took a part of her wealth and built a magnificent church. When it was finished and the candles were lighted, she knelt at the altar and prayed that, for her pious gift, God would grant her life upon this Earth as long as her church should stand.

The years went by. Her relatives died. Her old friends, her acquaintances, and all her old servants were laid in their graves. But she, who had made such an evil wish, did not die. Generation after generation grew up and were strangers to her. She did not go to see anyone, and no one came to see her. She wasted away in a long dotage, abandoned and alone. Her senses grew dull, and she was like someone asleep, but not like a dead person. Every Christmas Eve life flashed up in her for a moment, and she got back the use of her voice. Then she would order her new servants to put her in an oak coffin, and carry it to the graveyard by the church. The minister was asked to come and receive her commands. They laid her in the coffin, and brought it to the church. As she wished, every Christmas night the minister came through the choir up to the coffin and raised the coffin lid for the weary old lady who lay there without finding rest.

"Is my church still standing?" she would ask in a tremulous voice, and when the minister answered, "It still stands," she would give a deep sigh and sadly fall back in her coffin. The minister closed down the lid and came again on next Christmas Eve, and the next, and again and again.

Now there is no stone of the church left standing, no trace of the buried dead. A large whitethorn grows in the field there, and it blooms every spring as a sign of the resurrection of life. It is said that it grows on the spot where they placed the coffin of the highborn lady, and where her dust at last became dust of this earth.

VII

There is an old saying that when our Lord drove the rebellious angels out of heaven, He let some of them fall among the hills, where they still live and are called hobgoblins, or trolls. They always flee in terror when they hear thunder, which they believe is the wrath of Heaven. Others fell down in the alder marshes. These are called elves, and among them the women are very handsome to look at, but they are not to be trusted. Their backs are as hollow as a baker's dough trough. Others fell down in old farms and houses. These became dwarfs and goblins. Sometimes they have dealings with men, and many strange stories are told about them.

In Jutland, a hobgoblin lived with many other trolls in a large hill. One of his daughters was married to the village blacksmith, who was a bad man. He beat his wife until at last she tired of it. Just as he was about to beat her one day, she took a horseshoe and broke it upon him. She had such tremendous strength that she could easily have broken him in pieces too. He thought about this, and did not beat her again, but gossip spread the story abroad, and the country people no longer respected her. Now that they knew her to be the troll's daughter, no one in the parish would have anything to do with her. And the hobgoblin heard of this. One Sunday, the blacksmith, his wife, and other parishioners were in the churchyard, waiting for the parson. The blacksmith's wife looked out over the bay, where fog was rising.

"Here comes father," she said, "and he is angry." He came, and angry he was.

"Will you throw them to me, or would you rather do the catching?" he asked, and looked with greedy eyes upon the church people.

"I'll do the catching," she said, for she knew very well that he would not handle them gently if they fell in his hands. The hobgoblin seized one after another, and flung them over the roof of the church, while his daughter stood on the far side and caught them as gently as she could. From that time on, she got along very nicely with the parishioners. They were afraid of the hobgoblin and his many fellow trolls, who were scattered about the country. The best people could do was to avoid quarreling with him and try to turn his acquaintance to their profit. Everyone knew that trolls had big kettles full of gold, and it was well worthwhile to get a handful of this money. But to do so they had to be as clever and tricky as the farmer of whom I shall tell you. I shall tell you also of the farmer's boy, who tended pigs and was even cleverer than his master.

The farmer had a hill among his fields, which he did not want to leave idle. So he plowed it, but the hobgoblin who lived under the hill came out and asked him:

"How dare you plow my roof?"

"I didn't know it was your roof," the farmer said, "but it is neither to your advantage nor to mine for us to allow the land to lie idle. Let me plow and plant. The first year you may take what is growing above the ground, and I shall reap what grows in the earth. The next year we will change around." The bargain was made, and the first year the farmer planted carrots. The second year he sowed wheat. The hobgoblin got the tops of the carrots and the roots of the wheat. In this way they lived in harmony.

But it happened that there was to be a christening at the farmer's house. He was greatly embarrassed, because he could not very well avoid inviting a hobgoblin with whom he was on such good terms. But if the troll should accept his invitation, the farmer would get a bad name with the minister and with all the other people in the parish. Clever though the farmer usually was this time he didn't know what to do. He mentioned his troubles to the boy who tended his pigs and who was even more clever than he.

"I will help you," the boy said. He took a large bag and went out to the hill where the hobgoblin lived. He knocked and was let in. Then he said that he came to invite the hobgoblin to the christening. The hobgoblin accepted the invitation and promised to come.

"I suppose I'll have to give a christening present, won't I?"

"They usually do," said the boy, and opened his bag. The troll poured money into it. "Is that enough?"

The boy lifted the bag, and said, "Most people give as much." When all the gold in the big money kettle had been poured into the bag, the boy said, "Nobody gives more—most less."

"Tell me now," said the hobgoblin, "what honored guests are you expecting?"

"Three parsons and a bishop," said the boy.

"That's fine. Such gentlemen care only for eating and drinking. They won't bother me. Who else will come?"

"Mother Mary is expected."

"Hm, hm! But I think there will still be a little place for me behind the stove. And who else will be there?"

"Well, there's the Lord."

"Hm! Hm! Hm! You don't say so! But such extremely distinguished guests usually come late and leave early. While they are there I'll just step out for a moment. What sort of music will you have?"

"Drum music," said the boy. "The Lord has ordered a heavy thunder of drum music, to which we shall dance. Drum music it will be."

"Oh, isn't that dreadful!" the hobgoblin cried. "Thank your master for his invitation, but I prefer to stay at home. Doesn't he know that thundering and drumming terrify me and all of my people? Once, when I went for a walk in my younger days, the thunder began drumming, and one of the drumsticks thumped my thigh so hard that the bone cracked. I'll have no more of that sort of music, so just give the farmer my thanks and my present."

The boy took the bag on his back and brought his master a fortune along with the troll's best wishes.

We have many such legends, but those we have told here ought to be enough for today!

LUCKY PEER (1870)

I

In the most fashionable street in the city stood a fine old house; the wall around it had bits of glass worked into it, so that when the sun or the moon shone it looked as if it were covered with diamonds. That was a sign of wealth, and there was great wealth inside. It was said that the merchant was a man rich enough to put two barrels of gold into his best parlor and could even put a barrel of gold pieces, as a savings bank against the future, outside the door of the room where his little son was born.

When the baby arrived in the rich house, there was great joy from the cellar up to the garret; and up there, there was still greater joy an hour or two later. The warehouseman and his wife lived in the garret, and there, too, at the same time, a little son arrived, given by our Lord, brought by the stork, and exhibited by the mother. And there, too, was a barrel outside the door, quite accidentally; but it was not a barrel of gold—it was a barrel of sweepings.

The rich merchant was a very kind, fine man. His wife, delicate and always dressed in clothes of high quality, was pious and, besides, was kind and good to the poor. Everybody rejoiced with these two people on now having a little son who would grow up and be rich and happy, like his father. When the little boy was baptized he was called Felix, which in Latin means "lucky," and this he was, and his parents were even more so.

The warehouseman, a fellow who was really good to the core, and his wife, an honest and industrious woman, were well liked by all who knew them. How lucky they were to have their little boy; he was called Peer.

The boy on the first floor and the boy in the garret each received the same amount of kisses from his parents and just as much sunshine from our Lord; but still they were placed a little differently—one downstairs, and one up. Peer sat the highest, way up in the garret, and he had his own mother for a nurse; little Felix had a stranger for his nurse, but she was good and honest—that was written in her service book. The rich child had a pretty baby carriage, which was pushed about by his elegantly dressed nurse; the child from the garret was carried in the arms of his own mother, both when she was in her Sunday clothes and when she had her everyday things on, and he was just as happy.

Both children soon began to observe things; they were growing, and both could show with their hands how tall they were and say single words in their mother tongue. They were equally handsome and petted, and equally fond of sweets. As they grew up, they both got an equal amount of pleasure out of the merchant's horses and carriages. Felix was allowed to sit by the coachman, along with his nurse, and look at the horses; he would fancy himself driving. Peer was allowed to sit at the garret window and look down into the yard when the master and mistress went out to drive; and when they had left, he would place two chairs, one in front of the other, up there in the room, and so he would drive himself; he was the real coachman—that was a little more than fancying himself to be the coachman.

They got along splendidly, these two; yet it was not until they were two years old that they spoke to each other. Felix was always elegantly dressed in silk and velvet, with bare knees, after the English style. "The poor child will freeze!" said the family in the garret. Peer had trousers that came down to his ankles, but one day his clothes were torn right across his knees, so that he got as much of a draft and was just as much undressed as the merchant's delicate little boy. Felix came along with his mother and was about to go out through the gate when Peer came along with his and wanted to go in.

"Give little Peer your hand," said the merchant's wife. "You two should talk to each other."

And one said, "Peer!" and the other said, "Felix!" Yes, and that was all they said at that time.

The rich lady coddled her boy, but there was one who coddled Peer just as much, and that was his grandmother. She was weak-sighted, and yet she saw much, more in little Peer than his father or mother could see; yes, more than any person could.

"The sweet child," she said, "is surely going to get on in the world. He was born with a gold apple in his hand; I can see it even with my poor sight. Why, there is the shining apple!" And she kissed the child's little hand. His parents could see nothing, and neither could Peer; but as he grew to have more understanding, he liked to believe it.

"That is such a story, such a fairy tale, that Grandmother tells!" said the parents.

Yes, Grandmother could tell stories, and Peer was never tired of hearing always the same ones. She taught him a psalm and the Lord's Prayer as well, and he could say it, not as gabble but as words that meant something; she explained every single sentence in it to him. He gave particular thought to what Grandmother said about the words, "Give us this day our daily bread"; he was to understand that it was necessary for one to get wheat bread, for another to get black bread; one must have a great house when he had many people in his employ; another, in small circumstances, could live quite as happily in a little room in the garret. "So each person has what he calls 'daily bread.'"

Peer, of course, had his good daily bread—and the most delightful days, too, but they were not to last forever. The sad years of war began; the young men were to go away, and the older men as well. Peer's father was among those who were called in; and soon afterward it was heard that he had been one of the first to fall in battle against the superior enemy.

There was bitter grief in the little room in the garret. The mother cried; the grandmother and little Peer cried; and every time one of the neighbors came up to see them, they talked about "Pappa," and then they cried all together. The widow, meanwhile, was given permission to stay in her garret flat, rent free, during the first year, and afterward she was to pay only a small rent. The grandmother stayed with the mother, who supported herself by washing for several "single, elegant gentlemen," as she called them. Peer had neither sorrow nor want. He had plenty of food and drink, and Grandmother told him stories, such strange and wonderful ones about the wide world, that he asked her, one day, if the two of them might not go to foreign lands some Sunday and return home as prince and princess, wearing gold crowns.

"I am too old for that," said Grandmother, "and you must first learn a good many things and become big and strong; but you must always be a good and affectionate child—as you are now."

Peer rode around the room on hobbyhorses; he had two such horses. But the merchant's son had a real live horse; it was so small that it might well have been called a baby horse, which, in fact, Peer called it, and it never could become any bigger. Felix rode it in the yard; yes, and he even rode it outside the gate, when his father and a riding master from the king's stable were with him. For the first half hour, Peer had not liked his horses and hadn't ridden them, for they were not real; and then he had asked his mother why he could not have a real horse like little Felix had, and his mother had said, "Felix lives down on the first floor, close by the stables, but you live high up under the roof. One cannot have horses up in the garret except like those you have. You should ride on them."

And so now Peer rode—first to the chest of drawers, the great mountain with its many treasures; both Peter's Sunday clothes and his mother's were there, and there were the shining silver dollars that she laid aside for rent; then he rode to the stove, which he called the black bear; it slept all summer long, but when winter came it had to be useful, to warm the room and cook the meals.

Peer had a godfather who usually came there every Sunday during the winter and got a good warm meal. Things had gone wrong for him, said the mother and the grandmother. He had begun as a coachman. He had been drinking and had fallen asleep at his post, and that neither a soldier nor a coachman should do. He then had become a cabman and driven a cab, or sometimes a carriage, and often for very elegant people. But now he drove a garbage wagon and went from door to door, swinging his rattle, "snurre-rurre-ud!" and from all the houses came the servant girls and housewives with their buckets full, and turned these into the wagon; rubbish and junk, ashes and sweepings, were all thrown in.

One day Peer came down from the garret after his mother had gone to town. He stood at the open gate, and there outside was Godfather with his wagon. "Would you like to take a drive?" he asked. Yes, Peer was willing to indeed, but only as far as the corner. His eyes shone as he sat on the seat with Godfather and was allowed to hold the whip. Peer drove with real live horses, drove right to the corner. Then his mother came along; she looked rather dubious, for it was not very nice to see her own little son riding on a garbage wagon. She told him to get down at once. Still, she thanked Godfather; but at home she forbade Peer to drive with him again.

One day he again went down to the gate. There was no Godfather there to tempt him with a drive, but there were other temptations. Three or four small street urchins were down in the gutter, poking about to see what they could find that had been lost or had hidden itself there. Frequently they had found a button or a copper coin, but frequently, too, they had cut themselves on a broken bottle, or pricked themselves with a pin, which just now was the case. Peer simply had to join them, and when he got down among the gutter stones he found a silver coin.

Another day he was again down digging with the other boys; they only got dirty fingers; he found a gold ring, and then, with sparkling eyes, showed off his lucky find; whereupon the others threw dirt at him and called him Lucky Peer. They wouldn't permit him to be with them anymore when they poked in the gutter.

Back of the merchant's yard there was some low ground that was to be filled up for building lots; gravel and ashes were carted and dumped out there, great heaps of it. Godfather helped deliver it in his wagon, but Peer was not allowed to drive with him. The street urchins dug in the heaps, dug with a stick and with their bare hands; they always found one thing or another that seemed worth picking up.

Then little Peer came along. They saw him and cried, "Get away from here, Lucky Peer! And when, despite this, he came closer, they threw lumps of dirt at him. One of these struck against his wooden shoe and crumbled to pieces. Something shining rolled out, and Peer picked it up; it was a little heart made of amber. He ran home with it. The other boys did not notice that even when they threw dirt at him he was a child of luck.

The silver coin he had found was put away in his savings bank. The ring and the amber heart were shown to the merchant's wife downstairs, because the mother wanted to know if they were lost articles that should be returned to the police.

How the eyes of the merchant's wife shone on seeing the ring! It was her own engagement ring, one that she had lost three years before! That's how long it had lain in the gutter. Peer was well rewarded, and the money rattled in his little box. The amber heart was a cheap thing, the lady said; Peer might just as well keep that. At night the amber heart lay on the bureau, and the grandmother lay in bed.

"My, what is it that burns so!" she said. "It looks as if a small candle is lighted there." She got up to see, and it was the little heart of amber—yes, Grandmother, with her weak sight, frequently saw more than anyone else could see. She had her own thoughts about it. The next morning she took a narrow, strong ribbon, drew it through the opening at the top of the heart, and put it around her little grandson's neck.

"You must never take it off, except to put a new ribbon into it, and you must not show it to the other boys, either, for then they would take it from you, and you would get a stomachache!" That was the only painful sickness little Peer had known so far. There was a strange power, too, in that heart. Grandmother showed him that when she rubbed it with her hand and a little straw was put next to it, the straw seemed to be alive and was drawn to the heart of amber and would not let go.

II

The merchant's son had a private tutor who taught him his lessons and who took walks with him, too. Peer was also to have an education, so he went to public school with a great number of other boys. They played together, and that was much more fun than going along with a tutor. Peer would not have changed places with him.

He was a lucky Peer, but Godfather was also a lucky peer, although his name was not Peer. He won a prize in the lottery of two hundred dollars on a ticket he shared with eleven others. He immediately bought some better clothes, and he looked very well in them. Luck never comes alone; it always has company, and so it did this time. Godfather gave up the garbage wagon and joined the theater.

"What's that!" said Grandmother. "Is he going into the theater? As what?"

As a machinist. That was an advancement. He became quite another person; and he enjoyed the plays very much, although he always saw them from the top or from the side. Most wonderful was the ballet, but that gave him the hardest work, and there was always danger of fire. They danced both in Heaven and on Earth. That was something for little Peer to see; and one evening when there was to be a dress rehearsal of a new ballet, in which everyone was dressed and made up as on the opening night when people pay to see all the magnificence, he had permission to bring Peer with him and put him in a place where he could see the whole show.

It was a Biblical ballet—Samson. The Philistines danced about him, and he tumbled the whole house down over them and himself; but there were both fire engines and firemen on hand in case of any accident.

Peer had never seen a stage play, not to mention a ballet. He put on his Sunday clothes and went with Godfather to the theater. It was just like a great drying loft, with many curtains and screens, big openings in the floor, lamps, and lights. There were so many tricky nooks and corners everywhere, from which people appeared, just as in a great church with its gallery pews. Peer was seated down where the floor slanted steeply and was told to stay there until it was all finished and he was sent for. He had three sandwiches in his pocket, so that he need not starve.

Soon it grew lighter and lighter; then up in front, just as if straight out of the earth, there came a number of musicians with both flutes and violins. In the seats next to Peer sat people dressed in street clothes; but there also appeared knights with gold helmets, beautiful maidens in gauze and flowers, even angels all in white, with wings on their backs. They seated themselves upstairs and downstairs, on the floor and in the balcony seats, to watch what was going on. They were all members of the ballet, but Peer did not know that. He thought they belonged in the fairy tales his grandmother had told him about. There then appeared a woman, and she was the most beautiful of all, with a gold helmet and spear; she seemed to be above all the others, and sat between an angel and a troll. Ah, how much there was to see! And yet the ballet had not even begun.

Suddenly everything became quiet. A man dressed in black moved a little fairy wand over all the musicians, and then they began to play; the music made a whistling sound through the theater, and the whole wall in front began to rise. One looked into a flower garden, where the sun shone and all the people danced and leaped. Such a wonderful sight Peer had never imagined. There were soldiers marching, and there was war, and there was a banquet, and there were the mighty Samson and his lover. But she was as wicked as she was beautiful; she betrayed him. The Philistines plucked his eyes out; he was forced to grind in the mill and to be mocked and insulted in the great banquet hall; but then he took hold of the heavy stone pillars that held up the roof and shook them and the whole house; it fell, and there burst forth wonderful flames of red and green fire.

Peer could have sat there his whole life long and looked on, even if the sandwiches were all eaten—and they were all eaten.

Now here was something to tell about when he got home. It was impossible to get him to go to bed. He stood on one leg and laid the other on the table—that was what Samson's lover and all the other ladies had done. He made a treadmill out of Grandmother's chair and upset two chairs and a pillow over himself to show how the banquet hall had come down. He showed this—yes, and he even presented it with the music that belonged to it; there was no talking in the ballet. He sang high and low, with words and without words, and it was quite incoherent. It was like a whole opera. The most noticeable thing of all, meanwhile, was his beautiful, bell-clear voice, but no one spoke of that.

Peer previously had wanted to be a grocer's boy, to be in charge of prunes and powdered sugar. Now he found there was something much more wonderful, and that was to get into the Samson story and dance in the ballet. A great many poor children had taken that road, said the grandmother, and had become fine and honored people; yet no little girl of her family would ever be permitted to do so; but a boy—well, he stood more firmly. Peer had not seen a single one of the little girls fall down before the whole house fell, and then they all fell together, he said.

III

Peer wanted to, and felt he must, be a ballet dancer.

"He gives me no rest!" said his mother. At last, his grandmother promised to take him to the ballet master, who was a fine gentleman and had his own house, like the merchant. Would Peer ever be that rich? Nothing is impossible for our Lord. Peer had been born with a gold apple; luck had been laid in his hands—perhaps it was also in his legs.

Peer went to the ballet master and knew him at once; it was Samson himself. His eyes had not suffered at all at the hands of the Philistines. That was only acting in the play, he was told. And Samson looked kindly and pleasantly at him, and told him to stand up straight, look right at him, and show him his ankle. Peer showed his whole foot and leg, too.

"So he got a place in the ballet," said Grandmother.

This was easily arranged with the ballet master; but before that, his mother and grandmother had spoken with several understanding people—first with the merchant's wife, who thought it a good career for a handsome, honest boy like Peer, but without any future. Then they had spoken with Miss Frandsen; she knew all about the ballet, and at one time, in Grandmother's younger days, she had been the most beautiful danseuse at the theater; she had danced goddesses and princesses, had been cheered and applauded wherever she had gone; but then she had grown older—we all do—and so no longer had she been given principal parts; she'd had to dance behind the younger ones; and when finally her dancing days had come to and end, she had become a wardrobe woman and dressed the others as goddesses and princesses.

"So it goes!" said Miss Frandsen. "The theater road is a delightful one to travel, but it is full of thorns. Jealousy grows there! Jealousy!"

That was a word Peer did not understand at all; but he came to understand it in time.

"No force or power can keep him from the ballet," said his mother.

"A pious Christian child, that he is," said Grandmother.

"And well brought up," said Miss Frandsen. "Well formed and moral! That I was in my heyday."

And so Peer went to the dancing school and got some summer clothes and thin-soled dancing shoes to make himself lighter. All the older girl dancers kissed him and said that he was a boy good enough to eat.

He had to stand up, stick his legs out, and hold onto a post so as not to fall, while he leaned to kick, first with his right leg, then with his left. It was not nearly so difficult for him as it was for most of the others. The ballet master patted him and said that he would soon be in the ballet; he was to play the child of a king who was carried on shields and wore a gold crown. This was practiced at the dancing school and rehearsed at the theater itself.

The mother and grandmother had to see little Peer in all his glory, and when they saw this, they both cried, although it was such a happy occasion. Peer, in all his pomp and glory, did not see them at all; but he did see the merchant's family, who sat in the loge nearest the stage. Little Felix was with them, in his best clothes. He wore buttoned gloves, just like a grown-up gentleman, and although he could see perfectly well, he looked through an opera glass the whole evening, just like a grown-up gentleman. He looked at Peer, and Peer looked at him; Peer was a king's child with a crown of gold. This evening brought the two children into closer relationship with one another.

A few days later, when they met each other at home in the yard, Felix went up to Peer and told him he had seen him when he was a prince. He knew very well that he was not a prince any longer, but then he had worn a prince's clothes and a gold crown. "I shall wear them again on Sunday," said Peer.

Felix did not see him Sunday, but he thought about it the whole evening. He would have liked very much to have been in Peer's place; he had not heard Miss Frandsen's warning that the road of the theater was a thorny one and that jealousy grew along it; nor did Peer know this yet, but he would very soon learn it.

His young companions, the dancing children, were not at all so good as they ought to be, although they often played angels and had wings on them. There was a little girl, Malle Knallerup, who always—when she was dressed as a page and Peer was a page—stepped maliciously on the side of his foot, so as to dirty his stockings. There was a wicked boy who always was sticking pins in his back; and one day he ate Peer's sandwiches—by mistake; but that was impossible, for Peer had meat balls on his sandwiches, and the other boy had only bread without butter; he could not have made a mistake.

It would be impossible to recite all the annoyances that Peer endured in two years, and the worst was yet to come.

There was a ballet performed called *The Vampire.* In it the smallest dancing children were dressed as bats, wearing gray, knitted tights that fitted snugly to their bodies; black gauze wings were stretched from their shoulders. They were to run on tiptoe, as if they were light enough to fly, and then they were to whirl around on the floor. Peer could do this especially well; but his trousers and jacket, all of one piece, were old and worn and could not stand the strain. So just as he whirled around before the eyes of all the people, there was a rip right down his back, straight from his neck down to where the legs are fastened in, and all of his short white shirt could be seen. All the people laughed. Peer felt it and knew what had happened; he whirled and whirled, but it grew worse and worse. People laughed louder and louder; the other vampires laughed with them and whirled into him, and all the more dreadfully when the people clapped and shouted, "Bravo!"

"That is for the ripped vampire!" said the dancing children. And from then on they always called him Rippy.

Peer cried. Miss Frandsen comforted him. "It is only jealously," she said; and now Peer knew what jealousy was.

Besides the dancing school, they had a regular school at the theater where the children were taught arithmetic and writing, history and geography—yes, and they even had a teacher in religion, for it is not enough to know how to dance; there is something more important in the world than wearing out dancing shoes. Here, too, Peer was quick, the very quickest of all, and got plenty of good marks; but his fellow students still called him Rippy. They were only teasing him; but at last he could not stand it any longer, and he swung and hit one of the boys, so that he was black and blue under the left eye and had to have grease paint on it in the evening when he appeared in the ballet. Peer got a scolding from the dancing master, and a worse one from the sweeping woman, for it was her son he had "given a sweeping."

IV

A good many thoughts went through little Peer's head. And one Sunday, when he was dressed in his best clothes, he went out without saying a word about it to his mother or his grandmother, not even to Miss Frandsen, who always gave him good advice; he went straight to the orchestra conductor; he thought this man was the most important one there was outside the ballet. Cheerfully he stepped in and said, "I am at the dancing school, but there is so much jealousy there, and so I would rather be a player or a singer, if you would help me, please."

"Have you a voice?" asked the conductor, and looked quite pleasantly at him. "Seems to me I know you. Where have I seen you before? Wasn't it you who was ripped down the back?" And now he laughed. But Peer grew red; he was surely no longer Lucky Peer, as his grandmother had called him. He looked down at his feet and wished he were far away.

"Sing me a song!" said the conductor. "Come now, cheer up, my boy!" and he tapped him under the chin, and Peer looked up into his kind eyes and sang a song,

"Mercy for Me," which he had heard at the theater, in the opera Robert le Diable.

"That is a difficult song, but you did it pretty well," said the conductor. "You have an excellent voice—as long as it doesn't rip in the back!" and he laughed and called his wife. She also had to hear Peer sing, and she nodded her head and said something in a foreign tongue. Just at that moment the singing master of the theater came in; it was really to him Peer should have gone if he wanted to be a singer; now the singing master came to him, quite accidentally, as it were; he also heard him sing "Mercy for Me," but he did not laugh, and he did not look so kindly at him as the conductor and his wife; still it was decided that Peer should have singing lessons.

"Now he is on the right track," said Miss Frandsen. "One gets much farther with a voice than with legs. If I had had a voice, I would have been a great songstress and would perhaps have been a baroness by now."

"Or a bookbinder's wife," said Mother. "Had you become rich, you surely would have taken the bookbinder."

We do not understand that hint, but Miss Frandsen did.

Peer had to sing for her and sing for the merchant's family when they heard of his new career. He was called in one evening when they had company downstairs, and he sang several songs, among them "Mercy for Me." All the company clapped their hands, and Felix did, too; he had heard him sing before; in the stable Peer had sung the entire ballet of Samson, and that was the most delightful of all.

"One cannot sing a ballet," said the lady.

"Yes, Peer can," said Felix, and so they asked him to do it. He sang, and he talked; he drummed and he hummed; it was child's play, but fragments of well-known melodies came forth which really illustrated what the ballet was about. All the company found it very entertaining; they laughed and praised it, one louder than another. The merchant's wife gave Peer a huge piece of cake and a silver dollar.

How lucky the boy felt, until he discovered a gentleman who stood somewhat in the background and who looked sternly at him. There was something harsh and severe in the man's black eyes; he did not laugh; he did not speak a single friendly word; this gentleman was the singing master from the theater.

Next forenoon, Peer went to him, and he stood there quite as severe-looking as before.

"What was the matter with you yesterday!" he said. "Could you not understand that they were making a fool of you? Never do that again, and don't you go running about and singing at doors, either inside or outside. Now you can go. I won't give you any singing lesson today."

When Peer left, he was dreadfully downcast; he had fallen out of the master's good graces. On the contrary, the master was really more satisfied with him than ever before. In all the absurdity which he had seen him perform, there was really some meaning, something quite unusual. The boy had an ear for music and a voice as clear as a bell and of great compass; if it continued like that, then the little fellow's fortune was made.

Now began the singing lessons. Peer was industrious and Peer was clever. How much there was to learn, how much to know! The mother toiled and slaved to make an honest living, so that her son might be well dressed and neat and not look too shabby among the people to whom he now was invited. He was always singing and jubilant; they had no need at all of a canary bird, the mother said. Every Sunday he had to sing a psalm with his grandmother. It was delightful to hear his fresh voice lift itself up with hers. "It is much more beautiful than to hear him sing wildly!" That's what she called his singing when, like a little bird, his voice jubilantly gave forth with tones that seemed to come of themselves and make such music as they pleased. What tones there were in his little throat, what wonderful sounds in his little breast! Indeed, he could imitate a whole orchestra. There were both flute and bassoon in his voice, and there were violin and bugle. He sang as the birds sing; but man's voice is much more charming, even a little man's, when he can sing like Peer.

But in the winter, just as he was to go to the pastor to be prepared for confirmation, he caught cold; the little bird in his breast said, 'pip!' The voice was ripped like the vampire's backpiece.

"It is no great misfortune, after all," thought Mother and Grandmother. "Now he doesn't go singing, tra-la, so he can think more seriously about his religion."

His voice was changing, the singing master said. Peer must not sing at all now. How long would it be? A year, perhaps two; perhaps the voice would never come again. That was a great grief.

"Think only of your confirmation now," said Mother and Grandmother. "Practice your music," said the singing master, "but keep your mouth shut."

He thought of his religion, and he studied his music; it sang and resounded within him. He wrote entire melodies down in notes, songs without words. Finally he wrote the words, too.

"You are a poet, too, little Peer," said the merchant's wife, to whom he carried his text and music. The merchant received a piece of music dedicated to him, a piece without words. Felix got one, too; and, yes, Miss Frandsen also did, and that went into her scrapbook, in which were verses and music by two who were once young lieutenants but now were old majors on half pay; the book had been given by "a friend," who had bound it himself.

And Peer was confirmed at Easter. Felix presented him with a silver watch. It was the first watch Peer had owned; he felt that this made him a man, for now he did not have to ask others what time it was. Felix came up to the garret, congratulated him, and handed him the watch; he himself was not to be confirmed until the autumn. They took each other by the hand, these two children of the house, both the same age, born the same day and in the same house. And Felix ate a piece of the cake that had been baked in the garret for the occasion of the confirmation.

"It is a happy day with solemn thoughts," said Grandmother.

"Yes, very solemn!" said Mother. "If only Father had lived to see Peer today!"

The following Sunday all three of them went to Communion. When they came home from church they found a message from the singing master, asking Peer to come to see him; and Peer went. Some good news awaited him, and yet it was serious, too. While he must give up singing for a year, and his voice must lie fallow like a field, as a peasant might say, during that time he was to further his education, not in the capital, where every evening he would be running to the theater, from which he could not keep away, but he was to go 120 miles from home, to board with a schoolmaster who boarded a couple of other young men. There he was to learn language and science, which someday would be useful to him. The charge for a year's course was three hundred dollars, and that was paid by a "benefactor who does not wish his name to be known."

"It is the merchant," said Mother and Grandmother.

The day of departure came. A good many tears were shed, and kisses and blessings given; and then Peer rode the 120 miles on the railway, out into the wide world. It was Whitsuntide. The sun shone, and the woods were fresh and green; the train went rushing through them; new fields and villages were continually coming into view; country manors peeped out; the cattle stood in the pastures. Now they passed a station, then another, and market town after market town. At each stopping place there was a crowd of people, welcoming or saying good-bye; there was noisy talking, outside and in the carriages. Where Peer sat there was a lot of entertainment and chattering by a widow dressed in black. She talked about his grave, his coffin, and his corpse—meaning her child's. It had been such a poor little thing that there could have been no happiness for it had it lived. It had been a great relief for her and the little lamb when it had fallen asleep.

"I spared no expense on flowers on that occasion!" she said; "and you must remember that it died at a very expensive time, when the flowers had to be cut from potted plants! Every Sunday I went to my grave and laid a wreath on it with great white silk bows; the silk bows were immediately stolen by some little girls and used for dancing bows; they were so tempting! One Sunday I went there, and I knew that my grave was on the left of the main path, but when I got there, there was my grave on the right. 'How is this?' says I to the gravedigger. 'Isn't my grave on the left?'

"'No, it isn't any longer!' the gravedigger answered. 'Madam's grave lies there all right, but the mound has been moved over to the right; that place belongs to another man's grave.'

"'But I want my corpse in my grave,' says I, 'and I have a perfect right to say so. Shall I go and decorate a false mound, when my corpse lies without any sign on the other side? Indeed I won't!'

"'Then Madam must talk to the dean.'

"He is such a good man, that dean! He gave me permission to have my corpse on the right. It would cost five dollars. I gave that with a kiss of my hand and walked back to my old grave. 'Can I now be very sure that it is my own coffin and my corpse that is moved?'

"'That Madam can!' And so I gave each of the men a coin for the moving. But now, since it had cost so much, I thought I should spend something to make it beautiful, and so I ordered a monument with an inscription. But—will you believe it—when I got it, there was a gilded butterfly painted at the top. 'Why, that means Frivolity,' said I. 'I won't have that on my grave.'

"'It is not Frivolity, Madam; it is Immortality.'

"'I never heard that,' said I. Now, have any of you here in the carriage ever heard of a butterfly as a sign for anything but Frivolity? I kept quiet. I don't like long conversations. I composed myself, and put the monument away in my pantry. There it stood till my lodger came home. He is a student and has so many, many books. He assured me that it really stood for Immortality, and so the monument was placed on the grave."

And during all the chatter, Peer arrived at the station of the town where he was to live, and become just as wise as the student, and have just as many books.

V

Herr Gabriel, the honorable man of learning with whom Peer was to live as a boarding scholar, was at the railway station to call for him. Herr Gabriel was a man as thin as a skeleton, with great, shiny eyes that stuck out so very far that one was almost afraid that when he sneezed they would pop out of his head entirely. He was accompanied by three of his own little boys; one of them stumbled over his own legs, and the other two stepped all over Peer's feet in their eagerness to get a close view of him. Two larger boys were with them, the older about fourteen years, fair-skinned, freckled, and full of pimples.

"Young Madsen, who will be a student in about three years, if he studies! Primus, son of a dean." That was the younger, who looked like a head of wheat. "Both are boarders, studying with me," said Herr Gabriel. "Our small stuff," he called his own boys.

"Trine, bring the newcomer's trunk on your wheelbarrow. The table is set for you at home."

"Stuffed turkey!" said the other two young gentlemen boarders.

"Stuffed turkey!" said the "small stuff"; and again one of them fell over his own legs.

"Caesar, look after your feet!" exclaimed Herr Gabriel.

And they walked into town and then out of it. There stood a great half-tumbled-down timber house, with a jasmine-covered summerhouse, facing the road. Here Madam Gabriel waited with more "small stuff," two little girls.

"The new pupil," said Herr Gabriel.

"A most hearty welcome!" said Madam Gabriel, a youthful, well-fed woman, red and white, with spit curls and a lot of pomade on her hair.

"Good heavens, how grown-up you are!" she said to Peer. "Why, you are a fully developed gentleman already. I thought that you were like Primus or young Madsen. Angel Gabriel, it's a good thing the inner door is nailed. You know what I think." "Nonsense!" said Herr Gabriel. And they stepped into the room. There was a novel on the table, lying open, and a sandwich on it. One might have thought that it had been placed there as a bookmark—it lay across the open page.

"Now I must be the housewife!" And with all five of her children and the two boarders, she showed Peer through the kitchen, and the hallway, and into a little room, the windows of which looked out on the garden; that was to be his study and bedroom; it was next to Madam Gabriel's room, where she slept with all the five children; the connecting door, for decency's sake, and to prevent gossip "which spares nobody," had been nailed up by Herr Gabriel that very day, at Madam's express request.

"Here you can live just as if you were at your parents'. We have a theater, too, in the town. The pharmacist is the director of a private company, and we have traveling players. But now you are going to have your turkey." And so she showed Peer into the dining room, where the wash was drying on a line.

"That doesn't do any harm," she said. "It is only cleanliness, and that you are surely accustomed to."

So Peer sat down to eat the roast turkey while the children of the house—but not the two boarders, who had withdrawn—gave a dramatic show for the entertainment of themselves and the stranger. There had lately been a traveling company of actors in town, which had played Schiller's *The Robbers*. The two oldest boys had been immensely taken with it. And they now performed the whole play at home—all the parts, notwithstanding that they remembered only these words: "Dreams come from the stomach." But they were spoken by all the characters in different tones of voice. There stood Amelia, with heavenly eyes and a dreamy look. "Dreams come from the stomach!" she said, and covered her face with both her hands. Carl Moor came forward with a heroic stride and manly voice, "Dreams come from the stomach," and at that the whole flock of children, boys and girls, rushed in; they were all robbers, and murdered one another, crying out, "Dreams come from the stomach."

That was Schiller's *The Robbers*. This performance and stuffed turkey were Peer's first introduction into Herr Gabriel's house. He then went to his little chamber, where through the window, into which the sun shone warmly, he could see the garden. He sat down and looked out. Herr Gabriel was walking there, absorbed in reading a book. He came closer and looked in; his eyes seemed fixed upon Peer, who bowed respectfully. Herr Gabriel opened his mouth as wide as he would, stuck out his tongue, and let it wag from one side to the other right in the face of the astonished Peer, who could not understand why he was treated in such a manner. Whereupon Herr Gabriel left, but then turned back to the window and again stuck his tongue out of his mouth.

Why did he do that? He was not thinking of Peer, or that the panes of glass were transparent from the outside; he saw only the reflection of himself in them, and he wanted to look at his tongue, as he had a stomachache, but Peer did not know all this.

Early in the evening Herr Gabriel went into his room, and Peer sat in his. Much later in the evening he heard quarreling—female quarreling—in Madam Gabriel's bedroom.

"I am going up to Gabriel and tell him what rascals you are!"

"We will also go to Gabriel and tell him what Madam is!"

"I shall have a fit!" she cried.

"Who wants to see a woman in a fit! Four shillings!"

Then Madam's voice sank deeper, but was distinctly heard. "What will the young man in there think of our house when he hears all this vulgarity!" At that the quarrel subsided, but then again rose louder and louder.

"Period! *Finis*," cried Madam. "Go and make the punch; it's better to agree than to quarrel!"

And then it was still. The door opened, and the girls left, and then Madam knocked on the door to Peer's room.

"Young man, now you have some idea of what it is to be a housewife. You should thank Heaven that you don't have to bother with girls. I want to have peace, so I give them punch. I would gladly give you a glass—one sleeps so well after it—but no one dares go through the hallway door after ten o'clock; my Gabriel will not permit it. But you shall have some punch, nevertheless. There is a big hole in the door, stopped up with putty; I will push the putty out and put a funnel through the hole; you hold your waterglass under it, and I shall pour you some punch. Keep it a secret, even from my Gabriel. You must not worry him with household affairs."

And so Peer got his punch, and there was peace in Madam Gabriel's room, peace and quiet in the whole house. Peer went to bed, thought of his mother and grandmother, said his evening prayer, and fell asleep. What one dreams the first night one sleeps in a strange house has special significance, Grandmother had said. Peer dreamed that he took the amber heart, which he still constantly wore, laid it in a flowerpot, and it grew into a great tree, up through the ceiling and the roof; it bore thousands of hearts of silver and gold, so heavy that the flowerpot broke, and it was no longer an amber heart—it had become mold, earth to earth—gone, gone forever! Then Peer awoke; he still had the amber heart, and it was warm, warm against his own warm heart.

VI

Early in the morning the first study hours began at Herr Gabriel's. They studied French. At lunch the only ones present were the boarders, the children, and Madam. She drank her second cup of coffee here; her first she always took in bed. "It is so healthy when one is liable to spasms." She asked Peer what he had studied that day.

"French," he answered.

"It is an expensive language!" she said. "It is the language of diplomats and one used by distinguished people. I did not study it in my childhood, but when one is married to a learned man one gains from his knowledge, as one gains from his mother's milk. Thus, I have all the necessary words. I am quite sure I would know how to express myself in whatever company I happened to be."

Madam had acquired a foreign name by her marriage with a learned man. She had been baptized "Mette" after a rich aunt, whose heir she was to have been. She had got the name, but not the inheritance. Herr Gabriel rebaptized Mette as "Meta," the Latin word for *measure*. At the time of her wedding, all her clothes, woolen and linen, were marked with the letters M. G., Meta Gabriel; but young Madsen, who was a witty boy, interpreted the letters M. G. to be a mark meaning "most good," and he added a big question mark in ink, on the tablecloths, the towels, and the sheets.

"Don't you like Madam?" asked Peer, when young Madsen made him privately acquainted with this joke. "She is so kind, and Herr Gabriel is so learned."

"She is a bag of lies!" said young Madsen; "and Herr Gabriel is a scoundrel. If I were only a corporal, and he a recruit, oh, how I would discipline him!" And a bloodthirsty expression came to young Madsen's face; his lips grew narrower than usual, and his whole face seemed one great freckle.

There were terrible words to hear, and they gave Peer a shock; yet young Madsen had the clearest right to think that way. It was a cruel thing on the part of parents and teachers that a fellow had to waste his best time, delightful youth, on learning grammar, names, and dates, which nobody cares anything about, instead of enjoying his liberty relaxing and wandering about with a gun over his shoulder like a good hunter. "No, one has to be shut in and sit on a bench and look sleepily at a book; Herr

Gabriel wants that. And then one is called lazy and gets the mark 'passable'; yes, one's parents get letters about it; that's why Herr Gabriel is a scoundrel."

"He gives lickings, too," added little Primus, who agreed with young Madsen. This was not very pleasant for Peer to hear. But Peer got no lickings; he was too grown-up, as Madam had said. He was not called lazy, either, for that he was not. He had his lessons alone. He was soon well ahead of Madsen and Primus.

"He has ability!" said Herr Gabriel.

"And one can see that he has been to dancing school!" said Madam.

"We must have him in our dramatic club," said the pharmacist, who lived more for the town's private theater than for his pharmacy. Malicious people applied to him the old stale joke that he must have been bitten by a mad actor, for he was completely insane about the theater.

"The young student was born for a lover," said the pharmacist. "In a couple of years he could be Romeo; and I believe that if he were well made up, and we put a little mustache on him, he could very well appear this winter."

The pharmacist's daughter—"great dramatic talent," said the father; "true beauty," said the mother—was to be Juliet; Madam Gabriel had to be the nurse, and the pharmacist, who was both director and stage manager, would take the role of the apothecary, which was small but of great importance. Everything depended on Herr Gabriel's permission for Peer to play Romeo. This had to be worked through Madam Gabriel; one had to know how to win her over—and this the pharmacist knew.

"You were born to be the nurse," he said, and thought that he was flattering her exceedingly. "That is actually the most important part in the play," he continued. "It is the comedy role; without it, the play would be too sad to sit through. No one but you, Madam Gabriel, has the quickness and life that should sparkle here."

All very true, she agreed, but her husband would surely never permit the young student to contribute whatever time would be required to play the part of Romeo. She promised, however, to "pump" him, as she called it. The pharmacist immediately began to study his part, and especially to think about his make-up. He wanted to look almost like a skeleton, a poor, miserable fellow, and yet a clever man—a rather difficult problem. But Madam Gabriel had a much harder one in "pumping" her husband to give his permission. He could not, he said, answer for it to Peer's guardians, who paid for his schooling and board, if he permitted the young man to play in tragedy. We cannot conceal the fact, however, that Peer had the greatest desire to do it. "But it won't work," he said.

"It's working," said Madam; "only let me keep on pumping." She would have given him punch, but Herr Gabriel did not like to drink it. Married people are often different; this is said without any offense to Madam.

"One glass and no more," she thought. "It elevates the mind and makes one happy, and that's what we ought to be—it is our Lord's will with us."

Peer was to be Romeo; that was pumped through by Madam. The rehearsals were held at the pharmacist's. They had chocolate and "genii"—that is to say, small biscuits. These were sold at the bakery, twelve for a penny, and they were so exceedingly small, and there were so many, that it was considered witty to call them genii.

"It is an easy matter to make fun," said Herr Gabriel, although he himself often gave nicknames to one thing and another. He called the pharmacist's house "Noah's ark, with its clean and unclean beasts," and that was only because of the affection which was shown by that family toward their pet animals. The young lady had her own cat, Graciosa, which was pretty and soft-skinned; it would lie in the window, in her lap, on her sewing work, or run over the table spread for dinner. The wife had a poultry yard, a duck yard, a parrot, and canary birds—and Polly could outcry them all together. Two dogs, Flick and Flock, walked about in the living room; they were by no means perfume bottles, and they lay on the sofa and on the family bed.

The rehearsal began, and it was only interrupted a moment by the dogs slobbering over Madam Gabriel's new gown, but that was out of pure friendship and it did not spot it. The cat also caused a slight disturbance; it insisted on giving its paw to Juliet and sitting on her head and wagging its tail. Juliet's tender speeches were divided equally between cat and Romeo. Every word that Peer had to say was exactly what he wished to say to the pharmacist's daughter. How lovely and charming she was, a child of nature, who, as Madam Gabriel expressed it, was perfect for the role. Peer began to fall in love with her.

There surely was instinct or something even higher in the cat. It perched on Peer's shoulders as if to symbolize the sympathy between Romeo and Juliet. With each successive rehearsal Peer's fervor became stronger, more apparent; the cat became more confidential, the parrot and the canary birds noisier; Flick and Flock ran in and out. The evening of the performance came, and Peer was a perfect Romeo; he kissed Juliet right on her mouth.

"Perfectly natural!" said Madam Gabriel.

"Disgraceful!" said the Councillor, Herr Svendsen, the richest citizen and fattest man in the town. The perspiration poured from him; it was warm in the house, and warm within him as well. Peer found no favor in his eyes. "Such a puppy!" he said; "a puppy so long that one could break him in half and make two puppies of him."

Great applause—and one enemy! That was having good luck. Yes, Peer was a Lucky Peer. Tired and overcome by the exertions of the evening and the flattery shown him, he went home to his little room. It was past midnight; Madam Gabriel knocked on the wall.

"Romeo! I have some punch for you!"

And the funnel was put through the hole in the door, and Peer Romeo held his glass under.

"Good night, Madam Gabriel."

But Peer could not sleep. Everything he had said, and particularly what Juliet had said, buzzed through his head, and when he finally fell asleep he dreamed of a wedding—a wedding with Miss Frandsen! What strange things one can dream!

VII

"Now get that playacting out of your head," said Herr Gabriel the next morning, "and let's get busy with some science."

Peer had come near to thinking like young Madsen, that a fellow was wasting his delightful youth being shut in and sitting with a book in his hand. But when he sat with his book, there shone from it so many noble and good thoughts that Peer found himself quite absorbed in it. He learned of the world's great men and their achievements; so many had been the children of poor people: Themistocles, the hero, son of a potter; Shakespeare, a poor weaver's boy, who as a young man held horses outside the door of the theater, where later he was the mightiest man in poetic art of all countries and all time. He learned of the singing contest at Wartburg, where the poets competed to see who would produce the most beautiful poem—a contest like the old trial of the Grecian poets at the great public feasts. Herr Gabriel talked of these with especial delight. Sophocles in his old age had written one of his best tragedies and won the award over all the others. In this honor and fortune his heart broke with joy. Oh, how blessed to die in the midst of one's joy of victory! What could be more fortunate! Thoughts and dreams filled our little friend, but he had no one to whom he could tell them. They would not be understood by young Madsen or by Primus—nor by Madam Gabriel. Either she was either in a very good humor or was the sorrowing mother, in which case she was dissolved in tears.

Her two little girls looked with astonishment at her. Neither they nor Peer could discover why she was so overwhelmed with sorrow and grief.

"The poor children!" she said. "A mother is always thinking of their future. The boys can take care of themselves. Caesar falls, but he gets up again; the two older ones splash in the water tub; they ought to be in the navy, and would surely marry well. But my two little girls! What will their future be? They will reach the age when the heart feels, and then I am sure that whoever each of them falls in love with will not be at all after Gabriel's liking; he will choose someone they'll despise, and that will make them so unhappy. As a mother, I have to think about these things, and that is my sorrow and grief. You poor children! You will be so unhappy!" She wept.

The little girls looked at her. Peer looked at her and felt rather sad; he could think of nothing to say, so he returned to his little room, sat down at the old piano, and tones and fantasies came forth as they streamed through his heart.

In the early morning he went to his studies with a clear mind and performed his duties, for someone was paying for his schooling. He was a conscientious, right-minded fellow. In his diary he recorded each day what he had read and studied, and how late he had sat up playing the piano—always mutely, so that he wouldn't awaken Madam Gabriel. It never said in his diary, except on Sunday, the day of rest, "Thought of Juliet," "Was at the pharmacist's," "Wrote a letter to Mother and Grandmother." Peer was still Romeo and a good son.

"Very industrious!" said Herr Gabriel. "Follow that example, young Madsen! Or you'll fail!"

"Scoundrel!" said young Madsen to himself.

Primus, the Dean's son, suffered from sleeping sickness. "It is a disease," said the Dean's wife; he was not to be treated with severity.

The deanery was only eight miles away; wealth and comfort were there.

"That man will die a bishop" said Madam Gabriel. "He has good connections at the court, and the Deaness is a lady of noble birth. She knows all about heraldry—that means coats of arms."

It was Whitsuntide. A year had passed since Peer came to Herr Gabriel's house. He had gained much knowledge, but his voice had not come back; would it ever come?

The Gabriel household was invited to the Dean's to a great dinner and a ball later in the evening. A good many guests came from the town and from the manor houses about. The pharmacist's family was invited; Romeo would see his Juliet, perhaps dance the first dance with her.

The deanery was a well-kept place, whitewashed, and without any manure heaps in the yard, and it had a dovecote painted green, around which twined an ivy vine. The Deaness was a tall, corpulent woman; "Athene, Glaucopis," Herr Gabriel called her; "the blue-eyed," not "the ox-eyed," as Juno was called, thought Peer. There was a certain distinguished kindness about her, and an effort to have an invalid look; she probably had sleeping sickness just like Primus. She was in a light-blue silk dress and wore great curls; the one on the right side was fastened with a large medallion portrait of her great-grandmother, a general's wife, and the one on the left with an equally large bunch of grapes made of white porcelain.

The Dean had a ruddy, plump face, with shining white teeth, well suited to biting into a roast fillet. His conversation always consisted of anecdotes. He could converse with everybody, but no one ever succeeded in carrying on a conversation with him.

The Councillor, too, was there, and among the strangers from the manors was Felix, the merchant's son; he had been confirmed and was now a most elegant young gentleman, both in clothes and manners; he was a millionaire, they said. Madam Gabriel did not have courage enough to speak to him.

Peer was overjoyed at seeing Felix, who came to him in a very genial manner and said that he had brought greetings from his parents, who read all the letters Peer wrote home to his mother and grandmother.

The dancing began. The pharmacist's daughter was to dance the first dance with the Councillor; that was a promise she had made at home to her mother and to the Councillor. The second dance had been promised to Peer; but Felix came and took her with a good-natured nod.

"Permit me to have this one dance; the young lady will give her permission only if you say so."

Peer kept a polite face; he said nothing, and Felix danced with the pharmacist's daughter, the most beautiful girl at the ball. He also danced the next dance with her.

"You will grant me the supper dance?" asked Peer, with a pale face.

"Yes, the supper dance," she answered with her most charming smile.

"You surely will not take my partner from me?" said Felix, who stood close by. "That's not being very friendly. We two are old friends from town! You say that you are so glad to see me. Then you must allow me the pleasure of taking the lady to supper!" And he put his arm around Peer and laid his forehead jestingly against him. "Granted, isn't it? Granted!"

"No!" said Peer, his eyes sparkling with anger.

Felix gaily raised his arms and set his elbows akimbo, as if he were trying to look like a frog ready to leap. "You are perfectly right, young man! I would say the same if the supper dance were promised me, sir!" He drew back with a graceful bow to the young lady.

But shortly after, when Peer stood in a corner and adjusted his necktie, Felix returned, put his arms around his neck, and, with the most coaxing look, said, "Be bighearted! My mother and your mother and old grandmother will all say that is just like you. I am leaving tomorrow, and I will be terribly bored if I do not take the young lady to supper. My own friend, my only friend!"

Peer, as his only friend, could not resist that; he personally led Felix to the young beauty.

It was bright morning of the next day when the guests drove away from the Dean's. The Gabriel household was in one carriage, and the whole family went to sleep, except Peer and Madam.

She talked about the young merchant, the rich man's son, who was really Peer's friend; she had heard him say, "Skaal, my friend! To Mother and Grandmother!" There was something so "uninhibited, gallant in him," she said; "one saw at once that he is the son of rich people, or a count's child. That, the rest of us can't acquire. One must bow to that!"

Peer said nothing. He was depressed all day. At night, when bedtime had come and he lay in bed, sleep was chased away, and he said to himself, "One has to bow; one has to please!" That's what he had done; he had obeyed the rich young fellow, "because one is born poor, he is placed under obligation and subjection to these richly born people. Are they then better than we? And why were they created better than we?"

There was something vicious rearing up in him, something that his grandmother would be grieved at. He thought of her. "Poor Grandmother! You have also known what poverty is. Why has God permitted that?" And he felt anger in his heart, and yet at the same time he was conscious of having sinned in thoughts and words against the good God. He was grieved to think he had lost his child's mind; and his faith returned, as wholesome and rich as before. Happy Peer!

A week later a letter came from Grandmother. She wrote in the only way she could, mixing up big letters and small letters, but all her heart's love was in everything, big and small, that concerned Peer:

> My own sweet, blessed boy:
> I am thinking of you; I am longing for you, and so is your mother. She is getting along well; she takes washing. And the merchant's Felix came up to see us yesterday, with a greeting from you. You had both been at the Dean's ball, and you had been such a gentleman; but that you will always be, and make your old grandmother and your hardworking mother happy. She has something to tell you about Miss Frandsen.

And then followed a postscript from Peer's mother:

> Miss Frandsen is going to be married, the old thing. The bookbinder, Herr Hof, has been appointed court bookbinder, in accordance with his petition. He has a great new sign, "Court Bookbinder Hof." And she will become Madam Hof. It is an old love that does not rust, my sweet boy.
>
> YOUR MOTHER

Second Postscript: Grandmother has knitted you six pairs of woolen socks; you will get them at the first opportunity. I am also sending you a pork pie, your favorite dish. I know that you never get pork at Herr Gabriel's, since his wife is so afraid of what I have difficulty in spelling— "trichines." You must not believe in these, but just go ahead and eat.

Your Own Mother

Peer read the letter, and it made him happy. Felix was so good; what a great injustice he had done him! They had separated at the Dean's without saying good-bye to each other.

"Felix is better than I," said Peer.

VIII

In a quiet life, one day slips into the next, and month quickly follows month. Peer was already in the second year of his stay at Herr Gabriel's, who with great earnestness and determination, though Madam called it obstinacy, insisted that he should not again go on the stage.

Peer received from the singing master, who monthly paid the stipend for his instruction and support, a serious reminder not to think of the stage as long as he was placed there. And he obeyed; but his thoughts frequently traveled to the theater at the capital—they carried him, as if by magic, onto the stage there, where he was to have appeared as a great singer. Now his voice was gone, and it did not return, which often deeply grieved him. Who could comfort him? Neither Herr Gabriel nor Madam, but our Lord surely could. Consolation comes to us in many ways. Peer found it in sleep; he was indeed a Lucky Peer.

One night he dreamed that it was Whitsunday and he was out in the beautiful green forest, where the sun shone through the branches and where all the ground was covered with anemones and primrose. Then the cuckoo began, "Cuckoo!" "How many years shall I live?" asked Peer, for one always asks the cuckoo that, the first time in the year one hears it cuckoo; and the cuckoo answered, "Cuckoo!" but no more; it was silent.

"Shall I live only one more year?" asked Peer. "That is really too little. Be so good as to cuckoo again!" Then the bird began again, "Cuckoo! Cuckoo!" Yes, and it went on without stopping, and Peer cuckooed with it, as realistically as if he, too, were a cuckoo; but his notes were stronger and clearer. All the songbirds joined in the warbling. Peer sang their songs, but far more beautifully. He had all the clear voice of his childhood, and rejoiced in song; he was so happy at heart. And then he awoke, but with the assurance that the "soundboard" was still in him, that his voice still lived, and some bright Whitsun morning, would burst forth in all its freshness; and so he slept, happy in this assurance.

But in none of the following days, weeks, or months did he have any feeling of his voice returning.

Every bit of news he could get of the theater at the capital was a true feast for his soul; it was spiritual bread to him. Crumbs are also bread, and he received crumbs thankfully—the smallest bits of news.

There was a flax dealer's family living near the Gabriels'. The mother, a highly respectable housewife, lively and laughing, but without any acquaintance or knowledge of the theater, had been at the capital for the first time and was delighted with everything there, even with the people, who had laughed at all she had said, she assured—and that was very likely.

"Were you at the theater also?" asked Peer.

"That I was," replied the flax dealer's wife. "How I steamed! You should have seen me sit and steam in that heat!"

"But what did you see? What play?"

"I will tell you that," she said. "I shall give you the whole play. I was there twice. The first evening it was a talking play. Out came the princess—'Ahbe, dahbe! Abe, dabe!'—how she could talk! Next came a man—'Ahbe, dahbe! Abe, dabe!' And then down fell Madam. Now they began again. The prince—'Ahbe, dahbe! Abe, dabe!' Then down fell Madam. She fell down five times that evening. The second time I was there, it was all singing—'Ahbe, dahbe! Abe, dabe!' And then down fell Madam again. It so happened that a countrywoman was sitting next to me; she had never been in the theater, and thought the show was all over; but I, who now knew all about it, said that when I was there last, Madam fell down five times. The singing evening, she only did it three times. Yes, there you have both the plays, as true to life as I saw them."

Was it tragedy she had seen, since she said that Madam always fell down? Then it dawned on Peer what she meant. The great theater curtain that fell between the acts had a large female figure painted on it, a muse with the comic and the tragic masks. This was the Madam who fell down. That had been the real comedy; what they had said and sung had been only "Ahbe, dahbe! Abe, dabe!" to the flax dealer's wife; but it had been a great pleasure, and so it had been to Peer, too, and not less to Madam Gabriel, who had heard this recital of the plays. She had sat with an expression of astonishment and a consciousness of mental superiority, for the pharmacist had said that she, as the nurse, had "carried" Shakespeare's Romeo and Juliet. "Down fell the Madam," as explained by Peer, afterward became a witty byword in the house every time a child, a cup, or one or another piece of furniture fell on the floor in the house.

"That is the way proverbs and familiar sayings are created," said Herr Gabriel, who carried everything into the sphere of learning.

New Year's Eve, at the stroke of twelve, the Gabriels and their boarders stood, each with a glass of punch, the only one Herr Gabriel drank the whole year, because punch is bad for a weak stomach. They drank a toast, "Skaal," to the new year, and counted the strokes of the clock, "One, two—" to the twelfth stroke. "Down fell the Madam!" they said.

The new year rolled up and rolled along. By Whitsuntide, Peer had been two years in the house.

IX

Two years were gone, but the voice had not returned. How would the future be for our young friend?

He could always be a teacher in a school, opined Herr Gabriel; there was a livelihood in that, though nothing to be married on; however, that hadn't entered Peer's mind, no matter how large a place in his heart the pharmacist's daughter had.

"Be a teacher!" said Madam Gabriel; "a schoolmaster! Then you'll be the most boring individual on earth, just like my Gabriel. No, you were born for the theater. Be the greatest actor in the world; that is something more than being a teacher."

An actor! Yes, that was the goal.

He mentioned this in a letter to the singing master; he told of his longing and his hope. He longed most eagerly for the great city, where his mother and grandmother lived; he had not seen them for two long years. The distance was only 120 miles; by fast train, he could be there in six hours. Why had they not seen one another? That is easily explained. On his departure, Peer had given his promise to stay where he was being sent and not to think of a visit. His mother was busy enough with her washing and ironing; yet she had often thought of making the great journey, even if it would cost a good deal of money, but this never materialized. Grandmother had a horror of railways; to travel by rail was to tempt the Lord. Nothing could induce her to travel by steam; she was an old woman, and she was not going to travel until she traveled up to our Lord.

That she said in May, but in June the old woman would travel, and all alone, the 120 long miles, to the strange town, to strange people, and all to get to Peer. It would be a big occasion, yet the most dismal one that could occur to Mother and Grandmother.

The cuckoo had said "Cuckoo!" without end when Peer had asked it the second time, "How many years shall I live?" His health and spirits were good, and the future looked bright. He had received a delightful letter from his fatherly friend, the singing master. Peer was to go home, and they would see what could be done for him—what course he should take now that his voice was still gone.

"Appear as Romeo!" said Madam Gabriel. "Now you are old enough for the lover's part and have some flesh on your bones. You don't need to use make-up."

"Be Romeo!" said the pharmacist and the pharmacist's daughter.

Many thoughts went through his head and heart. But "Nobody knows what tomorrow will bring."

He sat down in the garden that stretched out to the meadow. It was evening, and there was moonlight. His cheeks burned; his blood was on fire; the air brought a delightful coolness. Over the moor hung a mist that rose and sank and made him think of the dance of the elfin maidens. Then into his mind came the old ballad about Knight Olaf, who rode out to ask the guests to his wedding, but was stopped by the elfin maidens, who drew him into their dance and play and thereby caused his death. It was a piece of folklore, an old poem. The moonlight and the mist over the moor formed pictures of it this evening.

Peer was soon in a state of half dreaming, looking out upon it all. The bushes seemed to have shapes of both humans and beasts; they stood motionless, while the mist rose like a great waving veil. Peer had seen something like this in a ballet at the theater, when elfin maidens were represented whirling and swaying with veils of gauze; but here it was far more charming and more wonderful. A stage as large as this, no theater could have; none had so clear an air, so shining a moonlight.

Right in front in the mist, there distinctly appeared a female shape; the one became three, and the three became many; hand in hand they danced; they were floating girls. The air bore them along to the hedge where Peer stood. They nodded to him; they spoke; it was like the sound of silver bells. They danced into the garden about him; they enclosed him in their circle. Without thought, he danced with them, but not their dance. He whirled about, as in the unforgettable vampire dance, but he didn't think of that; he really didn't think at all; he was completely overwhelmed by all the magnificent beauty he saw about him.

The moor was a sea, so deep and dark blue, with water lilies that were bright with all conceivable colors. Dancing over the waves, they carried him upon their veil to the opposite shore, where the old Viking burial mound had thrown aside its grassy turf and risen into a castle of clouds, but the clouds were of marble. Flowering trees of gold and costly stones twined about the mighty blocks of marble; each flower was a brilliantly colored bird that sang with a human voice. It was like a choir of thousands and thousands of happy children. Was it Heaven, or was it Elfin Hill?

The castle walls moved; they glided toward each other. They closed about him. He was inside, and the world of man was outside. He then felt anguish, a strange fear, as never before. There was no exit to be found, but from the floor way up to the roof, and from all the walls, there smiled at him lovely young girls; they were so lifelike to look at, and yet he thought: Are they but paintings? He wanted to speak to them, but his tongue found no words; his speech was completely gone; not a sound came from his lips. Then he threw himself upon the earth, more miserable than he had ever been.

One of the elfin maidens approached him; surely she meant well, for she had taken the shape he would most like to see; she looked like the pharmacist's daughter; he was almost ready to believe that it was she, but soon he saw that she was hollow in back and had only a beautiful front—open in the back, with nothing at all inside.

"One hour here is a hundred years outside," she said. "You have already been here a whole hour. Everyone you know and love outside these walls is dead. Stay with us! Yes, stay you must, or the walls will squeeze you until the blood flows from your brow!

And the walls trembled, and the air became like that of a glowing bake oven. He found his voice.

"O Lord, O Lord, have You forsaken me?" he cried from the depths of his soul.

Then Grandmother stood beside him. She took him in her arms; she kissed his brow; she kissed his mouth.

"My own sweet little one!" she said. "Our Lord will not forsake you; He forsakes none of us, not even the greatest sinner. God be praised and honored for all eternity!"

And she brought forth her psalmbook, the same one from which she and Peer had sung on many a Sunday. How her voice rang! How full were her tones! All the elfin maidens laid their heads down for a well-needed rest. Peer sang with Grandmother, as before he had sung every Sunday; how strange and powerful, yet how soft, his voice was all at once! The walls of the castle moved; they became clouds and mist. Grandmother walked with him out of the hill into the tall grass, where the glowworms gleamed and the moon shone. But his feet were so tired now he could not move them; he sank down on the turf; it was the softest bed; there he rested well and awoke to the sound of a psalm.

Grandmother sat beside him, sat by his bed in the little chamber in Herr Gabriel's house. The fever was over; health and life had returned. He had been deathly ill. They had found him in a faint on that evening down in the garden; a violent fever had followed. The doctor had thought that he would not get up from it, but would die, and they had written to his mother about it. She and Grandmother had wanted to, and felt they must, go to him; both had not been able to leave, and so the old grandmother had gone, and gone by the railway. "That I would only do for Peer," she said. "I did it in God's name; otherwise I would have had to believe that I flew with the evil ones on a broomstick on Midsummer Eve!"

X

The journey home was made with a glad and light heart. Grandmother deeply thanked our Lord that Peer was to outlive her. She had delightful traveling companions in the railway carriage—the pharmacist and his daughter; they talked about Peer, and loved Peer as if they were of the same family. He was to become a great actor, said the pharmacist. His voice had now returned, too, and there was a fortune in such a throat as his.

What a pleasure it was to the grandmother to hear such words! She lived on them; she believed them thoroughly. And then they arrived at the station in the capital, where the mother met her.

"God be praised for the railway!" said Grandmother, "and be praised, too, that I quite forgot I was on it! I owe that to these splendid people." And she pressed the hands of the pharmacist and his daughter. "The railway is a blessed discovery when one is through with it! One is in God's hands!"

And then she talked of her sweet boy, who was out of all danger and who lived with well-to-do people who kept two servant girls and a manservant. Peer was like a son in the house, and on the same footing with two children of distinguished families, one of whom was a dean's son. The grandmother had lodged at the post inn; it was terribly expensive, but then she had been invited to Madam Gabriel's; there she had stayed five days, and they were simply wonderful people, particularly the wife; she had urged her to drink punch, splendidly made but strong.

With God's help, Peer would be strong enough to come home to the capital in a month.

"He must have become very elegant and spoiled," said the mother. "He will not feel at home here in the garret. I am very happy that the singing master has invited him to stay with him. And yet," cried the mother, "it is awfully sad that one should be so poor that one's child cannot live in his own home!"

"Don't say those words to Peer!" said Grandmother. "You don't understand him as I do."

"But he must have food and drink, no matter how fine he has grown, and he shall not go hungry so long as I can move my hands. Madam Hof has told me that he can eat his dinner twice a week with her, now that she is well off. She has known both prosperity and hard times. She has told me herself that one evening, in the box at the theater where the old danseuses have a place, she felt sick. The whole day long she had only had water and a caraway-seed bun, and she was ill from hunger, and very faint. 'Water! water!' cried the others. 'No! Some food!' she begged. 'Food!' She needed something nourishing, and had not the least need of water. Now she has her own larder and a well-spread table."

Peer was still 120 miles away, but happy in the thought that he would soon be in the city and at the theater with all his dear old friends, whom now he would know how to value. Happiness sang and resounded within him and all about him; there was sunshine everywhere, in this happy time of youth, the time of hope and expectation. Every day he grew stronger; his good spirits and his color returned. But Madam Gabriel became very moved as the time for departure drew near.

"You are on your way to greatness; and there will be many temptations, for you are handsome—that you have become in our house. You are natural, just as I, and that will help when temptations come. One must not be too sensitive or unruly—sensitive like Queen Dagmar, who on Sunday laced her silk sleeves and then had pangs of conscience over such a minor thing; it should take more than that to affect one. I would never have grieved as Lucretia did. What did she stab herself for? She was pure and honest; she knew that, and everybody in the town knew that. What could she do about the misfortune which I won't talk about but which you at your age understand perfectly well? So she gave out a shriek and the dagger! That wasn't necessary at all. I would not have done it, and neither would you; we are both natural people; one should be natural at all times, and that you will continue to be in your artistic career. How happy I shall be to read about you in the papers! Perhaps sometime you will come to our little town and appear as Romeo, but I shall not be the nurse then. I shall sit in the parquet and enjoy myself."

Madam had a lot of washing and ironing done the week he went away, so Peer could go home with a clean wardrobe, as he had had on his arrival there. She drew a new, strong ribbon through his amber heart; that was the only thing she wanted as a "remembrance souvenir," but she did not get it.

From Herr Gabriel he received a French lexicon, the one he had used during his school hours, and it had marginal notes in Herr Gabriel's own hand. Madam Gabriel gave him roses and quaking grass. The roses would wither, but the grass would keep all winter if it wasn't put into the water but was kept in a dry place. And she wrote a quotation from Goethe on a kind of album leaf: *Umgang mit Frauen ist das Element guter Sitten.* She gave a translation of it: "Companionship with women is the foundation of good manners. Goethe."

"He was a great man!" she said. "If he had only not written Faust, for I don't understand it. Gabriel says so, too."

Young Madsen presented Peer with a not badly done drawing he had made of Herr Gabriel hanging from the gallows, with a birch rod in his hand, and the inscription, "A great actor's first conductor on the road of science." Primus, the Dean's son, gave him a new pair of slippers, which the Deaness herself had made, but so large that Primus could not fill them for a year or two yet. Upon the soles was written in ink, "A reminder of a sorrowing friend. Primus."

Herr Gabriel's entire household accompanied Peer to the train.

"It shall not be said that you left us sans adieu!" said Madam, and she kissed him at the railway station.

"I am not bashful!" she said. "When one does not do a thing secretly, one can do anything!"

The signal whistle blew—young Madsen and Primus shouted hurrahs; the "small stuff" joined in with them; Madam dried her eyes and waved with her pocket handkerchief; Herr Gabriel said only the word, "Vale!"

The villages and stations flew by. Were the people in them as happy as Peer? He thought of that, praised his good fortune, and thought of the invisible golden apple that Grandmother had seen lying in his hand when he was a child. He thought of his lucky find in the gutter and, above all, of his newfound voice and of the knowledge he had now acquired. He had become altogether another person. He sang inwardly with happiness; it took great self-control for him to keep from singing aloud in the car.

Now the towers of the city appeared, and the buildings began to show themselves. The train reached the station. There stood Mother and Grandmother, and someone with them, Madam Hof, well bound, Court Bookbinder Hof's wife, born Frandsen. Neither in want nor in prosperity did she forget her friends. She had to kiss him as his mother and his grandmother did.

"Hof could not come with me," she said, "he is home at work, binding a set of collected works for the king's private library. You have your good luck, and I have mine. I have my Hof and my own fireside corner with a rocking chair. Twice a week you are to eat with us. You will see my life at home; it is a complete ballet!"

Mother and Grandmother hardly had an opportunity to talk to Peer, but they looked at him, and their eyes shone with delight. Then he had to take a cab to get to his new home at the singing master's. They laughed and they cried.

"What a wonderful man he is!" said Grandmother.

"He still has such a kind face, just as when he went away," said Mother, "and that he will keep in the theater."

The cab stopped at the singing master's door, but the master was out; his old servant opened the door and showed Peer up to his room, where there were portraits of composers on the walls and a white plaster bust stood gleaming on the stove. The old man, a little dull, but trustworthiness itself, showed him the drawers in the bureau and hooks for him to hang his clothes on, and said he was very willing to shine his boots. Then the singing master arrived and welcomed Peer with a hearty handshake.

"This is the apartment!" he said. "Make yourself at home. You may use my piano in the living room. Tomorrow we will hear how your voice is. This is our castle warden, our housekeeper." And he nodded to the old servant. "All is in order. Carl Maria von Weber, on the stove there, has been whitened in honor of your coming; he was terribly dirty. But it isn't Weber that's up there, after all; it is Mozart. Where did he come from?"

"It is the old Weber," said the servant; "I carried him myself to the plasterer, and I brought him home again this morning."

"But this is a bust of Mozart, and not a bust of Weber."

"Pardon me, sir," said the servant; "it is the old Weber, who has been cleaned. The master does not recognize him now that he has been whitened." The plasterer could verify that.

But at the plasterer's he got the answer that Weber had been broken to pieces, and so he had given him Mozart instead; it was all the same on a stove.

The first day Peer was not to sing or play, but when our young friend came into the parlor, where the piano stood and the opera Joseph lay open upon it, he sang "My Fourteenth Spring," and sang with a voice that was as clear as a bell. There was something so sincere about it, so innocent, and yet so strong and full. The singing master's eyes were wet with tears. "That's the way it should be," he said, "and it will be even better. Now we shall close the piano. You need to rest."

"But I have promised my mother and grandmother to visit them tonight." And he hurried away. The setting sun shone over the home of his childhood; the bits of glass in the wall sparkled; it was like a diamond castle. Mother and Grandmother were waiting for him in the garret, a good many steps up, but he flew up, three stairs at a time, reached the door, and was received with kisses and embraces.

It was clean and tidy there in the little room. There stood the stove, the old bear, and the chest of drawers with the hidden treasure from his hobbyhorse days; on the walls hung the three familiar pictures, the king's portrait, a picture of our Lord, and Father's silhouette, cut out of black paper. It was an excellent side view of him, said Mother, but it would have been more like him if the paper had been white and red, for that he was. A wonderful man! And Peer was the very picture of him.

There was much to talk about, much to tell. They were to have a headcheese, and Madam Hof had promised to visit them later in the evening.

"But how is it that those two old people, Hof and Miss Frandsen, ever thought of getting married?" asked Peer.

"It has been in their thoughts these many years," said Mother. "You know, of course, that he was married. Well, he did it, they say, to irritate Miss Frandsen, who looked down on him when she was in her high and mighty state. His wife was wealthy, but she was very old, but lively, and on crutches! She could not die; he was waiting for it. It would not have surprised me if, like the man in the story, he had every Sunday put the old lady out in the open air, so our Lord could see her and remember to send for her."

"Miss Frandsen sat quietly by and waited," said Grandmother. "I never believed she would attain this. But last year Madam Hof died, and so Frandsen came to be the wife in the house."

At that moment, in came Madam Hof.

"We were talking about you," said Grandmother. "We were talking about your patience and reward."

"Yes," said Madam Hof. "It did not come in my youth, but one is always young enough, when one's health is good, says my Hof. He has the most charming flashes of wit. We were old, fine works, he says, both in one volume, and with a gilt top. I am so happy with my Hof and my corner by the fireside. A porcelain stove! There a fire is started in the evening, and it keeps warm all the next day. It is such a joy. It is as in the ballet of Circe's island. Do you remember me as Circe?"

"Yes, you were charming!" said Grandmother. "But how a person can change!" That was not at all said impolitely, and was not so taken. Then came the headcheese and the tea.

The next morning Peer paid a visit to the merchant's. The lady met him, pressed his hand, and asked him to take a seat by her. During their conversation he expressed his great gratitude; he knew that the merchant was his secret benefactor. The lady did not know it. "But it is like my husband," she said. "It is not worth talking about."

The merchant was almost angry when Peer mentioned this. "You are on the wrong track altogether," he said, as he closed the conversation and walked away.

Felix was a student and was to have a diplomatic career.

"My husband calls it madness," said the lady. "I have no opinion. Providence takes care of such things."

Felix did not show himself, for he was taking a lesson at his fencing master's.

At home Peer told how he had thanked the merchant, but that he would not receive this thanks.

"Who told you that he was, what you call him, your benefactor?" asked the singing master.

"My mother and my grandmother did," answered Peer.

"Well, then it must be he."

"You know about it?" said Peer.

"I know, but you will not find out from me. And from now on, we shall sing an hour here at home every morning."

XI

Once a week there was quartet music. Ears, soul, and thought were filled with the grand musical poems of Beethoven and Mozart. It had been a long time since Peer had heard good and well-played music. It was as if a kiss of fire traveled down his spine and shot through all his nerves. His eyes filled with tears. Every musical evening here at home was a festive evening to him, which made a deeper impression upon him than any opera at the theater, where something always disturbs one or imperfections are revealed. Sometimes the words do not come out right; they are so smoothed down in the singing that they are as intelligible to a Chinese as to a Greenlander; and sometimes the effect is weakened by faults in dramatic expression, and by a full voice sinking in places to the power of a music box or drawling out false tones. Lack of truthfulness in stage settings and costumes also is to be observed. All this was absent from the quartet. The music poems rose in all their grandeur; costly hangings decorated the walls in the concert room; here he was in the world of music, which its masters had created.

One evening, Beethoven's "Pastoral" Symphony was given by a great orchestra in the big public music hall. It was the andante movement, "the scene by the brook," that particularly, and with a strange power, stirred and excited our young friend. It carried him into the living, fresh woods; the lark and the nightingale rejoiced, and the cuckoo sang there. What beauty of nature; what a well spring of refreshment there was! From this hour he knew within himself that it was the picturesque music, in which nature was reflected and the emotions of human hearts were set forth, that struck deepest into his soul. Beethoven and Haydn became his favorite composers.

He often spoke with the singing master about this, and with each conversation the two became closer friends. How rich in knowledge this man was, as inexhaustible as

Mimir's well. Peer listened to him; just as eagerly as he had to Grandmother's fairy tales and stories as a little boy, he now listened to those of the world of music, and came to know what the forest and the sea told, what sounds in the old giant mounds, what every bird sings with its bill, and what the flower silently exhales in fragrance.

The hour devoted to his singing lesson every morning was an hour of true delight for master and pupil; every little song was sung with freshness, expression, and simplicity; most charmingly did he sing the Schubert series of *Travel Songs*. Both the melodies and the words were heard to their full advantage; they blended together; they exalted and illumined one another, as is fitting. Peer was undeniably a dramatic singer. His ability showed progress each month, each week, day by day.

Our young friend grew in a wholesome, happy way, knowing no want or sorrow. His was a rich and wonderful life, with a future full of blessings before him. His trust in mankind was never deceived; he had a child's soul and a man's endurance, and everywhere he was received with gentle eyes and a kind welcome. Day by day the relations between him and the singing master grew more heartfelt and confidential; the two were like an elder and a younger brother, and the younger had all the fervor and warmth of a young heart, which was understood and returned in full measure by the elder.

The singing master's personality was characterized by a southern ardor, and one saw at once that this man could hate vehemently or love passionately, and, fortunately, this last governed in him. He was, moreover, so situated by a fortune his father had left him that he did not need to work, unless it interested and pleased him to do so. Secretly he did a great deal of good in a sensible way, but didn't want people to thank him or to talk about it.

"If I have done anything," he said, "it was because I could and should have done it. It was my duty."

His old servant, "our warden," as he called him in jest, talked only with half a voice when he gave expression to his opinion about the master of the house. "I know what he has given away and done during years and days, and yet I don't know the half! The king ought to give him a star to wear on his breast. But he would not wear it; he would be furious, if I know him, should he be honored for his kind deeds. He is happy, more so than the rest of us, in whatever faith he has. He is just like a man out of the Bible."

And to that the old fellow gave additional emphasis, as if Peer could have some doubt.

He felt and understood well that the singing master was a true Christian in good deeds, an example for everyone; yet the man never went to church, and when Peer one day mentioned that the following Sunday he was going with his mother and his grandmother to our "Lord's table" and asked if the singing master ever did the same, the answer was, "No!" It seemed as if he wanted to say something more, as if, indeed, he had something to confide to Peer, but nothing was said.

One evening he read aloud from the newspaper about the beneficence of a couple of men, and that led him to speak of good deeds and their reward.

"When one does not think of it, it is sure to come. The reward for good deeds is like dates that are spoken of in the Talmud; they ripen late and then are sweet."

"Talmud?" asked Peer. "What sort of book is that?"

"A book," was the answer, "from which more than one seed of thought has been implanted in Christianity."

"Who wrote that book?"

"Wise men in the earliest times, wise men in various nations and religions. Here wisdom is preserved in a few words, as in Solomon's Proverbs. What kernels of truth! One reads here that men round about the whole earth, in all the centuries, have always been the same. 'Your friend has a friend, and your friend's friend has a friend; be discreet in what you say!' is found here. It is a piece of wisdom for all times. 'No one can jump over his own shadow!' is here, too, and, 'Wear shoes when you walk over thorns!' You ought to read this book. You will find in it the proof of culture more clearly than you find it in the layers of Earth. For me, as a Jew, it is, moreover, an inheritance from my fathers."

"Jew?" said Peer. "Are you a Jew?"

"Did you not know that? How strange that we two should not have spoken of it before today!"

Mother and Grandmother knew nothing about it, either; they had never thought anything about it, but always had known that the singing master was an honorable, wonderful man. It was through God's guidance that Peer had met him on his way; next to our Lord he owed him all his good fortune.

And now the mother divulged a secret that she had carried faithfully a few days only and that, under the pledge of secrecy, had been told her by the merchant's wife. The singing master must never know that this was revealed; it was he who had paid for Peer's support and education at Herr Gabriel's. From the evening when, at the merchant's house, he had heard Peer sing the ballet Samson, he alone had been his real friend and benefactor, but in secret.

XII

Madam Hof was expecting Peer at her house, and now he arrived there.

"Now you will meet my Hof," she said, "and you will meet my fireside corner. I never dreamed of this when I danced in Circe and The Rose Elf in Provence. Indeed, there are not many now who think of that ballet and of little Frandsen. 'Sic transit gloria in the Moon!'—that's what my Hof, who is a witty fellow, calls it in Latin, and he uses that phrase when I talk about my time of glory. He likes to poke fun at me, but he does it with a good heart."

The "fireside corner" was an inviting room with a low ceiling, a carpet on the floor, and portraits suitable for a bookbinder to have. There were pictures of Gutenberg, and of Franklin, of Shakespeare, Cervantes, Molière, and the two blind poets, Homer and Ossian. Lowest down hung one—enclosed in glass and a broad frame—of a danseuse, cut out of paper, with great gold spangles on a dress of gauze, the right leg lifted toward heaven, and with a verse written beneath:

Who captures all hearts by her dancing?
Who wears her wreath of art entrancing?
Miss Emilie Frandsen!

It was written by Hof, who wrote charming verse, especially comic verse. He had clipped the picture out himself and pasted and sewed it before he had married his first wife. For many years it had lain in a drawer; now it was displayed here in the poet picture gallery—"my fireside corner," as Madam Hof called her little room. Here Peer and Hof were introduced to each other.

"Isn't he a wonderful man?" she said to Peer. "To me he is just the most wonderful."

"Yes, on Sunday, when I am well bound in my new clothes," said Herr Hof.

"You are wonderful without any binding," she said, and then she tipped her head down as if she realized that she had spoken a little too childishly for one of her age.

"Old love does not rust," said Herr Hof. "An old house on fire burns down to the ground."

"It is as with the phoenix bird," said Madam Hof; "one rises up young again. Here is my paradise. I don't care to be any other place—except for an hour or so at your mother's and grandmother's."

"And at your sister's," said Herr Hof.

"No, Angel Hof; that is no longer a paradise. I must tell you, Peer, they live in small circumstances and amid big complications. One doesn't know what he dares say in that house. One doesn't dare mention the word 'darky,' for the eldest daughter is engaged to one who has some Negro blood in him. One doesn't dare say 'hunchback,' for that one of the children is. One doesn't dare talk about 'deficit'—my brother-in-law has been involved in such a mishap. One doesn't even dare say that he has been driving in the wood; 'wood' has an ugly sound, for Wood was the name of the fellow who broke his engagement with the youngest daughter. I don't like to go out and sit and keep my mouth shut. If I don't dare talk, I want to be in my own house and sit in my fireside corner. Were it not too sinful, as they say, I would gladly ask our Lord to let us live as long as my fireside corner holds out, for here one grows better. Here is my paradise, and this my Hof has given me."

"She has a gold mill in her mouth," he said.

"And you have gold grains in your heart," she said.

> Grind, grind what the bag will hold.
> Emilie is as pure as gold!

he said, as she tickled him under the chin.

"He wrote that verse at this very moment! It's good enough to be printed!"

"Yes, and handsomely bound!" he said.

That's how these two old folks amused each other.

A year passed before Peer began to study a role at the theater. He chose Joseph, but he exchanged it for the role of George Brown in the opera *The White Lady*. He quickly learned the words and music, and from Walter Scott's novel, which had furnished the material for the opera, he obtained a clear, full picture of the young, spirited officer who visits his native hills and comes to his ancestral castle without knowing it; an old song awakens recollections of his childhood; luck is with him, and he wins a castle and a wife.

What he read became like something he himself had lived—a chapter of his own life's story. The richly melodious music was entirely in keeping. A long, long time passed before the first rehearsals began. The singing master did not think that there was any hurry for him to make his appearance, but finally the day to start arrived. He was not merely a singer; he was an actor, and his whole personality was thrown into the role. The chorus and the orchestra applauded him loudly at the outset, and the opening night was looked forward to with the greatest expectation.

"One can be a great actor in a dressing gown at home," said a good-natured companion, "can be very great by daylight, but only so-so before the footlights in a packed house. Time will tell."

Peer had no fear, but had a burning desire for the eventful evening. The singing master, on the contrary, was extremely nervous. Peer's mother had not the courage to go to the theater; she would be ill with fear for her dear boy. Grandmother was sick and must stay at home, the doctor had said; but the faithful friend, Madam Hof, promised to bring news the very same evening of how it all went. She should and would be at the theater, even if she were dying.

How long that evening was! How the three or four hours stretched into eternity! Grandmother sang a psalm and prayed with Mother to the good God for their little Peer, that he might this evening also be Lucky Peer. The hands of the clock moved slowly.

"Now Peer is beginning," they said. "Now he is in the middle. Now he has finished." The mother and grandmother looked at each other, but they didn't say another word.

In the streets there was the rumbling of carriages; people were driving home from the theater. The two women looked down from the window; the people who were passing talked in loud voices; they had come from the theater; what they knew would bring either gladness or sadness up into the garret of the merchant's house.

At last someone came up the stairs. Madam Hof burst in, followed by her husband. She flung herself about the neck of the mother and grandmother, but didn't say a word. She wept and sobbed.

"Lord God!" said Mother and Grandmother. "How did everything go for Peer?"

"Let me weep!" said Madam Hof, who was so moved, so overcome. "I cannot bear it. Ah, you dear people, you cannot bear it, either!" And her tears streamed down.

"Have they hissed him off?" cried Mother.

"No, not that!" said Madam Hof. "They have—oh, that I should live to see it!" Then both Mother and Grandmother wept.

"Be calm, Emilie," said Herr Hof. "Peer has conquered! He has triumphed! They clapped so much that the house nearly tumbled down! I can still feel it in my hands. It was one storm of applause from the first row to the gallery. The entire royal family clapped, too. Really, it was what one may call a redletter day in the annals of the theater. It was more than talent—it was genius."

"Yes, genius!" said Madam Hof. "Those are my words. God bless you, Hof, because you said them for me! You good people, never would I have believed that one could both sing and act like that, though I have lived through a theater's whole history." She cried again; Mother and Grandmother laughed, while tears still ran down their cheeks.

"Now sleep well on that," said Herr Hof. "Come along, Emilie. Good night, good night!"

They left the garret room and two happy people there. These two were not alone long. The door opened, and Peer, who hadn't promised to come before the next forenoon, stood in the room. He well knew how the old people had followed him in their thoughts, how ignorant, too, they still must be of his success, and when driving by the house with the singing master, he had stopped outside; with the light still burning up in the garret, he had felt he must go to them.

"Splendid, glorious, superb! All went well!" he exclaimed jubilantly, and kissed his mother and his grandmother. The singing master nodded with a beaming face and pressed their hands.

"And now he must go home and have some rest," he said. And the late visit was over.

"Our Father in Heaven, how gracious and good you are!" said these two poor women. They talked far into the night about Peer. Everywhere in the great city people talked about him—the young, handsome, wonderful singer. Lucky Peer had gone that far.

XIII

With great fanfare, the morning paper told of the debut as something out of the ordinary, the drama critic reserving his privilege of expressing his opinion in a following issue. The merchant invited Peer and the singing master to a grand dinner. It was an observance—a testimony of his and his wife's interest in the young man, who had been born in the house, in the same year and on the very same day as their own son.

The merchant made a beautiful speech and proposed a toast to the singing master, the man who had found and polished this "precious stone," a name one of the prominent papers had called Peer. Felix sat by his side and was the soul of gaiety and affection. After dinner he brought out his own cigars; they were better than the merchant's. "He can afford to get them," said the latter; "he has a rich father." Peer did not smoke—a great fault, but one which could be remedied easily enough.

"We must be friends," said Felix. "You have become the lion of the town! All the young ladies, and the old ones, too, for that matter, you have taken by storm. You are lucky with everything, I envy you, especially in that you can go in and out over there at the theater, among all the little girls."

To Peer that did not seem anything very worthy of envy.

He received a letter from Madam Gabriel. She was in a state of ecstasy over the splendid accounts in the papers of his debut and over what he would become as an artist. She and the girls had drunk a toast to him with punch. Herr Gabriel also had a share in his honor, and was quite sure that he, beyond most others, could pronounce foreign words correctly. The pharmacist ran about town and reminded everyone that it was at their little theater they had first seen and admired his talent, which now for the first time was recognized in the capital. "The pharmacist's daughter would surely be irritated," added Madam, "now that he could propose to baronesses and countesses." The pharmacist's daughter had been in too much of a hurry and given in too soon, for a month earlier she had become betrothed to the fat Councillor. The banns had been published, and they were to be married on the twentieth of the month.

It was just the twentieth of the month when Peer received this letter. He felt as if he had been pierced through the heart. At that moment it became clear to him that, during all the vacillation of his soul, she had been his steadfast thought. He cared more for her than anyone else in the world. Tears came into his eyes; he crumpled the letter in his hand. It was the first great grief of heart he had known since he had heard, with Mother and Grandmother, that his father had fallen in the war. He thought that all happiness was gone, that his future would be empty and sorrowful. The sunlight no longer beamed from his youthful face; the sunshine was put out in his heart.

"He doesn't look well," said Mother and Grandmother. "It is the hard work at the theater."

They could both see that he was not the same as before, and the singing master saw it, too.

"What is the matter?" he said. "May I not know what troubles you?"

At that his cheeks turned red, his tears flowed afresh, and he told him about his sorrow, his loss.

"I loved her so deeply!" he said. "Only now, when it is too late, is it really clear to me!"

"Poor, grieved friend! I understand you so well. Weep freely, and as soon as you can, hold onto the thought that whatever happens in the world happens for the best. I, too, have known and felt what you now are feeling. I, like you, once loved a girl; she was intelligent, pretty, and fascinating; she was to be my wife. I could offer good her good circumstances, and she cared for me; but one condition had to be met before the marriage; her parents required it, and she required it: I must become a Christian!"

"And that you would not?"

"I could not. One cannot, with an honest conscience, jump from one religion to another without sinning either against the one he takes leave of or the one he steps into. "

"Have you no faith?" said Peer.

"I have the God of my fathers. He is a light for my feet and my understanding." They sat in silence for a while. Then the hands of the singing master touched the keys, and he played an old folk song. Neither of them sang the words; perhaps each was deep in his own thoughts.

Madam Gabriel's letter was not read again. She never dreamed what sorrow it had brought.

A few days later a letter arrived from Herr Gabriel; he also wished to offer his congratulations and "a commission," which perhaps was the real reason for the letter. He asked Peer to buy a little porcelain figure, namely, Amor and Hymen, Love and Marriage. "It is all sold out here in town," he wrote, "but can easily be bought in the capital. The money is enclosed with this. Send the thing as quickly as possible; it is a wedding present for the Councillor, at whose marriage I was with my wife." Moreover, Peer was told: "Young Madsen never will become a student; he has left the house and has painted the walls with embarrassing remarks against the family. A bad subject, that young Madsen. *Sunt pueri pueri, pueri puerilia tractant!* i.e., 'Boys are boys, and boys do boyish things.' I translate it since you are not a Latin scholar." And with that Herr Gabriel's letter closed.

XIV

Frequently, when Peer sat at the piano, there sounded tones in it that stirred within his breast and head. The tones rose into melodies, which now and then carried words along with them; they could not be separated from the melodies. Thus several little poems that were rhythmic and full of feeling came into being. They were sung in a subdued voice. It was as if they, shy and afraid of being heard, were gliding along in loneliness.

> *Everything passes, like the wind that blows;*
> *There is nothing lasting here.*
> *From your cheek will fade the rose,*
> *As well as smile and tear.*
>
> *Why be burdened with pain and grief?*
> *Away with your trouble and sorrow,*
> *For everything goes, fades like the leaf;*
> *Time and man pass with the morrow.*
>
> *All vanishes, everything goes,*
> *Your youth, your hope, and your friend.*
> *Everything passes, like the wind that blows,*
> *Never to return, only to end!*

"Where did you get that song and melody?" asked the singing master, who by chance saw the words and music written down.

"It came of itself, that and all these. They will never fly farther into the world."

"A downcast spirit sets out flowers, too," said the singing master, "but a downcast spirit dares not give advice. Now we must set sail and steer toward your next debut. What do you say to Hamlet, the melancholy young Prince of Denmark?"

"I know Shakespeare's tragedy," said Peer, "but not yet Thomas' opera."

"The opera should be called *Ophelia*," said the singing master. In the tragedy, Shakespeare has made the queen tell us of Ophelia's death, and this has become the high light in the musical rendering. One sees before his eyes, and feels in the tones, what before we could learn only from the narrative of the queen.

> *There is a willow grows aslant a brook,*
> *That shows his hoar leaves in the glassy stream;*
> *There with fantastic garlands did she come*
> *Of crow-flowers, nettles, daisies, and long purples*
> *That liberal shepherds give a grosser name,*
> *But our cold maids do dead men's fingers call them:*
> *There, on the pendent boughs her coronet weeds*
> *Clambering to hang, an envious sliver broke;*
> *When down her weedy trophies and herself*
> *Fell in the weeping brook. Her clothes spread wide,*
> *And, mermaid-like, awhile they bore her up:*

Which time she chanted snatches of old tunes,
As one incapable of her own distress...

The opera brings all this before our eyes. We see Ophelia; she comes out playing, dancing, singing the old ballad about the mermaid who entices men down beneath the river, and while she sings and plucks the flowers the same tones are heard from the depths of the stream; they sound in the voices of the chorus alluringly from the deep water; she listens; she laughs; she draws near the brink; she holds onto the overhanging willow and stoops to pluck the white water lilies; gently she glides out onto them and, singing, reclines on their broad leaves; she swings with them and is carried by the stream out into the deep, where, like the broken flower, she sinks in the moonlight, with the mermaid's melody welling forth about her.

In this great scene it is as if Hamlet, his mother, his uncle, and the dead, avenging king were created only to make the frame for this exquisite picture. We do not get Shakespeare's Hamlet, just as in the opera *Faust* we do not get Goethe's Faust. The speculative is no material for music. It is the love element in both these tragedies that elevates them to musical poems.

The opera of Hamlet was presented on the stage. The actress who had Ophelia's part was admirable, and the death scene was very effective, while Hamlet himself received sympathetic greatness on this evening, a fullness of character that grew with each scene in which he appeared. Furthermore, people were astonished at the extent of the singer's voice, at the freshness shown in the high as well as in the deep tones, and that he, with and equal brilliancy of power, could sing Hamlet and George Brown.

In most of the Italian operas the singing parts are each like a canvas on which the gifted singer or songstress puts his or her soul and genius, and with the varied, wavy colors creates the form the poem requires. How much more glorious they must be able to reveal themselves when the music is composed and carried out through thought centered upon the character; and this Gounod and Thomas have understood.

That evening at the theater, the character of Hamlet was given flesh and blood, and he raised himself into the position of the leading personage in the opera. Unforgettable was the night scene on the ramparts, where Hamlet, for the first time, sees his father's ghost—the scene in the castle, before the stage that has been erected, where he flings out the words that are drops of poison—the terrible meeting with his mother, where the father's ghost stands with avengeful attitude before the son—and finally, what power in his voice, what tones, at Ophelia's death! She was the sympathetic lotus flower upon the deep, dark sea; its waves rolled with a mighty force into the soul of the spectators. That evening Hamlet became the leading figure. The triumph was complete. "From whom did that boy get it?" said the merchant's rich wife, as she thought of Peer's parents and his grandmother up in the garret. The father had been a warehouseman, good and honorable, and had fallen as a soldier on the field of honor—the mother, a washerwoman—but that does not give the son culture; he had grown up in a charity school—and how much knowledge could a provincial schoolmaster give him in a period of two years?

"It is genius!" said the merchant. "Genius—that is born of God's grace."

"Most certainly!" said his wife. And she folded her hands as she talked to Peer. "Do you really feel humble in your heart at what you have received? Heaven has been inconceivably gracious to you! Everything is given you. You do not know how gripping your Hamlet is! You simply cannot imagine it! I have heard that many great poets do not themselves know the glory of what they have given; the philosophers must reveal it to them. Where did you get your conception of Hamlet?"

"I have thought about the character, have read a great deal of what has been written about Shakespeare's work, and then on the stage I have tried to put life into the person and his surroundings. I give my share, and our Lord gives the rest."

"Our Lord!" she said with a half-reproving look. "Do not use that name in such a manner! He gave you ability, but you surely do not believe that he has anything to do with the theater and opera!"

"Yes, most certainly!" said Peer courageously. "He has a pulpit there, too, and most people listen more there than in church!"

She shook her head. "God is with us in everything good and beautiful, but let us be careful not to take his name in vain. It is a gift of grace for one to be a great artist, but it is still better to be a good Christian." Felix, she felt, would never have compared the theater and the church before her, and she was glad.

"Now you have fallen out with Mamma!" said Felix, laughing.

"That was so far from my thoughts!"

"Don't trouble yourself about it. You will get into her good graces again next Sunday when you go to church. Stand outside her pew, and look up to the right, for there, in the balcony pew, is a little face which is worth looking at—the widow baroness' charming daughter. This is a well-meant bit of advice, and I'll give you some more. You cannot live where you are now. Move into a larger apartment—with a decent stairway!—or, if you won't leave the singing master, then let him live in better style. He has means enough, and you have a pretty good income. You must give a party, too, an evening supper. I could give it myself, and will do so, but you can invite a few of the little dancing girls. You're a lucky fellow! But I believe, Heaven help me, that you don't yet understand how to be a young man!"

Peer did understand it exactly, in his own way. With his full, warm, young heart, he was in love with art; she was his bride; she returned his love and lifted him into gladness and sunshine. The depression that had crushed him evaporated soon; gentle eyes looked upon him, and everyone met him in a friendly and cordial manner. The amber heart, which he still wore constantly on his breast, where Grandmother once had hung it, was certainly a talisman; yes, so he thought, for he was not quite free from superstition—a childlike faith, one may call it. Every nature that has genius in it has something of this and looks to and believes in its star. Grandmother had shown him the power that lay in the heart how it could draw things to itself. His dream had shown him a tree growing out of his amber heart, bursting through ceiling and roof and bearing thousands of hearts of silver and gold; that surely meant that in the heart, in his own warm heart, lay the power of his art, whereby he had won and still would win thousands upon thousands of hearts.

Between him and Felix there was undoubtedly a kind of sympathy, different as they were from each other. Peer assumed that the difference between them lay in that

Felix, as the rich man's son, had grown up amid temptations and desires and could afford to taste them.

He had, on the contrary, been more fortunately placed as a poor man's son.

Both of these two children of the house had since gained prominence. Felix would soon be a gentleman in waiting to the royal court, and that is the first step toward becoming a chamberlain; then one has a gold key behind. Peer, always lucky, already had the gold key of genius in his hand, though it was invisible—the key that opens all the treasures of Earth, and all hearts, too.

XV

It was still wintertime. The sleigh bells jingled, and the clouds carried snowflakes in them, but wherever a sunbeam burst through them, it announced that spring was near. In the young heart there was a fragrance and a song that flowed out in picturesque tones and found expression in words:

> *The snow is still upon the earth;*
> *O'er the lake, skaters race in mirth.*
> *The trees are frost-rimmed, full of crows;*
> *But tomorrow perhaps the winter goes. .*
> *The sun breaks through the sky of gray;*
> *Spring is in town; it's like a summer day.*
> *The willow's woolen gloves fall from the tree.*
> *Strike up, musicians, for a merry spree!*
> *Sing, little birds! All voices blend!*
> *For now the winter has come to an end!*
>
> *Oh, to be kissed by the warming sun!*
> *Come, pluck violets and primrose—what fun!*
> *It's as if the forest its breath were holding,*
> *While in the night each leaf is unfolding.*
> *The cuckoos sing; you know their song.*
> *Hear them sing that your life will be long.*
> *The world is young, so be young with the young!*
> *With thankful heart and merry tongue,*
> *Sing of spring! All voices blend!*
> *For never does youth come to an end!*
>
> *Never does youth come to an end!*
> *Life on Earth is a magic blend,*
> *Of sunshine and storm, joy and pain.*
> *Within our hearts a world was lain;*
> *It vanishes not like a shooting star,*
> *For man is the image of God afar.*
> *God and nature remain ever young.*
> *Teach us, O Spring, the song you've long sung.*
> *Every little bird sings; all voices blend—*
> *For never does youth come to an end!*

"That is a complete musical painting," said the singing master, "and well adapted for chorus and orchestra. It is the best yet of your emotional compositions. You certainly must learn thorough bass, although it is not your destiny to be a composer."

Young music friends soon introduced the song at a great concert, where it attracted attention but aroused no expectations. Our young friend's career was open before him. His greatness and importance lay not only in the sympathetic tones of his voice, but in his remarkable dramatic talent as well; this he had shown as George Brown and as Hamlet. He very much preferred the regular opera to the light opera. It was contrary to his sound, natural sense to go from song to talk and back to song.

"It is," he said, "as if one were going from marble steps onto wooden steps, sometimes even onto mere henroosts, and then back onto marble. The whole poem should live and breathe in its passage through tones."

The music of the future, as the new movement in opera is called, and for which Wagner, in particular, is a banner-bearer, had a defender and admirer in our young friend. He found here characters so clearly drawn, passages so full of thought, and the entire action characterized by forward movement, without any standstill or frequent recurrence of melodies. "It is most unnatural to include those long arias."

"Yes," said the singing master. "But how they, in the works of most of the great masters, stand out as a most important part of the whole! That is as it should and must be. If the lyric has a home in any place, it is in the opera." And he mentioned in *Don Giovanni*, Don Ottavio's aria, "Tears, cease your flowing." "How much it is like a beautiful lake in the woods, by whose bank one rests and enjoys the music that streams through it! I bow to the ingenuity that lies in this new musical movement, but I do not dance with you before that golden calf. Either it is not your heart's real opinion that you express, or else it is not quite clear to you."

"I will appear in one of Wagner's operas," said our young friend. "If I cannot express my meaning in words, I will do so by my singing and acting!"

The choice made was Lohengrin, the young mysterious knight who, in the boat drawn by the swan, glides over the river Scheldt to fight for Elsa of Brabant. Who had ever sung and acted so well the first song of the meeting, the love song in the bridal chamber, and the song of farewell when the Holy Grail's white dove hovers about the young knight who came, conquered, and vanished? This evening was, if possible, another step forward in the artistic greatness and significance of our young friend; and to the singing master it was a step forward in the recognition of the music of the future.

"Under certain conditions," he said.

XVI

At the great yearly exhibition of paintings, Peer and Felix met one day, before the portrait of a pretty young lady, the daughter of the widow baroness, as the mother was generally called; the latter's salon was the rendezvous for the world of distinction and for everyone of importance in art and science. The young baroness was in her sixteenth year, an innocent, beautiful child. The picture was a good likeness and done with artistic skill.

"Step into the hall nearby," said Felix. "There stands the young beauty herself with her mother."

They stood engrossed in viewing a painting of characterization. It represented a field where two young married people were riding on the same horse, holding onto one another. The chief figure, however, was a young monk who was looking at the two happy travelers. There was a sorrowful, dreamy look on the young man's face; one could read his thoughts in it, the story of his life—an aim missed, great happiness lost! Happiness in human love he had not won.

The elder baroness saw Felix, who respectfully greeted her and the beautiful daughter, Peer showed the same customary politeness. The widow baroness knew him immediately from having seen him on the stage, and after speaking to Felix she said some friendly, obliging words to Peer as she pressed his hand.

"I and my daughter belong to your admirers."

How perfectly beautiful the young girl was at this moment! She looked with her gentle, clear eyes almost gratefully at him.

"I see in my house," said the widow baroness, "so many of the most distinguished artists. We common people stand in need of a spiritual airing. You will be heartily welcome. Our young diplomat," she pointed to Felix, "will bring you along the first time, and afterward I hope that you will find the way yourself."

She smiled at him. The young girl reached out her hand naturally and cordially, as if they had long known each other.

Late in the autumn, on a cold, sleety evening, the two young men went to the baroness' home, the two born in the rich merchant's house. It was weather for driving and not walking for the rich man's son and the first singer on the stage. Nevertheless, they walked, well wrapped up, with galoshes on their feet and Bedouin caps on their heads.

It was like entering a complete fairyland to come from the raw air into this home that displayed such luxury and good taste. In the vestibule, before the carpeted stairs, there was a great display of flowers among bushes and fan palms. A little fountain splashed water into a basin, which was surrounded by tall callas.

The great salon was magnificently lighted, and a large part of the company had already gathered. It soon became very crowded. People stepped on silk trains and laces, amid the humming, sonorous mosaic of conversation, which, on the whole, was the least worthwhile of all the splendor there.

Had Peer been a vain fellow, which he was not, he could have imagined that it was a party for him, so cordial was the reception he received from the lady of the house and the beaming daughter. Young and elderly ladies, yes, and gentlemen, too, paid him many compliments.

There was music. A young author read a well-written poem. There was singing, and tactfulness was shown in that no one urged our young and honored singer to make the affair complete. The lady of the house was a most attentive hostess, brilliant and genial, in that elegant salon.

That was his introduction into the great world, and our young friend was soon also one of the select group in the choice family circle. The singing master shook his head and laughed.

"How young you are, dear friend," he said, "that it can please you to be with these people! In a way they are good enough, but they look down on us plain citizens. For some of them it is only a matter of vanity, an amusement, and for others a sort of sign of exclusive culture, when they receive into their circle artists and the lions of the day. These belong in the salon much as the flowers in a vase; they decorate and then they are thrown away."

"How harsh and unreasonable!" said Peer. "You do not know these people; you do not want to know them!"

"No," answered the singing master. "I don't feel at home among them, nor do you, either. That they all remember and know. They pat you and look at you just as they pat and look at a racehorse that is expected to win a wager. You belong to another race than they. They will let you go when you are no longer in the fashion. Don't you understand that? You are not proud enough. You are vain, and you show that by seeking these people's company.

"How very differently you would talk and judge," said Peer, "if you knew the widow baroness and a few of my friends there."

"I shall not come to know them," said the singing master.

"When is the engagement to be announced?" asked Felix one day. "Is it the mother or the daughter?" And he laughed. "Don't take the daughter, for then you'll have all the young nobility against you, and I, too, shall be your enemy, and the deadliest one!"

"What do you mean?" asked Peer.

"You are indeed the favorite. You can go in and out at all hours. With the mother, you'd get money and belong to a good family."

"Stop your joking," said Peer. "There is nothing amusing to me in what you say."

"It is not supposed to be amusing," said Felix. "It is a most serious matter, for you surely wouldn't let her grace sit and weep and be a double widow!"

"Leave the baroness out of this conversation," said Peer. "Make fun over me if you want to, but over me alone, and I will answer you!"

"No one will believe that it is a love match on your side," continued Felix. "She is a little outside of the line of beauty. True, one does not live on intellect alone!"

"I thought you had more refinement and good sense," said Peer, "than to talk so disrespectfully of a lady you should esteem and whose house you visit, and I can't bear to listen to you any longer!"

"What are you going to do about it?" asked Felix. "Do you want to fight?"

"I know that you have learned that, and I have not, but I can learn!" And he left Felix.

A couple of days later the two children of the house met again, the son from the first floor and the son from the garret. Felix talked to Peer as if no break had come between them. He answered courteously, but curtly, too.

"What is the matter now!" said Felix. "We two were a little irritable recently, but one must have his little joke, which doesn't necessarily mean one is flippant. I don't like to bear a grudge, so let us forgive and forget."

"Can you forgive yourself the manner in which you spoke of a lady to whom we both owe great respect?"

"I spoke very frankly!" said Felix. "In high society one can also talk with a razor edge, but no one takes that very seriously; it is the salt for the tasteless, everyday fish dinner, as the poet calls it. We are all just a little spiteful. You can also let a drop fall, my friend, a little drop of innocence that smarts!"

Soon they were seen arm in arm again. Felix well knew that more than one pretty young lady who otherwise would have passed him by without looking at him now noticed him because he was walking with the "idol of the stage." The footlights always cast a glamour over the theater's hero and lover, and it still shines about him when he shows himself on the street, in daylight, though it is more or less extinguished then. Most of the artists of the stage are like swans; one should see them in their element, not on the paving stones or the public promenade. There are exceptions, however, and to these belonged our young friend. His personality off the stage never disturbed the conception one had of him as George Brown, or Hamlet, or Lohengrin. To many a young heart these poetical and musical figures were the artist himself and rose to the exaltation of their ideal. He knew that this was the case and found a sort of pleasure in it. He was happy in his art and with the talents he possessed; still a shadow would come over the happy young face, and then from the piano would sound the melody to the words:

All vanishes, everything goes,
Your youth, your hope, and your friend.
Everything passes, like the wind that blows,
Never to return, only to end!

"How mournful!" said the widow baroness. "You have good fortune in full measure. I know no one who is as fortunate as you."

"Call no one fortunate before he is in his grave, the wise Solon said," he replied, and smiled through his seriousness. "It would be wrong, a sin, if I were not thankful and happy in my heart. I am that. I am thankful for what is entrusted to me, but I myself set a different value on this than others do. It is a beautiful piece of fireworks that soars forth and then goes out! So it is with the stage actor's work. The everlasting shining stars may be forgotten for the meteors of a moment, but when these are extinguished, there is no lasting trace of them other than what may be found in old records. A new generation does not know and cannot picture to itself those who delighted their grandfathers from the stage; the youth of today perhaps applauds the luster of brass as fervently and loudly as the old folks once did the luster of pure gold. Far more fortunately placed than the performing artist are the poet, the sculptor, the painter, and the composer. They often experience trying conditions in the struggle of life and miss the merited appreciation, while those who exhibit their works live in luxury and in arrogance born of idolatry.

"Let the mob stand and admire the bright-colored cloud and forget the sun; the cloud vanishes, but the sun shines and beams for new generations."

He sat at the piano and improvised with a richness of thought and a power such as he never before had shown. "Wonderfully beautiful!" broke in the widow baroness. "It was as if I heard the story of a whole lifetime. You gave your heart's song in the music."

"I thought of the *Thousand and One Nights*," said the young girl, "of the lamp of fortune, of Aladdin!" And she looked at him with innocent, tearful eyes.

"Aladdin!" he repeated.

That evening was the turning point in his life. A new chapter surely began.

What happened to him during this fast-moving year? His fresh color left his cheeks, though his eyes shone far more clearly than before. He passed sleepless nights, but not in wild orgies, in revels and drinking, as so many artists. He became less talkative, but more cheerful.

"What is it that fills you so?" said his friend, the singing master. "You do not confide everything to me!"

"I think of how fortunate I am!" he replied. "I think of the poor boy! I think of—Aladdin!"

XVII

Measured by the expectations of a poor-born child, Peer now led a prosperous, pleasant life. He was so well off that, as Felix once had said, he could give a big party for his friends. He thought of it, and thought of his two earliest friends, his mother and his Grandmother. For them and himself he provided a festival.

It was wonderful spring weather, and the two old people were going to drive with him out of town and see a little country place that the singing master had recently bought. As he was seating himself in the carriage, a woman came along humbly clad, about thirty years old; she had a note recommending her, signed by Madam Hof.

"Don't you know me?" she said. "Little Curlyhead, they used to call me. The curls are gone; there is so much that is gone; but there are still good people left. We two have appeared together in the ballet. You have become better off than I. You have become a great man. I am now separated from two husbands and no longer at the theater."

The note requested a sewing machine for her.

"In what ballet have we two performed together?" asked Peer.

"In the *Tyrant of Padua*," she replied. "We were both pages, in blue velvet and berets. Don't you remember little Malle Knallerup? I walked right behind you in the procession."

"And stepped on the side of my foot!" said Peer, laughing.

"Did I?" she said. "Then I took too long a step. But you have gone far ahead of me. You have understood how to use your head instead of your legs." And she looked coquettishly at him with her melancholy face, quite sure she had paid him a witty compliment. Peer was a generous fellow. She should have the sewing machine, he promised. Little Malle had indeed been one of those who in particular had driven him out of the ballet into a more fortunate career.

He was soon outside the merchant's house, and he then ascended the stairs to his mother's and his grandmother's. They were in their best clothes, and by chance they had a visit from Madam Hof, who was at once invited to drive with them; whereupon she had quite a struggle with herself, which ended in her sending a note to Herr Hof to inform him that she had accepted the invitation.

"Such fine greetings Peer gets!" she said.

"How stylishly we are driving!" said Mother.

"And in such a beautiful, comfortable carriage," said Grandmother.

Near the town, close to the royal park, stood a cozy little house, surrounded by vines and roses, hazels, and fruit trees. Here the carriage stopped. This was the country house. They were received by an old woman well acquainted with Mother and Grandmother; she had often helped them with their washing and ironing.

The garden was inspected, and the house was inspected. There was one particularly charming thing—a little glasshouse with beautiful flowers in it. It was connected with the sitting room; the sliding door between could be pushed right into the wall.

"That is just like a coulisse on the stage," said Madam Hof. "It moves by hand. And one can sit here just as in a bird cage, with chickweed all about. It is called a winter garden."

The bedroom was equally delightful in its way. There were long, heavy curtains at the windows, soft carpets, and two armchairs so comfortable that Mother and Grandmother must try them.

"One would get very lazy sitting in them," said Mother.

"One loses his weight," said Madam Hof. "Indeed, here you two music people can rest comfortably after your theatrical labors. I have also known what they are! Yes, believe me, I can still dream of doing high kicks, and Hof does high kicks by my side! Is it not charming—'two souls and one thought!'"

"The air is fresher here, and there is more room than in the two small rooms up in the garret," said Peer with beaming eyes.

"That there is," said Mother. "Still, home is nice, too. There you were born, my sweet boy, and there I lived with your father."

"It is better here," said Grandmother. "Here you have a whole mansion. I do not begrudge you and that noble man, the singing master, this home of peace."

"Then I do not begrudge you this, Grandmother, and you, my dear blessed mother! You two shall always live here, and not, as in town , walk up so many steps and be in such narrow and small quarters. You shall have a servant to help you and shall see me as often as in town. Are you happy about it? Are you content with it?"

"What is all this the boy stands here and says!" said Mother.

"The house, the garden—it's all yours, Mother, and yours, Grandmother! To be able to give you this is what I have striven for. My friend the singing master has faithfully helped me with getting it ready."

"What is all this you are saying, child!" exclaimed the mother. "You want to give us a gentleman's mansion! You sweet boy! Yes, you would do it if you could!"

"I am serious," he said. "The house is yours and Grandmother's." He kissed them both, and they burst into tears. Madam Hof shed just as many. "It is the happiest moment of my life!" exclaimed Peer, as he embraced all three of them.

And now they had to see everything all over again, since it was their own. They now had that beautiful little glasshouse in which to put their five or six pot plants from the garret roof. Instead of a little cupboard, they had here a great roomy pantry, and the kitchen was a complete, warm little chamber. The chimney had an oven and cooking stove; it looked like a great, shining flatiron, said Mother.

"Now you have a fireside corner just like I have!" said Madam Hof. "This is magnificent! You have attained all that people can attain on this Earth, and you, too, my own, popular friend!"

"Not all!" said Peer.

"The little wife will come along!" said Madam Hof. "I have her already for you!

I feel sure I know who she is! But I shall keep my mouth shut. You wonderful man! Isn't all this like a ballet!" She laughed with tears in her eyes, and so did Mother and Grandmother.

XVIII

To write the text and music for an opera, and be the interpreter of his own work on the stage, was a great and happy aim. Our young friend had a talent in common with Wagner, in that he could construct the dramatic poem himself; but did he, like Wagner, have the fullness of musical emotion to create a musical work of any significance?

Courage and doubt alternated in him. He could not dismiss this persistent thought of his. For years and days it had shone in his mind as a picture of fancy; now it was a possibility, his life's goal. Many free fancies were welcomed at the piano as birds of passage from that Land of Perhaps. The little ballads and the characteristic spring song gave promise of the still undiscovered land of tone. The widow baroness saw in them the sign of promise, as Columbus saw it in the fresh green weed that the currents of the sea bore toward him before he saw the land itself on the horizon.

Land was there! The child of fortune should reach it. A word thrown out was the seed of thought. She, the young, pretty, innocent girl, had spoken the word— Aladdin. Our young friend was a child of fortune like Aladdin; it shone within him.

With understanding and delight he read and reread the beautiful Oriental story. Soon it took dramatic form; scene after scene grew into words and music, and the more it grew, the richer the music thoughts became. At the close of the work it was as if the well of tone were now for the first time pierced, and all the abundant fresh water streamed forth. He then recomposed his work, and in stronger form, after months, arose the opera *Aladdin*.

No one knew of this work; no one had heard as much as a single bar of it, not even the most sympathetic of all his friends, the singing master. No one at the theater, when in the evening the young singer entranced his public with his voice and his masterful acting, had any idea that the young man who seemed so to live and breathe in his role lived far more intensely—yes, and for hours afterward lost himself in a mighty work of music that poured from his own soul.

The singing master had not heard a bar of the opera *Aladdin* before it was put on his table for examination, complete in notes and text. What judgment would be passed? Assuredly a strong and just one. The young composer passed from highest hope to the thought that the whole thing was only a self-delusion.

Two days passed by, and not a word was exchanged about this important matter. Finally, the singing master stood before him with the score in his hands, which he now knew. There was a peculiar seriousness spread over his face that did not indicate his thoughts.

"I had not expected this," he said. "I had not believed it of you. Indeed, I do not yet have a clear judgment, so I dare not express it. Here and there are faults in the instrumentation, faults that can easily be corrected. There are single things, bold and novel, that one must hear under proper conditions. As there is in Wagner a certain influence of Carl Maria von Weber, so there is noticeable in you a breath of Haydn.

That which is new in what you have given is still rather remote to me, and you yourself are too near for me to be the right judge. I would rather not judge. I will embrace you!" he burst out, beaming with happiness. "How have you been able to do this!" And he embraced him in his arms. "Happy man!"

A rumor soon spread through the city, via the newspapers and gossip, about the new opera by the popular young singer.

"He's a poor tailor who cannot put together a child's coat out of the scraps left over on his board," said one and another.

"Write the text, compose it, and sing it himself!" was also said. "That is a three-storied genius. But he really was born still higher—in a garret!"

"There are two at it, he and the singing master," they said. "Now they'll begin to beat the signal drum of the partnership of mutual admiration!"

The opera was given out for study. Those who took part would not give any opinion. "It shall not be said that it is judged from the theater," they remarked; and almost everyone put on a serious face that did not show any expectation.

"There are a good many horns in the piece," said a young trumpeter. "If only he doesn't run a horn into himself!"

"It has genius; it is brilliant, full of melody and character!" That was also said.

"Tomorrow at this time," said Peer, "the scaffold will be raised. The judgment is, perhaps, already passed."

"Some say that it is a masterpiece," said the singing master, "others, that it is a mere patchwork."

"And where lies the truth?"

"Truth!" said the singing master. "Yes, tell me where. Look at that star up there. Tell me exactly where its place is. Shut one eye. Do you see it? Now look at it with the other only. The star has shifted its place. When each eye in the same person sees so differently, how differently must the great multitude see!"

"Happen what may," said our young friend, "I must know my place in the world, understand what I can and must create, or give up."

The evening came, the evening of decision. A popular artist was to be exalted to a higher place or humiliated in his gigantic, vain effort.

Success or failure! The matter concerned the whole city. People stood all night in the street before the ticket office, to obtain seats. The house was crammed full. The ladies came with great bouquets; would they be carried home again or thrown at the victor's feet?

The widow baroness and the young, beautiful daughter sat in a box above the orchestra. There was a stir in the audience, a murmuring, a movement, which stopped at once as the leader of the orchestra took his place and the overture began.

Who does not remember Hanselt's piece, "*Si l'oiseau j'étais*," which is like a twittering of birds? This was somewhat similar; there were jubilant, playing children, happy child voices mingling; the cuckoo cuckooed with them; the thrush sang. It was the play and jubilation of the innocent child mind—the mind of Aladdin. Then a thunderstorm rolled in; Noureddin displayed his power; a flash of deadly lightning split the mountain. Gentle, beckoning tones followed; a sound came from the enchanted grotto, where the lamp shone in the petrified cavern, while the wings of mighty spirits brooded over it. Now, in the tones of a French horn, sounded a psalm, which was as gentle and soft as if it were coming from the mouth of a child; a single horn was heard, and then another; more and more were blended in the same tones and rose in fullness and power, as if they were the trumpets of the judgment day. The lamp was in Aladdin's hand, and then there swelled forth a sea of melody and grandeur such as only the ruler of spirits and the masters of music can create.

The curtain rolled up in a storm of applause that sounded like a fanfare under the conductor's baton. A grown-up, handsome boy was playing; he was so big and yet so innocent; it was Aladdin, who leaped about among the other boys. Grandmother would at once have said, "That is Peer as he played and jumped about between the stove and the chest of drawers at home in the garret. He is not a year older in his soul!"

With what faith and sincerity he sang the prayer Noureddin bade him offer before he stepped down into the rocky cavern to obtain the lamp! Was it the pure, religious melody or the innocence with which he sang that enchanted all the listeners? The applause would not cease.

It would have been a profane thing to have repeated the song. It was demanded, but it was not given. The curtain fell; the first act was over.

Every critic was speechless; people were overcome with gladness and, in their appreciation, were certain of enjoying the rest of the evening.

A few chords sounded from the orchestra, and the curtain rose. The strains of music, as in Gluck's *Armida* and Mozart's *Magic Flute*, arrested the attention of everyone as the scene was disclosed, the scene in which Aladdin stood in the wonderful garden. Soft, subdued music sounded from flowers and stones, from springs and deep caverns, different melodies blending in one great harmony. An air of spirits was heard in the chorus; it was now far off, now near, swelling in might and then dying away. Arising from this harmony, and supported by it, was the song monologue of Aladdin—what one indeed calls a great aria, but so entirely in keeping with character and situation that it was a necessary dramatic part of the whole. The resonant, sympathetic voice, the intense music of the heart, subdued all listeners and seized them with a rapture that could not rise higher when he reached for the lamp of fortune that was embraced by the song of the spirits.

Bouquets rained down from all sides; a carpet of living flowers was spread out before his feet.

What a moment of life for the young artist—the highest, the greatest! A mightier one could never again be granted him, he felt. A wreath of laurel touched his breast and fell down in front of him. He had seen from whose hand it had come. He saw the young girl in the box nearest the stage, the young baroness, rising like a spirit of beauty, loudly rejoicing over his triumph.

A fire rushed through him; his heart swelled as never before; he bowed, took the wreath, pressed it against his heart, and at the same moment fell backward. Fainted? Dead? What was it? The curtain fell.

"Dead!" resounded through the house. Dead in the moment of triumph, like Sophocles at the Olympian games, like Thorvaldsen in the theater during Beethoven's symphony. An artery in his heart had burst, and as by a flash of lightning his days here were ended, ended without pain, ended in an earthly triumph, in the fulfillment of his mission on Earth. Lucky Peer! More fortunate than millions!

WHAT THE WHOLE FAMILY SAID (1870)

What did the whole family say? Well, listen first to what little Marie said.

It was little Marie's birthday, the most wonderful of all days, she imagined. All her little boy friends and girl friends came to play with her, and she wore her prettiest dress, the one Grandmother, who was now with God, had sewn for her before she went up into the bright, beautiful Heaven. The table in little Marie's room was loaded with presents; there was the prettiest little kitchen, with everything that belongs to a kitchen, and a doll that could close its eyes and say "Ouch!" when you pinched its stomach; yes, and there was also a picture book, with the most wonderful stories, to be read when one could read! But to have many birthdays was more wonderful than all the stories in the book.

"Yes, it's wonderful to be alive," said little Marie. And her godfather added that it was the most beautiful of all fairy tales.

In the next room were both her brothers; they were big boys, one of them nine years old, the other eleven. They thought it was wonderful to be alive, too; that is, to live in their own way, not to be a baby like Marie, but to be real smart schoolboys, to get As on their report cards, to have friendly fights with their comrades, to go skating in the winter and bicycling in the summer, to read about the days of knighthood, with its castles, its drawbridges, and its dungeons, and to hear about new discoveries in Central Africa. On the latter subject, however, one of the boys felt very sad in that he feared everything might be discovered before he grew up, and then there would be no adventure left for him. But Godfather said, "Life itself is the most wonderful adventure, and you have a part in it yourself."

These children lived on the first floor of the house; in the flat above them lived another branch of the family, also with children, but these all had long since been shaken from their mother's apron strings, so big were they; one son was seventeen, and another twenty, but the third one was very old, said little Marie; he was twenty-five, and engaged to be married. They were all very well off, had nice parents, good clothes, and were well educated, and they knew what they wanted. "Look forward," they said. "Away with all the old fences! Let's have an open view into the wide world! That's the greatest thing we know of! Godfather is right—life is the most wonderful fairy tale!"

Father and Mother, both older people—naturally, they would have to be older than the children—said, with smiling lips and smiling eyes and hearts, "How young these young people are! Things usually don't happen in this world just as they expect them to, yet life goes on. Life is a strange and wonderful adventure."

On the next floor—a little closer to Heaven, as we say when people live in an attic— lived Godfather. He was old, and yet so young in mind, always in a good humor, and he certainly could tell stories, many and long ones. He had traveled the world over, and his room was filled with pretty tokens from every country. Pictures were hung from ceiling to floor, and some of the windowpanes were of red or yellow glass; if one looked through them, the whole world lay in sunshine, however gray the weather might be outside. Green plants grew in a large glass case, and in an enclosure therein swam goldfish; they looked at one as if they knew many things they didn't care to talk about. There was always a sweet fragrance of flowers, even in the wintertime. And then a great fire blazed in the fireplace; it was such a pleasure to sit and look into it and hear how it crackled and spat.

"It refreshes old memories to me," said Godfather. And to little Marie there seemed to appear many pictures in the fire.

But in the big bookcase close by stood real books; one of these Godfather often read, and this he called the Book of Books; it was the Bible. In it was pictured the history of the world and the history of all mankind, of the creation, the flood, the kings, and the King of Kings.

"All that has happened and all that will happen is written in this book," said Godfather; "so infinitely much in one single book! Just think of it! Yes, everything that a human being has to pray for is entered there, and said in a few words in the prayer 'Our Father'! It is the drop of mercy! It is the pearl of comfort from God. It is laid as a gift on the baby's cradle, laid on the child's heart. Little child, keep it safely; don't ever lose it, however big you may grow, and you will never be left alone on life's changeful way; it will shine within you and you will never be lost!"

Godfather's eyes radiated joy. Once, in his youth, they had wept, "and this was also good," he said. "That was a time of trial, when everything looked dark and gray. Now I have sunshine within me and around me. The older one grows, the clearer one sees, in both prosperity and misfortune, that our Lord always is with us and that life is the most beautiful of all fairy tales, and this he alone can give us—and so it will be into eternity."

"Yes, it is wonderful to be alive!" said little Marie.

So said also the small and the big boys, as well as Father and Mother and the whole family—but first of all, Godfather, who had had so much experience and was the oldest of them all. He knew all stories, all the fairy tales. And it was right from the bottom of his heart that he said, "Life is the most wonderful fairy tale of all!"

GREAT-GRANDFATHER (1870)

Great-grandfather was so lovable, wise and good. All of us looked up to Great-grandfather. As far back as I can remember, he was really called "Father's Father," and "Mother's Father" as well, but when my Brother Frederick's little son came along he was promoted, and got the title of "Great-grandfather." He could not expect to go any higher than that.

He was very fond of us all, but he did not appear to be fond of our times. "Old times were the good times," he used to say. "Quiet and genuine they were. In these days there's too much hurrying and turning everything upside down. The young folk lay down the law, and even speak about the kings as if they are their equals.

Any ne'er-do-well can sop a rag in dirty water and wring it out over the head of an honorable man."

Great-grandfather would get angry and red in the face when he talked of such things, but soon he would smile his kindly, sympathetic smile, and say, "Oh, well! I may be a bit wrong. I belong to the old days, and I can't quite get a foothold in the new. May God guide us and show us the right way to go."

When Great-grandfather got started on the old days, it seemed to me as if they came back. I would imagine myself riding along in a gilded coach, with footmen in fine livery. I saw the guilds move their signs and march in procession with their banners aloft, preceded by music. And I attended the merry Christmas festivities, where people in fancy dress played games of forfeit.

True enough, in the old days dreadfully cruel and horrible things used to be done. There was torture, rack and wheel, and bloodshed, but even these horrible things had an excitement about them that fascinated me. But I also thought of many pleasant things. I used to imagine how things were when the Danish nobility freed the peasants, and when the Danish Crown Prince abolished slave trading. It was marvelous to hear Great-grandfather talk of all these things, and to hear him tell of the days of his youth. But I think the times even earlier than that were the very best times of all—so mighty and glorious.

"They were barbarous times," Brother Frederick said. "Thank heaven we are well rid of them." He used to say this right out to Great-grandfather. This was most improper, I know, but just the same I always had great respect for Frederick. He was my oldest brother, and he used to say he was old enough to be my father—but then he was always saying the oddest things. He had graduated with the highest honors, and was so quick and clever in his work at Father's office that Father meant to make him a partner before long. Of us all, he was the one with whom Great-grandfather talked most, but they always began to argue, for they did not get along well together. They did not understand each other, those two, and the family said they never would, but even as young as I was, I soon felt that they were indispensable to each other. Great-grandfather would listen with the brightest look in his eyes while Frederick spoke of or read aloud about scientific progress, and new discoveries in the laws of nature, and about all the other marvels of our times.

"The human race gets cleverer, but it doesn't get better," Great-grandfather would say. "People invent the most terrible and harmful weapons with which to kill and injure each other."

"Then the war will be over that much sooner," Frederick would tell him. "No need now for us to wait seven years for the blessings of peace. The world is full-blooded, and it needs to be bled now and then. That is a necessity."

One day Frederick told him of something that actually happened in a small country and in our own times. The mayor's clock—the large one on the town hall—kept time for the whole town and for everyone who lived there. The clock did not run very well, but that didn't matter nor did it keep anyone from looking to it for the time. But by and by railroads were built in that country, and in all countries railroads run by the clock. One must therefore be sure of the time and know it exactly, or there will be collisions. At the railroad station they had a clock that was absolutely reliable, and exactly in accord with the sun. But as the mayor's was not, everyone went by the railroad clock.

I laughed, and thought the story a funny one, but Great-grandfather did not laugh. He became very serious.

"There is a profound meaning in what you have told me," he declared, "and I understood the thought that prompted you to tell me the story. There's a moral in the clockwork. It reminds me of another clock—my parents' simple, old-fashioned Bornholm clock, with lead weights. It measured out the time of their lives and of my childhood. Perhaps it didn't run any too well, but it ran just the same. We would look at the hour hand and believe in it, with never a thought about the works inside. In those days the machinery of government was like that old clock. Everybody believed in it and only looked at the hour hand. Now government machinery is like a clock in a glass case, so that one can look directly into the works and see the wheels turning and whizzing around. Sometimes we become quite frightened over this spring or that wheel, and then I wonder how it is possible for all these complicated parts to tell the right time. I have lost my childish belief in the rightness of the old clock. That is the weakness of this age."

Great-grandfather would talk on until he became quite angry. He and Frederick could not agree, yet they could not bear to be separated—"just like old times and new." Both of them felt this—and so did our whole family—when Frederick was to set out on his journey to faraway America. It was on business for the company, so the journey had to be made. To Great-grandfather, it was a sad parting, and it seemed a long, long journey—all the way across a great ocean, and to the other side of the globe.

"You shall get a letter from me every fortnight," Frederick promised. "And faster than any letter can go, you shall hear from me by telegraph. The days will be like hours, and the hours like minutes."

By telegraph we received Frederick's greeting to us from England, just as he boarded the steamship. Sooner than any letter could reach us, even though the swift sailing clouds had been our postman, came greetings from America, where Frederick had landed only a few hours before.

"What a glorious and divine inspiration has been granted our age," said Great-grandfather. "It is a true blessing to the human race."

"And it was in our country," I said, "that the natural principle underlying the telegraph was first understood and stated. Frederick told me so."

"Yes," Great-grandfather said, and he kissed me. "Yes, and I once looked into the kindly eyes that were the first to see and understand this marvelous law of nature— his were the eyes of a child, like yours—and I have shaken his hand." Then he kissed me again.

More than a month had gone by, when a letter came from Frederick with the news that he was engaged to a beautiful and lovable young lady. He was sure that everyone in our family would be delighted with her, and he sent us her photograph. We looked at it first with our bare eyes, and then with a magnifying glass, for the advantage of photographs is not only that they stand close inspection through the strongest glass, but that then you see the full likeness even better. No painter has ever been able to do that, even in the greatest of the ages past.

"If only this discovery had been made earlier, then we could have seen the world's greatest and most illustrious men, face to face. How gentle and good this young girl looks," Great-grandfather said, and stared through the glass.

"Now I know her face, and I shall recognize her the moment she comes in the door."

But that very nearly failed to happen. Fortunately, at home we did not hear of the danger until it had passed.

After a safe and pleasant trip, the young couple reached England. From there, they were to come by steamship to Copenhagen. When they came in sight of the Danish coast—the white sand dunes along the western shore of Jutland—a heavy sea arose and dashed the ship against the shore. The enormous waves threatened to break the grounded ship in pieces.

No lifeboat could reach them. Night fell, but out of the darkness burst a brightly flashing rocket from the shore. It shot far out over the grounded ship and brought a line to those on board. Once this connection between ship and shore was made fast, a rescue buoy was carefully drawn through the rough, tumultuous sea, to the shore. In it was a lovely young woman, safe and sound, and marvelously happy when she and her young husband again stood together on the shore. Every soul on board was saved before the break of day.

Here in Copenhagen we were sound asleep, dreaming neither of grief nor of danger. When we were gathered at the breakfast table, we heard a rumor that an English steamship had been wrecked on the west coast. We grew heartsick with anxiety, but within an hour we received a telegram from those who were dear to us. Frederick and his young bride were saved—they would soon be with us.

Everyone cried, and I cried too. Great-grandfather cried and clasped his hands. I am sure he gave thanks for the age in which we live, for that very day he gave two hundred dollars toward raising a monument to Hans Christian Oersted. When Frederick came home with his bride, and heard of it, he said, "That was right, Great-grandfather. Now let me read to you what Oersted wrote, a great many years ago, about the old times and the new."

THE GREAT SEA SERPENT (1871)

There was a little sea fish of good family, the name of which I don't remember; that the more learned will have to tell you. This little fish had eighteen hundred brothers and sisters, all the same age; they didn't know their father or mother, so they had to care for themselves and swim about on their own, but that was a lot of fun. They had plenty of water to drink—the entire ocean. They didn't think about their food; that was sure to come their way. Each did as he pleased; each would have his own story, but then none of them thought about that.

The sun shone down into the water, making it light and clear. It was a world full of the strangest creatures, some of them enormously big, with great, horrible mouths that could sallow all the eighteen hundred brothers and sisters, but none of them thought about that, either, for none of them had ever been swallowed.

The little ones swam together, close to one another, as the herring and the mackerel swim. As they were swimming along at their best and thinking of nothing in particular, there sank from above, down into the midst of them, with a terrifying noise, a long, heavy thing which seemed to have no end to it; further and further it stretched out, and every one of the small fish that it struck was crushed or got a crack from which he couldn't recover. All the fishes, the small and the big as well, were thrown into a panic. That heavy, horrible thing sank deeper and deeper and grew longer and longer, extending for miles—through the entire ocean. Fishes and snails, everything that swims, everything that creeps or is driven by the currents, saw this fearful thing, this enormous unknown sea eel that all of a sudden had come from above.

What kind of thing was it? Yes, we know! It was the great telegraph cable that people were laying between Europe and America.

There were great fear and commotion among all the rightful inhabitants of the ocean where the cable was laid. The flying fish shot up above the surface as high as he could, and the blowfish sped off like a gunshot across the water, for it can do that; other fishes went to the bottom of the ocean with such haste that they reached it long before the telegraph cable was seen down there, and they scared both the codfish and the flounder, who lived peacefully at the bottom of the ocean and ate their neighbors. A couple of the starfish were so frightened that they turned their stomachs inside out, but in spite of that they lived, for they can do that. Many of the lobsters and crabs got out of their fine shells and had to leave their legs behind.

In all this fright and confusion, the eighteen hundred brothers and sisters had all become separated, never again to know or even meet each other, excepting ten of them who had remained at the same place; and after these had held themselves still for a couple of hours, they recovered from their first fright and began to be curious. They looked about; they looked up and they looked down, and there in the deep they thought they saw the frightful thing that had scared them, scared everyone, big and little. There it lay along the bottom of the ocean, extending as far as they could see; it was quite thin, but then they didn't know how thick it could make itself or how strong it was. It lay very quiet, but that, they thought, could be a trick.

"Let it lie where it is! It doesn't concern us," said the most cautious of the little fish.

But the very smallest one of them insisted on gaining some knowledge as to what that thing might be. It had come down from above, so above one could best find out about it.

And so they swam up to the surface, where there was calm weather. There they met a dolphin, which is a sort of jumping jack, an ocean rover, that can turn somersaults in the water. As these have eyes to see with, he must have seen what had happened and should know all about it. They inquired, but the dolphin had only been thinking of himself and his somersaults, had seen nothing, and didn't know what to answer, so he kept quiet and looked proud.

Thereupon they turned to the seal who had just ducked down; he was more polite, although seals eat small fishes, for today he had had his fill. He knew a little more than the dolphin.

"Many a night I have rested on a wet rock and looked far inland, miles away from here; there live some sneaky creatures who, in their language, are called people; they plot against us, but often we slip away from them, which I know how to do, and that is what the sea eel has done, too. He has been in their power, up there on the earth, for a long, long time, and from there they carried him off on a ship to bring him across the ocean to a distant land. I saw what trouble they had, but they could manage him, because he had become weak on the earth. They laid him down in coils and circles; I heard how he 'ringled' and 'rangled' when they put him down, but still he got away from them. They held onto him with all their might; many hands held fast, but still he slipped away from them and reached the bottom; there he lies now, for a while at least, I think."

"He is rather thin!" said all the little fish.

"They have starved him," said the seal, "but he will soon be himself again, fat and big around. I suppose he is the great sea serpent that people are so afraid of and talk so much about. I had never seen him before and never believed he existed, but now I do; I'm sure he's the sea serpent!" And with that the seal dove down.

"How much he knew! How much he talked!" said all the little fish. "We have never been so enlightened before! If only it isn't all a lie!"

"We could swim down and investigate," said the smallest fish. "On the way, we can hear what others think about it."

"We're not going to move a fin to find out anything more!" said the others, and swam away.

"But I'm going to," said the smallest, and plunged down into deep water.

But the little fish was a considerable distance from the place where "that long sunken thing" lay. He looked and searched in a direction down in the deep water. Never before had he imagined the world to be so big. The herring swam in great masses, each school of them shining like a mighty boat of silver; the mackerel also swam together and looked even more magnificent. There were fishes of all shapes and with markings in all colors. Jellyfish, like half-transparent flowers, simply lay back and let the currents carry them along. Great plants grew up from the bottom of the ocean, as did fathom-high grass and palm-shaped trees, every leaf beset with shining shellfish.

At last the little fish saw a long, dark streak way down and swam toward it; but it was neither fish nor cable; it was the gunwale of a large sunken vessel, the upper and lower decks of which had been broken in two by the force of the ocean. The little fish swam inside, where the many people who had perished with the sinking of the ship had since been washed away, except for two—a young woman lay stretched out with a little child in her arms. The water rocked them to and fro, and they seemed to be asleep. The little fish became quite frightened, for he didn't know that they never again could awaken. Seaweed hung like cultivated foliage over the rail above the fair forms of mother and child. It was so quiet there, so lonely. The little fish hurried away as fast as he could, out to where the water was clearer and there were fishes to see. He hadn't gone far when he met a young and terribly large whale.

"Don't swallow me!" said the little fish. "I'm so small that I'm not even a tiny bite, and it's a great pleasure for me to live!"

"What do you want way down here, where your kind never comes?" asked the whale.

So the little fish told of the strange long eel, or whatever that thing was, which had sunk and scared even the most courageous of ocean creatures.

"Ho, ho!" said the whale, and drew in such a lot of water that he had to make an enormous waterspout when he came to the surface for a breath. "Ho, ho!" he said, "so that was the thing that tickled my back when I turned around! I thought it was a ship's mast that I could use for a back scratcher! However, it wasn't in this location; no, that thing is much farther out. I'll investigate it, though; I have nothing else to do."

And so he swam forth, the little fish following, but not too close, for there would be a powerful stream where the big whale shot through the water.

They met a shark and an old sawfish. These two had also heard of the strange sea eel that was so long and thin; they hadn't seen it, but they wanted to.

Then a catfish appeared. "I'm coming with you!" he said, and took the same course. "If the great sea serpent isn't thicker than a cable, then I'll bite it in two with one bite!" And he opened his mouth and showed his six rows of teeth. "I can bite dents in a ship's anchor, so I can easily bite through that stem!"

"There it is!" said the big whale. "I can see it!" He thought he saw better than the others. "See how it rises, see how it sways, bends, and curves!"

However, this was not the sea serpent, but an exceptionally large eel, who was many yards long, and came closer.

"I've seen him before," said the sawfish. "He's never made much fuss in the ocean here or frightened any big fishes."

And so they talked to him about the new eel and asked if he wanted to join them on their voyage of discovery.

"If that eel is longer than I," said the sea eel, "then something unfortunate will happen."

"That it will!" said the others. "There are enough of us not to have to tolerate it." And then they hurried along.

But now, directly in their way, there appeared a strange monster, bigger than them all. It looked like a floating island that could not hold itself up. It was a very old whale. His head was overgrown with seaweed, his back beset with barnacles and so many oysters and mussels that his black skin was entirely covered with white spots.

"Come along, old fellow," they said. "A new fish has come that we will not tolerate!"

"I'd rather lie where I am," said the old whale. "Leave me in peace. Let me lie. Oh, my, oh, my! I suffer from a dreadful sickness. The only relief I have is when I go up to the surface and get my back above it; then the big, nice birds come and pick at me, and that feels so good, as long they don't drive their beaks in too far; often they go right into my blubber. Just see for yourself! There is a complete skeleton of a bird stuck in my back. That bird struck his claws in too deep and couldn't get loose when I went down to the bottom. Now the little fishes have eaten him. Just see how he looks, and how I look! I have a sickness!"

"That's just imagination!" said the other whale. "I am never sick. No fish is sick!"

"I beg your pardon!" said the old whale. "The eel has a skin disease, the carp has smallpox, and all of us have intestinal worms!"

"Nonsense!" said the shark, and didn't care to hear more; nor did the others; they had something else to do.

Finally, they came to the place where the telegraph cable lay. It had a very long resting place indeed at the bottom of the ocean, from Europe to America, over sandbanks and sea mud, rocky formations and sea-plant wilderness, and, yes, entire forests of coral. The currents down there change, and whirlpools twist around; fishes crowd each other and swim in flocks greater than the countless multitudes of birds that people see when birds of passage are in flight. There are a commotion, a splashing, a humming, and a rushing; a little of that rushing still remains to haunt the big, empty conch shells when we hold them to our ears.

Yes, now they came to the place.

"There lies the animal!" said the big fishes, and the little one said so, too.

They saw the cable, its beginning and end beyond their horizon. Sponges, polyps, and seaweed swayed from the ground, rising and falling over the cable, so that now it was hidden and then visible again. Sea porcupines, snails, and worms moved over it. Gigantic spiders, with whole fringes of vermin on them, crawled along the cable. Dark-blue "sea sausages," or whatever the creatures are called that eat with their entire bodies, lay beside it and smelled this new animal that had come down to lie at the bottom of the ocean. Flounders and codfish turned about in the water, in order to hear what was said from all sides. The starfish, who could hold himself down in the mud and keep his eyes outside, lay and stared to see what would come of all this confusion. The telegraph cable lay motionless. But life and thought were in it; human thoughts went through it.

"That thing is cunning," said the whale. "It's able to hit me in the stomach, and that's my weak point!"

"Let's feel our way," said a polyp. "I have long arms; I have limber fingers. I have touched it. Now I'll feel it a little more firmly." And then he stretched his longest and most flexible arms down to the cable and around it. "It has no scales!" said the polyp. "It has no skin! I don't believe it will ever bear young ones!"

The sea eel laid down alongside the telegraph cable and stretched himself as far as he could. "That thing is longer than I am!" he said. "But it isn't length that counts; one must have skin, stomach, and flexibility!" The whale—that is, the young, strong whale—dove down deeper than he ever had been. "Are you a fish or a plant?" he asked the cable. "Or are you only some piece of work from above that can't thrive down here among us?"

But the telegraph cable didn't answer; it had no means of contacting anyone at such a location. Thoughts were going through it, people's thoughts, which in a single second were heard from land to land, many hundreds of miles apart.

"Will you answer, or do you want to be broken?" asked the fierce shark, and all the other big fishes asked the same. "Will you answer, or do you want to be broken?"

The cable didn't move, but it had its own private thoughts, which it had a right to have, considering that it was filled with other's thoughts. "Let them break me; then I'll be hauled up and put in order again—that has happened to others of my kind who were in shallower waters." And so it didn't answer; it had something else to do; it telegraphed and thereby did its just duty at the bottom of the sea.

Up above, the sun was going down, as people say. It blazed like the reddest fire, and all the clouds in the heavens glowed with a fiery hue, each more magnificent than the other.

"Now we're getting the red lighting," said the polyps, "and we may be able to see the thing better, if necessary."

"At it! At it!" shouted the shark, showing all his teeth.

"At it! At it!" said the swordfish, and the whale, and the sea eel. They rushed forward, the shark leading, but just as he was about to bite the cable, the swordfish, out of pure anxiety, ran his saw right into the back of the shark; that was a great mistake, and the shark had no strength left to bite. Everything became muddled in the mud. Big fishes, little fishes, "sea sausages," and snails ran into one another, ate each other—clashed and gnashed. The cable lay still and attended to its own business, as one should do.

The dark night brooded above; but in the ocean the millions and millions of small living creatures lighted it. Crawfish, not even as big as a pinhead, gave out light. It is quite wondrous, but now that's the way it is.

The ocean creatures looked at the telegraph cable. "What is that thing, and what isn't it?" Yes, that was the question.

Presently an old sea cow appeared. People call these mermaids or mermen. This one was a she, and had a tail and two short arms to splash with; she wore seaweed and parasites over her breasts and head, and she was proud of this.

"Are you seeking knowledge and wisdom?" she said. "I am the only one who can give you this; but in return I demand that you guarantee safe pasturage on the bottom of the ocean for me and mine. I am a fish like you are, but I am also a crawling animal, through practice. I am the wisest in the ocean; I know about everything that moves down here and about all that goes on up above. That thing you are pondering over is from above, and whatever falls down from up there is dead, or will be dead, and powerless; let it lie there for what it is. It's only a man-made invention."

"I believe there is more to it than that!" said the little fish.

"Hold your tongue, mackerel!" said the big sea cow.

"Stickleback!" said the others, and that was even more insulting.

And the sea cow explained further to them that this alarming thing, which, as a matter of fact, hadn't uttered a single sound, was in its entirety nothing more than some new device from the dry land, and she delivered a little lecture about people's deceitfulness. "They want to catch us," she said; "that's all they live for. They stretch out nets for us, and come with bait on hooks to tempt us. That thing there is some sort of big string that they think we are going to bite. They are so stupid! But we are not! Don't touch that junk; in time it will unravel and all turn to dust and mud. Everything that comes from up there cracks and breaks—is good for nothing!"

"Good for nothing!" said the other ocean creatures, and held onto the sea cow's opinion, so as to have an opinion.

The little fish, however, had his own thoughts. "Perhaps that enormously long, thin serpent is the most wonderful fish in the ocean. I have a feeling it is."

"The most wonderful," say we humans, too, and we say it with knowledge and assurance.

The great sea serpent has long been the theme of song and story. It was conceived and born by man's ingenuity and laid on the bottom of the ocean, stretching from the eastern to the western lands, and carrying messages as swiftly as light flashes from the sun to our earth. It grows, grows in power and length, grows year after year, through all oceans, around the world; it is beneath the stormy seas and the glass-clear waters, where the skipper, as if sailing through transparent air, looks down and sees crowds of fishes resembling many-colored fireworks.

Deepest down of all lies the outstretched serpent, a blessed Midgard snake, which bites its own tail as it encircles Earth. Fishes and other sea creatures clash with it; they do not understand that thing from above. People's thoughts rush noiselessly, in all languages, through the serpent of science, for both good and evil; the most wondrous of the ocean's wonders is our time's—

GREAT SEA SERPENT.

"DANCE, DANCE, DOLL OF MINE!" (1871)

Yes, this is a song for very small children!" declared Aunt Malle. "As much as I should like to, I cannot follow this 'Dance, Dance, Doll of Mine!'"

But little Amalie could; she was only three years old, played with dolls, and brought them up to be just as wise as Aunt Malle.

There was a student who came to the house to help her brothers with their lessons, and he frequently spoke to little Amalie and her dolls; he spoke differently from anyone else, and the little girl found him very amusing, although Aunt Malle said he didn't know how to converse with children—their little heads couldn't possibly grasp that silly talk. But little Amalie did. Yes, the student even taught her the whole song, "Dance, Dance, Doll of Mine!" and she sang it to her three dolls; two were new, one a girl doll and the other a boy doll, but the third doll was old; her name was Lise-moér. She also heard the song, and was even in it.

Dance, dance, doll of mine!
Girl doll's dress is very fine.
Boy doll is a dandy, too;
He wears gloves and hat and shoe;
White pants, blue coat, him adorn;
On his toe he has a corn.
He is fine and she is fine.
Dance, dance, doll of mine!

Old doll's name is Lise-moér;
She is from the year before;
Hair is new; it's made of flax,
Forehead polished up with wax.
Young again, not old and done.
Come along, my cherished one,
Let us dance a fast gavotte;
To watch it is worth a lot.

Dance, dance, doll of mine!
Watch your steps and get in line;
One foot forward; watch your feet.
Dancing makes you slender, sweet.
Bow and twist and turn around;
That will make you hale and sound.
What a sight it is to see!
You are doing fine, all three.

And the dolls understood the song; little Amalie understood it, and so did the student, but then he had written it himself and said it was excellent. Only Aunt Malle didn't understand it; she had passed over the fence of youth. "Silly song!" she said.

But not little Amalie! She sings it. It is from her that we know it.

THE GARDENER AND THE
NOBLE FAMILY (1872)

About four miles from the city stood an old manor house with thick walls, towers, and pointed gables. Here lived, but only in the summer season, a rich and noble family. Of all the different estates they owned, this was the best and the most beautiful; on the outside it looked as if it had just been cast in a foundry, and the inside was made for comfort and ease. The family coat of arms was carved in stone over the gate; beautiful roses climbed about the arms and the balconies; the courtyard was covered with grass; there were red thorn and whitethorn, and many rare flowers even outside the greenhouse.

The owners of the manor house also had a very skillful gardener. It was a pleasure to see the flower garden, the orchard, and the vegetable garden. A part of the manor's original old garden was still there, consisting of a few boxtree hedges cut so that they formed crowns and pyramids. Behind these stood two old, mighty trees, almost always without leaves, and one might easily think that a storm or a waterspout had scattered great lumps of dirt on their branches, but each lump was a bird's nest. Here, from time immemorial, a screaming swarm of crows and rooks had built their nests; it was a regular bird town, and the birds were the owners, the manor's oldest family—the real lordship! The people below meant nothing to them; they tolerated these crawling creatures, even if every now and then they shot with their guns, making the birds' backbones shiver, so that every bird flew up in fear and cried, "Rak! Rak!"

The gardener often spoke to the noble family about cutting down the old trees; they did not look well, and by taking them away, they might also get rid of the shrieking birds, which then would probably look for another place. But the family did not want to give up either the trees or the swarm of birds; that was something the manor could not lose, something from the olden times, which should never be forgotten.

"Why, those trees are the birds' heritage by this time, so let them keep them, my good Larsen!" Larsen was the gardener's name, but that is of very little consequence to this story.

"Haven't you space enough to work in, little Larsen? Have you not the flower garden, the greenhouse, the orchard, and the vegetable garden?"

Yes, those he had, and he cared for them; he kept them in order and cultivated them with affection and ability, and that the noble family knew; but they did not conceal from him that they often saw flowers and tasted fruits in other people's homes that surpassed what they had in their garden, and that made the gardener sad, for he always wished to do his best and really did his best. He was goodhearted and a good and faithful worker.

One day the noble family sent for him and told him, very kindly, that the day before, at some distinguished friend's home, they had eaten apples and pears that were so juicy and so well flavored that they and all the other guests had expressed their admiration. It was doubtful if the fruits were native, but they ought to be imported and grown here, provided the climate would permit it. It was known that they had been bought from the finest fruit dealer in the city, and it was decided that the gardener was to go there and find out where these apples and pears came from and then order some slips for grafting. The gardener knew the fruit dealer well, because he was the very person to whom he sold the superfluous fruit that grew in the manor garden.

And the gardener went to town and asked the dealer where he got those highly praised apples and pears. "Why, they are from your own garden," said the fruit dealer, and showed him both the apples and pears, which he recognized immediately.

How happy the gardener felt! He hurried back to the family and told them that both the apples and the pears were from their own garden. That they couldn't believe! "That's not possible, Larsen! Can you get a written guarantee to that effect from the fruit dealer?"

Yes, that he could, and a written guarantee he brought.

"That certainly is remarkable!" said the noble family.

Now every day great dishes filled with wonderful apples and pears from their own garden were set on the table. Bushels and barrels of these fruits were sent to friends in the city and outside the city; yes, even to foreign lands. This afforded great pleasure; yet the family added that the last two summers had, of course, been remarkably good for tree fruits and these had done very well all over the country.

Some time passed. The family were dinner guests at court. The next day they sent for the gardener. At the royal table they had eaten melons, very juicy and wonderfully flavored, from their majesties' greenhouse.

"You must go to the court gardener, my good Larsen, and let him give you some seeds of those precious melons."

"But the court gardener got his melon seeds from us!" said the gardener, very pleased.

"Then that man knows how to bring the fruit to a higher perfection!" answered the family. "Each melon was splendid."

"Well, then, I really can feel proud!" said the gardener. "I must tell your lordship that the court gardener had had bad luck with his melons this year, and when he saw how beautiful ours looked, and then tasted them, he ordered three of them for the castle."

"Larsen, don't try to tell us that those were melons from our garden."

"I really believe so," said the gardener.

And he went to the court gardener, from whom he got a written guarantee to the effect that the melons on the royal table were from the manor. This was really a big surprise to the family, and they did not keep the story to themselves; the written guarantee was displayed, and melon seeds were sent far and wide, as grafting slips had been earlier.

These slips, the family learned, had taken and begun to bear fruit of an excellent kind. This was named after the family manor, and the name became known in English, German, and French. This, no one had expected. "Let's hope the gardener won't get big ideas about himself," said the family.

But he took it in a different way; he would strive now to be known as one of the best gardeners in the country and to produce something superior out of all sorts of garden stuff every year. And that he did. But often he was told that the very first fruits he brought out, the apples and the pears, were, after all, the best, that all later variations were very inferior to these. The melons were very good, to be sure, though, of course, they belonged to another species; his strawberries might be called delicious, but no better than those grown by other gardeners, and when one year his radishes did not turn out very well, they spoke only of the unsuccessful radishes and not about all the other fine products he had developed.

It almost seemed as if the family felt a relief in saying, "It didn't go well this year, little Larsen!" Yes, they seemed quite happy when they said, "It didn't go well this year!"

Twice a week the gardener brought fresh flowers up to their drawing room, always arranged with such taste and artistry that the colors seemed to appear even brighter.

"You have good taste, Larsen," said the noble family, "but that is a gift from our Lord, not from yourself!"

One day the gardener brought a large crystal bowl; in it floated a water-lily leaf upon which was laid a beautiful blue flower as big as a sunflower.

"The lotus of Hindustan!" exclaimed the family.

They had never seen a lotus flower before. In the daytime it was placed in the sunlight and in the evening under artificial light. Everyone who saw it found it remarkably beautiful and unusual; yes, even the most highborn young lady in the country, the wise and kindhearted princess, said so. The family considered it an honor to present her with the flower, and the princess took it with her to the castle. Then they went down to their garden to pick another flower of the same kind, but none was to be found. So they sent for the gardener and asked him where he got the blue lotus flower.

"We have been looking for it in vain," they said. "We have been in the greenhouses and round about the flower garden!"

"Oh, no, it's not there," said the gardener. "It is only a common flower from the vegetable garden; but, look, isn't it beautiful! It looks like a blue cactus, and yet it is only the flower of the artichoke!"

"You should have told us that immediately!" said the noble family. "Naturally, we supposed it was a rare, foreign flower. You have ridiculed us to the young princess!

She saw the flower in our house and thought it was beautiful; she didn't know the flower, although she knows her botany well, but then, of course, that science has nothing to do with kitchen herbs. How could you do it, Larsen! To place such a flower in our drawing room is enough to make us ridiculous!"

And the gorgeous blue flower from the vegetable garden was taken out of the drawing room, where it didn't belong; yes, and the noble family apologized to the princess and told her that the flower was only a kitchen herb that the gardener had had the idea of exhibiting, and that he had been severely reprimanded for it.

"That was a shame, and very unfair," said the princess. "He has really opened our eyes to a magnificent flower we otherwise would have paid no attention to; he has shown us beauty where we didn't expect to find it. As long as the artichoke is in bloom, our court gardener shall daily bring one of them up to my private room!"

And this was done.

The noble family told the gardener that he could again bring them a fresh artichoke flower.

"It is really beautiful!" they said. "Highly remarkable!" And the gardener was praised.

"Larsen likes that," said the noble family. "He is like a spoiled child."

In the autumn there was a terrific storm. During the night it increased so violently that many of the large trees in the outskirts of the wood were torn up by the roots, and to the great grief of the noble family—yes, they called it grief—but to the gardener's delight, the two big trees with all the birds' nests blew down. Through the storm one could hear the screaming of the crows and the rooks as they beat their wings against the manor windows.

"Now, of course, you are happy, Larsen!" said the noble family. "The storm has felled the trees, and the birds have gone off into the forest. There is nothing from olden times left to see here; every sign and reference has disappeared; it makes us very sad!"

The gardener said nothing, but he thought of what he had long had in his mind, how he could make use of that wonderful, sunny spot, now at his disposal; it could become the pride of the garden and the joy of the family.

The large trees, in falling, had crushed the very old boxtree hedges with all their fancy trimmings. Here he put in a multitude of plants, native plants from the fields and the woods. What no other gardener had ever thought of planting in a manor garden, he planted, giving each its appropriate soil, and sunlight or shadow, according to what the individual plant required. He gave them loving care, and everything grew magnificently.

The juniper tree from the heaths of Jutland rose in shape and color like the Italian cypress; the shiny, thorny Christ's-thorn, evergreen, in the cold of winter and the sun of summer, was beautiful to behold. In the foreground grew ferns of various species; some of them looked as if they were children of the palm tree, others as if they were parents of the pretty plant we call Venushair. Here stood the neglected burdock, so pretty in its freshness that it can be outstanding in a bouquet. The burdock stood in a dry place, but further down, in the moist soil, grew the coltsfoot, also a neglected plant and yet very picturesque with its enormous leaf and its tall stem. Six feet tall, with flower after flower, like an enormous, many-armed candelabra, rose the mullein, just a mere field plant. Here grew the woodruff, the primrose, and the lily of the valley, the wild calla and the fine three-leaved wood sorrel. It was all wonderful to see.

In the front, in rows, grew very tiny pear trees from French soil, fastened to steel wires; by getting plenty of sun and good care they soon bore fruit as large and juicy as in their own country. In place of the two old leafless trees was set a tall flagpole from which Dannebrog—the flag of Denmark—proudly flew; and close by stood another pole, around which the hop tendril twisted and wound its fragrant flower cones in the summer and at harvesttime, but on which in the winter, according to an old custom, oat sheaves were hung, so that the birds could have a good meal during the happy Christmastime.

"Our good Larsen is getting sentimental in his old age," said the family, "but he is true and faithful to us!"

At New Year's, one of the city illustrated papers published a picture of the old manor; it showed the flagpole and the oat sheaves for the birds at the happy Christmastime, and the paper commented that it was a beautiful thought to uphold and honor this old custom, so appropriate to the old manor.

"Anything that Larsen does," said the noble family, "they beat the drum for. He is a lucky man. We should almost be proud to have him!"

But they were not a bit proud of it; they knew they were the masters of the manor, and they could dismiss Larsen, but that they wouldn't do. They were good people, and there are many good people of their kind in the world—and that is fortunate for all the Larsens.

Yes, that is the story of the gardener and the noble family. Now you may think about it!

THE CRIPPLE (1872)

There was an old manor house where a young, splendid family lived. They had riches and many blessings; they liked to enjoy themselves, and yet they did a lot of good. They wanted to make everybody happy, as happy as they themselves were.

On Christmas Eve a beautifully decorated Christmas tree stood in the large old hall, where fire burned in the fireplaces and fir branches were hung around the old paintings. Here gathered the family and their guests; here they sang and danced.

The Christmas festivities had already been well under way earlier in the evening in the servants' quarters. Here also stood a large fir tree, with lighted red and white candles, small Danish flags, swans and fishing nets cut out of colored paper and filled with candies and other sweets. The poor children from the parish had been invited, and each had its mother along. The mothers didn't pay much attention to the Christmas tree, but looked rather at the Christmas table, where there lay woolen and linen cloths for dresses and trousers. Yes, the mothers and the older children looked at this; only the smallest children stretched out their hands toward the candles, the tinsel, and the flags. This whole gathering had come early in the afternoon; they had been served Christmas porridge and roasted goose with red cabbage. Then when the Christmas tree had been looked over and the gifts distributed, each got a small glass of punch and apple-filled *æbleskiver.*

When they returned to their own humble rooms, they talked about the "good living," by which they meant the good food they had had, and the presents were again thoroughly inspected.

Now, among these folks were Garden-Kirsten and Garden-Ole. They were married, and earned their lodging and their daily bread by weeding and digging in the manor house garden. At every Christmas party they received a goodly share of the gifts, but then they had five children, and all five of them were clothed by the wealthy family.

"Our masters are generous people," they said. "But then they can afford it, and they get pleasure out of it."

"The four children received some good clothing to wear," said Garden-Ole, "but why is there nothing here for the Cripple? They always used to think of him, too, even if he wasn't at the party."

It was the eldest of the children they called the Cripple, although his name was Hans. When little, he had been the most able and the liveliest child, but all of a sudden he had become "loose in the legs," as they called it. He could neither walk nor stand, and now he had been lying in bed for nearly five years.

"Yes, I got something for him, too," said the mother. "But it's nothing much; it is only a book for him to read!"

"That won't make him fat!" said the father.

But Hans was happy for it. He was a very bright boy who enjoyed reading, but who also used his time for working, doing as much as he, who always had to lie bedridden, could, to be of some benefit. He was useful with his hands, knitted woolen stockings, and, yes, even whole bedcovers. The lady at the manor house had praised him and bought them. It was a book of fairy tales Hans had received; in it there was much to read and much to think about.

"It is of no use here in this house," said the parents, "but let him read, for it passes the time, and he can't always be knitting stockings."

Spring came; green leaves and flowers began to sprout, and the weeds, too, as one may call the nettles, even if the psalm speaks so nicely about them:

> *If every king, with power and might,*
> *Marched forth in stately row,*
> *They could not make the smallest leaf*
> *Upon a nettle grow.*

There was much to do in the manor house garden, not only for the gardener and his apprentices, but also for Garden-Kirsten and Garden-Ole.

"It's a lot of hard work," they said. "No sooner have we raked the walks, and made them look nice, than they are stepped on again. There is such a run of visitors at the manor house. How much it must cost! But the owners are rich people!"

"Things are strangely divided," said Ole. "We are our Lord's children, says the pastor. Why such a difference, then?"

"That comes from the fall of man!" said Kirsten.

In the evening they talked about it again, while Cripple-Hans was reading his book of fairy tales. Hard times, work, and toil had made the parents not only hard in the hands but also hard in their judgment and opinion.

They couldn't understand, and consequently couldn't explain, the matter clearly, and as they talked they became more peevish and angry.

"Some people are prosperous and happy; others live in poverty. Why should we suffer because of our first parents' curiosity and disobedience! We would not have behaved as those two did!"

"Yes, we would!" said Cripple-Hans all of a sudden. "It is all here in this book!"

"What's in the book?" asked the parents.

And Hans read for them the old fairy tale about the woodcutter and his wife. They, too, argued about Adam's and Eve's curiosity, which was the cause of their misfortune also. The king of the country then came by. "Follow me home," he said, "and you shall be as well off as I, with a seven-course dinner and a course for display. That course is in a closed tureen, and you must not touch it, for if you do, your days of leisure are over!" "What can there be in the tureen?" said the wife. "That's none of our business," said the husband. "Well, I'm not inquisitive," said the woman, "but I would like to know why we don't dare lift the lid; it must be something delicious!" "I only hope there is nothing mechanical about it," said the man, "such as a pistol shot, which goes off and awakens the whole house!" "Oh, my!" said the woman, and she didn't touch the tureen. But during the night she dreamed that the lid lifted itself, and from the tureen came an odor of the most wonderful punch, such as is served at weddings and funerals. In it lay a large silver coin bearing the following inscription, "If you drink of this punch, you will become the two richest people in the world, and all other people will become beggars!" Just then the woman awoke and told her husband about her dream. "You think too much about that thing," he said. "We could lift it gently," said the woman. "Gently," said the man. And the woman lifted the lid very, very gently. Then two small, sprightly mice sprang out and disappeared into a mousehole. "Good night," said the king. "Now you can go home and lie in your own bed. Don't blame Adam and Eve anymore; you two have been just as inquisitive and ungrateful!"

"Where has that story in the book come from?" said Garden-Ole. "It sounds as if it were meant for us. It is something to think about."

The next day they went to work again, and they were roasted by the sun and soaked to the skin by the rain. Within them were grumbling thoughts as they pondered over the story.

The evening was still light at home after they had eaten their milk porridge.

"Read the story about the woodcutter to us again," said Garden-Ole.

"But there are so many other beautiful stories in this book," said Hans, "so many you don't know."

"Yes, but those I don't care about!" said Garden-Ole. "I want to hear the one I know!"

And he and his wife heard it again.

More than one evening they returned to that story.

"It doesn't quite make everything clear to me," said Garden-Ole. "It's the same with people as it is with sweet milk when it sours; some becomes fine cheese, and the other, only the thin, watery whey; so it is with people; some are lucky in everything they do, live high all their lives, and know no sorrow or want."

This Cripple-Hans heard. His legs were weak, but his mind was bright. He read for them from his book of fairy tales, read about "The Man without Sorrow and Want." Yes, where could he be found, for found he must be! The king lay on his sickbed and could not be cured unless he wore the shirt that had belonged to, and been worn on the body of, a man who could truthfully say that he had never known sorrow or want. A command was sent to every country in the world, to all castles and manors, to all prosperous and happy people. But upon thorough questioning, every one of them was found to have known sorrow and want. "I haven't!" said the swineherd, who sat laughing and singing on the edge of the ditch. "I'm the happiest person!" "Then give us your shirt," said the messengers. "You will be paid for it with half of a kingdom." But he had no shirt at all, and yet he called himself the happiest person!

"He was a fine fellow!" shouted Garden-Ole, and he and his wife laughed as they hadn't laughed for years.

Then the schoolmaster came by.

"How pleased you are!" he said. "That is unusual in this house. Have you won a prize in the lottery?"

"No, it isn't that sort of pleasure," said Garden-Ole. "It is because Hans has been reading to us from his book of fairy tales; he read about 'The Man without Sorrow and Want,' and that fellow had no shirt. Your eyes get moist when you hear such things, and from a printed book, at that! Everyone has a load to carry; one is not alone in that. That, at least, is a comfort!"

"Where did you get that book?" asked the schoolmaster.

"Our Hans got it at Christmastime over a year ago. The manor house family gave it to him. They know he likes reading and, of course, that he is a cripple. At the time, we would rather have seen him get two linen shirts. But that book is unusual; it can almost answer one's thoughts."

The schoolmaster took the book and opened it.

"Let's have the same story again," said Garden-Ole. "I don't quite get it yet. And then he must also read the one about the woodcutter."

These two stories were enough for Ole. They were like two sunbeams pouring into that humble room, into the oppressed thoughts that had made them cross and grumbly. Hans had read the whole book, read it many times. The fairy tales carried him out into the world, where he, of course, could not go because his legs would not carry him. The schoolmaster sat beside his bed; they talked together, and both of them enjoyed it.

From that day on, the schoolmaster visited Hans often when his parents were at work, and every time he came it was a great treat for the boy. How attentively he listened to what the old man told him—about the size of the world and about its many countries, and that the sun was nearly half a million times larger than Earth and so far away that a cannon ball in its course would take twenty-five years to travel from the sun to Earth, while the light beams could reach Earth in eight minutes. Of course, every studious schoolboy knew all that, but to Hans this was all new, and even more wonderful than what he had read in the book of fairy tales.

Two or three times a year the schoolmaster dined with the manor house family, and on one of these occasions he told of how important the book of fairy tales was in the poor house, how alone two stories in it had been the means of spiritual awakening and blessing, that the sickly, clever little boy had, through his reading, brought meditation and joy into the house. When the schoolmaster departed from the manor house, the lady pressed two shiny silver dollars in his hand for little Hans.

"Father and Mother must have them," said the boy, when the schoolmaster brought him the money.

And Garden-Ole and Garden-Kirsten both said, "Cripple-Hans, after all, is also a profit and a blessing to us!"

A couple of days later, when the parents were away at work at the manor house, the owners' carriage stopped outside; it was the kindhearted lady who came, happy that her Christmas gift had afforded so much comfort and pleasure to the boy and his parents. She brought fine bread, fruit, and a bottle of sweet syrup, but what was still more wonderful, she brought him, in a gilded cage, a little blackbird which whistled quite charmingly. The bird cage was placed on the old cabinet close by the boy's bed; there he could see and hear the bird; yes, and people way out on the highway could hear it sing.

Garden-Ole and Garden-Kirsten didn't return home until after the lady had driven away. Even though they saw how happy Hans was, they thought there would only be trouble with the present he had received.

"Rich people don't think very clearly," they said. "Now we have that to look after. Cripple-Hans can't do it. In the end, the cat will get it!"

Eight days went by, and still another eight days. During that time the cat was often in the room without frightening the bird, to say nothing of not harming it.

Then one day a great event occurred. It was in the afternoon, while the parents and the other children were at work, and Hans was quite alone. He had the book of fairy tales in his hand and was reading about the fisherman's wife who got her wishes fulfilled; she wished to be king, and that she became; she wished to be emperor, and that, too, she became; but then she wished to be the good Lord—and thereupon she again sat in the muddy ditch she had come from.

Now that story had nothing whatsoever to do with the bird or the cat, but it happened to be the story he was reading when this occurrence took place; he always remembered that afterward.

The cage stood on the cabinet, and the cat stood on the floor and stared, with its yellow-green eyes, at the bird. There was something in the cat's look that seemed to say, "How beautiful you are! I'd like to eat you!" That Hans understood; he could read it in the cat's face.

"Get away, cat!" he shouted. "You get out of this room!"

It looked as if the cat were getting ready to leap. Hans couldn't reach it and had nothing to throw at it but his greatest treasure, the book of fairy tales. This he threw, but the cover was loose and flew to one side, while the book itself, with all its leaves, flew to the other side. The cat slowly stepped backward in the room and looked at Hans as if to say, "Don't get yourself mixed up in this matter, little Hans! I can walk and I can jump. You can do neither."

Hans was greatly worried and kept his eyes on the cat, while the bird also became uneasy. There wasn't a person he could call; it seemed as if the cat knew that, and it prepared itself to jump again. Hans shook his bedcover at it—he could, remember, use his hands—but the cat paid no attention to the bedcover. And after Hans had thrown it without avail, the cat leaped up onto the chair and onto the sill; there it was closer to the bird.

Hans could feel his own warm blood rushing through his body, but that he didn't think of; he thought only about the cat and the bird. The boy could not get out of bed without help; nor, of course, could he stand on his legs, much less walk. It was as if his heart turned inside him when he saw the cat leap straight from the window onto the cabinet and push the cage so that it overturned. The bird fluttered about bewilderedly in the cage.

Hans screamed; a great shock went through him. And without thinking about it, he sprang out of bed, moved toward the cabinet, chased the cat down, and got hold of the cage, where the bird was flying about in great fear. Holding the cage in his hand, he ran out of the door, onto the road. Then tears streamed from his eyes, and joyously he shouted, "I can walk! I can walk!" He had recovered the use of his limbs. Such a thing can happen, and it had indeed happened to Hans.

The schoolmaster lived nearby, and to him he ran on his bare feet, clad only in his shirt and jacket, and with the bird in the cage.

"I can walk!" he shouted. "Oh, Lord, my God!" And he cried out of sheer joy.

And there was joy in the house of Garden-Ole and Garden-Kirsten. "We shall never live to see a happier day," said both of them.

Hans was called to the manor house. He had not walked that road for many years. The trees and the nut bushes, which he knew so well, seemed to nod to him and say, "Good day, Hans! Welcome back out here!" The sun shone on his face and right into his heart.

The owners of the manor house, that young, blessed couple, let him sit with them, and looked as happy as if he were one of their own family. But the happiest of the two was the lady, for she had given him the book of fairy tales and the little songbird. The bird was now dead, having died of fright, but it had been the means of getting his health back. And the book had brought the awakening to him and his parents; he still had it, and he wanted to keep it and read it, no matter how old he became. Now he also could be of help to his family. He wanted to learn a trade; most of all he wanted to be a bookbinder, "because," he said, "then I can get all the new books to read!"

Later in the afternoon the lady called both his parents up to her. She and her husband had talked about Hans—he was a fine and clever boy, with a keen appreciation of reading and a capacity for learning. Our Lord always rewards the good.

That evening the parents were really happy when they returned home from the manor house, especially Kirsten.

But the following week she cried, for then little Hans went away. He was dressed in good, new clothes. He was a good boy, but now he must travel far away across the sea, go to school, and learn Latin. And many years would pass before they would see him again.

The book of fairy tales he did not take with him, because his parents wanted to keep that in remembrance. And the father often read from it, but only the two stories, for those he understood.

And they had letters from Hans, each one happier than the last. He lived with nice people, in good circumstances. But best of all, he liked to go to school; there was so much to learn and to know. He only wished to live to be a hundred years old, and eventually to become a schoolmaster.

"If we could only live to see it!" said the parents, and held each other's hands.

"Just think of what has happened to Hans!" said Ole. "Our Lord thinks also of the poor man's child! And to think that this should have happened to the Cripple! Isn't it as if Hans might have read it for us from the book of fairy tales!"

THE GATE KEY (1872)

Every key has a history, and there are many kinds of keys—a chamberlain's key, a watch key, Saint Peter's key. We could tell you about all the keys; but now we will only tell about the Councillor's gate key.

It had come into being at a locksmith's, but it might well have believed it had been made by a blacksmith, the way the man had worked on it with hammer and file. It was too large for one's trouser pocket, so it had to be put into the overcoat pocket. There it often lay in utter darkness; yet it had its own special hanging place on the wall, beside a childhood silhouette of the Councillor, in which he looked like a dumpling dressed in a frilled shirt.

It is said that every human being acquires in his character and conduct something from the astrological sign under which he has been born, such as the Bull, the Virgin, or Scorpion, as they are called in the almanacs. The Councillor's wife never mentioned the names of any of these; she said that her husband was born under the sign of the "Wheelbarrow," for he always had to be pushed on. His father had pushed him into an office; his mother had pushed him into matrimony; and his wife had pushed him on to become a councillor; the latter fact, however, she did not mention, being a good, sensible sort of woman who kept quiet in the right place and spoke and pushed in the right place.

He was now along in years—"well proportioned," as he said himself—a well-read man, good-natured, and "key wise" as well, which is something we shall better understand later. He was always in a good humor, loved all mankind, and liked to talk to everybody. If he went into the city, it was difficult to get him home again when his wife was not with him to push him along. He simply had to talk to every acquaintance he met; he had a lot of acquaintances, and this often made him late for dinner. Mrs. Councillor would sit at the window and watch for him. "Here he comes," she would say to the maid; "put the pot on the fire. Now he has stopped to speak to somebody, so take the pot off, or the food will be cooked too much. Now he is finally coming, so put the pot on again!"

But then he wouldn't come, after all. He would stand right under the windows of the house and nod up to her, and if an acquaintance happened to come by then, he could not keep from saying a few words to him; if while he was talking to this one, another one came by, he would take hold of the first by the buttonhole, clasp the other's hand, and shout to a third who wanted to pass by.

This was a heavy trial for the patience of the Councillor's wife. "Councillor! Councillor!" she would shout. "Yes, indeed, that man was born under the sign of the 'Wheelbarrow'; he won't move unless he is being pushed."

He was very fond of visiting bookshops and looking at books and periodicals. He would give his bookseller a small amount of money for the privilege of reading the new books at home, which meant he had permission to cut the leaves of the books along the side but not across the top, for then they could not be sold as new. He was a living newspaper, but a harmless one, and knew everything about engagements, weddings, and funerals, book talk, and town talk. Yes, and he even gave out mysterious hints regarding matters no one else knew anything about. This mysterious information came from the gate key.

The Councillor and his wife had lived in their own house since young and newly married, and they'd had that very same gate key since then; but in those days they hadn't yet come to know of its unusual powers, and not until much later had they learned of these.

It was at the time of King Frederick VI. Copenhagen had no gas then; it had only train-oil lamps; it had no Tivoli Gardens, no Casino Theater, no streetcars, and no railways. It had very few public amusements, compared with what it now has. On Sundays one would go for a walk, out beyond the city gates, to the Assistants' Churchyard, read the inscriptions on the graves, sit down in the grass, eat from one's food basket, and drink a glass of schnapps; or one would go to Frederiksberg, where in front of the palace military music was played; and many people would go to see the royal family rowing about in the small, narrow canals of the park, with the old king himself steering the boat, and he and the queen greeting everyone, without distinction of rank. Well-to-do families from the city would come to this place and drink their afternoon tea. They could get hot water at a small farmhouse in the field outside the park, but they had to bring their own tea service along.

One sunny Sunday afternoon the Councillor and his wife went out to the park, the servant girl walking in front with the tea service, a basket of food, and a "sip of Spendrup's Liqueur."

"Bring the gate key," Mrs. Councillor had said, "so we can get in by ourselves when we return; you know, they lock the gate here at nightfall, and the bell cord was broken this morning! It will be late before we get home! After we've been in Frederiksberg Park, we are going to the Casorti's theater at Vesterbro to see the pantomime, *Harlequin, Chief of the Thrashers*. You see them come down in a cloud; it costs two kroner a person."

And so they went to Frederiksberg, heard the music, saw the royal barges with their waving banners, saw the old king and the white swans. After drinking some very good tea, they hurried away; yet they did not arrive at the theater on time.

The rope-dance act was finished, the dance on stilts was finished, and the pantomime had started; as always, they were too late, and that was the Councillor's fault; every moment on the road, he had stopped to speak to an acquaintance. Within the theater he also found several good friends, and when the performance was over, he and his wife were obliged to accompany a family home at Vesterbro, to enjoy a glass of punch; they would stop for only ten minutes. But this was extended to a whole hour. They talked and talked. Especially entertaining was a Swedish baron, or, perhaps, he was German, for the Councillor hadn't quite caught which—but, on the other hand, the trick with the key that the baron taught him he caught and always remembered. This trick was extraordinarily interesting! He could get the key to answer everything that one asked it, even questions pertaining to the most secret matters. The Councillor's gate key was particularly suitable for performing this trick; its bit was heavy, and this part had to hang downward. The baron let the handle of the key rest on the forefinger of his right hand. There it hung loosely and lightly, and every pulsebeat in his finger could put it into motion and make it swing; and if this failed to happen, the baron understood how unnoticeably to make it turn as he wished. Every turn denoted a letter of the alphabet, and as many letters as desired, from A on through the alphabet, could be indicated by the key. When the first letter of a word was revealed, the key would turn to the opposite side; then the next letter would be sought, and in that manner one got whole words, sentences, and answers to questions. It was all a fake, but at any rate provided amusement; this was the Councillor's first thought, but he did not retain it; he became very engrossed in the key.

"Husband! Husband!" cried Mrs. Councillor. "The Westgate closes at twelve o'clock! We won't get through; we have only a quarter of an hour in which to hurry there."

They had to hurry indeed; several persons who were going into the city soon got ahead of them. They finally approached the outside guardhouse as the clock was striking twelve and the gates were being slammed shut. A number of people were locked out, and among these were the Councillor and his wife, with their servant girl, tea service, and empty food basket. Some stood there greatly frightened, while others were very annoyed, each reacting in his own manner. What could be done? Fortunately, an ordinance had been passed of late that one of the city gates, the Northgate, should not be locked at night, and there pedestrians were allowed to slip through the guardhouse into the city.

The road to the Northgate was by no means short, but the weather was fine, the sky bright with starlight and shooting stars; the frogs were croaking in the ditches and ponds. The party began singing and sang one song after another, but the Councillor did not sing; nor did he look up at the stars or even look at his own feet. He then fell down at the edge of the ditch, the full length of his body alongside it. One might have thought that he had had too much to drink; but it was not the punch, it was the key that had gone to his head and kept on turning there. They finally reached the Northgate guardhouse, slipped across the bridge and into the city.

"Now I am happy again," said the Councillor's wife. "Here's our gate."

"But where is the gate key," said the Councillor. It was neither in the back pocket nor in the side pocket.

"Good gracious!" cried the Councillor's wife. "Haven't you got the key? You must have lost it after letting the Baron use it for the key trick. How will we get in now? You know the bell cord was broken this morning, and the watchman doesn't have a key to our home. We are in a hopeless situation!"

The servant girl began to cry. The Councillor was the only one who showed presence of mind.

"We must break in a windowpane at the grocer's downstairs!" he said, "get him up, and then we can get into the building."

He broke one pane; he broke two. "Petersen!" he shouted, as the put the handle of his umbrella in through the windowpanes. Whereupon the grocer's daughter began to scream loudly. The grocer threw open the door of his shop and shouted, "Watchman!" And before he had a chance to see and recognize the Councillor's family and let them in, the watchman blew his whistle, and in the next street another watchman answered and whistled. People appeared in the windows. "Where is the fire? Where is the cause of all the excitement?" they asked, and were still asking such questions even after the Councillor was in his room. There he removed his overcoat—and in it lay the gate key, not in the pocket, but inside the lining; it had slipped through a hole that should not have been in the pocket.

From that night on, the gate key held a unique and great importance, not only when it was taken out in the evening, but also when remaining at home, for in either case the Councillor would show how clever he was by making the key answer questions. He would think of the most likely answer and then pretend to let the key give it. Finally, he himself came to believe in the power of the key.

That was not so of the Pharmacist, however, a young man closely related to the Councillor's wife. The Pharmacist had a good head, a critical mind; he had, as mere schoolboy, sent in critical articles on books and the theater, but without his signature, which is always important. He was what one calls a *bel esprit,* but he by no means believed in spirits, and, least of all, key spirits.

"Yes, I believe, I believe," he said, "blessed Mr. Councillor, I believe in gate keys and all key spirits as firmly as I believe in that new science which is beginning to become known of the table dance and the spirits in old and new furniture. Have you heard about that? I have! I have doubted—you know I am a skeptic—but I have been converted by reading—in a quite reliable foreign paper—a dreadful story. Councillor, can you imagine! I will give you the story as I read it. Two clever children had seen their parents raise the spirits in a large dining-room table. The little ones were alone and decided they would try, in the same manner, to rub life into an old chest of drawers. Life came, for a spirit was awakened; but it did not tolerate the commands of mere children; it arose, and the chest of drawers creaked; it then shot out the drawers, and with its wooden legs put each of the children in a separate drawer. The chest of drawers then ran off with them, out the open door, down the stairs, into the street, and over to the canal, where it jumped out into the water and drowned both the children. Their little bodies were given Christian burial, but the chest of drawers was taken to the town hall, tried for murder, and burned alive in the marketplace! I have read this," said the Pharmacist, "in a foreign paper; it is not something I have invented myself. This is the truth, and may the key take me if it isn't! I swear to it—on my oath!"

The Councillor found that such talk was all too much like a coarse joke. The two could never speak agreeably about the key. The Pharmacist was key ignorant.

The Councillor made progress in his key knowledge; the key was his diversion and channel of wisdom.

One evening, as the Councillor was getting ready to go to bed and was half undressed, there was a knock on the front door. It was the shopkeeper from downstairs who was calling at this late hour; he, too, was half undressed, but he had suddenly had a thought, he said, which he was afraid he would not be able to retain through the night.

"It is my daughter Lotte-Lene I must talk about. She is a beautiful girl, and has been confirmed, and now I would like to see her well provided for."

"But I am not as yet a widower!" said the Councillor, and chuckled, "and I have no son to offer her."

"You must understand me, Councillor," said the man from downstairs. "She can play the piano, and she can sing; you must be able to hear her upstairs. You have no idea of all the things that little girl is able to do; she can talk and entertain people. She is made for the stage, and that is a good course for pretty girls of good families to take; they may even have an opportunity to marry a count, though neither I nor Lotte-Lene are thinking of that. She can indeed sing and play the piano, so the other day I took her up to the singing school. She sang; but she doesn't have a beer bass, as I call it in women, nor does she shriek those very high canary-bird notes which they now demand in singers, and so they advised her strongly against pursuing that career. Well, I thought, if she can't become a singer, she can always become an actress; that only requires the ability to speak. Today I talked about it to the instructor as they call him. 'Is she well read?' he asked. 'No,' I said, 'not at all.' 'But it is necessary for an actress to be well read!' said he. She still has time for that, was my opinion; and then I went home. She can go to a rental library and read what is to be had there, I thought.

"But then tonight, while I was undressing, it occurred to me—why rent books when one can borrow them? The Councillor has plenty of books; let her read them; there is enough reading here for her, and it could be hers gratis!"

"Lotte-Lene is a nice girl," said the Councillor, "a beautiful girl! She shall have books to read. But has she what one calls grit and spirit—aptitude—genius? And, what is equally important, has she luck with her?"

"She has twice won in the lottery," said the grocer from downstairs. "Once she won a clothes cabinet, and another time six pairs of bed sheets; that I call luck, and that she has!"

"I shall ask the key," said the Councillor. And he placed the key on his right forefinger, and on the grocer's right forefinger as well, and then the key swung and gave out letter after letter.

The key said, "Victory and luck!" And so Lotte-Lene's future was decided.

The Councillor at once gave her two books to read, *Dyveke* and Knigge's *Social Intercourse*.

That night marked the beginning of a closer acquaintance between Lotte-Lene and the Councillor and his wife. She would come upstairs to the couple, and the Councillor found her to be a sensible girl; she believed in him and the key. The Councillor's wife saw something childish and innocent in the frankness with which she would at every moment show her great ignorance. The couple was fond of her, he in his way and she in hers, and Lotte-Lene was fond of them.

"It smells so lovely upstairs," Lotte-Lene would say. There was an odor, a fragrance, an apple fragrance, in the hallway, where the Councillor's wife had put away a whole barrel of graystone apples. There was also an incense odor of roses and lavender throughout all the rooms. "There is something refined in that!" Lotte-Lene would say.

Then, too, her eyes were pleased by the many pretty flowers the Councillor's wife always had. Even in the middle of winter, lilacs and cherry-tree slips bloomed here. The leafless twigs were cut off and put into water and in the warm room soon bore leaves and flowers.

"One would have thought that all life was gone from these naked branches, but see how they rise from the dead. It has never occurred to me before," said Lotte-Lene, "how wonderful nature is!"

And the Councillor let her look at his "key book," in which were written strange things the key had said—even about the half of an apple cake that had disappeared from the cupboard on the very evening that the servant girl had had her sweetheart there for a visit. The Councillor had asked his key. "Who has eaten the apple cake, the cat or the sweetheart?" and the key had replied, "The sweetheart." The Councillor had already thought so before asking the key; and the servant girl had confessed, "That cursed key knows everything!"

"Yes, isn't it strange!" said the Councillor. "That key, that key! And about Lotte-Lene it has said, 'Victory and luck.' That we shall see! I swear to it."

"That's wonderful" said Lotte-Lene.

The Councillor's wife was not so confident, but she did not express her doubts when her husband was within hearing distance. She later told Lotte-Lene in confidence that the Councillor, when a young man, had been quite taken with the theater. Had someone pushed him a little in that direction, he surely would have become an actor; his family, however, had pushed him in the opposite direction. But he had still aspired to the stage, and to further that ambition he had written a play.

"This is a great secret that I am entrusting you with, little Lotte-Lene. The play was not bad; it was accepted at the Royal Theater, and then hissed out, and no one has since heard of it, for which I am glad. I am his wife and know him. Now you want such a career, too. I wish you all that is good, but I don't think that things will work out as predicted; I don't believe in the gate key."

Lotte-Lene believed in it, and in that belief she was united with the Councillor. Within their hearts they had a mutual understanding, in all honor and chastity.

The girl had many qualifications that the Councillor's wife valued. Lotte-Lene knew how to make starch from potatoes, make silk gloves from old silk stockings, and recover her silk dancing shoes, although she could afford to buy all her clothes new. She had, as the grocer said, pennies in the table drawer and credit notes in her money safe. She would make just the wife for the Pharmacist, thought the Councillor's wife, but she did not say so, and of course didn't permit the key to say anything about it. The Pharmacist was going to settle down soon and have his own pharmacy in one of the nearest and largest provincial towns.

Lotte-Lene was continually reading *Dyveke* and Knigge's *Social Intercourse*. She kept the two books for two years, and by the end of that time she had learned one, *Dyveke*, by heart—all the parts, although she wished to play only one, that of Dyveke; she did not, however, want to appear at first in the capital, where there is so much envy, and where they would not have her, anyway. She wanted to start her artistic career, as the Councillor called it, in one of the country's large provincial towns. Now that, strangely enough, turned out to be the same place where the youthful Pharmacist had settled down as the youngest of the town's pharmacists.

The great, long-awaited night came on which Lotte-Lene was to make her debut and have "victory and luck," as the key had said. The Councillor was not there, for he lay in his bed, and his wife was nursing him; he had to have warm napkins and camomile tea; the napkins about his body and the tea in his body.

While the couple was absent from the *Dyveke* performance, the Pharmacist was there, and wrote a letter about it to his relative, the Councillor's wife.

"Dyveke's ruff was the best thing about it," he wrote. "If I had had the Councillor's gate key in my pocket, I would have pulled it out and used it as a whistle; she deserved it, and the key deserved it, because of its nasty lie about her 'victory and luck.'"

The Councillor read the letter. It was all spitefulness, he said, key hatred, aimed at that innocent girl. And as soon as he was out of bed and was himself again, he sent a short but poisonous note to the Pharmacist, who in turn replied as if he had seen only jest and good humor in the whole epistle. He thanked him for this and for any future contribution to the revelation of the incomparable worth and significance of keys; next he confided to the Councillor that, apart from his activities as an apothecary, he was writing a great key novel in which all the characters were keys and keys alone. A gate key naturally was the central character and—patterned after the Councillor's gate key—was gifted with prophetic vision and second sight; around this all the other keys had to revolve—the old chamberlain's key, experienced in the splendor and festivity of the court; the watch key, small, refined, and distinguished, but worth only a few pennies at the ironmonger's; the key to the church pew, which counted itself among the clergy, and which, from remaining one night in its keyhole in the church, could see ghosts; the larder key, the wine-cellar key, and the coal-cellar key all appeared, and bowed before, and turned around, the gate key. The sunbeams brightened it into silver, and the wind, that spirit of the Earth, entered its body and made it whistle!

It was the key of all keys; it was the Councillor's gate key. It was now the key of the heavenly gate itself; it was the papal key; it was infallible!

"Wickedness!" said the Councillor. "Great wickedness!"

He and the Pharmacist never saw each other again—except once, and that was at the funeral of the Councillor's wife.

She was the first to die. There was sorrow and emptiness in the house. Even the slips of cherry which had thrown out fresh roots and flowers seemed to mourn and fade away; they stood forgotten, for she was not there to tend them.

The Councillor and the Pharmacist walked behind her coffin, side by side, as the two nearest relations of the departed. This was not the time, nor were they in the mood, for quarreling. Lotte-Lene tied the mourning crepe around the Councillor's hat. She was living in the house again, having long since returned without victory and luck in her career. Yet that still might come; Lotte-Lene had a future before her; the key had said so, and the Councillor had said so.

She went up to him. They talked about the departed and they wept, for Lotte-Lene was tenderhearted; but when they talked about the art, Lotte-Lene felt strong. "Life in the theater is charming," she said, "but there is so much nonsense and envy! I would rather go my own way. Myself first, then art!"

Knigge had told the truth in his chapter about actors; that she was aware of; the key had not told the truth, but she never spoke of this to the Councillor; she was fond of him. Besides, the gate key was his comfort and relief during the whole year of mourning. He gave it questions, and it gave him answers.

And when the year had passed, and he and Lotte-Lene were sitting together one inspiring evening; he asked the key, "Will I marry, and whom will I marry?" No one pushed him, but he pushed the key, and it answered, "Lotte-Lene!"

So it was said, and Lotte-Lene became Mrs. Councillor.

"Victory and luck!"

And these words had been said before—by the gate key.

AUNTY TOOTHACHE (1872)

Where did we get this story? Would you like to know?
We got it from the basket that the wastepaper is thrown into.

Many a good and rare book has been taken to the delicatessen store and the grocer's, not to be read, but to be used as wrapping paper for starch and coffee, beans, for salted herring, butter, and cheese. Used writing paper has also been found suitable.

Frequently one throws into the wastepaper basket what ought not to go there.

I know a grocer's assistant, the son of a delicatessen store owner. He has worked his way up from serving in the cellar to serving in the front shop; he is a well-read person, his reading consisting of the printed and written matter to be found on the paper used for wrapping. He has an interesting collection, consisting of several important official documents from the wastepaper baskets of busy and absent-minded officials, a few confidential letters from one lady friend to another—reports of scandal which were not to go further, not to be mentioned by a soul. He is a living salvage institution for more than a little of our literature, and his collection covers a wide field. He has the run of his parents' shop and that of his present master and has there saved many a book, or leaves of a book, well worth reading twice.

He has shown me his collection of printed and written matter from the wastepaper basket, the most valued items of which have come from the delicatessen store. A couple of leaves from a large composition book lay among the collection; the unusually clear and neat handwriting attracted my attention at once.

"This was written by the student," he said, "the student who lived opposite here and died about a month ago. He suffered terribly from toothache, as one can see. It is quite amusing to read. This is only a small part of what he wrote; there was a whole book and more besides. My parents gave the student's landlady half a pound of green soap for it. This is what I have been able to save of it."

I borrowed it, I read it, and now I tell it.

The title was:

AUNTY TOOTHACHE

I

Aunty gave me sweets when I was little. My teeth could stand it then; it didn't hurt them. Now I am older, am a student, and still she goes on spoiling me with sweets. She says I am a poet.

I have something of the poet in me, but not enough. Often when I go walking along the city streets, it seems to me as if I am walking in a big library; the houses are the bookshelves; and every floor is a shelf with books. There stands a story of everyday life; next to it is a good old comedy, and there are works of all scientific branches, bad literature, and good reading. I can dream and philosophize among all this literature.

There is something of the poet in me, but not enough. No doubt many people have just as much of it in them as I, though they do not carry a sign or a necktie with the word "Poet" on it. They and I have been given a divine gift, a blessing great enough to satisfy oneself, but altogether too little to be portioned out again to others. It comes like a ray of sunlight and fills one's soul and thoughts; it comes like the fragrance of a flower, like a melody that one knows and yet cannot remember from where.

The other evening I sat in my room and felt an urge to read, but I had no book, no paper. Just then a leaf, fresh and green, fell from the lime tree, and the breeze carried it in through the window to me. I examined the many veins in it; a little insect was crawling across them, as if it were making a thorough study of the leaf. This made me think of man's wisdom: we also crawl about on a leaf; our knowledge is limited to that only, and yet we unhesitatingly deliver a lecture on the whole big tree—the root, the trunk, and the crown—the great tree comprised of God, the world, and immortality—and of all this we know only a little leaf!

As I was sitting there, I received a visit from Aunty Mille. I showed her the leaf with the insect and told her of my thoughts in connection with these. And her eyes lit up.

"You are a poet!" she said. "Perhaps the greatest we have. If I should live to see this, I would go to my grave gladly. Ever since the brewer Rasmussen's funeral, you have amazed me with your powerful imagination."

So said Aunty Mille, and she then kissed me.

Who was Aunty Mille, and who was Rasmussen the brewer?

II

We children always called our mother's aunt "Aunty"; we had no other name for her.

She gave us jam and sweets, although they were very injurious to our teeth; but the dear children were her weakness, she said. It was cruel to deny them a few sweets, when they were so fond of them. And that's why we loved Aunty so much.

She was an old maid; as far back as I can remember, she was always old. Her age never seemed to change.

In earlier years she had suffered a great deal from toothache, and she always spoke about it; and so it happened that her friend, the brewer Rasmussen, who was a great wit, called her Aunty Toothache.

He had retired from the brewing business some years before and was then living on the interest of his money. He frequently visited Aunty; he was older than she. He had no teeth at all—only a few black stumps. When a child, he had eaten too much sugar, he told us children, and that's how he came to look as he did.

Aunty could surely never have eaten sugar in her childhood, for she had the most beautiful white teeth. She took great care of them, and she did not sleep with them at night!—said Rasmussen the brewer. We children knew that this was said in malice, but Aunty said he did not mean anything by it.

One morning, at the breakfast table, she told us of a terrible dream she had had during the night, in which one of her teeth had fallen out.

"That means," she said, "that I shall lose a true friend!"

"Was it a false tooth?" asked the brewer with a chuckle. "If so, it can only mean that you will lose a false friend!"

"You are an insolent old man!" said Aunty, angrier than I had seen her before or ever have since.

She later told us that her old friend had only been teasing her; he was the finest man on Earth, and when he died he would become one of God's little angels in Heaven.

I thought a good deal of this transformation and wondered if I would be able to recognize him in this new character.

When Aunty and he had been young, he had proposed to her. She had settled down to think it over, had thought too long, and had become an old maid, but always remained his true friend.

And then Brewer Rasmussen died. He was taken to his grave in the most expensive hearse and was followed by a great number of folks, including people with orders and in uniform.

Aunty stood dressed in mourning by the window, together with all of us children, except our little brother, whom the stork had brought a week before. When the hearse and the procession had passed and the street was empty, Aunty wanted to go away from the window, but I did not want to; I was waiting for the angel, Rasmussen the brewer; surely he had by now become one of God's bewinged little children and would appear.

"Aunty," I said, "don't you think that he will come now? Or that when the stork again brings us a little brother, he'll then bring us the angel Rasmussen?"

Aunty was quite overwhelmed by my imagination, and said, "That child will become a great poet!" And this she kept repeating all the time I went to school, and even after my confirmation and, yes, still does now that I am a student.

She was, and is, to me the most sympathetic of friends, both in my poetical troubles and dental troubles, for I have attacks of both.

"Just write down all your thoughts," she said, "and put them in the table drawer! That's what Jean Paul did; he became a great poet, though I don't admire him; he does not excite one. You must be exciting! Yes, you will be exciting!"

The night after she said this, I lay awake, full of longings and anguish, with anxiety and fond hopes to become the great poet that Aunty saw and perceived in me; I went through all the pains of a poet! But there is an even greater pain—toothache—and it was grinding and crushing me; I became a writhing worm, with a bag of herbs and a mustard plaster.

"I know all about it," said Aunty. There was a sorrowful smile on her lips, and her white teeth glistened.

But I must begin a new chapter in my own and my aunt's story.

III

I had moved to a new flat and had been living there a month. I was telling Aunty about it.

"I live with a quiet family; they pay no attention to me, even if I ring three times. Besides, it is a noisy house, full of sounds and disturbances caused by the weather, the wind, and the people. I live just above the street gate; every carriage that drives out or in makes the pictures on the walls move about. The gate bangs and shakes the house as if there were an earthquake. If I am in bed, the shocks go right through all my limbs, but that is said to be strengthening to the nerves. If the wind blows, and it is always blowing in this country, the long window hooks outside swing to and fro, and strike against the wall. The bell on the gate to the neighbor's yard rings with every gust of wind.

"The people who live in the house come home at all hours, from late in the evening until far into the night; the lodger just above me, who in the daytime gives lessons on the trombone, comes home the latest and does not go to bed before he has taken a little midnight promenade with heavy steps and in iron-heeled shoes.

"There are no double windows. There is a broken pane in my room, over which the landlady has pasted some paper, but the wind blows through the crack despite that and produces a sound similar to that of a buzzing wasp. It is like the sort of music that makes one go to sleep. If at last I fall asleep, I am soon awakened by the crowing of the cocks. From the cellarman's hen coop, the cocks and hens announce that it will soon be morning. The small ponies, which have no stable, but are tied up in the storeroom under the staircase, kick against the door and the paneling as they move about.

"The day dawns. The porter, who lives with his family in the attic, comes thundering down the stairs; his wooden shoes clatter; the gate bangs and the house shakes. And when all this is over, the lodger above begins to occupy himself with gymnastic exercises; he lifts a heavy iron ball in each hand, but he is not able to hold onto them, and they are continually falling on the floor, while at the same time the young folks in the house, who are going to school, come screaming with all their might. I go to the window and open it to get some fresh air, and it is most refreshing—when I can get it, and when the young woman in the back building is not washing gloves in soapsuds, by which she earns her livelihood. Otherwise it is a pleasant house, and I live with a quiet family!"

This was the report I gave Aunty about my flat, though it was livelier at the time, for the spoken word has a fresher sound than the written.

"You are a poet!" cried Aunty. "Just write down all you have said, and you will be as good as Dickens! Indeed, to me, you are much more interesting. You paint when you speak. You describe your house so that one can see it. It makes one shudder. Go on with your poetry. Put some living beings into it—people, charming people, especially unhappy ones."

I wrote down my description of the house as it stands, with all its sounds, its noises, but included only myself. There was no plot in it. That came later.

IV

It was during wintertime, late at night, after theater hours; it was terrible weather; a snowstorm raged so that one could hardly move along.

Aunty had gone to the theater, and I went there to take her home; it was difficult for one to get anywhere, to say nothing of helping another. All the hiring carriages were engaged. Aunty lived in a distant section of the town, while my dwelling was close to the theater. Had this not been the case, we would have had to take refuge in a sentry box for a while.

We trudged along in the deep snow while the snowflakes whirled around us. I had to lift her, hold onto her, and push her along. Only twice did we fall, but we fell on the soft snow.

We reached my gate, where we shook some of the snow from ourselves. On the stairs, too, we shook some off, and yet there was still enough almost to cover the floor of the anteroom.

We took off our overcoats and boots and what other clothes might be removed. The landlady lent Aunty dry stockings and a nightcap; this she would need, said the landlady, and added that it would be impossible for my aunt to get home that night, which was true. Then she asked Aunty to make use of her parlor, where she would prepare a bed for her on the sofa, in front of the door that led into my room and that was always kept locked. And so she stayed.

The fire burned in my stove, the tea urn was placed on the table, and the little room became cozy, if not as cozy as Aunty's own room, where in the wintertime there are heavy curtains before the door, heavy curtains before the windows, and double carpets on the floor, with three layers of thick paper underneath. One sits there as if in a well-corked bottle, full of warm air; still, as I have said, it was also cozy at my place, while outside the wind was whistling.

Aunty talked and reminisced; she recalled the days of her youth; the brewer came back; many old memories were revived.

She could remember the time I got my first tooth, and the family's delight over it. My first tooth! The tooth of innocence, shining like a little drop of milk—the milk tooth!

When one had come, several more came, a whole rank of them, side by side, appearing both above and below—the finest of children's teeth, though these were only the "vanguard," not the real teeth, which have to last one's whole lifetime.

Then those also appeared, and the wisdom teeth as well, the flank men of each rank, born in pain and great tribulation.

They disappear, too, sometimes every one of them; they disappear before their time of service is up, and when the very last one goes, that is far from a happy day; it is a day for mourning. And so then one considers himself old, even if he feels young.

Such thoughts and talk are not pleasant. Yet we came to talk about all this; we went back to the days of my childhood and talked and talked. It was twelve o'clock before Aunty went to rest in the room nearby.

"Good night, my sweet child," she called. "I shall now sleep as if I were in my own bed."

And she slept peacefully; but otherwise there was no peace either in the house or outside. The storm rattled the windows, struck the long, dangling iron hooks against the house, and rang the neighbor's backyard bell. The lodger upstairs had come home. He was still taking his little nightly tour up and down the room; he then kicked off his boots and went to bed and to sleep; but he snores so that anyone with good ears can hear him through the ceiling.

I found no rest, no peace. The weather did not rest, either; it was lively. The wind howled and sang in its own way; my teeth also began to be lively, and they hummed and sang in their way. An awful toothache was coming on.

There was a draft from the window. The moon shone in upon the floor; the light came and went as the clouds came and went in the stormy weather. There was a restless change of light and shadow, but at last the shadow on the floor began to take shape. I stared at the moving form and felt an icy-cold wind against my face.

On the floor sat a figure, thin and long, like something a child would draw with a pencil on a slate, something supposed to look like a person, a single thin line forming the body, another two lines the arms, each leg being but a single line, and the head having a polygonal shape.

The figure soon became more distinct; it had a very thin, very fine sort of cloth draped around it, clearly showing that the figure was that of a female.

I heard a buzzing sound. Was it she or the wind which was buzzing like a hornet through the crack in the pane?

No, it was she, Madam Toothache herself! Her terrible highness, *Satania Infernalis*! God deliver and preserve us from her!

"It is good to be here!" she buzzed. "These are nice quarters—mossy ground, fenny ground! Gnats have been buzzing around here, with poison in their stings; and now I am here with such a sting. It must be sharpened on human teeth. Those belonging to the fellow in bed here shine so brightly. They have defied sweet and sour things, heat and cold, nutshells and plum stones; but I shall shake them, make them quake, feed their roots with drafty winds, and give them cold feet!"

That was a frightening speech! She was a terrible visitor!

"So you are a poet!" she said. "Well, I'll make you well versed in all the poetry of toothache! I'll thrust iron and steel into your body! I'll seize all the fibers of your nerves!"

I then felt as if a red-hot awl were being driven into my jawbone; I writhed and twisted.

"A splendid set of teeth," she said, "just like an organ to play upon! We shall have a grand concert, with jew's-harps, kettledrums, and trumpets, piccolo-flute, and a trombone in the wisdom tooth! Grand poet, grand music!"

And then she started to play; she looked terrible, even if one did not see more of her than her hand, the shadowy, gray, ice-cold hand, with the long, thin, pointed fingers; each of them was an instrument of torture; the thumb and the forefinger were the pincers and wrench; the middle finger ended in a pointed awl; the ring finger was a drill, and the little finger squirted gnat's poison.

"I am going to teach you meter!" she said. "A great poet must have a great toothache, a little poet a little toothache!"

"Oh, let me be a little poet!" I begged. "Let me be nothing at all! And I am not a poet; I have only fits of poetry, like fits of toothache. Go away, go away!"

"Will you acknowledge, then, that I am mightier than poetry, philosophy, mathematics, and all the music?" she said. "Mightier than all those notions that are painted on canvas or carved in marble? I am older than every one of them. I was born close to the Garden of Paradise, just outside, where the wind blew and the wet toadstools grew. It was I who made Eve wear clothes in the cold weather, and Adam also. Believe me, there was power in the first toothache!"

"I believe it all," I said. "But go away, go away!"

"Yes, if you will give up being a poet, never put verse on paper, slate, or any sort of writing material, then I will let you off; but I'll come again if you write poetry!"

"I swear!" I said; "only let me never see or feel you any more!"

"See me you shall, but in a more substantial shape, in a shape more dear to you than I am now. You shall see me as Aunty Mille, and I shall say, 'Write poetry, my sweet boy! You are a great poet, perhaps the greatest we have!' But if you believe me and begin to write poetry, then I will set music to your verses and play them on your mouth harp. You sweet child! Remember me when you see Aunty Mille!"

Then she disappeared.

At our parting I received a thrust through my jawbone like that of a red-hot awl; but it soon subsided, and then I felt as if I were gliding along the smooth water; I saw the white water lilies, with their large green leaves, bending and sinking down under me; they withered and dissolved, and I sank, too, and dissolved into peace and rest.

"To die, and melt away like snow!" resounded in the water. "To evaporate into air, to drift away like the clouds!"

Great, glowing names and inscriptions on waving banners of victory, the letters patent of immortality, written on the wing of an ephemera, shone down to me through the water.

The sleep was deep, a sleep now without dreams. I did not hear the whistling wind, the banging gate, the ringing of the neighbor's gate bell, or the lodger's strenuous gymnastics.

What happiness!

Then came a gust of wind so strong that the locked door to Aunty's room burst open. Aunty jumped up, put on her shoes, got dressed, and came into my room. I was sleeping like one of God's angels, she said, and she had not the heart to awaken me.

I later awoke by myself and opened my eyes. I had completely forgotten that Aunty was in the house, but I soon remembered it and then remembered my toothache vision. Dream and reality were blended.

"I suppose you did not write anything last night after we said good night?" she said. "I wish you had; you are my poet and shall always be!"

It seemed to me that she smiled rather slyly. I did not know if it was the kindly Aunty Mille, who loved me, or the terrible one to whom I had made the promise the night before.

"Have you written any poetry, sweet child?"

"No, no!" I shouted. "You are Aunty Mille, aren't you?"

"Who else?" she said. And it *was* Aunty Mille.

She kissed me, got into a carriage, and drove home.

I wrote down what is written here. It is not in verse, and it will never be printed.

Yes, here ended the manuscript.

My young friend, the grocer's assistant, could not find the missing sheets; they had gone out into the world like the papers around the salted herring, the butter, and the green soap; they had fulfilled their destiny!

The brewer is dead; Aunty is dead; the student is dead, he whose sparks of genius went into the basket. This is the end of the story—the story of Aunty Toothache.

WHAT OLD JOHANNE TOLD (1872)

The wind whistles in the old willow tree. It is as if one were hearing a song; the wind sings it; the tree tells it. If you do not understand it, then ask old Johanne in the poorhouse; she knows about it; she was born here in the parish.

Many years ago, when the King's Highway still lay along here, the tree was already large and conspicuous. It stood, as it still stands, in front of the tailor's whitewashed timber house, close to the ditch, which then was so large that the cattle could be watered there, and where in the summertime the little peasant boys used to run about naked and paddle in the water. Underneath the tree stood a stone milepost cut from a big rock; now it is overturned, and a bramblebush grows over it.

The new King's Highway was built on the other side of the rich farmer's manor house; the old one became a field path; the ditch became a puddle overgrown with duckweed; if a frog tumbled down into it, the greenery was parted, and one saw the black water; all around it grew, and still grow, "muskedonnere," buckbean, and yellow iris.

The tailor's house was old and crooked; the roof was a hotbed for moss and houseleek. The dovecote had collapsed, and starlings built their nests there. The swallows hung nest after nest on the house gable and all along beneath the roof; it was just as if luck itself lived there.

And once it had; now, however, this was a lonely and silent place. Here in solitude lived weak-willed "Poor Rasmus," as they called him. He had been born here; he had played here, had leaped across meadow and over hedge, had splashed, as a child, in the ditch, and had climbed up the old tree. The tree would raise its big branches with pride and beauty, just as it raises them yet, but storms had already bent the trunk a little, and time had given it a crack. Wind and weather have since lodged earth in the crack, and there grow grass and greenery; yes, and even a little serviceberry has planted itself there.

When in spring the swallows came, they flew about the tree and the roof and plastered and patched their old nests, while Poor Rasmus let his nest stand or fall as it liked. His motto was, "What good will it do?"—and it had been his father's, too.

He stayed in his home. The swallows flew away, but they always came back, the faithful creatures! The starling flew away, but it returned, too, and whistled its song again. Once Rasmus had known how, but now he neither whistled nor sang.

The wind whistled in the old willow tree then, just as it now whistles; indeed, it is as if one were hearing a song; the wind sings it; the tree tells it. And if you do not understand it, then ask old Johanne in the poorhouse; she knows about it; she knows about everything of old; she is like a book of chronicles, with inscriptions and old recollections.

At the time the house was new and good, the country tailor, Ivar Ölse, and his wife, Maren, moved into it—industrious, honest folk, both of them. Old Johanne was then a child; she was the daughter of a wooden-shoemaker—one of the poorest in the parish. Many a good sandwich did she receive from Maren, who was in no want of food. The lady of the manor house liked Maren, who was always laughing and happy and never downhearted. She used her tongue a good deal, but her hands also. She could sew as fast as she could use her mouth, and, moreover, she cared for her house and children; there were nearly a dozen children—eleven altogether; the twelfth never made its appearance.

"Poor people always have a nest full of youngsters," growled the master of the manor house. "If one could drown them like kittens and keep only one or two of the strongest, it would be less of a misfortune!"

"God have mercy!" said the tailor's wife. "Children are a blessing from God; they are such a delight in the house. Every child is one more Lord's prayer. If times are bad, and one has many mouths to feed, why, then a man works all the harder and finds out ways and means honestly; our Lord fails not when we do not fail."

The lady of the manor house agreed with her; she nodded kindly and patted Maren's cheek; she had often done so, yes, and had kissed her as well, but that had been when the lady was a little child and Maren her nursemaid. The two were fond of each other, and this feeling did not wane.

Each year at Christmastime winter provisions would arrive at the tailor's house from the manor house—a barrel of meal, a pig, two geese, a tub of butter, cheese, and apples. That was indeed an asset to the larder. Ivar Ölse looked quite pleased, too, but soon came out with his old motto, "What good will it do?"

The house was clean and tidy, with curtains in the windows, and flowers as well, both carnations and balsams. A sampler hung in a picture frame, and close by hung a love letter in rhyme, which Maren Ölse herself had written; she knew how to put rhymes together. She was almost a little proud of the family name Ölse; it was the only word in the Danish language that rhymed with *pölse* (sausage). "At least that's an advantage to have over other people," she said, and laughed. She always kept her good humor, and never said, like her husband, "What good will it do?" Her motto was, "Depend on yourself and on our Lord." So she did, and that kept them all together. The children thrived, grew out over the nest, went out into the world, and prospered well.

Rasmus was the smallest; he was such a pretty child that one of the great portrait painters in the capital had borrowed him to paint from, and in the picture he was as naked as when he had come into this world. That picture was now hanging in the king's palace. The lady of the manor house saw it, and recognized little Rasmus, though he had no clothes on.

But now came hard times. The tailor had rheumatism in both hands, on which great lumps appeared. No doctor could help him—not even the wise Stine, who herself did some "doctoring."

"One must not be downhearted," said Maren. "It never helps to hang the head. Now that we no longer have father's two hands to help us, I must try to use mine all the faster. Little Rasmus, too, can use the needle." He was already sitting on the sewing table, whistling and singing. He was a happy boy. "But he should not sit there the whole day long," said the mother; "that would be a shame for the child. He should play and jump about, too."

The shoemaker's Johanne was his favorite playmate. Her folks were still poorer than Rasmus'. She was not pretty. She went about barefooted, and her clothes hung in rags, for she had no one to mend them, and to do it herself did not occur to her—she was a child, and as happy as a bird in our Lord's sunshine.

By the stone milepost, under the large willow tree, Rasmus and Johanne played. He had ambitious thoughts; he would one day become a fine tailor and live in the city, where there were master tailors who had ten workmen at the table; this he had heard from his father. There he would be an apprentice, and there he would become a master tailor, and then Johanne could come to visit him; and if by that time she knew how to cook, she could prepare the meals for all of them and have a large apartment of her own. Johanne dared not expect that, but Rasmus believed it could happen. They sat beneath the old tree, and the wind whistled in the branches and leaves; it seemed as if the wind were singing and the tree talking.

In the autumn every single leaf fell off; rain dripped from the bare branches. "They will be green again," said Mother Ölse.

"What good will it do?" said her husband. "New year, new worries about our livelihood."

"The larder is full," said the wife. "We can thank our good lady for that. I am healthy and have plenty of strength. It is sinful for us to complain."

The master and lady of the manor house remained there in the country over Christmas, but the week after the new year, they were to go to the city, where they would spend the winter in festivity and amusement. They would even go to a reception and ball given by the king himself. The lady had bought two rich dresses from France; they were of such material, of such fashion, and so well sewn that the tailor's Maren had never seen such magnificence. She asked the lady if she might come up to the house with her husband, so that he could see the dresses as well. Such things had surely never been seen by a country tailor, she said. He saw them and had not a word to say until he returned home, and what he did say was only what he always said, "What good will it do?" And this time he spoke the truth.

The master and lady of the manor house went to the city, and the balls and merrymaking began. But amid all the splendor the old gentleman died, and the lady then, after all, did not wear her grand dresses. She was so sorrowful and was dressed from head to foot in heavy black mourning. Not so much as a white tucker was to be seen. All the servants were in black; even the state coach was covered with fine black cloth.

It was an icy-cold night; the snow glistened and the stars twinkled. The heavy hearse brought the body from the city to the country church, where it was to be laid in the family vault. The steward and the parish bailiff were waiting on horseback, with torches, in front of the cemetery gate. The church was lighted up, and the pastor stood in the open church door to receive the body. The coffin was carried up into the chancel; the whole congregation followed. The pastor spoke, and a psalm was sung. The lady was present in the church; she had been driven there in the black-draped state coach, which was black inside as well as outside; such a carriage had never before been seen in the parish.

Throughout the winter, people talked about this impressive display of grief; it was indeed a "nobleman's funeral."

"One could well see how important the man was," said the village folk. "He was nobly born and he was nobly buried."

"What good will it do him?" said the tailor. "Now he has neither life nor goods. At least we have one of these."

"Don't speak such words!" said Maren. "He has everlasting life in the Kingdom of Heaven."

"Who told you that, Maren?" said the tailor. "A dead man is good manure, but this man was too highborn to even do the soil any good; he must lie in a church vault."

"Don't speak so impiously!" said Maren. "I tell you again he has everlasting life!"

"Who told you that, Maren?" repeated the tailor. And Maren threw her apron over little Rasmus; he must not hear that kind of talk. She carried him off into the peathouse and wept.

"The words you heard over there, little Rasmus, were not your father's; it was the evil one who was passing through the room and took your father's voice. Say your Lord's Prayer. We'll both say it." She folded the child's hands. "Now I am happy again," she said. "Have faith in yourself and in our Lord."

The year of mourning came to an end. The widow lady dressed in half mourning, but she had whole happiness in her heart. It was rumored that she had a suitor and was already thinking of marriage. Maren knew something about it, and the pastor knew a little more.

On Palm Sunday, after the sermon, the banns of marriage for the widow lady and her betrothed were to be published. He was a woodcarver or a sculptor; just what the name of his profession was, people did not know; at that time not many had heard of Thorvaldsen and his art. The future master of the manor was not a nobleman, but still he was a very stately man. His was one profession that people did not understand, they said; he cut out images, was clever in his work and young and handsome. "What good will it do?" said Tailor Ölse.

On Palm Sunday the banns were read from the pulpit; then followed a psalm and Communion. The tailor, his wife, and little Rasmus were in church; the parents received Communion while Rasmus sat in the pew, for he was not yet confirmed. Of late there had been a shortage of clothes in the tailor's house; the old ones had been turned, and turned again, stitched and patched. Now they were all three dressed in new clothes, but of black material—as at a funeral. They were dressed in the drapery from the funeral coach. The man had a jacket and trousers of it; Maren, a high-necked dress; and Rasmus, a whole suit to grow in until confirmation time. Both the outside and inside cloth from the funeral carriage had been used. No one needed to know what it had been used for before, but people soon got to know.

The wise woman, Stine, and a couple of other equally wise women, who did not live on their wisdom, said that the clothes would bring sickness and disease into the household. "One cannot dress oneself in cloth from a funeral carriage without riding to the grave." The wooden-shoemaker's Johanne cried when she heard this talk. And it so happened that the tailor became more and more ill from that day on, until it seemed apparent who was going to suffer that fate. And it proved to be so.

On the first Sunday after Trinity, Tailor Ölse died, leaving Maren alone to keep things together. She did, keeping faith in herself and in our Lord.

The following year Rasmus was confirmed. He was then ready to go to the city as an apprentice to a master tailor—not, after all, one with ten assistants at the table, but with one; little Rasmus might be counted as a half. He was happy, and he looked delighted indeed, but Johanne wept; she was fonder of him than she had realized. The tailor's wife remained in the old house and carried on the business.

It was at that time that the new King's Highway was opened, and the old one, by the willow tree and the tailor's, became a field path, with duckweed growing over the water left in the ditch there; the milepost tumbled over, for it had nothing to stand for, but the tree kept itself strong and beautiful, the wind whistling among its branches and leaves.

The swallows flew away, and the starlings flew away, but they came again in the spring. And when they came back the fourth time, Rasmus, too, came back to his home. He had served his apprenticeship, and was a handsome but slim youth. Now he would buckle up his knapsack and see foreign countries; that was what he longed for. But his mother clung to him; home was the best place! All the other children were scattered about; he was the youngest, and the house would be his. He could get plenty of work if he would go about the neighborhood—be a traveling tailor and sew for a fortnight at this farm and a fortnight at that. That would be traveling, too. And Rasmus followed his mother's advice.

So again he slept beneath the roof of his birthplace. Again he sat under the old willow tree and heard it whistle. He was indeed good-looking, and he could whistle like a bird and sing new and old songs.

He was well liked at the big farms, especially at Klaus Hansen's, the second richest farmer in the parish. Else, the daughter, was like the loveliest flower to look at, and she was always laughing. There were people who were unkind enough to say that she laughed simply to show her pretty teeth. She was happy indeed, and always in the humor for playing tricks; everything suited her.

She was fond of Rasmus, and he was fond of her, but neither of them said a word about it. So he went about being gloomy; he had more of his father's disposition than his mother's. He was in a good humor only when Else was present; then they both laughed, joked, and played tricks; but although there was many a good opportunity, he did not say a single word about his love. "What good will it do?" was his thought. "Her parents look for profitable marriage for her, and that I cannot give her. The wisest thing for me to do would be to leave." But he could not leave. It was as if Else had a string fastened to him; he was like a trained bird with her; he sang and whistled for her pleasure and at her will.

Johanne, the shoemaker's daughter, was a servant girl at the farm, employed for common work. She drove the milk cart in the meadow, where she and the other girls milked the cows; yes, and she even had to cart manure when it was necessary. She never came into the sitting room and didn't see much of Rasmus or Else, but she heard that the two were as good as engaged.

"Now Rasmus will be well off," she said. "I cannot begrudge him that." And her eyes became quite wet. But there was really nothing to cry about.

There was a market in the town. Klaus Hansen drove there, and Rasmus went along; he sat beside Else, both going there and coming home. He was numb from love, but he didn't say a word about it.

"He ought to say something to me about the matter," thought the girl, and there she was right. "If he won't talk, I'll have to frighten him into it."

And soon there was talk at the farm that the richest farmer in the parish had proposed to Else; and so he had, but no one knew what answer she had given.

Thoughts buzzed around in Rasmus' head.

One evening Else put a gold ring on her finger and then asked Rasmus what that signified.

"Betrothal," he said.

"And with whom do you think?" she asked.

"With the rich farmer?" he said.

"There, you have hit it," she said, nodding, and then slipped away.

But he slipped away, too; he went home to his mother's house like a bewildered man and packed his knapsack. He wanted to go out into the wide world; even his mother's tears couldn't stop him.

He cut himself a stick from the old willow and whistled as if he were in a good humor; he was on his way to see the beauty of the whole world.

"This is a great grief to me," said the mother. "But I suppose it is wisest and best for you to go away, so I shall have to put up with it. Have faith in yourself and in our Lord; then I shall have you back again merry and happy."

He walked along the new highway, and there he saw Johanne come driving with a load of rubbish; she had not noticed him, and he did not wish to be seen by her, so he sat down behind the hedge; there he was hidden—and Johanne drove by.

Out into the world he went; no one knew where. His mother thought, "He will surely come home again before a year passes. Now he will see new things and have new things to think about, but then he will fall back into the old folds; they cannot be ironed out with any iron. He has a little too much of his father's disposition; I would rather he had mine, poor child! But he will surely come home again; he cannot forget either me or the house."

The mother would wait a year and a day. Else waited only a month and then she secretly went to the wise woman, Stine Madsdatter, who, besides knowing something about "doctoring," could tell fortunes in cards and coffee and knew more than her Lord's Prayer. She, of course, knew where Rasmus was; she read it in the coffee grounds. He was in a foreign town, but she couldn't read the name of it. In this town there were soldiers and beautiful ladies. He was thinking of either becoming a soldier or marrying one of the young ladies.

This Else could not bear to hear. She would willingly give her savings to buy him back, but no one must know that it was she.

And old Stine promised that he would come back; she knew of a charm, a dangerous charm for him; it would work; it was the ultimate remedy. She would set the pot boiling for him, and then, wherever in all the world he was, he would have to come home where the pot was boiling and his beloved was waiting for him. Months might pass before he came, but come he must if he was still alive. Without peace or rest night and day, he would be forced to return, over sea and mountain, whether the weather were mild or rough, and even if his feet were ever so tired. He would come home; he had to come home.

The moon was in the first quarter; it had to be for the charm to work, said old Stine. It was stormy weather, and the old willow tree creaked. Stine, cut a twig from it and tied it in a knot. That would surely help to draw Rasmus home to his mother's house. Moss and houseleek were taken from the roof and put in the pot, which was set upon the fire. Else had to tear a leaf out of the psalmbook; she tore out the last leaf by chance, that on which the list of errata appeared. "That will do just as well," said Stine, and threw it into the pot.

Many sorts of things went into the stew, which had to boil and boil steadily until Rasmus came home. The black cock in old Stine's room had to lose its red comb, which went into the pot. Else's heavy gold ring went in with it, and that she would never get again, Stine told her beforehand. She was so wise, Stine. Many things that we are unable to name went into the pot, which stood constantly over the flame or on glowing embers or hot ashes. Only she and Else knew about it.

Whenever the moon was new or the moon was on the wane, Else would come to her and ask, "Can't you see him coming?"

"Much do I know," said Stine, "and much do I see, but the length of the way before him I cannot see. Now he is over the first mountains; now he is on the sea in bad weather. The road is long, through large forests; he has blisters on his feet, and he has fever in his bones, but he must go on."

"No, no!" said Else. "I feel so sorry for him."

"He cannot be stopped now, for if we stop him, he will drop dead in the road!"

A year and a day had gone. The moon shone round and big, and the wind whistled in the old tree. A rainbow appeared across the sky in the bright moonlight.

"That is a sign to prove what I say," said Stine. "Now Rasmus is coming."

But still he did not come.

"The waiting time is long," said Stine.

"Now I am tired of this," said Else. She seldom visited Stine now and brought her no more gifts. Her mind became easier, and one fine morning they all knew in the parish that Else had said "yes" to the rich farmer. She went over to look at the house and grounds, the cattle, and the household belongings. All was in good order, and there was no reason to wait with the wedding.

It was celebrated with a great party lasting three days. There was dancing to the clarinet and violins. No one in the parish was forgotten in the invitations. Mother Ölse was there, too, and when the party came to an end, and the hosts had thanked the guests, and the trumpets had blown, she went home with the leavings from the feast.

She had fastened the door only with a peg; it had been taken out, the door stood open, and in the room sat Rasmus. He had returned home—come that very hour. Lord God, how he looked! He was only skin and bone; he was pale and yellow.

"Rasmus!" said his mother. "Is it you I see? How badly you look! But I am so happy in my heart to have you back."

And she gave him the good food she had brought home from the party, a piece of the roast and of the wedding cake.

He had lately, he said, often thought of his mother, his home, and the old willow tree; it was strange how often in his dreams he had seen the tree and the little barefooted Johanne. He did not mention Else at all. He was ill and had to go to bed.

But we do not believe that the pot was the cause of this, or that it had exercised any power over him. Only old Stine and Else believed that, but they did not talk about it.

Rasmus lay with a fever—an infectious one. For that reason no one came to the tailor's house, except Johanne, the shoemaker's daughter. She cried when she saw how miserable Rasmus was.

The doctor wrote a prescription for him to have filled at the pharmacy. He would not take the medicine. "What good will it do?" he said.

"You will get well again then," said his mother. "Have faith in yourself and in our Lord! If I could only see you get flesh on your body again, hear you whistle and sing; for that I would willingly lay down my life."

And Rasmus was cured of his illness, but his mother contracted it. Our Lord summoned her, and not him.

It was lonely in the house; he became poorer and poorer. "He is worn out," they said in the parish. "Poor Rasmus." He had led a wild life on his travels; that, and not the black pot that had boiled, had sucked out his marrow and given him pain in his body. His hair became thin and gray. He was too lazy to work. "What good will it do?" he said. He would rather visit the tavern than the church.

One autumn evening he was staggering through rain and wind along the muddy road from the tavern to his house; his mother had long since gone and been laid in her grave. The swallows and starlings were also gone, faithful as they were. Johanne, the shoemaker's daughter, was not gone; she overtook him on the road and then followed him a little way.

"Pull yourself together, Rasmus."

"What good will it do?" he said.

"That is an awful saying that you have," said she. "Remember your mother's words, 'Have faith in yourself and in our Lord.' You do not, Rasmus, but you must, and you shall. Never say, 'What good will it do?' for then you pull up the root of all your doings."

She followed him to the door of his house, and there she left him. He did not stay inside; he wandered out under the old willow tree and sat on a stone from the overturned milepost.

The wind whistled in the tree's branches; it was like a song: it was like talk.

Rasmus answered it; he spoke aloud but no one heard him except the tree and the whistling wind.

"I am getting so cold. It is time to go to bed. Sleep, sleep!"

And he walked away, not toward the house, but over to the ditch, where he tottered and fell. Rain poured down, and the wind was icy cold, but he didn't feel this. When the sun rose, and the crows flew over the bulrushes, he awoke, deathly ill. Had he laid his head where he put his feet, he would never have arisen; the green duckweed would have been his burial sheet.

Later in the day Johanne came to the tailor's house. She helped him; she managed to get him to the hospital.

"We have known each other since we were little," she said. "Your mother gave me both ale and food; for that I can never repay her. You will regain your health; you will be a man with a will to live!"

And our Lord willed that he should live. But he had his ups and downs, both in health and mind.

The swallows and the starlings returned, and flew away, and returned again. Rasmus became older than his years. He sat alone in his house, which deteriorated more and more. He was poor, poorer now than Johanne.

"You have no faith," she said, "and if we do not believe in God, what have we? You should go to Communion," she said; "you haven't been since your confirmation."

"What good will it do?" he said.

"If you say that and believe it, then let it be; the Master does not want an unwilling guest at his table. But think of your mother and your childhood. Once you were a good, pious boy. Let me read a psalm to you."

"What good will it do?" he said.

"It always comforts me," she answered.

"Johanne, you have surely become one of the saints." And he looked at her with dull, weary eyes.

And Johanne read the psalm, but not from a book, for she had none; she knew it by heart.

"Those were beautiful words," he said, "but I could not follow you altogether. My head feels so heavy."

Rasmus had become an old man. But Else, if we may mention her, was no longer young, either; Rasmus never mentioned her. She was a grandmother. Her granddaughter was an impudent little girl.

The little one was playing with the other children in the village. Rasmus came along, supporting himself on his stick. He stopped, watched the children play, and smiled to them, old times were in his thoughts. Else's granddaughter pointed at him. "Poor Rasmus!" she shouted. The other little girls followed her example. "Poor Rasmus!" they shouted, and pursued the old man with shrieks. It was a gray, gloomy day, and many others followed. But after gray and gloomy days, there comes a sunshiny day.

It was a beautiful Whitsunday morning. The church was decorated with green birch branches; there was a scent of the woods within it, and the sun shone on the church pews. The large altar candles were lighted, and Communion was being held. Johanne was among the kneeling, but Rasmus was not among them. That very morning the Lord had called him.

In God are grace and mercy.

Many years have since passed. The tailor's house still stands there, but no one lives in it. It might fall the first stormy night. The ditch is overgrown with bulrush and buck bean. The wind whistles in the old tree; it is as if one were hearing a song; the wind sings it; the tree tells it. If you do not understand it, ask old Johanne in the poorhouse.

She still lives there; she sings her psalm, the one she read for Rasmus. She thinks of him, prays to our Lord for him—she, the faithful soul. She can tell of bygone times, of memories that whistle in the old willow tree.

THE FLEA AND THE PROFESSOR (1872)

There was an aëronaut, and things went badly with him. His balloon burst, hurled him out, and went all to pieces. Just two minutes before, the aëronaut had sent his boy down by parachute—wasn't the boy lucky! He wasn't hurt, and he knew enough to be an aëronaut himself, but he had no balloon and no means of getting one.

Live he must, so he took to sleight-of-hand tricks and to throwing his voice, which is called ventriloquism. He was young and good-looking. When he grew a mustache and wore his best clothes, he might well have been mistaken for the son of a nobleman. Ladies found him handsome and one young lady was so taken by his charm and dexterity that she eloped with him to foreign lands. There he called himself "The Professor"—he could scarcely do less.

He continually thought about how to get himself a balloon and sail through the air with his little wife. But they still lacked the means to do so.

"That will come yet," he said.

"Oh, if only it would," said she.

"We are still young people," he said, "and I'm a Professor."

"Crumbs are also bread!"

She helped him all she could, and sat at the door to sell tickets for his entertainments. In the wintertime this was a chilly sort of pleasure. She also helped him with one of his acts. He would put her into a table drawer—a large table drawer—and she would creep into the back drawer. From in front she was not to be seen, and as far as the audience was concerned she was invisible. But one evening, when he pulled out the drawer she was invisible to him too. She was not in the front drawer, not in the back one, and not in the whole house. She was nowhere to be seen or heard, and that was her contribution to the entertainment.

She never came back. She was tired of it all, and he became tired of it, too. He lost his good humor and could not laugh or make jokes, so people stopped coming to see him. His earnings fell off and his clothes wore out, until at last all that he had was a large flea, an heirloom from his wife; that's why he liked it so well. He trained the flea and taught it to perform—to present arms and to fire off a cannon. Of course, it was a very small cannon.

The Professor was proud of the flea, and the flea was proud of himself. He had learned a thing or two and had human blood in him. He had been to the largest cities. Princes and princesses had seen him and given him high praise, which was printed in the newspapers and on the billposters. He knew he was a famous flea who could support a Professor, yes, a whole household.

Proud he was and famous he was. Yet when he and the Professor traveled they went by fourth-class railway carriages, which took them along just as quickly as those of the first-class. They made a secret pledge to each other that they would never separate. Neither of them would marry. The flea would remain a bachelor and the Professor a widower. That made them even.

"Where one has the best luck," said the Professor, "one ought not go back a second time." He was a student of human nature, which is a science in itself. At length he had traveled through all countries except the savage ones, and to those he decided to go. There they eat Christian men. The Professor knew this, but then he was not much of a Christian, and the flea was not much of a man, so he thought they might venture successfully into the wilds, and make a lot of money.

They traveled by steamship and they traveled by sailboat. The flea performed his trick along the way in exchange for free passage, and thus they came to the country of savages. Here a little princess ruled the land. She was only eight years old, but she ruled just the same. She had taken away the power from her papa and mamma, for she had a will of her own and was uncommonly beautiful, and uncommonly rude.

As soon as the flea presented arms and fired off his cannon, she took such a fancy to him that she cried, "Him or nobody!" She fell madly in love with the flea, and she was already a madcap in all other respects.

"My sweet, level-headed little child—" her papa said, "if only there were some way to make a man of him."

"Leave that to me, old fellow," said she, which was no way for a little princess to talk to her papa, but then she was a savage. She set the flea on her fair hand:

"Now you are a man, ruling with me, but you must do what I want you to do, or I shall kill you and eat the Professor."

The Professor had a large room to live in, with walls made of sugar cane. He could have licked them, but he didn't care for sweets. He had a hammock to sleep in, and that reminded him of being in a balloon, where he had always wanted to be. He thought of this continually.

The flea lived with the princess. He sat upon her delicate hand or on her fair neck.

She had taken a hair from her head and made the Professor fasten it to the flea's leg, and kept it tied to the big red coral pendant which hung from the tip of her ear. What a delightful time the princess did have, and the flea, too, she thought.

The Professor was not so delighted. He was a traveler who liked to ride from town to town and to read in the newspapers about how persevering and ingenious he had been to teach the flea tricks of human behavior. Day in and day out he lay lazily in his hammock. He ate good food: fresh bird's eggs, elephants' eyes, and fried giraffes' legs. Cannibals do not live entirely on human flesh. No, that is a special delicacy!

"Shoulder of child with pepper sauce," said the princess's mamma, "is the most delicate."

The Professor was bored with it all and preferred to leave this savage land, but his flea he must take with him, for it was his wonder and his bread and butter. How could he catch it? How could he get hold of it? This was not an easy thing to do. He racked his wits, and at last he declared:

"Now I have it! Papa of the princess, give me something to do. Let me teach your people to present themselves before Your Royal Highness. This is what is known as culture in the great and powerful nations of Earth."

"Can I learn to do that too?" the princess's papa asked.

"It's not quite proper," the Professor told him, "but I shall teach your Savage Papaship to fire off a cannon. It goes off with a bang. One sits high in the air, and then off it goes or down you come."

"Let me bang it off," the princess's papa begged. But in all the land there was no cannon, except the one the flea had brought with him—and that was so tiny.

"I shall cast a bigger one," said the Professor. "Just give me the means to do so. I must have fine silk cloth, a needle and thread, and rope and cordage, besides stomach drops for the balloon. Stomach drops blow a person up so easily and give one the heaves. They are what make the report in the cannon's stomach."

"By all means." The princess's papa gave him everything that he asked. The whole court and all the populace gathered together to see the casting of the big cannon. The Profesor did not call them until he had the ballon all ready to be filled and to go up. The flea sat there upon the princess's hand and looked on as the ballon was filled. It swelled out and became so violent that they could scarcely hold it down.

"I must take it up in the air to cool it off," said the Professor, who took his seat in the basket that hung underneath.

"But—I cannot steer it alone; I must have a trained companion to help me. There is no one here who can do that except the flea."

"I am not at all willing to permit it," said the princess, but she held out her hand and gave the flea to the Professor, who placed it on his wrist.

"Let go the lines and ropes!" he shouted. "Now the balloon is going up." They thought he said "the cannon." So the balloon went higher and higher, up above the clouds and far away from that savage land.

The little princess, her family, and all of her subjects sat and waited. They are waiting there still, and if you don't believe this, just you take a journey to the country of savages. Every child there is talking about the Professor and the flea, whom they expect back as soon as the cannon cools off.

But they won't be back. They are at home here with us. They are in their native land. They travel by rail, first-class, not fourth. For they have a great success, an enormous balloon. Nobody asks them how they got their balloon, or where it came from. They are wealthy folk now—oh, most respectable folk—the flea and the Professor.

CROAK! (1926)

All the birds of the forest were sitting upon the branches of the trees, which had quite enough leaves; and yet the birds were unanimous in their desire for more leaves—the "leaves" of a journal; a new, good journal was what they longed for—a critical newspaper such as humans have so many of, so many that half of them would be sufficient.

The songbirds wanted a music critic, each for his own praise—and for criticism (where it was needed) of the others. But they, the birds themselves, could not agree on an impartial critic.

"It must be a bird, though," said the Owl, who had been elected president by the assembly, for he is the bird of wisdom. "We ought not elect anyone from another branch of animals, except perhaps from the sea. There fish fly, like birds in the sky, but that, of course, is our only relationship. However, there are quite enough animals to select from between fish and birds."

Then the stork took the floor and rattled from his beak, "There are indeed beings between fish and birds. The children of the marsh, the Frogs—I am voting for them. They are extremely musical, and their choir singing is like church bells in a lonely wood. I get an urge to travel," said the Stork, "a tickling under my wings, when they begin to sing."

"I am also voting for the Frogs," said the Heron. "They are neither bird nor fish, but still they live with the fishes and sing like the birds."

"Now that's the musical part," said the Owl. "But the paper must speak of all the beauties of the forest. We must have coworkers. Let each of us consider everyone in his family."

Then the little Lark sang out cheerfully and prettily, "The Frog should not be the editor of the paper—no, it should be the Nightingale!"

"Stop your chirping!" said the Owl. "I am hooting for order! I know the Nightingale. We are both night birds. Each bird sings with his own beak. Neither he nor I ought to be elected, because the paper would become an aristocratic or philosophic newspaper, a beau monde paper, run by high society. It must also be an organ for the common man."

They agreed that the paper should be called *Morning Croak* or *Evening Croak*—or just *Croak*. They unanimously voted for the latter.

It would fill a long-felt need in the forest. The Bee, the Ant, and the Gopher promised to write about industrial and engineering activities, in which they had great insight. The Cuckoo was nature's poet. Not counted among the songbirds, he was, however, of the greatest importance to the common man. "He always praises himself; he is the vainest of all birds, and yet not much to look at," said the Peacock.

Then the Flesh Flies paid a visit to the editor in the forest. "We offer our services. We know people, editors, and human criticism. We lay our larva in the fresh flesh—and then it decays within twenty-four hours. We can destroy a great talent, if necessary, in the editor's service. If a paper is the spokesman for a party, it dares to be rude; and if one loses a subscriber, one will get sixteen in return. Be cruel, give nicknames, put them in a pillory, whistle through your fingers like a gang of young radicals, and you become a power in the state."

"Such an air rover!" said the Frog about the Stork. "I actually looked up to him when I was little and felt a trembling admiration. And when he walked in the marsh and spoke of Egypt, my imagination carried me to wonderful foreign lands. Now he doesn't impress me anymore—that is all just an echo in my memory.

"I have become wiser, rational, important—I write critical articles in *Croak*. I am what, in the most correct and proper writing and speech of our language, is called a Croaker!

In the human world there is also that sort. I have written a piece about it on the back page of our paper."

THE PENMAN (1926)

There once was a man who held an office that required good penmanship. While he filled the office ably otherwise, he was incapable of good penmanship. So he advertised in the newspaper for someone with a fine handwriting; and so many applied that the applications could have filled a whole bucket. But one was all he needed. And so he chose the first he came to, one with a script as beautiful as that of the finest writing machine. The man in office was an excellent writer. And when his writings appeared in the handsome lettering, everyone said, "That is beautifully written."

"That's my work," said the fellow, whose mind wasn't worth a penny.

And after hearing such praise for a whole week, he became so conceited that he wanted to be the man in office himself. He really would have made a fine writing teacher, and would have looked well in his white necktie at ladies' tea parties. But that wasn't what he wanted; he wanted to outwrite all the other writers. And he wrote about painters and sculptors, about composers and the theater. He wrote an awful lot of nonsense, and when it was too dreadful, he would write the following day that it had been a misprint. As a matter of fact, everything he wrote was a misprint, but the sad part was that his only asset, his beautiful handwriting, couldn't be seen in print.

"I can break; I can make! I'm a hell of a fellow, sort of a little god, and not so little, at that!"

This was a lot of silly talk. And that he finally died of. On his death a flowery obituary appeared in the newspaper. Now, wasn't that a sorry tale—his being painted in glowing terms by a friend who really could write stories?

Despite the good intentions of his friend, his life story, with all its nastiness, clamoring, and prattle, became a very sad fairy tale indeed.

FOLKS SAY— (1949)

Folks often say one thing and mean another. Folks say so much that means so little. Folks say— Folks say— Yes, there is a lot of slander, but also a lot of innocent talk. Both seriousness and humor hide under that saying.

Folks say that the age of miracles is past, but that is not true. The age of miracles is still with us, in our souls; it is there that revelations come to man. Although the world may seem arid and desolate, God's fountain of mercy spouts forth within it. Life flourishes, and through inspired music, through poetry and science, God will unfold miracles for us until the Judgment Day.

Folks say that our feelings and thoughts arise from the motions and vibrations of our nerves—now inspiration, now happiness, now pain. Each one of us is but an instrument. Yes, indeed, but who touches the strings and makes them vibrate and tremble? God's invisible spirit.

Folks say funny things, and often with four cents' worth of malice. Folks say that once there was a lady who dreamed that all her teeth had fallen out, and that she remarked, "Now I'll lose one of my friends." But they said it must have been a false friend, for all the lady's teeth were false!

Folks say that when Sarah married the Philistine king Abimelech, she said to her husband, "We will call our son Isaac," for that meant in their language: "Folks will laugh." Old Sarah knew human nature. She knew folks' opinions—and they haven't changed since Sarah's time.

Folks say—and this is supposed to be quite true—that the other day one of the severe art critics stood by the seashore watching the waves.

"This is superb," he said, "superb and right!" And our Lord took off his hat and answered, "Thank you, Herr Professor!"

Folks say— Yes, folks say— But let that be enough, at least for today.

THE POOR WOMAN AND THE LITTLE CANARY BIRD (1949)

There was a miserably poor woman. She was very sad, for she had nothing to eat, and her husband was dead and had to be buried, but she was so poor that she could not afford to buy a coffin. And no one would help her, not a single person, and so she wept and prayed to the good Lord to help her, for he is so good to us all.

The window was open, and a tiny little bird flew into the room. It was a canary bird that had escaped from its cage and flown over all the rooftops, and now, having come in through the poor woman's window, it sat by the head of the dead man and sang so beautifully. It was as if it wanted to say to the woman, "You must no be so sad. Can't you hear how happy I am!"

And the poor woman took some bread crumbs in her hand and called to the little bird. It hopped over to her and ate the crumbs. It was so sweet.

Then there was a knock on the door. A woman entered, and when she saw the little canary bird that had flown in through the window, she said, "This is surely the bird that was written about in the newspaper today. It has flown away from some people down the street."

And so the miserably poor woman went to the people with the little bird, and they were very happy to see it again. They asked her where she had found it, and she told them it had flown in through her window, had sat by her dead husband, and had sung so beautifully that she had stopped crying, although she was so poor she could not buy a coffin for her husband and had nothing at all to eat.

And the people felt very sorry for her. They were so good, and so happy to have the bird back. They bought a coffin for her dead husband and said to the poor woman that she must come to their home every day and eat and drink with them. She was very happy, and thanked the good Lord for having sent the little canary bird to her when she had been so sad.

URBANUS (1949)

In a cloister there lived a young man named Urbanus, who was pious and studious. He was entrusted with the keys to the cloister's book collection and faithfully guarded this treasure. He wrote many beautiful books and frequently studied the Holy Scriptures and other works.

Then one day Urbanus, who had been reading the writings of the Apostle Paul, found in the Bible: "For a thousand years in Thy sight are but as yesterday when it is past, and as a watch in the night." This impressed the young man as being quite impossible; he could not believe it, and he was tormented by doubt and ponderous thoughts.

It so happened that one morning the monk walked down from the gloomy library and out into the beautiful, sunlit cloister garden, and found a little, gaily colored wood bird sitting on the ground looking for a few grains of corn. Presently it flew up onto a branch, where it sang most strangely and wonderfully.

The little bird was not at all shy, and it permitted the monk to come very close. He would have liked to catch it, but the bird flew off, from tree to tree. The monk followed it, and it sang continuously with a clear and lovely voice. But the young monk could not catch it, although he pursued it for a considerable distance, from the cloister garden into the wood.

He finally gave up and returned to the cloister, but what he saw looked strangely changed to him. Everything had become extended, larger and more beautiful, both the buildings and the garden, and instead of the low, little old cloister church stood a mighty cathedral with three towers. The monk thought this strange and almost magical. And when he reached the cloister gate and hesitantly pulled the bell cord, he was met by a gatekeeper who was a complete stranger to him and who astoundedly drew away from him.

As the monk walked through the cloister cemetry, he noticed many, many tombstones that he did not remember having seen before.

And when he approached the cloister brethren they all drew away from him horrified.

Only the abbot, but not the abbot he had known—another, younger one, completely unknown to him—stood still, and pointing the crucifix toward him, he said, "In the name of the Crucified, who are you, unsaintly soul who has risen from the grave, and what are you searching for among us the living?"

At that the monk shuddered, and with downcast eyes, he staggered like a senile old man. And, look, he had a long, silver-white beard that reached down below his belt, where the bunch of keys to the locked bookcases still hung.

With shy reverence the monks led the curious-looking stranger to the abbot's seat.

There the abbot gave the library key to a young monk, who opened the library door and brought forth a handwritten chronicle in which one could read that a monk named Urbanus had completely vanished some three hundred years previously. No one knew if he had escaped or had met with an accident.

"Oh, wood bird! Was it your song!" said the stranger with a sigh. "I followed you and listened to your song for less than three minutes, and in the meantime three centuries went by. You have sung for me the song about eternity, the eternity I could not understand. But now I understand, and worship you, O Lord, in the dust. I am but a grain of dust," he said, bowing his head, and his body vanished into dust.